TAMI HOAG
Three Great Novels

The Thrillers

Tami Hoag
The Thrillers

Ashes to Ashes
Dust to Dust
Dark Horse

ORION

This omnibus edition first published in Great Britain in 2003 by Orion Books
an imprint of The Orion Publishing Group
Orion House, 5 Upper St Martin's Lane, London WC2H 9EA

A CIP catalogue record for this book is
available from the British Library

ISBN (trade paperback) 0 75286 005 4

Typeset by Deltatype Ltd,
Birkenhead, Merseyside

Printed and bound in Great Britain by
Clays Ltd, St Ives plc

Contents

Ashes to Ashes

Author's Note and Acknowledgments

My thanks and heartfelt gratitude first and foremost to Special Agent Larry Brubaker, FBI, for so generously sharing his time and expertise. I state unequivocally he was *not* the pattern for Vince Walsh! (Sorry about that, Bru.) I will also note here that between beginning this book and finishing it, a number of changes have taken place in the FBI units formerly – and within this story – known as Investigative Support and CASKU (Child Abduction Serial Killer Unit). Now under the blanket heading of the National Center for the Analysis of Violent Crime, the agents in this unit no longer work sixty feet below ground at the FBI Academy in Quantico. Literally moving up in the world, they get to have windows in their new place. Not as interesting for writers, but the agents appreciate it.

My sincere gratitude also to the following law enforcement and legal services professionals for graciously giving their time to answer my many questions. As always, I've done my best to bring a feeling of authenticity to the jobs depicted within this book. Any mistakes made or liberties taken in the name of fiction are my own.

Frances James, Hennepin County Victim/Witness Program
Donna Dunn, Olmsted County Victim Services
Sergeant Bernie Martinson, Minneapolis PD
Special Agent in Charge Roger Wheeler, FBI
Lieutenant Dale Barsness, Minneapolis PD
Detective John Reed, Hennepin County Sheriff's Office
Andi Sisco: A million thanks for making connections for me! You're a star.
Diva Karyn, aka Elizabeth Grayson: Special thanks for some inspired suggestions regarding a particularly gruesome fetish used herein. Who says suspense writers have cornered the market on disgusting knowledge?
Brain Dead author Eileen Dreyer: Thanks for the usual support, technical and otherwise.
Diva Bush, aka Kim Cates: For more of the same.
And special thanks, Rocket, for your support, empathy, encouragement, and the occasional necessary kick in the ass. Misery loves company.

1

Some killers are born. Some killers are made. And sometimes the origin of desire for homicide is lost in the tangle of roots that make an ugly childhood and a dangerous youth, so that no one may ever know if the urge was inbred or induced.

He lifts the body from the back of the Blazer like a roll of old carpet to be discarded. The soles of his boots scuff against the blacktop of the parking area, then fall nearly silent on the dead grass and hard ground. The night is balmy for November in Minneapolis. A swirling wind tosses fallen leaves. The bare branches of the trees rattle together like bags of bones.

He knows he falls into the last category of killers. He has spent many hours, days, months, years studying his compulsion and its point of origin. He knows what he is, and he embraces that truth. He has never known guilt or remorse. He believes conscience, rules, laws, serve the individual no practical purpose, and only limit human possibilities.

'Man enters into the ethical world through fear and not through love.' – Paul Ricoeur, Symbolism of Evil.

His True Self adheres only to his own code: domination, manipulation, control.

A broken shard of moon glares down on the scene, its light faint beneath the web of limbs. He arranges the body to his satisfaction and traces two intersecting Xs over the left upper chest. With a sense of ceremony, he pours the accelerant. Anointing the dead. Symbolism of evil. His True Self embraces the concept of evil as power. Fuel for the internal fire.

'Ashes to ashes.'

The sounds are ordered and specific, magnified by his excitement. The scrape of the match against the friction strip, the pop as it bursts with flame, the whoosh of the fire as it comes alive and consumes. As the fire burns, his memory replays the earlier sounds of pain and fear. He recalls the tremor in her voice as she pleaded for her life, the unique pitch and quality of each cry as he tortured her. The exquisite music of life and death.

For one fine moment he allows himself to admire the drama of the tableau. He allows himself to feel the heat of the flames caress his face like tongues of desire. He closes his eyes and listens to the sizzle and hiss, breathes deep the smell of roasting flesh.

Elated, excited, aroused, he takes his erection out of his pants and strokes himself hard. He brings himself nearly to climax, but is careful not to ejaculate. Save it for later, when he can celebrate fully.

His goal is in sight. He has a plan, meticulously thought out, to be executed with perfection. His name will live in infamy with all the great ones – Bundy, Kemper, the Boston Strangler, the Green River Killer. The press here has already given him a name: the Cremator.

It makes him smile. It makes him proud. He lights another match and holds it just in front of him, studying the flame, loving the sinuous, sensuous undulation of it. He brings it closer to his face, opens his mouth, and eats it.

Then he turns and walks away. Already thinking of next time.

Murder.

The sight burned its impression into the depths of her memory, into the backs of her eyeballs so that she could see it when she blinked against the tears. The body twisting in slow agony against its horrible fate. Orange flame a backdrop for the nightmare image.

Burning.

She ran, her lungs burning, her legs burning, her eyes burning, her throat burning. In one abstract corner of her mind, she was the corpse. Maybe this was what death was like. Maybe it *was* her body roasting, and this consciousness was her soul trying to escape the fires of hell. She had been told repeatedly that was where she would end up.

In the near distance she could hear a siren and see the weird flash of blue and red lights against the night. She ran for the street, sobbing, stumbling. Her right knee hit the frozen ground, but she forced her feet to keep moving.

Run run run run run run –

'Freeze! Police!'

The cruiser still rocked at the curb. The door was open. The cop was on the boulevard, gun drawn and pointed straight at her.

'Help me!' The words rasped in her throat.

'Help me!' she gasped, tears blurring her vision.

Her legs buckled beneath the weight of her body and the weight of her fear and the weight of her heart that was pounding like some huge swollen thing in her chest.

The cop was beside her in an instant, holstering his weapon and dropping to his knees to help. Must be a rookie, she thought dimly. She knew fourteen-year-old kids with better street instincts. She could have gotten his weapon. If she'd had a knife, she could have raised herself up and stabbed him.

He pulled her up into a sitting position with a hand on either shoulder. Sirens wailed in the distance.

'What happened? Are you all right?' he demanded. He had a face like an angel.

'I saw him,' she said, breathless, shaking, bile pushing up the back of her throat. 'I was there. Oh – Jesus. Oh – shit. I saw him!'

'Saw who?'

'The Cremator.'

2

'Why am I always the one in the wrong place at the wrong time?' Kate Conlan muttered to herself.

First day back from what had technically been a vacation – a guilt-forced trip to visit her parents in hell's amusement park (Las Vegas) – she was late for work, had a headache, wanted to strangle a certain sex crimes sergeant for spooking one of her clients – a screw-up *she* would pay for with the prosecuting attorney. All that and the fashionably chunky heel on a brand new pair of suede pumps was coming loose, thanks to the stairs in the Fourth Avenue parking ramp.

Now this. A twitcher.

No one else seemed to notice him prowling the edge of the spacious atrium of the Hennepin County Government Center like a nervous cat. Kate made the guy for late thirties, no more than a couple of inches past her own five-nine, medium-to-slender build. Wound way too tight. He'd likely suffered some kind of personal or emotional setback recently – lost his job or his girlfriend. He was either divorced or separated; living on his own, but not homeless. His clothes were rumpled, but not castoffs, and his shoes were too good for homeless. He was sweating like a fat man in a sauna, but he kept his coat on as he paced around and around the new piece of sculpture littering the hall – a symbolic piece of pretension fashioned from melted-down handguns. He was muttering to himself, one hand hanging on to the open front of his heavy canvas jacket. A hunter's coat. His inner emotional strain tightened the muscles of his face.

Kate slipped off her loose-heeled shoe and stepped out of the other one, never taking her eyes off the guy. She dug a hand into her purse and came out with her cell phone. At the same instant, the twitcher caught the interest of the woman working the information booth twenty feet away.

Damn.

Kate straightened slowly, punching the speed-dial button. She couldn't dial security from an outside phone. The nearest guard was across the broad expanse of the atrium, smiling, laughing, engaged in conversation with a mailman. The information lady came toward the twitcher with her head to one side, as if her cotton-candy cone of blond hair were too heavy.

Dammit.

The office phone rang once ... twice. Kate started moving slowly forward, phone in one hand, shoe in the other.

'Can I help you, sir?' the information woman said, still ten feet away. Blood was going to wreck the hell out of her ivory silk blouse.

The twitcher jerked around.

'Can I help you?' the woman asked again.

... fourth ring ...

A Latina woman with a toddler in tow cut through the distance between Kate and the twitcher. Kate thought she could see the tremors begin – his body fighting to contain the rage or the desperation or whatever was driving him or eating him alive.

... fifth ring. 'Hennepin County attorney's office –'

'Dammit!'

The movement was unmistakable – planting the feet, reaching into the jacket, eyes going wider.

'Get down!' Kate shouted, dropping the phone.

The information woman froze.

'Someone fucking pays!' the twitcher cried, lunging toward the woman, grabbing hold of her arm with his free hand. He jerked her toward him, thrusting his gun out ahead of her. The explosion of the shot was magnified in the towering atrium, deafening all ears to the shrieks of panic it elicited. Everyone noticed him now.

Kate barreled into him from behind, swinging the heel end of her shoe against his temple like a hammer. He expelled a cry of startled shock, then came back hard with his right elbow, catching Kate in the ribs.

The information woman screamed and screamed. Then lost her feet or lost consciousness, and the weight of her falling body jerked down on her assailant. He dropped to one knee, shouting obscenities, firing another round, this one skipping off the hard floor and going God knew where.

Kate fell with him, her left hand clutching the collar of his coat. She couldn't lose him. Whatever beast he'd had trapped inside was free now. If he got away from her, there'd be a hell of a lot more to worry about than stray bullets.

Her nylons giving her no purchase on the slick floor, she scrambled to get her feet under her, to hang on to him as he fought to stand. She swung the shoe again and smacked him in the ear. He twisted around, trying to backhand her with the gun. Kate grabbed his arm and forced it up, too aware as the gun went off again that there were more than twenty stories of offices and courtrooms above.

As they struggled for control of the gun, she hooked a leg around one of his and threw her weight against him, and suddenly they were falling, down and down, tumbling over each other down the biting metal treads of the escalator to the street level – where they were met by half a dozen shouts of 'Freeze! Police!'

Kate looked up at the grim faces through the haze of pain and muttered, 'Well, it's about damn time.'

'Hey, look!' one of the assistant prosecutors called from his office. 'It's Dirty Harriet!'

'Very funny, Logan,' Kate said, making her way down the hall to the county attorney's office. 'You read that in a book, didn't you?'

'They have to get Rene Russo to play you in the movie.'

'I'll tell them you said so.'

Aches bit into her back and hip. She had refused a ride to the emergency room. Instead, she had limped into the ladies' room, combed her mane of red-gold hair into a ponytail, washed off the blood, ditched her ruined black tights, and gone back to her office. She didn't have any wounds worth an X-ray or stitches, and half the morning was gone. The price of being a tough: She would have to make do tonight with Tylenol, cold gin, and a hot bath, instead of real painkillers. She could already tell she was going to be sorry.

The thought occurred to her that she was too old to be tackling lunatics and riding them down escalators, but she stubbornly resisted the idea that forty-two was too old for anything. Besides, she was only five years into what she termed her 'second adulthood'. The second career, the second stab at stability and routine.

The only thing she had wished for all the way home from the weirdness of Las Vegas was a return to the nice, normal, relatively sane life she had made for herself. Peace and quiet. The familiar entanglements of her job as a victim/witness advocate. The cooking class she was determined not to fail.

But no, she had to be the one to spot the twitcher. She was always the one who had to spot the twitcher.

Alerted by his secretary, the county attorney opened his office door for her himself. A tall, good-looking man, Ted Sabin had a commanding presence and a shock of gray hair, which he swept back from a prominent widow's peak. A pair of round steel-rimmed glasses perched on his hawkish nose gave him a studious look and helped camouflage the fact that his blue eyes were set too deep and too close together.

While he had once been a crack prosecutor himself, he now took on only the occasional high-profile case. His job as head honcho was largely administrative and political. He oversaw a bustling office of attorneys trying to juggle the ever-increasing workload of the Hennepin County court system. Lunch hours and evenings found him moving among the Minneapolis power elite, currying connections and favor. It was common knowledge he had his eye on a seat in the US Senate.

'Kate, come in,' he invited, the lines of his face etched deep with concern. He rested a big hand on her shoulder and guided her across the office toward a chair. 'How are you? I've been brought up to speed about what happened downstairs this morning. My God, you could have been killed! What an astonishing act of bravery!'

'No, it wasn't,' Kate protested, trying to ease away from him. She slipped into the visitor's chair and immediately felt his gaze on her bare thighs as she crossed her legs. She tugged discreetly at the hem of her black skirt, wishing to hell she'd found the spare panty hose she'd thought were in her desk drawer. 'I just reacted, that's all. How's Mrs Sabin?'

'Fine.' The reply was absent of thought. He focused on her as he hitched his pinstriped trousers and perched a hip on the corner of his desk. 'Just reacted? The way they taught you at the Bureau.'

He was obsessed with the fact that she had been an agent in what she now deemed a past life. Kate could only imagine the lewd fantasies that crawled like slugs through his mind. Dominatrix games, black leather, handcuffs, spanking. *Bleeehhhh.*

She turned her attention to her immediate boss, the director of the legal services unit, who had taken the chair next to hers. Rob Marshall was Sabin's opposite image – doughy, dumpy, rumpled. He had a head as round as a pumpkin, crowned with a thinning layer of hair cropped so short, it gave more the appearance of a rust stain than a haircut. His face was ruddy and ravaged by old acne scars, and his nose was too short.

He'd been her boss for about eighteen months, having come to Minneapolis from a similar position in Madison, Wisconsin. During that time they had tried with limited success to find a balance between their personalities and working styles. Kate flat-out didn't like him. Rob was a spineless suckup and he had a tendency to micromanage that rubbed hard against her sense of autonomy. He found her bossy, opinionated, and impertinent. She took it as a compliment. But she tried to let his concern for victims offset his faults. In addition to his administrative duties, he often sat in on conferences with victims, and put in time with a victim's support group.

He squinted at her now from behind a pair of rimless glasses, his mouth pursing as if he'd just bitten his tongue. 'You could have been killed. Why didn't you just call for security?'

'There wasn't time.'

'Instinct, Rob!' Sabin said, flashing large white teeth. 'I'm sure you and I could never hope to understand the kind of razor-sharp instincts someone with Kate's background has honed.'

Kate refrained from reminding him yet again that she had spent most of her years with the FBI at a desk in the Behavioral Sciences Unit at the National Center for the Analysis of Violent Crime. Her days in the field were longer ago than she cared to remember.

'The mayor will want to give you an award,' Sabin said brightly, knowing he would get in on the photo op.

Publicity was the last thing Kate wanted. As an advocate, it was her job to hold the hands of crime victims and witnesses, to shepherd them through the justice system, to reassure them. The idea of an advocate being chased down by media hounds was likely to spook some of her clients.

'I'd rather she didn't. I don't think it's the best idea for someone with my job. Right, Rob?'

'Kate's right, Mr Sabin,' he said, flashing his obsequious smile – an expression that often overtook his face when he was nervous. Kate called it the bootlicker's grin. It made his eyes nearly disappear. 'We don't want her picture in the paper ... all things considered.'

'I suppose not,' Sabin said, disappointed. 'At any rate, what happened this morning isn't why we've called you in, Kate. We're assigning you a witness.'

'Why all the fanfare?'

Most of her client assignments were automatic. She worked with six prosecuting attorneys and caught everything they charged – the exception being homicides. Rob assigned all homicides, but an assignment never warranted anything more than a phone call or a visit to her office. Sabin certainly never involved himself with the process.

'Are you familiar with the two prostitute murders we've had this fall?' Sabin asked. 'The ones where the bodies were burned?'

'Yes, of course.'

'There's been another one. Last night.'

Kate looked from one grim face to the other. Behind Sabin she had a panoramic view of downtown Minneapolis from twenty-two stories up.

'This one wasn't a prostitute,' she said.

'How did you know that?'

Because you'd never take time out of your day if it was.

'Lucky guess.'

'You didn't hear it on the street?'

'On the street?' Like he was in a gangster movie. 'No. I wasn't aware there'd been a murder.'

Sabin walked around behind his desk, suddenly restless. 'There's a chance this victim was Jillian Bondurant. Her father is Peter Bondurant.'

'Oh,' Kate said with significance. Oh, no, this wasn't just another dead hooker. Never mind that the first two victims had fathers somewhere too. This one's father was *important*.

Rob shifted uncomfortably in his chair, though whether it was the case or the fact that he insisted on wearing his pants too small around the waist was unclear. 'Her driver's license was left near the body.'

'And it's been confirmed that she's missing?'

'She had dinner with her father at his home Friday night. She hasn't been seen since.'

'That doesn't mean it's her.'

'No, but that's the way it worked with the first two,' Sabin said. 'The ID left with each hooker's body matched up.'

A hundred questions shot through Kate's mind, questions about the crime scene, about what information the police had released about the first two murders and what had been held back. This was the first she'd heard about the IDs being left at the scene. What did that mean? Why burn the bodies beyond recognition, yet leave the victim's identity right there?

'I assume they're checking dental records,' she said.

The men exchanged looks.

'I'm afraid that's not an option,' Rob said carefully. 'We have a body *only*.'

'Jesus,' Kate breathed as a chill ran through her. 'He didn't decapitate the others. I never heard that.'

'No, he didn't,' Rob said. He squinted again and tipped his head a little to one side. 'What do you make of it, Kate? You've had experience with this kind of thing.'

'Obviously, his level of violence is escalating. It could mean he's gearing up for something big. There was some sexual mutilation with the others, right?'

'The cause of death on the other two was ruled strangulation by ligature,' Sabin said. 'I'm sure I don't need to tell you, Kate, that while strangulation is certainly a violent enough method of murder, a decapitation will throw this city into a panic. Particularly if the victim was a decent, law-abiding young woman. My God, the daughter of one of the most prominent men in the state. We need to find this killer fast. And we can make that happen. We've got a witness.'

'And this is where I come in,' Kate said. 'What's the story?'

'Her name is Angie DiMarco,' Rob said. 'She came running out of the park just as the first radio car arrived.'

'Who called it in?'

'Anonymous caller on a cell phone, I'm told,' Sabin said. His mouth tightened and twisted as if he were sucking at a sore tooth. 'Peter Bondurant is a friend of the mayor's. I know him as well. He's beside himself with grief at the idea that this victim is Jillian, and he wants this case solved ASAP. A task force is being put together even as we speak. Your old friends at the Bureau have been called. They're sending someone from the Investigative Support Unit. We clearly have a serial killer on our hands.'

And a prominent businessman up your butts.

'Rumors are already flying,' Sabin muttered darkly. 'The police department has a leak big enough to drain the Mississippi.'

The phone on his desk was lighting up like the switchboard on a disease telethon, though it never audibly rang.

'I've spoken with Chief Greer and with the mayor,' he continued. 'We're grabbing this thing by the short hairs right now.'

'That's why we've called you in, Kate,' Rob said, shifting in his chair again. 'We can't wait until there's been an arrest to assign someone to this witness. She's the only link we have to the killer. We want someone from the unit attached to her right away. Someone to sit with her during police interviews. Someone to let her know not to talk to the press. Someone to maintain the thread of contact between her and the county attorney's office. Someone to keep tabs on her.'

'It sounds like what you want is a baby-sitter. I've got cases ongoing.'

'We'll shift some of your caseload.'

'Not Willis,' she said, then grimaced. 'As much as I'd like to dump him. And absolutely not Melanie Hessler.'

'I could take Hessler, Kate,' Rob insisted. 'I sat in on the initial meeting. I'm familiar with the case.'

'No.'

'I've worked with plenty of rape victims.'

'No,' she said as if she were the boss and the decision was hers to make. Sabin looked annoyed. 'What case is this?'

'Melanie Hessler. She was raped by two men in the alley behind the adult bookstore she works in downtown,' Kate explained. 'She's very fragile, and she's terrified about the trial. She couldn't take me abandoning her – especially not to a man. She needs me. I won't let her go.'

Rob huffed a sigh.

'Fine,' Sabin declared impatiently. 'But this case is priority one. I don't care what it takes. I want this lunatic out of business. Now.'

Now that the victim would garner more than a minute and a half on the six o'clock news. Kate had to wonder how many dead prostitutes it would have taken to get Ted Sabin to feel that same level of urgency. But she kept the question to herself and nodded, and tried to ignore the sense of dread that settled in her stomach like a lead weight.

Just another witness, she told herself. Just another case. Back to the usual, familiar entanglements of her job.

Like hell.

A dead billionaire's daughter, a case full of politicos, a serial killer, and someone winging in from Quantico. Someone from ISU. Someone who hadn't been there five years ago, she had to hope – but knew that hope was a flimsy shield.

Suddenly, Las Vegas didn't seem so bad after all.

3

'This happened in the night. It was dark. How much could she have seen?' Kate asked.

The three of them walked together through the underground concourse that ran beneath Fifth Street and connected the government center to the depressing Gothic stone monstrosity that housed the Minneapolis city government offices and the Minneapolis police department. The underground corridor was busy. No one was going out onto the street voluntarily. The gloomy morning had turned dour as a leaden sky sank low above the city and let loose with a cold, steady rain. November: a lovely month in Minnesota.

'She told the police she saw him,' Rob said, trundling along beside her. His legs were short for his body, and hurrying gave him the toddling gait of a midget, even though he was of average height. 'We have to hope she saw him well enough to identify him.'

'I'd like a composite sketch in time for the press conference,' Sabin announced.

Kate ground her molars. Oh, yeah, this was going to be a peach of a case. 'A good sketch takes time, Ted. It pays to get it right.'

'Yes, well, the sooner we get a description out there, a picture out there, the better.'

In her mind's eye she could envision Sabin wringing information out of the witness, then tossing her aside like a rag.

'We'll do everything we can to expedite the situation, Mr Sabin,' Rob promised. Kate shot him a dirty look.

The city hall building had at one time in its history been the Hennepin County courthouse, and had been constructed with a sense of sober grandiosity to impress visitors. The Fourth Street entrance, which Kate seldom had cause to pass through, was as stunning as a palace, with a marble double grand staircase, incredible stained glass, and the enormous *Father of the Waters* sculpture. The main body of the building had always reminded her of an old hospital with its tiled floor and white marble wainscoting. There was forever a vacant feeling about the place, although

Kate knew it was all but bursting at the seams with cops and crooks, city officials and reporters and citizens looking for justice or a favor.

The criminal investigative division of the PD had been crammed into a gloomy warren of rooms at the end of a cavernous hall while remodeling went on in their usual digs. The reception area was cut up with temporary partitions. There were files and boxes stacked everywhere, beat-up dingy gray metal file cabinets had been pushed into every available corner. Tacked to the wall beside the door into the converted broom closet that now housed sex crimes investigators was a sign that proclaimed:

TURKEY WAKE!
NOVEMBER 27
PATRICK'S
1600 HRS

Sabin gave the receptionist a dismissive wave and took a right into the homicide offices. The room was a maze of ugly steel desks the color of dirty putty. Some desks were occupied, most were not. Some were neat, most were awash in paperwork. Notes and photographs and cartoons were tacked and taped to walls and cabinets. A notice on one side of the door ordered: HOMICIDE − LOCK UP YOUR GUNS!

Telephone receiver pressed to his ear, Sam Kovac spotted them, scowled, and waved them over. A twenty-two-year veteran, Kovac had that universal cop look about him with the requisite mustache and cheap haircut, both sandy brown and liberally threaded with silver.

'Yeah, I realize you're dating my second wife's sister, Sid.' He pulled a fresh pack of Salems from a carton on his desk and fumbled with the cellophane wrapper. He had shed the jacket of his rumpled brown suit and jerked his tie loose. 'That doesn't entitle you to inside information on this murder. All that'll get you is my sympathy. Yeah? Yeah? She said that? Well, why do you think I left her? Uh-huh. Uh-huh. Is that right?'

He bit at the tab on the cigarette wrapper and ripped the pack open with his teeth. 'You hear that, Sid? That's the sound of me tearing you a new one if you print a word of that. You understand me? You want information? Come to the press conference with everybody else. Yeah? Well, same to you.'

He slammed the receiver down and turned his scowl on the county attorney. His eyes were the green-brown of damp bark, bloodshot, and hard and bright with intelligence. 'Damn newsies. This is gonna get uglier than my aunt Selma, and she has a face that could make a bulldog puke.'

'Do they have Bondurant's name?' Sabin asked.

'Of course they do.' He pulled a cigarette from the pack and let it dangle from his lip as he rummaged through the junk on his desk. 'They're all over this like flies on dog crap,' he said, glancing back at them over his shoulder. 'Hi, Kate − Jesus, what happened to you?'

'Long story. I'm sure you'll hear it at Patrick's tonight. Where's our witness?'

'Down the hall.'

'Is she working with the sketch artist yet?' Sabin asked.

Kovac blew air between his lips and made a sound like a disgusted horse. 'She's not even working with *us* yet. Our citizen isn't exactly overjoyed to be the center of attention here.'

Rob Marshall looked alarmed. 'She's not a problem, is she?' He flashed the bootlicker's smile at Sabin. 'I suppose she's just shaken up, Mr Sabin. Kate will settle her down.'

'What's your take on the witness, Detective?' Sabin asked.

Kovac snatched up a Bic lighter and a messy file and started for the door. World-weary and nicked up, his build was at once solid and rangy, utilitarian rather than ornamental. His brown pants were a little baggy and a little too long, the cuffs puddling over the tops of his heel-worn oxfords.

'Oh, she's a daisy,' he said with sarcasm. 'She gives us what's gotta be a stolen out-of-state driver's license. Tells us she's living at an apartment in the Phillips neighborhood but she's got no keys for it and can't tell us who has. If she hasn't got a sheet, I'll shave my ass and paint it blue.'

'So, you ran her and what?' Kate asked, forcing herself to keep pace with him, so that Sabin and Rob had to fall in behind. She had learned long ago to cultivate friendships with the cops who worked her cases. It was to her advantage to have them as allies rather than adversaries. Besides, she liked the good ones, like Kovac. They did a hard job for little credit and not enough pay for the plain old-fashioned reason that they believed in the necessity of it. She and Kovac had built a nice rapport in five years.

'I tried to run the name she's using today,' he qualified. 'The fucking computer's down. Swell day this is gonna be. I'm on nights this rotation, you know. I oughta be home in bed. My *team* is on nights. I hate this team-concept crap. Give me a partner and leave me the hell alone. You know what I mean? I got half a mind to transfer out to sex crimes.'

'And turn your back on all this fame and glamour?' Kate teased, bumping him with a subtle elbow.

He gave her a look, tilting his head down in conspiracy. A spark of wry humor lit his eyes. 'Shit, Red. I like my stiffs uncomplicated, you know.'

'I've heard that about you, Sam,' she joked, knowing he was the best investigator in the PD, a straight-up good guy who lived the job and hated the politics of it.

He huffed a laugh and pulled open the door to a small room that looked into another through the murky glass of a one-way mirror. On the other side of the glass, Nikki Liska, another detective, stood leaning against one wall, eyes locked in a staredown with the girl who sat on the far side of the fake-woodgrain table. A bad sign. The situation had already become adversarial. The table was littered with soda cans and paper coffee cups and doughnut chunks and fragments.

The sense of dread in Kate's belly gained a pound as she stared through the glass. She put the girl at maybe fifteen or sixteen. Pale and thin, she had a button nose and the lush, ripe mouth of a high-priced call girl. Her face was a narrow oval, the chin a little too long, so that she would probably look defiant without trying. Her eyes tilted at an exotic Slavic angle, and looked twenty years too old.

'She's a kid,' Kate declared flatly, looking to Rob with confusion and accusation. 'I don't do kids. You know that.'

'We need you to do this one, Kate.'

'Why?' she demanded. 'You've got a whole juvenile division at your disposal. God knows they deal with murder on a regular basis.'

'This is different. This isn't some gang shoot-'em-up we're dealing with,' Rob said, seemingly relegating some of the most violent crime in the city to the same category as shoplifting and traffic mishaps. 'We're dealing with a serial killer.'

Even in a profession that dealt with murder as a matter of routine, the words *serial killer* struck a chord. Kate wondered if their bad guy was aware of that, if he reveled in the idea, or if he was too completely bound up in his own small world of hunting and killing. She had seen both types. All their victims ended up equally dead.

She turned from her director and looked again at the girl who had crossed paths with this latest predator. Angie DiMarco glared at the mirror, resentment pulsing from her in invisible waves. She picked up a fat black pen from the table and very deliberately drew the cap end slowly back and forth along her full lower lip in a gesture that was both impatient and sensuous.

Sabin gave Kate his profile as if he were posing for a currency engraver. 'You've dealt with this kind of case before, Kate. With the Bureau. You have a frame of reference. You know what to expect with the investigation and with the media. You may well know the agent they send from the Investigative Support Unit. That could be helpful. We need every edge we can get.'

'I studied victims. I dealt with dead people.' She didn't like the anxiety coming to life inside her. Didn't like having it, didn't want to examine its source. 'There's a big difference between working with a dead person and working with a kid. Last I heard, dead people were more cooperative than teenagers.'

'You're a witness advocate,' Rob said, his voice taking on a slight whine. 'She's a witness.'

Kovac, who had propped himself up against the wall to watch the exchange, gave her a wan smile. 'Can't pick your relatives or your witnesses, Red. I would have liked Mother Teresa to come running out of that park last night.'

'No, you wouldn't,' Kate returned. 'The defense would claim she had cataracts and Alzheimer's, and say anyone who believes a man can rise from the dead three days after the fact is a less than credible witness.'

Kovac's mustache twitched. 'Scum lawyers.'

Rob looked bemused. 'Mother Teresa's dead.'

Kate and Kovac rolled their eyes in unison.

Sabin cleared his throat and looked pointedly at his watch. 'We need to get going with this. I want to hear what she has to say.'

Kate arched a brow. 'And you think she'll just tell you? You don't get out of the office enough, Ted.'

'She'd damn well better tell us,' he said ominously, and started for the door.

Kate stared through the glass for one last moment, her eyes meeting those of her witness, even though she knew the girl couldn't see her. A teenager. Christ, they could just as well have assigned her a Martian. She was nobody's mother. And there was a reminder she didn't need or want.

She looked into the girl's pale face and saw anger and defiance and experience no kid that age should have. And she saw fear. Buried beneath everything else, held as tight inside her as a secret, there was fear. Kate didn't let herself acknowledge what it was inside her own soul that let her recognize that fear.

In the interview room, Angie DiMarco flicked a glance at Liska, who was looking at her watch. She turned her eyes back to the one-way glass and slipped the pilfered pen inside the neckline of her sweater.

'A kid,' Kate muttered as Sabin and Rob Marshall stepped out into the hall ahead of her. 'I wasn't even good at being one.'

'That's perfect,' Kovac said, holding the door open for her. 'Neither is she.'

Liska, short, blond, and athletic with a boy's haircut, rolled away from the wall and gave them all a weary smile as they entered the interview room. She looked like Tinker Bell on steroids – or so Kovac had declared when he christened her with the nickname Tinks.

'Welcome to the fun house,' she said. 'Coffee, anybody?'

'Decaf for me and one for our friend at the table, please, Nikki,' Kate said softly, never taking her eyes off the girl, trying to formulate a strategy.

Kovac spilled himself into a chair and leaned against the table with one arm, his blunt-tipped fingers scratching at chocolate sprinkles that lay scattered like mouse turds on the tabletop.

'Kate, this is Angie DiMarco,' he said casually. 'Angie, this is Kate Conlan from the victim/witness program. She's being assigned to your case.'

'I'm not a case,' the girl snapped. 'Who are they?'

'County Attorney Ted Sabin and Rob Marshall from victim/witness.' Kovac pointed to one and then the other as the men took seats across the table from their prized witness.

Sabin gave her his best Ward Cleaver expression. 'We're very interested in what you have to say, Angie. This killer we're after is a dangerous man.'

'No shit.' The girl turned back to Kovac. Her glare homed in on his mouth. 'Can I have a smoke?'

He pulled the cigarette from his lips and looked at it. 'Hell, *I* can't even have one,' he confessed. 'It's a smoke-free building. I was going outside with this.'

'That sucks. I'm stuck in this fucking room half the fucking night and I can't even have a fucking cigarette!'

She sat back and crossed her arms over her chest. Her brown hair was oily and parted down the middle, falling loose around her shoulders. She wore too much mascara, which had smudged beneath her eyes, and a faded Calvin Klein denim jacket that had once belonged to someone named Rick. The name was printed in indelible ink above the left breast pocket. She kept the jacket on despite the fact that the room was warm. Security or hiding needle tracks, Kate figured.

'Oh, for godsake, Sam, give her a cigarette,' Kate said, shoving up the sleeves of her sweater. She took the vacant chair on the girl's side of the table. 'And give me one too, while you're at it. If the PC Nazis catch us, we'll all go down together. What're they gonna do? Ask us to leave this rat hole?'

She watched the girl out of the corner of her eye as Kovac shook two more cigarettes out of the pack. Angie's fingernails were bitten to the quick and painted metallic ice blue. Her hand trembled as she took the gift. She wore an assortment of cheap silver rings, and two small, crude ballpoint tattoos marred her pale skin – a cross near her thumb, and the letter A with a horizontal line across the top. A professional job circled her wrist, a delicate blue ink bracelet of thorns.

'You've been here all night, Angie?' Kate asked, drawing on the cigarette. It tasted like dried shit. She couldn't imagine why she had ever taken up the habit in her college days. The price of cool, she supposed. And now it was the price of bonding.

'Yes.' Angie fired a stream of smoke up at the ceiling. 'And they wouldn't get me a lawyer either.'

'You don't need a lawyer, Angie,' Kovac said congenially. 'You're not being charged with anything.'

'Then why can't I blow this shithole?'

'We got a lot of complications to sort out. For instance, the matter of your identification.'

'I *gave* you my ID.'

He pulled it from the file and handed it to Kate with a meaningful lift of his eyebrows.

'You're twenty-one,' Kate read deadpan, flicking ashes into an abandoned cup of oily coffee.

'That's what it says.'

'It says you're from Milwaukee –'

'*Was.* I left.'

'Any family there?'

'They're dead.'

'I'm sorry.'

'I doubt it.'

'Any family here? Aunts, uncles, cousins, half-related circus freaks? Anyone at all we could call for you – to help you through this?'

'No. I'm an orphan. Poor me.' She bluffed a sarcastic laugh. 'Trust me, I don't need any family.'

'You've got no permanent address, Angie,' Kovac said. 'You have to realize what's happened here. You're the only one who can identify a killer. We need to know where you're at.'

She rolled her eyes in the way only teenage girls can, imparting both incredulity and impatience. 'I *gave* you my address.'

'You gave me the address for an apartment you don't have keys for and you can't tell me the name of who it is you're staying with.'

'I *told* you!'

She pushed up out of her chair and turned away from Kovac, the cigarette in her hand raining ashes on the floor. The blue sweater she wore beneath her jacket was either cropped short or shrunken, revealing a pierced navel and another tattoo – three drops of blood falling into the waistband of her dirty jeans.

'Her name is Molly,' she said. 'I met her at a party and she said that I could crash at her place until I get my own.'

Kate caught the hint of a tremor in the girl's voice, the defensive body language as she pulled in on herself and turned away from them. Across the room, the door opened and Liska came in with the coffee.

'Angie, no one's trying to jam you up here,' Kate said. 'Our first concern is that you're safe.'

The girl wheeled on her, her eyes dark blue and glittering with anger. 'Your *concern* is that I testify against this psycho Cremator creep. You think I'm nuts? He'll track me down and kill me too!'

'Your cooperation is imperative, Angie,' Sabin said with authority. The man in command. 'You're our only witness. This man has killed three women that we know of.'

Kate shot a dagger look at the county attorney.

'Part of my job is to see to it that you're safe, Angie,' she explained, keeping her voice even and calm. 'If you need a place to stay, we can make that happen. Do you have a job?'

'No.' She turned away again. 'I been looking,' she added almost defensively. She gravitated toward the corner of the room, where a dirty backpack had been discarded. Kate was willing to bet everything the kid owned was in that bag.

'It's tough coming into a new town,' Kate said quietly. 'Don't know your way around. Don't have any connections. Hard to get set up, get your life going.'

The girl bowed her head and chewed at a thumbnail, her hair swinging down to obscure her face.

'It takes money to set yourself up,' Kate went on. 'Money to eat. Money for a place. Money for clothes. Money for everything.'

'I get by.'

Kate could imagine just how. She knew how it worked with kids on the street. They did what they had to do to survive. Beg. Steal. Sell a little dope. Turn a trick or two or ten. There was no shortage of depraved human scum in the world more than willing to prey on kids with no homes and no prospects.

Liska set the steaming coffee cups on the table and leaned down to murmur in Kovac's ear. 'Elwood tracked down the building manager. The guy says the apartment's vacant and if this kid is living there, then he wants a five-hundred-dollar deposit or he'll press charges for criminal trespass.'

'What a humanitarian.'

'Elwood says to him, "Five hundred? What's that? A buck a cockroach?"'

Kate absorbed the whispered remarks, her eyes still on Angie 'Your life's tough enough right now without having to become a witness to a murder.'

Head still down, the girl sniffed and brought the cigarette to her lips. 'I didn't see him kill her.'

'What *did* you see?' Sabin demanded. 'We need to know, Miss DiMarco. Every minute that passes is crucial to the investigation. This man is a serial killer.'

'I think we're all aware of that, Ted,' Kate conceded with a razor's edge in her voice. 'You really don't have to remind us every two minutes.'

Rob Marshall twitched hard. Sabin met her gaze, his own impatience showing. He wanted a revelation before he bolted for his meeting with the mayor. He wanted to be able to step in front of the cameras at the press conference and give the monster loose among them a name and a face and announce that an arrest was imminent.

'Angie seems to be having some difficulty deciding whether to cooperate or not,' he said. 'I think it's important she realize the gravity of the situation.'

'She watched someone set a human body on fire. I think she understands the gravity of the situation perfectly.'

In the corner of her eye, Kate could see she had caught the girl's attention. Maybe they could be friends living on the street together after Sabin fired her for challenging him in front of an audience. What was she thinking? She didn't even want this mess in her lap.

'What were you doing in that park at that hour of night, Angie?' Rob asked, mopping at his forehead with a handkerchief.

The girl looked him square in the face. 'Minding my own fucking business.'

'You can take your coat off if you want,' he said with a brittle smile.
'I don't want.'

His jaw clenched and the grin became more of a grimace. 'That's fine. If you want to keep it on, that's fine. It just seems hot in here. Why don't you tell us in your own way how you came to be in that park last night, Angie.'

She stared at him with venom in her eyes. 'I'd tell you to kiss my ass, but you're so fucking ugly, I'd make you pay in advance.'

His face flushed as red as a bad rash.

A beeper went off and everyone in the room except the witness reached for theirs. Sabin scowled darkly as he read the message in the display window of his. He checked his watch again.

'Did you get a good look at the man, Angie?' Rob asked in a tight voice. 'You could be such a help here. I know you've gone through something terrible –'

'You don't know shit,' the girl snapped.

A vein popped out in Rob's left temple and sweat beaded on his shiny forehead.

'That's why we're asking you, kiddo,' Kate said calmly. She blew a lazy stream of smoke. All the time in the world. 'Did you get a good look at the guy?'

Angie studied her for a moment, the time and the silence stretching, then looked to Sabin to Liska to Kovac, and back to Rob Marshall. Gauging. Assessing.

'I saw him in the flames,' she said at last, dropping her gaze to the floor. 'He lit the body on fire and he said, "Ashes to ashes."'

'Would you know him if you saw him again?' Sabin demanded.

'Sure,' she murmured, bringing the cigarette to her lips for one final drag. The tip of it glowed like an ember from hell against the pale white of her face. When she spoke again, it was on a breath of smoke. 'He's the devil.'

'What was that about?' Kate went on the offensive the second they stepped from the interview room into the hall.

Sabin turned on her, his expression furious. 'I was about to ask you the same thing, Kate. We need this girl's cooperation.'

'And you think you're going to get it by coming down on her like a ton of bricks? In case you didn't notice, she wasn't responding.'

'How could she respond with you butting in every time I started making some headway?'

'Force meets resistance, Ted. And it's my job to butt in – I'm an advocate,' she said, realizing she was inviting the wrath of a very powerful man. He had the power to take her off this case.

I should be so lucky, she thought. Already this investigation had the makings of a world-class cluster fuck. She couldn't possibly want to be stuck in the middle of it.

'You're the one who dragged me into this,' she said. 'You want me to be this girl's friend, remember? That's going to be a tough enough job without you setting us up as a group force against her.

'She has to want to tell us what she saw. She has to believe we'll take care of her. Do you honestly think she trusts you not to take what she has to give and cut her loose? How do you think a kid like Angie ends up in a mess like this in the first place?'

'You didn't want this case because she's a kid,' Sabin said irritably. 'Now suddenly you're an authority.'

'You wanted me on this because of my expertise, my frame of reference,' she reminded him. 'Then you have to trust me to do the job. I know how to interview a witness.'

Sabin dismissed her by turning to Kovac. 'You said the girl was apprehended fleeing the scene?'

'Not exactly.'

'She ran out of the park as the first unit arrived,' he said impatiently. 'She was running away from a burning body. That makes her a suspect. Shake her down. Rattle her. Threaten her. Scare the truth out of her. I don't care how you do it. I've got a meeting in two minutes with the chief and the mayor. The press conference is set for five. I want a description of a killer by then.'

He walked away from them, straightening his jacket, moving his shoulders like a boxer who'd just gone five rounds. Kate looked to Kovac, who made a sour face.

'See the kind of shit I have to put up with?' he said.

'*You?*' Kate sniffed. 'He could fire my ass. And still I don't care if he's on his way to a tryst with Janet Reno. Power doesn't give him license to harass a witness – or for you to do it for him. If you run over this kid with hobnail boots, I'll make your life a misery, Sam.'

Kovac grimaced. 'Jesus, Kate, the big dog says toss her in the can. What am I gonna do? Thumb my nose at him? He'll have my *cojones* in his nutcracker for Christmas.'

'I'll use 'em for tennis.'

'Sorry, Kate. You're overruled. Sabin can castrate me *and* my pension. Look on the bright side: The tank'll be like Club Med to this chick.'

Kate turned to her boss for support. Rob shifted his weight from one foot to the other. 'These circumstances are extraordinary, Kate.'

'I realize that. I also realize that if this kid hadn't watched our psycho light up one of those hookers, there wouldn't be a press conference pending and Ted Sabin wouldn't even know her name. But that doesn't change what she saw, Rob. It doesn't change who she is or how she needs to be handled. She expects to be treated badly. It gives her an excuse to be uncooperative.'

His expression was a cross between wry and wrenched. 'I thought you didn't want this case.'

'I don't,' Kate said flatly. 'I have no personal desire to be ass deep in alligators, but if I'm in this thing, then I'm in it all the way. Let me do my job with her or assign me elsewhere. I won't be a puppet and I won't have my hands tied. Not even by his high and mightiness.'

It was a bluff of sorts. She may not have wanted the job, but she was the best advocate for the job – or so Ted Sabin thought. Sabin with his hard-on for the idea of her as an FBI agent. As much as the obsession disgusted her, Kate knew it gave her a certain amount of leverage with him and therefore with Rob.

The real question was: What would it cost her? And why should she care enough to pay the price? She could smell the stench of this case a block away, could feel the potential entanglements touching her like the tentacles of an octopus. She should have cut and run. If she'd had any sense. If she hadn't looked past Angie DiMarco's defenses and glimpsed the fear.

'What's Sabin gonna do, Rob?' she questioned. 'Cut off our heads and set us on fire?'

'That's not even remotely funny.'

'I didn't mean for it to be. Have some backbone and stand up to him, for Christ's sake.'

Rob sighed and discreetly pried a thumb inside the waistband of his slacks. 'I'll talk to him and see what I can do. Maybe the girl will come up with an ID from the mug books by five,' he said without hope.

'You must still have connections in Wisconsin,' Kate said. 'Maybe you can get a line on her, find out who she really is.'

'I'll make some calls. Is that all?' he asked pointedly.

Kate pretended innocence. She was well aware of her tendency to lead the dance, and perfectly unapologetic about it where her boss was concerned. He never inspired her to follow.

Rob walked away looking defeated.

'Ever the man of action, your boss,' Kovac said dryly.

'I think Sabin keeps his *cojones* in a jar in his medicine cabinet.'

'Yeah, well, I don't want mine added to the collection. See if you can get something out of this kid besides lies and sarcasm before five.' He clamped a hand on Kate's shoulder in congratulation and consolation. 'Way to go, Red. The job's all yours.'

Kate frowned as she watched him retreat to the men's room. 'And I ask yet again: Why do I always have to be the one in the wrong place at the wrong time?'

4

Supervisory special agent John Quinn walked out of the jetway and into the Minneapolis-St Paul airport. It looked like nearly every other airport he'd ever seen: gray and cheerless, the only sign of emotion rising above the grim and travel-weary being the celebration of a family welcoming home a boy with a buzz cut and a blue air force uniform.

He felt a flicker of envy, a feeling that seemed as old as he was – forty-four. His own family had been geared for contention, not celebration. He hadn't seen them in years. Too busy, too distant, too detached. Too ashamed of them, his old man would have said . . . and he would have been right.

He spotted the field agent standing at the edge of the gate area. Vince Walsh. According to the file, he was fifty-two with a solid record. He would retire in June. He looked an unhealthy sixty-two. His complexion was the color of modeling clay, and gravity had pulled the flesh of his face down, leaving deep crevices in his cheeks and across his forehead. He had the look of a man with too much stress in his life and no way out but a heart attack. He had the look of a man who would rather have been doing something other than picking up some hotshot mind hunter from Quantico.

Quinn forced his energy level up along with the corners of his mouth. React accordingly: look apologetic, nonaggressive, nonthreatening; just a touch of friendliness, but not overly familiar. His shoulders were drooping naturally with fatigue; he didn't bother to square them up. 'You're Walsh?'

'You're Quinn,' Walsh declared flatly as Quinn started to pull his ID from the interior pocket of his suit coat. 'Got luggage?'

'Just what you see.' A bulging garment bag that exceeded regulation carry-on dimensions and a briefcase weighed down with a laptop computer and a ream of paperwork. Walsh made no offer to take either.

'I appreciate the ride,' Quinn said as they started down the concourse. 'It's the quickest way for me to get right in the game. Eliminates me driving around lost for an hour.'

'Fine.'

Fine. Not a great start, but there it was. He'd work the guy around as they went. The important thing here was to hit the ground running. The case was the priority. Always the case. One after another, on top of another, with another and another around the bend . . . The fatigue shuddered down through him, giving his stomach a kick as it went.

They walked in silence to the main terminal, took the elevator up one floor, and crossed over the street to the parking ramp where Walsh had left his Taurus parked illegally in a handicapped slot. Quinn dumped his stuff in the trunk and sat back for the ride out to the highway. Cigarette smoke had permeated the car's interior and gave the beige upholstery the same gray cast as the car's driver.

Walsh reached for a pack of Chesterfields as they hit state highway five. He hooked his lip over the cigarette and pulled it out of the pack. 'You mind?'

He flicked a lighter without waiting for a reply.

Quinn cracked the window a slit. 'It's your car.'

'For seven more months.' He lit up, sucked in a lungful of tar and nicotine, and stifled a cough. 'Christ, I can't shake this damn cold.'

'Filthy weather,' Quinn offered. Or lung cancer.

The sky seemed to press down over Minneapolis like an anvil. Rain and forty-three degrees. All vegetation had gone dormant or had died and would stay that way until spring – which he suspected was a depressingly long way off in this place. At least in Virginia there were signs of life by March.

'Could be worse,' Walsh said. 'Could be a goddamn blizzard. Had one here on Halloween a few years back. What a mess. Must have been ten feet of snow that winter and it wasn't gone till May. I hate this place.'

Quinn didn't ask why he stayed. He didn't want to hear the common litany against the Bureau or the common complaints of the unhappily married man with in-laws in the vicinity, or any other reason a man like Walsh hated his life. He had his own problems – which Vince Walsh would not want to hear about either. 'There's no such place as Utopia, Vince.'

'Yeah, well, Scottsdale comes close enough. I never want to be cold again as long as I live. Come June, I'm out of here. Out of this place. Out of this thankless job.'

He glanced at Quinn with suspicion, as if he figured him for some Bureau stoolie who would be on the phone to the special agent in charge the second he was left alone.

'The job can wear on a man,' Quinn commiserated. 'The politics is what gets to me,' he said, picking the hot nerve with unerring accuracy. 'Working in the field, you get it from both ends – the locals *and* the Bureau.'

'That's a fact. I wish to hell I could have blown out of here for good yesterday. This case is gonna be nothing but one kick in the ass after another.'

'Has that started already?'

'You're here, aren't you?'

Walsh picked up a file folder from the seat between them and handed it over. 'The crime scene photos. Knock yourself out.'

Quinn took the file without taking his dark eyes off Walsh. 'You have a problem with me being here, Vince?' he asked bluntly, softening the question with an expression that was part I'm-your-buddy smile, part confusion that he didn't feel. He'd been in this situation so many times, he knew every possible reaction to his arrival on the scene: genuine welcome, hypocritical welcome, cloaked annoyance, open hostility. Walsh was a number three who would have claimed he said exactly what he thought.

'Hell no,' he said at last. 'If we don't nail this scumbag ASAP, we're all gonna be running around with targets on our backs. I got no problem with you having a bigger one than me.'

'It's still your case. I'm here as support.'

'Funny. I said the same thing to the homicide lieutenant.'

Quinn said nothing, already starting to lay out a team strategy in his mind. It looked like he might have to work around Walsh, although it seemed unlikely that the ASAC (assistant special agent in charge) here would have assigned a less than stellar agent to this case. If Peter Bondurant could make top dogs in Washington bark, the locals weren't apt to antagonize the man. According to the faxes, Walsh had a solid rep that spanned a lot of years. Maybe a few too many years, a few too many cases, a few too many political games.

Quinn already had a picture of the political situation here. The body count was three – just meeting the official standard to be considered serial murders. Ordinarily he would have been consulted by phone at this stage – if he was consulted at all. In his experience, locals usually tried to handle this kind of thing themselves until they were slightly deeper in dead bodies. And with a case load of eighty-five, he had to prioritize worst to least. A three-murder case rarely made his travel schedule. His physical presence here seemed unnecessary – which aggravated his frustration and his exhaustion. He closed his eyes for two seconds, reining the feelings back into their corral.

'Your Mr Bondurant has friends in very high places,' he said. 'What's the story with him?'

'He's your basic nine-hundred-pound gorilla. Owns a computer outfit that has a lot of defense contracts – Paragon. He's been making noises about moving it out of state, which has the governor and every other politician in the state lining up to kiss his ass. They say he's worth a billion dollars or more.'

'Have you met him?'

'No. He didn't bother to go through our office to get to you. I hear he went straight to the top.'

And in a matter of hours the FBI had Quinn on a plane to Minneapolis. No consideration to the normal assignment of cases by region. No consideration to the cases he had ongoing. None of the usual bureaucratic bullshit entanglements over travel authorizations.

He wondered sourly if Bondurant had asked for him by name. He'd been in the spotlight a hell of a lot in the last year. Not by his own choosing. The press liked his image. He fit their profile of what a special agent from the Investigative Support Unit should look like: athletic, square-jawed, dark, intense. He took a good picture, looked good on television, George Clooney would play him in the movies. Some days the image was useful. Some days he found it amusing. More and more it was just a pain in the ass.

'He didn't waste any time,' Walsh went on. 'The girl's not even cold yet. They don't even know for a fact it's his kid – what with the head gone and all. But you know, people with money don't screw around. They don't have to.'

'Where are we at with the ID on the victim?'

'They've got her DL. They're going to try to get her fingerprints, but the hands were pretty badly burned, I'm told. The ME has requested Jillian Bondurant's medical history regarding any distinguishing marks or broken bones to see if anything matches up. We know the body is the right size and build. We know Jillian Bondurant had dinner with her father Friday night. She left his house around midnight and hasn't been seen since.'

'What about her car?'

'No one's found it yet. Autopsy's scheduled for tonight. Maybe they'll get lucky and be able to match the body's stomach contents with the meal Bondurant and her father had that night, but I doubt it. She'd have had to have been killed almost right away. That's not how this sicko operates.

'The press conference is at five – not that the press is waiting for it,' he went on. 'They've been all over the air with the story. They've already given this scumbag a nickname. They're calling him the Cremator. Catchy, huh?'

'I'm told they're drawing correlations to some murders from a couple of years ago. Is there any connection?'

'The Wirth Park murders. No connection, but a couple of similarities. Those victims were black women – and one Asian transvestite he got by mistake. Prostitutes or supposed prostitutes – and this guy's first two vics were prostitutes. But there's always someone killing prostitutes. They're easy targets. Those vics were mostly black and these are white. That right there points to a different killer – right?'

'Sexual serial killers generally stay within their own ethnic group, yes.'

'Anyway, they got a conviction on one of those Wirth Park murders and closed the books on the others. They got their killer, there just wasn't enough physical evidence to go to trial on all the cases. Besides, how many life sentences can a guy serve?

'I talked to one of the homicide dicks this morning,' Walsh said, crushing out the stub of his cigarette in the filthy ashtray. 'He says there's no doubt about it, this is definitely a different scumbag. But to tell you the truth, I don't know much more about these murders than you. Until this morning all they had were two dead hookers. I read about them in the paper just like everyone else. I sure as hell know the other guy never cut anybody's head off. That's a new twist for this neck of the woods.'

The dark play on words struck him belatedly, and he made a little huffing sound and shook his head at the bad joke.

Quinn looked out the window at the gray and the rain, the winter-dead trees as black and bleak as if they'd been charred, and observed a moment of sympathy for the nameless, faceless victims not important enough to warrant anything but a label. In their lives they had known joy and sorrow. On the way to their deaths they had likely known terror and pain. They had families and friends who would mourn them and miss them. But the press and society at large whittled their lives and their deaths down to the lowest, lowliest common denominator: two dead hookers. Quinn had seen a hundred . . . and he remembered every one.

Sighing, he rubbed at the dull headache that had taken up semipermanent residence in his frontal lobes. He was too tired for the kind of diplomacy needed at the start of a case. This was the kind of tired that went to the marrow of his bones and weighed him down like lead. There had been too many bodies in the last few years. Their names scrolled through his mind at night when he tried to sleep. Counting corpses, he called it. Not the kind of thing that inspired sweet dreams.

'You want to go to your hotel first or to the office?' Walsh asked.

As if what he wanted had anything to do with it. What he wanted in life had gone out of sight for him long ago.

'I have to go to the crime scene,' he said, the unopened folder of photographs as heavy as a steel plate on his lap. 'I need to see where he left her.'

The park looked like a campsite the day after a Cub Scout jamboree. The charred ground where the fire had been, the yellow tape strung from tree to tree like bunting to fence off the area; the dead grass trampled down, leaves pressed into the ground like wet paper cutouts. Crumpled paper coffee cups had blown out of the trash can that sat just off the blacktop trail on the hillside and skittered across the ground.

Walsh parked the car and they got out and stood on the blacktop, Quinn scanning the entire area from north to south. The crime scene was slightly below them in a shallow bowl of ground that had afforded excellent cover. The park was studded with trees, both deciduous and evergreen. By dead of night this would be a small world all its own. The nearest residences – neat middle-class single-family homes – were well away from the crime scene, the skyscrapers of downtown Minneapolis several miles to the north. Even the small service lot where they were parked was obscured from view by trees and what was likely a beautiful row of lilacs in the spring – camouflage to hide a small locked utility shed and the park maintenance vehicles that came and went as needed.

Their UNSUB (unknown subject) had likely parked here and carried the body down the hill for his little ceremony. Quinn looked up at the sodium vapor security light that topped a dark pole near the utility shed. The glass had been shattered, but there were no visible fragments of it on the ground.

'We know how long that light's been out?'

Walsh looked up, blinking and grimacing as the rain hit him in the face. 'You'll have to ask the cops.'

A couple of days, Quinn bet. Not long enough that the park service would have gotten around to fixing it. If the damage was the work of their man in preparation for his midnight call . . . If he had come here in advance, knocked out the light, cleaned up the glass to help avoid detection of the vandalism and thereby improve his odds that the security light would not be replaced quickly . . . if all of that was true, they were dealing with a strong degree of planning and premeditation. And experience. MO was learned behavior. A criminal learned by trial and error what to do and what not to do in the commission of his crimes. He improved his methods with time and repetition.

Ignoring the rain that pelted down on his bare head, Quinn hunched his shoulders inside his trench coat and started down the hill, conscious that the killer would have taken this route with a body in his arms. It was a fair distance – fifty or sixty yards. The crime scene unit would have the exact measurements. It took strength to carry a dead weight that far. The time of death would have determined how he had carried her. Over the shoulder would have been easiest – if rigor had not yet set in, or if it had come and gone already. If he had been able to carry her over his shoulder, then his size could vary more; a smaller man could accomplish the task. If he had to carry her in his arms, he would had to have been larger. Quinn hoped they would know more after the autopsy.

'What did the crime scene unit cover?' he asked, the words coming out of his mouth on a cloud of steam.

Walsh hustled along three paces behind him, coughing. 'Everything. This whole section of park, including the parking area and the utility shed. The homicide guys called in their own Bureau of Investigation crime scene people and the mobile lab from the Minnesota Bureau of Criminal Apprehension as well. They were very thorough.'

'When did this rain start?'

'This morning.'

'Shit,' Quinn grumbled. 'Last night – would the ground have been hard or soft?'

'Like a rock. They didn't get any shoe prints. They picked up some garbage – scraps of paper, cigarette butts, like that. But hell, it's a public park. The stuff could have come from anyone.'

'Anything distinguishing left at the first two scenes?'

'The victims' driver's licenses. Other than that, nothing to my knowledge.'

'Who's doing the lab work?'

'BCA. Their facilities are excellent.'

'I've heard that.'

'They're aware they can contact the FBI lab if they need help or clarification on anything.'

Quinn pulled up just short of the charred ground where the body had been left, a thick, dark sense of oppression closing tight around his chest as it always did at a crime scene. He had never tried to discern whether the feeling was anything as mystical or romantic as the notion of a malingering sense of evil, or something as psychologically profound as displaced guilt. The feeling was just a part of him. He supposed he should have welcomed it as some proof of his humanity. After all the bodies he'd seen, he had yet to become totally hardened.

Then again, he might have been better off if he had.

For the first time, he opened the folder Walsh had given him and looked at the photographs someone had had the foresight to slip into plastic protectors. The tableau presented might have made the average person recoil. Portable halogen lights had been set up near the body to illuminate both the night and the corpse, giving the photo a weirdly artistic quality. As did the charring of the flesh, and the melted fabric of the woman's clothing. Color against the absence of color; the fanciful vibrance of a triangle of undamaged red skirt against the grim reality of its wearer's violent death.

'Were the others wearing clothes?'

'I don't know.'

'I'll want to see those photos too. I'll want to see everything they've got. You have my list?'

'I faxed a copy to the homicide detectives. They'll try to have it all together for the task force meeting. Hell of a sight, isn't it?' Walsh nodded to the photograph. 'Enough to put a person off barbecue.'

Quinn made no comment as he further studied the photo. Because of the heat of the fire, the muscles and tendons of the limbs had contracted, pulling the victim's arms and legs into what was technically known as a pugilistic attitude – a position that suggested animation. A suggestion made macabre by the absence of the head.

Surreal, he thought. His brain wanted to believe he was looking at a discarded mannequin, something that had been dragged too late out of the incinerator at Macy's. But he knew what he was looking at had been flesh and bone, not plastic, and she had been alive and walking around three days earlier. She had eaten meals, listened to music, talked with friends, attended to the boring minutiae of the average life, never imagining that hers was nearly over.

The body had been positioned with the feet pointing toward downtown, which Quinn thought might have been more significant if the head had also been posed or buried nearby. One of the more infamous cases he had studied years before had included the decapitation of two victims. The killer, Ed Kemper, had buried the heads in the backyard of his family home, beneath his mother's bedroom window. A sick private joke, Kemper had later admitted. His mother, who had emotionally abused him from boyhood, had 'always wanted people to look up to her,' he'd said.

The head of this victim had not been found and the ground was too hard for the killer to have buried it here.

'There're a lot of theories on why he's burning them,' Walsh said. He bounced a little on the balls of his feet, trying unsuccessfully to keep the cold from knifing into his bones. 'Some people think he's just a copycat of the Wirth Park murders. Some people think it's symbolism: Whores of the world burn in hell – that kind of thing. Some think he's trying to obscure the forensic evidence and the victim's identity at the same time.'

'Why leave the DL if he doesn't want them identified?' Quinn said. 'Now he takes this one's head. That makes her pretty damn hard to recognize – he didn't have to burn her up. And still he leaves the driver's license.'

'So you think he's trying to get rid of trace evidence?'

'Maybe. What's he use for an accelerant?'

'Alcohol. Some kind of high-test vodka or something.'

'Then the fire is more likely part of his signature than it is part of his MO,' Quinn said. 'He might be getting rid of trace evidence, but if that's all he wanted, why wouldn't he just use gasoline? It's cheap. It's easily had with little or no interaction with another person. He chooses alcohol for an emotional reason rather than a practical one. That makes it part of the ritual, part of the fantasy.'

'Or maybe he's a big drinker.'

'No. A drinker doesn't waste good booze. And that's exactly what he'd call this: a waste of good liquor. He may be drinking prior to the hunt. He may drink during the torture and murder phase. But he's no drunk. A drunk would make mistakes. Sounds like this guy hasn't made any so far.'

None that anyone had noticed, at any rate. He thought again of the two hookers whose death had preceded this woman's and wondered who had caught their cases: a good cop or a bad cop. Every department had its share of both. He'd seen cops shrug and sleepwalk through an investigation if they didn't feel the victim was worth their time. And he'd seen veteran cops break down and cry over the violent death of someone most taxpaying citizens wouldn't sit next to on the bus.

He closed the file. Rain ran down his forehead and dripped off the end of his nose.

'This isn't where he left the others, is it?'

'No. One was found in Minnehaha Park and one in Powderhorn Park. Different parts of the city.'

He would need to see maps, to see where each dumping site was in relation to the others, where each abduction had taken place – to try to establish both a hunting territory and a killing and/or dumping territory. The task force would have maps in their command center, posted and flagged with little redheaded pins. Standard op. There was no need to ask. His mind was already full of maps bristling with pins. Manhunts that ran together like tag-team events, and command centers and war rooms that all looked alike and smelled alike, and cops who tended to look alike and sound alike, and smell like cigarettes and cheap cologne. He couldn't separate the cities anymore, but he could remember every single one of the victims.

The exhaustion poured through him again, and he wanted nothing more than to lie down right there on the ground.

He glanced over at Walsh as the agent fell into another spasm of deep, phlegm-rattling coughing.

'Let's go,' Quinn said. 'I've seen enough here for now.' He'd seen enough, period. And yet it took him another moment to move his feet and follow Vince Walsh back to the car.

5

The tension in the mayor's conference room was high and electric. Grim excitement, anticipation, anxiety, latent power. There were always those who saw murder as tragedy and those who sensed career opportunity. The next hour would sort out one type from the other, and establish the power order of the personalities involved. In that time Quinn would have to read them, work them, decide how to play them, and slot them into place in his own scheme of things.

He straightened his back, squared his aching shoulders, lifted his chin, and made his entrance. Show time. The heads turned immediately as he walked in the door. On the plane he had memorized the names of some of the principal players here, scouring the faxes that had come into the office before he'd left Virginia. He tried to recall them now, tried to sort them from the hundreds of others he'd known in hundreds of conference rooms across the country.

The mayor of Minneapolis detached herself from the crowd when she spotted him, and came toward him with purpose, trailing lesser politicians in her wake. Grace Noble resembled nothing so much as an operatic Valkyrie. She was fifty-something and large, built like a tree trunk, with a helmet of starched blond hair. She had no upper lip to speak of, but had carefully drawn herself one and filled it in with red lipstick that matched her suit.

'Special Agent Quinn,' she declared, holding out a broad, wrinkled hand tipped with red nails. 'I've been reading all about you. As soon as we heard from the director, I sent Cynthia to the library for every article she could find.'

He flashed what had been called his *Top Gun* smile – confident, winning, charming, but with the unmistakable glint of steel beneath it. 'Mayor Noble. I should tell you not to believe everything you read, but I find there is an advantage to having people think I can see into their minds.'

'I'm sure you don't have to be able to read minds to know how grateful we are to have you here.'

'I'll do what I can to help. Did you say you'd spoken with the director?'

Grace Noble patted his arm. Maternal. 'No, dear. Peter spoke with him. Peter Bondurant. They're old friends, as it happens.'

'Is Mr Bondurant here?'

'No, he couldn't bring himself to face the press. Not yet. Not knowing . . .' Her shoulders slumped briefly beneath the weight of it all. 'My God, what this will do to him if it *is* Jillie . . .'

A short African American man with a weightlifter build and a tailored gray suit stepped up beside her, his eyes on Quinn. 'Dick Greer, chief of police,' he said crisply, thrusting out his hand. 'Glad to have you on board, John. We're ready to *nail* this creep.'

As if he would have anything to do with it. In a metropolitan police department the chief was an administrator and a politician, a spokesman, an idea man. The men in the trenches likely said Chief Greer couldn't find his own dick in a dark room.

Quinn listened to the list of names and titles as the introductions were made. A deputy chief, a deputy mayor, an assistant county attorney, the state director of public safety, a city attorney, and a pair of press secretaries – too damn many politicians. Also present were the Hennepin County sheriff, a detective from the same office, a special agent in charge from the Minnesota Bureau of Criminal Apprehension with one of his agents, the homicide lieutenant from the PD – representatives from three of the agencies that would comprise the task force.

He met each with a firm handshake and played it low key. Midwesterners tended to be reserved and didn't quite trust people who weren't. In the Northeast he would have given more of the steel. On the West Coast he would have turned up the charm, would have been Mr Affable, Mr Spirit of Cooperation. Different horses for different courses, his old man used to say. And which one was the real John Quinn – even he didn't know anymore.

'. . . and my husband, Edwyn Noble,' the mayor finished the introductions.

'Here in a professional capacity, Agent Quinn,' Edwyn Noble said. 'Peter Bondurant is a client as well as a friend.'

Quinn's attention focused sharply on the man before him. Six five or six six, Noble was all joints and sinew, an exaggerated skeleton of a man with a smile that was perfectly square and too wide for his face. He looked slightly younger than his wife. The gray in his hair was contained to flags at the temples.

'Mr Bondurant sent his attorney?' Quinn said.

'I'm Peter's personal counsel, yes. I'm here on his behalf.'

'Why is that?'

'The shock has been terrific.'

'I'm sure it has been. Has Mr Bondurant already given the police his statement?'

Noble leaned back, the question physically putting him off. 'A statement regarding what?'

Quinn shrugged, nonchalant. 'The usual. When he last saw his daughter. Her frame of mind at the time. The quality of their relationship.'

Color blushed the attorney's prominent cheekbones. 'Are you suggesting Mr Bondurant is a suspect in his own daughter's death?' he said in a harsh, hushed tone, his gaze slicing across the room to check for eavesdroppers.

'Not at all,' Quinn said with blank innocence. 'I'm sorry if you misunderstood me. We need all the pieces of the puzzle we can get in order to form a clear picture of things, that's all. You understand.'

Noble looked unhappy.

In Quinn's experience, the parents of murder victims tended to camp out at the police department, demanding answers, constantly underfoot of the detectives. After the description Walsh had given of Bondurant, Quinn had expected to see the man throwing his weight around city hall like a mad bull. But Peter Bondurant had reached out and touched the director of the FBI, called out his personal attorney, and stayed home.

'Peter Bondurant is one of the finest men I know,' Noble declared.

'I'm sure Agent Quinn didn't mean to imply otherwise, Edwyn,' the mayor said, patting her husband's arm.

The lawyer's attention remained on Quinn. 'Peter was assured you're the best man for this job.'

'I'm very good at what I do, Mr Noble,' Quinn said. 'One of the reasons I'm good at my job is that I'm not afraid to *do* my job. I'm sure Mr Bondurant will be glad to hear it.'

He left it at that. He didn't want to make enemies of Bondurant's people. Offend a man like Bondurant and he'd find himself called on the carpet before the Bureau's Office of Professional Responsibility – at the very least. On the other hand, after having Peter Bondurant jerk him out here like a dog on a leash, he wanted it made clear he wouldn't be manipulated.

'We're running short on time, people. Let's take our seats and get started,' the mayor announced, herding the men toward the conference table like a first-grade teacher with a pack of little boys.

She stood at the political end of the table as everyone fell into rank, and drew breath to speak just as the door opened again and four more people walked in.

'Ted, we were about to start without you.' The mayor's doughy face creased with disapproval at his lack of punctuality.

'We've had some complications.' He strode across the room directly toward Quinn. 'Special Agent Quinn. Ted Sabin, Hennepin County attorney. I'm glad to meet you.'

Quinn rose unsteadily to his feet. His gaze glanced off the man's shoulder to the woman trailing reluctantly behind him. He mumbled an adequate reply to Sabin, shaking the county attorney's hand. A mustached cop stepped up and introduced himself. Kovac. The name registered dimly. The pudgy guy with them introduced himself and said something about having once heard Quinn speak somewhere.

'. . . And this is Kate Conlan with our victim/witness program,' Sabin said. 'You may –'

'We've met,' they said in unison.

Kate looked Quinn in the eye for just a moment because it seemed important to do so, to recognize him, acknowledge him, but not react. Then she glanced away, stifling the urge to sigh or swear or walk out of the room.

She couldn't say she was surprised to see him. There were only eighteen agents assigned to Investigative Support's Child Abduction/Serial Killer Unit. Quinn was the current poster boy for CASKU, and sexual homicide was his specialty. The odds had not been in her favor, and her luck today was for shit. Hell, she should have *expected* to see him standing in the mayor's conference room. But she hadn't.

'You've worked together?' Sabin said, not quite certain whether he should be pleased or disappointed.

An awkward silence hung for a second or three. Kate sank into a chair. 'Uh – yes,' she said. 'It's been a long time.'

Quinn stared at her. No one took him by surprise. Ever. He'd spent a lifetime building that level of control. That Kate Conlan could walk in the door and tilt the earth beneath his feet after all this time did not sit well. He ducked his head and cleared his throat. 'Yeah. You're missed, Kate.'

By whom? she wanted to ask, but instead she said, 'I doubt it. The Bureau is like the Chinese Army: The personnel could march into the sea for a year and there'd still be plenty of warm bodies to fill the posts.'

Oblivious of the discomfort at the other end of the table, the mayor brought the meeting to order. The press conference was less than an hour away. The politicians needed to get their ducks in a row. Who would speak first. Who would stand where. Who would say what. The cops combed their mustaches and drummed their fingers on the table, impatient with the formalities.

'We need to make a *strong* statement,' Chief Greer said, warming up his orator's voice. 'Let this creep know we *won't rest* until we get him. Let him know right up front we've got the FBI's leading profiler here, we've got the combined resources of *four* agencies working on this thing day and night.'

Edwyn Noble nodded. 'Mr Bondurant is establishing a reward of one hundred fifty thousand for information leading to an arrest.'

Quinn pulled his attention away from Kate and rose. 'Actually, Chief, I wouldn't advise any of that just yet.'

Greer's face pinched. Edwyn Noble glared at him. The collective expression from the political end of the table was a frown.

'I haven't had the opportunity to thoroughly go over the case,' Quinn began, 'which is reason enough to hold off. We need to get a handle on just who this killer might be, how his mind works. Making a blind show of strength at this point could be a move in the wrong direction.'

'And that would be based on what?' Greer asked, his bulky shoulders tensing beneath the weight of the chip he was carrying. 'You've said yourself, you haven't reviewed the case.'

'We've got a killer who's putting on a show. I've seen the photos from this last crime scene. He brought the body to a public place, intending to shock. He drew attention to the scene with a fire. This probably means he wants an audience, and if that's what he wants, we have to be careful of just how we give it to him.

'My advice is to hold off today. Minimize this press conference. Assure the public you're doing everything you can to identify and arrest the killer, but don't go into details. Keep the number of people behind the podium down – Chief Greer, Mayor Noble, Mr Sabin, that's it. Don't get into the specifics of the task force. Don't talk about Mr Bondurant. Don't bring up the FBI. Don't mention my name at all. And don't take any questions.'

Predictably, eyebrows went up all around the table. He knew from experience some of them had been expecting him to try to take the limelight: the FBI bully jumping in to grab the headlines. And undoubtedly, some of them wanted to show him off at the press conference like a trophy – *Look who we've got on our side: It's Super Agent!* No one ever expected him to downplay his role.

'At this stage of the game we don't want to set up an adversarial situation where he may see me as a direct challenge to him,' he said, resting his hands at his waist, settling in for the inevitable arguments. 'I'm in the background as much as I can be. I'll maintain a low profile with the media for as long as I can or until I deem it advantageous to do otherwise.'

The politicians looked crestfallen. They loved nothing so much as a public forum and the undivided attention of the media and thereby the masses. Greer obviously resented having his thunder stolen. The muscles in his jaw pulsed subtly.

'The people of this city are ready to panic,' the chief said. 'We've got three women dead, one of them *beheaded*. The phones in my office are ringing off the hook. A *statement* needs to be made. People want to know we're going after this *animal* with everything we've got.'

The mayor nodded. 'I'm inclined to agree with Dick. We've got business conferences in town, tourists coming in for plays, for concerts, for holiday shopping –'

'To say nothing of the anxiety of the general population over the growing crime rate in the city,' said the deputy mayor.

'It was bad enough with the two prostitute killings making the news,' a press secretary added. 'Now we've got the daughter of a very prominent citizen dead. People start thinking if it could happen to her, it could happen to anyone. News like this creates an environment of fear.'

'Give this guy a sense of importance and power and this city may well have a reason to panic,' Quinn said bluntly.

'Isn't it just as likely that minimizing the case in the media could enrage him? Drive him to commit more crimes in order to draw more attention to himself?' Greer questioned. 'How do you know coming out with a strong and public offensive won't scare him and flush him out?'

'I don't. I don't know what this guy might do – and neither do you. We need to take the time to try to figure that out. He's murdered three women that you know of, getting progressively bolder and more flamboyant. He won't scare easily, I can tell you that. We may eventually be able to draw him into the investigation – he's sure as hell watching – but we need to maintain tight control and keep our options open.' He turned toward Edwyn Noble. 'And the reward is too large. I'd advise you to cut it back to no more than fifty thousand to start.'

'With all due respect, Agent Quinn,' the lawyer said tightly, 'the choice is Mr Bondurant's.'

'Yes, it is, and I'm sure he feels information about his daughter's murder is worth any price. My reasoning is this, Mr Noble: People will come forward for a lot less than one hundred fifty thousand. An amount that extraordinary is going to bring in a flood of kooks and money-grubbing opportunists willing to sell their own mothers down the river. Start with fifty. Later we may want to use raising the amount as a strategic move.'

Noble breathed a measured sigh and pushed his chair back from the table. 'I'll need to speak with Peter about this.' He unfolded his long body and walked across the room to a side table with a telephone.

'We've got every reporter in the Twin Cities camped out on the steps of city hall,' the mayor pointed out. 'They're anticipating something more than a simple statement.'

'That's their problem,' Quinn said. 'You have to think of them as tools rather than guests. They're not entitled to the details of an ongoing investigation. You called a press conference, you didn't promise them anything.'

The mayor's expression suggested otherwise. Quinn tightened his grip on the fraying threads of his patience. *Play diplomat. Go easy. Don't lose your cool.* Christ, he was tired of it.

'Did you?'

Grace Noble looked to Sabin. 'We had hoped to have a composite sketch . . .'

Sabin cut a nasty look at Kate. 'Our witness is being less than cooperative.'

'Our witness is a scared kid who saw a psychopath set fire to a headless corpse,' Kate said sharply. 'The last thing on her mind is accommodating your timetable . . . sir.'

'She got a good look at the guy?' Quinn asked.

Kate spread her hands. 'She says she saw him. She's tired, she's afraid, she's angry – and rightfully so – at the treatment she's been given. Those factors tend not to create a spirit of cooperation.'

Sabin began to position himself for rebuttal. Quinn blocked the argument. 'Bottom line: We have no composite.'

'We have no composite,' Kate said.

'Then don't bring it up,' Quinn said, turning back to the mayor. 'Divert their attention to something else. Give them a photograph of Jillian Bondurant and one of her car and make an appeal for people to call the hotline if they've seen either one since Friday evening. Don't talk about the witness. Your first concern here has to be with how your actions and reactions will be perceived by the killer, not how they'll be perceived by the media.'

Grace Noble pulled in a deep breath. 'Agent Quinn –'

'I don't normally come into a case this early on,' he interrupted, the control slipping a little more. 'But since I'm here, I want to do everything I can to help defuse the situation and bring a swift and satisfactory conclusion to the investigation. That means advising you all on proactive investigative strategies and how to handle the case in the press. You don't have to listen to me, but I'm drawing on a wealth of past experience. The director of the FBI personally chose me for this case. You might want to consider why before you disregard my suggestions.'

Kate watched him as he took two steps back from the table and the argument, and turned his profile to her, pretending to look out the window. A subtle threat. He had established his own importance and now dared them to challenge it. He had attached the director of the FBI to his position and indirectly dared them to defy *him*.

Same old Quinn. She had known him as well as anyone could know John Quinn. He was a master manipulator. He could read people in a heartbeat and change colors like a chameleon. He played both adversaries and colleagues with the brilliance of Mozart at the keyboard, turning them to his side of an argument with charm or bullying or guile or the brute force of his intelligence. He was smart, he was sly, he was ruthless if he needed to be. And who he really was behind all the clever disguises and razor-sharp strategies – well, Kate wondered if *he* knew. She'd thought she had once upon a time.

Physically, he had changed some in five years. The thick, dark hair was salted with gray and cropped almost military short. He looked leaner, worn thin by the job. Ever the clothes-horse, he wore a suit that was Italian and expensive. But the coat hung a little loose off the broad shoulders, and the pants were a little baggy. The effect, though, created elegance rather than an eroding of his physical presence. The planes and angles of his face were sharp. There were circles under the brown eyes. Impatience vibrated in the air around him, and she wondered if it was real or manufactured for the moment.

Sabin turned toward her suddenly. 'Well, Kate, what do you think?'

'Me?'

'You worked for the same unit as Special Agent Quinn. What do you think?'

She could feel Quinn's eyes on her, as well as the gazes of everyone else in the room. 'No. I'm just the advocate here. I don't even know what business I have being at this meeting. John is the expert –'

'No, he's right, Kate,' Quinn said. He planted his hands on the tabletop and leaned toward her, his dark eyes like coals – she thought she could feel the heat of them on her face. 'You were a part of the old Behavioral Sciences Unit. You've got more experience with this kind of case than anyone else at this table besides me. What's your take?'

Kate stared at him, knowing her resentment had to be plain in her eyes. Bad enough to have Sabin put her on the spot, but for Quinn to do it struck her as a betrayal. But then, why she should have been surprised at that, she couldn't imagine.

'Regarding this case, I have no basis on which to form an educated opinion,' she began woodenly. 'However, I am well aware of Special Agent Quinn's qualifications and expertise. Personally, I think you would be making a mistake not to follow his advice.'

Quinn looked to the mayor and the chief of police.

'You can't unring a bell,' he said quietly. 'Put too much information out there now, there's no taking it back. You can call another press conference tomorrow if you need to. Just give the task force this chance to muster their resources and get a running start.'

Edwyn Noble returned from his phone call, his face sober. 'Mr Bondurant says he'll do whatever Agent Quinn suggests. We'll set the reward at fifty thousand.'

The meeting adjourned at four forty-eight. The politicos moved into the mayor's office for last-minute preparations before facing the press. The cops gathered in a cluster at the far end of the conference room to talk about setting up the task force.

'Sabin isn't happy with you, Kate,' Rob said in a tone of confidentiality, as if anyone else in the room would be interested.

'I'd say Ted Sabin can kiss my ass, but he'd be on his knees in a heartbeat.'

Rob blushed and frowned. 'Kate –'

'He dragged me into this, he can live with the consequences,' she said, moving toward the door. 'I'm going to go check on Angie. See if she's come up with anything from the mug books yet. You're going to the press conference?'

'Yes.'

Good. She had a witness to spring while everyone else was looking the other way. Where to take the girl was the next problem. She belonged in a juvenile facility, but they had as yet been unable to prove she was a juvenile.

'So you worked with Quinn?' Rob said, still with the voice of secrecy, following her toward the door. 'I heard him speak at a conference once. He's very impressive. I think his focus on victimology is dead on.'

'That's John all right. *Impressive* is his middle name.'

Across the room, Quinn turned away from his conversation with the homicide lieutenant and looked at her, as if he'd picked up her comment on his radar. At the same instant, Rob Marshall's pager beeped and he excused himself to use the phone, looking disappointed at the lost opportunity to speak with Quinn again.

Kate wanted no such opportunity. She turned away and started again for the door as Quinn came toward her.

'Kate.'

She glared at him and jerked her arm away as he moved to take hold of her.

'Thanks for your help,' he said softly, ducking his head in that way he had that made him seem boyish and contrite when he was neither.

'Yeah, right. Can I have the cervical collar concession tomorrow when you march in here and tell them to challenge this son of a bitch in order to trap him?'

He blinked innocently. 'I don't know what you mean, Kate. You know as well as I do how important it is to be proactive in a situation like this – when the time is right.'

She wanted to ask him if he was talking about the killer or the politicians, but she stopped herself. Quinn's proactive theories extended to all aspects of his life.

'Don't play your little mind games with me, John,' she whispered bitterly. 'I didn't mean to help you. I didn't offer you anything. You took, and I don't appreciate it. You think you can just manipulate people like pawns on a chessboard.'

'The end justified the means.'

'It always does, doesn't it?'

'You know I was right.'

'Funny, but that doesn't make you seem any less of a jerk to me.' She took a step back toward the door. 'Excuse me. I've got a job to do. You want to make power plays, you leave me out of the game plan, thank you very much.'

'Good to see you too, Kate,' he murmured as she walked away, thick red-gold hair swinging softly across her back.

It struck Quinn only belatedly that she had a nasty bruise on her cheek and a split lip. He'd seen her as he remembered her: as an ex-friend's wife ... as the only woman he'd ever truly loved.

6

The crowd is large. The Twin Cities are overrun with reporters. Two major daily newspapers, half a dozen television stations, radio stations too numerous to keep track of. And the story has brought in still more reporters from other places.

He has captured their attention. He relishes the sense of power that brings. The *sounds* in particular excite him – the urgent voices, the angry voices, the scuffle of feet, the whirl of camera motor drives.

He wishes he hadn't waited so long to go public. His first murders were private, hidden, far between in both time and space, the bodies left buried in shallow graves. This is so much better.

The reporters jockey for position. Videographers and photographers set the perimeter of the gathering. Blinding artificial lights give the setting an otherworldly white glow. He stands just outside the media pack with the other spectators, caught on the fringe of a headline.

The mayor takes the podium. The spokeswoman for the community expressing the collective moral outrage against senseless acts of violence. The county attorney parrots the mayor's remarks and promises punishment. The chief of police makes a statement regarding the formation of a task force.

They take no questions, even though the reporters are clamoring for confirmation of the victim's identity and for the gruesome details of the crime, like scavengers drooling for the chance to pick the carcass after the predator's feast. They bark out questions, shout the word *decapitation*. There are rumors of a witness.

The idea of someone watching the intimacy of his acts excites him. He believes any witness to his acts would be aroused by those acts, as he was. Aroused in a way just beyond understanding, as he had been as a child locked in the closet, listening to his mother having sex with men he didn't know. Arousal instinctively known as forbidden, irrepressible just the same.

Questions and more questions from the media.

No answers. No comment.

He sees John Quinn standing off to one side among a group of cops, and feels a rush of pride. He is familiar with Quinn's reputation, his theories. He has seen him on television, read articles about him. The FBI has sent their best for the Cremator.

He wants the agent to take the podium, wants to hear his voice and his thoughts, but Quinn doesn't move. The reporters seem not to recognize him standing out of reach of the spotlight. Then the principals walk away from the podium, surrounded by uniformed police officers. The press conference is over.

Disappointment weighs down on him. He had expected more, wanted more. Needs more. He had predicted *they* would need more.

With a jolt he realizes he has been waiting to react, that for a moment he allowed his feelings to hinge on the decisions of others. Unacceptable behavior. He is *pro*active, not *re*active.

The reporters give up and hurry for the doors. Stories to write, sources to pump. The small crowd in which he stands begins to break up and move. He moves with them, just another face.

'Let's go, kiddo. We're out of here.'

Angie looked up from the mug books on the table, wary, her stringy hair hiding half her face. Her gaze darted from Kate to Liska as she rose from her chair, as if she were expecting the detective to pull a gun and prevent her escape. Liska's attention was on Kate.

'You got the okay to go? Where's Kovac?'

Kate looked her in the eye. 'Yeah ... uh, Kovac's tied up with the lieutenant at the press conference. They're talking task force.'

'I want in on that,' Liska said with determination.

'You should. A case like this makes careers.' And breaks them, Kate thought, wondering just how much trouble she was making for herself springing Angie DiMarco – and how much trouble she would be making for Liska.

The end justifies the means. She thought of Quinn. At least her goal was noble rather than self-serving manipulation.

Rationalization: the key to a clear conscience.

'Are the cameras rolling?' Liska asked.

'Even as we speak.' Kate watched out of the corner of her eye as her client palmed a Bic lighter someone had left on the table and slipped it into her coat pocket. Christ. A kid *and* a kleptomaniac. 'Seems like a good time to split.'

'Run for it while you can,' Liska advised. 'You're a double bonus today. I hear your name attached to a certain act of heroic lunacy at the government center this morning. If the newsies don't nail you for one thing, they'll nail you for another.'

'My life is much too exciting.'

'Where are you taking me?' Angie demanded as she came to the door, slinging her backpack over one shoulder.

'Dinner. I'm starving, and you look like you've been starving for a while.'

'But your boss said –'

'Screw him. I want to see somebody lock Ted Sabin in a room for a day or two. Maybe he'd develop a little empathy. Let's go.'

Angie shot one last glance at Liska and scooted out the door, hiking her backpack up as she hurried after Kate.

'Will you get in trouble?'

'Do you care?'

'It's not my problem if you get fired.'

'That's the spirit. Listen, we've got to go up to my office. If anyone stops me on the way, do us both a favor and pretend we're not together. I don't want the media putting two and two together, and you don't want them knowing who you are. Trust me on that one.'

Angie gave her a sly look. 'Could I get on *Hard Copy*? I hear they pay.'

'You fuck this up for Sabin and he'll get you on *America's Most Wanted*. That is if our friendly neighborhood serial killer doesn't put you on *Unsolved Mysteries* first. If you don't hear anything else I tell you, kiddo, hear this. You do *not* want to be on television, you do *not* want your picture in a newspaper.'

'Are you trying to scare me?'

'I'm just telling you how it is,' she said as they entered the concourse to the government center.

Kate put on her don't-fuck-with-me face and walked as quickly as she could, considering the aches and stiffness from her morning wrestling match were beginning to sink in deep. Time was a-wasting. If the politicians took John's advice and somehow managed to contain themselves, the press conference would break up fast. Some of the reporters would dog Chief Greer, but most would split between the mayor and Ted Sabin, liking their odds better with elected officials than with a cop. Any minute now the concourse could be swarming with them.

If they followed Sabin into the concourse and caught sight of her, if someone called her name or pointed her out within earshot of the ravenous pack, she was bound to get cornered about the government center gunman. Eventually someone might make the mental leap and connect her to rumors of a witness in the latest homicide, and then the last few hours would truly deserve listing in the annals of all-time shitty days. Somewhere on the lower third of the list, she figured, leaving plenty of room above for the string of rotten days to come.

But luck was with her for once today. Only three people tried to intercept her on their way to the twenty-second floor. All making clever comments on Kate's morning heroics. She brushed them off with a wry look and a smart remark, and never broke stride.

'What's that about?' Angie asked as they got off the elevator, her curiosity overcoming her show of indifference.

'Nothing.'

'He called you the Terminator. What'd you do? Kill somebody?' The question came with a look that mixed disbelief with wariness with a small, grudging flicker of admiration.

'Nothing that dramatic. Not that I haven't been tempted today.' Kate keyed the access code into the security panel beside the door to the legal services department. She unlocked the door to her own office and motioned Angie inside.

'You know, you don't *have* to take me anywhere,' the girl said, flopping into the spare chair. 'I can take care of myself. It's a free country and I'm not a criminal . . . or a kid,' she added belatedly.

'Let's not even touch on that subject for the moment,' Kate suggested, glancing through her unopened mail. 'You know what the situation is here, Angie. You need a safe place to stay.'

'I can stay with my friend Michele –'

'I thought her name was Molly.'

Angie pressed her mouth into a line and narrowed her eyes.

'Don't even try to bullshit me,' Kate advised – for all the good it would do. 'There is no friend, and you don't have a place to crash in the Phillips neighborhood. That was a nice touch, though, picking a rotten neighborhood. Who would claim they lived there if they didn't?'

'Are you calling me a liar?'

'I think you've got your own agenda,' Kate said calmly, her attention on a memo that read: *Talked w/Sabin. Wit to Phoenix House – RM.* Permission. Odd Rob hadn't mentioned this in the mayor's office. The note was in a receptionist's hand. No time notation. The decision had probably come just before the press conference. All that subterfuge on her part for nothing. Oh, well.

'An agenda that probably centers on staying out of jail or a juvenile facility,' she went on.

'I'm not a –'

'Save it.'

She hit the message button on her phone and listened to the voices of the impatient and the forlorn who had tried to reach her during the afternoon. Reporters hot on the trail of the government center shootout heroine. She hit fast forward through each of them. Mixed in with the news hounds was the usual assortment. David Willis, her current pain-in-the-butt client. A coordinator of a victims' rights group. The husband of a woman who had allegedly been assaulted, though Kate had the gut feeling it was a scam, that the couple was looking to score reparation money. The husband had a string of petty drug arrests on his record.

'Kate.' The gruff male voice coming from the machine made her flinch. 'It's Quinn – um – John. I, ah, I'm staying at the Radisson.'

As if he expected her to call. Just like that.

'Who's that?' Angie asked. 'Boyfriend?'

'No, um, no,' Kate said, scrambling to pull her composure together. 'Let's get out of here. I'm starving.'

She drew in a long breath and released it as she pushed to her feet, feeling caught off guard, something she had always worked studiously to avoid. Another offense to add to the list against Quinn. She couldn't let him get to her. He'd be here and gone. A couple of days at most, she figured. The Bureau had sent him because Peter Bondurant had friends in high places. It was a show of good faith or ass kissing, depending on your point of view.

He didn't need to be here. He wouldn't be here long. She didn't have to have any contact with him while he was here. She wasn't with the Bureau anymore. She wasn't a part of this task force. He had no power over her.

God, Kate, you sound like you're afraid of him, she thought with disgust as she turned her Toyota 4Runner out of the parking ramp onto Fourth Avenue. Quinn was past history and she was a grown-up, not some adolescent girl who'd broken up with the class cool guy and couldn't bear to face him in home room.

'Where are we going?' Angie asked, dialing the radio to an alternative rock station. Alanis Morissette whining at an ex-boyfriend with bongos in the background.

'Uptown. What do you want to eat? You look like you could use some fat and cholesterol. Ribs? Pizza? Burgers? Pasta?'

The girl made the snotty shrug that had driven parents of teenagers from the time of Adam to consider the pros and cons of killing their young. 'Whatever. Just as long as there's a bar. I need a drink.'

'Don't push it, kid.'

'What? I have a valid driver's license.' She flopped back against the seat and put her feet up against the dash. 'Can I bum a smoke?'

'I don't have any. I quit.'

'Since when?'

'Since 1981. I fall off the wagon every once in a while. Get your feet off my dashboard.'

The big sigh as she rearranged herself sideways in the bucket seat. 'Why are you taking me to dinner? You don't like me. Wouldn't you rather go home to your husband?'

'I'm divorced.'

'From the guy on the answering machine? Quinn?'

'No. Not that it's any of your business.'

'Got kids?'

A beat of silence before answering. Kate wondered if she would ever get over that hesitation or the guilt that inspired it. 'I have a cat.'

'So do you live in Uptown?'

Kate cut her a sideways look, taking her eyes briefly off the heavy rush hour traffic. 'Let's talk about you. Who's Rick?'

'Who?'

'Rick – the name on your jacket.'

'It came that way.'

Translation: name of the guy she stole it from.

'How long have you been in Minneapolis?'

'A while.'

'How old were you when your folks died?'

'Thirteen.'

'So you've been on your own how long?'

The girl glared at her for a beat. 'Eight years.' That was lame.

Kate shrugged. Worth a shot. 'So what happened to them? Accident?'

'Yeah,' Angie said softly, staring straight ahead. 'An accident.'

There was a story in there somewhere, Kate thought as she negotiated the twisted transition from 94 to get to Hennepin Avenue. She could probably guess at some of the key plot ingredients – alcohol, abuse, a cycle of unhappy circumstances, and dysfunction. Virtually every kid on the street had lived a variation of that story. So had every man in prison. Family was a fertile breeding ground for the kind of psychological bacteria that warped minds and devoured hope. Conversely, she knew plenty of people in law enforcement and social work who came from that same set of circumstances, people who had come to that same fork in the road and turned one way instead of the other.

She thought again of Quinn, even though she didn't want to.

The rain had thickened to a misty, miserable fog. The sidewalks were deserted. Uptown, contrary to its name, was some distance south of downtown Minneapolis. A gentrified area of shops, restaurants, coffee bars, art house movie theaters, it centered on the intersection of Lake Street and Hennepin. Just a stone's throw – and a world – west of the tough Whittier neighborhood, which in recent years had become the territory of black gangs, driveby shootings, and drug raids.

Uptown was edged to the west by Lake Calhoun and Lake of the Isles, and was currently inhabited by yuppies and the terribly hip. The house Kate had grown up in and now owned was just two blocks off Lake Calhoun, her parents having purchased the solid prairie-style home decades before the area became trendy.

Kate chose La Loon as their destination, a pub away from the lively Calhoun Square area, parking in the nearly empty side lot. She wasn't in the mood for noise or a crowd, and knew both could be used as a shield by her dinner companion. Just being a teenager was enough of a barrier to overcome.

Inside, La Loon was dark and warm, all wood and brass with a long, old-fashioned bar and few patrons. Kate shunned a booth in favor of a corner table, where she took the corner chair, which gave her a view of the entire dining room. The paranoid seat. A habit Angie DiMarco had already picked up for herself. She didn't sit across from Kate with her back to the room; she took a side seat with her back to a wall so she could see anyone approaching the table.

The waitress brought menus and took drink orders. Kate longed for a stout glass of gin, but settled for chardonnay. Angie ordered rum and Coke.

The waitress looked at Kate, who shrugged. 'She's got ID.'

A look of sly triumph stole across Angie's face as the waitress walked away. 'I thought you didn't want me to drink.'

'Oh, what the hell,' Kate said, digging a bottle of Tylenol out of her purse. 'It's not like it's going to corrupt you.'

The girl had clearly expected a confrontation. She sat back, a little bemused, slightly disappointed. 'You're not like any social worker I ever knew.'

'How many have you known?'

'A few. They were either bitches or so goody-goody, I wanted to puke.'

'Yeah, well, plenty of people will tell you I qualify on one count.'

'But you're different. I don't know,' she said, struggling for the definition she wanted. 'It's like you've been around or something.'

'Let's just say I didn't come into this job via the usual route.'

'What's that mean?'

'It means I don't sweat the small stuff and I don't take any shit.'

'If you don't take any shit, then who beat you up?'

'Above and beyond the call of duty.' Kate tossed the Tylenol back and washed it down with water. 'You should see the other guy. So, any familiar faces in those mug books today?'

Angie's mood shifted with the subject, her pouty mouth turning down at the corners, her gaze dropping to the tabletop. 'No. I would have said.'

'Would you?' Kate muttered, earning a sullen glance. 'They'll want you to work with the sketch artist in the morning. How do you think that'll go? Did you see him well enough to describe him?'

'I saw him in the fire,' Angie murmured.

'How far away were you?'

Angie traced a gouge mark in the tabletop with one bitten fingernail. 'I don't know. Not far. I was cutting through the park and I had to pee, so I ducked behind some bushes. And then he came down the hill . . . and he was carrying that –'

Her face tightened and she bit her lip, hanging her head lower, obviously in the hope that her hair would hide the emotion that had rushed to the surface. Kate waited patiently, keenly aware of the girl's rising tension. Even to a streetwise kid like Angie, seeing what she had seen had to be an unimaginable shock. The stress of that and the stress of what she had been through at the police station, compounded by exhaustion, would all have to eventually take a toll.

And I want to be there when the poor kid breaks down, she thought, never pleased with that aspect of her job. The system was supposed to champion the victim, but it often victimized them again in the process. And the advocate was caught in the middle – an employee of the system, there supposedly to protect the citizen who was being dragged into the teeth of the justice machine.

The waitress returned with their drinks. Kate ordered cheeseburgers and fries for both of them and handed the menus back.

'I – I didn't know what he was carrying,' Angie whispered when the waitress was out of earshot. 'I just knew someone was coming and I needed to hide.'

Like an animal that knew too well the night was stalked by predators of one kind or another.

'A park's a scary place late at night, I suppose,' Kate said softly, turning her wineglass by the stem. 'Everybody loves to go in daylight. We think it's so pretty, so nice to get away from the city. Then night comes, and suddenly it's like the evil forest out of *The Wizard of Oz*. Nobody wants to be there in the dead of night. So what were you doing there, Angie?'

'I told you, I was just cutting through.'

'Cutting from where to where at that hour?' She kept her tone casual.

Angie hunkered over her rum and Coke and took a long pull on the straw. Tense. Forcing the anger back up to replace the fear.

'Angie, I've been around. I've seen things even you wouldn't believe,' Kate said. 'Nothing you tell me could shock me.'

The girl gave a humorless half-laugh and looked toward the television that hung above one end of the bar. Local news anchor Paul Magers was looking grave and handsome as he related the story of a madman run amok in the county government center. They flashed a mug shot and told about the recent breakup of the man's marriage, his wife having taken their children and gone into hiding in a shelter a week before.

Precipitating stressors, Kate thought, not surprised.

'Nobody cares if you were breaking the law, Angie. Murder overrules everything – burglary, prostitution, poaching squirrels – which I personally consider a service to the community,' she said. 'I had a squirrel in my attic last month. Vermin menace. They're nothing but rats with furry tails.'

No reaction. No smile. No overblown teenage outrage at her callous disregard for animal life.

'I'm not trying to lean on you here, Angie. I'm telling you as your advocate: The sooner you come clean about everything that went down last night, the better for all concerned – yourself included. The county attorney has his shorts in a knot over this case. He tried to tell Sergeant Kovac he should treat you as a suspect.'

Alarm rounded the girl's eyes. 'Fuck him! I didn't do anything!'

'Kovac believes you, which is why you're not sitting in a cell right now. That and the fact that I wouldn't allow it. But this is serious shit, Angie. This killer is public enemy number one, and you're the only person who's seen him and lived to tell the tale. You're in the hot seat.'

Elbows on the table, the girl dropped her face into her hands and mumbled between her fingers, 'God, this sucks!'

'You've got that right, sweetie,' Kate said softly. 'But here's the deal, plain and simple. This nut job is going to go on killing until somebody stops him. Maybe you can help stop him.'

She waited. Held her breath. Willed the poor kid over the edge. She could see through the bars of Angie's fingers: the girl's face going red with the pressure of holding the emotions in. She could see the tension in the thin shoulders, feel the anticipation that thickened the air around her.

But nothing in this situation was going to be plain or simple, Kate thought as her pager began to shrill inside her purse. The moment, the opportunity, was gone. She swore silently as she dug through the bag, cursing the inconvenience of modern conveniences.

'Think about it, Angie,' she said as she rose from her chair. 'You're *it*, and I'm here to help you.'

That makes me IT by association, she thought as she headed to the pay phone in the alcove by the bathrooms.

No. Nothing about this would be plain or simple.

7

'What the hell did you do with my witness, Red?' Kovac leaned against the wall of the autopsy suite, the receiver of the phone jammed between his shoulder and his ear. He slipped a hand inside the surgical gown he wore over his clothes, pulled a little jar of Mentholatum from his jacket pocket, and smeared a gob around each nostril.

'I thought it'd be nice to treat her like a human being and feed her a real meal as opposed to the crap you give people at the cop shop,' Kate said.

'You don't like doughnuts? What kind of American are you?'

'The kind who has at least a partial grasp of the concept of civil liberties.'

'Yeah, fine, all right, I get it.' He plugged his free ear with a finger as the blade of a bone saw whined against a whetstone in the background. 'Sabin asks, I'm gonna tell him you nabbed her before I could throw her in the slammer – which is true. Better your lovely tit in a wringer than my johnson.'

'Don't worry about Sabin. I've got his okay on a memo.'

'Do you have a picture of him signing it? Is it notarized?'

'God, you're a raving paranoid.'

'How do you think I've lived this long on the job?'

'It wasn't from kissing ass and following orders. That's for damn sure.'

He had to laugh. Kate called a spade a spade. And she was right. He handled his cases as he thought best, not with an eye to publicity or promotion. 'So where are you taking the angel after this grand feast?'

'The Phoenix House, I'm told. She belongs in a juvie facility, but there you go. I've got to put her somewhere, and her ID says she's an adult. Did you get a Polaroid of her?'

'Yeah. I'll show it around juvenile division. See if anyone knows her. I'll give a copy to vice too.'

'I'll do the same on my end of things if you get me a copy.'

'Will do. Keep me posted. I want a short leash on that chick.' He raised his voice briefly as water pounded into a stainless steel sink. 'I gotta go. Dr Death is about to crack open our crispy critter.'

'Jesus, Sam, you're so sensitive.'

'Hey, I gotta cope. You know what I'm saying.'

53

'Yeah, I know. Just don't let the wrong people hear you doing it. Is the task force set up?'

'Yeah. As soon as we get the brass out of our hair, we'll be good to go.' He looked across the room to where Quinn stood in discussion with the ME and Hamill, the agent from the BCA, all of them in surgical gowns and booties. 'So what's the story with you and the Quantico hotshot?'

There was the briefest of hesitations on the other end of the line. 'What do you mean?'

'What do you mean, what do I mean? What's the deal? What's the story? What's the history?'

Another pause, just a heartbeat. 'I knew him, that's all. I was working on the research side in Behavioral Sciences. The people in BSU and Investigative Support regularly cross paths. And he used to be a friend of Steven's – my ex.'

This tossed in at the end, as if he might believe it was an afterthought. Kovac filed it all away for future rumination. *Used to be* a friend of Steven's. There was more to that story, he thought as Liska came toward him from the crowd around the corpse, looking impatient and nauseated. He gave Kate his pager number and instructions to call, and hung up.

'They're ready to rock and roll,' Liska said, pulling a travel-size jar of Vicks VapoRub from the pocket of her boxy blazer. She stuck her nose over the rim and breathed deep.

'God, the smell!' she whispered as she turned and fell in step with him, heading back toward the table. 'I've had floaters. I've had drunks in Dumpsters. I once had a guy left in the trunk of a Chrysler over the Fourth of July weekend. I never smelled anything like this.'

The stench was an entity, a presence. It was an invisible fist that forced its way into the mouths of all present, rolled over their tongues, and jammed at the backs of their throats. The room was cold, but not even the constant blast of clean, frigid air from the ventilation system or the cloying perfume of chemical air fresheners could kill the smell of roasted human flesh and organs.

'Nothing like posting Toasties,' Kovac said.

Liska pointed a finger at him and narrowed her eyes. 'No internal-organ jokes or I puke on your shoes.'

'Wimp.'

'And I'll kick your ass later for calling me that.'

There were three tables in the room, the ones at either end occupied. They walked past one as an assistant eased a plastic bag full of organs back into the body cavity of a man with thick yellow toenails. A scale hung over each table, like the kind for weighing grapes and sweet peppers in the supermarket. These were for weighing hearts and brains.

'Did you want me to start the party without you?' the ME queried with an arch of her brow.

Maggie Stone was generally considered by her staff to have a few nuts

54

rattling loose in the mental machine. She suspected everyone of everything, rode a Harley Hog in good weather, and had been known to carry weapons. But when it came to the job, she was the best.

People who had known her in her tamer years claimed her hair was naturally mouse brown. Sam had never been good at remembering such details for long, which was one of many reasons he had two ex-wives. He did notice Dr Stone, on the far side of forty, had recently gone from flame-red to platinum. Her hair was chopped short and she wore it in a style that looked as if she'd just rolled out of bed and gotten a bad scare.

She stared at him as she adjusted the tiny clip-on microphone at the neck of her scrub suit. Her eyes were a spooky translucent green.

'Get this bastard,' she ordered, pointing a scalpel at him, the implication in her tone being that if he didn't, she would. She then turned her attention to the charred body that lay on the stainless steel table, curled up like a praying mantis. A deep calm settled over her.

'Okay, Lars, let's see if we can't straighten her out a bit.'

Moving to one end of the table, she took hold of the corpse firmly but gently while her assistant, a hulking Swede, took hold of the ankles and they began to pull slowly. The resulting sound was like snapping fried chicken wings.

Liska turned away with a hand over her mouth. Kovac stood his ground. On the other side of the table, Quinn's expression was granite, his eyes on the body that had yet to give up its secrets. Hamill, one of two agents from the BCA assigned to the task force, cast his gaze up at the ceiling. He was a small, tidy man with a runner's wire-thin body and a hairline that was rapidly falling back from a towering forehead.

Stone stood back from the table and picked up a chart.

'Dr Maggie Stone,' she said quietly for the benefit of the tape, though she appeared to be addressing the deceased. 'Case number 11–7820, Jane Doe. Caucasian female. The head has been severed from her body and is currently missing. The body measures 55 inches in length and weighs 122 pounds.'

The measurement and weight had been obtained earlier. A thorough set of X-rays and photographs had been taken, and Stone had gone over the body carefully with a laser to illuminate and collect trace evidence. She now went over every inch of the body visually, describing in detail everything she saw, every wound, every mark.

The burned clothing remained on the corpse. Melted to the body by the heat of the fire. A cautionary tale against wearing synthetic fabrics.

Stone made note of the 'severe trauma' to the victim's neck, speculating the damage had been done by a blade with a serrated edge.

'Postmortem?' Quinn asked.

Stone stared at the gaping wound as if she were trying to see down into the dead woman's heart. 'Yes,' she said at last.

Lower down on the throat were several telltale ligature marks – not a single red furrow, but stripes that indicated the cord had been loosened and tightened over the course of the victim's ordeal. This was likely the manner of death – asphyxiation due to ligature strangulation – though it would be difficult to prove because of the decapitation. The most consistent indicator of a strangulation death was a crushed hyoid bone at the base of the tongue in the upper part of the trachea – above the point of decapitation. Nor was there any opportunity to check the eyes for petechial hemorrhaging, another sure sign of strangulation.

'He played with the others this way?' Quinn asked, referring to the multiple ligature marks on the throat.

Stone nodded and moved down the body.

'Is this roughly the same amount of fire damage as the other bodies?'

'Yes.'

'And the others were clothed.'

'Yes. After he killed them, we believe. There were wounds on the bodies with no corresponding damage to the clothing – what clothing wasn't destroyed by the fire.'

'And not in their own clothes,' Kovac said. 'Stuff the killer picked out for them. Always synthetic fabrics. Fire melts the fabric. Screws trace evidence on the body.'

Undoubtedly it meant more to the mind hunter, he thought with a twinge of impatience. As valuable as he knew profiles of murderers could be, the flatfoot cop in him held the reservation that the brainiacs sometimes gave these monsters a little too much credit. Sometimes killers did things just for the hell of it. Sometimes they did things out of curiosity or pure evil or because they knew it would jam up the investigation.

'We gonna get any fingerprints?' he asked.

'Nope,' Stone said as she examined the back of the left hand. The top layer of skin had turned a dirty ivory color and was sloughing off. The underlayer was red. Knuckle bones gleamed white where the skin had seared away entirely.

'Not good ones anyway,' she said. 'My guess is he positioned the body with the hands crossed over the chest or stomach. The fire instantly melted the blouse and the resulting goo melted into the fingertips before the tendons in the arms began to constrict and pull the hands away from the body.'

'Is there any chance of separating the fabric residue from the fingertips?' Quinn asked. 'The fabric itself might bear an impression of the friction ridges.'

'We don't have the capability here,' she said. 'Your people back in Washington might be game to try. We can detach the hands, bag them, and send them in.'

'I'll have Walsh call ahead.'

Coughing like he had tuberculosis, Walsh had begged off from the autopsy. There was no need for the whole task force to attend. They would all be briefed in the morning and would all have access to the reports and photographs.

Stone moved methodically down the length of the body. The victim's legs were bare, the skin seared and blistered in an irregular pattern where the accelerant had burned away in a flash.

'Ligature marks at the right and left ankles,' she said, her small, gloved hands moving tenderly, almost lovingly, over the tops of the victim's feet – as much emotion as she would show during the process.

Kovac took in the appearance of the wounds the bindings had made around the victim's ankles, trying hard not to picture this woman tied to a bed in some maniac's chamber of horrors, struggling so frantically to get free that the ligatures had cut grooves into her flesh.

'The fibers have already gone to the BCA lab,' Stone said. 'They seemed consistent with the others – a white poly-propylene twine,' she specified for the benefit of Quinn and Hamill. 'Tough as hell. You can buy it in any office supply store. The county buys enough every month to wrap around the moon. It's impossible to trace.

'Deep lacerations in a double-X pattern to the bottoms of both feet.' She went on with the exam. She measured and catalogued each cut, then described what appeared to be cigarette burns to the pad of each toe.

'Torture or disfigurement to conceal her identity?' Hamill wondered aloud.

'Or both,' Liska said.

'Looks like all of this was done while she was alive,' Stone said.

'Sick bastard,' Kovac muttered.

'If she got free, she couldn't have run,' Quinn said. 'There was a case in Canada a few years ago where the victim's Achilles tendons were severed for the same reason. Did the other victims have similar wounds?'

'They had each been tortured in a variety of ways,' Stone answered. 'Neither exactly the same. I can get you copies of the reports.'

'That's already being taken care of, thank you.'

There was no hope of removing the victim's clothing without taking skin with it. Stone and her assistant snipped and peeled, coaxing the melted fibers gently away with forceps, Stone swearing under her breath every few minutes.

Anticipation tightened in Kovac's gut as the destroyed blouse and a layer of flesh were worked away from the left side of the chest.

Stone looked across the body at him. 'Here it is.'

'What?' Quinn asked, moving to the head of the table.

Kovac stepped in close and surveyed the killer's handiwork. 'The detail we've managed to keep away from the stinking reporters. This pattern of stab wounds – see?'

A tight cluster of eight marks, half an inch to an inch in length, perforated the dead woman's chest roughly in the vicinity of the heart.

'The first two had this,' Kovac said, glancing at Quinn. 'They were both strangled and the stabbing was done after the fact.'

'In that exact pattern?'

'Yep. Like a star. See?' Holding his hand three inches above the corpse, he traced the pattern in the air with his index finger. 'The longer marks form one X. The shorter marks form another. Smokey Joe strikes again.'

'Other similarities too,' Stone said. 'See here: amputation of the nipples and areola.'

'Postmortem?' Quinn asked.

'No.'

Stone looked to her assistant. 'Lars, let's turn her over. See what we find on the other side.'

The body had been positioned on its back before being set ablaze. Consequently, the fire damage was contained to the front side. Stone removed the undamaged pieces of clothing and bagged them for the lab. A piece of red spandex skirt. A scrap of chartreuse blouse. No underwear.

'Uh-huh,' Stone murmured to herself, then glanced up at Kovac. 'A section of flesh missing from the right buttock.'

'He did this with the others too?' Quinn asked.

'Yes. With the first victim he took a chunk from the right breast. With the second, it was also the right buttock.'

'Eliminating a bite mark?' Hamill speculated aloud.

'Could be,' Quinn said. 'Biting certainly isn't unusual with this kind of killer. Any indication of bruising in the tissue? When these guys sink their teeth in, it isn't any love nip.'

Stone took up her little ruler to measure the wounds precisely. 'If there was any bruising, he's cut it out. There's considerable muscle gone.'

'Jesus,' Kovac muttered with disgust as he stared at the shiny dark red square on the victim's body, the flesh cut out precisely with a small sharp knife. 'Who does this guy think he is? Hannibal Fucking Lecter?'

Quinn gave him a look from the headless end of the body. 'Everybody's got a hero.'

Case number 11–7820, Jane Doe, Caucasian female, had no organic reason to die. She had been healthy in all respects. Well fed, carrying the extra ten or fifteen pounds most people did. Although what her last meal had been, Dr Stone had not been able to determine. If this was Jillian, she had digested the dinner she'd eaten with her father before her death. Her body was free of disease and natural defect. Stone had judged her to be between the ages of twenty and twenty-five. A young woman with most of her life ahead of her – until she crossed the path of the wrong man.

This type of killer rarely chose a victim who was ready to die.

Quinn reviewed this fact as he stood on the wet tarmac of the morgue's delivery bay. The damp cold of the night seeped into his clothes, into his muscles. Fog hung like a fine white shroud over the city.

There were too damn many victims who were young women: pretty young women, ordinary young women, women with everything going for them, and women with nothing in their lives but a sliver of hope for something better. All of them broken and wasted like dolls, abused and thrown away as if their lives had meant nothing at all.

'Hope you're not attached to that suit,' Kovac said as he walked up, fishing a cigarette out of a pack of Salem Menthols.

Quinn looked down at himself, knowing the stench of violent death had permeated every fiber of his clothing. 'Professional hazard. I didn't have time to change.'

'Me neither. Used to drive my wives crazy.'

'Wives – plural?'

'Consecutive, not concurrent. Two. You know how it is – the job and all . . . Anyway, my second wife used to call them corpse clothes – whatever I had to wear to a really putrid death scene or an autopsy or something. She made me undress in the garage, and then you'd think she'd maybe burn the clothes or stick 'em in the trash or something, 'cause she sure as hell wouldn't let me wear them again. But no. She'd box the stuff up and take it to the Goodwill – on account of it still had wear in it, she'd say.' He shook his head in amazement. 'Underprivileged people all over Minneapolis were walking around smelling like dead bodies, thanks to her. You married?'

Quinn shook his head.

'Divorced?'

'Once. A long time ago.'

So long ago, the brief attempt at marriage seemed more like a half-remembered bad dream than a memory. Bringing it up was like kicking a pile of ashes, stirring old flecks of emotional debris inside him – feelings of frustration and failure and regret that had long since gone cold. Feelings that came stronger when he thought of Kate.

'Everybody's got one,' Kovac said. 'It's the job.'

He held the cigarettes out, Quinn declined.

'God, I gotta get that smell out of my mouth.' Kovac filled his lungs and absorbed the maximum amount of tar and nicotine before exhaling, letting the smoke roll over his tongue. It drifted away to blend into the fog. 'So, you think that's Jillian Bondurant in there?'

'Could be, but I think there's a chance it's not. The UNSUB went to a hell of a lot of trouble to make sure we couldn't get prints.'

'But he leaves Bondurant's DL at the scene. So maybe he nabbed Bondurant, then figured out who she was and decided to hang on to her, hold her for ransom,' Kovac speculated. 'Meanwhile, he picks up another woman and offs her, leaves Bondurant's DL with the body to show what might happen if Daddy doesn't cough up.'

Kovac narrowed his eyes as if he were playing the theory through again for review. 'No ransom demand we know of, and she's been missing since Friday. Still, maybe . . . But you don't think so.'

'I've never seen it happen that way, that's all,' Quinn said. 'As a rule, with this type of murder you get a killer with one thing on his mind: playing out his fantasy. It's got nothing to do with money – usually.'

Quinn turned a little more toward Kovac, knowing this was the member of the task force he most needed to win over. Kovac was the investigative lead. His knowledge of these cases, of this town, and the kind of criminals who lived in its underbelly would be invaluable. Trouble was, Quinn didn't think he had the energy left to pull out the old I'm-just-a-cop-like-you routine. He settled for some truth, instead.

'The thing about profiling is that it's a proactive tool based on the reactive use of knowledge gained from past events. Not a perfect science. Every case could potentially present something we've never seen before.'

'I hear you're pretty good though,' the detective conceded. 'You nailed that child-killer out in Colorado right down to his stutter.'

Quinn shrugged. 'Sometimes all the pieces fit. How long before you can get your hands on Bondurant's medical records for comparison with the body?'

Kovac rolled his eyes. 'I oughta change my name to Murphy. Murphy's Law: nothing's ever easy. Turns out, most of her medical records are in *France*,' he said as if France were an obscure planet in another galaxy. 'Her mom divorced Peter Bondurant eleven years ago and married a guy with an international construction firm. They lived in France. The mother's dead, stepfather still lives there. Jillian came back here a couple of years ago. She was enrolled at the U – University of Minnesota.'

'The Bureau can help get the records via our legal attaché offices in Paris.'

'I know. Walsh is already on it. Meantime, we'll try to talk to anyone who was close to Jillian. Find out if she had any moles, scars, birthmarks, tattoos. We'll get pictures. We haven't turned up any close friends yet. No boyfriend anyone knows of. I gather she wasn't exactly a social butterfly.'

'What about her father?'

'He's too distraught to talk to us.' Kovac's mouth twisted.

' "Too distraught" – that's what his lawyer says. If I thought somebody whacked my kid, I'd be fucking distraught, all right. I'd be climbing all over the cops. I'd be living in their back pockets, doing anything I could to nail the son of a bitch.' He cocked an eyebrow at Quinn. 'Wouldn't you?'

'I'd turn the world upside down and shake it by its heels.'

'Damn right. I go over to Bondurant's house to break the news this might be Jillian. He gets a look like I'd hit him in the head with a ball bat. "Oh, my God. Oh, my God," he says, and I think he's gonna puke. So I don't think much of it when he excuses himself. The son of a bitch goes and calls his lawyer and he never comes out of his study again. I spend the next hour talking to Bondurant via Edwyn Noble.'

'And what did he tell you?'

'That Jillian had been to the house Friday night for dinner and he hadn't seen her since. She left around midnight. A neighbor corroborates. The couple across the street were just getting home from a party. Jillian's Saab pulled onto the street just as they turned onto the block at eleven fifty.

'Peter Filthy Fucking Rich Bondurant,' he grumbled. 'My luck. I'll be writing parking tickets by the time this thing is through.'

He finished his cigarette, dropped it on the tarmac, and ground out the butt with the toe of his shoe.

'Too bad DNA tests take so damn long,' he said, jumping back to the matter of identification. 'Six weeks, eight weeks. Too damn long.'

'You're checking missing persons reports?'

'Minnesota, Wisconsin, Iowa, the Dakotas. We've even called Canada. Nothing fits yet. Maybe the head'll turn up,' he said with optimism the way he might hope for the return of a pair of eyeglasses or a wallet.

'Maybe.'

'Well, enough of this shit for tonight. I'm starving,' he said abruptly, pulling his suit coat shut as if he had confused hunger for cold. 'I know a place with great Mexican take-out. So hot it burns the corpse taste out of your mouth. We'll swing by on the way to your hotel.'

They walked away from the delivery bay as an ambulance pulled up. No lights, no siren. Another customer. Kovac fished his keys out of his pocket, looking at Quinn from the corner of his eye. 'So, you knew our Kate?'

'Yeah.' Quinn stared into the fog, wondering where she was tonight. Wondering if she was thinking about him. 'In another lifetime.'

8

Kate eased her aching body down into the old claw-foot tub and tried to exhale the tension she had stored up during the day. It worked its way from the core of her through her muscles in the form of pain. She envisioned it rising from the water with steam and the scent of lavender. The brass wire tray that spanned the tub before her held a Bad Monday-size glass of Bombay Sapphire and tonic. She took a deep drink, lay back, and closed her eyes.

The stress management people frowned on alcohol as an answer to tension and preached that it would set a person on the road to alcoholism and doom. Kate had been up and down the road to doom. She figured if she was ever to become an alcoholic, it would have happened years before. Five years before. It hadn't, and so tonight she drank gin and waited for the pleasant numbness it would bring.

For just the briefest of moments the montage of faces from that bleak period of her life flashed through her mind's eye: Steven's changing face over the passing of that terrible year – distant, cold, angry, bitter; the doctor's regret, worn tired and bland by too many tragedies; her daughter's sweet face, there and gone in a single painful heartbeat; Quinn's face – intense, compassionate, passionate ... angry, dispassionate, indifferent, a memory.

It never failed to amaze her, the sudden sharpness of that pain as it stabbed through the cotton batting of time. A part of her wished fervently it would dull, and another part of her hoped that it never would. The endless cycle of guilt: the need to escape it and the equally desperate need to cling to it.

She opened her eyes and stared at the window beyond the foot of the tub. A rectangle of night peered in above the half-curtain, blackness beyond the steamed glass.

She had at least healed over the surface of the old wounds and moved on with her life, which was as much as anyone could ever honestly hope to do. But how easily torn, that old scar tissue. How humbling the reality that she hadn't really grown past that pain attached to the memory of John Quinn. She felt like a fool and a child, and blamed the element of surprise.

She would do better tomorrow. She would have a clear head and keep her focus. She would allow no surprises. There was no sense in dredging up the past when the present demanded all her attention. And Kate Conlan had never been anything if not sensible ... with the exception of a few brief months during the worst year of her life.

She and Steven had grown apart. A tolerable situation, had all things remained equal. Then Emily had contracted a virulent strain of influenza, and in a matter of days their sweet, sunny child was gone. Steven had blamed Kate, feeling she should have recognized the seriousness of the illness sooner. Kate had blamed herself despite the doctors' assurances that it wasn't her fault, that she couldn't have known. She had been so in need of someone to hold her, someone to offer comfort and support and absolution ...

Pulling the end of the towel over her shoulder from the towel bar behind her, she dabbed at her eyes, wiped her nose, then took another drink. The past was out of her control. She could at least delude herself into believing she had some control of the present.

She steered her thoughts to her client. Idiotic word – *client*. It implied the person had chosen her, hired her. Angie DiMarco would have done neither. What a piece of work that kid was. And Kate was far too experienced in the ways of the real world to believe there was a heart of gold under all that. There was more likely something warped and mutated by a life less kind than that of the average stray cat. How people could bring a child into the world and let her come to this ... The notion brought indignation and an unwelcome stab of jealousy.

It wasn't her job, really, finding out who Angie DiMarco was or why she was that sadly screwed-up person. But the more she knew about a client, the better able she was to understand that client, to act and react accordingly. To manipulate. To get what Sabin wanted out of the witness.

Draining the tub, she dried off, wrapped herself in a fat terry robe, and took the last of her drink to the small antique writing desk in her bedroom. Her feminine sanctuary. Peach tones and rich deep green gave the room a sense of warmth and welcome. Nanci Griffith's quirky sweet voice drifted from the speakers of the small stereo system on the bookshelf. Thor, the Norwegian forest cat who held dominion over the house, had claimed Kate's bed as his rightful throne and lay in all his regal, hairy splendor dead center on the down comforter. He gazed at her with the bored supremacy of a crown prince.

Kate curled a leg beneath her on the chair, pulled a sheet of paper from a cubbyhole in the desk, and began to write.

Angie DiMarco

Name? Probably phony. Belongs to some woman in Wisconsin. Get someone to run it through Wisconsin DMV.

Family dead – figuratively or literally?
Abuse? Likely. Sexual? Strong probability.

Tattoos: multiple – professional and amateur.
Significance?
Significance of individual designs?
Body piercing: fashion or something more?

Compulsive behaviors: Nail biting. Smokes.
Drinks: How much? How often?
Drugs? Possibly. Thin, pale, unkempt. But seems too focused in
    behavior.

She could make only a thumbnail sketch of Angie's personality. Their time together had been too brief and too strongly influenced by the stress of the situation. Kate hated to think what conclusions some stranger would draw of *her* if she were thrust in a similar position. Stress triggered those old fight-or-flight instincts in everyone. But understanding didn't make the kid any more pleasant to deal with.

Luckily, the woman who ran the Phoenix House was accustomed to a wide range of bad attitudes. Residents at the house were women who had chosen or been forced down some of life's rougher roads and now wanted out.

Angie had been less than appreciative for the roof over her head. She had lashed out at Kate in a way that struck Kate as being way out of proportion.

'So what if I don't want to stay here?'

'Angie, you've got no place else to go.'

'You don't know that.'

'Don't make me go through this again,' Kate said with an impatient sigh.

Toni Urskine, director of the Phoenix, lingered in the doorway for that much of the exchange, watching with a frown. Then she left them to have it out in the otherwise deserted den, a small room with cheap paneling and cast-off furnishings. Mismatched rummage sale 'art' on the walls gave the place the ambience of a fleabag hotel.

'You have no permanent address,' Kate said. 'You tell me your family is dead. You haven't managed to come up with a single real-live person who would take you in. You need a place to stay. This is a place to stay. Three squares, bed, and bath. What's the problem?'

Angie swatted at a stained throw pillow on a worn plaid love seat. 'It's a fucking sty, that's the problem.'

'Oh, excuse me, you've been living at the Hilton? Your fake address wasn't in this good a house.'

'You like it so much, then you stay here.'

'I don't have to stay here. I'm not the homeless witness to a murder.'

'Well, I don't fucking want to be!' the girl cried, her eyes shining like crystal, sudden tears poised to spill down her cheeks. She turned away from

Kate and jammed the heels of her hands against her eyes. Her thin body curled in on itself like a comma.

'No, no, no,' she mewed softly to herself. 'Not now . . .'

The swift break in emotions caught Kate flatfooted. This was what she had wanted, wasn't it? To have the hard shell crack. Now that it had, she wasn't quite sure what to do about it. She hadn't been expecting the break to come now, over this.

Hesitantly, she stepped toward the girl, feeling awkward and guilty. 'Angie . . .'

'No,' the girl whispered more to herself than to Kate. 'Not now. Please, please . . .'

'You don't have to be embarrassed, Angie,' Kate said softly, standing close, though she made no attempt to touch the girl. 'You've had a hell of a day. I'd cry too. I'll cry later. I'm no good at it – my nose runs, it's gross.'

'Why c-c-can't I j-j-just stay with you?'

The question came from way out in left field, hit Kate square in the temple, and stunned her to her toes. As if this girl had never been away from home. As if she had never stayed among strangers. She'd likely been living on the street for God only knew how long, doing God only knew what to survive, and suddenly this dependence. It didn't make sense.

Before Kate could respond, Angie shook her head a little, rubbed the tears from her face with the sleeve of her jacket, and sucked in a ragged breath. That fast the window of opportunity shut and the steel mask was back in place.

'Never mind. Like you fucking care what happens to me.'

'Angie, I care what happens to you or I wouldn't have this job.'

'Yeah, right. Your job.'

'Look,' Kate said, out of energy for the argument, 'it beats sleeping in a box. Give it a couple of days. If you hate it here, I'll see about making some other arrangements. You've got my cell phone number. Call me if you need me or if you just need to talk. Anytime. I meant what I said – I'm on your side. I'll pick you up in the morning.'

Angie said nothing, just stood there looking sullen and small inside her too-big denim jacket that belonged to someone else.

'Try to get some sleep, kiddo,' Kate said softly.

She had left the girl standing in the den, staring out a window at the lights of the house next door. The poignant picture brought a sense of sympathy to Kate. The symbolism of a kid on the outside of a family looking in. A child with no one.

'This is why I don't work with kids,' she said now to the cat. 'They'd just ruin my reputation as a hard-ass.'

Thor trilled deep in his throat and rolled onto his back, offering his hairy belly for rubbing. She complied, enjoying the contact with another living being who appreciated and loved her in her own way. And she thought of Angie DiMarco lying awake in the night, in a house filled with strangers, the one connection in her life that meant anything to anyone being her connection to a killer.

A blinking message light greeted Quinn as he let himself into his room at the Radisson Plaza Hotel. He tossed the sack of Mexican take-out in the wastebasket beneath the writing table, called room service, and ordered wild rice soup and a turkey sandwich he probably wouldn't eat. His stomach couldn't deal with Mexican anymore.

He stripped out of his clothes, crammed everything but his shoes into a plastic laundry bag, tied the bag shut, and set it by the door. Someone down in laundry was in for an unpleasant surprise.

The water pounded out of the shower head like a hail of bullets, as hot as he could stand it. He scrubbed his hair and body and let the water work on the knots in his shoulders, then he turned and let it pelt him in the face and chest. Images from the day tumbled through his head, out of order: the meeting, Bondurant's lawyer, the rush to the airport, the crime scene tape fluttering around the trunks of sturdy maple trees, Kate.

Kate. Five years was a long time. In five years she had established herself in a new career, she had a new life – which she deserved after all that had gone wrong in Virginia.

And what had he built in five years besides his reputation and a lot of unused vacation time?

Nothing. He owned a town house and a Porsche and a closet full of designer suits. He socked the rest of his money away for a retirement that would probably end in a massive coronary two months after he left the Bureau because he had nothing else in his life. If the job didn't kill him first.

He turned the water off, climbed out of the shower, and toweled himself dry. He had an athlete's body, solid, roped with muscle, leaner than it used to be – the reverse of most men in their mid-forties. He couldn't remember when his enjoyment of food had become indifference. Once upon a time he had considered himself a gourmet cook. Now he ate because he had to. The exercise he used to burn off tension burned off all the calories as well.

The greasy, spicy smell of the discarded Mexican food was permeating the bedroom. A smell preferable to a burned corpse, though he knew from experience it wouldn't be so welcome when it turned stale and he woke up to it at three in the morning.

The thought brought on a tumble of unpleasant memories of other hotel rooms in other cities and other dinners bought to fight off the aftertaste and smell of death. Of lying awake, alone in a strange bed in the middle of the night, sweating like a horse from nightmares, his heart racing.

The panic hit him in the gut like a sledgehammer, and he sat down on the edge of the bed in sweat pants and a gray FBI Academy T-shirt. He put his head in his hands for a moment, dreading the attack – the hollowness, the dizziness; the tremors that started in the core of him and rattled outward, down his arms and legs; the sense that there was nothing left of who he really was, the fear that he wouldn't know the difference.

He cursed himself and reached down deep for the strength to fight it off as he had done again and again in the last year. Or was it two now? He measured time by cases, measured cases by bodies. He had a recurring dream that he was locked away in a white room, pulling the hair out of his head one by one and naming each after the victims, pasting the hairs to the wall with his saliva.

He clicked the television on for noise to drown out the voice of fear in his head, then dialed the phone for his voice-mail messages.

Seven calls regarding other cases he had dragged here with him: a string of robberies and torture murders of gay men in Miami; the poisoning deaths of five elderly women in Charlotte, North Carolina; a child abduction case in Blacksburg, Virginia, that had, as of 8:19 P.M. eastern standard time, become a homicide with the discovery of the little girl's body in a wooded ravine.

Goddamn, he should have been there. Or maybe he should have been in rural Georgia, where a mother of four had been beaten to death with a ball peen hammer in a fashion reminiscent of three other murders in the last five years. Or maybe he should have been in England, consulting with Scotland Yard on the case that had turned up nine mutilated bodies in the yard of an abandoned slaughterhouse, the eyes gouged out of each and the mouths sewn shut with waxed thread.

'Special Agent Quinn, this is Edwyn Noble —'

'And you got this number how?' Quinn asked aloud as the message played.

He wasn't thrilled with Noble's in with this investigation.

Being married to the mayor gave him a foot in the door no other lawyer in the city would have had. Being Peter Bondurant's attorney forced the door open wider.

'I'm calling on behalf of Mr Bondurant. Peter would very much like to meet with you tomorrow morning if possible. Please give me a call back tonight.'

He left the number, then a seductive taped voice informed Quinn he had no further messages. He recradled the receiver with no intention of picking it up again to call Noble. Let him stew. If he had something pertinent to the case, he could call Kovac or Fowler, the homicide lieutenant. Quinn called no one back, preferring to wait until after he didn't eat his dinner.

The ten o'clock news led with the latest murder, flashing taped footage of the crime scene unit combing over the dumping site in the park, then going to the tape of the press conference. A photo of Jillian Bondurant came up with another of her red Saab. A good three and a half minutes of coverage, total. The average news story ran less than half that.

Quinn dug the files for the first two murders out of his briefcase and stacked them on the writing desk. Copies of investigative reports and crime scene photos. Autopsy reports, lab reports, initial and follow-up investigative reports. News clippings from both the *Minneapolis Star Tribune* and the *St Paul Pioneer Press*. Descriptions, and photos of the crime scenes.

He had stated very clearly he wanted no information on possible suspects if there were any, and none had been included. He couldn't let anyone's speculation about a possible suspect cloud his judgment or steer his analysis in one direction or another. This was yet another reason he would have preferred to put the profile together from his office in Quantico. Here he was too close; the case was all around him. The personalities involved in the cases could spur reactions he would not have looking at a collection of adjectives and facts. There was too much worthless input, too many distractions.

Too many distractions – like Kate. Who hadn't called and had no reason to really. Except that they had once shared something special . . . and walked away from it . . . and let it die . . .

Nothing in a man's life had the power to be quite so distracting as the irreparable past. The only cure he had found for the past was to try to control the present, which meant pouring himself into the case at hand. Focus with intensity on maintaining control of the present. And on maintaining control of his sanity. And when the nights stretched long – as they all did – and his mind raced with the details of a hundred murders, he could feel his grip slipping on both.

Angie sat at the head of the small, hard twin bed, her back pressed into the corner so that she could feel the nubby plaster wall biting through the baggy flannel shirt she had chosen to sleep in. She sat with her knees pulled up beneath her chin, her arms wrapped tight around her legs. The door was closed, she was alone. The only light coming in through the window came from a distant streetlamp.

The Phoenix was a house for women 'rising to a new beginning'. So said the sign on the front lawn. It was a big, rambling old house with squeaky floors and no frills. Kate had brought her there and dumped her among the ex-hookers and ex-dopers and women trying to escape boyfriends who beat the shit out of them.

Angie had looked in at some of them watching TV in a big living room full of ratty furniture, and thought how stupid they must be. If there was one thing she had learned in life, it was that you could escape circumstance, but you could never escape who you were. Your personal truth was a shadow: There was no denying it, no changing it, and no getting rid of it.

She felt the shadow sweep over her now, cold and black. Her body trembled and tears rose in her eyes. She had been fighting it off all day, all night. She had thought it was going to swallow her whole right in front of Kate – an idea that only added to the panic. She couldn't lose control in front of anyone. Then they'd know that she was crazy, that she was defective. They'd ship her off to the nuthouse. She'd be alone then.

She was alone now.

The tremor began at the very core of her, then opened up wider and wider into a weird, hollow feeling. At the same time, she felt her consciousness shrinking and shrinking until she felt as if her body was just a shell and she was a tiny being locked inside it, in danger of falling off a ledge into some dark chasm inside and never being able to climb out.

She called this feeling the Zone. The Zone was an old enemy. But as well as she knew it, it never failed to terrify her. She knew if she didn't fight it off, she could lose control, and control was everything. If she didn't fight it off, she could lose whole blocks of time. She could lose herself, and what would happen then?

It shook her now, and she started to cry. Silently. Always silently. She couldn't let anyone hear her, she couldn't let them know how afraid she was. Her mouth tore open, but she strangled the sobs until her throat ached. She pressed her face against her knees, closing her eyes tight. The tears burned, fell, slid down her bare thigh.

In her mind, she could see the burning corpse. She ran from it. She ran and ran but didn't get anywhere. In her mind, the corpse became her, but she couldn't feel the flames. She would have welcomed the pain, but she couldn't conjure it up with just her mind. And all the while she felt herself growing smaller and smaller inside the shell of her body.

Stop it! Stop it! Stop it! She pinched her thigh hard, digging the ragged edge of her fingernails into the skin. And still she felt herself being sucked deeper and deeper into the Zone.

You know what you have to do. The voice unfurled in her mind like a black ribbon. She shivered in response to it. It twined itself through vital parts of her, a strange matrix of fear and need.

You know what you have to do.

Frantically, she pulled her backpack to her, fumbled with the zipper, and dug through an inner pocket for the thing she needed. Her fingers curled around the box cutter, which was disguised as a small plastic key.

Shaking, choking back the sobs, she crawled to a wedge of light on the bed and shoved up the left sleeve of the flannel shirt, exposing a thin white arm that was striped with narrow scars, one beside another and another, lining her arms like bars in an iron fence. The razor emerged from the end of the box cutter like a serpent's tongue and she drew it across a patch of tender skin near her elbow.

The pain was sharp and sweet, and seemed to short-circuit the panic that had electrified her brain. Blood blossomed from the cut, a shiny black bead in the moonlight. She stared at it, mesmerized as the calm flowed through her.

Control. Life was all about control. Pain and control. She had learned that lesson long ago.

'I'm thinking of changing my name,' he says. 'What do you think of Elvis? Elvis Nagel.'

His companion says nothing. He picks up a pair of panties from the pile in the box and presses them to his face, burying his nose in the crotch and sniffing deep the scent of pussy. Nice. Smell is not as good a stimulant as sound for him, but still . . .

'Get it?' he says. 'It's an anagram. Elvis Nagel – Evil's Angel.'

In the background, three televisions are running videotapes of the local six o'clock newscasts. The voices blend together in a discordant cacophony he finds stimulating. The common thread that runs through them all is urgency. Urgency breeds fear. Fear excites him. He especially enjoys the sound of it. The tight, quivering tension underlying a controlled voice. The erratic changes in pitch and tone in the voice of someone openly afraid.

The mayor appears on two screens. The ugly cow. He watches her speak, wondering what it might be like to cut her lips off while she is still alive. Maybe make her eat them. The fantasy excites, as his fantasies always have.

He turns up the volume on the televisions, then crosses to the stereo system set into the bookcase, selects a cassette from the rack, and slips it into the machine. He stands in the center of the basement room, staring at the televisions, at the furrowed brows of anchormen and the faces of the people at the press conference shot from three different angles, and lets the sounds wash over him – the voices of the reporters, the background echo in the cavernous hall, the urgency. At the same time from the stereo speakers comes the voice of raw, unvarnished fear. Pleading. Crying for God. Begging for death. His triumph.

He stands in the center of it. The conductor of this macabre opera. The excitement builds inside him, a huge, hot, swelling, sexual excitement that builds to a crescendo and demands release. He looks to his companion for the evening, considering, but he controls the need.

Control is all. Control is power. *He* is the action. *They* are the reaction. He wants to see the fear in all their faces, to hear it in their voices – the police, the task force, John Quinn. Especially Quinn, who hadn't even bothered to speak at the press conference, as if he wanted the Cremator to think he didn't warrant his personal attention.

He will have Quinn's attention. He will have their respect. He will have whatever he wants because he has control.

He turns the televisions down to a dull mumble but leaves them on so he won't return to silence. Silence is something he abhors. He turns off the stereo system but pockets a microcassette recorder loaded with a tape.

'I'm going out,' he says. 'I've had enough of you. You're boring me.'

He goes to the mannequin he has been playing with, trying different combinations of the clothes of his victims.

'Not that I don't appreciate you,' he says quietly.

He leans forward and kisses her, putting his tongue in her open mouth.

Then he lifts the head of his last victim off the shoulders of the mannequin, puts it back into its plastic bag, takes it to the refrigerator in the laundry room, and sets it carefully on a shelf.

The night is thick with fog and mist, the streets black and gleaming wet in the glow of the streetlights. A night reminiscent of the Ripper's London. A night for hunting.

He smiles at the thought as he drives toward the lake. He smiles wider as he presses the play button on the microcassette recorder and holds the machine against his ear, the screams a twisted metamorphosis of a lover's whispered words. Affection and desire warped into hatred and fear. Two sides of the same emotions. The difference is control.

9

'If the newsies find us here, I'll eat my shorts,' Kovac declared, turning around in a circle in the middle of the floor.

One wall was papered in a montage of naked women engaged in various erotic pursuits, the other three in cheap red flocked paper that best resembled moth-eaten velvet.

'Something tells me you could have gotten that done here for you,' Quinn remarked dryly. He sniffed the air, identifying the smells of mice, cheap perfume, and damp underwear. 'For a bargain price.'

'The newsies find us here, our careers are toast,' Elwood Knutson said. The big homicide sergeant pulled a giant ceramic penis out of a drawer behind the counter and held it up for all to see.

Liska made a face. 'Jesus, Sam. You sure know how to pick 'em.'

'Don't look at me! You think I hang out in massage parlors?'

'Yeah.'

'Very funny. These lovely accommodations are courtesy of Detective Adler, Hennepin County Sheriff's Office. Chunk, take a bow.'

Adler, a chunk of muscle with ebony skin and a tight cap of steel-gray curls, gave a sheepish grin and a wave to the rest of the task force. 'My sister works for Norwest Banks. They foreclosed on the building after sex crimes shut the place down last summer. The location is perfect, the price is right – meaning free – and the press lost interest in the place after the hookers moved out. No one's going to suspect this is where we're meeting.'

Which was the main point, Quinn thought as he followed Kovac down the narrow hall, the detective turning on lights in the succession of four smaller rooms – two on either side of the hall. It was essential that the task force be allowed to do their jobs without interruption or distraction, without having to run a gauntlet of reporters. A place where the case could be contained and leaks kept to a minimum.

And if the leaks continued, Elwood was right. The press would roast their careers on a public bonfire.

'I love it!' Kovac declared, striding back down the hall to the front room. 'Let's set up.'

Liska wrinkled her nose. 'Can we hose it down with Lysol first?'

'Sure, Tinks. You can redecorate the place while the rest of us are solving these murders.'

'Oh, fuck you, Kojak. I hope you're the first to catch the cooties from the toilet seat.'

'Naw, that'll be Bear Butt in there with the *Reader's Digest*. Cooties see his hairy ass and come running. He's probably got a whole civilization living in that pelt.'

Elwood, who was roughly the size and shape of a small grizzly, raised his head with dignity. 'On behalf of hairy people everywhere, I take umbrage.'

'Yeah?' Kovac said. 'Well, take your umbrage outside and grab some stuff. We're burning daylight.'

Two unmarked utility vans from the PD fleet were parked in the alley, loaded with the necessary office furniture and equipment. All of it was carried into the former Loving Touch Massage Parlor, along with boxes of office supplies, a coffeemaker, and, most important, the boxes containing the files on all three murders attributed to the killer the detectives privately called Smokey Joe.

Quinn worked alongside the others. Just one of the guys. Trying to blend into another team like a free agent cleanup hitter drifting from one baseball park to another. Brought in by management to hit a dinger in the big game, then cut loose and sent on to the next crucial moment. The jokes felt forced, the attempts at camaraderie false. Some of these people would feel they knew him by the time all this was over. They wouldn't really know him at all.

Still, he went through the motions as he always did, knowing none of the people around him could tell the difference – the same way people working side by side with this serial killer wouldn't know or suspect. People in general had a myopic view of their own small worlds. They focused on what was important to them. The rotting soul of the guy in the next cubicle didn't matter to them – until his disease touched their lives.

In short order, the Loving Touch had been transformed from a brothel to a tactical war room. By nine o'clock the entire task force had assembled: six detectives from the Minneapolis PD, three from the Sheriff's Office, two from the state Bureau of Criminal Apprehension, Quinn, and Walsh.

Walsh looked like he had malaria.

Kovac briefed them on all three murders, finishing with the autopsy of the Jane Doe victim, complete with photographs that had been rushed through the lab for processing and enlarging.

'We'll have some of the preliminary lab results today,' he said as he passed the gruesome pictures around the table. 'We've got a blood type – O positive – which happens to be Jillian Bondurant's – and a gazillion other people's.

'I want you to note the photographs of wounds where sections of flesh have been cut from the body. We had similar wounds on the first two vics. We're speculating the killer may be cutting away bite marks. But with this latest, he might have cut away any identifying marks that could prove or disprove the victim's identity: scars, moles, et cetera.'

'Tattoos,' someone said.

'Bondurant's father is unaware of Jillian having any tattoos. According to his lawyer, he couldn't come up with any distinguishing marks at all. Jillian had been out of his life for about half of hers, so I guess it's not surprising. We're trying to come up with photographs of her in a bathing suit or something, but no luck so far.

'We're proceeding on the assumption that Jillian Bondurant is the vic,' he said, 'but staying open to other possibilities. There've been a few calls to the hotline, people claiming they've seen her since Friday, but none of them have panned out yet.'

'Are you going to bring up the K word?' asked Mary Moss from the BCA. She looked like a soccer mom from the suburbs in a turtleneck and tweed blazer. Oversize glasses dominated her oval face. Her thick gray-blond pageboy seemed in need of a serious thinning.

'There haven't been any ransom demands that we know of,' Kovac said, 'but it's not beyond the realm.'

'Big Daddy Bondurant sure never jumped to the kidnapping conclusion,' Adler said. 'Anyone find that strange besides me?'

'He heard about the driver's license found with the body and accepted the probability the body was hers,' Hamill concluded.

Adler spread hands the size of catcher's mits. 'I say again: Anyone find that strange besides me? Who wants to believe their child is the decapitated victim of a homicidal maniac? Man as rich as Bondurant, isn't he gonna think kidnapping before murder?'

'Is he talking yet?' Elwood asked, chowing down a bran muffin as he perused the autopsy photos.

'Not to me,' Kovac said.

'I don't like the smell of that either.'

'His attorney called me last night and left a message,' Quinn said. 'Bondurant wants to see me this morning.'

Kovac stepped back, nonplussed. 'No shit? What'd you tell him?'

'Nothing. I let him hang overnight. I don't particularly want to meet him at this stage of the game, but if it helps you get a foot in his door . . .'

Kovac smiled like a shark. 'You need a lift over to the Bondurant house, don't you, John?'

Quinn tipped his head, wincing. 'Do I have time to call and up my life insurance?'

Laughter erupted around the table. Kovac made a face.

'He gave me a lift from the morgue last night,' Quinn explained. 'I thought I'd be going back in a black bag.'

'Hey,' Kovac barked with false annoyance. 'I got you there in one piece.'

'Actually, I think my spleen is over on Marquette somewhere. Maybe we can pick it up on the way.'

'He's been here a day and already he's got your number, Sam,' Liska joked.

'Yeah, like you should talk, Tinks,' someone else countered.

'I drive like Kovac only when I've got PMS.'

Kovac held up a hand. 'Okay, okay, back to business. Back to the bite marks. We ran that feature through the database back when we were looking at the first murder, searching for any known offenders in the metro – murderers or sex offenders – who had bitten or cannibalized victims, and came up with a list. We also ran it through VICAP and came up with another list.' He lifted a sheaf of computer printouts.

'How long before we can confirm or deny this body is Bondurant's?'

Gary 'Charm' Yurek of the PD had been designated media spokesman for the task force, giving the line of official bullshit to the press every day. He had a face worthy of a soap star. People tended to become distracted by the utter perfection of his smile and miss that he hadn't really told them anything.

Kovac looked now to Walsh. 'Vince, any word on the girl's health records?'

Walsh hacked a phlegm-rattling cough, shaking his head. 'The Paris office is tracking them down. They've been trying to contact the stepfather, but he's somewhere between construction sites in Hungary and Slovakia.'

'Apparently, she's been the picture of health since her return to the States,' Liska said. 'She's had no serious injuries or illness, nothing to warrant X-rays – except her teeth.'

'He screwed us up but good taking her head,' Elwood complained.

'You come up with any ideas on that, John?' Kovac asked.

'Could be he meant to jam up the investigation. Could be that the body isn't Jillian Bondurant and he's sending some kind of message or playing a game,' Quinn suggested. 'Maybe he knew the victim – whoever she was – and decapitated her to depersonalize her. Or the decapitation could be the new step in the escalation of his violent fantasies and how he plays them out. He could be keeping the head as a trophy. He could be using it to further act out his sexual fantasies.'

'Judas,' Chunk muttered.

Tippen, another of the sheriff's detectives, scowled. 'You're not exactly narrowing it down.'

'I don't know enough about him yet,' Quinn said evenly.

'What *do* you know?'

'Basics.'

'Such as?'

He looked to Kovac, who motioned him to the head of the table.

'This is *not* by any means the completed analysis. I want that made clear. I did a quick read-through of the reports last night, but it takes more than a couple of hours to build a solid, accurate profile.'

'Okay, you've covered your ass,' Tippen said impatiently. 'So who do you think we're looking for?'

Quinn held his temper in check. It was nothing new to have a skeptic in the crowd. He had learned long ago how to play them, how to pull them around a little at a time with logic and practicality. He leveled his gaze on Tippen, a lean, homely man with a face like an Irish wolfhound – all nose and mustache and shaggy brows over sharp, dark eyes.

'Your UNSUB is a white male, probably between the ages of thirty and thirty-five. Sadistic sexual serial killers hunt within their own ethnic group as a rule.' Pointing to the close-ups of wounds from the crime scene photos, he said, 'You've got a very specific pattern of wounds, carefully repeated on each victim. He's spent a long time perfecting this fantasy. When you find him you'll find a collection of S&M pornography. He's been into it for a long while. The sophistication of the crimes, the care taken to leave no usable physical evidence, suggests maturity and experience. He may have an old record as a sex offender. But record or no, he's been on this course from when he was in his late teens or early twenties.

'He likely started with window peeping or fetish burglaries – stealing women's underwear and so forth. That may still be a part of his fantasy. We don't know what he's doing with the victims' clothing. The clothes he dresses them in after he's killed them are clothes he's chosen for them from his own source.'

'You suppose he played with Barbie dolls as a kid?' Tippen said to Adler.

'If he did, you can bet they ended up with limbs missing,' Quinn said.

'Jesus, I was kidding.'

'No joke, Detective. Aberrant fantasies can begin as young as five or six. Particularly in a home with sexual abuse or open sexual promiscuity going on – which is almost a sure bet in this case.

'He's likely murdered long before your first victim and gotten away with it. Escaping detection will make him feel bold, invulnerable. His presentation of the bodies in a public area where he could have been seen and where the bodies would certainly be found is risky and suggests arrogance. It also suggests the type of killer who can be drawn to the investigation. He wants attention, he's watching the news, clipping articles from the paper.'

'So Chief Greer was right yesterday when he said we should make a statement to this creep,' Kovac said.

'He'll be just as right today or tomorrow, when we're ready to make a move.'

'And it looks like your idea,' Tippen muttered.

'I'll be happy to let you suggest it to the brass, Detective,' Quinn said. 'I don't give a rat's ass who gets credit. I don't want my name in the paper. I don't want to see myself on TV. Hell, I'd just as soon be doing this job in my office sixty feet underground back in Quantico. I have one objective here: helping you nail this son of a bitch and take him out of society forever and ever, amen. That's all this is about for me.'

Tippen dropped his gaze to his notepad, a nonbeliever still.

Kovac huffed a little sigh. 'You know, we got no time for fence pissing. I'm sure no one in the general public gives a rip which one of us has the biggest dick.'

'I have,' Liska chirped, snatching the giant ceramic penis away from Elwood, who had set it on the table as a centerpiece. She held it up as proof of her claim.

Laughter broke the tension.

'Anyway,' Quinn went on, sliding his hands into his pants pockets and cocking a leg, settling in, subtly letting Tippen know he wasn't going anywhere and wasn't bothered by his opinions. 'We have to be careful about how we draw him in. I'd suggest starting with a heavily publicized community meeting held in a location central between the dumping sites. You're asking for help, for community participation. It's nonaggressive, nonthreatening. He can come into that scenario feeling anonymous and safe.

'It won't be easy to trick him unless his arrogance gets out of hand. He's organized. He's of above-average intelligence. He's got a job, but it may be beneath his capabilities. He knows the city parks system, so if you haven't done so already, you'll want to get a parks service employee roster, see if anyone has a criminal record.'

'Already happening,' Kovac said.

'How do you know he has a job at all?' Tippen challenged. 'How do you know he's not some drifter, familiar with the parks because that's where he hangs out?'

'He's no drifter,' Quinn said with certainty. 'He's got a house. The crime scenes are not the death scenes. The women were abducted, taken someplace, and held there. He needs privacy, a place where he can torture his victims without having to worry about anyone hearing.

'Also, he may have more than one vehicle. He probably has access to a Suburban-type truck or a pickup. A basic package, older, dark in color, fairly well kept. Something to transport the bodies in, a vehicle that wouldn't seem out of place pulling into the service lot of a city park. But this may not be what he's picking them up in, because a big vehicle would be conspicuous and memorable to witnesses.'

'How do you know he's an underachiever?' Frank Hamill asked.

'Because that's the norm for this type of killer. He has a job because it's necessary. But his energies, his *talents,* are applied to his hobby. He spends a lot of his time fantasizing. He lives for the next kill. A corporate CEO wouldn't have that kind of free time.'

'Even though they're mostly psychopaths,' someone joked.

Quinn flashed a shark smile. 'Be glad some of them like their day jobs.'

'What else?' Liska asked. 'Any guesses on appearance?'

'I've got mixed feelings on this because of the conflicting victimology.'

'Hookers go for cash, not flash,' Elwood said.

'And if all three victims were hookers, I'd say we're looking for a guy who's unattractive, maybe has some kind of problem like a stutter or a scar, something that would make it difficult for him to approach women. But if our third vic is the daughter of a billionaire?' Quinn arched a brow.

'Who knows what she might have been into.'

'Is there any reason to think she was involved in prostitution?' Quinn asked. 'On the surface she wouldn't seem to have much in common with the first two victims.'

'She doesn't have a record,' Liska said. 'But then, her father is Peter Bondurant.'

'I need more extensive victimology on all three women,' Quinn said. 'If there's any kind of common link between them, that's a prime spot for you to start developing a suspect.'

'Two hookers and a billionaire's daughter – what could they possibly have in common?' Yurek asked.

'Drugs,' Liska said.

'A man,' Mary Moss offered.

Kovac nodded. 'You two want to work that angle?'

The women nodded.

'But maybe the guy just nabbed these women from behind,' Tippen suggested. 'Maybe he didn't need to finesse them. Maybe he picked them because they were in the wrong place at the wrong time.'

'It's possible. It just doesn't feel that way to me,' Quinn said. 'He's too smooth. These women just vanished. No one saw a struggle. No one heard a scream. Logic tells me they went with him willingly.'

'So where's Bondurant's car?' Adler asked. Jillian's red Saab had yet to be located.

'Maybe *she* picked *him* up,' Liska said. 'It's the nineties. Maybe he's still got her car.'

'So we're looking for a killer with a three-car garage?' Adler said. 'Hell, I am in the wrong line of work.'

'You want to start whacking ex-wives for a living, you could fill the damn garage with Porsches,' Kovac joked.

Liska punched him in the arm. 'Hey! *I'm* an ex-wife.'

'Present company excluded.'

Quinn took a long drink of his coffee while the jokes ran through the group. Humor was a safety valve for cops, releasing measured bursts of pressure the job built up inside them. The members of this team were standing at the start of what would undoubtedly be a long, unpleasant gauntlet. They would need to squeeze a joke in wherever they could. The better their rapport as a unit, the better for the investigation. He usually tossed in a few jokes himself to bend the image of the straitlaced G-man.

'Sizewise,' he went on, 'he'll probably be medium height, medium build – strong enough to tote a dead body around but not so big as to seem a physical threat when he's approaching his victims. That's about as much as I can give you for now.'

'What? Can't you just close your eyes and conjure up a psychic photograph or something?' Adler said, only half joking.

'Sorry, Detective,' Quinn said with a grin and a shrug. 'If I were psychic, I'd be making my living at the racetrack. Not a psychic cell in my body.'

'You would have if you was on TV.'

'If we were on TV, we'd have solved these crimes in an hour,' Elwood said. 'TV is why the public gets impatient with an investigation that lasts more than two days. The whole damn country lives on TV time.'

'Speaking of TV,' Hamill said, holding up a videocassette. 'I've got the tape from the press conference.'

A television with a built-in VCR sat atop a wheeled metal cart near the head of the table. Hamill loaded the cassette and they all sat back to watch. At Quinn's request, a videographer from the BCA special operations unit had been stationed discreetly among the cameramen from the local stations with instructions to capture not the event, but the people gathered to take it in.

The voices of the mayor, Chief Greer, and the county attorney droned in the background as the camera scanned the faces of reporters and cops and news photographers. Quinn stared at the screen, tuned to pick up the slightest nuances of expression, the glint of something knowing in a pair of eyes, the hint of something smug playing at the corners of a mouth. His attention was on the people at the periphery of the crowd, people who seemed to be there by accident or coincidence.

He looked for that intangible, almost imperceptible something that set a detective's instincts on point. The knowledge that their killer might have been standing there among the unsuspecting, that he could have been looking at the face of a murderer without knowing, stirred a deep sense of frustration within. This killer wouldn't stand out. He wouldn't appear to be nervous. He wouldn't have the wild-eyed edginess that would give him away as disorganized offenders often did. He'd killed at least three women and gotten away with it. The police had no viable leads. He had nothing to worry about. And he knew it.

'Well,' Tippen said dryly. 'I don't see anyone carrying an extra head with them.'

'We could be looking right at him and not know it,' Kovac said, hitting the power button on the remote control. 'But if we come up with a possible suspect, we can go back and look again.'

'We gonna get that composite from the wit today, Sam?' Adler asked.

Kovac's mouth twisted a little. 'I sure as hell hope so. I've already had calls from the chief and Sabin about it.' And they would ride his ass until they got it. He was the primary. He ran the investigation and took the heat. 'In the meantime, let's make assignments and hit the bricks before Smokey Joe decides to light up another one.'

Peter Bondurant's home was a sprawling old Tudor with an expensive view of Lake of the Isles beyond its tall iron bar fence. Tall bare-branched trees studded the lawn. One broad wall of the stucco home was crazed with a network of vines, dry and brown this time of year. Just a few miles from the heart of Minneapolis, it discreetly displayed signs of city life paranoia along the fence and on the closed driveway gate in the form of blue-and-white security company signs.

Quinn tried to take it all in visually and still pay attention to the call on his cell phone. A suspect had been apprehended in the child abduction in Blacksburg, Virginia. The CASKU agent on site wanted to confirm a strategy for the interrogation. Quinn was sounding board and guru. He listened, agreed, made a suggestion, and signed off as quickly as he could, wanting his focus on the matter at hand.

'The man in demand,' Kovac remarked as he swung the car into the drive too fast and hit the brakes, rocking to a stop beside the intercom panel. His gaze moved past Quinn to the news vans parked on either side of the street. The occupants of the vans stared back.

'Lousy vultures.'

A voice crackled from the intercom speaker. 'Yes?'

'John Quinn, FBI,' Kovac said with drama, flashing a comic look at Quinn.

The gate rolled open, then closed behind them. The reporters made no move to rush in. Midwestern manners, Quinn thought, knowing full well there were places in this country where the press would have stormed the place and demanded answers as if they had a right to tear apart the grief that belonged to the victim's family. He'd seen it happen. He'd seen promotion-hungry reporters dig through people's garbage for scraps of information that could be turned into speculative headlines. He'd seen them crash funerals.

A black Lincoln Continental polished to a hard shine sat in the driveway near the house. Kovac pulled his dirt-brown Caprice alongside the luxury car and turned the key. The engine rattled on pathetically for half a minute.

'Cheap piece of crap,' he muttered. 'Twenty-two years on the job and I get the worst fucking car in the fleet. You know why?'

'Because you won't kiss the right ass?' Quinn ventured.

Kovac huffed a laugh. 'I'm not kissing anything that's got a dick on the flip side.' He chuckled to himself as he dug through a pile of junk on the seat, finally coming up with a mini cassette recorder, which he offered to Quinn.

'In case he still won't talk to me . . . By Minnesota law, only one party to a conversation needs to grant permission to tape that conversation.'

'Hell of a law for a state full of Democrats.'

'We're practical. We've got a killer to catch. Maybe Bondurant knows something he doesn't realize. Or maybe he'll say something that won't ring a bell with you because you're not from here.'

Quinn slipped the recorder into the inside breast pocket of his suit coat. 'The end justifies the means.'

'You know it.'

'Better than most.'

'Does it ever get to you?' Kovac asked as they got out of the car. 'Working serial murders and child abductions twenty-four/seven. I gotta think that'd get to me. At least some of the stiffs I get deserved to get whacked. How do you cope?'

I don't. The response was automatic – and just as automatically unspoken. He didn't cope. He never had. He just shoveled it all into the big dark pit inside him and hoped to hell the pit didn't overflow.

'Focus on the win column,' he said.

The wind cut across the lake, kicking up whitecaps on water that looked like mercury, and chasing dead leaves across the dead lawn. It flirted with the tails of Quinn's and Kovac's trench coats. The sky looked like dirty cotton batting sinking down on the city.

'I drink,' Kovac confessed amiably. 'I smoke and I drink.'

A grin tugged at Quinn's mouth. 'And chase women?'

'Naw, I gave that up. It's a bad habit.'

Edwyn Noble answered the door. Lurch with a law degree. His expression froze at the sight of Kovac.

'Special Agent Quinn,' he began as they moved past him into an entry hall of carved mahogany paneling. A massive wrought iron chandelier hung from the second-story ceiling. 'I don't remember you mentioning Sergeant Kovac when you called.'

Quinn flashed him innocence. 'Didn't I? Well, Sam offered to drive me, and I don't know my way around the city, so . . .'

'I've been wanting to talk to Mr Bondurant myself anyway,' Kovac said casually, browsing the artwork on display in the hall, his hands stuffed into his pockets as if he were afraid of breaking something.

The lawyer's ears turned red around the rim. 'Sergeant, Peter's just lost his only child. He'd like to have a little time to collect himself before he has to be subjected to any kind of questioning.'

'Questioning?' Kovac's brows arched as he glanced up from a sculpture of a racehorse. He exchanged a look with Quinn. 'Like a suspect? Does Mr Bondurant think we consider him a suspect? Because I don't know where he would have gotten that idea. Do you, Mr Noble?'

Color streaked across Noble's cheekbones. 'Interview. Statement. Whatever you'd like to call it.'

'I'd like to call it a conversation, but, hey, whatever you want.'

'What I want,' came a quiet voice from beyond an arched doorway, 'is to have my daughter back.'

The man who emerged from the dimly lit interior hall was half a foot shy of six feet, with a slight build and an air of neatness and precision even in casual slacks and a sweater. His dark hair was cropped so close to his skull it

81

looked like a fine coating of metal shavings. He stared at Quinn with serious eyes through the small oval lenses of wire-framed glasses.

'That's what we all want, Mr Bondurant,' Quinn said. 'There may still be a chance of making that happen, but we'll need all the help we can get.'

The straight brows drew together in confusion. 'You think Jillian might still be alive?'

'We haven't been able to conclusively determine otherwise,' Kovac said. 'Until we can positively identify the victim, there's a chance it's not your daughter. We've had some unsubstantiated sightings –'

Bondurant shook his head. 'No, I don't think so,' he said softly. 'Jillie is dead.'

'How do you know that?' Quinn asked. Bondurant's expression was somber, tormented, defeated. His gaze skated off somewhere to Quinn's left.

'Because she was my child,' he said at last. 'I can't explain it any better than that. There's a feeling – like a rock in my gut, like some part of me died with her. She's gone.

'Do you have children, Agent Quinn?' he asked.

'No. But I've known too many parents who've lost a child. It's a terrible place to be. If I were you, I wouldn't be in any hurry to get there.'

Bondurant looked down at Quinn's shoes and breathed a sigh. 'Come into my study, Agent Quinn,' he said, then turned to Kovac, his mouth tightening subtly. 'Edwyn, why don't you and Sergeant Kovac wait for us in the living room?'

Kovac made a sound of dissatisfaction.

Concern tightened the lawyer's features. 'Perhaps I should sit in, Peter. I –'

'No. Have Helen get you coffee.'

Clearly unhappy, Noble leaned toward his client across the hall like a marionette straining against its strings. Bondurant turned and walked away.

Quinn followed. Their footfalls were muffled by the fine wool of a thick Oriental runner. He wondered at Bondurant's strategy. He wouldn't talk to the police, but he banished his attorney from a conversation with an FBI agent. It didn't make sense if he was trying to protect himself. Then again, anything incriminating he said in the absence of his attorney would be worthless in court, audiotape or no audiotape.

'I understand you have a witness. Can she identify the man who did this?'

'I'm not at liberty to discuss that,' Quinn said. 'I'd like to talk about you and your daughter, your relationship. Forgive me for being blunt, but your lack of cooperation with the police thus far comes across as puzzling at best.'

'You think I'm not reacting in the typical way of a parent of a murdered child? *Is there* a typical reaction?'

'*Typical* is maybe not the word. Some reactions are more common than others.'

'I don't know anything that would be pertinent to the case. Therefore, I have nothing further to tell the police. A stranger abducted and murdered my daughter. How could they expect me to have any information relevant to such a senseless act?'

Bondurant led the way into a spacious office and closed the door. The room was dominated by a massive U-shaped mahogany desk, one wing of which was devoted to computer equipment, one to paperwork. The center section was meticulously neat, the blotter spotless, every pen and paper clip in its place.

'Take your coat off, Agent Quinn. Have a seat.' He gestured a thin hand toward a pair of oxblood leather chairs while he went around the desk to claim his own place in a high-backed executive's throne.

Putting distance and authority between them, Quinn thought, shrugging out of his topcoat. *Putting me in my place.* He settled into a chair, realizing immediately that it squatted just a little too low to the ground, just enough to make its occupant feel vaguely small.

'Some maniac murdered my daughter,' Bondurant said again calmly. 'In the face of that, I can't really give a good goddamn what anyone thinks of my behavior. Besides, I *am* helping the investigation: I brought you here.'

Another reminder of the balance of power, softly spoken. 'And you're willing to talk to me?'

'Bob Brewster says you're the best.'

'Thank the director for me the next time you speak to him. Our paths don't cross that often,' Quinn returned, deliberately unimpressed by the man's implied cozy familiarity with the director of the FBI.

'He says this type of murder is your specialty.'

'Yes, but I'm not a hired gun, Mr Bondurant. I want to be very clear on that. I'll do what I can in terms of building a profile and advising as to investigative techniques. If a suspect is brought in, I'll offer an interview strategy. In the event of a trial, I'll testify as an expert witness and offer my expertise to the prosecution regarding the questioning of witnesses. I'll do my job, and I'll do it well, but I don't work for you, Mr Bondurant.'

Bondurant absorbed this information expressionless. His face was as bony and severe as his attorney's, but without the relief of the too-wide smile. A hard mask, impossible to see past.

'I want Jillian's killer caught. I'll deal with you because you're the best and because I've been told I can trust you not to sell out.'

'Sell out? In what way?'

'To the media. I'm a very private man in a very public position. I hate the idea that millions of strangers will know the intimate details of my daughter's death. It seems like it should be a very private, personal thing – the ending of a life.'

'It should be. It's the *taking* of a life that can't be kept quiet – for everyone's sake.'

'I suppose what I really dread isn't people knowing about Jillie's death so much as their ravenous desire to tear apart her life. And mine – I'll admit that.'

Quinn shifted in his chair, casually crossing his legs, and offered the barest hint of a sympathetic smile. Settling in. The I-could-be-your-friend guise. 'That's understandable. Has the press been hounding you? It looks like they're camped out front.'

'I refuse to deal with them. I've pulled in my media relations coordinator from Paragon to handle it. The thing that angers me most is their sense of entitlement. Because I'm wealthy, because I'm prominent, they think they have some right to invade my grief. Do you think they parked their news vans in front of the homes of the parents of the two prostitutes this maniac killed? I can assure you they didn't.'

'We live in a society addicted to sensationalism,' Quinn said. 'Some people are deemed newsworthy and some are considered disposable. I'm not sure which side of the coin is worse. I can just about guarantee you the parents of those first two victims are sitting at home wondering why news vans *aren't* parked in front of their houses.'

'You think they'd like people to know how they failed as parents?' Bondurant asked, a slim shadow of anger darkening his tone. 'You think they'd like people to know why their daughters became whores and drug addicts?'

Guilt and blame. How much of that was he projecting from his own pain? Quinn wondered.

'About this witness,' Bondurant said again, seeming a little shaken by his last near-revelation. He moved a notepad on his desk a quarter of an inch. 'Do you think she'll be able to identify the killer? She doesn't sound very reliable.'

'I don't know,' Quinn said, knowing exactly where Bondurant had gotten his information. Kovac was going to have to do his best to plug that leak, which would mean stepping on some very sensitive, influential toes. The victim's family was entitled to certain courtesies, but this investigation needed as tight an environment as possible. Peter Bondurant couldn't be allowed total access. He in fact had not been ruled out as a viable suspect.

'Well . . . we can only hope . . .' Bondurant murmured.

His gaze strayed to the wall that held an assortment of framed photographs, many of himself with men Quinn had to assume were business associates or rivals or dignitaries. He spotted Bob Brewster among the crowd, then found what Bondurant had turned to: a small cluster of photographs on the lower left-hand corner.

Quinn rose from his chair and went to the wall for a closer inspection. Jillian at various stages of her life. He recognized her from a snapshot in the case file. One photograph in particular drew his eye: a young woman out of place in a prim black dress with a white Peter Pan collar and cuffs. Her hair was cut boyishly short and bleached nearly white. A striking contrast to the dark roots and brows. Half a dozen earrings ornamented one ear. A tiny ruby studded one nostril. She resembled her father in no way at all. Her body, her face, were softer, rounder. Her eyes were huge and sad, the camera catching the vulnerability she felt at not being the politely feminine creature of someone else's expectations.

'Pretty girl,' Quinn murmured automatically. It didn't matter that it wasn't precisely true. The statement was made for a purpose other than flattery. 'She must have felt very close to you, coming back here from Europe for college.'

'Our relationship was complicated.' Bondurant rose from his chair and hovered beside it, tense and uncertain, as if a part of him wanted to go to the photographs but a stronger part held him back. 'We were close when she was young. Then her mother and I divorced when Jillie was at a vulnerable age. It was difficult for her – the antagonism between Sophie and me. Then came Serge, Sophie's last husband. And Sophie's illness – she was in and out of institutions for depression.'

He was silent for a stretch of time, and Quinn could feel the weight of everything Bondurant was omitting from the story. What had precipitated the divorce? What had driven Sophie's mental illness? Was the distaste in Bondurant's voice when he spoke of his successor bitterness over a rival or something more?

'What was she studying at the university?' he asked, knowing better than to go directly for the other answers he wanted. Peter Bondurant wouldn't give up his secrets that easily, if he gave them up at all.

'Psychology,' he said with the driest hint of irony as he stared at the photo of her in the black dress and bleached boy-cut, the earrings and pierced nose and unhappy eyes.

'Did you see her often?'

'Every Friday. She came for dinner.'

'How many people knew that?'

'I don't know. My housekeeper, my personal assistant, a few close friends. Some of Jillian's friends, I suppose.'

'Do you have additional staff here at the house or just the housekeeper?'

'Helen is full-time. A girl comes in to help her clean once a week. There's a grounds crew of three who come weekly. That's all. I prefer my privacy to a staff. My needs aren't that extravagant.'

'Friday's usually a hot night on the town for college kids. Jillian wasn't into the club scene?'

'No. She'd grown past it.'

'Did she have many close friends?'

'Not that she spoke about with me. She was a very private person. The only one she mentioned with any regularity was a waitress at a coffee bar. Michele something. I never met her.'

'Did she have a boyfriend?'

'No,' he said, turning away. French doors behind his desk led out to a flagstone courtyard of vacant benches and empty planters. He stared through the glass as if he were looking through a portal into another time. 'Boys didn't interest her. She didn't want temporary relationships. She'd been through so much . . .'

His thin mouth quivered slightly, and a deep pain came into his eyes. The strongest sign of inner emotion he had shown. 'She had so much life ahead of her,' he murmured. 'I wish this hadn't happened.'

Quinn quietly moved in alongside him. His voice was low and soft, the voice of sad experience and understanding. 'That's the hardest thing to cope with when a young person dies – especially when they've been murdered. The unfulfilled dreams, the unrealized potential. The people close to them – family, friends – thought they had so much time to make up for mistakes, plenty of time down the road to tell that person they loved them. Suddenly that time is gone.'

He could see the muscles of Bondurant's face tighten against the pain. He could see the suffering in the eyes, that hint of desperation at the knowledge the emotional tidal wave was coming, and the fear that there might not be enough strength to hold it back.

'At least you had that last evening together,' Quinn murmured. 'That should be some comfort to you.'

Or it could be the bitter, lasting reminder of every unresolved issue left between father and daughter. The raw wound of opportunity lost. Quinn could almost taste the regret in the air.

'How was she that night?' he asked quietly. 'Did she seem up or down?'

'She was –' Bondurant swallowed hard and searched for the appropriate word '– herself. Jillie was always up one minute and down the next. Volatile.'

The daughter of a woman in and out of institutions for psychiatric problems.

'She didn't give any sign something was bothering her, that she was worried about anything?'

'No.'

'Did you discuss anything in particular, or argue about –'

Bondurant's explosion was sudden, strong, surprising. 'My God, if I'd thought there was anything wrong, if I'd thought something was going to happen, don't you think I would have stopped her from leaving? Don't you think I would have kept her here?'

'I'm sure you would have,' Quinn said softly, the voice of compassion and reassurance, emotions he had stopped giving out in full measure long ago because it took too much from him and there was no one around to help him refill the well. He tried to keep his focus on his underlying motive, which was to get information. Manipulate, coax, slip under the guard, draw out the truth a sliver at a time. Get the info to get the killer. Remember that the first person he owed his allegiance to was the victim.

'What did you talk about that night?' he asked gently as Bondurant worked visibly to gather his composure.

'The usual things,' he said, impatient, looking out the window again. 'Her classes. My work. Nothing.'

'Her therapy?'

'No, she –' He stiffened, then turned to glare at Quinn.

'We need to know these things, Mr Bondurant,' Quinn said without apology. 'With every victim we have to consider the possibility that some part of their life may have a link to their death. It may be the thinnest thread that ties one thing to the other. It might be something you don't think could be important at all. But sometimes that's all it takes, and sometimes that's all we have.

'Do you understand what I'm telling you? We'll do everything in our power to keep details confidential, but if you want this killer apprehended, you have to cooperate with us.'

The explanation did nothing to soften Bondurant's anger. He turned abruptly back to the desk and pulled a card from the Rolodex. 'Dr Lucas Brandt. For all the good it will do you. I'm sure I don't have to tell you that anything Jillian related to Lucas as a patient is confidential.'

'And what about anything she related to you as her father?'

His temper came in another quick flash, boiling up and over the rigid control. 'If I knew anything, *anything* that could lead you to my daughter's murderer, don't you think I would tell you?'

Quinn was silent, his unblinking gaze steady on Peter Bondurant's face, on the vein that slashed down across his high forehead like a bolt of lightning. He pulled the Rolodex card from Bondurant's fingers.

'I hope so, Mr Bondurant,' he said at last. 'Some other young woman's life may depend on it.'

'What'd you get?' Kovac asked as they walked away from the house. He lit a cigarette and went to work sucking in as much of it as he could before they reached the car.

Quinn stared down the driveway and past the gate where two cameramen stood with eyes pressed to viewfinders. There was no long-range audio equipment in sight, but the lenses on the cameras were fat and long. His period of anonymity was going into countdown.

'Yeah,' he said. 'A bad feeling.'

'Jeez, I've had that from the start of this deal. You know what a man like Bondurant could do to a career?'

'My question is: Why would he want to?'

''Cause he's rich and he's hurting. He's like that guy with the gun in the government center yesterday. He wants someone else to hurt. He wants someone to pay. Maybe if he can make someone else miserable, he won't feel his own pain so much. You know,' he said in that offhand way he had, 'people are nuts. So what'd he say? Why won't he talk to us locals?'

'He doesn't trust you.'

Kovac straightened with affront and tossed his cigarette on the driveway. 'Well, fuck him!'

'He's paranoid about details leaking to the media.'

'Like what details? What's he got to hide?'

Quinn shrugged. 'That's your job, Sherlock. But I got you a place to start.'

They climbed into the Caprice. Quinn pulled the cassette recorder from his coat pocket and laid it on the seat between them with the Rolodex card on top of it.

Kovac picked up the card and frowned at it. 'A shrink. What'd I tell you? People are nuts. *Especially* rich people – they're the only ones who can afford to do anything about it. It's like a hobby with them.'

Quinn stared up at the house, half expecting to see a face at one of the windows, but there was no one. All the windows were blank and black on this dreary morning.

'Was there ever any mention in the press about either of the first two victims being drug users?' he asked.

'No,' Kovac said. 'One used to be, but we held it back. Lila White. "Lily" White. The first vic. She was a basehead for a while, but she got herself straightened out. Went through a county program, lived at one of the hooker halfway houses for a while – only that part didn't take, I guess. Anyway, the drug angle didn't develop. Why?'

'Bondurant made a reference. Might have just been an assumption on his part, but I don't think so. I think either he knew something about the other victims or he knew something about Jillian.'

'If she was using anything around the time of her death, it'll show up in the tox screen. I went through her town house. I didn't see anything stronger than Tylenol.'

'If she was using, you might have a connection to the other victims.' And thereby a possible connection to a dealer or another user they could develop into a suspect.

The feral smile of the hunter on a fresh scent lifted the corners of Kovac's mustache. 'Networking. I love it. Corporate America thinks they're on to something new. Crooks have been networking since Judas sold Jesus Christ down the river. I'll call Liska, have her and Moss nose around. Then let's go see what Sigmund Fraud here has to say about the price of loose marbles.' He tapped the Rolodex card against the steering wheel. 'His office is on the other side of this lake.'

10

'So what do you think of Quinn?' Liska asked.

Mary Moss rode shotgun, looking out the window at the Mississippi. Barge traffic had given up for the year. Along this stretch, the river was a deserted strip of brown between ratty, half-abandoned industrial and warehouse blocks. 'They say he's hot stuff. A legend in the making.'

'You've never worked with him?'

'No. Roger Emerson usually works this territory out of Quantico. But then, the vic isn't usually the daughter of a billionaire captain of industry with contacts in Washington.

'I liked the way he handled Tippen,' Moss went on. 'No bully-boy, I'm-the-fed-and-you're-a-hick nonsense. I think he's a quick study of people. Probably frighteningly intelligent. What'd you think?'

Liska sent her a lascivious grin. 'Nice pants.'

'God! Here I was being serious and professional, and you were looking at his ass!'

'Well, not when he was talking. But, come on, Mary, the guy's a total babe. Wouldn't you like a piece of that if you could get it?'

Moss looked flustered. 'Don't ask me things like that. I'm an old married woman! I'm an old married *Catholic* woman!'

'As long as the word *dead* doesn't figure into that description, you're allowed to look.'

'Nice pants,' Moss muttered, fighting chuckles.

'Those big brown eyes, that granite jaw, that sexy mouth. I think I could have an orgasm watching him talk about proactive strategies.'

'Nikki!'

'Oh, that's right, you're a married woman,' Liska teased. 'You're not allowed to have orgasms.'

'Do you talk this way when you're riding around with Kovac?'

'Only if I want to get him crazy. He twitches like a gigged frog. Tells me he doesn't want to know anything about my orgasms, that a woman's G spot should just remain a mystery. I tell him that's why he's been divorced twice. You should see how red he gets. I love Kovac – he's such a guy.'

Moss pointed through the windshield. 'Here it is – Edgewater.'

The Edgewater town homes were a collection of impeccably styled buildings designed to call to mind a tidy New England fishing village – gray clapboard trimmed in white, cedar shake roofs, six-over-six paned windows. The units were arranged like a crop of wild mushrooms connected by meandering, landscaped paths. All of them faced the river.

'I've got the key to Bondurant's unit,' Liska said, piloting the car into the entrance of the town house complex, 'but I called the caretaker anyway. He says he saw Jillian leaving Friday afternoon. I figure it won't hurt to talk to him again.'

She parked near the first unit and she and Moss showed their badges to the man waiting for them on the stoop. Liska pegged Gil Vanlees for mid-thirties. He was blond with a thin, weedy mustache, six feet tall, and soft-looking. His Timberwolves starter jacket hung open over a blue security guard's uniform. He had that look of a marginal high school jock who had let himself go. Too many hours spent watching professional sports with a can in his hand and a sack of chips beside him.

'So, you're a detective?' His small eyes gleamed at Liska with an almost sexual excitement. One was blue and one the odd, murky color of smoky topaz.

Liska smiled at him. 'That's right.'

'I think it's great to see women on the job. I work security down at the Target Center, you know,' he said importantly. 'Timberwolves, concerts, truck pulls, and all. We've got a couple gals on, you know. I just think it's great. More power to you.'

She was willing to bet money that when he was sitting around drinking with the boys, he called those women names even she wouldn't use. She knew Vanlees's type firsthand. 'So you work security there and look after this complex too?'

'Yeah, well, you know my wife – we're separated – she works for the management company, and that's how we got the town house, 'cause I'm telling you, for what they charge for these places . . . It's unreal.

'So I'm kind of like the super, you know, even though I'm not living here now. The owners here count on me, so I'm hanging in until the wife decides what to do. People have problems – plumbing, electrical, whatnot – I see it gets taken care of. I've got the locksmith coming to change the locks on Miss Bondurant's place this afternoon. And I keep an eye out, you know. Unofficial security. The residents appreciate it. They know I'm on the job, that I've got the training.'

'Is Miss Bondurant's unit this way?' Moss inquired, gesturing toward the river, leaning, hinting.

Vanlees frowned at her, the small eyes going smaller still. 'I talked to some detectives yesterday.' As if he thought she might be an impostor with her mousy-mom looks, not the real deal like Liska.

'Yeah, well, we're following up,' Liska said casually. 'You know how it is.' Though he clearly didn't have a clue other than what he'd picked up watching *NYPD Blue* and reading cheesy detective magazines. Some people would cooperate better when they felt included. Others wanted all kinds of assurances neither the crime nor the investigation would taint their lives in any way.

Vanlees dug a ring of keys out of his jacket pocket and led the way down the sidewalk. 'I applied to the police department once,' he confided. 'They had a hiring freeze on. You know, budgets and all.'

'Jeez, that's tough,' Liska said, doing her best Frances McDormand in *Fargo* impersonation. 'You know, it seems like we always need good people, but that budget hang-up, that's a kicker . . .'

Vanlees nodded, the man in the know. 'Political BS – but I don't need to tell you, right?'

'You got that right. Who knows how many potential great cops like yourself are working other jobs. It's a shame.'

'I could have done the job.' Years-old bitterness colored his tone like an old stain that wouldn't quite wash out.

'So, did you know this Bondurant girl, Gil?'

'Oh, sure, I saw her around. She never had much to say. Unfriendly type. She's dead, huh? They wouldn't say it for sure on the news, but it's her, right?'

'We've got some questions unanswered.'

'I heard there was a witness. To what – that's what I'm wondering. I mean, did they see him kill her or what? That'd be something, huh? Awful.'

'I can't really get into it, you know?' Liska said, apologetic. 'I'd like to – you being in a related field and all – but you know how it is.'

Vanlees nodded with false wisdom.

'You saw her Friday?' Moss asked. 'Jillian Bondurant?'

'Yeah. About three. I was here working on my garbage disposal. The wife tried to run celery through it. What a mess. Little Miss College Graduate. You'd think she'd have more brains than to do that.'

'Jillian Bondurant . . .' Moss prompted.

He narrowed his mismatched eyes again. 'I was looking out the kitchen window. Saw her drive out.'

'Alone?'

'Yep.'

'And that was the last time you saw her?'

'Yeah.' He turned back to Liska. 'That nutcase burned her up, didn't he? The Cremator. Jeez, that's sick,' he said, though morbid fascination sparked bright in his expression. 'What's this town coming to?'

'Your guess is good as mine.'

'I think it's the millennium. That's what I think,' he ventured. 'World's just gonna get crazier and crazier. The thousand years is over and all that.'

'*Millennium,*' Moss muttered, squinting down at a terra-cotta pot of dead chrysanthemums on the deck of Jillian Bondurant's small front porch.

'Could be,' Liska said. 'God help us all, eh?'

'God help us,' Moss echoed sarcastically.

'Too late for Miss Bondurant,' Vanlees said soberly, turning the key in the brass lock. 'You need any help here, Detective?'

'No, thanks, Gil. Regulations and all . . .' Liska turned to face him, blocking his entrance to the house. 'Did you ever see Miss Bondurant with anyone in particular? Friends? A boyfriend?'

'I saw her dad here every once in a while. He actually owns the unit. No boyfriend. A girlfriend every once in a while. A friend, I mean. Not *girlfriend* – at least I don't think so.'

'One particular girl? You know her name?'

'No. She wasn't too friendly either. Had a mean look to her. Almost like a biker chick, but not. Anyway, I never had anything to do with her. She – Miss Bondurant – was usually alone, never said much. She didn't really fit in here. Not too many of the residents are students, and then she dressed kind of strange. Army boots and black clothes and all.'

'Did she ever seem out of it to you?'

'Like on drugs, you mean? No. Was she into drugs?'

'I'm just covering my bases, you know, or else my lieutenant . . .'

She let the suggestion hang, the impression being that Vanlees could empathize, blood brother that he was. She thanked him for his help and gave him her business card with instructions to call if he thought of anything that might be helpful to the case. He backed away from the door, reluctant, craning his neck to see what Moss was doing deeper into the apartment. Liska waved good-bye and closed the door.

'Eew, Christ, let me go take a shower,' she whispered, shuddering as she came into the living room.

'Jeez, you didn't like him, then, Margie?' Moss said with an exaggerated north country accent.

Liska made a face at her and at the odd combination of aromas that hung in the air – sweet air freshener over stale cigarette smoke. 'Hey, I got him talking, didn't I?'

'You're shameless.'

'In the line of duty.'

'Makes me glad I'm menopausal.'

Liska sobered, her gaze on the door. 'Seriously, those cop wanna-bes creep me out. They always have an authority thing. A need for power and control, and a deep-seated poor self-image. More often than not, they've got a thing against women. Hey!' She brightened again suddenly. 'I'll have to bring this theory to the attention of Special Agent Quite Good-looking.'

'Hussy.'

'I prefer *opportunist*.'

Jillian Bondurant's living room had a view of the river. The furnishings looked new. Overstuffed nubby sofa and chairs the color of oatmeal. Glass-topped rattan coffee table and end tables dirty with the fine soot of fingerprint dust left behind by the Bureau of Investigation team. An entertainment center with a large televison and a top-line stereo system. In one corner a desk and matching bookshelves held textbooks, notebooks, everything pertaining to Jillian's studies at the U, all of it ridiculously neat. Along another wall sat the latest in shiny black electronic pianos. The kitchen, easily seen from the living room, was immaculate.

'We'll need to find out if she had maid service.'

'Not the digs of the average flat-broke college student,' Liska said. 'But then, I gotta think nothing much about this kid was average. She had a pretty atypical childhood trotting all over Europe.'

'And yet she came back here for college. What's with that? She could have gone anywhere – to the Sorbonne, to Oxford, to Harvard, to Southern Cal. She could have gone somewhere warm and sunny. She could have gone somewhere exotic. Why come here?'

'To be close to Daddy.'

Moss walked the room, her gaze scanning for anything that might give a clue about their victim. 'I guess that makes sense. But still . . . My daughter Beth and I have a great relationship, but the second that girl graduated high school, she wanted out of the nest.'

'Where'd she go?'

'University of Wisconsin at Madison. My husband isn't Peter Bondurant. She had to fly somewhere with tuition reciprocity,' Moss said, checking through the magazines. *Psychology Today* and *Rolling Stone*.

'If my old man had a billion bucks and would spring for a place like this, I'd want to spend time with him too. Maybe I can get Bondurant to adopt me.'

'Who was here yesterday?'

'They sent a couple of uniforms after the body was found with Bondurant's DL – just to make sure she wasn't here, alive and oblivious. Then Sam came over with Elwood to look around. They canvassed the neighbors. Nobody knew anything. He picked up her address book, credit card receipts, phone bills, and a few other things, but he didn't come up with any big prizes. Gotta think if she had a drug habit, the B of I guys would have found something.'

'Maybe she carried everything with her in her purse.'

'And risk losing her stash to a purse snatcher? I don't think so. Besides, this place is way too clean for a druggie.'

Two bedrooms with two full-size baths on the second level. In her small house in St Paul, Liska had the cozy pleasure of sharing one small crummy bathroom with her sons, ages eleven and nine. She made good pay as a detective, but things like hockey league and orthodontists cost bucks, and the child support her ex had been directed by the courts to pay was laughable. She often thought she should have had sense enough to get knocked up by a rich guy instead of by a guy *named* Rich.

Jillian's bedroom was as eerily tidy as the rest of the house.

The queen-size bed had been stripped bare by the B of I team, the sheets taken to the lab to be tested for any sign of blood or seminal fluid. There was no discarded clothing draped over chairs or trailing on the floor, no half-open dresser drawers spilling lingerie, no pile of abandoned shoes – nothing like Liska's own crowded room she never had the time or desire to clean. Who the hell ever saw it but herself and the boys? Who ever saw Jillian Bondurant's room?

No snapshots of a boyfriend tucked into the mirror above the oak dresser. No photos of family members. She pulled open the drawers in the nightstands that flanked the bed. No condoms, no diaphragm. A clean ashtray and a tiny box of matches from D'Cup Coffee House.

Nothing about the room gave away any personal information about its occupant – which suggested to Liska two possibilities: that Jillian Bondurant was the princess of repression, or that someone had come through the house after her disappearance and sanitized the place.

Matches and the smell of cigarettes, but every ashtray in the place was clean.

Vanlees had a key. Who else could they add to that list? Peter Bondurant. Jillian's mean-looking girlfriend? The killer. The killer now had Jillian's keys, her address, her car, her credit cards. Kovac had immediately put a trace on the cards to catch any activity following the girl's disappearance Friday night. So far, nothing. Every cop in the greater metro area had the description and tag numbers on Bondurant's red Saab. Nothing yet.

The master bath was clean. Mauve and jade green with decorative soaps no one was supposed to actually use. The shampoo in the bathtub rack was Paul Mitchell with a sticker from a salon in the Dinkydale shopping center. A possible source of information if Jillian had been the kind to confess all to her hairdresser. There was nothing of interest in the medicine cabinet or beneath the sink.

The second bedroom was smaller, the bed also stripped. Summer clothes hung in the closet, pushed out of the master bedroom by the rapid approach of another brutal Minnesota winter. Odds and ends occupied the dresser drawers – a few pair of underpants: black, silky, size five; a black lace bra from Frederick's of Hollywood: skimpy, wash-worn, 34B; a pair of cheap black leggings with a hole in one knee, size S. The clothes were not folded, and Liska had the feeling they did not belong to Bondurant.

The friend? There wasn't enough stuff to indicate a full-time roommate. The fact that this second bedroom was being used discounted the idea of a lover. She went back into the master suite and checked the dresser drawers again.

'You coming up with anything?' Moss asked, stepping into the bedroom doorway, careful not to lean against the jamb, grimy with fingerprint powder.

'The willies. Either this chick was incredibly anal or a phantom house fairy got here before anyone else. She went missing Friday. That gave the killer a good two days with her keys.'

'But there've been no reports of anyone unknown or suspicious coming around.'

'So maybe the killer wasn't unknown or suspicious. I wonder if we could get a surveillance team to watch the place for a couple days,' Liska mused. 'Maybe the guy'll show up.'

'Better chance he's already been here and gone. He'd be taking a big risk coming back after the body had been found.'

'He took a pretty big risk lighting up that body in the park.'

Liska pulled her cell phone out of a coat pocket and dialed Kovac's number, then listened impatiently while it rang unanswered. Finally she gave up and stuffed the phone back in her pocket. 'Sam must have left his coat in the car again. He oughta wear that phone on a chain like a trucker's wallet. Well, you're probably right anyway. If Smokey Joe wanted to come back here, he'd do it after he'd killed her but before her body had been discovered. And if he's been here already, maybe his prints are being run even as we speak.'

'We should get that lucky.'

Liska sighed. 'I found some clothes that probably belong to a girlfriend in the second bedroom, found the name of Jillian's hair salon and a book of matches for a coffeehouse.'

'D'Cup?' Moss said. 'I found one too. Should we try it on for size?'

Liska smirked. 'A D cup? In my ex-husband's dreams. You know what I found in his sock drawer once?' she said as they walked down into the living room together. 'One of those dirty magazines full of women with big, huge, giant, gargantuan tits. I'm talking hooters that would hang to your knees. Page after page of this. Tits, tits, tits the size of the *Hindenburg*. And men think *we're* bad because we want six inches to *mean* six inches.'

Moss made a sound between a groan and a giggle. 'Nikki, after a day with you, I'm going to have to go to confession.'

'Well, while you're there, ask the priest what it is about boys and boobs.'

They let themselves out of the apartment and locked the place behind them. The wind blew down the river, sweeping along the scents of mud and decaying leaves and the metallic tinge of the city and the machines that inhabited it. Moss pulled her jacket tight around her. Liska shoved her hands deep in her pockets and hunched her shoulders. They walked back to the car, complaining in advance about how long winter was going to be. Winter was always too long in Minnesota.

As they backed out of the parking slot, Gil Vanlees stood looking out the door of the house he no longer lived in, watching them with a blank expression until Liska raised a hand and waved good-bye.

'Why don't we try again, Angie?' the forensic artist said gently.

His name was Oscar and he had a voice the consistency of warm caramel. Kate had seen him lull people nearly to sleep with that voice: Angie DiMarco wasn't about to be lulled.

Kate stood behind the girl and a good six feet back, near the door. She didn't want her own impatience compounding Angie's nervousness. The girl sat in her chair, squirming like a toddler in a pediatrician's waiting room, unhappy, uncomfortable, uncooperative. She looked like she hadn't slept well, though she had taken advantage of the bathroom facilities at the Phoenix and showered. Her brown hair was still limp and straight, but it was clean. She wore the same denim jacket over a different sweater and the same dirty jeans.

'I want you to close your eyes,' the artist said. 'Take a slow, deep breath and let it out –'

Angie heaved an impatient sigh.

'– slooowly . . .'

Kate had to give the man credit for his tolerance. She personally felt on the verge of slapping someone, anyone. But then, Oscar hadn't had the pleasure of picking up Angie from Phoenix House, where Toni Urskine had yet again unleashed her frustration with the Cremator cases on Kate.

'Two women brutally murdered and nothing gets done because they were prostitutes. My God, the police even went so far as to say there was no threat to the general public – as if these women didn't count as citizens of this city! It's outrageous!'

Kate had refrained from attempting to explain the concept of high-risk and low-risk victim pools. She knew too well what the reaction would be – emotional, visceral, without logic.

'The police couldn't care less about women who are driven by desperation into prostitution and drugs. What's another dead hooker to them – one less problem on the street. A millionaire's daughter is murdered and suddenly we have a crisis! My God, a *real* person has been victimized!' she had ranted sarcastically.

Kate made an effort to loosen the clenching muscles in her jaw even now. She had never liked Toni Urskine. Urskine worked around the clock to keep her indignation cooking at a slow burn. If she or her ideals or 'her victims', as she called the women at the Phoenix, hadn't been slighted outright, she would find some way of perceiving an insult so she could climb up on her soapbox and shriek at anyone within hearing distance. The Cremator murders would give her fuel for her own fire for a long time to come.

Urskine had a certain amount of justification for her outrage, Kate admitted. Similar cynical thoughts about these cases had run through Kate's own mind. But she knew the cops had been working those first two murders, doing the best they could with the limited manpower and budget the brass allowed for the average violent death.

Still, the only thing she'd wanted to say to Toni Urskine that morning was 'Life's a bitch. Get over it.' Her tongue still hurt from biting it. Instead, she'd offered, 'I'm not a cop, I'm an advocate. I'm on your side.'

A lot of people didn't want to hear that either. She worked with the police and was considered guilty by association. And there were plenty of times when the cops looked at her and saw her as an enemy because she worked with a lot of bleeding-heart liberals who spent too much time bad-mouthing the police. Stuck in the middle.

Good thing I love this job, or I'd hate it.

'You're in the park, but you're safe,' Oscar said gently. 'The danger is past, Angie. He can't hurt you now. Open your mind's eye and look at his face. Take a good long look.'

Kate moved slowly to a chair a few feet from her witness and eased herself down. Angie caught Kate's steady gaze and shifted the other way to find Oscar watching her too, his kindly eyes twinkling like polished onyx in a face that was drowning in hair – a full beard and mustache and a bushy lion's mane worn loose around his thick shoulders.

'You can't see if you won't look, Angie,' he said wisely.

'Maybe I don't want to see,' the girl challenged.

Oscar looked sad for her. 'He can't hurt you here, Angie. And all you have to look at is his face. You don't have to look inside his mind or his heart. All you have to see is his face.'

Oscar had sat across from a lot of witnesses in his time, all of them afraid of the same two things: retribution by the criminal sometime in the vague future, and the more immediate fear of having to relive the crime over and over. Kate knew a memory or a nightmare could cause as much psychological stress as an event taking place in real time. As evolved as people liked to believe the human race had become, the mind still had difficulty differentiating between actual reality and perceived reality.

The silence went on. Oscar looked at Kate.

'Angie, you told me you'd do this,' she said.

The girl scowled harder. 'Yeah, well, maybe I changed my mind. I mean, what the hell's in it for me?'

'Keeping safe and taking a killer off the street.'

'No, I mean *really*,' she said, suddenly all business. 'What's in it for me? I hear there's a reward. You never said anything about a reward.'

'I haven't had time to talk to anyone about it.'

'Well, you'd better. 'Cause if I'm gonna do this, then I damn well want something for it. I deserve it.'

'That remains to be seen,' Kate said. 'So far you haven't given us squat. I'll check into the reward. In the meantime, you're a witness. You can help us and we can help you. Maybe you don't feel ready for this. Maybe you don't think your memory is strong enough. If that's what's really going on here, then fine. The cops have mug books stacked to the rafters. Maybe you'll run across him in there.'

'And maybe I can just get the fuck out of here.' She shoved herself up out of the chair so hard, the legs scraped back across the floor.

Kate wanted to choke her. This was why she didn't work juvenile: Her tolerance for drama and bullshit was too low.

She studied Angie, trying to formulate a strategy. If the kid really wanted to leave, she would leave. No one was barring the door. What Angie wanted was to make a scene and have everyone fuss over her and beg her to come back. Begging was not an option as far as Kate was concerned. She wouldn't play a game where she didn't have a shot at control.

If she called the kid's bluff and Angie walked, Kate figured she could just as well follow the girl out the door. Sabin would put her career through the shredder if she lost his star and only witness. She was already on her second career. How many more could she have?

She rose slowly and went to lean against the doorjamb with her arms crossed.

'You know, Angie, I gotta think there's a reason you told us you saw this guy in the first place. You didn't have to say it. You didn't know anything about a reward. You could have lied and told us he was gone when you came across the body. How would we know any different? We have to take your word for what you saw or didn't see. So let's cut the crap, huh? I don't appreciate you jerking me around when I'm on your side. I'm the one who's standing between you and the county attorney who wants to toss your ass in jail and call you a suspect.'

Angie set her jaw at a mulish angle. 'Don't threaten me.'

'That's not a threat. I'm being straight with you because I think that's what you want. You don't want to be lied to and screwed over any more than I do. I respect that. How about returning the favor?'

The girl gnawed on a ragged thumbnail, her hair swinging down to obscure her face, but Kate could tell she was blinking hard, and felt a swift wave of sympathy. The mood swings this kid inspired were going to drive her to Prozac.

'You must think I'm a real pain in the ass,' Angie said at last, her lush mouth twisting at one corner in what looked almost like chagrin.

'Yeah, but I don't consider that a fatal or irreversible flaw. And I know you've got your reasons. But you've got more to be afraid of if you don't try to ID him,' Kate said. 'Now you're the only one who knows what he looks like. Better if a couple hundred cops know too.'

'What happens if I don't do it?'

'No reward. Other than that, I don't know. Right now you're a potential witness. If you decide that's not what you are, then it's out of my hands. The county attorney might play rough or he might just cut you loose. He'll take me out of the picture either way.'

'You'd probably be glad.'

'I didn't take this job because I thought it would be simple and pleasant. I don't want to see you alone in all this, Angie. And I don't think that's what you want either.'

Alone. Goose bumps chased themselves down Angie's arms and legs. The word was a constant hollowness in the core of her. She remembered the feeling of it growing inside her last night, pushing her consciousness into a smaller and smaller corner of her mind. It was the thing she feared most in the world and beyond it. More than physical pain. More than a killer.

'*We'll leave you alone. How would you like that, brat? You can be alone forever. You just sit in there and think about it. Maybe we'll never come back.*'

She flinched at the remembered sound of the door closing, the absolute darkness of the closet, the sense of aloneness swallowing her up. She felt it rising up inside her now like a black ghost. It closed around her throat like an unseen hand, and she wanted to cry, but she knew she couldn't. Not here. Not now. Her heart began beating harder and faster.

'Come on, kiddo,' Kate said gently, nodding toward Oscar. 'Give it a shot. It's not like you've got anything better to do. I'll make a phone call about that reward money.'

The story of my life, Angie thought. *Do what I want or I'll leave you. Do what I want or I'll hurt you.* Choices that weren't choices.

'All right,' she murmured, and went back to the chair to give instructions on drawing a portrait of evil.

11

The building that housed the offices of Dr Lucas Brandt, two other psychotherapists, and two psychiatrists was a Georgian-style brick home of gracious proportion. Patients seeking treatment here probably felt more like they were going to high tea than to pour out their innermost secrets and psychological dirty laundry.

Lucas Brandt's office was on the second floor. Quinn and Kovac were left to cool their heels in the hall for ten minutes while he finished with a patient. Bach's Third Brandenburg Concerto floated on the air as soft as a whisper. Quinn stared out the Palladian window that offered a view of Lake of the Isles and part of the larger Lake Calhoun, both as gray as old quarters in the gloom of the day.

Kovac prowled the hall, checking out the furniture. 'Real antiques. Classy. Why is it rich crazies are classy and the kind I have to haul into jail just want to piss on my shoes?'

'Repression.'

'What?'

'Social skills are founded and couched in repression. Rich crazies want to piss on your shoes too,' Quinn smiled, 'but their manners hold them back.'

Kovac chuckled. 'I like you, Quinn. I'm gonna have to give you a nickname.' He looked at Quinn, taking in the sharp suit, considering for a moment, then nodded. 'GQ. Yeah, I like that. GQ, like the magazine. G like in G-man. Q like in Quinn.' He looked enormously pleased with himself. 'Yeah, I like that.'

He didn't ask if Quinn liked it.

The door to Brandt's business office opened, and his secretary, a petite woman with red hair and no chin, invited them in, her voice a librarian's whisper.

The patient, if there had been one, must have escaped out the door of the second room. Lucas Brandt rose from behind his desk as they entered the room, and an unpleasant flash of recognition hit Kovac. *Brandt.* The name had rung a bell, but he wouldn't have equated the Brandt of his association with the Brandt of *Neuroses of the Rich and Famous*.

They went through the round of introductions, Kovac waiting for that same recognition to dawn on Brandt, but it didn't – which served only to further sour Kovac's mood. Brandt's expression was appropriately serious. Blond and Germanically attractive with a straight nose and blue eyes, he was of medium build with a posture and presence that gave the impression he was bigger than he really was. *Solid* was the word that came to mind. He wore a trendy silk tie and a blue dress shirt that looked professionally ironed. A steel-gray suit coat hung on one of those fancy-ass gentleman's racks in the corner.

Kovac smoothed a hand self-consciously over his J. C. Penney tie. 'Dr Brandt. I've seen you in court.'

'Yes, you probably have. Forensic psychology – a sideline I picked up when I was first starting out,' he explained for Quinn. 'I needed the money at the time,' he confessed with a conspiratorial little smile that let them in on the joke that he didn't need it now. 'I found I enjoyed the work, so I've kept a hand in it. It's a good diversion from what I see day to day.'

Kovac arched a brow. 'Take a break from rich girls with eating disorders and go testify for some scumbag. Yeah, there's a hobby.'

'I work for who needs me, Detective. Defense or prosecution.'

You work for who pulls his wallet out first. Kovac knew better than to say it.

'I'm due in court this afternoon, as a matter of fact,' Brandt said. 'And I've got a lunch date first. So, while I hate to be rude, gentlemen, can we get down to business here?'

'Just a few quick questions,' Kovac said, picking up the toy rake that went with the Zen garden on the credenza by the window. He looked from the rake to the box as if he expected it was for digging up cat feces.

'You know I can't be of much help to your investigation. Jillian was my patient. My hands are tied by doctor-patient confidentiality.'

'Your patient is dead,' Kovac said bluntly. He picked up a smooth black stone from the sand and turned to lean back against the credenza, rolling the stone between his fingers. A man settling in, making himself comfortable. 'I don't think her expectations for privacy are quite what they were.'

Brandt looked almost amused. 'You can't seem to make up your mind, Detective. Is Jillian dead or not? You implied to Peter she may still be alive. If Jillian is alive, then she still has the expectation of privacy.'

'There's a high probability the body found is Jillian Bondurant's, but it's not a certainty,' Quinn said, moving back toward the conversation, taking the reins diplomatically from Kovac. 'Either way, we're working against the clock, Dr Brandt. This killer will kill again. That's an absolute. Sooner rather than later, I think. The more we can find out about his victims, the closer we will be to stopping him.'

'I'm familiar with your theories, Agent Quinn. I've read some of your articles. In fact, I think I have the textbook you coauthored somewhere on those shelves. Very insightful. Know the victims, know their killer.'

'That's part of it. This killer's first two victims were high risk. Jillian doesn't seem to fit the mold.'

Brandt sat back against the edge of his desk, tapped a forefinger against his lips, and nodded slowly. 'The deviation from the pattern. I see. That makes her the logical centerpiece to the puzzle. You think he's saying more about himself in killing Jillian than with the other two. But what if she were just in the wrong place at the wrong time? What if he didn't choose the first two because they were prostitutes? Perhaps all the victims were situational.'

'No,' Quinn said, studying the subtle, curious light of challenge in Brandt's eyes. 'There's nothing random in this guy's bag of tricks. He picked each of these women for a reason. The reason should be more apparent with Jillian. How long had she been seeing you?'

'Two years.'

'How had she come to you? By referral?'

'By golf. Peter and I are both members at Minikahda. An excellent place to make connections,' he confessed with a smile, pleased with his own clever business acumen.

'You'd make more if you lived in Florida,' Quinn joked. *Aren't we buddies – so smart, so resourceful.* 'The season here has to be – what? – all of two months?'

'Three if we have spring,' Brandt shot back, settling into the rhythm of repartee. 'A lot of time spent in the clubhouse. The dining room is lovely. You golf?'

'When I get the chance.' Never because he enjoyed it. Always as an opportunity for a contact, a chance to get his ideas through to his SAC or the unit chief, or supposed downtime with law enforcement personnel he was working cases with across the country. Not so different from Lucas Brandt after all.

'Too bad the season's over,' Brandt said.

'Yeah,' Kovac drawled, 'damned inconsiderate for this killer to work in November, if you look at it that way.'

Brandt flicked him a glance. 'That's hardly what I meant, Detective. Though, now that you've brought it up, it's a shame you didn't catch him this summer. We wouldn't be having this conversation.

'Anyway,' he said, turning back to Quinn. 'I've known Peter for years.'

'He doesn't strike me as a very social man.'

'No. Golf is serious business with Peter. Everything is serious with Peter. He's very driven.'

'How did that quality impact his relationship with Jillian?'

'Ah!' He held up a finger in warning and shook his head, still smiling. 'Crossing the line, Agent Quinn.'

Quinn acknowledged the breach with a tip of his head.

'When did you last speak with Jillian?' Kovac asked.

'We had a session Friday. Every Friday at four.'

'And then she'd go over to her father's house for supper?'

'Yes. Peter and Jillian were working very hard on their relationship. They'd been separated for a long time. A lot of old feelings to deal with.'

'Such as?'

Brandt blinked at him.

'All right. What about a general statement, say, about the root of Jillian's problems? Give us an impression.'

'Sorry. No.'

Kovac gave a little sigh. 'Look, you could answer a few simple questions without breaching anyone's trust. For instance, whether or not she was on any medication. We need to know for the tox screen.'

'Prozac. Trying to even out her mood swings.'

'Manic depressive?' Quinn asked.

The doctor gave him a look.

'Did she have any problem with drugs that you knew of?' Kovac tried.

'No comment.'

'Was she having trouble with a boyfriend?'

Nothing.

'Did she ever talk about anyone abusing her?'

Silence.

Kovac rubbed a hand over his mouth, petting his mustache. He could feel his temper crumbling like old cork. 'You know this girl two years. You know her father. He considers you a friend. You could maybe give us a direction in this girl's murder. And you waste our time with this bullshit game – pick and choose, hot and cold.'

Quinn cleared his throat discreetly. 'You know the rules, Sam.'

'Yeah, well, fuck the rules!' Kovac barked, flipping a book of Mapplethorpe photographs off the end table. 'If I was a defense attorney waving a wad of cash, you can bet he'd find a loophole to ooze through.'

'I resent that, Detective.'

'Oh, well, yeah, I'm sorry I hurt your feelings. Somebody tortured this girl, Doctor.' He pushed away from the credenza, his expression as hard as the stone he shot into the wastebasket. The sound was like a .22 popping. 'Somebody cut her head off and kept it for a souvenir. If I knew this girl, I think I would care about who did that to her. And if I could help catch the sick bastard, I would. But you care more about your social status than you care about Jillian Bondurant. I wonder if her father realizes that.'

He gave a harsh laugh as his pager went off. 'What the hell am I saying? Peter Bondurant doesn't even want to believe his daughter could be alive. The two of you probably deserve each other.'

The pager trilled again. He checked the readout, swore under his breath, and went out of the office, leaving Quinn to deal with the aftermath.

Brandt managed to find something amusing in Kovac's outburst. 'Well, that was quick. It generally takes the average cop a little longer to lose his temper with me.'

'Sergeant Kovac is under a great deal of stress with these murders,' Quinn said, moving to the credenza and the Zen garden. 'I apologize on his behalf.'

The stones in the box had been arranged to form an X, the sand raked in a sinuous pattern around them. His mind flashed on the lacerations in the victim's feet – a double X pattern – and on the stab wounds to the victim's chest – two intersecting Xs.

'Is the pattern significant?' he asked casually.

'Not to me,' Brandt said. 'My patients play with that more than I do. I find it calms some people, encourages the flow of thought and communication.'

Quinn knew several agents at the NCAVC who kept Zen gardens. Their offices were sixty feet below ground – ten times deeper than the dead, they joked. No windows, no fresh air, and the knowledge that the weight of the earth pressed in on the walls were all symbolic enough to give Freud a hard-on. A person needed something to relieve the tension. Personally, he preferred to hit things – hard. He spent hours in the gym punishing a punching bag for the sins of the world.

'No apology needed on Kovac's behalf.' Brandt bent down to pick up the Mapplethorpe book. 'I'm an old hand at dealing with the police. Everything is simple to them. You're either a good guy or a bad guy. They don't seem to understand that I find the boundaries of my professional ethics frustrating at times too, but they are what they are. You understand.'

He set the book aside and sat back against his desk, his hip just nudging a small stack of files. The label read BONDURANT, JILLIAN. A microcassette recorder lay atop the file, as if perhaps he had been at work or would still work on his notes from his last session with her.

'I understand your position. I hope you understand mine,' Quinn said carefully. 'I'm not a cop here. While our ultimate goal is the same, Sergeant Kovac and I have different agendas. My profile doesn't require the kind of evidence admissible in court. I'm looking for impressions, feelings, gut instinct, details some would consider insignificant. Sam's looking for a bloody knife with fingerprints. You see what I mean?'

Brandt nodded slowly, never taking his eyes from Quinn's. 'Yes, I believe I do. I'll have to think about it. But at the same time, you should consider that the problems Jillian brought to me may have had nothing whatsoever to do with her death. Her killer may not have known anything at all about her.'

'And then again, he might have known the one thing that set him off,' Quinn said. He took a business card from a slim case in his breast pocket and handed it to Brandt. 'This is my direct line at the Bureau office downtown. I hope to hear from you.'

Brandt set the card aside and shook his hand. 'With due consideration for the circumstances, it was a pleasure meeting you. I have to confess, I'm the one who suggested your name to Peter when he told me he wanted to call your director.'

Quinn's mouth twisted as he started for the door. 'I'm not so sure I should thank you for that, Dr Brandt.'

He left the office through the reception area, glancing at the woman waiting on the camelback sofa with her feet perfectly together and her red Coach bag balanced on her knees, her expression a carefully blank screen over annoyance and embarrassment. She didn't want to be seen there.

He wondered how Jillian had felt coming here and confiding all to one of her father's sycophants. Had it been a choice or a condition of Peter's support? She'd shown up every week for two years, and only God and Lucas Brandt knew why. And very possibly Bondurant. Brandt could preen for them and display his ethics like a peacock fanning his tail feathers, but Quinn suspected Kovac was right: When it came down to it, Brandt's first obligation would be to himself. And keeping Peter Bondurant happy would go a long way toward keeping Lucas Brandt happy.

Kovac was waiting in the foyer on the first floor, staring in puzzlement at an abstract painting of a woman with three eyes and breasts growing out the sides of her head.

'Jesus Christ, that's uglier than my second wife's mother – and she could break a mirror from fifty feet away. You suppose they hang it there just to give their crazies an extra little tweak on the way in and out?'

'It's a Rorschach test,' Quinn said. 'They're looking to weed out the guys who think it's a woman with three eyes and breasts on the sides of her head.'

Kovac frowned and stole a last look at the thing before they stepped outside.

'One phone call from Brandt and my sorry butt's in a sling,' he groused as they descended the steps. 'I can hear my lieutenant now – "What the hell were you thinking, Kovac?" Jesus, Brandt'll probably sic the chief on me. They're probably in the same fucking backgammon league. They probably get manicures together. Greer'll get up on a ladder, rip my head off, and shout down the hole – "What the hell were you thinking, Kovac? Thirty days without pay!" '

He shook his head. 'What the hell was I thinking?'

'I don't know. What the hell were you thinking?'

'That I *hate* that guy, that's what.'

'Really? I thought we were playing good cop–bad cop.'

Kovac looked at him over the roof of the Caprice. 'I'm not that good an actor. Do I look like Harrison Ford?'

Quinn squinted. 'Maybe if you lose the mustache...'

They slid into the car from their respective sides, Kovac's laugh dying as he shook his head. 'I don't know what I'm laughing about. I know better than to go off like that. Brandt yanks my chain, that's all. I'm kicking myself because I didn't place him until I saw him. I just wasn't expecting...'

No excuse was a good excuse. He blew air between his lips and stared out the windshield through the naked fingerling branches of a dormant bush to the lake in the distance.

'You know him from a case?' Quinn asked.

'Yeah. Eight or nine years ago he testified for the defense in a murder case I worked. Carl Borchard, nineteen, killed his girlfriend after she tried to break up with him. Choked her. Brandt comes in with this sob story about how Borchard's mother abandoned him, and how this stress with his girlfriend pushed him over a line. He tells the jury how we all should pity Carl, 'cause he didn't mean it and he was so remorseful. How he wasn't really a killer. It was a crime of passion. He wasn't a danger to society. Blah, blah, blah. Boo-hoo-hoo.'

'And you knew different?'

'Carl Borchard was a whiny, sociopathic little shit with a juvenile sheet full of stuff the prosecutors couldn't get admitted. He had a history of acting out against women. Brandt knew that as well as we did, but he wasn't on our payroll.'

'Borchard got off.'

'Manslaughter. First adult offense, reduced sentence, time served, et cetera, et cetera. The little creep barely had time to take a crap in prison. Then they send him to a halfway house. While he's living at this halfway house he rapes a woman in the next neighborhood and beats her head in with a claw hammer. Thank you, Dr Brandt.

'You know what he had to say about it?' Kovac said with amazement. 'He was in the *Star Tribune* saying he thought Carl had "exhausted his victim pool" with the first murder, but, hey, shit happens. He went on to say he couldn't really be held accountable for this little blunder because he hadn't been able to spend all that much time with Borchard. Fucking amazing.'

Quinn absorbed the information quietly. The feeling that he was getting too close to this case pressed in on him again. He felt the people in it crowding around him, standing too close for him to really see them. He wanted them back and away. He didn't want to know anything about Lucas Brandt, didn't want to have a personal impression of the man. He wanted what Brandt could give him from an arm's length. He wanted to go lock himself in the neat, paneled office the SAC had given him in the building on Washington Avenue downtown. But that wasn't the way things were going to work here.

'I know something else about your Dr Brandt,' he said as Kovac started the car and put it in gear.

'What's that?'

'He was standing in the background at the press conference yesterday.'

'There he is.'

Kovac hit the freeze button on the remote control. The picture jerked and twitched as the VCR held the tape in place. To the side of the press mob, standing with a pack of suits, was Brandt. A muscle at the base of

Kovac's diaphragm tightened like a fist. He punched the play button and watched the psychologist tip his head and say something to the man next to him. He froze the picture again.

'Who's that he's talking to?'

'Ahh . . .' Yurek tipped his head sideways for a better angle. 'Kellerman, the public defender.'

'Oh, yeah. Worm Boy. Call him. See if Brandt and him were together,' Kovac ordered. 'Find out if Brandt had any legit reason to be there.'

Adler raised a brow. 'You think he's a suspect?'

'I think he's an asshole.'

'If that was against the law, the jails would be full of lawyers.'

'He jerked me around this morning,' Kovac complained. 'Him and Bondurant are too cozy, and Bondurant's jerking us around too.'

'He's the victim's father,' Adler pointed out.

'He's the victim's *rich* father,' Tippen added.

'He's the victim's rich, *powerful* father,' Yurek, Mr Public Relations, reminded all.

Kovac gave him a look. 'He's part of a murder investigation. I've gotta run this investigation as tight as any other. That means we look at everybody. Family always comes under the microscope. I want to step on Brandt a little, let him know we're not just a pack of tame dogs Peter Bondurant can order around. If he can give us anything on Jillian Bondurant, I want it. And I also want to step on him because he's a fucking tick.'

'This smells like trouble, Kojak,' Yurek sang.

'It's a murder investigation, Charm. You want to consult Emily Post?'

'I want to come out of it with my career intact.'

'Your career is investigating,' Kovac returned. 'Brandt had a connection to Jillian Bondurant.'

'You got any reason other than not liking him to think this prick shrink would off two hookers and decapitate a patient?' Tippen asked.

'I'm not saying he's a suspect,' he snapped. 'He saw Jillian Bondurant Friday. He saw her every Friday. He knows everything we need to know about this vic. If he's withholding information on us, we have a right to squeeze him a little.'

'And make him squeal privilege.'

'He's already singing that song. Skate around it. Stay on the fringes. If we can so much as get him to mention the name of Jillian's boyfriend, that's something we didn't have before. As soon as we confirm the DB is Jillian, then there's no longer an expectation of privacy and we can lean on Brandt for details.

'Something else I don't like about this jerk,' Kovac added, pacing beside the table, the wheels of his brain spinning. 'I don't like that he's been associated with God knows how many criminals. I want a list of every violent offender he's ever testified for or against.'

'I'll get it,' Tippen offered. 'My ex works in records for the felony courts. She hates my guts, but she'll hate this killer more. I'll look good by comparison.'

'Man, that's sad, Tip.' Adler shook his head. 'You barely rank above the scumbags.'

'Hey, that's a step up from when she filed the papers.'

'And Bondurant,' Kovac said, drawing another chorus of groans. 'Bondurant won't talk to us, and I don't like that. He told Quinn he was worried about his privacy. Can't imagine why,' he added with a sly grin, pulling the mini-cassette recorder out of his coat pocket.

The five members of the task force present crowded around to listen. Liska and Moss were still out doing victim background. The feds had returned to the FBI offices. Walsh was working through the list VICAP had provided of similar crimes committed in other parts of the country. He would be calling agents in other Bureau field offices, and calling contacts he had in various law enforcement agencies through his affiliation with the FBI's National Academy program that offered training to law enforcement professionals outside the Bureau. Quinn had sequestered himself to work on Smokey Joe's profile.

The tape of Bondurant's conversation with Quinn played out. The detectives listened, barely breathing. Kovac tried to picture Bondurant, needing to see the man's face, needing the expressions that went with the mostly expressionless voice. He had gone over the conversation with Quinn, and had Quinn's impressions. But questioning someone via a third party was a lot like trying to have sex with someone who was in another room – a lot of frustration and not much satisfaction.

The tape played out. The machine shut itself off with a sharp click. Kovac looked from one team member to the next. Cop faces: stern with ingrained, guarded skepticism.

'That skinny white boy's hiding something,' Adler said at last, sitting back in his chair.

'I don't know that it has anything to do with the murder,' Kovac said. 'But I'd say he's definitely holding something back on us about Friday night. I want to re-canvass the neighbors and talk to the housekeeper.'

'She was gone that night,' Elwood said.

'I don't care. She knew the girl. She knows her boss.'

Yurek groaned and put his head in his hands.

'What's your problem, Charm?' Tippen asked. 'All you have to do is tell the newsies we have no comment at this time.'

'Yeah, on national television,' he said. 'The big dogs smelled this shit and came running. I've got network news people ringing my phone off the hook. Bondurant is news all by himself. Bondurant plus a decapitated, burned corpse that may or may not be his daughter is the kind of stuff that transcends Tom Brokaw, headlines *Dateline,* and sells tabloids by the truckload. Sniff too hard in Peter Bondurant's direction, get the press leaning that way, I'm telling you, he'll blow. We'll be hip deep in lawsuits and suspensions.'

'I'll work on Bondurant and Brandt,' Kovac said, knowing he'd have to do a hell of a lot better job of it than he'd done that morning. 'I'll take the heat, but I need people working them peripherally, talking to friends, acquaintances, and so forth. Chunk, you and Hamill checking around Paragon? Working the disgruntled-employee angle?'

'Got a meeting out there in thirty.'

'Maybe we can talk to someone who knew the girl in France,' Tippen suggested. 'Maybe the feds can dig up someone over there. Let us in on some of her back story. The kid was screwed up for a reason. Maybe some friend over there knows if this reason has a name.'

'Call Walsh and see what he can do. Ask him if there's any word yet on those medical records. Elwood, did you get anything back from Wisconsin on the DL our witness is running around with?'

'No wants, no warrants. I called information to get a phone number – she doesn't have one. I contacted the post office – they say she moved and left no forwarding address. Strike three.'

'She give us a sketch yet?' Yurek asked.

'Kate Conlan brought her in this morning to work with Oscar,' Kovac said, rising. 'I'm gonna go see what's what right now. We'd better pray to God that girl has a Polaroid memory. A break on this thing now could save all our asses.'

'I'll need copies ASAP for the press,' Yurek said.

'I'll get it to you. What time are you set to play *America's Most Wanted*?'

'Five.'

Kovac checked his watch. The day was running double time and they didn't have much to show for it yet. That was the hell of getting an investigation this size off the ground. Time was of the essence. Every cop knew that after the first forty-eight hours of an investigation, the odds of solving a murder dropped off sharply. But the amount of information that needed to be gathered, collated, interpreted, and acted upon at the start of a multiple murder investigation was staggering. And just one piece ignored could be the one piece that turned the tide.

His pager trilled. The readout gave his lieutenant's number.

'Everyone who can, meet back here at four,' he said, grabbing his coat off the back of his chair. 'If you're out, check in with me on the cell phone. I'm outta here.'

'She didn't seem very sure of herself, Sam,' Oscar said, leading him to a tilt-top drawing table in a small office made smaller by a pack rat's clutter. Papers, books, magazines, filled all available space in precarious towers and piles. 'I led her through it as gently as I could, but she was resistant at the core.'

'Resistant as in lying or resistant as in scared?'

'Afraid. And as you well know, fear can precipitate prevarication.'

'You've been into the thesaurus again, haven't you, Oscar?'

A beatific smile peeked through the copious facial hair. 'Education is the wellspring of the soul.'

'Yeah, well, you'll be drowning in it, Oscar,' Kovac said, impatient, digging a lint-ridden Mylanta tablet out of his pants pocket. 'So, let's see the masterpiece.'

'I consider it a work in progress.'

He peeled back the opaque protective sheet, revealing the pencil sketch Twin Cities residents had been promised by their top elected and appointed officials. The suspect wore a dark, puffed-up jacket – hiding his build – over a hooded sweatshirt, hood up, hiding the color of his hair. Aviator sunglasses hid the shape of his eyes. The nose was nondescript, the face of medium width. The mouth was partially obscured by a mustache.

Kovac's stomach did a slow roll. 'It's the fucking Unabomber!' he snapped, wheeling on Oscar. 'What the hell am I supposed to do with this?'

'Now, Sam, I told you it was a work in progress,' Oscar said in that low, slow voice.

'He's wearing *sunglasses*! It was fucking midnight and she's got him wearing sunglasses!' Sam ranted. 'Judas fucking priest! This could be anyone. This could be no one. This could be *me,* for godsake!'

'I'm hoping to work with Angie a little more,' the artist said, unperturbed by Kovac's temper. 'She doesn't believe she has the details in her memory, but I believe she does. She has only to release her fear and clarity will come. Eventually.'

'I don't have *eventually,* Oscar! I've got a goddamn press conference at five o'clock!'

He blew out a breath and turned a circuit around the artist's small, cramped, cluttered workspace, looking around as if he wanted to find something to throw. Christ, he sounded like Sabin, wanting evidence on demand. He had been telling himself all day not to count on that lying, thieving little piece of baggage he had to call a witness, but beneath the cynicism, he'd been praying for a dead-on, got-you-by-the-balls-now composite. Twenty-two years on the job and the optimist in him still lived. Amazing.

'I'm working on a version without the mustache,' Oscar said. 'She seemed uncertain about the mustache.'

'How can she be uncertain about a *mustache*! He either had one or he didn't! Fuck! Fuck, fuck, fuck!'

'I won't release it today, that's all,' he said mostly to himself. 'We'll hold off, get the girl back in here tomorrow, and try to get some better detail.'

From the corner of his eye, he could see Oscar drop his head a little. He looked to be retreating into his beard. Kovac stopped his pacing and looked at him square.

'We can do that, can't we, Oscar?'

'I'll be pleased to work with Angie again tomorrow. I'd like nothing better than to help her unblock her memory flow. Confronting memory is the first step to neutralizing its negative power. As for the other, you'll have to take it up with Chief Greer. He was in here an hour ago to get a copy.'

'She saw his face for two minutes in the light of a burning corpse, Sam,' Kate said, leading him into her office, not sure the small space would hold him. When he was wound, Kovac was a barely contained column of energy that required perpetual motion.

'She looked directly at the face of a murderer in bright light. Come on, Red. Wouldn't you think the details would be branded, so to speak, in her memory?'

Kate sat back against her desk, crossing her ankles, careful to keep her toes out of Kovac's way. 'I think her memory might improve dramatically with the application of a little cash,' she said dryly.

'What!'

'She got wind of Bondurant's reward and wants a chunk. Can you blame her, Sam? The kid's got nothing. She's got no one. She's been living on the street, doing God knows what to survive.'

'Did you explain to her that rewards go out *on conviction*? We can't convict somebody we can't catch. We can't catch somebody we don't have a clue what the hell he looks like.'

'I know. Hey, you don't have to preach to me. And – word of warning – don't preach to Angie either,' Kate said. 'She's on the fence, Sam. We could lose her. Figuratively and literally. You think life's a bitch now, imagine what'll happen if your only witness skips.'

'What are you saying? Are you saying we should stick someone on her?'

'Unmarked, low-key, and well back. You set a uniform on the curb in front of the Phoenix, it's only going to make matters worse. She already thinks we're treating her like a criminal.'

'Lovely,' Kovac drawled. 'And what else would her highness require?'

'Don't bust my chops,' Kate ordered. 'I'm on your side. And stop pacing, you'll make yourself dizzy. You're making *me* dizzy.'

Kovac pulled in a deep breath and leaned back against the wall, directly across from Kate.

'You knew what to expect from this girl, Sam. Why are you surprised by this? Or did you just want that composite to be a dead ringer for one of your exes?'

His mouth twisted with chagrin. He rubbed a hand across his face and wished for a cigarette. 'I got a bad feeling about this deal, Kate,' he admitted. 'I guess I was hoping for the witness fairy to touch our little Miss Daisy with her wand. Or poke her with it. Or hold it to her head like a gun. I hoped that maybe the kid would be scared enough to tell the truth. Oscar tells me fear precipitates prevarication.'

'He's been reading those pop psychology books again, hasn't he?'

'Or something.' He heaved a sigh. 'Bottom line: I need something to kick-start this investigation or I'll have to go digging in some nasty shitholes. I guess I was hoping this was it.'

'Hold the sketch back a day. I'll bring her in again tomorrow. See if Oscar can apply his mystic powers and draw something out of her – no pun intended.'

'I don't think I'll be able to hold it back. Big Chief Little Dick got his hands on the sketch before me. He'll want to run with it. He'll want to present it at the press conference himself.

'Goddamn brass,' he grumbled. 'They're worse than kids with a case like this. Everybody wants the credit. Everybody wants their face on the news. They all have to look important, like they've got shit to do with the investigation besides get in the way of the real cops.'

'That's what's really grating on you, Sam,' Kate pointed out. 'It's not the sketch, it's your natural resistance to working under supervision.'

He scowled at her. 'You been reading Oscar's books too?'

'I have a college degree in brain picking,' she reminded him. 'What's the worst that happens if the sketch goes out and it isn't totally accurate?'

'I don't know, Kate. This mope barbecues women and cuts their heads off. What's the worst that could happen?'

'He won't be offended by the sketch,' Kate said. 'He's more likely to be amused, to think he's outsmarted you again.'

'Ahh, so then he'll feel more invincible and be empowered to go out and whack another one! Swell!'

'Don't be such a fatalist. You can use this to your advantage. Ask Quinn. Besides, if the sketch is even partially accurate, you might get something off it. Maybe someone out there will remember seeing a similar individual near a truck. Maybe they'll remember a partial license plate, a dent in a fender, a guy with a limp. You know as well as I do, luck plays into an investigation like this in a big way.'

'Yeah, well,' Kovac said, reluctantly pushing himself away from the wall. 'We could use a truckload. Soon. So where's the sunshine girl now?'

'I had someone take her back to the Phoenix. She's not happy about that.'

'Tough.'

'Ditto,' Kate said. 'She wants a hotel room or an apartment or something. I want her with people. Isolation isn't going to open her up. Plus, I'd like someone keeping an eye on her. Did you go through that backpack she carries around?'

'Liska checked it out. Angie was steamed, but, hey, she came running away from a headless corpse. We couldn't risk her going psycho and pulling a knife on us. The uniform picked her up should have done it at the scene, but he was all shook up thinking about Smokey Joe. Stupid rookie. He screws up that way with the wrong mutt, he'll get himself whacked.'

'Did Nikki find anything?'

He pursed his lips and shook his head. 'What are you thinking? Drugs?'

'I don't know. Maybe. Her behavior is all over the map. She's up, she's down, she's tough, she's on the verge of tears. I start to think something's off about her, then I stop and think: My God, look what she's been through. Maybe she's remarkably stable and sane, all things considered.'

'Or maybe she needs a score,' Kovac speculated, moving toward the door. 'Maybe that's what she was doing in that park at midnight. I know some guys in narcotics. I'll reach out, see if maybe they know this kid. We got nothing else on her yet. Wisconsin had nothing.'

'I talked to a Susan Frye in our juvenile division,' Kate said. 'She's been at this forever. She's got a great network. Rob is checking his contacts in Wisconsin. In the meantime, I need to get Angie some kind of perk, Sam. A show of appreciation. Can you kick her something out of petty cash as an informant?'

'I'll see what I can do.'

Another duty to add to his long list. Poor guy, Kate thought. The lines in his face seemed deeper today. He had the weight of the city on those sturdy shoulders. His suit jacket hung limp on him, as if he had somehow drawn the starch out of it to supplement his draining energy.

'Listen, don't worry about it,' she said as she pulled the door open. 'I can weasel it out of your lieutenant myself. You've got better things to do.'

Halfway out the door, he turned and gave her a lopsided smile.

'What gave you that idea?'

'Just a hunch.'

'Thanks. You're sure you're not too busy tackling armed gunmen?'

'Heard about that, did you?' Kate made a face, not comfortable with the attention yesterday's incident had gotten her. She'd turned down half a dozen requests for interviews and made too many trips to the ladies' room to dab makeup over the bruises.

'Wrong place, wrong time, that's all. The story of my life,' she said dryly.

Kovac looked thoughtful, as if he were considering saying something profound, then shook his head a little. 'You're a wonder, Red.'

'Hardly. I've just got a guardian angel with a sick sense of humor. Go fight the fight, Sergeant. I'll take care of the witness.'

12

The traffic annoys him. He takes 35W south out of downtown to avoid traffic lights and the tedious twists and turns of the alternate route. Stop-and-go traffic until he wants to abandon the car and walk down the shoulder, randomly pulling people out of their vehicles and beating their heads in with a tire iron. It amuses him that other motorists are likely entertaining the same fantasy. They have no idea that the man sitting in the dark sedan behind them, beside them, in front of them, could act on that fantasy without turning a hair.

He looks at the woman in the red Saturn beside him. She is pretty, with Nordic features and white-blond hair done in a voluminous, airy, tousled style that has been sprayed into place. She catches him looking, and he smiles and waves. She smiles back, then makes a gesture and a funny face at the traffic snarled ahead of them. He shrugs and grins, mouths, 'What can you do?'

He imagines that face drawn tight and pale with terror as he leans down over her with a knife. He can see her bare chest rise and fall in time with her shallow breathing. He can hear the tremor in her voice as she begs him for her life. He can hear her screams as he cuts her breasts.

Desire stirs deep in his groin.

'Probably the most crucial factor in the development of a serial rapist or killer is the role of fantasy.' – John Douglas, Mindhunter.

His fantasies have never shocked him. Not in childhood, when he would think of what it might be like to watch a living thing die, what it would be like to close his hands around the throat of a cat or the kid down the block and hold the power of life and death literally within his grasp. Not in adolescence, when he would think of cutting the nipples from his mother's breasts, or cutting out her larynx and smashing it with a hammer, or cutting out her uterus and throwing it into the furnace.

He knows that for killers such as himself, these thoughts are a sustained part of the internal processing and cognitive operations. They are, in effect, natural for him. Natural, and, therefore, not deviant.

He exits on 36th and drives west on tree-lined side streets toward Lake Calhoun. The blonde is gone and the fantasy with her. He thinks again of the afternoon press briefing, both amused and frustrated. The police had a sketch – this amused him. He stood there in the crowd as Chief Greer held up the drawing that was supposed to be a rendition of him so accurate that people would recognize him at a glance on the street. And when the briefing had ended, all those reporters had walked right past him.

The frustration has its source in John Quinn. Quinn made no appearance at the briefing, and has made no official statement, which seems a deliberate slight. Quinn is too wrapped up in his deduction and speculation. He is probably focusing all his attention on the victims. Who they were and what they were, wondering why they were chosen.

'In a sense the victim shapes and molds the criminal . . . To know one we must be acquainted with the complementary partner.' – Hans von Hentig.

Quinn believes this too. Quinn's textbook on sexual homicide is among many on his shelf. *Seductions of Crime* by Katz, *Inside the Criminal Mind* by Samenow, *Without Conscience* by Hare, *Sexual Homicide: Patterns and Motives* by Ressler, Burgess, and Douglas. He has studied all of them and more. A voyage of self-exploration.

He turns onto his block. Because of the way the lakes lie in this part of town, the streets immediately around them are often irregular. This one has a bend in it that gives the houses larger lots than usual. More privacy. He parks the car on the concrete apron outside the garage and gets out.

Night has inked out what meager daylight there had been earlier. The wind is blowing out of the west and bringing with it the scent of fresh dog shit. The smell hits his nostrils a split second before the sound of rapid-fire toy-dog barking.

Out of the darkness of the neighbor's yard darts Mrs Vetter's bichon frise, a creature that looks like a collection of white pompoms sewn loosely together. The dog runs to within five feet of him, then stops and stands its ground, barking, snarling like a rabid squirrel.

The noise instantly sets off his temper. He hates the dog. He especially hates the dog now because it has triggered the return of his foul mood from the traffic jam. He wants to kick the dog as hard as he can. He can imagine the high-pitched yip, the animal's limp body as he picks it up by the throat and crushes its windpipe.

'Bitsy!' Mrs Vetter shrieks from her front step. 'Bitsy, come here!'

Yvonne Vetter is in her sixties, a widow, an unpleasant woman with a round, sour face and a shrill voice. He hates her in a deeply visceral way, and thinks of killing her every time he sees her, but something equally deep and fundamental holds him back. He refuses to examine what that feeling is, and becomes angrier imagining what John Quinn would make of it.

'Bitsy! Come here!'

The dog snarls at him, then turns and runs up and down the length of the garage, stopping to pee on the corners of the building.

'Bit-sy!!'

A pulse begins to throb in his head and warmth floods his brain and washes down through his body. If Yvonne Vetter crosses the lawn now, he will kill her. He will grab her and smother her screams with the newspapers he holds. He will quickly pull her into the garage, smash her head against the wall to knock her out, then kill the dog first to stop its infernal barking. Then he will let loose his temper and kill Yvonne Vetter in a way that will satiate a vicious hunger buried deep within him.

She begins to descend the front steps of her house.

The muscles across his back and shoulders tighten. His pulse quickens.

'Bit-sy!! Come now!!'

His lungs fill. His fingers flex on the edge of the newspapers.

The dog barks at him one last time, then darts back to its mistress. Fifteen feet away, Vetter bends down and scoops the dog into her arms as if he were a child.

Opportunity dies like an unsung song.

'He's excited tonight,' he says, smiling.

'He gets that way when he's inside too much. He doesn't like you either,' Mrs Vetter says defensively, and takes the dog back to her house.

'Fucking bitch,' he whispers. The anger will vibrate within him for a long while, like a tuning fork still trembling long after it's been struck. He will play through the fantasy of killing Yvonne Vetter again and again and again.

He goes into the garage, where the Blazer and a red Saab sit, and enters the house through a side door, eager to read about the Cremator in the two newspapers. He will cut out all stories pertaining to the investigation and make photocopies of them, because newsprint is cheap and doesn't hold up over time. He has taped both the network evening news and the local evening news, and will watch for any mention of the Cremator.

The Cremator. The name amuses him. It sounds like something from a comic book. It conjures images of Nazi war criminals or B-movie monsters. The stuff of nightmares.

He is the stuff of nightmares.

And like the creatures of childhood nightmares, he goes to the basement. The basement is his personal space, his ideal sanctuary. The main room is outfitted with an amateur sound studio. Walls and ceiling of sound-absorbing acoustic tile. Flat carpet the color of slate. He likes the low ceiling, the lack of natural light, the sensation of being in the earth with thick concrete walls around him. His own safe world. Just like when he was a boy.

He goes down the hall and into the game room, holding the newspapers out in front of him to admire the headlines.

'Yes, I am famous,' he says, smiling. 'But don't feel bad. You'll be famous soon too. There's nothing quite like it.'

He turns toward the pool table, holding the newspapers at an angle so that the naked woman bound spread-eagle on it can glance at the headlines if she wants to. She stares, instead, at him, her eyes glassy with terror and tears. The sounds she makes are not words, but the most basic vocalizations of that most basic emotion – fear.

The sounds touch him like electrical currents, energizing him. Her fear gives him control of her. Control is power. Power is the ultimate aphrodisiac.

'Soon you'll be a part of this headline,' he says, running a finger beneath the bold black print on page one of the *Star Tribune*. '*Ashes to Ashes.*'

Day slipped into evening, into night. Quinn's only indicator was his watch, which he seldom checked. There were no windows in the office he'd been given, only walls, which he'd spent the day papering with notes, often with the telephone receiver sandwiched between ear and shoulder, consulting on the Blacksburg case, where the suspect seemed on the brink of confession. He should have been there. His need for control fostered the conceit that he could prevent all mistakes, even though he knew that wasn't true.

Kovac had offered him space at what the task force had unofficially dubbed the Loving Touch of Death offices. He had declined. He needed separation, isolation. He couldn't be there when a dozen cops were tossing theories and suspect names like a chopped salad. He already felt tainted as it was.

Now word was out that John Quinn had been brought on board the Cremator case. Kovac had called with the bad news after the press briefing. It was only a matter of hours before he would have to deal with the media himself.

Damn, he'd wanted more time. He had these next few hours. He should have settled in and lost himself, but he couldn't seem to. Exhaustion pulled at him. His ulcer was burning. He was hungry and knew he needed fuel to keep his brain running, but he didn't want to waste the time going out. There was too much information and the buzz of too much caffeine swarming in his head. And there was a familiar sense of restlessness vibrating deep within – the urgency that came with every on-site case, compounded this time by mitigating circumstances and intrusive, fragmented memories from the past. Compounded again by a feeling that had been creeping up on him more and more and more lately – fear. The fear that he wouldn't make a difference in the case fast enough. The fear that he would screw up. The fear that the fatigue pressing down on him would suddenly be too much. The fear that what he really wanted was to just walk away from it all.

Needing to move to escape the emotions, he began to pace back and forth in front of the wall of notes, taking in snatches of them at a glance. The faces of Bondurant and Brandt blew around inside his head like leaves.

Peter Bondurant was holding back more than he was giving them.

Lucas Brandt had a license to keep secrets.

Quinn wished he'd never met either of them. He should have argued harder against coming here so early in the investigation, he thought, rubbing at a knot in his right shoulder. The issue was control. If he walked onstage with his strategy mapped out, he had the upper hand.

That methodology applied to more than just this case. It was how he ran his whole life – from dealing with the bureaucracy on the job, to dealing with the Chinese people who ran the mailbox place where he kept a box, to buying his groceries. In any and all situations and relationships, control was key.

Kate slipped into the back of his mind, as if to taunt him. How many times over the years had he replayed what had happened between them, adjusting his own actions and reactions to get a different outcome? More times than he would admit. Control and strategy were his watchwords. He'd had neither where Kate was concerned. One minute they'd been acquaintances, then friends, then in over their heads. No time to think, too tangled up in the moment to have any perspective, drawn together by a need and a passion that was stronger than either of them. And then it was over, and she was gone, and . . . nothing. Nothing but regrets that he had let lie, sure that they both would eventually see it was for the best.

It *was* for the best. For Kate anyway. She had a life here. She had a new career, friends, a home. He should have had sense enough to back away from all that, leave well enough alone, but the temptation of opportunity lured him like a crooked finger and a seductive smile. And the force of all those regrets pushed him from behind.

He supposed five years was a long time to carry regrets, but he'd carried others longer. Cases not solved, trials lost, a child-killer who had slipped away. His marriage, his mother's death, his father's alcoholism. Maybe he never let anything go. Maybe that was why he felt so hollow inside: There was no room left for anything but the dried detritus of his past.

He swore under his breath, disgusted with himself. He was supposed to be delving into the mind of a criminal, not his own.

He didn't remember sitting back against the desk, had no idea how many minutes he'd lost. He rubbed his big hands over his face, licked his lips, and caught the phantom taste of scotch. An odd psychological quirk, and a need that would go unfulfilled. He didn't allow himself to drink. He didn't allow himself to smoke. He didn't allow himself much. If he added regret to that list, what would he have left?

He walked to the section of wall where he had taped up brief notes on the Cremator's victims, scrawled in his own hand in colored markers. All caps. Tight, with a hard right-hand slant. The kind of handwriting that made graphologists raise their brows and give him a wide berth.

Photographs of all three women were taped above his notes. A three-ring binder lay open on the desk, filled with page after page of neatly typed reports, maps, scale drawings of the crime scenes, crime scene photographs, autopsy protocols – his portable bible of the case. But he found it helpful to lay out some of the basic information in a more linear way, and thus the notes on the wall and the photographs of three smiling women – gone now from this world, their lives snuffed out like candles, their dignity torn violently from them.

Three white women. All between the ages of twenty-one and twenty-three. Height varied from five five to five nine. Body types ranged from large-boned Lila White to petite Fawn Pierce to average Jane Doe/Jillian Bondurant.

Two prostitutes and a college student. They had lived in different parts of town. The hookers worked two different neighborhoods as a rule, neither of which was frequented by Jillian Bondurant. Lila and Fawn may have crossed paths occasionally, but it was highly unlikely Jillian would have frequented any of the same bars or restaurants or stores.

He had considered the drug connection, but they had nothing to support it so far. Lila White had gotten straight after entering a county program more than a year ago. Fawn Pierce had never been known to use, although she'd had a reputation for the occasional days-long bender on cheap vodka. And Jillian? No drugs had been found in her home, none in her system. She had no criminal record relating to drug use. As yet, no anecdotal stories of drug use.

'You think they'd like people to know why their daughters became whores and drug addicts?'

He could still hear the bitterness in Peter Bondurant's voice. Where had it come from?

Jillian was the piece that didn't fit in the puzzle of these crimes. She was the one that skewed the profile. There was a common type of killer who preyed on prostitutes. Prostitutes were high-risk victims, easy pickings. Their killers tended to be socially inadequate, under-employed white males who had a history of humiliating experiences with women and sought to get back at the gender by punishing what they considered to be the worst of the lot.

Unless Jillian had led a secret life as a hooker . . . Not beyond the realm, he supposed, but so far there were no indications Jillian had had a single boyfriend, let alone a list of johns.

'Boys didn't interest her. She didn't want temporary relationships. She'd been through so much . . .'

What had she been through? Her parents' divorce. Her mother's illness. A stepfather in a new country. What else? Something deeper? Darker? Something that pushed her into therapy with Lucas Brandt.

'. . . You should consider that the problems Jillian brought to me may have had nothing whatsoever to do with her death. Her killer may not have known anything at all about her.'

'But I'll bet you a dollar he did, Dr Brandt,' he said softly, staring at the snapshot of the girl. He could feel it in his gut. Jillian was the key. Something in her life had put her in the crosshairs of this killer. And if they could find out what that something was, then they might have a hope in hell of catching the son of a bitch.

He went back to the desk and flipped through the binder pages to the section of photographs: eight-by-ten color prints, neatly labeled as to subject matter. The crime scenes: general shots, lay-of-the-land shots, body position from various angles, close-ups of the burned, defiled women. And from the ME's office: general and close-up shots of the victims before and after clean-up at the morgue, autopsy photographs, close-up shots of wounds. Wounds inflicted before death – indicative of a sexual sadist. Wounds inflicted after death – which were more fetishistic than sadistic, intrinsic to the killer's fantasies.

Sophisticated fantasies. Fantasies he'd been developing for a long, long time.

He paged slowly through the close-ups of the wounds, examining every mark the killer had left, lingering on the stab wounds to the victims' chests. Eight stab wounds clustered in a group, longer wounds alternating with shorter in a specific pattern.

Of all the gruesome aspects of the murders, this bothered him most. More than the burning. The burning seemed more for show, making a public statement. *Ashes to ashes.* A symbolic funeral, the end of his connection to the victim. These stab wounds meant something more personal, intimate. What?

A cacophony of voices filled Quinn's head: Bondurant's, Brandt's, the medical examiner's, Kovac's; cops and coroners and experts and agents from hundreds of past cases. All of them with an opinion or a question or an ax to grind. All of them so loud he couldn't hear himself think anymore. And the fatigue only seemed to magnify the noise until he wanted to beg someone to turn it off.

The Mighty Quinn. That was what they called him back in Quantico. If they could see him now . . . Feeling as if he might choke on the fear of missing something or turning the investigation in the wrong way.

The system was on overload, and he was the one at the switch – and there was the most frightening thought: that only he could make things change, and he wouldn't make things change because as awful as this was, the alternative scared him even more. Without the job, there was no John Quinn.

A fine trembling started deep within him and subtly worked its way out into his arms. He fought against it, hating it, tightening his biceps and triceps, trying to force the weakness back down inside him. Eyes squeezed shut, he dropped to the floor and began push-ups. Ten, twenty, thirty, more, until his arms felt as if the skin would burst open, unable to contain the straining muscle mass, until the pain burned the noise out of his mind and all he could hear was the pounding of his own pulse. And then he forced himself to his feet, breathing hard, warm and damp with sweat.

He focused on the photograph before him, seeing not the torn flesh or the blood or the corpse; seeing only the pattern of the wound. X over X.

'Cross my heart,' he murmured, tracing a fingertip over the lines. 'Hope to die.'

'A serial killer stalks the streets of Minneapolis. Today, Minneapolis police released a composite sketch of the man who may have brutally slain three women, and *that* is our top story tonight . . .'

The women of the Phoenix House sat in, on, and around the mismatched assortment of chairs and couches in the living room, their attention on the broad-shouldered, square-jawed anchor of the Channel Eleven news. The camera cut to film footage of the afternoon press briefing, the chief of police holding up the sketch of the Cremator, then the screen was filled with the sketch itself.

Angie watched from the doorway, her attention on the women. A couple of them weren't much older than she was. Four were in their twenties. One was older, fat, and ugly. The fat one wore a sleeveless top because the furnace had gone haywire and the house was as hot and dry as a desert. Her upper arms were flabby and fish-belly white. Her stomach rested on her thighs when she sat down.

Angie knew the woman had been a hooker, but she couldn't imagine a man ever being hard up enough to pay to have sex with her. Men liked pretty girls, young girls. Didn't matter how old or ugly the man was, they all wanted pretty girls. That was Angie's experience. Maybe that was why Fat Arlene was there. Maybe she couldn't get a man to pay her, and the Phoenix was her retirement home.

A redhead who had the thin, pale, bruised look of an addict started to cry when photographs of the three murder victims came onscreen. The other women pretended not to notice. Toni Urskine, who ran the Phoenix, perched on the arm of the redhead's chair, leaned down, and touched her shoulder.

'It's okay,' she said softly. 'It's okay to cry. Fawn was your friend, Rita.'

The redhead pulled her bony bare feet up onto the seat of her chair and buried her head against her knees, sobbing. 'Why'd he have to kill her that way? She didn't hurt nobody!'

'There's no making sense of it,' another one said. 'It could have been any of us.'

A fact that was clear to all of them, even the ones who tried to deny it.

Fat Arlene said, 'You gotta be smart about who you go with. You gotta have a sense about it.'

A black woman with ratty dreadlocks shot her a mean glare. 'Like you get to pick and choose. Who wanna tie your fat ass down? See all that fat jiggling like Jell-O while he cut you up.'

Arlene's face went red and squeezed tight, eyes disappearing in the round mounds of cheeks and puffy brows. She looked like a chow chow Angie had seen once. 'You can just shut your hole, you bony bitch!'

Looking angry, Toni Urskine left the crying redhead and moved toward the middle of the room, holding her hands up like a referee. 'Hey! None of that! We've got to learn to respect and care for one another. Remember: group esteem, gender esteem, *self*-esteem.'

Easy for her to say, Angie thought, slipping back from the door. Toni Urskine had never had to go down on some old pervert to get enough money for a meal. She was little miss do-gooder, in her casual-chic outfits from Dayton's and a hundred-dollar hairdo by Horst. She drove up to this crappy house in her Ford Explorer from some beautiful home out in Edina or Minnetonka. She didn't know what it did to a person inside to find out she was worth only twenty-five bucks.

'We *all* care about these murder victims,' Urskine said passionately, dark eyes shining, her sharp-featured face aglow. 'We *all* are angry that the police have done virtually nothing until now. It's an outrage. It's a slap in the face. It's the city of Minneapolis telling us the lives of women in desperate circumstances mean nothing. We need to be angry about that, not angry with each other.'

The women listened, some intent, some halfheartedly, some pretending not to.

'I think what we need here is involvement. We need to be proactive,' Urskine said. 'We'll go down to city hall tomorrow. The press can hear our side of it. We'll get copies of the composite sketch and canvass . . .'

Angie backed away from the door and moved silently down the hall. She didn't like it when people started talking about the Cremator case. The Phoenix women weren't supposed to know who she was or that she was involved in the case, but Angie always got the tense feeling that the other women would look at her and somehow figure out she was the mystery witness. She didn't want anyone to know.

She didn't want it to be true.

Sudden tears filled her eyes and she rubbed her hands against them. No show of emotion. If she showed what she felt, then someone would see a weakness in her, or a need, or the madness that sucked her into the Zone and made her cut herself. No one would understand that the blade severed the connection to insanity.

'Is everything all right?'

Startled, Angie jerked around and stared at the man standing in the open doorway to the basement. Late thirties, good-looking, dressed in tan chinos and a Ralph Lauren Polo shirt to work on the furnace. He had to be some relation to Toni Urskine. Sweat and dirt streaked his face. He worked a gray rag between hands dark with grime and something the color of blood.

He glanced down as Angie did and looked back up with a crooked smile. 'The old furnace in this place,' he said by way of explanation. 'I keep it running with willpower and rubber bands.'

'Greggory Urskine,' he said, sticking out his hand.

'You cut yourself,' Angie said, not accepting the gesture, her gaze still on the smear of blood that crossed his palm.

Urskine looked at it and rubbed the rag over it, chuckling in that nervous way people sometimes have when they are trying to make a good impression. Angie just stared at him. He looked a little like Kurt Russell, she thought: a wide jaw and small nose, tousled sandy hair. He wore glasses with silver wire rims. He had cut himself that morning shaving his upper lip.

'Aren't you hot in that jacket?' he asked.

Angie said nothing. She was sweating like a horse, but the sleeves of her sweater were too short and didn't cover all the scars on her arms. The jacket was a necessity. If she got any money out of Kate, she was going to buy herself some clothes. Maybe something brand new and not from the Goodwill or a thrift shop.

'I'm Toni's husband – and handyman,' Urskine said. He narrowed his eyes. 'I'm guessing you're Angie.'

Angie just stared at him.

'I won't tell anyone,' Urskine said in a confidential tone. 'Your secret's safe with me.'

It seemed like he was making fun of her somehow. Angie decided she didn't like him, handsome or not. There was something about the eyes behind the expensive designer glasses that bothered her. Like he was looking down at her, like she was a bug or something. She wondered idly if he had ever paid a woman for sex. His wife seemed like the kind of woman who thought sex was dirty. Saving women from having to do it was Toni Urskine's mission in life.

'We're all very concerned about this case,' he went on, looking serious. 'The first victim – Lila White – was a resident here for a while. Toni took it hard. She loves this place. Loves the women. Works like a trooper for the cause.'

Angie crossed her arms. 'And what do you do?'

Again with the flashing smile, the nervous chuckle. 'I'm an engineer at Honeywell. Currently on leave so I can help fix this place up before winter – and finally finish my master's thesis.'

He laughed like that was some kind of big joke. He didn't ask Angie what she did, even though not all of the women in this place were hookers. He was looking at her stomach, at the navel ring and tattoos revealed as her too-small sweater crept up. She cocked a hip, flashing a little more skin, and wondered if he was thinking he might want her.

He glanced back up at her. 'So, they've got a good chance of catching this guy, thanks to you,' he said as a half-statement, half-question. 'You actually saw him.'

'No one's supposed to know that,' Angie said bluntly. 'I'm not supposed to talk about it.'

End of conversation. She ignored the closing niceties, backed away from him, then headed up the stairs. She felt Greggory Urskine's eyes on her as she went.

'Uh, good night, then,' he called as she disappeared into the darkness of the second story.

She went to the room she shared with a woman whose ex-boyfriend had held her down and cut all her hair off with a hunting knife because she refused to give him her AFDC check so he could buy crack. The woman's kids were in foster care now. The boyfriend had skipped to Wisconsin. The woman had been through drug rehab and come out of it with a need to confess. Therapy did that to some people. Angie had been too smart to let it happen to her.

Don't tell your secrets, Angel. They're all that make you special.

Special. She wanted to be special. She wanted not to be alone. It didn't matter that there were other people in this house. None of them were here *with* her. She didn't belong. She'd been dropped here like an unwanted puppy. Fucking cops. They wanted things from her, but they didn't want to give her anything back. They didn't give a shit about her. They didn't care about what she might want from them.

At least Kate was halfway honest, Angie thought as she paced the room. But she couldn't forget that Kate was still one of *them*. It was Kate Conlan's job to try to wedge open her defenses so the cops and the county attorney could get what they wanted. And that would be the end of it. She wasn't really a friend. Angie could count the only friends she'd ever had on one hand and have fingers left over.

She wanted one tonight. She wanted not to be stuck in this house. She wanted to belong somewhere.

She thought of the woman burning in the park, thought of where that woman had belonged, and wondered fancifully what would happen if she just took that woman's place. She would be a rich man's daughter. She would have a father and a home and money.

She'd had a father once: She had the scars to prove it. She'd had a home: She could still smell the sour grease in the kitchen, could still remember the big, dark closets with the doors that locked from the outside. She'd never had money.

She went to bed with her clothes on and waited until the house was quiet and her roommate was snoring. Then she slipped out from under the covers and out of the room, down the stairs, and out of the house through the back door.

The night was windy. Clouds rolled across the sky so fast, it looked almost like time-lapse photography. The streets were empty except for the occasional car rolling down one of the big cross streets going north and south. Angie headed west, jittery, skittish. The feeling that she was being watched constantly scratched at the back of her neck, but when she looked over her shoulder, there was no one.

The Zone was chasing her like a shadow. If she kept walking, if she had a purpose, focused on a goal, maybe it wouldn't catch her.

The houses along the way were dark. Tree limbs rattled in the wind. When she came to the lake, it was as black and shiny as an oil slick. She stuck to the dark side of the street and walked north. People in this neighborhood would call the cops if they saw someone out walking this late at night.

She recognized the house from the news reports – like something from England with a big iron fence around it. She turned and climbed the hill to the back side of the property, the big trees giving her cover. Hedges blocked the view of the house three seasons of the year, but their leaves were gone now, and she could look through the tangle of fine branches.

A light was on inside the house, in a room with fancy glass-paned doors that let out onto a patio. Angie stood at the fence, careful not to touch it, and gazed into Peter Bondurant's backyard. She looked past the swimming pool and the stone benches and the wrought iron tables and chairs that hadn't yet been taken into storage for the winter. She looked at the amber glow in the window and the figure of a man sitting at a desk, and wondered if he felt as alone as she did. She wondered if his money gave him comfort now.

Peter rose from the desk and moved around his office, restless, tense. He couldn't sleep, refused to take the pills his doctor had prescribed and had delivered to the house. The nightmare was alive in his mind: the orange brilliance of the flames, the smell. When he closed his eyes he could see it, feel the heat of it. He could see Jillian's face: the shock, the shame, the heartbreak. He could see her face floating free, the base of her throat ragged and bloody. If his mind was filled with images like these when he was awake, what would he see if he went to sleep?

Going to the French doors, he stared out at the night, black and cold, and imagined he felt eyes staring back. *Jillian.* He thought he could feel her presence. The weight of it pressed against his chest as if she had wrapped her arms around him. Even after death she wanted to touch him, cling to him; desperate for love, the meaning of it for her skewed and warped.

A strange, dark arousal flickered deep inside him, followed by disgust and shame and guilt. He turned away from the window with an animal roar and flung himself at his desk, sweeping everything from the tidy surface. Pens, Rolodex, paperweights, files, appointment book. The telephone jingled a protest. The lamp hit the floor, the bulb bursting with an explosive *pop!*, casting the room into darkness.

The final bright flash of light remained in Peter's eyes, twin flares of orange that moved as he moved. Flames he couldn't escape. Emotion was a rock in his throat, lodged there, hard and jagged. He felt a pressure within his eyeballs, as if they might burst, and he wondered wildly if he might not still see the flames anyway.

A harsh, dry choking sound rasped from him as he stumbled in the dark to a floor lamp, tripping over the things he'd knocked from the desk. Calmer in the light, he began to pick up the mess. He put the things back one at a time, aligning them precisely. This was what he had to do: Put his life back together with seamless precision, smooth the tears in the surface and go on, just as he had when Sophie had taken Jillian and left him all those years ago.

He picked up the appointment book last and found it opened to Friday. *Jillian: dinner,* written in his own precise hand. It sounded so innocent, so simple. But nothing was ever simple or innocent with Jillie. No matter how hard she tried.

The phone rang, startling him from the dark memories.

'Peter Bondurant,' he said as if this were normal business hours. In the back of his mind he was trying to remember if he'd been expecting a call from overseas.

'Daddy dearest,' the voice sang softly, seductively. 'I know all your secrets.'

13

'We're going to look like asses if we have to release another composite,' Sabin complained, prowling behind his desk. His lower lip jutted out like a sulky two-year-old's, an odd contrast to the sharp sophistication of his image. Ready to deal with the press at a moment's notice, he had decked himself out in a pewter-gray suit with a tie two shades darker and a French-blue shirt. Very dapper.

'I don't see how it reflects badly on your office, Ted,' Kate said. 'Chief Greer was the one who jumped the gun.'

He frowned harder and gave her a meaningful look. 'I know whose fault this is.'

'You can't blame the witness,' Kate said, knowing full well he meant to blame *her*.

'I'm told she's not been very cooperative,' Edwyn Noble said with concern, wedging his way into the discussion. He sat in a visitor's chair, his body too long for it, the legs of his dark trousers hiking up above bony ankles and nylon socks.

Kate stared at him, half a dozen stinging remarks on the tip of her tongue, not the least of which was *'What the hell are you doing here?'* Of course, she knew what he was doing there. His presence skirted the bounds of propriety, but she had already run the argument through her head and knew what the outcome would be. The county attorney's office ran victim/witness services. Peter Bondurant was the immediate family of a victim – if the dead woman proved to be his daughter – and therefore entitled to be kept informed as to the disposition of the case. Edwyn Noble was Bondurant's envoy. Et cetera, et cetera.

She looked at Noble as if he were something she might scrape off her shoe. 'Yes, well, there's always some of that going around.'

The inference struck the bull's-eye. Noble sat up a little straighter in the too-small chair, his eyes going cold.

Rob Marshall moved between them as peacemaker, the bootlicker's grin stretching across his moon face. 'What Kate means is that it's not unusual for a witness to such a brutal crime to become a little reluctant.'

Sabin huffed. 'She's not reluctant for the reward money.'

'The reward will go out only upon conviction,' Noble reminded them, as if it would take his client that long to scrape the cash together. As if Bondurant might be half hoping to get out of it altogether.

'This office does not buy witnesses,' Sabin proclaimed. 'I told you I wanted her dealt with, Kate.'

He made her sound like a paid assassin. 'I *am* dealing with her.'

'Then why did she not spend Monday night in jail? I told Kovac to treat her like a suspect. Scare her a little.'

'But you –' Kate began, confused.

Rob gave her a warning look. 'We still have that option in our pocket, Ted. Trying Phoenix House first might soften her up, give the girl the impression that Kate is on her side. I'm sure that's what you had in mind, isn't it, Kate?'

She glared at her boss, openmouthed.

Sabin was pouting. 'Now this sketch fiasco.'

'It's not a fiasco. No one should've seen the sketch yesterday,' Kate argued, turning away from Rob before she could go for his throat. 'Ted, you pressure this kid, she'll walk. Get tough with her, she'll develop a real mean case of amnesia. I guarantee it. You and I both know you have nothing to hold her on with relation to the murder. You couldn't even get her arraigned. A judge would bounce it out of the courtroom like a Super Ball, and you'd be left with egg on your face and no witness.'

He rubbed his chin as if he already felt the yolk drying.

'She's a vagrant. That's against the law.'

'Oh, yeah, that'll look good in the papers. *Teenage Murder Witness Charged for Homelessness.* Next time you run for office, you can bill yourself as the Simon Legree candidate.'

'My political life is not an issue here, Ms Conlan,' he snapped, suddenly stiff and steely-eyed. 'Your handling of this witness is.'

Rob looked at Kate with an expression that questioned her sanity. Kate looked to Edwyn Noble. *Not an issue. In a pig's eye.*

She could have pushed Sabin a little now and gotten herself reassigned. She could have confessed a total inability to deal with this witness and been out from under the burden that was Angie DiMarco. But the second Kate thought it, she saw herself leaving the girl at the mercy of the assembled wolves, and couldn't do it. The memory was too fresh of Angie standing in the ratty den at the Phoenix, sudden tears in her eyes, asking Kate why she couldn't go home with her.

She rose, discreetly smoothing the wrinkles from the front of her skirt. 'I'm doing my best to get the truth out of this girl. I know that's everyone's goal. Give me a chance to work her my way, Ted. Please.' She wasn't above giving him the hopeful, wide-eyed look if it would sway his mood. He didn't have to fall for it if he didn't want to. The word *mercenary* crawled through her mind, leaving a small trail of slime.

'She's not the kid next door,' she went on. 'She's had a tough life and it's made her a tough person, but I think she wants to do the right thing here. It won't do anyone any good to get impatient at this stage of the game. If you want corroboration of my opinion, ask Quinn. He knows as much about dealing with witnesses in this kind of case as I do,' Kate said, thinking turnabout was fair play. John owed her one. At least.

Noble cleared his throat politely. 'What about hypnosis? Will you try that?'

Kate shook her head. 'She'll never go for it. Hypnosis requires trust. This kid hasn't got any. Oscar's as mystical as she's going to sit still for.'

'I hate to play devil's advocate,' the attorney said, unfolding himself from the chair, 'but how are we to know the girl saw anything at all? It sounds to me as if she's the type to do anything for money. Perhaps the reward is her only goal.'

'And she set her sights on that goal before she knew it would even exist?' Kate said. 'If that's the case, then she's worth more than she ever was to this case because she'd have to be psychic. No reward was offered after the first two murders.'

She glanced at her watch and swore under her breath. 'I'm afraid you gentlemen will have to excuse me. I have to be at a hearing in a few minutes and my victim's probably already panicking because I'm not there.'

Sabin had come around the desk to lean back against it with his arms crossed and his stern face on. Kate recognized the pose from the profile *Minnesota Monthly* had done on him a year earlier. Not that she discounted his power or his willingness to use it. Ted Sabin hadn't gotten where he was by being anybody's fool or pretty boy.

'I'll give you more time with this girl, Kate.' He made it sound as if he were doing so grudgingly, even though the whole arrangement had been his idea. 'But we need results, and we need them quickly. I thought you of all the advocates in your office would understand that.'

'She's working with Oscar again this afternoon,' she said, moving toward the door.

Sabin came away from his desk and walked with her, resting his hand between her shoulder blades. 'You'll be through in court in time to be there with her?'

'Yes.'

'Because I'm sure Rob can juggle something and have someone else take care of this hearing.'

'No, sir. The hearing won't take long,' she promised with a pained smile. 'Besides, I wouldn't wish this particular client on any of my colleagues. They know where I live.'

'Maybe we should have Agent Quinn sit in on this session with Oscar and the girl,' he suggested.

The hand on her back had a knife in it suddenly.

'I don't see how that would be helpful.'

'No, you were right, Kate,' he argued. 'This witness isn't ordinary. And as you said, Quinn has a great deal of experience. He might be able to pick up on something, suggest a strategy. I'll call him.'

Kate stepped out the door and stood there as it closed behind her. 'Me and my big mouth.'

'Kate –' Rob Marshall began in a low voice. Kate wheeled on him as he slipped out into the hall.

'You weasel,' she accused in a harsh whisper. It was all she could do to keep from grabbing him by the ears and shaking him. 'You gave me the go-ahead to take Angie to the Phoenix. Now you stand in there and give Sabin the impression it was all *my* doing! I thought you'd cleared it with him. That's what I told Kovac. And I accused Kovac of being paranoid for not trusting it.'

'I broached the subject of the Phoenix with him –'

'But he didn't go for it.'

'He didn't say no.'

'Well, he sure as hell didn't say yes.'

'He had his mind on other things. I knew taking her there was how you would want to play it, Kate.'

'Don't try to put this off on me. You took some initiative for a change. Can't you at least own up to it?'

He breathed heavily through his too-short nose and his face turned a dull red. 'Kate, does it *ever* cross your mind that I'm your superior?'

She closed her mouth on the rejoinder that came to mind, and scraped together what respect she could. 'I'm sorry. I'm angry.'

'And I'm your boss. *I'm* in charge,' he said. She could hear the frustration in his voice.

'I don't envy you that job,' she said dryly. 'I ought to really antagonize you. You could take me off this powder keg. But I don't want off it,' she admitted. 'Must be the Swedish masochist in me.'

'You're exactly who I want with this witness, Kate,' he said. He pushed his glasses up on his nose and smiled like a man with a toothache. 'Now who's the masochist?'

'I'm sorry. I don't like being made to feel like a pawn, that's all.'

'Focus on the outcome. We got what we wanted.'

His relationship with Sabin was intact. Her apparent overstepping of boundaries would be written off to her well-known arrogance, Sabin would forgive her because he had the hots for her, and Rob came off looking like a diplomat, if not a leader. Once again the end justified the means. Nothing hurt but her pride.

'I'm not averse to conspiracy, you know,' she said, still miffed. She'd had every intention of stealing Angie away from Sabin's clutches, and she would never in a million years have let Rob Marshall in on the plan. That was what was really grating on her – that Rob had one-upped her. She never wanted to think he was more clever than her or more shrewd or her superior in any way. A hell of an attitude to have toward her boss.

'Have you heard anything back from your friends in Wisconsin yet?' she asked.

'Nothing yet.'

'It'd be nice to know who the hell this kid is. I feel like I'm working with a blindfold on.'

'I've got the videotape of Angie's interviews,' he said, setting his hands at his middle. 'I thought it might be helpful to sit down together and go over it. Maybe we could bring Quinn into that too. I'd like to hear his opinion.'

'Yeah, why not?' Kate said, resigning herself. 'Let me know when you set it up. I have to get to court.'

Some days it just seemed the better option to stay home and hit her thumb with a hammer. At least that was a pain from which she could easily recover. John Quinn was another matter altogether.

'I was afraid you weren't coming,' David Willis said with no small amount of accusation. He rushed up to Kate as she made her way around the knots of lawyers in the hall outside the criminal courtrooms.

'I'm sorry I'm late, Mr Willis. I was in a meeting with the county attorney.'

'About *my* case?'

'No. Everything is ready to go for your case.'

'I'm not going to have to testify, right?'

'Not today, Mr Willis.' Kate steered her client toward the courtroom. 'This is just a hearing. The prosecutor, Mr Merced, will be presenting just enough evidence to have the court bind Mr Zubek over for trial.'

'But he won't call me as a surprise witness or anything?' He looked half terrified, half hopeful at the prospect.

Somehow, Kate knew this was just how David Willis had looked in his high school yearbook back in the seventies: out-of-date crew cut and nerd glasses, pants that were an odd shade of green and an inch too high-waisted. People had probably assaulted him regularly all his life.

For the occasion of the hearing, he had worn the black horn-rimmed glasses that had been broken in the course of his assault. They were held together in two places by adhesive tape. His left wrist was encased in a molded plastic cast, and he wore a cervical collar like a thick turtleneck.

'Surprise witnesses happen only on *Matlock,*' Kate said.

'Because I'm just not ready for that. I'm going to have to work myself up to that, you know.'

'Yes, I think we're all aware of that, Mr Willis.' Because he had called every day for the last week to remind them: Kate, Ken Merced, Ken's secretary, the legal services receptionist.

'I won't be in any physical danger, will I? He'll be in handcuffs and leg irons, right?'

'You'll be perfectly safe.'

'Because, you know, situational stress can push people over the edge. I've been reading up on it. I've been religiously attending the victims' group you set me up with, Ms Conlan, and I've been reading everything I can get my hands on about the criminal mind, and the psychology of victims, and post-traumatic stress disorder – just the way you told me to do.'

Kate often recommended her clients educate themselves as to what to expect of their own reactions and emotions following a crime. It gave them a sense of understanding and a small feeling of control. She didn't recommend it as an all-consuming hobby.

Knowing Willis would want to be close to the action, she chose the first row in the gallery behind the prosecution's table, where Ken Merced was going over some notes. Willis bumped into her as she stopped to indicate the row, then tripped over his own feet trying to move aside and gallantly motion Kate in ahead of him.

Kate shook her head as she stepped into the row and took a seat. Willis fumbled with the cheap briefcase he'd brought with him. Filled with news clippings about his case, Polaroids taken of him in the ER after the attack, brochures on victims' groups and therapists, and a hardcover copy of *Coping After the Crime*. He pulled out a yellow legal pad and prepared to take notes of the proceedings – as he had at every meeting Kate had had with him.

Merced turned to them with a pleasant poker face. 'We're all set, Mr Willis. This won't take long.'

'You're certain you won't need me to testify?'

'Not today.'

He gave a shuddering sigh. 'Because I'm not ready for that.'

'No.' Merced turned back toward the table. 'None of us are.'

Kate sat back and tried to will the tension out of her jaw as Willis became engrossed in making his preliminary notes.

'You always were a secret soft touch.'

The low whisper rumbled over her right shoulder, the breath caressing the delicate skin of her neck. Kate jerked around, scowling. Quinn leaned ahead on his chair, elbows braced on his knees, dark eyes gleaming, that little-boy-caught-with-his-hand-in-the-cookie-jar smile firmly and calculatingly in place.

'I need to talk to you,' he murmured.

'You have my office number.'

'I do,' he admitted. 'However, you seem not to want to answer my messages.'

'I'm a very busy person.'

'I can see that.'

'Don't mock me,' she snapped.

David Willis grabbed hold of her forearm and she turned back around. The side door had opened, and O. T. Zubek entered the courtroom with his lawyer, a deputy trailing after them. Zubek was a human fireplug, squat with thick limbs and a protruding belly. He wore a cheap navy-blue suit that showed a dusting of dandruff on the shoulders, and a baby-blue knit shirt underneath, untucked and too snug around the middle. He looked right at Willis and scowled, his face the doughy caricature of a cartoon tough guy with a blue-shadowed jaw.

Willis stared at him, bug-eyed for a second, then twisted toward Kate. 'Did you see that? He threatened me! That was threatening eye contact. I perceived that as a threat. Why isn't he in handcuffs?'

'Try to stay calm, Mr Willis, or the judge will have you removed from the courtroom.'

'*I'm* not the criminal here!'

'Everyone knows that.'

The judge entered from chambers and everyone rose, then sat again. The docket number and charges were read, the prosecution and defense attorneys stated their names for the record, and the probable-cause hearing was under way.

Merced called his first witness, a pear-shaped man who serviced Slurpee machines at 7-Eleven stores in the greater Twin Cities metropolitan area. He testified he had heard Willis arguing with Zubek about the condition of a delivery of Hostess Twinkies and assorted snack cakes in the store Willis managed, and that he had seen the two come tumbling down the chips aisle, Zubek striking Willis repeatedly.

'And did you hear who started this *alleged* argument?' the defense attorney questioned on cross-examination.

'No.'

'So for all you know, Mr Willis may have provoked the argument?'

'Objection. Calls for speculation.'

'Withdrawn. And did you see who threw the first punch in this *so-called* attack?'

'No.'

'Might it have been Mr Willis?'

Willis trembled and twitched beside Kate. 'I didn't!'

'Shhh!'

Merced sighed. 'Your honor . . .'

The judge frowned at the defense attorney, who had come costumed as a bad used-car salesman. He looked seedy enough that he might have been Zubek's cousin. 'Mr Krupke, this is a hearing, not a trial. The court is more concerned with what the witnesses saw than with what they did not see.'

'Not exactly the Richmond Ripper case, is it?' Quinn murmured in Kate's ear. She gave him the evil eye over her shoulder. The stiffness in her jaw began radiating down into her neck.

Merced's second witness corroborated the testimony of the Slurpee mechanic. Krupke went through the same cross, with Merced voicing the same objections, and the judge getting crankier and crankier. Willis fidgeted and recorded copious notes in tiny bold print that said frightening things about the inner workings of his mind. Merced entered into evidence the security surveillance tape showing much of the fight, then rested his case.

Krupke had no witnesses and put on no defense.

'We don't dispute that an altercation took place, your honor.'

'Then why are you wasting my time with this hearing, Mr Krupke?'

'We wanted to establish that events may not have taken place *exactly* as Mr Willis claims.'

'That's a lie!' Willis shouted.

The judge cracked his gavel. The bailiff frowned at Willis but didn't move from his post. Kate put a vise grip on her client's arm and whispered furiously, 'Mr Willis, be quiet!'

'I suggest you listen to your advocate, Mr Willis,' the judge said. 'You'll have your turn to speak.'

'Today?'

'No!' the judge snorted, turning his glare on Merced, who spread his hands and shrugged. He turned back to the defense. 'Mr Krupke, write me a check for two hundred dollars for wasting my time. If you had no intention of disputing the charges, you should have waived rights and asked for a trial date at the arraignment.'

The date for the trial was set and the proceedings were over. Kate breathed a sigh of relief. Merced got up from the table and collected his papers. Kate leaned across the bar and whispered, 'Can't you get this guy to cop, Ken? I'd rather gouge my eyes out than sit through a trial with this man.'

'Christ, I'd pay Zubek to take a plea if it wouldn't get me disbarred.'

Krupke asked someone to lend him a pen so he could write out the check for contempt of court. Willis looked around like he had just awakened from a nap and had no idea where he was.

'That's it?'

'That's it, Mr Willis,' Kate said, standing. 'I told you it wouldn't take long.'

'But – but –' He swung his blue-casted arm in the direction of Zubek. 'They called me a liar! Don't I get to defend myself?'

Zubek leaned over the rail, sneering. 'Everyone can see what a shitty job you do of that, Willis.'

'We should leave now,' Kate suggested, handing Willis his briefcase. The thing weighed a ton.

He fumbled with the case and his notepad and pen as she herded him toward the aisle. Kate was more concerned with what she was going to do about Quinn. He had already moved into the aisle and was backing toward the door, his gaze on her, trying to get her to look at him. Sabin must have called him the second she was out of the office.

'But I don't understand,' Willis whined. 'There should have been more. He hurt me! He hurt me and he called me a liar!'

Zubek twitched his shoulders like a boxer and made a Bluto face. 'Weanie wuss.'

Kate saw Quinn's reaction the second the war cry curdled up out of David Willis. She spun around as Willis launched himself at Zubek, swinging. The briefcase hit Zubek in the side of the head like a frying pan and knocked him backward across the defense table. The locks sprung and the contents exploded out of the briefcase.

Kate hurled herself at Willis as he drew his arm back to swing again. She grabbed both his shoulders, and the two of them tumbled headfirst over the bar and into a sea of table legs and chairs and scrambling people. Zubek was squealing like a stuck pig. The judge was shouting at the bailiff, the bailiff was shouting at Krupke, who was screaming at Willis and trying to kick him. His wingtip connected with Kate's thigh, and she swore and kicked back, nailing Willis.

It seemed to take forever for order to be restored and for Willis to be hauled off her. Kate sat up slowly, muttering a string of obscenities under her breath.

Quinn squatted down in front of her, reached out, and brushed a rope of red-gold hair back behind her ear. 'You really ought to come back to the FBI, Kate. This job's going to be the death of you.'

'Don't you dare be amused at me,' Kate snapped, surveying the damage to herself and her clothes. Quinn leaned back against her desk, watching as she plucked at a hole in her stockings that was big enough to put her fist through. 'This is my second pair of good tights this week. That's it. I'm giving up skirts.'

'The men in the building will have to wear black armbands,' Quinn said. He held his hands up in surrender as she shot him another deadly glare. 'Hey, you always had a nice set of pegs on you, Kate. You can't argue.'

'The subject is inappropriate and irrelevant.'

He gave her innocence. 'Political correctness prohibits one old friend from complimenting another?'

She straightened slowly in her chair, forgetting about the ruined tights. 'Is that what we are?' she asked quietly. 'Old friends?'

He sobered at that. He couldn't look her in the eye and be glib about the past that lay behind them and between them. The awkwardness was a palpable entity.

'That's not exactly the way we parted company,' she said.

'No.' He moved away from the desk, sticking his hands in his pants pockets, pretending an interest in the notices and cartoons she had tacked up on her bulletin board. 'That was a long time ago.'

Which meant what, she wondered. That it was all water under the bridge? While a part of her wanted to say yes, there was another part of her that held those bitter memories in a fist. For her, nothing was forgotten. The idea that it might be for him upset her in a way she wished weren't so. It made her feel weak, a word she never wanted associated with her.

Quinn looked at her out of the corner of his eye. 'Five years is a long time to stay mad.'

'I'm not mad at you.'

He laughed. 'The hell you're not. You won't return my phone calls. You don't want to have a conversation with me. Your back goes up every time you see me.'

'I've seen you what – twice since you got here? The first time you used me to get your way, and the second time you made fun of my job –'

'I did not make fun of your job,' he protested. 'I made fun of your client.'

'Oh, that makes all the difference,' she said with sarcasm, conveniently forgetting that everyone made fun of David Willis, including her. She stood, not wanting him looking down on her any more than their height difference allowed. 'What I do here is important, John. Maybe not in the same way as what you do, but it *is* important.'

'I'm not disagreeing with you, Kate.'

'No? As I recall, when I decided to leave the Bureau, you told me I was throwing my life away.'

The reminder struck a spark, and old frustration came alive in his dark eyes. 'You threw away a solid career. You had what? Fourteen, fifteen years in? You were a tremendous asset to the BSU. You were a good agent, Kate, and –'

'And I'm a better advocate. I get to deal with people while they're still alive. I get to make a difference for them one-on-one, help them through a hard time, help them empower themselves, help them take steps to make a difference in their own lives. How is that not valuable?'

'I'm not against you being an advocate,' Quinn argued. 'I was against you leaving the Bureau. Those are two separate issues. You let Steven push you out –'

'I did not!'

'The hell you didn't! He wanted to punish you –'

'And I didn't let him.'

'You cut and ran. You let him win.'

'He didn't win,' Kate returned. 'His victory would have been in crushing the life out of my career one drop of blood at a time. I was supposed to stick around for that just to show him how tough I was? What was I supposed to do? Transfer and transfer until he ran out of cronies in his ol' boy network? Until I ended up at the resident agency in Gallup, New Mexico, with nothing to do but count the snakes and tarantulas crossing the road?'

'You could have fought him, Kate,' he insisted. 'I would have helped you.'

She crossed her arms and arched a brow. 'Oh, really? As I remember it, you didn't want much to do with me after your little run-in with the Office of Professional Responsibility.'

'That had nothing to do with it,' he said angrily. 'The OPR never scared me. Steven and his petty little bureaucratic bullshit games didn't scare me. I was tied up. I was juggling maybe seventy-five cases including the Cleveland Cannibal –'

'Oh, I know all about it, John,' she said caustically. 'The Mighty Quinn, bearing the weight of the criminal world on your shoulders.'

'What's that supposed to mean?' he demanded. 'I've got a job and I do it.'

And to hell with the rest of the world, thought Kate, *including me*. But she didn't say it. What good would it do now? It wouldn't change history as she remembered it. And it wouldn't help to argue that he surely did give a damn what the OPR put in his file. There was no sense arguing that to Quinn the job was everything.

Long story short: She'd had an affair that had delivered the death blows to a marriage already battered beyond recognition. Her husband's retaliation had forced her out of her career. And Quinn had walked away from the wreck and lost himself in his first love – his work. When push had come to shove, he stepped back and let her fall. When she turned to go, he hadn't asked her not to.

In five years he hadn't called her once.

Not that she'd wanted him to.

The argument had drawn them closer together one step at a time. He was near enough now that she could smell the faint hint of a subtle aftershave. She could sense the tension in his body. And fragments of a thousand memories she'd locked away came rushing to the surface. The strength of his arms, the warmth of his body, the comfort he had offered that she had soaked up like a dry sponge.

Her mistake had been in needing. She didn't need him now.

She turned away from him and sat back on the desk, trying to convince herself that it wasn't a sign of anything that they'd fallen so readily into this argument.

'I've got a job to do too,' she said, looking pointedly at her watch. 'I suppose that's why you showed up. Sabin called you?'

Quinn let out the air he'd held in his lungs. His shoulders dropped three inches. He hadn't expected the emotions to erupt so easily. It wasn't like him to let that happen. Nor was it like him to abandon a fight until he won. The relief he felt in doing so was strong enough to induce embarrassment.

He retreated a step. 'He wants me to sit in with you and your witness when she comes back to work on the sketch.'

'I don't care what he wants,' Kate said stubbornly. 'I won't have you there. This girl is hanging with me by a thread. Somebody whispers the letters *FBI* and she'll bolt.'

'Then we won't mention those letters.'

'She can smell a lie a mile off.'

'She'll never have to know I'm there. I'll be a mouse in the corner.'

Kate almost laughed. Yeah, who would notice Quinn? Six feet of dark, handsome masculinity in an Italian suit. Naw, a girl like Angie wouldn't notice him at all.

'I'd like to get a sense of this girl,' he said. 'What's your take on her? Is she a credible witness?'

'She's a foul-mouthed, lying, scheming little bitch,' Kate said bluntly. 'She's probably a runaway. She's maybe sixteen going on forty-two. She's had some hard knocks, she's alone, and she's scared spitless.'

'The well-rounded American child,' Quinn said dryly. 'So, did she see Smokey Joe?'

Kate considered for a moment, weighing all that Angie was and was not. Whatever the girl hoped to gain in terms of a reward, whatever lies she may have told, seeing the face of evil was for real. Kate could feel the truth in that. The tension in the girl every time she had to retell the story was something virtually impossible to fake convincingly. 'Yes. I believe she did.'

Quinn nodded. 'But she's holding back?'

'She's afraid of retaliation by the killer – and maybe by the cops too. She won't tell us what she was doing in that park at midnight.'

'Guesses?'

'Maybe scoring drugs. Or she might have turned a trick somewhere nearby and was cutting across the park to get back to whatever alley she'd been sleeping in.'

'But she doesn't have a record?'

'None that anyone's been able to find. We're flashing her picture around sex crimes, narcotics, and the juvie division. No bites yet.'

'A woman of mystery.'

'Pollyanna she ain't.'

'Too bad you can't get her prints.'

Kate made a face. 'We'd have them now if I'd let Sabin get his way. He wanted Kovac to arrest her Monday and let her sit in jail overnight to put the fear of God in her.'

'Might have worked.'

'Over my dead body.'

Quinn couldn't help but smile at the steel in her voice, the fire in her eyes. Clearly, she felt protective of her client, lying, scheming little bitch or not. Kovac had commented to him that while Kate was the consummate professional, she protected her victims and witnesses as if they were family. An interesting choice of words.

In five years she hadn't remarried. There was no snapshot of a boyfriend on the shelves above her desk. But inside a delicate silver filigree frame was a tiny photo of the daughter she had lost. Tucked back in the corner, away from the paperwork, away from the casual glance of visitors, almost hidden even from her own gaze, the cherubic face of the child whose death she carried on her conscience like a stone.

The pain of Emily's death had nearly crushed her. No-nonsense, unflappable Kate Conlan. Grief and guilt had struck her with the force of a

Mack truck, shattering her, stunning her. She'd had no idea how to cope. Turning to her husband hadn't been an option because Steven Waterston had readily shoveled his own sense of guilt and blame onto Kate. And so she had turned to a friend . . .

'And if you tell Sabin it might have worked,' she continued, 'the dead body in question will be yours. I told him you'd back me up on this, John, and you'd damn well better. You owe me one.'

'Yeah,' he said softly, the old memories still too close to the surface. 'At least.'

14

Located in the Lowry Hill area, just south of the tangle of interstate highways that corralled downtown Minneapolis, D'Cup was the kind of coffeehouse funky enough for the artsy crowd and just clean enough for the patrons of the nearby Guthrie Theater and Walker Art Center. Liska walked in and breathed deep the rich aroma of exotic imported beans.

She and Moss had split the duties for the day, needing to cover as much ground as they could. Mother Mary with her twenty-some years of maternal experience, had taken the unenviable task of talking with the families of the first two victims. She would open the old wounds as gently as possible. Liska had gladly taken the job of meeting with one of Jillian Bondurant's only known friends: Michele Fine.

Fine worked at D'Cup as a waitress and sometimes sang and played guitar on the small stage wedged into a corner near the front window. The three customers in the place sat at small tables near the window, absorbing the weak sunlight filtering in after three days of November gloom. Two older men – one tall and slender with a silver goatee, one shorter and wider with a black beret – sipped their espressos and argued the merits of the National Endowment for the Arts. A younger blond man with bug-eye gargoyle sunglasses and a black turtleneck nursed a *grande* something-or-other and worked a newspaper crossword puzzle. A cigarette smoldered in the ashtray beside his drink. He had the thin, vaguely seedy look of a struggling actor.

Liska went to the counter, where a hunky Italian-looking guy with a wavy black ponytail was pressing grounds into the fine cone-shaped basket of an espresso machine. He glanced up at her with eyes the color of dark Godiva chocolate. She resisted the urge to swoon. Barely. She wasn't as successful in resisting the automatic counting of the weeks since she'd had sex. Moss would have told her mothers of eleven- and nine-year-old boys weren't supposed to have sex.

'I'm looking for Michele.'

He nodded, shoved the basket into place on the machine, and cranked the handle around. 'Chell!'

Fine came through the archway that led into a back room carrying a tray of clean Fiestaware coffee cups the size of soup bowls. She was tall and thin with a narrow, bony face bearing several old scars that made Liska think she must have been in a car accident a long time ago. One curled down at one corner of her wide mouth. Another rode the crest of a high cheekbone like a short, flat worm. Her dark hair had an unnatural maroon sheen, and she had slicked it back against her head and bound it at the nape of her neck. The length of it bushed out in a kinky mass fatter than a fox tail.

Liska flashed her ID discreetly. 'Thanks for agreeing to meet with me, Michele. Can we sit down?'

Fine set the tray aside and pulled her purse out from under the counter. 'You mind if I smoke?'

'No.'

'I can't seem to stop,' she said, her voice as rusty as an old gate hinge. She led the way to a table in the smoking section, as far away from the blond man as possible. 'This whole business with Jillie ... my nerves are raw.'

Her hand was trembling slightly as she extracted a long, thin cigarette from a cheap green vinyl case. Puckered, discolored flesh warped the back of her right hand. Tattooed around the scar, an elegant, intricately drawn snake coiled around Fine's wrist, its head resting on the back of her hand, a small red apple in its mouth.

'Looks like that was a nasty burn,' Liska said, pointing to the scar with her pen as she flipped open her pocket notebook.

Fine held her hand out, as if to admire it. 'Grease fire,' she said dispassionately. 'When I was a kid.'

She flicked her lighter and stared at the flame, frowning for a second. 'It hurt like hell.'

'I'll bet.'

'So,' she said, snapping out of the old memories. 'What's the deal? No one will say for sure that Jillie's dead, but she is, isn't she? All the news reports talk about "speculation" and "likelihood", but Peter Bondurant is involved and giving a reward. Why would he do that if it wasn't Jillie? Why won't anyone just *say* it's her?'

'I'm afraid I'm not at liberty to comment. How long have you known Jillian?'

'About a year. She comes in here every Friday, either before or after her session with her shrink. We got to know each other.'

She took a deep pull on her cigarette and exhaled through teeth set wide apart. Her eyes were hazel, too narrow and too heavily lined with black, the lashes stubby and crusty with mascara. A mean look, Vanlees had called it. Nikki thought *tough* was a better word.

'And when was the last time you saw Jillian?'

'Friday. She stopped in on her way to see the psychic vampire.'

'You don't approve of Dr Brandt? Do you know him?'

She squinted through the haze of smoke. 'I know he's a money-sucking leech who doesn't give a damn about helping anyone but himself. I kept telling her to dump him and get a woman therapist. He was the last thing she needed. All he was interested in was keeping his hand in Daddy's pocket.'

'Do you know why she was seeing him?'

She looked just over Liska's shoulder and out the window. 'Depression. Unresolved stuff with her parents' divorce and her mom and her stepfather. The usual family shit, right?'

'Glad to say I wouldn't know. Did she tell you specifics?'

'No.'

Lie, Nikki thought. 'Did she ever do drugs that you know of?'

'Nothing serious.'

'What's that mean?'

'A little weed once in a while when she was wired.'

'Who'd she buy it from?'

Fine's expression tightened, the scars on her face seeming darker and shinier. 'A friend.'

Meaning herself, Liska figured. She spread her hands. 'Hey, I'm not interested in busting anybody's ass over a little weed. I just want to know if Jillian could have had an enemy in that line.'

'No. She hardly ever did it anyway. Not like when she lived in Europe. She was into everything there – sex, drugs, booze. But she kicked all that when she came here.'

'Just like that? She comes over here and lives like a nun?'

Fine shrugged, tapping off her cigarette. 'She tried to kill herself. I guess that changes a person.'

'In France? She tried to kill herself?'

'That's what she told me. Her stepfather locked her up in a mental hospital for a while. Ironic, seeing as how she was going crazy because of him.'

'How's that?'

'He was fucking her. She actually believed he was in love with her for a while. She wanted him to divorce her mother and marry her.' She related the information in an almost offhand manner, as if that kind of behavior were the norm in her world. 'She ended up taking a bunch of pills. Stepdaddy had her put away. When she got out, she came back here.'

Liska scribbled the news in a personal shorthand no one but she could read, excitement making it all the more illegible. She'd hit the mother lode of dirt here. Kovac would love it. 'Did her stepfather ever come here to see her?'

'No. The suicide thing freaked him out, I guess. Jillie said he never even came to see her in the loony bin.' She sighed a cloud of smoke and stared off past the blond guy. 'It's sad what passes for love, isn't it?'

'What kind of mood was she in Friday?'

The bony shoulders lifted and fell. 'I don't know. Kind of wired, I guess.

It was busy in here. We didn't have time to talk. I told her I'd call her Saturday.'

'And did you?'

'Yeah. Got the machine. I left a message, but she never called back.'

She stared out the window again, but without seeing anything in the street. Looking back to the weekend. Wondering if anything she could have done differently might have prevented a tragedy. Nikki had seen the expression many times. Tears washed across Michele Fine's mean eyes and she pressed her wide, scarred mouth into a line.

'I just figured she stayed over at her dad's,' she said, her throat tightening on the words. 'I thought about trying to catch her Sunday, but then . . . I just didn't. . . .'

'What'd you do Sunday?'

She wagged her head a little. 'Nothing. Slept late. Walked around the lakes. Nothing.'

She pressed her free hand over her mouth and squeezed her eyes shut, fighting for composure. Color flooded her pale face as she held her breath against the need to cry. Liska waited a moment.

The old guys were arguing now about performance art.

'How is pissing in a bottle full of crucifixes art?' Beret Man demanded.

The goatee spread his hands. 'It makes a statement! Art makes a statement!'

The blond guy turned his paper over to the want ads and snuck a look at Michele. Liska gave him the cop glare and he went back to his reading.

'What about the rest of the weekend?' she asked, coming back to Fine. 'What'd you do after work Friday night?'

'Why?' The suspicion was instantaneous, edged with affront and a little bit of panic.

'It's just routine. We need to establish where Jillian's family and friends were in case she might have tried to contact them.'

'She didn't.'

'You were home, then?'

'I went to a late movie, but I have a machine. She would have left a message.'

'Did you ever stay over at Jillian's apartment?'

Fine sniffed, wiped her eyes and nose with her hand, and took another ragged puff on her cigarette. Her hand was shaking. 'Yeah, sometimes. We wrote music together. Jillie won't perform, but she's good.'

In and out of present tense when she talked about her friend. That was always a difficult transition for people to make after a death.

'We found some clothes in the dresser of the second bedroom that didn't look to be hers.'

'That's my stuff. She's way the hell over by the river. Sometimes we'd sit up late working on a song and I'd just stay over.'

'Do you have a key to her place?'

'No. Why would I? I didn't live there.'

'What kind of housekeeper is she?'

'What difference does that make?'

'Neat? Sloppy?'

Fine fussed, impatient with what she didn't understand. 'Sloppy. She left stuff everywhere – clothes, dishes, ashtrays. What difference does it make? She's dead.'

She ducked her head then, and reddened and struggled as another wave of emotion hit on the heels of that final statement. 'She's dead. He burned her. Oh, God.' A pair of tears squeezed through her lashes and splashed on the paper place mat.

'We don't know for a fact that anything's happened to her, Michele.'

Fine abandoned her cigarette in the ashtray and put her face in her hands. Not sobbing, but still struggling to choke the emotions back.

'Maybe she left town for a few days,' Liska said. 'We don't know. Do you?'

'No.'

'Do you know of anyone who would want to hurt Jillian?'

She shook her head.

'She have a boyfriend? Ex-boyfriend? A guy who was interested in her?'

'No.'

'How about yourself? Got a boyfriend?'

'No,' she answered, looking down at the smoldering butt in the ashtray. 'Why would I want one?'

'Jillian ever say anything about a man bothering her? Watching her, maybe? Hitting on her?'

Her laugh this time was bitter. 'You know how men are. They all look. They all think they have a shot. Who pays any attention to the losers?'

She sniffed and pulled in a deep breath, then let it go slowly and reached for another cigarette. Her nails were bitten to the quick.

'What about her relationship with her father? They get along?'

Fine's mouth twisted. 'She adores him. I don't know why.'

'You don't like him?'

'Never met him. But he controls her, doesn't he? He owns the town house, pays for school, picks the therapist, pays for the therapist. Dinner every Friday. A car.'

It sounded like a sweet deal to Liska. Maybe she *could* get Bondurant to adopt her. She let the subject drop. It was beginning to sound like if it had a penis, Michele didn't like it.

'Michele, do you know if Jillian had any distinguishing marks on her body: moles, scars, tattoos?'

Fine gave her a cross look. 'How would I know that? We weren't lovers.'

'Nothing obvious, then. No scar on her arm. No snake tattooed around her wrist.'

'Not that I ever noticed.'

'If you were to look around Jillian's apartment, would you know if things were missing? Like if she'd packed some clothes and gone somewhere?'

She shrugged. 'I guess.'

'Good. Let's see if we can take a ride.'

While Michele Fine squared an hour's absence with her boss, the Italian stallion, Liska stepped out of the coffeehouse, pulled her cell phone out of her pocket, and dialed Kovac.

The air was crisp, a stiff breeze blowing, as was common for November. Not a bad day. A paler imitation of the glorious weather of late September and early October that made Minnesota rival any state in the union for perfection. Her boys would be out on their bikes after school, trying to squeeze in every last wheelie they could before the snow flew and the sleds came out of storage. They were lucky that hadn't happened already.

'Moose Lodge,' the gruff voice barked in her ear.

'Can I speak to Bullwinkle? I hear he's got a dick as long as my arm.'

'Christ, Liska. Is that all you ever think about?'

'That and my bank balance. I can't get enough either way.'

'You're preaching to the choir. What have you got for me?'

'Besides the hots? A question. When you went through Jillian's town house Monday, did you take a tape out of the answering machine?'

'It was digital. No messages.'

'This friend of hers says she called Saturday and left a message. So who erased it?'

'Ooo, a mystery. I hate a mystery. Get anything else?'

'Oh, yeah.' She looked through the window back into the coffee shop. 'A tale to rival Shakespeare.'

'She was putting her life back together,' Lila White's mother insisted. Her expression had the hard look of someone grown stubborn in the telling and retelling of a lie. A lie she wanted too badly to believe in and couldn't deep down in her heart.

Mary Moss felt a deep sadness for the woman.

The White family lived in the small farming community of Glencoe, the kind of place where gossip was a common hobby and rumors cut like broken glass. Mr White was a mechanic at a farm implement dealership. They lived on the edge of town in a neat rambler with a family of concrete deer in the front yard and a swingset out back. The swingset was for the grandchild they were raising: Lila's daughter, Kylie, a towheaded four-year-old blessedly immune to the facts of her mother's death. For now.

'She called us that Thursday night. She'd kicked the drugs, you know. It was the drugs that dragged her down.' The features of Mrs White's lumpy face puckered, as if the bitterness of her feelings left a taste in her mouth. 'It's all the fault of that Ostertag boy. He's the one got her started on the drugs.'

'Now, Jeannie,' Mr White said with the weariness of pointless repetition. He was a tall, raw-boned man with eyes the color of washed-out denim. He had farmer's creases in his face from too many years of squinting under a bright sun.

'Don't Jeannie me,' his wife snapped. 'Everyone in town knows he peddles drugs, and his parents walk around pretending their shit don't stink. It makes me sick.'

'Allan Ostertag?' Moss said, referring to her notes. 'Your daughter went to high school with him?'

Mr White sighed and nodded, enduring the process, waiting for it to be over so they could start the healing again and hope this was the last time the wounds would have to be reopened. His wife went on about the Ostertags. Moss waited patiently, knowing that Allan Ostertag was not and had never been a viable suspect in Lila White's murder, and was, therefore, irrelevant to her. He was not irrelevant to the Whites.

'Had she mentioned seeing anyone in particular last summer?' she asked when the rant ended. 'A steady boyfriend? Someone who might have been a problem to her?'

'We've answered all these questions before,' Jeannie White said impatiently. 'It's like you people don't bother to write anything down. Course it didn't matter when it was just our girl dead,' she said, the sarcasm as pointed as a needle. 'We didn't see no task force on the news when it was just our Lila murdered. The police never cared –'

'That's not true, Mrs White.'

'They never cared when that drug dealer beat her up last fall neither. They never even bothered to have a trial. It's like our girl didn't count.' The woman's eyes and throat filled with tears. 'She wasn't important enough to anyone but us.'

Moss offered apologies, knowing they wouldn't be accepted. No explanation could penetrate the hurt, the imagined insult, the anger, the pain. It didn't matter to the Whites that an individual murder was, by necessity, handled differently from a string of related murders. It mattered to them that the child they had loved had fallen down one of life's darker paths. It mattered to them she had died a prostitute. That was how she would be remembered by the world, when she was remembered at all. Victim number one, convicted prostitute and drug addict.

The Whites probably saw the headlines in their sleep. The hopes they had held for their daughter to turn her life around had died unfulfilled, and no one else in the world cared that Lila had wanted to become a counselor or that she had been a B student in high school or that she had often cried her heart out over not being able to raise her own child.

In the file folder on the passenger seat of Moss's car were snapshots of Lila and Kylie in the Whites' backyard. Smiling and laughing, and wearing party hats for Kylie's fourth birthday. Photos of mother and daughter splashing in a green plastic wading pool. Three weeks later someone had tortured the life from Lila White, desecrated her body and set it on fire like a pile of garbage.

Victim number one, convicted prostitute and drug addict.

Moss went through the reassurances in her own mind. The police couldn't form a task force for every homicide in the city. Lila White's murder had been investigated fully. Sam Kovac had caught the case, and Kovac's reputation was that he did his best for every victim, regardless of who or what they had been in life.

Still, she couldn't help but wonder – as Jeannie White had wondered aloud – how differently things might have turned out if Jillian Bondurant had been victim number one.

The locks had been changed on Jillian Bondurant's town house at Edgewater and a new key delivered to the PD. Liska worked the shiny new key into the dead bolt and opened the door. She went to the bedrooms with Michele Fine and watched as Fine looked through the closets, pausing now and again to linger briefly over something that struck a memory for her.

'Jesus, it's eerie,' she said, looking around. 'Seeing the place so clean.'

'Jillian didn't have a cleaning service?'

'No. Her old man tried to give her maid service as a present once. He's the most anal man on the planet. Jillie said no. She didn't want people going through her stuff.'

'I don't see anything missing,' she said finally.

As she stood at Jillian's dresser, her gaze drifted across the few objects there: a mahogany jewelry box, some scented candles in mismatched holders, a small porcelain figurine of an elegant woman in a flowing blue dress. She touched the figurine carefully, her expression wistful.

As Fine gathered her few clothing items from the guest bedroom, Liska walked down the steps and took in the main rooms at a glance, seeing the place differently from before she'd met Jillian's friend. It should have been a mess, but it wasn't. She'd never known a killer to offer maid services as part of the package, but someone had cleaned the place up. Not just wiped it down to get rid of prints. Cleaned it, folded and put away clothes, washed the dishes.

Her thoughts turned back to Michele Fine and Jillian as friends. They must have seemed an unlikely pair: a billionaire's daughter and a coffeehouse waitress. If there had been a ransom demand to Peter Bondurant, the relationship would have automatically fallen under scrutiny. Even without it, the suspicions flashed through Liska's mind out of habit.

Considered and dismissed. Michele Fine was cooperating fully. Nothing she had said or done seemed out of place. Her grief appeared genuine, and was colored with the shades of anger and relief and guilt Liska had encountered time and again in the people a murder victim left behind.

Still, she would run Michele Fine's name through the computer and see if anything kicked up.

She crossed the living room to the electronic piano. Jillian Bondurant had written music but was too shy to perform. That was the kind of detail that made her a real person in a way that knowing she was Peter Bondurant's daughter did not. The sheet music stacked neatly on the stand was classical. Another contradiction in Jillian's image. Liska lifted the padded seat and glanced through the collection there: folk, rock, alternative, New Age –

'Hold it right there!'

Her first impulse was to go for her gun, but she held herself bent over at the piano stool, breathing through her mouth. Slowly, she turned her head and relief swept through her, her temper hot on its heels.

'It's me, Mr Vanlees. Detective Liska,' she said, straightening. 'Put the gun down, please.'

Vanlees stood just inside the doorway in his security guard's uniform, a Colt Python clutched in his hands. Liska wanted to pull the gun away from him and smack him in the head with it.

He blinked at her and lowered the weapon, a barely sheepish grin pulling at his mouth. 'Oh, jeez, Detective, I'm sorry. I didn't know you were coming over. When I saw there was someone moving around over here, I thought the worst. You know, tabloid reporters have been coming around. I hear they'll steal anything that's not nailed down.'

'You didn't recognize my car, then?' Liska said with a little too much edge.

'Uh, I guess I didn't. Sorry.'

Like hell, she thought. Wanna-bes like Vanlees took note of everything about the cops they encountered in the real world. She would have bet he had her tag number written down somewhere. He sure as hell recognized the make and model. This little show had been about impressing her. Gil Vanlees: Man of Action. On his toes. On the job. Ever diligent. *God help us all.*

Liska shook her head. 'That's quite the gun you've got there, Gil,' she said, moving toward him. 'Don't suppose I've got to ask if you've got a permit for it?'

The eyes went a little cold and the smile sagged out of his face. He didn't like having her reprimand him. He didn't want to be reminded his uniform wasn't the real deal. He stuck the nose of the Python under his belt and eased the gun into place alongside his gut.

'Yeah, I got a permit.'

Liska forced a smile. 'That's some piece of hardware. Not really a good idea to come up behind people with it, Gil. You never know what might happen. Reflexes a little too sharp that day and you blow somebody away. That'd be a bad deal all the way around, you know.'

He wouldn't meet her eyes now, like a kid being scolded for getting into his father's tools.

'You say reporters have been nosing around here? No one's been in the house though, right?'

His attention shifted further away, and he frowned harder. Liska glanced over her shoulder. Michele Fine stood at the bottom of the steps with her messy pile of black clothing clutched to her. She looked offended by Vanlees's presence.

'Mr Vanlees?' Liska prompted, turning back to him as Michele went into the kitchen. 'No one's been in the house that you know of, right?'

'Right.' He moved back a step toward the door, his hand resting on the butt of the Python. He kept his gaze on Michele, watching her as she dumped her clothes on the counter that divided kitchen and eating area. 'I gotta go,' he said glumly. 'I was just keeping an eye out, that's all.'

Liska followed him out onto the stoop. 'Hey, Gil, I'm sorry if I snapped at you back there. You got the drop on me. Shook me up, you know.'

He didn't bite this time. She had questioned his honor, impugned his status as a peer, bruised his ego. The rapport she had built two days ago teetered on its foundation. She had expected it to hold up better, and found its fragility telling. Another point to bring up with Quinn: Vanlees's self-image.

He barely looked at her, pouting. 'Sure. No problem.'

'I'm glad you're keeping an eye out,' she said. 'You heard about the community meeting tonight, right? You might want to drop by that if you get a chance.'

Liska watched him walk away, wondering. From a distance Vanlees looked like a city cop in his blue-over-black uniform. It would be an easy thing for a guy in a uniform to get a woman to stop for him, talk to him. All three of Smokey Joe's victims had vanished with no report of a scream, no suspicious activity in the area. On the other hand, no one had mentioned seeing a uniform in the vicinity either.

'I'm ready.'

She started a little at Michele Fine's announcement, and turned to find her standing in the doorway, her clothes crammed into a plastic bag from Rainbow Foods.

'Right. Great. I'll drive you back.'

She locked up the house, Fine waiting for her at the bottom of the steps. Vanlees had disappeared down the winding path, but not from Liska's mind.

'You know that guy?' she asked as they settled into the car.

'Not personally,' Fine said, hugging her Rainbow bag as if it were an infant. 'Like I said before, who pays any attention to the losers?'

No one, Liska thought as she put the car in gear. And while no one was paying any attention to them, the losers were allowed to brood and fantasize and imagine getting back at all the women who didn't want them and would never love them.

15

'So, what do you think, John?' Sabin asked. 'Is the girl holding back on us?'

They sat in a conference room in the county attorney's offices: Quinn, Sabin, Kate, and Marshall. Quinn looked at Kate, sitting across from him with her jaw set and fire in her eyes, plainly telegraphing violence if he stepped on the wrong side of this argument. Just another minefield to cross. He kept his gaze on hers.

'Yes.' The fire flared brighter. 'Because she's afraid. She's probably feeling that the killer somehow knows what she's doing, as if he's watching her when she's talking with the police or describing him to your sketch artist. It's a common phenomenon. Isn't that right, Kate?'

'Yes.' A banked fire in the eyes now. Reserving the right to burn him later. He liked it too much that she could still feel that strongly about him. Negative emotion was still emotion. Indifference was the thing to dread.

'A sense of omniscient evil,' Marshall said, nodding wisely. 'I've seen it time and again. It's fascinating. Even the most logical, sensible victims experience it.'

He played with the VCR remote, running the tape back to the beginning of Angie DiMarco's initial interview, which had occurred within an hour of her being picked up. They had already gone through it. Freezing the tape at significant points, when Marshall and Sabin would then turn and stare at Quinn, waiting for a revelation like the disciples sitting at the feet of Christ.

'She's clearly terrified here,' Marshall said, repeating with authority what Quinn had said the first time they'd run through it. 'You can see her shaking. You can hear it in her voice. You're absolutely right, John.'

John. My buddy, my pal, my colleague. The familiarity rubbed Quinn the wrong way, even though it was something he purposely cultivated. He was tired of people pretending to know him, and even more tired of the people overly impressed with him. He wondered how impressed Rob Marshall would be to know he woke up in the middle of most nights, shaking and sick because he couldn't handle it anymore.

Marshall edged up the volume at a point where the girl lost her temper and shouted, voice quavering, 'I don't *know* him! He set a fucking body on fire! He's some kind of fucking psycho!'

'She's not faking that,' he pronounced quietly, squinting hard at the television screen, as if that would sharpen his myopic vision and allow him to see into the girl's mind.

Sabin looked displeased, as though he had been hoping for some excuse to put the girl on the rack. 'Maybe she'd feel *safer* behind bars.'

'Angie hasn't done anything wrong,' Kate snapped. 'She never had to admit she even saw this creep. She needs our help, not your threats.'

Color started creeping up from the county attorney's collar.

'We don't want an adversarial situation here, Ted,' Quinn said calmly. Mr Laid Back. Mr Coolheaded.

'The girl set herself up that way,' Sabin argued. 'I had a bad feeling about her the minute I set eyes on her. We should have called her bluff right off the bat. Let her know we're not screwing around here.'

'I think you handled her perfectly,' Quinn said. 'A kid like Angie doesn't trust the system. You needed to give her a friend, and Kate was the ideal choice. She's genuine, she's blunt, she's not full of crap and phony sympathy. Let Kate handle her. You won't get anything out of her with threats. She expects threats; they'll just bounce off her.'

'If she doesn't give us something we can use, there's nothing to handle,' Sabin came back. 'If she can't give us anything, then there's no point in wasting county resources on her.'

'It's not a waste,' Kate insisted.

'What do you think here, John?' Marshall asked, pointing to the screen with the remote. He had run the tape back again. 'Her use of personal pronouns – *I don't know* him. He's *some kind of psycho*. Do you think it could be significant?'

Quinn blew out a breath, impatience creeping in on his temper.

'What's she going to call the guy – it?'

One corner of Kate's mouth twitched.

Marshall sulked. 'I've taken courses in psycholinguistics. The use of language can be very telling.'

'I agree,' Quinn offered, recovering diplomatically. 'But there is such a thing as overanalyzing. I think the best thing you can do with this girl is step back and let Kate deal with her.'

'Dammit, we need a break,' Sabin said almost to himself. 'She barely added anything to that sketch today. She stood right there and looked at the guy, and the picture she gives us could be anybody.'

'It might be all her mind is allowing her to see,' Kate said. 'What do you want her to do, Ted? Make something up just so you believe she's trying harder?'

'I'm sure that's not what Mr Sabin was suggesting, Kate,' Marshall said with disapproval.

'I was being facetious to make a point, Rob.'

'She's valuable to the investigation regardless,' Quinn said. 'We can use the threat of her. We can leak things to the press. Make it sound like she's told us more than she has. We can use her any number of ways. At this point she doesn't have to be a Girl Scout and she doesn't have to have total recall.'

'My fear here is that she's lying about the whole thing,' Sabin admitted, Edwyn Noble's skepticism having taken root.

Kate tried not to roll her eyes. 'We've been over that. It doesn't make any sense. If all she wanted was money, she would have booked it out of that park Sunday night and never said a word until the reward was offered.'

'And if the only thing on her mind was the money,' Quinn added, 'then she'd be going out of her way to give us details. In my experience, greed outranks fear.'

'What if she's involved in some way?' Marshall suggested. 'To try to throw us off track or to get inside info –'

Kate glared at him. 'Don't be absurd. If she was involved with this creep, then she'd be giving us a detailed sketch of a phantom to chase. And she isn't privy to any information the Cremator can't read in the paper.'

Marshall looked down at the table. The rims of his ears turned hot pink.

'She's a scared, screwed-up kid,' Kate said, rising. 'And I have to get back to her before she sets my office on fire.'

'Are we done here?' Marshall asked pointedly. 'I guess we are. Kate has spoken.'

She looked at him with undisguised dislike and walked out.

Sabin watched her go – his eyes on her ass, Quinn thought – and when she was out the door said, 'Was she this headstrong at the Bureau?'

'At least,' Quinn said, and followed her out.

'You're defecting too?' she said as he caught up with her. 'You didn't want to stay and let Rob suck up to you? It's what he's best at.'

He flashed her a grin. 'You don't think much of your boss. Not that that's anything new.'

'You don't think much of him either.' Kate cast a precautionary glance back over her shoulder. 'Rob Marshall is an obsequious, fussy little ass-kissing toad. But, in all fairness, he genuinely cares about the job we do and he tries to do it justice.'

'Yes, well, he *is* trained in psycholinguistics.'

'He's read your book.'

Quinn raised his brows. 'There are people who haven't?'

The reception area outside the secured boundaries of the major prosecution unit was vacant. The receptionist had slipped away from her post behind a sheet of bulletproof glass. Stacks of the new Yellow Pages had been left on the floor. The latest issue of *Truth & Justice* lay on the end table with half a dozen outdated news magazines.

Kate blew out a breath and turned to face him. 'Thank you for backing me up.'

Quinn winced. 'Did it really hurt that much? God, Kate.'

'I'm sorry. I'm not like you, John. I hate the game-playing that goes on in a case like this. I didn't want to have to ask for your help at all. But I suppose the least I could do is show some genuine gratitude.'

'Not necessary. All I had to do was tell the truth. Sabin wanted a second opinion and he got it. You were right. That should make you happy,' he said dryly.

'I don't need you to tell me I was right. And as for what would make me happy: nothing much to do with this case.'

'Including my being here.'

'I'm not having this conversation with you,' she said flatly.

She walked out the door into the hall and took a left, going toward the atrium balcony. There wasn't another soul on the floor. Twenty-plus stories filled with people and not one of them convenient for a buffer. She knew Quinn was right behind her. And then he was beside her, his hand on her arm as if he still had some right to touch her.

'Kate, I'm sorry,' he said softly. 'I'm not trying to pick a fight. Really.'

He was standing too close, the dark eyes too big, the lashes long and thick and pretty – an almost feminine feature in a face that was quintessentially rugged and male. The kind of face to make the average woman's heart skip. Kate felt something tighten in her chest as she drew a breath. The knuckle of his thumb pressed against the outer swell of her breast. They both became aware of the contact at the same instant.

'Kate, I –'

His pager went off and he swore under his breath and let go of her. Kate stepped away and leaned a hip against the balcony railing, crossing her arms over her chest and trying to ignore the feelings his touch had aroused. She watched him as he checked the display, swore again, and traded the pager for a slim cell phone from the pocket of his suit jacket.

The natural light that poured in through the south end of the atrium brought out the gray in his close-cropped hair. She wondered against her will if there was a woman back in Virginia worrying about his health and the level of stress he shouldered day in and day out.

'Goddammit, McCleary, can't you go two hours on this case without a fucking crisis?' he barked into the phone, then listened for a minute. 'There's a lawyer involved. Shit . . . There's nothing you can do about it now. The interview is screwed . . . Back off and go over the evidence again. See if there's anything you can blow out of proportion. What about the tests on that pad of paper? . . . Well, he doesn't know you haven't got it. For godsake, use it! . . . No, I'm not coming down. I'm tied up here. Handle it.'

Snapping the phone shut, he heaved a sigh and absently rubbed a hand against his stomach.

'I thought you'd be unit chief by now,' Kate said.

'They offered. I declined. I'm no administrator.'

But he was the natural leader for CASKU just the same. He was the resident expert the rest of the team would turn to. He was the control freak who believed no job could be handled as effectively without him being in charge of it. No, Quinn wouldn't relinquish his field duties for the unit chief's post. Instead, he would essentially do both jobs. The perfect answer for the man obsessed with his work and with his need to save humanity from its darker side.

'What kind of caseload are you carrying?' Kate asked.

He shrugged it off. 'The usual.'

Which was more than anyone else in the unit. More than any one person could humanly deal with, unless he had no other life. There had been times she had labeled his obsession ambition, and other times she had looked past the obvious and caught a glimpse of him standing at the edge of a deep, dark internal abyss. Dangerous thinking, because her instinctive response was to want to pull him back from that edge. His life was his own. She didn't even want him here.

'I have to get back to Angie,' she said. 'She won't be happy I abandoned her. I don't know why I care so much,' she grumbled.

'You always liked a challenge,' he said, offering her a hint of a smile.

'I ought to have my head examined.'

'Can't help there, but how about dinner?'

Kate almost laughed out of incredulity rather than humor. Just like that – *how about dinner?* Two minutes ago they'd been sniping at each other. Five years and a load of emotional baggage between them, and . . . *and what? He's over it and I'm not?*

'I don't think so. Thanks anyway.'

'We'll talk about the case,' he said, backpedaling. 'I've got some ideas I'd like to bounce off you.'

'That's not my job. I'm not with the BSU anymore,' she said, moving toward the door into victim/witness services. The need to escape was so strong, it was embarrassing. 'The BCA has an agent who's taken the behavioral analysis course and –'

'– is currently in Quantico for eight weeks at the National Academy.'

'You can bring in another agent if you want. You've got all of CASKU to call on for backup, to say nothing of every expert and pioneer in the field. You don't need me.'

With quick fingers she punched the code into the key panel beside the door.

'*You* were an expert in the field,' he reminded her. 'It's victim analysis –'

'Thanks for helping out with Sabin,' she said as the lock relinquished its grip and she turned the knob. 'I've got to get back to my office before my witness steals all my good pens.'

Angie moved around Kate's office, restless, curious, jumpy. Kate was pissed off about the sketch. She'd hardly said a word all the way back from the police department.

Guilt pricked Angie like so many tiny needles. Kate was trying to help her, but she had to look out for herself. The two didn't necessarily go together. How was she supposed to know what to do? How was she supposed to know what was right?

You're nothing but a fuckup! You never do anything right!

'I'm trying,' she whispered.

Stupid little bitch. You never listen.

'I'm *trying*.'

Scared was what she was, but she would never speak the word, not even in her mind. The Voice would feed on her fear. The fear would feed on the Voice. She could feel both forces gaining strength inside her.

I'll give you something to be scared of.

She clamped her hands over her ears, as if she might be able to shut out the voice that echoed only in her mind. She rocked herself for a minute, eyes wide open, because if she closed them she would see things she didn't want to see again. Her past was like a bad movie playing over and over and over in her mind, always right there, ready to pull to the surface emotions better left buried deep. Hate and love, violent anger, violent need. Hate and love, hate and love, *hateandlove* – all one word for her. Feelings so intertwined they were inseparable, like the tangled limbs of two animals attacking each other.

The fear swelled a little larger. The Zone was zooming in.

You're afraid of everything, aren't you, crazy little bitch?

Trembling, she stared at the fliers tacked to Kate's bulletin board. She read the titles, trying to focus on something before the Zone could sweep in and suffocate her. *Community Resources for Crime Victims, Rape Crisis Center, The Phoenix: Women Rising to a New Beginning.* Then the titles blurred and she sat down, breathing just a little too hard.

What the hell was taking Kate so long? She'd left with no explanation, said nothing more than that she'd be back in a few minutes, which was – how many minutes ago? Angie looked around for a clock, found it, then couldn't remember what time it had been when Kate had left her. Hadn't she looked at the clock then? Why couldn't she remember?

Because you're stupid, that's why. Stupid and crazy.

She began to shiver. It felt like her throat was closing. There was no air in this stupid little room. The walls were pressing in on her. She tried to swallow as tears flooded her eyes. The Zone was zooming in. She could feel it coming, could feel the change in the air pressure around her. She wanted to run, but she couldn't outrun the Zone or the Voice.

So do something. Make it stop, Angel. You know how to make it stop.

Frantic, she shoved the sleeves of her jacket and sweater up and scratched a stubby thumbnail along the thin white lines of the scars, turning them pink. She wanted to get at the cut she'd opened yesterday, to make it bleed again, but she couldn't get her sleeve up that high and she didn't dare take her coat off for fear someone would come in and catch her. Kate had told her to wait there, that she would be back in a few minutes. The minutes were ticking by.

She'll know how crazy you are then, Angel.
The Zone was zooming in . . .
You know what to do.
But Kate was coming back.
Do it.
The shaking started.
Do it.
The Zone was zooming in . . .
Do it!
She didn't dare take the box cutter out of her backpack. How would she explain it? She could stick it in her pocket –

The panic was setting in. She could feel her mind begin to fracture just as her desperate gaze hit on the dish of paper clips on Kate's desk.

Without hesitation, she grabbed one and straightened it, testing the end with her fingertip. It wasn't as sharp as the razor. It would hurt more.

Coward. Do it!

'I hate you,' she muttered, fighting the tears. 'I hate you. I hate you.'

Do it! Do it!

'Shut up! Shut up! Shut up!' she whispered, the pressure building in her head until she thought it would burst.

She dragged the piece of wire across an old scar on her wrist where the skin was as thin and white as paper. She cut parallel to a fine blue vein, and waited for her tear-blurred vision to fill with blood. Rich and red, a thin liquid line.

The pain was strong and sweet. The relief was immediate. The pressure lifted. She could breathe again. She could think.

She stared at the crimson ribbon for a moment, some lost part of her deep, deep inside wanting to cry. But the overwhelming sensation was relief. She set the paper clip aside and wiped the blood away with the bottom of her sweater. The line bloomed again, bringing an extra wave of calm.

She drew her thumb down along the cut, then looked at the way the blood had smeared into the whorls and between the ridges of the pad. Her fingerprint, her blood, her crime. She stared at it for a long time, then raised her thumb to her mouth and slowly licked it off. She felt a kind of release that was almost sexual. She had conquered the demon and consumed it. She drew her tongue along the cut, taking up the last few beads of red.

Still slightly weak-kneed and light-headed, she pulled her sleeve into place and got up from the chair to move around the office. She took in every detail and committed it to memory.

Kate's thick wool coat hung on a wall rack with a funky black crushed-velvet hat. Kate had cool taste in clothes for a woman her age. Angie wanted to try the hat on, but there was no mirror to look in to see it.

A small cartoon on the bulletin board showed a lawyer grilling a witness – a groundhog. '*So, Mr Groundhog, you claim you saw your shadow that day. But isn't it true you have a drinking problem?*'

The desk drawers were locked. There was no purse in sight. She tried the file cabinet, thinking she might find her own file, but that too was locked.

As she fingered through the papers on the desk, she was struck by how she had been in such a state of panic just a few minutes ago and now she felt strong and in control, just as she had slipping out of and back into Phoenix House undetected. She hated that part of her that let the Zone take over. She hated how weak that part of her was. She knew she could be strong.

I make you strong, Angel. You need me. You love me. You hate me.

The fresh strength let her ignore the Voice.

She flipped through the Rolodex and stopped on the name *Conlan*. Frank and Ingrid in Las Vegas. Kate's parents, she guessed. Kate would have normal parents. A father who went to work in a suit. A mother who made pot roast and baked cookies. Not the kind of mother who did drugs and slept around. Not the kind of father who didn't give a shit about his kids, who left and left them at the mercy of the jerks their mother brought home. Kate Conlan's parents loved Kate like normal people loved their kids. Kate Conlan had never been locked in a closet or whipped with a wire hanger or forced to go down on her stepfather.

Angie pulled the card from the Rolodex, tore it into tiny pieces, and stuffed the pieces into her jacket pocket.

A stack of mail sat unopened in the in basket. Another stack sat in the out basket. Angie picked the envelopes up and sorted through them. Three official pieces of correspondence in Hennepin County Government Center envelopes. One bright yellow envelope addressed by hand to someone named Maggie Hartman, the return address on a gold foil label in the upper left corner: Kate Conlan.

She memorized the address and put the envelopes back, her attention moving on to the collection of tiny angel statues she had spotted the first time she'd come into the office. They sat scattered atop the shelving unit on the desk. Each was different: glass, brass, silver, pewter, painted. None was more than an inch high. Angie singled out the one made of painted pottery. She had black hair and dots of turquoise on her dress. Gold edged her wings and circled her head in a halo.

Angie held the statue close and stared at its round face with black dots for eyes and a crooked little smile. She looked happy and innocent, simple and sweet.

Everything you're not, Angel.

Knowing better than to acknowledge the deep sadness that yawned inside her heart, Angie turned away from the desk, slipping the angel into her coat pocket just as the doorknob rattled. An instant later Kate came into the room.

'Where the hell have you been?' Angie demanded.

Kate looked at her, checking the instant retort before it could get to her tongue. 'Damage control' was the most diplomatic thing she could say. 'Sorry it took so long.'

Instantly Angie's bravado faded. 'I did the best I could!'

Kate doubted that was the truth, but there was nothing to gain in saying so. What she needed to do was figure out how to get the whole story out of this kid. She dropped into her chair, unlocked the desk, and took a bottle of Aleve out of the pencil drawer. She shook out two, downed them with cold coffee and a grimace, then paused to consider the possibility that her charming charge might poison her.

'Don't worry about the sketch,' she said, rubbing at the tension in the back of her neck. The tendons stood out like steel rods. She swept her gaze discreetly across the desk. An automatic check that was second nature after she'd left a client alone in her office. One of her angels was missing.

Angie settled uneasily on the visitor's chair, leaning her arm on the desk. 'What's going to happen?'

'Nothing. Sabin is frustrated. He needs something big and he was hoping you'd be it. He talked about cutting you loose, but I talked him out of it. For now. If he decides you're a scam artist just trying to collect reward money, he'll cut you loose and I won't be able to help you. If you go to a tabloid and try to give them something more than what you've given the cops, Sabin will throw your ass in jail, and no one will be able to help you.

'You're between a rock and hard place here, Angie. And I know your first instinct is to pull everything inside you and shut the rest of the world out, but you have to remember one thing: That secret you're holding, you share it with one other person – and he'll kill you for it.'

'I don't need you scaring me.'

'God, I hope not. The man you saw tortures women, kills them, and sets their bodies on fire. I hope that scares you more than anything I could say.'

'You don't know what scared is,' Angie accused, her voice bitter with memories. She sprang up out of the chair and began to pace, chewing hard on a thumbnail.

'Then tell me. Tell me something, Angie. Anything I can toss Sabin and the cops to back them off. What were you doing in the park that night?'

'I told you.'

'You were cutting through. From where? From what? If you'd been with someone, don't you realize he might have seen this guy too? He might have caught a glimpse of a car. He could, at the very least, confirm your side of things and at the most he could help us catch this monster.'

'What do you think?' Angie demanded. 'You think I'm a whore? You think I was there fucking some john for pocket money? I told you what I was doing there. So that means you think I'm a whore *and* a liar. Fuck you.'

She was out the door that fast, with Kate right behind her.

'Hey! Don't give me that bullshit,' Kate ordered, catching hold of the girl's arm, the thinness of it almost startling her.

Angie's expression held as much surprise as anger. This wasn't how it was supposed to go. This wasn't how the umpteen social workers she'd seen in her young life would have reacted.

'What?' Kate demanded. 'You thought I'd go contrite and apologize? "Oh, gee, I offended Angie! She must never have done anything bad to stay alive on the streets!" ' She feigned wide-eyed shock, one hand on her cheek, then dropped the act in a heartbeat. 'You think I just rode in on the turnip wagon? I know what goes on in the big bad world, Angie. I know what women with no homes and no jobs are forced to do to survive.

'Yes, frankly, I *do* think you were in that park fucking some john for pocket money. And I know damn well you're a liar. You're a thief too. What I'm telling you is this: *I don't care.* I'm not judging you. I can't do anything about what happened to you before you came into my life, Angie. I can only help you with what's happening now and with what's going to happen. You're drowning in this thing and *I want to help you.* Can you get that through your thick head and quit fighting me?'

The silence was absolute for a second as they stood there in the hall of legal services, staring at each other – one angry, one wary. Then a phone rang in someone's office, and Kate became aware of Rob Marshall looking out his door down the hall. She kept her attention on Angie, and prayed to God Rob would keep his nose out of it. The bleakness in the girl's eyes was enough to break Kate's heart.

'Why would you care what happens to me?' Angie asked quietly.

'Because no one else does,' Kate said simply.

Tears rose in the girl's dark blue eyes. The truth of what Kate had said was right there. No one had ever cared a damn about Angie DiMarco, and she didn't dare trust that someone would start now.

'All I have to gain is a congratulatory pat on the ass from Ted Sabin,' Kate said, pulling a scrap of humor up through the thicker emotions. 'Believe me, that's not my motivation.'

Angie stared at her for another moment, weighing options, the weight of those options pressing down hard on her. A single tear rolled down her cheek. She drew a shallow, shaky breath.

'I don't like doing it,' she whispered in a child's voice, her lower lip trembling.

Slowly and carefully, Kate put an arm around Angie's shoulders and drew the girl to her, the need to give comfort so strong, it frightened her. Someone had brought this child into the world, not wanting her for any reason other than to punish her for their mistakes. The injustice burned in Kate's chest. *This is why I don't do kids,* she thought. *They make me feel too much.*

The girl's body shuddered as she let go a fraction more of the emotion that was threatening to crush her. 'I'm sorry,' she whispered. 'I'm so sorry.'

'I know, kiddo,' Kate murmured thickly as she patted Angie's back. 'I'm sorry too. Let's go sit down and talk about it. These damn heels. My feet are killing me.'

16

'You can't believe some of the stuff coming in over the hotline,' Gary Yurek said, carrying a thick file and a pad of paper to the table in the Loving Touch of Death war room. 'They actually had a woman call in to say she thinks her neighbor is the Cremator because her *dog* doesn't like him!'

'What kind of dog?' Tippen called.

'American scumbag spaniel,' Elwood said, pulling out a chair. 'A hearty, cheerful breed known for digging up corpses and cavorting merrily with cadaver parts.'

'Sounds like you, Elwood.' Liska punched him in the arm as she passed.

'Hey, my hobbies are my own business.'

'Any more sightings of Jillian Bondurant?' Hamill asked.

Yurek looked disgusted. 'Yeah, a Jiffy Lube mechanic in Brooklyn Park whose every third word was *reward*.'

Quinn took a seat at the table, his head throbbing, his mind trying to go in too many directions at once. Kate. Kate's witness. Bondurant. The profile he was struggling with. The Atlanta case. The Blacksburg case. The calls backing up on his voice mail about a dozen others. Kate. Kate...

His brain wanted a cup of coffee, but his stomach was saying no in strong and painful language. He fished a Tagamet out of his pocket and washed it down with Diet Coke. Mary Moss handed him a packet of photographs.

'Lila White's parents gave them to me. I don't see how they'll help, but it was important to them. The pictures were taken just a few days before her murder.'

'Progress reports!' Kovac called, shrugging out of his topcoat and juggling three files as he came to the head of the table. 'Anything on the parks employees?'

'Found a convicted child-molester who lied about his record on his application,' Tippen said. 'Other than that, no red flags on the permanent staff. However, the parks department also gets work crews of misdemeanor offenders doing community service time. We're getting a list.'

'Jillian's phone records don't show anything out of the ordinary,' Elwood said. 'Calls to her father, to her shrink, to this friend Tinks went to see. Nothing unusual in the last couple of weeks. I've requested the records from her cell phone service, but their computers were screwed up, so I don't have that yet.'

'We've got a list of employees fired from Paragon in the last eighteen months,' Adler said. 'None of them stood out as being particularly vindictive toward Peter Bondurant. We ran their names through the system and came up with petty shit.'

'One guy convicted of soliciting a prostitute,' Hamill said. 'But that was a one-time, bachelor-party situation. He's married now. Spent last weekend at his in-laws'.'

'That could drive *me* to murder,' Tippen quipped.

'One guy with a third-degree-assault charge. He attacked his manager when he got the news Paragon was giving him the ax,' Adler said. 'That was nine months ago. He's moved out of town. Lives in Cannon Falls now and works in Rochester.'

'How far is that?' Quinn asked.

'Cannon Falls? Half an hour, forty-five minutes.'

'An easy drive. He's not off the hook.'

'Our Rochester field agent is checking him out,' Hamill said.

'In general,' Adler went on, 'no one who works for Bondurant seems particularly fond of him, but no one had anything bad to say about him either – with one notable exception. Bondurant started Paragon back in the late seventies with a partner – Donald Thorton. He bought Thorton out in 'eighty-six.'

'About the time of his divorce,' Kovac said.

'Exactly the time of the divorce. He paid Thorton top dollar – more than, according to some. Thorton developed serious problems with booze and gambling, and ran his Caddie into Lake Minnetonka in 'eighty-nine. Lake patrol fished him out before he drowned, but not before he sustained serious brain damage and a spinal cord injury. His wife blames Bondurant.'

'How so?'

'She wouldn't say over the phone. She wants a face-to-face.'

'I'll take it,' Kovac said. 'Anyone has something bad to say about Mr Billionaire can be my friend.'

Walsh raised one hand, covering his mouth with the other while he tried to cough up part of a lung. When he finally drew breath to speak, his face was purple. 'I've been on the phone with the legal attaché's office in Paris,' he said in a thin, strained voice. 'They're checking out the stepfather – Serge LeBlanc – with Interpol and with the French authorities. But I'd say he's a dead end. Come all the way over here to off two hookers and then his stepdaughter? I don't think so.'

'He could have hired it done,' Tippen offered.

'No,' Quinn said. 'This is classic sadistic sexual homicide. The killer had his own agenda. He doesn't do it for money. He does it because he gets off on it.'

Walsh pulled a nasty-looking handkerchief out of his pocket and stared into it, contemplating a sneeze. 'LeBlanc is plenty pissed off about the inquiries, and not being too cooperative. He says he'll release Jillian's dental records – which will do us no good. He'll release any X-rays she's ever had taken, but that's it. He won't let the whole file go.'

Kovac's face lit up. 'Why is that? What's he trying to hide?'

'Maybe the fact that he had sex with her, drove her to a suicide attempt, then had her committed,' Liska offered, looking pleased to have scooped the boys. She filled them in on what she had learned from Michele Fine.

'I also asked Fine to stop in and get fingerprinted so we can eliminate her prints from the ones found in Jillian's apartment. And, by the way, somebody definitely cleaned the place up over the weekend. Fine says Jillian was a slob. The place is way too clean and the friend says there was no maid service.'

'Maybe the killer was in her house that night,' Adler speculated. 'Didn't want to leave any trace.'

'I can see he'd wipe the place for prints,' Elwood said. 'But tidy up? That doesn't make sense.'

Quinn shook his head. 'No. If he was there, he wouldn't have cleaned up. If anything, he would have made it worse as a sign of disrespect to his victim. He would have trashed the place, maybe urinated or defecated somewhere obvious.'

'So, we got us another mystery,' Kovac said. He turned to Liska again. 'You ran Fine through the system?'

'No wants, no warrants, no record. No boyfriend, she says, and I'd believe that. She says she and Jillian weren't lovers. There's a dope connection there somewhere. Small-time, I'd say.'

'But it might be worth digging on,' Moss said. 'Lila White had connections too. One of them beat the snot out of her last fall.'

'Willy Parrish,' Kovac said. 'He was a guest of the county at the time of White's murder. Had no connection to Fawn Pierce.'

'I also checked the guy White's parents blame for hooking her on drugs in the first place,' Moss said. 'A Glencoe local named Allan Ostertag. No convictions. Strictly small-time. Works as a salesman at his father's car dealership. He can be accounted for all this last weekend.'

'Jillian and Fine wrote music together,' Quinn said, jotting himself a note. 'What kind of music?'

'Folky alternative stuff,' Liska said. 'Man-hating female angst bullshit, I'd guess from my impression of Fine. She's a real trip. Alanis Morissette with PMS.'

'So where's the music?' Quinn asked. 'I'd like to see it.'

'Super G-man and talent scout on the side,' Tippen remarked snidely.

Quinn cut him a look. 'Music is personal, intimate. It reveals a lot about the person who wrote it.'

Liska's brow knitted as she thought. 'I saw sheet music, like you'd buy in a store. I didn't see anything handwritten.'

'See if the friend has copies,' Kovac suggested.

'I will, but I think Vanlees is the direction we should be sniffing. The guy's got a screw loose, and he fits John's preliminary profile pretty well.'

'Criminal background?' Quinn asked.

'Nothing serious. A slew of parking tickets and a couple of misdemeanors three or four years ago. Trespass charges and a DUI – all spread out over a period of eighteen months or so.'

'Trespass?' The word raised a flag in Quinn's mind. 'Was that the original charge or did he plead down from something else?'

'Final outcome.'

'Dig deeper. A lot of Peeping Toms bargain down their first couple of offenses. They seem too pathetic to be worth charging out on a low-end sex crime. Check out the tickets too. Check the locations the tickets were issued in relation to the address of the trespass charges.'

Tippen leaned toward Adler. 'Yeah, we might have a serial weanie wagger on our hands.'

'They all start somewhere, Tippen,' Quinn said. 'The Boston Strangler started out looking in windows, jerking off, and some asshole cop shrugged that off too.'

The detective started to come up out of his chair. 'Hey, fu –'

'Put 'em back in your pants, guys,' Kovac ordered. 'We got no time to get out the yardstick. Tinks, find out if this mutt did his community service in the parks.'

'And find out what kind of car he's driving,' Quinn added.

'Will do. I made a point of telling him about the meeting tonight. I'm betting he shows.'

'Speaking of,' Kovac said. 'I want everyone there by seven-thirty. We'll have surveillance units from the BCA and from narcotics pulling plate numbers off the cars in the parking lot. Yurek will be our master of ceremonies. I want the rest of you in the crowd, and for God's sake, try not to look like cops.'

'Except the cover boy,' Tippen said, holding up a copy of the day's *Star Tribune* with the headline *FBI's Top Profiler on the Case.* 'You might get two headlines in a row, Slick.'

Quinn frowned, reining in his temper, fighting the urge to put his fist in Tippen's mouth. Christ, he knew better than to let jerks like Tippen yank his chain. He'd dealt with a hundred of them in the last year alone. 'I don't want a headline. I'll say a few words, but I'll keep it brief and I'll keep it vague.'

'Just like you have with us?'

'What do you want me to tell you, Tippen? That the killer will be wearing one red shoe?'

'It'd be something. What the hell have you given us so far for our tax dollars? An age range, the possible description of two vehicles the guy may

163

or may not drive. That he slept with his mother and jacked off with porno magazines? Big deal.'

'It will be if you get a suspect. And I don't believe I ever said anything about him sleeping with his mother.'

'Tip reliving his childhood.'

'Fuck you, Chunk.'

'Maybe,' Quinn said, watching the homely sheriff's detective just to see him twitch. 'The UNSUB, that is. It's likely there was inappropriate sexual behavior both in the home in general and toward this man specifically when he was a child. His mother was probably promiscuous, possibly a prostitute. His father was a weak or absent figure. Discipline was inconsistent, swinging from nonexistent to extreme.

'He was a bright kid, but in trouble a lot at school. He couldn't relate to other kids. His mind was full of thoughts of domination and control of his peers. He was cruel to animals and to other children. He started fires, he stole things. He was a pathological liar at an early age.

'In high school he had trouble concentrating because of his addiction to his sexual fantasies, which were already becoming violent. He got into trouble with authority figures, maybe had run-ins with the police. His mother smoothed over the problems, rationalized for him, got him off the hook, thereby reinforcing a pattern where he was never held accountable for his destructive actions toward others. This empowered him and encouraged him to try even more extreme behavior. It also reinforced a lack of respect for his mother.'

Tippen raised his hands. 'And unless the guy sitting next to me tonight turns and says, "Hi, my name is Harry. My mother had sex with me when I was a kid," it's all just so much crap.'

'I think *you're* full of crap, Tippen,' Liska said. 'When I'm digging up stuff on Vanlees, if I see any of these red flags, I can use them.'

'The analysis is a tool,' Quinn said. 'You can make it work for you or you can leave it in the toolbox.

'When you're in the crowd tonight, watch for anyone who seems overstimulated – excited or nervous or too conscious of the people around them. Listen for anyone who seems to have too great a command of the facts of the case, anyone who seems unusually familiar with police work. Or you can take Detective Tippen's approach and wait for someone to tell you he fucked his mother.'

'G, you know what you can do with that smart mouth?' Tippen said, rising again.

Kovac stepped between them. 'Take yours over to Patrick's and stick a sandwich in it, Tippen. Go now, before you piss me off and I tell you not to come back.'

A sour look twisted Tippen's face. 'Oh, fuck this,' he muttered, grabbing his coat and walking away.

Kovac looked askance at Quinn. A phone was ringing in one of the rooms down the hall. The rest of the task force began to disperse, everyone wanting to grab a bite or a drink before the big event.

'Being a good cop and being an asshole are not exclusive,' Liska said, pulling on her coat.

'You talking about him or me?' Quinn said with chagrin.

'Hey, Sam!' Elwood called. 'Come take a look at this.'

'Tippen's a jerk, but he's a good detective,' Liska said.

'It's all right.' Quinn gave an absent smile as he slipped his trench coat on. 'Skepticism makes for a good investigator.'

'You think so?' She narrowed her eyes and looked at him sideways, then laughed and popped him on the arm. 'Just a little cop humor. So, we've got some more background on Jillian and the two hookers. You want to sit down over dinner and go over it? Or maybe after the meeting tonight we could get a drink somewhere . . .'

'Hey, Tinks,' Kovac barked as he strode back into the room with a fistful of fax paper. 'No hitting on the fed.'

Liska reddened. 'Go bite yourself, Kojak.'

'You'd pay money to see that.'

'I'd throw pennies at your ugly butt.'

He hooked a thumb in her direction as she walked away and gave Quinn a wry look. 'She's crazy about me.'

Liska flipped him off over her shoulder.

Kovac shrugged and turned to business. 'You up for a ride, GQ? I need an extra hammer in my toolbox.'

'What's the occasion?'

His eyes were as bright as a zealot's as he held up the fax. 'Jillian Bondurant's cell phone records. She made two phone calls after midnight Saturday morning – *after* she left the old homestead. One to the headshrinker and one to Daddy Dearest.'

He saw them coming. Standing in the immaculate music room beside the baby grand piano that held a small gallery of framed photos of Jillian as a small child, he saw the car pull up at the gate. A dirt-brown domestic piece of junk. Kovac.

The intercom buzzed. Helen hadn't left yet. She was in the kitchen preparing his dinner. She would get the buzzer and she would let Kovac in because he was with the police, and like every older middle-class American woman in the country, she would not defy the police.

Not for the first time he thought he should have brought his personal assistant in from Paragon to guard his gates both figuratively and literally, but he didn't want another person that close to him now. Bad enough to have Edwyn Noble at his heels every time he turned around. He had purposely sent his media relations coordinator away from him to deal with the news and sensation seekers, who insisted on crowding his gate nevertheless.

Car doors. Quinn walked around from the passenger's side, an elegant figure, head up, shoulders square. Kovac, disheveled, hair sticking up in back, finished a cigarette and dropped it on the driveway. His trench coat flapped open in the wind.

Peter stared at the photographs for another minute. Jillian, too serious at the keyboard. Always something dark and turbulent and sad in her eyes. Her first recital. And her second, and third. Dressed up in frilly frocks that had never suited her – too innocent and prim, representative of the kind of carefree girlishness his daughter had never possessed.

He left the room as the doorbell sounded, shutting the door on that segment of his regret as voices sounded in the front hall.

'Is he in?' Quinn.

Helen: 'I'll see if he's available. Have you had any new developments in the case?'

'We're working on some things.' Kovac.

'Did you know Jillian very well?' Quinn.

'Oh, well –'

'You've been given instructions to reach me through my attorney,' Peter said by way of greeting.

'Sorry about that, Mr Bondurant,' Kovac said, blatantly unrepentant. 'John and I were just on our way over to the community meeting we've set up to try to help catch your daughter's killer, and we decided to swing by kinda spur-of-the-moment like to run some things by you. Hope it's not a bad time.'

Bondurant leveled a heavy look at him, then turned to his housekeeper. 'Thank you, Helen. If you're finished in the kitchen, why don't you head home?'

The housekeeper looked worried that she'd screwed up. Quinn watched Bondurant as the woman started back toward the kitchen. The stress of the last few days was telling on him. He looked as if he hadn't eaten or slept. All dark circles and sunken cheeks and a pallor that was unique to people under tremendous pressure.

'I don't have anything useful to say to you,' he declared, impatient. 'My daughter is dead. I can't do anything to change that. I can't even bury her. I can't even make funeral arrangements. The medical examiner's office won't release the body.'

'They can't release the body without a positive ID, Mr Bondurant,' Quinn said. 'You don't want to bury a stranger by mistake, do you?'

'My daughter was a stranger to me,' he said enigmatically, wearily.

'Really?' Kovac said, moving slowly around the foyer, like a shark circling. 'Here I thought she might have been telling you all about who she really was when she called you that night – *after* she left here. After you said you never heard from her again.'

Bondurant stared at him. No denial. No apology.

'What'd you think?' Kovac demanded. 'Did you think I wouldn't find that out? Do you think I'm a moron? Do you think I've gotta have a fucking FBI shield in order to have a brain?'

'I didn't think it was relevant.'

Kovac looked astounded. 'Not relevant? Maybe she gave a clue where she was when she made the call. That would give us an area to canvass for witnesses. Maybe there was a voice in the background, or a distinguishing sound. Maybe the call was interrupted.'

'No on all counts.'

'Why did she call?'

'To say goodnight.'

'And is that the same reason she'd call her shrink in the middle of the night?'

No reaction. No surprise, no anger. 'I wouldn't know why she called Lucas. Their relationship as doctor and patient was none of my business.'

'She was your daughter,' Kovac said, pacing fast, the frustration building. 'Did you think it wasn't any of your business when her stepfather was fucking her?'

Direct hit. At last, Quinn thought, watching anger fill Peter Bondurant's thin face. 'I've had all I want of you, Sergeant.'

'Yeah? Do you suppose that's what LeBlanc said to Jillian that drove her to try to kill herself back in France?' Kovac taunted, reckless, skating on a thin edge.

'You bastard.' Bondurant made no move toward him, but held himself rigid. Quinn could see him trembling.

'*I'm* a bastard?' Kovac laughed. 'Your daughter's maybe dead and you don't bother to tell us jack shit about her, and *I'm* the bastard? That's rich. John, do you fucking believe this guy?'

Quinn gave the big sigh of disappointment. 'We don't ask these questions lightly, Mr Bondurant. We don't ask them to hurt you or your daughter's memory. We ask because we need the whole picture.'

'I've told you,' Bondurant said in a low, tight voice, the fury cold and hard in his eyes. 'Jillian's past has nothing to do with this.'

'I'm afraid it does. One way or another. Your daughter's past was a part of who she was – or who she *is*.'

'Lucas told me you'd insist on that. It's ludicrous to think Jillian somehow brought this on herself. She was doing so well –'

'It's not your job to try to dissect this, Peter,' Quinn said, shifting to the personal. *I'm your friend. You can tell me.* Giving him permission to let go of the control slowly and voluntarily. Quinn could see the logical part of Bondurant's mind arguing with the emotions he kept so firmly boxed. He was wound so tight that if Kovac pushed him hard enough and he snapped, it would be like suddenly loosing a high-tension wire – no control at all. Bondurant was smart enough to realize that and anal enough to dread the possibility.

'We're not saying it was Jillian's fault, Peter. She didn't ask for this to happen. She didn't deserve to have this happen.'

A sheen of tears glazed Bondurant's eyes.

'I realize this is difficult for you,' Quinn said softly. 'When your wife left, she took your daughter to a man who abused her. I can imagine the kind of anger you must have felt when you found out.'

'No, you can't.' Bondurant turned away, looking for some kind of escape but not willing to leave the hall.

'Jillian was an ocean away, in trouble, in pain. But everything was over by the time you found out, so what could you do? Nothing. I can imagine the frustration, the anger, the feeling of impotence. The guilt.'

'I couldn't do anything,' he murmured. He stood beside a marble-topped table, staring at a sculpture of ragged bronze lilies, seeing a past he would rather have kept locked away. 'I didn't know. She didn't tell me until after she'd moved back here. I didn't know until it was too late.'

With a trembling hand he touched one of the lilies and closed his eyes.

Quinn stood beside him, just encroaching on Bondurant's personal space. Near enough to invite confidence, to suggest support rather than intimidation. 'It's not too late, Peter. You can still help. We have the same goal – finding and stopping Jillian's killer. What happened that night?'

He shook his head. Denying what? There was a sense of something – guilt? shame? – emanating from him almost like an odor. 'Nothing,' he said. 'Nothing.'

'You had dinner. She stayed till midnight. What happened that made her call Brandt? She must have been upset about something.'

Still shaking his head. Denying what? Her emotional state, or just refusing to answer? Shaking off the questions as unacceptable because the answers would open a door he didn't want to go through? The daughter who had come back to him after all those years had not come back the innocent child she had been. She had come back different, damaged. How would a father feel? Hurt, disappointed, ashamed. Guilty because he hadn't been there to prevent what had driven his daughter to try to end her own life. Guilty because of the shame he felt when he thought of her as damaged, as less than perfect. Emotions tangled and dark, tied in a knot that would take the skill of a surgeon to unravel. He thought of the photograph in Bondurant's office: Jillian, so unhappy in a dress meant for another kind of girl.

Kovac came up on Bondurant's right. 'We're not out to hurt Jillian. Or you, Mr Bondurant. We just want the truth.'

Quinn held his breath, never taking his eyes off Bondurant. A moment passed. A decision was made. The scales tipped away from them. He could see it in Peter Bondurant's face as his hand slipped from the ragged bronze lily and he pulled everything inside him tight, and closed that inner door that had slipped ajar.

'No,' Bondurant said, his face a vacant, bony mask as he reached for the receiver of the sleek black telephone that sat beside the sculpture. 'You won't get the chance. I won't have my daughter's memory dragged through the mud. If I see one word in one paper about what happened to Jillian in France, I'll ruin you both.'

Kovac blew out a breath and moved away from the table. 'I'm just trying to solve these murders, Mr Bondurant. That's my only agenda here. I'm a simple guy with simple needs – like the truth. You could ruin me in a heartbeat. Hell, anything I ever had that was worth anything at all went to one ex-wife or the other. You can squash me like a bug. And you know what? I'll still want that truth, 'cause that's the way I am. It'll be easier on all of us if you give it to me sooner rather than later.'

Bondurant just stared at him, stone-faced, and Kovac just shook his head and walked away.

Quinn didn't move for a moment, watching Bondurant, trying to measure, trying to read. They had been so close to drawing him out ... 'You brought me here for a reason,' he said softly, one-on-one, man-to-man. He pulled a business card from his pocket and laid it on the table. 'Call me when you're ready.'

Bondurant hit a direct dial button on the phone and waited.

'One last question,' Quinn said. 'Jillian liked to write music. Did you ever hear her perform? Ever see any of her stuff?'

'No. She didn't share that with me.'

He looked away as someone answered on the other end of the line. 'This is Peter Bondurant. Put me through to Edwyn Noble.'

He stood in the hall and waited for a long time after the rude rumble of Kovac's car had died away. Just stood there in the silence, in the gloom. Time passed. He didn't know how much. And then he was walking down the hall to his office, his body and mind seemingly working independent of each other.

One floor lamp burned low in a corner of the room. He didn't turn on more. Night had crept up into the late afternoon and stolen the clear light that had fallen in through the French doors earlier in the day. The room had a gloomy cast to it that suited his mood.

He unlocked his desk, took a sheet of music from it, and went to stand by the window to read, as if the farther the words were away from the light, the less harsh their reality.

Love Child

I'm your love child
Little girl
Want you more than all the world
Take me to that place I know
Take me where you want to go

Got to make you love me
Only one way how
Daddy, won't you love me
Love me now
Daddy, I'm your love child
Take me now

JB

17

The meeting is in his honor, in a manner of speaking. He sits in the crowd, watching, listening, fascinated and amused. The people around him – he estimates 150, many of them with the media – have come here because they fear him or are fascinated by him. They have no idea the monster is sitting beside them, behind them, shaking his head as they comment on the frightening state of the world and the vicious mentality of the Cremator.

He believes some of them actually envy the Cremator his boldness, though they will never admit it. None of them have the nerve, the clarity of vision, to act on their fantasies and release the dark power within.

The meeting comes to order, the spokesman of the task force stating the alleged purpose of the meeting, which is a lie. The meeting is not to inform, or even to offer the community a show of action. The purpose of the meeting is Quinn's.

'More important in this ongoing cycle of murders, I told them, was to begin going proactive, using police efforts and the media to try to lure the guy into a trap. For example, I suggested the police might set up a series of community meetings to "discuss" the crimes. I was reasonably certain the killer would show up at one or more of these.' – John Douglas, Mindhunter.

The purpose of the meeting is to trap him, and yet he sits here, cool and calm. Just another concerned citizen. Quinn is watching the crowd, looking for him, looking for something most people won't recognize: the face of evil.

'People expect evil to have an ugly face, a set of horns. Evil can be handsome. Evil can be ordinary. The ugliness is internal, a black, cancerous rot that consumes conscience and moral fiber and the controls that define civilized behavior, and leave an animal hiding behind the normal facade.' – John Quinn, in an interview with People *magazine, January 1997.*

In his sharp tailored gray suit, Quinn is obviously a cut above the local stiffs. He has the bored, superior expression of a *GQ* model. This stirs anger – that

Quinn has finally deigned to acknowledge him in public, and he looks as if he couldn't be less interested.

Because you think you know me, Quinn. You think I'm just another case. Nothing special. But you don't know the Cremator. Evil's Angel. And I know you so well.

He knows Quinn's record, his reputation, his theories, his methods. In the end, he will have Quinn's respect, which will mean more to Quinn than it does to him. His dark, true self is above the need for approval. Seeking approval is weak, reactive, induces vulnerability, invites ridicule and disappointment. Not acceptable. Not allowed on the dark side.

He recites his credo in his mind: *Domination. Manipulation. Control.*

Lights flash and camera motors whir as Quinn takes the podium. The woman sitting next to him begins to cough. He offers her a Life Saver and thinks about cutting her throat for disrupting his concentration.

He thinks about doing it here, now – grabbing a fistful of blond hair, pulling her head back, and in one quick motion slicing through her larynx and her jugular and her carotid – all the way back to her spine. The blood will flood out of her in a gushing wave, and he will melt back through the hysterical crowd and slip away. He smiles at the thought and thumbs off a piece of candy for himself. Cherry – his favorite.

Quinn assures the people the full services of the Bureau are at the disposal of the task force. He talks about the VICAP computers, NCIC and the NCAVC, ISU and CASKU. Reassurance through confusion. The average person can't decipher the alphabet soup of modern law enforcement agencies and services. Most people don't know the difference between the police department and the sheriff's office. They know only that acronyms sound important and official. The people gathered here listen with rapt attention and sneak glances at the person sitting beside them.

Quinn gives away only the barest details of the profile he's building, experience allowing him to make a little information seem like the mother lode. He speaks of the common killer of prostitutes: an inadequate loser who hates women and chooses what he deems the worst of the lot to exact revenge for the sins of his mother. Quinn speculates this is not an entirely accurate profile of the Cremator, that this killer is special – highly intelligent, highly organized, clever – and it is going to take the diligence of not only the law enforcement community, but of the community itself to catch him.

Quinn is right about one thing – there is nothing common about the Cremator. He is superior rather than inadequate. He cares so little about the woman who spawned him, he could never be inspired to revenge against her memory.

And yet, in the back of his mind he hears her voice berating him, criticizing him, taunting him. And the anger, ever banked, begins to heat. Goddamn Quinn and his Freudian bullshit. He doesn't know anything about the power and euphoria in taking a life. He has never considered the exquisite music of pain and fear, or how that music elevates the musician. The killing has nothing to do with any feelings of inadequacy of his common self, and everything to do with power.

On one far side of the room, the contingent from the Phoenix House take up their chant: 'Our lives matter too!'

Toni Urskine introduces herself and starts in. 'Lila White and Fawn Pierce were forced by circumstance into prostitution. Are you saying they deserved what happened to them?'

'I would never suggest that,' Quinn says. 'It's simply a fact that prostitution is a high-risk profession compared to being an attorney or an elementary-school teacher.'

'And so they're considered expendable? Lila White's murder didn't rate a task force. Lila White had been a resident of the Phoenix House at one time. No one from the Minneapolis Police Department has come to reinvestigate her death. The FBI didn't send anyone to Minneapolis for Fawn Pierce. One of our current residents was a close friend of Ms Pierce. No one from the Minneapolis Police Department has *ever* interviewed her. But Peter Bondurant's daughter goes missing and suddenly we have network news coverage and community action meetings.

'Chief Greer, in view of these facts, can you honestly say the city of Minneapolis gives a damn about women in difficult circumstances?'

Greer steps up to the podium, looking stern and strong. 'Mrs Urskine, I assure you every *possible* measure was taken to solve the murders of the first two victims. We are *redoubling* our efforts to seek out and find this *monster*. And we *will not rest* until the monster is *caught*!'

'I want to point out that Chief Greer isn't using the term *monster* literally,' Quinn says. 'We're not looking for a raving lunatic, foaming at the mouth. For all appearances, he's an ordinary man. The monster is in his mind.'

Monster. A word ordinary people misapply to creatures they don't understand. The shark is labeled a monster when in fact it is simply efficient and purposeful, pure in its thought and in its power. So, too, the Cremator. He is efficient and purposeful, pure in thought and in power. He doesn't waver in action. He doesn't question the compulsion. He gives himself over wholly to the needs of his Dark Self, and in that complete surrender rises above his common self.

'At this instant, when the victims were dying at their hands, many serial killers report an insight so intense that it is like an emotional quasar, blinding in its revelation of truth.' – Joel Norris, Serial Killers.

'Special Agent Quinn, what are your theories regarding the burning of the bodies?'

The question came from a reporter. The danger with these open community meetings was having them turn into press conferences, and a press conference was the last thing Quinn wanted. He needed a controlled situation – for the purpose of the case, and for himself. He needed to give out just enough information, not too much. A little speculation, but nothing that could be construed by the killer as arrogance. He needed to condemn the killer, but be certain to weave into that condemnation a certain kind of respect.

A direct challenge could result in more bodies. Play it too soft and Smokey Joe might feel he needed to make a statement. More bodies. A wrong word, a careless inflection – another death. The weight of that responsibility pressed against his chest like a huge stone.

'Agent Quinn?'

The voice hit him like a prod, jarring him back to the moment. 'The burning is this killer's signature,' he answered, rubbing a hand against his forehead. He was hot. There wasn't enough air in the room. His head was pounding like a hammer against an anvil. The hole in his stomach lining was burning bigger. 'Something he feels compelled to perform to satisfy some inner need. What that need might be, only he knows.'

Pick a face, any face, he thought as he looked out at the crowd. After all the years and all the cases and all the killers, he sometimes thought he should have been able to recognize the compulsion to kill, to see it like an unholy aura, but it didn't work that way. People made much of the eyes of serial killers – the stark, flat emptiness that was like looking down a long, black tunnel where a soul should have been. But a killer like this one was smart and adaptable, and no one except his victims would see that look in his eyes until he stood for his mug shot.

Any face in the crowd could be the mask of a killer. One person in this group might listen to the descriptions of the crimes, smell the fear in this room, and feel elated, aroused. He had actually seen killers get erections as their monstrous exploits were related to a stunned and sickened jury.

The killer would be here with his own agenda. To gauge, to judge, to plan his next move. To enjoy the fuss being made over him. Maybe he would come forward as a concerned citizen. Maybe he would want the thrill of knowing he could stand within their grasp, then walk away. Or maybe he would choose his next victim from the women in this room.

Quinn's gaze went automatically to Kate as she slipped in the door at the back of the room. He scanned her face, careful not to linger, even though he wanted to. He wanted it too much, and she wanted nothing to do with him. He'd taken that hint once. He sure as hell should have been smart enough to take it now. He had a case to focus on.

'What about the religious overtones?'

'There may not be any as far as he's concerned. We can only speculate. He could be saying "sinners burn in hell". Or it could be a cleansing ceremony to save their souls. Or it could be that he deems burning the bodies the ultimate disrespect and degradation.'

'Isn't it your job to narrow down the possibilities?' another reporter called out. Quinn almost looked for Tippen in the crowd.

'The profile isn't complete,' he said. *Don't tell me my job. I know my job, asshole.*

'Is it true you were pulled off the Bennet child abduction in Virginia to work this case?'

'What about the South Beach gay murders?'

'I have a number of ongoing cases at any given time.'

'But you're here because of Peter Bondurant,' another stated. 'Doesn't that reek of elitism?'

'I go where I'm sent,' he said flatly. 'My focus is on the case, not where the orders came from or why.'

'Why hasn't Peter Bondurant been formally questioned?'

Chief Greer stepped up to the podium to put the official shut-down on that line of inquiry, to expound on Peter Bondurant's virtues in front of Edwyn Noble and the Paragon PR person who had attended on Bondurant's behalf.

Quinn stepped back beside Kovac and tried to breathe again. Kovac had his cop face on, the eyes hooded and flat, taking in far more than anyone in the audience would have imagined.

'You see Liska's mutt sitting next to her?' he said under his breath. 'He came in uniform, for chrissake.'

'That would be handy for getting his victims to go with him,' Quinn said. 'He's got a petty record that might be something more.'

'He's connected to Jillian Bondurant,' Kovac said.

'Have Liska ask him in for a sit-down.' Quinn wished for that rush of gut instinct that this might be the guy, but that sense had abandoned him, and he felt nothing. 'Let it sound like a consultation. We're asking for his assistance, we want his take on things, his opinion as a trained observer. Like that.'

'Kiss his wanna-be ass. Jeez.' Kovac's mustache twitched with distaste. 'You know, he's not far off that piece-of-shit drawing we've got.'

'Neither are you. Get a Polaroid when he comes in. Build a photo array for the witness. Maybe she'll tag him.'

Greer finished his talk with a final dramatic plea for the public's assistance in the case, and pointed out detectives Liska and Yurek as being available to take information tonight. As soon as he declared the meeting over, the reporters started in like a pack of yapping dogs. The crowd instantly became a moving mass of humanity, some drifting toward the door, some moving toward the end of the room, where Toni Urskine from the Phoenix House was trying to rally support for her cause.

Kate wedged her way to the front of the pack, her attention on Kovac. As Kovac stepped toward her, Edwyn Noble moved in on Quinn like the specter of death, his wide mouth set in a hard line. Lucas Brandt stood beside him, hands in the pockets of his camel-hair topcoat.

'Agent Quinn, can we have a word in private?'

'Of course.'

He led them away from the podium, away from the press, into the kitchen of the community center, where industrial-sized coffeepots lined the red Formica countertop, and a hand-lettered sign taped above the sink read PLEASE WASH YOUR CUPS!

'Peter was very upset by your visit this evening,' Noble began.

Quinn raised his brows. 'Yes, I know. I was there.' He slipped his hands into his pockets and leaned back against the edge of the counter. Mr Relaxation. All the time in the world. He gave a thin smile. 'The two of you sat through this meeting to tell me that? Here I thought you were just another pair of concerned citizens.'

'I'm here to represent Peter's interests,' Noble said. 'I think you should know he's talking about calling Bob Brewster. He's extremely displeased that you seem to be wasting valuable time –'

'Excuse me, Mr Noble, but I know my job,' Quinn said calmly. 'Peter doesn't have to like the way I do it. I don't work for Peter. But if Peter is unhappy, then he can feel free to call the director. It won't change the fact that Jillian made two phone calls after she left his home that night, or that neither Peter nor you, Dr Brandt, bothered to mention that to the police. Something was going on with Jillian Bondurant that night, and now she may be dead. Certain questions need to be answered one way or another.'

The muscles in Brandt's square jaw flexed. 'Jillian had problems. Peter loved his daughter. It would kill him to see her past and the difficulties she'd had splashed across the tabloids and paraded before America on the nightly news.'

Quinn abruptly straightened away from the counter, putting himself into Brandt's space, frowning into his face. 'I'm not in the business of selling cases to the media.'

Noble spread his hands. The peacemaker, the diplomat. 'Of course not. We're simply trying to be as discreet about this as possible. That's why we're talking to you rather than to the police. Peter and Lucas and I have discussed this, and we feel that you may be able to steer the rudder of the case, so to speak. That if we could satisfy you with regard to the calls Jillian made that night, the matter could be put to rest.'

'What about your ethics?' Quinn asked, still looking at Brandt.

'A small sacrifice to the greater good.'

His own, Quinn suspected.

'I'm listening.'

Brandt took a breath, bracing himself for this breach of his patient's trust. Somehow Quinn didn't think it bothered his conscience nearly as much as defying Peter Bondurant would bother him socially and financially.

'Jillian's stepfather had contacted her several times in the past few weeks, implying he wanted to mend their relationship. Jillian had very complicated, very mixed feelings toward him.'

'Would she have wanted to resume some kind of relationship with him?' Quinn asked. 'Her friend implied Jillian had been in love with him, that she wanted him to divorce her mother for her.'

'Jillian was a very unhappy, confused girl when she was involved with Serge. Her mother had always been jealous of her, from Jillie's infancy. She was starving for love. I'm sure you know people will go to terrible lengths to get it – or, rather, to get what will pass for love for them.'

'Yes. I've seen the result in crime scene photographs. Why was the stepfather never prosecuted?'

'No charges were ever brought. LeBlanc had brainwashed her,' Noble said with disgust. 'Jillian refused even to talk to the police.'

'Peter had hoped that in moving back to Minnesota and getting therapy, she had put it all behind her,' Brandt said.

'And had she?'

'Therapy is a long, ongoing process.'

'And then LeBlanc started calling her again.'

'Friday night she decided to tell Peter about it. Naturally, he was upset. He was frightened for Jillie. She'd been doing so well.' Another strategically placed sigh. 'Peter has difficulty expressing emotion. His concern came out as anger. They ended up arguing. Jillie was upset when she left. She called me from her car.'

'Where was she?'

'In a parking lot somewhere. She didn't really say. I told her to go back to Peter and talk it through, but she was embarrassed and hurt, and in the end she just called him,' Brandt said. 'That's the whole story. It's as simple as that.'

Quinn doubted him on both counts. What Lucas Brandt had just told him was by no means the whole story, and nothing about Jillian Bondurant's life or death would prove to be simple.

'And Peter couldn't have just told this story to Sergeant Kovac and me four hours ago when we were standing in his foyer.'

Noble cast a nervous glance over his shoulder at the closed door on the other side of the room, as if he were waiting for the reporters to ram it down and storm in, microphones thrust before them like bayonets.

'It isn't easy for Peter to talk about these things, Agent Quinn. He's an intensely private man.'

'I realize that, Mr Noble,' Quinn said, casually fishing a peppermint out of his pocket. He spoke as he unwrapped it. 'The trouble with that is that this is a murder investigation. And in a murder investigation, there's no such thing as privacy.' He set the wrapper on the counter and popped the candy in his mouth. 'Not even if your name is Peter Bondurant and you have the ear of the director of the FBI – not as long as it's my case.'

'Well,' Edwyn Noble said, stepping back, his long face as cold and hard as marble. 'It may not be your case much longer.'

They left looking like spoiled children who would immediately run home and tell on him. They would tell Bondurant. Bondurant would call Brewster. Brewster might call and reprimand him, Quinn supposed. Or he might simply have the ASAC pull him off the case and send him on to another stack of bodies somewhere else. There was always another case. And another . . . and another . . . And what the hell else did he have to do with his life?

He watched as Noble and Brandt worked their way toward the exit, reporters dogging their heels.

'What was that about?' Kovac asked.

'Heading us off at the pass, I think.'

'Kate says our wit came clean with her. Little Mary Sunshine says she was in the park that night earning a Jackson doing the hokey-pokey with some loser.'

'This loser have a name?'

Kovac snorted. 'Hubert Humphrey, he tells her. BOLO: republican asshole with a bad sense of humor.'

'That narrows it down,' Quinn said dryly.

The television crews were packing up lights and cameras. The last of the crowd was drifting out. The party was over, and with it went the adrenaline that had elevated his heart rate and tightened his nerves. He actually preferred the tension because it fended off the depression and the sense of being overwhelmed and exhausted and confused. He preferred action, because the alternative was to be alone in his hotel room with nothing but the fear to keep him company. The fear that he wasn't doing enough, that he was missing something; that despite the accumulated knowledge from a thousand or more cases, he had lost his feel for the job and was just stumbling around like a newly blinded man.

'Of course, she didn't get a license number,' Kovac went on. 'No address. No credit card receipt.'

'Can she describe him?'

'Sure. He was about four inches long and made a sound like a meat grinder when he came.'

'That'll be an interesting lineup.'

'Yeah. Just another pathetic yuppie with an SUV and a wife who won't give him a blow job.'

Quinn looked at him sharply. 'A what?'

'A wife who –'

'The other part. He was driving what?'

'A sport utility vehi –' Kovac's eyes rounded and he threw down the cigarette he had been about to light. 'Oh, Jesus.'

He moves with the last of the crowd out of the doors of the community center, picking up bits and pieces of conversation about himself.

'I wish they would have talked more about the burning.'

'I mean, the FBI guy says this killer looks and acts like anyone else, but how can that be? Setting bodies on fire? That's nuts. He's gotta be nuts.'

'Or just smart. The fire destroys evidence.'

'Yeah, but cutting someone's head off is nuts.'

'Don't you think the fire is symbolic?' he asks. 'I think maybe the guy has some kind of religious mania. You know: *ashes to ashes* and all that.'

'Maybe.'

'I'll bet when they catch him, the cops find out he had some kind of religious fanatic stepfather or something. A mortician, maybe,' he says, thinking of the man who had been involved with his mother during much of his youth. The man who had believed he had been charged by God to redeem her through sexual subjugation and beatings.

'Sick bastard. Going around torturing and killing women because of his own inadequacies. Should have been drowned in a sack at birth.'

'And these creeps always put everything off on their mothers. Like they have no minds of their own.'

He wants to grab the two women saying these things. Grab them by their throats, scream his name in their purpling faces, and crush their windpipes with his bare hands. The anger is now a living flame, blue-centered and hot.

'I've read about that Quinn. He's brilliant. He caught that child-killer out in Colorado.'

'He can interrogate me anytime he wants,' the other woman says. 'George Clooney's got nothing on him.'

They laugh, and he wants to pull a claw hammer out of the air and smash their skulls in with it. He feels the heat of the fire in his chest. His head is throbbing. The need is a fever just beneath the surface of his skin.

Outside the community center, the parking lot is in a state of gridlock. He goes to the car and leans back against it, crossing his arms.

'No point trying!' he calls to one of the uniform cops directing traffic. 'Might as well wait it out.'

The idiot. Who in this picture is inadequate? Not the Cremator, but those who look for him and look at him and see a common man.

He watches others exit the building and come out onto the sidewalk. The yellow-white floodlight washes over them. Some are citizens. Some are cops assigned to the task force. Some he recognizes.

Quinn emerges from a side door toward the back of the building – a spot the media had chosen to ignore. He rushes out with no overcoat and stands just out of cover of the shadows in the doorwell, hands on hips, shoulders square, his breath clouding the air as he looks around.

Looking for me, Agent Quinn? The inadequate loser with the mother complex? The mental monster. You're about to find out what a monster really is.

The Cremator has a plan. The Cremator will be a legend. The killer who broke John Quinn. The ultimate triumph for the ultimate killer over the ultimate hunter of his kind.

He slides behind the wheel of the car he has driven here, starts the motor, adjusts the heater, and curses the cold. He needs a warmer hunting ground. He backs the car out of the slot and follows a silver Toyota 4Runner out of the parking lot and into the street.

18

Kate piloted the 4Runner carefully into the narrow, ancient garage that sat just off the alley behind her house. During the winter months she regularly dreamed of an attached garage, but then spring would come and the backyard perennial beds would bloom and she would forget about the hassle of tromping through the snow, and the danger of walking in a dark alley in a city with a disturbing number of sex crimes.

The wind scrambled and scattered the dead leaves that lay in a drift along the side of the neighbor's garage. A little shiver snaked down Kate's back, and she paused to turn and stare back into the darkness behind her – just in case. But it was only her natural paranoia compounded by the knowledge that the meeting she had just attended had been staged for the sole purpose of baiting a serial killer.

Old feelings from her days in the BSU came rushing back.

Memories of unspeakable crimes that were the topics of casual conversation around the water cooler. Serial murder had been such an ingrained part of her world, that kind of idle talk hadn't seemed strange to her until toward the end of her career – after Emily died. Death had then suddenly taken on a more personal quality, and she had lost the veneer of detachment that was necessary for people in law enforcement. Finally, she hadn't been able to stand it anymore.

She wondered how John still did . . . *if* he did. He'd looked pale tonight, gaunt and gray in the harsh lights. Back in the old days, his coping strategy had been overwork. He didn't have to deal with feelings if he was too busy to face them. That probably hadn't changed. And what did she care if it had or not?

She slid the key into the back-door dead bolt and paused again before turning it, the hair rising up on the back of her neck. Slowly, she turned, straining to see past the reach of the motion-detector light into the shadowed corners of the yard. It struck her then that she'd left her cell phone in the truck. In the truck, across the yard in the creepy garage.

Screw it. She could pick up any messages from the house phone. If there was a God, none of her clients would have a crisis tonight. And she could settle into a hot tub with a glass of her favorite coping method. This case might kill her, but at least she'd die clean and pleasantly numb.

No maniac rushed to push his way in the door behind her, and no maniac waited in the kitchen with a butcher knife. Thor ran in to complain loudly at the late dinner hour. Kate tossed her purse on the counter and clicked on the small television to catch the news. With one hand she unbuttoned her coat, with the other she reached into the fridge for the cat food and then the bottle of Sapphire.

The lead story on the ten o'clock news was the meeting. There was a clip of the crowd – Toni Urskine and her Phoenix women prominent in the shot – Chief Greer thumping the podium, and John looking grave as he spoke about the Bureau's role in the investigation.

Grave and handsome. The camera had always loved his face. He had aged hard, and even that looked good on him – the lines fanning out beside his eyes, the gray in his close-cropped hair. His physical, sexual appeal hit her on a basic level she couldn't block, and could only pretend to ignore.

Then it was back to the anchor, who rehashed the facts of the cases while photographs of Peter and Jillian Bondurant filled one corner of the screen. Reward and hotline information followed, and they were on to the next hot topic: beat cops warming themselves these chilly nights in the strip clubs downtown.

Kate left the news to Thor and wandered into the dining room, flipping on the old mission-style chandelier she had salvaged and rewired herself, thinking about the Bondurant connection and how Jillian did or didn't fit the victim profile.

'Damn you, John,' she muttered.

'We'll talk about the case. I've got some ideas I'd like to bounce off you.'

'It's not my job. I'm not with BSU anymore.'

'You were an expert in the field . . .'

And he had access to every expert in the field. He didn't need her.

She hung her coat on the back of a chair and sat down at the oak table she'd refinished that first summer after she'd left the Bureau. She had been wound, wired, still reeling from Emily's death and the wreck of both her marriage and her relationship with Quinn. Life as she knew it had ended, and she had to start over again. Alone, except for the ghosts.

She'd never told anyone close to her about Quinn, not her sister or her parents. They didn't know her resignation from the Bureau had come under a cloud of scandal. She couldn't have adequately explained the connection she'd felt to Quinn as Steven had drifted away from her on a tide of grief and anger. Even severed, that connection had been too precious to share with people who wouldn't understand. And her parents wouldn't have understood any more than any of her colleagues back in Quantico had.

She'd had an affair, cheated on her husband. She was a villain. That was what people wanted to believe – the worst and most sordid. No one wanted to know how alone she'd felt, how in need of comfort and support she'd been. They didn't want to hear about the powerful pull of something far beyond physical attraction that had drawn her to John Quinn – and him to her. People preferred to believe the worst because it seemed less apt to touch their own lives.

And so Kate had kept her secret to herself – and the guilt and regret and heartache that were part and parcel of the deal. And she'd built that new life a block at a time, careful to give it a good foundation and balance. The job was eight to five most days. Clients came and went. She got to help them in specific ways, and then their lives moved on and out of hers. Her involvement was finite and manageable.

Even as she thought that, she saw Angie in her mind's eye, and took a long pull on the Sapphire. She remembered the girl's tears, the tough kid, the street kid, curled in on herself and crying like the child she would never admit she was. Scared and embarrassed and ashamed – and she would never admit that either.

Kate had kneeled at Angie's feet, maintaining contact with one hand – touching the girl's hand or her knee or stroking her head as she doubled over and tried to hide her face. And the whole time, the same loop of emotions, the same chain of thoughts, played through Kate's mind – that she was nobody's mother, that this connection she was making to this girl was more than Kate wanted and less than Angie needed.

But the stark truth was that Kate was all she had. The ball was in her court and there was no one else to dump it to. There wasn't another advocate in the office who would stand up to Ted Sabin. There weren't that many who would stand up to Angie.

The story the girl told was short and sad and sordid. She had got picked up on Lake Street and dumped out in the park, a disposable sex toy for a man who never even asked her name. He paid her twenty when the going rate was thirty-five, told her to call a cop when she complained, shoved her out of his vehicle, and drove away. He left her there in the middle of the night like an unwanted kitten.

The image of her standing there alone, disheveled, smelling of sex, with a crumpled twenty in her pocket stuck in Kate's mind. Abandoned. Alone. Her life stretching out in front of her like forty miles of bad road. She couldn't have been more than fifteen or sixteen. Not that much older than Emily would have been if she had lived.

The tears rose up in a sneak attack. Kate took another sip of the gin and tried to swallow the knot down with it. There was no time for crying and no point in it. Emily was gone and Angie was no substitute. She didn't even want a substitute. The sudden sense of emptiness could be dodged or numbed. She was an old hand at it. Put the pain back in its box. Keep those walls up high. God forbid anyone see over them . . . herself included.

The fatigue and the alcohol pulled at her as she got up and headed for the den. She had to check her messages. And she wanted to call the Phoenix to make one last connection with Angie for the night – to strengthen the connection that had been made that afternoon.

She refused to let herself think of the girl sitting alone in her room at the Phoenix, feeling vulnerable and afraid and disappointed in herself for reaching out. She refused to think that she should have tried harder to make that connection go deeper.

The entry hall was lit by a streetlight half a block away, the illumination coming soft and silver through a pair of sidelights Kate kept meaning to get rid of. It was a simple matter to break a sidelight and get into a house. That reminder unfailingly came at night just before she went upstairs to bed.

A lamp burned low in the library-cum-office, a room she had left much the way she remembered it from childhood, when her father had been a midlevel executive for Honeywell. Cluttered and masculine with a sturdy oak desk and a couple of hundred books lining the walls, it smelled of leather upholstery and the faintest memory of good cigars. The message light on the answering machine flickered like a flame, but the phone rang before she could hit the playback button.

'Kate Conlan.'

'Kovac. Get your fanny to the Phoenix, Red. Our witness is missing. We'll meet you there.'

'I should have stayed,' Kate said, pacing the ratty den of the Phoenix with her hands on her hips. 'Goddammit, I should have stayed.'

'You can't be with 'em twenty-four/seven, Red,' Kovac said, lighting a cigarette.

'No,' she muttered, turning a furious glare on the narcotics dick Kovac had borrowed to keep an eye on Angie while she was at the Phoenix – a grubby-looking skinny guy in an army jacket with the name Iverson stenciled over the pocket. 'That was *your* job.'

'Hey.' He held up his hands to ward her off. 'I was here, but I was told *you* didn't want me too close. She must have slipped out the back.'

'Well, duh. Where did you think she would "slip out"? By definition, that sorta rules out the front door, doesn't it?'

The narc tipped his head back and swaggered toward Kate, cocky and mean, an attitude that played well with dealers and hypes. 'I didn't ask for this lame fucking job, and I don't have to take a bunch of shit from a fucking social worker.'

'Hey!' Quinn barked.

Kate stopped Iverson in his tracks with a look and closed the distance between them herself. 'You lost the only witness we had, asshole. You don't want to answer to me? Fine. How about the chief? How about the county attorney? Why don't you tell the mayor how you lost the only witness to the burning of Peter Bondurant's daughter's body because you're a hot-shit narc and you think baby-sitting is beneath you?'

Iverson's face went purple to the rims of his ears. 'Fuck this,' he said, backing off. 'I'm out of here.'

Kovac let him walk out. The front door squeaked open and slammed shut, the sound reverberating in the cavernous hall.

'Every superior in the chain is gonna ream his ass,' he said with a sigh. 'He won't be able to sit down on the street sweeper they assign him to tomorrow.'

Kate began to pace again. 'Did she leave or was she taken?'

'Iverson said her stuff is gone from her room and there's no sign of forced entry at the back. There was another resident here the whole time. She told him she didn't see or hear anything. Quinn and I got here just ahead of you. We haven't looked for ourselves yet.'

Kate shook her head at her own stupidity. 'I'd actually made some progress with her. I should have stayed.'

'What time did you drop her off?'

'I don't know. It must have been after eight. She told me about the john in the park late this afternoon, but then she was embarrassed and upset, and I didn't want to push it. I took her to City Center for something to eat, and let her do a little shopping.'

'Lieutenant Fowler came up with some dough for her?'

Kate made a face and waved the question off. The money had come out of her own pocket, but it didn't matter. 'Then I brought her back here.'

Angie growing quieter and quieter the closer they got to the Phoenix. Slipping back inside the tough shell. *And I let her,* Kate thought.

'I dropped her off and went on to the meeting to tell you – oh, shit. I should have stayed.'

'Who else was here when you let her off?'

'Gregg Urskine – but he was going to the meeting – and one other woman. I don't know who. I didn't see her. Gregg told me she was here. I didn't want Angie alone.'

It was too easy to imagine Angie in this big old house, all but alone.

If Smokey Joe had any way of knowing where she was ... His three victims had vanished with no sign of a struggle. There and gone, simply, easily. And Angie DiMarco claimed she could identify him.

That fast, that easily, the girl was gone. One careless decision ...

'I blew it, and now we've lost her.'

Kate knew the emotions suddenly threatening to swamp her were out of proportion, but she didn't seem able to pull them back. She felt vaguely ill, slightly dizzy. The aftertaste of gin was like metal in her mouth.

She felt Quinn come up behind her, knew it was he without looking. Her body was still attuned to his. There was a disconcerting thought: that the physical magnetism hadn't faded in all this time.

'It isn't your fault, Kate,' he said softly.

He put a hand on her shoulder, his thumb unerringly finding the knot of tension in her trapezius and rubbing at it in an old, familiar way. Too familiar. Too comforting.

'It doesn't matter now,' she said, turning away stiffly. 'What matters is finding her. So let's start looking.'

They went upstairs to the room Angie had been sharing with another Phoenix resident. The walls of the room were a nasty shade of yellow, the old woodwork dark with age and varnish. As it was all through the house, the furniture was mismatched and ill proportioned.

Angie's bed was a wad of unmade sheets. The shopping bag from their excursion to City Center lay in the midst of the mess, tissue tumbling out of it, the jeans and sweater she'd bought nowhere in sight. The dirty backpack was conspicuously absent, suggesting the girl had flown the coop of her own accord.

Sitting on the nightstand beside the cheap glass lamp was a tiny statue of an angel.

Kate picked it up and looked at it: an inch-high piece of pottery she'd bought for five bucks from a Navajo woman on the plaza in Santa Fe. She had slipped the old woman's five-year-old granddaughter an extra dollar for carefully wrapping the doll in tissue, her little brow furrowed as she concentrated on the importance of her task. Watching the little girl, she'd thought of Emily and, to her extreme embarrassment, had nearly started to cry.

'You know something about that?' Quinn asked softly, standing too close again.

'Sure. She stole it off my desk today.' She touched the gold-painted halo on the angel's dark head. 'I have a collection of guardian angels. Ironic, huh? I don't really believe in them. If there were such things as guardian angels, then you and I wouldn't have jobs, and I wouldn't have lost my daughter, and we wouldn't have kids living lives like Angie's.

'Stupid,' she said, rubbing the angel's wings gently between her fingers. 'I wish she'd taken this with her.'

The statue slipped from her grasp and fell to the old rug beside the bed. Kate knelt down to get it, putting her left hand down on the floor for balance. Her heart thumped hard in her chest, and she sat back against her heels as she raised the same hand, turning it palm up.

'Oh, Jesus,' she breathed, staring at the smear of blood.

Quinn swore, grabbing her hand, pulling it closer to the light.

Kate pulled away from him, twisting around, crouching low and straining to see against the dark wood of the old floor. The angle had to be perfect. The light had to hit it just right . . . Iverson hadn't seen it because he hadn't been looking hard enough.

'No,' she muttered, finding another droplet, then a smear where someone had tried to hastily clean up. *I should have stayed with her.*

The trail led to the hall. The hall led to the bathroom.

Panic fell like stone in Kate's stomach. 'Oh, God, no.'

I should have stayed with her.

She stumbled to her feet and down the hall, all senses magnified, the pounding of her heart like a jackhammer in her ears.

'Don't touch anything!' Kovac yelled, coming behind her.

Kate pulled up short of the bathroom door, which stood ajar, and allowed Kovac to bump it open with his shoulder. He pulled a ballpoint pen from his coat pocket and flipped on the light.

The room was awash in brain-bending hot pink, orange, and silver foil wallpaper from the seventies. The fixtures were older, the two-inch floor tiles long past being white. Dotted with blood. A fleck here. A smeared stain there.

Why didn't I stay with her?

'Come out in the hall, honey,' Quinn said, setting his hands on Kate's shoulders as Kovac moved to pull back the shower curtain.

'No.'

She held her ground, trembling, the breath held tight in her lungs. Quinn slipped an arm around her, ready to pull her out as Kovac drew the shower curtain back.

There was no body. Angie wasn't lying dead in the tub. Still Kate's stomach turned and a wave of cold washed over her. Quinn's arm tightened around her and she sagged back against him.

Blood streaked the tiled wall in pale smudges, like a faded fingerpainting. A thin line of water tinted rusty with diluted blood led from the center of the tub to the drain.

Kate pressed a hand across her mouth, smearing the blood on her palm across her chin.

'Shit,' Kovac breathed, backing away from the tub.

He went to the plastic hamper beside the sink and opened it gingerly with the same pen he had used to turn on the light.

'Hey, Kojak,' Elwood said, sticking his big head in the door. 'What's up?'

'Call the crime scene guys.' He pulled one towel and then another from the hamper, both of them wet and bloody. 'Looks like we've got us a crime scene.'

19

Toni Urskine entered the front room still dressed to impress in slim black slacks and a cardinal-red blazer over a white blouse with an elaborate cravat. The fire of righteous indignation burned bright in her eyes.

'I don't appreciate those police cars out front. Could they at least turn their lights off? This is a neighborhood, Sergeant, and our neighbors are none too gracious about us being here as it is.'

'I'm sorry for the disruption, Ms Urskine,' Kovac said dryly. 'Abductions, murders, they're a big damn pain in the ass, I know.'

A redhead with the thin, brittle look of a crack addict came into the room behind Toni Urskine, followed by Gregg Urskine, who looked like a model for Eddie Bauer in scuffed work boots, jeans, and a flannel shirt open at the throat to reveal a white T-shirt. He put a hand on the redhead's back and urged her forward.

'This is Rita Renner. Rita was here with Angie tonight after I left.'

'I wasn't really with her,' Renner said in a small voice. 'I was watching TV. I saw her go upstairs. She was in the bathroom for a long time – I could hear the water running. We're not supposed to take long showers.'

'And what time did you notice the shower stop running?'

'I didn't. I fell asleep on the couch. I didn't wake up until the news.'

'And in the time you were awake, did you see or hear anyone else in the house – other than Angie?'

'Not after Gregg left.'

'No doors opening, closing? No footsteps? No nothing?'

Renner shook her head, staring at her feet.

'She's already told you she didn't hear or see anything,' Toni Urskine said impatiently.

Kovac ignored her. 'Why didn't you go to the meeting with the others?'

Toni Urskine stiffened. 'Is Rita under suspicion of something, Sergeant?'

'Just curious.'

Nervous, Renner looked from one Urskine to the other, as if seeking some kind of invisible sign for permission to speak. 'I don't like crowds,' she said apologetically. 'And, then, it's hard for me, you know. Because of Fawn.'

'Rita and Fawn Pierce – or, as you call her, victim number two – were good friends.' Toni put a supportive arm around Renner's bony shoulders. 'Not that anyone in your investigation cares.'

Kovac held back a scowl. 'I'm sorry about the oversight. I'll have a detective come by tomorrow for an interview. My priority tonight is Angie DiMarco. We need to find her.'

'You don't think this killer came in here and took her, do you?' Toni asked with sudden alarm.

'Don't be ridiculous,' Gregg said, trying to smile away the edge in his voice. 'No one broke in.'

His wife turned on him with a venomous look. 'I'm not ridiculous. Anyone could have come in here. I've been asking you for months to install new locks and seal off that old storm cellar door.'

Urskine contained his embarrassment to a dull blush. 'The storm cellar door is locked from the inside.'

Kovac looked to Elwood. 'Check it out.'

'I'll show you,' Urskine offered, starting for the door, eager to get away from his wife.

Kate held him up with a question. 'Gregg, did Angie say anything to you before you left for the meeting?'

He gave the nervous laugh, and she thought what an annoying habit that was, on a par with the Rob Marshall bootlicker's grin.

'Angie never has anything to say to me. She avoids me like the plague.'

'What time did you leave for the meeting?' Kovac asked.

Urskine's brows went up above the rims of his glasses. 'Am *I* under suspicion of something?' he asked, pretending to be amused.

Toni glared at Kovac. 'We're being punished, Gregg. Can't you see that? The police don't appreciate having attention called to their shortcomings.'

Kovac gave her the cop eyes. 'I'm just trying to get our time line straight, ma'am. That's all.'

'I left not long after Kate,' Gregg said. 'I must have gotten to the meeting about – what, honey? – eight thirty, quarter to nine?'

'Something like that,' his wife said, pouting. 'You were late.'

'I was working on the furnace.' A muscle flexed in Urskine's jaw, and he turned again to Elwood. 'I'll show you that cellar door now.'

'Are we free to go, Sergeant?' Toni Urskine asked. 'It's been a very long evening.'

'You're telling me,' Kovac muttered, waving them off.

Kate followed them out of the room, but took a right to the front door, leaving Toni Urskine to rant to her captive audience of residents gathered in the living room.

OUR LIVES MATTER TOO. The banner stretched across the front porch of the Phoenix, the oilcloth crackling as the wind picked up.

'It's going to snow,' she said, burying her hands in her coat pockets and hunching her shoulders, not against the weather, but against a cold that was internal. She wandered to the far end of the porch, almost out of reach of the yellow bug light that hadn't been changed at summer's end, away from the traffic that came and went through the front door.

If Toni Urskine was unhappy with two cruisers parked at the curb, she would be livid soon, Kate thought as the crime scene people parked their van on the front lawn. Uniforms had already begun KOD duty – knocking on doors in search of a neighbor who might have seen a strange car, or a man on foot, or a man carrying something, or a man and a young woman together – anything that might give them a time frame or a lead. Despite the late hour, the neighborhood homes were well lit, and the occasional figure could be seen at a window, pulling the drapes back to look out.

'Kate, we don't *know* what happened,' Quinn said.

'Well, I think it's safe to say Angie didn't cut herself shaving her legs.'

A tremor went through her as she saw the blood again in her mind. The blood on the floor, the blood-streaked tile, the bloody towels. She stiffened against the nauseating weakness seeping through her muscles.

Gotta be tough, Kate. Put those feelings in a box. Put the box in its proper cubicle. Keep the walls intact.

'Looks this way to me,' she said around the knot in her throat. 'He slips into the house through the back. Grabs her upstairs. There's a struggle, judging by the bloody handprints in the tub – I'm guessing they're Angie's. Maybe he kills her, or maybe he just starts the job – probably the first. And he lets her bleed out in the tub, otherwise there would have been more mess elsewhere. He wants to make it look like she just left, so he tries to clean up, but he's in a hurry and he does a poor job of it. Still, even the poor job he did would have bought him some time if we hadn't come looking tonight.'

'How did he know she was here?'

'I don't know. She felt like he was watching her. Maybe he was.'

'And how does all this go down with no one hearing, no one seeing anything?'

'He'd already managed to grab, torture, and murder three women without anyone hearing or seeing a thing. Rita Renner was asleep on the first floor with the television going. It's a big house.'

Quinn shook his head. 'It doesn't feel right.'

'Why not? Because you wanted him to be at the meeting?'

He sat back against the railing, shoulders hunched inside his trench coat. 'He could still have been at the meeting. We're only a few blocks away, and the meeting was over half an hour before Kovac and I started over here. My question is, why would he risk it? The girl hadn't given the cops anything worthwhile – not a name, not a decent composite, she pulled nothing from the mug books. Why would he risk this?'

'To show us he can,' Kate said. 'What a nose-thumbing. The night of the meeting intended to draw him out, he slips into a house and takes the only witness to his crimes. A killer like this one, he'll have a hard-on the size of a Louisville Slugger over that. You know it.'

Quinn looked over as one of the evidence guys carried a vacuum cleaner into the house.

'Why *did* you come here tonight?' Kate asked. 'Kovac never said.'

'When you told him about Angie and her john in the park Sunday night, you mentioned the guy was in an SUV. I think there's a good chance Smokey Joe is transporting his bodies to the parks in a truck of some kind. Something resembling a parks department vehicle. Possibly an SUV.'

Kate felt her stomach turn. A chill pebbled her flesh from head to toe. 'Oh, God, John. You don't think he was her customer?'

'It would be right on target. He hates women, particularly the sexually promiscuous variety. He's got a dead one in the back of his truck. He picks up another and takes her to his dumping grounds to have sex with her. This excites him. That excitement reminds him of the thrill and stimulation of the kill. At the same time he's mentally asserting domination and control over the woman he's with. The secret knowledge that he could do to his current partner what he did to his victim but chooses not to gives him a sense of control both over her and over his compulsion to kill.'

'That decision not to kill bolsters his sense of power. And everything is building toward the burning ceremony – the completion of the cycle,' Kate finished.

'Looks good on paper.'

'Angie said the guy shoved her out of his truck and she watched him drive away. From where he left her, he would have had to have doubled around to that back lot in a hurry in order for her to have seen him burning that body.'

Quinn moved his shoulders. 'It's still just a theory.'

A theory from a man who knew more about sexually sadistic killers than perhaps anyone else in the country. Kate stared out into the darkness, watching the cloud of her breath float away.

'But if it was the same guy, why wouldn't she have told me? And why wouldn't she give us a better composite? She saw this john up close and personal.'

'Those are questions only she can answer.'

'And she can't answer them now,' Kate said quietly. 'It was so hard for her to tell me about it this afternoon. From the beginning of this mess, she'd talk so tough, give so much attitude, but when she finally told me about this john, it was like she was ashamed. She kept saying that she didn't like doing it, that she was so sorry. And she cried and cried.'

Her own emotions threatened to rise up at the memory, just as they had that afternoon with Angie.

'You like this girl,' Quinn declared.

She huffed a breath. 'What's to like? She's a lying, thieving, foul-mouthed prostitute.'

'And she needs you,' he said simply.

'Yeah, well, look what that got her.'

'This isn't your fault, Kate.'

'I should have stayed with her.'

'You couldn't have known this would happen.'

'She was at a vulnerable point,' she reasoned. 'I should have stayed with her if for no other reason than to get something out of her. But I didn't because –'

She choked herself off, not wanting to admit it. Not here. Not to Quinn. He knew her too well – or once had. He knew every raw spot in her soul. He'd held her more times than she could count when she'd been so racked with the pain and guilt of Emily's death that the anguish was beyond sound. He had given her comfort and offered his strength and soothed her with his touch. She couldn't let him do that now, and she didn't want to find out that maybe he wouldn't try.

'She's not Emily, Kate.'

Kate sucked in a breath as if he'd slapped her and turned sharply to glare at him. 'I'm well aware of that. My daughter is dead.'

'And you still blame yourself. After all this time.'

'As far as I know, there's no statute of limitations on guilt.'

'It wasn't your fault. And neither is this.'

'Emily was my daughter, my responsibility. Angie is my client, my responsibility,' she argued stubbornly.

'How many of your clients do you take home with you?' Quinn demanded, moving away from the railing, closer to her.

'None, but –'

'How many of your clients do you stay with around the clock?'

'None, but –'

'Then there's no reason for you to think you should have been with her.'

'She needed me and I wasn't here.'

'But anytime you get a chance to punish yourself, by God, you're right there,' Quinn said, old anger of his own rising up sharp and pure. He could remember too well the frustration of trying to separate Kate from her sense of culpability in Emily's death. He could remember too well the need to shake her and hold her close at once, because that was exactly what he was feeling now.

She stood before him, fierce and angry and defensive. And beautiful. And vulnerable. He wanted to protect her from the pain she would inflict on herself. And she would fight him tooth and nail every step of the way.

'I'm taking responsibility – as if you don't know anything about that,' she said bitterly, toe to toe with him. 'The Mighty Quinn, curing the cancer of modern society. Singlehandedly rooting out all evil. You carry the world around on your shoulders as if you were sole guardian, and you have the gall to stand there and criticize me? My God, you're amazing!'

Shaking her head, she started past him for the front steps.

'Where are you going?' He reached for her as if to touch her. She stepped aside, giving him a look that could have frozen water at fifty paces.

'I'm going to do something. I'm not sitting here biting my fingernails all night. On the slim chance Angie left here under her own power, the least I can do is help look for her.'

Hands in her coat pockets, digging for her keys, she trotted down the steps and headed for her truck. Quinn glanced at the front door of the Phoenix. He was of no use here. And the sight of Kate walking away triggered his panic. Foolish thought. She didn't want him there, didn't want him, period. She was sure as hell better off without him. If he'd been a stronger man, he would have let it go at that.

But he wasn't feeling strong, and he wouldn't be here more than a few days, a week. Where was the harm in stealing a little time with her? Just to be near her. A fresh memory to put away with the old ones, to take out when the solace of his life threatened to swallow him whole.

'Kate!' he called, jogging after her. 'Wait. I'm going with you.'

She arched a brow imperiously. 'Did I invite you?'

'Two pairs of eyes looking are better than one,' he argued.

Kate told herself to say no. She didn't need him poking at old wounds. She did a mean enough job of that herself. Then she thought of the way he'd put his arms around her upstairs, ready to pull her away from the horror they hadn't found on the other side of that shower curtain, ready to hold her up if she needed it, giving her his own strength to lean against. She thought of how easily she'd let him do that, and knew she should say no.

He watched her, the dark eyes intent, the lines of his face serious, then he dredged up half a charming smile from somewhere, and she felt something clutch in her chest exactly as it had all those years before. 'I promise not to be a jerk. And I'll let you drive.'

She sighed and turned toward the 4Runner, punching the button on the keyless remote. 'Well, I believe half of that.'

They made the rounds of the places on Lake Street where the nocturnal creatures passed the hours between dusk and dawn. Pool halls, bars, and all-night diners. A homeless shelter full of women with children. A Laundromat where a wino with a thick halo of filthy gray hair sat in one of the plastic bucket chairs and stared out the windows until the slightly more fortunate night clerk chased him back onto the street.

No one had seen Angie. Half of them barely glanced at the photograph. Kate refused to think about the lack of results. She hadn't expected results, she had expected to pass time. She couldn't decide which had to be more like penance: spending the night pounding the pavement in this rotten part of town or sitting home drinking gin until she couldn't see the bloodstains in her head anymore.

'I need a drink,' she said as they walked into a place called Eight Ball's. The interior was obscured by a fog bank of cigarette smoke. The sharp clack of billiard balls colliding was underscored by Jonny Lang's blues wailing from the juke – *Lie to Me*.

'You missed last call a while ago, gorgeous,' the bartender said. He was the size of a minivan with a shaved head and a woolly Fu-Manchu mustache. 'Name's Tiny Marvin. How 'bout something strong and black like me?'

Quinn flashed his ID and a no-nonsense G-man look.

'Damnation. It's Scully and Mulder,' Tiny Marvin said, unimpressed, as he pulled a coffeepot off its warmer.

Kate planted her butt on a barstool. 'Coffee's fine, thanks.'

There were maybe a dozen serious players at the pool tables. A pair of hookers served as ornamentation, looking bored and impatient at the downtime. One caught an eyeful of Quinn and nudged the other, but neither made a move to get closer.

Tiny Marvin squinted at Quinn. 'Hey, man, didn't I see you on TV? For real?'

'We're looking for a girl,' Quinn said.

Kate slid the Polaroid across the bar, expecting Marvin to give it as little attention as every other bartender had. He picked it up with fingers as short and thick as Vienna sausages and squinted harder.

'Yeah, she been in here.'

Kate sat up straighter. 'Tonight?'

'Naw, Sunday night, around ten thirty, eleven. Came in to warm up, she said. Jailbait. I chased her skinny white ass outta here. I mean, consenting adults is one thing, man – you know what I mean? That child's trouble. I don't want no part of that shit.'

'Did she leave with anybody?' Quinn asked.

'Not from here she didn't. She went back on the street and walked up and down for a while. Then I start feeling bad – like, what if she was my niece or something, and I found out some hard-ass threw her out on the street? Man, I'd bust his hard ass. So I go to tell her she can have a cup of coffee if she wants, but she's got a ride and they're going down the road.'

'What kind of car?' Kate asked.

'Some kind of truck.'

Her heart started to beat a little harder, and she looked to Quinn, but his attention was still on Tiny Marvin.

'Don't suppose you got the plates?'

'Hey, man, I ain't no neighborhood watch commander.'

'It didn't bother you the guy was breaking the law,' Kate said.

Tiny Marvin frowned at her. 'Look, I take care of what goes on in here, Scully. Rest of the world ain't my problem. The girl was doing what hookers do. Wasn't none of my business.'

'And if she'd been your niece?'

Quinn gave her a warning look and spoke again to the bartender. 'Did you see the driver?'

'Didn't look. I just thought, man, what about his sorry ass, picking up a kid like that. The world's a cold, sick place – you know what I'm saying?'

'Yeah,' Kate muttered, picking up the snapshot of Angie from the bar, looking at the pretty, exotic face, the frowning mouth, the angry eyes that had seen too much. 'I know exactly what you're saying.'

She put the photo back in her purse, tossed a buck on the bar for the coffee she hadn't touched, and walked out. The snow had started in flurries, the clouds sending down a handful at a time on gusts of cold wind. The street was deserted, the sidewalks empty, the dingy storefronts dark except for the bail-bonds place across the street.

She leaned back against the building and wished the wind would blow away the feelings that were stacking up inside her. They'd about reached the back of her throat and she couldn't even begin to swallow them down.

She knew too much about the world to let its injustices and cruelties get to her too easily. Of course a bartender in a pool hall on Lake Street wouldn't be overly concerned about the life of a hooker, young or not. He saw it every day and never looked too closely. He had his own life to worry about.

It hit Kate hard only because she knew the next chapter to the story. The ride that had taken Angie DiMarco away from Eight Ball's had taken her to a crime scene, and the driver of that nondescript truck might have been a killer. Even if he'd been just another pathetic loser willing to pay for sex, he'd delivered her to a rendezvous with a fate that may just have gotten her killed.

Quinn came out of the pool hall, eyes narrowed against the cold and wind as he flipped up the collar of his trench coat.

'Kovac says: "Good police work, Red." If you ever want to give up the soft life, he'll put a word in for you.'

'Yeah? Well, I've always wanted to work nights, weekends, and holidays up to my ass in dead bodies. Now's my big chance.'

'He's sending a team out to talk to the bartender and whoever else they can find. If they can come up with somebody who remembers more about the vehicle, or saw the driver that night, they've got something to run with.'

Kate pulled her coat closed up around her throat and stared across the empty street at the bail-bonds place. A red neon light glowed through the barred window: CHECKS CASHED HERE.

'Timing is everything,' she said. 'If Angie hadn't been standing on this street at the exact moment that truck pulled up, I'd be home in bed, and you'd be digging in someone else's boneyard.'

She laughed at herself and shook her head, the wind catching a rope of hair and whipping it across her face. 'As long as I've been around, I still shake my fist at chance. How stupid is that?'

'You always took the prize for stubborn.' Quinn reached out automatically to brush her hair back, his fingertips grazing her cheek. 'A cynic is a disappointed idealist, you know.'

'Is that what happened to you?' she tossed back.

'I never saw life as ideal.'

She knew that, of course. She knew about his life, about the abusive alcoholic father, and the grim years growing up in working-class Cincinnati. She was one of the few people he had allowed to see in that window.

'But that never saved you from disappointment,' she said quietly.

'The only thing that can save you from disappointment is hopelessness. But if you don't have hope, then there's no point in living.'

'And what's the difference between hope and desperation?' she asked, thinking of Angie, wondering if she dared hope.

'Time.'

Which might have already run out for Angie DiMarco, and which had run out for the two of them years earlier. Kate felt disappointment sink down through her. She wanted to lay her head against Quinn's shoulder and feel his arms slip around her. Instead, she pushed away from the wall and started for the 4Runner parked down by the Laundromat. The homeless guy was looking in her back window as if considering it for his night's accommodations.

'I'll drop you off at your hotel,' she said to Quinn.

'No. I'll ride home with you and call a cab. Tough as you are, I don't want you going home alone, Kate. It's not smart. Not tonight.'

If she'd been feeling stronger, she might have argued just on principle, but she wasn't feeling strong, and the memory of phantom eyes watching her as she'd let herself in her back door just hours before was still too fresh.

'All right.' She hit the remote lock. The alarm system on the truck beeped loudly, sending the homeless guy scuttling back into the doorwell of the Suds-O-Rama. 'But don't try anything funny, or I'll sic my cat on you.'

20

'Anything on the house-to-house yet?' Kovac asked, lighting a cigarette.

Tippen hunched his bony shoulders. 'A lot of people pissed off about having cops pounding on their doors in the middle of the night.'

They stood on the front porch of the Phoenix, huddled under a jaundice-yellow bug light. The B of I van was still on the yard. The yard had been cordoned off to create a media-free zone.

The press had swooped in like a flock of vultures, suspiciously in sync. Kovac squinted through the smoke and the falling snow, staring out at the end of the sidewalk, where Toni Urskine was being interviewed in the eerie glow of portable lights.

'How much you wanna bet I pull the phone records for this dump tonight I find calls to WCCO, KSTP, and KARE?' he muttered.

'Raking publicity off crime and tragedy,' Elwood said, pushing his goofy-looking felt hat down on his head. 'It's the American way. All this media exposure, you can bet the donations will come rolling in.'

'She even hints what's going on here is connected to our witness, I can just bend over and grab my ankles,' Kovac groused. 'The brass pricks will be lining up behind me.'

'Better make nice with her, Sam,' Liska suggested, bouncing up and down on the balls of her feet to keep warm. 'Or I could loan you a tube of K-Y Jelly.'

'Jeez, Tinks.' Distaste rippled across Kovac's face. He turned to Elwood. 'What've we got in the basement? What's the story with that cellar door?'

'Door's locked from the inside. We've got what looks like some bloodstains on the floor. Not a lot. Urskine says it's nothing, that he cut himself working on the furnace a few nights ago.'

Kovac made a growling sound low in his throat and looked to Liska again. 'What about your mutt, Vanlees?'

'Can't find him. I wanted to follow him from the meeting, but between the crowd and the traffic getting out there, I lost him.'

'He's not working tonight? He came to the meeting in his uniform.'

'I'll bet he sleeps in that uniform,' she said. 'Ever ready to save the public from ticket scalpers and unruly basketball fans. He's got a cheap apartment over on Lyndale, but he's not in it. I finally talked to his soon-to-be ex-wife. She tells me he's house-sitting for someone. She doesn't know who and couldn't give a shit.'

'Hey, he wants to be a cop, he might as well start out with one divorce under his belt,' Tippen said.

'She give any indication he's into anything kinky?' Kovac asked.

'Oh, you'll love this,' she said, eyes brightening. 'I asked her about that misdemeanor trespass conviction eighteen months ago. Quinn was right. Ol' Gil had the hots for some woman his wife works with. He got caught trying to sneak a peek at her in her panties.'

'And he's still working security?' Kovac said.

'He kept it quiet, pleaded down, no one paid attention. He claimed it was all a big misunderstanding anyway.'

'Yeah,' Tippen sneered. ' "It was all a big mistake, your honor. I was just driving along, minding my own business, when I was struck by an uncontrollable urge to play spank the monkey." '

'I like this guy, Sam,' Liska said. 'His wife had nothing but disdain for him. She hinted their sex life was nonexistent when they were together. If that's true, he could be an even better fit to Quinn's profile. A lot of these guys are sexually inadequate with their partners.'

'Is that the voice of experience?' Tippen dug.

'Well, I haven't been sleeping with you, so I guess not.'

'Fuck you, Tinker Bell.'

'What part of no don't you understand?'

'I'll put a car outside his apartment,' Kovac said. 'I want him downtown ASAP. See if you can't track down this house he's sitting. Somebody's gotta know where he is. Call his boss, call the wife again. Tonight. Get the names of his friends. Call them.'

'I'll help with that,' Moss said.

'Annoy everybody who knows him,' Kovac said. 'That'll get back to him and rattle him. Did you find out what he's driving?'

'A maroon GMC Jimmy.'

Kovac felt like someone had punched him in the diaphragm. 'A bartender on Lake Street spotted our witness Sunday night getting into a dark-colored truck or SUV. This was the john she did in the park before she came across victim number three.'

'Did she name this john?' Adler asked.

'No.'

'Would Vanlees have had any way of knowing the girl was staying here?' Moss asked.

Liska shook her head. 'I don't see how, unless he somehow managed to tail her here from downtown. Seems unlikely.'

'Who all *did* know the witness was here?' Adler asked.

'Us, Sabin, the vic/wit people, the brass cupcake out there –' Kovac hooked a thumb in Toni Urskine's direction '– and the husband. The mayor, Bondurant's people –'

'And a partridge in a pear tree,' Elwood finished.

'One of the other victims had a connection to this place,' Moss pointed out.

'And when she turned up croaked back when, we interviewed everybody at the house, checked records, alibis, known associates, yadda, yadda, yadda,' Kovac said. 'I remember the body was found on a Friday. She'd been out of here six months or more. I make it over here on Sunday to see if she was still tight with anyone. The Urskines are gone to some cabin up north, so I can't talk to them, right? Monday morning, eight o'clock, Toni Urskine's on the horn to the lieutenant, demanding he ream me a new one because I hadn't called her yet.'

'Now we get to do it all again for a fresh batch of hookers,' Tippen groaned. 'Like we need more fucking paperwork to do.'

'Hey, that's why they pay you slave wages and treat you like dirt,' Kovac said.

'Here I thought it was something personal.'

'Okay. Who wants to hit Lake Street?' Kovac asked. 'See if you can find anyone who might have seen the DiMarco girl get in that truck Sunday night? If you can get a plate number, I'll kiss you full on the mouth.'

'That ain't no incentive, Kojak,' Adler said.

'Let Tippen do it,' Liska said. 'He might find a girlfriend.'

'Send Charm,' Tippen said. 'The hookers will pay *him*.'

'The two of you,' Kovac said, pointing to Yurek and Tippen both. 'You're the perfect pair.'

'God's Gift and the Mercy Fuck,' Liska snickered.

Tippen jerked the end of the scarf around her throat. 'You'll get it one of these days, Liska.'

'Not if I stay more than three inches away from you.'

'Hit the bricks,' Kovac ordered. 'Time's awastin' and this case is starting to cook. No pun intended. Let's get this dirtbag before he lights someone else's fire.'

'That's a hell of a cat,' Quinn remarked, regarding Thor as Thor regarded him from the front hall table. 'But I think I could take him.'

The cat had to be twenty pounds. Fantastic tufts of hair sprouted from his ears. His whiskers looked a foot long. He tucked his chin back into a great ruff of fur and made a sound like 'hmmm' deep in his throat. He raised his hind leg up behind his ear in a yoga move and licked his butt.

Quinn made a face. 'Guess I know what he thinks of me.'

'Don't take it personally,' Kate said. 'Thor is above the petty considerations of mere humans.'

She hung her coat in the hall closet and nearly reached for a second empty hanger, but stopped herself.

'Thanks for your help tonight,' she said, closing the door and leaning back against it. 'I was less than gracious about the offer, but I know it's not your job to investigate.'

'Or yours.'

'True, but I needed to do something proactive. You know I can't bear to just sit back and let things happen. What about you? It wasn't your job to go to the Phoenix with Kovac.'

'This case has been anything but normal.'

'Because of Peter Bondurant. I know.' She stroked a hand over Thor. The cat gave her a look of affront, hopped down, and trotted away, belly hanging low to the ground.

'Money changes all the rules,' Kate said. 'There's not a politician in the Cities who wouldn't bend over backward to kiss Peter Bondurant's ass, then tell him it smells like a rose. Because he's got money and they want him to keep it here. Because of that his attorney can sit in on meetings with Sabin, and he can have the ear of the mayor, and of the director of the FBI, no less. I'll bet Lila White's parents couldn't get past Director Brewster's secretary. If it would even occur to them to try.'

'Now you're sounding like Toni Urskine, saying there's no equal justice under the law.'

'It's a lovely ideal we both know doesn't hold water in the real world. Money can and does buy justice – and injustice – every day.'

'Still, I guess I can't blame Bondurant. What parent wouldn't do everything in their power to get their child back?' she said, her expression somber. 'I would have made a deal with the devil himself when Em got sick. In fact, I believe I tried,' she confessed, forcing a lopsided smile. 'No takers. Shook my faith in evil.'

Her pain was still a palpable thing, and Quinn wanted to pull her into his arms and invite her to divide it between the two of them, like old times.

'Bondurant's money didn't stop his daughter's death either,' he said. 'If that body is Jillian's. He's convinced it is.'

'Why would he want to believe that?' Kate asked, bewildered by the notion. She had been so violently resistant to the news of Emily's death that even after a nurse had taken her into the room to see her daughter's body, to touch the cold little hand, to feel for herself there was no pulse, no breath, she had insisted it wasn't true.

'What an odd man,' she said. 'I was surprised to see him at the meeting tonight. He's been keeping such a low profile.'

The offhand remark hit Quinn like an invisible fist. 'You saw Bondurant at the meeting? Are you sure?'

'Sure looked like him to me,' Kate said. 'I saw him on my way out. I thought it was strange he wasn't with his camp, but it was clear he didn't want any attention. He was dressed down like one of the common folk in a parka and a crumpled-looking hat, trying to look anonymous, slipping out the back with the rest of the crowd.'

Quinn frowned. 'I can't get a handle on him. I'd say he's being uncooperative, but he's the one who brought me in, then he turns around and refuses to answer questions. He's one contradiction after another.'

'Christ, I can't believe I didn't see him there.'

'You weren't looking for him,' Kate said reasonably. 'You were looking for a killer.'

And did I miss him too? Quinn wondered, rubbing harder at the sudden searing pain in his gut. What else had he missed? Some subtle sign: a look, a squint, the hint of a smile. And if he'd seen it, would Angie DiMarco be in bed at the Phoenix right now? Logically, he thought no. But catching a killer like this one required something more than logic. It required instinct, and it seemed that he was feeling around in the dark through a blanket for his these days.

'I can't shake the feeling that his daughter is the key to this whole thing,' he said. 'If she's the third vic. Smokey Joe deviated from the pattern with that one. Why? With the first two, he burned the bodies but didn't try to make them unrecognizable in any other way. With number three he obliterates her fingertips and the soles of her feet. He takes her head. He makes it as difficult as possible to identify her.'

'But he left her driver's license.'

'Why do both?'

'Maybe the first as part of the torture,' Kate suggested. 'As part of the depersonalization. He reduced her to no one. He doesn't care if we know who she is after she's dead, so he leaves the DL as if to say "Hey, look who I killed." But maybe he wanted this victim to feel like nobody in those last few moments of her life, let her die thinking no one would be able to identify her or take care of her body or mourn her.'

'Maybe,' Quinn said. 'And maybe this extreme depersonalization is the deviation in his pattern because he knew Jillian. If, for instance, we can develop this security guard who lived at Jillian's town house complex, we might speculate he killed the two prostitutes for practice, projecting his feelings for Jillian onto them. But that didn't satisfy his need, so he does Jillian, goes overboard, keeps her head because he wants to own her.

'Or maybe the killer takes the head because that body *isn't* Jillian Bondurant and he wants us to believe it is. But that's definitely her DL, and if the body isn't her, then how'd Smokey Joe get it?' he asked. 'We know this is no kidnapping. It's been days with no call, no ransom demand – at least that we know of. Bondurant won't allow a tap on his phone – another odd bit of behavior on his part.'

'And if Jillian is alive,' Kate said, 'then where is she and how is she tied to all this?'

'I don't know. And there doesn't seem to be anyone who knew Jillian willing or able to tell us. This case gives me a bad feeling, Kate.'

'The kind you should see a doctor for?' she asked with a pointed look to the hand he was rubbing against his stomach. 'You keep doing that.'

He killed the gesture. 'It's nothing.'

Kate shook her head. 'You've probably got a hole in your stomach lining big enough to drive a Buick through. But God forbid you admit it. Think what that would do to the Quinn mystique. It would bring you down to the level of Superman with his weakness for kryptonite. How embarrassing.'

She wanted to ask if he had talked to anyone in Psych Services, but she knew it would be a waste of breath. Every other agent in Investigative Support could line up at the shrink's door and no one would bat an eye. Stress disorders were the norm in the unit. Everyone understood. They saw too much, got too deep into the heads of victims and killers in case after horrific case. They saw the worst the world had to offer every day, and made life-and-death decisions based on an inexact science: their own knowledge of human behavior. But John Quinn would never admit to bending beneath the strain of that. Vulnerability did not become a legend well.

'Bullets don't really bounce off you, John,' she said quietly.

He smiled as if she had amused him in some small, endearing way, but he wouldn't meet her eyes. 'It's nothing.'

'Fine.' If he wasn't taking care of himself, that was his problem – or the problem of some faceless woman back in Virginia, not hers. 'I'm having that drink now. You want something before you go? Maalox? Mylanta? A roll of Tums to chew on for the cab ride?'

She headed for the kitchen, kicking herself for giving him the opportunity to linger, then rationalized it was payback. She owed him for tonight. Besides, he looked like he could do with a drink.

Of course, she knew he wouldn't allow himself one. He was too conscious of the alcoholism that ran rampant both in his family and in his profession. As much as he may have needed to douse the frustration and the tension the job induced, the risk of drowning was too high.

'Great house,' he said, following her to the kitchen.

'I bought it from my parents when they lost their minds and moved to Las Vegas.'

'So you really did come home.'

From the shattered mess that had been her life in Virginia to a house with warm memories and a sense of security. The house would have substituted its comfort for the comfort of her family – whom he doubted she had ever told the whole story. When everything had broken in Quantico, she'd been embarrassed and ashamed. It still hurt him to think of it. What they'd had together had been a connection deeper than any other he'd ever known, but not deep enough or strong enough to survive the stress of discovery and disapproval and Kate's predisposition to guilt.

He watched her now as she moved around the kitchen, getting a cup from the cupboard and a box of herbal teabags, her long hair falling down her back in a wave of red-gold. He wanted to stroke a hand over it, rest that hand at the small of her back.

He had always seen her femininity, her vulnerability. He doubted many people looked at Kate and thought she might need protecting. Her strength and tenacity were what others noted. But just behind that wall was a woman not always so certain as she seemed.

'How are you, Kate?'

'Hmm? What?' She turned toward him from the microwave, her brow knit in confusion. 'I'm tired. I'm upset. I've lost a witness –'

Stepping close, Quinn put a finger to her lips. 'I don't mean with the case. It's been five years. How are you, really?'

Kate's heart thumped hard against her sternum. Answers log-jammed in her throat. Five years. The first was remembered as a pain so sharp, it stole her breath. The second had been like trying to relearn how to walk and talk after a stroke. Then came the third and the fourth and another after that. In that time she'd built a career, made a home for herself, done some traveling, settled into a nice, safe rut. But the answers that rushed to mind were other words.

How are you? Empty. Alone. Walled off.

'Let's not play that game,' she said softly. 'If you'd really wanted to know, it wouldn't have taken you five years to ask.'

She heard the regret in those words and wished them back. What was the point now, when all they would have was a few days. Better to pretend there'd been no fire at all than to poke at the ash and stir up the dust of memories. The timer went off on the microwave, and she turned her back to him and busied herself making a cup of tea.

'You told me that was what you wanted,' he said. 'You wanted out. You wanted a clean break. You wanted to leave, to start over. What was I supposed to do, Kate?'

Ask me not to go. Go with me. The answers were right there, as fresh as yesterday and just as futile. By the time she'd left Virginia, the anger and the pain had taken them past the point of his asking her not to go. And she knew without having to ask that he would never have left Investigative Support to go with her. The job was who John Quinn was. He was bound to it in a way he would never be bound to a woman. And, God, how it still hurt to think that.

'What were you supposed to do? Nothing,' she whispered. 'You did it well.'

Quinn moved in close behind her, wanting to touch her, as if that might magically erase the time and the trouble that had passed between them. He wanted to tell her the phone worked both ways, but he knew she would never have backed away from her pride or the insecurity it covered. A part of him had been relieved that she had never called, because he would then have had to face himself in life's big mirror and finally answer the question of whether or not there was enough left in him to build a lasting relationship. His fear of the answer had kept him running from that question for a long, long time.

And now he stood here, an inch away from the better part of his past, knowing he should let it lie. If he hadn't had enough to give a relationship five years ago, he sure as hell didn't have any more now.

He raised a hand to touch her hair, his memory of its texture meeting the silk of reality. He let his hand rest on her shoulder, his thumb finding the familiar knot of tension there.

'Do you regret it, Kate? Not the way it ended, but *us*.'

Kate squeezed her eyes shut. She had a truckload of regret she had to move out of her way every day in order to get on with her life. But she had never been able to find it in her to regret turning to him. She regretted she had wished for more. She regretted he hadn't had more to give. But she couldn't think of a single touch, a single kiss, a single night in his arms, and regret a second of it. He had given her love and understanding, passion and compassion, tenderness and comfort when she had needed so badly, when she had hurt so much, when she had felt so alone. How could she regret that?

'No,' she said, turning and holding the steaming mug of tea between them. 'Here. It's good for what ails you.'

He took the cup and set it aside.

'I don't regret us,' he said. 'There were times when I thought I should, but I didn't, and I don't.'

His fingertips touched her cheek and slid back into her hair, and he leaned down and touched his mouth to hers. Need, sharp and bitter and sweet, instantly sprang up inside her. Her lips moved against his out of memory and longing. A perfect fit. The perfect balance of pressure and passion. Their tongues tangled, seeking, searching, tasting, touching, deepening the kiss and the emotions it evoked. Her heart beat hard against the wall of her chest and his. She was instantly aware of a tenderness in her breasts, a longing for the touch of his hand, his mouth, a need for a connection beyond this simple act. His arms tightened around her. She could feel him hard against her belly as he pressed against her.

He would be here a matter of days, her fading logic reminded her. He had come for a case, not because he needed her or missed her or wanted to resolve what they had walked away from. All of that was incidental.

'No,' she said softly as he raised his head. 'I don't regret it. But that doesn't mean I'll go through it again, John. I'm not here for your convenience.'

'You think that's what I expect?' he asked, hurt. 'You think I expect you to go to bed with me because you're handy and you know what I like? I thought you knew me better than that, Kate.' His voice dropped low and rough, and skimmed across her heart like a callused hand. 'My God, you're the only person who ever knew me.'

'Well, at least I thought I did,' Kate murmured. 'It seemed at the end there we didn't know each other very well at all.'

He sighed and stepped back.

'Let's just call ourselves old friends and leave it at that, huh?' she said around the knot in her throat. 'You didn't come here for me, John. You would have done that years ago if it was what you wanted. I'll go call you that cab.'

21

The house was dark. The neighborhood was dark. People living on Lake of the Isles kept civilized hours. In Kovac's neighborhood there was always a light on somewhere – people coming in late, going to work early, watching infomercials.

Kovac parked on the street at the edge of Bondurant's property and made a complete circuit of the place on foot through the fresh snow. Fresh, *wet* snow. Heavy and sticky, it clung to his pant legs and worked down into his shoes, but he ignored it, his attention on the mansion that seemed to loom even larger in the dark than in the light. Security lights marked entrances on the back side. There were no lights visible in the house. If Peter Bondurant was watching TV, learning how to get buns of steel, he was in some windowless room in the heart of his home.

Some home. It looked like something out of medieval England, like someplace that would have a torture chamber in the basement. For all he knew, it *did* have.

Christ, wouldn't that be just his luck? He'd have to be the one to tell the world billionaire Peter Big Deal Bondurant was a homicidal lunatic. The mayor would have his throat cut and dispose of his body in the footings of the new jail. The bigwigs wanted a killer caught, all right. And this killer would preferably be a bug-eyed, drooling ex-con from Wisconsin.

Circling back around to his car, he kicked the snow off his legs and feet, slid in behind the wheel, and started the engine, setting the anemic heater to full blast. The bones in his feet and ankles and shins had absorbed the cold into their marrow, and it was now making its way up his legs like mercury in a thermometer.

He dug his cell phone out from under a pile of junk on the seat and dialed Bondurant's home number. Quinn had called to tell him Kate had spotted Bondurant in the back at the meeting, hiding out among the common folk. The guy was a twitch. He was holding out on them about that last night with Jillian, and God knew what else.

The phone rang.

It burned his ass that Bondurant got special treatment, was privy to information, didn't have to come downtown to make a statement. It was wrong. They should have been able to rattle his cage same as anyone else's.

On the fifth ring the answering machine picked up and an emotionless voice gave instructions. Kovac left his name and number, and a request for a return call.

He put the car in gear, rolled up to the intercom panel at the security gate, and hit the buzzer. No one responded. He sat there for another five minutes, leaning on the buzzer again and again, well schooled in how to be an asshole to get someone's attention. No one ever responded.

A prowl car from a private security company came by and a weightlifter in a spiffy uniform asked to see his ID. Then he was alone again, left to stare up at Peter Bondurant's house and wonder what secrets hid inside.

Some people didn't answer their phones when they rang after midnight. Not the parents of missing children. Maybe Peter Bondurant never answered his gate buzzer, and was, even at that moment, cowering in his bed, waiting for a mob of the desperate poor to burst in and loot his house. But he hadn't been the one to call in the security car. Routine driveby, the weightlifter had said.

Kovac stared at the house and let seventeen years of experience tell him there was no one in. Peter Bondurant was not at home in the dead of this night when their witness had gone missing. Peter Bondurant, who demanded answers but refused to give any. Peter Bondurant, who had fought with his daughter the night she disappeared, then lied about it. Peter Bondurant, who had the power to crush a cop's career like an empty beer can.

I'm probably a moron for sitting here, he thought. Vanlees was their hot ticket. Vanlees looked to fit Quinn's profile. He had a history. He'd known Jillian, had access to her town house. He even drove the right kind of vehicle.

But there was still something off about Peter Bondurant. He could feel it like hives just under his skin, and come hell or high water, he was going to find out what.

He sighed, shifted his weight to a new uncomfortable position, and settled in, lighting a cigarette. What the hell did he need with a pension anyway?

The corpses floated above him like logs. Naked, rotting bodies. Torn, hacked apart, riddled with holes. Decomposing flesh shredded away from the wounds. Fish food. Eels swam in and out of the bodies through the gaping holes.

Quinn looked up at the bodies from below, trying to identify each one by name in the dim blue watery light. He was out of oxygen. His lungs were burning. But he couldn't go to the surface until he had identified every body and named the killer that went with each.

The bodies bobbed and shifted position. Decaying limbs fell away from torsos and sank toward him. Below him, a bed of lush green weeds caught at his feet like the tentacles of a squid.

He needed to think hard. Names. Dates. Facts. But he couldn't remember all the names. He didn't know all the killers. Random facts raced through his head. The bodies seemed to be multiplying, kept drifting and bobbing. He was running out of air.

He couldn't breathe, couldn't think.

He struck out with his arms, trying to grab hold of anything that might help pull him up. But the hands he caught hold of were cold and dead, and held him under. The bodies and his responsibility to them held him under. He had to think hard. He could solve the puzzles if only the pieces would stop moving, if only his thoughts would stop racing, if only he could breathe.

The bodies shifted again above him, and he could see Kate's face on the other side of the surface, looking down at him. Then the bodies shifted again and she was gone.

Just as it felt as if his lungs were starting to bleed, he gave one last hard kick and broke the surface of the water and the dream, gasping for air, coming up off the bed. Sweat drenched his body, ran off the end of his nose and down the valley of his spine.

He staggered away from the bed, his legs weak beneath him, and fell into the chair by the writing desk, shaking now as the air chilled him. Naked, shaking, sweating, sick, the taste of bile and blood bitter in his mouth.

He sat doubled over the wastebasket, his focus not entirely on the writhing fire in his belly. As ever, there was the sound of that inner voice that always found him wanting, and never hesitated to kick him when he was down. It told him he didn't have time for this shit. He had cases to work, people depending on him; if he lost his focus and fucked up, people could die. If he fucked up bad enough, if anyone found out what a mess his head was, that he'd lost his nerve and his edge, he'd be out of a job. And if he didn't have the job, he didn't have anything, because it wasn't just what he did, it was all he was, all he had.

The dream was nothing new, nothing to shake over, nothing to waste his energy on. He had any number of variations on that one. They were all stupidly simple to interpret, and he always felt vaguely embarrassed for having them at all. He didn't have time for it.

He could hear exactly what Kate would have to say about that. She would give him the sharp side of her tongue and another lecture on Superman, then try to make him drink herbal tea. She would try to mask her concern and her maternal instincts with the wise-ass sarcasm that seemed so much safer and more familiar and more in character with the image others had of her. She would pretend he didn't know her better.

And then she'd call him a cab and shove him out of her house.

'Let's just call ourselves old friends and leave it at that, huh? You didn't

come here for me, John. You would have done that years ago if it was what you wanted.'

That was what she thought, that he hadn't come because he didn't want her. Maybe that was what she wanted to think. She was the one who had walked away. It justified her action to believe there'd been no reason to stay.

Still feeling weak, he went to the window that looked out on a wedge of downtown Minneapolis and an empty street filling with snow.

What he wanted. He wasn't sure what that even was anymore. He didn't allow himself to want outside the scope of the job. A lead, a piece of evidence, a fresh insight to help pry open a killer's head. He could want those things. But what was the point in wanting what couldn't be had?

The point was whether or not to allow himself hope.

'The only thing that can save you from disappointment is hopelessness. But if you don't have hope, then there's no point in living.'

His own words. His own voice. His own wisdom. Coming right back around to bite him in the ass.

He didn't ask the point of his life. He lived to work and he worked to live. He was as simple and pathetic as that. That was the Quinn machine of perpetual function. The trouble was he could feel the wheels coming loose. What would happen when one came off altogether?

Closing his eyes, he saw the corpses again, and felt the panic wash down through him, a cold, internal acid rain. He could hear his unit chief demanding answers, explanations, prodding for results. *'The director chewed my tail for half an hour. Bondurant isn't the guy to piss off, John. What the hell's wrong with you?'*

Tears burned his eyes as the answer called up from the hollow in the center of his chest: *I've lost it.* His edge, his nerve, his instincts. He felt it all torn asunder and scattered to too many parts of the country. He didn't have the time to go hunting for the pieces. He could only pretend he was intact and hope not too many people caught on.

'Are you getting anywhere with this? Have they developed a suspect? You know what they're looking for, don't you? It's pretty straightforward, isn't it?'

Sure it was. If you looked at the murders of two prostitutes and ignored the fact that Peter Bondurant's daughter may or may not have been the third victim. If you pretended Peter Bondurant's behavior was normal. If you didn't have a hundred unanswered questions about the enigma that was Jillian Bondurant. If this was simply about the murder of prostitues, he could have pulled a profile out of a textbook and never left Quantico.

But if this were simply about the murders of two prostitutes, no one would ever have called his office.

Giving up on the notion of sleep, he brushed his teeth, took a shower, pulled on sweat pants and his academy sweatshirt. He sat down at the desk with the murder book and a bottle of antacid, drinking straight out of the bottle as he browsed through the reports.

Wedged in between pages was the packet of photographs Mary Moss had gotten from Lila White's parents. Pictures of Lila White alive and happy, and laughing at her little girl's birthday party. Her lifestyle had aged her beyond her years, but he could easily see the pretty girl she had once been before the drugs and the disillusioned dreams. Her daughter was a doll with blond pigtails and a pixie's face. One shot captured mother and daughter in bathing suits in a plastic wading pool, Lila on her knees with the little girl hugged close in front of her, both of them smiling the same crooked smile.

It had to break her parents' hearts to look at this, Quinn thought. In the baby's face they would see their daughter as she had been when her world was simple and sunny and full of wonderful possibility. And in Lila's face they would see the lines of hard lessons learned, disappointment, and failure. And the hope for something better. Hope that had been rewarded with a brutal death not long after these photographs had been taken.

Quinn sighed as he held the picture under the lamplight, committing Lila White's image to memory: the style of her hair, the crooked smile, the slight bump in the bridge of her nose, the curve where her shoulder met her neck. She would join the others who haunted his sleep.

As he went to set the picture aside, something caught his eye and he pulled it back. Half obscured by the strap of her swimming suit was a small tattoo on her upper right chest. Quinn found his magnifying glass and held the snapshot under the light again for closer scrutiny.

A flower. A lily, he thought.

With one hand he flipped through the murder book to the White autopsy photos. There were about a third of the photos of the victim believed to be Jillian Bondurant. Still, he found what he was looking for: a shot showing a section of flesh missing from Lila White's upper right chest – and no tattoo in sight.

Kate sat curled into the corner of the old green leather sofa in her study, another glass of Sapphire on the table beside her. She'd lost count of its number. Didn't care. It took the sharp corners off the pain that assaulted her on several different fronts. That was all that mattered tonight.

How had her life taken such a sudden left turn? Things had been going so smoothly, then BAM! Ninety degrees hard to port, and everything fell out of the neat little cubicles into a jumbled mess that came up to her chin. She hated the feeling that she didn't have control. She hated the idea of her past rear-ending her. She'd been doing so well. Focus forward, concentrate on what was ahead of her for the day, for the week. She tried not to think too much about the past. She tried never to think about Quinn. She never *ever* allowed the memory of his mouth on hers.

She lifted a hand and touched her lips, thinking she still felt the heat of him there. She took another drink, thinking she could still taste him.

She had more important things to think about. Whether or not Angie was still alive. Whether or not they had a hope in hell of getting her back. She'd made the dreaded call to Rob Marshall to inform him of the situation.

He had the unenviable task of passing the news on to the county attorney. Sabin would spend the rest of the night contemplating methods of torture. Tomorrow Kate figured she would be burned at the stake.

But a confrontation with Ted Sabin was the least of her worries. Nothing he could do to her could punish her more than she would punish herself.

Every time she closed her eyes she saw the blood.

I should have stayed with her. If I'd been there for her, she would still be alive.

And every time she thought that, Angie's face morphed into Emily's, and the pain bit deeper and held on harder. Quinn had accused her of being a martyr, but martyrs suffered without sin, and she took full blame. For Emily. For Angie.

If she'd just gone into the house with the girl . . . If she'd just pressed a little harder to get a little closer . . . But she'd pulled back because a part of her didn't want to get that close or care that much. Christ, this was why she didn't do kids: They needed too much and she was too afraid of the potential for pain to give it.

'And I thought I was doing so well.'

She rose from the couch just to see if she could still stand without aid, and went to the massive old oak desk that had been her father's. She picked up the phone and dialed the number for her voice mail, feeling the lump form in her throat before she punched the code to retrieve the messages. She'd listened three times already. She skipped through messages from David Willis and her cooking instructor to hit the one she wanted.

10:05 P.M., the mechanical voice announced. A long silence followed the tone.

10:08 P.M. Another long silence.

10:10 P.M. Another long silence.

She had left the cell phone in the truck. Hadn't wanted to go back out to get it because she was spooked. Any callers could leave a message. She'd check her voice mail later, she remembered thinking.

If those calls had come from Angie . . .

But there was no way of knowing, and nothing to do but wonder and wait.

The call came into Hennepin County 911 dispatch at 3:49 A.M. A car fire. Kovac listened with one ear out of habit. He was cold to the bone. His feet felt like blocks of ice. Snow blew in the window he had kept cracked open to prevent carbon monoxide poisoning. Maybe he should set *this* car on fire. The heat could thaw his blood out, and the powers that ruled the motor pool could move him up to something better – like a Hyundai with a hamster wheel under the hood.

And then came the address, and adrenaline instantly burned off the chill.

They'd sure as hell drawn Smokey Joe out with the meeting, all right. He gunned the engine and rocked the car away from the curb and onto the street half a block down from Peter Bondurant's empty house.

Their killer had just lit up his fourth victim . . . in the parking lot of the community center where the meeting had been held.

22

Kate ran out the back door with her coat half on, half off. She had managed to pull on a pair of snow boots, but the heavy soles were little help as she hit the ice on the steps. An involuntary shriek raked her throat as she tumbled down into the yard, where what looked to be half a foot of wet snow cushioned her landing. She didn't even allow herself to catch her breath, but kept her legs moving and pushed herself upright.

Kovac had called on his way to the community center where the meeting had been held. A car fire in the parking lot. Reports of someone in the vehicle.

Angie.

No one knew at this point, of course, but the thought that it could be Angie burned in Kate's mind as she ran for the garage, fumbling in her pocket for her keys.

Quinn had given her an earful of his opinion on her garage.

Terrible location. Poorly lit. Left her vulnerable. All of which was true, but she didn't have time to think about it. Anyone wanting to mug her or rape her would just have to wait.

God help her if she got pulled over en route, she thought as she hit the light switch. She probably had no business getting behind the wheel of a vehicle at all, but she wasn't waiting for a ride. No one was on the streets this time of night anyway. It wasn't five minutes to that community center.

She was halfway to the 4Runner before she realized the garage light hadn't come on.

The realization held her up a step, a fraction of a second in which time all her senses sharpened and her heart gave an exaggerated thump. She hit the key for the remote lock, and the truck's interior lit up. *Keep moving,* she thought. If she kept moving, she wasn't allowing an opportunity for anyone to stop her. A ridiculous notion, but she grabbed on to it, yanked the door of the truck open, and hauled herself up into the driver's seat.

In a quick succession of moves, she locked the doors, started the engine, punched on the four-wheel drive, and put the truck in gear. It rocked back into the snow, pulling to the left. The exterior mirror missed disaster by a fraction of an inch. The back bumper kissed the neighbor's privacy fence, then she was rolling forward, the engine revving loudly. She pulled the wheel too hard as she hit the street and skidded sideways, just whispering past the front end of a black Lexus parked on the street.

Stupid to rush, she thought, fighting the sense of desperation, trying to lighten her foot on the accelerator. Whoever it was in that burning car would not be going anywhere, but still the urgency burned in her veins, in her gut. If there was any chance of discounting her fear – and thereby absolving herself of one stone of guilt – she wanted to grab it.

The street in front of the community center was clogged with emergency vehicles, red, white, and blue lights rolling like so many carnival rides. Mixed in among them were the omnipresent news vans, spilling reporters and cameramen and equipment. The house-to-house canvass had already begun, rousing neighbors from their beds. Overhead, a state patrol chopper cruised above the rooftops, spotlight washing down on lawns and shining in windows, flashing briefly over a pair of K-9 dogs and their officers.

If Smokey Joe had driven the car to the lot to set it ablaze, then it followed that he had left on foot. There was a good chance he lived in or near this neighborhood. Not five minutes from Kate's, though she didn't let herself think about that now.

She slid the 4Runner in behind the KMSP van, slammed it into park, and abandoned it sitting cockeyed to the curb. Despite the hour, some of the neighbors had come out of their homes to get the scoop and to further clutter the periphery of the scene. One of them could have been the killer, come back to recharge his batteries watching the resulting chaos his act had touched off. There was no way of knowing, and Kate had set her priority elsewhere. She dodged through the gathering throng, bumping shoulders, pushing, shoving.

Her eyes were on the emergency personnel working inside a circle of uniformed cops some distance away from the burned-out car. The paramedics swarmed around the victim, snapping off rapid-fire medicalese.

One of the uniforms caught Kate by the arm as she tried to pass, and held her back.

'Sorry, ma'am. Authorized personnel only.'

'I'm with victim services. I've got ID.'

'This one ain't gonna need you. He's toast.'

'He?'

The cop shrugged. 'It. Who can tell?'

Kate's stomach double-clutched. *Oh, Jesus, Angie.* 'Where's Kovac?'

'He's busy, ma'am. If you'll just step over to the side –'

'Don't "little lady" me,' Kate snapped. 'I've got cause to be here.'

'I can vouch for her, Officer,' Quinn said, holding up his ID. 'Better let her go before you lose a hand.'

The cop scowled at the order and at the FBI ID, but relinquished his hold. Kate bolted for the paramedics. Four steps closer, then Quinn caught her from behind and pulled her up short, holding tight as she fought to twist away from him.

'Let me go!'

'Let's find out what Kovac knows. If this is Smokey Joe, then there should be an ID around here somewhere.'

'No. I have to see!'

'It's going to be bad, Kate.'

'I know that. I've seen it before. God, what *haven't* I seen?'

Nothing. She'd spent years poring over photographs of unspeakable horror. She knew every evil thing one human being could do to another. Still, there was nothing quite like the stark, raw reality of an actual crime scene. Photographs never captured the sounds, the electricity in the air, the smell of death.

The smell of burnt flesh was horrific, and it hit her in the face like a club, the sensation it caused something akin to pain. Her stomach, already rolling on anxiety and half a tank of gin, pitched its contents up the back of her throat, and she nearly turned and vomited. It felt as if her knees turned to water. She couldn't understand why she didn't fall, then realized Quinn had hold of her again, his arms wrapped around her from behind. She sank back against him and made a mental note to chide herself for it later.

Of the hundreds of victims she'd seen, none had potentially been someone she'd known.

Hideously charred and half melted, the body lay on one side, limbs bent and fused into a sitting position. The heat of the fire had to have been incredible. The hair was gone, the nose was gone; the lips were twisted and burned away, revealing the teeth in a macabre grimace. The sternum was exposed, white bone shining where the thin layer of flesh had been seared away. The uniform had been right: At a glance there was no determining gender, except that the scraps of fabric that clung to the back of the body might have once been women's clothing – a piece of pink sweater, a swatch of skirt.

A burly paramedic with soot on his face looked up and shook his head. 'This one's for the bonepicker. She was long gone before we got here.'

Kate's head swam. She kept trying to think of what to do, how to know if it was Angie. The ideas seemed to bend and elongate and swoop through her brain.

Dental records were out of the question. They didn't know who the hell Angie DiMarco was or where she had come from. There were no parents who could give them dental records or medical records that might have pointed out old bone fractures to look for when the body was X-rayed. There were no personal effects to pick through.

Earrings. Angie wore earrings.

The ears of the corpse had been burned down to charred nubs.

Rings. She had half a dozen, at least.

The hands of the corpse were black and curled like monkey's paws. It looked as if there were fingers missing.

A shudder went through Kate that had nothing to do with the cold. Quinn drew her away a step at a time.

'I don't know,' she mumbled, still staring at the body. The toes were pointed like a gymnast's, a result of tendons constricting. 'I don't know.'

She was shaking so badly, Quinn could feel it through her heavy wool coat. He pulled her out of the traffic flow and pushed her hair from her face, tipping her head back so that she had to look up. Her face was ashen beneath the sodium vapor lights of the parking lot. She stared up at him, her eyes glassy with shock and dread. He wanted nothing more at that moment than to pull her close and hold her tight.

'Are you all right, honey?' he asked gently. 'Do you need to sit down?'

She shook her head, looking away from him to the ambulance crew, to the fire engines, to the glare of lights around the television people. 'I – no – um – oh, God,' she stammered, her breath coming too hard and too fast. Her eyes found his again and her mouth trembled. 'Oh, God, John, what if it's her?'

'If it's her, you didn't put her there, Kate,' he said firmly.

'Rotten kid,' she muttered, fighting tears. 'This is why I don't do kids. Nothing but trouble.'

He watched her fight, knowing she wasn't half as tough as she pretended to be, knowing she had no one in her life to turn to and lean against. Knowing she probably wouldn't have chosen him for the job now. Knowing all those things, he whispered, 'Hey, come here,' and drew her close.

She offered no resistance – strong, independent Kate. Her head found his shoulder and she fitted against him like his missing half. Familiar, comfortable, perfect. The noise and commotion of the crime scene seemed to recede into the distant background. He stroked a hand over her hair and kissed her temple, and felt complete for the first time in five years.

'I'm here for you, sweetheart,' he whispered. 'I've got you.'

'Is it her?' Rob Marshall scuttled toward them on his too-short legs. He was bundled into a fat down parka that appeared to be creeping up around his ears; a stocking cap sat tight on his round head.

At the sound of his voice, Kate stiffened, straightened, moved a step away from Quinn. He could almost see her reining in the emotions and hastily reconstructing the wall around them.

'We don't know,' she said, her voice husky. She cleared her throat and swiped a gloved finger beneath one eye. 'The body is unrecognizable. No one's found an ID yet that we know of.'

Rob looked past her to the paramedics. 'I can't believe this is happening. You think this is her, don't you? You think this is your witness.'

Your witness, Kate noted. He was already distancing himself from the disaster, the same way he'd distanced himself from the decision to take Angie to the Phoenix in the first place. The miserable toad.

'How did this happen?' he demanded. 'I thought you were watching out for her, Kate.'

'I'm sorry. I told you on the phone I was sorry. I should have stayed with her.' The admission grated now because it was a concession to her boss, and she automatically wanted to disagree with him.

'We chose you for this case for a reason.'

'I'm well aware of that.'

'Your background, the strength of your personality. For once I thought your stubbornness would actually work to my benefit –'

'You know, I'm blaming myself enough for both of us, Rob,' she said. 'So you can just get off my back, thank you very much.'

'Sabin is furious. I don't know how I'll placate him.'

The witness was hers to lose, the peace was his to make. Kate could already hear him whining and wheedling to Sabin, taking her name in vain every chance he got.

'I'm sure you'll be fine,' she snapped, too angry for prudence. 'Just get down on your knees and pucker up like you always do.'

Rob's whole being quaked in a spasm from his feet up, the fury erupting from his mouth. 'How dare you speak that way to me! How dare you! You've lost the witness. Maybe gotten her killed –'

'We don't know that,' Quinn intervened.

'– and still you have the gall to talk to me that way! You've never shown me an ounce of respect. Even now. Even after *this*. I can't believe you! You fucking bitch!'

'Back off,' Quinn ordered. He stepped between them and knocked Rob in the sternum hard with the heel of his hand. Rob stumbled backward, lost his footing in the snow, and landed on his butt.

'Why don't you go take a look at what Kate's just seen,' Quinn said, not bothering to offer a hand up. 'Get a fresh perspective as to what's important here right now.'

Rob scrambled to his feet, muttering, jerked around and stomped toward the ambulance, dusting the snow off his jacket with quick, angry movements.

'Dammit, John, *I* wanted to knock him on his ass,' Kate said.

'Then I probably just saved your job for you.'

The sudden possibility that her career might indeed be in danger struck Kate belatedly. God, why *wouldn't* Rob fire her? He was right: She'd never given him more than the barest requirement of respect. Never mind that he hadn't earned it. He was her boss.

She watched him as he stood near the ambulance with a mittened hand over his mouth. The crew was preparing to put the body in a bag. When he came back, his face looked both waxy and flushed.

'That's – that's – horrific,' he said, breathing heavily through his mouth. He pulled off his glasses and wiped his face with a mitten. 'Incredible.' He swallowed a couple of times and shifted his weight from one foot to the other. 'That smell . . .'

'Maybe you should sit down,' Kate suggested.

Rob partially unzipped his coat and tugged down on the bottom. His gaze was still on the ambulance. 'Incredible . . . horrible . . .'

The search helicopter swept near, blades pounding the air like the wings of a giant hummingbird.

'He's challenging us, isn't he? The Cremator,' he said, looking to Quinn. 'Taking the girl. Doing this here, where the meeting was held.'

'Yes. He wants to make us look like fools while he makes himself look invincible.'

'I'd say he's doing a damn good job of it,' Rob said, staring across the way as the paramedics loaded the corpse into the ambulance.

'Anybody can look like a genius if they have all the answers ahead of time,' Quinn said. 'He'll screw up eventually. They all do. The trick is to get it to happen sooner rather than later. And to get him by the balls the instant he stumbles.'

'I'd like to be around to see that happen.' Rob wiped his face again and adjusted the parka. 'I'll go call Sabin,' he said to Kate. 'While we still work for him.'

Kate said nothing. Her silence had nothing to do with the county attorney or the suddenly precarious disposition of her job.

'Let's go find Kovac,' she said to Quinn. 'See if they've found the driver's license yet.'

Kovac stood arguing jurisdiction with an African American woman in a dark parka with ARSON printed across the back. The car, smallish and red, was the centerpiece in a ring of portable lights. The fire had gutted it and blown out the windshield. The driver's door hung open, twisted by the tools the rescue squad had used to wrench it free. The interior was a mess of ash, melted plastic, and dripping foam fire retardant. The driver's seat had been eaten away, the flames leaving nothing but a carcass of distorted springs.

'It's an arson, Sergeant,' the woman insisted. 'It's up to *my* office to determine the cause.'

'It's a homicide, and I could give a shit about the cause of the fire,' Kovac returned. 'I want B of I in that car to get whatever evidence your people haven't already fucked up.'

'On behalf of the Minneapolis Fire Department, I apologize for trying to put out a fire and save a life. Maybe we'll get that straight before someone sets *your* car on fire.'

'Marcell, I should be so lucky someone sets that piece of crap on fire.'

As crime scenes went, this one was a disaster, Kate knew. Called to a fire, the firefighters didn't worry about trampling the scene. Their job was saving lives, not finding out who might have taken one. And so they ruined car doors and sprayed foam over any trace evidence that might have survived inside.

'The thing's already burned to a crisp,' Kovac said to the arson investigator. 'What's *your* hurry? Me, I got a flame-throwing fruitloop running around killing women.'

'Maybe this was an accident,' Marcell shot back. 'Maybe this has nothing to do with your killer and you're standing here arguing with me and wasting our time for nothing.'

'Sam, we got the plates back.' Elwood waded toward him through the snow. He waited until he was near enough for confidentiality, even though there was no hope of keeping this news under wraps for long. 'It's a 'ninety-eight Saab registered to Jillian Bondurant.'

The arson investigator saluted Kovac and stepped out of his way. 'As pissing contests go, Sergeant, you just wrote your name in the snow.'

The B of I Team swarmed over the burned-out Saab like vultures cleaning an elephant carcass. Kate sat behind the wheel of Kovac's car and watched, feeling numb and exhausted. The body – whoever she was – had been transported to HCMC. Someone else's corpse had just been knocked to number two on Maggie Stone's itinerary for the day that would soon be dawning.

Quinn opened the passenger door and climbed in on a cold breath of air. Snow clung to his dark head like dandruff. He rubbed a gloved hand over it.

'It's pretty clear the fire was set on the driver's side,' he said. 'It burned hottest and longest there. The dashboard and steering wheel are melted. Our two best bets for fingerprints gone.'

'He's escalating,' Kate said.

'Yes.'

'Changing his MO.'

'To make a point.'

'He's building toward something.'

'Yes. And I'd give everything I have to know what and when.'

'And why.'

Quinn shook his head. 'I don't care why anymore. There are no valid reasons. There are only excuses. You know all the contributing factors as well as I do, but you also know not all kids with abusive parents grow up to abuse, and not all kids with emotionally distant mothers grow up to kill. At some point in time a choice is made, and once it's made, I don't care why, I just want the bastards off the planet.'

'And you've appointed yourself responsible for catching them all.'

'It's a shit job, but what else have I got going for me?' He flashed the famous Quinn smile, worn around the edges now, running on too little sleep and too much stress.

'You don't need to be here now,' Kate said, feeling the fatigue and the pressure in every muscle of her body. 'They'll fill you in at the morning briefing. You look like you could use a couple hours' sleep.'

'Sleep? I gave that up. It was taking the edge off my paranoia.'

'Careful with that, John. They'll pull you out of CASKU and stick you in *The X-Files*.'

'I am better-looking than David Duchovny.'

'Far and away.'

Funny, she thought, how they fell back into the old patterns of teasing, even now, even after all that had gone on tonight. But then, it was familiar and comforting.

'You don't need to be here either, Kate,' he said, going serious.

'Yes, I do. I'm the closest thing Angie DiMarco has to someone who cares about her. If that body turns out to be hers, the least I can do is miss a little sleep to hear the news.'

She expected another lecture from Quinn on her lack of culpability, but he didn't say anything.

'Do you think there's any chance that body is Jillian Bondurant?' she asked. 'That she wasn't victim number three, and she did this to herself?'

'No. Self-immolation is rare, and when it does happen, the person usually wants an audience. Why would Jillian come here in the dead of night? What's her connection to this place? Nothing. We'll know for certain if it's Jillian after the autopsy, seeing as we can compare dental records this time, but I'd say the chances this is her and the fire was self-inflicted are nil.'

Kate turned up the corners of her mouth in a pseudo-smile. 'Yeah, I know all that. I was just hoping that corpse might be someone I wasn't responsible for.'

'I'm the one who called the meeting, Kate. Smokey Joe did this to say "Fuck you, Quinn." Now I get to wonder what set him off. Should I have been harder on him? Should I have tried to pretend I feel sympathy for him? Should I have stroked his ego and made him out as a genius? What did I do? What *didn't* I do? Why didn't I know better? If he was at the meeting, if he was sitting right there in front of me, why didn't I see him?'

'Guess your super X-ray vision that allows you to see what evil lurks in the hearts of men is on the fritz.'

'Along with your ability to foresee the future.'

This time the smile was genuine, if sad. 'We're a pair.'

'Used to be.'

Kate stared at him, seeing the man she'd known and loved, and the man the intervening years had turned him into. He looked tired, haunted. She wondered if he saw the same in her. It was humbling to admit that he ought to. She'd fooled herself into believing she was fine. But that was all it had been: an act, a ruse. She had fully realized that truth an hour ago as she stood in the warm shelter of his arms. It had been like suddenly having back a crucial part of herself she had spent years refusing to acknowledge was missing.

'I loved you, Kate,' he said softly, his dark gaze holding hers. 'Whatever else you think of me, and of the way things came apart, I loved you. You can doubt everything else about me. God knows, I do. But don't doubt that.'

Something fluttered inside Kate. She refused to name it. It couldn't be hope. She didn't want to hope for anything with regard to John Quinn. She preferred annoyance, indignation, a dash of anger. But none of that was what she really felt, and she knew it, and he would know it as well. He'd always been able to read the slightest shadow that crossed her mind.

'Damn you, John,' she muttered.

Whatever else she might have said was lost as Kovac's face appeared suddenly at Quinn's window. Kate started and swore, then lowered the window from the control panel on the driver's door.

'Hey, kids, no making out,' he quipped. 'It's after curfew.'

'We're trying to save ourselves from hypothermia,' Quinn said. 'I have a toaster that gives off more warmth than this heater.'

'Did you find the DL?' Kate asked.

'No, but we found this.' He held up a microcassette tape inside a clear plastic case. 'It was on the ground about fifteen feet from the car. It's a pure damn miracle one of the firemen didn't squash it.

'It's probably some reporter's notes from the meeting,' he said. 'But you never know. Every once in a blue moon we find evidence there is a God. I've got a player somewhere on the seat there.'

'Yeah, that and the Holy Grail,' Kate muttered as she dug through the junk on the seat: reports, magazines, burger wrappers. 'Are you living in this car, Sam? There are shelters for people like you, you know.'

She came up with the player and handed it to Quinn. He popped the cassette out and carefully inserted the one Kovac handed him on the end of a ballpoint pen.

What came from the tiny speaker ran through Kate like a spike. A woman's screams, thick with desperation, interspersed with breathless, broken pleas for mercy that would never be delivered. The cries of someone enduring torture and begging for death.

Not proof there was a God, Kate thought. Proof there wasn't.

23

Elation. Ecstasy. Arousal. These are the things he feels in his triumph, stirred into the darker emotions of anger and hatred and frustration that burn constantly inside him.

Manipulation. Domination. Control. His power extends beyond his victims, he reminds himself. He exercises the same forces over the police and over Quinn.

Elation. Ecstasy. Arousal.

Never mind the rest. Focus on the win.

The intensity is overwhelming. He is shaking, sweating, flushed with excitement as he drives toward the house. He can smell himself. The odor is peculiar to this kind of excitement – strong, musky, almost sexual. He wants to wipe his armpits with his hands and rub the sweat and the scent all over his face, into his nostrils, lick it from his fingers.

He wants to strip and have the woman in his fantasies lick it all from his body. From his chest and his belly and his back. In his fantasy she ends up on her knees before him, licking his balls. His erection is huge and straining and he shoves it into her mouth and fucks her mouth, slapping her every time she gags on him. He comes in her face, then forces her down on her hands and knees and penetrates her anally. His hands around her throat, he rapes her viciously, choking her between screams.

The images excite him, arouse him. His penis is stiff and throbbing. He needs release. He needs to hear the sounds that are as sharp and beautiful as finely honed blades. He needs to hear the screams, that raw, pure quality of sound that is terror, and to pretend the screams come from the woman in his mind. He needs to hear the building crescendo as a life reaches its limit. The fading energy absorbed greedily by death.

He digs a hand into his coat pocket for the tape and finds nothing.

A wave of panic sweeps over him. He pulls to the curb and searches all pockets, checks the seat beside him, checks the floor, checks the cassette player. The tape is gone.

Anger burns through him. Huge and violent. A wall of rage. Cursing, he slams the car into gear and pulls back onto the street. He's made a mistake. Unacceptable. He knows it won't be fatal. Even if the police find the tape, even if they are able to lift a fingerprint from it, they won't find him. His prints are in no criminal database. He hasn't been arrested since his juvenile days. But the very *idea* of a mistake infuriates him because he knows it will give the task force and John Quinn encouragement, when he wants only to crush them.

His triumph is now diminished. His celebration ruined. His erection has gone soft, his cock shriveling to a pathetic nub. In the back of his mind he can hear the sneering voice, the disdain as the fantasy woman gets up and walks away from him, bored and disinterested.

He pulls into the driveway, hitting the remote control for the garage door. The anger is a snake writhing inside him, oozing poison. The sound of toy-dog barking follows him into the garage. That goddamn mutt from next door. His night ruined, now this.

He gets out of the car and goes to the trash bin. The garage door is descending. The bichon makes eye contact with him, yapping incessantly, bouncing backward toward the lowering door. He pulls a dropcloth out of the garbage and turns toward the dog, already imagining scooping the dog up, then swinging the makeshift bag hard against the concrete wall again and again and again.

'Come on, Bitsy, you rotten little shit,' he murmurs in a sweet tone. 'Why don't you like me? What have I ever done to you?'

The dog growls, a sound as ferocious as an electric pencil sharpener, and holds his ground, glancing back toward the door now less than a foot from sealing his fate.

'Do you know I've killed little rat dogs like you before?' he asks, smiling, stepping closer, bending down. 'Do you think I smell like evil?'

He reaches a hand toward the dog. 'That's because I am,' he murmurs as the dog lunges toward him, teeth bared.

The grinding of the garage door mechanism stops.

The dropcloth falls, muffling the yip of surprise.

24

Kate was still shaking when they reached her house. Quinn had insisted on seeing her home for the second time that night, and she hadn't argued. The memory of the screams echoed in her head. She heard them, faint but constant, as she slipped wordlessly from the truck and left the garage, as she fumbled with the keys for the back door, as she passed through the kitchen to the hall and turned the thermostat up.

Quinn was behind her like a shadow the whole time. She expected him to say something about the burned-out light in the garage, but if he did, she didn't hear him. She could hear only the whoosh of her pulse in her ears, the magnified rattle of keys, Thor meowing, the refrigerator humming . . . and beneath all that, the screams.

'I'm so cold,' she said, going into the study, where the desk lamp still burned and a chenille throw lay in a heap on the old sofa. She glanced at the answering machine – no blinking light – and thought of the hang-up calls that had come to her cell phone at 10:05, 10:08, 10:10.

A half-empty glass of Sapphire and tonic sat on the blotter, the ice long melted. Kate picked it up with a shaking hand and took a swallow. The tonic had gone flat, but she didn't notice, didn't taste anything at all. Quinn took the glass from her hand and set it aside, then turned her gently by the shoulders to face him.

'Aren't you cold?' she prattled on. 'It takes forever for the furnace to heat this place. I should probably have it replaced – it's old as Moses – but I never think of it until the weather turns.

'Maybe I should start a fire,' she suggested, and immediately felt the blood drain from her face. 'Oh, God, I can't believe I said that. All I can smell is smoke and that horrible – Jesus, what an awful –'

She swallowed hard and looked at the glass that was now out of easy reach.

Quinn laid a hand against her cheek and turned her face toward him. 'Hush,' he said softly.

'But –'

'Hush.'

As carefully as if she were made of spun glass, he folded his arms around her and drew her close against him. Another invitation to lean on him, to let go. She knew she shouldn't. If she let go for even a second now, she would be lost. She needed to keep moving, keep talking, *do something*. If she let go, if she went still, if she didn't occupy herself with some mindless, meaningless task, the tide of despair would sweep over her, and then where would she be?

Without defense in the arms of a man she still loved but couldn't have.

The full import of that answer was heavy enough to strain what little strength she had left, ironically tempting her further to take the support Quinn offered for now.

She had never stopped loving him. She had just put it away in a lockbox in her secret heart, never to be taken out again. Maybe hoping it would wither and die, but it had only gone dormant.

Another chill washed over her, and she let her head find the hollow of his shoulder. With her ear pressed against his chest, she could hear his heart beat, and she remembered all the other times, long ago, when he had held her and comforted her, and she had pretended what they had in a stolen moment might last forever.

God, she wanted to pretend that now. She wanted to pretend they hadn't just come from a crime scene, and her witness wasn't missing, and that Quinn had come here for her instead of the job he had always put first.

How unfair that she felt so safe with him, that contentment seemed so close, that looking at her life from the vantage point of his arms, she could suddenly see all the holes, the missing pieces, the faded colors, the dulled senses. How unfair to realize all that, when she had decided it was better not to need anyone, and certainly best not to need him.

She felt his lips brush her temple, her cheek. Against the weaker part of her will, she turned her face up and let his lips find hers. Warm, firm, a perfect match, a perfect fit. The feeling that flooded her was equal parts pain and pleasure, bitter and sweet. The kiss was tender, careful, gentle – asking, not taking. And when Quinn raised his head an inch, the question and the caution were in his eyes, as if her every want and misgiving had passed to him through the kiss.

'I need to sit down,' Kate murmured, stepping back. His arms fell away from her and the chill swept back around her like an invisible stole. She grabbed the glass off the desk as she went to the couch and wedged herself into a corner, pulling the chenille throw into her lap.

'I can't do this,' she said softly, more to herself than to him. 'It's too hard. It's too cruel. I don't want that kind of mess to clean up when you go back to Quantico.' She sipped at the gin and shook her head. 'I wish you hadn't come, John.'

Quinn sat down beside her, forearms on his thighs. 'Is that what you really wish, Kate?'

Tears clung to her lashes. 'No. But what does it matter now? What I wish has never had any bearing on reality.'

She finished the drink, set the glass aside, and rubbed her hands over her face.

'I wished Emily would live, and she didn't. I wished Steven wouldn't blame me, but he did. I wished –'

She held short on that. What was she supposed to say? That she'd wished Quinn had loved her more? That they had married and had children and lived in Montana, raising horses and making love every night? Fantasies that should have belonged to someone more naive. Christ, she felt like a fool for even having such thoughts and stowing them away in a dusty corner of her mind. She sure as hell wasn't going to share them and risk looking more pathetic.

'I've wished a lot of things. And wishing never made them so,' she said. 'And now I'll wish to close my eyes and not see blood, to close my ears and not hear screams, to close out this nightmare and go to sleep. And I might as well wish for the moon.'

Quinn laid a hand on her shoulder, his thumb finding the knot of tension in the muscle and rubbing at it. 'I'd give you the moon, Kate,' he said. An old, familiar line they had passed back and forth between them like a secret keepsake. 'And unhook the stars and take them down, and give them to you for a necklace.'

Emotions stung her eyes, burning away the last of her resolve to hold strong. She was too tired and it hurt too much – all of it: the case, the memories, the dreams that had died. She buried her face in her hands.

Quinn put his arms around her, guided her head to his shoulder once more.

'It's all right,' he whispered.

'No, it isn't.'

'Let me hold you, Kate.'

She couldn't bring herself to say no. She couldn't bear the idea of pulling away, of being alone. She'd been alone too long. She wanted his comfort. She wanted his strength, the warmth of his body. Being in his arms, she felt a sense of being where she belonged for the first time in a long time.

'I never stopped loving you,' he whispered.

Kate tightened her arms around him, but didn't trust herself to look at him.

'Then why did you let me go?' she asked, the pain just beneath the surface of her voice. 'And why did you stay away?'

'I thought it was what you wanted, what you needed. I thought it was best for you. You didn't exactly beg my attention at the end.'

'You were tied up with the OPR because of me –'

'Because of Steven, not because of you.'

'Semantics. Steven wanted to punish you because of me, because of *us*.'

'And you wanted to hide because of us.'

She didn't try to deny it. What they'd had in their secret love had been so special: the kind of magic most people wished for and never found, the kind of magic neither of them had ever known before. But when the secrecy had finally been broken, no one had seen that magic. Under the harsh light of public scrutiny, their love had become an affair, something tawdry and cheap. No one had understood; no one had tried; no one had wanted to. No one had seen her pain, her need. She wasn't a woman drowning in grief, shut out by a husband who had turned distant and bitter. She was a slut who had cheated on her grieving husband while their daughter was barely cold in the ground.

She couldn't say her own sense of guilt hadn't reflected back some of those same feelings, even though she knew better. It had never been in her to lie, to cheat. She'd been raised on a combination of Catholic guilt and Swedish self-reproof. And the wave of self-condemnation from Emily's death and her own sense of breached morality had come up over her head, and she hadn't been able to surface – especially not when the one person she would have reached to for help had backed away, wrestling with anger and pain of his own.

The memory of that turmoil pushed her now to her feet again, restless, not liking the emotions that came with the memories.

'You might have come after me,' she said. 'But between the OPR and the job, suddenly you were never there.

'I thought you loved the job more than me,' she admitted in a whisper, then offered Quinn a twisted half-smile. 'I thought maybe you finally figured out I was more trouble than I was worth.'

'Oh, Kate . . .' He stepped close, tipped her head back, and looked in her eyes. His were as dark as the night, shining and intense.

Hers brimmed with the uncertainty that had always touched him most deeply – the uncertainty that lay buried beneath layers of polish and stubborn strength. An uncertainty he recognized perhaps as being akin to his own, the thing he hid and feared in himself.

'I let you go because I thought that was what you wanted. And I buried myself in work because it was the only thing that dulled the hurt.

'I've given everything I ever was to this job,' he said. 'I don't know if there's anything left of me worth having. But I know I've never loved it – or anything, or anyone – the way I loved you, Kate.'

Kate said nothing. Quinn was aware of time slipping by, of a tear sliding down her cheek. He thought of how they'd come apart, and all the time they'd lost, and knew it was more complicated than a simple lack of communication. The feelings, the fears, the pride, and the pain that had wedged between them had all been genuine. So sharp and true that neither of them had ever found the nerve to face them down. It had been easier to just let go – and that had been the hardest thing he'd ever done in his life.

'We're a pair,' he whispered, echoing what she'd said in Kovac's car. 'What did you feel, Kate? Did you stop needing me? Did you stop loving me? Did you –'

She pressed trembling fingers to his lips, shaking her head. 'Never,' she said, so softly the word was little more than a thought. 'Never.'

She had hated him. She had resented him. She had blamed him and tried to forget him. But she had never stopped loving him. And what a terrifying truth that was – that in five years the need had never died, that she'd never felt anything close to it. Now it rose within her like an awakening flame burning through the exhaustion and the fear and everything else.

She leaned up to meet his lips with hers. She tasted his mouth and the salt of her own tears. His arms went around her and crushed her to him, bending her backward, fitting her body against his.

'Oh, God, Kate, I've needed you,' he confessed, his mouth brushing the shell of her ear. 'I've missed you so.'

Kate kissed his cheek, ran a hand over the short-cropped hair. 'I've never needed anyone the way I needed you ... need you ...'

He caught the distinction, and stood back to look at her for a moment. He didn't ask if she was sure. Afraid she might answer, Kate supposed. And so was she. There was no certainty in her. There was no logic, no thought of anything beyond the moment, and the tangle of raw feelings, and the need to lose herself with Quinn ... only with him.

She led him upstairs by the hand. He stopped her three times to kiss her, touch her, bury his face in her hair. In her bedroom they helped each other undress. Tangled hands, impatient fingers. His shirt on the back of a chair, her skirt in a puddle on the floor. Never losing contact with each other. A caress. A kiss. An anxious embrace.

For Kate, Quinn's touch was a memory overlapping real time. The feel of his hand on her skin was imprinted on her mind and in her heart. It drew to the surface the desire she had known only with him. Instantly, in a warm rush and a sweet ache. As if they'd been apart five days instead of five years.

Her breath caught at the feel of his mouth on her breast, and shuddered from her as his hand slipped between her legs, and his fingers found her wet and hot. Her hips arched automatically to the angle they'd found so many times before, so very long ago.

Her hands traveled over his body. Familiar territory. Ridges and planes of muscle and bone. Smooth, hot skin. The valley of his spine. His erection straining against her, as hard as marble, as soft as velvet. His thick, muscular thigh urging her legs farther apart.

She guided him into her, felt the absolute thrill of him filling her perfectly, the same as she had felt every single time they'd ever made love. The sensation, the wonder of it, had never dulled, only sharpened. For him as well as for her. She could see it in his eyes as he looked down at her in the lamplight: the intense pleasure, the heat, the surprise, the hint of desperation that came from knowing this magic happened only with each other.

The last made her want to cry. He was the one, the only one. The man she'd married, whose child she'd borne, had never come close to making her feel what John Quinn made her feel with his mere presence in the room.

She held him tighter, moved against him stronger, dug her fingernails into his back. He kissed her deeply, possessively, with his tongue, with his teeth. He moved into her with building force, then pulled himself back, gentled, eased them both away from the edge.

Time lost all meaning. There were no seconds, only breaths and murmured words; no minutes, just the ebb and flow of pleasure. And when the end finally came, it was with an explosion of emotion running head-on from each extreme of the spectrum. And then came an odd mix of peace and tension, contentment and completion and wariness, until exhaustion overrode all else, and they fell asleep in each other's arms.

25

'Listen up!'

Kovac leaned heavily on the end of the table in the Loving Touch of Death war room. He had been home long enough to fall asleep on a kitchen chair while waiting for the coffee to brew. He hadn't showered or shaved, and imagined he looked like a bum in the same limp, wrinkled suit he'd worn the day before. He hadn't had time to even change his shirt.

Everyone on the team was showing similar signs of wear. Dark circles under bloodshot eyes. Deep frown lines etched into pale faces.

The room stank of cigarettes, sweat, and bitter coffee over the original aromas of mice and mildew. A portable radio on the counter tuned to WCCO competed with a ten-inch television tuned to KSTP, both on to catch the latest reports the media had to offer. Photos from the car fire and of victim number four had been hastily pinned to one of the boards, so fresh from the developing trays, they were curling in on themselves.

'The media is going nuts with the stuff from last night,' Kovac said. 'Smokey Joe lights up a vic practically under our noses, and we look like we've been sitting around picking our toenails. I've already had the chief and Lieutenant Fowler on me like a couple of trick riders this morning. Long story short: If we can't make something happen fast, we'll all be on jail duty doing body cavity searches.'

'That'd be the closest thing to sex Tip's had in years,' Adler said.

Tippen fired a paper clip at him from a rubber-band slingshot. 'Very funny. Let me start with you, Chunk. Mind if I use a crowbar?'

Kovac ignored them. 'We managed to keep word of that cassette tape away from them.'

'Thank God none of them found it,' Walsh said, contemplating the state of his handkerchief. 'They'd be playing it on every station in town.'

Kovac hadn't been able to get the sound of those screams out of his head. The idea of that tape playing into every house in the Twin Cities was enough to make his stomach roll.

'The tape is at the BCA lab,' he said. 'Some techno-geek is going over it, trying to pick up background noise and the like. We'll see what he has to say later. Tinks, did you find Vanlees?'

Liska shook her head. 'No go. It seems the only close friend he's got is whoever he's house-sitting for. And he sure won't be making any new ones soon. Mary and I managed to piss off everyone he knows, calling up in the middle of the night. One guy said Vanlees was bragging on this house though. He thought it sounded like it might be Uptown or thereabouts. Near a lake.'

'I've got a car sitting on his Lyndale apartment,' Kovac said. 'Another one at the Target Center, and one at the Edgewater town houses. And every cop in town is looking for his truck.'

'We've got no probable cause to arrest him,' Yurek pointed out.

'You won't need it,' Quinn said, walking into the middle of the conversation. Flecks of snow melted in his hair. He shrugged out of his trench coat and tossed it on the counter. 'It's not an arrest. We're asking for his assistance. If this guy is Smokey Joe, then he's feeling cocky and smug. He made us look like idiots last night. The idea of the cops asking him for help will have enormous appeal to his ego.'

'We don't want to lose the guy on a technicality, that's all,' Yurek pointed out.

'The first person to screw up that way, I will personally shoot in the kneecaps,' Kovac promised.

'So, G,' Tippen said, eyes narrowed. 'You think this guy is it?'

'He fits the picture pretty well. We'll get him in here and have a chat, then I'd recommend a bumper-lock surveillance. Make him sweat, see what we can get him to do. If we can rattle him, get him to spook, doors will open. If things fall right, we'll end up with cause for a search warrant.'

'I'll head over to the Edgewater,' Liska said. 'I'd like to be on hand, try to put him at ease, get his guard down.'

'How did he seem at the meeting last night?' Quinn asked.

'Fascinated, a little excited, full of theories.'

'Do we know where he was Sunday night?'

'The ever-popular home alone.'

'I want to be there when you get him in the box,' Quinn said. 'Not in the room, but watching.'

'You don't want to question him?'

'Not right off the bat. We'll have you in there, and someone he's never seen before. Probably Sam. I'll come in later.'

'Beep me as soon as you've got him,' Kovac said as a phone rang in the background. Elwood got up to answer it. 'Tip, Charm, did you find anybody who saw the DiMarco girl get in a truck Sunday night?'

'No,' Tippen said. 'And the going rate for that answer is ten bucks. Unless you're Charm. In which case, you can get that answer and a blowjob for a smile.'

Yurek gave him a dirty look. 'Like it's some kind of treat to get the clap for free.'

'It is for Tip,' Liska pointed out.

'Charm! Telephone!' Elwood called.

'Stay on it,' Kovac ordered. 'Get some fliers printed off with the girl's picture and a picture of a GMC Jimmy. Ask Lieutenant Fowler about a reward. Chances are someone just hanging out in that area at that time of night will be willing to turn in his mother for a couple hundred bucks.'

'Will do.'

'Someone diplomatic has to go to the Phoenix and talk again to this hooker that knew the second vic,' Kovac went on.

'I'll do it,' Moss offered.

'Ask her if Fawn Pierce had a tattoo,' Quinn said, forcing himself to sit ahead. He rubbed at a knot in the back of his neck. 'Lila White had a tattoo exactly where that chunk of flesh was missing from her chest. Smokey Joe may be an art lover. Or an artist.'

'Where'd you get that?' Tippen asked, skeptical, as if maybe Quinn had just pulled it down out of the sky.

'I did something no one else bothered to do: I looked,' he said bluntly. 'I looked at the photographs Lila White's parents gave Agent Moss. They were taken days before her death. If it turns out Fawn Pierce had a tattoo removed by the killer, you'll need to find where both women got them done and check out the parlors and everyone associated with them.'

'Do we know if Jillian Bondurant had any tattoos?' Hamill asked.

'Her father says none he knew of.'

'Her friend, Michelle Fine, claims not to know of any either,' Liska said. 'And I think she'd know. She's a walking scratch pad herself.'

'Did she ever come in to get printed?' Kovac asked, digging through a messy stack of notes.

'I haven't had time to check.'

A cell phone rang, and Quinn swore and got up from the table, digging in the pocket of his suit coat.

Adler pointed at the television, where scenes from the car fire filled the screen. 'Hey, there's Kojak!'

The sun guns washed Kovac's skin out to the color of parchment. He frowned heavily at the cameras and shut down the questions with a stiff rendition of 'The investigation is sensitive and ongoing. We have no comment at this time.'

'You need to lose that mustache, Sam,' Liska said. 'You look like Mr Peabody from Rocky and Bullwinkle.'

'Any mutilation on the latest vic?' Tippen called from the coffeepot.

'Autopsy's scheduled for eight,' Kovac said, checking his watch. Seven forty. He turned to Moss. 'Rob Marshall from legal services will meet you at the Phoenix. That's the brass making public nice-nice with the Urskines after the Bitch Queen of the North kicked up that stink last night.

'Personally, don't care how offended they are. I want someone to have a heart-to-heart with Vampira's mate at the station later today. Mary, ask him to come in, and be vague when they demand to know why. Routine procedure, like that. And ask if they have a credit card receipt or canceled check from the cabin they were in the weekend Lila White was killed.

'Gregg Urskine was one of the last people to see our witness last night. The first vic was a guest of theirs. The second was a friend of one of their current hookers. That's too many close calls for me,' Kovac declared.

'Toni Urskine will be on the phone to every news outlet in the metro,' Yurek cautioned.

'If we're polite, that only makes her look bad,' Kovac said. 'We're being thorough, leaving no stone unturned. That's what Toni Urskine wanted.'

'Did we get anything from the meeting last night?' Hamill asked.

'Nothing of use to us from the cars,' Elwood said. 'Just the videotape.'

Kovac checked his watch again. 'I'll look at it later. Doc'll be sharpening her knives. You with me, GQ?'

Quinn held up a hand in acknowledgment and signed off on his call. They grabbed their coats and went out the back way.

The snow had covered the filth of the alley – including Kovac's car – camouflaging tire hazards like broken Thunderbird and Colt 45 malt liquor bottles, which covered the ground in these downtown alleys like dead leaves. Kovac pulled a brush out from under a pile of junk in the backseat and swept off the windshields, the hood, and the taillights.

'You got back to your hotel all right last night?' he asked as they slid into their seats and he turned the engine over. ''Cause I sure could've taken you. It's not that much out of my way.'

'No. I was fine. It was fine,' Quinn said, not looking at him. He could feel Kovac's gaze on him. 'Kate was so upset over that tape, I wanted to make sure she was all right.'

'Uh-huh. Was she? All right?'

'No. She thinks that body was her witness, that those screams were the screams of her witness being tortured. She blames herself.'

'Well, it's probably a good thing you saw her home, then. What'd you do? Catch a cab downtown?'

'Yeah,' he lied, the morning scene playing through his mind.

Waking up and looking at Kate across the pillow in the faint light, touching her, watching those incredible clear gray eyes open, seeing the uncertainty there. He would rather have been able to say making love had solved all their problems, but that wasn't true. It had given them some solace, reconnected their souls, and complicated everything. But, God, it had been like returning to heaven after years in purgatory.

Now what? The unspoken question had hung between them awkwardly as they'd cleaned up, gotten dressed, grabbed bagels, and hustled out the door. There had been no morning afterglow touching, kissing, lingering passion. There had been no time to talk, not that he could have gotten Kate to. Her first tendency when feeling cornered was to retreat within herself, shut the door, and stew. God knew he wasn't much better.

She'd dropped him off at the Radisson. He'd shaved too hastily, thrown on a fresh suit, and run out the door, late.

'I tried to call you this morning,' Kovac said, putting the car in reverse but keeping his foot on the brake. 'You didn't answer.'

'Must have been in the shower.' Quinn stayed poker-faced. 'Did you leave a message? I didn't take time to check.'

'Just wanted to see how Kate was doing.'

'Then why didn't you call her?' Quinn asked, his temper tightening. He looked at Kovac and turned the conversation around on a dime. 'You know, if you'd shown this much interest in the White murder back when, we may not be here right now.'

Kovac flushed. More with guilt than anger, Quinn thought, though the cop played the latter. 'I did that case by the numbers.'

'You took the express lane, Sam. How else do you explain missing that tattoo?'

'We asked. I'm sure we did. We must have,' Kovac said, certain, then less so, then not at all. He craned his neck and looked out the back window as he let his foot off the brake. 'Maybe we didn't ask the right person. Maybe no one had noticed the goddamn thing.'

'Her parents are a couple of square pegs from a farming town. You think they wouldn't have noticed their daughter had a calla lily tattooed on her chest? You think none of her regular johns noticed it?'

Kovac gunned the engine, rocked the car out of its spot too fast, then hit the brakes too hard. The Caprice slid on the slick wet snow and the back bumper met the corner of a trash Dumpster with a nasty thud.

'Shit!'

Quinn winced, then relaxed, his attention still on Kovac. 'You never checked the Urskines' alibi when Lila White was killed.'

'I didn't make them produce the receipt. What motive did they have to kill the woman? None. Besides, Toni Urskine was kicking up such a stink that we weren't trying hard enough . . .'

'I read the reports,' Quinn said. 'You worked the case hard for a week, then less and less and less. Same thing with Fawn Pierce.'

Kovac cracked the window open, lit a cigarette, and blew the first lungful outside. The Caprice still sat cockeyed, ass up against the Dumpster. Liska came out of the building and pointed at him, shaking her head, then climbed into her car.

'You've seen enough of these cases to know how it works,' he said. 'A hooker buys it, the department is about as concerned as if someone had run over a stray dog. Tag 'em, bag 'em, give 'em the no-frills investigation. If the case isn't solved fast, it gets pushed to the back burner to make way for the taxpaying citizens getting murdered by jealous husbands and crack-crazed carjackers.

'I did what I could while I could,' he said, staring out the windshield at the falling snow.

'I believe you, Sam.' Though Quinn thought Kovac did not entirely believe himself. The regret was etched in the lines of his weathered face. 'It's just too bad for those other three victims that it wasn't enough.'

'How long had you known Fawn Pierce?' Mary Moss asked.

In the den of the Phoenix House, she sat down at one end of a pea-green couch, silently inviting Rita Renner to take the other end, creating a certain sense of intimacy. A spring poked her in the butt.

'About two years,' Renner said, so softly Mary reached out to the small tape recorder on the coffee table and pushed it closer. 'We met downtown and we just got to be friends.'

'You worked the same territory?'

She glanced up at Toni Urskine, who sat on the arm of the couch, a hand resting reassuringly on Renner's shoulder. Then she looked to Rob Marshall, who hovered on the other side of the coffee table, looking impatient to be somewhere else. His left leg was jiggling like an idling motor.

'Yeah,' she said. 'We worked around the strip clubs and the Target Center.'

Her voice sounded as if it were coming from another dimension. So quiet and mousy, dressed in old jeans and a flannel shirt, she hardly looked the picture of a woman strutting her stuff for the horny sleazeballs that trolled the seedier streets of Minneapolis, looking to pay for sex. But then, this was the 'reformed' Rita Renner, not the woman who had been arrested for possession and found to keep her crack pipe in her vagina. What a difference sobriety had made.

'Did she have any enemies? Did you ever see anybody hassle her on the street?'

Renner looked confused. 'Every night. That's the way men are,' she said, glancing under her lashes at Rob. 'She got raped once, you know. People don't think you can rape a hooker, but you can. The cops caught the guy and he went away, but not for raping Fawn. He did some woman accountant in a parking ramp downtown. That's what he went away for. They didn't even want Fawn to testify. Like it didn't matter what he done to her.'

'Testimony about other possible crimes committed by a defendant isn't admissible in court, Ms Renner,' Rob said. 'That seems unfair, doesn't it?'

'It sucks.'

'Someone should have explained that to Ms Pierce. Do you know if she ever met with anyone from victim/witness services?'

'Yeah. She said it was a bunch of shit. She was supposed to go back a few times, but she never did. All they wanted to do was rehash it all.'

'Restating the events is crucial to the healing process,' Rob stated. He smiled in a way that seemed awkward and made his little pig eyes disappear. 'I highly recommend it to all my clients. In fact, I recommend they tape record themselves talking about their experience over a period of time, so they can actually hear the changes in their emotions and attitudes as they heal. It can be very cathartic.'

Renner just stared at him, her head a little to one side, like a small bird contemplating something new and strange.

Mary stifled a sigh of impatience. Having someone not in law enforcement 'helping' with an interview was about as helpful as an extra pinkie finger. 'Do you know of anyone in particular who might have wanted to hurt Fawn?'

'She said some guy had been calling her. Bugging her.'

'When was this?'

'Couple days before she died.'

'Did this guy have a name?'

'I don't remember. I was pretty strung out at the time. One of her johns, I guess. Can't you check the phone records?'

'It would work only if *she* called *him*.'

Renner frowned. 'It's not in a computer somewhere?'

'If you knew the guy's name, we could check *his* phone records.'

'I don't know.' Tears came to her eyes and she looked up at Toni Urskine, who patted her shoulder again. 'Fawn called him the Toad. I remember that.'

'Unfortunately, I don't think that'll be the name he uses with the phone company,' Rob Marshall said.

Toni Urskine gave him a pointed look. 'There's no need to get snide. Rita is doing the best she can.'

Rob scrambled to recover. 'Of course she is. I didn't mean to imply otherwise,' he said with a nervous smile, which he turned to Rita Renner. 'Can you recall any conversation you had with Fawn about this . . . Toad? If you could replay a conversation in your mind, it might come to you.'

'I don't know!' Renner whined, twisting one shirttail around her hand. 'I was on the rock then. And – and – why would I remember anyway? It wasn't like she was scared of him or anything.'

'That's okay, Rita. It might come to you later,' Moss said. 'Can you tell me if Fawn had any tattoos?'

Renner looked at her, confused again by the sudden change of direction. 'Sure, a couple. Why?'

'Can you tell me where they were on her body?'

'She had a rose on her ankle, and a shamrock on her stomach, and a pair of lips with a tongue sticking out on her butt. Why?'

Moss was saved from finding the noncommittal lie, as Gregg Urskine chose that moment to enter the room with a coffee tray. Picking up her tape recorder from the table, she rose and smiled apologetically.

'I'm afraid I can't stay. Thank you for the thought.'

'You don't want to warm up before you go back out into the cold, Detective?' Urskine asked, looking pleasant and vacuous.

'No time, but thanks.'

'I suppose there's extra pressure today,' Toni Urskine said with a hint of malicious pleasure. 'With everything that happened last night, the task force is looking exceptionally inept.'

'We're doing everything we can,' Moss said. 'In fact, Sergeant Kovac asked me to have you stop by the station later today, Mr Urskine, with a copy of your receipt for the inn you were staying at the weekend Lila White was murdered.'

Toni Urskine shot off the couch, her face flaming. 'What! That's outrageous!'

'It's a formality,' Moss assured. 'We're just crossing all our *t*s and dotting all our *i*s.'

'It's harassment, that's what.'

'A simple request. Of course, you're under no obligation to comply at this time. Sergeant Kovac didn't see the need for a warrant, considering how strongly you both feel about the thoroughness of the investigation.'

Gregg Urskine gave a nervous laugh, his attention on Toni. 'It's okay, honey. I'm sure I can find the receipt. It's not a problem.'

'It's an outrage!' Toni snapped. 'I'm calling our attorney. We've been nothing but conscientious citizens in all of this, and *this* is how we're treated! You can leave now, Ms Moss. Mr Marshall,' she added, including Rob as an afterthought.

'I think what we have here is a simple communication problem,' Rob said with the nervous grin. 'If my office can in any way facilitate –'

'Get out.'

Gregg Urskine reached out. 'Now, Toni –'

'Get out!' she shrieked, batting his hand away without even looking.

'We're only trying to do the best job for the victims, Mrs Urskine,' Moss said quietly. 'I thought that was what you wanted. Or is that only when the cameras are rolling?'

'Have you had a chance to talk to your friend in Milwaukee?' Kate asked. 'You faxed her the picture, right?'

'Yes, on the second. No, on the first,' Susan Frye answered.

Kate thanked God she had chosen to call rather than walk to the woman's office. Her frustration and impatience would have shown, she knew. Stress had shredded the veneer of manners, leaving all the emotional nerve endings exposed and raw. At this point, she thought, one wrong answer might drive her over the edge, and she'd wind up like the guy with the gun in the atrium.

'She's been tied up with a trial,' Frye said. 'I'll call and leave her a message.'

'Today.' Kate realized too late the word had come out as an order rather than as a question. 'Please, Susan? I'm in a world of hurt with this kid. I don't know what Rob was thinking. He should have assigned her to someone on your side of the fence. I don't do kids. I don't know how. And now she's gone –'

'I heard she might be dead,' Frye said bluntly. 'Don't they think she's the victim from last night?'

'We haven't heard for certain.' Kate mouthed the word *bitch* after. Some friend, swinging for the low blow. 'Even if it's true, we have to know who the kid is – was – so we can try to contact her family.'

'I'll guarantee you right now, Kate, you won't find any who could give a damn or she never would have ended up in this mess. Poor kid would have been better off aborted in the first trimester.'

The callousness of that statement struck Kate hard as she thanked Susan Frye for her dubious assistance and hung up the phone. It made her wonder what exactly had brought Angie DiMarco into the world – chance? fate? love? the desire for a check from Aid to Families with Dependent Children? Had her life gone wrong from conception, or had the mistakes come later, like tarnish slowly growing on silver that had been minted shiny and bright?

Her gaze went to the little picture of Emily in the pocket of her overhead cupboard. A beautiful small life, luminous with the promise of the future. She wondered if Angie had ever looked that innocent, or if her eyes had always held the weary bitterness of a bleak existence.

'Poor kid would have been better off aborted in the first trimester.'

But Angie DiMarco was living out her sad life, while Emily's had been taken.

Kate bolted out of her chair and began to pace the tiny space that was her office. If she didn't lose her mind by the end of the day, it was going to be a miracle.

She had fully expected a command to Sabin's office first thing, or, at the very least, an order to Rob's office for a formal dressing-down for the things she'd said in the parking lot the previous night. No such call had come ... yet. And so she had tried to fend off thoughts of Angie being dead by taking proactive measures to find out about the girl's life. But every time she so much as slowed down her thought process, she heard the screams from the tape.

And every time she tried to think of something else entirely, she thought of Quinn.

Not wanting Quinn in her mind, she sat down again, grabbed the telephone receiver, and dialed another number. She had other clients to think of. At least she did until Rob fired her.

She called David Willis and got a very long, overly detailed explanation of how to leave a message on his machine. She tried her rape victim at home with similar results, then tried her at work and was told by the manager of the adult bookstore that Melanie Hessler had been fired.

'As of when?' Kate demanded.

'As of today. She's had too many absences.'

'She's suffering from post-traumatic stress,' Kate pointed out. 'Because of a crime committed against her on *your* property, I might add.'

'That wasn't *our* fault.'

'Post-traumatic stress has been ruled a disability by the courts, and therefore falls under the Americans with Disabilities Act.' She sank her teeth into the sense of injustice, almost glad for the chance to tear into someone. 'If you discriminate against Melanie on the basis of this disability, she can sue you out of existence.'

'Listen, lady,' the manager said, 'maybe you ought to talk to Melanie about this before you go around threatening people, 'cause I don't think she's all that bent out of shape about it. I haven't heard boo from her all week.'

'I thought you said you fired her.'

'I did. I left it on her machine.'

'You *fired* her on her answering machine? What kind of rotten coward are you?'

'The kind that's hanging up on you, bitch,' he said, slamming down the receiver.

Kate hung up absently, trying to think when she had last spoken to Melanie Hessler. A week ago at most, she thought. BC – before the Cremator case. There hadn't been time to call her since. Angie had taken up all her time. It seemed too long now that she thought of it. Melanie's calls had become more frequent as the trial drew closer and her nerves wound tighter and tighter.

'I haven't heard boo from her all week.'

Kate supposed she might have gone out of town, but Melanie would have let her know. She checked in as if Kate were her parole officer. This felt wrong. The court, in its infinite wisdom, had seen fit to release Melanie's attackers on bail, but the cops had been good about keeping tabs on them, with the detective in charge of the case staying on top of the situation.

I'm just spooked about everything because of Angie, Kate thought. There was probably no cause for alarm. Still, she followed her instincts, picked up the phone again, and dialed the detective in sex crimes.

He'd heard nothing from their victim either, but knew that one of her perps had been picked up over the weekend for assaulting a former girlfriend. Kate explained what she knew and asked him to drop by Melanie Hessler's house, just to check.

'I'll head over that way after lunch.'

'Thanks, Bernie. You're a peach. I'm probably just being paranoid, but . . .'

'Just because you're paranoid doesn't mean life's not out to get you.'

'True. And my luck isn't exactly on high tide here.'

'Hang in there, Kate. Things can always get worse.'

Cop humor. She couldn't quite appreciate it today.

She tried to turn her attention to a stack of paperwork, but turned away from it and pulled Angie's file instead, hoping she might see something in it that would prompt an idea for some kind of action. Sitting in this office, waiting, was going to make her brain explode.

The file was woefully thin. More questions than answers. Could the girl have left the Phoenix herself? If so, where had the blood come from? She flashed on the scene in the bathroom: the bloody handprint on the tile, the diluted blood trickling down the tub drain, the bloody towels in the hamper. More blood than any reasonable explanation could account for.

But if Smokey Joe had come for her, how had he found her, and how was it Rita Renner had heard nothing – no doors, no struggle, no nothing?

More questions than answers.

The phone rang, and Kate picked it up, half hoping, half dreading to hear Kovac on the other end of the line with news of the autopsy on victim number four.

'Kate Conlan.'

The polished voice of a secretary delivered unwelcome news of another variety. 'Ms Conlan? Mr Sabin would like to see you in his office now.'

26

'So, is this Sergeant Kovac coming or what?'

Liska checked her watch as she walked back into the interview room. It was almost noon and the room was uncomfortably hot. Vanlees had been waiting almost an hour, and he wasn't liking it.

'He's on his way. He should be here anytime now. I called him the minute you said you'd come talk, Gil. He really wants to get your take on things regarding Jillian. But, you know, he's over at that autopsy – the woman that got lit up last night. That's why he's running late. It won't be much longer.'

She'd given him that line at least three times, and he was clearly tired of hearing it.

'Yeah, well, you know I want to help, but I got other things to do,' he said. He sat across the table from her wearing work clothes – navy pants and shirt. Like a janitor might wear, Liska thought. Or like a cop uniform with no embellishments. 'I've got to work this afternoon –'

'Oh, you're squared with that.' She waved off his concern. 'I called your boss and cleared it. Didn't want you getting into trouble for being a good citizen.'

He looked as if he didn't like that idea much either. He shifted on his chair. His gaze went to the mirror on the wall behind Liska. 'You know we have one of those at the Target Center, back in the offices. Anybody on the other side?'

Liska blinked innocence. 'Why would there be anybody on the other side? It's not like you're under arrest. You're here to help us.'

Vanlees stared at the glass.

Liska turned and stared at it too, wondering how she must look to Quinn. Like some worn-out barfly in a smoky lounge, no doubt. If the bags under her eyes got any bigger, she was going to need a luggage cart to carry them. The middle of a serial murder investigation was not the time to want to impress anyone with her fresh good looks.

'So you heard about the fourth victim,' she said, turning back to Vanlees. 'That's some balls this guy has, lighting her up in that parking lot, huh?'

'Yeah, like he's trying to send a message or something.'

'Arrogant. That's what Quinn says. Smokey Joe's flipping us off.'

Vanlees frowned. 'Smokey Joe? I thought you called him the Cremator.'

'That's what the press calls him. To us, he's Smokey Joe.' She leaned across the table to suggest intimacy. 'Don't tell anyone I told you that. It's supposed to be just an inside cop thing – you know?'

Vanlees nodded, hip to the ways of the cop world. Cool with the inside secrets. Mr Professional.

'She's good,' Quinn said, watching through the glass. He and Kovac had been standing there twenty minutes, biding their time, watching, waiting, letting Gil Vanlees's nerves work on him.

'Yeah. No one ever suspects Tinker Bell will work them over.' Kovac sniffed at the lapel of his suit and made a face. 'Jesus, I stink. Eau de autopsy with a hint of smoke. So what do you think of this mutt?'

'He's twitchy. I think we can scare him a little here, then ride his tail from the second he leaves. See what he does. If he spooks hard enough, you might get a search warrant out of it,' Quinn said, his eyes never leaving Vanlees. 'He fits in a lot of ways, but he's not the sharpest knife in the drawer, is he?'

'Maybe he just plays it stupid so people expect less of him. I've seen that more than once.'

Quinn made a noncommittal sound. As a rule, the type of killer they were looking for went out of his way to show off what brains he had. That vanity was a common downfall. Invariably, they were not as smart as they wanted to believe, and screwed up trying to show off to the cops.

'Let him know you know about the window peeping,' Quinn said. 'Press on that nerve. He won't like it. He won't want cops thinking he's a pervert. And if he's held to the usual pattern, if he's looked in windows, he's maybe tried fetish burglaries. These guys work their way up. Fish in that pond a little.

'Keep him off balance,' he suggested. 'Let him think you might do something crazy, that you're fighting with yourself to keep control. The case and the brilliance of this killer are pushing you to the edge. Suggest it, don't admit it. Put all your acting skills to use.'

Kovac jerked his tie loose and mussed his hair. 'Acting? You'll want to give me the fucking Oscar.'

'Do they know yet who the vic is?' Vanlees asked.

The *vic.*

'I heard they found her ID during the autopsy,' Liska said. 'Kovac wouldn't tell me about it, except to say it made him sick. He said he wants to find this sick son of a bitch and stick something in him.'

'It was *in her body?*' Vanlees said with a mix of horror and fascination. 'I read about a case like that once.'

'You read true crime?'

'Some,' he admitted cautiously. 'It gives me insights.'

Into what? Nikki wondered. 'Yeah, me too. So what was the guy's story?'

'His mother was a prostitute, and because of that he hated prostitutes, and so he killed them. And he always stuck something in their –' He caught himself and blushed. 'Well, you know . . .'

Liska didn't blink. 'Vagina?'

Vanlees looked away and shifted on his chair again. 'It's really hot in here.'

He picked up a glass, but it was empty and so was the plastic pitcher on the table.

'What do you suppose the killer gets out of that?' Liska asked, watching him closely. 'Sticking things in a woman's vagina. You think it makes him feel tough? Powerful? What?

'Is it disrespect on an adult level?' she posed. 'It always strikes me as something a snotty brat little boy would do – if he knew what a vagina was. Like sticking beans up his nose, or wanting to poke the eyes out of a dead cat in the road. It seems juvenile somehow, but on this job I see grown men do it all the time. What's your take on that, Gil?'

He frowned. A single bead of sweat skimmed down the side of his face. 'I don't have one.'

'Well, you must, all the studying and true crime reading you've done. Put yourself in the killer's place. Why would you want to stick some foreign object up a woman's vagina? Because you couldn't do the job with your dick? Is that it?'

Vanlees had turned pink. He wouldn't look at her. 'Shouldn't Kovac be here by now?'

'Any minute.'

'I gotta use the men's room,' he mumbled. 'Maybe I should go do that.'

The door swung open and Kovac walked in – hair mussed, tie jerked loose, rumpled suit hanging on him like a wet sack. He scowled at Liska, then turned it on Vanlees.

'This is him?'

Liska nodded. 'Gil Vanlees, Sergeant Kovac.'

Vanlees started to offer his hand. Kovac stared at it as if it were covered with shit.

'I got four women hacked up like Halloween pumpkins and burned to a crisp. I'm in no mood to fuck around. Where were you last night between the hours of ten and two A.M.?'

Vanlees looked as if he'd been hit in the face. 'What – ?'

'Sam,' Liska said with annoyance. 'Mr Vanlees came in to give us some insight on –'

'I want his insight on last night between ten and two. Where were you?'

'Home.'

'Home where? I understand your wife threw you out for wagging your willy at a friend of hers.'

'That was a misunderstanding –'

'Between you and your johnson, or between you and this broad whose windows you were looking in?'

'It wasn't like that.'

'It never is. Tell me, how much time did you spend looking in Jillian Bondurant's windows?'

His face was crimson now. 'I didn't –'

'Oh, come on. She was kind of a hot little ticket, wasn't she? Curvy. Exotic. Dressed a little provocatively – those filmy little dresses and combat boots and dog collars and shit like that. A guy might want a piece of that – especially if the home fires went out, you know what I'm saying?'

'I don't like what you're saying.' Vanlees looked to Liska. 'Do I need a lawyer? Should I have a lawyer here?'

'Jesus, Sam,' Liska said, disgusted. She turned to Vanlees. 'I'm sorry, Gil.'

'Don't apologize for me!' Kovac snapped.

Vanlees looked warily from one to the other. 'What is this? Good cop–bad cop? I'm not stupid. I don't need to take this shit.'

He started to get out of his chair. Kovac lunged toward him, wild-eyed, pointing at him with one hand and slamming the other on the tabletop. 'Sit! Please!'

Vanlees dropped back into the chair, his face washing white. Making an obvious show to control himself, Kovac pulled himself back one step and then another, lifting his hands and lowering his head, breathing heavily through his mouth.

'Please,' he said more quietly. 'Please. Sit. I'm sorry. I'm sorry.'

He paced for a minute between the table and the door, watching Vanlees out of the corner of his eye. Vanlees was looking at him the way he might look at a wild gorilla had he found himself accidentally locked in the pen with one at the Como Park Zoo.

'Do I need a lawyer?' he asked Liska again.

'Why would you need a lawyer, Gil? You haven't done anything wrong that I know of. You're not under arrest. But if you think you need one . . .'

He looked between the two detectives, trying to figure out if this was some kind of trick.

'I'm sorry,' Kovac said as he pulled a chair out at the end of the table and sat down. Shaking his head, he fished a cigarette out of his shirt pocket, lit it, and took a long drag.

'I've had about three hours of sleep all week,' he said on a breath of smoke. 'I've just come from one of the worst autopsies I've seen in years.' He shook his head and stared at the table. 'What was done to this woman –'

He let the silence drag, smoking his cigarette as if they were all in the break room taking their fifteen minutes away from the desk. Finally, he stubbed it out on the sole of his shoe and dropped the butt in an empty coffee cup. He rubbed his hands over his face and combed his mustache with his thumbs.

'Where is it you're living now, Gil?' he asked.

'On Lyndale –'

'No. I mean this friend you're house-sitting for. Where is that?'

'Over by Lake Harriet.'

'We'll need an address. Give it to Nikki here before you go. How long you been doing that – house-sitting?'

'Off and on. The guy travels a lot.'

'What's he do?'

'He imports electronics and sells them over the Internet. Computers and stereos, and stuff like that.'

'So why don't you just bunk in with him all the time and dump the apartment?'

'He's got a girlfriend. She lives with him.'

'She there now?'

'No. She travels with him.'

'So, how about you, Gil? You seeing anybody?'

'No.'

'No? You been separated for a while. A man has needs.'

Liska made a sound of disgust. 'Like you think a woman doesn't?'

Kovac gave her a perturbed look. 'Tinks, your needs are common knowledge. Would you pretend for a minute you're not liberated and go get us some more water? It's hotter than hell in here.'

'I don't mind the heat,' she said. 'But the way you smell could turn the stomach of a sewer rat. Jeez, Sam.'

'Just get the water.'

He shrugged out of his suit jacket and let it fall inside out over the back of his chair as Liska left grumbling. Vanlees watched her go, unhappy.

'Sorry about the stink,' Kovac said. 'You ever wanted to know what a charred dead body smells like, now's your chance. Breathe deep.'

Vanlees just looked at him.

'So, you never answered my question, Gil. Do you pay for it? You like hookers? You see a lot of them around where you work. Pay them enough, you can do what you like. Some of them will even let you knock 'em around a little, if you're into that. Tie them down, stuff like that.'

'Detective Liska said you wanted to talk to me about Ms Bondurant,' Vanlees said stiffly. 'I don't know anything about those other murders.'

Kovac paused, rolling up his shirtsleeves and gave him the cop stare. 'But you know something about Jillian's murder?'

'No! That's not what I meant.'

'What *do* you know about Jillian, Gil?'

'Just how she was around the Edgewater, that's all. My take on her. Like that.'

Kovac nodded and sat back. 'So how was she? She ever come on to you?'

'No! She mostly kept her head down, didn't talk much.'

'She didn't talk to anyone or she didn't talk to you? Maybe she didn't like the way you watched her, Gil,' he said, poking once again at the sore spot.

Sweat beaded on Vanlees's forehead. 'I didn't watch her.'

'Did you flirt with her? Come on to her?'

'No.'

'You had a key to her place. You ever go in there when she wasn't around?'

'No!' The denial did not come with eye contact.

Kovac went for another of Quinn's hunches. 'Ever dig through her panty drawer, maybe take a souvenir?'

'No!' Vanlees shoved his chair back from the table and got to his feet. 'I don't like this. I came in here to help you. You shouldn't treat me like this.'

'So help me, Gil,' Kovac said with a nonchalant shrug. 'Give me something I can use. You ever see a boyfriend hanging around her place?'

'No. Just that friend of hers – Michele. And her father. He came over sometimes. He owns her place, you know.'

'Yeah, I suppose. The guy's as rich as Rockefeller. You ever think maybe this deal with Jillian was a kidnapping? Someone wanting to tap in to the father lode, so to speak? You ever see any suspicious characters hanging around, scoping out the place?'

'No.'

'And you've been hanging around enough to notice, isn't that right?'

'I work there.'

'Not exactly, but what the hay – saying so gives you just cause to be there, check out the various apartments, maybe do a little lingerie shopping.'

Purple in the face, Vanlees declared, 'I'm leaving now.'

'But we've barely started,' Kovac protested.

The door swung open again and Liska came in with the water. Quinn held the door and came in behind her. In contrast to Kovac, he looked crisp and fresh except for the dark circles under his eyes and the lines etched deep beside them. His face was a hard, emotionless mask. He took a paper cup from Liska, filled it with water, and drank it down slowly before he said a word. Vanlees's gaze was on him the whole time.

'Mr Vanlees, John Quinn, FBI,' he said, holding out his hand.

Vanlees was quick to accept the gesture. His hand was wide and clammy with stubby fingers. 'I've read about you. It's an honor to meet you.'

He took his seat again as Quinn went to the chair directly across from him. Quinn slipped his dark suit jacket off and hung it neatly on the back of the chair. He smoothed his gray silk tie as he sat down.

'You know a little about me, do you, Mr Vanlees?'

'Yeah. Some.'

'Then you probably have some idea how my mind works,' Quinn said. 'You probably know what conclusion I might draw looking at the history of a man who wanted to be a cop but couldn't cut it, a man with a history of window peeping and fetish burglary –'

Vanlees's face dropped. 'I'm not – I didn't –'

Liska picked up the Polaroid camera sitting on the table and quickly took his picture.

Vanlees jumped as the flash went off. 'Hey!'

'A man whose wife has evicted him and criticizes his sexual abilities,' Quinn went on.

'What? She said what?' Vanlees sputtered. His expression now was a mix of torment and embarrassment and disbelief. A man caught awake in a nightmare. He came out of the chair once more to pace. Circles of sweat ringed the armpits of his dark shirt. 'I can't believe this!'

'You knew Jillian Bondurant,' Quinn went on without emotion. 'You were watching her.'

He denied it again, shaking his head, his eyes on the floor as he paced. 'I didn't. I don't care what that bitch told you.'

'What bitch is that?' Quinn asked calmly.

Vanlees stopped and looked at him. 'That friend of hers. She said something about me, didn't she?'

'That friend whose name you didn't know?' Liska asked. She stood between Quinn and Kovac, looking tough. 'You told me you didn't know her. But you said her name not five minutes ago, Gil. Michele. Michele Fine. Why would you lie to me about knowing her?'

'I didn't. I don't know her. Her name just slipped my mind, that's all.'

'And if you'd lie to me about a little thing like that,' Liska said, 'I've got to wonder what else you'd lie about.'

Vanlees glared at them, red in the face, tears in his eyes, mouth quivering with temper. 'Fuck you people. You've got nothing on me. I'm leaving. I came here to help you and you treat me like a common criminal. Fuck you!'

'Don't sell yourself short, Mr Vanlees,' Quinn said. 'If you're the man we're looking for, there's nothing common about you.'

Vanlees said nothing. No one stopped him from throwing open the door. He stormed out, his steps hurried as he made for the men's room down the hall.

Kovac leaned against the doorjamb, watching. 'Touchy guy.'

'Almost like he has something to feel guilty about.' Liska looked up at Quinn. 'What do you think?'

Quinn watched Vanlees bull the men's room door open with his shoulder, already reaching for his fly with his other hand. He adjusted the knot in his tie and stroked a hand down the strip of silk. 'I think I'll go freshen up.'

The stench in the men's room was hot and fresh. Vanlees was not at the urinals. One pair of thick-soled black work shoes showed beneath the stalls. Quinn went to the sinks, turned on a faucet, filled his cupped hands, and rinsed his face. The toilet flushed and a moment later Vanlees emerged, sweaty and pale. He froze in his tracks at the sight of Quinn.

'Everything all right, Mr Vanlees?' Quinn asked without real concern as he dried his hands on a paper towel.

'You're harassing me,' he accused.

Quinn raised his brows. 'I'm drying my hands.'

'You followed me in here.'

'Just making sure you're all right, Gil.' *My buddy, my pal.* 'I know you're upset. I don't blame you. But I want you to realize this isn't personal. I'm not after *you* personally. I'm after a killer. I have to do what I have to do to make that happen. You understand that, don't you? What I'm after is the truth, justice, nothing more, nothing less.'

'I didn't hurt Jillian,' Vanlees said defensively. 'I wouldn't.'

Quinn weighed the statements carefully. He never expected a serial killer to admit to anything. Many of them spoke of their crimes in the third person, even after they had been proven guilty beyond any doubt. And many referred to the side of themselves that was capable of committing murder as a separate entity. The evil twin syndrome, he called it. It enabled those with some small scrap of conscience to rationalize, to push the guilt away from themselves and onto their dark side.

The Gil Vanlees standing before him wouldn't kill anyone. But what about his dark side?

'Do you know someone who would hurt Jillian, Gil?' he asked.

Vanlees frowned at his feet. 'No.'

'Well, in case you think of someone.' Quinn held out a business card.

Vanlees took it reluctantly and looked at the front and the back, as if searching for some tiny homing device imbedded in the paper.

'We need to stop this killer, Gil,' Quinn said, giving him a long, level stare. 'He's a bad, bad guy, and I'll do whatever I have to do to put him away. Whoever he is.'

'Good,' Vanlees murmured. 'I hope you do.'

He slipped the card into his breast pocket and left the men's room without washing his hands. Quinn frowned and turned back to the sink, staring at himself hard in the mirror, as if he might be able to see some sign in his own visage, some secret sure knowledge that Gil Vanlees was the one.

The pieces were there. If they all fit together right . . . If the cops could come up with just one piece of evidence . . .

Kovac came in a moment later and reeled backward at the lingering smell. 'Jeez! What'd that guy eat for breakfast – roadkill?'

'Nerves,' Quinn said.

'Wait'll he figures out there's a cop on his tail every time he turns around.'

'Let's hope he bolts. If you can get in his truck, you might hit pay dirt. Or maybe he's just another pathetic loser who's a couple of clicks to the right of killing anybody. And the real Smokey Joe is sitting home right now, jerking off as he listens to one of his torture tapes.'

'Speaking of, the techno-geek at the BCA called,' Kovac said. 'He thinks we'll want to come listen to that tape from last night now that he's played with it.'

'Could he pull out the killer's voice?'

'*Killers*, plural,' Kovac said soberly. 'He thinks there's two of them. And get this. He thinks one is a woman.'

Kate walked into Sabin's office, thinking it had been just a matter of days since the meeting that had brought her into this case. In some ways it seemed like a year. In that span of days, her life had changed. And it wasn't over yet. Not by a long shot.

Sabin and Rob rose from their chairs. Sabin looking tired and dour. Rob sprang up. His small eyes seemed too bright in his pumpkin head, and he looked as if he had a temperature. The fever of self-righteous indignation.

'So where's the guy with the black hood and the ax?' Kate asked, stopping behind the chair intended for her.

Sabin frowned as if she'd just spoiled his opening line.

Rob looked to him. 'See? That's exactly what I'm talking about!'

'Kate, this is hardly the time for cracking jokes,' Sabin said.

'Was I joking? I've managed to lose the only witness in the biggest murder investigation the Cities have seen in years. You're not giving me the ax? After last night, I'm surprised Rob isn't holding it himself.'

'Don't think I wouldn't like to be,' Rob said. 'You're entirely too flip, Kate. I've had it with your attitude toward me. You have no respect.'

She turned to Sabin, discounting her boss without saying a word. 'But . . . ?'

'But I'm intervening, Kate,' Sabin said, taking his seat. 'This is a highly charged situation. Tempers are running high all around.'

'But she *always* treats me like this!'

'Stop whining, Rob,' Sabin ordered. 'She's also the best advocate you've got. You know it. You suggested her for this assignment for very specific reasons.'

'Need I remind you, we no longer have a witness?'

Sabin glared at him. 'No, you don't need to remind me.'

'Angie was my responsibility,' Kate said. 'No one is more sorry about this than I am. If I could do anything – If I could go back to yesterday and do something differently –'

'You delivered the girl to the Phoenix last night yourself. Isn't that right?' Sabin said in his prosecutor's voice.

'Yes.'

'And the house was supposedly under surveillance by the police. Isn't that right?'

'Yes.'

'Then I blame this nightmare on them. Whatever became of the girl – whether she was taken or left on her own – is their fault, not yours.'

Kate glanced at her watch, thinking the autopsy was long over by now. If there had been any definitive proof the body in the car last night was Angie's, Sabin would know.

'I want you to remain available to the case, Kate –'

'Do we know –' she began, her heart rate picking up as she struggled to phrase the question, as if the answer would depend on how she put it. 'The victim in the car – have you heard one way or the other?'

Rob gave her a nasty look. 'Oh, didn't one of your police buddies call you from the morgue?'

'I'm sure they're a little busy today.'

'The victim's driver's license was found during the autopsy.' He drew a breath to deliver the news fast and hard, then seemed to think better of it. At that hesitation, Kate felt her nerves tighten. 'Maybe you should sit down, Kate,' he said, overly solicitous.

'No.' Already chills were racing up and down her body, raising goose bumps in the wake. Her fingers tightened on the back of the chair. 'Why?'

Rob no longer looked smug or angry. His expression had gone carefully blank. 'The victim was Melanie Hessler. Your client.'

27

'I'm sorry,' Rob said.

His voice sounded far away. Kate felt all the blood drain from her head. Her legs gave way beneath her. She went down on one knee, still holding on to the back of the chair, and scrambled to stand again just as quickly. Emotions swirled through her like a cyclone – shock, horror, embarrassment, confusion. Sabin came around from behind his desk to take her arm as Rob stood staring, flatfooted and awkward, four feet away.

'Are you all right?' Sabin asked.

Kate sank down on the chair, for once not minding when he put his hand on her knee. He knelt beside her, looking at her with concern.

'Kate?'

'Um – no,' she said. She felt dizzy and weak and ill, and suddenly nothing seemed quite real. 'I – ah – I don't understand.'

'I'm sorry, Kate,' Rob said again, coming forward suddenly, looking as if it had just occurred to him that he should do something now that it was too late. 'I know you were very protective of her.'

'I just tried to call her,' Kate said weakly. 'I should have called her Monday, but suddenly there was Angie, and everything just got away from me.'

Images of Melanie Hessler played through her mind in a montage. An ordinary, almost shy woman with a slight build and a bad home perm. Working in an adult bookstore embarrassed her, but she needed the job until she could scrape together enough money to go back to school. A divorce had left her with no cash and no skills. The attack she had suffered months ago had left her fragile – damaged emotionally, psychologically, physically. She had become chronically fearful, skittish, waiting for her attackers to come after her again – a common fear among rape victims. Only it wasn't the men who had raped her Melanie had to fear, as it turned out.

'Oh, Jesus,' Kate said, putting her head in her hands.

She closed her eyes and saw the body, charred and horrible, disfigured, twisted, shrunken, stinking, violated, mutilated. Kate had held Melanie's hand and comforted her as she had related the awful details of her rape, the deep sense of shame and embarrassment she had felt, the confusion that such a terrible thing should have happened to her.

Melanie Hessler, who had been so frightened of being hurt again. Tortured, brutalized, burned beyond recognition.

And in the back of her mind, Kate could hear the store manager's voice: *'I haven't heard boo from her all week.'*

When had the son of a bitch taken her? How long had he kept her alive? How long had she begged for death, all the while wondering what kind of God could make her suffer that way?

'Dammit.' Kate let the anger well up, trying to draw strength from it. 'Goddammit.'

Rob's voice came to her again through the maze of her thoughts. 'Kate, you know it would help you to talk about what you're feeling now. Let it out. You knew Melanie. You'd helped her through so much. To think of her the way you saw her last night –'

'Why?' she demanded of no one in particular. 'Why would he choose her? I don't understand how this happened.'

'It probably had to do with her working in that adult bookstore,' Rob offered.

Rob knew the case as well as she did. He had sat in on several meetings with Melanie, had gone over the tapes of those meetings with Kate, and suggested a support group for Melanie.

Tapes.

'Oh, God,' Kate whispered, her strength draining again in a rush. 'That tape. Oh, my God.' She doubled over, putting her head in her hands.

'What tape?' Rob asked.

The screams of pain, of fear, of torment and anguish. The screams of a woman she had known, a woman who had trusted her and looked to her for support and protection within the justice system.

'Kate?'

'Excuse me,' she mumbled, pushing unsteadily to her feet. 'I have to go be sick.'

The dizziness tilted her one way and then another, and she grabbed what solid objects she could as she went. The ladies' room seemed a mile away. The faces she encountered en route were blurred and distorted, the voices warped and muted and slurred.

One of her clients was dead. One was missing. She was the only common link between them.

Crouching beside a toilet, holding her hair back with one hand, she lost what little she'd eaten, her stomach trying to reject not only the food, but the images and ideas she had just been force-fed in Ted Sabin's office, and the thoughts that were now seeping like poison through her brain. *Her client, her responsibility. She was the only link . . .*

When the spasms stopped, she sank down on the floor of the stall, feeling weak and clammy, not caring where she was, not feeling the cold of the floor through her slacks. The tremors that shook her body came not from the cold, but from shock and from a heavy black sense of foreboding that swept over her soul like a storm cloud.

One of her clients was dead. Tortured, murdered, burned. One was missing, a hastily wiped trail of blood left behind.

She was the only common link between them.

She had to be logical, think straight. It was coincidence, certainly. How could it be anything else? Rob was right: Smokey Joe had chosen Melanie because of her connection to the adult bookstore that happened to be in the same part of town frequented by hookers like the first two victims. And Angie had already been connected to the killer when Kate had been assigned the case.

Still that black cloud hovered, pressing down on her. A strange instinctive reaction she couldn't shake.

Too much stress. Too little sleep. Too much bad luck. She leaned her head back against the wall and tried to force her brain to move past the images from the crime scenes last night.

Do something.

The directive that had gotten her through every crisis she'd ever faced. *Don't just sit there. Do something.* Action countered helplessness, regardless of outcome. She had to move, go, think, *do something.*

The first thing she wanted to do was call Quinn, an instinctive urge she immediately defied. Just because they'd spent a night together didn't mean she could lean on him. There had been no guarantee of a future in those few hours. She didn't know that she even wanted to hope for a future with him. They had too much of a past.

At any rate, this wasn't the time to think about it. Now that she knew Angie hadn't been the victim in the car, there was still some hope the girl was alive. There had to be something she could do to help find her.

She hauled herself up off the floor, flushed the john, and left the stall. A woman in a prissy, snot-green suit stood at one of the sinks, redoing her already perfect makeup, tubes and jars spread out on the counter. Kate gave her a wan smile and moved two sinks down to wash her hands and face.

Making a cup of her hand, she rinsed her mouth out. She looked at herself in the mirror, the makeup woman just in the fringe of her peripheral vision. She looked like hell – bruised up, beat up, dragged down, pale. She looked exactly the way she felt.

'This job will be the death of you, Kate,' she muttered to her reflection.

Brandishing a mascara wand, Makeup Woman paused to frown at her.

Kate flashed her a lunatic smile. 'Well, I guess they can't start that competency hearing without me,' she said brightly, and walked out.

Rob waited for her in the hall, looking embarrassed to be within proximity of a women's toilet. He pulled a handkerchief out of his hip pocket and dabbed at his forehead. Kate scowled at him.

'What?' she demanded. 'Now that Sabin's out of earshot, you're going to tell me how Melanie Hessler's death is somehow my fault? If I'd turned her case over to you on Monday, that would have somehow prevented her from falling into the hands of this sick son of a bitch?'

He faked a look of affront. 'No! Why would you say such a thing?'

'Because maybe that's what I'm thinking,' she admitted, going to the railing overlooking the atrium. 'I think nobody can do my job as well as I can. But I didn't do my job, and now Melanie's dead.'

'Why would you think you could have prevented what happened?' He stared at her with a mix of bemusement and resentment. 'You think you're Wonder Woman or something? You think everything is about you?'

'No. I just know that I should have called her and I neglected to do so. If I had, at least someone would have known and cared she was missing. She didn't have anyone else.'

'And so she was your responsibility,' he said. 'Like Angie.'

'The buck has to stop somewhere.'

'With you. Kathryn the Great,' he said with a hint of bitter sarcasm.

Kate lifted her chin and gave him the imperious glare. 'You were quick enough to dump the blame on me last night,' she pointed out. 'I don't get you, Rob. You tell me I'm just the person you want for this case, then you turn around and whine about the way I work it. You want to blame me for what's gone wrong, but you don't want me to accept that blame.'

'What's your problem?' she asked. 'Does my taking responsibility somehow screw up your strategy with Sabin? If I'm willing to take the blame, you can't be contrite and obsequious on my behalf. Is that it?'

The muscles of his wide jaw worked and something nasty flashed in his small eyes. 'You'll live to regret the way you treat me, Kate. Maybe not today. Maybe not tomorrow. But one day –'

'You can't fire me today, Rob,' she said. 'Sabin won't let you. And I'm in no mood to play your little posturing games. If you have a point for being here right now, please get to it. I have a job to do – at least for the next few hours.'

His eyes narrowed to slits and he moved his weight from foot to foot. His face grew darker. She'd pushed too hard, crossed a line she might not be able to get back over with a simple apology and a promise to behave, but she wasn't about to back down from him now.

'The police want you to go over Melanie's interview tapes to see if she mentioned something that might be pertinent to this case,' he said stiffly. 'I thought it would be too much for you, considering,' he went on with the affected tone of the wounded martyr. 'I was going to offer to help.'

'*Was?* Does that mean the offer has been rescinded because you've decided I'm an ungrateful bitch after all?'

He gave her an unpleasant smile, his eyes disappearing behind the lenses of his glasses. 'No. I won't let your attitude interfere with my job. We'll listen to the tapes together. You listen for things that seem out of place to you because you knew her. I'll listen objectively from a linguistics angle. Meet me in my office in five minutes.'

Kate watched him waddle off, thinking that she hated him almost as much as she was going to hate doing this job.

'Why can't I just stick an ice pick in my forehead?' she muttered to herself, and fell in step after him.

'This tape is a copy,' the BCA tech explained.

They – Kovac, Quinn, Liska, and a skinny guy Kovac called Ears – crowded together around a bank of black-faced electronics equipment studded with an amazing array of knobs and levers and lights and gauges.

'The quality of the sound is much better than you'd ever get off a microcassette recorder,' Ears said. 'In fact, I'd say the killer actually had a mike clipped to the victim, or stationed very close to her. That would account for the distortion in the screams. It would also explain why the other voices are so indistinct.'

'You're sure there are two voices?' Quinn asked, the ramifications of that possibility filling his brain.

'Yes. Here, listen.'

The tech punched a button and adjusted a knob. A scream filled the small room, all four people tensing against it as if it were a physical assault.

Quinn fought to focus not on the emotions within the scream, but on the individual components of sound, trying to eliminate the human factor and his own human reaction to it. Reliving their crimes was a crucial component of a serial killer's life cycle – fantasy, violent fantasy, facilitators to murder, murder, fantasy, violent fantasy, and on and on, around and around.

Cheap technology made it as easy as the flick of a switch and the focus of a lens for them to play back something more perfect than a memory. Cheap technology combined with the killer's egotistic need had also made for a lot of damning evidence in recent years. The trick for cops and prosecutors was to stomach hearing and seeing it. Bad enough to see the aftermath of crimes like these. Having to watch or listen to them in progress could take a horrible toll.

Quinn had watched or listened to one after another, after another, after another . . .

Ears turned one knob down and pushed two small levers up. 'Coming up here. I've isolated and muted the victim's voice and pulled out the others. Listen close.'

No one so much as took a breath. The screams faded into the background and a man's voice, soft and indistinct said, '. . . Turn . . . do it . . .' followed by white noise, followed by an even less distinct voice that said, '. . . Want to . . . of me . . .'

'That's as good as it gets,' Ears said, punching buttons, running the tape back. 'I can make it louder, but the voices won't be any more distinguishable. They were too far away from the mike. But by the readings I'm seeing, I'd say the first one is a man and the second one is a woman.'

Quinn thought of the stab wounds to each victim's chest, the distinct pattern: long wound, short wound, long wound, short wound . . . *Cross my heart, hope to die* . . . A pact, a pledge, a covenant. Two knives – the light flashing off one and then the other as they descended in a macabre rhythm.

Those wounds made sense now. He should have thought of it himself: two knives, two killers. It wasn't as if he hadn't seen it happen before. But he sure as hell didn't want to have to see it again, he realized as resistance rose like panic up through his chest.

Murder didn't get any darker or more twisted than when the killers were a couple. The dynamics of that kind of relationship epitomized the sickest extremes of human behavior. The obsessions and compulsions, the fears and sadistic fantasies of two equally disturbed people tangled like a pair of vipers trying to devour each other.

'Will you play with the tape some more, Ears?' Kovac asked. 'See if you can't pull out a few more words from one or both of them? I'd like to know what they're talking about.'

The tech shrugged. 'I'll try, but I'm not making any promises.'

'Do what you can. The career you save could be mine.'

'Then you'll owe me *two* cases of beer I'll never see in this lifetime.'

'Crack this for me, I'll send you a lifetime supply of Pig's Eye.'

Quinn led the way back into the hall, already trying to sort through the tangle in his head in order to take his attention away from the tight feeling in his throat. Concentrate on the problem at hand, not the problem inside. Try not to think that just when he was beginning to feel they were making some progress, the number of killers multiplied, like something in a nightmare.

Kovac brought up the rear, shutting the door behind him.

'There's a wrinkle we didn't need,' he complained. 'Bad enough looking for one psycho. Now I get to tell the bosses we're looking for two of them.'

'Don't tell them,' Quinn said. 'Not right away. I need to think about this.'

He put his back to the wall as if he intended to stand right there until the answer came to him.

'What's it do to the profile if he's got a partner?' Liska asked.

'What's it do to the profile if he's got a partner and his partner is a woman?' Quinn asked back.

'Complicates the hell out of my life,' Kovac said.

The hall was dark with a low ceiling and not much traffic this time of day. Two women in lab coats walked past, engrossed in a conversation about office politics. Quinn waited until they were out of earshot.

'Are they equal partners, or is the woman what we call a "willing victim"? Is she participating because she likes it, or because she feels she has to for one reason or another – she's afraid of him, he controls her, whatever.' He turned to Liska. 'Does Gil Vanlees have a girlfriend?'

'Not that I've heard about. I asked his wife, his boss, coworkers. Nothing.'

'Did you ask the wife about Jillian Bondurant? Whether she knew Jillian, whether she thought her husband knew her a little too well?'

'She said he liked to look at anything with tits. She didn't single out Jillian.'

'What are you thinking?' Kovac asked.

'I'm thinking it's bothered me all along that we've never gotten a positive ID on the third victim. Why the decapitation? The extra mutilation of the feet? Now using Jillian's car to burn the fourth victim. Why so much emphasis on Jillian?' Quinn asked. 'We know she was an unhappy, troubled girl. What more permanent escape from an unhappy life than death – real or symbolic.'

'You think that could be Jillian's voice on the tape,' Liska said. 'You think she could be Vanlees's partner?'

'I've said all along the key to this thing is Jillian Bondurant. She's the piece that doesn't fit. It just never hit me until now that maybe she isn't just the key. Maybe she's a killer.'

'Jesus,' Kovac said. 'Well, it was a decent career while it lasted. Maybe I can take over Vanlees's job, chasing groupies away from the stage door at the Target Center.'

He glanced at his watch and tapped its face. 'I gotta go. I've got a date with the wife of Peter Bondurant's ex-partner. Maybe I'll find out something about Jillian there.'

'I want to talk to this friend of hers – Michele Fine. See if she has copies of the music she wrote with Jillian. We could get some insights to her state of mind, maybe even to her fantasy life through her lyrics. I also want to find out what Fine's take on Vanlees is.'

'She doesn't have one,' Liska said. 'I asked her the day we were at the apartment and we saw him. She said, "Whoever notices the losers?"'

'But predators recognize their own kind,' Quinn said. He turned to Kovac. 'Who's on Vanlees?'

'Tippen and Hamill.'

'Perfect. Have them go ask him if this friend whose house he's staying at imports recording equipment, video cameras, stuff like that.'

Kovac nodded. 'Will do.'

'There are a couple of possibilities to consider other than Vanlees,' Quinn pointed out. 'If the relationship between Smokey Joe and his partner is about control, domination, power, then we have to look at Jillian's life and ask ourselves what men have held that kind of sway over her. I can name two that we know of.'

'Lucas Brandt and Daddy Dearest,' Kovac said with a grim look.

'Great. We may finally be on to something, and it's that the daughter of the most powerful man in the state is a sicko freak murderer – and maybe she gets it from Dad. I just get all the luck.'

Liska patted his arm as they started down the hall. 'You know what they say, Sam. You can't pick your relatives or your serial killers.'

'I've got a better one,' Quinn said as the myriad ugly possibilities for the close of this case flashed through his head. 'It ain't over till it's over.'

28

D'Cup was mostly empty with the same pair of old geezers in beret and goatee arguing about pornography today, and a different struggling artist contemplating his mediocrity by the window with a three-dollar latte at hand.

Michele Fine had called in sick. Liska gleaned this information from the Italian stallion behind the bar and made a mental note to start a daily cappuccino habit. Never mind D'Cup was miles out of the way to anything in her life. That was actually part of the allure.

'Did you know her friend at all?' Quinn asked. 'Jillian Bondurant?'

The Roman god pursed his full lips and shook his head. 'Not really. I mean, she came in here a lot, but she wasn't very sociable..Very internal, if you know what I mean. She and Chell were tight. That's about all I know besides what I've read in the papers.'

'Did you ever see her in here with anyone else?' Quinn tried.

'Michele or Jillian Bondurant?'

'Jillian.'

'Can't say that I did.'

'What about Michele? She have a boyfriend?'

He didn't seem to like that question, like maybe they were getting too personal and he was thinking he should take a stand for the Fourth Amendment. Liska pulled out the Polaroid of Vanlees and held it out.

'You ever see either one of them with this guy? Or the guy in here alone?'

Studly squinted at the photo the way people do in an effort to improve both their memory and their vision. 'Nah. He doesn't look familiar.'

'What about their music?' Quinn asked. 'Michele said they performed here sometimes.'

'Chell sings and plays the guitar on open-mike nights. I know they wrote some stuff together, but I couldn't tell you who contributed what. Jillian never performed. She was a spectator. She liked to watch other people.'

'What kind of music?' Quinn asked.

'The edgy feminist folk thing. Lots of anger, lots of angst, kind of dark.'

'Dark in what way?'

'Bad relationships, twisted relationships, lots of emotional pain.'

He said it as if he were saying 'the usual', with a certain air of boredom. A commentary on modern life.

Quinn thanked him. Liska ordered a mocha to go and tipped him a buck. Quinn smiled a little as he held the door.

'Hey,' Liska said. 'It never hurts to be kind.'

'I didn't say anything.'

'You didn't have to.'

The snow was still coming down. The street in front of the coffeehouse was a mess. Lanes invisible, drivers had adopted a survival-of-the-fittest mentality. As they watched, a purple Neon nearly lost its life to an MTC bus.

'You're pretty good at this cop stuff,' Liska said, digging the car keys out of her coat pocket. 'You should consider giving up the glamour of CASKU and the FBI for the relative ignominy of the Minneapolis homicide unit. You get to be hassled by the brass, abused by the press, and ride around in a piece-of-shit car like this one.'

'All that and I'd get to live in this weather too?' Quinn turned up his collar against the wind and snow. 'How can I resist an offer like that?'

'Oh, all right,' Liska said with resignation as she climbed behind the wheel. 'I'll throw in all the sex you want. But you have to promise to want a lot.'

Quinn chuckled and looked out the back window at the traffic. 'Tinks, you're something.'

Michele Fine's apartment was less than a mile away, in a slightly seedy neighborhood full of sagging old duplexes and square, ugly apartment buildings that housed an inordinate number of parolees and petty criminals on probation, according to Liska.

'Vanlees's apartment on Lyndale is just a few blocks south of here,' she said as they picked their way up the sidewalk, stepping in the rut others had stomped into the wet snow. 'Don't you just love a coincidence like that?'

'But they seemed not to know each other when you were at the apartment?'

She thought back to the scene, furrowing her brow. 'Not more than in passing. They didn't speak. Do you really think she might have caught him looking in Jillian's windows?'

'That was a shot in the dark, but it sure got a rise out of your boy. The thing I'm wondering is, if she caught him doing something like that, why wouldn't she have told you about it?'

'Good question.' Liska tried the building's security door, finding it unlocked. 'Let's go get an answer.'

The elevator smelled of bad Chinese takeout. They rode up to the fourth floor with an emaciated hype who huddled into one corner, trying to look inconspicuous and eye Quinn's expensive trench coat at the same time. Quinn gave him a flat stare and watched the sweat instantly bead on the man's pasty forehead. When the doors opened, the hype hung back in the elevator and rode it back down.

'You must be something at a poker table,' Liska said.

'No time for it.'

She arched a brow, blue eyes shining invitingly. 'Better watch out. All work and no play makes John a dull boy.'

Quinn ducked her gaze, mustering a sheepish smile. 'I'd put you to sleep, Tinks.'

'Well, I doubt that, but if you need to prove it scientifically . . .'

She stopped in front of Fine's door and looked at him. 'I'm just giving you a hard time, you know. The sad truth is, you strike me as a man who has someone on his mind.'

Quinn rang the bell and stared at the door. 'Yeah. A killer.' Though for the first time in a very long time, his thoughts were not entirely on his work.

As if Liska had given him permission, he flashed on Kate. Wondered how she was doing, what she was thinking. He wondered if she had yet gotten his message that the victim in the car had not been her witness. He hated the idea of her blaming herself for what had happened, and he hated even more the idea of her boss blaming her. It made his protective instincts rise up, made him want to do something more violent to Rob Marshall than knock him on his ass. He wondered if Kate would be amused or annoyed to know that.

He rang the bell again.

'Who is it?' a voice demanded from inside the apartment.

Liska stood in view of the peephole. 'Sergeant Liska, Michele. I need to ask you a couple more questions about Jillian.'

'I'm sick.'

'It'll only take a minute. It's very important. There's been another murder, you know.'

The door opened a crack, and Fine peered out at them from the other side of the safety chain. The wedge of space framed the scarred portion of her narrow, angular face. 'That's got nothing to do with me. I can't help you.'

She saw Quinn then, and her gaze hardened with suspicion.

'Who's he?'

'John Quinn, FBI,' Quinn said. 'I'd like to talk with you a little about Jillian, Ms Fine. I'm trying to get a better idea of who she was. I understand you and she were close friends.'

The seconds ticked past as she stared at him, sizing him up in a way that seemed odd for a waitress in a trendy coffee bar. It was more the look of someone who had seen too much of the streets. As she raised her hand to undo the safety chain, he caught a glimpse of the snake tattooed around her wrist.

She opened the door and stepped back reluctantly.

'You haven't heard from her since Friday?' Quinn asked.

Fine gave him a look of suspicion and dislike. 'How could I hear from her?' she asked bitterly, her eyes filling. 'She's dead. Why would you ask me something like that?'

'Because I'm not as certain about it as you seem to be.'

'What the hell are you talking about?' she demanded, looking frustrated and confused. 'It's all over the news. Her father is offering a reward. What kind of game are you trying to play?'

Quinn let her hang as he looked around the room. The apartment was vintage seventies – original, not retro – and he figured nothing had been changed or dusted since. The woven drapes looked ready to rot off their hooks. The couch and matching chair in the small living room were square, brown and orange plaid, and worn nubby. Dog-eared travel magazines lay on the cheap coffee table like abandoned dreams beside an ashtray brimming with butts. Everything had been permeated by the smell of cigarette and pot smoke.

'I don't need you trying to fuck with my mind,' Fine said. 'I'm sick. I'm sick about Jillian. She was my friend –' Her voice broke and she looked away, her mouth tightening in a way that emphasized the scar hooking down from the one corner. 'I'm – I'm just sick. So, whatever you want, ask for it and get the hell out of my life.'

She plucked up her smoke and sidestepped away, hugging her free arm across her middle. She was an unhealthy kind of thin, Quinn thought, pale and bony. Maybe she really was sick. She wore a huge, ratty black cardigan sweater, and beneath it a grimy white T-shirt, so small it looked as if it had been intended for a child. Her legs looked as skinny as pegs in worn black leggings. Her feet were bare on the filthy carpet.

'So, what have you got?' Liska asked.

'Huh?'

'You said you were sick. What have you got?'

'Uhhh ... the flu,' she said absently, looking at the television, where a grotesquely obese woman appeared to be telling Jerry Springer all about her relationships with the pockmarked dwarf and the black transexual sitting on either side of her. Fine picked a fleck of tobacco off her tongue and flicked it in the direction of the screen. 'Stomach flu.'

'You know what I hear is good for nausea?' Liska said, deadpan. 'Marijuana. They're using it for chemotherapy patients. Of course, it's otherwise illegal . . .'

The threat was subtle. Maybe just enough to weigh in their favor if Fine found herself struggling with the idea of cooperation.

Fine stared at her with flat eyes.

'The other day – when we ran into the caretaker at Jillian's place,' Liska said. 'You didn't have much to say about him.'

'What's to say?'

'How well did Jillian know him? Were they friends?'

'No. She knew him enough to call him by name.' She went to the postage-stamp-sized dining table, sat down, and propped herself against it as if she didn't have enough strength to sit up on her own. 'He had his eye on her.'

'In what way?'

Fine looked at Quinn. 'In the way men do.'

'Did Jillian ever say he was hitting on her, watching her, anything like that?' Liska asked.

'You think he killed her.'

'What do you think, Michele?' Quinn asked. 'What's your take on the guy?'

'He's a loser.'

'Did you ever have any kind of run-in with him?'

She lifted a shoulder as thin as a bird's wing. 'Maybe I told him to fuck off once or twice.'

'Why?'

'Because he was staring at us. Like maybe he was picturing us naked together. Fat bastard.'

'And what did Jillian say about it?'

Another shrug. 'She said once if that was the biggest thrill of his life, let him stare.'

'She never said anything to you about him bothering her.'

'No.'

'She ever mention anything to you about feeling like she was being watched or followed, anything like that?'

'No. Even though she was.'

Liska looked at her sharply. 'How's that?'

'Her father and that Nazi shrink of hers watched her like hawks. Her father had a key to her apartment. Sometimes we'd get to her place and he'd be waiting for her inside. Talk about invasion of privacy.'

'Did it bother Jillian when he did that?'

Michele Fine's mouth twisted in a strange little bitter smile, and she looked at the ashtray as she stubbed out her cigarette. 'No. She was Daddy's girl, after all.'

'What's that mean?'

'Nothing. She just let him pull her strings, that's all.'

'She told you about her relationship with her stepfather. Did she ever say anything to you about her relationship with her father?'

'We didn't talk about him. She knew what I thought about him trying to control her. The subject was out of bounds. Why?' she asked matter-of-factly. 'Do you think he was trying to fuck her too?'

'I don't know,' Quinn said. 'What do you think?'

'I think I never met a man who wouldn't take a piece of ass if he got the chance,' she said, deliberately brazen, her gaze sliding down Quinn's body to his groin. He let her look, waited her out. Finally her eyes returned to his. 'If he was, she never said it in so many words.'

Quinn helped himself to the chair at the end of the small table, sitting down and settling in as if he meant to stay for supper. He looked again around the apartment, noting that there was very little in the way of ornamentation, nothing homey, nothing personal. No photos. The only thing that appeared to be well taken care of was the small stack of stereo and recording equipment in the far corner of the living room. A guitar was propped nearby.

'I understand you and Jillian wrote music together,' he said. 'What was Jillian's part of that?'

Fine lit another cigarette and blew smoke at the cheap chandelier. Quinn's gaze caught again on the snake tattooed around her wrist, twisting around the scars that had been seared into the flesh there long ago. The serpent from the Garden of Eden, a small red apple in its mouth.

'Sometimes lyrics,' she said, smoke drifting through the gap between her front teeth. 'Sometimes music. Whatever she felt like. Whatever I felt like.'

'Have you published anything?'

'Not yet.'

'What did she like to write about?'

'Life. People. Relationships.'

'Bad relationships?'

'Is there another kind?'

'Did she keep copies of the stuff you'd written?'

'Sure.'

'Where?' Liska asked.

'In her apartment. In the piano bench and the bookcase.'

'I didn't find anything there the other day.'

'Well, that's where it was,' Fine said defensively, blowing another stream of smoke.

'Do you have any copies I could look at?' Quinn asked. 'I'd like to read her lyrics, see what they have to say about her.'

'Poetry is a window to the soul,' Fine said in an odd, dreamy tone. Her gaze drifted away again, and Quinn wondered just what she was on and why. Had the alleged murder of Jillian Bondurant pushed her over some mental edge? It seemed she had been Jillian's only friend. Perhaps Jillian had been hers. And now there was no one – no friend, no writing partner, nothing but this crappy apartment and a dead-end job.

'That's what I'm counting on,' he said.

She looked right at him then, homely and slightly exotic, greasy dark hair scraped back from her face, vaguely familiar – as every face in the world seemed to be to him after so many cases. Her small eyes seemed suddenly very clear as she said, 'But does it reflect who we are or what we want?'

She got up and went across the room to a set of shelves made from cinder blocks and wood planks, and came back sorting through a file folder. Quinn rose and reached out for it, and Fine twisted away, giving him a look from beneath her lashes that was almost coquettish.

'It's the window to my soul too, Mr Fed. Maybe I don't want you peeking.'

She held out half a dozen pieces of sheet music. Her fingernails had been bitten to the quick. Then she hugged the folder to her belly, an action that emphasized her small breasts beneath the tight T-shirt. She wasn't wearing a bra.

Liska put her briefcase on the table, popped it open, and produced a fingerprint kit. 'We still need your prints, Michele. So we can eliminate them from all the prints taken in Jillian's town house. I knew you hadn't made it in to do that, busy as you are and all.'

Fine stared at the ink pad and print card, wary and unhappy.

'It'll take only a minute,' Liska said. 'Have a seat.'

Fine fell down on her chair and offered her hand reluctantly.

'When was the last time you heard from Jillian?' Quinn asked.

'I saw her Friday before her session with the mind fucker,' Michele said as Liska rolled her thumb across the ink pad and pressed it to a card.

'She didn't call you Friday night?'

'No.'

'She didn't come to see you?'

'No.'

'Where were you around midnight, one o'clock?'

'In bed. Naked and alone.' She looked up at him from under her lashes. Sultry.

'Seems odd, don't you think?' Quinn asked. 'She'd had a fight with her father. She was upset enough to run out of his house. But she didn't try to contact her best friend.'

'Well, Agent Quinn,' she said, the voice of sad experience. 'I learned a long time ago, you can never really know what's in another person's heart. And sometimes that's just as well.'

Kovac jammed the Caprice into a Police Vehicles Only slot on the Fifth Street side of City Hall and abandoned it. Swearing a blue streak, he tried to run through the plow-made snowdrift covering the curb, sinking to his knee in one spot. Stumbling, staggering, he got over the hump and hurried up the steps and into the building. Breathing like a bellows. Heart working too hard to pump blood and adrenaline through arteries that probably looked like the inside of bad plumbing pipes.

Christ, he was going to have to get himself in shape if he wanted to survive another case like this one. Then again, his career wasn't likely to survive this one.

The hall was full of angry women who turned on him in a tide as he tried to negotiate his way to the criminal investigative division. It wasn't until he was swamped in the middle of them that he saw the protest signs bobbing above their heads: OUR LIVES MATTER TOO! JUSTICE: A PHOENIX RISING.

Their voices came at him in a barrage, like two dozen shotguns going off at once.

'Police harassment!'

'Only the Urskines want true justice!'

'Why don't you find the *real* killer!'

'That's what I'm trying to do, sister,' Kovac snapped at the woman blocking his path with a bitter scowl and a belly the size of a beer keg. 'So why don't you move the wide load and let me get on with it?'

That was when he noticed the media. Flashes went off left and right. *Shit.*

Kovac kept moving. The only rule of survival in a situation like this: Shut your mouth and keep moving.

'Sergeant Kovac, is it true you ordered Gregg Urskine's arrest?'

'No one is under arrest!' he shouted, forging through the mob.

'Kovac, has he confessed?'

'Was Melanie Hessler your mystery witness?'

Leak in the ME's office, he thought, shaking his head. That was what was wrong with this country – people would sell their mothers for the right money, and never think twice about the consequences to anyone else.

'No comment,' he barked, and pushed his way past the last of them.

He negotiated the clutter of boxes and file cabinets into homicide, hanging a right at Lieutenant Fowler's makeshift office. Toni Urskine's voice raked over his nerve endings like a serrated knife on raw meat.

'. . . And you can rest assured every station, every paper, every reporter who will listen to me, will hear about it! This is an absolute outrage! *We* have been victimized by these crimes. *We* have lost friends. *We* have suffered. And this is how we're treated by the Minneapolis Police Department after we've bent over backward to cooperate!'

Kovac ducked through the door into the offices. Yurek jumped up from his desk, telephone receiver stuck to the side of his face, and made wild eye contact with Kovac, holding up a hand to keep him in the general vicinity. Kovac held up for five seconds, motor running, the excitement he had brought with him into the building like currents of energy humming through his arms, his legs, his veins and arteries. He bounced up and down on the balls of his feet like a boy who had to pee.

'I've got places to go and people to rake over the coals, Charm.'

Yurek nodded and said into the phone, 'I'm sorry, ma'am. I have to go now. I have an emergency situation here. I'm sorry. Yes, someone will get back to you. I'm sorry, ma'am.'

He came around his desk, shaking his head. 'These people are driving me batshit. There's a woman insisting her neighbor is the Cremator, and not only has he brutally murdered four women, she thinks he killed *and ate* her dog.'

'I got time for this shit like I got time for root canal,' Kovac snapped. 'Is Quinn here?'

'He just got back. He's watching Urskine's interview,' Yurek said, falling in step beside Kovac, heading for the interview rooms. 'I just got a call from upstairs –'

'And the woman with the dead poodle is the mayor? That's how frigging weird this case is.'

'No, before the dog lady. You're wanted in the mayor's office. They tried to get you on your cell phone.'

'Dead battery. And you didn't see me. The battleax can wait. I've got a big damn fish to fry. I've got Jonah's goddamn whale.'

Worry creased Yurek's perfect brow. 'What do you mean, "big fish"? Where've you been?'

Kovac didn't answer, his mind already on the confrontation ahead. Quinn stood near the one-way glass, looking dead on his feet as he stared through to the next room, where Gregg Urskine sat across the table from Elwood.

'We paid cash. I couldn't find the receipt,' Urskine said, exasperated, fighting to keep that pleasant yuppie smile hanging on his face. 'Do you keep all your receipts, Sergeant? Could you find a receipt for something you did months ago?'

'Yes, I could. I keep a simple but efficient home filing system,' Elwood said conversationally. 'You never know when you might need a record of something. For tax purposes, for an alibi –'

'I don't need an alibi.'

'I know someone who does,' Kovac said, snagging Quinn's attention. 'You want to take another ride?'

'What's up?'

'I just talked to Mrs Donald Thorton, Peter Bondurant's ex-partner. You want to know how the emotionally unstable Sophie Bondurant got custody of Jillian in the divorce? You'll love this,' he promised sarcastically.

'I'm almost afraid to ask.'

'She threatened to expose him to the court and to the media. For molesting Jillian.'

29

'Oh, God,' Yurek groaned with dread.

Kovac wheeled on him. 'What now? You want me to pretend I don't know Bondurant was molesting his daughter?'

'*Allegedly* molesting –'

'You think I don't know I've just stepped in it up to my ass?'

'I think you'd better hear what the mayor wants.'

'I could give a rat's –'

'She wants you in her office to give Mr Bondurant a personal briefing on the status of the case. They're up there waiting for you now.'

The room fell silent for a heartbeat, then Elwood's calm voice came over the speaker again from the interview room next door. 'Have you ever paid for sex, Mr Urskine?'

'No!'

'No offense intended. It's just that working around all those women who've sold their bodies professionally might give rise to a certain curiosity. So to speak.'

Urskine shoved his chair back from the table. 'That's it. I'm leaving. If you want to speak to me again, you can do it through my attorney.'

'All right,' Kovac said to Quinn, nerves and anticipation knotting in his stomach. 'Let's go give the mayor and Mr Bondurant the big update. I'll fill you in on the way.'

'I'm sure you can understand Peter's need for closure in this matter,' Edwyn Noble said to Chief Greer. 'Do we have any kind of time frame as to when the body may be released?'

'Not *specifically*.' Greer stood near the head of the mayor's conference table, feet slightly spread, hands clasped before him, like a soldier at ease, or a bouncer with an attitude. 'I have a call in to Sergeant Kovac. I understand he's waiting to hear from the FBI lab on some tests. *Possibly* after those are completed, which could be *any* day –'

'I want to bury my daughter, Chief Greer.' Bondurant's voice was tight. He didn't look at the chief, but seemed to be staring into a dimension only he could see. He had ignored the offer of a seat, and moved restlessly

268

around the conference room. 'The thought of her body sitting in some refrigerated locker like so much meat ... I want her back.'

'Peter darling, we understand,' Grace Noble said. 'We feel your pain. And I can assure you, the task force is doing everything possible to solve this –'

'Really? Your lead detective has spent more time harassing me than he's spent pursuing any suspects.'

'Sergeant Kovac can be a bit gruff,' Greer said. 'But his record in homicide speaks for itself.'

'At the risk of sounding glib, Chief Greer,' Edwyn Noble said, 'Sergeant Kovac's record notwithstanding, what has he done for us lately? We have another victim. The killer seems to be thumbing his nose, not only at the task force, but at the city. Does Sergeant Kovac even have a viable suspect at this point?'

'Lieutenant Fowler tells me someone was questioned earlier today.'

'Who? A legitimate suspect?'

Greer frowned. 'I'm not at liberty –'

'She was *my daughter*!' Peter shouted, the rage in his voice reverberating off the walls. He turned away from the stares of the others and put his hands over his face.

The mayor pressed a hand to her ample bosom, as if the sight was causing her chest pains.

'If someone has been brought in,' Noble said, the voice of reason, 'then it will be only a matter of hours before the press reveals that information. That isn't a comment on the security of your force, per se, Chief. It's simply impossible to eliminate all leaks in a case of this magnitude.'

Greer looked from Bondurant's lawyer to Bondurant's lawyer's wife – his boss. Unhappy and unable to see any escape routes, he sighed heavily. 'The caretaker from Ms Bondurant's town house complex.'

The intercom buzzed, and Grace Noble answered it from the phone on the side table. 'Mayor Noble, Sergeant Kovac and Special Agent Quinn are here to see you.'

'Send them in, Cynthia.'

Kovac was through the door almost before the mayor finished her sentence, his eyes finding Peter Bondurant like a pair of heat-seeking missiles. Bondurant looked thinner than he had the day before, his color worse. He met Kovac's gaze with an expression of stony dislike.

'Sergeant Kovac, Agent Quinn, thank you for joining us,' the mayor said. 'Let's all have seats and talk.'

'I'm not going into particulars of the case,' Kovac stated stubbornly. Neither would he sit down and be a still target for Bondurant or Edwyn Noble.

No one sat.

'We understand you have a suspect,' Edwyn Noble said.

Kovac gave him the eagle eye, then turned it on Dick Greer and thought *cocksucker*.

'No arrests have been made,' Kovac said. 'We're still pursuing all avenues. I've just been down an interesting one myself.'

'Does Mr Vanlees have an alibi for the night my daughter went missing?' Bondurant asked sharply. He looked at Kovac as he paced back and forth along the table, passing within a foot of him.

'Do *you* have an alibi for the night your daughter went missing, Mr Bondurant?'

'Kovac!' the chief barked.

'With all due respect, Chief, I'm not in the habit of giving up my cases to anybody.'

'Mr Bondurant is the father of a victim. There are extenuating circumstances.'

'Yeah, a few billion of them,' Kovac muttered.

'Sergeant!'

'Sergeant Kovac believes I should be punished for my wealth, Chief,' Bondurant said, still pacing, staring at the floor now. 'He perhaps believes I deserved to lose my daughter so I could know what real suffering is.'

'After what I heard today, I believe you never deserved to have a daughter at all,' Kovac said, eliciting a gasp from the mayor. 'You sure as hell deserved to lose her, but not in the way she's lost now. That is to say if she's dead at all – and we're nowhere near ready to say that she is.'

'Sergeant Kovac, I hope you have a very good explanation for this behavior.' Greer moved toward him aggressively, drawing his weightlifter's shoulders up.

Kovac stepped away from him. His full attention was on Peter Bondurant. And Peter Bondurant's attention was on him. He stopped his pacing, an instinctive wariness in the narrowed eyes, like an animal sensing danger.

'I had a long talk today with Cheryl Thorton,' Kovac said, and watched what color Peter Bondurant had leach away. 'She had some very interesting things to say about your divorce from Jillian's mother.'

Edwyn Noble looked startled. 'I fail to see what relevance –'

'Oh, I think it could be very relevant.' Kovac still stared hard at Bondurant.

Bondurant said, 'Cheryl is a bitter, vindictive woman.'

'You think so? After she's kept her mouth shut all this time? I'd say you're an ungrateful son of a bitch –'

'Kovac, that's enough!' Greer shouted.

'Hardly,' Kovac said. 'You want to kiss the ass of a child-molester, Chief, that's your business. I won't do it. I don't give a shit how rich he is.'

'Oh!' Grace Noble exclaimed, pressing her hand to her chest again.

'Maybe we should take this downstairs,' Quinn suggested mildly.

'Fine by me,' Kovac said. 'We've got an interview room all warmed up.'

Bondurant had begun to tremble visibly. 'I *never* abused Jillian.'

'Maybe you think you didn't.' Kovac circled slowly around him, moving

away from Greer, keeping Bondurant's eyes on him and putting his back to
his lawyer. 'A lot of pedophiles convince themselves they're doing the kid a
favor. Some even confuse fucking little kids with love. Is that what you
made yourself believe?'

'You son of a bitch!'

Bondurant launched himself, grabbing Kovac by the lapels and running
him backward across the room. They crashed into a side table and sent a
pair of brass candlesticks flying like bowling pins.

Kovac held back the urge to roll Bondurant over and pound the shit out
of him. After what he'd heard today, he dearly wanted to, and maybe he
could have if they'd crossed paths in a dark alley. But men like Peter
Bondurant didn't frequent dark alleys, and rough justice never touched
them.

Bondurant got in one good swing, glancing his knuckles off the corner of
Kovac's mouth. Then Quinn grabbed him by the back of the collar and
pulled him away. Greer rushed in between them like a referee, arms spread
wide, eyes rolling white in his dark face.

'Sergeant Kovac, I think *you* should step *outside,*' he said loudly.

Kovac straightened his tie and jacket. He wiped a smear of blood away
from the corner of his mouth, and a smirk twisted his lips as he looked at
Peter Bondurant.

'Ask him where he was last night at two o'clock in the morning,' he said.
'While someone was setting his daughter's car on fire with a mutilated dead
woman inside it.'

'I won't even dignify that with a comment.' Bondurant said, fussing with
his glasses.

'Jesus, you're just the cat's ass, aren't you?' Kovac said. 'You get away
with child abuse. You get away with assaulting an officer. You're into this
case like a bad infection. You think you might get away with murder if you
want to?'

'*Kovac!*' Greer screamed.

Kovac looked to Quinn, shook his head, and walked out.

Bondurant jerked out of Quinn's hold. 'I want him off the case! I want
him off the force!'

'Because he's doing his job?' Quinn asked calmly. 'It's his job to
investigate. He can't help what he finds, Peter. You're killing the messenger.'

'He's not investigating the case!' he shouted, pacing again, gesturing
wildly. 'He's investigating *me*. He's harassing me. I've lost my daughter, for
God's sake!'

Edwyn Noble tried to take hold of his arm as he passed. Bondurant
twisted away. 'Peter, calm down. Kovac will be dealt with.'

'I think we should deal with what Sergeant Kovac found, don't you?'
Quinn said to the lawyer.

'It's nonsense,' Noble snapped. 'There's nothing to the allegation
whatsoever.'

'Really? Sophie Bondurant was an emotionally unstable woman. Why would the courts award her custody of Jillian? More to the point, why wouldn't you fight her, Peter?' Quinn asked, trying to establish eye contact with Bondurant.

Bondurant kept moving, highly agitated, sweating now, pale in the way that made Quinn think he might be ill.

'Cheryl Thorton says the reason you didn't fight was that Sophie threatened to expose you for molesting Jillian.'

'I *never* hurt Jillian. I wouldn't.'

'Cheryl has always blamed Peter for her husband's accident,' Noble said bitterly. 'She didn't want Donald to sell out of Paragon. She punished him for it too. Drove him to drink. She's the one who caused the accident – indirectly – but she blames Peter.'

'And this bitter, vindictive woman never said anything until now about this alleged abuse?' Quinn said. 'That would be hard to imagine if not for the generous monthly payments Peter sends to the convalescent home where Donald Thorton is spending the last of his life.'

'Some people would call that generosity,' Noble said.

'And some people would call it blackmail. Some people would say Peter was buying Cheryl Thorton's silence.'

'They'd be wrong,' Noble stated unequivocally. 'Donald and Peter were friends, partners. Why shouldn't he see to it the man's needs are taken care of?'

'He took very good care of him in the buyout of Paragon – which, coincidentally, went on about the same time as the divorce,' Quinn continued. 'The deal might have been considered overly generous on Peter's part.'

'What was he supposed to do?' Noble demanded. 'Try to steal the company from the man who'd helped him build it?'

Bondurant, Quinn noticed, had stopped talking, and now confined his pacing to the corner by the window. Retreating. His head was down and he kept touching his hand to his forehead as if feeling for a fever. Quinn moved casually toward him, neatly cutting his pacing area in half. Subtly crowding his space.

'Why didn't you fight Sophie for custody, Peter?' he asked softly, an intimate question between friends. He kept his own head down, his hands in his pants pockets.

'I was taking over the business. I couldn't handle a child too.'

'And so you left her to Sophie? A woman in and out of mental institutions.'

'It wasn't like that. It wasn't as if she was insane. Sophie had problems. We all have problems.'

'Not the kind that make us kill ourselves.'

Tears filled the man's eyes. He raised a hand as if to shade his eyes from Quinn's scrutiny.

'What did you and Jillian argue about that night, Peter?'

He shook his head a little, moving now in a tight, short line. Pacing three steps, turning, pacing three steps, turning . . .

'She'd gotten a call from her stepfather,' Quinn said. 'You were angry.'

'We've been over this,' Edwyn Noble said impatiently, clearly wanting to get between Quinn and his client. Quinn turned a shoulder, blocking him out.

'Why do you keep insisting Jillian is dead, Peter? I don't know that she is. I think she may not be. Why would you say that she is? What did you fight about that night?'

'Why are you doing this to me?' Bondurant whispered in a tortured voice. His prim, tight-lipped mouth was quivering.

'Because we need to know the truth, Peter, and I think you're holding back pieces of the puzzle. If you want the truth – as you say you do – then you have to give those pieces to me. Do you understand? We need to see the whole picture.'

Quinn held his breath. Bondurant was on the edge. He could feel it, see it. He tried to will him over it.

Bondurant stared out the window at the snow, still now, looking numb. 'All I wanted was for us to be father and daughter –'

'That's enough, Peter.' Noble stepped in front of Quinn and took his client by the arm. 'We're leaving.'

He glared at Quinn. 'I thought we understood each other.'

'Oh, I understand you perfectly, Mr Noble,' Quinn said. 'That doesn't mean I'm interested in playing on your team. I'm interested in two things only: the truth, and justice. I don't know that you want either.'

Noble said nothing. He led Bondurant from the room like a caretaker with a sedated patient.

Quinn looked to the mayor, who had finally taken a seat herself. She looked partly stunned and partly reflective, as if trying to sort through old memories for any that might have implicated Peter Bondurant in something she would never have suspected. Chief Greer looked like a man in the early stages of diverticulitis.

'That's the thing about digging holes,' Quinn said. 'There are no assurances you'll find what you want – or want what you find.'

By five o'clock every news agency native to and camped in the Twin Cities had the name of Gil Vanlees. The same media that would plaster that name in print and fill television screens with bad photographs of the man would point fingers at the police department for leaking information.

Quinn had no doubt where the leak had sprung, and it pissed him off. Bondurant's people having the kind of access they had tainted the case. And in the light of Kovac's revelation that afternoon, Bondurant's meddling took on an even darker quality.

No one had leaked *that* story to the press. Not even the allegedly bitter, vindictive Cheryl Thorton, whose brain-damaged husband was supported by Peter Bondurant. He wondered exactly how much money it took to hold a grudge like that at bay for a decade.

What had gone on in the lives of Jillian and her mother and father in that pivotal time of the divorce? he wondered in his windowless room at the FBI offices. From the start, Bondurant had struck him as a man with secrets. Secrets about the present. Secrets about the past. Secrets as dark as incest?

How else would Sophie Bondurant have gotten custody of Jillian? Unstable as she was. Powerful as Peter was.

He flipped through the casebook to the crime scene photos of the third murder. Certain aspects of the murder gave the impression the killer and victim may have known each other. The decapitation when none of the other victims had been decapitated, the extreme depersonalization. Both suggested a kind of rage that was personal. But what of the latest theory that the killer worked with a partner, a woman? That didn't fit Peter Bondurant. And what of the thought that perhaps the woman involved was Jillian Bondurant herself?

A history of sexual abuse would fit the profile of a woman involved in this type of crime. She would have a skewed view of male-female relationships, of sexual relationships. Her partner was likely older, some twisted suggestion of a father figure, the dominant partner.

Quinn thought of Jillian, of the photograph in Bondurant's office. Emotionally troubled, with low self-esteem, a girl unhappily pretending to be something she wasn't in order to please. To what lengths might she go to find the approval she craved?

He thought of her involvement with her stepfather – supposedly consensual, but these things never really are. Children need love and can be easily manipulated by that need. And if Jillian had escaped an abusive relationship with her father, only to be coerced into another by her stepfather, that would have reinforced every warped idea she had of relationships with men.

If Peter had abused her.

If Jillian wasn't a dead victim, but a willing victim.

If Gil Vanlees was her partner in this sickness.

If Gil Vanlees was a killer at all.

If if if if . . .

Vanlees seemed a perfect fit – except he didn't strike Quinn as having the brain power to outsmart the cops for this long, or the balls to play the kind of taunting game this killer played. Not the Gil Vanlees he'd seen in that interview room today. But he knew from experience people could have more than one side, and that a dark side that was capable of killing the way the Cremator killed was capable of anything, including disguising itself very, very well.

He pictured Gil Vanlees in his mind and waited for that twist in his gut that told him this was the guy. But the feeling didn't come. He couldn't remember the last time it had. Not even after the fact, after a killer had been caught and fit his profile point by point. That sense of knowing didn't come anymore. The arrogance of certainty had abandoned him. Dread had taken its place.

He flipped farther into the murder book, to the fresh photographs from Melanie Hessler's autopsy. As with the third victim, the wounds inflicted both before and after death had been brutal, unspeakably cruel, worse than with the first two victims. As he looked at the photographs he could hear the echo of the tape recording in his head. Scream after scream after scream.

The screams ran into one another and into the cacophony that filled his nightmares, growing louder and louder. The sound swelled and expanded in his brain until he felt as if his head would burst and the contents run out in a sickly gray ooze. And all the while he stared at the autopsy photographs, at the charred, mutilated thing that had once been a woman, and he thought of the kind of rage it took to do that to another person. The kind of poisonous, black emotions kept under tight control until the pressure became too much. And he thought of Peter Bondurant and Gil Vanlees and a thousand nameless faces walking the streets of these cities just waiting for that main line of hate to blow and push them over the edge.

Any of them could have been this killer. The necessary components resided in a great many people, and needed only the proper catalyst to set them off. The task force was putting its money on Vanlees, based on circumstance and the profile. But all they had was logic and a hunch. No physical evidence. Could Gil Vanlees have been that careful, that clever? They had no witness to put him with any of the victims. Their witness was gone. They had no obvious connection between all four victims or anything tying Vanlees to any victim other than Jillian – if Jillian was a victim.

If this. If that.

Quinn dug a Tagamet out of his pants pocket and washed it down with Diet Coke. The case was crowding in on him; he couldn't get perspective. The players were too close around him, their ideas, their emotions, bleeding into the cold facts that were all he needed for his analysis.

The professional in him still wished for the distance of his office in Quantico. But if he had stayed in Quantico, then he and Kate would have remained in the past tense.

On impulse, he grabbed up the telephone receiver and dialed her office number. On the fourth ring her machine picked up. He left his number again, hung up, picked up again, and dialed her home line with the same result. It was seven now. Where the hell was she?

Instantly he flashed on the decrepit garage in the dark alley behind her house and muttered a curse. Then he reminded himself – as Kate herself would surely do – that she had gotten along just fine without him for the past five years.

He could have used her expertise tonight, to say nothing of a long, slow kiss and a warm embrace. He turned back to the casebook and flipped to the victimologies, looking for the one thing he felt he'd missed that would tie it all together and point the finger.

The notes on Melanie Hessler were in his own hand, sketchy, too brief. Kovac had set Moss to the task of gathering the information on the latest of the Cremator's victims, but she had yet to bring him anything. He knew she'd worked in an adult bookstore – which, in the killer's mind, likely put her into the same category as the two hookers. She'd been attacked in the alley behind the store just months before, but the two men who had raped her had solid alibis and were not considered suspects in her death.

It was sad to think how each of these women had been victimized repeatedly in their brief lives. Lila White and Fawn Pierce in a profession and a lifestyle that specialized in abuse and degradation. White had been assaulted by her drug dealer just last summer. Pierce had been hospitalized three times in two years, the victim of her pimp once, once a mugging victim, and once a rape victim.

Jillian Bondurant's victimization had taken place behind the closed doors of her home. If Jillian was a victim.

He turned back to the photographs of victim number three once again and stared at the stab wounds to her chest. The signature. Long wound, short wound, long wound, short wound, like the arms of a star or the petals of a gruesome flower. *I love you, I love you not. Cross my heart, hope to die.*

He thought of the faint voices on the tape.

'. . . *Turn . . . do it . . .*'

'. . . *Want to . . . of me . . .*'

Too easily he could picture the killers standing on either side of their victim's warm, lifeless body, each with a knife, taking turns punching their signature into the woman's chest, sealing the pact of their partnership.

It should have horrified him to think it, but it wasn't the worst thing he'd ever seen. Not by a long way. Mostly it left him numb.

That made him shudder.

A man and a woman. He scrolled through the possibilities, considering people known to be attached to the victims in some way. Gil Vanlees, Bondurant, Lucas Brandt. The Urskines – possibilities there. The hooker who had been at the Phoenix last night when the DiMarco girl had disappeared – and claimed not to have seen or heard a thing, who had also known the second victim. Michele Fine, Jillian's only friend. Strange and shaky. Scarred – physically and emotionally. A woman with a long, dark story behind her, no doubt – and no good alibi for the night Jillian went missing.

He reached for the sheet music Fine had handed over to him and wondered about Jillian's compositions she'd kept to herself.

Outsider

Outside

On the dark side
Alone
Looking in
On a whim
Want a home

Outsider
In my blood
In my bones
Can't have
What I want
Doomed to roam
All alone
On the outside

Let me in
Want a friend
Need a lover
Be with me
Be my boy
Be my father

Outsider
In my blood
In my bones
Can't have
What I want
Doomed to roam
All alone
On the outside

Knuckles cracked against the door, and Kovac stuck his head in without waiting for an invitation.

'Can you smell it?' he asked, letting himself in. He leaned back against Quinn's wall of notes, suit rumpled, lip swollen where Peter Bondurant had popped him, tie askew. 'Cooked goose, burned ass, toast.'

'You're out,' Quinn said.

'Give the man a cigar. I'm off the task force. They'll name my successor at a press conference sometime tomorrow.'

'At least Bondurant didn't get you thrown off the force altogether,' Quinn said. 'You played bad cop a little too hard this time, Sam.'

'Bad cop,' Kovac said with disgust. 'That was me, and I meant every word of it. I'm fed up to my back teeth with Peter Bondurant, and his money and his power and his people. What Cheryl Thorton told me pushed me over the edge. I just kept thinking about the dead women nobody cared about, and Bondurant playing with the case like it was his own personal live game of Clue. I kept thinking about his daughter and how she should have had such a great life, but instead – dead or alive – she's fucked up forever, thanks to him.'

'*If* he molested her. We don't know what Cheryl Thorton said is true.'

'Bondurant pays her husband's medical bills. Why would she say something that rotten against the man if it wasn't true?'

'Did she give any indication she thinks Peter killed Jillian?'

'She wouldn't go that far.'

Quinn held out the sheet of music. 'Make what you want of that. It could say you're on a hot trail.'

Kovac scowled as he read the lyrics of the song. 'Jesus.'

Quinn spread his hands. 'Could be sexual or not. Might refer to her father or her stepfather or not mean anything at all. I want to talk more with her friend Michele. See if she has an interpretation – if she'll give it to me.'

Kovac turned and looked at the photographs Quinn had taped up. The victims when they were alive and smiling. 'There's nothing I hate more than a child-molester. That's why I don't work sex crimes – even if they do get better hours. If I ever worked sex crimes, I'd be in the tank so fast, I'd get whiplash. I'd get my hands on some son of a bitch who raped his own kid, and I'd just fucking kill him. Get 'em out of the gene pool, you know what I'm saying?'

'Yeah, I do.'

'I don't know how a man can look at his own daughter and think, "Hey, I gotta have me some of that." '

He shook his head and dug a cigarette out of the pack in the breast pocket of his limp white shirt. The FBI offices were nonsmoking, but Quinn said nothing.

'I've got a daughter, you know,' Kovac said, exhaling his first lungful. 'Well, you *don't* know. Hardly anyone knows. From my first marriage, which lasted about a minute and a half after I joined the force. Gina. She's sixteen now. I never see her. Her mother remarried with embarrassing haste and moved to Seattle. Some other guy got to be her dad.' He moved his shoulders and looked at the pictures again. 'Not so different from Bondurant, huh?' he said, his mouth twisting. The shoulders sagged on a long sigh. 'Christ, I hate irony.'

Quinn could see the regret in his eyes. He'd seen it many times in many faces across the country. The job took a toll, and the people who were willing to pay it didn't get nearly enough in return.

'What're you going to do about the case?' he asked.

Kovac looked surprised by the question. 'Work the damn task force, that's what. I don't care what Little Dick says. It's my case, I'm lead. They can *name* whoever they want.'

'Your lieutenant won't reassign you?'

'Fowler's on my side. He put me on the support team on the QT. I'm supposed to keep my head down and my mouth shut.'

'How long has he known you?'

'Long enough to know better.'

Quinn found a weary laugh. 'Sam, you're something.'

'Yeah, I am. Just don't ask too many people what.' Kovac grinned, then it faded away. He dropped the last of his cigarette into an empty Diet Coke can. 'It's no ego trip, you know. I don't need my name in the paper. I don't care what goes in my jacket. I've never looked for a promotion, and I sure as hell don't expect to ever see another.

'I want this scumbag,' he said with steel in his voice. 'I should've wanted him this bad when Lila White was killed, but I didn't. Not that I didn't care about her, but you were right: I went through the motions. I didn't hang in, didn't dig hard enough. When it didn't wrap up fast, I let it slide 'cause the brass was on my case and she was a hooker and hookers get whacked every once in a while. Hazard of the profession. Now we're up to four. I want Smokey Joe's ass on a platter before the body count goes up again.'

Quinn listened as Kovac said his piece, and nodded at the end of it. This was a good cop standing in front of him. A good man. And this case would break his career more easily than it would make it – even if he solved the mystery. But especially if the answer to the question turned out to be Peter Bondurant.

'What's the latest on Vanlees?' he asked.

'Tippen's riding his tail like a cat on a mouse. They pulled him over on Hennepin to ask about his buddy, the electronics dealer. Tip says the guy about shit his pants.'

'What about the electronics?'

'Adler checked out the guy's Web page. He specializes in computers and related gizmos, but if it plugs into a wall, he can get it for you. So there's nothing to say that he isn't up to his ears in recording equipment. I wish we could get a search warrant for his house, but there isn't a judge in the state who'd give us one based on what we've got on this mutt – which is nothing.'

'That bothers me,' Quinn admitted, tapping a pen against the file on Vanlees. 'I don't think Gil's the brightest bulb in the chandelier. He's a good fit to the profile on a lot of points, but Smokey Joe is smart and he's bold, and Vanlees seems to be neither – which also makes him a perfect fall guy.'

Kovac fell into a chair as if the weight of this latest concern made the burden all suddenly too much for him. 'Vanlees is connected to Jillian, *and* to Peter. I don't like that. I keep having this nightmare that Bondurant is Smokey Joe, and that no one will listen to me and no one else will look at him, and the son of a bitch will get away with it.

'I try to dig on him a little and he damn near gets me fired. I don't like it.' He pulled out another cigarette and just ran his fingers over it, as if he hoped that alone might calm him. 'And then I think, "Sam, you're an idiot. Bondurant brought in Quinn." Why would he do that if he was the killer?'

'For the challenge,' Quinn said without hesitation. 'Or to get himself caught. I'd go with the first in this case. He'd get off on knowing I'm here and unable to spot him. Outsmarting the cops is big with this killer. But if Bondurant is Smokey Joe, then who's his accomplice?'

'Jillian,' Kovac offered. 'And this whole thing with her murder is a sham.'

Quinn shook his head. 'I don't think so. Bondurant believes his daughter is dead. Believes it more strongly than we do. That's no act.'

'So we're back to Vanlees.'

'Or the Urskines. Or someone we haven't even considered.'

Kovac scowled at him. 'Some help you are.'

'That's why they pay me the big bucks.'

'My tax dollars at work,' he said with disgust. He hung the cigarette on his lip for a second, then took it away. 'The Urskines. How twisted would that be? They whack two of their hookers, then do a couple of citizens in order to make a political point.'

'And to push suspicion away from themselves,' Quinn said. 'No one considers the person trying to draw attention.'

'But to snatch the witness staying in their house? That's titanium balls.' Kovac tipped his head, considering. 'I bet Toni Urskine can grow hair on hers.'

Quinn went to his wall of notes and scanned them, not really reading the words, just seeing a jumble of letters and facts that tangled in his mind with the theories and the faces and the names.

'Any word on Angie DiMarco?' he asked.

Kovac shook his head. 'No one's seen her. No one's heard from her. We're flashing her picture on television, asking people to call the hotline if they've seen her. Personally, I'm afraid finding someone else in that car last night was just postponing the inevitable. But, hey,' he said, dragging himself up out of his chair, 'I am, as my second wife used to call me, the infernal pessimist.'

He yawned hugely and consulted his watch.

'Well, GQ, I'm calling it. I can't remember the last time I slept in a bed. That's my goal for the night – if I don't pass out in the shower. How about you? I can give you a ride back to your hotel.'

'What for? Sleep? I gave that up. It was cutting into my anxiety attacks,' Quinn said, ducking his gaze. 'Thanks anyway, Sam, but I think I'll stick to it awhile yet. There's something here I'm just not seeing.' He gestured to the open casebook. 'Maybe if I stare at it all a little longer . . .'

Kovac watched him for a few moments without saying anything, then nodded. 'Suit yourself. See you in the morning. You want me to pick you up?'

'No. Thanks.'

'Uh-huh. Well, goodnight.' He started through the door, then looked back in. 'Say hello to Kate for me. If you happen to talk to her.'

Quinn said nothing. He did nothing for a full five minutes after Kovac left, just stood there thinking Kovac had a hell of an eye. Then he went to the phone and dialed Kate's number.

30

'Kate, it's me. Uh – John. Um, I'm at the office. Give me a call if you get the chance. I'd like to go over some points in these victimologies with you. Get your take. Thanks.'

Kate stared at the phone as the line went dead and the message light began to flash. A part of her felt guilty for not picking up. A part of her felt relieved. At the core she ached at the lost opportunity to touch him in some way. A bad sign, but there it was.

She was exhausted, stressed out, overwhelmed, feeling as low as she had in years ... and she wanted John Quinn's arms around her. She hadn't taken his call precisely for that reason. She was afraid.

What a rotten, unwelcome feeling it was.

The office was silent. She and Rob were the only ones left in their section. Rob sequestered in his office down the hall, no doubt writing a long and virulent report to file in her personnel jacket. On the other side of the reception area, in the county attorney's offices, there were any number of assistant prosecutors at work preparing for court, strategizing and researching and writing briefs and motions. But for the most part the building was empty. For all intents and purposes, she was alone.

Her nerves were raw from spending hours listening to the voice of her dead client confessing her fears of being hurt, her fears of being raped, of being killed, of dying alone, and Kate's own voice reassuring her, promising to look out for her, to get her help, fostering a false security that had ultimately failed Melanie Hessler in the worst possible way.

Rob had insisted on playing the tapes over and over, stopping and rewinding in sections, asking Kate the same questions over and over. As if any of it would make any difference at all. The cops didn't want to hear about the subtle nuances of Melanie's speech. All they wanted to know was if Melanie had expressed a fear of anyone in particular in the last few weeks of her life.

He'd been punishing her, Kate knew. She hated him for it, but she refused to break. As much as it tore at her to hear those tapes, she sat there and took it hour after hour, fielding all his little digs.

'She really trusted you, Kate ... It's clear she looked up to you, Kate ...

Poor woman, she was so afraid . . . Think of that: Her worst nightmare came true . . . Think how terrifed she must have been . . . This must be very hard for you, Kate . . . You must feel terrible . . . Especially after what happened with Angie . . .'

On and on and on. Sly little slivers slipped under the skin with the mastery of an acupuncturist, but meant to hurt, twisted just so the barb would catch.

Finally, he'd hit the nerve one time too many. As he fiddled with the buttons on the tape player to rewind an interview for the third time, Kate stood, leaned across the table, and pressed stop.

'You've made your point. You've had your revenge. Enough is enough,' she said quietly.

'I don't know what you're talking about.' He said it almost as a taunt, without a speck of sincerity. He wouldn't look directly at her.

'You know, of all the many things I despise about you, Rob, that would have to be at the top of my list. You're a passive-aggressive little shit, and I'd say you'd fire me for saying so, but I'm sure that would be too direct for you.

'If by some miracle you find the balls to do it, fine. I'd just as soon stay here. I like this office. I like most of the people I work with. But I'm damn good at what I do, and I can get another job in a heartbeat. I won't take you trying to manipulate me and punish me and make me play your little passive-aggressive mind games.'

'Apologize,' he said through gritted teeth. Planting his hands on the table, he pushed up out of his chair, breathing hard. 'Apologize for what you just said to me.'

Kate stepped back and gave him a long, cool look. 'Fine. I'll apologize. I'm sorry I don't like you, Rob. I'm sorry I can't respect you. If I thought you deserved it, I'd be your champion till the day I die. But you haven't earned my respect, and I won't just give it to you.

'Now you'll excuse me,' she went on. 'Because I've just had the third worst twenty-four hours of my life and I feel like I'm on the verge of a psychotic breakdown. I'm going home. Call if you don't want me to come back.'

He hadn't said a word as she walked out. At least she hadn't heard him for the pulse roaring in her ears. She had expected him to throw one of his little hissy fits, and God knew she probably deserved to have him fire her, but there simply wasn't any tact left in her. All pretense of manners and social bullshit had been scraped away, leaving nothing but raw emotion.

She felt it flooding through her still, as if some vital artery had ruptured inside her. She felt as if she might choke on it, drown in it.

And all she wanted was to find Quinn and fall into his arms.

She'd worked so hard to put her life back together, piece by piece on a new foundation, and now that foundation was shifting. No. Worse – she'd discovered it was built directly over the fault line of her past, just covering up. Not new, not stronger, just a lie she'd told herself every day for the last five years: that she didn't need John Quinn to feel complete.

Tears welled in her eyes, and despair yawned through her, leaving her aching and empty and alone and afraid. And God, she was so tired. But she choked the tears back and put one foot in front of the other. Go home, regroup, have a drink, try to sleep. Tomorrow was another day.

She pulled her coat on, scooped up her file on Angie, grabbed her mail and her messages and the faxes that had piled up in the tray during the day, and dumped it all into her briefcase. She reached to turn the desk lamp off, but her hand strayed to the shelves, and she plucked out the little framed photo of Emily.

Sweet, smiling little cherub in a sunny yellow dress. The future bright before her. Or so anyone with ordinary human arrogance would have thought. Kate wondered if tucked away somewhere in someone's old shoe box there might be a similar photograph of Angie DiMarco . . . or Melanie Hessler . . . Lila White, Fawn Pierce, Jillian Bondurant.

Life didn't come with any guarantee. There'd never been a promise made that couldn't be broken. She knew that firsthand. She'd made too many with the best of intentions, then watched them crack and come apart.

'I'm sorry, Em,' she whispered. She pressed the picture to her lips for a goodnight kiss, then tucked the frame back into its hiding place, where the cleaning woman would find it and dig it back out.

She let herself out of the office and locked the door behind her. A vacuum cleaner was running in the office across from hers. Down the hall, Rob Marshall's door was closed. He might still have been there, plotting how to screw her out of her severance pay. Or he might have gone home to – to what? She didn't even know if he had a girlfriend – or a boyfriend, for that matter. Thursday could have been his bowling league night for all she knew about him. He didn't have any close personal friends within the department. Kate had never socialized with him outside the obligatory office Christmas party. She wondered now if he had someone to go home to and complain to about that bitch from the office.

The snow had finally stopped, she noticed as she took the skyway to the Fourth Street ramp. Six inches total, she'd heard someone say. The street below was a mess that city crews would clear away overnight, though this time of year they might decide to leave it and hope for a couple of warm days to save the city some money for the storms that were sure to come in the next few months.

She pulled her keys out and folded them into her fist, the longest, sharpest one protruding between her index and middle fingers – a habit she'd developed living in the DC suburbs. The ramp was well lit, but not busy this time of night, and it always made her edgy walking around in it alone. More so tonight, after all that had gone on. Between the murders and the lack of sleep, her paranoia was running high. A shadow falling between cars, the scrape of a footstep, the sudden thump of a door – her nerves twisted tight every time. The 4Runner seemed a mile away.

Then she was in it, doors locked, motor running, heading home, one layer of tension peeling away. She tried to focus on letting the knots out of her shoulders. Pajamas, a drink, and bed. She'd drag her briefcase there with her and sit propped up by pillows on the sheets still rumpled from lovemaking.

Maybe she would change the sheets.

The enterprising guy from down the block kept a blade on the front of his pickup five months a year and supplemented his income plowing driveways. He had plowed the alley. Kate would write him a check and leave it in his mailbox tomorrow.

She drove into the garage, remembering too late the burned-out light. Swearing under her breath, she dug the big flashlight out of her glove compartment, then climbed down from the truck, juggling too much stuff.

The smell hit her nose just a second before her foot hit the soft, squishy pile.

'Oh, shit!' Literally. 'Shit!'

'Kate?'

The voice came from toward the house. Quinn's voice.

'I'm in here!' she called back, fumbling with the briefcase and the flashlight and her purse.

'What's wrong? I heard you swearing,' he said, coming in.

'I just stepped in a pile of shit.'

'What – Jesus, I smell it. That must have been some dog.'

The flashlight clicked on and she shined it down at the mess. 'It couldn't have been a dog. The door was shut. Gross!'

'That looks human,' Quinn said. 'Where's your shovel?'

Kate flashed the beam of light at the wall. 'Right there. My God, you think someone came into my garage and did this?'

'You have a more viable theory?' he asked.

'I just can't imagine why anyone would do that.'

'It's a sign of disrespect.'

'I know that. I mean, why to me? Who do I know who would do something that strange, that primitive?'

'Who've you pissed off lately?'

'My boss. But somehow I can't envision him squatting in my garage. Nor would I want to.' She limped outside with him, stepping only with the toe of her soiled boot, trying not to smear more feces on her garage floor.

'Do your clients know where you live?'

'If any of them do, it's not because I gave them the information. They have my office number – which forwards to my house machine after hours – and they have my cell phone number for emergencies. That's it. My home number is unlisted, not that that would necessarily stop anyone from finding me. It isn't that hard to do if you know how.'

Quinn dumped the mess between the garage and the neighbor's privacy fence. He cleaned the shovel off in a snowbank while Kate tried to do the same with her boot.

'This is just the exclamation point at the end of my day,' she grumbled as they went back into the garage to put the shovel away. She shone the light around to see if anything was missing. Nothing seemed to be.

'Have you had any odd things happen lately?'

She laughed without humor. 'What about my life lately *isn't* odd?'

'I mean vandalism, hang-up calls, strange mail, anything like that?'

'No,' she said, then automatically thought of the three hang-up calls last night. God, was it just last night? She'd attributed them to Angie. That made the most sense to her. The idea of a stalker had never occurred. It still didn't seem a possibility.

'I think you should park on the street,' Quinn said. 'This might have been some transient going through the neighborhood, or it might have been some kid playing a joke, but you can't be too careful, Kate.'

'I know. I will – starting tomorrow. How long have you been here?' Kate asked as they started for the house.

'Not long enough to have to do *that*.'

'That's not what I meant.'

'I just got here. I tried calling you at the office. I tried calling here. I went to the office – you were gone. So I took a cab. Did you get my messages?'

'Yes, but it was late and I was tired. It's been a rotten, rotten day, and I just wanted out of there.'

She let them in the back door and Thor greeted them with an indignant meow. Kate left her boots in the entry, dropped her briefcase on a kitchen chair, and went directly to the fridge to pull out the cat food.

'You weren't avoiding me?' Quinn said, shrugging out of his coat.

'Maybe. A little.'

'I was worried about you, Kate.'

She set the dish down on the floor, stroked a hand over the cat, and straightened with her back to Quinn. Just that one little sentence brought the volatile emotions swirling once more to the surface, brought tears to her eyes. She wouldn't let him see them if she could help it. She would choke them back down if she could. He was inviting her to need him. She wanted to so badly.

'I'm sorry,' she said. 'I'm not used to anyone caring –'

Christ, what a poor choice of words. She wasn't used to anyone caring about her anymore. The truth, but it made her sound pathetic and wretched. It made her think of Melanie Hessler – missing for a week without anyone caring enough to find out why.

'She was my client,' she said. 'Melanie Hessler. Victim number four. I managed to lose two in one night. How's that for a record?'

'Oh, Kate.' He came up behind her and slipped his arms around her, folding his warmth and his strength around her. 'Why didn't you call me?'

Because I'm afraid of needing you. Because I'm afraid of loving you.

'Nothing you could do about it,' she said.

Quinn turned her in his arms and brushed her hair back from her face, but he didn't try to make her look at him. 'I could have done this,' he murmured. 'I could have come and put my arms around you and held you for a while.'

'I don't know that that would have been such a good idea,' she said quietly.

'Why not?'

'Because. You're here to work a case. You've got more important things to do.'

'Kate, I love you.'

'Just like that.'

'You know it's not "just like that".'

She stepped away from him, instantly missing the contact. 'I know that we went five years without a word, a note, nothing. And now in a day and a half we're in love again. And in a week you'll go. And then what?' she said, moving restlessly, hands on her hips. 'What am I thinking?'

'Apparently, nothing good.'

Kate could see that she'd hurt him, which hadn't been her intent at all. She cursed herself for being so clumsy with such fragile feelings, but she was out of practice, and she was so afraid, and fear made her awkward.

'I'm thinking about every time in those five years that I wanted to pick up the phone but didn't,' Quinn said. 'But I'm here now.'

'By chance. Can't you see how that scares me, John? If not for this case, would you ever have come? Would you ever have called?'

'Would you?'

'No,' she said without hesitation, then softer and softer, shaking her head. 'No ... no ... I've had enough pain to last me a lifetime. I wouldn't have gone looking for it. I don't want any more. I'd rather not feel anything at all. And you make me feel *so much*,' she said, her throat tightening. 'Too much. And I don't trust it all not to just disappear.'

'No. No.' He caught hold of her by the arms and held her in front of him. 'Look at me, Kate.'

She wouldn't, didn't dare, wanted to be anywhere but right there in front of him on the brink of tears.

'Kate, look at me. It doesn't matter what we would have done. It matters that we're here now. It matters that we feel exactly what we felt back then. It matters that making love to you this morning was the most natural, perfect thing in the world – as if we'd never been apart. That's what matters. Not the rest of it.'

'I love you. I do,' he murmured. 'That's what matters. Do you love me?'

She nodded, head down, as if she were ashamed to admit it. 'I always did.'

Tears slipped down her cheeks. Quinn caught them with his thumbs and brushed them away.

'That's what matters,' he whispered. 'Anything else we can work around.

'My life has been so empty since you left, Kate. I tried to fill the hole with work, but the work just ate away more of me, and the hole just got bigger and bigger, and I kept digging like crazy, trying to backfill. Lately, I've been feeling like there's nothing left. I blamed the job, thought I'd given away so many pieces of myself to it that I don't know who I am anymore. But I know exactly who I am when I'm with you, Kate. That's what's been missing all this time – the part of me I gave to you.'

Kate stared at him, knowing he meant what he said. Quinn might have been a chameleon when it came to the job, changing colors at will to get the result he wanted, but he had never been less than honest with her in their relationship – at least until the end of it, when both of them had pulled the armor tight around bruised hearts. And she knew what it cost him to open himself up that way. Vulnerability was not something John Quinn did well. It was something Kate tried never to do at all herself. But she felt it now inside her, pushing hard at the gate.

'Have you noticed how our timing really sucks?' she said, winning a smile from him. He knew her well enough to realize she was trying to back them both away from this edge. A little joke to slacken the tension. A subtle sign that she wasn't ready, didn't have the strength to deal with it all just then.

'Oh, I don't know,' he said, easing his arms around her. 'I think right now you need to be held, and I need my arms around you. So that's working out pretty well.'

'Yeah, I guess.' She let herself put her head on his shoulder. *Resigned* was the word that came to mind, but she didn't fight it. She was too tired to fight, and she did indeed need to be held. She didn't get many opportunities these days. Her own fault, she knew. She told herself she was too busy to date, that she didn't need the complication of a man in her life right now, when the truth was that there was only one man for her. She didn't want any other.

'Kiss me,' he whispered.

Kate raised her head and invited his mouth to settle on hers, parted her lips, and invited the intimacy of his tongue on hers. As with every kiss they had ever shared, she felt a glowing warmth, a sense of excitement, but also a sense of contentment deep within her soul. She felt as if she had been unconsciously holding her breath, waiting for this, and could now relax and breathe again. A sense of rightness, of completeness.

'I need you, Kate,' Quinn whispered, dragging his mouth across her cheek to her ear.

'Yes,' she whispered, the need pounding inside her like waves against rock. The need speaking above the fear that this would all end in heartache in a day or a week.

He kissed her again, deeper, harder, hotter, letting the reins out on the hunger racing through him. She could feel it in his muscles, in the heat of him; she could taste it in his mouth. His tongue thrust against hers even as he dropped one hand down her back and pulled her hips tight against his, letting her feel just how much he wanted her. She groaned deep in her throat, as much at the stunning depth of the need as at the feel of him hard against her.

Breaking the kiss, he leaned back from her and stared at her, his eyes hard and bright and dark, his lips slightly parted. He was breathing hard.

'My God, I need you.'

Kate took his hand and led him to the hall. At the foot of the stairs, Quinn pulled her to him again for another kiss, still hotter and deeper, more urgent. He pressed her back against the wall. His hands caught the bottom of her black sweater and pulled it up between them, exposing her skin to the air, to his touch, giving him access to her breasts. She gasped as he pulled the cup of her bra aside and filled his hand with her. It didn't matter where they were. It didn't matter that anyone going by could have glimpsed them through the sidelights at her front door. That fast her desire for him outstripped all sense. There was only need, primal and fierce.

She gasped again as his mouth found her nipple. She cradled his head and arched into the contact. She lifted her hips away from the wall as he shoved her snug knit skirt up and stripped down her black tights. Suddenly there was no case, no past, nothing but the need and feel of his fingers exploring her, stroking her, finding her most sensitive flesh, sliding into her.

'John. Oh, God, John,' she breathed, her fingers digging into his shoulders. 'I need you. I need you now.'

He straightened and kissed her quick and hard, twice, then looked up the stairs and back at her, then over his shoulder at the open door to her study, where the desk lamp cast an amber glow that just reached the old leather couch.

In the next moment they were beside the couch, Quinn stripping her sweater over her head, Kate impatiently pulling at his tie. In a few rough moves their clothes were off and abandoned on the floor. They sank down, tangled together on the couch, breath catching at the coldness of the leather. And then the sensation was forgotten, gone, burned away by the heat of their bodies and the heat of their passion.

Kate wrapped her long legs around him, took him into her body in one smooth stroke. He filled her perfectly, completely, physically and deep within her soul. They moved together like dancers, each body exquisitely complementing the other, the passion building like a powerful piece of music, building to a tremendous crescendo.

Then they were over the peak and free-falling, holding each other tight, murmuring words of comfort and assurance Kate already feared wouldn't hold up to the pressures of reality. But she didn't try to dispel the myth or break the promise of 'everything will be all right.' She knew they both wanted to believe it, and they could in those few quiet moments before the real world came back to them.

She knew that John needed to give that promise. He had always had a strong compulsion to protect her. That had always touched her deeply – that he could see the vulnerabilities in her when no one else, not even her husband, could. They had always recognized the secret needs in each other, had always seen each other's secret heart, as if they had always been meant for each other.

'I haven't made out on this couch since I was seventeen,' she said softly, looking into his eyes in the glow of the lamplight. They lay on their sides, pressed close together, almost nose to nose.

Quinn smiled like a shark. 'What was the guy's name – so I can go and kill him.'

'My caveman.'

'I am with you. I always was.'

Kate didn't comment, though she instantly called to mind the ugly scene of Steven confronting her and John in his office. Steven choosing the weapons he used best: cruel words and threats. Quinn taking it and taking it until Steven turned on her. A broken nose and some dental work later, her husband had taken the war to a new playing field and done his best to ruin both their careers.

Quinn caught a finger beneath her chin and brought her head up so he could look into her eyes. He knew exactly what she was remembering. She could see it in his face, in the lowered line of his brow. 'Don't,' he warned.

'I know. The present is screwed up enough. Why dredge up the past?'

He stroked his hand down her cheek and kissed her softly, as if the gesture would seal off the door to those memories. 'I love you. Now. Right now. In the present – even if it is screwed up.'

Kate burrowed her head under his chin and kissed the hollow at the base of his throat. There was that part of her that wanted to ask what they were going to do about it, but she kept her mouth shut for once. It didn't matter tonight.

'I'm sorry about your client,' Quinn said. 'Kovac says she worked in an adult bookstore. That's probably the connection for Smokey Joe.'

'Probably, but it spooked me,' Kate admitted, absently stroking a hand down his bare back – all lean muscle and hard bone, too thin. He wasn't taking care of himself. 'A week ago I didn't have anything to do with this case. Today I've lost two clients to it.'

'You can't blame yourself for this one, Kate.'

'Of course I can. I'm me.'

'Where there's a will there's a way.'

'I don't *want* to,' she protested. 'I just wish I'd called Melanie on Monday, like I usually do. If I hadn't been so preoccupied with Angie, I would have been concerned that I hadn't heard from her. She'd become emotionally dependent on me. I seemed to be her sole support network.

'I know this sounds odd, but I wish I had at least worried about her. The thought of her being caught in a nightmare like that with no one waiting for her, wondering about her, concerned for her . . . It's too sad.'

Quinn hugged her close and kissed her hair, thinking she had a heart as soft as butter behind the armor. It was all the more precious to him because she tried so hard to hide it from everyone. He had seen it all along, from the first time he'd ever met her.

'You couldn't have prevented this from happening,' he said. 'But you may be able to help her now.'

'In what way? By reliving my every conversation with her? Trying to pick out clues to a crime she couldn't have known would be committed against her? That's how I spent my afternoon. I would rather have spent the day poking myself in the eye with a needle.'

'You didn't get anything off the tapes.'

'Anxiety and depression, culminating with a row with Rob Marshall that could have me reading want ads soon.'

'You're pushing your luck there, Kate.'

'I know, but I can't seem to help it. He knows just how to punch my buttons. What do you have for me to do? Could I stretch it into a new career?'

'It's your old career. I brought you copies of the victimologies. I keep having the feeling that I'm looking right at the key we need and not seeing it. I need fresh eyes.'

'You have all of CASKU and Behavioral Sciences at your disposal. Why me?'

'Because you need to,' he said simply. 'I know you, Kate. You need to do something, and you're as qualified as anyone in the Bureau. I've forwarded everything to Quantico, but you're right here, and I trust you. Will you take a look?'

'All right,' she answered, for exactly the reason he'd said: because she needed to. She'd lost Angie. She'd lost Melanie Hessler. If there was something she could do to try to balance that out, she would.

'Let me put some clothes on.' She pulled the chenille throw around her as she sat up.

Quinn scowled. 'I knew there'd be a downside.'

Kate gave him a wry smile, then went to her desk, where the light was blinking on the answering machine. She was a vision in the amber glow of the desk lamp, her hair flame red, the curve of her back a sculptor's dream. It made him ache just to look at her. How incredibly lucky he was to get a second chance.

A petulant voice whined from the machine, 'Kate, it's David Willis. I *need* to speak with you. Call me tonight. You *know* I'm not home during the day. I feel like you're deliberately avoiding me. *Now* – when my confidence level is *so* low. I *need* you –'

Kate hit the button to forward to the next message. 'If they were all like him, I'd get a job at Wal-Mart.'

The next message was from the leader of a businesswoman's group, asking her to speak at a meeting.

Then next a long silence.

Kate met Quinn's sober stare with one of her own. 'I had a couple of those last night. I thought they might be Angie. I wanted to believe it might be.'

Or it might be whoever had Angie, Quinn thought. Smokey Joe. 'We need to put a tap on your phone, Kate. If he's got Angie, he's got your number.'

He could see that hadn't occurred to her. He saw the flash of surprise followed by annoyance with herself for having missed it. But of course Kate wouldn't think of herself as a possible victim. She was strong, in control, in charge. But not invulnerable.

Quinn got up from the couch and went to her, still naked, and put his arms around her.

'God, what a nightmare,' she whispered. 'Do you think she could still be alive?'

'She could be,' he said, because he knew Kate needed to hear it. But he also knew that she was as aware of the odds and the horrible possibilities as he was. She knew as well as he did Angie DiMarco might still be alive, and that they might have been kinder hoping she was not.

> *I am dead*
> *My need alive*
> *Keeps me going*
> *Keeps me hoping*
> *Will he want me?*
> *Will he take me?*
> *Will he hurt me?*
> *Will he love me?*

The words cut at him. The music clawed at his senses. He played the tape anyway. Letting it hurt, needing to feel.

Peter sat in his office, the only light coming in through the window, just enough to turn black to charcoal, gray to ash. The anxiety, the guilt, the longing, the pain, the need, the emotions he could seldom grasp and never express, were trapped inside him, the pressure building until he thought his body would simply explode and there would be nothing left of him except fragments of tissue and hair stuck to the walls and the ceiling and the glass of the photographs of him with the people he had deemed important in his life in the last decade.

He wondered if any part of him would touch the pictures of Jillie crowded down into one small corner of the display. Out of the way, not calling any attention. Subtle shame – of her, of his failure, his mistakes.

'. . . *We need to know the truth, Peter, and I think you're holding back pieces of the puzzle. . . . We need to see the whole picture.'*

Dark pieces of a disturbing picture he didn't want anyone to see.

The surge of shame and rage was like acid in his veins.

I am dead
My need alive
Keeps me going
Keeps me hoping
Will he want me?
Will he take me?
Will he hurt me?
Will he love me?

The sound of the phone was like a razor slicing along his nerves. He grabbed the receiver with a trembling hand.

'Hello?'

'Da-ddy, Da-ddy, Da-ddy,' the voice sang like a siren. 'Come see me. Come give me what I want. You know what I want. I want it now.'

He swallowed hard at the bile in his throat. 'If I do, will you leave me alone?'

'Daddy, don't you love me?'

'Please,' he whispered. 'I'll give you what you want.'

'Then you won't want me anymore. You won't like what I have in store. But you'll come anyway. You'll come for me. Say you'll come.'

'Yes,' he breathed.

He was crying as he hung up, tears scalding his eyelids, burning his cheeks, blurring his vision. He opened the lower right-hand drawer of his desk, took out a matte black Glock nine-millimeter semiautomatic, and slipped it gently into the black duffel bag at his feet. He left the room, the duffel bag hanging heavy in his hand. Then he left the house and drove out into the night.

31

'What's your dream job?' Elwood asked.

'Technical consultant to a cop movie, set in Hawaii and starring Mel Gibson,' Liska said without hesitation. 'Turn the motor on. I'm cold.' She shivered and burrowed her hands down into her coat pockets.

They sat in an employee lot near the Target Center, watching Gil Vanlees's truck by the white glow of the security light. Like the vultures they were often compared to, reporters circled the block around the building and sat in the many small parking lots scattered around it, waiting. They had been on Vanlees like ticks as soon as his name had been leaked in connection with Jillian Bondurant's murder.

Vanlees had yet to leave the building. Groupies lingering after the Dave Matthews Band concert required his full attention. Word from detectives inside the Target Center was that management had kept him behind the scenes – afraid of a lawsuit from Vanlees if they dismissed him based on suspicion alone, afraid of lawsuits from the public if they let him work as usual and something went awry. Press passes had been handed from music critics to crime reporters, who had roamed the halls, looking for him.

The radio crackled. 'Coming your way, Elwood.'

'Roger.' Elwood hung up the handset and chewed thoughtfully on his snack. The whole car smelled of peanut butter. 'Mel Gibson is married and has six children.'

'Not in my fantasy he doesn't. Here he comes.'

Vanlees came lumbering through the gate. Half a dozen reporters swarmed after him like a cloud of gnats. Elwood ran the window down to catch their voices.

'Mr Vanlees, John Quinn has pegged you as a suspect in the Cremator murders. What do you have to say about that?'

'Did you murder Jillian Bondurant?'

'What did you do with her head? Did you have sex with it?' Elwood sighed heavily. 'It's enough to put you off the First Amendment.'

'Assholes,' Liska complained. 'They're worse than assholes. They're the bacteria that gather in assholes.'

Vanlees had no comment for the reporters. He kept moving, having quickly learned that rule of survival. When he was directly in front of their car, Elwood cranked the key and started the engine. Vanlees bolted sideways and hurried on toward his truck.

'A nervous, antisocial individual,' Elwood said, putting the last of his sandwich in a plastic evidence bag as Vanlees fumbled with his keys at the door of his truck.

'The guy's a twitch,' Nikki said. '*My* twitch. Do you think I'll get anything out of it if we nail him for these murders?'

'No.'

'Be brutally honest, why don't you? I don't want to hold any false expectations.'

Vanlees gunned his engine and pulled out of his slot, scattering the reporters. Elwood eased in behind him, then turned the headlights on bright for an instant.

'A commendation would look good on my résumé when I send it off to Mel Gibson's people.'

'The credit will go to Quinn,' Elwood said. 'The media is enamored of mind hunters.'

'And he looks great on television.'

'He could be the next Mel Gibson.'

'Better – he's not losing his hair.'

They sat behind Vanlees as he waited to pull onto First Avenue, and rolled out right behind him, causing an oncoming car to hit the brakes and the horn.

'Think Quinn would hire me as a technical adviser when he goes Hollywood?' Liska asked.

'It seems to me advising isn't your true goal,' Elwood observed.

'True. I'd rather have a participatory role, but I don't think that'll happen. I think he's haunted. Doesn't he seem haunted to you?'

'Driven.'

'Driven *and* haunted. Double whammy.'

'Very romantic.'

'If you're Jane Eyre.' Liska shook her head. 'I don't have time for driven *or* haunted. I'm thirty-two. I've got kids. I need Ward Cleaver.'

'He's dead.'

'My luck.'

They stayed on the truck's tail, negotiating the maze of streets going toward Lyndale. Elwood checked the rearview, grumbling.

'We look like a funeral procession. There must be nine loads of newsies behind us.'

'They'll get everything on videotape. Put away the nightsticks and saps.'

'Police work just isn't the fun it used to be.'

'Watch him in here,' Liska said as they came to the worst of the confusing tangle of streets. 'We might get him on a traffic violation. I break nine laws every time I drive through here.'

Gil Vanlees didn't break any. He kept his speed a fraction under the limit, driving as if he were carrying a payload of eggs in crystal cups. Elwood stayed on the truck's tail, riding Vanlees's bumper a little too close, violating his space, goading him.

'What do you think, Tinks? Is he the guy, or is this the Olympic Park bombing all over again?'

'He fits the profile. He's hiding *something*.'

'Doesn't make him a killer. Everybody's hiding something.'

'I would have liked a chance to find out what, without a pack of reporters at our heels. He'd be an idiot to try anything now.'

'They might not be at our heels long,' Elwood said, checking the rearview again. 'Look at this son of a bitch.'

An older Mustang hatchback came up alongside them on the left, two men in the front seat, their focus on Vanlees's pickup.

'That's balls,' Liska said.

'They probably think we're the competition.'

The Mustang sped up, passing them, coming even with Vanlees, the passenger's window rolling down.

'Son of a bitch!' Elwood yelled.

Vanlees sped up. The car stayed with him.

Liska grabbed the handset and radioed their position, calling for backup and reporting the tag number on the Mustang. Elwood grabbed the dash light off the seat, slapped it onto the bracket, and turned it on. Ahead of them, the passenger in the car was leaning out the window with a telephoto lens.

Vanlees gunned ahead. The car raced even with him.

The flash was brilliant, blinding.

Vanlees's truck swerved into the Mustang, knocking it ass end into the next lane, directly into the path of an oncoming cab. There was no time for even the screech of tires, no time for brakes, just the horrific sound of tons of metal colliding. The photographer was thrown as the cars hit. He tumbled across the street like a rag doll that had been flung out a window. A ball of flame rolled through the Mustang.

Liska saw it all in slow motion – the crash, the fire, Vanlees's truck ahead of them swerving to the curb, one wheel jumping up, the front bumper taking out a parking meter. And then time snapped back to real speed, and Elwood swung the Lumina past the truck and dove into the curb at an angle, cutting off the escape route. He slammed the car into park and was out the door. Liska clutched the handset in a trembling fist and called for ambulances and a fire truck.

Some of the cars that had been tailing them pulled to the side.

Several raced past, making Elwood dodge them as he ran for the burning wreck. Liska shoved her door open and went for Vanlees as he tumbled out of his pickup. She could smell the whiskey on him two feet away.

'I didn't do it!' he shouted, sobbing.

Camera flashes went off like strobes, illuminating his face in stark white light. Blood ran from his nose and his mouth where his face had evidently met with the steering wheel. He threw his arms up to block the glare and spoil the shots. 'Goddammit, leave me alone!'

'I don't think so, Gil,' Liska said, reaching for his arm. 'Up against the truck. You're under arrest.'

'Now I know how they break spies with sleep deprivation,' Kovac said, striding toward Gil Vanlees's truck, which was still hung up on the curb. 'I'm ready to transfer to records so I can get some sleep.'

Liska scowled at him. 'Come crying to me when you have a nine-year-old look up at you with big teary blue eyes and ask why you didn't come to his Thanksgiving pageant at school when he was playing a Pilgrim and everything.'

'Jesus, Tinks,' he growled, hanging a cigarette on his lip. The apology was in his eyes. 'We shouldn't be allowed to breed.'

'Tell it to my ovaries. What the hell are you doing here anyway?' she asked, turning him away from the reporters. 'Trying to get yourself fired altogether? You're supposed to lie low.'

'I'm bringing you coffee.' The picture of innocence, he handed her a steaming foam cup. 'Just trying to support the first team.'

Even as he said it, his gaze was roaming to Vanlees's truck.

The truck was surrounded by uniformed cops and the crime scene team setting up to do their thing. Portable lights illuminated it from all angles, giving the scene the feel of a photo shoot for a Chevy ad. The totalled cars sitting in the middle of the street were being dealt with by tow trucks.

Reporters hung around the perimeter of the scene, backed off by the uniforms, their interest in the accident made all the more keen by their own involvement in the drama.

'Any word on your replacement?' Liska asked.

Kovac lit a cigarette and shook his head. 'I put in a word for you with Fowler.'

She looked surprised. 'Wow, thanks, Sam. You think they'll listen?'

'Not a chance. My money's on Yurek because they can scare him. So what's the latest here?'

'Vanlees is at HCMC getting looked at before we haul his sorry ass downtown. I think he broke his nose. Other than him, we've got one dead, one critical, one in good condition.' Liska leaned back against the car she and Elwood had been riding in. 'The driver of the Mustang is toast. The cabbie broke both ankles and cracked his head, but he'll be okay. The photographer is in surgery. They think his brain is bleeding. I wouldn't be too optimistic. Then again, I wouldn't have said he had a brain, doing what he was doing.'

'Do we know who these guys are – were?'

'Kevin Pardee and Michael Morin. Freelancers looking to score with an exclusive photo. Life and death in the age of tabloid news. Now they're the headline.'

'How'd Vanlees get behind the wheel if he was drunk enough you could smell it on him?'

'You'd have to ask the reporters that. They were the ones crowded around him as he left the building. All our people had to watch him from a distance or spark a lawsuit for harassment.'

'Ask the reporters,' Sam grumbled. 'They'll be the first ones to raise questions about *our* negligence. Scumsuckers. How's Elwood?'

'Burned his hands pretty bad trying to get Morin out of the car. He's at the hospital. Singed his eyebrows off too. Looks pretty damn goofy.'

'He looked goofy to start with.'

'Vanlees registered .08 on the Breathalyzer. Lucky for us. I was able to impound the truck. Gotta inventory everything in it,' she said with a shrug, blinking false innocence. 'Can't know what we might find.'

'Let's hope for a bloody knife under the seat,' Kovac said. 'He looks like he'd be that stupid, don't you think? Christ, it's cold. And it's not even Thanksgiving.'

'Bingo!' called one of the crime scene team.

Kovac jumped away from the car. 'What? What'd you get? Tell me it's got blood on it.'

The criminalist stepped back from the driver's door. 'The economy self-gratification kit,' she said, turning around, holding up a copy of *Hustler* and one very disgusting pair of black silk women's panties.

'The pervert's version of the smoking gun,' Kovac said. 'Bag it. We may just have the key to unlock this mutt's head.'

'What's the word on getting a warrant to search Vanlees's place?' Quinn asked, shrugging out of his trench coat. He wore the same suit he'd had on the night before, Kovac noticed. Heavily creased.

Kovac shook his head. 'Based on what we've got, not a chance in hell. Not even with Peter Bondurant's name attached to the case. We went over every inch of that truck and didn't come up with anything that would tie him directly to any of the murder victims. We might get lucky with the panties – a few weeks from now when the DNA tests come back. We can't even run the tests now. The underpants are just part of the inventory of his stuff at this point. We don't know who they belonged to. We can't say he stole them. And whacking off ain't a crime.'

'You hear that, Tippen?' Liska said. 'You're in the clear.'

'I heard those were your panties, Tinks.'

'Tinks wears panties?' Adler said.

'Very funny.'

They stood in a conference room at the PD, the task force minus Elwood, who had refused to go home and was now sitting with Vanlees in an interview room down the hall.

'Why couldn't he be dumb enough to keep a bloody knife under the seat?' Adler asked. 'He looks like he'd be that stupid.'

'Yeah,' Quinn agreed. 'That bothers me. We're not exactly dealing with a brainiac here – unless he's got multiple personalities and one of the alters keeps the brain to himself. What do we know about his background, other than his more recent escapades?'

'I'm checking it,' Walsh said. His voice was almost gone, choked off by his cold and his pack-a-day habit.

'Nikki and I have both talked with his wife,' Moss said. 'Should I see if she'll come down?'

'Please,' Quinn said.

'She's gotta know if her husband's this kind of a sick pervert,' Tippen said.

Quinn shook his head. 'Not necessarily. It sounds like she's the dominant partner in that relationship. He's likely kept his hobby a secret from her, partly out of fear, partly as an act of defiance. But if he's got a female partner – and we think he has – then who is she? The wife is clean?'

'Jillian?' Liska ventured.

'Possibly. Has the wife given any indication she thought he might have a girlfriend?'

'No.'

Quinn checked his watch. He wanted Vanlees waiting just long enough to get nervous. 'You get anything back on Michele Fine's prints?'

'Nothing in Minnesota.'

'Has Vanlees called a lawyer?'

'Not yet,' Liska said. 'He's got his logic going. He says he's not calling a lawyer because an innocent man doesn't need one.'

Tippen snorted. 'Christ, how'd he ever find his way out of St Cloud?'

'Dumb luck. I told him we weren't charging him right off on the accident. I told him we needed to sit down and sort through what happened before we could determine negligence, but that we had to hold him on the DUI. He can't decide if he should be relieved or pissed.'

'Let's go to it before he makes up his mind,' Quinn said. 'Sam – you, Tinks, and me. We work him like before.'

'I wouldn't if I were you, Sam,' Yurek cautioned. 'Fowler, Little Dick, Sabin, and that assistant prosecutor Logan – they're all there to observe.'

'Fuck me,' Kovac said with abject disgust.

Liska arched a brow. 'Will you respect me afterward?'

'Do I respect you now?'

She kicked him in the shin.

'Charm,' he said to Yurek through his teeth. 'If you were me, I wouldn't be in this mess.'

Greer, Sabin, Logan, and Fowler stood in the hall outside the interview room, waiting. At the sight of Kovac, Fowler got an expression as if he were having angina. Greer's eyes bugged out.

'What are you doing here, Sergeant?' he demanded. 'You've officially been removed from the task force.'

'My request, Chief,' Quinn said smoothly. 'We've already established a certain way of dealing with Mr Vanlees. I don't want to change anything at this point. I need him to trust me.'

Greer and Sabin looked sulky; Logan, impatient. Fowler pulled a roll of Tums out of his pocket and thumbed one off.

Quinn dismissed the topic before anyone could think to defy him. He held the door for Liska and Kovac, and followed them in.

Gil Vanlees looked like a giant raccoon. Both eyes had blackened in the hours since the accident. He had a split lip and a wide strip of adhesive tape across his nose. He stood at one end of the room with his hands on his hips, looking pissed and nervous.

Elwood sat in a chair with his back against the wall. Both hands were bandaged. His face was seared red. Without eyebrows his expression seemed one of perpetual unpleasant surprise.

'I hear you had a little accident, Gil,' Kovac said, falling into a chair at the table.

Vanlees pointed a finger at him. 'I'm gonna sue. You people harassed me, you let the press harass me –'

'You got behind the wheel of a truck with a snootful,' Kovac said, lighting a cigarette. 'Did I buy it for you? Did I pour it down your throat?'

'Your people let me get behind that wheel,' Vanlees began with all the sanctimonious indignation of a master at rationalization. He shot a quick, nervous glance at Elwood.

Kovac made a face. 'Next thing you're gonna tell me it's my fault you killed Jillian Bondurant and those other women.'

Vanlees reddened, his eyes teared. He made a sound like a man straining on the toilet. 'I *didn't*.' He turned on Liska then. 'You told me this was about the accident. You're such a lying little cunt!'

'Hey!' Kovac barked. 'Sergeant Liska's doing you a favor. You killed someone last night, you fucking drunk.'

'That wasn't my fault! That son of a bitch shot a flash off in my face! I couldn't see!'

'That's what Sergeant Liska says. She was there. She's your witness. You want to call her a cunt again? I was her, I'd feed you your dick for dinner, you sorry sack of shit.'

Vanlees looked at Liska, contrite.

'Liska says you're innocent as a vestal virgin,' Kovac went on, 'and that you don't want a lawyer. Is that right?'

'I haven't done anything wrong,' he said, sulking.

Kovac shook his head. 'Wow. You've got a broad definition of reality there, Gil. We've got you dead to rights on the DUI – which is wrong by law. I know you were looking in Jillian Bondurant's windows. That would be considered wrong.'

Vanlees sat down, chair turned sideways to the table, presenting his back to Kovac and to the people on the other side of the one-way glass. He rested his forearms on his thighs and looked at the floor. He looked prepared to sit there all night without saying another word.

Quinn studied him. In his experience it wasn't the innocent man who refused counsel, it was the man with something on his conscience he wanted to unload.

'So, were those Jillian's panties we pulled out from under your driver's seat, Gil?' Kovac asked bluntly.

Vanlees kept his head down. 'No.'

'Lila White's? Fawn Pierce's? Melanie Hessler's?'

'No. No. No.'

'You know, I wouldn't have guessed it looking at you, but you're a complex individual, Gil,' Kovac said. 'Multilayered – like an onion. And every layer I peel away smells worse than the last. You look like an average Joe. Peel one layer back and – oh! – your wife's leaving you! Well, that's not so unusual. I'm a two-time loser myself. Peel another layer back and – jeez! – she's leaving you because you're a window peeper! No, wait, you're not just a window peeper. You're a weenie wagger! You're just one big, bad progessive joke. You're a drunk. You're a drunk who drives. You're a drunk who drives and gets somebody killed.'

Vanlees hung his head lower. Quinn could see the man's swollen mouth quivering.

'I didn't mean to. I couldn't see,' Vanlees said in a thick voice. 'They won't leave me alone. That's *your* fault. I didn't do anything.'

'They want to know what happened to Jillian,' Kovac said. 'I want to know what happened to her too. I think there was something more going on between you than what you're telling us, Gil. I think you had the hots for her. I think you were watching her. I think you stole those panties out of her dresser so you could whack off with them and fantasize about her, and I'm gonna prove it. We already know the panties are her size, her brand,' he bluffed. 'It's just a matter of time before we get the DNA match. A few weeks. You'd better get used to those reporters, 'cause they're gonna be on you like flies on roadkill.'

Vanlees was crying now. Silently. Tears dripping onto the backs of his hands. He was trembling with the effort to hold them back.

Quinn looked to Kovac. 'Sergeant, I'd like to have a few moments alone with Mr Vanlees.'

'Oh, sure, like I got nothing better to do,' Kovac complained, getting up. 'I know where this is going, Quinn. You G-men want it all to yourself. Fuck that. His ass is mine.'

'I just want a few words with Mr Vanlees.'

'Uh-huh. You don't like the way I talk to this piece of cheese. You're sitting there thinking I should go easy on him on account of his prostitute mother used to beat his bare ass with a wire hanger or some such psychobabble bullshit. Fine. I'll see you in the headlines, I'm sure.'

Quinn said nothing until the cops had gone out, and then he said nothing for a long time. He took a Tagamet and washed it down with water from the plastic pitcher on the table. Casually, he turned his chair perpendicular to Vanlees's, leaned ahead, rested his forearms on his thighs, and sat there some more, until Vanlees glanced up at him.

'More of that good cop–bad cop shit,' Vanlees said, pouting. 'You think I'm a dumb shit.'

'I think you watch too much TV,' Quinn said. 'This is the real world, Gil. Sergeant Kovac and I don't have identical agendas here.

'I'm not interested in headlines, Gil. I've had plenty. You know that. I get them automatically. You know all I'm interested in, right? You know about me. You've read about me.'

Vanlees said nothing.

'The truth and justice. That's it. And I don't care what the truth turns out to be. It's not personal with me. With Kovac, everything is personal. He's got you in his crosshairs. All I want to know is the truth, Gil. I want to know your truth. I get the feeling you've got something heavy on your chest, and maybe you want to get it off, but you don't trust Kovac.'

'I don't trust you either.'

'Sure you do. You know about me. I've been nothing but up front with you, Gil, and I think you appreciate that on some level.'

'You think I killed Jillian.'

'I think you fit the profile in a lot of respects. I admit that. Moreover, if you look at the situation objectively, you'll agree with me. You've studied this stuff. You know what we look for. You know some of your pieces fit the puzzle. But that doesn't mean I believe you killed her. I don't necessarily believe Jillian is dead.'

'What?' Vanlees looked at him as if he thought Quinn might have lost his mind.

'I think there's a lot more to Jillian than first meets the eye. And I think you may have something to say about that. Do you, Gil?'

Vanlees looked at the floor again. Quinn could feel the pressure building in him as he weighed the pros and cons of answering truthfully.

'If you were watching her, Gil,' Quinn said very softly, 'you're not going to get in trouble for that. That's not the focus here. The police will gladly let that go in trade for something they can use.'

Vanlees seemed to consider that, never thinking, Quinn was sure, that the 'something' they were looking for could in turn be used against him. He was thinking of Jillian, of how he might cast some odd light on her and away from himself, because that was what people tended to do when they found themselves in big trouble – blame the other guy. Criminals regularly blamed their victims for the crimes committed against them.

'You were attracted to her, right?' Quinn said. 'That's not a crime. She was a pretty girl. Why shouldn't you look?'

'I'm married,' he mumbled.

'You're married, you're not dead. Looking is free. So you looked. I don't have a problem with that.'

'She was ... different,' Vanlees said, still staring at the floor but seeing Jillian Bondurant, Quinn thought. 'Kind of ... exotic.'

'You told Kovac she didn't come on to you, but that's not exactly true, is it?' Quinn ventured, still speaking softly, an intimate chat between acquaintances. 'She was aware of you, wasn't she, Gil?'

'She never said anything, but she'd look at me in a certain way,' he admitted.

'Like she wanted you.' A statement, not a question, as if it came as no surprise.

Vanlees shied away from that. 'I don't know. Like she wanted me to know she was looking, that's all.'

'Kind of mixed signals.'

'Yeah. Mixed signals.'

'Did anything come of it?'

Vanlees hesitated, struggled. Quinn waited, held his breath.

'I just want the truth, Gil. If you're innocent, it won't hurt you. It's just between us. Man to man.'

The silence stretched.

'I – I know it was wrong,' Vanlees murmured at last. 'I didn't really mean to do it. But I was checking the yards one night, making the rounds –'

'When was this?'

'This summer. And ... I was there ...'

'At Jillian's house.'

He nodded. 'She was playing the piano, wearing a silky robe that wanted to fall off her shoulder. I could see her bra strap.'

'So you watched her for a while,' Quinn said, as if it was only natural, any man would do it, no harm.

'Then she slipped the robe off and stood up and stretched.'

Vanlees was seeing it all in his mind. His respiration rate had picked up, and a fine sheen of sweat misted his face. 'She started moving her body, like a dance. Slow and very ... erotic.'

'Did she know you were there?'

'I didn't think so. But then she came to the window and pulled the cups of her bra down so I could see her tits, and she pressed them right to the glass and rubbed against it,' he said in a near whisper, ashamed, thrilled. 'She – she licked the window with her tongue.'

'Jesus, that must have been very arousing for you.'

Vanlees blinked, embarrassed, looked away. This would be where parts of the story would go missing. He wouldn't tell about getting an erection or taking his penis out and masturbating while he watched her. Then again, he didn't have to. Quinn knew his history, knew the patterns of behavior, had seen it over and over in the years of studying criminal sexual behavior. He wasn't learning anything new here about Gil Vanlees. But if the story was true, he was learning something very significant about Jillian Bondurant.

'What'd she do then?' he asked softly.

Vanlees shifted on his chair, physically uncomfortable. 'She – she pulled her panties down and she . . . touched herself between her legs.'

'She masturbated in front of you?'

His face flushed. 'Then she opened the window and I got scared and ran. But later I went back, and she had dropped her panties out the window.'

'And those are the panties the police found in your truck. They *are* Jillian's.'

He nodded, bringing one hand up to his forehead as if to try to hide his face. Quinn watched him, trying to gauge him. Truth or a tale to cover his ass for having the underwear of a possible murder victim in his possession?

'When was this?' he asked again.

'Back this summer. July.'

'Did anything like that ever happen again?'

'No.'

'Did she ever say anything about it to you?'

'No. She almost never talked to me at all.'

'Mixed signals,' Quinn said again. 'Did that make you mad, Gil? That she would strip in front of you, masturbate in front of you, then pretend like nothing happened. Pretend like she hardly knew you, like you weren't good enough for her. Did that piss you off?'

'I didn't do anything to her,' he whispered.

'She was a tease. If a woman did that to me – got me hard and hot for her, then turned it off – I'd be pissed. I'd want to fuck her good, make her pay attention. Didn't you want to do that, Gil?'

'But I never did.'

'But you wanted to have sex with her, didn't you? Didn't some part of you want to teach her a lesson? That dark side we all have, where we hold grudges and plan revenge. Don't you have a dark side, Gil? I do.'

He waited again, the tension coiled tight inside him.

Vanlees looked bleak, defeated, as if the full import of all that had happened tonight had finally sunk in.

'Kovac is going to try to hang that murder on me,' he said. 'Because those panties are Jillian's. Because of what I just told you. Even when she was the bad one, not me. That's what's going to happen, isn't it?'

'You make a good suspect, Gil. You see that, don't you?'

He nodded slowly, thinking.

'Her father was there, at the town house,' he mumbled. 'Sunday morning. Early. Before dawn. I saw him coming out. Monday his lawyer gave me five hundred dollars not to say anything.'

Quinn absorbed the information in silence, weighing it, gauging it. Gil

Vanlees was ass deep in alligators. He might say anything. He might say he'd seen a stranger, a vagrant, a one-armed man near Jillian's apartment. He chose to say he'd seen Peter Bondurant, and that Peter Bondurant had paid him to shut up.

'Early Sunday morning,' Quinn said.

Vanlees nodded. No eye contact.

'Before dawn.'

'Yes.'

'What were you doing around there at that hour, Gil? Where were you that you saw him – and that he saw you?'

Vanlees shook his head this time – at the question or at something playing through his own mind. He seemed to have aged ten years in the last ten minutes. There was something pathetic about him sitting there in his security guard's uniform, the wanna-be cop playing pretend. The best he could do.

He spoke in a small, soft voice. 'I want to call a lawyer now.'

32

Kate sat on the old leather couch in her study, curled into one corner, warding off the old house's morning chill with black leggings, thick wool socks, and a baggy old sweatshirt she hadn't worn in years. Quinn had given it to her back when. The name of the gym he frequented was stitched across the front. That she'd kept it all this time should have told her something, but then, she'd always been selectively deaf.

She had pulled it out of her closet after Quinn had gone to meet with the task force, freshening it in the clothes drier for a few minutes, and putting it on while it was still warm, pretending it was his warmth. A poor substitute for the feel of his arms around her. Still, it made her feel closer to him somehow. And after a night in his arms, the need for that was strong.

God, what an inconvenient time to rediscover love. But given their professions and their lives, what choice did they have? They were both too aware that life held no guarantees. Too aware that they had already given up too much time they could never get back because of fear and pride and pain.

Kate imagined she could look down from the height of another dimension and see the two of them as if that time had passed. Her time spent focusing myopically on the minutiae of building a 'normal' life for herself with a job and hobbies and people she saw socially at the requisite functions and holidays. Nothing deeper. Going through the motions, pretending not to mind the numbness in her soul. Figuring it was preferable to the alternative. Quinn's time poured into the job, the job, the job. Taking on more responsibility to fill the void, until the weight of it threatened to crush him. Crowding his brain with cases and facts until he couldn't keep them straight. Giving away pieces of himself and masking others until he couldn't remember what was genuine. Exhausting the well of strength that had once seemed almost bottomless. Wearing his confidence in his abilities and his judgment as threadbare as the lining of his stomach.

Both of them denying themselves the one thing they had needed most to heal after all that had happened: each other.

Sad, what people could do to themselves, and to each other, Kate thought, her gaze skimming across the pages of the victimologies she had spread out on the coffee table. Four more lives fucked up and ruined before they had ever met the Cremator. Five with Angie. Ruined because they needed love and couldn't find anything but a twisted, cheap replica. Because they wanted things out of their reach. Because it seemed easier to settle for less than work for more. Because they believed they didn't deserve anything better. Because the people around them who should have, didn't believe they deserved better either. Because they were women, and women are automatic targets in American society.

All of those reasons made a victim.

Everyone was a victim of something. The difference in people was what they did about it – succumb or rise above and move beyond. The women whose pictures lay before her would not be given that choice again.

Kate leaned over the coffee table, skimming her gaze across the reports. She had called the office to say she was taking some personal time. She'd been told Rob was out as well, and that office speculation was that they had beaten each other up and didn't want anyone to see the bruises. Kate said it was more likely Rob was still working on his written complaint to put in her personnel file.

At least she was free of him for the day. Which would have been a sweet deal if not for the photographs she had to look at of burned and mutilated women, and if not for all the emotions and depressing realities that those photographs evoked.

Everyone was a victim of something.

This group presented a depressing laundry list. Prostitution, drugs, alcohol, assault, rape, incest – if what Kovac had been told about Jillian Bondurant was true. Victims of crime, victims of their upbringing.

From a distance, Jillian Bondurant would have seemed to have been the anomaly because she wasn't a prostitute or in any sex-associated profession, but from the standpoint of her psychological profile, she wasn't all that far removed from Lila White or Fawn Pierce. Confused and conflicted feelings about sex and about men. Low self-esteem. Emotionally needy. Outwardly, she would seem not to have had as hard a life as a streetwalking prostitute because she wasn't as vulnerable to the same kind of crime and open violence. But there was nothing easy about suffering in silence, covering up pain and damage to save face for the family.

Quinn said there was considerable doubt that Jillian was dead at all, but that didn't mean she wasn't a victim. If she was Smokey Joe's accomplice, she was just a victim of another sort. The Cremator himself had been a victim once. Victimization as a child was one of many components that went into making a serial killer.

Everyone was a victim of something.

Kate turned to her own notes about Angie. Spare. Mostly hunches, things she had learned in her years of studying people to see what shaped their minds and their personalities. Abuse had shaped Angie DiMarco. Likely from a very early age. She expected the worst of people, dared them to show it to her, to prove her right. And that had undoubtedly happened again and again, because the kind of people who lived in Angie's world tended to live down to expectations. Angie included.

She expected people to dislike her, to distrust her, to cheat her, to use her, and made certain that they did. This case had been no exception. Sabin and the police had wanted nothing more than to use her, and Kate had been their tool. Angie's disappearance was an inconvenience to them, not a tragedy. If not for her status as a witness, no one on earth would have posted a reward or flashed her photograph on television asking 'Have you seen this girl?' Even then, the police were not putting forth a tremendous search effort to find her. The energies of the task force were all dedicated to finding the suspect, not the AWOL witness.

Kate wondered if Angie might have seen the spots on the news. She would have enjoyed the notoriety, the attention. She might secretly have pretended to believe someone actually cared about her.

'Why would you care what happens to me?' the girl had asked as they stood in the hall outside Kate's office.

'Because no one else does.'

And I didn't care enough, Kate thought with a heavy heart. She'd been afraid to. Just as she had been afraid to let John back into her life. Afraid to feel that deeply. Afraid of the pain that kind of feeling could bring with it.

What a pathetic way to live. No – that wasn't living, that was simply existing.

Was the girl alive? she wondered, getting up from the couch to prowl the room. Was she dead? Had she been taken? Had she just left?

Am I being unrealistic to think there's even a question here?

She'd seen the blood for herself. Too much of it for a benign explanation.

But how could Smokey Joe have known where she was? What were the chances of his having spotted her at the PD and followed her to the Phoenix? Slim. Which would mean he would have to have found out some other way. Which meant he either had some in with the case . . . or an in with Angie.

Who had known where Angie was staying? Sabin, Rob, the task force, a couple of uniforms, the Urskines, Peter Bondurant's lawyer – and therefore Peter Bondurant.

The Urskines, who had known the first victim and had a peripheral connection to the second. They hadn't known Jillian Bondurant, but her connection to these crimes had given Toni Urskine a platform for her cause.

Gregg had been there at the house Wednesday night when Kate had left Angie off. Just Gregg and Rita Renner, who gave all the appearances of being an Urskine puppet. Rita Renner, who had been friends with Fawn Pierce.

Kate had known the Urskines for years. While Toni might drive someone to kill, she couldn't imagine the couple practising that hobby themselves. Then again, no one in Toronto had ever suspected the Ken and Barbie killers, and that couple had committed murders so hideous, veteran cops had broken down and wept on the witness stand during the trial.

God, what a sinister thought – that the Urskines might take women in, using kindness and caring as a front for a sadistic hunting game. But surely they wouldn't be so stupid as to prey on their own clientele. They would be automatic suspects. And if the man Angie had seen in the park that night had been Gregg Urskine, then she would have recognized him at the Phoenix, wouldn't she?

Kate thought of the vague description the girl had given of Smokey Joe, the almost nondescript sketch, trying to make some sense of it all. Had she been so reluctant, so vague, because she was frightened, as Kate had suspected? Or because – as Angie said – it was dark, he wore a hood, it happened so fast? Or did her motivation lie elsewhere?

The task force had a hot suspect, Kate knew. Quinn was probably interviewing him right now. The caretaker from Jillian's town house complex. He had no inside connection to the case, but she supposed he could have known Angie if she had ever trolled for johns in the area around the Target Center, where he worked as a security guard.

But it didn't make sense for Angie to have a connection to the killer. If she knew him and wanted him caught, she would have given him up. If she knew him and didn't want him caught, she would have given a clear description of a phantom for the cops to chase.

And if she hadn't seen anything at all in the park that night, why would she say she had? For three squares and a place to stay? For attention? Then it would have made more sense for her to be cooperative rather than difficult.

Everything about this kid was a mystery inside a puzzle wrapped in an enigma.

Which is why I don't do kids.

But this one was – had been – her responsibility, and she would find out the truth about her or die trying.

'Poor choice of words, Kate,' she muttered, heading upstairs to change clothes.

Twenty minutes later, she was out the back door. It had snowed another inch during the night, giving the landscape a clean dusting of fresh white powder, coating the back steps . . . where a pair of boots had left tracks.

Quinn had gone out the front this morning, to a waiting cab. The tracks were too small to be his, at any rate. They were more the size of Kate's feet, though that didn't necessarily establish gender.

Carefully staying to one side of them, Kate followed the tracks down the stairs to the yard. The trail led past the end of her garage and down the far side, down the narrow corridor between the building and the neighbor's weathered-gray privacy fence, to the side entrance of the garage. All the doors were closed.

A chill ran through her. She thought back to last night and someone defecating in the garage. She thought of the suddenly burned-out light, the feeling Wednesday night that someone had been watching her as she'd made her way from the garage to the house.

She looked around, down the deserted alley. Most of the neighbors had fences that hid the first stories of their homes from view. Second-story windows looked black and empty. The neighborhood was full of white-collar professionals, most of whom left for work by seven thirty.

Kate backed away from the garage, heart pumping, hand digging in her bag for her cell phone. Moving toward the house, she pulled the phone out, flipped it open, and punched the power button. Nothing happened. The battery had died in the night. The inconvenience of modern convenience.

She kept her eyes on the garage, thought she saw a movement through the side window. Car thief? Burglar? Rapist? Disgruntled client? Cremator?

She stuffed the phone back in her bag and pulled out her house keys. She let herself in, locked herself in, and breathed again.

'I need this like I need the plague,' she muttered, going into the kitchen. She put her tote and her purse on the table and started to slip out of her coat, when the sound registered in her brain. The low, feral growl of a cat. Thor was under the table, snarling, ears flat.

The fine hair rose up on the back of Kate's neck, and with it the itchy feeling of being watched.

Options raced through her mind. She had no idea how close the person might be behind her, or how close they might be to the door. The phone was on the wall on the other end of the room – too far away.

Casually opening the tote, she looked inside with an eye for a weapon. She didn't carry a gun. The canister of pepper spray she had carried for a while had expired and she'd thrown it out. She had a plastic bottle of Aleve, a packet of Kleenex, the heel from the shoe she'd ruined Monday. She dug a little deeper and found a metal nail file, palmed that, and slipped it into her coat pocket. She knew her escape routes. She would turn, confront, break right or left. Plan set, she counted to five and turned around.

The kitchen was empty. But framed by the doorway to the dining room, sitting on one of Kate's straight-backed oak chairs, was Angie DiMarco.

'He confesses to having Jillian Bondurant's underpants, and you don't think he's the guy?' Kovac said, incredulous.

His temper had a direct effect on his driving, Quinn noticed.

The Caprice roared down 94, rocking like a clown car. Quinn braced his feet in the floor well, knowing his legs would snap like toothpicks in the crash. Of course, it probably wouldn't matter, because he would be dead. This piece-of-crap car would crumple like an empty beer can.

'I'm just saying there are some things I don't like,' he said. 'Vanlees doesn't strike me as a team player. He lacks the arrogance to be the top dog, and the sadistic male is virtually always the dominant partner in a couple that kills. The woman is subservient to him, a victim who counts herself lucky not to be the one he's murdering.'

'So this time it's reversed,' Kovac insisted. 'The woman runs the show. Why not? Moss and Liska say his wife had him pussy-whipped.'

'His mother probably did too. And yes, it's often a domineering or manipulative or otherwise influential woman in his past or present a sexual sadist is killing symbolically when he kills his victims. That all fits, but there are holes too. I wish I could say I just look at him and like him for these murders, but I'm not feeling that bolt of lightning.'

But then, that feeling had more or less deserted him in recent years, he reminded himself. Doubt had become more the rule than the exception, so what the hell did he know anymore? Why should he trust his instincts now?

Kovac swerved the car across three lanes to the exit he wanted. 'Well, I can tell you, the powers that be like this guy fine. You talk about lightning. They're all getting a goddamn thunderstorm in their pants over Vanlees. He's got a history, he fits the profile, he has a connection to Jillian, access to hookers, and he's not Peter Bondurant. If they can find a way to charge him, they will. If they can, they'll do it in time for the press conference today.'

And if Vanlees wasn't the guy, they ran the risk of pushing the real killer into proving himself again. The thought made Quinn ill.

'Vanlees says Peter was in Jillian's place predawn Sunday morning, and sent Noble on Monday to pay him to keep his mouth shut,' he said, drawing a frighteningly long stare from Kovac. The Caprice began to drift toward a rusted-out Escort in the next lane.

'Jesus, will you watch the road!' Quinn snapped. 'How do they give out driver's licenses in this state? You save up bottle caps or something?'

'Beer-can tabs,' Kovac replied, returning his attention to the traffic. 'So Bondurant was the one who cleaned up Jillian's house and erased the messages on the answering machine.'

'I'd say so – if Vanlees is telling the truth. And I think it's a safe bet then that Peter is the reason you didn't find any of Jillian's own musical compositions. He might have taken them because they revealed something about his relationship with Jillian.'

'The sexual abuse.'

'Possibly.'

'Son of a bitch,' Kovac muttered. 'Sunday morning. Smokey Joe didn't light up the body until midnight. Why would Bondurant go to her place Sunday morning, wipe the place down, take the music, if he didn't already know she was dead?'

'Why would he wipe the place down at all?' Quinn asked. 'He owns the town house. His daughter lived there. His fingerprints wouldn't be out of place.'

Kovac cut him a glance. 'Unless they were bloody.'

Quinn braced a hand against the dash as a tow truck cut in front of them and Kovac hit the brakes. 'Just drive, Kojak. Or we won't live long enough to find out.'

With rumors of a suspect in custody, the media circus had begun anew on the street in front of Peter Bondurant's house. Videographers roamed the boulevard, taking exterior shots of the mansion while on-air talent did their sound checks. Quinn wondered if anyone had even bothered to call the families of Lila White or Fawn Pierce.

Two Paragon security officers stood at the gate with walkie-talkies. Quinn flashed his ID and they were waved through to the house. Edwyn Noble's black Lincoln was parked in the drive with a steel-blue Mercedes sedan beside it. Kovac pulled in behind the Lincoln, so close the cars were nearly kissing bumpers.

Quinn gave him a look. 'Promise you'll behave yourself.'

Kovac played it innocent. He had been relegated to the role of driver and wasn't to leave the car. He wasn't to cross Peter Bondurant's field of vision. Quinn had kept Gil Vanlees's revelation to himself, as an added precaution. The last thing he needed was Kovac bulling his way into this.

'Take your time, GQ. I'll just be sitting here reading the paper.' He picked up a copy of the *Star Tribune* from the pile of junk on the seat. Gil Vanlees took up half the front page – headline story, sidebar, and a bad photograph that made him look like Popeye's archnemesis, Bluto. Kovac's eyes were on the house, scanning the windows.

Noble met Quinn at the door, frowning, looking past him to the Caprice. In the car, Kovac had his newspaper open. He held it in such a way as to give Edwyn Noble the finger.

'Don't worry,' Quinn said. 'You managed to get the best cop on the case busted to chauffeur.'

'We understand Vanlees has been taken into custody,' the attorney said as they went into the house, ignoring Kovac as an unworthy topic.

'He was arrested on a DUI. The police will hold him as long as they can, but at the moment they don't have any evidence he's the Cremator.'

'But he had . . . something of Jillian's,' Noble said with the awkwardness of a prude.

'Which he says Jillian gave to him.'

'That's preposterous.'

'He tells a very interesting story. One that includes you and a payoff, by the way.'

Fear flashed cold in the lawyer's eyes. Just for an instant. 'That's absurd. He's a liar.'

'He hasn't exactly cornered the market there,' Quinn said. 'I want to speak with Peter. I have some questions for him regarding Jillian's state of mind that night and in general.'

The lawyer cast a nervous glance at the stairs. 'Peter isn't seeing anyone this morning. He isn't feeling well.'

'He'll see me.' Quinn started up the stairs on his own, as if he knew where he was going. Noble hurried after him.

'I don't think you understand, Agent Quinn. This business has taken a terrible toll on his nerves.'

'Are you trying to tell me he's what? Drunk? Sedated? Catatonic?'

Noble's long face had a mulish look when Quinn glanced over his shoulder. 'Lucas Brandt is with him.'

'That's even better. I'll kill two birds.'

He stepped aside at the top of the stairs and motioned for Noble to lead the way.

The antechamber of Peter Bondurant's bedroom suite was the showcase of a decorator who likely knew more about the house than about Peter. It was a room fit for an eighteenth-century English lord, all mahogany and brocade with dark oil hunting scenes in gilt frames on the walls. The gold damask wing chairs looked as if no one had ever sat in them.

Noble knocked softly on the bedroom door and let himself in, leaving Quinn to wait. A moment later, Noble and Brandt came out together. Brandt had his game face on – even, carefully neutral. Probably the face he wore in the courtroom when he testified for whoever was paying him the most money that day.

'Agent Quinn,' he said in the hushed tones of a hospital ward. 'I understand you have a suspect.'

'Possibly. I have a couple of questions for Peter.'

'Peter isn't himself this morning.'

Quinn lifted his brows. 'Really? Who is he?'

Noble frowned at him. 'I think Sergeant Kovac has been a bad influence on you. This is hardly the time to be glib.'

'Nor is it the time for you to play games with me, Mr Noble,' Quinn said. He turned to Brandt. 'I need to speak with him about Jillian. If you want to be in the room, that's fine by me. Even better if you want to offer your opinion as to her mental and emotional state.'

'We've been over that issue.'

Quinn ducked his head, using a sheepish look to cover the anger. 'Fine, then don't say anything.'

He started toward the door as if he would just knock Brandt on his ass and walk over him.

'He's sedated,' Brandt said, standing his ground. 'I'll answer what I can.'

Quinn studied him with narrowed eyes, then cut a glance to the lawyer. 'Just curious,' he said. 'Are you protecting him for his own good, or for yours?'

Neither batted an eye.

Quinn shook his head. 'It doesn't matter – not to me anyway. All I'm interested in is getting the whole truth.'

He told the story Vanlees had given him about the window-peeping incident.

Edwyn Noble rejected the tale with every part of him – intellectually, emotionally, physically – reiterating his opinion of Vanlees as a liar. He paced and clucked and shook his head, denying every bit of it except the idea that Vanlees had been looking in Jillian's window. Brandt, on the other hand, stood with his back to the bedroom door, eyes downcast, hands clasped in front of him, listening carefully.

'What I want to know, Dr Brandt, is whether or not Jillian was capable of that kind of behavior.'

'And you would have told Peter this story and asked Peter this question? About his child?' Brandt said with affront.

'No. I would have asked Peter something else entirely.' He cut a look at Noble. 'Like what he was doing at Jillian's apartment before dawn on Sunday that was worth paying off a witness.'

Noble drew his head back, offended, and started to open his mouth.

'Save it, Edwyn,' Quinn advised, turning back to Brandt.

'I told you before, Jillian had a lot of conflicted emotions and confusion regarding her sexuality because of her relationship with her stepfather.'

'So the answer is yes.'

Brandt held his silence. Quinn waited.

'She sometimes behaved inappropriately.'

'Promiscuously.'

'I wouldn't call it that, no. She would . . . provoke reactions. Deliberately.'

'Manipulative.'

'Yes.'

'Cruel?'

That one brought his head up. Brandt stared at him. 'Why would you ask that?'

'Because if Jillian isn't dead, Dr Brandt, then there's only one logical thing she can be: a suspect.'

33

The kid looked like hell, Kate thought – pale as death, her eyes glassy and bloodshot, her hair greasy. But she was alive, and the relief Kate felt at that was enormous. She didn't have to bear the weight of Angie's death. The girl was alive, if not well.

And sitting in my kitchen.

'Angie, God, you scared the hell out of me!' Kate said. 'How did you get in? The door was locked. How'd you even know where I live?'

The girl said nothing. Kate edged a little closer, trying to assess her condition. Bruises marred her face. Her full lower lip was split and crusted with blood.

'Hey, kiddo, where've you been?' she asked. 'People were worried about you.'

'I saw your address on an envelope in your office,' the girl said, still staring, her voice a flat hoarse rasp.

'Very resourceful.' Kate moved closer. 'Now if only we could get you to use your talents for the good of humankind. Where've you been, Angie? Who hurt you?'

Kate was at the doorway now. The girl hadn't moved on the chair. She wore the same jeans she'd worn from day one, now with dark stains that looked like blood on the thighs, the same dirty jean jacket that couldn't have been warm enough in this weather, and a dingy blue sweater Kate had seen before. Around her throat she wore a set of choke marks – purple bruises where fingers had pressed hard enough to cut off her wind and the blood supply to her brain.

A ghost of a bitter smile twisted Angie's mouth. 'I've had worse.'

'I know you have, sweetie,' Kate said softly. It wasn't until she started to crouch down to take a closer look that Kate saw the utility knife in the girl's lap – a razor-blade nose on a sleek, thick, gray metal handle.

She straightened away slowly and took a half-step back. 'Who did this to you? Where've you been, Angie?'

'In the Devil's basement,' she said, finding some kind of sour amusement in that.

'Angie, I'm going to call an ambulance for you, okay?' Kate said, taking another step back toward the phone.

Instantly, tears filled the girl's eyes. 'No. I don't need an ambulance,' she said, nearly frantic at the prospect.

'Someone's done a number on you, kiddo.' Kate wondered where that someone might be. Had Angie escaped and come here on her own, or had she been brought here? Was her abductor in the next room, watching, waiting? If she could get on the phone, she could dial 911 and the cops would be here in a matter of minutes.

'No. Please,' Angie begged. 'Can't I just stay here? Can't I just be here with you? Just for a while?'

'Honey, you need a doctor.'

'No. No. No.' The girl shook her head. Her fingers curled around the handle of the utility knife. She held the blade against the palm of her left hand.

Blood beaded where the tip of the blade bit her skin.

The phone rang, shattering the tense silence. Kate jumped.

'Don't get it!' Angie shouted, holding her hand up, dragging the knife down inch by inch, opening the top layer of flesh, drawing blood.

'I'll *really* cut myself,' she threatened. 'I know how to do it.'

If she meant it, if she brought that blade down a few inches to her wrist, she could bleed out before Kate finished the call to 911.

The ringing stopped. The machine in the den was politely informing whoever to leave a message. Quinn? she wondered. Kovac with some news? Rob calling to fire her? She imagined him capable of leaving that message, just as Melanie Hessler's boss had.

'Why would you want to cut yourself, Angie?' she asked. 'You're safe now. I'll help you. I'll help you get through this. I'll help you get a fresh start.'

'You didn't help me before.'

'You didn't give me much chance.'

'Sometimes I like to cut myself,' Angie admitted, face downcast in shame. 'Sometimes I need to. I start to feel . . . It scares me. But if I cut myself, then it goes away. That's crazy, isn't it?' She looked up at Kate with such forlorn eyes, it nearly broke her heart.

Kate was slow to answer. She'd read about girls who did what Angie was describing, and, yes, her first thought was that it was crazy. How could people mutilate themselves and not be insane?

'I can get you help, Angie,' she said. 'There are people who can teach you how to deal with those feelings without having to hurt yourself.'

'What do they know?' Angie sneered, her eyes shining with contempt. 'What do they know about "dealing with" anything? They don't know shit.'

Neither do I, Kate thought. God, why hadn't she just called in sick Monday?

She considered and discarded the idea of trying to wrestle the knife away from the girl. The potential for disaster was too great. If she could keep her talking, she might eventually persuade her into putting it down. They had all the time in the world – provided they were alone.

'Angie, did you come here by yourself?'

Angie stared at the knife blade as she delicately traced it along the blue lines of the tattoo near her thumb, the letter A with a horizontal line crossing the top of it.

'Did someone bring you?'

'I'm always alone,' she murmured.

'What about the other night, after I took you back to the Phoenix? Were you alone then?'

'No.' She dug the point of the blade into the tattooed blood droplets on the bracelet of thorns that encircled her wrist. 'I knew he wanted me. He sent for me.'

'Who wanted you? Gregg Urskine?'

'Evil's Angel.'

'Who is that?' Kate asked.

'I was in the shower,' she said, eyes glazed as she looked back on the memory. 'I was cutting myself. Watching the blood and the water. Then he sent for me. Like he smelled my blood or something.'

'Who?' Kate tried again.

'He wasn't happy,' she said ominously. In eerie contrast, a sly smirk twisted her mouth. 'He was mad 'cause I didn't follow orders.'

'I can see this is a long story,' Kate said, watching the blood drip from Angie's hand to her dining room rug. 'Why don't we go in the other room and sit down? I can get a fire going in the fireplace. Warm you up. How's that sound?'

Distract her from her knife play. Get her out of sight of one telephone and near another, so that one way or another a call might get placed. The phone/fax in the den had 911 on the speed dial. If she could get Angie settled on the couch, she could sit on the desktop, work the phone off the hook, punch the button. It might work. It sure as hell beat standing there, watching the girl bleed.

'My feet are cold,' Angie said.

'Let's go in the other room. You can take those wet boots off.'

The girl looked at her with narrowed eyes, raised her bleeding hand to her mouth and dragged her tongue along one wound. 'You go first.'

In front of a psychotic with a knife, possibly going toward some waiting lunatic serial killer. Great. Kate started for the den, walking almost sideways, trying to keep one eye on Angie, one scouting ahead, trying to keep the conversation going. Angie clutched the knife in her hand, ready to use it. She walked a little bent over, with her other arm braced across her stomach, obviously in some pain.

'Did Gregg Urskine hurt you, Angie? I saw the blood in the bathroom.'

She blinked confusion. 'I was in the Zone.'

'I don't know what that means.'

'No, you wouldn't.'

Kate led the way into the den.

'Have a seat.' She motioned to the couch where she and Quinn had made love not that many hours before. 'I'll get the fire going.'

She thought of using the poker as a weapon, but discarded that idea immediately. If she could get the knife away from Angie by trickery, it would be preferable to violence for many reasons, not the least of which would be Angie's state of mind.

Angie wedged herself into a corner of the couch and began tracing over the bloodstains on her jeans with the point of the knife.

'Who choked you, Angie?' Kate asked, going to the desk. A fax had come in. The call she hadn't answered.

'A friend of a friend.'

'You need a better class of friends.' She eased a hip onto the desktop, her eyes on the fax – a copy of a newspaper article from Milwaukee. 'Did you know this guy?'

'Sure,' the girl murmured, staring at the fire. 'So do you.'

Kate barely heard her. Her attention was riveted on the fax the legal services secretary had forwarded with a note saying, *Thought you'd want to see this right away.* The article was dated January 21, 1996. The headline read: *Sisters Exonerated in Burning Death of Parents.* There were two poor, grainy photographs, made worse by the fax. But even so, Kate recognized the girl in the photo on the right. Angie DiMarco.

Peter sat in his bedroom, in a small chair by the window, the black duffel bag in his lap, his arms wrapped around it. He was wearing the same clothes he had worn in the night – black slacks and sweater. The slacks were dirty. He had vomited on the sweater. The sour smell of puke and sweat and fear hung around him like a noxious cloud, but he didn't care to change, didn't want to shower.

He imagined he was pale. He felt as if all the blood had been drained out of him. What flowed through his veins now was the acid of guilt, burning, burning, burning. He imagined it might burn him alive from the inside out, turn all his bones to ash.

Edwyn had come to tell him about the arrest of the caretaker, Vanlees, and had found him in the music room, smashing the baby grand piano with a tire iron. Edwyn had called Lucas. Lucas had come with a little black bag full of vials and needles.

Peter had refused the drugs. He didn't want to feel numb. He'd spent too much of his life feeling numb, ignoring the lives of the people around him. Maybe if he'd dared to feel something sooner, things wouldn't have come to this. Now all he could feel was the searing pain of remorse.

Looking out the window, he watched as Kovac nudged the nose of his car against the bumper of Edwyn's Lincoln, then backed up and turned around.

A part of him felt relief that John Quinn was leaving. A part of him felt despair.

He had listened to the conversation on the other side of the door. Noble and Brandt making excuses for him, lying for him. Quinn asking the definitive question: Were they protecting him for his sake or for their own?

Time passed as he sat in the chair, thinking back, reliving all of it from Jillian's birth, on through his every devastating mistake, to this moment and beyond. He stared out the window, not seeing the news vans, the reporters waiting for an appearance by him, a sound bite from him. He hugged the duffel bag and rocked from side to side, coming to the only conclusion that made sense to him.

Then he checked his watch, and waited.

Kate stared at the fax, a chill running from the top of her head down her entire body. Her brain picked out key words: *burning deaths, mother, stepfather, drinking, drugs, foster care, juvenile records, history of abuse.*

'What's wrong with you?' Angie asked.

'Nothing,' Kate said automatically, tearing her gaze from the article. 'I just felt a little dizzy for a minute there.'

'I thought maybe *you* were in the Zone.' She smiled like a pixie. 'Wouldn't that be funny?'

'I don't know. What's the Zone like?'

The smile vanished. 'It's dark and empty and it swallows you whole and you feel like you'll never get out, and no one will ever come to get you,' she said, her eyes bleak again. Not empty but bleak, afraid, full of pain – which meant there was still something in her to save. Whatever had happened to her in a childhood that culminated with the suspicious deaths of her parents, some scrap of humanity had survived. And it had survived the last days in 'the Devil's basement', wherever that was.

'But sometimes it's a safe place too,' she said softly, staring at the blood that ran in rivulets all over her left hand, back and front and around her wrist. 'I can hide there . . . if I dare.'

'Angie? Will you let me get a cold cloth for your hand?' Kate asked.

'Don't you like to see my blood? I do.'

'I'd rather not see it dripping on my carpet,' Kate said with a hint of her usual wry tone, more to spark some fire in Angie than out of any real concern for the rug.

Angie stared at her palm for a moment, then raised it to her face and wiped the blood down her cheek in a loving caress.

Kate eased away from the desk and backed toward the door.

The girl looked up at her. 'Are you going to leave me?'

'No, honey, I'm not going to leave you. I'm just going to get that wet cloth.' And call 911, Kate thought, moving another step toward the door, afraid now to leave the girl for fear of what she might do to herself.

The doorbell rang as she stepped into the hall, and she froze for a second.

A face appeared at one of the sidelights, a round head above a puffed-up down jacket, trying to peer in through the sheer curtain. Rob.

'Kate, I know you're home,' he said, petulant, knocking, his face still pressed to the window. 'I can see you standing there.'

'What are you doing here?' Kate asked in a harsh whisper, pulling the door open.

'I heard from the office you weren't going in. We need to talk about this –'

'You can't pick up a telephone?' she started, then caught herself and waved off the argument. 'This isn't the time –'

Rob looked stubborn. He moved a little closer. 'Kate, we *need* to talk.'

Kate clamped her teeth against a sigh of exasperation. 'Could you lower your voice?'

'Why? Is it a neighborhood secret you're trying to avoid me?'

'Don't be an ass. I'm not avoiding you. I've got a situation here. Angie's shown up and she's in a very fragile mental state.'

His little pig eyes rounded. 'She's *here*? What is she doing here? Have you called the police?'

'Not yet. I don't want to make things worse. She's got a knife and she's willing to use it – on herself.'

'My God. And you haven't taken it away from her, Ms Superwoman?' he said sarcastically as he pushed past her into the hall.

'I'd rather keep all my appendages attached, thanks.'

'Has she hurt herself?'

'So far, it's just surface cuts, but one will need stitches.'

'Where is she?'

Kate motioned to the den. 'Maybe you can distract her while I call 911.'

'Has she told you where she's been? Who took her?'

'Not exactly.'

'If she goes to a hospital, she'll clam up out of resentment. It could be hours or days before we get the information out of her,' he said in an urgent tone. 'The police have made an arrest. The press conference is starting soon. If we can get her to tell us what happened, we can call Sabin before it's over.'

Kate crossed her arms and considered. She could see Angie still sitting on the couch, drawing patterns with her fingertip on the palm of her bloody hand. If paramedics came and hauled her away, she would react badly, that was a sure bet. On the other hand, what would they be doing to her? Trying to drag what they wanted out of her while she sat bleeding and vulnerable.

Trying to catch a killer.

She heaved a sigh. 'All right. We try, but if she gets serious with that knife, I'm calling.'

Rob squinted at her. The toothache smile. 'I know it pains you, Kate, but sometimes I *am* right. You'll see this is one of those times. I know exactly what I'm doing.'

'What's *he* doing here?' Angie blurted out the words as if they gave her a bad taste in her mouth.

Rob gave her the toothache smile too. 'I'm just here to help, Angie,' he said, sitting back against the desk.

She gave him a long, hard stare. 'I doubt it.'

'It looks like you've had a little trouble since we saw you last. Can you tell us about that?'

'You want to hear about it?' she asked, eyes narrowed, her hoarse voice sounding almost seductive. She raised her hand and slowly licked the blood from her palm again, her gaze locked on his. 'You want to know who did this to me? Or do you just want to hear about the sex?'

'Whatever you want to tell us about, Angie,' he said evenly. 'It's important for you to talk about it. We're here to listen.'

'I'm sure you are. You like to hear about other people's pain and suffering. You're a sick little fuck, aren't you?'

A muscle ticked in Rob's cheek. He held on to his excuse for a smile, but it looked more like he was biting a bullet.

'You're trying my patience, Angie,' he said tightly. 'I'm sure that's not what you really want to do. Is it?'

The girl looked away toward the fire for so long that Kate thought she would never speak again. Maybe she'd gone to the Zone she'd talked about. She held the utility knife in her right hand, pressing the fingertips against the blade.

'Angie,' Kate said, moving behind the couch, casually picking up the chenille throw from the back of it as she went. 'We're trying to help you.'

She sat on the arm of the unoccupied end, holding the blanket loosely in her lap.

Tears gleamed in Angie's eyes and she shook her head. 'No, you're not. I wanted you to, but you're not. You just want what I can tell you.' Her swollen mouth twisted into a bitter smile. 'The funny thing is, you think you're getting what you want, but you are *so* wrong.'

'Tell us what happened that night at the Phoenix,' Rob prompted, trying to draw her attention back to him. 'Kate dropped you off. You went upstairs to take a shower ... Did someone interrupt you?'

Angie stared at him, slowly scratching the tip of the blade along her thigh over and over.

'Who came to take you, Angie?' Rob pressed.

'No,' she said.

'Who came to take you?' he asked again, enunciating with emphasis.

'No,' she said, glaring at him. 'I won't do it.'

The blade of the knife bit deeper. Sweat glistened on her pale face in the firelight. The denim shredded. Blood bloomed bright red in the tears.

Kate felt ill at the sight. 'Rob, stop it.'

'She needs to do this, Kate,' he said. 'Angie, who came to take you?'

'No.' Tears streaked down Angie's battered face. 'You can't make me.'

'Let her alone.' Kate moved off her perch. Christ, she had to do something before the girl cut herself to ribbons.

Rob's stare was locked on Angie. 'Tell us, Angie. No more games.'

Angie glared at him, shaking visibly now.

'Where did he take you? What did he do to you?'

'Fuck you!' she spat out. 'I'm not playing your game.'

'Yes, you are, Angie,' he said, his voice growing darker. 'You will. You don't have a choice.'

'Fuck you! I hate you!'

Shrieking, she came up off the couch, arm raised, knife blade flashing.

Kate moved fast, flinging the chenille throw to cover the knife and diving into Angie from the side almost simultaneously. The girl howled as they crashed to the floor, knocking into the coffee table and scattering the victimology reports.

Kate held her down as she struggled, the first wave of relief washing through her. Rob picked up the knife, closed the blade, and put it in his pocket.

Angie was sobbing. Kate moved onto her knees and pulled the girl into her arms to hold her.

'It's all right, Angie,' she whispered. 'You're safe now.'

Angie pushed free, staring at her, incredulous and furious. 'You stupid bitch,' she rasped. 'Now you're dead.'

34

'The sharks smell blood in the water,' Quinn commented as they watched the mob gather for the press conference.

Kovac scowled. 'Yeah, and some of it is mine.'

'Sam, I can guarantee you, with Vanlees on the block, they could give a shit about you.'

The idea seemed to further depress Kovac. It did nothing for Quinn either. Having Bondurant's people leak information about Vanlees to the press was bad enough, but to have the police talk openly to the press about Gil Vanlees at this point was dangerously premature. He'd said so to the mayor, Greer, and Sabin. That they were choosing to ignore his advice was beyond his control. And yet he could feel the anxiety singeing another hole in the wall of his stomach.

He was the one who had come up with the initial profile, which Vanlees fit, nearly to a T. In retrospect he thought he shouldn't have been so quick to offer an opinion. The possibility of tandem killers changed everything. But the press and the powers running the show had Vanlees now, and were all too happy to sink their teeth into him.

The mayor had chosen the grand Fourth Street entrance for the setting of the press conference. A cathedral of polished marble with an impressive double staircase and stained glass panels. The kind of place where politicians could stand on the stairs above the common folk and look important, where the glow of the marble seemed to reflect off their skin and make them seem more radiant than the average citizen.

Quinn and Kovac watched from a shadowed alcove as the television people set up and the newspaper people jockeyed for status spots. On the stairs, the mayor and Sabin conferred as the mayor's assistant brushed lint from her suit. Gary Yurek was deep in conversation with Chief Greer, Fowler, and a pair of captains who seemed to have come out of the woodwork for the photo op. Quinn would join the circus in a moment and give his two cents' worth to the throng, trying to give the announcement of a suspect in custody a cautionary spin, which almost no one would listen to. They would rather listen to Edwyn Noble spin lies for Peter Bondurant, which was almost certainly what he was doing standing with a reporter for MSNBC.

There was no sign of Peter. Not that Quinn had expected him – not after this morning, and not with the possibility of incest allegations seeping out into the news pool. Still, he couldn't help but wonder at Bondurant's mental state, and what exactly had brought Lucas Brandt running with his little black bag. Jillian's supposed demise, or the revelation of what might have happened all those years ago?

'Charm,' Kovac said with derision, staring at Yurek. 'Destined for a corner office. They love him upstairs. A million-dollar smile on lips he won't hesitate to use to kiss ass.'

'Jealous?' Quinn asked.

He made one of his faces. 'I was made for chewing ass, not kissing it. What do I need with a corner office, when I can have a crappy little desk in a crappy little cubicle with no decent file cabinets?'

'At least you're not bitter.'

'I was born bitter.'

Vince Walsh heralded his arrival with a phlegm-rattling coughing fit. Kovac turned and looked at him.

'Jesus, Vince, hack up a lung, why don't you?'

'Goddamn cold,' Walsh complained. His color had the odd yellow cast of an embalmed body. He offered Kovac a manila envelope. 'Jillian Bondurant's medical records – or what of them LeBlanc would release. There are some X-rays. You want to take them or you want me to drop them off with the ME?'

'I'm out, you know,' Kovac said even as he took the envelope. 'Yurek's boss now.'

Walsh sucked half the contents of his sinuses down the back of his throat and made a sour face.

Kovac nodded. 'Yeah, that's what I said.'

Peter waited until the press conference was under way to enter the building. A simple matter of calling Edwyn on his cell phone from the car. Noble had no way of knowing he wasn't still at home. Peter had dismissed from the house the employees Edwyn had posted to keep an eye on him. They had gone without argument. He was the one who paid their wages, after all.

He came into the hall, holding the duffel bag in his arms, his gaze scanning the backs of five dozen heads. Greer was at the podium, going on in his overly dramatic way about the qualifications of the man he had chosen to succeed Kovac as head of the task force. Peter didn't care to hear it. The task force was no longer of any interest to him. He knew who had killed Jillian.

The press shouted questions. Flashes went off like so many star bursts. Peter worked his way along one side of the crowd, moving toward the stairs, feeling as if he were invisible. Maybe he was. Maybe he was already a ghost.

All his life he had felt a certain emptiness in his soul, a hole nothing had ever been able to fill. Maybe he had been eroding away from the inside out for so long that the essence of what made him human had all leeched away, making him invisible.

Quinn saw Bondurant coming. Oddly, no one else seemed to. No one looked closely enough, he supposed. Their focus was on the podium and the latest batch of bullshit they wanted to spread on the news and in the papers. And there was the fact that he looked vaguely seedy – unshaven, unkempt – not the Peter Bondurant of finely tailored suits, every hair in place.

His skin looked so pale, it was nearly translucent. His face was gaunt, as if his body were devouring itself from within. His eyes met Quinn's, and he stopped behind the camera people and stood there, a black duffel bag in his arms.

Quinn's instincts went on point – just as Greer invited him to step to the podium.

The glare of the lights blocked his view of Bondurant. He wondered if Kovac had spotted him.

'I want to stress,' he began, 'that the interview of a possible suspect does not end the investigation.'

'Do you believe Vanlees is the Cremator?' a reporter called out.

'It wouldn't be prudent for me to comment on that one way or the other.'

He tried to shift to an angle where he could see Bondurant again, but Bondurant was gone from the spot where he had last been. His nerves tightened.

'But Vanlees fits the profile. He knew Jillian Bondurant –'

'Isn't it true he had articles of her clothing in his possession when he was arrested?' another asked.

Damn leaks, Quinn thought, his attention focused more on getting Bondurant back in his sights than on the reporters. What was he doing here on his own, and looking like a vagrant?

'Special Agent Quinn . . . ?'

'No comment.'

'Do you have *anything* to say about the Bondurant case?'

'I killed her.'

Peter stepped out from behind a cameraman at the foot of the stairs and turned to face the crowd. For a moment no one but Quinn realized the admission had come from him. Then he raised a nine-millimeter semiautomatic handgun to his head, and awareness ran back through the crowd in a wave.

'I killed her!' Peter cried louder.

He looked stunned by his own confession – bug-eyed, stark white, openmouthed. He looked at the gun with terror, as if someone else were holding it. He went up the stairs sideways, eyes darting to the crowd, to the people near the podium: Mayor Noble, Chief Greer, Ted Sabin – all of whom backed away, staring at him as if they'd never seen him before.

Quinn held his spot at the podium.

'Peter, put the gun down,' he said firmly, the microphone picking up his voice and broadcasting it to the hall.

Bondurant shook his head. His face was quivering, twitching, contorting. He clutched the duffel bag to him with his left arm. Behind him Quinn could see two uniformed officers moving into place with guns drawn and held low.

'Peter, you don't want to do this,' he said quietly, calmly, shifting subtly away from the podium.

'I ruined her life. I killed her. It's my turn.'

'Why here? Why now?'

'So everyone will know,' he said, his voice choked. 'Everyone will know what I am.'

Edwyn Noble moved from the front of the crowd toward the stairs. 'Peter, don't do this.'

'What?' Bondurant asked. 'Damage my reputation? Or yours?'

'You're talking nonsense!' the lawyer demanded. 'Put down the gun.'

Peter didn't listen. His anguish was an almost palpable thing. It was in the sweat that ran down his face. It was in the smell of him. It was in the air he exhaled too quickly from his lungs.

'This is my fault,' he said, the tears coming harder. 'I did this. I have to pay. Here. Now. I can't stand it anymore.'

'Come with me, Peter,' Quinn said, stepping a little closer, offering his left hand. 'We'll sit down and you can tell me the whole story. That's what you want, isn't it?'

He was aware of the whir of motor drives as photographers shot frame after frame. The video cameras were running as well, some likely running live feeds to their stations. All of them recording this man's agony for their audiences.

'You can trust me, Peter. I've been asking you for the truth from day one. That's all I want: the truth. You can give it to me.'

'I killed her. I killed her,' he mumbled over and over, tears streaming down his cheeks.

His gun hand was trembling badly. Another few minutes and his own burning muscles would make him lower it. If he didn't blow his head off first.

'You sent for me, Peter,' Quinn said. 'You sent for me for a reason. You want to give me the truth.'

'Oh, my God. Oh, my God!' Bondurant sobbed, the struggle within himself enormous, powerful, tearing him apart. His whole right arm was shaking now. He cocked the hammer back.

'Peter, no!' Quinn ordered, going for him.

The gun exploded. Shouts and screams echoed with the shot. A fraction of a second too late, Quinn grabbed hold of Bondurant's wrist and forced it up. Another shot boomed. Kovac rushed up behind Peter, the uniforms right behind him, and pulled the gun out of his hand.

Bondurant collapsed against Quinn, sobbing, bleeding, but alive. Quinn lowered him gently to the marble steps. The first shot had cut at an angle above his temple and plowed out a furrow of flesh and hair two inches long on its way to the second floor of the building. Gunpowder residue blackened the skin. He dropped his head between his knees and vomited.

The sound level in the hall was deafening. Photographers rushed forward for better angles. Edwyn Noble shoved past two of them to get to his boss.

'Don't say anything, Peter.'

Kovac gave the attorney a look of disgust. 'You know, I think it's a little late for that.'

Ted Sabin took the podium and called for order and calm. The mayor was crying. Dick Greer snapped at his captains. The cops went about their jobs, dealing with the gun, clearing a path for the EMTs.

Quinn crouched beside Peter, hand still on the man's wrist, feeling his pulse race out of control. Quinn's own heart was pumping hard. A fraction of an inch, a steadier hand, and Peter Bondurant would have blown his brains out in front of half the country. An event to be broadcast on the nightly news with the disclaimer: We warn you – what you are about to see may be disturbing . . .

'You have the right to remain silent, Peter,' he began quietly. 'Anything you say may be used against you in court.'

'Must you do this now?' Noble asked in a harsh whisper. 'The press is watching.'

'They were watching when he came onstage with a loaded gun too,' Quinn said, tugging at the duffel bag Peter had smuggled the gun in. Bondurant, sobbing uncontrollably, tried to hold on to it for a moment, then let go. His body crumpled into a bony heap.

'I think people have already let too many rules slide where Peter is concerned,' Quinn said.

He handed the bag to Vince Walsh. 'It's heavy. He may have more weapons in it.'

'You have the right to have your attorney present at questioning,' Kovac continued the Miranda warning, pulling out handcuffs.

'Jesus God!' came the hoarse exclamation. Quinn looked up to see Walsh drop the duffel bag and grab the side of his neck, his face purple.

The paramedics said later he was dead before he hit the ground . . . right beside the bag that carried Jillian Bondurant's decapitated head.

35

Kate stepped back from Angie, not trying to decipher what the girl had said. She was breathing hard, and she'd cracked her elbow on the coffee table on the fall to the floor. She rubbed it now as she tried to get her thoughts clear. Angie sat on her knees, keening like a banshee, hitting herself in the head with her bloody hands over and over again. Blood soaked the thighs of her jeans and oozed out through the slits she had cut with the knife.

'My God,' Kate murmured, shaken by the sight. She backed into the desk, turned to the phone.

Rob stood three feet away, staring at the girl with a peculiar kind of interest, as if he were a scientist watching a specimen.

'Talk to us, Angie,' he said softly. 'Tell us what you're feeling.'

'Jesus Christ, Rob,' Kate snapped as she picked up the receiver. 'Leave her alone! Go in the kitchen and get some wet towels.'

He went instead to Angie, pulled a six-inch black leather sap from his coat pocket, and struck her across the back. The girl screamed and fell over sideways, arching her back as if to try to escape the pain.

Kate stood stunned, staring at her boss with her mouth hanging open. 'W-what . . . ?' she began, then swallowed and started again, her pulse racing. 'What the hell is wrong with you?' she asked, breathless with astonishment.

Rob Marshall turned his gaze on her with undisguised hate. His eyes nearly glowed with it. The stare ran through Kate like a sword. She could feel the contempt roll off him in hot waves, could smell it rising, sour and vile from his pores. She stood there, time elongating, instincts coming alive even as she realized her phone was dead.

'You have no respect for me, Kate, you fucking cunt,' he said in a low, growling voice.

The words and the hatred behind them hit her like a fist, stunning her for a moment, then shaking her as the pieces fell into place.

'Who choked you, Angie? Did you know this guy?'

'Sure . . . So do you . . .'

'. . . It's all right, Angie. You're safe now.'

'You stupid bitch. Now you're dead.'

328

Rob Marshall? No. The idea seemed almost laughable. Almost. Except that the phone had been working before he showed up, and he was standing before her with a weapon in his hand.

She put the receiver down.

'I've had it with you,' he said bitterly. 'Picking, picking, picking. Bitching, bitching, bitching. Belittling me. Looking down your nose at me.'

He stood on the victimology reports that had scattered on the floor. *Everyone is a victim of something.* She'd had that thought half a dozen times that morning when she'd been going over the reports, but she hadn't examined it closely enough.

Lila White had been a victim of an assault.

Fawn Pierce had been a victim of rape.

Melanie Hessler, another rape victim.

At some time or other they had all dealt with victim/witness services. The only one who didn't fit was Jillian Bondurant.

'But you're an *advocate* for victims, for God's sake,' she murmured.

An advocate who, because of his position, listened to account after account of people – largely women – being victimized, brutalized, beaten, raped, degraded . . .

How many times had he made her sit through the replaying of Melanie Hessler's interview tapes? Rob listening intently, running the tape back, replaying pieces over and over.

In her mind she was suddenly in Kovac's car at the Hessler crime scene, listening to the microcassette the killer had dropped. Melanie Hessler begging for her life, screaming in agony, begging for death.

She thought of Rob going to look at the charred body, coming back agitated, seemingly upset. But what she had mistaken for distress had in fact been excitement.

Oh, my God.

Bile rose up the back of her throat as every rotten thing she'd ever said to him scrolled through her memory.

Oh, God, I'm dead.

'I'm sorry,' she said, options racing through her mind. The front door was just ten feet down the hall.

Disgust crossed Rob's face in a spasm. He squeezed his eyes nearly shut, looking as if he'd just caught wind of an open sewer. 'No, you're not. You're not sorry about the way you've treated me. You're sorry I'm going to kill you for it.'

'Angie, run!' Kate shouted. She grabbed the fax machine off the desk, jerking the power cord out the back, and flung the machine at Rob. It hit him in the chest and knocked him off balance.

She bolted for the door, slipping on one of the victimology reports – a mistake that cost her a precious fraction of a second. Rob grabbed at her, caught hold of a coat sleeve with one hand, and swung wildly with the sap.

Even through the thick wool of her coat collar, Kate felt the weight of it as it struck her shoulder. Heavy, deadly, serious. If he caught her in the head, she would go down like a rock.

She shied sideways, eluding his grasp, then used his own momentum to shove him into the hall. Grabbing his left arm and twisting it up behind him as he came past, she ran him into the hall table and bolted away before the crash was over, running for the front door that suddenly seemed a mile away.

Rob let out a roar and tackled her from behind. They hit the floor hard, Kate crying out as her right arm twisted unnaturally beneath her and she felt the sickening tear of muscles in her shoulder.

Pain swept through her like a fire. She ignored it as best she could as she tried to kick free and scramble to the door. Rob wrapped a fist in her hair and jerked her head back, hitting her with his fist on the right side of her head. Her vision blurred, her ear rang like a bell and burned like a son of a bitch. Knife-sharp pain shot out across her face and down her jaw.

'You bitch! You bitch!' he screamed over and over.

And then his hands were around her throat and he was choking her, and his screams faded from her head. She fought automatically, frantically, clawing at his hands, but his fingers were short and thick and strong.

She couldn't breathe, felt like her eyes were going to burst, felt like her brain was swelling.

With the last bit of sense she could grab, Kate forced herself to go limp. Rob continued to squeeze for seconds that seemed like an eternity, then slammed her head down on the floor. She knew he was ranting but couldn't make out the words as the blood roared back up to her brain. She tried not to suck in the great gulps of oxygen she wanted and needed so desperately. She tried not to let her mind stall out. She had to keep thinking – and not of the crime scene she had visited, not of the charred body of her client, not of the autopsy photos of four women this man had tortured and mutilated.

'You think I can't do anything right!' Rob raved, pushing himself up off her. 'You think I'm an idiot! You think you're better than everyone and I'm just a nothing!'

Not able to see him, Kate inched her left hand toward her coat pocket.

'You're such a fucking bitch!' he screamed, and kicked her, too immersed in his ranting to hear her grunt of pain as his boot connected with her hip.

Kate ground her teeth together and concentrated on moving the hand, half an inch at a time, into her coat pocket.

'You don't know *me*,' Rob declared. He grabbed something from her hall table and threw it. Whatever it was, it crashed somewhere in the vicinity of the kitchen. 'You don't know anything about *me*, about my *True Self*.'

And she would never have suspected. God in heaven, she'd worked beside this man for a year and a half. Never once would she have thought he was capable of this. Never once had she questioned his motives for choosing his profession. On the contrary, his being an advocate for victims – so ready to listen to them, so ready to spend time with them – had been his one redeeming quality. Or so she had believed.

'You think I'm nobody,' he yelled. '*I AM SOMEBODY! I AM EVIL'S ANGEL! I AM THE FUCKING CREMATOR!* Now what do you think of me, Ms Bitch?'

He crouched down beside her and rolled her onto her back. Kate kept her eyes nearly shut, barely seeing more than a blur of colors between her lashes. Her hand was in her pocket, fingers sliding around the shaft of the metal nail file.

'I saved you for last,' he said. 'You're going to beg me to kill you. And I'm going to love doing it.'

36

'What happened that night, Peter?' Quinn asked.

They sat in a small, dingy white room in the bowels of the city hall building, near the booking area of the adult detention center. Bondurant had waived his rights and refused to go to the hospital. A paramedic had cleaned the bullet wound to his scalp right there on the stairs where he had tried to end it all.

Edwyn Noble had thrown a holy fit, insisting to be present during questioning, insisting on sending Peter directly to a hospital whether he wanted to go or not. But Peter had won out, swearing in front of a dozen news cameras he wanted to confess.

Present in the room were Bondurant, Quinn, and Yurek. Peter had wanted only Quinn, but the police had insisted on having a representative present. Sam Kovac's name was not mentioned.

'Jillian came to dinner,' Peter said. He looked small and shrunken, like a longtime heroin junkie. Pale, red-eyed, vacant. 'She was in one of her moods. Up, down, laughing one minute, snapping the next. She was just like that – volatile. Like her mother. Even as a baby.'

'What did you fight about?'

He stared across the room at a rosy stain on the wall that might have been blood before someone tried to scrub it away. 'School, her music, her therapy, her stepfather, us.'

'She wanted to resume her relationship with LeBlanc?'

'She'd been speaking with him. She said she was thinking of going back to France.'

'You were angry.'

'Angry,' he said, and sighed. 'That's not really the right word. I was upset. I felt tremendous guilt.'

'Why guilt?'

He took a long time formulating his answer, as if he were pre-choosing each word he would use. 'Because that was my fault – what happened with Jillian and LeBlanc. I could have prevented it. I could have fought Sophie for custody, but I just let go.'

'She threatened to expose you for molesting Jillian,' Quinn reminded him.

'She threatened to *claim* I had molested Jillian,' Peter corrected him. 'She had actually coached Jillie on what to say, how to behave in order to convince people it was true.'

'But it wasn't?'

'She was my child. I could never have done anything to hurt her.'

He thought about that answer, his composure cracking and crumbling. He covered his mouth with a trembling hand and cried silently for a moment. 'How could I have known?'

'You knew Sophie's mental state,' Quinn pointed out.

'I was in the process of buying out Don Thorton. I had several huge government contracts pending. She could have ruined me.'

Quinn said nothing, letting Bondurant sort through it himself, as he had undoubtedly done a thousand times in the last week alone.

Bondurant heaved a defeated sigh and looked at the table. 'I gave my daughter to a madwoman and a child molester. It would have been kinder to kill her then.'

'What happened Friday night?' Quinn asked again, drawing him back to the present.

'We argued about LeBlanc. She accused me of not loving her. She locked herself in the music room for a time. I let her alone. I went into the library, sat in front of the fire, drank some cognac.

'About eleven thirty she came into the room behind me, singing. She had a beautiful voice – haunting, ethereal. The song was obscene, disgusting, perverse. It was everything Sophie had coached her to say about me all those years ago: the things I had supposedly done to her.'

'That made you angry.'

'It made me sick. I got up and turned to tell her so, and she was standing in front of me naked. "Don't you want me, Daddy?" she said. "Don't you love me?" '

Even the memory astonished him, sickened him. He bent over the wastebasket that had been set beside his chair and retched, but there was nothing left in his stomach. Quinn waited, calm, unemotional, purposely detached.

'Did you have sex with her?' Yurek asked.

Quinn glared at him.

'No! My God!' Peter said, outraged at the suggestion.

'What happened?' Quinn asked. 'You fought. She ended up running out.'

'Yes,' he said, calming. 'We fought. I said some things I shouldn't have. She was so fragile. But I was so shocked, so angry. She ran and put her clothes on and left. I never saw her alive again.'

Yurek looked confused and disappointed. 'But you said you killed her.'

'Don't you see? I could have saved her, but I didn't. I let her go the first time to save myself, my business, my fortune. It's my fault she became who she did. I let her go Friday night because I didn't want to deal with that, and now she's dead. I killed her, Detective, just as surely as if I had stabbed her in the heart.'

Yurek skidded his chair back and got up to pace, looking like a man who'd just realized he'd been cheated in a shell game. 'Come on, Mr Bondurant. You expect us to believe that?' He didn't have the voice or the edge to play bad cop – even when he meant it. 'You were carrying your daughter's head in a bag. What is that about? A little memento the *real* killer sent you?'

Bondurant said nothing. The mention of Jillian's head upset him, and he began focusing inward again. Quinn could see him slipping away, allowing his mind to be lured to a place other than this ugly reality. He might go there and not come back for a long time.

'Peter, what were you doing in Jillian's town house Sunday morning?'

'I went to see her. To see if she was all right.'

'In the middle of the night?' Yurek said doubtfully.

'She wouldn't return my calls. I left her alone Saturday on Lucas Brandt's advice. By Sunday morning ... I had to do something.'

'So you went there and let yourself in,' Quinn said.

Bondurant looked down at a stain on his sweater and scratched at it absently with his thumbnail. 'I thought she would be in bed ... then I wondered whose bed she *was* in. I waited for her.'

'What did you do while you were waiting?'

'Cleaned,' he said, as if that made perfect sense and wasn't in any way odd. 'The apartment looked like – like – a sty,' he said, lip curling with disgust. 'Filthy, dirty, full of garbage and mess.'

'Like Jillian's life?' Quinn asked gently.

Tears swelled in Bondurant's eyes. The cleaning had been more symbolic than for sanitary purposes. He hadn't been able to change his daughter's life, but he could clean up her environment. An act of control, and perhaps of affection, Quinn thought.

'You erased the messages on her machine?' he asked.

Bondurant nodded. The tears came harder. Elbows on the table, he cupped his hands around his eyes.

'There was something from LeBlanc?' Quinn ventured.

'That son of a bitch! He killed her as much as I did!'

He curled down toward the tabletop, sobbing hard, a terrible braying sound tearing from the center of his chest up his throat. Quinn waited him out, thinking of Peter coming across Jillian's music as he straightened and tidied. The music may even have been his primary reason for going there, after the incident in his study Friday night, but Peter, out of guilt, would now claim Jillian's welfare had been the priority.

Quinn leaned forward and laid his hand on Bondurant's wrist across the table, establishing a physical link, trying to draw him back into the moment. 'Peter? Do you know who really killed Jillian?'

'Her friend,' he said in a thin, weary voice, his mouth twisting at the irony. 'Her one friend. Michele Fine.'

'What makes you believe that?'

'She was trying to blackmail me.'

'Was?'

'Until last night.'

'What happened last night?' Quinn asked.

'I killed her.'

Edwyn Noble was on Quinn the second he stepped out the door of the interview room.

'Not one word of that will be admissible in court, Quinn,' he promised.

'He waived his rights, Mr Noble.'

'He's clearly not competent to make those decisions.'

'Take it up with a judge,' Sabin said.

The lawyers turned on each other like a pair of cobras. Yurek pulled aside the assistant prosecutor, Logan, to talk about a warrant for Michele Fine's home. Kovac stood ten feet down the hall, leaning against the wall, not smoking a cigarette. The lone coyote.

'Need a ride, GQ?' he said with a hopeful look.

Quinn made a very Kovac-like face. 'I am definitely now a confirmed masochist. I can't believe I'm going to say this, but, let's go.'

They ran the media gauntlet out of the building, Quinn offering a stone-faced 'No comment' to every query hurled at him. Kovac had left his car on the Fourth Avenue side of the building. Half a dozen reporters followed them the whole way. Quinn didn't speak until Kovac put the car in gear and roared away from the curb.

'Bondurant says he shot Michele Fine and left her body in the Minneapolis Sculpture Garden. She'd been trying to blackmail him with some of Jillian's more revealing pieces of music, and with the things Jillian had allegedly confessed to her. Last night was supposed to be the big payoff. He'd bring the money, she'd hand over the music, the tapes she had, et cetera.

'At that point, he didn't know she'd been involved in Jillian's murder. He said he was willing to pay to keep the story under wraps, but he took a gun with him.'

'Sounds like premeditation to me,' Kovac said, slapping the dash-mount light on the bracket.

'Right. Then Michele shows up with the stuff in a duffel bag. Shows him some sheet music, a couple of cassettes, zips the bag shut. They make the trade. She starts to go, not thinking he'll look in the bag again.'

'Never assume.'

Quinn braced himself and held on to the door as the Lumina made a hard right on a red light. Horns blared.

'He looked. He shot her in the back and left her where she fell.'

'What the hell was she thinking, giving him the head?'

'She was thinking she'd be long gone before he called the cops,' Quinn speculated. 'I noticed travel magazines at her apartment when Liska and I were there the other day. I'll bet she would have gone straight to the airport and got on a plane.'

'What about Vanlees? Did he say anything about Vanlees?'

Quinn held his breath as Kovac cut between an MTC bus and a Snap-On Tool van. 'Nothing.'

'You don't think she was working alone?'

'No. We know she didn't kill on her own. She wouldn't have tried the blackmail on her own either. Willing victims of a sexual sadist are virtual puppets. Their partner holds the power, he controls them through physical abuse, psychological abuse, sexual abuse. No way she did this on her own.'

'And Vanlees was in custody by the time this went down.'

'They probably had the plan in place and she followed through without knowing where he was. She would have been afraid not to. *If* he's the guy.'

'They knew each other.'

'You and I know each other. We haven't killed anyone. I have a hard time seeing Vanlees manipulating anyone at that level. He fits the wrong profile.'

'Who, then?'

'I don't know,' Quinn said, scowling at himself rather than at Kovac gunning the accelerator and nearly side-swiping a minivan. 'But if we've got Fine, then we've got a thread to follow.'

Four radio cars had arrived ahead of them. The Minneapolis Sculpture Garden was an eleven-acre park dotted with more than forty works by prominent artists, the feature piece being a fifty-two-foot-long spoon holding a nine-and-a-half-foot-tall red cherry. The place had to be a bit surreal in the best of times, Quinn thought. As a crime scene it was something out of *Alice's Adventures in Wonderland*.

'Report from the local ERs,' Yurek called as he climbed out of his car. 'No gunshot wounds meeting Michele Fine's description.'

'He said they met at the spoon,' Quinn said as they walked quickly in that direction.

'He's sure he hit her?' Kovac asked. 'It was dark.'

'He says he hit her, she cried out, she went down.'

'Over here!' one of the uniforms called, waving from near the bridge of the spoon. His breath was like a smoke signal in the cold gray air.

Quinn broke into a jog with the others. The news crews wouldn't be far behind.

'Is she dead?' Yurek demanded as he ran up.

'Dead? Hell,' the uniform said, pointing to a large cherry-red bloodstain in the snow. 'She's gone.'

37

Rob caught Kate by the hair and began to pull her up. Kate's fingers closed around the metal nail file in her pocket. She waited. This might be the best weapon she would get her hands on. But she had to use it accurately, and she had to use it at the perfect moment. Strategies ran through her head like rats in a maze, each desperate for a way out.

Rob slapped her face, and the taste of blood bloomed in her mouth like a rose.

'I know you're not dead. You keep underestimating me, Kate,' he said. 'Even now you taunt me. That's very stupid.'

Kate hung her head, curling her legs beneath her. He wanted her frightened. He wanted to see it in her eyes. He wanted to smell it on her skin. He wanted to hear it in her voice. That was his thing. That was what he soaked up listening to the tapes of victims – his own victims and the victims of others. It sickened her to think how many victims had poured their hearts out to him, him feeding his sick compulsions on their suffering and their fear.

Now he wanted her afraid, and he wanted her submissive. He wanted her sorry for every time she'd ever mouthed off to him, for every time she'd defied him. And if she gave him what he wanted, his sense of victory would only further fuel his cruelty.

'I will be your master today, Kate,' he said dramatically.

Kate raised her head and gave him a long, level, venomous stare, screwing up her courage as she sucked at the cut in her mouth. He would make her pay for this, but it seemed the way to go.

Very deliberately, she spit the blood in his face. 'The hell you will, you miserable little shit.'

Instantly furious, he swung at her with the sap. Kate ducked the blow and launched herself upward, bringing her right elbow up under his chin, knocking his teeth together. She pulled the nail file and stabbed it into his neck to the hilt just above his collarbone.

Rob screamed and grabbed at the file, falling back, crashing into the hall table. Kate ran for the kitchen.

If she could just get out of the house, get to the street. Surely he would have disabled her car somehow, or blocked it in. To get help, she had to get to the street.

She dashed through the dining room, knocking chairs over as she ran past. Rob came behind her, grunting as he hit something, swearing, spitting the words out between his teeth like bullets.

He couldn't outrun her on his stubby legs. He seemed not to have a gun. Through the kitchen and she was home free. She'd run to the neighbor across the street. The graphic designer who had his office in his attic. He was always home.

She burst into the kitchen, faltered, then pulled up, her heart plummeting.

Angie stood just inside the back door, tears streaming down her face, a butcher's knife in her hand – pointed directly at Kate's chest.

'I'm sorry. I'm sorry. I'm sorry,' she sobbed, shaking badly.

Suddenly, the conversation that had taken place between Angie and Rob in the den took on a whole new dimension. Pieces of the truth began to click into place. The picture they made was distorted and surreal.

If Rob was the Cremator, then it was Rob Angie had seen in the park. Yet the man in the sketch Oscar had drawn at her instruction looked no more like Rob Marshall than he looked like Ted Sabin. She had sat across from him in the interview room, giving no indication . . .

In the next second Rob Marshall was through the door behind her and six ounces of steel packed in sand and bound in leather connected with the back of her skull. Her legs folded beneath her and she dropped to her knees on the kitchen floor, her last sight: Angie DiMarco.

This is why I don't do kids. You never know what they're thinking.

Then everything went dark.

The travel magazines were still scattered on Michele Fine's coffee table with pages folded and destinations circled with notations in the margins. *Get a tan! Too $$$. Nightlife!*

The murderer as a tourist, Quinn thought, turning the pages.

When the police checked with the airlines, they might find she had booked flights to one or more of those locations. If they were very lucky, they would also find matching flights booked in the name of her partner. Whoever he was.

With the amount of blood at the scene in the sculpture garden, it seemed highly unlikely Fine had taken herself out of the park. Gil Vanlees had been in custody. Both Fine and the money Peter Bondurant had brought to the scene and subsequently walked away from were gone.

The cops swarmed over the apartment like ants, invading every cupboard, crack, and crevice, looking for anything that might give them a clue as to who Fine's partner in murder was. A scribbled note, a doodled phone number, an envelope, a photograph, something, anything. Adler and

Yurek were canvassing the neighbors for information. Did they know her? Had they seen her? What about a boyfriend?

The main living areas of the apartment looked exactly as they had the day before. Same dust, same filthy ashtray. Tippen found a crack pipe in an end table drawer.

Quinn went down the hall, glancing into a bathroom worthy of a speedtrap gas station, and on to Michele Fine's bedroom. The bed was unmade. Clothes lay strewn around the room like outlines where dead bodies had fallen. Just as in the rest of the apartment, there were no personal touches, nothing decorative – except in the window that faced south and the back side of another building.

'Look at the sun catchers,' Liska said, moving across the room.

They hung from hooks on little suction cups stuck to the window.

Hoops about three inches in diameter, each holding its own miniature work of art. The light coming through them gave the colors a sense of life. The air from a register above the window made them quiver against the glass like butterfly wings, and fluttered the decorations that were attached to each – a piece of ribbon, a pearl button on a string, a dangling earring, a finely braided lock of hair . . .

Liska's face dropped as she stopped beside Quinn, the realization hitting her.

Lila White's calla lily. Fawn Pierce's shamrock. A mouth with a tongue sticking out. A heart with the word 'Daddy'. There were half a dozen.

Tattoos.

The tattoos that had been cut from the bodies of the Cremator's victims. Stretched tight in little craft hoops, drying in the sun. Decorated with mementos of the women they had been cut from. Souvenirs of torture and murder.

38

His triumph is at hand. His crowning glory. His finale – for now, for this place. He has arranged the Bitch on the table to his satisfaction and bound her hands and feet to the table legs with plastic twine he has pilfered from the mailroom at the office. A length of it is wrapped around the Bitch's throat with long free ends trailing for him to wrap around his fists. For mood lighting he has brought candles down to the basement from other parts of the house. He finds the flames very sensual, exciting, erotic. That excitement is heightened by the smell of gasoline heavy in the air.

He stands back and surveys the tableau. The Bitch under *his* absolute control. She is still clothed because he wants her conscious for her degradation. He wants her to feel every second of her humiliation. He wants to capture it all on tape.

He loads the microcassette recorder with a fresh tape and sets it on a black vinyl barstool with a ripped seat. He doesn't worry about fingerprints. The world will shortly discover the Cremator's 'true' identity.

He sees no reason not to carry through with the plan. Michele might be out of the picture, but he still has Angie. If she passes her test, he might take her with him. If she fails, he will kill her. She isn't Michele – his perfect complement. Michele, who would do anything he asked if she thought compliance would make him love her. Michele, who had followed his lead in the torture games, who had encouraged him to burn the bodies, and reveled in her tattoo arts and crafts.

He misses her as much as he can miss anyone. With a vague detachment. Mrs Vetter will miss her horrid little dog more.

Angie watches him as he unties the leather roll that holds all his favorite tools and spreads it out on the table. She looks like something from a teenage slasher movie. Her clothes are disheveled, the thighs of her jeans shredded and blood-soaked. She still holds the butcher knife from the kitchen and surreptitiously pricks the end of her thumb with the point of it and watches the blood bead. Crazy little bitch.

He looks at the choke marks on her throat, thinks about all the ways she has defied him during the execution of his Great Plan. Making him look stupid during her first interview, refusing to give the name of the bar where he'd picked her up that night to lend credibility to her story. Refusing to describe the Cremator to the sketch artist the way he had instructed her to. He had spent considerable time creating the image of a phantom killer in his mind. The girl had willfully given a description so vague it might fit half the men in the Twin Cities – including the hapless Vanlees. The idea of Vanlees getting credit as the Cremator makes him furious. And, even after the beatings he'd given her since Wednesday, she had refused him his perfect moment of revelation in Kate's living room.

'*Who came to take you, Angie?*'

'*No.*'

'*Who came to take you?*'

'*No. I won't do it.*'

'*Angie, who came to take you?*'

'*No. You can't make me.*'

She had been coached to say 'Evil's Angel'. No matter that he hadn't taken her, that Michele had been the one who'd saved the stupid little slut from slicing herself to ribbons in the shower, who'd cleaned up the mess and slipped the two of them out the back door of the house. The girl had her instructions and she defied them openly.

He decides he will kill her after all, despite her cooperation in the kitchen. She is too unpredictable.

He will kill her here. After the Bitch is dead. He pictures himself in a frenzy, wild with the euphoria of killing the Bitch. He sees himself throwing the girl onto the table, on top of the bloody, mutilated body, tying her there, fucking her, choking her, stabbing her in the face over and over and over and over. Punishing her exactly as he plans to punish the Bitch.

He will kill them both, then burn them together, here, and burn the house as well. He has already set the stage for the fire, pouring the accelerant – gas from a can he put in the Bitch's garage himself the night he shit on the floor.

The fantasy of the murders he is about to commit excites him as fantasies always have – intellectually, sexually, fundamentally. The pattern of the mind of his breed: fantasy, violent fantasy; then facilitators that trigger action: murder. The natural cycle of his life – and his victims' death.

Decision made, he turns his thoughts to the matter at hand: Kate Conlan.

Consciousness returned for Kate in fits and starts, like a television with bad reception. She could hear but not see. Then she had some blurred vision, but nothing more than a horrific ringing in her ears. The only clear, constant signal was pain hammering at the back of her skull. She felt sick with it. She couldn't seem to move her arms or legs and wondered if Rob had broken her neck or severed her spinal cord. Then she realized she could still feel her hands, and that they hurt like hell.

Tied.

The ceiling tile, the smell of dust, the vague sense of dampness. The basement. She was tied spread-eagle on the old Ping-Pong table in her own basement.

Another scent – out of place – came to her, thick, oily and bitter. *Gasoline.*

Oh, sweet Jesus.

She looked at Rob Marshall standing at the foot of the table, staring at her. Rob Marshall, a serial killer. The incongruity made her want to believe she was just having a nightmare, but she knew better. She'd seen too much when she was an agent. The stories were stacked up in her memory like files in a cabinet. The NASA engineer who had kidnapped hitchhikers and drained their blood to drink it. The electronics technician, a married father of two, who kept chosen body parts of his victims in his meat freezer in his garage. The young Republican law student who volunteered at a suicide hotline and turned out to be Ted Bundy.

Add to the stack the victim advocate who chose his own victims from the department's client list. She felt like a fool for not having seen it, even though she knew a killer as sophisticated as Smokey Joe was one of nature's perfect chameleons. Even now she didn't want to think of Rob Marshall as being that clever.

He had taken his coat off, revealing a gray sweater soaked at the throat with blood from where she'd stabbed him with the nail file. An inch in the right direction and she would have hit his jugular.

'Did I miss anything?' she asked, her voice rusty from the choking he'd given her.

She could see the surprise in his face, the confusion. Score one for the victim.

'Still with the smart mouth,' he said. 'You don't learn, bitch.'

'Why should I? What will you do, Rob? Torture and kill me?' She tried desperately to keep the fear out of her voice. She felt as if it had her by the throat, then remembered with another jolt of adrenaline the ligature marks on the throats of his victims. 'You'll do that either way. I might as well have the satisfaction of calling you a dickless loser to your face.'

Standing to one side of the table, backlit by candles, butcher knife in hand, Angie sucked in a breath and made a piteous sound in her throat. She clutched the knife to her as if it were a treasured toy to comfort herself.

Rob's face hardened. He pulled a penknife from his pocket and jabbed it, all the way to the handle, into the bottom of Kate's right foot, and she learned very quickly and painfully the price he was going to make her pay for the strategy she'd chosen.

Kate cried out and her whole body convulsed against the restraints that bit deep into the skin of her wrists and ankles. When she fell back, the bindings seemed to have stretched to give her slightly more mobility.

She pulled her mind back together by focusing on Angie, thinking of the look she'd seen in the girl's eyes earlier, when she'd been struck by the thought that Angie's eyes weren't empty, that as long as there was some light in the darkness, there was still hope. She thought of the way the girl had started to go after Rob with the utility knife.

'Angie, get out!' she rasped. 'Save yourself!'

The girl flinched and glanced nervously at Rob.

'She'll stay,' he snapped, stabbing the knife into her foot again, winning another cry from Kate. 'She's mine,' he said, eyes glowing with the intoxication he achieved from inflicting pain.

'I don't think so.' Kate sucked in a sharp breath. 'She's not stupid.'

'No, you're the stupid one,' he said, backing away a step. He pulled a long taper from the candelabrum he'd taken from her dining room and set on the clothes drier.

'Because I know the kind of pathetic, warped excuse for a human being you are?'

'How pathetic am I now, bitch?' he demanded, dragging the flame of the candle from toe to toe on her right foot.

Instinctively, Kate kicked at the source of her torment, knocking the candle from his hand. Rob pounced on it, swearing, disappearing from view at the end of the table.

'Stupid bitch!' he cursed frantically. 'Stupid fucking bitch!'

The scent of the gasoline pressed over Kate's nose and mouth, and she shuddered at the notion of burning alive. The terror was like a fist in the base of her throat. The pain where Rob had already burned her was like a live thing, as if her foot had ignited and now the flames would shoot up her leg.

'What's the matter, Rob?' she asked, fighting the need to cry. 'I thought you liked fire. Are you afraid of it?'

He scrambled to his feet, glaring at her. '*I am the Cremator!*' he shouted, the candle clutched in his fist. She could see his increasing agitation in his respiration rate, in the quick jerkiness of his movements. This wasn't going the way it had in his fantasies.

'*I am superior!*' he shouted, wild-eyed.

'I am Evil's Angel! *I* hold *your life* in *my* hands! I am *your* god!'

Kate channeled her pain into her anger. 'You're a leech. You're a parasite. You're *nothing*.'

She was probably goading him into stabbing her forty-seven times, cutting her larynx out and running it down the garbage disposal. Then she thought of the photographs of his other victims, of the tape of Melanie Hessler, of the hours of torture, rape, repeated strangulation.

She'd take her chances. Live by the sword, die by the sword.

'You make me sick, you spineless little shit.'

That was the truth. It made her want to vomit to think she'd worked beside him day in and day out, and every time his mind wandered it wandered to fantasies of abuse and brutality and murder – the very things they tried to help their clients live through and get past.

He paced at the foot of the table, muttering under his breath, as if he might be speaking to voices in his head, though Kate thought it unlikely he heard any. Rob Marshall wasn't psychotic. He was perfectly aware of everything he did. His actions were a conscious choice – though, if he were caught, he would probably try to convince the authorities otherwise.

'You can't get it up without the domination, can you?' Kate pressed on. 'What woman would have you if you didn't tie her down?'

'Shut up!' he screamed. 'Shut the fuck up!'

He threw the candle at her, missing her head by three feet. He rushed up alongside her, grabbed a boning knife off the table beside her and jammed the point of it against her larynx. Kate swallowed reflexively, felt the tip of the steel bite into her skin.

'I'll cut it out!' he shouted in her face. 'I'll fucking cut it out! I'm so sick of your bitching! I'm so sick of your voice!'

Kate closed her eyes and tried not to swallow again, holding herself rigid as he started to push the small, sharp blade into her throat. Terror tore through her. Instinct told her to jerk away. Logic told her not to move. And then the pressure stopped, eased away.

Rob stared at the tape recorder he'd left on the old barstool. He may not have wanted to hear her criticism of him, but he wanted to listen to her screams as he had listened to the screams and cries and pleading of all his victims. In fact, with her, he probably wanted it more. If he cut her voice out, he couldn't get that. If he couldn't get that, the act of killing her lost its meaning.

'You want to hear it, don't you, Rob?' she asked. 'You want to be able to listen later and hear the exact moment I became frightened of you and gave you control. You don't want to give that up, do you?'

He picked up the tape recorder and held it close to her mouth. He put down the knife, picked up some pliers, and grabbed hold of the tip of her breast, squeezing brutally. Even through the buffer of her sweater and bra, the bite was sharp, then excruciating, making her scream. When he finally let go, he stepped back with a vicious smile and held up the cassette recorder.

'There,' he said. 'I've got it.'

It seemed an eternity passed before the white noise faded from Kate's head. She was breathing as if she'd run the four-hundred-yard dash, sweating, shaking. The haze cleared from her vision and she was looking at Angie, the girl still standing in the same spot, clutching the knife to her. Kate wondered if she'd gone catatonic. Angie was her only hope, the weakest link in Rob's scenario. She needed the girl with her, lucid and able to act.

'Angie,' Kate croaked. 'He doesn't own you. You can fight him. You've *been* fighting him, haven't you?' She thought of the scene that had played out upstairs – Rob wanting Angie to describe what he'd done to her after taking her from the Phoenix House, Angie refusing, defying him, taunting him. She'd done it before – in the offices.

Rob's face reddened. 'Quit talking to her!'

'Afraid she might turn on you, Rob?' Kate asked with not nearly the attitude she'd had five minutes earlier.

'Shut up. She's mine. And you're mine too, bitch!'

He lunged at her, grabbed hold of the neck of her sweater and tore at it with his hands, trying without success to rip it. Swearing, sputtering, flustered, embarrassed, he fumbled for another knife among the array of tools he had so carefully laid out on the table.

'You don't own her any more than you own me,' Kate said, glaring at him, straining against the bonds. 'And you will *never, ever* own me, you toad.'

'Shut up!' he screamed again. He turned and slapped her across the mouth with the back of his hand. 'Shut up! Shut up! You fucking bitch!'

The knives clattered together and he came away with a big one. Kate sucked in what she imagined might be her last breath and held it. Rob grabbed the neck of her sweater again and cut through it with the knife, violently rending the fabric with big, jagged tears. The tip of the knife bit into her breast, skipped along her belly, nicked the point of her hip.

'I'll show you! I'll show you! Angie!' he barked, swinging toward the girl. 'Come here! Come here, now!'

He didn't wait. He rushed around the end of the table, grabbed the girl by the arm, and dragged her back to Kate.

'Do it!' he said in her ear. 'For Michele. You want to do this for Michele. You want Michele to love you, don't you, Angie?'

Michele? Wild card, Kate thought, a fresh wave of terror flashing through her. Who the hell was Michele, and what did she mean to Angie? How could she fight an enemy she'd never seen?

Tears ran down Angie's face. Her lower lip was quivering. She clutched the butcher knife with both trembling hands.

'Don't do it, Angie,' Kate said, her voice vibrating with fear. 'Don't let him use you this way.'

She couldn't know if the girl even heard her. She thought of what Angie had told her about the Zone, and wondered if she was going into that place now, to escape this nightmare. And what then? Would she act on autopilot? Was the Zone a dissociative state? Had it allowed her to participate in Rob's kills before?

She jerked again at the restraints, stretching the plastic another fraction of an inch.

'Do it!' Rob shouted against the side of Angie's face. 'Do it, you stupid cunt! Do it for your sister. Do it for Michele. You want Michele to love you.'

Sister. The headline went through Kate's mind like a comet: *Sisters Exonerated in Burning Death of Parents.*

Pig eyes popping from his ugly round head, Rob screamed with frustration and raised the knife he held. '*Do it!!*'

Light hit a blinding starburst off the blade as it plunged through the air and into the hollow of Kate's shoulder just as she managed to twist her body a crucial few inches. The tip of the blade hit bone and glanced off, and the pain was like lightning striking her.

'Do it!' Rob screamed at Angie, striking her in the back of the head with the handle of the bloody knife. 'You worthless whore!'

'*No!*' the girl cried.

'*Do it!!*'

Sobbing, Angie brought the knife up.

'We got a hit on Fine's prints in Wisconsin,' Yurek said, stepping into the bedroom doorway.

The crime scene unit was removing the tattoo fetishes from the window, carefully folding tissue paper around each and sliding each into its own small paper sack.

'Her real name is Michele Finlow. She's got a handful of misdemeanors and a sealed juvenile record.'

Kovac arched a brow. 'Is skinning people a misdemeanor in Wisconsin?'

'The state that brought us Ed Gein and Jeffrey Dahmer,' Tippen remarked.

'Hey, aren't you from Wisconsin, Tip?' one of the crime scene guys asked.

'Yeah. Menominie. Wanna come to my house for Thanksgiving?'

Quinn stuck a finger in his free ear and listened to Kate's home number ring unanswered for the third time in twenty minutes. Her machine should have picked up. He disconnected and tried her cell phone. It rang four times, then passed him on to her message service. Her clients called her on the cell phone. Angie DiMarco had the number. Kate wouldn't let it go unanswered. Not as responsible as she felt for Angie.

He rubbed a hand against the fire in his belly.

Mary Moss joined the group. 'One of the neighbors down the hall says she sometimes saw Michele with a stubby, balding guy with glasses. She didn't get a name, but she says he drives a black SUV that once rear-ended the car of the guy in 3F.'

'Yes!' Kovac said, pumping one arm. 'Smokey Joe, you're toast.'

'Hamill is talking right now with Mr 3F to get the insurance info.'

'We can bust the Cremator in time for the six o'clock news and still make Patrick's for happy hour,' Kovac said, grinning. 'This is turning into my kind of day.'

Hamill hustled into the apartment, dodging crime scene people. 'You won't believe this,' he said to the task force at large. 'Michele Fine's boyfriend was Rob Marshall.'

'Holy shit.'

Quinn grabbed Kovac by shoulder and shoved him toward the door. 'I have to get to Kate. Give me the keys. I'm driving.'

'Do it! do it!'

Angie let out a long, distorted scream that sounded very far away in her own ears, like a wail coming down a long, long tunnel. The Zone loomed up beside her, a yawning black mouth. And on the other side, the Voice had come to life.

You stupid little slut! Do what I tell you!

'I can't!' she cried.

'DO IT!'

The fear was like a softball in her throat, closing off her air, gagging her, choking her.

No one loves you, crazy little bitch.

'You love me, Michele,' she mewed, not sure if she had spoken the words aloud or if they existed only in her head.

'DO IT!'

DO IT!

She stared down at Kate.

The Zone moved over her. She could feel the hot breath of it. She could fall into it and never come out. She would be safe.

She would be alone. Forever.

'DO IT!'

You know what to do, Angel. Do what you're told, Angel.

Her whole body was shaking.

Coward.

'You can save Michele, Angie. Do this for Michele.'

She looked down at Kate, at the place on her chest where she was supposed to stick the knife. Just as Michele had. She'd seen her sister do it. *He* had made her watch as they stood on either side of the dead woman, one stabbing and then the other, making their pact, sealing their bond, pledging their love. It had frightened her and made her sick. Michele had laughed at her, then given her to *him* for sex.

He hurt her. She hated him. Michele loved him. She loved Michele.

Nobody loves you, crazy little bitch.

That was all she'd ever wanted, someone to care about her, someone to keep her from being alone. All she'd ever gotten was use and abuse. Even from Michele, who had kept her from being alone. But Michele loved her. Love and hate. Love and hate. Lovehate, lovehate, lovehate. There was no line between them for her. She loved Michele, wanted to save her. Michele was all she had.

'DO IT! KILL HER! KILL HER!'

She looked down at Kate, straining against the ties, terror in her face.

'*Why do you care what happens to me?*'

'*Because no one else does.*'

'I'm sorry,' she whimpered.

'Angie, don't!'

'Stab her. Now!'

The pressure inside her was tremendous. The pressure from outside was more. She felt as if her bones would collapse and the weight of it would crush her, and the Zone would suck up the mess and she would be gone forever.

Maybe that would be just as well. At least then she wouldn't hurt anymore.

'Do it or I let your fucking cunt sister die!' he shouted. 'Do it or I'll finish Michele in front of you! DO IT!'

She loved her sister. She could save her sister. She raised the knife.

'NO!'

Kate sucked in a breath and braced herself, never taking her eyes off Angie.

The girl let out an unearthly shriek as she raised the butcher knife with both hands above her head, then twisted her body and plunged the knife into Rob Marshall's neck.

Blood sprayed in a geyser as she jerked the blade out. Blood on the wall, on the bed, on Kate, spraying like a loose fire hose. Rob jerked back, astonished, grabbing at the wound, blood gushing through his fingers.

Angie went on screaming, plunging the knife again, stabbing his hand, stabbing his chest. She followed him as he staggered backward, trying to escape. He tried to call out for help or for mercy and choked on his own blood, the sound gurgling in his throat. His knees buckled, and he fell against the clothes drier, knocking the candelabrum to the floor.

Angie stepped back then and stared at him for a moment, as if she had no idea who he was or how he had come to fall to the floor with the last of his life's blood pumping out of him as he gurgled and gagged. Then she looked at the knife, dripping blood, her hands covered and sticky with it, and slowly she turned toward Kate.

Quinn drove with no regard for the laws of the road or of physics, driven himself by a growing sense of panic in his gut. Kovac hung on, braced himself, screamed more than once as Quinn swept the Caprice around and between cars.

'If he's smart, he's already blown town,' Kovac said.

'Smart's got nothing to do with it,' Quinn said above the roar of the engine. 'He brought Kate on the case as part of his game. He killed Melanie Hessler because she was Kate's client. He left a calling card in Kate's garage the other night. He won't leave town without finishing the thing between them.'

He could see the hall light on as the car skidded to a stop in front of Kate's house. The light glowed through the sheers at the goddamn sidelights she should have known better than to have. Quinn slammed the Caprice into park before it fully stopped, and the transmission made an ominous sound. He was out of the car before it could stop rocking, running for the house as a pair of radio cars screamed up the street. He thundered onto the porch and pounded on the door, tried the handle. Locked.

'Kate! Kate!'

He pressed his face to the glass of one sidelight. The hall table sat askew. Things had tumbled over on it and off it. The rug was cockeyed.

'Kate!'

The shout that came from somewhere in the house went through him like steel. 'No!'

Quinn grabbed the mailbox, ripped it off the wall, and smashed out the sidelight just as Kovac ran up onto the porch. Another few seconds and they were in. His eyes went to a smear of blood on the wall near the den.

'Kate!'

Her cry came from somewhere deep in the house. 'Angie! NO!'

Angie turned the knife in her bloody hands, staring at the blade. She let the tip of it kiss the fragile skin of her wrist.

'Angie, no!' Kate shouted, straining against the ties. 'Don't do it! Please don't do it! Come cut me loose. Then we'll get you some help.'

She couldn't see Rob, but knew he lay crumpled on the floor near the drier. She could hear gurgling sounds coming from his throat. He had knocked the candelabrum over as he crashed, and the flames had found some of the gasoline he must have poured around while Kate had been unconscious. It ignited with a *whoosh*.

The flames would follow the trail of fuel in search of more fuel. The basement was crammed with possibilities – boxes of junk her parents had saved and abandoned, stuff she'd been meaning to throw out but hadn't gotten to, the obligatory half-empty cans of paint and other hazardous chemicals.

'Angie. Angie!' Kate said, trying to pull the girl's focus to her. Angie, who stood looking into the face of her own death.

'Michele won't love me,' the girl murmured, looking at the man she had just killed. She sounded disappointed in herself, like a small child who had written on the wall in crayon, then realized there would be a bad consequence.

'Kate!' Quinn's bellow sounded above.

Angie seemed not to hear the shouts or the thunder of big male feet. She pressed the blade of the knife lengthwise against the shadow of a vein in her wrist.

'Kate!'

She tried to shout 'In the basement!' but her voice seized up so she barely heard herself. The flames caught hold of a box of clothes destined, oddly enough, for the Phoenix, and leapt with enthusiasm – far too near the table. Kate jerked at her bindings, succeeding only in pulling them even tighter around her wrists and ankles. She was losing the feeling in her hands.

She tried to clear her throat to speak. Smoke rolled thick and black from the boxes.

'Angie, help me. Help me and I'll help you. How's that for a deal?'

The girl stared at the knife.

The smoke detector at the top of the stairs finally blew, and the thunder of feet homed in on it.

Angie pressed the blade a little harder against her wrist. Tiny beads of blood surfaced like little jewels in a bracelet.

'No, Angie, please,' Kate whispered, knowing the girl couldn't have heard her if she'd shouted.

Angie looked at her square in the face, and for the first time since Kate had met her she looked like exactly what she was: a child. A child no one had ever wanted, had ever loved.

'I hurt,' she said.

'Call the fire department!' Quinn shouted at the head of the stairs. 'Kate!'

'Joh –' Her voice cracked and she began to cough. The smoke rolled along the ceiling toward the stairwell and the new source of fresh air.

'Kate!'

Quinn led the way down the stairs with a .38 Kovac had lent him, his fear obliterating all known rules of procedure. As he dropped below the cloud of smoke, his focus was instantly on Kate, bound hand and foot on a table, her sweater cut open, blood pooling on her skin. And then his attention went to the girl beside the table: Angie DiMarco with a butcher knife in her hands.

'Angie, drop the knife!' he shouted.

The girl looked up at him, the light in her eyes fading away. 'Nobody loves me,' she said, and in one quick, violent motion slashed her wrist to the bone.

'NO!' Kate screamed.

'Jesus!' Quinn charged across the room, leading with the gun.

Angie dropped to her knees as the blood gushed from her arm. The knife fell to the floor. Quinn kicked it aside and dropped to his knees, grabbing the girl's arm with a grip like a C-clamp. Blood pumped between his fingers. Angie sagged against him.

Kate watched with horror, not even acknowledging Kovac as he cut her loose. She rolled off the table onto feet she could no longer feel, and fell in a heap. She had to scramble to Angie on her knees. Her hands were as useless as clubs, swollen and purple, and she couldn't make her fingers move. Still, she wrapped her arms around the girl.

'We have to get out of here!' Quinn shouted.

The fire had begun licking its way up the steps. A uniformed officer fought it down with an extinguisher. But even as he cleared the stairs, the flames were working their way across the basement, following the trail of gasoline, pouncing on everything edible in its path.

Quinn and a uniform took Angie up the basement steps and out the back door. Sirens were screaming out on the street, a couple of blocks away yet.

He passed the girl off to the uniform and ran back to the house as Kovac came with Kate leaning heavily against him, both of them coughing as thick black smoke rolled up behind them, acrid with the smell of chemicals.

'Kate!'

She fell against him and he scooped her up in his arms.

'I'm going back for Marshall!' Kovac shouted above the roar. The fire had come up through the floor and found the river of gasoline Rob had poured through the house.

'He's dead!' Kate yelled, but Kovac was gone. 'Sam!'

One of the uniforms charged in after him.

The sirens blasted out front, fire trucks bulling their way down the narrow street. Quinn negotiated the back steps with Kate in his arms and hustled down the side of the house to the front yard and the boulevard. He lowered her into the backseat of Kovac's car just as an explosion sounded from the bowels of the house and windows on the first floor shattered. Kovac and the uniform staggered away from the back corner of the house and fell to their hands and knees in the snow. Firemen and paramedics rushed toward them and toward the house.

'Are you all right?' Quinn asked, staring into Kate's eyes, his fingers digging into her shoulders.

Kate looked up at her house, flames visible now through the windows of the first floor. Behind Kovac's car, Angie was being loaded into an ambulance. The fear, the panic she had fought to keep at bay during the ordeal, hit her belatedly in a pounding wave.

She turned back to Quinn, shaking. 'No,' she whispered as the flood of tears came. And he folded her into his arms and held her.

39

'I *never* liked him,' Yvonne Vetter said to the uniformed officer who stood guard outside Rob Marshall's garage door. She was huddled into a lumpy wool coat that made her look misshapen. Her round, sour face squinted up at him from beneath an incongruously jaunty red beret. 'I called your hotline *several* times. I believe he cannibalized my Bitsy.'

'Your what, ma'am?'

'My Bitsy. My sweet little dog!'

'Wouldn't that be *animal*ized?' Tippen speculated.

Liska cuffed him one on the arm.

The task force would get the first look around Rob's chamber of horrors before the collection of evidence began. The videographer followed right behind them. Even as they entered the house, the news crews were pulling up to the curbs on both sides of the street.

It was a nice house on a quiet street in a quiet neighborhood. An extra-large tree-studded lot near one of the most popular lakes in the Cities. A beautifully finished basement. Realtors would have been drooling over the opportunity to sell it if not for the fact Rob Marshall had tortured and murdered at least four women there.

They started in the basement, wandering through a media room equipped with several televisions, VCRs, stereo equipment, a bookcase lined with video- and audiotapes.

Tippen turned to the videographer. 'Don't shoot the stereo equipment yet. I really need a new tuner and tape deck.'

The videographer immediately turned the camera on the recording equipment.

Tippen rolled his eyes. 'It was a *joke*. You techno-geeks have no sense of humor.'

The camera guy turned his lens on Tippen's ass as he walked away.

A headless mannequin stood in one corner of the room decked out in a skimpy see-through black lace bra and a purple spandex miniskirt.

'Hey, Tinks, you could pick up some new outfits,' Tippen called, eyeballing a sticky-looking residue on the shoulders of the mannequin. Possibly blood mixed with some other, clearer fluid.

Liska continued down the hall, checking out a utility room, moving on. Her boys would have loved this house. They talked endlessly about getting a house like their friend Mark had, with a cool rec room in the basement – where they could escape Mom's scrutiny – with a pool table and a big-screen TV.

There was a pool table here in the room at the end of the hall. It was draped with bloodstained white plastic, and there was a body on it. The smell of blood, urine, and excrement hung thick in the air. The stench of violent death.

'Tippen!' Liska hollered, bolting for the table.

Michele Fine lay twisted at an odd angle on her back, staring up at the light glaring in her face. She didn't blink. Her eyes had the flat look of a corpse's. Her mouth hung open, drool crusted white in a trail down her chin. Her lips moved ever so slightly.

Liska bent close, laying two fingers on the side of Fine's neck to feel for a pulse, unable to detect one.

'. . . elp . . . me . . . elp . . . me . . .' Fragments of words on the thinnest of breaths.

Tippen jogged in and stopped cold. 'Shit.'

'Get an ambulance,' Liska ordered. 'She may just live to tell the tale.'

40

'I didn't want to help,' Angie said softly.

It didn't sound like her voice. The thought drifted through her drug-fogged brain on a cloud. It sounded like the voice of the little girl inside her, the one she always tried to hide, to protect. She stared at the bandage on her left arm, the desire to pull it off and make the wound bleed lurking at the dark edge of her mind.

'I didn't want to do what *he* said.'

She waited for the Voice to sneer at her, but it was strangely silent. She waited for the Zone to zoom up on her, but the drugs held it off.

She sat at a table in a room that wasn't supposed to look like part of a hospital. The blue print gown she wore had short sleeves and exposed her thin, scarred arms for all to see. She looked at the scars, one beside another and another, like bars in a prison cell door. Marks she had carved into her own flesh. Marks life had carved into her soul. A constant reminder so she could never forget exactly who and what she was.

'Was Rob Marshall the one who took you to the park that night, Angie?' Kate asked quietly. She sat at the table too, beside Angie with her chair turned so that she was facing the girl. 'Was he the john you told me about?'

Angie nodded, still looking down at the scars. 'His Great Plan,' she murmured.

She wished the drugs would fog the memories, but the pictures were clear in her head, like watching them on television. Sitting in the truck, knowing the dead woman's body was in the back, knowing that the man at the wheel had killed her, knowing Michele had been a part of that too. She could see them stabbing her over and over, could see the sexual excitement in them growing with every thrust of the knives. Michele had given her to *him* afterward, and he had taken her again that night in the park, excited because of the dead woman in the back and because of his Great Plan.

'I was supposed to describe someone else.'

'As the killer?' Kate asked.

'Someone he made up. All these details. He made me repeat them over and over and over.'

Angie picked at a loose thread on the edge of her bandage, wishing blood would seep up through the layers of white gauze. The sight would comfort her, make her feel less terrible about sitting beside Kate. She couldn't look her in the face after all that had happened.

'I hate him.'

Present tense, Kate thought. As if she didn't know he was dead, that she had killed him. Maybe she didn't. Maybe her mind would allow her that one consolation.

'I hate him too,' Kate said softly.

Facts about Rob and the Finlow sisters were coming out of Wisconsin and piecing together into a terrible, sordid story America received new episodes of every night on the news. The lurid quality of lover-killers and the fall of a billionaire made for juicy ratings bait. Michele Finlow, who had lingered for ten hours after being found in Rob's basement, had filled in some of the blanks herself. And Angie would supply what fragments her mind would allow.

Daughters of two different men and a mother with a history of drug abuse and assorted domestic misery, Michele and Angie had been in and out of the child welfare system, never finding the care they needed. Children falling through the cracks of a system that was poor at best. Both girls had juvenile records, Michele's being longer and more inclined to violent behavior.

Kate had read the news accounts of the fire that had killed the mother and stepfather. The general consensus of the investigators on the case was that one or both of the girls had started it, but there hadn't been enough evidence to take to court. One witness had recalled seeing Michele calmly standing in the yard while the house burned, listening to the screams of the two people trapped inside. She had, in fact, been standing too near a window, and was burned when the window exploded and the fire rolled outside to consume fresh oxygen. The case had brought Rob Marshall into their lives via the court system. And Rob had brought the girls to Minneapolis.

Love. Or so Michele had called it, though it was doubtful she had any real grasp of the meaning of the word. A man in love didn't leave his partner to die a horrible death alone in a basement while he skipped the country, which was exactly what Rob would have done.

Peter Bondurant's bullet had struck Michele in the back, severing her spinal cord. Rob, who had been watching from a distance, had waited for Bondurant to leave, then picked her up and took her back to his home. Any gunshot wound brought into an ER had to be reported to the police. He hadn't been willing to risk that not even to save the life of this woman who allegedly loved him.

He'd left her there on the table, where they had played out their sick, sadistic fantasies; where they had killed four women. Left her paralyzed, bleeding, in shock, dying. He hadn't even bothered to cover her with a blanket. The payoff money had been recovered from Rob's car.

According to Michele, Rob had fixated on Jillian out of jealousy, but Michele had put him off. Then on that fateful Friday night Jillian had called from a pay phone after the battery in her cell phone had gone dead. She wanted to talk about the fight she'd had with her father. She needed the support of a friend. Her friend had delivered her to Rob Marshall.

'Michele loves him,' Angie said, picking at the bandage. A frown curved her mouth and she added, 'More than me.'

But Michele was all she had, her only family, her surrogate mother, and so she had done whatever Michele had asked. Kate wondered what would happen in Angie's mind when she was finally told Michele was dead, that she was alone – the one thing she feared the most.

There was a soft rap at the door, signifying Kate's allotted time as a visitor was up. When she left she would be grilled by the people sitting on the other side of the observation window – Sabin, Lieutenant Fowler, Gary Yurek, and Kovac – back in good graces after scoring news time as a hero at Kate's fire – a photo of him and Quinn carrying her out the back door of her house had graced the cover of both papers in the Cities and made *Newsweek*. They believed she was here at their request. But she hadn't asked their questions or pressed for the answers. She hadn't come to this locked psychiatric ward to exploit Angie Finlow. She hadn't come as an advocate to see a client. She had come to see someone she had shared an ordeal with. Someone whose life would be forever tied to hers in a way no one else's ever would be.

She reached along the tabletop and touched Angie's hand, trying to keep her in the present, in the moment. Her own hands were still discolored and puffy, the ligature marks on her wrists covered by her own pristine white bandages. Three days had passed since the incident in her house.

'You're not alone, kiddo,' Kate whispered softly. 'You can't just save my life and breeze out of it again. I'll be keeping my eye on you. Here's a little reminder of that.'

With the skill of a magician, she slipped the thing from her hand to Angie's. The tiny pottery angel Angie had stolen from her desk, then left behind at the Phoenix.

Angie stared at the statue, a guardian angel in a world where such things did not truly exist – or so she had always believed. The need to believe now was so strong, it terrified her, and she retreated to the shadowed side of her mind to escape the fear. Better to believe in nothing than wait for the inevitable disappointment to drop like an ax.

She closed her hand around the statue and held it like a secret. She closed her eyes and shut her mind down, not even aware of the tears that slipped down her cheeks.

Kate blinked back tears of her own as she rose slowly and carefully. She stroked a hand over Angie's hair, bent, and pressed the softest of kisses to the top of her head.

'I'll be back,' she whispered, then gathered her crutches and hobbled toward the door, muttering to herself. 'Guess maybe I'll have to stop saying I don't do kids, after all.'

The idea came with a wave of emotions she simply didn't have the strength to deal with today. Luckily, she would have a lot of tomorrows to work on them.

As she went into the hall, the door to the observation room opened and Sabin, Fowler, and Yurek spilled out, looking frustrated. Kovac followed with a look-at-these-clowns smirk. At the same time, a short, handsome Italian-looking man in a thirty-five-hundred-dollar charcoal suit steamed down the hall toward them with Lucas Brandt and a scowl.

'Have you been speaking with the girl without her counsel present?' he demanded.

Kate gave him the deep-freeze stare.

'You can't proceed with this until her competency has been determined,' Brandt said to Sabin.

'Don't tell me my job.' Sabin's shoulders hunched as if he might bring his fists up. 'What are you doing here, Costello?'

'I'm here to represent Angie Finlow at the request of Peter Bondurant.'

Anthony Costello, sleazeball to the rich and famous.

Kate almost laughed. Just when she thought nothing could amaze her . . . Peter Bondurant paying for Angie's legal counsel. Retribution for shooting her sister in the back? Good PR for a man who would stand to face charges of his own? Or maybe he simply wanted to make up for the mess his daughter's life had become by helping Angie out of the mess her life had always been. Karma.

'Anything she told you is privileged,' Costello barked at her.

'I'm just here to see a friend,' Kate said, hobbling away to let the men duke it out.

A new act for the media circus.

'Hey, Red!'

She turned and stopped as Kovac came toward her. He looked as if he'd fallen asleep at the beach. His face was the bright red of a bad sunburn. His eyebrows were a pair of pale hyphens, singed short. The requisite cop mustache was gone, leaving him looking naked and younger.

'How do you like them apples?' he croaked, fighting off a coughing fit. The aftereffects of smoke inhalation.

'Curiouser and curiouser.'

'Quinn back yet?'

'Tomorrow.'

He had gone back to Quantico for the wrap-up and to put in for his first holiday in five years – Thanksgiving.

'So you're coming tonight?'

Kate made a face. 'I don't think so, Sam. I'm not feeling very social.'

'Kate,' he said on a disapproving growl. 'It's Turkey Wake! I'm the damn bishop, for Christ's sake! We've got a lot to celebrate.'

True, but a rousing, ribald roast of a rubber chicken with a mob of drunken cops and courthouse personnel didn't seem the way to go for her. After all that had happened, after the media she'd had to face in the last few days, interaction was the last thing she wanted.

'I'll catch it on the news,' she said.

He heaved a sigh, giving up, sobering for the real reason he had broken away from the pack. 'It's been a hell of a case. You held your own, Red.' A hint of his usual wry grin canted his mouth. 'You're okay for a civilian.'

Kate grinned at him. 'Up yours, Kojak.' Then she hobbled closer, leaned forward, and kissed his cheek. 'Thanks for saving my life.'

'Anytime.'

A warm front had moved into Minnesota the day before, bringing sun and temperatures in the high fifties. The snow was nearly gone, re-exposing dead yellow lawns and leafless bushes and dirt. Ever conscious of the length of winter once it settled in with serious intent, the citizens of Minneapolis had emerged from early hibernation on bicycles and Rollerblades. Small packs of power-walking old ladies trooped down Kate's block on the way to the lake, slowing to gawk at the blackened exterior of her home.

Most of the damage had been contained to the basement and first floor. The house would be salvaged, repaired, restored, and she would try not to think too much about what had happened there every time she had to go to the basement. She would try not to stand at the washing machine and think of Rob Marshall lying dead and burned to a charred black lump on her floor.

There were tougher jobs ahead than selecting new kitchen cabinets.

Kate picked her way through the charred mess that had been the first floor. A buddy of Kovac's who had done a lot of arson investigation had gone through the structure for her, telling her where she could and couldn't go, what she should and shouldn't do. She wore the yellow hardhat he'd given her to protect herself from falling chunks of plaster. On one foot she wore a thick-soled hiking boot. Over the bandages on the other foot was a thick wool sock and a heavy-duty plastic garbage bag.

She sorted through the debris with long-handled tongs, for things worth keeping. The job depressed her beyond tears. Even with the timely arrival of the fire department, the explosion of paint and solvents in the basement had damaged much of the first floor. And what the fire hadn't ruined, the fire hoses had.

The loss of ordinary possessions didn't bother her. She could buy another television. A sofa was a sofa. Her wardrobe was smoke-damaged, but insurance would buy her another. It was the loss of things richly steeped in memories that hurt. She'd grown up in this house. The thing that now looked like a pair of burned tree stumps had been her father's desk. She could remember crawling into the knee well during games of hide-and-seek with her sister. The rocking chair in the living room had belonged to her great-aunt. Photograph albums holding a lifetime's worth of memories had burned, melted, or been soaked, then frozen and thawed again.

She picked up what was left of an album with pictures of Emily and started to page through, tears coming as she realized the photographs were mostly ruined. It was like losing her child all over again.

She closed the book and held it to her chest, looking around through the blur at the devastation. Maybe this wasn't the day to do this job. Quinn had tried to talk her out of it on the phone. She had insisted she was strong enough, that she needed to do something positive.

But she wasn't strong enough. Not in the way that she needed to be. She felt too raw, too tired, emotions too close to the surface. She felt as if she'd lost more than what the fire had taken. Her faith in her judgment had been shaken. The order of her world had been upended. She felt very strongly that she should have been able to prevent what had happened.

The curse of the victim. Second-guessing herself. Hating her lack of control of the world around her. The test was whether a person could rise above it, push past it, grow beyond the experience.

She carried the photo album outside and set it in a box on the back steps. The backyard was awash in yellow-orange light as the sun began its early exit from the day. The grainy light fell like mist on her winter-dead garden in the far corner of the yard, and a statue she had forgotten to put away for the season – a fairy sitting on a pedestal, reading a book. With nothing but dead stems around it, it looked far too exposed and vulnerable. She had the strangest urge to pick it up and hold it like a child. Protect it.

Another wave of emotion pushed tears up in her eyes as she thought again of Angie looking so small and so young and so lost sitting in the too-big hospital gown, her gaze on the tiny guardian angel statue in her hand.

A car door slammed out front and she peered around the corner of the house to see Quinn walking away from a cab. Instantly her heart lifted at the sight of him, at the way he looked, the way he moved, the frown on his face as he looked up at the house without realizing she was watching him. And just as instantly her nerves tightened a notch.

They hadn't seen much of each other in the days since the fire. The wrap-up of the case had taken much of Quinn's time. He'd been in demand by the media as they had insisted on rehashing, analyzing and re-analyzing every aspect of it. And then the official summons back to Quantico, where he had several cases coming to a head at once. Even their phone conversations had been brief, and both of them had skated around the big issues of their relationship. The case had brought him to Minneapolis. The case had brought them together. The case was over. Now what?

'I'm out back!' Kate called.

Quinn fixed his gaze on her as he came up the walk beside the house. She looked ridiculous and beautiful in a hardhat and a green canvas coat that was a bit too big for her. Beautiful, even battered and bruised and shaken from the inside out.

He'd almost lost her. Again. Forever. The idea struck him with the force of a hammer to the solar plexus about every five minutes. He'd almost lost her in part because he hadn't been able to see right in front of him the monster he was supposed to know as well as any man on earth.

'Hey, pretty,' he said. He dropped his bags on the ground, took her into his arms, and kissed her – not in a sexual way, but in a way that gave them both comfort. The hardhat tipped back on her head and fell off, letting her hair cascade down her back. 'How's it going?'

'It sucks. I hate it,' she said plainly, Kate-style. 'I liked my house. I liked my stuff. I had to start over once. I don't want to have to do it again. But life says, "Tough bounce", and what are my options? Take it on the chin and keep marching.'

She gave a shrug and broke eye contact. 'Better than the deal Angie got. Or Melanie Hessler.'

Quinn took her stubborn chin in his hand and turned her face back to his. 'Are you beating yourself up, Kathryn Elizabeth?'

She nodded and let him wipe the tears from her cheeks with his thumbs.

'So am I,' he confessed, and found a wry smile. 'We're a pair. Think how great the world would be if you and I really did control it.'

'We'd do a better job of it than whoever has the job now,' she promised, then shivered. 'Or I'd blow it, and people I cared about would get hurt.'

'Well, here's an ugly rumor I heard today: We're only human. Mistakes come with the territory.'

Kate knitted her brow. 'Human?' She took his hand and led him to the old weathered cedar garden bench. 'You and I? Who told you that? Let me go melt their brain with death rays.'

They sat, and his arm automatically went around her shoulders, just as her head automatically found his shoulder.

'Hey, you. You're early,' she said.

'Well, I didn't want to miss Turkey Wake,' he said, deadpan. 'Happy to see me?'

'Not after that answer.'

He laughed and brushed a kiss against her temple. They sat in silence for another few minutes, staring at the blackened back door of the house where Quinn and Kovac had carried her out.

'I came back here and built this very specific life,' Kate said softly. 'Thinking if I did it that way, I could have control of it, and bad things wouldn't happen. How's that for naive?'

Quinn shrugged. 'I thought if I could grab my world by the balls, I could ride all the demons out of it. But it doesn't work that way. There's always another demon. I can't count them all anymore. I can't keep them straight. Hell, I can't even see them right in front of me.'

Kate could hear the hint of desperation underlying the toughness, and knew his faith in his abilities had been shaken too. The Mighty Quinn. Always right, always sure, moving forward like an arrow. She had always loved his unfailing strength, had always admired his bullheadedness. She loved him as much for his vulnerability.

'No one saw this coming, John. I hated the guy from the day he took the job, and not even I suspected *this*. We see what we expect to see. Scary, considering what can lie beneath the surface.'

She stared at the garden, dead and brown, surreal in the fading light. 'Imagine the most horrific, repulsive cruelty one human being can commit against another. Someone's out there doing it right now. I don't know how you stand it anymore, John.'

'I don't,' he admitted. 'You know how it is when you first come on the job? Everything gets to you. You have to toughen up. You have to get that emotional armor on. Then you reach a point when you've seen so much, nothing gets to you, and you start to wonder about your humanity. Stay at it long enough, the armor starts to corrode, the evil starts to eat through it, and you're back where you started, only you're older and tired, and you know you can't slay all the dragons no matter how hard you try.'

'And then what?' Kate asked quietly.

'And then you either step aside, or you eat your gun, or you drop in your tracks like Vince Walsh.'

'On the surface that choice would seem like a no-brainer.'

'Not when the job is all you've got. When you bury yourself in it because you're too afraid to go and get the life you really want. Portrait of me for the last five years,' he said. 'No more. As of today, I am officially on leave. Time to drain the strain, get my head screwed on straight.'

'Decide what you want,' Kate offered to the list.

'I know what I want,' he said simply.

He turned to her on the bench and took her hands in his. 'I need something good in my life, Kate. I need something beautiful and warm. I need you. I need us. What do you need?'

Kate looked at him, her destroyed home in her peripheral vision, and thought, of all things, of the phoenix rising from the ashes. The events that had brought them to this place in this time may have been devastating, but here was their chance for a new beginning. Together.

For the first time in five years she felt a sense of warm, sweet peace in place of the hard, aching emptiness she'd grown almost numb to. She had spent the years without him, merely existing. It was time to live. After all the death, literal and metaphorical, it was time for both of them to live.

'I need your arms around me, John Quinn,' she said, smiling softly. 'Every day and every night of my life.'

Quinn let out a pent-up breath, a grin splitting his handsome face. 'Took you long enough to answer.'

He took her into his arms carefully, mindful of her wounds, and held her close. He imagined he could feel her heart beat even through the heavy canvas of her coat.

'You've got my heart, Kate Conlan,' he said, burying his cold nose in the thick silk of her hair. 'You've had it all this time. I lived too long without it.'

Kate smiled against his chest, knowing *this* was home – his embrace, his love.

'Well, tough, John Quinn,' she said, gazing up at him in the last light of sunset. 'I'm not giving it back.'

Dust to Dust

To the very good friends
who helped me through a very bad time:
Bob, Betsy, Jessie and, as always, the Divas

Acknowledgments

The author wishes to thank the following people for their help and support in the making of this book:

Special Agent Larry Brubaker, FBI (retired); Sergeant Mark Lenzen, Homicide unit, Minneapolis Police Department; Sergeant Mike Carlson, Homicide unit, Minneapolis Police Department; Commander Thomas Reding, Internal Affairs, St Paul Police Department; Robert Crais; Eileen Dreyer; Nita Taublib; Beth de Guzman; and Andrea Cirillo.

PROLOGUE

It is stunning how quickly it happens. How little time it takes to go from trouble to tragedy. Seconds. Mere seconds without air and the brain begins to shut down. No time to struggle. No time to panic even.

Like a boa constrictor choking the life from its prey, the noose tightens and tightens. It makes no difference what thoughts explode in the brain. *Move! Grab the rope! Get air!* The commands don't make it down the neural pathways to the muscles of the arms. Coordination is gone.

The sturdy rope makes a tearing sound as the weight of his body stretches it. The beam creaks.

His body turns slightly this way and that. The arms pull upward in hideous, slow-motion spasms. A macabre marionette's dance – arms moving up and down; hands twitching, twisting, bending; fingers curling. The knees try to draw upward, then straighten again. Posturing: a sign of brain damage.

The eerie contortions go on and on. The seconds stretch as the death dance continues. A minute. Two. Four. The rope and beam creak in the otherwise silent room. The eyes are open but vacant. Mouth moves in a final, futile gasp for air. The most acute, exquisite split second of life: the final heartbeat before death.

And then it is over.

At last.

The flash explodes in a brilliant burst of white light and the scene is frozen in time.

1

'They oughta hang the son of a bitch came up with this shit,' Sam Kovac groused, digging a piece of nicotine gum out of a crumpled foil pack.

'The gum or the wrapper?'

'Both. I can't open the damn package and I'd rather chew on a cat turd.'

'And that would taste different from a cigarette how?' Nikki Liska asked.

They moved through a small throng of people in the wide white hall. Cops heading out onto the steps of the Minneapolis city hall for a cigarette, cops coming back in from having a cigarette, and the odd citizen looking for something for their tax dollar.

Kovac scowled down at her from the corner of one eye. Liska made five-five by sheer dint of will. He always figured God made her short because if she had the size of Janet Reno she'd take over the world. She had that kind of energy – and attitude out the wazoo.

'What do you know about it?' he challenged.

'My ex smoked. Lick an ashtray sometime. That's why we got divorced, you know. I wouldn't stick my tongue in his mouth.'

'Jesus, Tinks, like I wanted to know that.'

He'd given her the nickname – Tinker Bell on Steroids. Nordic blond hair cut in a shaggy Peter Pan style, eyes as blue as a lake on a sunny day. Feminine but unmistakably athletic. She'd kicked more ass in her years on the force than half the guys he knew. She'd come onto homicide – Christ, what was it now? – five or six years ago? He lost track. He'd been there himself almost longer than he could remember. All of his forty-four years, it seemed. The better part of a twenty-three-year career, for certain. Seven to go. He'd get his thirty and take the pension. Catch up on his sleep for the next ten years. He sometimes wondered why he hadn't taken his twenty and moved on. But he didn't have anything to move on to, so he stayed.

Liska slipped between a pair of nervous-looking uniforms blocking the way in front of the door to Room 126 – Internal Affairs.

'Hey, that was the least of it,' she said. 'I was more upset about where he wanted to put his dick.'

Kovac made a sound of pain and disgust, his face twisting.

Liska grinned, mischievous and triumphant. 'Her name was Brandi.'

The Criminal Investigative Division offices had been newly refurbished. The walls were the color of dried blood. Kovac wondered if that had been intentional or just trendy. Probably the latter. Nothing else in the place had been designed with cops in mind. The narrow, gray, two-person cubicles could just as well have housed a bunch of accountants.

He preferred the temporary digs they'd had during the remodeling: a dirty, beat-up room full of dirty, beat-up desks, and beat-up cops getting migraines under harsh white fluorescent lights. Homicide crammed into one room, robbery down the way, half the sex crimes guys wedged into a broom closet. That was atmosphere.

'What's the status on the Nixon assault?'

The voice stopped Kovac in his tracks as effectively as a hook to the collar. He bit a little harder on the Nicorette. Liska kept moving.

New offices, new lieutenant, new pain in the ass. The homicide lieutenant's office had a figurative revolving door. It was a stop on the way for upwardly mobile management types. At least this new one – Leonard – had them back working partners instead of like the last guy, who'd tortured them with some bullshit high-concept team crap with rotating sleep-deprivation schedules.

Of course, that didn't mean he wasn't an asshole.

'We'll see,' Kovac said. 'Elwood just brought in a guy he thinks is good for the Truman murder.'

Leonard flushed pink. He had that kind of complexion, and short, white-gray hair like duck fuzz all over his head. 'What the hell are you doing working the Truman murder? That's what? A week ago? You're up to your ass in assaults since then.'

Liska came back then, wearing her cop face. 'We think this guy's a two-fer, Lou. He was maybe in on Nixon *and* Truman. I guess the Nation wants to start calling the Bloods the Dead Presidents.'

Kovac laughed at that – a cross between a bark and a snort. 'Like these dickheads would know a president if he pissed on them.'

Liska looked up at him. 'Elwood's got him in the guest room. Let's go before he uses the L word.'

Leonard stepped back, frowning. He had no lips, and ears that stuck out perpendicular to his head like a chimpanzee's. Kovac had nicknamed him the Brass Monkey. He was looking as if solving a murder would ruin his day.

'Don't worry,' Kovac said. 'There's more assaults where that one came from.'

He turned away before Leonard could react, and headed for the interview room with Liska.

'So this guy was in on Nixon too?'

'Beats me. Leonard liked it.'

'Brass asshole,' Kovac grumbled. 'Someone should take him out and show him the fucking sign on the door. It still says "Homicide", doesn't it?'

'Last I looked.'

'All he wants is to clear assaults.'

'Assaults are the homicides of tomorrow.'

'Yeah, that'd make a great tattoo. I know just where he can put it.'

'But you'd need a miner's hat to read it. I'll get you one for Christmas. Give you something to hope for.'

Liska opened the door and Kovac preceded her into the room, which was about the size of a spacious coat closet. The architect would have described it as 'intimate'. In keeping with the latest theories on how to interview scumbags, the table was small and round. No dominant side. Everybody equal. Pals. Confidants.

No one was sitting at it.

Elwood Knutson stood in the near corner, looking like a Disney cartoon bear in a black felt bowler. Jamal Jackson had the opposite corner, near the totally useless and empty built-in bookcase, and beneath the wall-mounted video camera, which was required by Minnesota law to prove they weren't beating confessions out of suspects.

Jackson's attitude hung on him as badly as his clothes. Jeans that would have fit Elwood were slipping off his skinny ass. A huge down coat in Nation black and red colors puffed up around his upper body. He had a lower lip as thick as a garden hose, and he stuck it out at Kovac.

'Man, this is bogus. I din' off no-body.'

Kovac lifted his brows. 'No? Gee, there must be some mistake.' He turned to Elwood and spread his hands. 'I thought you said he was the guy, Elwood. He says he's not the guy.'

'I must have been mistaken,' Elwood said. 'My profuse apologies, Mr Jackson.'

'We'll have a radio car take you back home,' Kovac said. 'Maybe have them announce over the bullhorn to your 'hood that we didn't mean to bring you in. That it was all a big mistake.'

Jackson stared at him, the lip moving up and down.

'We can have them announce specifically that we know you weren't really involved in the murder of Deon Truman. Just so there's no mistake what we had you in for. We don't want a lot of bad rumors going around about you on account of us.'

'Fuck you, man!' Jackson shouted, his voice jumping an octave. 'You trying to get me killed?'

Kovac laughed. 'Hey. You said you didn't do it. Fine. I'll send you home.'

'An' the brothers think I talk to you. Next thing, my ass is horizontal. Fuck that!'

Jackson paced a little, pulling at the short braids that stuck up in all directions on his head. His hands were cuffed together in front of him. He gave Kovac the eye.

'You put me in jail, motherfucker.'

'Can't do it. And here you asked so nice. Sorry.'

'I am *under arrest*,' Jamal insisted.

'Not if you didn't do anything.'

'I done plenty.'

'So now you're confessing?' Liska said.

Jackson looked at her, incredulous. 'Who the hell is she? Your girlfriend?'

'Don't insult the lady,' Kovac said. 'You're telling us you capped Deon Truman.'

'The fuck I am.'

'Then who did?'

'Fuck you, man. I ain't telling you jack.'

'Elwood, see that the man gets home in style.'

'But I'm *under arrest*!' Jackson wailed. 'Put me in jail!'

'Fuck you,' Kovac said. 'Jail's overcrowded. It's not a goddamn hotel. What'd you pick him up on, Elwood?'

'I believe it was loitering.'

'Petty misdemeanor.'

'The fuck!' Jackson shouted, outraged. He pointed at Elwood with both index fingers. 'You saw me selling crack! Right there on the corner of Chicago and Twenty-sixth.'

'He have crack on him when you arrested him?' Kovac asked.

'No, sir. He did have a pipe.'

'I ditched the goods!'

'Possession of drug paraphernalia,' Liska said, unimpressed. 'Big deal. Cut him loose. He's not worth our time.'

'Fuck you, bitch!' Jamal said, swaggering toward her. 'I wouldn't let you suck my cock.'

'I'd rather gouge my eyes out with a rusty nail.' Liska advanced on him, blue glare boring into him like a pair of cold lasers. 'Keep it in your pants, Jamal. If you live long enough, maybe you'll find some nice guy in prison to do it for you.'

'He's not going to prison today,' Kovac announced impatiently. 'Let's wrap this up. I got a party to go to.'

Jackson made his move as Kovac started to turn for the door. He pulled one of the loose shelves out of the bookcase and rushed Kovac from behind. Caught back on his heels, Elwood shouted an obscenity and jumped too late. Kovac swung around in time to catch the corner of the shelf, the board slicing a gash above his left eyebrow.

'Shit!'

'Dammit!'

Kovac went down on his knees, his vision lacy with a spiderweb of black. The floor felt like rubber beneath him.

Elwood grabbed Jackson's wrists and jammed his arms upward, and the board went flying, a corner of it gouging the new wall.

Then Jackson screamed and went down suddenly, his left knee buckling beneath him. Halfway down he screamed again, back arching. Elwood jumped back, wide-eyed.

Liska rode Jackson down from behind, her knee in the middle of his back as his face hit the floor.

The door opened and half a dozen detectives stood with guns drawn. Liska raised a short black ASP tactical baton, looking surprised and innocent.

'Gosh, look what I found in my coat pocket!'

She leaned down over Jamal Jackson's ear and murmured seductively, 'Looks like I'll get to fulfill one of your wishes, Jamal. You're under arrest.'

'Looks kind of faggy.'

'Is that the voice of authority, Tippen?'

'Fuck you, Tinks.'

'Is that a no or wishful thinking?'

Laughter erupted around the table, the kind of raw, hard laughter that came from people who saw too much ugliness on a day-to-day basis. Cop humor was rude and biting because the world they lived in was a crude and savage place. They had no time or patience for Noel Coward repartee.

The group had snagged a coveted corner table at Patrick's, an Irish-named bar owned and run by Swedes. On an ordinary day the pub – strategically located equidistant between the Minneapolis Police Department and the Hennepin County Sheriff's Office – was packed belly to butt with cops this time of day. Day-shift cops gearing down and loading up for life off the job. Retired cops who'd found they couldn't socialize with regular humans once they'd left the job. Dog-watch guys grabbing dinner and camaraderie, killing time before they were up for their tour.

This was not an ordinary day. The usual crowd had been augmented by PD brass, city politicos, and newsies. Unwelcome additions that put an extra layer of tension in the air that was already blue with smoke and language. A news crew from one of the local stations was setting up near the front window.

'You should've insisted on real stitches. The old-fashioned kind,' Tippen went on.

He tapped the ash off his cigarette and raised it to his lips for a long drag, his attention narrowed on the camera crew. He had a face like an Irish wolfhound: long and homely with a bristly gray mustache and fiercely intelligent dark eyes. A detective with the Sheriff's Office, he had been a member of the task force that had worked the Cremator murders a little more than a year before. Some of the task force members had become the kind of friends who did this – met in a bar to drink and talk shop and insult one another.

'Then he ends up with a big ugly Frankenstein scar,' Liska said. 'With the butterfly clamp, he gets a neat, thin scar – the kind women find sexy.'

'Sadistic women,' Elwood commented.

Tippen curled his lip. 'Is there another kind?'

'Sure. The kind who go out with you,' Liska said. 'Masochists.'

Tippen flicked a corn chip at her.

Kovac regarded himself critically in the mirror of Liska's compact. The split in his forehead had been cleaned and patched by an overworked resident in the Hennepin County Medical Center ER, where gangbangers were regularly patched up or zipped into body bags. He'd been embarrassed to go there with anything less than a gunshot wound, and the young woman had given him the attitude that treating anything less was beneath her. Sexual attraction hadn't been a part of the picture.

He assessed the damage with a critical eye. His face was a quadrangle punctuated with stress lines, a couple of scars, and a hawkish, crooked nose that made a nice accompaniment to the crooked, sardonic mouth lurking beneath the requisite cop mustache. The hair was more gray than brown. Once a month he paid an old Norwegian barber ten bucks to cut it, which probably accounted for the fact that it tended to stand up.

He'd never been handsome in the *GQ* sense of the word, but he'd never sent women running either – at least not because of his looks. One more scar wasn't going to matter.

Liska studied him as she sipped her beer. 'It gives you character, Sam.'

'It gives me a headache,' he groused, handing the compact back to her. 'I already had all the character I needed.'

'Well, I'd kiss it and make it better for you. But I already kneecapped the guy who did it. I think I've done my part.'

'And you wonder why you're single,' Tippen remarked.

Liska blew him a kiss. 'Hey, love me, love my ASP. Or in your case, Tip, kiss my ASP.'

The front door swung open and a gust of cold air swept in, along with a new pack of patrons. Every cop's eye in the place went instantly flat, and the tension level cranked a notch. The cop collective guarding against outsiders.

'The man of the hour,' Elwood said, as recognition rippled through the crowd and a cheer went up. 'Come to hobnob with the unwashed masses before his ascension.'

Kovac said nothing. Ace Wyatt stood in the doorway in a double-breasted camel-hair topcoat, looking like Captain America, master of all he surveyed. Square jaw, white smile, groomed like a fucking game-show host. He probably tipped his hairstylist ten bucks and got a complimentary blowjob from the shampoo girl.

'Is he wearing makeup?' Tippen asked under his breath. 'I heard he gets his eyelashes dyed.'

'That's what happens when you go Hollywood,' Elwood said.

'I'd be willing to suffer the indignity,' Liska said sarcastically. 'Did you hear the kind of money he's getting for that show?'

Tippen took a long pull on his cigarette and exhaled. Kovac looked at Captain Ace Wyatt through the cloud. They'd worked on the same squad for a time. It seemed a hundred years ago. He'd just made the move from robbery to homicide. Wyatt was the top dog, already a legend, and angling to become a star on the brass side of things. He'd succeeded handsomely within the department, then branched out into television – maintaining his office as a CID captain and starring in a Minneapolis cross between *America's Most Wanted* and a motivational infomercial. The show, *Crime Time*, was going national.

'I hate that guy.'

He reached for the Jack he wasn't supposed to mix with his painkillers and tossed back what was left of it.

'Jealous?' Liska needled.

'Of what? Being a prick?'

'Don't sell yourself short, Kojak. You're as big a prick as any man here.'

Kovac made a growl at the back of his throat, suddenly wanting to be anywhere but here. Why in hell had he come? He had three parts of a concussion, and a perfect excuse to beg off and go home. So there was nothing to go home to – an empty house with an empty aquarium in the living room. The fish had all died of neglect while he'd pulled nearly seventy-two hours straight on the Cremator case. He hadn't bothered to replace them.

Sitting at a party for Ace Wyatt, he was as big a masochist as any woman Tippen had ever dated. He'd finished his drink. As soon as Wyatt's posse cleared the door, he could make his way through the crowd and slip out. Maybe go down to the bar where the Fifth Precinct cops hung out. They could give a shit about Ace Wyatt.

In the instant he made the decision, Wyatt spotted him and zeroed in with a blinding grin, a quartet of minions trailing after him. He wove through the crowd, touching hands and shoulders like the Pope giving cursory blessings.

'Kojak, you old warhorse!' he shouted above the din. He took hold of Sam's hand in a powerful grasp.

Kovac came up out of his chair, the floor seeming to shift beneath his feet. The aftereffects of his close encounter with the board, or the mix of drugs and booze. It sure as hell wasn't his thrill at Wyatt's attention. The asshole, calling him Kojak. He hated the nickname. People who knew him well mostly used it to grind him.

One of the minions came in close with a Polaroid and the flash damn near blinded him.

'One for the scrapbook,' the minion said, a thirty-something cover-boy type with shiny black hair and cobalt-blue eyes. He had the looks for a part in a low-end prime-time drama.

'I heard you took another one for the cause!' Wyatt bellowed, grinning. 'Jesus, quit while you're ahead. Quit while you still *have* a head!'

'Seven to go, Slick,' Kovac said. 'Hollywood's not beating my door down. Congratulations, by the way.'

'Thanks. Taking the show national is a chance to make a big difference.'

To the Ace Wyatt bank account, Kovac thought, but he didn't say it. What the hell. He'd never had a taste for designer suits or a weekly manicure. He was just a cop. That was all he'd ever wanted to be. Ace Wyatt had always set his sights on bigger, better, brighter, faster; reaching for the brass rings of life – and catching every goddamn one of them.

'Glad you could make it to the party, Sam.'

'Hey, I'm a cop. Free food, free booze – I'm there.'

Wyatt's gaze was already roaming for a more important hand to shake. The pretty-boy minion caught his attention and directed it toward the television camera. The Wyatt grin brightened by a couple hundred watts.

Liska popped up out of her chair like a jack-in-the-box and stuck her hand out before Wyatt could move on. 'Captain Wyatt. Nikki Liska, homicide. It's a pleasure. I enjoy your show.'

Kovac cocked a brow at her. 'My partner. Blond ambition.'

'You lucky old dog,' Wyatt said with good-natured chauvinism.

The muscles flexed in Liska's jaws as if she was swallowing something unpleasant. 'I think your idea of strengthening the link between communities and their police forces through the show and the Internet is a brilliant innovation.'

Wyatt soaked up the praise. 'America is a multimedia culture,' he said loudly, as the TV reporter – a brunette in a bright red blazer – edged in close with a microphone. Wyatt turned fully toward the camera, bending down to hear the woman's question.

Kovac looked to Liska with disapproval.

'Hey, maybe he'll give me a job as a technical consultant. I could be a technical consultant,' she said with a mischievous quirk to her lips. 'That could be my stepping-stone to working on Mel Gibson movies.'

'I'll be in the john.'

Kovac made his way through the mob that had come in to drink Ace Wyatt's booze and chow down on spicy chicken wings and deep-fried cheese. Half the people here had never met Wyatt, let alone worked with him, but they would gladly celebrate his retirement. They would have celebrated the devil's birthday for an open bar.

He stood at the back of the main room and surveyed the scene, made all the more surreal by the Christmas decorations reflecting the glare of the television lights. A sea of people – a lot of the faces familiar – yet he felt acutely alone. Empty. Time to get seriously hammered or leave.

Liska was hovering around Wyatt's people, trying to make nice with the main minion. Wyatt had moved to shake the hand of an attractive, serious-looking blonde who seemed vaguely familiar. He put his left hand on her shoulder and bent to say something in her ear. Elwood was cutting a swath through the buffet. Tippen was trying to flirt with a waitress who was looking at him as if she'd just stepped in something.

It'd be last call before they missed him. And then missing him would be just a fleeting thought.

Where's Kovac? Gone? Pass the beer nuts.

He started for the door.

'You were the best fuckin' badge on the job!' a drunken voice bellowed. 'The man who don't think so can talk to me! Come on! Come on! I'd give Ace Wyatt my goddamn legs!' he shouted.

The drunk sat in a wheelchair that teetered on the top of three shallow steps leading down to the main bar, where Wyatt stood. The drunk had no legs to give. His had been useless for twenty years. There was nothing left of them but spindly bone and atrophied muscle. In contrast, his face was full and red, his upper body a barrel.

Kovac shook his head and took a step toward the wheelchair, trying to catch the old man's attention.

'Hey, Mikey! No one's arguing,' he said.

Mike Fallon looked at him without recognition, his eyes glassy with tears. 'He's a fucking hero! Don't try to say different!' he said angrily. He swung an arm in Wyatt's direction. 'I love that man! I love that man like a son!'

The old man's voice broke on the last word, his face contorting with an inner pain that had nothing to do with the amount of Old Crow he'd put away in the past few hours.

Wyatt lost his glamour grin and started toward Mike Fallon just as Fallon's left hand landed on the wheel of his chair. Kovac leapt forward, crashing into another drunk.

The chair pitched down the steps and spilled its occupant. Mike Fallon hit the floor like a sack of potatoes.

Kovac pushed the drunk aside and hustled down the steps. The crowd had cleared back in surprise. Wyatt stood frozen ten feet away, frowning as he stared down at Mike Fallon.

Kovac dropped down to one knee. 'Hey, Mikey, let's get you off your face. You've got it confused with your ass again.'

Someone righted the wheelchair. The old man rolled over onto his back and made a pathetic attempt to sit up, flopping on the floor like a beached seal, tears pouring down the sides of his face. A guy Kovac knew from robbery took one side while Kovac took the other, and together they hoisted Fallon back into his chair.

The people standing nearby turned away, embarrassed for the old man. Fallon hung his head in abject humiliation – a sight Kovac had never wished to see.

He'd known Mike Fallon since day one on the job. Back then, every patrol cop in Minneapolis had known Iron Mike. They had followed his example and his orders. And a good lot of them had cried like babies when Mike Fallon was gunned down. But to see him like this – broken in every way – was a heartbreak.

Kovac knelt beside the wheelchair and put a hand on Fallon's shoulder. 'Come on, Mike. Let's call it a night, huh? I'll drive you home.'

'You all right, Mike?' Ace Wyatt asked woodenly, stepping up at last.

Fallon held a shaking hand out to him but couldn't bring himself to look up, even when Wyatt took hold. His voice was tight and raw. 'I love you like a brother, Ace. Like a son. More. You know, I can't say —'

'You don't have to say, Mike. Don't.'

'I'm sorry. I'm sorry,' the old man mumbled over and over, bringing his other hand up to cover his face. Snot ran in an elastic string from his nose to his lap. He had wet his pants.

In his peripheral vision, Kovac could see the newsies creeping in like vultures.

'I'll see he gets home,' he said to Wyatt as he rose.

Wyatt stared down at Mike Fallon. 'Thanks, Sam,' he murmured. 'You're a good man.'

'I'm a fucking sap. But what else have I got to do with my time?'

The blond had vanished, but the brunette from TV sidled up to Wyatt again. 'Is this Mike Fallon? Officer Fallon from the Thorne murder back in the seventies?'

The black-haired minion appeared like the devil's familiar and pried the woman away with a serious something whispered in her ear.

Wyatt collected himself and turned away, waving off the reporters with a look of disapproval. 'Just a little accident, folks. Let's move on.'

Kovac looked down at the man sobbing in the wheelchair.

Let's move on.

2

'Yeah, this is why I hired a sitter tonight,' Liska said. 'So I could cart a drunk home. I got enough of that when I was a uniform.'

'Quit bitching,' Kovac ordered. 'You could have said no, *partner.*'

'Sure. And look bad in front of Mr Community Service. I just hope he took note of my selflessness and remembers when I hit him up for a job on his program,' she said, teasing.

'Looked to me like you were trying to hit up the assistant for something else.'

Liska reached across and slugged his arm, trying not to laugh. 'I was not! What do you take me for?'

'What would *he* take you for? There's the real question.'

'He wouldn't.'

'He didn't. There's a difference.'

Liska pretended to pout. 'He's obviously gay.'

'Obviously.'

They drove in silence for a few blocks as the windshield wipers swiped at the snow coming down. Mike Fallon was propped up in a corner of the backseat, smelling of urine, snoring.

'You worked with him, huh?' Liska said, nodding to their passenger.

'Everybody worked with Iron Mike when I came on. He was the original warhorse. Always above and beyond the call. 'Cause it was right, he'd say. That's what being a cop is supposed to be about. And he's the one takes a slug in the spine. It's never some lazy shit just putting in his hours till the pension comes.'

'There's no such thing as fair.'

'There's a news flash. At least he nailed the mutt who shot him.'

'That was the Thorne murder.'

'You remember it?'

'I was a child at the time, Methuselah.'

'Twenty years ago?' he scoffed. 'You were probably busy making out with the captain of the football team.'

'Wide receiver,' she countered. 'And let me tell you, they didn't call him Hands for nothing.'

'Jeez,' Kovac grumbled, the corner of his mouth twitching against a chuckle. 'Tinks, you're something else.'

'Someone has to break your moods. You're too content to wallow in them.'

'Look who's talking –'

'So what was the story with Thorne?'

'Bill Thorne was a cop. Rode patrol for years. I didn't know him. I was new on the job at the time. He lived in a neighborhood over by the old West High School, where a bunch of cops lived back then. So Mike's patrolling the neighborhood, sees something doesn't look right at Thorne's place. He calls it in, then goes up to the house himself.'

'He should have waited for backup.'

'Yeah, he should have. Major mistake. But Thorne's car was there. It was a neighborhood full of cops. Anyway, there was a handyman who'd been working in the neighborhood. A drifter. Thorne had tried to run him off a couple of times, but the wife felt sorry for him and paid him to wash windows. Turned out Thorne was right – the guy was bad news. He broke into the house and raped the wife.

'Thorne had been scheduled to work that night, but he stopped back at the house for something. The mutt had found a gun and he used it on Thorne. Killed him.

'Then Mike showed up and went in. The bad guy shot. Mike shot back. Nailed the guy, but he went down. Ace Wyatt lived across the street at the time. At some point Thorne's wife called him, hysterical. He kept Mike alive until the ambulance got there.'

'That explains tonight.'

'Yeah,' Kovac said, pensive again. 'Part of it, anyway.'

There was a lot of story between Iron Mike Fallon, fallen hero, and old Mike Fallon, pathetic alcoholic. The profession was too full of sad stories and sadder drunks.

The one in the backseat tipped over and puked on the floor as Kovac pulled up in front of Fallon's house.

Kovac groaned and hit his forehead on the steering wheel.

Liska opened her door and looked at him. 'No good deed goes unpunished. I'm not cleaning that up, *partner.*'

From the outside, the house was small and tidy in a neighborhood of small, tidy houses. Inside was a different story. Fallon's wife had died years before. Cancer. He lived here alone. The place smelled of old man and fried onions.

The rooms were spare, the furnishings kept to a minimum to make way for Mike's wheelchair. An odd mix of worn junk and state-of-the-art. A high-end massage recliner sat front and center in the living room, pointed at a thirty-one-inch color television. The couch was a relic from the seventies. The dining room looked as if it hadn't been used in two decades, and was probably exactly as Mrs Fallon had left it, with the exception of the booze bottles on the table.

Twin beds nearly filled the little bedroom – one stacked with piles of clothes, the other a tangle of sheets. Dirty laundry had been thrown in the general vicinity of an overflowing hamper. A bottle of Maker's Mark bourbon sat on the nightstand beside a jelly-jar glass sporting the likeness of Barney the Dinosaur. On the other end of the room, the dead wife's dresser was lined with family photos, half a dozen of them turned facedown.

'I'm sorry. I'm so sorry,' Mike muttered as Kovac went about the job of putting him in bed.

Liska found a laundry basket and took the discarded clothes away, nose wrinkled, but not complaining.

'Forget it, Mike. It's nothing we all haven't done once in a while,' Kovac said.

'Christ, I pissed myself.'

'Don't worry about it.'

'I'm sorry. Where ya workin', Sam?'

'Homicide.'

Fallon gave a weak, derisive, drunken laugh. 'Fuckin' big shot. Too good for a uniform.'

Kovac heaved a sigh and straightened, his gaze landing on the photographs across the room. Fallon had two sons. The younger – Andy – was a cop. He'd worked robbery for a while. His were the photos turned down on the dresser, Kovac discovered as he turned them up.

Good-looking kid. Athletic, handsome. There was a shot of him in a baseball uniform. He was built like a shortstop: compact, cat-like. Another photo showed him in his police uniform, graduating from the academy. Mike Fallon's pride and joy, carrying on the family tradition.

'How's Andy doing?'

'He's dead,' Fallon mumbled.

Kovac turned abruptly. 'What?'

Fallon turned his face away. He looked frail in the lamplight, his skin as pale and wrinkled as old parchment. 'He's dead to me,' he said softly. Then he closed his eyes and passed out.

The sadness and finality of Mike Fallon's words haunted Kovac all the way back to Patrick's, where he left Liska to catch the last of the party. He dropped her at the curb and drove on through empty side streets filling with snow, away from downtown to his own slightly shabby neighborhood.

Old trees dominated the boulevard, their roots buckling the sidewalks like an LA freeway after an earthquake. The houses were crammed shoulder to shoulder, some big and square and cut up into apartments, some smaller. One side of the street was lined with a motley assortment of cars, the other side clear for snow removal.

The house just east of Kovac's was decorated for Christmas to within an inch of its life. It appeared to sag beneath the burden of colored lights. A plastic Santa and reindeer were mounted on the roof. Another Santa was crawling down the chimney. A third stood on the lawn, contemplating the others, while two feet away the wise men were about to visit the Christ child in a manger. The entire yard was spotlit.

Kovac trudged up the sidewalk to his house and went inside, not bothering to turn on lights. Plenty spilled in from next door. His home was not so different from Mike Fallon's in that it was short on furniture. The last divorce had left him with the castoffs, which he had never bothered to replace or add to. He was himself a castoff, so it seemed only fitting. His biggest indulgence in the last five years had been the aquarium. A sorry attempt to bring other living creatures into his home.

There were no photographs of children or family. Two failed marriages seemed nothing to brag about. He had a lot of bad memories and a daughter he hadn't seen since her infancy. She was dead to him in a way, he supposed. But it was more as if she had never existed. After the divorce, her mother had remarried with embarrassing haste, and the new family had moved to Seattle. Kovac hadn't watched his daughter grow up or play sports or follow him into law enforcement. He had trained himself not to think about the lost opportunities . . . most of the time.

He went upstairs to his bedroom, but the bed didn't interest him. His head was throbbing. He sat down in the chair by the window and looked out at the garish light show next door.

He's dead to me, Mike Fallon had said about his son.

What would prompt a man to say such a thing about a child who had clearly been the pride of his life? Why would he cut that tie when he had so little else?

Kovac dug his Nicorette gum out of his pocket and tossed it in the wastebasket, reached into the nightstand drawer for a half-empty pack of Salems, and lit one up.

Who was gonna tell him not to?

3

The photograph has a fake quality to it. Most people would have glanced at it, felt an immediate burst of horror, then quickly decided it was some kind of sick joke.

The photographer is not most people.

As the artist considers the portrait, there is an initial sense of shock, but what follows immediately on its heels is a strange, complicated mix of emotions: horror, fascination, relief, guilt. And beneath that layer, another darker dimension of feeling: a certain sense of excitement . . . a sense of control . . . a sense of power. Feelings that are frightening, sickening.

There is tremendous power in taking a life. To take a life: the phrase implies to take the energy of another living creature and add it to one's own life force. The idea is seductive in a sinister way. Addictive to a certain type of individual: the kind who kills for sport.

I'm not that. I could never be that.

Even as the pledge is made, memories of another death flash frame by frame through the memory: violence, movement, blood, white noise roaring in the ears, a deafening internal scream that can't be heard. Then silence and the stillness, and the terrible realization: *I did that.*

And the sense of excitement . . . and power . . .

The dark feelings move through the soul like a snake, sinuous and shiny. The conscience shudders in its wake. Fear rises like a flood tide.

The photographer stares at the captured image of a corpse dancing on the end of a rope, the image reflected in a mirror, the mirror scrawled with the single word. *Sorry.*

So sorry.

4

'Andy Fallon is dead.'

Liska met Kovac with the news at the door into the CID offices.

The breath went out of him. 'What?'

'Andy Fallon is dead. A friend found him this morning. It looks like suicide.'

'Jesus,' Kovac muttered, feeling as disoriented as he had this morning when he'd rolled out of bed too fast for his throbbing head. In the back of his mind he saw Mike Fallon, frail and white; heard him say the words. *He's dead to me.* 'Jesus.'

Liska stared up at him, expectant.

He shook himself mentally. 'Who's up?'

'Springer and Copeland,' she said, glancing sideways for eavesdroppers. '*Were* up. Past tense. I figured you'd want it, so I grabbed it.'

'I don't know if I should thank you or wish your parents had practiced better birth control,' Kovac grumbled, heading toward their cubicle.

'Did you know Andy?'

'No. Not really. I met him a couple of times. Suicide. Man, I don't want to be the one to tell Mike.'

'You'd rather some uniform do it? Or someone from the ME's office?' Liska said with disapproval.

Kovac blew out a breath and closed his eyes for a second as the burden settled on his shoulders. 'No.'

Fate had tied him to Iron Mike years ago, and again last night. The least he could do was maintain some continuity for the old man. Let the news come from a familiar face.

'Don't you think we should jump on it?' Liska said, glancing around for Copeland and Springer. 'Try to keep a lid on things. Andy being on the job and all.'

'Yeah,' Kovac said, glancing at the blinking light on his phone. 'Let's blow this joint before Leonard saddles us with another "murder of tomorrow".'

Andy Fallon lived in a one-and-a-half-story house just north of the trendy district known as Uptown. Home to the upwardly mobile and the stylishly hip, Uptown was, in fact, south of downtown, which had never made any sense to Kovac. 'Uptown' in the sense of being too chic for the likes of him, he supposed. The business center was an area of reclamations and renovations – coffee bars, yuppie restaurants, and art house movie theaters. Homes on the west side, near Lake of the Isles and Lake Calhoun, went for a premium. Fallon's was just far enough north and east to be affordable on a single cop's salary.

Two radio cars sat at the curb out front. Liska marched ahead up the sidewalk, always eager for a new case. Kovac trailed behind, dreading this one.

'Wait'll you get a load of this,' said the uniform who met them at the door. 'It's one for the scrapbook.'

His tone was almost snide. He'd been at it too long, had grown numb to the sight of dead people to the point where they were no longer people to him – they were bodies. All cops got that way or they got off the street before they could lose their minds. Death simply couldn't affect them in a personal way every time they encountered it. Kovac knew he was surely no exception. But this time would be different. It already was.

Liska gave the cop the flat look all detectives mastered early on in their career. 'Where's the body?'

'Bedroom. Upstairs.'

'Who found him?'

'A "friend",' the uniform said, again with the snide tone, making the quotation marks with his fingers. 'He's in the kitchen, crying.'

Kovac looked at the name tag, leaning in, crowding him. 'Burgess?'

'Yeah,' he said, visibly resisting the urge to step back.

Liska scribbled his name and badge number in her notebook.

'You were first on the scene?' Kovac said.

'Yeah.'

'You used that mouth to talk to the guy found the body?'

Burgess frowned, suspicious. 'Yeah . . .'

Kovac took another small step into the cop's space. 'Burgess, are you always such a fucking asshole or is today special?'

The cop colored, his features growing taut.

'Keep the mouth in check,' Kovac ordered. 'The vic was a cop, and so's his old man. Show some respect.'

Burgess pressed his lips together and took a step back, eyes cold. 'Yes, sir.'

'I don't want anyone coming in here unless they've got a badge or they're from the ME. Got that?'

'Yes, sir.'

'And I want a log of every name, badge number, and the time they walk in the door and walk back out. Can you manage that?'

'Yes. Sir.'

'Ooh, he didn't like that,' Liska whispered gleefully as they left Burgess at the door and headed toward the back of the house.

'Yeah? Fuck him.' Kovac glanced down at her. 'Andy Fallon was queer?'

'Gay,' she corrected. 'How would I know? I don't hang out with IA rats. What do you take me for?'

'You really want to know?' Kovac asked, then, 'He worked IA? No wonder Mike said the kid was dead to him.'

The kitchen was hunter green with pristine white woodwork and had everything in its place. It was the kitchen of someone who knew how to do more than run the microwave – commercial range, pots hanging from the iron rack above a granite-topped island loaded with big-ass knives in a wood block.

On the far side of the room, at a round table nestled into a bay window, sat the 'friend', head in hands. A good-looking guy in a dark suit. Red hair, stylishly cut. A rectangular face full of sharp angles and freckles. The freckles stood out against skin washed ashen by stress and by the cold gray light spilling in the windows. He barely glanced up as they walked into the room.

Liska flashed her ID and introduced them. 'We understand you found the body, Mr –'

'Pierce,' he said hoarsely, and sniffed. 'Steve Pierce. Yes. I . . . found him.'

'We know this is terribly upsetting for you, Mr Pierce, but we'll need to talk to you when we finish. Do you understand?'

'No,' he said, shaking his head. 'I don't understand any of this. I can't believe it. I just can't believe it.'

'We're sorry for your loss,' Liska said automatically.

'He wouldn't do this,' he mumbled, staring at the tabletop. 'He wouldn't do this. It's just not possible.'

Kovac said nothing. A sense of dread built in his chest as they climbed the stairs.

'I've got a bad feeling about this, Tinks,' he muttered, pulling on latex gloves. 'Or maybe I'm having a heart attack. That'd be my luck. I finally quit smoking and I have a heart attack.'

'Well, don't die at the scene,' Liska said. 'The paperwork would be a big pain in the ass.'

'You're full of sympathy.'

'Better than what you're full of. You're not having a heart attack.'

The second floor of the house had probably been open attic space at one time, but had been nicely converted to a master suite. Joist beams had been left exposed, creating a loft effect. A lovely, private place to die, Kovac thought, taking in the scene at a glance.

The body hung from a traditional rope noose just a few feet beyond the four-poster bed. The rope looped over a ceiling beam and was tied off somewhere at the head of the bed frame, that end of it hidden by the bedding. The bed was neatly made, hadn't been slept in or even sat upon. Kovac noted these things in the back of his mind, his concentration on the victim. He flashed on the photographs he'd turned over on the dresser in Mike Fallon's bedroom the night before: the handsome young man, the star athlete, the fresh-faced new cop with Mike beaming proudly beside him. He could see that same academy graduation photograph sitting on Andy Fallon's dresser. *Good-looking kid,* he remembered thinking.

Now the handsome face was discolored, distorted, purple and bloated, the mouth frozen in a kind of sneer. The eyes were half-open and cloudy. He'd been there a while. A day or so, Kovac guessed from the apparent lack of rigor, the tautness of the skin, the smell. The sickly sweet aroma of beginning decay commingled with stale urine and feces. In death, the muscles had relaxed, bladder and bowel discharging on the floor.

The body was nude. His arms hung at his sides, hands curled into fists held slightly forward of the hips. Dark spots dotted the knuckles – lividity, the blood settling in the lowest levels of the extremities. The feet, no more than a few inches off the floor, were swollen and deep purple as well.

Kovac squatted down, took hold of an ankle, and pressed his thumb against the flesh for a moment, then let go. He watched for the skin to blanch, but nothing happened. The blood had clotted long before. The leg was cold to the touch.

An oak-framed full-length mirror was propped against the wall some ten feet in front of the corpse. The body was reflected fully, the reflection distorted by the angle of the mirror. The word *Sorry* had been written on the glass with something dark.

'I always figured these IA guys for kinky.'

Kovac looked to the two uniforms standing ten feet away, smirking at the mirror. The cops were a pair of buzz-cut no-necks, the bigger one having a head as square as a concrete block. Their name tags read 'Rubel' and 'Ogden'.

'Hey, Dumb and Dumber,' Kovac snapped. 'Get the hell outta my death scene. What the fuck's the matter with you? Tromping all over the place.'

'It's a suicide,' the uglier one said, as if that mattered.

Kovac felt his face flush. 'Don't tell me what's what, Moose. You don't know dick. Maybe in twenty years you'll have a right to an opinion. Now get the fuck outta here. Go downstairs and secure the zone. I don't want anyone coming closer than the street. And keep your big fat yaps shut. Where there's a corpse, there's newsies. I read one word about this,' he said, pointing to the reflection in the mirror, 'I'll know who gets reamed new ones. You got me?'

The officers glanced at each other sullenly, then headed for the stairs.

'IA rat offs himself,' the ugly one said under his breath. 'So what's the crime? Looks like a service to everyone, you ask me.'

Kovac stared at the body. He could see Liska snooping around, making notes of every detail, sketching the room, the placement of the furniture and of anything that might be deemed significant. They took turns at that job – keeping the notes at the scene. It was his turn to shoot the preliminary Polaroids.

He started with the room itself, then slowly moved in on the body, photographing it from all angles. Each flash burned an imprint on his memory – the dead thing that had been Mike Fallon's son; the beam from which the noose hung; the Reebok exercise steps that sat just behind the body, near enough to have been what Andy Fallon had used for his big dismount into the hereafter; the mirror. *Sorry.*

Sorry. Yes, it was.

Had Andy Fallon been sorry? About what? Or had someone else scrawled the word?

The furnace blower kicked on, and the corpse began to twist slightly like a giant rotting piñata. The reflection in the mirror was a macabre dance partner.

'I never understand people who get naked to commit suicide,' Liska said.

'It's symbolic. Shedding their earthly skin.'

'Nobody is finding me naked.'

'Maybe he didn't commit suicide,' Kovac said.

'You think someone could have done this to him? Or forced him to do it? Murder by hanging is rare.'

'What's with the mirror?' Kovac asked, though it wasn't a question to him.

Liska studied the naked corpse for a moment, then looked to the mirror, catching a slice of her own reflection with that of Andy Fallon.

'Oh, man,' she said quietly. 'Autoerotic misadventure? I've never had one before.'

Kovac said nothing, trying to imagine what he would tell Mike. Bad enough to have to explain autoerotic asphyxiation to strangers, which he had done a couple of times in his career. But how did you tell a tough, hard-line, old-time cop that his son had been trying to get himself off by cutting off his oxygen supply, and had strangled himself in the process?

'But why the message?' Liska wondered aloud. '*Sorry* says suicide to me. Why would he write that if he was doing this just to get off?'

Kovac touched a hand to the top of his throbbing head and winced. 'You know, some days it just doesn't pay to get out of bed.'

'Yeah, well . . . Here's your option,' Liska said, nodding to the body. 'Doesn't look too sweet to me. I always figure a bad day living beats any day dead.'

'Fuck me,' Kovac muttered.

Liska squatted down in front of the mirror to examine the letters more closely. She looked at Kovac's reflection. 'Not in front of a corpse. I'm not that kind of girl.'

'You know what I mean.'

'I do.' She rose slowly, dropped the act, and touched his arm, looking up at him with earnest blue eyes. 'I'm sorry, Sam. Like ol' Iron Mike doesn't have it bad enough.'

Kovac stared at his partner for a moment, stared at the small hand on his coat sleeve and briefly considered taking hold of it. Just for the comfort of contact with another human. She wore no rings – so as not to confuse potential suitors, she said. Her fingernails were short and unpolished.

'Yeah,' he whispered.

Below them there was a shout, then a sudden loud crash, followed by more shouting. Liska ran down the stairs like a mountain goat. Kovac pounded down behind her.

Rubel was trying to haul Steve Pierce off Ogden's prone body. 'Off him!' Rubel shouted.

In a rage, Pierce shrugged him off and took a swing at Ogden, connecting, by the sound of the thump and the grunt. Rubel grabbed Pierce again, hooking a thick arm around his throat and dragging him up and back, screaming in his ear.

'I said, off him!'

Ogden, scrambling to get his legs under himself, slipped on the polished wood. Shards of broken glass and china crunched beneath his thick cop brogues. He grabbed the edge of the china cabinet they had crashed into and hauled himself up, rattling everything left in it. His face was mottled and his nose was bleeding. He swiped a hand under it, eyes widening in disbelief. He had to have forty pounds on Steve Pierce.

'You're under arrest, asshole!' he yelled, pointing a bloody finger at Pierce.

'Let him go!' Liska shouted at Rubel.

Pierce's face had gone purple above the choke hold. Rubel released him and Pierce dropped to his knees, wheezing. He gasped and looked up at Ogden with venom in his eyes. 'You son of a bitch!'

'Nobody's under arrest,' Kovac declared, stepping between them.

'I want them out of here!' Pierce demanded hoarsely, fighting his way to his feet. His eyes gleamed with tears and fury. 'Get them out of here!'

'You –' Ogden started.

Kovac hit him in the chest with the heel of his hand. It was like slapping a slab of granite. 'Shut up! Outta here!'

Rubel stalked past and Ogden fell in step, fuming. Kovac dogged their heels into the living room.

'What the hell did you say to him?'

'Nothing,' Rubel returned.

'I was talking to the other ox. You said something stupid, didn't you? Christ, what a question! I might as well ask if shit is brown,' Kovac said with disgust.

'He attacked me,' Ogden said indignantly. 'He assaulted an officer.'

'Yeah?' Kovac said tightly, getting in his face. 'You want to go there, Ogden? You want to make a report detailing this little fiasco? You want Mr Pierce there to give a statement? You want your supervisor reading what a dickhead you are?'

Sulking, the officer pulled a dingy handkerchief out of his pocket and dabbed it under his nose.

'You're gonna be lucky he doesn't call the citizens' commission and sue the department,' Kovac said. 'Now get outta here and go do your jobs.'

Rubel led the way out the front door, jaw set, eyes narrow. Ogden hustled up alongside him to the street, bloody rag held to his nose with one hand, the other gesticulating as he tried to impress something on his partner, who didn't want to hear.

The crime scene van pulled up behind the radio car at the curb. A pair of shitty compacts swarmed in from opposite directions like buzzards. Newsies. Kovac felt his lip start to curl. He stepped back into the house, catching Burgess reaching for a stack of videocassettes on a shelf beside the television.

'Don't touch anything!' Kovac snapped. 'Get out on the lawn and keep the reporters away. "No comment" – do you think you can manage that, or is it too many syllables?'

Burgess ducked his head.

'And I want every license plate on the block noted and run. Got that?'

'Yessir,' the cop said through his teeth as he went out.

'Where do they get these guys?' Kovac asked as he went back to the kitchen.

'They breed them up north as pack animals,' Liska said, meeting him at the archway into the room. 'Ogden made a crack about one less fag. Pierce lost it. Who can blame him?'

'Great,' Kovac muttered. 'Let's hope he doesn't decide to get vocal about it. Bad enough Andy Fallon's dead. We don't need to broadcast to the whole metropolitan area which way his willy waggled.'

The crime scene team came through then, toting their cases and cameras. The scene would be photographed again and videotaped. The area of the death scene would be dusted for prints. If there was any evidence to gather, it would be photographed, its exact position measured and noted; it would be logged and marked and packaged with great care taken to establish the chain of custody so that its every moment could be accounted for. And all the while Andy Fallon's body would hang there, waiting for the arrival of the ME's people.

Kovac briefed the senior criminalist and directed them upstairs.

Liska had herded Steve Pierce back to the kitchen table. He sat like a man who wanted to pace, one hand rubbing his throat. Ogden's blood stained his knuckles. He had pulled his tie loose and undone his collar. The black suit was limp and rumpled.

'Mind if we sit down, Steve?' Kovac asked.

Pierce made no reply. They sat anyway. Kovac produced a microcassette recorder from his pocket, turned it on, and placed it on the table.

'We'll make a recording of our conversation here, Steve,' he explained casually. 'So that we're sure we've got all the details straight when we get back to the station to write our reports. Is that all right with you?'

Pierce nodded wearily, dragging a hand back through his hair.

'I'll need you to answer out loud, Steve.'

'Yes. Sure. Fine.' He tried to clear his throat. Distress etched lines beside his mouth. 'Will they . . . take him down now?' he asked, his voice closing off on the last words.

'The medical examiner's people will do that,' Liska explained.

He looked at her as if it had only just dawned on him there would have to be an autopsy. His eyes filled again and he looked out the window at the snow in the backyard, trying to compose himself.

'What do you do for a living, Steve?' Kovac asked.

'Investments. I'm with Daring-Landis.'

'Do you live here? In this house?'

'No.'

'What brought you here this morning?'

'Andy was supposed to meet me for coffee at the Uptown Caribou yesterday. He wanted to talk to me about something. He didn't show. He didn't answer my calls. I was concerned so I came by.'

'What was your relationship with Andy Fallon?'

'We're friends,' he said. Present tense. 'From college. Buddies. You know.'

'Suppose you tell us,' Kovac said. 'What kind of buddies?'

Pierce's brow creased. 'You know, out for beer and pizza, the occasional basketball game. Get together for *Monday Night Football.* Guy stuff.'

'Nothing more . . . intimate?'

Kovac watched his face carefully. Pierce colored from the collar up.

'What are you suggesting, Detective?'

'I'm asking if the two of you had a sexual relationship,' Kovac said with calm bluntness.

Pierce looked as if his head might burst. 'I'm straight. Not that it's any of your business.'

'There's a dead body upstairs,' Kovac said. 'That makes everything my business. What about Mr Fallon?'

'Andy's gay,' Pierce said, resentment bitter in his eyes. 'Does that make it all right that he's dead?'

Kovac spread his hands. 'Hey, I don't care who plugs what in where. I just need a frame of reference for my investigation.'

'You have a real way with words, Detective.'

'You said Andy wanted to talk something over with you,' Liska prompted, diverting his attention to her. Allowing Kovac to watch every facial tic. 'Do you know what?'

'No. He didn't say.'

'When did you last speak with him?' Kovac asked.

Pierce cut him a sideways look, the resentment lingering.

'Um, Friday, I guess it was. My fiancée was busy that night so I swung by to see Andy. We hadn't seen much of each other lately. I came by to suggest we get together for coffee or something. Catch up.'

'So the two of you were supposed to meet yesterday, but Andy was a no-show.'

'I called a couple of times, got the machine. He never called back. I decided to swing by. See if everything was all right.'

'Why wouldn't you just think he was busy? Maybe he had to go to work early.'

Pierce glared at him. 'Pardon me for being concerned about my friends. I guess I should just be an asshole like you. I could be at my desk now. I could have saved myself the trouble of seeing –'

He cut himself off as the image rose in his memory again. His face was still red but with a waxy sheen to it now as he looked out the window, as if the sight of the snow, white and serene, might cool and soothe him.

'How'd you get into the house?' Kovac asked. 'You have a key?'

'The door wasn't locked.'

'Had he talked about suicide? Had he seemed depressed?' Liska asked.

'He had seemed . . . frustrated. A little down, yes, but not to the point that he'd kill himself. I just won't believe that. He wouldn't have done something like that without trying to reach out to someone first.'

That was what the survivors always wanted to think at first. Kovac knew from experience. They always wanted to believe the loved one would have asked for help before taking that fatal step. They never wanted to think they might have missed a sign. If it turned out Andy Fallon *had* committed suicide, at some point Steve Pierce would start wondering if there hadn't been a dozen signs and he'd missed them all because he was selfish or scared or blind.

'Down about what?'

Pierce made a helpless gesture. 'I don't know. Work. Or maybe his family. I know there'd been some strain between him and his dad.'

'What about other relationships?' Liska asked. 'Was he involved with anyone?'

'No.'

'How can you be sure?' Kovac asked. 'You weren't living here. You weren't seeing each other. You just got together for the occasional cup o' joe.'

'We were friends.'

'Yet you don't really know what was bothering him. You don't really know how depressed he might have been.'

'I knew Andy. He would *not* have killed himself,' Pierce insisted, his patience wearing thin.

'Aside from the door being unlocked,' Liska said, 'did anything seem to be missing or out of place?'

'Not that I noticed. I wasn't looking, though. I came to find Andy.'

'Steve, did you ever know Andy to practice any unusual sexual rituals?' Kovac asked.

Pierce shot up out of his chair, sending it skidding backward. 'You people are *unbelievable!*' He jerked around as if scanning the kitchen for a witness or a weapon.

Kovac remembered the knives on the island and the rage in Pierce's face as he'd pounded Ogden. He got up and put himself between Pierce and the knife block.

'This isn't personal, Steve. It's our job,' he said. 'We need the clearest picture we can get.'

'You're a bunch of fucking sadists!' Pierce shouted. 'My friend is *dead* and –'

'And I didn't know him from Adam,' Kovac said reasonably. 'And I don't know *you* from Adam. For all I know, you might have killed him yourself.'

'That's absurd!'

'And you know what?' Kovac went on. 'I find a dead guy hanging naked, watching himself in a mirror . . . Call me a prude, but that strikes me odd. You know, I gotta think maybe this guy was into something a little out of the ordinary. But maybe you're into that too. Maybe you don't bat an eye at shit like that. What do I know? Maybe you choke yourself to get off every other day. Maybe you play spank the monkey with a cattle prod. If you do, if you and Fallon were involved in something like that together, you're better off telling us now, Steve.'

Pierce was crying now, tears streaming, the muscles in his face straining as if he was fighting to hold in all the raw emotions ripping through him. 'No.'

'No, you weren't involved in that kind of thing, or no, you won't tell us?' Kovac prodded.

Pierce closed his eyes and hung his head. 'God, I can't believe this is happening.' The burden of it all suddenly too much, he sank down to the floor on his knees and curled forward, his head in his hands. 'Why is this happening?'

Kovac watched him, a feeling of weary, familiar remorse coming over him. He squatted down beside Steve Pierce and put a hand on his shoulder.

'That's what we want to find out, Steve,' he said softly. 'You may not always like the way we do it. And you may not like what we find. But in the end, that's all we want – the truth.'

Even as he said it, Kovac knew that when they found the truth, no one was going to want it. There simply wasn't going to be a good reason for Andy Fallon to be dead.

5

Mike Fallon's house looked somehow more alone in the cold gray light of day. Night had a way of enveloping a neighborhood; homes seemed to huddle together like a flock with only slips of velvet darkness between them. By day, they were separated and isolated by light and driveways and fences and snow.

Kovac looked up at the house and wondered if Mike already knew. People sometimes did. As if a shock wave had somehow rippled out from the death scene, reaching them faster than the speed of sound, or the speed of the messenger.

He's dead to me.

He doubted Mike Fallon would remember saying those words, but they still rang in Kovac's ears as he sat alone in the car. He had dropped Liska at the station to get a running start on the investigation. She would contact Andy Fallon's IA supervisor to find out what he'd been working on, what his attitude had been lately. She would get his jacket sent up from personnel, find out if he'd been making any use of the department shrink.

Kovac would've traded places with her in a heartbeat, except the sense of obligation was too strong. He cursed himself for a sap and got out of the car. Some days life just sucked when you were a decent human being.

He peered into the house through a narrow, rectangular window in the front door. The living room seemed shabbier than it had the night before. The walls needed paint. The sofa should have seen the back door of Goodwill years ago. A strange contrast to the massage chair and big-screen TV.

He rang the doorbell and knocked for good measure, then waited, impatient, trying not to wonder what a stranger would think of *his* living room with the empty fish tank. Someday he'd have to get around to getting a life outside the job.

His hands fidgeted at his coat pockets. He dug out a stick of Juicy Fruit, his nerves quivering at the base of his neck like ants just beneath his skin. He knocked again. Flashes of last night popped in his memory – Mike Fallon, the old cop, broken, discarded, depressed, drunk. . . . There was no sign of life within the house. No motion. No sound.

Sinking in snow halfway up his shins, he went around to the side of the house, looking for a bedroom window. Wouldn't that be a story for the six o'clock news? Father-son cop suicides. Paul Harvey would probably pick that one up to depress all of America over lunch tomorrow. Pointless death over chicken salad and Big Macs.

He found a ladder in the tiny garage that was bursting at the seams with the usual life's accumulation of barely used junk. A nearly new Subaru Outback tricked out for a handicapped driver took up most of the space. Some other cop must have returned it from Patrick's back lot after the party, or someone else had taken Mike to the bar, then melted into the woodwork when the trouble started. Someone who didn't want a drunk puking in his backseat.

The shade was up on Mike Fallon's bedroom window. Mike lay on his back on the bed, arms flung out, head turned to one side, mouth hanging open like a busted gate. Kovac held his breath and looked for some sign of Fallon's heart beating beneath his thin T-shirt.

'Hey, Mikey!' he shouted, knocking on the window.

Fallon didn't flinch.

'Mike Fallon!'

The old man jolted on the second round of pounding, eyes slitting open, resentful of the light. He made a raw sound of fear at the sight of the face pressed to his window.

'Mike, it's Sam Kovac!'

Fallon rocked himself up in the bed, hawking up a night's worth of phlegm.

'What the fuck are you doing?' he shouted. 'Are you out of your fucking head?'

Kovac cupped his hands around the sides of his face so he could see better. 'You gotta let me in, Mike. We need to talk.' His breath fogged the glass and he wiped the moisture away with his coat sleeve.

Fallon scowled and waved him off. 'Leave me alone. I don't need to hear it from you.'

'Hear what?'

'Last night. Bad enough I did it. I don't need my nose rubbed in it.'

He looked pathetic sitting there in his underwear like a derelict Humpty-Dumpty: the barrel body and the twig legs, beard stubble and bloodshot eyes. He brushed over the flattop, wincing, pressing gingerly.

'Just let me in, will you?' Kovac said. 'It's important.'

Fallon squinted at him, trying to size it up. No one hated a surprise more than a cop.

Finally, he lifted a hand in defeat. 'There's a key under the mat in back.'

'A key under the mat.' Kovac set it on the counter and cocked a look at the old man. 'Jeez, Mike. You used to be a cop. You oughta know better.'

Fallon ignored him. The kitchen smelled of bacon grease and fried onions. The curtains were stiff with age. The countertops were lined with cups and glasses and plates and cereal boxes, and a giant jar of Metamucil with prescription bottles clustered around it like white-capped toadstools. All the doors had been taken off the lower cupboards, exposing the contents: boxes of instant potatoes, canned vegetables, about a case of Campbell's soup.

Fallon hadn't bothered with pants. He rolled around the small room in his chair, his hairy, atrophied legs pushed to one side, out of the way. He ferreted out a bottle of Tylenol from the pharmacy on the counter, and got himself a glass of water from the door of the refrigerator.

'What's so damned important?' he demanded gruffly, though Kovac could see the tension in Fallon's shoulders, as if he was bracing himself. 'I got a hangover could drop a cow.'

'Mike.' Kovac waited until Fallon turned and looked at him, then took a deep breath. 'Andy's dead. I'm sorry.'

Blunt. Just like that. People always thought they had to lead in to bad news with platitudes, but that wasn't the way. All that did was give the recipient a chance to panic at the many horrible possibilities. He had learned long ago to just say it and get it over with.

Fallon looked away, his jaw working.

'We don't know yet what happened.'

'What do you mean, you don't know what happened?' Fallon demanded. 'Was he shot? Was he stabbed? Was it a car accident?' He worked up a temper, anger being more comfortable, more familiar than grief. A flush began at the base of his throat and pushed upward. 'You're a detective. Somebody's dead. You can't tell me how they got that way? Jesus H.'

Kovac let it roll off. 'It might have been an accident. Or it might have been suicide, Mike. We found him hanging. I wish I didn't have to tell you, but there it is. I'm really sorry.'

Sorry. As Andy had been. He could see the word on the mirror over the reflection of Andy Fallon. Naked. Dead. Bloated. Rotting. *Sorry* didn't mean a whole lot in the face of that.

Mike seemed to deflate and shrivel. Tears filled his small red eyes and spilled down his cheeks like glass beads.

'Oh, Jesus,' he said. A plea, not a curse. 'Oh, dear Jesus.'

He brought a trembling hand to his mouth. It was the size of a canned ham but looked fragile, the skin thin and spotted. A sound of terrific pain wrenched free of his soul.

Kovac looked away, wanting to allow the man at least that much privacy. This was the worst part of being the messenger: trespassing on those first acute moments of grief, moments that should not be witnessed by anyone.

That, and knowing he would have to intrude on the grief with questions.

Fallon abruptly spun his chair around and wheeled out of the room. Kovac let him go. The questions could wait. Andy was already dead, most likely by his own hand, purposely or not. What difference would ten minutes make?

He leaned against the counter and counted the bottles of pills. Seven brown prescription bottles for the treatment of everything from indigestion to arrhythmia to insomnia to pain. Prilosec, Darvocet, Ambien. At least Mike had plenty of chemicals to help him get through this.

'Damn you! Damn you!'

The shouts were accompanied by a crash and the sound of glass breaking. Kovac bolted out of the kitchen and down the short hall.

'Damn you!' Mike Fallon screamed, smashing a framed picture against the edge of the dresser. The cheap metal frame bent like modeling clay. Glass sprayed out across the dresser.

'Mike! Stop it!'

'Damn you!' the old man cried again, swinging his arms and the shattered frame, flinging broken glass across the room. 'Damn you!'

Kovac thought the curses might be for him at this point as he grabbed Mike Fallon's wrist. The picture frame flew across the room like a Frisbee, crashing against the wall and falling to the hardwood floor. Fallon continued to fight, the strength in his upper body amazing for a man his age. His free arm flailed across the top of the dresser, sending more picture frames to the floor. Kovac got behind the wheelchair, bending at an awkward angle to try to restrain the man. Wailing, Fallon threw his head back and butted him hard on the bridge of the nose. Blood came in an instant gush.

'Dammit, Mike, stop it!' The blood ran down his chin and onto Fallon's shoulder, his ear, his hair.

Sobbing, the old man flung himself against the dresser top, then back. Back and forth, back and forth. The energy ran out of him little by little with each motion, until he laid his face on the dresser amid the shards of glass, and moved only his hands. Pounding, pounding, slapping, slapping, tapping, tapping.

Kovac stepped back, wiping his bloody nose on his coat sleeve as he fumbled for a handkerchief. He went over to where the first of the destroyed frames had landed and tried to nudge it over with his foot. His shoes and the bottoms of his pants legs were soaked from stomping through the snow, but the cold only began to register now that he'd seen the evidence. He couldn't feel his toes inside his shoes.

Handkerchief crammed against his nostrils to stem the flow of blood, he squatted down and picked up the picture with his free hand. Andy Fallon's academy graduation. Andy beaming, Mike beside him in the wheelchair, a jagged line now cutting between them like a lightning bolt.

He shook off the last of the glass and tried to bend the frame back into shape.

'Mike,' he said quietly. 'Last night you said Andy was dead to you. What did you mean by that?'

Fallon kept his head on the dresser, his gaze on nothing, empty. He didn't answer. Kovac had to stare at him a moment to be certain the old man hadn't just died on him. That would have been the cap on the damn day – and it wasn't even two o'clock yet.

'The two of you were having problems?' he prompted.

'I loved that kid,' Fallon said weakly, still not moving. 'I loved him. He was my legs. He was my heart. He was everything I couldn't be.'

But . . .

The word hung in the air, unspoken. Kovac had a feeling he knew where it would lead. He looked around at the scattered photographs of Andy Fallon. Handsome and athletic. And gay.

A hard-ass old-timer like Mike wouldn't have taken it well. Hell, Kovac didn't know how well *he* would have taken it if it had been his kid.

'I loved him,' Mike murmured. 'He ruined everything. He's ruined everything.'

His face pinched tight as he looked inward, seeing the pain in its brightest light. He flushed red with the effort to hold the tears back – or maybe to push them out. Hard to say which would have been more difficult for a man like Iron Mike.

Kovac dabbed absently at his nose, then stuffed the handkerchief in his coat pocket. Quietly, he picked up all the photographs and stacked them on the dresser so they would be there when the anger subsided and the need for memories set in.

The questions were there, lined up in the front of his mind, automatic, orderly, routine. *When was the last time you spoke to Andy? Did he talk to you about what he was working on? What was his mental state the last time you saw him? Did he ever talk about suicide? Had he been depressed? Did you know his friends, his lovers?*

None of those questions made it to his lips. Later.

'Is there anyone you'd like me to call, Mike?'

Fallon didn't respond. The grief had surrounded him like a force field. He wasn't hearing anything but the voice of regret in his head, wasn't feeling any pain but that in the deepest part of his soul. He was oblivious to everything external, including the bits of glass that cut into his cheek.

Kovac let out a long, slow breath, his gaze falling on one photograph that still lay on the floor, half under the dresser. He pulled it out and looked at a past that seemed as far away as Mars. The Fallons all together before one tragedy after another had torn them apart. Mike and his wife and their two boys.

'I'll call your other son, if you want,' he offered.

'I don't have another son,' Mike Fallon said. 'One shut me out years ago, and I shut out the other. Helluva deal, huh, Kojak?'

Kovac looked at the photograph for another moment, then set it on top of the others. Fallon's admission left him feeling hollow inside, an echo of the old man's emotions. Or maybe the emotions were his own. He was no less alone in his life than Mike Fallon.

'Yeah, Mikey. It's a helluva deal.'

Liska stood in the hall, staring at the door to Room 126. Internal Affairs. The name conjured up images of interrogation rooms with bare lightbulbs and SS officers with narrowed eyes and rubber truncheons.

The Rat Squad. She'd had little cause to associate with them in her career, had never been investigated by them. She knew the job of IA was to root out bad cops, not to persecute the good ones. But the fear and loathing were instinctive things for most cops. Cops hung together, protected one another. IA turned on their own. Like cannibals.

For Liska, the aversion went deeper.

In the Minneapolis PD, IA was for fast-track, brownnose, brass types. People destined for management. People born to be hated by their peers. The kind who had regularly gotten pushed down on the playground as kids, and ran to the teacher every time. The kind of people who inspired neither admiration nor loyalty.

Liska thought of Andy Fallon hanging in his bedroom, and wondered who might have turned on him.

She went into the IA offices before she could balk again. There were no human heads mounted on pikes. No manacles bolted to the wall. At least not in the reception area.

'Liska, homicide,' she said, badging the receptionist. 'I'm here to see Lieutenant Savard.'

She made the receptionist for early fifties. Plump and unsmiling, the woman asked no questions, which was likely a requirement of the job. She buzzed the lieutenant.

There were three offices off the reception area – one dark, one closed and lit, one open and lit. Looking in the last one, she could see a thin suit-and-tie standing behind the desk and frowning, deep in conversation with a short guy with chopped platinum hair and a neon-green parka.

'. . . don't appreciate being passed around,' Neon whined, his voice just high enough to irritate. 'This has been a nightmare from the start. Now you're telling me the case is being reassigned.'

'In point of fact, the case is closed. I'll be your contact should you need one. That's purely out of courtesy on the part of the department. I'm afraid there's nothing I can do about the change in personnel,' the suit explained. 'The circumstances are beyond our control. Sergeant Fallon is no longer with us.'

The suit caught Liska's gaze then. He frowned harder, came around the desk, and closed the door.

'Lieutenant Savard is expecting you,' the receptionist said in the hushed tone of a funeral director.

Savard's office was immaculate. None of the usual cop clutter. A place for everything and everything in its place. The same could be said of the lieutenant. She stood behind her perfectly neat desk in a perfectly tailored black pantsuit. Forty or thereabouts, with perfectly symmetrical features and perfect porcelain skin. Her ash-blond hair was perfectly coiffed in chin-length waves ingeniously cut to appear careless, but likely requiring a cosmetology degree to style every day.

Liska resisted the self-conscious urge to reach up and touch her own boy-short crop.

'Liska, homicide,' she said by way of introduction, not offering her hand. 'I'm here about Andy Fallon.'

'Yes,' Savard murmured, almost as if she were talking to herself. 'Of course.'

She seemed too feminine to live up to her rep, Liska thought. Amanda Savard had been described as tough and smooth, sharp and cold as a tungsten steel blade.

Liska helped herself to a seat. Cool, casual, in control. A good front anyway. She pulled out her notebook and pen.

'It's a terrible tragedy,' Savard said, easing into her seat with care. As if she had a bad back but didn't want to show it. Her hand trembled slightly as she reached for her coffee cup. 'I liked Andy. He was a good kid.'

'What kind of cop was he?'

'Dedicated. Conscientious.'

'When did you last see him?'

'Sunday evening. We needed to talk some things over in relation to a case he'd been working. He hadn't been pleased with the outcome.'

'And where did you go?'

'His home.'

'Isn't that a little intimate?'

Savard didn't bat an eye. 'Andy was gay. I was in Uptown doing some Christmas shopping. I called and asked him if I could drop by.'

'What time was that?'

'Around eight. I left around nine-thirty.'

'Did he say anything about expecting someone else?'

'No.'

'And what was his frame of mind when you left?'

'He seemed fine. We had talked everything through.'

'But he didn't come in for work yesterday?'

'No. He had asked to take Monday as a personal day. Christmas shopping, he said. If I'd had any idea . . .' She looked away, taking a few seconds to tighten the straps on her composure.

'Had he given any indication of having emotional problems recently?'

Savard released a delicate sigh, seemingly lost in the stark beauty of a black-and-white winterscape photograph that hung on one wall.

'Yes. He'd been quiet. Down. He'd lost some weight. I knew he was having some problems with a case. And I knew he was dealing with some stress in his personal life. But I didn't think he was a risk to himself. Andy did a good job of internalizing.'

'Was he seeing the shrink?'

'Not that I was aware of. I wish now I had been stronger in suggesting that.'

'You *had* suggested it?'

'I make it clear to my people the department psychologist is there for a reason. Internal Affairs can be a tough row to hoe. There's a considerable amount of job stress.'

'Yeah, I guess ruining other cops could have its drawbacks,' Liska muttered, scribbling in her pad.

'Cops ruin themselves, Sergeant,' Savard said, a hint of the steel glinting now in her voice. 'We stop them from ruining other people's lives. We provide a necessary service here.'

'I didn't mean to imply that you didn't.'

'Of course you did.'

Liska shifted on her chair, her gaze sliding away from Savard's cold green eyes.

'I've lost a good investigator,' Savard said. 'And I've lost a young man I liked a lot. Do you think I don't feel that, Sergeant? Do you think IA rats have ice water in their veins?'

Liska stared down at her lap. 'No, ma'am. I'm sorry.'

'I'm sure you are. You're sitting there wondering if I'll complain to your lieutenant.'

Liska said nothing because Savard was exactly right. She was more concerned about how this screw-up would affect her career than how it might have upset Savard personally. Sad but true. She put her career first when she wasn't busy sticking her foot in her mouth. Habitual behavior – on both counts. Professional ambition was one part of the survivor mentality that had kept her head above water all her life. The other was an unfortunate tendency that had hindered her progress more than once.

'Don't worry, Sergeant,' Savard said wearily. 'My skin is thicker than that.'

After an uncomfortable moment, Liska said, 'Do you think Andy Fallon killed himself?'

Savard's brow furrowed delicately. 'Do you think something else? I was told Andy hung himself.'

'He was found hanging, yes.'

'My God, you don't think he was –' The lieutenant broke off before she could say the word. *Murdered.* She had a homicide detective sitting in front of her.

'It may have been an accident,' Liska said. 'We can't rule out autoerotic asphyxiation. At this point, we don't know what might have happened.'

'An accident,' Savard repeated, dropping her lashes. 'That would be terrible too, but it's certainly better than any of the alternatives. No matter what, hanging isn't an easy way to die.' Her hand settled briefly at the base of her throat, then moved away.

'I figure any way to die isn't fun,' Liska said. 'Hanging's quick at least. It doesn't take long before you lose consciousness. A couple of minutes.'

The thought of what those couple of minutes would be like struck them both at the same moment. Liska swallowed.

'What was he working on? This case you talked about Sunday night? What was that about?'

'I'm not at liberty to say.'

'I'm investigating a death, Lieutenant. What if Andy Fallon didn't kill himself? What if he's dead because of one of his cases?'

She waited for Savard to cave, seeing no sign that would happen before the end of the decade.

'Sergeant Liska, Andy had been depressed,' Savard pointed out calmly. 'He was found hanging. I'm assuming his home was undisturbed, right? People don't say "suspected suicide" if the door's been kicked in and the stereo is missing.

'I don't see a crime, Sergeant,' she went on. 'I see a tragedy.'

'It's that no matter what,' Liska said. 'The details are for me to sort out. I'm only trying to do my job, Lieutenant. I'd like to see Andy's case files and notes.'

'That's out of the question. We'll wait until we hear what the ME has to say.'

'It's Christmastime,' Liska pointed out. 'The suicides are stacking up like cordwood. It could be days before they get to Fallon.'

Savard didn't blink.

'An IA investigation is a serious thing, Sergeant. I don't want details getting out unless it's absolutely necessary. Someone's career could be damaged.'

'I thought that was your goal,' Liska said, getting to her feet.

She closed her notebook, stuck it in her jacket pocket, and made a little face. 'Shit. There goes that tone again. Sorry,' she said without remorse. 'Well, while you're telling my lieutenant how flip I am, toss in the fact that you don't want to cooperate with a death investigation, Lieutenant Savard. Maybe he'll have better luck persuading you than I have.'

She made a mock salute and walked out.

The receptionist didn't so much as look up. The door was still closed on the suit's office. Liska could hear the tone of an argument but not the content. Whatever Neon Man had come here for involved Andy Fallon. The case was being reassigned.

She went out into the hall and looked up and down. Deserted – for the moment at least. The building often gave that impression, even though the place was full of cops and criminals, city officials and citizens. She went to the water fountain across the hall from 126 and waited.

Maybe three minutes went by before the door opened and Neon came out. His face was a shade of red that clashed badly with his parka. He crossed to the water fountain, ran some water on his fingers, and pressed them delicately to his cheeks. He breathed deliberately through pursed lips, visibly working to calm down.

'Frustrating place, huh?' Liska said.

Neon's head snapped around. His green eyes were bright, clear and translucent, and suspicious.

'I didn't get what I went in there for either,' Liska confided, moving closer. 'Feel free to hate them. Everyone hates IA. I hate them, and I work here.'

'All the more reason, isn't it?' he said. 'It certainly is hateful from what I've seen.'

Liska squinted at him. 'You a cop? A narc? I'd know you otherwise.'

He was no more a cop than her paperboy, but she scored points asking. Up close, she was surprised to find that he was barely as tall as she was – and three inches of that were the soles of a very funky pair of shoes. *Petite* was the best word to describe him. He wore mascara and lip gloss, and had five earrings in one ear.

'Just a concerned citizen,' he said, glancing up and down the hall.

'And what is it you're concerned about?'

'Injustice.'

'You've come to the right place. Theoretically.' She dug a card out of her jacket pocket and handed it to him. 'Maybe you're just talking to the wrong people.'

Neon took the card. His manicure was better than hers. He looked at the card as if he were trying to memorize it.

'Maybe,' he said, and slipped it into his coat pocket and walked away.

6

Neil Fallon had forsaken not only his father but the city as well. Kovac drove west on the broad speedway multilanes of 394, which thinned down to four lanes, then two, then two with no shoulders, the last a narrow ribbon of road that wound around the fingers of Lake Minnetonka. On other tributaries of asphalt around this lake stood old mansions that had been built by lumber barons and industrialists, and new mansions built in recent years by professional athletes and rock stars. But here the strips of land were too meager for ostentation. Cabins perched on the banks, crouching beneath towering pines. Some were summer places, some fishing shacks that should have seen a wrecking ball a decade or two past, others were modest year-round homes.

Andy Fallon's brother owned a motley collection of cabins congregated on a wedge of land between the lake and a crossroads. Fallon's Bar and Bait Shop squatted nearest the road, a building not much bigger than a three-car garage, with green shingle siding and too-small windows that made the place look as if it were squinting. The windows were glowing with neon advertising Miller's and Coors and live bait.

The thought of a late lunch shriveled and died in Kovac's empty belly.

He wheeled the piece-of-shit Chevy Caprice into the small, frozen parking lot, turned off the engine, and listened to it rattle on. He'd been driving the same car out of the department fleet for more than a year. In that time, no mechanic had been able to cure its hiccups or make the heater give more than a token effort. He had requested a different vehicle, but the paperwork had gone into a bureaucratic black hole, and no one on that end would return his phone calls. His driving record might have had something to do with it, but he preferred to think he was getting fucked over. Gave him an excuse to be pissed off.

A pool table dominated much of the floor space in the bar. Walls paneled with old barn wood were hung with dozens of photographs of people — presumably customers — holding up fish. The television over the tiny bar was showing a soap. A lumpy woman with thin brown hair and a cigarette hanging from her mouth stood inside the horseshoe-shaped bar drying a beer mug with a dingy cloth. *Mental note to Kovac: Drink out of the bottle.*

On the consumer side of the bar, an old lake rat with half his teeth sat on a stool, a filthy red ball cap at a jaunty angle on his head.

'Hope would never do that to Bo,' the woman scoffed. 'He's the love of her goddamned life.'

'*Was*,' the lake rat corrected. 'Ain't you been paying attention, Maureen? Stephano planted a microchip in her brain makes her fucking evil. Evil Gina, that's what they call her now.'

'That's crap,' Maureen proclaimed, half an inch of ash glowing red on the end of her cigarette.

Kovac cleared his throat. 'Neil Fallon?'

The woman gave him the head-to-toe. 'What are you selling?'

'Bad news.'

'He's out back.'

Some friend.

She nodded him toward the kitchen door.

The kitchen was as cramped as a carnival concession stand and stank of rancid grease and sour washrags. Or maybe that damp scent came from dead minnows. Kovac kept his hands in the pockets of his topcoat and the coat pulled tightly around him. He tried not to wonder where Neil kept the live bait.

Fallon stood in the open mouth of a big storage shed. He looked like old Mike twenty-some years previous: built like a bull with a meaty, ruddy face and a bit of a downward hook to his mouth. He looked at Kovac coming across the yard, pulled a welder's mask down over his face, and went back to work on the runner of a snowmobile. Sparks arced away from the torch like a tiny fireworks display, bright against the gloom of the shed.

'Neil Fallon?' Kovac called above the roar. He pulled his shield out of his pocket and held it up, staying out of range of the sparks. 'Kovac. Minneapolis PD.'

Fallon stepped back, turned the torch off, and raised the mask. His face was blank. 'He's dead.'

Kovac stopped a yard from the snowmobile. 'Someone called you?'

'No. I just always knew they'd send a cop to tell me, that's all. You were more his family than I ever was.' He pulled a red bandanna out of his coveralls pocket and wiped sweat from his face, despite the fact that the afternoon temperature was in the low twenties. 'So what was it? His heart? Or did he get drunk and fall out of the goddamn chair?'

'I'm not here about your father,' Kovac said.

Neil looked at him as if he'd started speaking Greek.

'I'm here about Andy. He's dead. I'm sorry.'

'Andy.'

'Your brother.'

'Jesus Christ, I know he's my brother,' Fallon snapped.

He set the welding torch aside on a workbench, hands fumbling at the task, then at the thick, grimy welder's gloves. He jerked the mask off his head and threw it as if it burned him. It landed with a crash amid a stack of old gas cans.

'He's dead?' he said, short of breath. 'How is he dead? How can he be dead? He can't be.'

'It looks like suicide. Or an accident.'

'Suicide?' Fallon repeated. 'Fuck.' Breathing harder, he went to a rusty metal locker beside the workbench, took out a half-empty bottle of Old Crow, and drank two good glugs of it. Then he put the bottle down and bent over with his hands on his knees, muttering a long string of curses. 'Andy.' He spat on the ground. 'Suicide.' He spat again. 'Jesus.' He took two steps out the door and puked in the snow.

Everyone reacted differently.

Kovac dug around in his coat pocket and came up with a piece of Nicorette. Shit.

'Jesus,' Fallon muttered. He came back and sat down on a stool fashioned from a tree trunk. He set the bottle of Old Crow between his feet. 'Andy.'

'Were you close?' Kovac asked, leaning back against the workbench.

Fallon shook his head and scraped his fingers back through thick hair the color of old rust. 'Once, I guess. Or maybe never. He spent a lot of time looking up to me when we were little kids 'cause I was older, tougher. 'Cause I stood up to the old man. But he was always Iron Mike's favorite. I wasted a lot of time hating him for that.'

He made it sound as if he had given up the hate long ago, but there was still a trace of bitterness in his voice, Kovac noted. In his experience, family resentments were seldom set aside entirely, if at all. Instead people tossed a cover over them and ignored them, like an ugly old piece of furniture.

'Looked like he was the all-American kid, all right,' he said, poking at the old wound. 'The star athlete. The good student. Followed in the old man's footsteps.'

Fallon looked down at the floor, his mouth a tight, hard line. 'He was everything the old man wanted in a son. That's what Mike thought anyway. I was none of it.'

He reached inside the open zipper of his coveralls and dug a cigarette and a lighter out of his shirt pocket. On the first long exhale he muttered, 'Fuck 'em.' Then he huffed a humorless laugh, picked up the Old Crow, and took another swig.

'Did you see much of each other?' Kovac asked.

Fallon wagged his head, though Kovac wasn't certain if he was answering in the negative or still trying to shake off the news.

'He came by now and then. He liked to fish a little. He keeps his gear here. Stores his boat in the winter. It's like a token sibling thing, I guess. Like he thinks it's his duty to patronize my business. Andy's big on duty.'

'When did you last speak with him?'

'He stopped by Sunday, but I didn't talk to him. I was busy. I had a guy here to buy a snowmobile.'

'When was the last time you had a serious conversation?'

'Serious? A month or so ago, I guess.'

'What about?'

Fallon's lips twisted. 'He wanted to tell me he was coming out of the closet. That he was a fag. Like I needed to hear that.'

'You didn't know he was gay?'

'Sure I did. I knew it years ago. High school. I just knew it. It wasn't something he had to tell me.' He took another snort of the Crow, then pulled on the cigarette. 'I told the old man so once. Way back when. Just because I was pissed off. Sick of it. Sick of "Why can't you be more like your brother?"'

He laughed loudly then, as if at a hilarious joke. 'Man. He damn near broke my jaw, he hit me so hard. I'd never seen him so mad. I could've said the Virgin Mary was a whore and he wouldn't have been half that mad. I sinned against the golden child. If he hadn't been in that chair, he'd have kicked my ass blue.'

'How did Andy seem when he told you?'

Fallon thought about it for a moment. 'Intense,' he said at last. 'I guess it was a trauma for him. He'd told Mike. That must've been a scene and a half. I would've gone back to see that. I couldn't believe the old man didn't stroke out.'

He sucked on the cigarette, dropped the butt on the floor, and crushed it out with the toe of his work boot. 'It was strange, though, you know? I felt sorry for Andy. I know all about disappointing the old man. He didn't.'

'Had you seen him since?'

'A couple of times. He came out to ice fish. I let him have one of my shacks. We had a drink one other time. I think he wanted us to be like brothers again, but, shit, what did we have in common besides the old man? Nothing.

'How'd Mike take this?' Fallon asked quietly, staring at the floor. 'Andy being dead.' He blew out a breath of smoke through flared nostrils. 'He sent you out here? He couldn't call me to tell me himself. Couldn't bring himself to admit the perfect son didn't turn out to be so fucking perfect after all. That's Mike. If he can't be right, he'll be an asshole.'

Taking the bottle of Old Crow by the throat, he pushed to his feet and headed out the door. 'Fuck 'em.'

Kovac followed, hunching into his coat. It was getting colder, a damp kind of cold that bit to the bone. His head hurt and his nose was throbbing.

Fallon stepped around the corner of the shed and stopped, staring between the shitty little fishing cabins he rented out in the summer. The buildings squatted near the shore of Minnetonka, but there was no shore to speak of this time of year. Snow drifted across land and ice, making one nearly indistinguishable from the other. The landscape was a sea of white stretching out toward an orange horizon.

'How'd he do it?'

'Hung himself.'

'Huh.'

Just that: *Huh.* Then he stood there some more while the wind blew a fine mist of white from one side of the lake to the other. No denial or disbelief. Perhaps he hadn't known his brother as well as Steve Pierce had. Or maybe he'd wished his brother dead in the past and so had less trouble accepting his death by any means.

'When we were kids, we played cowboys,' he said. 'I was always the one that got strung up. I was always the bad guy. Andy always played the sheriff. Funny how things turn out.'

They said nothing for another few moments. Kovac imagined Fallon was seeing those old memories play out before him. Two little boys, their whole lives ahead of them, in two-dollar cowboy hats, riding on broomsticks. Bright futures stained dark by the jealousies and strains and disappointments of growing up.

The images of childhood faded into the memory of Andy Fallon hanging naked from a rafter.

'Mind if I have a belt of that?' he asked, nodding toward the bottle.

Fallon handed it over. 'Aren't you on duty?'

'I'm always on duty. It's all I've got,' Kovac admitted. 'I won't tell the brass if you don't.'

Fallon turned back toward the lake. 'Hey, fuck 'em.'

The neighbor was in his yard harvesting burned-out Christmas bulbs when Kovac pulled up. Kovac stopped halfway up the walk to watch him as he unscrewed a light from the Virgin Mary's halo and stuffed it into a garbage bag.

'Half of them could burn out and it'd still be like living next door to the sun,' Kovac said.

The neighbor stared at him with a mix of offense and apprehension, clutching the garbage bag to his chest. He was a small man of about seventy with a hard-boiled look and small mean eyes. He wore a red plaid bomber cap with the flaps hanging down like hound's ears.

'Where's your Christmas spirit?' he demanded.

'I lost it about the fourth night I didn't get any sleep on account of your fucking lights. Can't you put that shit on a timer?'

'Shows what you know,' the neighbor huffed.

'I know you're a lunatic.'

'You want me to cause a power surge? That's what would happen turning these lights on and off. Power surge. Could black out the whole block.'

'We should be so lucky,' Kovac said, and went up the sidewalk and into his house.

He turned the television on for company, radiated some left-over lasagne, sat on the couch, and picked at dinner. He wondered if Mike Fallon was sitting in front of his big-screen television tonight, trying to eat, trying to temporarily hide from his grief in the ruts of routine.

During the course of his career in homicide, Kovac had watched a lot of people straddle that awkward line between normalcy and the surreal reality of having violent crime disrupt their lives. He never thought much about it, as a rule. He wasn't a social worker. His job was to solve the crime and move on. But he thought about it tonight because Mike was a cop. And maybe for a few other reasons.

Abandoning the lasagne and *Dateline*, he went to his desk and rummaged around in a drawer, digging out an address book that hadn't seen the light of day in half a decade. His ex-wife was listed under her first name. He dialed the number and waited, then hung up when an answering machine picked up. A man's voice. The second husband.

What would he have said anyway? *I had a dead body today and it reminded me I have a kid.*

No. It reminded him he didn't have anyone.

He wandered back into the living room with the empty fish tank and Stone Phillips on the TV. Too much like old Iron Mike sitting in his massage chair in front of the big screen, alone in the world with nothing but bitter memories and soured hopes. And a dead son.

Most of the time Kovac believed he was happier without a real life. The job was a safe place. He knew what to expect. He knew who he was. He knew where he fit in. He knew what to do. He'd never been good at any of that without the badge.

There were worse fates than being a career cop. Most of the time he loved the work, if not the politics that went with it. He was good at it. Not fancy, not flashy. Not in the flamboyant way Ace Wyatt had been, grabbing headlines and sticking out his granite jaw for any passing camera. But good in the way that counted.

'Stick with what you do best,' he muttered, then turned his back on his dinner, grabbed his coat, and left.

Steve Pierce lived in a brick duplex on a drab street too close to the freeway in Lowry Hill. The neighborhood was full of yuppies and artsy types with money to renovate the old brownstones. But this portion had been chopped up into odd little angles when the major traffic arteries of Hennepin and Lyndale had been widened years ago, and it remained fragmented not only physically but psychologically as well.

Steve Pierce's neighbors had no gaudy Christmas displays draining the Northern States Power supply. Everything was tasteful and moderate. A wreath here. A swag there. As much as Kovac hated his neighbor, he thought he liked this even less. The street had the feel of a place where the inhabitants were not connected in any way, not even by animosity.

He fit right in tonight.

He sat in his car, parked across and down the street from Pierce's, waiting, thinking. Thinking Andy Fallon probably didn't leave his doors unlocked. Thinking Steve Pierce seemed to know a lot and yet nothing about his old buddy. Thinking there was more to that story and Steve Pierce didn't want to tell it.

People lied to the cops all the time. Not just bad guys or the guilty. Lying was an equal opportunity activity. Innocent people lied. Mothers of small children lied. Pencil-neck paper pushers lied. Blue-haired grannies lied. Everyone lied to the cops. It seemed to be embedded in the human genetic code.

Steve Pierce was lying. Kovac had no doubt about that. He just had to narrow the field of possible lies and decide if any of them were significant to Andy Fallon's death.

He pulled a pack of Salems out from under the passenger's seat, held it under his nose, and breathed deeply, then put the cigarettes back and got out of the car.

Pierce answered the door in sweatpants and a U of M hockey jersey, the smell of good scotch hovering around him like cologne, and a cigarette dangling from his lip. In the hours since his discovery of Andy Fallon's corpse, his physical appearance had degraded to the look of a man who had been battling a terminal illness for a very long time. Gaunt, ashen, red-eyed. One corner of his mouth curled up in a sneer as he pulled the cigarette and exhaled.

'Oh, look. It's the Ghost of Christmas Present. Did you bring your rubber truncheon this time? 'Cause, you know, I don't feel like I've been abused enough for one day. I find my best friend dead, get in a fight with Hulk Hogan in a cop uniform, and get harassed by a dickhead detective. The list just doesn't go on long enough. I could go for a little torture.'

He made his eyes and mouth round with feigned shock. 'Oops! My secret is out now! S and M. Shit!'

'Look,' Kovac said. 'This hasn't been my favorite day either. I got to go tell a man I used to look up to that his son probably killed himself.'

'Did he even listen?' Pierce asked.

'What?'

'Mike Fallon. Did he even listen when you told him about Andy?'

Kovac's brow creased. 'He didn't have much choice.'

Pierce stared past him at the dark street, as if some part of him still clung to a tattered scrap of fantasy that Andy Fallon would materialize from the gloom and come up the walk. The weight of reality defeated him. He flicked the cigarette butt out the door.

'I need a drink,' he said, and he turned and walked away from the open door.

Kovac followed him, taking the place in with a glance. Dramatic colors and oak furniture of some retro style he couldn't have named on a bet. What he knew about decorating wouldn't dot an *i*, but he recognized quality and big price tags. The walls of the hall were a patchwork of artsy photographs in white mats and thin black frames.

They went into a den with dark blue walls and fat leather armchairs the color of a fielder's glove. Pierce went to a small wet bar in one corner and freshened his glass from a bottle of Macallan. Fifty bucks a bottle. Kovac knew because he had been asked to kick in a few so the department could buy a bottle for the last lieutenant when he left. He'd personally never paid more than twenty dollars for a bottle of booze in his life.

'Andy's brother told me Andy stopped by about a month ago to come out of the closet,' Kovac said, leaning a hip against the bar. Pierce frowned at that and made a task of wiping imaginary condensation off the soapstone counter. 'I guess it didn't go well with the old man, huh?'

'What was the point of telling him?' Pierce's voice tightened with anger he was trying hard to camouflage. 'Sure, Dad, I'm still the same son who made you so proud in all those ball games,' he said with heavy sarcasm to the room at large. 'I just like it up the ass, that's all.'

He tipped back the scotch and drank it like apple juice. 'Jesus, what did he expect? He should have just let well enough alone. Let the old man see what he wanted to see. That's all people really want anyway.'

'How long had you known Andy was gay?'

'I don't know. I didn't mark it on the calendar,' Pierce said, walking away.

'A month? A year? Ten years?'

'A while.' Impatient. 'What difference does it make?'

'Coming out – was that something he'd saved for his family? Everyone else in his life knew? His friends, his coworkers?'

'It wasn't like he was a queen or something,' Pierce snapped. 'It wasn't anybody's business unless Andy wanted it to be. We roomed together in college. He told me then. I didn't care. It didn't matter. More chicks for me, right? Major competition out of the dating pool.'

'Why'd he tell them now?' Kovac asked. 'His father, his brother? What brought that on? People don't just up and spill their guts. Something pushes them to it.'

'Is there a point to this? Because if there's not, I'd sooner just sit here alone and drink myself into unconsciousness.'

'You don't strike me as someone wanting to sit down, Steve,' Kovac said. He pushed away from the bar to lean against one of the fat leather chairs. It smelled like a fielder's mitt too. That probably cost extra.

Pierce held himself stiff before Kovac's scrutiny. People even lied with their body language – or tried to. That was seldom as successful as the verbal variety.

'Your friend took a big step coming out,' Kovac said. 'And he landed on his chin, at least with his father. That kind of rejection might push a person. A person like Andy, close to his dad, wanting to please him –'

'No.'

'He wrote an apology on the mirror. Why would he do that if he was just playing around, just getting himself off?'

'I don't know. He just wouldn't have killed himself, that's all.'

'Or maybe the note on the mirror wasn't Andy's,' Kovac suggested. 'Maybe Andy had a boyfriend over. Maybe they were having a little game, something went wrong. . . . The boyfriend got scared. . . . Do you happen to know the names of any of his partners?'

'No.'

'None? You being best pals and all? That seems strange.'

'I wasn't interested in his sex life. It didn't have anything to do with me.' He took a drink of the scotch and stared sullenly at an electrical outlet on the other side of the room.

'This morning you told me he wasn't seeing anybody. Like maybe you *were* interested.'

'Which reminds me,' Pierce said. 'We've had this conversation before, Detective. I don't care to relive the experience.'

Kovac spread his hands. 'Hey, you seem like a man with something he wants to get off his chest, Steve. I'm just giving you an outlet here, you know what I mean?'

'I know that I don't have anything of value to tell you.'

Kovac smoothed a hand over his mustache and down his chin. 'You're sure?'

Keys rattled in the front door, giving Pierce the opportunity to escape. Kovac followed him to the front hall. A drop-dead blonde had let herself in and was stepping out of a pair of low boots even as she set take-out bags on the hall table.

Garlic chicken and Mongolian beef. Kovac's stomach growled, and he remembered the lasagne on his coffee table with a fondness it didn't deserve.

'I told you, I don't feel like eating, Joss.'

'You need to eat something, sweetie,' the blonde chided gently, slipping out of her coat. Her features were beautifully sculpted, eyes impossibly large. Her shoulder-length hair looked like pale gold silk. 'I was hoping the aroma might revive your appetite.'

She hung the coat on an oak hall tree, which looked a hundred years old and worth a small fortune. When she turned around, she caught sight of Kovac for the first time and stiffened her back. She looked as unhappy as a queen finding an uninvited peasant in her chambers. Regal in her bearing and her disdain. Even in her stocking feet, she was as tall as Pierce and looked athletic. She dressed with the conservative flair of someone born to money – expensive fabrics, traditional style; tawny wool slacks and a navy-blue blazer, an ivory turtleneck sweater that looked incredibly soft.

Kovac flashed his badge at her. 'Kovac. Homicide. I'm here about Andy Fallon. Sorry to disrupt your evening, ma'am.'

'Homicide?' she said with wary surprise, her eyes going wider. They were brown, like Bambi's. 'But Andy wasn't murdered.'

'We need to be as sure of that as you, Miss . . .'

'Jocelyn Daring,' she said, but didn't offer her hand. 'I'm Steven's fiancée.'

'And the boss's daughter,' Kovac ventured.

'You're out of line, Kovac,' Pierce warned.

'Sorry,' Kovac said. 'You'll get that a lot with me. Inappropriate is my middle name. I guess I wasn't brought up right.'

The look Jocelyn Daring gave him could have freeze-dried coffee. Kovac didn't care. He was busy thinking that Steve Pierce was an up-and-comer for Daring-Landis, and that up-and-comers for Daring-Landis probably needed to be straight arrows with skeleton-free closets.

The fiancée put her hand on Steve Pierce's arm in a gesture that struck Kovac as both possessive and reassuring. She kept her eyes on Kovac. 'Is there really any reason for you to be here now, Detective? Steven's had a terrible shock today. We'd like to have some time alone to process the grief. Besides, it's hardly his fault Andy committed suicide.'

Pierce didn't even look at her. His stare was directed across the hall and through the open doorway of the den – or into another dimension. It wasn't difficult to imagine what he was seeing. The question was what it meant to him, and whether the weight of the emotion pressing in on him had anything to do with guilt. If it did, what kind of guilt.

'I just had some questions, that's all,' Kovac said. 'Trying to get a clear picture of who Andy was, who his friends were, what might have pushed him to the edge – provided he stepped over it voluntarily. You know, trying to find out if he'd had any recent disappointments, ended relationships, personal setbacks of any kind.'

Jocelyn Daring opened the slim black purse she'd set on the table beside the food and extracted a business card. Her fingers were long and elegant, the nails gleamed like sheer pearl. The square-cut diamond on her left ring finger could've choked a goat.

'If you have any more questions, why don't you call first?' she suggested.

Kovac took the card in at a glance and raised a brow. 'A lawyer?'

'Steven told me about the way you treated him this morning, Detective. I won't allow that to happen again. Do you understand me?'

Pierce still wasn't looking at her. Kovac nodded. 'Yeah. I'm a little slow, but I think I'm beginning to see how things are.'

He moved past them to the door, then paused with his hand on the knob and looked back at them. Jocelyn Daring had moved in front of Steve Pierce again, putting herself between Kovac and her fiancé-client, protecting him.

'Did you know Andy Fallon, Ms Daring?' Kovac asked.

'Yes,' she said simply. No tears. No strain of grief.

'My condolences on your loss,' Kovac said, and let himself out into the cold.

7

Small and unremarkable, Liska's house sat shoulder to shoulder with half a dozen like it on a street in a neighborhood of St Paul that had no name. 'Near Grand Avenue' was what people who lived there liked to say, because Grand Avenue was just that: grand. Lined with beautiful restored mansions of former lumber barons. The governor's mansion was on Grand Avenue. Not even the fact that the governor was a former professional wrestler could bring the neighborhood down. St Paul's version of Uptown, the heart of the Grand Avenue area was a trendy stretch of boutiques and upscale restaurants.

Liska's neighborhood was a lot like Andy Fallon's – just far enough outside the chic radius to be affordable on a single income. Theoretically, Liska's ex paid child support, which was supposed to ease the financial burden of single motherhood. But what Speed Hatcher had been ordered by the court to pay and what he actually came across with were two very different figures.

That's what she got for marrying a narc. Narcs lived too close to the edge too much of the time; the line between who they were on the job and who they were in civilian life often blurred very badly. For Speed, the line no longer existed. He liked that edge too well.

In retrospect, Liska knew she had caught glimpses of that wildness in him from the first, when they'd both still been in uniform. She admitted it was part of what had attracted her to him. That and a dazzling smile and a great ass. But while wildness might have been a desirable trait in a lover, it was not in a father. The smile could make her take him back only so many times. The ass, it turned out, had been a serious liability. Too many other women wanted to get their hands on it.

She shuffled the Polaroids of Andy Fallon and wondered if his lovers had felt the same way. Fallon had been a knockout before rigor set in. The kind of looks that made women lament same-sex attraction.

She spread the photographs on her living room coffee table, with a copy of the *St Paul Pioneer Press* at the ready to cover them if one of the boys wandered in, though it was late and both Kyle and R.J. had been in bed for an hour. It wasn't unknown for one or the other to come out bleary-eyed in his pajamas and snuggle up to her on the couch while she tried to unwind with Letterman or a book.

A part of her wished that would happen now so she could put the pictures out of her head and try to be a normal human being for a while. She had a headache and her jaw throbbed from grinding her teeth. The cap on the day had been getting cornered by Lieutenant Leonard while she'd waited for Kovac to show – which he hadn't. Jamal Jackson was making noise about suing her for brutality. He didn't have a case, but that wouldn't stop him from hooking up with some slimy ACLU lawyer and making her life a misery until the case was thrown out of court. The report would go in her jacket whether the charges were substantiated or not. Next she'd have IA on her case while she tried to dig into theirs.

Great. If the incident had happened a week ago, she might have met Andy Fallon before he became a corpse.

She studied the photographs, not feeling the shock or revulsion an ordinary person would have. She had been toughened past that initial instinctive response long ago. She looked at them as a cop, searching for what they could tell her. Then the thought occurred that Andy Fallon had been twelve once, just like Kyle, her oldest.

A tremor of fear rattled through her, slipping past her guard because she was tired. The worry that she didn't spend enough quality time with the boys was always in her mind, chewing at the edge of her consciousness. Their lives seemed to be set at fast-forward. The boys were swamped with school and Scouts and hockey. She was overburdened with work and trying to keep the house and put food on the table and sign permission slips and show up for parent-teacher meetings and attend to the thousand other business details of motherhood. They were all so exhausted, there was little energy left for one another at the end of the day. How was she supposed to know if one of them might be slipping through the cracks?

She'd read that experimentation with autoerotic asphyxiation was not uncommon among adolescent boys. Every year a fair portion of teen deaths written off as suicides were in fact autoerotic accidents. At twelve, Kyle was still more interested in Nintendo than girls, but puberty was right around the corner. Liska wanted to sneak around that corner and beat the shit out of puberty with her ASP.

She tried not to think about it as she focused on Andy Fallon. If his death was an accident, then why the note on the mirror? If this kind of sexual practice was a habitual thing for him, would Steve Pierce have known about it? Probably not, if they were just buddies. If they were more than that . . . If Pierce was lying, was he lying to protect Fallon's memory or to protect himself?

The *Diagnostic and Statistical Manual of Mental Disorders, Fourth Edition* – aka the DSM-IV – was on the table, open to page 529 and the heading 'Sexual Masochism'. Amazing the things people learned to do to get themselves off. The fantasies ranged from rape to bondage to being spanked to being peed on to wearing a diaper. Halfway down the page she found what she was looking for.

> *One particularly dangerous form of Sexual Masochism, called 'hypoxy-philia,' involves sexual arousal by oxygen deprivation. . . . Oxygen-depriving activities may be engaged in alone or with a partner. Because of equipment malfunction, errors in placement of the noose or ligature, or other mistakes, accidental deaths sometimes occur. . . . Sexual Masochism is usually chronic, and the person tends to repeat the same masochistic act.*

Alone or with a partner. Pierce's initial response to the question of Fallon's sexual habits had been indignation, but indignation could be used to cover any number of other emotions: embarrassment, fear, guilt. Steve Pierce professed to be straight. Maybe he was trying to hide the fact that he really wasn't, or that he had dabbled on the other side of that line. Or maybe he was telling the truth and Andy Fallon had other partners. Who?

They needed to find out more about Andy Fallon's private life. If he'd been lucky, there would be one to uncover. Anyone looking into Liska's private life would have had a short glance at nothing. She couldn't remember the last decent date she'd had. She never socialized with anyone but cops, and cops made lousy boyfriends as a rule. On the other hand, men with normal jobs found her a little too intimidating. The idea of a girlfriend who could handle a tactical baton and a nine-millimeter handgun was a bit much for the average Joe. So what was a girl to do? And when was a mother of two to do it?

She sensed the presence at her front door a split second before she heard the faint rattle of the lock being opened. Adrenaline surged through her. She came up off the couch in a heartbeat, eyes never leaving the door, hand reaching for the cordless phone. She wished it was her gun, but the gun remained locked in a cabinet when she was home – a necessary precaution for the safety of the boys and their friends. The ASP, however, was never far out of reach. Her right hand closed on the cushioned handle and she snapped her wrist in a well-practiced move to extend the steel rod to its full length.

She moved to the hinged side of the door as it began to ease open, and took a position with the baton.

A Cartman hand puppet popped into view, the *South Park* character craning its fat head around the door to look up at her.

'Hey, lady, you gonna shoot my ass?'

Relief and anger poured through Liska in a hot-cold mix that prickled her skin.

'Goddammit, Speed, I *ought* to shoot your ass! One of these days I'm going to plug you through that door and let you bleed out on the front step. It'd serve you right.'

'Is that any way to talk to the father of your children?' he asked, slipping inside and closing the door behind him. Not for the first time, Liska wished she didn't have to let him have a key. She didn't like him coming and going from her life and the boys' lives at will, but neither did she want a hostile relationship with him – for the sake of Kyle and R.J. Speed was an asshole, but he was their father and they needed him.

'The boys up?'

'It's eleven-thirty, Speed. No one should be up. Kyle and R.J. and I live in the real world, where people have to get up in the morning.'

He shrugged and tried to look innocent. Other women would have fallen for it. Liska was too familiar with the expression and the lack of sincerity behind it.

'What do you really want?'

He grinned the wicked grin of a romance-novel pirate. He must have been working a case, she thought. Though his blond hair was cropped almost military-short, he hadn't shaved in a few days. He wore a filthy old army field coat hanging open over faded, paint-spattered jeans and an old black sweatshirt. Despite all this, he looked sexy as hell. But she had long ago become immune.

'I could say I want you,' he said, moving toward her.

'Yeah,' Liska said, unimpressed. 'And I could still coldcock you. Give me a reason.'

The smile dropped off. Just like that.

'I can't drop by to leave a toy for my kids?' he said, pulling the puppet off his hand. 'What the hell's the matter with you, Nikki? You have to be such a bitch about everything?'

'You break into my house at eleven-thirty, scare the shit out of me, and expect me to be happy to see you? What's wrong with that picture?'

'I didn't break in. I have a key.'

'Yeah, you have a key. Do you have a fucking telephone? Could you use that once in a while instead of just blowing in like a tornado?'

Speed didn't bother to answer. He never answered questions he didn't like. He put the Cartman puppet down on the coffee table and picked up one of the Polaroids of Andy Fallon.

'This the kind of shit you leave around for my kids to see?'

'*Your* kids,' she muttered, snatching the photograph out of his hand. 'Like you did anything but provide the raw materials – and only half of that. How is it they're never *your* kids when they're sick or need new clothes or they're having trouble?'

'Do I need to hear this?' he asked, making a face.

'You came to my house. You hear whatever I want to say.'

'Dad!'

R.J. was across the room before the exclamation died. He flung himself at his father, wrapping his arms around Speed's legs. Liska scrambled to put down the ASP and pull the newspaper over it and the Fallon Polaroids, even though no one was paying the least attention to her.

'R.J., my man!' Speed grinned and high-fived his youngest, pulling free of the boy's embrace to squat down in front of him.

'I wanna be called Rocket now,' R.J. said, rubbing the sleep from one eye. His blond hair stood up in little tufts at the crown of his head. His Minnesota Vikings pajamas, inherited from Kyle, were too big for him. 'I wanna have a nickname like you, Dad.'

'Rocket. I like it,' Speed declared. 'Seriously cool, little man.'

The hand puppet was discovered and the two males went into a five-minute riff on *South Park*. Liska's fuse grew shorter and shorter.

'R.J., it's really late,' she said, hating to do it and hating Speed for making her into the bad guy with his mere presence. He breezed in and out of the boys' lives as he chose, all excitement and fun and adventure. As custodial parent, Liska felt she provided little of that and all of the discipline and drudgery. 'You have school tomorrow.'

Her son looked up at her with duplicates of her own blue eyes, angry and disappointed. 'But Dad just got here!'

'Then be mad at Dad. He's the one who thought it'd be a great idea to come over in the middle of the night when everyone's supposed to be sleeping.'

'*You're* not sleeping,' R.J. pointed out.

'I'm not ten either. When you get to be thirty-two you can stay up half the night working and taking Tagamet too. So you've got that to look forward to.'

'I'm gonna work undercover and be a narc like Dad.'

'You're gonna be undercover in bed in two minutes, mister.'

R.J. and Speed exchanged a look that locked Liska out of the loop. Speed shrugged. 'I'm outranked, Rocket. Better call it a night.'

'Can I take Cartman with me?'

'Sure.' He ruffled the boy's hair, his attention already shifting from his son to his ex.

Liska bent down to brush a kiss to R.J.'s cheek, but he ducked away and retreated down the hall, talking to the puppet in a cartoon voice and making farting noises. When he was out of sight and earshot, she glared at Speed.

'You are such a shit,' she hissed, straining to keep her voice down when she wanted to rail at him. 'You didn't come here to see R.J. –'

'Rocket.'

'– or Kyle. Now you've got R.J. all wound up. He won't sleep half the night.'

'Sorry.'

'No, you're not. You never are,' she said bitterly. 'What do you want, Speed? I'll bet it isn't to pay me the money you owe me.'

He pulled in a big breath. 'Next week. I promise,' he said with well-rehearsed contrition. 'I'm in the middle of something right now, but next week –'

'Save it. Pack up the act and make it a road show, why don't you,' Liska said, flipping the paper off the Polaroids. She gathered the pictures into a stack. 'It's been a very long day. I'd like to go to bed now, if you don't mind.'

Speed said nothing for a minute, then reached out and tapped a finger against the top photograph.

'Anyone I know?' he asked quietly. 'I heard one of yours offed himself. Is this him?'

'Looks that way. An IA guy. You wouldn't know him.'

They had both started out in uniforms in St Paul; Speed had stayed but she had gone across the river to Minneapolis. He knew a lot of Minneapolis cops – mainly the narcs and some of the homicide dicks – but he had no reason to know Andy Fallon. No one went out of their way to meet the people from Internal Affairs.

He slipped the picture out of her hand and examined it closely. 'Hell of a way to check out. I guess IA guys don't know how to shoot a gun, huh?'

'Who knows what goes on in people's heads,' Liska said.

There had been a time in their marriage when they had shared details of cases and helped each other work things through. She thought of those as the Golden Moments, that brief period of time before infidelity and professional rivalry pulled apart the fabric of their relationship.

'Maybe it wasn't his choice,' she said.

'Jesus, you homicide dicks.' He tossed the picture back down on the coffee table. 'It's a no-brainer, Nikki. Why torment yourself looking at these? The guy did himself. Hanging is suicide or an accident, not murder. Write it off and move on.'

'When the ME says let it go, I'll let it go. Not before,' she said, as much to be stubborn as anything. 'That's my job. That's the way I am.'

'Yeah. Well, you don't need to bring it home with you.'

'Don't accuse me of corrupting *your* children,' she said sourly. 'You heard R.J. He wants to be a narc. Can't get much lower than that.'

'Sure he could. He could be IA. Look how they wind up.'

Liska didn't look at the photo as he held it up. She didn't have to. 'All right. Enough pleasant chitchat for one evening. It's been . . . the usual. You know where the door is.'

Speed didn't move. He put on his yes-I-can-be-an-adult face. Liska sighed.

'You know, I came over here to see how you were doing,' he confessed. 'I heard you caught this one, Nikki. I thought it might be tough – because he was a cop, because he was IA. Because of your old man and all.'

'My father didn't kill himself,' Liska said too quickly, too defensively. The mistake left her feeling vulnerable.

'I know that, but the whole IA thing . . .'

'This has nothing to do with that,' she said flatly.

Speed considered his options. She could see him thinking, trying to figure how to play it. How to play her.

He spread his hands. The friend, just offering a suggestion. 'Still . . . Well, you can dump it as soon as the ME says suicide. Or you could pass it off now. A case like this hardly needs two detectives. Dump it on Kojak.'

Wrong tack. Liska bristled at the implication that she wasn't tough enough to handle it. 'What's it to you? I caught the case and I'll work it till it's over.'

'Fine. I just . . .' He blew out a long-suffering sigh and dragged a hand back over his head. 'I still care about you, Nikki, that's all. We have a history. That means something . . . even to an asshole like me.'

Liska said nothing. She trusted neither her voice nor the tangle of emotions knotting together inside her. His concern was unexpected and she was unprepared for the way it made her feel – vulnerable, needy. Not words she wanted associated with herself.

Speed reached inside his jacket, dug out a cigarette, and dangled it from his lip.

'Well,' he said softly, lifting a hand to touch her cheek. 'Don't say I never tried to do anything for you.'

Liska stepped aside, turned her face away.

'Yeah,' he said, letting his hand fall. 'I know where the door is. See you around, Nikki.'

He had his hand on the doorknob before she could make herself speak.

'Uh . . . Speed . . . thanks for your concern. But I'm fine. I can handle it. It's just another case.'

'Sure. Whatever. You'll be off it in a day and a half.'

He gave her one last long look, and Liska had the feeling he wanted to say something more. But he didn't. And then he was gone.

She locked the dead bolt behind him and turned out the lights. She gathered up the photographs of Andy Fallon and went to her bedroom to secure them in her briefcase. Then she checked on the boys, who were both pretending to be asleep, brushed her teeth, changed into an oversize T-shirt from the FBI National Academy, and went to bed so she could stare at the ceiling and watch the past whirl around in her memory like a carousel.

The junior high father-daughter dance. She was thirteen and mortified. Embarrassed. Guilt sat in her stomach like a huge, jagged rock because of the other emotions. Her father stood stiffly beside her, eyes downcast, as ashamed as she was to have people see him. A stocky man with piercing blue eyes, the left side of his face slack and drooping, as if all the nerves had been snipped with scissors. People staring at them – not only because of her father's face but because of the stories they'd heard: the implications of corruption in the police department, cops stealing drug money, an Internal Affairs investigation . . .

None of it was true, Nikki knew. She seemed to believe that more strongly than her father did, which made her angry. He was innocent. Why wouldn't he fight harder to prove it? Why wouldn't he spit in their faces? Deny, defy, take action. Instead, he went around in public with his head down in order to shield both his shame and the Bell's palsy the stress had induced. Words like *weak* and *spineless* drifted through his daughter's mind like dirt in a dust-bowl breeze. As each one crossed her mind, the feeling of guilt deepened and the resentment sharpened.

The investigation had dragged on for nearly eighteen months, petering out to nothing in the end. No charges had been brought. Everyone was supposed to forget and forgive. By then, Thomas Liska's health had begun to seriously deteriorate. Two years later he died of pancreatic cancer.

It was a very long night.

8

The body has been discovered.

Suicide. Accident. Tragedy.

The word *murder* has not been mentioned.

Is it really murder if dictated by necessity, if accompanied by remorse?

Sorry . . .

There is a sense of unease from knowing other people are now aware, even though they don't suspect. As if strangers are invading what should have remained private. The intimacy of death had been shared by just the two of them. The aftermath would be a public event.

That somehow cheapens the experience.

Andy Fallon stares out from the photograph, the last spark of life dying in the half-opened eyes, tongue coming out through the parted lips. The expression seems to take on an accusatory quality.

Sorry . . .

The photograph, cradled in one hand, is raised to the lips, the image of the death mask kissed.

Sorry . . .

But even as the apology is offered, the excitement rises.

9

Liska stormed into the cubicle, her face pinched with temper, cheeks pink with cold. Kovac watched her with dread because he knew the look and what it meant for the quality of his day. Still, he didn't move as she bore down on him. She slugged his left upper arm as hard as she could. It was like being hit with a ball peen hammer.

'Ouch!'

'*That* was for ditching me last night,' she announced. 'I waited for you, and because I waited for you, Leonard cornered me and gave me the third degree about the Nixon assault and how Jamal Jackson couldn't be tied to it in any way. Now he's got it in his head that Jackson can somehow claim false arrest and use it in his suit against the department.'

'What suit?' he asked, rubbing the sore spot.

'The suit Jackson's threatening. Brutality. Against me.'

Kovac rolled his eyes. 'Oh, for Christ's sake. We've got the video of him beaning me. Let him try to sue. If Leonard thinks Jackson has a case, he's got his head so far up his ass we should call the people at Guinness. It's gotta be some kind of record.'

'I know,' Liska said, calming. She tossed her purse in a deep desk drawer and dropped her briefcase in her chair. 'I'm sorry I belted you. I had a rotten night. Speed came by. I didn't get much sleep.'

'Oh, jeez. I'm not gonna have to hear about sex, am I?'

Liska's face went dark again, and she lunged across the cubicle and popped him a second time in exactly the same spot.

'Ouch!'

Elwood stuck his huge head around the side of the half-wall. 'Do I need to call the police?'

'Why?' Liska demanded, shrugging out of her coat. 'Is being a knothead a crime now?'

Kovac rubbed his arm. 'I guess I said the wrong thing.'

'Again,' Elwood added. 'Did she do that to your nose?'

Kovac tried to catch his reflection in the dark screen of his computer monitor, though he already knew how it looked: puffy and red and lumpy as an old drunk's. At least it wasn't broken for the umpteenth time.

'Physical abuse of men by women,' Elwood said. 'One of society's great taboos. Victim Services can probably hook you up with a support group, Sam. Should I call Kate Conlan?'

Kovac threw a pen at him. 'Why don't you go take a flying leap?'

Liska settled into her chair and swiveled toward him, looking sullen and maybe just a little contrite. 'I didn't get any sleep because my brain preferred to remain awake, dwelling on what an asshole my ex is, among other fine topics. What happened to your nose? Iron Mike didn't want to hear his son was into kinky sex?'

'It was an accident,' Kovac said. 'He took the news hard. He and Andy had had a split, probably about a month ago when Andy decided to tell him he preferred DC to AC. That's not an easy thing for a father to face, I guess. What'd you get from IA?'

'The cold shoulder. Lieutenant Ice Bitch gave me a lot of attitude and no information. She claims she doesn't want to compromise an IA investigation. Someone's career might get damaged.'

'I thought that was their goal.'

Liska shrugged. 'She was at Fallon's home Sunday night between eight and nine-thirty, discussing a case he was unhappy about. She says he seemed fine when she left. She did tell me he'd been depressed. She hadn't ordered him to see the shrink, but she'd suggested he do it.'

'Do we know if he took her up on it?'

'Confidential information.'

'No one's gonna talk until the ME's done,' Kovac said. 'They're all holding out to hear *suicide*, and then they won't have to talk at all, and to hell with anyone who wants to know why this kid killed himself. If that's what he did.'

Liska picked up a fat pen with a plastic bloodshot eyeball glued to one end. One of many odd treasures in their cubicle. They bought them for each other as a running joke. Kovac's most prized possession was a very realistic fake finger that looked as if it had been separated from its hand with a hacksaw. He liked to surprise people with it, leaving it in file folders, booby-trapping desks with it. It was the strangest thing a woman had ever given him – and, oddly, it brought him the most simple enjoyment. Two failed marriages to 'normal' women, and he got the biggest kick out of a chick who gave him imitation severed body parts. What did that say?

'You going to the autopsy?' Liska asked.

'What's the point? Bad enough seeing the kid dead. I don't need to watch him get carved up for no good reason. His brother told me Andy came to see him about a month ago. He was coming out of the closet. He'd told Mike, and it hadn't gone well.'

'That timing would coincide with his apparent depression.'

'Yeah. It sure smells like suicide,' he said. 'The crime scene guys didn't come up with anything unusual that I've heard about.'

'No, they didn't, but the grapevine says otherwise,' Liska said. 'Tippen told me it was the hot gossip at Patrick's last night. That they came up with all kinds of sex toys and gay pornography. Now, where do you think a rumor like that might have started?'

Kovac scowled. 'With the Three Stooges in uniform. Where'd you see Tippen this early?'

'Caribou Coffee. He has a really ugly double espresso habit.'

'Real cops are supposed to drink the sludge in the break room pot. It's tradition.'

'Christmas is a tradition,' Liska corrected him. 'Bad coffee is avoidable.'

'The thing that bothers me with the whole sex angle is this,' she went on. 'What if Andy Fallon *was* into S and M? Let's say he and a pal are playing around with erotic rope tricks and something goes wrong. Fallon dies. The partner panics and leaves the scene. That's a crime in my book. Man two: depraved indifference. At least.'

'I've been thinking about that too,' Kovac said. 'I went to see Steve Pierce last night. He seems like a man with something heavy on his chest.'

'What'd he have to say?'

'Nothing much. We were interrupted by his fiancée: the lovely Ms Jocelyn Daring, attorney-at-law.'

Liska's brows went up under her bangs. 'Daring as in Daring-Landis?'

'I made that assumption. No one corrected me.'

Liska gave a low whistle. 'There's an interesting twist. Anything back yet from latent prints?'

'No, but we can expect to find Pierce's prints. They were friends.'

Liska's phone rang and she turned to answer it.

Kovac turned back to his computer and hit the power switch. He figured he'd get a jump on the preliminary report on Andy Fallon's death. A week or so after the autopsy they would get the ME's reports. He would call the morgue sooner than that to hear about the tox screens and to try to speed the report process along.

Lieutenant Leonard appeared suddenly at the cubicle. 'Kovac. My office. Now.'

Liska kept her head down as she spoke on the phone, avoiding eye contact. Kovac bit back a big sigh and followed Leonard.

One wall of the lieutenant's office was dominated by a huge calendar dotted with round colored stickers. Red for open homicides, black for when the case cleared. Orange for open assaults, blue for when they closed. Color-coordinated crime fighting. Neat and tidy. The shit they taught these guys in management class.

Leonard went behind his desk and stood with his hands on his hips and a frown on his mug face. He was wearing a tweedy brown sweater over a shirt and tie. The sleeves of the sweater were too long. The overall picture made Kovac think of a sock monkey he'd had as a kid.

'You'll have a preliminary report from the ME on the Fallon kid later today.'

Kovac gave his head a little shake, as if he had water in his ear. 'What? I was told it could be four or five days before they even got to him.'

'Someone called in a favor. On account of Mike Fallon,' Leonard added. 'He's a department hero. No one wants him suffering more than he has to because of this. What with the circumstances surrounding the suicide...'

His lipless mouth squirmed like a worm. Distasteful business: naked suicide with kinky sexual overtones.

'Yeah,' Kovac said. 'Damned inconsiderate of the kid to off himself that way. If that's what happened. It's an embarrassment to the department.'

'That's a secondary consideration, but it's a valid one,' Leonard said defensively. 'The media is all too happy to make us look bad.'

'Well, this would do the trick. First it's downtown beat cops spending their shifts in strip clubs. Now this. We got us a regular Sodom and Gomorrah down here.'

'You can keep that comment to yourself, Sergeant. I don't want anyone talking to the media with regards to this case. I'll give the official statement later today. "Sergeant Fallon's untimely death was a tragic accident. We mourn his loss and our thoughts are with his family." ' He recited the lines he'd memorized, trying them out for size and impact.

'Dry, brief, to the point,' Kovac critiqued. 'Sounds good, as long as it's true.'

Leonard stared at him. 'Do you have any reason to believe it *isn't* true, Sergeant?'

'Not at the moment. It'd be nice to have a couple of days to tie up the loose ends. You know, like an investigation. What if it was a sex game gone wrong? There could be an issue of culpability.'

'Do you have any proof anyone else was at the scene?'

'No.'

'And you've been told he was having problems with depression, that he was seeing the department shrink?'

'Uh ... yeah,' Kovac said, figuring it was a half-truth, at least.

'He had ... *issues*,' Leonard said, uncomfortable with the topic.

'I know he was gay, if that's what you mean.'

'Then don't stir the pot,' Leonard snapped. Taking a sudden interest in the paperwork on his desk, he sat down and opened a file folder. 'There's nothing to be gained in it. Fallon killed himself either accidentally or on purpose. The sooner we all move on, the better. You've got cases open.'

'Oh, yeah,' Kovac said dryly. 'My murders of tomorrow.'

'Your what?'

'Nothing, sir.'

'Tie this up and get back on the Nixon assault. The county attorney is riding me like a jockey on that one. Gang violence is a priority.'

Yeah, Kovac thought, heading back toward the cubicle, *keep those gang stats down to placate the city council*. The odd, unexplained death of a cop could be shrugged off.

He told himself he should be happy. He didn't want the Fallon case dragging on any more than Leonard did, though for different reasons. Leonard could give a shit about Iron Mike. He'd probably never even met the man. Leonard's concern was the department. Kovac wanted it over for Mike's sake – same as whoever had called in the marker with the ME. Yet that fist of tension Kovac didn't want to acknowledge held firm in the pit of his belly, as familiar to him as a lover's touch. More so, considering how long it had been since he'd had a lover.

Liska shoved his coat at him. 'You need a cigarette, don't you, Sam?'

'Hello? I'm quitting. Big fucking help you are.'

'Then you should get a lot of fresh air. To clean the crud out of your lungs.'

She stepped in close and gave him a meaningful look. He followed when she turned for the door.

'Fallon's over,' he said, pulling on his topcoat as they left the office.

Liska looked at him the same way he'd looked at Leonard, only more so.

'The autopsy's a done deal.'

'What?'

'Everyone expects a suicide ruling. Only they'll call it accidental, just to go easy on Mike. We'll have a preliminary report today and a benediction from Leonard. No one upstairs wants Mike – or the department – to be further embarrassed by the sordid details.'

'Yeah, I bet not,' Liska said, suddenly looking pale.

She didn't speak again until they were outside. Kovac didn't ask for an explanation. They'd been together long enough that he could read her easily. A partnership on the job was an intimacy – not in the sexual sense, but psychologically, emotionally. The more in tune with each other, the better they could work a case. His partnership with Liska was as good as any he'd had. They understood each other, respected each other.

He walked beside her through a maze of halls and out a little-used door on the north side of the building. The sun was out, brilliant and blinding on the snow. The sky was the pale blue of a robin's egg. A deceptively pretty day with a windchill factor in the teens. There was no one else on this set of steps, which caught no sunlight and all the wind. People flocked instead to the south side like arctic birds searching for warmth.

Kovac winced as the cold slapped him in the face. He jammed his hands down in his coat pockets and turned a hunched shoulder to the wind.

'Leonard told you Fallon was over,' Liska said.

'Wrap it up and close it.'

'Who made that autopsy happen so fast?'

'Someone higher on the food chain.'

Liska looked up the street, the muscles in her jaw tensing. The wind fluttered through her short hair and brought moisture to her eyes. He could sense he wasn't going to like what she was working up to tell him.

'So what bug's up your ass?' he asked irritably. 'It's colder than my second wife's mother out here.'

'I just had a call from someone who claims to have known what Andy Fallon was working on.'

'Does this someone have a name?'

'Not yet. But I saw him yesterday in the IA offices. Another dissatisfied customer.'

The fist in Kovac's belly pressed knuckles-down and started to grind. 'And what does he claim Fallon was working?'

She looked up at him. 'A murder.'

'Murder?' Kovac said with disbelief. 'Since when does IA touch a murder? No way. A felony always goes to the division, on account of IA can't find their own asses in a dark room. How could Fallon be working a murder and us not know about it? That's bullshit.'

'He could have if we thought it was closed,' Liska said. 'Remember Eric Curtis?'

'*Curtis?* The off-duty patrol cop? The mutt that did him is sitting in jail. What was his name? Vermin?'

'Verma. Renaldo Verma.'

'A string of robbery-assaults. Gay victims. He did – what? Three or four in eighteen months.'

'Four. Two of the vics died. Curtis was last.'

'Same MO as the others, right? Bound, beaten, robbed.'

'Yes, but Eric Curtis was a cop,' Liska pointed out.

'So?'

'So he was a cop and he was gay. According to my mystery man, months before his death, Curtis had complained to IA about harassment on the job because of his sexual preference.'

'And you're saying maybe a cop killed him because of it?' Kovac said. 'Jesus, Tinks. You want to believe that, maybe you ought to apply for Fallon's job.'

'Fuck you, Kojak,' she snapped. 'I hate IA. I hate what they do to people. I hate them like you can't know. But Eric Curtis was a cop, and he was gay, and now he's dead. Andy Fallon was looking into it, he was gay, and now *he's* dead,' she said, not liking the sound of it herself by the scowl on her face. And still, she stood up to him, toe to toe, and pressed her point. That was Liska: no job too mean or too ugly. She stepped up to the plate and swung at whatever she had to.

'And I just got told the book is all but closed on Fallon,' Kovac said, looking out at the street.

'You don't like it either, Sam,' Liska said quietly. 'You can feel it in your gut, can't you?'

He didn't answer her right away. He let it all roll through his head like a movie while the carillon in the city hall clock tower began to mark the hour with 'White Christmas'.

'No,' he said at last. 'I don't like anything about this.'

They were both silent for a moment. Cars rolled by on Fourth Street. The wind howled down the tunnels created by the buildings, snapping the flags on the federal building across the street.

'Andy Fallon probably killed himself,' Liska said. 'There wasn't anything at the scene to say he didn't. This guy that just called me. Who's to say he gives a shit about Andy Fallon? Maybe the Curtis murder is just his ax to grind and he thinks we'll get into it through the back door. . . . But what if it's not, Sam? We're all Andy Fallon has. And Mike. You taught me that – who do we work for?'

'The victim,' he murmured, that bad feeling still heavy in the bottom of his stomach.

They worked for the victim. He'd grounded that into countless trainees. The victims couldn't speak for themselves. It was up to the detective to ask all pertinent questions, to dig and prod, and turn over rocks until he found the truth. Sometimes it was easy. And sometimes it wasn't.

'What's it gonna hurt to ask a few more questions?' he said, knowing it sounded too much like something for the Famous Final Words file.

'I'll take the morgue.' Liska hugged her coat around her as she turned back for the door. 'You take IA.'

'I've already spoken with your partner, Sergeant,' Lieutenant Savard said, barely glancing up at him as she sorted through a pile of reports on her desk. 'And, in case you haven't been informed, Andy Fallon's death is being ruled an accident.'

'In record time,' Kovac said.

The IA lieutenant gave him her undivided attention at that. The green of her eyes was almost startling. Clear and cold, staring out from beneath brows several shades darker than the ash blond of her hair. The contrast intensified the sharp seriousness of her expression. He had to think she scared the shit out of a lot of cops with that look.

He'd been around too long to feel fear. He was numb to it. Or maybe he was just stupid.

He sat in the chair across the desk from her, ankles crossed. He'd done a brief stint in IA himself a hundred years ago, back when the department had been run by a real cop, not some brass-polisher looking to shine his way up the chain of command. He hadn't been ashamed to work the job. He had no love for bad cops. But he hadn't liked it either.

In those days there hadn't been any lieutenants on the force who looked like this one.

'Damn decent of them to do the slicing and dicing so quick, don't you think?' he said. 'Seeing how backed up they are at the morgue this time of year. They've got bodies stacked up like Yule logs, for Christ's sake.'

'Professional courtesy,' Savard said curtly.

Kovac caught himself watching her lips. They were the perfect shape of an archer's bow, with a sheer coat of lipstick.

'Yeah, well,' he said, 'I feel like I kinda owe old Mike the same courtesy, you know? Do you know him? Mike Fallon?'

The eyes went back to the papers. 'I know of him. I spoke with him on the phone today and gave him my condolences.'

'Yeah, you're too young. You wouldn't have been around in the days of Iron Mike. You must be – what? Thirty-seven, thirty-eight?'

She looked at him as if she had a mouthful of bitters. 'That would be none of your business, Sergeant. And just a word of advice. If you're going to try to guess a woman's age, err on the side of youth.'

Kovac winced. 'Was I that far off?'

'No. You were that close. I'm vain. Now, if you don't mind . . .' She lifted some of the papers and rattled them. The subtle reminder to leave.

'I just have a couple of questions.'

'You don't need questions or answers to them. You have no case to investigate.'

'But I have Mike,' he reminded her. 'I'm just trying to piece some things together for him. It's a tough thing for a parent to lose a child. If it helps for me to fill him in on Andy's last days, then I'll do that. That doesn't seem too much to ask, do you think?'

'It is if you want confidential information from an Internal Affairs investigation,' Savard said, pushing her chair back from the desk.

She had tried the cool dismissal. Now she would try to herd him out. Kovac stayed seated for a moment, just to irk her, just to let her know he wouldn't give up that easily. She came around the desk to show him the door. He waited until she was near his chair, then he stood, making her hesitate. She took a half-step back, frowning, retreating and not liking it.

'I know about the Curtis thing,' Kovac bluffed.

'Then you know you don't need to speak with me after all, don't you?'

A wry smile tugged at one corner of his mouth. 'You didn't ride in here on the equal rights bandwagon, did you, Lieutenant?'

'Believe me, I'm more than qualified for my job, Sergeant Kovac.'

There was something like amusement in her voice, but it was darker. Irony, maybe. He couldn't begin to imagine why, or where it came from, or why she would allow him to hear it. It wasn't important to him now, but he filed the curiosity in his brain, just in case he might need it later.

He crossed his arms and sat back against the edge of her desk as she made a move toward the door. Irritation flashed in the green eyes. Temper brought a tint of color to her cheeks. This, he thought, was what television wanted lady lieutenants to look like: classy, sleek, stylish in a steel-gray pantsuit. Cool, controlled, sexy in an understated way.

Too classy for you, Kovac, he thought. A lieutenant. Jesus. Why was he even looking?

'Did you know Andy Fallon was gay?' he asked.

'His personal life was none of my business.'

'That's not what I asked.'

'Yes, he told me he was gay.'

'Before you went to his house Sunday night?'

'You're pressing your luck here, Sergeant,' Savard said. 'I've already told you, I'm not going to answer your questions. Do you really want me to speak to your lieutenant about this?'

'You can call him, but he's busy practicing his it-was-a-tragic-accident-now-drop-it speech.'

'He should be practicing it on you.'

'I've already given him my critique – there's no beat and you can't dance to it. He should keep his day job as a petty bureaucrat and forget about politics.'

'I'm sure your opinion means a great deal to him.'

'Yeah. Exactly nothing,' he said. 'Yours will mean more, if you decide to go that way. He'll ask me in his office and tell me to do my job the way he says or get suspended. Thirty days without pay. And all because I'm trying to do something decent for another cop. Life sucks, some days harder than others. But what am I supposed to do? Hang myself?'

Savard's face darkened. 'That wasn't funny, Sergeant.'

'It wasn't meant to be. I'm sure you know it was meant to make you see Andy Fallon in your head again. I can show you the Polaroids if you want.' He pulled one out of his inside breast pocket and held it up like a magician doing a card trick. 'It's a hell of a thing to see, isn't it?'

The blood drained out of the lieutenant's face. She looked as if she wanted to hit him with something. 'Put it away.'

Kovac flipped it over and looked at it with the dispassion of someone who had seen hundreds of such photographs. 'You knew him. You had a connection to him. You're sorry he's dead. Think how his old man feels.'

'Put it away,' she said again. There was the barest hint of a tremor in her voice as she added, 'Please.'

He slipped the Polaroid back into his coat pocket. 'Do you care enough to help lay a father's doubts to rest?'

'Does Mike Fallon have doubts about Andy's death being an accident?' she asked.

'Mike has doubts about who Andy was.'

She moved away from him, silent for a moment, thinking, considering. 'No one knows anyone. Not really. Most of us don't even know ourselves.'

Kovac watched her, intrigued by the sudden turn to philosophy. She seemed reflective rather than defensive.

'I know exactly who I am, Lieutenant,' he said.

'And who are you, Sergeant Kovac?'

'I'm exactly what you're looking at,' he answered, lifting his arms to the sides. 'I'm a flatfoot, a straight-line cop in a cheap suit from J.C. Penney. I'm a walking, talking stereotype. I eat bad food, drink too much, and smoke – though I'm trying to quit and think I should score character points for that. I don't run marathons or do tai chi or compose opera in my free time. If I have a question, I ask it. People don't always like that, but fuck 'em – pardon my language, another bad habit I won't be shed of. Oh, yeah – and I'm stubborn as hell.'

Savard arched a brow. 'Let me guess. You're divorced?'

'Twice, but that won't stop me from trying again. Under the cheap suit beats the heart of a hopeless romantic.'

'Is there any other kind?'

Kovac chose not to answer. The better part of valor.

'So, I want to do this for Mike,' he said. 'Ask around about his kid, try to put together a picture he can live with. Will you help me with that?'

Savard thought about that for a moment, digested it, dissected it, weighed the pros and cons.

'Andy Fallon was a good investigator,' she said at last. 'He always tried hard. Sometimes he tried too hard.'

'What does that mean? Too hard?'

'Just that the job was everything to him. He worked too hard and took failures too much to heart.'

'Had he had a failure lately? The Curtis case?'

'Officer Curtis's killer is sitting in jail awaiting sentencing.'

'Renaldo Verma.'

'If you know that, then you should know there is no case ongoing in this department regarding Eric Curtis.'

'I guess not, what with your investigator being dead and all.'

'The case was dead before Andy.'

'Had Curtis complained about harassment?'

Savard said nothing.

Kovac felt his patience slip. 'Look, I can go to the gay and lesbian officers' liaison. Curtis would have told them before he came to IA. But then I'll come back here, and I gotta think you've already seen enough of me to last you.'

'Yes,' she said, letting the answer hang a moment. 'Officer Curtis had filed a complaint some time before his death. Because of that there was some IA interest when he was murdered. But the evidence pointed to no one but Verma, and the case ended with Verma's plea agreement.'

'And the names of the officers in question?'

'Will remain confidential.'

'I can dig them up.'

'You can dig all you want,' Savard said. 'But you won't do it here. The case is closed and I have no reason to reopen it.'

'Why was Fallon so upset if the killer is sitting in jail?'

'I don't know. Andy had a lot on his mind this last month or so. Only he could tell you what or why. He didn't confide in me. And I don't care to

432

speculate. No one can know another person's heart. There are too many barriers.'

'Sure you can.' Kovac met her eyes with an even gaze that tried to see past her barriers. Without luck, he acknowledged. Those walls were thick. A woman didn't get where she was by letting weaknesses show.

'You just have to be willing to chip away the bullshit,' he said. 'Me, I'm knee-deep in it half the time. I don't even mind the smell anymore.'

The lieutenant said nothing, though Kovac had the impression she had much to say, that words were building up inside her like water behind a dam. He could sense the tension in her. But in the end she stepped away from him.

'Take your pickax and chip elsewhere, Sergeant Kovac.' She pulled the door open, offering him the view of the outer office. 'I've told you as much as I'm going to tell you.'

Kovac took his time going to the door. When he was even with Amanda Savard, he stopped – just a hair inside her comfort zone. Close enough to catch the subtle hint of her perfume. Close enough to see the pulse beat beneath the delicate skin in the hollow at the base of her throat. Close enough to feel something like electricity hum just under his skin.

'You know, somehow I don't think so, Lieutenant,' he said softly. 'Thank you for your time.'

10

Renaldo Verma was an oily rat of a man. Slight of build, he had the sinewy, boiled-down look of a longtime crack addict, which he was. It was difficult to imagine him overpowering anyone, let alone a police officer. Yet he had pled guilty to murder in the second degree for beating a man to death with a baseball bat. His record ran the gamut from soliciting to drugs, from burglary to robbery. Assault and murder were recent additions to his repertoire, but he had shown a flair for both. He had fallen into a pattern of robbery and assault that shared traits beyond MO. The mind hunters liked to call it 'signature', acts committed during the crime that were unnecessary to the completion of the crime but fulfilled some inner need. He might eventually have graduated to serial killer had he been better at eluding capture.

Verma came into the interrogation room with a swagger to his gait, as if he had something to be cocky about. He took his seat opposite Kovac and immediately reached for the pack of Salems on the table. His hands were long and bony, like the paws of a rodent, the skin marked with lesions that were likely a sign of AIDS.

'I hadn't ought to be speaking to you without my lawyer,' he said, and blew smoke out his nostrils. His nose was thin and long, with a pair of bumps along the bridge. A pencil-thin mustache rode his long upper lip like a dirty shadow. He had an affected, somewhat effeminate way of speaking, and an elaborate body language. His whole upper body swayed and bent and twisted as he spoke, as if he were listening to ballroom dance music in his head.

'So call your lawyer,' Kovac said, rising. 'But I don't have time for that bullshit. By the time he gets here, I'll be long gone and you'll get stuck with the bill.'

'Taxpayers get stuck with that bill,' Verma said, snickering, his bony shoulders collapsing together as his chest caved in. 'What do I care?'

'Yeah, I can see you don't give a rat's ass about anything,' Kovac said. 'So you'll only feed me what you think I want to hear because you're looking for a trade. Only it's too late for a trade. You made your bed with the county attorney. It's in the pen in St Cloud.'

'No, it ain't,' Verma said with smug confidence, wagging a finger at Kovac. 'It's in Oak Park Heights. I ain't going to that slab of granite way the fuck north. That place is medieval. I'm going to the Heights. That's part of the deal. I got friends in the Heights.'

Kovac pulled a folded sheet of paper from the inside pocket of his suit coat, consulted it as if it were something more important than the receipt for his dry cleaning, put it back. 'Yeah, well, whatever you think.'

Verma narrowed his eyes in suspicion. 'What do you mean? We did the deal. The deal is done.'

Kovac shrugged, indifferent. 'Whatever. I want to talk to you about the Eric Curtis murder.'

'I didn't do it.'

'You know how many mutts say that?' Kovac countered. 'Every last frigging one of 'em. Do I need to point out this ain't the Ritz-Carlton we're sitting in?'

'I copped to the Franz murder. And I didn't mean to kill him.'

'Of course not. How were you to know the human head can take only so much beating?'

'I didn't *go there* to kill him,' Verma clarified, pouting.

'Oh, I see. It was his fault for being at home when you came by to rob him. He was clearly an idiot. You should be commended for taking him out of the gene pool.'

Verma stood up. 'Hey, I don't need you on my ass, Kovac.'

'Yeah, I'm sure you've got some big homey back in lockup to cover that for you. Think he'll go up to St Cloud too? Or will you have to get back in the dating game?'

Verma pointed the cigarette at him, ash raining down on the tabletop. 'I am *not* going to St Cloud. You talk to my attorney.'

'Your attorney, the overworked, underpaid servant of Hennepin County? Yeah, I'll look him up. See if he remembers your name.' He stood up, went around the table, and put a hand on Verma's bony shoulder. 'Have a seat, Mr Vermin.'

Verma's butt hit the chair with a thud. He crushed out the cigarette on the tabletop and lit another.

'I didn't kill no cop.'

'Uh-huh. So the county attorney charged that out just for the hell of it? Just 'cause he wanted some poor grunt in his office to do more paperwork?' Kovac made a face as he slid back down on his own chair. 'Give me a break. He charged it out because it fit you to a *T*. Same MO as the others.'

'So? You never heard of a copycat?'

'You don't strike me as a role model.'

'Yeah? So how come I got the deal?' Verma asked smugly. 'They didn't have shit on me for that murder. No prints. No witnesses.'

'No? Well, you're the fucking Shadow, aren't you? So if you didn't do Curtis, how come you had his watch in your apartment?'

'It was a shock to me,' Verma insisted. 'I sure as hell didn't put it there. Fucking Timex. Why would I steal that?'

'Takes a lickin' and keeps on tickin',' Kovac said. 'That could come in handy where you're going. You knew Eric Curtis,' he went on. 'He ran you in for soliciting – twice.'

Verma shrugged, pursing his lips and lowering his lashes coyly. 'No hard feelings. Last time I offered him a freebie. He was cute. He said, "Maybe some other time." Wish he would have taken me up.'

'So you dropped by his place for the rain check. One thing led to another . . .'

'No,' Verma said firmly. He looked Kovac in the eye as he drew hard on the cigarette. The smoke came out in a forceful stream directed at Kovac's chest. 'Look, Kojak, those other cops tried to stick me with that Curtis murder, and they couldn't. The county attorney tried, and he couldn't.'

He leaned across the table, trying to look seductive. It made Kovac's skin crawl. 'I know you're hard for it,' he murmured, 'but you can't stick it in me either.'

'I'd rather stick it in a light socket.'

Verma threw himself back in the chair and laughed dementedly. 'Spoken like a man who doesn't know what he's missing.'

'Believe me, I'm not missing it.'

Verma snickered, then stuck his tongue out as far as he could and waggled it obscenely. 'You don't want me to suck you off, Kojak? Maybe stick my tongue in your ass?'

'Jesus Christ.' Kovac shoved his chair back from the table. He pulled a brown muffler from the pocket of the overcoat he had hung over the back of the chair, went across the room to the corner where the video camera hung, and draped the scarf over it.

Verma sat up straight, one hand fluttering at the base of his throat. 'Hey, man, what you do that for?'

'Uh-oh, Renaldo!' Kovac whispered, wide-eyed, as he came back toward the table. 'I don't think that video camera is working anymore!'

Verma tried to scuttle off the chair, but Kovac caught him by the back of the neck and held him firmly in place, leaning down over his shoulder from behind.

'The only thing I want to put up your ass is the toe of my shoe,' he said softly. 'Cut the crap, Vermin. You think I don't have people in St Cloud who owe me favors?'

'I'm not going to –' The pressure tightened on his neck, cutting him off. His shoulders came up to his ears.

'My sister's kid is a guard up there,' Kovac lied. 'He's a big dumb fuck straight off the dairy farm. Not too bright, but he's loyal as a dog. Too bad about his temper.'

'Okay! Okay!'

Kovac let him go and went back to his seat.

'Can't blame me for trying,' Verma pouted, reaching for the Salems. Kovac pulled them out of reach, shook one out, and lit up, telling himself it was a tactical move rather than caving in.

'You've got that rugged thing going on,' Verma said, playing coy. 'So hot.'

'Vermin . . .'

'What?' he asked with a great show of exasperation. 'What d'you want from me, Kojak? You want me to cop to Curtis? Fuck you. The deal is done and I didn't do him. The county attorney didn't press it 'cause they got shit. But they'll let it hang on my rep. They'll say they got me cold for Franz and saved the state some money on a trial. And that's okay by me. Won't do me no harm to have the boys at the Heights think I did a cop. But I didn't do Curtis. You want to know who did Curtis, you ask your homicide sergeant Springer. He knows who did Curtis.'

Kovac let that hang in the air for a moment, as if maybe he hadn't even been paying attention. He looked off into the middle distance, smoking, wondering how sick it was to actually enjoy the feel of tar and nicotine settling in his lungs.

'Yeah?' he said at last, turning back to Verma. 'Then why didn't he nail the son of a bitch?'

'On account of the son of a bitch was another cop.'

'Says you.'

'Says that good-looking boy from Internal Affairs.'

'I don't know who you mean,' Kovac said, nerves tightening.

'Lean muscle, pretty, like a Versace model.' Verma closed his eyes and hummed to himself. 'Yummy.'

'Uh-huh. So this IA weasel comes around and talks to you. He tells you balls-out he thinks a cop whacked Curtis?'

Verma stuck out his lower lip and slouched. Kovac wanted to smack him.

'Yeah, I thought so,' he said. 'What'd he ask you about?'

Verma shrugged. 'This and that. Stuff about the murder. Stuff about after the murder. The investigation – I use the term loosely.'

'And you told him what?'

'Why don't you ask him?'

''Cause I'm asking you. You oughta be happy about that, Renaldo. You rank above IA. Then again, so does the clap.'

'I tell him I didn't kill Curtis and I don't care how many cops want me to say different. Not him. Not Springer. Not the uniform.'

'What uniform?'

'The one gave me this,' he said, pointing to the higher of the two bumps on the bridge of his nose. 'Said I was resisting.'

'I apologize on behalf of the department,' Kovac said without remorse. 'This uniform have a name?'

'Big dude,' Verma said. 'Studly Steroid, I called him. He didn't like it. His partner called him B.O. He didn't seem to mind *that*,' he complained, flinging up a hand in disgust. 'But I guess that was short for something besides the way he smelled. I read his name on his chest just before he knocked me out. Ogden.'

'Ogden,' Kovac repeated, the flashback coming so fast it damn near made his head swim: Steve Pierce wrestling on the floor of Andy Fallon's kitchen with a human moose. The moose stumbling to his feet with blood gushing from his nose.

Ogden.

'Verma got a deal because your people fucked up,' Chris Logan said bluntly as he dug through a drift of paperwork on his desk. 'Talk to Cal Springer about chain of evidence. Ask him if he knows dick about the specifics of a search warrant.'

'Something was funky about the evidence?' Kovac stayed on his feet near the door of Logan's small office, ready to bolt with the prosecutor, who was due in court in five minutes.

Logan swore under his breath, still staring down at the mess on his desk, hands on his hips. He was a tall, athletic type. Early thirties, with good looks and a big chip on his shoulder. A tough guy with a law degree and a quick temper.

He was a good prosecutor. Ted Sabin's sword arm, seeing as the county attorney rarely tried a case himself.

'Everything was wrong,' Logan mumbled.

He dove for the wastebasket sitting beside his desk, tearing through crumpled paper, discarded candy wrappers, mutilated bags from half a dozen take-out places in the skyway system that connected into the government center. He came up with a yellow wad the size of a softball, spread it out, and scanned the handwriting. After a moment he blew out a sigh of relief and rolled his eyes heavenward. He crammed the paper into the briefcase and headed for the door.

Kovac followed, then matched him stride for stride.

'I'm due in court,' Logan said, weaving his way through the population in the hall outside the county attorney's offices.

'I don't have a lot of time, myself,' Kovac said. He wondered if Savard had followed through on her threat to call his boss. She was too tough a read to say for sure one way or the other. Who could say how long before Leonard yanked him in for the Big Talk.

They stepped into an empty elevator and Kovac badged the people trying to get on behind them.

'Police business, folks. Sorry,' he said, hitting the CLOSE DOOR button with his free hand.

Logan looked unhappy, but then, he looked that way a lot of the time.

'Everything we had was circumstantial,' he said. 'Prior association, motive, Verma's MO. But there were no witnesses placing Verma at or near the scene, and there was no forensic evidence. No prints. No fibers. No bodily fluids. Verma had jacked off at the other crime scenes. Not with Curtis. We don't know why. Maybe something made him leave the scene early. Maybe he couldn't get it up. Who knows? It could have been anything.'

'So, what was the deal with the watch?' Kovac asked as the elevator landed and the doors pulled back to reveal a human hive of activity.

The hall outside the courtrooms was perpetually packed with wheeler-dealers, shysters, losers, the frightened, the bewildered. All summoned to feed themselves into the machine of the Hennepin County justice system.

'So, some idiot uniform claimed he found it on Verma's dresser, but the whole deal stank to high heaven,' Logan said, angling for a courtroom door. 'It was O.J. and the fucking bloody glove all over again. No way we were getting it admitted. And in light of the last few lawsuits against your department, Sabin didn't even want to try.'

'Even though the vic was a cop,' Kovac said with disgust.

Logan shrugged, heading for the counsel table nearest the best air vent in the room. 'We couldn't have won the case. The city didn't want another lawsuit. What was the point of pressing for it? We got Verma to cop to Franz. He's going away.'

'On murder two.'

'Piggybacked on assault with intent, on felony robbery. It's no lightweight stretch. Besides, he killed Franz with Franz's own baseball bat. Weapon of opportunity. How could we argue premeditation?'

'Was there ever any feeling Verma didn't do Curtis? That maybe he really was being railroaded?'

'There were some rumors Curtis had been harassed by other patrol cops because he was gay. But it didn't add up to murder, and the circumstantial case spelled out VERMA in big fat caps.'

Kovac sighed and looked around the room. The bailiff was joking with the clerk. The defense attorney, a squat woman with a frizzy gray bun and huge clear-rimmed glasses, set her mega-briefcase on the defense counsel table and came over to Logan with a hopeless smirk on her face.

'Last chance for a deal, Chris.'

'In your dreams, Phyllis,' Logan said, hauling a file as thick as the Bible out of his case. 'No breaks on kiddie porn freaks.'

'Too bad you don't feel as strongly about murderers,' Kovac said, and walked away.

'Why'd you go to Verma?' Liska asked, plucking a french fry from the red plastic basket Kovac's food had come in. She was late. He'd ordered without her. 'Lying sack of shit,' she added.

'You've met him?'

'No.' She swiped a second fry through the puddle of ketchup on his plate. 'They're all lying sacks of shit. That's my sweeping generalization of the day.'

'You want something?' he asked, hailing the waitress.

'No. I'll just eat yours.'

'The hell you will. You owe me ninety-two thousand french fries as it is. You never get your own.'

'They're too fattening.'

'What? They're less fattening if I order them?'

She flashed him a grin. 'That's right. And besides, you're gonna gain weight 'cause you're quitting smoking. I'm doing you a favor. Why'd you go to Verma?'

Kovac sat back from the burger, his appetite souring. He'd chosen Patrick's out of habit, and regretted it. As always, the place was populated by cops. He had claimed a booth in the rear and put his back to the corner. He felt a little that way – cornered. He didn't like what Verma had told him or what Logan had alluded to; didn't like the knowledge that if he were to pursue this look into Andy Fallon's life, most of the other players would be cops, and there was a fair chance not all of them would be good.

'Because if IA was involved in the Curtis thing, I can't say why. Savard wouldn't tell me,' he said, keeping his voice in the low register of confidences. 'Maybe they were looking into the actual murder, like your guy said. Or maybe they were looking at the investigation. I wanted a feel for it before I went to Springer for answers.'

'Cal Springer couldn't find shit in a cow pasture,' Liska proclaimed, then ordered a Coke from a slouchy waitress. 'But I've never heard anyone say he's rotten.'

'He's an idiot,' Kovac declared. 'Pompous prick. He spends more time trying to organize union socials than he does on his caseload. Still, this Curtis thing looked like a slam-dunk. Even Springer shouldn't have been able to screw it up. But Verma says he didn't do it.'

Liska made her eyes and mouth round. 'No! An innocent man in jail!'

'Yeah, he's pure as the driven snow,' Kovac said with heavy sarcasm. 'But here's the deal. He claims a cop threw down Eric Curtis's watch in his place. Ogden.'

Liska's brow furrowed. 'Ogden? From yesterday?'

'The one and only. An allegation like that would bring IA in. Logan told me the situation smelled so bad, Sabin didn't want to touch it. And Ted Sabin doesn't smell blood in the water, then climb out of the pool. Especially considering Curtis was a cop.'

'Curtis was a *gay* cop,' Liska reminded him. 'Who was a victim of a criminal targeting openly gay men. You think the mayor and her stooges want a media spotlight on that?'

Kovac conceded the point with a shift of his eyebrows.

'Verma also claims it was a cop did Curtis.'

'So why didn't we ever hear about any of this?' Liska asked, clearly perturbed to have been left out of the loop.

'That's a good question. IA only got involved within the last month or so.

440

Verma's been in the can at least two. Maybe no one knew IA was looking. Springer sure as hell wouldn't broadcast the news if he knew about it. The ass-pucker factor would be so extreme as to render him incapable of speech.' He actually found a chuckle for the thought. 'Ha! IA after Cal Springer. That's funny.'

Liska didn't join in the merriment, but Kovac didn't notice.

'Maybe no one knew until Andy Fallon told them,' she said.

'Can you set up a meeting with your mystery man and get us some details?'

Liska pulled a face. 'He has to call me. He wouldn't give me his number this morning. He seemed nervous.'

'They'd have his name and number in IA, by the sound of what you heard in there yesterday.'

'But IA won't give it to us. We can't even ask. Our case is officially closed.'

'It's closed when I sign off on it,' Kovac said, realizing with no great enthusiasm that he had gone territorial. The case was his. He didn't want anyone telling him how to run it or when to stop it or anything else. He ran a case until he was satisfied. He was a long way from being satisfied.

'It won't be that simple this time,' Liska said. 'Guess who made Andy Fallon's corpse leapfrog the line waiting at the morgue?'

Kovac scowled. 'I'm not gonna like this, am I?'

'Guaranteed.'

He heaved a sigh and shoved his plate across the table to her. 'Ah, shit. Who?'

Liska cut away the chewed-on part of the burger, then picked up the sandwich and took a big bite, ketchup oozing at the corner of her mouth. She wiped it away with a napkin and looked him in the eye.

'Ace Wyatt.'

Kovac growled. 'That cocksucker.'

'Doing a favor for Mike.'

'Yeah. Throwing his weight around. He sure as hell didn't do us a favor.'

He took a pull on his beer and looked around the room, remembering it as it had been the night of Ace Wyatt's retirement party: over-festive, crowded, hot, smoky. He saw Mike Fallon on the floor, the tight expression on Ace Wyatt's face.

He considered the burden of having a man owe you his life, and having that man never let you forget it. The obligation never ended. Ace Wyatt was still saving Mike Fallon, calling in favors. It was likely Wyatt's influence that had gotten Andy Fallon's death ruled accidental rather than a straight-out suicide, sparing Mike that burden and freeing up Andy's life insurance.

'Did you get the reports?' he asked. 'Did Stone have them done?'

'Stone didn't do the autopsy. Upshaw did.'

'Upshaw? Who the hell is Upshaw?'

'Some new guy. Kinda cute, if you go for the type who has his hands in a

441

dead body all day. I'll pass, thanks,' Liska said, then polished off the last of the burger.

'Did you notice anything else about him? Like if he has half a brain?'

'At least half, I'd say. He wasn't drooling. Whether or not he knows his shit – too soon to tell.'

'Great.'

'The preliminary report says Fallon died of asphyxia. No other significant wounds to the body. No signs of a struggle.'

'Had he had sex?'

'Upshaw said he didn't find any seminal fluid where it shouldn't have been. So if it was a game gone wrong, they were practicing safe sex or saving the main event for last. Or it wasn't about sex at all.'

'Tox screens in?'

'No paperwork yet, but I called and talked to Barkin. He says Fallon had a low level of alcohol in his bloodstream: point oh-four. And a barbiturate, something called zolpidem, which is a sleeping pill also known by the brand name Ambien. That would be more consistent with suicide than a sex game, although the amounts were by no means lethal, even in combination. Plenty of people dope themselves up for the big deed. Now, if they'd found Rohypnol or something, that would be a different story. No one plans to date-rape themselves, except maybe a lonely masochist.'

Kovac frowned at a memory that wouldn't quite come clear. 'Did anyone check out what was in Andy Fallon's medicine cabinet?'

'No reason to at the time.'

'I want to know.'

'You won't get a warrant.'

'What do I need with a warrant? Who's going to object?'

Liska shrugged and sucked on the straw of her Coke, her gaze scanning the room. She sat back, face impassive, but eyes suddenly hard and sharp.

'What?' Kovac asked.

'Here comes Cal Springer. Looks like he ate too many jalapeños and can't fart.'

Springer moved through the crowd like a wooden figure, muscles taut with anger, face pink with temper or cold or both. He had a long, flat face with a long, hooked nose, the look crowned by a mop of unruly brown-gray curls. His gaze lit on Kovac and he rushed forward, barreling into the slouchy waitress. She spilled a beer and swore, and Springer ruined his entrance with awkward apologies.

Kovac shook his head. 'Hey, Cal, I heard you knock the ladies out. I didn't know they meant it literally.'

Springer jabbed a finger at him. 'What were you doing with Renaldo Verma?'

'We did the tango and had a cigarette.'

'His lawyer was all over me this afternoon. No one cleared that meeting with him. Or with me.'

'No one had to clear it with him. Verma agreed to see me. He could have called the lawyer if he wanted. And since when do I have to ask you for permission to wipe my ass?'

'That's my case.'

'And it's over. You're out. What's the big deal?'

Springer glanced around like a man about to disclose sensitive state secrets. 'It's not over.'

'Oh, on account of IA?' Kovac asked loudly.

Springer looked sick.

'They don't have a case against you, do they?' Liska asked. 'I mean, you're not the one who threw down the watch, are you, Cal?'

'I didn't do anything.'

'Consistent with your usual investigative techniques,' Kovac said. 'If that's a crime, you'd better bend over and kiss your ass good-bye.'

Springer glared at him. 'I ran a clean investigation. I worked that case by the book. Verma has no call coming after me. IA neither.'

'Then why are you wasting your time trying to ream me a new one?' Kovac asked.

Springer took a breath and held it tight for a couple of seconds, like a man trying to force something from his body by straining. 'Stay out of it, Kovac. It's over. The case is closed and everything with it.'

'Well, make up your mind, Cal. Is it over or isn't it?' Kovac said, watching him, wondering. He could see Liska watching Springer too, though her expression held a certain tension, as if it caused her distress to watch Cal Springer battle his nerves.

'The IA lieutenant told me there's nothing ongoing with the Curtis murder,' Kovac said. 'Not today, anyway. Her investigator's dead.'

'I know,' Springer murmured, glancing away, the red draining from his face. 'I heard. Suicide. Too bad.'

'So they say.'

Springer looked at him again. 'What's that mean?'

Kovac shrugged. 'Nothing. Figure of speech.'

Springer weighed that for a moment, weighed his options. In the end, his shoulders sagged and the air leaked out of his lungs.

'Look,' he said. 'I can't have IA on my ass. I'm running for union delegate.'

'Having IA on you oughta make you a shoo-in.'

'Only if guys like you bothered to vote. I've got bigger plans for my life than you do, Kovac. I care about what goes in my jacket. Please don't fuck that up for me.'

Kovac watched him walk away, watched him bang into the same waitress he'd run into on his entrance, his mind clearly not in Patrick's bar.

'By the book,' Kovac scoffed. 'What book do you suppose that is? *Practical Homicide Investigation For Dummies*?'

Liska didn't answer him. She had turned sideways in the booth to watch

Springer go, but she seemed to be looking at something a whole lot farther away. *Maybe light-years*, he thought. He reached across the table and poked her shoulder.

'Hey, that was a good one,' he said. 'Deserving of recognition.'

'Lay off him, Sam,' she said, turning back around. 'Springer's square. He doesn't deserve what IA might do to him for no good reason.'

'If he knows something, I want it.'

'I'll get it.'

Kovac watched her. She dodged his gaze. She looked fourteen and in possession of a burdensome secret. Knowledge of the football captain drinking beer and smoking cigarettes. She reached tentatively for the last french fry and traced the end of it through the coagulating glob of ketchup.

'Is something up with you?' he asked quietly.

Her mouth twisted into a semblance of her smart-ass smirk. 'Sure,' she said. 'My hormones. Wanna do something about that?'

'If your hormones are up because of Cal Springer, I want to hose you down with ice water.'

'Please. I just ate,' she said with disgust. 'It's been a long day. On top of a long night. I should go home.'

'I thought you didn't want anything to do with IA.'

'I don't,' she said, busying herself gathering her things. 'How's that stop me from getting what Springer has? He doesn't want anything to do with them either.'

'Suit yourself.' Liska was entitled to a mystery or two, he supposed, though he didn't like the idea.

He got up and tossed some bills on the table, then grabbed his coat off the hook on the end of the booth. 'I'm going to go see what Andy Fallon kept in his medicine chest.'

'Sam Kovac, Round-the-Clock Detective.'

'What else have I got to do with my time?'

'Nothing, apparently. Don't you ever want something more?' she asked, sliding out of the booth.

'Naw.' He ignored the image of Amanda Savard that came to mind. That was too ludicrous to even consider as a fantasy. 'If you never want anything, then you can't be disappointed when you don't get it.'

11

The parking garage had been named for a cop who had been murdered in cold blood in a pizza place on Lake Street. This thought always came to Liska when it was late and she was going in alone to find her car, or when she was tired and looking at the future with a jaundiced eye. She scored on all counts tonight. Rush hour had passed, the ramp seemed deserted, and her mood was dark. Kovac had gone back to the office to get the key to Fallon's house. She had blown off his offer to walk her to her car.

The hair prickled on the back of her neck. She stopped abruptly and turned around, glaring into the gloom. Sound bounced around and echoed in the concrete labyrinth, making it difficult to identify the source. The slam of a car door could be a level above or below. The scrape of a foot could be at the end of the row. Or right behind you. Parking ramps were a favorite of muggers and rapists. Vagrants, most of them drunk or mentally ill, liked the ramps for shelter and to use as public toilets when they got kicked out of places like the downtown public library.

Liska's breath burned in her lungs as she waited and watched, turning slowly, one hand slipping inside her coat and finding the butt of her gun at her waist.

She saw no one, heard nothing of any significance. Maybe she was just being edgy, but she had just cause. She had spent her day inquiring about the deaths of two cops. She felt as if someone had put a pillow over her head and beat her with a tire iron. She wanted her home, her sweats, her boys, a few hours to ignore the fact that she had volunteered to dig around in an IA shitpile.

'That was a blond moment,' she muttered, releasing the gun and digging her keys out of her coat pocket.

Now she had to figure a way to sweet-talk information out of Cal Springer. Christ. Without barfing. Tall order.

It was hard to figure Springer for being in on anything dirty. He was seldom allowed in on lunch, let alone a conspiracy, but there was no denying the smell of fear on him. It was a scent memory that tumbled her all the way back to her father. She hated it.

'Why couldn't I have listened to my mother?' she muttered. 'Learn a trade, Nikki. Cosmetology. Food service. Aim high. Get a job you can wear a nice skirt for. Meet the man of your dreams.'

The dark blue Saturn that served as traveling office and taxi sat at the end of the row, next to the wall, in a spot too dark for her liking now that night had fallen. Nose out, poised for a quick getaway. She hit the button on the keyless remote and swore under her breath. Nothing happened. No click of locks releasing. No flash of lights. The thing had been on the fritz for weeks, sometimes working, sometimes not. Liska, on the other hand, seemed *always* to be working and never had the time to take it in. It seemed too small an inconvenience to bother with. Until she was alone in a dark parking ramp.

A thump and a scrape froze her in her tracks a second time. On another level of the ramp she could hear the squeal of protest from a steering column being cranked too far in one direction. On this level, she could feel a presence. Another human. The awareness vibrated in her nerve endings. She didn't go through the bullshit rationalization most women did in a situation where they felt unease. Instincts were to be trusted above the teachings of an allegedly polite society. If she felt something was wrong, then something was probably wrong.

'Hey! Who's there?' she demanded, turning slowly. The tough chick. The come-over-here-and-I'll-kick-your-ass voice. Her heart rate had picked up fifteen extra beats per minute.

She sidled toward the car, key in her left hand, the right one reaching again for the gun, slipping it from the belt holster. With the tip of the key, she felt for the lock, missing once, twice. Her gaze remained up, scanning left to right, right to left, catching – Something. Someone. The shadowed side of a concrete column that seemed a bit too thick, a little distorted.

Liska blinked and tried to refocus. Too dark. It might have been something or nothing.

The key found the lock. She eased down into the Saturn, shut the door, hit the power lock button, and got no response. She cursed the car and started the engine, hit the lock button again, and this time was rewarded by the thump of locks engaging. Her gaze was still on the column fifty feet away. She could detect no motion, but the feeling of another living creature being there, watching her, lingered.

Time to go.

She tossed her briefcase on the passenger side, amid the debris of working motherhood, a mess that looked even worse than usual and spilled from the seat to the floor. Junk mail, a Burger King bag, a couple of magazines, one of the boys' stray sneakers, some plastic action figures. And a whole lot of broken glass.

Nine more extra beats a minute.

The passenger's side window was gone, reduced to a thousand bits that lay scattered on the seat and floor, mixed in with the junk mail and the Burger King bag, and the magazines and R.J.'s stray sneaker and the plastic action figures. It was probably the work of some junkie, Liska told herself. Probably her phantom in the shadows, who was now hiding, waiting for her to go so he could knock in someone else's window in search of valuables to hock. That was the likely explanation.

She started the engine and put the car in gear. She would drive down to street level and call for a radio car from the well-lit area near the attendant's booth.

A red dash light caught her eye, telling her to service the engine soon.

'Yeah. How about you service *my* engine soon?' she grumbled, easing the car out of the slot.

Her headlights hit the column. Nothing. No one. She tried to let go of the suspicion as she exhaled, but the tension wouldn't dissipate.

She looked to the rearview mirror as she passed the column and caught a glimpse of something. Half the figure of a man standing near a sedan three cars away, back toward where she had been parked.

Nothing strange about a person in a parking garage. Every car had one sooner or later. Usually they opened doors and turned on lights. This one didn't. He stepped out of sight. Liska abandoned the mirror and looked over her left shoulder. Her right hand rested on her gun on the seat beside her: a neat little Sig Sauer, sized to fit her small hand and still knock the shit out of a charging bull.

Where had he come from? She'd been watching and listening for another person to the point of straining her eyes and ears. No one had walked that far into the ramp after her without her knowing.

'Hey!'

The voice struck like a bullet. Liska snapped her head around to the right to see a man lunging toward the car, his head and upper body thrusting through the window frame.

'Hey!' he shouted again. His face was like something carved out of a stump with a penknife. Craggy, dirty. Yellow teeth. Filthy beard. Wild, dark eyes. 'Gimme five dollars!'

Liska gunned the engine. The tires shrieked against the concrete. The man screamed in rage, rough hands grabbing hold of the front passenger's seat by the stems of the headrest. Liska brought the Sig up and swung it toward his face.

'Get outta my car! I'm a cop!'

The man's mouth tore open and a sound of rage roared up out of him on a foul breath.

Liska stabbed the Sig at him, half an inch from his mouth. 'Let go, asshole!'

With one hand, she cranked the wheel left and hit the brakes, sending the Saturn into a skid. One of the back panels hit a minivan, and the drunk lost his grip on the headrest and was flung out the window.

Liska jammed the car into park, jumped out the door, and ran around the hood, leading with the Sig in a stiff-arm grip. The drunk lay crumpled

447

near the back door of a filthy seventies Cadillac, still as death, eyes closed. Shit, that was all she needed – to have killed somebody. The parking ramp booth attendant ran up the ramp from the level below: a fat guy in a bad uniform with a too-small parka open to let his beer gut lead the way.

'Jeez, lady!' he exclaimed between gulps of air. It was twenty degrees and he was sweating like a racehorse, limp brown hair matted to his big head. His eyes bugged as he caught sight of the gun, and he raised his arms.

'I'm a cop,' Liska said. 'He's under arrest. Is there any security on duty?'

'Uh ... he's on a break.'

'Great. At the strip joint down the block, right?'

The attendant opened and closed his mouth a couple of times. Liska checked the drunk for signs of life. His breathing was regular and he had a good pulse. There was no blood she could see. She pulled a pair of handcuffs out of her coat pocket and snagged one of his wrists.

'You got a cell phone on you?' she asked, glancing at the attendant.

'Yes, ma'am.'

'Call nine-one-one. We need police and an ambulance.'

He looked ready to dive for cover. 'Yes, ma'am. I thought you said *you're* a cop.'

'Just do it.'

The drunk cracked open a bloodshot eye and tried to focus on her. 'You're a boy,' he declared. 'Gimme five dollars.'

Liska glared at him. 'You have the right to remain silent. Use it.'

She snapped the other cuff to the back door handle of the Caddie. Then she went back to the Saturn and dug a huge Maglite patrolman's flashlight out of the glove compartment. The thing weighed three pounds and doubled as a club. The attendant was still standing with his hands up as she came out of the car.

Liska glared at him. 'Why aren't you calling?'

'I didn't want to make any sudden moves.'

'Oh, for God's sake.'

She snapped on the Maglite with her left hand, dug the Sig back out of her pocket, and started back up the ramp.

'Where are you going?' the attendant called.

'To look for the boogie man. Go make that call, Slick.'

It was nearly ten o'clock by the time Liska pulled into her own driveway, exhausted and disgusted. More so when she saw Speed's car blocking her way into the garage. It didn't matter that she couldn't actually get her car in the garage because of the accumulation of junk. It was a matter of principle.

She sat in the Saturn, freezing, the heater not able to compete against the cold rushing in the busted window. She'd found no trace of her phantom in the ramp. The uniforms had taken custody of the drunk – Edward Gedes – and followed the ambulance to HCMC, where they would kill time drinking coffee and flirting with the nurses in the ER as they waited for

Edward to get checked out. There wasn't much to charge him with unless they could prove he was the one who broke the window, and Liska didn't see that happening. Her gut told her it *hadn't* happened. Maybe Gedes had busted the window, then waited for her to come so he could try to jump through it like a trick pony, but she didn't think so.

Nothing had been missing from the car, not that she kept anything of real value in it. No one had broken in to steal R.J.'s Jesse Ventura action figure. The glove compartment had not been ransacked. The stereo hadn't been touched. She almost wished it had been. The theft of something would have made the broken window make sense. The only thing in the car that had been disturbed had been her junk mail. Someone willing to break into a car in a public garage now had her home address.

The phantom in the shadows.

Why her car, of all the cars in the ramp?

She gathered her stuff and trudged to the house. No one noticed her entrance. A battle was being waged in her living room. In one corner a tent had been fashioned from a blanket. Dining room chairs had been dragged in and overturned to make a fort near the Christmas tree. Their faces streaked with camo paint, the boys were running around in their pajamas, waving plastic light sabers, making enough noise to wake the dead. Her ex-husband was crouched behind the recliner, wearing a bathrobe over his clothes, a black rag tied around his head, a glow-in-the-dark samurai sword in hand.

'Welcome home, Mom,' Liska said, slinging her purse onto the dining room table. 'Did you have a good day? Not really,' she answered herself. 'But thank you for asking. I'm just glad to be home where everything is peaceful and orderly, and I feel loved by all.'

Kyle reacted first, stopping in his tracks, the grin dropping off his face as he looked from his mother to his father and back. Two years older than R.J., he remembered the hostilities at the end of the marriage, and was sensitive to the tension that remained between his parents.

'Hi, Mom,' he said, glancing down at the toy in his hand and setting it aside, as if he were embarrassed to be caught having fun. He had his father's heartbreaker looks, but a seriousness lacking in Speed's genes.

'Hi, Big Guy.' Liska went to him, brushed his hair back, and kissed his forehead. Kyle looked at the floor.

R.J. squealed like a wild pig and ran around in circles, swinging his saber with reckless abandon, stubbornly refusing to acknowledge his mother's presence. Anger burned a familiar path through her as she turned her gaze on her ex.

'Hey, Speed, fancy meeting you here. Again. You're almost acting like you're a father or something. Where's Heather?'

'I sent her home,' he said, straightening out of his crouch. 'Why should you pay a sitter if you don't have to? I had some time tonight.'

'That's very considerate of you to think of my financial situation,' she said, wanting badly to add, *especially considering you never bother to contribute to the cause.* But she bit her tongue for the boys' sake.

'It's way past bedtime, boys,' she said, playing the bad guy again and resenting Speed for it. 'Go wash your faces and brush your teeth, please.'

Kyle started from the room. R.J. stared at her with big eyes, then gave a bloodcurdling shout and leapt in the air, twisting and flailing his arms and legs in his best Ninja impersonation.

Kyle went and grabbed his arm. 'Knock it off, Rockhead,' he said in his sternest voice. Liska didn't reprimand him.

'I realize you made a career of truancy,' she told Speed after the boys had left the room, 'but your sons actually attend school. They need a certain amount of sleep for that.'

'One late night won't kill them, Nikki.'

'No.'

But why did you have to pick tonight? she wanted to say, except she was afraid she might burst into tears if she did. She was too worn out for Speed tonight, and Kovac's burger was a long time past. She rubbed her face with her hands and walked away from him, back through the dining room and into the kitchen, where she began rummaging through one of the lower cupboards.

She could see Speed strike a pose in the doorway. He had shed the bathrobe, revealing a black Aerosmith T-shirt stretched taut across his chest and clinging to his flat belly. The short sleeves strained around upper arms thick with well-cut muscle. He looked as if he'd been pumping iron in a serious way. He pulled the rag off his head and ruffled his short hair, making it stand up in tufts.

'You want to talk about it?' he asked.

'Since when do we talk about anything?'

He shrugged. 'So we start tonight.'

'I don't want to start anything tonight.'

She pulled a box of translucent blue trash bags from the cupboard and scrutinized one for size and durability. 'It'll do for now.'

'Do for what?'

'Someone busted the side window out of my car tonight. Makes for a drafty ride doing sixty on the freeway.'

'Goddamn junkies,' he muttered. 'They steal anything?'

'Nope.'

'They just broke the window?'

'And rummaged through the junk mail on the front seat.'

'You're sure it was junk? No credit card statements? No cell phone bill? Nothing like that?'

'Nothing like that.'

'Didn't touch the stereo?'

'What's to touch? I drive a Saturn. It's got a radio. Who would want it?'

Speed frowned. 'I don't like that they didn't take anything.'

'Me neither.' She pulled the junk drawer open and dug around for a roll of duct tape. 'I wish they had taken the car. The engine light is coming on. With my luck, it has some terminal illness.'

'You working anything that someone might want to find you?' he asked, coming to the counter where she stood compulsively folding the trash bag into the smallest square possible.

Liska thought of Neon Man, and Cal Springer, and IA, and the uniform Ogden and two dead cops. She shook her head, looking down at the bag. 'Nothing special.'

He's standing too close, she thought. *I don't want him that close. Not tonight.*

'I hear the ME ruled on your IA guy,' he said. 'Accident, huh?'

Liska shrugged a little and fingered a frayed piece of tape. 'The insurance pays out that way.'

'You think something else?'

'Doesn't matter what I think. Leonard says it's closed.'

'It matters if you're going to keep digging on it. What are you thinking? That he bought it because of an investigation? You think some rotten cop lynched him? That's pretty fucking out there, Nikki. What could be going on in the Minneapolis PD that would push someone that far off the ledge?'

'I don't think anything,' she said impatiently. 'And I'm not in on what goes on in IA. It doesn't matter anyway. The lieutenant signed off on it.'

'So it's closed,' he said. 'You're out of it. That's gotta be a relief.'

'Sure,' she said without conviction. She could feel him watching her, waiting for what she wasn't saying.

'Nikki . . .'

There was frustration in his voice, and maybe a little longing. Maybe more than a little. Or maybe she just wanted to think it. He touched her chin and she looked up at him, holding her breath. Many things about their relationship had turned sour in the last few years, but never the physical aspect. He had always – and to her eternal despair, probably would always – excited her physically. Chemistry didn't care about jealousies or rivalries or infidelities.

'Are you guys gonna kiss?'

'R.J.,' Liska said as Speed exhaled heavily. 'You don't ask people questions like that. It's rude.'

'So?'

He hadn't quite rubbed all the camo paint off his face. She bent down and kissed a smudge on his forehead.

'So I love you,' she said. 'Time for bed.'

'But Dad –'

'Was just leaving,' she said, giving Speed a pointed look.

R.J. scowled. 'You *always* make him leave.'

'Come on, Rocket,' Speed said, scooping R.J. up and over his shoulder. 'I'll tuck you in and tell you about the time I busted Big Ass Baxter.'

Liska watched them leave the kitchen, part of her wanting to follow. Not because she wanted to give any impression they had a normal family life. She wanted to follow because she was jealous of the rapport Speed had with the boys. That didn't seem a healthy thing to indulge. No more than her need for her ex-husband's touch.

She picked up the duct tape and garbage bag and went out the kitchen door, glad for the slap of cold night air.

'How stylish,' she muttered as she taped the bag over the broken-out window. Nothing like a little duct tape to class up a car.

The neighborhood was quiet. The night was clear and crisp with a sky full of more stars than she could see from this spot in the city. Her neighbor on this side of her house worked for United Way. On the other side was a couple who'd been with 3M for a collective thirty-some years. None of them had ever seen a dead guy hanging from a rafter. Standing in the middle of the neighborhood, Liska felt suddenly alone, set apart from normal humans by the experiences she had had and would have. Set apart tonight by violence that had been directed at her.

Someone she didn't know and couldn't identify had her address.

She looked down the driveway to the street. Any car going by ... Any pair of eyes watching from the dark ... Any strange sound outside her bedroom window ...

Vulnerability was not a familiar or welcome feeling. It went through her and over her like the chill of an illness. The anticipation of fear. A kind of weakness. A sense of powerlessness. A sense of isolation.

She wanted to kick someone.

'Alone at last.'

Liska startled and spun around, voice recognition coming a split second before she came face-to-face with the source. 'Dammit, Speed! How have you lived this long?'

'I don't know. I expected you to kill me a long time ago.' His grin lit up the dark.

'You're lucky I wasn't holding a gun,' she said.

'I'm probably still lucky you're not holding a gun.'

He stuffed his hands in the pockets of the old jacket he was wearing and dug out a pack of Marlboros and a lighter. He fired one up.

'I wouldn't shoot you now,' she said. 'I want this night to be over. If I shot you, I'd have to be up till dawn with the arrest and the booking and all of that. It's not worth it.'

'Gee, thanks.'

'I'm tired, Speed. Can you say goodnight now?'

He took a long pull on the cigarette and exhaled, looking down the driveway to the street as a dark nondescript sedan crept past and kept going. Liska watched it out of the corner of her eye and pulled her coat tighter around her.

'You'll call someone and get that window fixed tomorrow?' Speed said, flaking ash off his cigarette as he gestured toward her car.

'I'm on the phone mentally, even as we speak.'

''Cause that garbage bag just screams white trash.'

'Thanks for your concern over my safety.'

'You're the mother of my children.'

'That speaks volumes about my judgment, doesn't it?'

'Hey.' He looked straight at her and flicked the cigarette on the snow. 'Don't say you regret the boys.'

Liska met his gaze. 'I don't regret the boys. Not for half a heartbeat.'

'But you regret us.'

'Why are you doing this?' she asked wearily. 'It seems a little late for remorse and bargaining, Speed. Our marriage has been dead a very long time.'

Speed pulled his keys out of his pocket and sorted out the one he needed. 'Regret's a waste of time. Live for the moment. You never know which one will be your last.'

'And on that cheery note . . .' Liska turned toward the house.

He caught her by the arm as she went past. He was thinking he might try to kiss her. She could see it in his eyes, feel it in the tension of his body. But she didn't want it, and she supposed he could see and feel that too.

'Take care, Nikki,' he said softly. 'You're too brave for your own good.'

'I'm what I need to be,' she said.

He found a sad smile for that and let go of her. 'Yeah. Too bad I was never what you needed.'

'I wouldn't say never,' she said, but she didn't look at him. She kept her eyes on the ground.

She didn't watch him walk away, but she watched him back out the driveway and turn onto the street. She stood there until the red glow of his taillights was a faded memory. And then she was alone again, she thought as she stared at her patchwork car window. Or so she hoped.

She went up the back steps and into the house. She locked the door and turned out the light. And as she retreated to her bedroom, alone, a dark sedan rolled past on the street . . . for the second time.

12

Andy Fallon's house was a dark spot in the neighborhood, the only glow the reflection of the neighbor's porch lights off the yellow police line tape that crossed the front door.

Kovac detached the tape and let himself in with the key. There was always a lingering sense of violation about a house that had been gone through by a crime scene unit. The place had been probed and examined and trooped through by a dozen or more strangers, without the blessing of the homeowner. Personal items had been touched, the sanctity of privacy raped. Judgments had been passed, remarks made. All of that seemed to hang in the air like a sour smell. And yet Kovac tried to return to a home after the fact if it was possible, to walk the rooms and get a feel for who the victim had been before he or she had become a corpse.

He started with the living room, with the Christmas tree – a Fraser fir decorated with small clear lights and a red bead garland. It was a beautiful tree that had the smell of fake pine scent. Kneeling, he checked the tags on the few wrapped gifts, noting names. Most were from Andy Fallon, yet to be delivered to Kirk and Aaron and Jessica . . . He would cross-reference the first names against Fallon's address book and try to get a line on the friends. He would do the same with the Christmas cards that filled a basket on the coffee table.

Moving on to the entertainment center, he scanned the titles on the spines of the videotape cassettes. *Miracle on 34th Street. Holiday Inn. It's a Wonderful Life* – a movie that began with a man wanting to kill himself, but concluded with all the usual nauseating sap of a Hollywood happy ending. No angel named Clarence had saved Andy Fallon from his fate. In Kovac's experience, there was never an angel around when you needed one.

He passed through the dining room on his way to the stairs. The room appeared unused, as most dining rooms were.

The master bath at the head of the stairs was loaded with the usual assortment of stuff a man needed on a daily basis. There were no towels in the hamper. If there had been, the towels could have been checked for hairs and body fluids, the detritus sent off for DNA comparisons. If Fallon's death had been an obvious murder – or ruled a murder – he could have had the crime scene people clean the drain traps in the sinks, checking for hairs. In his experience, that kind of trace evidence never made a case, but it was always welcomed by the prosecutors as more rocks in their pile. But this case was officially closed, and no one would be fishing pubic hairs out of Andy Fallon's bathtub.

A brown prescription bottle of Zoloft sat on a shelf in the medicine cabinet. Antidepressant. Dr Seiros. Kovac noted all pertinent information and left the bottle on the shelf. Beside it was a bottle of Tylenol and one of melatonin. No Ambien.

The smell of death lingered in the bedroom over a layer of room freshener. The room had been dusted for latent prints, and a fine, ashy residue was left behind on the dresser and nightstands. Other than that, the room was as neat as a new hotel room. The blue spread was smoothed impeccably over the four-poster. Kovac peeled it back at one corner. Clean sheets. Unlike his father, Andy Fallon had no piles of soiled clothing, no jelly jars with half an inch of evaporating whiskey. His closet was neat. He folded his underwear and matched his socks in the dresser drawers.

On the nightstand beside the bed was a hardcover book about a young man's ill-fated trek into the Alaskan wilderness. Probably depressing enough to warrant an extra Zoloft or two. In the drawer was a Walkman, half a dozen tapes for relaxation and meditation, a couple of honey-lemon cough drops. The table on the other side held an array of squat ivory candles in a hammered metal bowl. Matchboxes from various restaurants and bars were in the drawer with a bottle of K-Y personal lubricant.

Kovac closed the drawer and looked around the room and thought of Andy Fallon. The good son. Fastidious. No trouble. Always striving to excel. Keeping his secrets tucked away in metaphorical drawers and closets. On the dresser was the same photograph Mike had smashed in his fit of grief: Andy's graduation from the police academy. Tucked back in a corner, out of harm's way. A memory Andy Fallon had preserved and refreshed every day of his life, despite the strain between him and his old man.

Sadness ran down through Kovac like a slow rain, draining energy. Maybe this was why he'd never tried harder to be something beyond a cop. He'd seen too many families torn like rotten drapes. Ruined by unrealistic or unrealized expectations. No one could ever let well enough alone. It was human nature to want more, to want better, to want what was out of reach.

He filled his lungs with air and paused as he started to leave the room. The faint scent of stale cigarette smoke caught his nostrils. From his own clothes, he thought at first, then tested the air again. No. It was a scent beneath a masking scent. A woodsy air freshener over burned tobacco. Faint but there.

There were no ashtrays in the room. No half-empty packs. He hadn't seen any evidence of a smoker in any other part of the house. The crime scene people weren't allowed to smoke at a scene.

Steve Pierce was a smoker. Kovac thought again of his impression that

Pierce had something heavy sitting on his chest. He thought of the doe-eyed Ms Daring.

His attention turned back to the bed. Neatly made. Clean sheets. Hadn't even been sat on. Didn't that seem strange? Fallon had been found hanging just a few feet from the bed with his back to it. It seemed to Kovac a man might prepare the scene for his suicide or for a sex game, then sit down to think it through before putting his head in a noose.

He went and stood in the spot where Fallon's body had been hanging and checked the distance to the bed. Only one or maybe two small steps apart. He scowled at his reflection in the full-length mirror. *Sorry.*

The word was still there. They had found the marker that had probably been used to write it. Nothing special. A black Sharpie permanent marker left lying on the dresser. Kovac made a mental note to call and ask about fingerprints on it.

They had made a ten card of Pierce's prints Tuesday in the kitchen downstairs – for elimination purposes. Standard op. Pierce hadn't been happy about it. Because he knew his prints could be found in this bedroom? On the front of the nightstand drawer with the K-Y lube in it? On a bedpost? On the mirror? On that black Sharpie?

It wasn't a tough scenario to put together: Pierce and Fallon were secret lovers who liked to play on the dark side. The game went wrong, Fallon died, Pierce panicked. Or maybe it wasn't as innocent as that. Maybe Fallon wanted Pierce to make a commitment and dump the fiancée. Maybe Steve Pierce had seen his cushy future at Daring-Landis circling the drain as Fallon threatened to expose him. Maybe Steve Pierce had come back Tuesday morning to check his tracks, then called the cops and put on the face of the shocked best friend.

He took one last look around the bedroom, then headed back downstairs. In the kitchen, he checked the cupboards for prescription bottles. None. Nor were there any used glasses on the counter. The dishwasher had been run with half a load: three plates, some silverware, an assortment of glasses and coffee mugs. Two wineglasses. Off the kitchen, a washer and dryer sat in an alcove behind a pair of louvered doors. Inside the washer: towels and sheets, molded to the sides of the tub.

Either Andy Fallon had wanted his house in order before he died or someone else had wanted it in order afterward. The second possibility made Kovac's nerves hum.

There were two bedrooms on the main floor, down the hall from the stairs to the second story. The smaller was a guest room that held nothing of interest. The larger had been converted into a home office with a modest desk, bookshelves, and a couple of filing cabinets. Kovac clicked on the desk lamp and went through the desk drawers, careful to see but not to disturb.

A lot of cops he knew kept old case files. He had a basement full himself. If there was a God, Andy Fallon would have kept a duplicate file on his investigation of the Curtis murder. If he had, chances were good he would have it filed under *C* like a good little anal retentive IA automaton.

The first of the file cabinets held personal financial information and tax returns. The second was the jackpot drawer. Neatly ordered manila folders, the tabs marked with last names printed in careful block letters followed by eight-digit case numbers. None bore the name Curtis. No Ogden. No Springer.

Kovac sat back in Andy Fallon's desk chair and let it swivel and dip. If the Curtis investigation had been Fallon's obsession, there should have been a file. The file cabinets hadn't been locked. Anyone could have pinched the thing and walked off with it. Ogden came to mind, though he didn't seem as though subterfuge would have been among his strengths. Busting concrete block with his forehead, yes. Clever sleight of hand, no. But then, there was no telling who might have been in and out of the house between Fallon's death and the discovery of his body. There was too much time unaccounted for, too many people in the neighborhood who minded their own business.

He played angles and odds in his mind, trying to scheme a way to get at the actual IA file, but nothing good came to mind. Every path was blocked by the lovely Lieutenant Savard. He couldn't get to the file without her, and she had no intention of letting him past her guard. In any respect.

He could see her plainly as she had looked standing beside the desk in her office. A face right off a Hollywood glossy from the days of black-and-white and Veronica Lake. And he somehow knew that what lay beneath those looks was a mystery worthy of any of the great detectives, real or fictional. That drew him in as much as the looks. He wanted to slip in the secret door and find out what made her tick.

'Like you got a shot, Kovac,' he mumbled, amazed by and embarrassed at himself. 'You and the IA lieutenant. Yeah, *that* could happen.'

It struck him then, as he wasted time with thoughts of a woman he couldn't have, that there was something missing from Andy Fallon's desktop. There was no computer. The printer cord with its wide, multi-pinned connector lay there like a flat-headed snake, its other end joined with an ink-jet printer. Kovac checked the drawers again, finding a box of blank diskettes. He pulled the drawer with the case files and found that each folder contained a diskette. He went to the bookcase and found, in the collection of instruction manuals for phone/fax, for printer, for stereo equipment, a manual for an IBM ThinkPad laptop computer.

'So where is it?' Kovac asked aloud.

As he considered possibilities, a sound pierced his consciousness – sharp, electronic, coming from another part of the house. A beep followed by the creak of a floorboard. He flicked off the desk lamp, plunging the room into darkness. His hand went automatically to the Glock in his belt holster as he moved to the door, waited for his eyes to adjust, then slipped into the hall.

Out of habit he had turned out the lights as he left each room during his search. Not wanting to attract attention from the neighbors. The only light now was muted and white, coming in through the glass panes in the front door. Enough to backlight the figure of a person.

Kovac pulled the Glock and leveled it in his right hand, located the hall light switch with his left.

The figure near the front door lifted a hand close to the face.

Kovac held his breath, waiting for the click of a trigger.

'Yes, it's me,' a man's voice. 'I'm at the house. I –'

'Freeze! Police!' Kovac yelled, hitting the switch.

The man started, letting out a cry, eyes going wide, then squinting against the light, free hand coming up as if to ward off bullets. A tinny voice squawked out of the cell phone in his hand.

'No, it's all right, Captain Wyatt,' he said, slowly lowering his free hand. The cell phone was still pressed to his ear. 'Just one of the city's finest, doing his job.'

Kovac took a good long look at the man before him, keeping the Glock out because he was pissed now and wanted to show it. He recognized the face from the party. Mr Too Handsome with the black hair and the smell of Ace Wyatt's ass on his breath.

'Hang up the phone,' Kovac ordered crossly.

Too Handsome stared at him. 'But it's –'

'Close the goddamn phone, Slick. What are you doing walking in here? This is a secure police scene.'

Wyatt's man clicked the little phone shut and slipped it into the inner breast pocket of an expensive charcoal topcoat. 'Captain Wyatt asked me to meet him here. You might think that would be reason enough –'

'You might think wrong, Slick,' Kovac snapped, coming forward, gun still in hand. 'I could have blown your pretty head off. You never heard of a doorbell?'

'Why would I ring the bell at a dead man's house?'

'Why would you come here at all?'

'Captain Wyatt's on his way with Mike Fallon. Mr Fallon has to select burial attire for his son,' he explained, using the kind of tone one might use on ignorant hired help. 'I work for Captain Wyatt. Gavin Gaines is my name, in case you get tired of calling me Slick.'

The smile was a little too self-amused, Kovac thought. College-educated pricks were his least-favorite kind.

'Should I assume the position?' Gaines asked, hands out at his sides. Outside a car door slammed.

'Don't be a smartass.' Kovac slid the Glock back into its holster. 'Like you can help it. What exactly do you do for Captain America?'

'Personal assistant, public relations, media liaison. Whatever he needs.' Translation: toady, gofer, suckup.

'He needs you to help get Mr Fallon in the house,' Kovac said, going to the door and opening it. 'Or will that muss the look?'

Gaines gritted the perfect teeth. 'Like I said, whatever he needs. I live to serve.'

It took the two of them to negotiate the steps with Fallon, Mike hanging on them, deadweight. Worse than when he had been drunk, Kovac thought. Grief had somehow increased his body mass; the desperation of it had sapped his strength. Ace Wyatt brought the wheelchair.

'Sam, I hear you nearly took out my right hand here,' Wyatt joked. Mr Congeniality.

'If you're paying him per brain cell, he probably owes you some change back,' Kovac said. 'He's a little short in the common-sense department.'

'What makes you say that? It's not as if Gavin was walking into a crime scene. He had no reason to expect anyone to be here. Why *are* you here, by the way?'

'Just doing the usual walk-through,' Kovac said. 'Looking for pieces.'

'You know Andy's death has been ruled an accident,' Wyatt said in a hushed tone, his gaze on Mike Fallon sitting slumped in his wheelchair. Gaines stood farther into the room, waiting with his hands folded in front of him and a thousand-yard stare going off in the direction of the Christmas tree. A look he'd probably picked up watching actors play Secret Service agents in the movies.

'So I heard,' Kovac said. 'That was big of you, Ace, moving things along the way you did.'

Wyatt missed the bite in Kovac's voice. 'Well, what was the point of prolonging Mike's misery? Whose interest would be served calling it suicide?'

'The insurance company. Fuck 'em.'

'Mike gave the department everything,' Wyatt said. 'His legs. His son. The least they can do is pay out the benefits and put a better face on it.'

'So you've seen to it.'

'My last great act as captain.' He flashed a tired version of the famous smile. His skin looked a little jaundiced under the hall light, and the lines at the corners of his eyes seemed chiseled deeper than two nights ago. No makeup.

His last great act. Fitting, Kovac thought, considering the case that had launched Ace Wyatt's stardom within the department had been the one that had brought Mike Fallon down.

'Where's my boy?' Mike roared.

Wyatt looked away.

Kovac squatted beside the chair. 'He's gone, Mikey. Remember? I told you.'

Fallon stared at him, face slack, eyes vacant. But he knew. He knew his son was gone, knew he was going to have to face it, deal with it, carry on. But if he could pretend for just a little while . . . An old man should be entitled to that.

'I can take care of selecting the clothes, if you'd like, Captain,' Gaines offered, moving toward the stairs.

'You want that, Mike?' Kovac asked. 'You want a stranger picking what your boy wears to the hereafter?'

'He won't go,' Fallon mumbled, bleak. 'He took his own life. That's a mortal sin.'

'You don't know that, Mikey. Might have been an accident, like the ME said.'

Fallon stared at him for several seconds. 'I know. I know what he was. I know what he did.'

His eyes filled and he started to shake. 'I can't forgive him, Sam,' he whispered, clutching Kovac's forearm. 'God help me. I can't forgive him. I hated him. I hated him for what he was doing!'

'Don't talk that way, Mike,' Wyatt said. 'You don't mean it.'

'Let him say what he needs to,' Kovac said shortly. 'He knows what he really means.'

'Why couldn't he just do like I said?' Fallon mumbled, talking to himself or his God – the one who kept a bouncer at heaven's gate to keep out gays and the suicidal and whoever else didn't fit within the confines of Mike Fallon's narrow mind. 'Why?'

Kovac touched the old man's head. A cop-to-cop benediction. 'Come on, Mikey. Let's go do it.'

They left the wheelchair at the foot of the stairs. Again, Kovac and Gaines carried Mike Fallon. Wyatt brought up the rear of the procession. They set the old man on the edge of the bed with his back to the mirror that bore the apology for his son's death. But there was nothing to do about the smell – a smell every cop knew too well.

Mike Fallon hung his head and began to cry silently, lost in the torment of wondering where it had all gone so wrong for his boy. Gaines went to the window and looked out. Wyatt stood at the foot of the bed and stared at the mirror, frowning.

Kovac went into the closet to pull out a couple of Andy Fallon's suits, and wondered who would do the chore for him when the time came.

'You like one of these, Mike?' he asked, coming out of the closet with a blue suit in one hand and a dark gray in the other.

Fallon didn't answer. He stared across the room at the photograph on the dresser. The one of Andy's graduation from the academy. A frozen split second of pride and joy.

'A man should never outlive his kids,' he said bleakly. 'He ought to die before they can break his heart.'

13

A man should never outlive his kids.

He shouldn't have.

He hadn't.

He can see the scene unfold before his eyes, as plainly as if two decades hadn't passed: The still night. The squeak of his shoes. The sound of his own breathing.

The house seems huge. A trick of the adrenaline rush. The back door stands ajar.

In the kitchen. White fluorescent under-counter lights humming like high-voltage wires. Pass through into darkness. Rooms dark, moon bright and beaming through windows. A silence that presses like fingers against his eardrums. Seconds that pass in slow motion.

He moves with athleticism. (The feeling is vivid, even though he hasn't been able to feel anything below his waist for twenty years. He remembers the tension in each and every muscle of his body – his legs, his back, the fingers of his left hand curled around the grip of his gun, the contractions of his heart.)

Then there it is. Surprise at the sight of something he can't quite remember. Death in a sudden blue-white flash. An explosion so loud. The power of it knocks him backward even as he shoots in reflex.

Officer down.

Blind. Deaf. Floating.

Disbelief. Panic. Release.

I'm dead.

He wishes he had stayed that way.

He stares in the darkness, listens to his own breathing, feels his own frailty, feels his own mortality, and wonders for the millionth time why he didn't check out that night. He has wished it often enough but has never done anything about it, has never found the nerve. Instead, he's stayed alive, steeping himself in bitterness and booze and drugs. Twenty years in purgatory. Never emerging because he won't look the demons in the face.

He faces one now. Even in his drugged state, he sees it clearly and recognizes it for what it is: the Demon of Truth. The Angel of Death.

It speaks to him calmly and quietly. He sees its mouth move, but the sound seems to come from within his own head.

Time to die, Mike. A man should never outlive his kids.

He stares at his old service revolver, a squat .38 with a big scar on the butt where the bullet that severed his spinal cord had cut deep on its way to his body. The gun they said he had killed his killer with that night, the last night of his career.

He hears a little cry of fear and guesses it must have come from his own body, though it sounds far away. His hands try to push at the wheels of his chair, as if his body were trying to escape the fate his mind has already accepted. Strange.

He wonders if it was this way for Andy – fear swelling as the noose tightened around his throat. God, the feelings that image sets loose inside him! Embarrassment, rage. Guilt and hate and love.

'I loved him,' he says, his speech slurred. Spittle runs down his chin from the corner of his mouth. 'I loved him, but I hated him! He did that. It was his own fault.'

Saying it is like plunging a knife into his chest over and over. Yet he can't stop saying it, thinking it, hating Andy, hating himself. What kind of man hates his own son? He cries again, a loud, agonized wail that rises and falls and rises and falls, like a siren's call. Only the demon hears him. He is alone in the world, alone in the night. Alone with his demon, the Angel of Death.

A man should never outlive his kids. He ought to die before they can break his heart. Or before he can break theirs. You killed him. You hated him. You killed him.

'But I loved him too. Don't you see?'

I saw what you did to him, how you broke his heart. He did everything for you, and you killed him.

'No. No,' he says, tasting tears. Panic and anguish swell like a tumor in the base of his throat. 'He wouldn't listen. I told him. I told him . . . Goddamn him,' he sobs. 'Goddamn fag.'

The pain tears out of him in a raw scream and he flails his arms at the demon, pawing like an animal.

You killed him.

'How could I do that?' he cried. 'My beautiful boy!'

You want free of it, Mike? End the pain.

End the pain. . . .

The voice is seductive, tempting. He cries out again, nearly choking on the fear as it thrusts up his throat.

End the pain.

It's a sin!

It's your redemption.

Do it, Mike.

End it.

The cold barrel of the service revolver kisses his cheek. His tears roll over the black steel.

End the pain.

After all these years.

Do it.

Sobbing, he opens his mouth and closes his eyes.

The flash is blinding. The explosion is deafening.

The deed is done.

Smoke drifts in sinuous strings in the silent air.

Time passes. A moment. Two. Respect for the dead.

Then another flash, and the whir of a motor drive.

The Angel of Death slips the photo in a pocket, turns and walks away.

14

She woke from a restless, dream-filled sleep and saw him. He stood beside her bed, backlit by the grainy light that seeped around the bathroom door: a huge, faceless silhouette with shoulders like mountain slopes.

Panic exploded like a bomb in her chest. Shards of it wedged in her throat, making her gasp for breath. It tore down through her stomach like shrapnel. The muscles in her arms and legs spasmed at the shock.

Run!

He raised both hands and let go of something as she started to come up off the mattress. She saw it coming as if in slow motion: the thick, twisting body of a snake. The colors of it were very clear to her: the creamy underside, the brown and black pattern on the back.

Arms flailing, she launched herself up and forward. For a split second, confusion tipped her brain this way and that. The world went pitch-black. She couldn't see. She couldn't feel. Her feet didn't seem to be under her, though she was running as hard as she could.

Something hit her on the side of her right eye and cheek. The force was like a sledgehammer connecting to her skull. Her neck snapped back and she thought she might have cried out. Then all motion stopped and she realized the thing that had hit her was the floor.

Oh, my God, I've broken my neck.

He's still in the room.

I can't move.

She felt consciousness ebb away like a slippery thing. She clawed at it with her will, forced her brain to continue functioning.

If she could move her legs . . . Yes.

If she could move her arms . . . Yes.

She pulled her arms in tight to her sides and slowly pushed up from the floor. Her head felt as heavy as a bowling ball, her neck as fragile as a broken toothpick. She sat back on her knees, cradling her face in her hands, pain coming like a pulse. Realization blinking on and off in her mind. Neon bright, then blackness. Neon bright, then blackness.

It wasn't real.

It didn't happen.

It hadn't been a dream, though, not really. More like a hallucination. She had been awake but not conscious. Night terrors, the experts called them. She was an expert by experience. Years and years of it.

Now came the familiar wave of despair. She wanted to cry but couldn't. The protective numbness had already begun to set in. She didn't welcome it, merely resigned herself to it, and slowly, unsteadily rose to her feet.

Still holding her head in one hand, she turned on the lamp on the dresser. There was no one in the room. The light reflected a warm glow off the creamy tone-on-tone striped wallpaper. The bed was empty, the curved upholstered headboard naked of its usual pile of pillows. She'd thrown the pillows to the floor on either side of the bed, and had knocked her water glass off the nightstand. A wet stain darkened the ivory rug. The alarm clock lay on the floor near the empty glass: 4:39 A.M.

Moving carefully, in pain, she went to the bed and pulled the covers off. There was no snake. In the logical part of her brain, she knew there had never been, yet her gaze scanned the floor. She half expected to see the dark, slender shape disappearing beneath the closet door.

She worked on regulating her respiration, the exercise nearly as familiar to her as breathing. Her head was pounding. Pain was like a knife in her neck. She felt sick to her stomach. She gradually became aware of a stickiness in the hand that cradled her head, and knew it was time to assess the damage.

Amanda Savard stared at herself in the bathroom mirror, dimly taking in the surroundings reflected around her image. Soft, elegant, feminine: the environment she had created for herself to give a sense of security and belonging. The same words generally described the image she presented the world, but now she looked as if she'd gone five rounds in a boxing ring. The area around her right eye was swollen from the impact of the fall, and bright red where skidding across the rug had burned her skin. The color blazed against the pallor of her face. She pressed two fingertips gently around the wounds, feeling for fractures, the pain making her breath hiss through her teeth.

How would she explain this? How could she hide it? Who would believe her?

She took a washcloth from the linen cupboard, wet it with cold tap water, and touched it to the raw spots, gritting against the urge to wince. She took three Tylenol and went back to the bedroom. Awkwardly she stripped off the nightshirt she'd sweat through, and pulled on an oversize sweatshirt and a pair of leggings.

The house was silent. Everything was normal according to the security system panel on the wall beside the bedroom door. She'd gone through her nightly ritual, checking locks before going up to bed. And still the sense of danger lingered. She knew from experience the only thing to do was to walk through the house and prove there was no intruder.

She took her gun from the drawer in the nightstand and went out into the hall, moving like a ninety-year-old woman. Room by room, every light in the house was turned on, every room checked, every window, every lock. All of the lights remained on. Light was a good thing. Light chased away the ghosts in the shadows. Those ghosts had been haunting her for so long, it was a wonder they still possessed the ability to frighten her. They were as familiar as family, and as deeply hated.

In her office, Kenny Loggins came on at the flick of a switch on the bookcase stereo system. A quiet, gentle song about the holidays and memories of home. The emotions it evoked in her were emptiness, loneliness, sadness, but she left the song on anyway.

She liked this small room at the back of her house. The space was cozy and felt safe, and looked out on her backyard, which was very private and dotted with birdfeeders. She lived in Plymouth, a suburb that bent and twisted around marshes and woods and Medicine Lake. It wasn't uncommon to see deer nosing around the feeders, though none was braving the security light tonight. Three photographs she'd taken of them through the window hung in small frames in the office. One held a ghost image, her own reflection in the glass superimposed over the animal as it stared at her.

She closed the blinds, too edgy to expose herself to the outside world. She needed to feel enclosed. Her bedroom was her sanctuary when she had to get away from work. The office was her sanctuary when she had to escape the shadows of her life.

There was no escape from anything tonight.

Her desk was neat, the shelves and cubbyholes above it well organized. Bills and papers properly filed, paper clips in a magnetic dish, pens in a cherrywood cup. There were no photographs and only a few mementos, including a badge kept in the far upper-right-hand nook of the shelves. Her constant reminder of why she had become a cop in the first place. She rarely looked at it, but she picked it out now and held it in her hand and stared at it for a long while, acid burning in her stomach.

Spread on the otherwise uncluttered surface of the desk was a copy of the *Minneapolis Star Tribune*, open to the pages most people skipped on their way to the sports. The piece that interested her was an inch long, stuck down near the bottom. DEATH RULED ACCIDENTAL. There wasn't even a photo.

That seemed a shame, she thought. He'd been so handsome. But to most of the metro area, he would never be anything more than a few lines of type, skimmed over and forgotten. Yesterday's news.

'I won't forget you, Andy,' she whispered.

How could I? I killed you.

Her hand closed tightly on the badge until the edges bit into her fingers.

Darkness still cloaked Minneapolis as Amanda Savard arrived at city hall. Most of the lights that shone in office windows facing the street were left on overnight. No one came in at this hour, which made it the perfect time for her to sequester herself in her office without being seen. The longer she could avoid that, the better. Though there would be no ducking the funeral in the afternoon. At least she would be able to get away with dark glasses for the occasion.

Even now, with little chance of running into another human, she wore black sunglasses with frames just large enough to cover the damage she'd done to herself. She had swathed her head in a wide black velvet scarf that wrapped around her neck and trailed dramatically back over her shoulders. Drama had not been her goal. Hiding was.

Her footfalls echoed in the empty hall, boot heels ringing against the old floor. The distance to Room 126 seemed to stretch out before her. Inside her gloves, her hands were sweating. She gripped her keys too hard. The adrenaline from the dream had never entirely burned off, the residue leaving her feeling both jittery and exhausted. Dizziness swam through her head at random moments. Her legs were weak and her head pounded. She couldn't turn her neck to the right, and she felt nauseated.

She put the key in the lock and pulled up short, the skin prickling on the back of her neck. But the hall was empty – what she could see of it. She passed through the Internal Affairs outer office without bothering to turn the light on, and went directly to her own office, where she'd left on the desk lamp.

Safe. For an hour or two. She hung the scarf and her coat on the wall-mounted rack near the door, and went around behind the desk. She slipped the sunglasses off to check her reflection in the mirror of her compact. As if there had been some chance of a miracle between home and here.

The burns around the right eye looked angry, red, shiny with antibiotic gel. There had been no hope of covering them with makeup, and no way to keep bandages in place. The area directly around the eye was puffy and bruised purple and black.

'That's a hell of a shiner.'

Savard bolted at the sound of the voice. She wanted to turn her back, but realized it was too late. Embarrassment and shame flooded her. Anger and resentment rushed in their wake. She grabbed the sunglasses and put them back on.

Kovac stood just inside her door looking like something out of a Raymond Chandler novel: long coat with the collar turned up, hands stuffed in the pockets, an old fedora slouching down over his forehead.

'I suppose getting popped in the face is a common hazard of working IA.'

'If you want to see me, Sergeant, make an appointment,' she said in the chilliest tone she could manage.

'I've already seen you.'

Something about the way he said it made her feel vulnerable. As if he had seen something more than just the physical evidence of what had happened to her, something deeper and more important.

'Did you go to a doctor for that?' he asked, coming closer. He pulled the fedora off and set it on her desk, then ran a hand back over his short hair. His gaze was narrow and zoomed in on the damage she'd done to herself. 'Nasty.'

'I'm fine,' she said, glad to have the desk as a buffer. She moved to the far end of it on the pretext of putting her compact away and stowing her purse in a drawer. The dizziness swirled through her and she kept one hand on the desktop to steady herself.

'And I should see the other guy, huh?' Kovac said.

'There was no other guy. I took a fall.'

'From what? A three-story building?'

'It's none of your business.'

'It is if someone did that to you.'

He was paid to protect and serve, as the saying went. It was nothing personal. She shouldn't have wanted it to be.

'I told you – I fell.'

He didn't believe her. She could see that. He was a cop, and a good one. She'd made it her business to find out. Sam Kovac had years of experience listening to the nuances of lies. And while she wasn't exactly lying, neither was she exactly telling the truth.

She watched Kovac's gaze slide to her left hand, in search of a ring. Wondering if there was an abusive husband. The only ring she wore was on her right hand. An emerald that had been passed down through the women in her mother's family for a hundred years.

'Believe me, Sergeant. I'm the last woman who would let a man get away with this,' she said.

He weighed the idea of saying something more, drew breath for it, then stopped himself.

'You didn't come here to see about my well-being.'

'I ran into Cal Springer last night,' Kovac said. 'You'll be proud to know he's still sweating bullets over your investigation.'

'I have no interest in Cal Springer. I told you, the Curtis case is closed. The investigation was full of mistakes, but none of the allegations of impropriety bore fruit. None that would stand up in court, at any rate.'

'Incompetency is Cal's forte, but he's too big a chickenshit for impropriety. What about Ogden? I hear he threw down Curtis's watch at Verma's place.'

'Can you prove it?'

'I can't. Could Andy Fallon? Ogden was on the scene when my partner and I got to Fallon's house on Tuesday.'

'No, he couldn't prove it. We closed the case,' she said, struggling to keep her focus over another wave of unsteadiness. Pain pounded her head like a hammer. 'He was moving on to other assignments.'

Not by choice. By order. Her order.

'Did Ogden know that?'

'Yes, he did. What was he doing there – at Andy's?'

'Sightseeing.'

'That's ghoulish.'

'Stupid too, but I don't think he's the brightest bulb in the chandelier to begin with.'

'Have you questioned him about his presence at the scene?'

'I have no right to question anyone, Lieutenant,' Kovac reminded her. 'The case is closed. A tragic accident. Remember?'

'I'm not likely to forget.'

'I assumed Ogden and his partner responded to the radio call. I had no reason to think he'd have any other motive to be there. Silly question – was there bad blood between him and Fallon? Had Ogden threatened him?'

'Not that I'm aware of. No more animosity than the usual, I should say.'

'You're all used to having people hate you.'

'So are you, Sergeant.'

'Not my own kind.'

She let that pass. 'Resentment comes with the territory. People who do bad things don't like to suffer the consequences of their actions. Bad cops are worse than criminals in that respect. They have the idea they can hide behind the badge. When it turns out they can't . . .

'I can check the case file,' she said, letting out a long, carefully measured breath. She felt hot and clammy with sweat. She needed to sit down, but she didn't want to show weakness in front of him, nor did she want him to think she would pull the case up on the computer while he waited. 'I don't expect to find anything. At any rate, you and I both know in our hearts that – despite what the ME ruled – Andy probably committed suicide.'

'I don't let my heart get involved, Lieutenant. I let my gut do my feeling for me.'

'You know what I mean. He wasn't murdered.'

'I know he's dead,' Kovac conceded stubbornly. 'I know he shouldn't be.'

'The world is full of tragedy, Sergeant Kovac,' she said, breathing a little too quickly. 'This is our piece of it for the week. Maybe it would make more sense to us if it were a crime, but it wasn't. That means we deal with it and move on.'

'Is that what you're doing?' he asked, moving to the end of the desk where she stood. 'Dealing with it?'

Savard got the feeling he wasn't talking about Andy Fallon anymore. He seemed to be looking at the marks on her face – what he could see of them around the sunglasses. She started to take a step back, but the floor didn't quite seem to be under her foot. Blackness closed in around her, and the dizziness came in a rippling wave.

Kovac moved quickly, catching her by the upper arms. She brought her hands up to his chest to steady herself.

'You need to see a doctor,' he insisted.

'No. I'll be fine. I just need to sit for a minute.'

She pushed against him, wanting free. He didn't let go. Instead, he turned her, and this time when her knees gave out, her butt hit her chair. Kovac pulled the sunglasses off her face and looked into her eyes.

'How many of me do you see?' he asked.

'One is plenty.'

'Follow my finger,' he ordered, moving it back and forth, then up and down in front of her face. His expression was grim. His eyes were a smoky shade of brown, a hint of blue in the depths. More interesting up close than from a distance, she thought absently.

'Jesus,' he muttered, staring at the area around her right eye. One big hand came up and cradled that side of her face gently, thumb pressing experimentally against the bones. 'Ten bucks says that scars.'

'It won't be my first,' she said softly.

His hand stilled. His gaze found hers, searching. She turned away.

'You need to see someone,' he said again, sitting back against her desk. 'You might have a concussion. This is the voice of experience talking.' He pointed to a butterfly clip holding together a gash over his left eye. The area surrounding it was mottled purple with a yellow tint.

'Did you have a concussion?' Savard asked. 'That might explain some things.'

'Naw. My head's like granite. Maybe you and I have something in common after all,' he said, as if he'd given the subject some thought.

'I imagine you have a job to do, Sergeant,' she said, moving her chair toward the desk and hoping the motion wouldn't make her dizzy enough to fall off or to vomit. Kovac didn't move. She didn't like the proximity at all. He could have lifted his hand and touched her hair, touched her face the way he had a moment ago.

She didn't like him behind the desk. That was her space. He had breached a defense, and she imagined he knew it.

'You don't want to talk about Andy Fallon,' he said quietly. 'Why is that, Lieutenant?'

She closed her eyes in frustration, then opened them. 'Because he's dead and I feel responsible.'

'You think you should have seen it coming. Sometimes you can't,' he said. 'Sometimes you're watching for one thing, and life belts you with a sucker punch out of nowhere.' He pantomimed a slow left hook that pulled up just short of her injured eye.

Savard stared at him. 'You probably have an actual murder to investigate,' she said, reaching for the telephone. 'I suggest you get to it.'

He watched as she dialed to get her messages. He didn't look happy, but then, she'd never seen him happy. Perhaps he never was.

Something else we have in common, Sergeant, she thought.

He went back around the desk reluctantly and picked up his hat.

'It's not always smart to be brave, Amanda,' he said quietly.

'You may call me Lieutenant Savard.'

His mouth hooked up on one corner. 'Yeah. I know. I just wanted to

470

hear how it sounded.' He paused. 'When you saw Andy Sunday night, did you have a glass of wine?'

'I don't drink. We had coffee.'

'Mmm. Did you know Andy changed his sheets and did his laundry before he killed himself?' he asked. 'Strange, huh?'

Savard said nothing.

'See you at the funeral,' he said, and walked out.

She watched him go, her messages playing to a deaf ear.

15

For forty years the uniforms had liked having breakfast at a place called Cheap Charlie's, which was located in the no-man's-land northeast of the Metrodome. Run-down, with a filthy fifties exterior, the place had spat in the face of progress, recession, gentrification, and everything else that might have changed it in the years it had existed. Cheap Charlie's had no need to change. Their clientele was cops. The decades could come and go, but cops would never change. Tradition was all.

Mike Fallon had probably eaten here as a rookie, Liska thought, looking at the place through the blue bag serving as her passenger's window. She had lucked out and caught a parking spot in the front just as a radio car was pulling out.

She had eaten here as a rookie. They had probably all been served by the same waitress, a woman called Cheeks. In her heyday, before modern photography, Cheeks had looked like a chipmunk with a full load of nuts in her mouth. All cheeks, no chin, and a button of a nose. In the intervening years, gravity had done its thing to the point that Jowls would have been a more appropriate nickname, but Cheeks had stuck.

She was working the counter this morning, a shrunken doll with slitted eyes and a leaning tower of dyed-black hair, pouring coffee and smoking a cigarette in defiance of all known health codes. Not one cop in the place would reprimand her, and the place was a sea of uniforms and mustaches. A lot of the detectives ate breakfast here as well. Kovac among them some days. Tradition.

She went to the counter and took a vacant stool beside Elwood Knutson, her gaze scanning the room.

'Elwood, I thought you were too enlightened to eat here.'

'I am,' he said, regarding a plate smeared with the remains of bacon and eggs. 'But I've decided to try the Protein Power diet, and I couldn't think of a better place for the required breakfast. See, it's so out, it's hip again. What's your excuse?'

'I haven't had a really good heartburn in a long time.'

'You're in for a treat.'

'Bingo,' she said to herself as she spotted Ogden. He had wedged himself into a booth at the back and had an expression on his face that suggested he hadn't had a proper bowel movement in too long. Because of the angles, she couldn't see his breakfast partner and the recipient of his sour scowl.

Elwood didn't turn, studying Liska instead. 'Something I should know about?'

'Something you might know about. Do you remember when that uniform Curtis was murdered off duty?'

'Yes. Part of a string of gay crimes. A serial killer in the making.'

'Supposedly. What do you know about gay-bashing in the department?'

Elwood nibbled thoughtfully on the end of a bacon strip. He wore a mouse-brown porkpie hat with the brim bent up in front.

'I know I find it deplorable to harass or discriminate on the basis of sexual preference,' he said. 'Who are we to choose for others? Love is rare –'

'Thank you. That's admirable. I'll send your mailing address to the ACLU,' Liska said dryly. 'We're not talking about you, Elwood.'

'Who are we talking about?'

She glanced around discreetly for eavesdroppers, hoping for a few. 'I'm talking about the uniforms. What's it like in the trenches? Department PC policy aside, what's the attitude among the rank and file? I heard Curtis had complained to IA about harassment. What was that about? Are they still letting Neanderthals into the club? I thought that went out with Rodney King and the LA riots.'

'Sadly, the job attracts them,' Elwood commented. 'It's the badge. It's like a shiny coin to a monkey.'

The uniform on the other side of Liska looked around her to give Elwood a dirty look.

'Might have been an orangutan in a past life,' Liska whispered. She took a sip of the coffee Cheeks had poured for her and was instantly reminded it was time to change the oil in the Saturn. 'Anyway, I know that Curtis investigation was a major cluster fuck.'

'That was Springer's. His conception was a cluster fuck.'

'That's true, but it was a uniform that screwed the pooch on that investigation, the way I hear it. Big dumb ox of a guy name of Ogden. You know him?'

'We don't travel in the same social circles, I'm afraid.'

'I'd be more afraid if you did,' Liska said, sliding from the stool.

She made her way toward the back of the diner, fielding greetings without looking, holding her gaze on Ogden. He still hadn't noticed her, and his conversation with the man she couldn't see was becoming more intense. She couldn't make out the words, but the anger was distinct. She wished she could have come in behind him and blindsided him, but the diner was too narrow. He finally saw her and straightened, nearly tipping over a glass of orange juice.

'I'd go with prune if I were you,' she said. 'I hear those steroids can stop a person up like concrete.'

'I don't know what you're talking about,' Ogden said. 'I'm no steroid juicer.'

A comeback stuck in Liska's mouth as she got her first look at Ogden's dining companion. Cal Springer. And he couldn't have looked more guilty if he had been caught with a hooker.

'Hey, Cal. Interesting company you keep. Is this how you don't look bad to IA? Hanging out with the guy they think screwed your case? Maybe people are wrong about you. Maybe you really are as dumb as you look.'

'Why don't you mind your own business, Liska?'

'I wouldn't be much of a detective, then, would I?' she pointed out. 'Look, Cal, I'm not on your ass here. I'm just saying it looks bad, that's all. You should think about these things if you want to be a political animal.'

He turned toward the window. No view there. The plate glass was fogged over with smoke and hot breath and airborne grease.

'Where's your partner these days, Cal?' Liska asked. 'I need to talk to him.'

'Vacation. Two weeks in Hawaii.'

'Lucky stiff.'

Springer looked as if he would have preferred two weeks in hell to this conversation.

Liska turned back to Ogden and asked him point-blank: 'How'd you and your partner come to be at the Fallon scene?'

Ogden scratched at his flattop. His scalp was fish-belly white between the fine, short hairs. 'Caught the call on the radio.'

'And you just happened to be in the neighborhood.'

'That's right.'

'Dumb luck. Well, that'd be the kind you'd have.'

Ogden's little eyes looked like BBs set in dough. He rolled the sloped shoulders back. 'I don't like your attitude, Liska.'

Liska laughed. '*You* don't like *my* attitude? Guess what, Ox,' she said, bending down to get in his face. 'You're a few evolutionary limbs below me in the cop tree. I can shit my attitude all over your head if I want and nobody will listen to you complain about it. Now, if *I* don't like *your* attitude – and I don't – *that's* a problem.

'Why were you there?' she asked again.

'I told you, we caught the call.'

'Burgess had the first response. Burgess was first on the scene.'

'We thought he might need help.'

'With a DB.'

'He was riding alone. He had to secure the scene.'

'So you and Rubel came and tromped all over it. And it was just a happy coincidence that the vic turned out to be the IA investigator that was on you for the Curtis screw-up.'

'That's right.'

Liska shook her head in amazement. 'Were you busting rocks with your head when they were passing out brains? What were you thinking? You want IA on you again?'

Ogden looked around, scowling at anyone he thought might be listening. 'We responded to a call. How were we supposed to know the DB was Fallon?'

'But when you found out, you stayed. You put your prints all over his house –'

'So? He offed himself. It wasn't like somebody did it for him.'

'You couldn't know that. You still don't know that. And it's *never* your call to make as long as you're in a uniform.'

'The ME ruled it,' he said. 'It wasn't a murder.'

'It wasn't a spectator sport either, but you couldn't resist, could you? Did you take a couple of Polaroids to share with the rest of the homophobes back in the locker room?'

Ogden slid out of the booth and stood up. Liska tried to hold her ground, but had to take a step back or be forced back. One big vein stood out in a zigzag on his forehead, like a lightning bolt. His eyes were cold and as flat as buttons. The chill of fear that went through her was instinctive, and that was frightening to her in and of itself. Fear was not a common companion.

'I don't answer to you, Liska,' he said in a tone that was both quiet and taut.

She met his glare with her own, knowing she was poking a stick at a bull. It might not have been the smartest tack, but it was the one she'd chosen and there was nothing to do now but ride it out. 'Fuck up another one of my crime scenes and you won't have to answer to anyone, Ogden. You won't be wearing a badge anymore.'

The vein pulsed like something in a horror movie, and color pushed up from his too-tight collar into his face.

'Hey, B.O., let's rock 'n' roll.'

Liska knew it had to be Ogden's partner, Rubel, coming toward them from the front of the diner. Still, she didn't turn away from Ogden. She sure as hell would never have turned her back on him. He couldn't seem to break his fixation on her. The rage within him swelled with every short breath. She could see it, feel it.

Liska's brain flashed on the crime scene photos from the Curtis murder. Rage. Overkill. A human skull smashed like a pumpkin.

People around them were staring now. Cal Springer got up from the booth and beat a path for the front door, narrowly missing banging shoulders with Rubel.

'B.O., come on. Let's do it,' Rubel ordered.

Ogden looked at him finally, and the tension snapped like a twig. Liska felt the air rush out of her lungs. Rubel gave her a once-over from behind a pair of mirrored shades.

He was definitely the better-looking of the two. Dark hair, square jaw, built like Michelangelo's *David* on steroids. He was the brains of the pair, she guessed, when he herded his partner toward the door. Hustling Ogden away from trouble, much as he had done that day at Fallon's.

She followed them out to the sidewalk. They were headed toward the corner parking lot across the street.

'Hey, Rubel!' she called. He turned and stared at her. 'I need to speak with you too. Alone. Come to the CID offices at the end of your shift.'

He didn't answer. His expression didn't change. He and Ogden walked away, the collective width of their shoulders taking up the entire sidewalk.

If Andy Fallon's death had not been ruled an accident or suicide, Ogden would have been high on the list of suspects. Was he stupid to have shown up at the scene? Maybe not. Responding to the dead body call had given him ample opportunity to legitimately put his fingerprints all over Andy Fallon's house.

How did you force a man to hang himself?

A chill went through her, and Liska knew it had little to do with the temperature and everything to do with the fact that she was looking at another cop and trying to see what was rotten about him.

The little bell rang on Cheap Charlie's door as it swung open behind her.

'Call me a stickler for details,' Elwood said, 'but I was of the impression we don't investigate closed cases.'

Liska watched the uniforms get into a cruiser. Rubel was the driver. Ogden rode shotgun. The car dipped down on its springs as he got in on the passenger's side.

'Who do we work for, Elwood?'

'Technically or figuratively?'

'Who do we work for, Elwood?'

Kovac had raised them all on this.

'The victim.'

'My employer hasn't properly notified me to terminate my services,' she said without any of her usual humor.

Elwood gave a big sigh. 'Tinks, for someone so determined to get ahead, you devote a lot of time to putting your backside in a crack.'

'Yeah,' she said, digging her car keys out of her coat pocket. 'I'm an oxymoron. Emphasis on the moron.'

16

The world is full of tragedy, Sergeant Kovac.

Savard's voice stayed in his head as he drove toward Mike Fallon's. His mind played the trick of making her sound breathy in a sexy way. It made the play of light and shadow on her face dramatic and soft, the look in her eyes full of mystery.

That part was true enough. Amanda Savard was a puzzle, and he'd always found puzzles too tempting. He was usually pretty good at them, but he knew instinctively this one would be more difficult than most, and the odds of any kind of payoff weren't good. She wouldn't appreciate his trying, that was for damn sure.

You may call me Lieutenant Savard.

'Amanda,' he said, just to be defiant. She wouldn't like knowing he was saying her name while he was alone any more than she liked it in her presence. Maybe less. She couldn't boss him around if she wasn't there to hear him, and control was her big thing. He wondered why, wondered what events had shaped her into the woman she was. 'What's your tragedy, Amanda?'

She didn't wear a wedding ring. There were no pictures of a significant other in her office. She didn't seem the type to troll bars for the kind of guy who could have given her that shiner.

He didn't buy the explanation of a fall. The placement of the wounds was too suspicious. Who took a fall and broke it with her face? The natural reaction to falling was to bring the hands out to hit first and save doing the kind of damage that had been done to her. She hadn't had a mark on her hands.

The idea of someone striking a woman made him sick and furious. The idea of this particular woman allowing it baffled him.

He set the questions aside as he pulled into Mike Fallon's driveway. There were no cars at the curb or in the drive. No one answered the doorbell.

Kovac pulled out his cell phone and dialed Mike's number from the scrap of paper he'd scribbled it on. The phone rang unanswered. That Mike was asleep or unconscious from tranquilizers or booze seemed a good bet, and either possibility suited Kovac fine. All he really wanted was a few minutes alone in the house.

He went around the side and checked the garage. The car was there. He went around to the back and took the key out from under the mat.

The house was silent. No distant sound of a television or radio or a shower running. The old man was probably dead to the world. He could have another five or ten minutes before he had to face the day he would bury his son.

Kovac went to the kitchen counter cluttered with the pharmaceuticals that kept Mike Fallon functioning in one way or another, and sorted through the bottles. Prilosec, Darvocet, Ambien.

Ambien, aka zolpidem. The barbiturate found in Andy Fallon's blood. Kovac stared at the bottle, a tight feeling in his chest. He popped the childproof cap and looked inside. Empty. The prescription was for thirty tablets with instructions to take one at bedtime as needed. The refill date was November 7.

It was probably just a coincidence that father and son had been using the same stuff to knock themselves out. Ambien was a common prescription sleep aid. But there had been no Ambien at Andy Fallon's house, and that seemed strange. If he'd taken the drug the night of his death, then where was the bottle? Not in the medicine cabinet, not in the garbage, not in the nightstand. Mike's bottle was empty, but he could have taken all the pills himself in accordance with the instructions. On the other hand, if 'as needed' meant once or twice a week, then there were a hell of a lot of pills unaccounted for.

Kovac let possibilities run through his mind, unchecked, uncensored. None of them pleasant, but then, that was the nature of his work and the bent of his mind because of the work. He couldn't afford to trust, to discount, to filter possibilities through a screen of denial the way most people did. He didn't feel badly about that. It didn't depress him, the way it did others in his line of work. The simple truth of the world was that people, even otherwise decent people, regularly did rotten things to other people, even to their own children.

Still, he couldn't come up with a scenario in which Mike Fallon played a direct role in his son's death. The old man's physical limitations made it impossible. He supposed Andy could have taken the pills from his father's stash, but that didn't ring true for him either. Or he could have gotten them from a friend. He thought again of the sheets and towels in the washing machine, of the few clean dishes in Andy's dishwasher.

'Hey, Mike! You up?' he called. 'It's Kovac!'

No answer.

He set the prescription bottle back on the counter and went out of the cramped little kitchen. The house had a stillness to it he didn't like, a sense of being vacant. Maybe Neil had come and carted Mike away already, but the funeral was hours away. Maybe Mike had other relatives who were, even now, giving him comfort and coffee and saying all the right things, but Kovac didn't think so. He'd known Mike Fallon only in the context of being alone. Isolated first by his toughness, then by his bitterness. It was hard to imagine anyone loving him the way people in close families loved one another. Not that Kovac knew much about it. His own family was scattered to the four winds. He never saw any of them.

He looked at the empty rooms of Mike Fallon's house and wondered if he was looking at his own future.

'Mike? It's Kovac,' he called again, turning down the short hall to the bedrooms.

The smell hit him first. Not overpowering, but unmistakable. Dread fell like an anvil on his chest. His heart beat up against it like a fist hammering on a door.

He swore under his breath, pulling the Glock from its holster. With his foot, he pushed open the door to the spare bedroom. Nothing. No one. Just empty twin beds with white chenille spreads, and a sepia-toned portrait of Jesus in a cheap metal frame on the wall.

'Mike?'

He moved toward Fallon's bedroom door, already knowing. The images of what he would find on the other side were rolling through his head. Still, he stood to the side as he turned the knob. He filled his lungs with air and pushed the door open with his foot.

The room was in the same state of disarray as when he had last seen it. The framed photographs Fallon had smashed were still piled where Kovac had left them. The bed was still unmade. The jelly glass still sat on the nightstand with a splash of whiskey in it. Dirty clothes still littered the floor.

Kovac stared at the empty room, at a loss for a moment, trying to clear the images he'd had from his head. The smell was stronger here, where he was standing. Blood and excrement and urine. The biting, metallic scent of gunpowder. The bathroom door was directly across from him. Closed.

He stood to the side and knocked, said Fallon's name again, though barely loud enough to hear himself. He turned the knob and pushed the door open.

The shower curtain looked as if someone had given birth on it. Bloody chunks of tissue and hair clung to it.

Iron Mike Fallon sat in his wheelchair, in his underwear, his head and shoulders flung backward, arms hanging out to the sides. The spindly, hairy, useless legs were canted over to the left. His mouth hung open and his eyes were wide, as if he had realized in the final instant that the reality of death was surprisingly different from the way he had imagined it would be.

'Aw, Mikey,' Kovac said softly.

Out of long habit, he came into the room carefully, taking in the details automatically, even as another part of his brain considered his own loss in this. Mike Fallon had broken him in, set a standard, became a legend to live up to. Like a father in a lot of ways. Better than, he supposed, considering

Mike's strained relationships with his own sons. It had been bad enough to see the old man soured and angry and pathetic. To see him dead in his underwear was the final indignity.

The back of his skull was gone, blown wide open. A flap of scalp clung to the crown of his head by a collection of bloody gray hairs. Brain matter and tiny bone fragments had splattered the floor. An old .38 service revolver lay on the floor to Fallon's right, flung there as his body had jerked in its death spasm.

Iron Mike Fallon, just another cop to end it all by his own hand with the gun he had carried to protect the public. God knew how many did it each year. Too many. They spent their careers as a part of a brotherhood but died alone – because none of them knew how to deal with the stress and every last one was afraid to tell anybody. It didn't matter if they'd turned in the badge. A cop was a cop until the day he died.

That day was today for Mike Fallon. The day his son would be buried.

A man should never outlive his kids, Kojak. He ought to die before they can break his heart.

Kovac touched two fingers to the old man's throat. A mere formality, though he'd known people who'd survived such wounds. Or rather, he'd known a few whose hearts had continued beating for a time because the damage had been done to some less useful part of the brain. It wasn't really survival.

Fallon was cool to the touch. Rigor was setting in in the face and throat, but not yet in the upper body. Based on that, Kovac put the time of death within the last five or six hours. Two or three in the morning. The loneliest hours of the night. The hours that seem to stretch endlessly when a man was lying awake, staring into the dark at the bleaker realities of his life.

Kovac went out of the room, out of the house, and stood on the back stoop, staring at nothing. He lit a cigarette and smoked it, his fingers stiffening in the cold. He had gloves in his pockets, but didn't bother to put them on. Sometimes it was good to hurt. Physical pain as an affirmation of life, as an acknowledgment of deeper suffering.

He wished for a glass of whiskey to toast the old man, but that would have to wait. He finished the cigarette and reached for his cell phone.

'This is Kovac, homicide. Send me the tag 'em and bag 'em boys. I've got a DB,' he said. 'And send the A team. He used to be one of ours.'

He had taken a seat on the front step, trench coat wrapped around his freezing ass, and was smoking a second cigarette by the time Liska rolled up.

'Jesus, Tinks, what're you trying to do? Bring down the neighborhood?' he called as she climbed out of the car. It was her own, the Saturn sporting a trash bag window.

'You think the neighborhood watch block commander will call the cops?' she asked, coming up the sidewalk.

'He'll probably gun you down in the street. Shoot first, ask questions later. America at the dawn of the new millennium.'

'If I'm lucky he'll hit the gas tank and toast the rotten thing. I could stand a break this week.'

'You and me both,' Kovac said. He nodded at the car as Liska came up the snow-packed steps, ignoring the clean wheelchair ramp. 'So what happened?'

She shrugged it off. 'Just another victim of the moral decline. In the Haaff ramp, no less.'

'World's going to hell on Rollerblades.'

'Keeps the paychecks coming.'

'Did they get anything?'

'Not that I could tell. There was nothing worth getting, except my address off some junk mail.'

Kovac frowned. 'I don't like that.'

'Yeah, well . . . Didn't your mother ever tell you you'll get hemorrhoids sitting on cold concrete?'

'Naw.' He got up slowly, stiffly. 'She told me I'd go blind beating off.'

'I didn't need that image in my head.'

'Beats what you'll see inside,' he said. He bent over to crush out the cigarette and dropped the butt off the side of the stoop, behind a juniper shrub.

Neither of them spoke for a moment as an awkward tension fell around them.

'I'm really sorry, Sam,' Liska said softly. 'I know he meant a lot to you.'

Kovac sighed. 'It's always the tough ones that eat their guns.'

Liska gave him a little shove. 'Hey, you do that to me, I'll revive you just so I can shoot you myself.'

He tried to smile but couldn't, so he looked away, to next door. Fallon's neighbor had plywood silhouettes of the three wise men on camels in front of their picture window, hot on the trail of the Christ child. A schnauzer was taking a whiz on one of the camels.

'I'm not that tough, Tinks,' he confessed. He felt as if all of that old armor had rusted and flaked away, layer by layer, leaving him exposed. Which was worse? Being too hard to feel, too remote to be touched, or being open to feel the touch of other people's lives and emotions, open to being hurt by that contact? Hell of a choice on a day like this. *Like trying to decide if you'd rather be stabbed or bludgeoned,* he thought.

'Good.' Liska put her hand on his back and leaned her head against his shoulder for a few seconds. The contact gave comfort, like something cool against a burn.

Better to be open, he decided, reflecting back on the original question. Even if it hurt more often than not. Sometimes it felt like this. He slipped his arm around his partner's shoulders and gave her a squeeze. 'Thanks.'

'Don't mention it. Really,' she teased, straight-faced, as she stepped away.

'I have a reputation to uphold. And speaking of people with reputations . . . Guess who was seen dining together this morning at that celebrity hot spot Chez Chuck.'

Kovac waited.

'Cal Springer and Bruce Ogden.'

'I'll be damned.'

'Strange bedfellows, huh?'

'Were they happy to see you?'

'Yeah, like they'd be happy to have head lice. My guess is it wasn't a planned meeting. Cal was sweating like a monk in a whorehouse. He bolted at the first chance.'

'He's pretty damn nervous for a man who's been cleared of any wrongdoing.'

'I'll say. And Ogden . . .' She looked out at the street as if she might find something there to compare him to. A garbage truck rumbled past. 'That guy's like a keg of nitro with a tricky detonator. I'd love a peek in his personnel jacket.'

'Savard told me she'll check Fallon's case file regarding the Curtis investigation. See what notes he might have made about Ogden, whether Ogden threatened him, that kind of thing.'

'But she wouldn't let you see the file.'

'No.'

'You're losing your touch, Sam.'

He huffed a laugh. 'What touch? I'm hoping she gets so sick of the sight of me she gives me what I want just to make me go away. Aversion therapy.'

'Well, I have to say, if I weren't such the tough cupcake, Ogden would have given me a little chill this morning,' Liska admitted. 'There we are, him getting in my face, and all I could think of was Curtis – beaten to death with a ball bat.'

Kovac turned it over in his head. 'You're thinking what if Ogden was the one harassing Curtis and went off on him for complaining to IA. But Ogden would never have been privy to the Curtis investigation if there'd been any beef about him harassing Curtis in the past. That shit only happens in the movies.'

'Yeah,' Liska said on a sigh. 'If you were Mel Gibson and I were Jodie Foster, that could happen.'

'Mel Gibson's short.'

'Okay. If you were . . . Bruce Willis.'

'He's short and bald.'

'Al Pacino?'

'Looks like someone dragged him down a gravel road behind a truck.'

Liska rolled her eyes. 'Jesus. Harrison Ford?'

'He's getting kind of old.'

'So are you,' Liska pointed out, then looked at the street again. 'Where's the CSU?' She bounced up and down a little on the balls of her feet. She wasn't wearing a hat, and the rims of her ears had turned bright pink in the cold.

'At a terminal domestic situation,' Kovac said. 'Get this. Common-law wife says she got fed up with the hubby raping her when she was passed out drunk – after nine years of it. She stabbed him in the chest, face, and groin with a busted vodka bottle.'

'Wow. Absolut homicide.'

'Good one. Anyway, they'll be a little while.'

'I'll do the Polaroids, then.' She held her hand out for his car keys so she could go get the camera.

By the book. Every violent death was processed like a homicide.

Kovac went back into the house with her and started making notes. There was a certain comfort in the routine, provided he didn't remind himself the victim had been his mentor once upon a lifetime ago. Liska made none of the usual dark jokes they used to take the edge off a horrific death scene. For a time the only sound was the click and whir of the camera as it spat out one gruesome photo after another. When he realized the sound had stopped, Kovac looked up from his notebook.

Liska was squatting down in front of Fallon, staring at him as if she expected him to answer some question she had asked telepathically.

'What?' Kovac asked.

She didn't answer, but stood and glanced from wall to wall in the narrow bathroom, then over her shoulder and back. Her brows puckered together and she made a little knot of her mouth. 'Why'd he back in?'

'Huh?'

'This room is narrow, besides the obstacles of the toilet and sink. Why'd he back in? That had to be tricky. Why bother?'

Kovac considered the old man and the question. 'He goes in frontwise, whoever opens the door opens it on the hamburger side of his head. Maybe he wanted to preserve a little dignity.'

'Then he might have had the consideration to put on some clothes, don't you think? Those skivvies don't exactly scream "Respect me".'

'Suicides don't always make sense. Someone's gonna take and eat a thirty-eight slug, he's not exactly in his right mind. And you know as well as I do – plenty of people off themselves in the can. You'd think they were gonna have to clean up the mess themselves.'

Liska said nothing. Her attention had gone to the floor, dingy vinyl that had been mostly white twenty years ago. Behind Fallon, the vinyl had taken a spray of blood flecked with bits of bone and chunks of brain matter that looked like overcooked macaroni. In front of him: nothing. The shower curtain was a mess; the door they had entered through was clean.

Anyone coming into – or going out of – the room had a clean path. No blood to step in or to mark fingerprints.

'If he'd been a billionaire with a young, pretty wife, I'd say you're on a hot scent, Tinks,' Kovac said. 'But he was a bitter old man in a wheelchair who just lost his favorite son. What'd he have left to live for? He was torn up about Andy, couldn't forgive himself for not forgiving the boy. So he rolled it in here, parked it, and capped himself. And he did it the way he did it to make a neat death scene – so none of us would come busting in here and step on his brain.'

Liska pointed the Polaroid at the .38 on the floor and snapped one last shot.

'That'll be his old service weapon,' Kovac said. 'When we look around, we'll find that he kept it in a shoe box in the back of his closet, 'cause that's where old cops always stash their guns.' He made a sharp, hard-edged smile. 'That's where I stash mine, if you want to come and take it away from me. We're pathetic creatures of pattern and habit.' He stared at Fallon. 'Some of us more pathetic than others.'

'You're sounding a little bitter yourself, Kojak,' Liska said, handing the snapshots to him.

He slipped them into the inside breast pocket of his topcoat. 'How can I look at this and not be?'

From another part of the house came the thump of an exterior door closing. Kovac gladly turned away from the corpse and started down the hall.

'It's about damn time,' he barked, then pulled up short at the same time Neil Fallon stopped dead in the archway between the living room and dining room.

He looked as if he'd been rolled. His hair stood up on one side, a purpling bruise crowned the crest of his right cheek, and his lip was split. The brown suit looked slept in. The cheap tie was askew and the top button of the white shirt undone. He couldn't have gotten the collar closed with a winch. He'd obviously bought the shirt a couple of neck sizes ago and hadn't had occasion to wear it since.

He gulped a couple of breaths, pumping himself up.

'Jesus Christ, he can't even leave *this* to me?' he said, his expression sliding from shock to anger. 'I can't even drive him to the goddamn funeral home? He's gotta have one of his own for that too? The son of a bitch –'

'He's dead, Neil,' Kovac said bluntly. 'Looks like he shot himself. I'm sorry.'

Fallon stared at him for a full minute, then shook his head in amazement. 'You're the regular Angel of Death, aren't you?'

'Just the messenger.'

Fallon turned around as if he might walk right back out the front door, but he just stood there with his hands on his hips, the bull shoulders rising and falling.

Kovac waited, thinking about another cigarette and that glass of whiskey he'd wanted earlier. He remembered the bottle of Old Crow Neil had had out in his shed the day he'd told him about his brother, and how they had stood out in the cold and shared it while they stared at the snow blowing across the frozen lake. It seemed a year ago.

'When did you last talk to Mike?' he asked, falling back on the routine, same as he always did.

'Last night. On the phone.'

'What time was that?'

Fallon started to laugh, a harsh, discordant sound. 'You're some piece of work, Kovac,' he said, starting to pace a small circle at the far end of the dining room table. 'My brother and my old man dead inside a week and you're giving me the fucking third degree. You're something. I hadn't seen the old man five times in the last ten years, and you think maybe I killed him. Why would I bother?'

'That's not why I asked, but as long as you've brought it up, I'll need to know for the record where you were this morning between midnight and four A.M.'

'Fuck you.'

'I think I'd remember that. Must have been someone else.'

'I was home in bed.'

'Got a wife or girlfriend to corroborate?'

'I've got a wife. We're separated.'

Fallon looked around as if searching for some neutral third party to witness what was happening to him now, but there was no one. He paced some more and shook his head, the anger and frustration building visibly.

He made a little lunge toward Kovac and bounced back, jabbing the air with a forefinger, a grimace contorting his face. 'I hated that old son of a bitch! I fucking hated him!'

Tears squeezed out of his tightly closed eyes and rolled over his cheeks. 'But he was my old man,' he said, and sucked in a quick breath. 'And now he's dead. I don't need any shit from you!'

He stopped pacing and bent over with his hands on his knees, as if he'd taken a blow to the stomach. He groaned in the back of his throat. 'Christ, I'm gonna be sick.'

Kovac moved to block the path to the bathroom, but Fallon went for the kitchen instead and straight out the back door.

Kovac started to follow, then pulled up as the head of the crime scene unit walked in the front door. Just as well. By the time he was able to join Neil Fallon on the back steps, any gastrointestinal pyrotechnics had subsided. Fallon stood leaning against the railing, staring at the backyard, sipping out of a slim metal flask. His skin looked slightly gray, his eyes rimmed in red. He didn't acknowledge Kovac's presence, but pointed to a naked oak tree in the far corner of the yard.

'That was the hanging tree,' he said without emotion. 'When Andy and I were kids.'

'Playing cowboys.'

'And pirates, and Tarzan, and whatever. He should have come back here

485

and done it. Andy hanging dead in the backyard, Iron Mike in the house with his head blown off. I could have come and parked my car in the garage and gassed myself.'

'How'd Mike sound last night on the phone?'

'Like an asshole, like always. "I wanna be at the goddamn funeral home by ten o'clock." ' The impersonation was less than flattering, but not less than accurate. ' "You can damn well be here on time." Fucking old prick,' he muttered, and swiped a gloved hand under his running nose.

'What time was that? I'm trying to get a frame for what happened when,' Kovac explained. 'We need it for the paperwork.'

Fallon stared at the tree and shrugged. 'I dunno. I wasn't paying attention. Maybe like nine or something.'

'Couldn't have been. I ran into him at your brother's house around nine.'

Fallon looked at him. 'What were you doing there?'

'Poking around. There's a couple of loose ends need tying up.'

'Like what? Andy hung himself. How can you have any doubts about that?'

'I like to know the why of things,' Kovac said. 'I'm funny that way. I want to look at what he was working on, what was going on in his personal life, things like that. Fill in the blanks, get the whole picture. You see?'

If Fallon saw, he didn't like it. He turned away and took another pull on the little flask.

'I'm used to people dying,' Kovac said. 'Drug dealers kill each other over money. Junkies kill each other over dope. Husbands and wives kill each other out of hate. There's a method to the madness. Someone like your brother buys it, a guy with everything going for him, I need to try to make some sense of it.'

'Good luck.'

'What'd you do to your face?'

Fallon tried to shake off the attention. He touched a hand to the bruise on his cheek as if to brush it away. 'Nothing. Mixed it up a little in the parking lot with a customer last night.'

'Over what?'

'He made a remark. I took exception and said something about his sexual preferences and a sheep. He took a swing and got lucky.'

'That's assault,' Kovac pointed out. 'You call the cops?'

Fallon gave a nervous laugh. 'That's a good one. He *was* a cop.'

'A cop? A city cop?'

'He wasn't in uniform.'

'How'd you know he was a cop?'

'Please. Like I can't spot one a mile off.'

'Did you get a name? A badge number?'

'Right. After he knocked me on my ass, I demanded his badge number. Anyway, I don't need the hassle of filing a report. He was just some asshole knew Andy. He made a crack. We took it outside.'

'What'd he look like?'

'Like half the cops in the world,' Fallon said impatiently. He slipped the flask into his coat pocket, pulled out a pack of cigarettes, and went about that ritual, fumbling with his gloves, fingers clumsy with cold – or with nerves. He swore to himself, got the thing lit, took a couple of hard puffs.

'Look, I wish I hadn't said anything. I don't want to do anything with it. I'd had a few myself. I got a mouth on me when I'm tanked.'

'Big guy? Little guy? White? Black? Old? Young?'

Fallon scowled and fidgeted. He looked as if his skin suddenly didn't fit him right. He wouldn't meet Kovac's gaze. 'I don't even know that I'd know him if I saw him again. It didn't mean anything. It's not important.'

'It could mean a hell of a lot,' Kovac said. 'Your brother worked Internal Affairs. He made enemies for a living.'

'But he killed himself,' Fallon insisted. 'That was what happened, right? He hung himself. The case is closed.'

'Everyone seems to want it to be.'

'But you don't?'

'I want the truth – whatever it might be.'

Neil Fallon laughed, then sobered, staring once again at the backyard – or back in time. 'Then you picked the wrong family, Kovac. The Fallons have never been very dedicated to the truth about anything. We lie to ourselves and about ourselves and about our lives. That's what we do best.'

'What's that supposed to mean?'

'Nothing. We're the all-American family, that's what. At least we were before two-thirds of us committed suicide this week.'

'Could anyone else at your place ID this guy from last night?' Kovac asked, more concerned for the moment with the notion of Ogden going way the hell out to Neil Fallon's bar and bait shop than he was with the crumbling dynamics of the Fallon family.

'I was working alone.'

'Other customers?'

'Maybe. Jesus,' Fallon muttered, 'I wish I'd told you I walked into a door.'

'You wouldn't be the first person to try it today,' Kovac said. 'So, was it before or after the donnybrook when you talked to Mike?'

Fallon blew smoke out his nose. Annoyed. 'After, I guess. What the hell difference does it make?'

'He was pretty out of it when I saw him. On sedatives or something. If you talked to him after that, I guess he had snapped out of it.'

'I guess. When it came to chewing my ass, he always rose to the occasion,' he said bitterly. 'Nothing was ever good enough. Nothing ever made up.'

'Made up for what?'

'That I wasn't him. That I wasn't Andy. You might have thought after he found out Andy was queer ... Well, he's dead now, so what's the difference? It's over. Finally.'

He looked at the oak tree once more, then threw the cigarette into the snow and checked his watch. 'I have to get to the funeral home. Maybe I can get one in the ground before the other turns cold.'

He gave Kovac a sideways look as he went to open the door. 'Don't take it personal, but I hope I never see you again, Kovac.'

Kovac didn't say anything. He stood on the stoop and looked back at the Fallon brothers' hanging tree, imagining two young boys with their lives ahead of them, playing good guys and bad guys; the bonds of brotherhood twining the paths of their lives, shaping their strengths and weaknesses and resentments.

If there was one thing from which people never recovered, it was childhood. If there was one tie that could never truly be broken, for good or for ill, it was to family.

He turned the thoughts over in his head like a bear turning over rocks to see what kind of grubs it might find. He thought about the Fallons and the jealousies and disappointments and anger among them. He thought about the faceless cop Neil Fallon had picked a fight with in the parking lot of the bar and bait shop.

Would Ogden have been stupid enough to go there? Why? Or maybe *stupid* was the wrong word. What would he stand to gain? Maybe that was the question.

Even as he pondered that, Kovac couldn't stop thinking that Neil Fallon hadn't even asked to see his father. The vic's family usually did. Most people would refuse to believe the bad news until they saw the body with their own eyes. Neil Fallon hadn't asked. And he hadn't taken a step toward the bathroom when he'd said he felt sick. He'd gone straight for the back door.

Maybe he'd wanted air. Maybe he hadn't asked to see his dead father because he wasn't the sort of person who needed the visual image to make the death real, or maybe because he couldn't stomach that kind of thing.

Or maybe they should be running tests for gunpowder residue on Neil Fallon's hands.

The back door opened and Liska stuck her head out. 'The vultures have landed.'

Kovac groaned. He'd bought some time calling in the request for the crime scene unit over his cell phone, but dispatch would have called the team over the radio, and every reporter in the metro area had a scanner. News of a dead body never failed to bring out the scavengers. According to the press, The People had a right to know about the tragedies of strangers.

'You want me to handle them?' Liska asked.

'No. I'll give them a statement,' he said, thinking about the life and times of Mike Fallon, the pain, the loss, the soured love and wasted chances. 'How's this? Life's a bitch and then you die.'

Liska arched a brow and spoke with heavy sarcasm. 'Yeah. There's a headline.'

She started to go back inside. Kovac stopped her with a question.

'Hey, Tinks, when you saw Ogden this morning, did he look like he'd been in a fight?'

'No. Why?'

'Next time you see him, ask him what the hell he was doing at Neil Fallon's bar last night. See if you get a rise.'

Liska looked unhappy. 'He was at Fallon's bar?'

'Maybe. Fallon claims some cop was out there making cracks, and they mixed it up in the parking lot.'

'Did he describe Ogden?'

'No. He dropped his little bomb, then clammed up. He acts like a man who's scared of something. Like retribution maybe.'

'Why would Ogden go all the way out there? What would be the point? Even if – God, *especially* if he had something to do with Andy Fallon or with the Curtis murder. Go out there and pick a fight with Neil Fallon? Not even Ogden is that stupid.'

'That's what I'm thinking. And the next logical question is, then why would Neil Fallon lie about it if it didn't happen?'

'Neil Fallon, whose father is sitting in the bathroom missing the back of his head?'

Neil Fallon, who was seething with long-held hard feelings. Neil Fallon, who had admitted to a quick, harsh temper. Neil Fallon, who resented his brother and hated his father, even after their deaths.

'Let's do a little digging on Mr Fallon,' Kovac said. 'Put Elwood on it, if he's not busy. I'll talk to some of Fallon's customers. See if anyone else saw this phantom cop.'

'Will do.'

Kovac took one last grim look at the hanging tree. 'Make sure the ME's people bag Mike's hands. We could be looking at a murder, after all.'

17

It wouldn't be a cop funeral like the ones shown on the six o'clock news. The church would not overflow with ranks of uniforms who had rolled in from all over the state. There would be no endless caravan of radio cars to the cemetery. No one was going to play 'Amazing Grace' on the bagpipes. Andy Fallon had not fallen in the line of duty. His death had not been heroic.

The place didn't even look like a church, Kovac thought as he left the car in the lot and walked toward the low brick building. Like most churches built in the seventies, it looked more like a municipal building. Only the thin, stylized iron cross on the front gave it away. That and the illuminated sign out near the boulevard.

ST MICHAEL'S
ADVENT: WAITING FOR A MIRACLE?
MASS WEEKDAYS: 7 A.M.
SATURDAY: 5 P.M.
SUNDAY: 9 A.M. & 11 A.M.

As if miracles were performed regularly at those scheduled hours. The hearse was sitting on the circle drive near the side entrance. No miracles for Andy Fallon. Maybe if he had come here Saturday at five . . .

The wind whipped Kovac's coat around his legs. He bent his head into it to keep his hat. The windchill was in the teens. Mourners moved toward the church from scattershot spots in the parking lot. Cop. Cop. Three civilians together – a man and two women in their late twenties. The cops were in plain clothes, and he didn't know them, but he could spot a cop as easily as Neil Fallon. It was in the carriage, in the demeanor, in the eyes, in the mustache.

The usual dirge was playing on the organ as they trailed one another into the building to loiter in the narthex. Kovac renewed his promise to himself not to have a funeral when he died. His pals could hoist a few for him at Patrick's, and maybe Liska could do something with his ashes. Toss them out on the steps of city hall to join the ashes of a thousand cigarettes smoked there by cops every day. Seemed fitting. He sure as hell wouldn't put people through this: standing around staring at one another, listening to god-awful organ music and choking on the smell of gladiolas.

He put his hat on the rack but kept his coat, and stood off to the side watching the civilians move as a trio to another small knot of their own kind. He would approach them later. Afterward. After they had all shared the experience of putting their friend in the ground. He wondered if any of them had been close enough to Andy Fallon to share a sexual paraphilia.

Impossible to tell. In his experience the most normal-seeming people could be involved in the weirdest shit. Andy Fallon's friends looked like the cream of their generation. Well dressed, clean-cut, their faces pale with grief beneath the fading red of wind-kissed cheeks. Couldn't say who was gay, who was straight, who was into S and M.

The doors opened again, and Steve Pierce held one back, letting Jocelyn Daring precede him in. They made a handsome couple in expensive black cashmere coats: Jocelyn a statuesque porcelain doll with every blond hair neatly swept back and held in place with a black velvet bow. She may not have felt the loss of her fiancé's best friend, but she knew how to dress the part. She appeared to be pouting. Pierce stood beside her near the coatrack with a thousand-yard stare. He didn't help her with her coat. She said something to him, and he snapped at her. Kovac couldn't make out the words, but his tone was sharp and her reaction was to intensify the pout. They didn't touch as they went into the church.

Not a happy couple.

Kovac went to the glass doors and looked in at the assembled mourners. The pews were chrome and black plastic chairs hooked one to the next. There were no kneelers, no creepy statues of the Virgin or the saints adorned with real human hair. There was nothing daunting about the place, no overriding sense of God glaring down on His terrified flock. Not like when Kovac had been a kid, when eating a burger on Friday during Lent was a sure pass to hell. He had feared and respected the church of his youth. This place was about as scary as going to a lecture at the public library.

Pierce and Daring had taken seats on the center aisle about halfway toward the front. Pierce rose abruptly and came back out, the girlfriend watching him all the way. He stared at the floor, digging a cigarette and a lighter from his coat pocket as he walked. Kovac moved away from the doors. Pierce didn't see him as he crossed the narthex and went outside.

Kovac followed and took a position three feet to Pierce's right on the broad concrete step. Pierce didn't look at him.

'I keep saying I'm quitting,' Kovac said, shaking one out of a pack of Salems. He hooked it with his lip and lit it with a Christmas Bic. Nothing says Christmas like lung cancer. 'But you know what? I never do. I like it. Everybody tries to make me feel guilty about it, and I buy into that. Like I think I deserve it or something. So then I say I'm quitting, but I never do.'

Pierce regarded him from the corner of his eye and lit his own cigarette with a slim brushed-chrome lighter that looked like a giant bullet. His hands were shaking. He returned his stare to the street and slowly exhaled.

'I guess that's just human nature,' Kovac went on, wishing he'd grabbed his hat on his way out. He could feel all his body heat rushing out the top of his head. 'Everybody carries around a load of shit they think they ought to feel guilty about. Like somehow that makes them a better person. Like there's some law against just being who you are.'

'There are plenty of laws against that,' Pierce said, still staring at the street. 'Depending on who you are.'

Kovac let that hang for a moment. Waited. Pierce had opened the door. Just a crack. 'Well, sure, if you're a prostitute or a drug dealer. Or did you mean something less obvious?'

Pierce blew out a stream of smoke.

'Like if you're gay,' Kovac suggested.

Pierce moved his shoulders and swallowed, Adam's apple bobbing. 'That would depend on who you ask.'

'I'm asking you. Do you think that's something a person should feel guilty about? Do you think it's something a person should hide?'

'Depends on the person. Depends on their circumstances.'

'Depends on whether he's engaged to the boss's daughter, for instance,' Kovac offered.

He watched as the missile hit the target square in the chest. Pierce actually took a step back.

'I believe I've already told you I'm not gay,' he said in a tight voice. His gaze darted from side to side, looking for eavesdroppers.

'You did.'

'Then you clearly didn't believe me.' Angrier.

Kovac took a slow pull on his smoke. All the time in the world.

'Would you care to ask my fiancée? Would you like us to videotape ourselves having sex?' Angrier. 'Any requests for positions?'

Kovac didn't answer.

'Would you like a list of my ex-girlfriends?'

Kovac just looked at him, letting the anger roll off him. And still it was visibly building in Pierce, a kind of frenetic excitement he was having difficulty containing.

'I've been a cop for a lot of years, Steve,' he said at last. 'I can tell when someone's holding something back on me. You're carrying a lot of extra weight.'

Pierce looked as if the blood vessels in his eyes might pop. 'I just lost my best friend since college. I found him dead. We were like brothers. You think one man can't grieve deeply for another without them being gay? Is that what your life is like, Sergeant? You wall yourself off for fear of what other people might think of you if they knew the truth?'

'I don't give a shit what anybody thinks of me,' Kovac said matter-of-factly. 'I got nothing riding on it. I'm not trying to impress anyone. I've seen too many people carry rocks around every day until the weight of it all drags them under and kills them one way or another. You've got a chance to unload one.'

'I don't need to.'

'He's going in the ground today. If you know something, it won't go in the ground with him, Steve. It'll hang around your neck until you take it off.'

'I don't know anything.' He gave a harsh laugh that came out on a cloud of smoke and warm breath in the cold air. 'I don't know a damn thing.'

'If you were there that night –'

'I don't know who Andy was fucking, Sergeant,' Pierce said bitterly, turning the heads of several people going into the church. 'But it wasn't me.'

The cords stood out in his neck. His face was as red as his hair. The blue eyes were narrow and filled with venom and tears. He threw his cigarette down and ground it out with the toe of an expensive oxford. 'Now, if you'll excuse me, I'm a pallbearer. I have to go move my best friend's corpse.'

Kovac let him go and finished his own smoke, thinking that a lot of people would have called him cruel for what he'd just done. He didn't think of it that way. He thought of Andy Fallon hanging dead from a rafter. What he did, he did for the victim. The victim was dead – there weren't many things crueler than death.

He crushed out the cigarette, then picked up both butts and deposited them in a plant pot near the door. Through the glass he could see the casket had been rolled into the narthex from a side hall. The pallbearers were being given instructions by a portly man from the funeral home.

Neil Fallon stood off to one side, looking blank. Ace Wyatt put a hand on the funeral director's shoulder and said something to him in confidence. Gaines, the über-assistant, hovered nearby, ready to step, fetch, or kiss an ass.

'Are you going in, Sergeant? Or are you watching from the cheap seats?'

Kovac focused on the faint reflection that had appeared beside his in the glass. Amanda Savard in her Veronica Lake getup. The glam sunglasses, the velvet scarf swathing her head. Not a getup, he thought, a disguise. There was a big difference.

'How's the head?' he asked.

'Nothing hurt but my pride.'

'Yeah. What's a little concussion to a tough cookie like you?'

'Embarrassing,' she said. 'I'd sooner you let the subject go.'

He almost laughed. 'You don't know me very well, Lieutenant.'

'I don't know you at all,' she said, taking hold of the door handle with a small gloved hand. 'Let's keep it that way.'

She may as well have waved a red flag. He wondered if she knew that – and if she did, then what game she was playing at.

You and the IA lieutenant. Yeah, right, Kovac.

'I don't let go,' he said, making her glance back at him over her shoulder. 'You might as well know that.'

Inscrutable behind the shades, she made no comment and went into the church. Kovac followed her. Glutton for punishment. The procession of casket and mourners had gone up the aisle. The organist was pounding out yet another depressing song of death.

Savard chose a seat in the back, in an otherwise empty row. She didn't so much as acknowledge Kovac as he slid in beside her. She didn't sing the required hymn, didn't join in the spoken prayers or responsories. She never took the sunglasses off or lowered the scarf or unbuttoned her coat. As if she were in a cocoon, the layers of clothing insulating her from the thoughts of the outside world. Wrapping her in her own thoughts about Andy Fallon.

Kovac watched her from the corner of his eye, thinking he had to be an asshole to tempt fate this way, to push her buttons. One word from her and he'd be suspended. On the other hand, it seemed not a bad idea to give the appearance of having aligned himself with IA for the moment. Not that anyone in this crowd seemed to care.

All focus – not simply that of Amanda Savard – seemed inward. No one really heard the priest, who hadn't known Andy Fallon at all, and could speak of him only because someone had filled him in. As with most funerals, it didn't matter what the presiding clergyman had to say anyway. What mattered was the panorama of memories playing through each person's head, the mental and emotional scrapbooks of experiences with the person lost.

As Kovac studied the faces, he wondered which, if any, hid memories of intimacies with Andy Fallon; memories of shared passions, of shared perversions. Which of these people might have helped Andy Fallon put a noose around his neck, then panicked when things went wrong? Which one knew that missing piece to the puzzle of Andy Fallon's state of mind: would he have killed himself?

Did any of them really care to know? The case had been closed. The priest was pretending the word *suicide* had never been mentioned in the same sentence with Andy Fallon's name. In another hour, Andy Fallon would be in the ground, buried, a fading memory.

The moment came for eulogies. Neil Fallon shifted in his seat, glancing furtively from side to side as if to see whether anyone was watching him not get up and speak at his only brother's funeral. Steve Pierce stared down at his feet, looking as if he was having trouble getting a deep breath. Kovac felt a similar pressure in his own chest as he waited. The mind hunters called emotionally charged situations such as this 'precipitating stressors,' triggers for actions, triggers for confessions, for testimonials. But this was Minnesota, a place where people were not naturally given to speaking openly about their emotions. The moment passed without drama.

Savard rose, slipped her coat off, and – sunglasses and scarf still in place –

walked with all the elegance and import of a queen to the front of the church. The priest stepped aside for her to take the lectern.

'I'm Lieutenant Amanda Savard,' she said in a tone that was at once quiet and authoritative. 'Andy worked for me. He was a fine officer, a dedicated and talented investigator, and a wonderful person. We are all richer for having known him and we are poorer for his untimely loss. Thank you.'

Simple. Eloquent. She came back to the pew with her head bowed. Mysterious. Kovac rose and stepped into the aisle to allow her back to her seat. People were staring. Probably at Savard. Probably wondering how a guy like him came to be sitting with a woman like her.

Kovac stared back, silently challenging. Steve Pierce met his gaze for just a moment, then looked away. Ace Wyatt rose and adjusted his shirt cuffs as he went to the lectern.

'Jesus Christ,' Kovac grumbled, then crossed himself as the woman sitting two rows ahead turned and gave him a dirty look. 'Can you believe this guy? Any excuse for a photo op.'

Savard lifted a brow at him.

'He'd hang his bare ass out a tenth-story window and fart the national anthem if he thought it'd get him publicity.'

One corner of Savard's perfect mouth curled in wry amusement. 'Captain Wyatt is a longtime acquaintance of mine.'

Kovac winced. 'Stepped right into that, didn't I?'

'Headfirst.'

'That's how I do most everything. That's why I look this way.'

'I knew Andy Fallon when he was a boy,' Wyatt began with all the dramatic talent of a community theater actor. The fact that he was about to become a star on national television was testimony to the declining standards of the American public. 'I didn't know Andy Fallon the man very well, but I know what he was made of. Courage and integrity and determination. I know this because I came up through the trenches with his old man, Iron Mike Fallon. We all knew Iron Mike. We all respected the man and his opinions, and feared his temper if we screwed up. A finer police officer I have never known.

'It is with deepest regret I have to announce Mike Fallon's passing late last night.'

A small gasp went through the crowd. Savard jerked as if she'd been hit with a cattle prod, her pale skin instantly turning paler. Her breathing turned quick and shallow.

Wyatt went on. 'Despondent over the death of his son . . .'

Kovac leaned down. 'Are you all right, Lieutenant?'

'Excuse me,' she said, standing abruptly.

Kovac rose to let her out. She pushed past him, nearly shoving him back into his chair. She wanted to run down the aisle and out of the church, and just keep on running. But she didn't. No one she passed gave her more than a passing glance, their collective attention on Wyatt at the lectern. No one else seemed to hear the pounding of her heart or the roaring of her blood in her veins.

She pushed open the glass door to the narthex and turned down the hall, seeking and finding the ladies' room. The light was dim and the room smelled of commercial air freshener. Ace Wyatt's voice was still in her head, bringing on a sense of panic. Then she realized it was coming from a speaker hung high on the wall.

She tore off the scarf and sunglasses, nearly crying out in pain as the earpiece dragged through the oozing rug burn. Eyes squeezed tight against the threatening flood of tears, she fumbled blindly for the faucets. The water exploded into the sink, splashing up on her. She didn't care. She scooped it with both hands and put her face in it.

Dizziness swirled through her brain, weakness drained her legs. She fell against the sink, clutching at the porcelain basin with one hand, reaching to brace against the wall with the other. She tried to will herself past the nausea, begged God to get her through it, ignored her convenient faith in a higher power she had ceased to believe in long ago.

'Please, please, please,' she chanted, doubled over, her head nearly in the sink. In her mind's eye she could see Andy Fallon staring at her with accusation and anger. He was dead. Now Mike Fallon.

Despondent over the death of his son . . .

'Lieutenant?' Kovac's voice sounded just outside the door. 'Amanda? You in there? Are you all right?'

Savard tried to push herself upright, tried to get a breath deep enough to speak with a steady voice. She couldn't quite manage either.

'Y-yes,' she said, wincing at the weakness of her tone. 'I'm fine. Thank you.'

The door swung open and Kovac came in without hesitation or regard for the modesty of any woman who might have been in the rest room. He looked fierce.

'I'm fine, Sergeant Kovac.'

'Yeah, I can see that,' he said, coming to her. 'Even better than when you were fine this morning, keeling over at your desk. Do you often feel the overwhelming urge to take a shower with your clothes on?' he asked, his gaze cutting from the wet tendrils of hair plastered to the sides of her face to the dark splotches of water on her suit.

'I was feeling a little dizzy,' she said, pressing a hand to her forehead. She took a slow breath through her mouth and closed her eyes for a second.

Kovac put a hand on her shoulder and she stiffened, telling herself she should bolt, telling herself not to. She looked at him via his reflection in the mirror and saw the concern in his dark eyes. She saw herself and was appalled by how vulnerable she appeared in that moment – pale and battered.

'Come on, LT,' he said softly, shortening her title to a nickname, 'let me take you to a doctor.'

'No.'

She should have told him to take his hand off her, but the weight of it was solid and strong and reassuring, even if she couldn't lean into it the way she wanted to, needed to. A shiver went through her. She shouldn't have wanted or needed anything, certainly not from this man.

She looked at the reflection of his hand on her shoulder. A big hand, wide, with blunt-tipped fingers. A working man's hands, she thought, regardless of the fact that Kovac's work was done with his mind and not his hands. His fingers tightened briefly.

'Well, at least let's get out of here,' he said. 'This damn air freshener is enough to choke a goat.'

'I can take care of myself,' Savard announced. 'Really. Thank you anyway.'

'Come on,' Kovac coaxed again, turning toward the door and neatly drawing her with him. Years of practice herding drunks and victims and people in various states of shock made it easy for him. 'I've got your coat in the hall.'

She pulled away, went back to the sink, and collected her sunglasses and carefully slid them on. The velvet scarf was wet in spots. She put it back on anyway, arranging it carefully, draping it just so. Kovac watched her.

'I thought you only knew Mike Fallon by reputation,' he said.

'That's right. I'd spoken to him, of course. About Andy.'

'Your reaction to the news of his death seems a little extreme, then.'

'I told you, I was feeling dizzy,' she said. 'The announcement of Mike Fallon's death didn't really have all that much to do with it. It's a tragedy, of course. . . .'

'The world's full of them, I hear.'

'Yes.'

Satisfied with the scarf, she walked past Kovac and out under her own steam. Show no weakness. Too late for that.

He had left her coat draped over a table piled with church bulletins. She picked it up and started to put it on, the pain in her neck and upper back grabbing hold and stopping her with only one arm in a sleeve. Kovac helped her on with it the rest of the way, standing a little too close behind her, trapping her between himself and the table.

'I know,' he said softly. 'You're fine. You could have done it yourself.'

Savard stepped sideways and ducked around him, heading across the narthex. The organ had started up again, and the acrid-sweet smell of incense burned the air.

'I'm not letting you drive away from here, Lieutenant,' Kovac said, falling into step beside her. 'If you're dizzy, you're not safe to be behind the wheel.'

'I'm fine. It's passed.'

'I'll give you a ride. I'm headed back to the station myself.'

'I'm going home.'

'Then I'll drop you off.'

'It's out of your way.'

He held the door for her. 'That's all right, the ride will give me the chance to ask you a couple of questions.'

'God, do you never stop?' she said through her teeth.

'No. Never. I told you – I don't let go. Not until I get what I want.'

His hand slipped around hers and she tried to jerk away, her heart jumping, eyes going wide behind the glasses. 'What do you think you're doing?'

He stared at her for a second, reading God knew what in her expression. Even with the scarf and glasses, she felt naked in front of him.

'Keys.'

As he said it, the muscles of her hand relaxed marginally and he slipped the key ring from her fingers. A major tactical error. She didn't want Kovac driving her home. She didn't want him in her house. She didn't want his interest. She was accustomed to a position of power, but even though she outranked him, Kovac had years and experience over her. Knowing that made her feel subordinate, like a little girl pretending at a job of great importance.

'If you have a question, ask it,' she said, folding her arms around herself. The wind was bitter and raw. The temperature had dropped in the hour they'd been in the church. The sun was already sagging in the winter-white sky. 'Then you'll give me my keys back, Sergeant.'

'Did Andy Fallon ever talk about his brother?'

'No.'

'Did he ever mention he was seeing someone – dating – or that he was having problems in his personal life?'

'I told you before – his personal life was none of my business. Why are you pursuing this, Sergeant?'

He tried to look innocent, but Savard doubted he had been able to pull that off even as an infant. There was a world-weariness to Kovac that surpassed his years by a thousand. 'I'm paid to investigate,' he said.

'To investigate *crimes*. There's been no crime I'm aware of.'

'Mike Fallon is minus half his head,' Kovac said. 'I'm gonna make damn sure somebody else didn't do that job for him before I walk away from it.'

Savard stared at him through the dark glasses. 'Why would you think anyone would murder Mike Fallon? Captain Wyatt said he took his own life.'

'Captain Wyatt was speaking prematurely. The investigation is ongoing. The body wasn't even stiff yet when I left the scene to come here.'

'It wouldn't make any sense for someone to murder Mike Fallon,' Savard argued.

'Who says it has to make any sense?' Kovac returned. 'Someone gets pissed off, loses their temper, strikes out. Boom, murder. Someone holds a grudge long enough, gets fed up on it, something strikes a spark. Bang, somebody's dead. I see it every damn day, Lieutenant.'

'Mr Fallon was in poor health. He'd just lost his son. I'm assuming the signs at the scene of his death pointed to suicide. Doesn't it seem more logical that he pulled the trigger himself than to think someone else might have done it?'

'Sure. But then, a clever killer might think that too,' Kovac pointed out.

'It must be slow in homicide these days,' Savard remarked, 'that one of their best detectives can spend all his time on non-cases.'

'The more I'm around the people involved with Andy and Mike Fallon, the less I consider these deaths "non-cases". You knew Andy. You claim to have cared about him. You want me to walk away from this if I think there's a chance he didn't put that noose around his neck himself? You want me to shrug it off if it looks like maybe Mike didn't stick that thirty-eight in his mouth without help? What kind of cop would I be if I did that?'

Behind them, the doors of the church swung open and the mourners came out, bundled against the cold and hurrying toward the parking lot. Kovac spotted Steve Pierce and Jocelyn Daring, Daring trying to put her arm through her fiancé's, Pierce shrugging her off. Not far behind them came Ace Wyatt and his toady. Wyatt looked impervious to cold, shoulders back, jaw out. He drew a bead on Kovac like a laser-sight missile.

'Sam,' he said in his serious TV voice, 'I understand you found Mike. My God, what a tragedy.'

'His death, or me finding him?'

'Both, I suppose. Poor Mike. He just couldn't take the burden. I think he felt a tremendous guilt over Andy's death, over the unresolved issues between them. It's too bad. . . .'

He looked to Savard and nodded. 'Amanda, good to see you, despite the occasion.'

'Captain.' Even with the shades on, Kovac could tell she was looking past Wyatt, not at him. 'Terrible news about Mike Fallon,' she said. 'I'm sorry to hear it. I know you and he had a history.'

'Poor Mike,' he said in a thick voice, looking away. He let a beat of silence pass, as if out of respect, then pulled in a cleansing breath. 'I see you know Sam.'

'Better than I'd care to,' she said, and reached out and took her keys from Kovac's hand. 'If you gentlemen will excuse me . . .'

'I was just telling the lieutenant how it struck me odd Mike would be so upset last night about Andy killing himself, that being a mortal sin and all, then go home after and eat his gun,' Kovac said, effectively holding Savard in place. 'Doesn't make sense, does it?'

'Who says it has to make sense?' Savard said sarcastically.

'Amanda's right,' Wyatt said. 'Mike wasn't in his right mind, was he?'

'He was barely coherent last I saw him,' Kovac said. 'How about you, Ace? You took him home. How'd he seem when you left him?'

Gaines looked pointedly at his watch. 'Captain . . .'

Wyatt made a face. 'I know, Gavin. The meeting with the PR people.'

'And miss the interment?' Kovac said. *There goes a photo op.* Somehow, he managed to have the sense not to say that.

'It's been postponed,' Gaines informed him. 'Some kind of equipment problem.'

'Ah. TFC technical difficulty,' Kovac said. 'Too Fucking Cold to dig the hole. Excuse my language, Lieutenant,' he said sweetly.

'I don't think there is an excuse for you, Sergeant Kovac,' she said dryly. 'And on that note, gentlemen, I'll say good-bye.'

She raised a hand in farewell and made her escape across the snowpacked lot. Kovac let her go, sensing that to try to stop her now, with witnesses around, would be crossing a line he'd come too close to as it was. He allowed himself to watch her for a second.

'Sam, you can't seriously be thinking Mike was murdered,' Wyatt said.

'I'm a homicide cop.' Kovac settled his hat on his head. 'I think everyone's murdered. It's my natural mind-set. What time was it when you left Mike?'

Gaines interrupted. 'Captain, if you'd like to go on to the meeting, I'll take care of this.'

'Do you eat his food and wipe his ass too?' Kovac asked, earning a cold look from the assistant.

'You're holding the captain from a very important meeting, Sergeant Kovac,' Gaines said curtly, subtly moving to put himself between them. 'I was there with Mr Fallon and the captain last night. I can answer your questions as well as Captain Wyatt.'

'There's no need, Gavin,' Wyatt said. 'By the time you bring the car around, Sam and I will be done.'

Kovac looked smug. 'Yeah, Slick, you run along and start the car. You and I can get together later and get your take on things over a latte. So you'll have that to look forward to.'

Gaines didn't like being bested, and didn't like being dismissed. The blue eyes were as cold as the concrete beneath their feet, the handsome jaw set. But he bowed to Wyatt's orders and hustled away toward a black Lincoln Continental.

'That's some elegant guard dog you've got yourself, Ace,' Kovac said.

'Gavin is my right hand. Ambitious, single-minded, fiercely loyal. I wouldn't be where I am without him. He's got a very bright future. He's a bit overzealous at times, but I could say the same about you, Sam. Unless I'm out of the loop – and I'm not – there wasn't anything about Mike's death to warrant suspicion of murder.'

Kovac stuffed his hands in his coat pockets and sighed. 'He was one of ours, Ace. Mike was special. Sure, maybe the legend was more special than the man, more important, but still . . . I feel like I owe him a good hard look. You know what I mean? You ought to, considering your own history with him.'

'It's hard to think the door's closing on that chapter of our lives. Hard to believe he's gone,' Wyatt said quietly, staring across the parking lot as exhaust billowed in a cold vapor cloud from the tailpipe of the Lincoln.

It had to be as much a relief to him as anything, Kovac thought. The night of the Thorne murder, all those years ago, had been the defining moment in the lives of Ace Wyatt and Mike Fallon. That night their lives had turned on a dime, never to be the same again, always to be linked by that moment that had made Mike Fallon a cripple and Ace Wyatt a hero. With Mike gone, the weight of that burden must have lifted, a sensation that would both relieve and confuse. How could there be an Ace Wyatt if there was no Mike Fallon to counterbalance?

'It was around ten-thirty when we left Mike's house,' Wyatt said. 'He was quiet. Wrapped up in his grief. I had no idea what he was thinking or I would have tried to stop him.' His mouth twisted with irony as the car pulled up. 'Or maybe that would have been the greater tragedy. He suffered a lot of years. Now it's over. Let him go, Sam. He's at peace now.'

Gaines got out of the car and went around to open the passenger door. Wyatt got in without another word, and the Lincoln was off in a cloud of exhaust. The Lone Ranger and Tonto riding off into the sunset.

Kovac stood on the curb a moment longer, the only one left of the group who had come to see Andy Fallon off to the hereafter. Even the priest had disappeared.

'Lone Ranger,' he muttered, and started across the frozen parking lot with his hands in his pockets and his shoulders hunched into the wind.

18

'Neil Fallon has a record.'

Kovac paused with his coat half off. 'That was fast.'

'Service with a smile,' Elwood said, peering over the cubicle.

Liska sat on her chair, her maniacal pixie look lighting her face. She was something when she caught a scent on a case, he thought. It was like an addiction with her. The excitement was so intense, it was just a few steps to the right of sexual. Kovac couldn't remember ever being that hot for the job, and the job was the one great love of his life. Maybe he needed to consider hormone therapy.

'He has a juvie record – sealed, of course, though I've put through a request to have a peek,' Liska said. 'He spent seven years in the army. I've requested his service records. The year he got out, he went away for assault. Three to five. He did eighteen months.'

'What'd he do?'

'Got in a fight at a bar. He put the guy in a coma for a week.'

'Temper, temper, Neil.'

Kovac finished taking off his coat and hooked it on the rack, thinking. The office was the usual buzzing hive of constant low-level activity. Phones rang, someone laughed. A multiply-pierced twenty-something thug with bleached, spiked hair and pants hanging off his ass was led past in cuffs and ushered into an interview room. In the days of Mike Fallon, someone would have kicked his ass for his fashion choices alone.

'So how'd he get a liquor license with a felony conviction on his sheet?' Kovac asked, sagging into his chair.

'He didn't,' Elwood said.

'Come around here, for chrissake,' Kovac groused. 'You're giving me a stiff neck.'

Liska grinned and pushed at his chair with the toe of her boot. 'You should be glad for the sensation.'

'Very funny.'

Elwood rounded the end of the cubicle, holding out a fax. 'The license on the bar was issued by the municipality of Excelsior in the name of Cheryl Brewster, who months later became Cheryl Fallon.'

'Ah, the estranged missus,' Kovac said.

'The soon to be ex-missus,' Liska corrected. 'I called her at home. She's a nurse. She works nights at Fairview Ridgedale. She says she's divorcing him, and it can't happen a moment too soon to suit her. Drunken, mean son of a bitch – just a sampling of the terms of endearment.'

'Gee, and I found him such an agreeable fellow,' Kovac said. 'So, the wife holds the liquor license. What happens when she dumps him?'

'Neil's shit-out-of-luck, that's what,' Liska said. 'They can sell the bar with the license, pending approval of the new owner by the powers that be in Excelsior. Neil could get himself a new front man, but that hasn't happened yet. Cheryl says he's trying to buy the rest of the business out and forget the liquor license, but he can't seem to get the cash together for that either. Even if he could, she says he can't make a living off the place without the bar, so . . .

'I asked her if she thought he'd try to borrow money from his family. She laughed and said that Mike wouldn't give Neil change for a dime, let alone enough money to buy out the business – even though she says she knows Mike had plenty.'

'We call that motive in the detective business,' Elwood pointed out.

'I wonder if he put the touch on Andy,' Kovac mused.

'He had told Cheryl he was going to see if Andy wanted to invest, but she didn't know what ever happened with that,' Liska said. 'We can ask Pierce. It's safe to think he might have advised Andy on his financial stuff.'

'But if Pierce thought Andy's brother might have had something to do with his death, why wouldn't he have said so?' Elwood asked.

Kovac nodded. 'Why not point the finger instead of acting like the weight's on his shoulders?

'Let's check through the notes on the canvass of Fallon's neighbors. See who we missed, make some follow-up calls. Maybe someone might recognize a car, or know he'd been seeing someone. Elwood, do you have time to run through Fallon's address book and check with the friends?'

'Will do.'

'We've got to redo part of the neighborhood canvass anyway,' Liska said. 'Why?'

'First time around, two of our little elves were Ogden and Rubel.'

Kovac groaned. 'Great. That's what we need, Ogden telling people they didn't see anything.'

'If a wit saw someone other than him or Rubel – like Neil Fallon or Pierce – even Ogden would have brains enough to bring it to our attention,' Liska said.

'So we have to hope the uniforms missed that someone.'

'Who missed who?' Leonard demanded, coming to an abrupt halt at the cubicle.

Kovac pretended to search for a file on his desk, covering the notes he'd made regarding Andy Fallon's death.

'The guy that beat up Nixon,' he said. 'Deene Combs's henchman. We have to hope his people missed scaring the shit out of someone who knows something about it.'

'Have you talked to that woman again? The one the cab driver saw going inside that building as the perp ran away.'

'Five times.'

'Talk to her again. She's the key. We know she knows something.'

'That's a dead end,' Kovac said. 'She'll take it to her grave.'

'If Nixon isn't going to rat the guy out himself, Chamiqua Jones isn't gonna do it for him,' Liska pointed out.

Leonard frowned at her. 'Talk to her again. Go to where she works. Today. I don't want these gangbangers thinking they can run wild.'

Kovac glanced at Liska, who looked down at the floor and crossed her eyes. The common logic regarding the Nixon assault was that Wyan Nixon had shorted his boss, Deene Combs, on a small-time drug deal and had been made an example by said boss, but no one was talking, including Nixon. The county attorney, who wanted to take a more publicly visible hard line against drug dealers, had pledged the county would press the charges if Nixon wouldn't. But without a witness, there was no case, and the cab driver hadn't seen enough to give a detailed description of the assailant.

'It's a black hole,' Kovac said. 'No one's going to testify to anything. What's the point?'

Leonard made his monkey frown. 'The point is, it's your job, Kovac.'

'I know my job.'

'Do you? It sounds to me that you've been redefining the parameters.'

'I don't know what you're talking about.'

'Fallon is closed. Leave it alone.'

'You heard about Mike?' Kovac said. The deliberate curveball, even as he wondered who had ratted him out to Leonard. His money was on Savard. She didn't want him hanging around, getting too close to her, threatening to breach the security of the walls she had so carefully erected around herself. Wyatt didn't give a shit what went on in Kovac's little world. All he cared about was getting to his next PR event.

Leonard looked confused. 'That he killed himself?'

'I'm not so sure that's what happened.'

'He ate his gun.'

'Looked that way.'

'There are a couple of red flags, Lieutenant,' Liska said. 'The positioning of the body, for instance.'

'You're saying the scene was staged?'

'Not staged, but a little too convenient. And there's no suicide note.'

'That doesn't mean anything. A lot of suicides don't leave notes.'

'The older son has some issues – and a record.'

'I want to dig a little,' Kovac said. 'Maybe Mike did whack himself, but what if he didn't? We owe him better than to let it slide because suicide was the easy answer.'

'Let's see what the ME has to say,' Leonard said grudgingly, unhappy with the idea of a slam dunk turning into a whodunit – especially this case, with Wyatt and the rest of the brass monkeys looking on. 'In the meantime, go see Chamiqua Jones. Today. I want the county attorney's office off my ass about Nixon.'

'I'd rather stick myself with needles than go to the Mall of America during the Christmas season.'

Kovac glanced over at Liska as he piloted the Caprice through rush hour traffic going east on 494. 'Where's your consumer spirit?'

'Dying from lack of oxygen down at the bottom of my bank account. Do you have any idea what kids want for Christmas nowadays?'

'Semiautomatic weapons?'

'R.J. gave me a list that looks like the inventory for Toys 'R' Us.'

'Look on the bright side, Tinks. He didn't send it to you from a juvenile detention center.'

'Whoever said it cost a million bucks to raise a kid through college did not take Christmas into account.'

Kovac negotiated a lane change around a snot-green Geo doing fifty with a white-knuckled balding guy at the wheel. Iowa plates.

'I-wegian farmers,' he growled. 'They don't know how to drive without a cornfield on either side of them.'

He cut across two lanes to catch the exit he wanted. His driving usually spurred remarks from Liska, but she said nothing, seeming lost in her thoughts of the holiday bearing down on them.

Kovac remembered the Christmas the year after his first wife had left. He'd sent gifts to their daughter. Stuffed animals. A rag doll. Shit like that. Things he'd hoped a little girl might like. The boxes had been returned unopened. He'd hauled the stuff to a Toys for Tots drop, then gone out and drunk himself into a stupor. He wound up in a fistfight with a Salvation Army Santa out in front of the government center, and got suspended for thirty days without pay.

'He's your kid,' he said. 'Get him something he really wants and quit your bitching. It's only money.'

Liska stared at him.

'What's he really want?' he asked, uncomfortable with her scrutiny.

'He wants me and Speed to get back together.'

'Jesus H. Any danger of that happening?'

She was silent half a beat too long as they drove into the mall's west-side ramp. Kovac looked over at her again.

'Has hell frozen over yet?' she asked defensively. 'Did I miss that on the news?'

'He's an asshole.'

'I don't need you to tell me that.'

'I'm just saying.'

Kovac parked and memorized the level and row number. One of 12,750 parking spaces on mall property. This was not the place to get lost.

The Mall of America was like a giant, elegant, four-tiered rat maze, the wide hallways teeming with frantic humans scurrying from one store to the next. The biggest mall in the United States – five hundred stores, two and a half million square feet of commercial space – and still there weren't enough retail outlets for those searching for the perfect item to wrap and have returned two days after Christmas. Human nature.

The noise from the Camp Snoopy amusement park at the mall's center was constant; the dull roar of roller coasters and the water flume ride, punctuated by shrieks of customers. A high school choir was assembling on risers in front of the entrance to Macy's, boys cutting up and girls wandering toward the windows of Lerner's as their director barked at them ineffectually.

They passed the three-story Lego Imagination Center with its twenty-five-foot Lego clock tower, huge Lego dinosaur, Lego space station, and a Lego blimp made from 138,240 Lego blocks hanging suspended above it all.

Kovac turned in at Old Navy with a jaundiced eye on a display of track pants and T-shirts and ugly quilted vests.

'Look at this shit.'

'Retro-seventies,' Liska said. 'Shirts in the all-my-clothes-shrunk-in-the-wash-but-I-wear-them-anyway style.'

'I thought it was ugly the first time around. Looking at this is like having a bad flashback on high school.'

The clerk Kovac badged was a girl with a lip ring, cat-eye glasses, and maroon hair that looked as if a five-year-old had hacked at it with a pinking shears. 'Is your manager around?'

'I'm the manager. Is this about that guy who's always hiding in the racks and flashing his thing at women?'

'No.'

'You ought to do something about him.'

'I'll put him on my list. Is Chamiqua Jones working?'

'Yes.' The girl's eyes looked big behind the glasses. 'What'd she do? She's never flashed a penis at anyone.'

'We've just got a couple questions,' Liska said. 'She's not in any trouble.'

Cat Eyes looked skeptical but made no comment as she led them toward the dressing rooms.

Chamiqua Jones was twenty-something, looked forty-something, and was built like a fifty-five-gallon drum with a rusty Brillo pad hairdo. She stood guard near the dressing rooms, directing would-be consumers and shoplifters.

'That door over there, honey.' She pointed a customer down the row, then shook her head and muttered under her breath as the customer walked away, 'Like you gonna get your fat white ass in them pants.'

She glanced at Kovac and Liska, then let herself into one of the dressing rooms to pick up a tangled pile of discarded jeans.

'You again.'

'Hey, Chamiqua.'

'I don't need this hassle on my job, Kovac.'

'Here I was missing you, and that's the greeting I get? I feel like we're getting to be old pals.'

Jones didn't smile. 'You gonna get my ass killed, that's what.'

'You still don't have anything to say about Nixon?' Liska said.

'The president? Nope. Nothing. I wasn't born yet. I hear he was a crook, but ain't they all?'

'Witnesses put you at the scene of the assault, Chamiqua.'

'That rag-head cab driver?' she said, carrying the jeans to a table. 'He lying. I never seen no assault. I told y'all before.'

'You didn't see a man jump Wyan Nixon and beat him with a tire iron.'

'No, ma'am. All I know 'bout Wyan Nixon is he is *bad* news. Especially for me.'

She folded the jeans with quick, practiced movements. Her hands were chubby, with short fingers and taut skin. They made Kovac think of small balloon animals. Her gaze darted twenty feet away to a stocky young man with a tight white spandex cap that looked like a condom for the skull. Kovac had never seen him before, but there was no mistaking what he was: muscle. A hundred eighty pounds of sociopathic meanness. He might have been sixteen or seventeen, but he was no kid. He stood near a rounder of polar fleece vests, turning it without looking, his flat, cold gaze on Chamiqua Jones.

'I'm very busy here,' she said, and went to unlock a dressing room with a key hanging from a neon-green plastic coil around her wrist.

Kovac turned his back to the muscle. 'We can offer you protection, Chamiqua. The county attorney wants Deene Combs behind bars.'

'Protection,' she snorted. 'What? You gonna send me on a bus to some flea-trap motel in Gary, Indiana? Hide me out?' She shook her head as she returned to the table with another pile of clothing. 'I'm a decent person, Kovac. I work two jobs. I'm raising three good kids. I want to live to see them through school, thank you very much. Wyan Nixon can look out for his own black ass. I'm looking out for mine.'

'If he wants to be a hard-ass, the county attorney can charge you as accessory after the fact,' Liska said, fishing. 'Obstruction of justice, failure to cooperate . . .'

Jones held her hands out in front of her, darting a glance at Condom Cap. 'Then you put the cuffs on me and take me away. I got nothing to say about Wyan Nixon or Deene Combs. I didn't see nothing.'

Kovac shook his head. 'Not today. See you around, Chamiqua.'

'I hope not.'

'Nobody loves me today,' Kovac complained.

Liska pulled out a business card and put it down on the stack of folded jeans. 'Call if you change your mind.'

Jones tore the card in two as they walked away.

'Who can blame her?' Kovac said under his breath, giving the skunk eye to Condom Cap as they passed.

'She's looking out for her kids,' Liska said. 'I'd do the same. It's not like she could take Deene Combs off the street, anyway. You know he didn't do Nixon himself. She could give up some piece of meat like that guy watching her and still get herself killed for her trouble, and for what? There's a thousand more where he came from.'

'Yeah. Let it go. One scumbag beats the shit out of another scumbag. That's one less scumbag on the street for a while. Who cares? Nobody cares.'

'Somebody has to care,' Liska corrected him. 'We have to care.'

Kovac looked at her. 'Because we're all that's standing between society and anarchy?'

Liska made a face. 'Please. Because our clearance rates count big-time toward promotion. Screw society. I have kids to put through college.'

Kovac laughed. 'Tinks, you never fail to put things in their proper perspective.'

'Someone has to keep you from getting morose.'

'I'm never morose.'

'You're always morose.'

'I'm not morose, I'm bitter,' he corrected her as they passed the Rainforest Café, where sounds of thunder and rain were playing over the speaker system, and one of the live parrots on display was screaming like a banshee. People lined up for that.

'There's a difference,' he said. 'Morose is passive. Bitter is active. Being bitter is like having a hobby.'

'Everyone needs a hobby,' Liska agreed. 'Mine is the mercenary pursuit of easy money.'

She veered to the entrance of Sam Goody, where a near-life-size cutout of Ace Wyatt stood with its arm protectively around a box full of videotapes titled *Pro-Active: A Police Professional's Tips on How Not to Become a Victim*. She put her sunglasses on and struck a pose beside the display.

'What do you think? Don't we look good together?' she said, grinning. 'Don't you think he needs a younger female partner to broaden his demographics? I'd wear a bikini if I had to.'

Kovac scowled at the cardboard Wyatt. 'Why don't you just go up to the third floor here and get a job at Hooters? Or you could walk Hennepin Avenue.'

'I'm a mercenary, not a prostitute. There's a difference.'

'No, there isn't.'

'Yes, there is. A mercenary doesn't use a vagina.'

'Jesus.' Kovac felt heat creep up his face. 'Don't you ever embarrass yourself?'

Liska laughed. 'With what? My mouth or my seemingly shameless quest for advancement?'

'I was raised not to talk about . . . those . . .' He flushed an even darker shade of red as they started back down the hall.

'Vaginas?'

Kovac gave her a furious look as passing shoppers turned to stare at them.

'That might help explain why you don't have one at your disposal,' Liska speculated. 'You need to open up, Sam. You need to get in touch with your feminine side.'

'If I could touch my own feminine side, I wouldn't need . . . one of those . . . at my disposal.'

'Good point. And you could have your own TV show – Hermaphrodite Homicide Detective. Think of the following that would have. You could stop being jealous of Ace Wyatt.'

'I'm not jealous of Ace Wyatt.'

'Yeah, right. And I'm Heather Locklear.'

'You're just hot for his assistant. That's what you're after,' Kovac said.

Liska rolled her eyes. 'Gaines? Please. He's gay.'

'Gay or not interested?'

'Same difference.'

Kovac laughed. 'Tinks, you're too much woman for him, either way. The guy's a prick. And Wyatt's a big asshole. They deserve each other.'

'Yeah, all that community service, helping people, working with victims . . . What a jerk.'

Kovac scowled darkly. 'All that publicity, all those promotions, all that Hollywood money. Ace Wyatt never did anything that didn't benefit Ace Wyatt.'

'He saved Mike Fallon's life.'

'And became a legend.'

'Yeah, I'm sure that was premeditated.'

Kovac made a face at the bad taste in his mouth.

'All right. He did one decent, selfless thing in his life,' he conceded as they pushed through the doors and were hit with cold air and exhaust. 'That doesn't mean he's not an asshole.'

'People are complex.'

'Yeah,' Kovac agreed. 'That's why I hate them. At least with a psychopath, you know where you stand.'

19

The shift had changed and Leonard had gone by the time they returned to the office, saving them from having to report their lack of success with Chamiqua Jones. Liska considered and discarded the idea of making phone calls from her desk. She couldn't shake the feeling that everyone around her was watching her, listening, straining to hear – all because the questions she needed to ask were about other cops.

She had always thought of herself as tough, able to take whatever the job dished out, but she would have preferred any kind of case to this, with the exception of a child killing. Nothing was worse than working a child's murder. As she gathered her stuff and left the office, she wondered what she would do if the road to advancement led through IA. Make another road.

The walk to the Haaff ramp was cold, the wind biting her cheeks and ears. The drive home wouldn't be much better. She hadn't been able to get an appointment with the glass replacement shop. Too bad the busted window diminished the chances of the car's being stolen. Her insurance would at least have paid for a loaner then.

The same fat attendant manned the booth. He recognized her and ducked his head, afraid to attract her attention. Liska rolled her eyes and felt in her pocket for the reassuring weight of her ASP. She had briefly considered parking elsewhere, but in the end had made herself go back to the scene of the crime. Climbing back on the horse – with an eye peeled for her perpetrator at the same time. If she was lucky, she could conquer her fear and make a collar all in one fell swoop, though it seemed unlikely her mystery man would still be hanging around. Unless he had chosen her specifically as his target.

Nothing stolen. Nothing disturbed but her mail . . .

Patrol had been instructed to take tours through the concrete maze of the ramp today. The show of a police presence in the form of the occasional radio car was meant to scare off the vagrants, who all had likely moved across the street to piss in the corners of the Gateway Municipal ramp and try all the car doors there in search of spare change.

The Saturn sat a third of the way down a mostly empty row, parked nose out. The plastic window was still intact. No one had broken any of the others. Liska walked past it, checking, scanning the area. This level of the ramp was quiet, half deserted. She went back to her car and let herself in. She locked the doors, started the engine and the heater, and dug her cell phone out of her purse. She punched in the number for the gay and lesbian officers' liaison and stared at the CHECK ENGINE light glowing red on her dash as the phone rang on the other end.

Rotten car. She was going to have to think about trading. Maybe in January, provided her finances survived Christmas. Maybe bite the bullet and trade up to an SUV. The extra room would be good for hauling the boys with their buddies and all their hockey gear. If she could squeeze Speed for the money he owed her . . .

'Hello?'

'Is this David Dungen?'

'Yes, it is.'

'David, this is Sergeant Liska, homicide. If this is a good time for you, I have a couple of questions you might be able to help me with.'

A cautious pause. 'Regarding what?'

'Eric Curtis.'

'About the murder? That case is closed.'

'I realize that. I'm looking into a related matter.'

'Have you spoken with Internal Affairs?'

'You know how they are. They don't want to untie the nice, neat bow, and they're not inclined to share anyway.'

'There's a reason for that,' Dungen said. 'These matters are sensitive. I can't just volunteer information to anyone who asks.'

'I'm not just anyone. I'm homicide. I'm not asking because I have some kind of morbid curiosity.'

'This has something to do with another case?'

'I'll be honest with you, David.' Use the first name. You're my pal. You can tell me anything. 'It's a fishing expedition at this point. If I get something I can take to my lieutenant . . .'

Dungen said nothing for a moment, then finally, 'I'll need to take your badge number.'

'I'll give it to you, but I don't want any paperwork on this. You understand?'

Again the pregnant pause. 'Why is that?'

'Because some people would sooner let sleeping dogs lie, if you know what I mean. I'm checking out some things regarding Curtis because someone asked me personally. I don't know that anything will come of it. I can't go to my boss with hunches and funny feelings. I need something real.'

He was silent for so long this time, Liska began to think she'd lost the connection.

'What's your number?' he asked at last.

Liska breathed deeply, silently letting go a sigh of relief. The smell of exhaust was strong. She cracked the window but left the engine running. It was too damn cold to shut it off. She gave Dungen her shield number, along with her phone number, and hoped to God he wouldn't call Leonard to check it out.

'All right,' he said, satisfied. 'What would you like to know?'

'I know Curtis had complained to IA he was being harassed by someone on the job. What do you know about that?'

'I know he'd gotten some hate letters. In the ransom-note style with letters cut out of magazines. "All faggots must die. That's why God invented AIDS." That was the gist of it. The usual homophobic vitriol with bad grammar and bad spelling.'

'Had to be a cop,' Liska said dryly.

'Oh, it was a cop. No question. Two of the letters were slipped into his locker. One was found in his car after his shift. The mailman smashed out the passenger's window to deliver it.'

Liska looked to her blue plastic window, a chill running through her. 'Did he have any idea who it was?'

'He said no. He'd ended a relationship several months prior, but he swore it wasn't the ex.'

'And the ex was someone in the department?'

'Yes, but the boyfriend wasn't out. That's one of the reasons he was an ex. Curtis wanted him to be honest about who he was.'

'Curtis was out.'

'Yes, but in a quiet way. He wasn't some flaming militant. He was just tired of living a lie. He wanted the world to be a place where people could be who they are without having to fear for their lives. Ironic that he was killed by a gay man.'

'Do you know who the ex was?'

'No. I know Curtis had changed patrol partners a couple of times, but that doesn't necessarily mean anything. He didn't suspect any of them. At any rate, it wasn't my business. I'm not an investigator. My business was to lodge his complaint and work as a liaison with Internal Affairs and with his supervisor.'

'Do you remember the names of his patrol partners?'

'He was riding with a guy named Ben Engle at the time. As for the others, I don't remember off the top of my head. He had no complaints with Engle. They seemed to get along well.'

'When he was found murdered, did you think it was the person who had sent the letters?'

'Well, yes, of course that was my first fear. It was terrible. I mean, we – that is to say, gay officers – we've all experienced harassment and prejudice to one degree or another. There are plenty of guys on the job with small brains and thick red necks. That whole weightlifting crowd comes readily to mind. But murder would have taken everything to a whole new, very ugly level. It was frightening to think. But that's not how it turned out, thank God.'

'You believe Curtis was killed by Renaldo Verma?'

'Yes. Don't you?'

'Some people aren't convinced.'

'Ah . . .' he said as if the lightbulb of awareness had just gone on. 'You've been talking to Ken Ibsen.'

The name meant nothing to her, but Liska put it to Neon Man's face. Dungen took her silence for agreement.

'There hasn't been a bigger conspiracy theorist since Oliver Stone,' he said.

'You think he's a kook?'

'I think he's a drama queen. He doesn't get enough stage time at the club he works. He has a history of filing lawsuits for sex discrimination and sexual harassment. He knew Eric Curtis – or claims to have known him – and so that gave him a reason to draw a bead on the department. And now he's come to you because Internal Affairs got tired of listening to his theories,' Dungen added.

'Actually, he came to me because the Internal Affairs officer he was working with was found dead.'

'Andy Fallon. Yes. That was too bad.'

'Did you know Fallon?'

'I spoke with him regarding his investigation. I didn't know him personally.'

'He was gay.'

'It's not a club, Sergeant. We don't all play together,' Dungen said. 'I suppose Mr Ibsen has found a way to incorporate Fallon's death into his latest theory. It's all a part of the larger conspiracy to cover up the menace of AIDS in the police department.'

'Curtis had AIDS?'

'He was HIV-positive. You didn't know that?'

'I'm new to the game. I've got some catching up to do,' Liska said, a part of her brain already reconfiguring the playing field, taking this new bomb into consideration. 'He was HIV-positive and he was still working the streets?'

'He hadn't told his supervisor. He came to me first. He was afraid he'd lose his job. I told him that couldn't happen. The department can't discriminate against an officer because of a medical condition. So says the Americans With Disabilities Act. Curtis would have been taken off the street and reassigned. Obviously, there's too great a risk – not the least of which is to the department in the form of potential lawsuits – having an HIV-positive officer on the street, having to deal with accident and injury situations, situations where the officer himself or herself might become injured and run the risk of infecting someone.'

'At the time he was being harassed, who else knew Curtis was HIV-positive? Would other uniforms have known?'

'To my knowledge, he hadn't told anyone. I told him he was obligated to inform everyone he'd been intimate with. I don't know if he did,' Dungen said. 'The killer couldn't have known. Who would be stupid enough to go after someone who was HIV-positive with a baseball bat?'

Liska could see the crime scene in her head. Blood everywhere, splattering the walls, the ceiling, lampshades; spraying everywhere as the killer struck Eric Curtis again and again with the baseball bat.

Who would knowingly expose himself to contact with contaminated blood?

Someone ignorant about the transmission of the disease or someone who didn't care. Someone arrogant enough to believe in his own immortality. Someone who was already infected.

'When was the last time Fallon spoke with you about the case?' she asked, rubbing a thumb against her right temple, where a headache was taking root. She buzzed her window back up, thinking it was letting in more fumes than oxygen. 'Recently?'

'No. The case was closed. The guy cut a deal. What's this about, Sergeant?' Dungen asked, suspicious. 'I thought Andy Fallon committed suicide.'

'Yeah,' Liska said. 'Just trying to find out why, that's all. Thank you for your time, David.'

One of the great tricks of interviewing people: know when to quit. Liska bailed on the phone call, and wondered again if it would come back around to bite her in the ass with Leonard. The idea made her feel nauseated. Or maybe that was the carbon monoxide, she thought, only half joking. She felt a little dizzy.

She turned off the engine and got out of the car, taking a big breath of cold air as she leaned against the roof of the Saturn.

'Sergeant Liska.'

The voice went through her like a blade. She turned abruptly to see Rubel twenty feet away. She hadn't heard the elevator, hadn't heard footfalls coming up the stairwell. It seemed as if he had simply materialized.

'I tried to catch you at your office,' he said. 'You'd already gone.'

'It's a little past the end of your shift, isn't it?'

He came steadily forward, looming larger and larger. Even without the mirrored shades he seemed to have no expression. 'Paperwork.'

'And you found me here ... how?'

He gestured to a black Ford Explorer across and down from the Saturn. 'Coincidence.'

My ass, Liska thought. Of all the parking spots in all the parking ramps in downtown Minneapolis ...

'Small world,' she said flatly. She leaned back against the car to offset the watery feeling in her legs, and slipped her hands into her coat pockets, curling her fingers around the handle of her ASP.

'What was it you wanted to talk to me about?' Rubel asked. He stopped just a few feet from her. A foot closer than she would have liked, which he probably knew.

'Like your pal B.O. didn't fill you in. Please.'

Rubel said nothing.

'You knew IA was looking at Ogden for fucking with evidence in the Curtis investigation –'

'That's over.'

'But you went to the investigator's house on a DB call anyway. Whose bright idea was that?'

'The call came over the radio. We were in the vicinity.'

'You're a regular magnet for coincidence.'

'We had no way of knowing the dead body was Fallon.'

'You knew it as soon as you got there. You should have hauled Ogden out of there. You seem to make a habit of saving his ass. Why didn't you do it when you got to Fallon's house?'

Rubel stared at her for a long, unnerving time. Liska's head pounded with the beat of her pulse. The nausea swirled in her stomach.

'If you suspect some impropriety on our part,' he said at last, 'why aren't you talking to IA about it?'

'Is that what you want me to do?'

'You won't because your case is closed. Fallon killed himself.'

'That doesn't mean it's over. It doesn't mean I won't still talk to your supervisor –'

'Go ahead.'

'How long have you been riding with Ogden?' Liska asked.

'Three months.'

'Who was he riding with before you?'

'Larry Porter. He left the department. Hired on with the Plymouth PD. You could get all this from our supervisor. If you wanted to talk to him.'

There was a hint of smugness in his tone, as if he knew she wouldn't go to his supervisor for fear it would get back to Leonard.

'You know, I'm trying to cut you a break here, Rubel,' she said irritably. 'I don't want bad blood with the uniforms. We need you guys. But we need you not to fuck up at a scene. A case can be made or broken on what happens at the scene. What if it turned out someone murdered Andy Fallon? You think a defense attorney isn't going to make us all look like assholes when he hears Ogden, of all people, was there stomping around?'

'You've made your point,' Rubel said calmly. 'It won't happen again.'

He started to walk away toward his truck.

'Your partner is a loose cannon, Rubel,' Liska said. 'If he has the kind of problems I think he has, you'd be smart to get yourself clear of that.'

Rubel looked at her over his shoulder. 'I know what I need to know,

Sergeant.' He looked at her car and said, 'You'd better get that window fixed. I'd have to pull you over for that.'

Liska watched him walk away and get in his truck. Gooseflesh pebbled the skin of her arms and raised the fine hairs on the back of her neck. The Explorer started with a rumble, exhaust billowing out the tailpipe. He backed out and drove away, leaving her alone again.

She couldn't decide who was scarier: Ogden with his steroid-pumped temper, or Rubel with his eerie calm. What a pair they made.

Breathing deeply for the first time since Rubel had startled her, she moved away from the Saturn and made herself walk, hoping to shake off the weird weakness that trickled down the muscles of her arms and legs. She looked at her garbage-bag window and wondered if she was being paranoid reading into Rubel's crack about getting it fixed. He wouldn't have to break into her car to get her address off her junk mail. Cops had any number of ways to easily come by that information.

But then, someone might have broken the window for another reason. Out of anger. To frighten her. As a setup to cast suspicion regarding any future crime against her on someone like the old drunk who had tried to jump in the car with her. None of the options was good.

As she stared at the window, she slowly became aware of something hanging down from the back end of the Saturn. A chunk of grungy snow, she thought. Another reason to hate winter: the filthy snow boogers that built up behind the tires and would freeze to the density of granite if not quickly removed.

But as Liska went back to kick the thing off, she realized that wasn't what she'd seen at all. What had caught her eye wasn't hanging behind the tire. It was hanging from the tailpipe.

The nausea surged up her esophagus as she bent down. The pain in her temples intensified. Dizzy, she had to brace a hand against the trunk as she squatted behind the car.

A filthy white rag had been stuffed into the tailpipe.

A cold sweat misted her skin.

For all intents and purposes, someone had just tried to kill her.

The cell phone in her pocket began to bleat. Shaking, Liska rose and leaned against the car as she dug the thing out and answered it.

'Liska, homicide.'

'Sergeant Liska, we need to meet.'

The voice was familiar. She put a name to it this time: Ken Ibsen.

'Where and when?'

20

'Hey, Red, I have a couple of questions about autoerotic asphyxiation.'

Kate Conlan stared at Kovac. Rene Russo might be this good-looking on her best day, he thought. She combed an errant strand of hair behind her ear. A wry smile pulled up one corner of her sexy mouth.

'I'm so flattered you thought of me, Sam. Come on in,' she said, stepping back from the door. 'John and I were just talking about indulging in some weird sex games.'

'I didn't need to know that.'

'You rang the doorbell. Let me take your coat.'

He stepped into the entry hall, scrubbing his shoes on the mat. 'The house looks great.'

'Thanks. I'm liking it out here in the 'burbs. It's nice having space,' Kate said. 'And there's the added benefit that no one's tried to murder me here, or died a hideous death in the basement.'

She tossed that out as if she were saying it was great not to have carpenter ants. *Oh, those pesky serial killers.* The truth was that she had come too damn close to becoming a victim herself instead of an advocate for victims, which was her job. Kovac had been on the scene that day, along with John Quinn. Kovac ended up with smoke inhalation. Quinn ended up with the girl.

The story of my life.

'You're something, Red.'

'Follow me to the inner sanctum,' she said, leading the way down a wide hall with a polished wood floor and red oriental rugs. An enormous hairy cat sat on the hall table. It reached out and tapped Kovac with a paw as he started past.

'Hey, Thor.'

The cat made a sound like a squeaky toy, jumped to the floor with a thump, and dashed down the hall ahead of them with his huge plume tail straight up in the air.

They went into a den with lots of light-stained pinewood paneling and dark green paint on the walls. A Christmas tree stood near a set of French doors that led outside. A fire crackled in a fieldstone fireplace. A big yellow

Lab puppy slept heavily on a pillow near the hearth. Thor the cat went to the puppy and stared at him with suspicion and disdain.

A pair of desks sat back-to-back on one side of the room, each fully equipped with computer, phone-fax machine, and the usual clerical clutter. John Quinn sat at one, intent on the computer screen.

'Look what the cat dragged in,' Kate said.

Quinn did, and grinned, pulling off a pair of reading glasses. 'Sam. Good to see you.'

'Don't be too thankful,' Kate said dryly. 'He wants to talk about his sex life. The joys of autoerotic adventures.'

Kovac blushed. 'I'm not *that* desperate.'

Quinn walked to him and shook his hand. Rugged and athletic, he looked younger now than when they had met during the Cremator case, more than a year past. There was an ease about Quinn he had not possessed then, and the haunted look was gone from the dark eyes. That was apparently what love and contentment could do for a person.

After the Cremator, Quinn had left the FBI, where he had been top gun among the mind hunters. Too many cases, too much death, too much stress had taken a toll on him. The Bureau had a history of running its best horses into the ground, and so they had done with Quinn – with Quinn's willing participation. But nearly losing Kate to a killer had been the wake-up call. Quinn had traded the Bureau for private consulting and teaching – and life with Kate. A sweet deal all the way around.

'Have a seat,' he offered, gesturing to a pair of fat couches in front of the fire. 'What are you working on, Sam?'

'An apparent suicide that was ruled an accident that might be something else.'

'The Internal Affairs guy?' Kate asked, handing Kovac a neat scotch. She sat down on the couch too close to Quinn, and put her stocking feet up on the coffee table.

'That's the animal.'

'He was found hanging, right?' Quinn asked. 'Was he nude?'

'Yes.'

'Any evidence of masturbatory activity?'

'No.'

'Fantasy, role-playing, bondage?'

'No, but there was a full-length mirror there so he could see his reflection,' Kovac said. 'Someone had written the word *Sorry* on the glass with a marker.'

Quinn's brow furrowed.

'Did he have any kind of protective padding positioned between the rope and his throat?' Kate asked. She herself had worked for the FBI in the old Behavioral Sciences unit – in a past life, as she said.

'No.'

Kate frowned. Quinn got up from the couch and went to a set of bookshelves on the far side of his desk.

'Most practitioners of autoerotic asphyxiophilia – the more sophisticated and experienced ones – won't risk the rope leaving a mark on their throat,' Kate said. 'How would they explain it to coworkers, family members, friends, et cetera.'

Kovac reached into the breast pocket of his suit coat. 'I've got some of the Polaroids.'

He laid them out on the coffee table. Kate looked at them without reaction, sipping at a gin and tonic from time to time.

'Did you find any videotapes with sexual subject matter?' Quinn asked, coming back to the couch with a couple of books and a videocassette.

'*Holiday Inn,*' Kovac said. 'I suppose some people could argue it's full of latent homosexual subtext or some such bullshit.'

'That's a little more subtle than I was thinking.' Quinn went to the television, punched on the VCR and the set, and loaded the tape.

'No porn – gay, straight, or otherwise. The vic was gay, by the way, if that matters.'

'It doesn't. There's no data suggesting this paraphilia is more a gay hobby than a straight one,' Quinn said. 'The reason I asked about videotapes is that a lot of people who indulge in this kind of thing will videotape themselves, so they can relive the fun later on.'

He came back to the couch, settled in next to Kate, and hit the play button on the remote. Kovac leaned forward with his forearms on his thighs and his eyes on the screen, studiously avoiding looking at Kate's hand, which settled casually on her husband's stomach.

The show that rolled across the screen was sordid and sad and pathetic. A man's home video of his own accidental death. A pudgy, balding guy with too much body hair, dressed in a black leather S and M harness. He set the stage carefully, checking the elaborate rigging of the rope, which hung in what looked to be a garage or storage shed. He had draped the background with white drop cloths and strategically placed a couple of female mannequins dressed in dominatrix garb. He spent three minutes taping a riding crop into the hand of one of his silent witnesses. INXS played in the background: 'Need You Tonight.'

When he was satisfied with the set, he walked to a full-length mirror and went through his own little play, complete with dialogue. He sentenced himself to punishment, pulled a black discipline mask over his head, and wrapped a long black silk scarf around his throat several times. Then he danced his way from the mirror toward his makeshift gallows, fondling himself, presenting himself to the mannequins. He mounted the step stool and put the noose around his neck. He stroked his erection and eased one foot and then the other off the step.

His toes were just touching the floor, a position he couldn't maintain for long. The noose tightened. He didn't realize he was in trouble yet. He was still playing out the fantasy. Then he began to struggle with his balance. He extended one foot back to step onto the stool. The stool skidded backward and the noose tightened as he tried to reach behind and hook the thing with his foot. He let go of his penis to grab for his safety rope, but he had twisted to one side in an effort to catch the stool and he couldn't quite reach the rope.

And then it was too late. That fast. Seconds, and his dance became something from a horror movie.

'See how quickly it all goes wrong?' Quinn said. 'A couple seconds too long, a slight miscalculation – it's all over.'

'Jesus,' Kovac muttered. 'You don't want to accidentally return this one to Blockbuster.'

Though Kovac knew this was from Quinn's tape library. His specialty was sexual homicide.

They sat there and watched a man die the way other people would sit through their neighbor's vacation video. When the guy stopped kicking and his arms pulled up and went back down for the last time, Quinn clicked the tape off. From start to finish, the hanging had taken less than four minutes.

'There's not always this much ceremony involved,' Quinn said. 'But it's not uncommon. Not that any of this is *common*. Rough estimate, you're probably looking at a confirmed thousand autoerotic deaths in this country every year, with maybe two or three times that that are missed calls, labeled suicide or something else.'

'But those are just the people who miscalculate and don't escape whatever contraption they've devised,' Kate said. 'Who knows how many actually practice the paraphilia and don't screw up. You haven't found any family or friends who suggested he was into this kind of thing?'

'The brother says they used to play hangman when they were kids. You know, cowboy stuff, war games, like that. Nothing kinky. But what about that angle? Have you ever seen family members involved in this kind of thing together?'

'There's not much I haven't seen, Sam,' Quinn said. 'I haven't seen that, but it could certainly happen. I never say never, 'cause just when I think I can't be shocked, someone comes up with something worse than I ever imagined. What's your read on the brother?'

'He's a redneck type. I don't make him for kinky sex, but I could be wrong. There was a lot of resentment for the younger brother.'

'What about friends?' Kate asked.

'The best friend says no, Fallon wasn't into kink, but the best friend is hiding something.'

'The best friend – a man or a woman?' Kate asked.

'Male, allegedly straight, engaged to someone prominent. The vic, like I said, was gay. He'd just come out to his family.'

'You think they might have been partners,' Quinn said.

'I think they could have been. That might explain the word on the mirror. Things got out of hand, went wrong, the friend panicked...'

Kate shook her head as she studied the Polaroids. 'I don't see this as a game. I still say he would have taken some precautions with his neck. It looks more like suicide.'

'Then why the mirror?' Quinn challenged.

'Self-humiliation.'

While they argued over details Kovac had wrestled with again and again, he flipped through the books Quinn had brought out: The *DSM-IV*, *Abnormal Psychology and Modern Life*, *The Handbook of Forensic Sexology*, *Autoerotic Fatalities*. A little light reading. He had already studied the photographs in the 'Modes of Death' chapter of *Practical Homicide Investigation*, which showed photo after photo of one dumb schmuck after another, dead in some elaborate invention of ropes and pulleys and vacuum cleaner hoses and plastic garbage bags – contraptions designed for bigger, better orgasms. Floaters on the shallow end of the gene pool. People surrounded with bizarre sex toys and sick pornography. People living in crappy basement apartments with no windows. Losers.

'He doesn't seem to fit in with this crowd,' Kovac said.

'You never see Rockefellers and Kennedys in these books,' Kate said. 'That doesn't mean they can't be just as sick or worse. It just means they're rich.'

Quinn agreed. 'The studies show this behavior crosses all socioeconomic lines. But you're right too, Sam. The scene strikes me as being wrong for AEA. It's too neat and tidy. And the absence of sexual paraphernalia ... The scene we're looking at doesn't fit. Any reason to believe it's not suicide?'

'Motives and suspects coming out my ears.'

'Murder by hanging is rare,' Quinn said. 'And damn hard to pull off without leaving tracks. Any defense wounds on the hands or arms?'

'Nope.'

'Contusions to the head?'

'No. I don't have the full report on the autopsy, but the doc who cut him didn't mention anything to Liska about a head wound,' Kovac said. 'Toxicology is back. He'd had a drink and taken a prescription sleeping pill – not an overdose, just a couple of pills.'

'That's sounding like suicide.'

'But there's no trace of a prescription bottle anywhere in his house. If he had a scrip, he didn't fill it at his usual pharmacy, nor was it written by his shrink.'

'He was seeing a psychiatrist?'

'Minor depression. He had a bottle of Zoloft in his medicine cabinet. I talked to the doc this afternoon.'

'Did the doctor consider him a candidate for suicide?' Kate asked.

'No, but he wasn't surprised either.'

'So you've got yourself a genuine whodunit,' Quinn said.

'Unfortunately, no one wants to hear about it. The case is closed. I'm hanging my ass out on a limb for a victim everyone wants buried. He'd be in the ground right now if it hadn't turned so fucking cold.'

He scooped the Polaroids up, returned them to his coat pocket, and pasted on a sorry smile for the couple sitting across from him. 'But, hey, what else have I got to do with my time? It's not like I have a life or anything.'

'I recommend getting one,' Quinn said, winking at Kate, who smiled at him with warmth and love.

Kovac stood up. 'All right. I'm out of here before the two of you embarrass yourselves.'

'I think we're embarrassing you, Sam,' Kate said, getting up from the couch.

'There's that too.'

Quinn and Kate saw him out together. His last image before the front door closed was the pair turning to walk back into their lovely home, each with an arm around the other. And damn if that didn't hurt, he thought as he started the car.

He hated admitting it, wished he could have lied to himself, but there it was: he'd been half in love with Kate Conlan for the better part of five years and had never done a damn thing about it. Because he wouldn't allow himself to try. Nothing ventured, nothing lost. What would a woman like her see in a guy like him?

He would never find out now. Facing that reality left a hollow feeling in the deepest part of his soul. There was no escape from it, sitting there in the dark. He'd never felt more alone.

Unbidden, Amanda Savard's face came to mind. Beautiful, battered, haunted by something he couldn't even guess at. He wanted to tell himself she was just a part of the puzzle, that that was his entire interest in her. But there were no lies in him tonight. The truth was right there, just under the surface. He wanted her.

Night was wrapped closer to the earth here than in the city. Kate and Quinn's house was technically in Plymouth, but it was more in the country than in a suburb. The drive was off a secluded side road. There was a small lake practically in their backyard. Few lights, less traffic. No distractions to keep him from looking too closely at what he was feeling tonight as he sat in his car on the side of the road.

Maybe there was an advantage to having a neighbor who lit up his yard like a cheap Vegas hotel after all.

21

Ken Ibsen couldn't shake the feeling someone was watching him, but then, that was nothing new. Ever since the start of this mess, he'd felt as if some giant malevolent eye had hovered above him, tracking his every move. And the worst of it was, it all seemed for nothing on his part. He had done his best to be a conscientious citizen and a good friend, and all he'd gotten for his trouble was ridicule and harassment. Eric was just as dead. The wrong man was sitting in jail for his murder, and no one cared he hadn't done it – apparently, including the convict. The world had gone stark raving mad.

Andy Fallon had been the only one interested in getting to the truth of what had happened to Eric, and now Fallon was dead. Ken counted himself lucky to be alive. Maybe it wasn't such a terrible thing having people think he was a flaming conspiracy nut.

But Liska seemed genuinely interested in the truth.

So where the hell was she?

She had agreed to meet him at 10:30. After his first show. He was due back onstage at 11:30. He checked the delicate watch he wore over his white kid glove, and sighed out a delicate stream of cigarette smoke. 10:55. It was a cold five-minute walk in heels back to the club, and he would have to touch up his lipstick. . . .

He wished now he'd told her to meet him backstage, but he hadn't wanted certain extra ears listening in. And the parking lot behind *Boys Will Be Girls* did too brisk a business in clandestine trysts, even in this cold. He didn't want Liska hearing the guy in the next car getting a blowjob while Ken tried to tell her about the organized hatred of gays in the Minneapolis Police Department. Credibility was a major issue. Bad enough that he would be meeting her in full costume.

He hoped she would see past the makeup and mascara, but then, that was the problem with people, wasn't it? Judgments were most often based on face value and stereotypes. Most of the people in this coffeehouse would have looked at him sitting here dressed as a woman and decided he was a transvestite/transsexual, the terms being interchangeable to the average heterosexual. He was neither. They would have a neat package of preconceived ideas about the way he would walk, the way he would talk, his likes, dislikes, talents. Some of their ideas would be right, but most would not.

What he was was a gay man with an exceptional voice and a talent for mimicry. He was a serious actor working at a ridiculous job because it paid well. He liked to shoot pool and wear jeans. He owned a Weimaraner dog, which he never dressed up in costumes. He preferred steak over quiche, and he couldn't stand Bette Midler.

Most people are more than their stereotypes.

He sipped his coffee and crossed his legs, staring back at the older man who was watching him from across the room. Just to be a jerk, he pursed his lips and sent the old fart an air kiss.

Instead of feeling conspicuous dressed as Marilyn Monroe, he felt safe hidden beneath the platinum wig and behind the thick stage makeup. He had slipped into the coffeehouse the back way and taken a back corner table to avoid the notice of the other customers. There weren't many. It was too cold to bother to go out on a weeknight. That suited Ken's plan – a public place without much of the public present.

Now all he needed was Liska.

He sipped his coffee and watched the door.

Liska swore a blue streak under her breath as she idled at yet another red light. She was late. She was shaken. She was angry. Tonight of all nights she hadn't been able to find a sitter who could stay late. She'd spent an hour and a half on the phone, calling everyone she could think of while Kyle complained that she'd promised to help him with his math, and R.J. expressed his displeasure in her by covering the dining room table with action figures, then dramatically sweeping them onto the floor.

In the end she'd called Speed. Grudgingly. Hating it. There was nothing worse to her than having to rely on him openly for anything. Especially when it came to the boys. She was supposed to be self-reliant, *had to be* self-reliant, *was* self-reliant. But instead, she felt inadequate, and a failure, and a poor mother. It frustrated her no end that had the circumstances been reversed, Speed would have done exactly the same thing and never batted an eye. He wouldn't have even bothered to go through the endless calls to the sitters, and he wouldn't have felt inadequate.

A huge, hot ball of emotion wedged in her throat, and tears burned her eyes. She'd caught him on his cell phone at the gym with every other ironhead in the department, and he had whined about having his workout interrupted. Liska doubted he had cut it short or skipped his shower. It had taken him for-fucking-ever to get to the house. Asshole. Now she was late.

The light changed and she gunned the Saturn around a Cadillac, cut him off, and took the next right fast. She didn't know how long Ibsen would wait. Drama queen that he was, he was playing the skittish informant to the hilt, refusing to tell her his tale over the phone, insisting on a face-to-face. She wanted to believe he had something valid to tell her. But given the mood she was in, she was more inclined to believe he'd turn out to be everything Dungen had said, and she would have put herself through this evening and risked her career, only to be proved a big idiot.

Still, beneath the simmering cynicism, Liska believed she was poking at a live hornet's nest rather than a dead case, and Ken Ibsen – kook or no kook – was a part of that. If he would wait five minutes more, she might find out just what his role in the drama could be.

She wasn't coming. He'd said it in his mind every two minutes for the last ten. In between, he'd distracted himself by doodling on a napkin, drawing a caricature of himself in costume, writing random notes.

Maybe she didn't believe him. Maybe she had spoken with that viper David Dungen, and he had poisoned her mind against him. Dungen, the traitor. Dungen, the puppet of the department higher-ups. He was nothing but a shill, a warm gay body willing to fill the token post of liaison. The Minneapolis Police Department cared nothing for the concerns of its gay officers.

Of course, Ken didn't know this from firsthand experience, but he was certain of it nevertheless. Eric had alluded to as much. The liaison post had been created to pay lip service to gay issues. Therefore, the department hadn't *really* cared about the harassment Eric had suffered. Therefore, the department had fostered the environment of hatred that had led to Eric's death. *Therefore*, Ken wrote on his napkin, underlining the word, the department should be held accountable in a wrongful death suit.

If only the court would recognize his right to file the suit. He was no blood relation to Eric Curtis. They hadn't been married – same-sex marriage was (unconstitutionally, to his way of thinking) against the law. Therefore, the court would hear nothing from him.

Sure, it was fine for Neanderthal cops to bludgeon people for their private preferences, but allow caring individuals to express their love . . . Not that he and Eric had been in love. They had been friends. Well . . . acquaintances, with the potential to be friends. Who knew what they might have become.

The bell above the coffeehouse door rang and Ken looked up from his doodling, hopeful, only to have his heart sink. The newest patron was a scruffy-looking guy in an old army fatigue jacket.

She wasn't coming.

Eleven-eighteen.

He put out his smoldering cigarette, stuffed the napkin he had written on into the pocket of his full-length faux leopard coat, and went out the back way.

Not that he liked going by way of the alleys. Drunks and drug addicts and the homeless traveled this maze of back routes, avoiding the cops. That was his reason as well. He'd been harassed by the police more than once for walking down the street in costume. Like any common street whore could do the kind of job he did. Idiots. And, naturally, they assumed any man in a blond wig and a dress was a prostitute. Then there was the fact that he hadn't exactly made a lot of friends among the patrol cops with his diligent pursuit of the truth in Eric's death.

It was awfully dark and creepy in this alley. The buildings created a sinister canyon of concrete. The darkness was broken only intermittently by weak bulbs over the back doors of dubious businesses. Every Dumpster, every empty box was a potential hiding place for a predator or a scavenger.

As if his thoughts had called up the devil, a shape suddenly loomed up at the end of a trash bin thirty feet down the alley. The end of a cigarette glowed red, an evil eye in the dark.

Ken's step faltered and he slipped on the rutted ice and had to catch himself against the side of a building. He swore as he felt a false nail tip give way. He would have to keep his gloves on for the next set. There wouldn't be any time to fix the fingernail. Damn Liska.

The figure down the alley didn't move. The business behind the specter was a tattoo parlor. The kind of place where the patrons got AIDS and hepatitis from dirty needles.

Ken dug around in the pocket of his coat for his pepper spray and kept walking, staying as far on the other side of the alley as possible. The club was two blocks away.

He held his breath with each step. He ran every day to stay in shape, and he was better than most women in the heels, but he didn't want to have to try sprinting in them.

He could feel the specter's gaze on him. He waited for the eyes to glow red, like a wolf's.

He drew even with the back door of the tattoo parlor, ready to bolt, hand sweating around the canister of pepper spray even in this cold. His heart seemed to be quivering in his chest behind the falsies.

God, he did not want to die in drag. In his mind's eye he could already see the crime scene photographs being passed around. He could hear the cops snickering. Maybe, if he wasn't killed tonight, he would go get a tattoo of his own: I Am Not A Transvestite.

The specter tossed the cigarette, the glowing ember an arc of light in the gloom, and lurched forward suddenly. Ken bolted. Hoarse laughter followed him as he slipped and skidded. His right ankle buckled beneath him and he fell, sprawling gracelessly. Pain hit him like so many hammers – both knees, one elbow, one hipbone, his chin. A cry wrenched out of him, sounding desperate and weak, dying against the brick and concrete.

He scrambled to get back on his feet, clawing at anything to pull himself up. He grabbed hold of the edge of a Dumpster and hauled himself up, slipping, banging against it. His nylons were ruined. He could feel cold and wet against bare skin. He heard stitching pop as his legs splayed and strained the seams of his dress.

He jerked his head around to look behind him. Still laughing, the specter turned and went back into the tattoo parlor. *Asshole.*

Ken leaned against the Dumpster, breathing hard, the air feeling like dry ice rasping down his throat.

Damn Liska. He had half a mind to send her his dry cleaning bill.

Limping, he started down the alley again. One shoe was missing a heel, and his ankle felt sprained. He touched a hand to his mouth and chin, and brought it away; the white glove was smeared with blood and dirt. Damn. If he needed stitches, his boss was going to have a hissy fit. Two blocks was looking a lot farther than it had in the beginning of the evening. And with the repairs he was going to have to make, there was no way he was making the last set.

The end of the alley was near. There was no traffic on the side street. A single dark car sat parked along the near curb. He could see the trunk and no more. He thought nothing of it until just a split second before the large, dark shadow of a man fell across the mouth of the alley, when the cold wash of a horrible premonition swept over him.

I'm going to die tonight.

The trunk of the car opened, the light illuminating a face in a dark ski mask. The man reached into the trunk and came out with a tire iron.

Ken Ibsen stopped and stood still, the moment seeming both real and surreal. Then he turned slowly, thinking to go back the way he'd come, after all. The better part of valor. The lesser of evils. But there was no going back. And there was no lesser evil. Another dark, faceless figure blocked the escape route behind him. A hulking silhouette with something in its hand.

He could feel evil emanating from them as they closed the distance from either side. Fear hit him like a bolt of lightning, and he screamed and pulled the pepper spray from his pocket, fumbling with the trigger. The attacker with the tire iron made one quick move, and Ken's arm flung out to the side, broken and useless. The canister clattered to the ground like a piece of trash.

He thought to run as the iron hit the side of his knee, and bone shattered like glass.

He thought to cry out for help, and felt his jaw crumble and his teeth spill like Chiclets from his mouth.

He thought, *I don't want to die in drag,* and everything went black.

Liska slid the Saturn to the curb in a no-parking zone a quarter of a block from the coffeehouse Ibsen had chosen for their meet. She was way late. Damn Speed for taking so long.

The few customers sat in knots of two or three, scattered as far away from each other as possible, wrapped up in their own conversations. No one looked up as Liska came in. She went directly to the bar, where the only visible employee was engrossed in a textbook as thick as the Yellow Pages.

'What are you learning?' she asked as she pulled her badge out of her purse.

The bartender looked up at her through a pair of trendy glasses. He had soulful brown eyes and the kind of thin, elegant face painters attributed to Jesus Christ. 'I'm learning that my father is spending a lot of money to send me through school so I can learn to make a great cappuccino.' He glanced at her badge. 'Are you here to arrest me for impersonating a med student?'

'Naw. I was supposed to meet someone here a little while ago. Short, slim guy with platinum hair.'

The med student shook his head. 'Haven't seen anyone like that. There was a transvestite dressed as Marilyn Monroe. He seemed like he was waiting for someone, but he left. Not a blind date, I hope.'

'No. How long ago did Marilyn leave?'

'Ten, fifteen minutes. Went out the back way. He works down at *Boys Will Be Girls.* They come in between sets sometimes. Otherwise I wouldn't know anything about that,' he hurried to add.

'A transvestite,' Liska muttered to herself, turning away. 'This night just gets better and better.'

Her big informant went around dressed up as Marilyn Monroe. Preachers and bankers seldom ended up as informants to crimes, she reminded herself. And when they did, it was because they were secretly perverts or thieves.

And her mother wondered why she didn't date more.

She went down the hall, past the bathrooms, to the back door of the coffeehouse. Med Student followed like a puppy.

'Do you know anyone at the county morgue?' he asked. ''Cause the way things are going, I'm thinking pathology might be best for me. No malpractice.'

'Sure, I know people,' Liska said. 'It's not a bad job if you can stand the smell.'

She pushed the door open and looked out. The alley was dark and wet and filthy. There should have been some rats and ragged orphans to complete the picture, she thought, and just then noticed a scavenger bent over something thirty feet down the way. He stood in a little puddle of light coming from over the back door of some other business. He started and stared back at her, like a coyote caught going through the garbage – wanting to run, but loath to give up the treasure. He moved just enough to allow the pale light to fall on his find, and the details of the scene began to register in Liska's brain: a woman's shoe, a bare leg, a glimpse of pale hair.

'Hey, you!' she shouted, drawing her weapon, moving so that the Dumpster gave her cover. 'Police! Step away from the body!'

'Call nine-one-one,' she said to Med Student. 'Request police and an ambulance. Tell them there's been an assault. Hurry.'

Coyote bolted. Liska was in gear instantly, running, shouting, leading with her weapon, wondering if he had a gun, if he would turn and use it. He tripped and staggered, lost precious seconds trying to get his feet back under him. Liska hit him running and rode him down to the ground, driving her knee into his back, grabbing a handful of coat collar and greasy hair in her left hand as she put her weapon on him with her right.

'You're under arrest, motherfucker! Don't move!'

'I didn't do nothing!'

The smell of cheap bourbon and diarrhea wafted from him in a noxious cloud. He tried to rise up and Liska banged him hard on the back of his skull with the butt of her Sig. 'I said don't move!'

'But I didn't do nothing!'

'If I had a dollar for every talking asshole who said that, I'd have a mansion and pool boy named Raoul.'

'Ask Beano! It was them other guys!'

'Shut up!'

Other guys.

She glanced back over her shoulder at the victim. She couldn't make out features, couldn't tell if the person was breathing. She cuffed Coyote's hands behind his back.

'Stay right here. Don't get up. Don't move.'

'But I didn't do it,' he whined.

'Say that again and I'll fucking shoot you. *Shut up!*'

He started to cry as she turned away and went back to the victim.

'Ma'am, are you all right?' she asked. A stupid question meant simply to elicit a response. A moan, a groan, something, anything.

She squatted down beside the body and reached under the matted mess of white-blond hair to try to find a pulse in the throat. At first, she thought what she was looking at was the back of the skull – a bloody mess of caved-in bone without features. Then the victim drew a shallow, shuddering breath; a horrible, wet, sucking sound; and she saw bubbles in the blood coming from what must have been a mouth.

'Oh, Jesus,' she whispered, finding the weak, thready pulse with shaking fingertips. With her other hand, she carefully brushed the hair back. It was a wig, and it pulled free with little pressure, revealing short platinum hair streaked with blood leaking from a skull fracture. Ken Ibsen.

He lay on the ground like a discarded rag doll, limbs bent at odd angles. In one hand he clutched a scrap of paper – a napkin. Liska slipped it from his twitching fingers and held it so that the faint light fell across it. Doodling. Probably what he'd done while he'd waited for her to show up. Random words and little drawings. One phrase caught her eye: *wrongful death.*

Med Student ran up, panting. 'They're on the way.'

Even as he said it, a siren sounded not too far in the distance.

'I brought a flashlight,' he said, and directed the beam on the face of the victim.

The flashlight hit the ground and bounced. Med Student turned and vomited, and began to reconsider medicine as a career.

22

She felt him behind her before she looked. Awareness rose inside her like a floodtide, lapping at the back of her throat, threatening to spill out of her mouth in a scream. Fear stiffened the muscles of her back, making it difficult to turn around. She felt as if she were wearing a straitjacket.

He stood in the shadows of the living room, the moonlight coming through the windows making his form clear, yet she couldn't make out his features at all. He didn't speak. He didn't move as long as she watched him. She wondered if he thought he could make himself invisible by being still. She had thought that when she was a child: *If I can be still, they won't see me.*

Conversely, she wondered whether if she pretended not to see him, he might disappear.

She walked away, trying not to hurry, and went into the dining room. She didn't hear him follow. She should have heard his shoes on the hardwood floor, but she heard nothing. Still, when she looked over her shoulder, he was there. He stood in the shadows of the hall, looking in.

She held her breath until it felt as if someone was strangling her. Then she realized with a jolt of raw panic that someone *was*. His large hands closed around her throat from behind, fingers pressing against the small, vital bones. She clawed at his hands and tried to jerk free. He pulled her back against him and tried to push her down to the floor. Adrenaline surged through her, and she broke his grip suddenly, gasping air into her lungs. She looked over her shoulder then, as she started to run, and saw him clearly: Andy Fallon, his face purple and bloated, eyes dull, tongue coming out of his mouth.

And then she was awake. She had leapt up off the couch, becoming conscious as her feet hit the floor. She stumbled, crashing into the antique steamer trunk that served as a coffee table. She clawed at her throat, scratching herself as her fingers tore at the high zippered neck of the sweater she wore. The soft cotton sweater she had put on because it made her feel cocooned and safe. She had sweat through it.

The tears came then, as she realized what had happened, as she thought of how many times she had gone through this, and wondered if it would ever end. She sank down to the floor on her knees and started to put her face in her hands, gasping as she touched the raw spots.

She was so tired. Physically, mentally, emotionally. Tired from the lack of sleep, and from the stress, and from the nightmares, and the guilt. God, all of it.

For just a moment, she wondered what it might be like to have someone there to hold her up as she shouldered the burdens of her life. Foolish fantasy. She was meant to be alone whether or not that was what she wanted. That was the thing about fate: it didn't ask for your opinion, didn't consider what you might want or need. And so she sat alone in the night, shaking from the strain and from the sweat now chilling on her skin. Trying not to cry because there was no point in it. Crying was just a waste of energy she couldn't afford – one of the few useful lessons her father had taught her.

She closed her eyes and started the breathing exercise to slow her heart rate and calm her nerves. Unbidden came the memory of a strong hand on her shoulder, solid strength beside her. She could see Sam Kovac's dark eyes looking at her reflection in the ladies' room mirror. She could feel his concern, hear it in his voice. For just a second she let herself imagine what it might have been like to turn toward him and rest her head on his chest, and have him put his arms around her.

Kovac was a rock, an anchor. He seemed so grounded, she doubted anything could knock him off balance. Not that she would ever find out. He was the last man she would allow to see inside her and try to tame the snakes in her head. She was destined to fight them alone, and she would. She had done so for a very long time. It was just that tonight . . . tonight she felt so tired, and so alone. . . .

She breathed a sigh and forced herself to her feet. She made the obligatory search of the downstairs rooms, walking through the silent house like a zombie, not really seeing anything, dimly aware that she was searching for something that couldn't be seen. She ended the search back in the living room, standing for a long time just staring at the wall of photographs she had taken over the years. Black-and-white, landscapes and still lifes. Beautiful, empty, bleak, stark. A projection of the photographer's inner self, a therapist would say.

Time slipped by unnoticed. She might have been standing there five minutes or an hour when the doorbell rang. The sound startled her so, she wondered if she had gone back under into that place of waking dreams and was now being shocked back out of it, or if this was part of the next nightmare and she wasn't really awake at all.

The bell rang again. Heart pounding, she went to the door and looked out through the peephole. Kovac stood on her front step. Not sure that her mind hadn't conjured the image, she pulled the door open.

'Your lights were on,' he said by way of explanation for being there.

Savard stared at him.

'I assumed you were up,' he said. 'Was I wrong about that?'

She touched her hair self-consciously, started to shield the wound around her eye, but stopped. She glanced down to see that she was actually wearing clothes. 'I . . . ah . . . fell asleep on the couch.'

'I'm sorry, then, if I got you up.'

'What do you want, Sergeant?'

He shifted from foot to foot, his hands in his coat pockets, his shoulders hunched. 'Getting in out of this cold would be a good start.'

Hugging herself against the night air, Savard went back into the hall, leaving him to follow. She checked her reflection in the mirror above the hall table and was appalled. Dark circles, pale skin, hair limp and messy. She looked battered and lost. Haunted. She would rather he *had* caught her naked, at least then he wouldn't have been paying enough attention to her face to wonder at her mental state.

'I'm not keeping you from anything – like a significant other?' he asked bluntly.

Not unless inner demons count, she thought. 'What are you doing here?'

'I was in the neighborhood.'

She caught his reflection in the mirror. He was looking at her, studying her, and she jerked around, the pain in her neck and shoulder making her wince. 'Plymouth is out of your jurisdiction.'

'I'm off duty. I have friends out here. John Quinn. You know him?'

'I know of him.'

'I had a couple of questions for him regarding your boy Andy. I'm still not convinced he died alone or by choice. Could have been an accident,' he conceded. 'But if it was an accident and he wasn't alone, then someone left the scene of a death, and I'd wanna know who, 'cause they got something to answer for, you know?'

Savard smoothed one hand over the wrinkles sleep had pressed into her top. She couldn't quite keep her other hand from touching her hair again. She hated him seeing her like this. *Vulnerable* – the word pulsed in her brain like a nerve that had been struck with a hammer.

'What did Mr Quinn have to say?' She couldn't seem to make herself look directly at him. As if he couldn't really see what a mess she was if they had no direct eye contact. *If I can be still, they won't see me. . . .*

'He had some thoughts,' Kovac said, moving to stay in front of her. 'I don't always take a lot of stock in that mind hunter stuff. You know, sometimes people do things just on account of they're rotten. Then again, sometimes a person's past can haunt him – or her – to the point of driving him to do things.'

'Profiling is a tool for hunting serial criminals,' Savard said. 'You're not dealing with a serial criminal. You're not dealing with a criminal at all.'

'The Fallon family might beg to differ, two of them being dead inside a week,' Kovac said. 'Anyway, as I was leaving his house, I remembered you, Lieutenant.'

'With regards to?'

'At the funeral, I forgot to ask if you'd looked up that case file. Fallon's investigation into the Curtis-Ogden thing.'

'Are you now going to try to tell me Ogden was Andy's secret gay lover, and that he's a potential serial killer? You're losing me, Sergeant.'

'I'm just trying to take in all the facts so I have as clear a picture as possible. I learned a long time ago, if an investigator gets tunnel vision on one aspect of a case, he runs the risk of missing crucial pieces of the puzzle. How can you know where everything fits if you can't see the big picture? So, did you look it up?'

She looked past the living room to her office, wanting to go in there and shut the door behind her. 'No. I didn't have a chance.'

Kovac moved into her line of vision again. 'Could we sit down? You look like you need to, Lieutenant. No offense.'

'Asking you to sit down would imply I don't mind you staying for an indefinite period of time,' Savard pointed out. 'I do mind.'

He shrugged off the insult. 'Then you sit. I'll stand. You look a little rocky.'

For the – what? – third time that day, he put his hands on her, and she allowed it. He guided her by the shoulders to the Windsor settee along the wall. She felt as small as a child, and fragile, and ineffectual. She could have just told him to leave, but there was that part of her that didn't want him to. Anger and frustration and shame coiled inside her with needs she rarely acknowledged having.

'You know, I looked for it at Andy's place,' Kovac said. 'I looked in his office there for a duplicate file on the Curtis-Ogden thing. I wanted to see what he was investigating, what his take on things might be, see if he'd been threatened, anything like that, anything that could give me some idea of his life, his state of mind. But there was no file, and his computer was gone. An IBM ThinkPad. You know anything about that? Did he leave it in his office downtown?'

'I don't know. I don't think so. Maybe he left it in his car. Maybe he'd lost it. Maybe it's in the shop. Maybe it had been stolen.'

'Maybe it was stolen by someone who didn't want something in it to be seen by someone like me.' He picked up a small carved Santa figurine from the hall table and studied it.

Savard sighed. 'I'll check the file in the morning. Is that all, Sergeant?'

'No.'

He set the figurine aside and came toward her, leaning down. He tipped her chin up and looked in her eyes. 'How are you feeling?'

I'm feeling my pulse in my throat. I'm feeling light-headed. I'm feeling vulnerable. God, there was that word again.

'I'm fine. I'm tired. I'd like to go to bed.'

He traced a forefinger slowly in front of her eyes, the same as he had done in her office that morning. Across and back. Up and down. His left hand still cupped her chin.

'No offense, LT,' he said softly, 'but for a beautiful woman, you look like hell.'

Savard arched a brow. 'Gee, why would I take offense at that?'

He didn't answer her. He was looking at the rug burn, taking in the lines of her face . . . still touching her chin. . . . His gaze lingered on her mouth. Her breath caught in her throat.

'You are, you know,' he whispered. 'Beautiful.'

She turned her face away, the air shuddering from her lungs. 'You should go now, Sergeant.'

'I should,' he admitted. 'Before you see to it I get suspended for paying you a compliment. But I want one thing first.'

Scraping together what was left of her strength, Savard managed to put on the imperious mask that was her everyday game face. It didn't make Kovac back off an inch.

'Call me Sam,' he said, one corner of his mouth crooking upward. 'Just to hear how it sounds.'

I can't want this, she thought, fear tightening in a knot in her stomach. *I can't want him. I can't need him.*

'You should go now . . . Sergeant Kovac.'

He did nothing for a moment, and she held her breath and tried without success to read his mind. Finally, his hand dropped away from her face. He stepped back and straightened.

'Call me,' he said. 'If you come up with anything from that case file.'

She rose to her feet, feeling unsteady, and banded her arms across her chest. Kovac paused at the door.

'Goodnight . . . Amanda.' He shrugged, the slight smile still pulling at his lips. 'What's another suspension to an old horse like me?'

Cold air rushed into the hall as he let himself out. Savard locked the door behind him and leaned against it, thinking of the warmth of his fingers against her skin. Tears stung her eyes.

She climbed the stairs slowly. The table lamp was already on in her bedroom, and would remain on all night. She changed into a nightgown and crawled into bed, took a drink from the glass on the nightstand, and washed down a sleeping pill. Then she lay down carefully on her left side, hugging the spare pillow to her, and waited for sleep, eyes wide open, feeling so alone it was an ache in the very center of her being.

Goodnight . . . Sam. . . .

23

Liska wished it was all a nightmare. All of it: that her informant was a transvestite in a coma, that she'd spent half the night freezing to the bone in a filthy alley, that Speed's car was in her drive and he was in the house, waiting.

She parked at the curb, trying to remember the snow emergency rules, fatalistically certain her car would be mowed down by a city snowplow and she would be fined, to add insult to injury. *Screw it*, she thought, climbing out of the car and trudging to the front door. At least she'd collect insurance and get a new vehicle. A used Chevette, perhaps, considering where her career would be headed in the near future.

The table lamp was on low and the television was showing an infomercial for Tae-Bo. Billy Blanks offering self-esteem and spiritual enlightenment through kickboxing. Speed and R.J. were asleep, side by side, in the recliner, unmistakably father and son. Their hair even stood up in the same places. R.J. was in Spiderman pajamas with feet. The Cartman hand puppet was tucked under one arm.

Liska stood looking at them, hating the emotions the sight awakened in her. Longing, regret, need. How unfair to be hit with that tonight, on the heels of everything else that had happened. She pressed a hand to her mouth and fought the feelings as if they were demons.

Damn you. She didn't know if she had spoken the words or just thought them, didn't know if she was cursing her ex-husband or herself.

Speed cracked an eye open and looked at her, then checked his son. Slowly and carefully, he eased himself from the chair and covered R.J. with a throw from the couch.

'Is it that bad?' he asked softly as he came toward her.

He was asking about the moment, about the way she was looking at him, the way she felt about him being here. But taking a page from his book, Liska chose to interpret the question the way she wanted, and applied it to the case. 'My drag queen informant is lying in ICU with a face only Picasso could love. According to two witnesses – one of whom was caught trying to steal valuables off the guy's body – he was attacked by ninjas with lead pipes.'

'Ninjas don't use lead pipes. Nunchuks, maybe.'

'Please don't be cute, Speed. I can't deal with it right now.'

'I thought you liked me cute. It's one of my better qualities.'

Liska just looked away.

'Hey, come on. It can't be all that bad, you're still standing.'

'It's worse than bad,' she whispered.

'You want to talk about it?'

Translation: Do you want to lean on me, confide in me, let me help carry the load?

Yes, but I won't let myself.

'Nikki,' he murmured, stepping too close. He touched her cheek with a warm hand, slid his fingers back through her short hair, and gathered her to him with his other arm. 'You don't always have to be the tough one.'

'Yes, I do.'

'You don't tonight,' he murmured, his lips brushing her temple.

A shudder rippled through her as she fought the urge to melt against him, to let him hold her up.

'What's the worst part of it?' he asked.

Knowing you'll let me down in the end. Fearing that maybe I'm wrong and you wouldn't, but I won't give you the chance to prove it because I'm tired of you hurting me.

She sniffed back tears and said, 'Thinking he ended up that way because I wasn't there in time.'

'The guy's a snitch, Nik. He got beat up because of that, not because of you.'

'But if I had been there –'

'He would have got it some other time.'

'I don't know if he'll live. I don't know if he'll want to,' she said. 'You should have seen what they did to him, Speed. It was horrible.'

'Don't do that to yourself, Nikki. You know better.'

A cop learned early on not to allow that kind of emotion. The road to madness was paved with guilt. Kovac had reminded her of the same when she had called him from the scene with news of Ibsen's assault. Still, it was hard not to place the blame at her own feet. Ibsen had been there waiting for her.

'They must have shattered every bone in his face,' she said. 'Broke his arm, his collarbone, ribs, one knee. They assaulted him anally with a pipe.'

'Jesus.'

She took a deep breath and made the confession that lay at the heart of it for her: 'And the worst part of it is, I think they were cops.'

Speed went still. She could feel his heart beat beneath her hand. 'God, Nikki, what are you into? Looking at other cops . . .'

'I don't want it to be true,' she said. 'I don't want any part of it. We're supposed to be the good guys. I don't want to be the one to prove otherwise.'

The idea was so abhorrent to her, it felt like a virus in her blood, and she shuddered against the intrusion. Speed tightened his arms around her. She allowed it. Because it was the middle of the night, and she felt very alone. Because it would be only for a moment. Because the feel and the smell of him were familiar. Because when he left, she would have to carry all the weight herself.

'I hate it,' she whispered, knowing she meant more than the case. That she hated feeling needy, that she hated always having to be tough, that she hated the contradictions, that she hated the tears that were burning her eyes and the conflicts she felt at being in the arms of her ex-husband.

'Why do you think they were cops?' he asked as softly as a lover whispering endearments.

'That's why he was meeting me – to talk about a rotten cop.'

'Maybe it was a random hate crime. Drag queens are unpopular in certain circles.'

She pulled away and gave him a look. 'Yeah, I believe in that kind of coincidence, and in Santa Claus and the Easter Bunny.'

She walked away from him to rearrange the blanket over her son, then went to the television and turned it off.

'Is this still about the dead IA guy?' Speed asked.

'Partly.' She almost laughed. 'It's about a closed murder with a convicted killer, and a closed suicide-slash-accident. Strange that someone should be beaten nearly to death over that, don't you think?'

'Who are you looking at?'

'A uniform. No one you know,' she said, then turned and looked at him with the scrutiny of a cop. He was in his stocking feet, in jeans that hung low on a flat belly, and a T-shirt that showed off an enviable physique. The cop in her resurfaced. 'Or maybe you do. You look like you've been pumping some iron lately. This guy's a serious lifter.'

'Does he come to the St Paul station house to do it?'

'You're working out at the station like a common cop?'

'It's free. I have enough obligations for my paycheck.'

'Can't imagine what they are,' Liska muttered. 'I never see any evidence of it.'

Speed opened his mouth to fire a retort, but Liska held up a hand to fend him off. R.J. was right there. Asleep, but who was to say how deeply or what sounds might penetrate his subconscious. She tried not to fight with Speed in front of the boys. She failed a lot, but she tried.

'Sorry,' she said. 'That was out of bounds. The fuse is a little short tonight, you know. What I meant to say was, I know a lot of the cops from both departments lift at that gym on University – Steele's. I thought you might have seen this guy there.'

He just stood there for a moment, working up his hurt feelings. She could see it in his face. R.J. did the same thing when he felt he'd been wronged. She could see him mentally reliving each slight, each sharp remark in order to reinforce his sense of affront.

'I said I'm sorry,' she reminded him.

'You know, I'm trying here, Nikki,' he said, the wounded martyr. 'I'm trying to help when I can with the boys. I told you I'd come up with some cash soon –'

'I know –'

'But you just have to keep at it with the digs, don't you? Why is that, Nikki? Is it that you really hate me that much? Or is it because maybe you're afraid you still have feelings for me?'

Bull's-eye, she thought. 'It's just habit.'

'Break it,' he said softly, his eyes locked on hers. He went to her, lifted a hand, and touched her cheek. 'I care about you, Nikki. I'm not afraid to say it, even if you are.'

He bent his head and touched his lips to hers, a soft kiss that lingered but didn't press for more. Liska's heart seemed to press up against the base of her throat.

'Be careful, Nikki,' he said as he stepped back.

Of the case or of you? she wanted to ask. Then she thought, *Both.*

'You make serious enemies when you turn on your own kind.'

'If this guy is what I think he is, he's not "my kind".'

That was how she had to look at it, she thought, as Speed went to the front entry, stepped into his hiking boots, and pulled on his coat. If Ogden was a killer, if he was the kind of animal who could beat a man, rape a man with a piece of pipe, then the fact that he carried a badge was the worst kind of offense.

'What do you have on him? Anything solid?'

She shook her head. 'Hunches, feelings. This drag queen was supposed to have something to fill me in. I think the cop's a juicer. If nothing else, maybe I can give him to the narcs,' she said, giving him a lopsided excuse for a smile as she went to the door.

'If the guy's doing steroids, his temper will be unpredictable,' he said. 'He's dangerous.'

'That's not exactly news to me. Anyway, thanks for watching the boys. And thanks for caring.'

'Thanks isn't what I'm after,' he said, catching her off guard. She barely had time to register the look in his eyes before his arms were around her and his mouth was on hers. Not soft this time. Hot, hungry, demanding. Her lips felt bruised when he pulled away.

He was out the door the next moment. She listened to the slam of a car door, the growl of a motor turning over. Only then did she touch two fingers to her lips.

'I need this like I need the plague,' she muttered.

She put a second throw over R.J., choosing not to disrupt his sleep, left the light on low, and went to bed herself, with no real hopes of sleep or dreams.

The clock was glowing 3:19 when the phone rang.

'Hello?'

The silence on the other end had the quality of a held breath. Or maybe the held breath was hers.

And then came a whisper that raised all the fine hairs on her arms. 'Let sleeping dogs lie.'

24

The photographs are lying on a narrow worktable, a cone of yellow light shining down on them from the desk lamp. The room is otherwise in darkness. The room is silent.

The photographs are in a neat row. Life exploding. Blood spray. Bone splinters. Still life. Lifeless. A study in destruction. A testimony to the fragility of the human body. Abstract. Violent. Sad and pathetic.

Too easily accomplished.

A necessary evil, but still . . . it should have been impossible. The concept should have so gone against the moral grain that execution would simply not have been possible.

Execution.

The word brings a rush of remembered emotions. Regret, loathing, relief, excitement. Fear. Fear of what had been done, of the rush of excitement in that final instant. Fear that something human, something civilized, something vulnerable could be replaced . . . or had been replaced long ago.

But then if that were true, sleep would have come easily instead of not at all.

25

Observation: an autopsy is not a good way to begin the day.

The thought rolled around in Kovac's head as he settled into his desk chair, a cup of bad coffee in hand. Liska was nowhere to be seen. The office was momentarily quiet. He had managed to slip in more or less unnoticed, and was glad for it. He needed a few minutes to reflect, to regroup. He pulled out Mike Fallon's death-scene Polaroids and spread them out on top of the paperwork he had been neglecting the last few days.

A nagging unease moved around the edges of his awareness, undefined, barely formed, a shadow. He could have called the case a slam-dunk suicide, and it would have been over, pending the paperwork from the ME. Except for that feeling, and the fact that Neil Fallon was starting to show as many rotten layers as a bad onion.

Kovac let his gaze wash over the pictures almost without focusing, hoping to see something he'd been missing. At the same time, hoping he would see nothing. The idea that Iron Mike had chosen to check himself out was definitely preferable to the alternative.

Viewed that way, he could almost think of the photographs as abstract art instead of pictures of a man he had known for twenty years. It was certainly easier to look at the pictures than it had been to stand in on the autopsy and see a personal acquaintance sliced and diced.

Maggie Stone, the Hennepin County ME, had performed the autopsy herself. Despite such eccentricities as carrying concealed weapons and changing hair color every six months, Stone was the best. When she said it was so, it was so. Kovac had known her for years. They had the kind of rapport that allowed him to ask for favors, such as standing in on an old friend's autopsy at the crack of dawn. Stone hadn't blinked an eye. To someone who spent her life cutting open the dead to extract their internal organs and their secrets, nothing much came as a shock.

And so Kovac had stood there in the autopsy suite, just out of the way as Stone and her assistant, Lars, moved around the stainless steel table, doing their thing. A hell of a way to kick off the morning.

Liska came into the cubicle looking grim, no color in her cheeks, despite the fact she had come in from outside, where the temperature was struggling toward the mid-teens. She said nothing as she put her purse in a drawer and slipped out of her coat.

'How's your snitch?'

'Looks like he'll live. Sort of. I just came from the hospital.'

'Is he conscious?'

'No. But he hasn't curled up like a fetus, so they're hopeful there's no serious brain injury. Broken bones will heal, and hey, who would mind having a colostomy, really?' she said sarcastically. 'And looking like the Elephant Man? A minor trade-off for not biting the big dirt sandwich.'

'You didn't do it to him, Tinks,' Kovac said evenly.

Liska didn't meet his eyes. 'I know. I'm dealing with it. I am. It's just that seeing him again . . .' She took a deep breath and let it go. 'If I had gotten there on time . . .'

'Feeling guilty won't change anything, kiddo. He made his own choices, and you did the best you could.'

She nodded. 'It's just frustrating, that's all. But I'll handle it.'

'I know you will. And you know I'm here when you need me.'

She looked at him with fondness and appreciation and a sheen of tears in her eyes. 'Thanks.'

'That's what partners do. We back each other up.'

'Don't make me cry, Kovac,' she said with a phony scowl. 'I'll have to hurt you.'

'Careful,' he warned. 'I might like it. I'm a lonely guy.' He paused. 'So, what's the word on the case? Are you in?'

'I have to talk to Leonard,' she said, and made a face. 'Ibsen was my informant. I was on the scene. I'm the one who got the call to leave it alone.'

'That call says dumb and dumber all over it. If it was a random assault, you never would have gotten a call after the fact.'

Liska agreed. 'Dumb as dirt. Now I've got something I can take to IA and use to get access to the files on the Curtis investigation. Why would anyone warn me off a closed case unless there was a damn good reason to open it back up?'

'Anything on the caller ID?'

'The number came back to a pay phone on the backside of nothing. So Deep Throat gets credit for having a couple of brain cells. I have no hope for witnesses of the call being placed.'

'And Ogden and Rubel – their alibi holds up?'

Liska made a sound of contempt. 'What alibi? They were shooting pool in Rubel's basement. And guess who was with them? Cal Springer.'

'That's cozy.'

'He'd probably swear they'd all been on the moon at the time if that was what the other two said, he's such a chickenshit. They must have pictures of him doing a goat,' Liska said with disgust. 'Anyway, Castleton was up for Ibsen's assault. He and the shift supervisor both said I'm welcome as second if Leonard clears it.'

'Leonard's gonna have your ass for digging around in IA business.'

Liska shrugged. 'Can I help it if the guy would only talk to me? According to what I've heard, the rest of the department had tuned him out. Nobody wanted to hear about his AIDS conspiracy theories.'

'Who has AIDS?'

'Eric Curtis was HIV-positive. Puts a new wrinkle into it, huh? What homophobe would beat a gay man to death and run the risk of coming into contact with contaminated blood?'

Kovac frowned, recalling his visit with the man credited with the Curtis homicide. 'Twenty says Verma has it.'

'But if Verma did it, then who's warning me off? He's in jail.'

They stared at each other for a moment, Kovac swiveling his chair.

'I still like Ogden for that,' he said.

'Me too. That's the way I'm playing it.'

'Be careful.'

She nodded. 'How'd Mike's autopsy go?'

'No big revelations so far. Nothing under his fingernails but dirt. He had some bruising on the back of his hands, but not conclusively defense wounds. The skin wasn't freshly broken, and we know he had taken a fall recently, which could explain any marks. For that matter, Stone couldn't swear the discoloration was genuine bruising. There was a lot of lividity in the hands because of the position of the body.'

'What about gunpowder residue?'

'Both hands. Doesn't mean somebody didn't force him to put the gun in his mouth, but we can't prove someone did either.'

'So we're nowhere with that,' Liska said. 'Stone will rule it a suicide.'

'She won't do anything till all the lab work comes back, and she promised me everything is backed up – to say nothing of the fact that paperwork regularly gets *mislaid*, if you know what I mean.'

Liska grinned. 'I think Doc Stone wouldn't mind getting *mislaid* by you, if you know what I mean.'

Kovac felt heat rise in his cheeks. In his mind's eye he flashed on Amanda Savard, not Maggie Stone. The look in her eyes when he'd cupped her chin in his hand: vulnerability. He forced a scowl. 'I'm not going to bed with any woman who dissects people for a living. Anyway, she'll buy us a little time, but we could do with a miracle about now. I also asked her to go back and look over Andy Fallon's autopsy. In case Upshaw doesn't know his ass.'

'Need a miracle?' Elwood asked, walking over to the cubicle. He wore a thick mohair sweater over a shirt and tie. It made him look like a woolly mammoth.

'I'd sell my soul,' Kovac said.

'That would be something of a contradiction, as miracles are associated with positive higher powers,' Elwood pointed out. 'You sell your soul to the devil.'

'You can give him my regards if you don't spill what you've got.'

'A neighbor saw Neil Fallon's truck parked in front of Mike's house late Wednesday night. One oh-nine, to be precise. I checked the reports on the neighbors the uniforms canvassed yesterday. They hit this house, but the owner was out. The cleaning lady answered the door. So I called, and bingo.'

Kovac vaulted up out of his chair.

'That's more like it.'

'They saw this truck pull up, but they didn't hear the gunshot?' Liska asked, dubious.

'An insomniac with hearing aids,' Elwood said. 'She's eighty-three. But she's sharp as a tack.'

'How's her eyesight?'

'Great with the Bausch and Lomb binoculars she keeps on her coffee table.'

'Light?'

'Floodlights on the corners of her home. She's a neighborhood watch commander. She didn't recognize the truck, but she got the license number.'

'Would she like my job after Leonard fires me?'

'Did she see him leave?' Kovac asked.

'One thirty-two.'

'That's earlier than the estimated TOD, but I'll take it.'

Kovac scooped the Mike Fallon Polaroids into a drawer and, looking into his blank computer monitor, tried to straighten his tie.

'Have Neil Fallon picked up for questioning,' he said to Elwood. 'I'll break the news to Leonard.'

'What the hell is this about?' Neil Fallon demanded.

A pair of uniforms had pulled him out of his shop to bring him in. His filthy coveralls looked like the same ones he wore the day Kovac had told him about his brother. His hands were dark with dirt and grease.

'Jesus Christ, my brother and my father are dead and – and – you drag me down here like a fucking criminal!' Fallon ranted as he paced hard in the tight confines of the interview room. The same room where Jamal Jackson had cracked Kovac in the head. 'No explanation. No apology –'

'You *are* a fucking criminal,' Kovac said, matter-of-fact. 'We know about the assault conviction, Neil. Did you think we wouldn't check? Now, how about you give *me* an explanation and an apology?'

He stood with his arms crossed and his back against the wall beside the two-way mirror, watching Fallon's reaction. Liska stood opposite him, against the other wall. Elwood had the door. No one availed themselves of the chairs at the friendly little round table. The red light glowed on the video camera.

Fallon glared at him. 'That was a long time ago, and it was bullshit besides. It was an accident.'

'You accidentally beat some guy into a coma in a bar fight?' Liska said. 'How does that work?'

'There was a fight. He fell and hit his head.'

Kovac looked over at Elwood. 'Isn't that what Cain said about Abel?'

'I believe so.'

'How about you apologize for lying to me yesterday, Neil?' Kovac said. 'How about you explain to me what you were doing at your father's house at one A.M. the same morning he died?'

Fallon ran out of gas abruptly. He tried to hold on to some of the anger in his expression. Beneath it was a layer of confusion, then suspicion, then fear. 'What are you talking about? I-I don't know what you're talking about.'

'Save it,' Liska advised. 'A neighbor of your father's put your truck in his driveway at one A.M.'

'You told me yesterday the last time you spoke with him was on the phone that night.' Kovac paused.

Fallon's eyes darted around the room as if he might see an explanation somewhere.

'Why would you lie to me like that, Neil? Were you embarrassed you couldn't convince your old man to fork over the money you need to pay off your ex? If that's what you talked about in the twenty-three-minute phone call placed from your bar at eleven oh-seven P.M.'

Fallon sucked in a short breath and then another, like an asthmatic on the verge of an attack. He rubbed the side of his neck with his thick, filthy hand.

Kovac shifted his weight lazily. 'You're getting that "oh, shit" look, Neil. Don't you think so, Tinks?'

'Oh, shit,' she said. 'It's sphincter spasm time, Neil.'

'Did you think I wouldn't call the phone company and request the local usage records on your phone?' Kovac asked. 'You must think I'm pretty fucking stupid, Neil.'

'Why would you do that?' Fallon asked, nervous. 'I'm not a suspect for anything. Jesus, my father just killed himself—'

'And I'm sick of hearing you remind me. I'm the one found him with his head blown half off. You think you need to keep reminding me of that? That's not an effective strategy, Neil.

'Someone dies a violent death like Mike did, it gets investigated,' Kovac said. 'You know the first people who get looked at? Family. 'Cause no one's got better motive to croak a person than a relative. You told me yourself: You hated Mike. Add to that the fact that you need money to pay off your soon-to-be ex, and that Mike wouldn't give it to you. That's called *motive*.'

The fear began to rise to the surface. Fallon's movements became jerky. Sweat misted his upper lip. He moved backward toward the corner with the built-in bookcase. All the shelves had been removed. 'But he was my old man. I wouldn't do that to him. He was my father.'

'And he spent thirty-some years telling you you weren't as good as your fag brother. That's what we call a *festering wound*.'

'He was a bastard,' Fallon declared. 'I won't say otherwise, but I didn't kill him. As for that bitch Cheryl, it's none of her goddamn business where I get the money. I'll pay her off.'

'Or you'll lose the business you've busted your hump for,' Liska said. 'Hell hath no fury like a bitter, vindictive woman. I should know, I am one.'

'I spoke with your ex,' Kovac said. 'She sounded like she's losing patience, ready to put the squeeze on you. Did you ask your brother for the money?'

He shook his head as if he'd taken a sharp smack in the ear, incredulous at this sudden downturn in his life. He looked from Liska to Kovac. 'You gonna say I killed him too?'

'We're not saying you killed anybody, Neil. We're just asking you questions pertinent to our case, that's all. That and pointing out how things look from the police perspective.'

'Stick your perspective up your ass, Kovac. Andy's not your case. That's over. Dead and buried. Ashes to ashes and dust to dust. The brass signed off.'

Kovac arched a brow. 'And you're trying to rub my face in that for what reason?'

'I'm just saying it's over.'

'But see, we have to look at an established pattern of behavior here, Neil. One member of the family offs himself, that's one thing. Two in a week? That's something else. You hated them both. You're going through a rough time emotionally and financially. We call those factors *precipitating stressors*. Stressors that might be enough to push a guy over the line. You have a record of violent behavior –'

'I didn't kill anybody.'

'What were you doing at Mike's house at that time of night?'

'I went to check on him,' Fallon said, his gaze sliding away. Absently, he touched his face just below the bruise on the crest of his cheek. 'We'd talked earlier. I didn't like the way he sounded.'

'The way he sounded or what he had to say?' Kovac asked. 'We know you'd been drinking. You told me so. You told me you were tanked enough to mix it up with a customer, the guy you made for a cop. Did your old man say something to piss you off?'

'It wasn't like that.'

'How wasn't it like that? You're gonna try to tell me now your family was like something out of *Ozzie and Harriet*?'

'No, but –'

'You told me Mike was always chewing your ass. How was this different? What did you talk about?'

'I told you yesterday – what time he wanted to be at the funeral home.'

'Yeah, you told me yesterday. Why didn't you tell me then you hadn't liked the way he sounded? You didn't say anything about having been concerned. In fact, if memory serves, you called him an old prick. Why didn't you tell me you'd been to the house to check on him?'

Fallon turned around in a slow circle, left hand massaging his forehead, right hand on his hip. 'He killed himself after I left,' he said, lowering his voice. 'I didn't do a very good job seeing to his needs, did I? His only living son . . .'

'What did he need? What did he say?'

Kovac waited and watched as Neil Fallon paced his little circle. His bull shoulders curled in as if he were fighting a pain in his stomach. His face was flushed. He held a shallow breath, then puffed it out, held it, puffed it out. He dug into the pocket of his coveralls and came out with a pack of Marlboros.

'Sorry, Mr Fallon,' Elwood said. 'We keep a smoke-free environment.'

Fallon glared at him and shook one out of the pack. 'So throw me out.'

Kovac moved toward him slowly. 'I don't think that conversation was about what Mike needed, Neil,' he said softly, shifting gears. 'I think it was more likely about what you need. I think you were drunk and pissed off when you called him, and you argued about the cash you need. And after that conversation, you got angrier and angrier, thinking about what you need and how your old man wouldn't give it to you, how he doted on Andy and shit all over you. And you got so mad, you got in your truck and you went to give it to him in his face.'

'He was half drunk, half wasted on pills,' Fallon muttered. 'I might as well have been talking to a turnip. He didn't give a shit what I had to say about anything. He never did.'

'He wouldn't give you the money.'

He shook his head and laughed. 'He wouldn't listen to the question. All he wanted to talk about was Andy. How much he loved Andy. How Andy let him down. How Andy couldn't let sleeping dogs lie.'

Kovac looked at Liska, who had straightened abruptly.

'He used those words?' she asked. ' "Let sleeping dogs lie"? Why would he say that?'

'I don't know,' he snapped. 'Because of Andy coming out of the closet, I suppose. If he'd kept it to himself he was queer, then the old man wouldn't have had to deal with it. "After all these years," he kept saying. Like it wasn't fair telling him now. Like either he should have told when he was ten or waited for the old man to die. Jesus.'

'That must have made you crazy,' Kovac said. 'You'd had a few. You'd mixed it up with that customer. You're there in the flesh and Andy's dead, but he's going on about Andy this and Andy that.'

'That's what I said to him. "Andy's dead. Can we bury him and move on?" '

He took a pull on his cigarette and blew the smoke out hard. His face had turned a deep red. He squinted to better picture the memory . . . or to keep tears at bay. He stared at the two-way mirror, not seeing it. 'I got right down in his face and I screamed at him – "Andy was a butt-fucking fag and I'm glad he's dead!" '

He shouted the words past the emotions that swelled in his throat. He covered his eyes with his left hand, the cigarette smoldering between his fingers.

'What'd he do?'

Fallon was crying, the tears sliding under his hand, tortured, broken sounds cracking from his mouth.

'What'd Mike do when you said that, Neil?'

'H-he h-hit m-me.'

'And what did you do then?'

'Oh, God . . .'

'What'd you do then, Neil?' Kovac prodded gently, stepping close.

'I h-hit h-him b-back. Oh, Christ!' He sobbed and bent over, putting both hands over his face. 'And now he's dead. They're both dead! Oh, God!'

Kovac took the cigarette from him, breathing in the smoke, craving one of his own. With regret, he put it out on the table, burning a black mark in the woodgrain surface.

'Did you kill him, Neil?' he asked softly. 'Did you kill Mike?'

Fallon shook his head, hands still over his face. 'No.'

'We can test your hands for gunpowder residue,' Liska said.

'We'll do what's called a neutron activation analysis,' Kovac explained. 'It won't matter how many times you've washed your hands since. Microscopic particles become embedded in your skin from the blowback. It shows up for weeks after.'

He was bluffing, playing the card as a scare tactic. The test could only show whether the person had come in contact with barium and antimony – components of gunpowder – and a million other mixtures, natural and man-made. Practically speaking, even a positive result would have little forensic value and less validity in a courtroom. Too much time had elapsed between the incident and the test. Defense attorneys made a living at arguing that time equaled contamination of evidence. Paid forensic expert witnesses would have a field day disputing the results. But Neil Fallon probably didn't know that.

A knock sounded at the door, and Elwood moved away from it. Lieutenant Leonard stuck his head in. A constipated expression hardened his face. 'Sergeant. Can I have a word?'

'I'm kind of in the middle of something here,' Kovac said impatiently.

Leonard just looked at him, eloquent in his silence. Kovac looked back at Neil Fallon and stifled a sigh. If he was going to confess to anything, this was the time to get it: while he was emotionally weak, before he had a chance to pull up the shields and regroup, before he could utter the L word.

Kovac felt like a pitcher being taken out of the game while he was still throwing heat.

He turned to Liska. 'Guess you're the closer,' he said under his breath.

'Sergeant . . .' Leonard said.

Kovac stepped out the door and followed him into the next room, where Leonard had been watching through the glass. The room was dark. A theater with a window for a movie screen. Ace Wyatt stood at the window with his arms crossed, looking through the murky pane at Neil Fallon. Wyatt gave Kovac the profile for another few seconds, then the heavy-things-on-my-mind look. It was the same expression plastered on billboards around the Twin Cities advertising his television show.

'Why are you doing this, Sam?' Wyatt asked. 'Hasn't this family suffered enough?'

'That depends. If it turns out this one killed the other two, then the answer would be no.'

'Did something happen at the autopsy I don't know about?'

'Why should you know anything about it?' Kovac challenged. 'Maggie Stone isn't in the habit of passing that kind of information around.'

Wyatt ignored the question, above the curiosity of the common street cop. 'You're treating him like you know for a fact Mike was murdered.'

'We've got good reasons,' Kovac said. He pulled the Polaroids out of his inside coat pocket and spread them out on the window ledge. 'First, he did it in the can. Lots of people do, but it had to be a hassle for him to get in there with the chair – backward, no less. Liska picked up on that. I thought maybe he wanted to leave us a neat death scene, but it makes more sense that somebody else wanted to leave us a neat death scene. When was the last time old Mike gave a shit about anyone else? The gun came out of the closet in his bedroom. Why wouldn't he just do it there? It's not like he was worried about making a mess. The place was a pigsty.

'Plus there's Neil Fallon's record, his history of problems with the old man, the fact that he lied about being at the house.'

'But the time he was there and the time of death don't line up,' Leonard pointed out.

'Other factors might have skewed the TOD,' Kovac said. 'Stone will tell you that.'

'But there wasn't anything conclusive in the autopsy to say murder, was there?' Wyatt asked.

Kovac lifted a shoulder, his eyes moving from the Polaroids to the interview room and back. Neil Fallon was sitting, both elbows on the table, his head in his hands. Liska stood beside him, leaning down.

'If something happened that night, you'd be better off telling us now, Neil,' she said quietly, like a friend. 'Get it off your chest. You're carrying a lot of weight there.'

Fallon shook his head. 'I didn't kill him.' His voice sounded tinny and far away as it came out of the television that was mounted on a wall bracket near the window. The camera in the interview room looked down on the parties involved, making them appear small and distorted.

'I hit him,' he said. 'I did that. I hit him in the face. My own father. And him in that goddamn chair. And now he's dead.'

'We'll do the neutron activation,' Kovac told Leonard and Wyatt. 'See if we can't scare something out of him.'

'And if you can't?' Leonard asked.

'Then I apologize for the inconvenience and we try something else.'

Wyatt frowned. 'Why not wait until you get word from Stone? There's no sense tormenting the man unnecessarily. Mike was one of ours –'

'And he deserves to have us do more than go through the motions,' Kovac said, his temper rising. 'You want I should just wave this one through, Ace? You want to go to Maggie Stone and try to get her to sign this one off as an accident too? Keep it all quiet so Iron Mike's legend isn't tarnished? Jesus. What if this hump capped him?'

'Kovac,' Leonard snapped.

Kovac shot him a glare. 'What? This is the homicide squad. We investigate violent deaths. Mike Fallon died a violent death, and we want to look the other way because we think he killed himself, because that could be us in the Polaroids in five years. Suicide makes too much sense to us, because we know what the job can do to a man, how it can leave him with nothing.'

'And maybe that's why you want to think it's something else, Sam,' Wyatt said. 'Because if Mike Fallon didn't kill himself, maybe you won't either.'

'No. I didn't want to see it. Liska put it in my face. I might have walked away from it. But she was right to dig at it, to look at it like any other shooting. There's too much going on here to just say what a shame.'

'I'm just thinking of showing due respect for his only remaining family,' Wyatt said. 'At least until the ME gives us something concrete.'

'Well, that's fine. And if you had any say in the matter, maybe I'd listen to you. But unless I had a dream, I was at your retirement party, Ace. What you think about my investigation doesn't amount to a hill of rat shit.'

Ace Wyatt's face went purple.

Leonard stepped up. 'You're out of line, Kovac.'

'What line is that? The ass-kissing line?' Kovac muttered as he walked away from the pair. Wyatt's toady, Gaines, stood in the back corner of the room, staring at him with the smug smirk of a classroom tattletale. Kovac gave him a look of distaste and turned back toward the window.

'If I was out of line, I'm sorry,' he said without sincerity. 'It's been a hell of a week.'

'No,' Wyatt said on a tight sigh. 'You're right, Sam. I don't have any say here. It's your investigation. If you want to punish Neil Fallon and invite a lawsuit against the department because you need some time on the shrink's couch, it's not my place to do anything about it. That *is* a shame, and I wish it didn't have to be that way.'

'Yeah, well, I wish for world peace and for the Vikings to win the Super

Bowl before I die,' Kovac said. 'You know how it is, Ace. Murder's an ugly business.'

'If that's what this is.'

'If that's what this is. And if that's what this is, then I'll nail the turd that did it. I don't care who it is.'

He went back to the window and stood watching.

'Are you right- or left-handed, Mr Fallon?' Elwood asked.

'Left.'

Elwood set a small kit of containers and cotton swabs on the table. Fallon stared at the test kit, straightening in his chair.

'We'll swab the back of your index finger and thumb with a five percent nitric acid solution,' Liska explained. 'It doesn't hurt.'

Kovac jerked his gaze to the photos of Mike Fallon's death scene.

'Jesus,' he whispered, picking up one Polaroid and then another, looking at them, then setting them aside. One after another. His pulse kicked up a notch.

'What?' Wyatt demanded.

The thing he had known was there but hadn't been able to see. He looked at the last of the photographs.

'Please hold out your left hand, Mr Fallon,' Elwood said, preparing a swab.

Neil Fallon started to reach out, his hand trembling visibly.

Kovac held the Polaroid up against the window. A split-screen image of father and son. Mike Fallon, a dead husk, bloody, half-beheaded; the gun that had killed him lying on the floor on the right side of his chair, apparently having fallen from his hand as life rushed out of him.

'Mr Fallon?'

The question mark in Elwood's voice caught Kovac's ear.

'Mr Fallon, I need you to hold out your hand.'

'No.'

Neil Fallon pushed his chair back from the table and stood up. 'No. I'm not doing it. I don't have to do it. I won't.'

'It's not a big deal, Neil,' Liska said. 'If you didn't shoot him.'

He moved back, shoving the chair aside, tipping it over. 'I didn't kill anybody. You think I did, then charge me or go fuck yourselves. I'm outta here.'

Elwood turned toward the window.

Kovac stared at the photograph as Neil Fallon stormed out of the interview room.

'Mike Fallon was left-handed,' he said, looking at Wyatt. 'Mike Fallon was murdered.'

26

'Mike Fallon was left-handed,' Kovac said. 'He's gonna kill himself, he takes the gun in his left hand.'

He pantomimed the action for the people assembled in Leonard's office: Leonard, Liska, Elwood, and Chris Logan from the county attorney's office. 'He supports the left hand with the right, sticks the barrel in his mouth, pulls the trigger. Bang! That's it. He's dead. The recoil pulls the arms away from the body. So maybe the gun is flung away from him. Or maybe it stays in the gun hand – the left hand – as that arm swings to the side. But there's no way it falls to the right side of the chair.'

'You're sure he was left-handed?' Logan asked. The prosecutor looked as if he'd been blown across the street from the government center by an arctic wind: dark hair mussed, cheeks red. The monobrow formed a dark V above his eyes.

'I'm sure,' Kovac said. 'I don't know why it didn't hit me at the scene. I guess because it made too much sense that Mike offed himself.'

'But his son would know he was left-handed.'

'Neil's left-handed too,' Kovac argued. 'So he helps the old man along to the next life, pulls back, sets the gun down with his left hand. That puts it on Mike's right.'

Logan's frown deepened. 'That's too thin. You have anything else? Fingerprints on the gun?'

'No. Mike's prints on the gun, but they're smudged. Like maybe someone had their hands on top of his.'

'*Maybe* doesn't cut it. Maybe his hands were sweating and he changed his grip repeatedly. Maybe the prints smudged as the gun slipped from his hands after he pulled the trigger.'

'A witness puts Neil Fallon at the scene that night,' Elwood said.

'And Fallon lied about it,' Kovac added.

'But it was two or three hours before the TOD, right?'

Liska took a turn. 'He didn't get along with Mike. Lots of pent-up resentment and jealousy. Mike wouldn't loan him the money he needed. Fallon admits to having argued with his father. He admits to having hit him.'

'But he doesn't admit to having killed him.'

Kovac swore. 'Is that what we have to do now? Serve every damn perp up on a platter to you guys? Dressed up like Christmas turkeys with signed confessions in their beaks?'

'You have to bring me more than what you've got. His lawyer's going to have him out of here in five minutes. You have motive, and that's it. You have opportunity that doesn't jibe with the ME's take on what happened. You've got no physical evidence, no witnesses. So the guy lied to you. Everybody lies to the cops.

'You don't have enough to hold him. I don't have enough to take to the grand jury. Put him at the scene when someone heard a gunshot. Find the old man's blood on his shoes. Something. Anything.'

'If Neil had his hands over Mike's on the gun, then he left his fingerprints on the old man's skin,' Liska pointed out.

'It'll be hard to pick up now,' Kovac said. 'Stone and Lars clipped the fingernails, examined the hands for defense wounds . . .'

'It's still worth a call,' she insisted. 'Ply her with your charm, Sam.'

Kovac rolled his eyes. 'How about a search warrant for Neil Fallon's place? So we can find the bloody shoes.'

'Type out an affidavit and go see Judge Lundquist with my blessing,' Logan said, checking his watch. 'I'm all for nailing this bastard if he killed the old man.' He shrugged into his coat. 'But the case has to stand up. Otherwise it's another cluster fuck for the press to turn their cameras on, and I'm not going to be the guy in the spotlight stomping on the burning bag of dog shit.

'I've got to go,' he announced. 'I'm due in judge's chambers.' He was out the door and gone before anyone could object.

'The downside to drawing the politically ambitious prosecutor,' Elwood said. 'He'll take only well-calculated risks he knows he can win.'

'Logan's smart,' Leonard interjected. 'The department can't take another fiasco.'

Translation: We fuck up and the brass is up Leonard's ass with a fire hose, Kovac thought. With Ace Wyatt orchestrating the charge from behind the scenes. And the shit storm would drench him and Liska. Elwood might escape, being on the periphery of the case.

'I'll get the affidavit,' Kovac said.

Liska's pager went off and she grabbed for her belt.

'Should we get a sheriff's unit to sit on Neil Fallon's place?' Elwood asked. 'They'll want in on the search. It's their jurisdiction.'

Leonard started to say something. Kovac spoke over him, ignoring the lieutenant's authority to run the case.

'Call Tippen. See what he can do for us. If anyone from the SO is coming to the party, I want it to be him.'

'Sam, I've gotta go,' Liska said. 'Ibsen's regained consciousness. Do you need me for the search?'

'No, go ahead.'

'The night-shift supervisor called me,' Leonard said loudly, bringing her up short of the door. 'I agreed you could be Castleton's second on the Ibsen assault. In case you were wondering.'

'Thanks, Lieutenant,' she said, trying unsuccessfully not to look sheepish. 'I meant to tell you. Ibsen is my informant.'

'Maybe when you get back, you can take five minutes to fill me in as to what he's been informing you about.'

'Sure, later.' She turned away from him, making big eyes at Kovac.

'Good luck, Tinks,' he said. 'I hope the guy has total recall and twenty-twenty night vision.'

'I'll be happy if he can do more than drool.'

'Regaining consciousness,' as it turned out, was something of an overstatement. Ibsen had cracked an eye partially open and moaned. The medical staff of the Hennepin County Medical Center ICU had responded by pumping him full of morphine.

He looked small and fragile and pathetic in the bed, swathed in bandages, wired to an array of machines. No one sat at his bedside praying for God to spare him. Not one person had come to see him, according to the ICU staff, even though his boss at *Boys Will Be Girls* had been notified, and had presumably told Ibsen's friends at the club. Apparently, he didn't have any. Then again, maybe the idea that he had been beaten to a pulp was enough to deter acquaintances from associating with him.

'Can you hear me, Mr Ibsen?' she asked for the third time.

He lay with his head turned toward her, eyes open but unfocused. Some people claimed conversation penetrated the brains of even the deeply comatose. Who was she to say it didn't?

'We'll get the people who did this to you,' she promised.

Cops. She felt sick to her stomach thinking it. Cops had done this damage. Cops had committed this crime, this sacrilege against the uniforms they wore. The damage didn't end with Ken Ibsen. It extended to the image of the department, to the trust the public was supposed to have in the officers they paid to protect them. She hated Ogden and Rubel for betraying that trust, and for undermining her belief in the community of cops that had been her second family most of her life.

She wasn't naive. She knew not all cops were good cops. There were plenty of assholes walking around with badges. But murder and attempted murder? At the very core of her being she still didn't want to believe it. Ken Ibsen was barely living proof that she would have to.

'They've got a hell of a lot to answer for,' she whispered, and turned away.

A uniform sat outside the door to Ibsen's room with a fishing magazine in his lap. Hess, according to the name tag. A fat guy waiting for retirement or a heart attack, whichever came first. He gave Liska the 'Oh, it's just a girl' smirk. She wanted to kick his chair. She wanted to yank the magazine out of his hands and beat him on the head with it. She could afford to do neither.

'What precinct are you out of, Hess?'

'Third.'

'Do you know why you were pulled downtown?'

He shrugged. ''Cause I was available to watch this guy.'

He didn't seem to have an interest in knowing why someone from the downtown station house didn't get the job. He was just glad for the time to bone up on his knowledge of bait and lures for walleye. Liska had insisted on people from outside, fearing that precinct camaraderie among the uniforms could put Ibsen at risk, just as it had compromised Andy Fallon's death scene with the first responding uniform letting Ogden and Rubel into the house. She didn't know that having a lump like Hess at the door might not be just as bad.

'Has Castleton been by?' she asked.

'No.'

'Anyone else from the department?'

'No.'

'Anyone besides doctors and nurses goes in that room, I'm to be notified immediately.'

'Uh-huh.'

'Someone goes in that room with him – I don't care who it is – get your ass out of that chair and watch through the glass. I could have killed him five times while you were sitting here debating jigs versus minnows.'

Hess pouted a little at that, not liking being told his job by a woman, certainly not one young enough to be his daughter.

'And see about getting a personality transplant while you're here,' Liska muttered under her breath as she walked away.

She rode the elevator down to street level, thinking of Ogden and Rubel, and how far they would go, whether they would be willing to try something here, in the hospital. That seemed too great a risk, but if they'd had something to do with the murder of Eric Curtis, if they'd had something to do with the death of Andy Fallon, if they were willing to do to another human being what had been done to Ken Ibsen, then there were no limits.

Then again, maybe they didn't want Ibsen dead. He was a more horrifying symbol alive, if what they wanted was to send a message to people not to fuck with them. She wondered why they had waited till now to do it. Why not when the investigation had been hot? Maybe Ibsen didn't worry them so much as did her interest in reopening the case. After all, no one had given Ibsen much credit to this point.

Great. That meant Ibsen was made an example for her, and she really was the reason he was now lying in a hospital bed.

They had to have been watching Ibsen to catch him in that alley, she thought. They were probably watching her. Omniscience seemed a tall order for that pair. But then, they weren't simply a pair, she reminded herself. Springer had corroborated their alibi. Dungen, the gay officers' liaison, had commented to her there was no shortage of anti-gay sentiment in the department. But how many cops would be willing to go so far as assault and murder? Or be willing to look the other way? She wished she didn't have to find out.

She left the elevator, head down, lost in thought, trying to prioritize the things she needed to do. She wanted to call Eric Curtis's last patrol partner. What was his name? Engle. And she had been appointed by Castleton to go to IA to get the scoop on Ibsen's conversations with them. She wanted to call Kovac to update him on Ibsen and get the latest on the search of Neil Fallon's property. He was probably in Judge Lundquist's chambers by now.

She dug her cell phone out of her pocket and glanced up, looking for a spot out of the traffic flow to stand. Rubel stood not ten feet down the hall, staring at her, blank-faced, out of uniform. The moment froze for a heartbeat, and she registered that he had something in his hand, then someone banged into her from behind. Rubel moved forward, sliding the mirrored shades in place with one hand and sliding the other into his coat pocket.

'What the hell are you doing here?' Liska blurted, stepping into his path.

'Flu shot.'

'Ibsen's under guard.'

'Why should I care about that? He doesn't have anything to do with me.'

'Yeah, I guess you're right,' she said. 'It was your partner he had plenty to talk about.'

Rubel shrugged. 'Ogden's clear. I guess IA didn't think the guy had anything worth hearing.'

'Somebody thought so. He'll be talking through what teeth he has left for a couple of months.'

'Like I told Castleton,' Rubel said, 'I wouldn't know anything about that. Ogden and Springer and I were playing pool in my basement.'

'That ranks right up there with "The dog ate my homework." '

'Innocent people don't live their lives having an alibi in mind,' he said, glancing over his shoulder back the way he'd come. 'If you'll excuse me, Sergeant –'

'Yeah, you and Ogden and your homophobic pals are a regular bunch of choirboys.' Liska wished she were tall enough to truly get in his face. As it was, he was looking over the top of her head.

'You know, it's not the Eric Curtises and Andy Fallons who bring shame on the department,' she said. 'It's no-neck thugs like you guys, thinking you should have free rein to crush out anyone who doesn't fit your narrow ideal of human perfection. You're the ones who ought to be run out of the department. And if I can find one shred of evidence against you, I'll burn your asses like a blowtorch.'

'That sounds like a threat, Sergeant.'

'Yeah? Call IA,' she said, and walked away down the hall Rubel had come from. She felt his eyes on her back until she turned the corner.

'Can I help you, miss?' a desk attendant asked.

Liska looked around. There was a small area of chairs with people waiting and looking miserable. The sign above the desk said LAB.

'Is this where I get my flu shot?'

'No, ma'am. Blood tests. You can get a flu shot in the ER. Go back down the hall the way you came and . . .'

Liska murmured a thank-you, tuned the woman out, and walked away.

'I'm suing the police department!' Neil Fallon ranted, his heavy boots screeching on the hard-packed snow as he paced a line back and forth to Kovac's left. He wore nothing on his head, and the wind howling across the lake had swept his hair into a frantic mess. Wild-eyed, veins bulging in his neck, he looked like a madman.

Kovac lit a cigarette, inhaled deeply, and exhaled a thin ribbon of smoke that was quickly dispatched. The windchill factor had to be fifteen below. 'You do that, Neil,' he said. 'It's a waste of money you already don't have, but hey, what do I care?'

'False arrest –'

'You're not under arrest.'

'Harassment –'

'We have a warrant. You're basically fucked here, Neil,' he said calmly.

The sun shone weak yellow light through a haze of blowing snow. The ice fishing houses that dotted the near end of the lake seemed to huddle together for warmth.

Fallon stopped, huffing and puffing, watching through the wide door as cops combed through the stuff in the cluttered workshop. The house had yielded nothing but proof that there was no woman living on the premises.

'I didn't kill anyone,' Fallon said emphatically.

Kovac watched him from the corner of his eye. 'Then you got nothing to worry about, Sport. Go have a beer.'

Tippen from the SO detectives unit stood to Kovac's right, also smoking, also staring into the cavernous mouth of the shed. The collar of his parka was up around his ears, a snowboarder's red-and-white-striped stocking cap perched on his head.

'I thought you quit smoking,' he said to Kovac.

'I did.'

'You're in serious denial, Sam.'

'Yeah, well . . . Anybody tell you you look like something out of Dr Seuss with that friggin' hat?'

'I do not like green eggs and ham, Sam I Am,' Tippen said, deadpan. 'Where's Liska?'

'You've got the hots for her.'

'I beg to differ. I was merely inquiring after a colleague.'

'Begging. Tinks'll like that. She's someplace warmer than here, working another angle.'

'Point Barrow, Alaska, is warmer than here.'

'What angle?' Fallon demanded.

'It doesn't concern you, Neil. She's got other cases.'

'I didn't kill my father.'

'So you've said.' Kovac kept his attention on the shed. Elwood was coming out, holding a pair of brown twill coveralls by the shoulders.

Fallon's whole body gave a jerk, as if he'd been given an electrical shock. 'That's not what you think.'

'And what am I gonna think, Neil?'

'I can explain that.'

'What do you think, Sam?' Elwood asked. 'It looks like blood to me.'

The coveralls were filthy. Spattered over the filth was what appeared to be dried blood and tissue.

Kovac turned to Neil Fallon. 'Here's what I think, Neil. I think you're under arrest. You have the right to remain silent. . . .'

Cal Springer had called in sick. Liska pulled into his driveway and stared at his house for a moment before turning off the engine. Cal and the missus lived in one of a multitude of cul-de-sacs in suburban Eden Prairie. The house was what realtors would call 'soft contemporary', meaning without style. Anyone coming home to this neighborhood from a night of barhopping would run the risk of walking into a neighbor's house and never knowing the difference until the alarm went off in the morning.

Still and all, it was a nice place, and Liska would have been happy to have something on a par with it. She wondered how Cal afforded it. He made good money at his grade and with the years he'd put in, but not this good. And she knew for a fact he had a daughter at St Olaf, a pricey private college down the road in Northfield. Maybe Mrs Cal brought home the big bacon. There was a thought: Cal Springer, kept man.

She went to the front door and rang the bell, then put her finger over the peephole.

'Who's there?' Springer's voice came through the door. He sounded as if the IRS was waiting to drag him away in chains for living above his means.

'Elana from Elite Escorts,' Liska called loudly. 'I'm here for your four o'clock spanking, Mr Springer!'

'Damn it, Liska!' The door swung open and Springer glared at her, then scanned for neighbors. 'Could you have a little consideration? I live here.'

'Well, duh. Why would I try to embarrass you in front of strangers?'

She ducked under Springer's arm and into the foyer, a place of colorless tile, colorless paint, and a colorless wood banister leading up the staircase to the second floor.

'Did you know you shouldn't have a staircase lead right to a door like this?' she asked. 'Your *feng shui* is thrown all to hell. All your good *chi* goes right out the door.'

'I'm sick,' Springer announced.

'That could be why. Lack of *chi*. They say that might have been what killed Bruce Lee. I read it in *In Style* magazine.' She gave him the cop once-over from head to toe, taking in the mussed hair, the gray skin, the bags sagging under bloodshot eyes. He looked like hell. 'Or that could just be what you get for running with the likes of Rubel and Ogden. Strange company for you, Cal, don't you think?'

'My friends are none of your business.'

'They are when I'm pretty sure they beat a man into a coma while you were allegedly playing pool with them.'

'They couldn't have done that,' he said, but he wasn't looking at her. 'We were at Rubel's.'

'Is that what Mrs Cal is going to tell me when I ask her?'

'She's not home.'

'She will be eventually.'

Liska tried to get in front of him. Springer kept turning. He was wearing baggy brown dress pants that had seen better days, and an ill-fitting gray St Olaf sweatshirt with sleeves shrunk halfway up his forearms. He couldn't even get dressing casually right.

'What's this got to do with you anyway?' he asked irritably.

'I'm Castleton's second on this assault. The vic was supposed to be meeting me. He had something interesting to tell me about the Curtis murder. And you know, now that someone went to all the trouble to shut him up, I'm all the more anxious to find out what it was he had to say. You know how I am with something like this, Cal. I'm like a terrier after a rat. I don't quit till I get it.'

Springer made a sound in the back of his throat and put his hand on his stomach. His gaze strayed to the open door of the half-bath that was tucked under the staircase.

'What are you doing, hanging with uniforms, Cal? You're a detective, for God's sake. And you must have – what? – fifteen years on them? No offense, but why would they want to hang with you?'

'Look, I told you – I'm not feeling well, Liska,' he said, glancing at the bathroom again. 'Could we have this conversation some other time?'

'After I drove way the hell out here?' she said, offended. 'You're some host. Nice house, though.'

She wandered to the edge of the foyer and looked into a living room with a stone fireplace and overstuffed couches. A tall Christmas tree was overly decorated with artsy-craftsy ornaments and too much tinsel. 'Taxes out here must be a killer, huh?'

'Why would you care?' Springer asked, exasperated.

'I wouldn't. I couldn't afford a place like this. How do you?'

She looked right at him, catching him unguarded for a second, seeing something bleak in his eyes. It struck her very clearly at that moment that Cal Springer was probably always playing catch-up in one way or another, and probably always falling a little short of expectations.

The sound of the garage door opening caught his attention and he looked a little sicker than he had a moment ago.

'That's my wife. Home from work.'

'Yeah? What's she do? Brain surgery? Oh, silly me,' Liska said. 'If she was a brain surgeon, she would have done something about your lack of good sense.'

'She's a teacher,' Springer said, hand worrying his belly.

'Oh, well, that explains the extravagant lifestyle. Those schoolteachers just rake in the dough.'

'We do well enough between us,' Springer said defensively.

Well enough to be up to his ass in debt, Liska thought. 'But a promotion wouldn't hurt, huh? 'Course, after the fuckup on Curtis, that's looking pretty dim. So you think to run for delegate and show the brass maybe you're management material. Right?'

'Calvin? I'm home.' The soft, sweet voice came from the kitchen. 'I got the Imodium.'

'We're in here, Patsy.'

'We?'

There was a rustle of grocery bags being set down, then a moment later Mrs Cal came into the foyer, looking like a stereotype of a middle-aged schoolteacher. A little plump, a little frumpy, big glasses, mousy hair.

'Nikki Liska, Mrs Springer.' Liska held her hand out.

'From work,' Cal specified.

'I think we met at a function once,' Liska said.

Mrs Cal looked confused. Or maybe apprehensive. 'Did you come out to check on Calvin? His stomach has just been a mess.'

'Yeah, well, actually, I had to ask him a couple of questions.'

Springer had moved behind his wife. His flat face looked made of wax. His focus seemed to be on some other dimension, one where he could see his life crumbling like so much old cheese.

Mrs Cal's brows knitted. 'Questions about what?'

'Do you know where Cal was last night around eleven, eleven-thirty?'

Mrs Cal's eyes filled with tears behind the too-big glasses. She glanced over her shoulder at her husband. 'What's this about?'

'Just answer her, Patsy,' Springer said impatiently. 'It's nothing.'

Liska waited, a weight in her chest, thinking of her own mother when IA had come to the house and asked questions. She knew that feeling of vulnerability; that sense of betrayal, of being turned on by your own kind.

'Calvin was out last night,' Patsy Springer said softly. 'With friends.'

Behind her, Springer rubbed a hand over his face and tried to stifle a sigh.

'No,' Liska said, her eyes on him. 'Those people Cal claims he was out with? They're not his friends, Mrs Springer. I hope for his sake you just told me a lie.'

'That's enough, Liska,' Springer said, stepping between them. 'You can't come into my home and call my wife a liar.'

Liska held her ground, took her gloves out of her coat pocket, and pulled them on, one and then the other.

'You weren't listening, Cal,' she said quietly. 'Get out in front of this before you get caught in the wheels. Nothing they've got on you is as bad as what they've done.'

'What's she talking about, Calvin?' There was fear in Mrs Cal's voice now.

Springer glared at Liska. 'Leave my house.'

Liska nodded, taking a final glance at the too-nice house, and a final look at Cal Springer, a man being eaten alive from the inside out.

'Think about it, Calvin,' she said. 'You know what they did to him. You probably know more than that. They wear the same badge you and I do, and that's just wrong. Be a man and stop them.'

Springer looked away, hand pressed to his belly, sweat misting his pale, ashen skin. He said nothing.

Liska walked out into the cold of the fading afternoon, got into the car, and headed east for Minneapolis, wanting nothing more than to be in her modest home with her sons.

27

'What are the odds that blood is Iron Mike's?' Tippen asked over a glass of beer.

They sat in Patrick's with the diehards who always gathered after first shift, and the Friday night get-loose-once-a-week bunch.

'Slim to none,' Kovac said. He took a handful of party mix from the bowl on the table and sorted out the peanuts and pretzels. He had long suspected the hard things masquerading as corn chips were, in fact, toenail clippings. 'He had to be in front of the old man when the gun went off. The mess went in the other direction. I think the blood on the coveralls is just what Neil Fallon says it's from – gutting fish. But that doesn't mean he didn't kill the old man. And now we've got him sitting in jail, where he can sweat and fret and decide to spill the story.'

'Being the weekend, we won't get lab results on the blood until Tuesday or Wednesday,' Elwood interjected. 'If he's got something to tell, I believe he'll let it go by Sunday night.'

'Confession on the Sabbath.' Tippen nodded with the wisdom of experience. 'Very symbolic.'

'Very Catholic,' Kovac corrected. 'That's how he was raised. Neil Fallon's no hard-case killer. If he did the old man, he won't be able to live with the guilt for long.'

'I don't know, Sam,' Tippen said. 'Don't we all harbor guilt for something? We carry it around our whole lives like ballast. Something to weigh us down and keep us from reaching for true happiness. It reminds us we're not worthy, gives us an excuse to underachieve.'

'Most of us didn't clip our own fathers. That kind of guilt rolls out,' Kovac said. 'Eventually.'

He rose from the booth, wishing he didn't have to.

'Where are you going?' Tippen demanded. 'It's your turn to buy.'

Kovac dug out his wallet and dropped some bills on the table. 'To see if I can't hasten the process along for someone.'

Someone down the block from Steve Pierce was having a Christmas party. Music and conversation and laughter escaped the town house as a fresh batch of guests arrived. Kovac leaned back against his car for a moment and watched as he finished his cigarette, then dropped the butt in the gutter and went to the door.

Lights shone in the windows of Pierce's duplex. His Lexus was in the drive. He might have walked down to the neighbor's party, but Kovac doubted it. Steve Pierce wouldn't join in the holiday festivities this year. It was damn hard to be merry and bright with the weight of loss and grief and guilt hanging around your neck. Kovac's hope was that the fiancée would be absent, leaving Pierce alone and vulnerable.

'Kick 'em when they're down,' he muttered, and rang the bell.

Time passed, and he rang it again. More guests arrived down the block. One of them, a guy wearing a red muffler, ran into the yard, threw an arm around a snowman, and began to sing 'Holly Jolly Christmas'.

'Jesus, you again,' Pierce muttered as he pulled the door open. 'Have you ever heard of a telephone?'

'I prefer that personal touch, Steve. Shows how much I care.'

Pierce looked worse than he had the night after he'd found Andy Fallon's body. He was wearing the same clothes. He stank of cigarettes and scotch and sweat – the kind of sweat from emotional upset. The smell of it was different from the smell of physical work, more sour and sharp. He had a short glass half-full of scotch in one hand and a cigarette hanging from his lip. He looked as if he hadn't shaved since the funeral.

'You care to throw my ass in jail,' he said.

'Only if you've committed a crime.'

Pierce laughed. He was close to drunk, but he probably wouldn't allow himself to cross over, to deaden the pain completely. Kovac suspected he wanted to hurt, and the scotch allowed him to maintain it at a tolerable level.

'Neil Fallon's in jail,' Kovac said. 'It looks like he might have killed the old man. I'd like to hear your take on that.'

'Well.' Pierce raised his glass. 'That calls for a toast. Come on in, Sergeant,' he invited as he walked away from the open door.

Kovac followed. 'A toast that Neil's in jail or that Mike's dead?'

'Two for one. They deserved each other.'

They went into the den with the dark blue walls. Kovac pulled the door shut behind him, to buy an extra minute or two if the girlfriend showed up.

'How well do you know Neil?'

Pierce took another glass from the small cupboard above the bar and splashed in some of the Macallan, then topped off his own glass.

'Well enough to know he's a thug. Angry, jealous, petty, mean. A chip off the old block.' He held the new glass out to Kovac. 'I used to tell Andy he must have gotten sent home from the hospital with the wrong family when he was a baby. I could never see how he came out of that pack of pit bulls. He was so decent, so good, so kind.'

His eyes reddened around the rims, and he went to the narrow window that looked out on the side of the house. The place next door was dark.

'He was so much better than they were,' he said, the sense of injustice and frustration thickening his voice. 'And yet he couldn't stop trying to win them over.'

Kovac sipped the scotch, realizing at first taste there was valid reason it cost fifty bucks a bottle. Molten gold might taste this smooth.

'He was his father's favorite for a long time,' he said, his eyes steady on Pierce. He eased around to the side of one of the leather armchairs for a better angle. 'I imagine it was pretty hard for him to take rejection from the old man.'

'He kept trying to make it up to him. As if he had something to be sorry for. He wanted the old man to understand something a guy like that will never grasp in a million years. I told Andy to let it go, that he couldn't change someone else's mind, but he wouldn't listen.'

'How was he going to make it up to him? What could be the trade-off?'

Pierce shrugged. 'There isn't one. That's just it. Andy thought maybe they could do something together. Write the old man's memoirs or something. He used to talk about that sometimes, that maybe if he knew more about the old man, he could understand him better, find some common ground with him. He wanted to know more about the shooting that put him in the chair, that being a defining moment in Mike's life. But the old man didn't appreciate the effort. He didn't want to talk about what happened. He didn't want to talk about his feelings. I doubt he had the right vocabulary for it. Personal enlightenment isn't high on the list for guys like Mike Fallon, or Neil.'

'And what about Neil?' Kovac asked. 'He claims it didn't have any impact on him when Andy came out.'

Pierce laughed. 'Sure. Smug asshole. He hated Andy already. He thought being the straight one gave him an advantage with the old man. He wasn't such a black sheep anymore. Homosexuality trumps being a felon in the redneck scheme of things.'

'Did Andy see much of him?'

'He tried to do macho, brotherly things with Neil from time to time. Hunting, fishing, that kind of thing. A complete waste of time. Neil didn't want to understand Andy or like Andy. Neil didn't want anything from Andy but money.'

'He'd asked Andy for money?'

'Sure. First he put it to him as an investment opportunity. I told Andy to forget it. Give Neil the money if he didn't care if he ever saw it again. As an investment? What a crock. Might as well flush the money down the john.'

'What did Andy do?'

'Put him off. Kept saying maybe later, hoping Neil would take the hint.' He drank some more of the scotch and muttered, 'Investment opportunity.'

'Did they ever fight, that you knew of?'

Pierce shook his head. He sucked the cigarette down to the filter and put the butt out against a corner of the windowpane. 'No. Andy wouldn't fight with him. He felt too guilty about being better than the average Fallon. Why? Do you think Neil killed him?'

'That door's still open.'

'I don't see it. Neil's not that clever. You would have caught him by now.'

'We have,' Kovac reminded him.

'Still . . . you know what I mean.' He went back to the bar and freshened his drink for the umpteenth time. 'Neil's the messy type, don't you think? Shooting, stabbing, blood and gore, devastation at the scene, fingerprints everywhere.'

'Maybe so.'

'He sure as hell wouldn't be sorry. Christ, he probably couldn't *spell* sorry. He's the one who should have died,' Pierce said bitterly, and drank more of the scotch, stirring up his anger, pouring fuel on the flames. 'Worthless excuse for a human being. It doesn't make sense that someone as good as Andy –'

Tears rushed up on him like a flash flood, and he choked on them and fought against them, and lost. He swore and threw his drink. The glass shattered against the bar top, spraying the immediate area with liquor and shards of crystal.

'God!' he cried, covering his head with his arms, as if fending off the blows of a higher power punishing him for his sins. He staggered from side to side, sobbing; dry, raw sounds tearing at his throat. 'Oh, God!'

Kovac waited, let him feel his pain, gave him time to look the demon in the face.

After a time, he said, 'You loved him.'

It sounded strange saying it to a man. But as he witnessed the depth of Steve Pierce's pain, he thought he should be so lucky to have another human being – male or female – care that deeply about him. Then again, maybe all he was seeing was guilt.

'Yes,' Pierce admitted in a tortured whisper.

Kovac put a hand on his shoulder, and Pierce shrank away.

'You had a relationship with him.'

'He wanted me to admit it, to come out. But I couldn't. People don't understand. They don't. Even when they say they do, they don't. I've seen it. I know what's said behind the back. The jokes, the snickering, the lack of respect. I know what happens. My career . . . everything I've worked for . . . I – I –' He choked himself off, as if the argument wasn't convincing even to his own ears. He sank down in one of the leather chairs, his face in his hands. 'He didn't understand. I couldn't . . .'

Kovac set his own drink aside. 'Were you there, Steve? The night Andy died?'

He shook his head and kept on shaking it, wagging it back and forth as he tried to collect himself.

'No,' he said at last. 'I told you, I saw him Friday night. Jocelyn's girlfriends had a wedding shower for her. I hadn't seen him in a month. We had fought about his coming out, and . . . We hadn't been together in a long time. Hadn't even spoken.'

'Was he seeing someone else?'

'I don't know. Maybe. I saw him at a bar one night with someone, but I don't know if there was anything to it.'

'Did you know him? This other guy?'

'No.'

'What'd he look like?'

'Like an actor. Dark hair, great smile. I don't know that they were really together.'

'What happened when you went to see him Friday night?'

'We fought again. He wanted me to tell Joss the truth.'

'You got angry.'

'Frustrated.'

'How long had you and Andy been involved?'

He made a vague motion with one hand. 'Off and on since college. At first, I thought it was just . . . experimentation . . . curiosity. But I kept . . . needing . . . and living this other life . . . and I couldn't see a way out of it. I'm engaged to Douglas Daring's daughter, for God's sake. We're getting married in a month. How could I . . . ?'

'You'd had that argument before.'

'Fifty times. We'd have that fight, break it off for a while, get back together, ignore the issue, he'd get depressed . . .'

He let the sentence trail off and sat there, slumped over like an old man, his expression bleak with pain and regret.

'Would he have told Jocelyn?' Kovac asked.

'No. He wasn't like that. It was up to me, my responsibility. And I wouldn't accept it.'

'Was he angry?'

'He was hurt,' he said, then fell silent for a moment. 'I don't want to believe he might have killed himself, because I don't want to believe I might have caused him to.'

His eyes filled again, and he closed them tight, squeezing the tears out between the lashes.

'But I'm afraid I did,' he whispered. 'I couldn't be man enough to admit what I am, and now maybe the person I loved most in the world is dead because of that. Then I *did* kill him. I loved him and I killed him.'

Silence hung between them for a moment, only the murmur of the stereo in the distant background. One of those soft pseudo-jazz stations that seem to play the same song continuously; same beat, same wimpy saxophone, same lazy trumpet. Kovac sighed and thought about what to do next. Nothing, he guessed. There was no point in pushing Pierce further. This was his secret, the weight around his neck. His punishment was to carry it around for the rest of his life.

'Will you tell Jocelyn?' Kovac asked.

'No.'

'That's a hell of a big lie to live, Steve.'

'It doesn't matter.'

'Maybe not to you, but don't you think she deserves something more?'

'I'll be a good husband, a good father, even. We make a stunning couple, don't you think? That's what Joss wants – her own life-size Ken doll to dress up and take out and play make-believe with. I'm very good at make-believe. I've played it most of my life.'

'And you'll get your partnership at Daring-Landis, and everyone will live miserably ever after.'

'No one will even notice.'

'It's the American way.'

'Are you married, Kovac?'

'Twice.'

'So you're an expert.'

'On the misery part. I finally figured out it was cheaper and easier to be miserable alone.'

They were silent again for a moment.

'You should tell her, Steve. For both your sakes.'

'No.'

Kovac saw the door to the hall swing open slowly, and a ripple of dread went through him. Jocelyn Daring stood in the doorway, still in her coat. He didn't know how long she had been standing there, but by the look on her face it had been long enough. Tears and mascara striped her cheeks. All the color had drained from her lips. Pierce looked at her and said nothing. Slowly her mouth pulled back into a trembling snarl.

'You stupid son of a bitch!' She spat the words out like so many bullets, then flew across the room, shrieking like a banshee, eyes wild with fury.

Kovac caught her around the waist as she launched herself at Pierce. She screamed and flailed, fists swinging, connecting with his forehead and splitting open the cut that had begun to heal. She kicked him and twisted out of his grasp, grabbing a pewter candlestick off the end table.

'You stupid son of a bitch!' she screamed again, swinging and hitting Pierce – who hadn't moved – a glancing blow off the side of his head. 'I told you not to talk to him! I told you! I told you!'

Kovac grabbed her again from behind and struggled, dragging her backward. Her body was taut and strong, and she was tall, and her fury was superhuman.

Pierce did nothing to defend himself. Blood ran in bright rivulets down the side of his head. He wiped at it with his fingertips and smeared some onto his cheek.

'I loved you! I loved you!' Jocelyn shouted, nearly incoherent. 'Why did you have to tell? I could have made it right.'

The fury ran out of her then, and she collapsed, sobbing. Kovac maneuvered her to a chair and eased her down into it. Body limp, she slipped down to the floor and curled into a ball, pounding her fist against the chair. 'I could have made it right. I could have . . .'

Kovac leaned down and pried the candlestick from her hand. Blood dripped from his own wound onto her sweater. Baby-blue cashmere.

'I think you're right, Sergeant,' Pierce said dimly, staring at his bloody hand. 'It probably is easier to be miserable alone.'

The neighbor had managed to find three square feet of yard not already occupied, and had added a new display to the montage: a lighted scoreboard counting down the hours and minutes to Santa's arrival.

Kovac stared at it for an indeterminate length of time, mesmerized by the ever-changing numbers, and wondered how bad the suspension would be if he were to be arrested for destruction of private property. How many glowing, garish icons to the overcommercialization of the holiday could he destroy before the damage toll took him over the line from petty misdemeanor to something worse? Could he plead a felony down and still keep his badge?

In the end, he didn't have the energy for vandalism, and simply went into his house. It was as empty as before, except for the stench of garbage that should have been left at the curb that morning.

Home sweet home.

He took off his coat, threw it over the back of the couch, and went into the half-bath off the hall to wash up and assess the damage. The gash above his left eye was angry-looking, crusted and smeared with dried blood. He should have gone to the ER to get it repaired, but he hadn't. He dabbed at it with a washcloth, wincing, then gave up and washed his hands and took three Tylenol.

In the kitchen, he opened the fridge, pulled out a half-eaten meatball sandwich, and sniffed at it. Better than the garbage . . .

Sandwich in hand, he leaned back against the counter and listened to the silence, the scene at Pierce's house replaying through his head. Jocelyn Daring, insane with rage and pain and jealousy, flying across the room.

I told you not to talk to him. . . . Why did you have to tell? . . . I loved you. I loved you.

Why did you have to tell? Strange wording, he thought. As if Pierce's homosexuality was a secret she had already known, even though Pierce hadn't told her and had had no intention of telling her.

He thought back to the night he'd first met her, the way she behaved toward Pierce – possessive, protective; the carefully blank look in her eyes when he'd asked her if she'd known Andy Fallon.

That's what Joss wants – her own life-size Ken doll to dress up and take out and play make-believe with. . . .

She was amazingly strong. Even now, Kovac's biceps ached from the effort to restrain her.

Pensive, he raised the sandwich to take an absent bite. His pager went off before he could taste-test for salmonella. The display showed Liska's cell phone number. He dialed her back and waited.

She answered the phone: 'House of Pain. We deliver.'

'Yeah. I'll take another smack in the head, and a kick in the teeth for dessert.'

'Sorry. No time for fun. But this'll make your day. Deene Combs just reached out and touched someone. One of Chamiqua Jones's kids is dead.'

28

'What happened to you?' Liska asked, frowning at Kovac as he climbed out of the car.

'A woman scorned.'

'You don't have a woman to scorn.'

'Why should that limit my chances at suffering?' he asked, taking in the scene.

Chamiqua Jones's neighborhood was shabby, the houses sagging old monsters built in the early part of the century and later cut up into apartments. But it was by no means a slum. The families who lived here were poor, but for the most part did their best to look out for one another. The gangs and the crack dealers were far worse enemies to them than to white suburbia.

And this was why, Kovac thought as they walked toward the gathering of cops and crime scene techs.

A small body lay in the street near a pile of snow. The body had been covered. The mound of dirty snow was splashed with blood. Chamiqua Jones stood off to one side, wailing, screaming, rocking, friends and neighbors trying to comfort and restrain her.

'The kids were playing on the snowbank,' Liska said. 'According to one of them, a car with three or four gangbangers pulled up, one stuck his head out the window and called the name Jones. When he saw which child reacted, he shot her. Caught her once in the face, two to the torso.'

'Aw, jeez.'

'Not exactly a subtle message.'

'Whose case?'

'Tom Michaels.'

At the mention of his name, Michaels looked up from a conversation with one of the uniforms, and immediately came toward them. Stocky and full of nervous energy, he wore his hair slicked straight back with a ton of goo to combat the fact that he looked about seventeen. It didn't work. He was a good cop.

'Sam, I knew you and Liska were on the Nixon assault,' he said. 'I figured you'd want a heads-up on this.'

'Thanks, I guess,' Kovac said. 'Any ID on the shooter?'

Michaels made a face.

Answer: no. And there wouldn't be. The Jones girl was dead because her mother had been asked to testify against one of Deene Combs's thugs. The neighborhood's leaders would make an angry show of demanding justice and daring citizens to stand up and fight back, but no one would. Not after this. And who the hell could blame them?

'I told you!'

The shout turned all their heads. Chamiqua Jones stormed toward them, her focus on Kovac, her eyes full of tears and pain and anger. She thrust a gloved finger at him.

'I told you you was gonna get me killed! Look what they did! Look what they did! They killed my child! They killed my Chantal! What you gonna do for me now, Kovac?'

'I'm sorry, Chamiqua,' Kovac said, knowing how horribly inadequate the apology was.

She glared at him and at Liska. 'You're sorry? My child is dead! I told you to leave me be, but you had to keep on. Testify, Chamiqua, you said. Tell what you saw or we'll put your black ass in jail, you said. I told you what would happen. I *told* you!'

She hit Kovac in the chest with both fists as hard as she could. He let her have her shot. Then she stepped back, glaring at him because it hadn't helped.

'I hate you!' she shouted.

Kovac said nothing. Chamiqua Jones didn't want to hear how rotten he felt, or how badly he wished this hadn't happened. She wouldn't forgive him or absolve him for doing his job, for following orders. It wouldn't impress her that he had become a cop because he wanted to help people, to try to do his little part to make the world a better, safer place. Chamiqua Jones didn't give a shit about him, except to hate him.

'Ms Jones, if there's anything we can do –' Liska began.

'You've done enough,' Jones said bitterly. 'Do you have children, Detective?'

'I have two boys.'

'Then you pray to God you don't ever have to feel what I'm feeling. That's what you can do.'

She turned away and went to where her daughter's body lay. No one tried to stop her.

'It's a pisser,' Michaels said quietly, watching as Jones pulled the cover back and touched her child's bloody head. 'If people could stand up and give us thugs like Combs, this wouldn't happen. But because this kind of thing happens, nobody wants to stand up.'

'We tried to tell Leonard to back off,' Kovac said. 'Come up with some other angle to get Combs. But Sabin thought if we could nail the guy from the Nixon assault, he could turn him for Combs.'

Michaels sniffed. 'Bullshit. No banger's gonna beat a guy's head in with a tire iron, then give up his boss.'

'You know it and I know it.'

'And Chamiqua Jones pays for it,' Liska said, not able to take her eyes away from the grieving mother.

'Whatever you need from us relating to the Nixon case, just ask,' Kovac said.

'And vice versa,' Michaels said.

Kovac put a hand on Liska's shoulder as Michaels went back to work. 'Life sucks, and the night's still young,' he said. 'Come on, Tinks. I'll buy you a cup of coffee. We can cry on each other's shoulders.'

'No, thanks,' she said absently, still watching Chamiqua Jones even as they started to walk away. 'I need to get home to my boys.'

Kovac put her in her car and watched her drive away, wishing he had someone to get home to.

A terrible sense of urgency chased Liska home. A feeling of dread, of impending doom. She couldn't escape the idea that while she had been paying her respects to the mother of a dead child, something horrible had happened to her own children. She drove fast, ignoring traffic laws and speed limits, feeling almost as if Chamiqua Jones's words to her had been a curse. That was stupid, she knew, but it didn't matter.

As a homicide detective, she encountered death on a regular basis. Like most cops, she had hardened herself to it long ago. That was the necessary route to maintain sanity. But there was no immunity to the effects of seeing a dead child. There was no escaping the emotions – the anger and sadness at how brief that young life had been, at the things that child would never experience; the heavy sense of guilt that the death could have been prevented somehow, some way. Adults could look out for themselves. Oftentimes an adult victim's life choices put the person in the situation that ended his life. But children never chose to be put at risk. Children were dependent on the adults in their lives to keep them safe.

Liska felt that burden now, as she turned off Grand Avenue and spotted her home. It was still standing. That was a good start. It hadn't been burned to the ground in her absence. It didn't matter that the sitter had told her so just ten minutes prior when she'd called home on her cell phone.

She pulled in the driveway, abandoned the car, and hurried to the house, fumbling with her keys.

The boys were in their pajamas, stretched out on their bellies in front of the television, mesmerized by the video game they were playing. Liska dropped her purse, toed her shoes off, and hurried across the room to them, ignoring the sitter's greeting. She fell down on her knees between them and scooped a boy into each arm, earning howls of protest.

'Hey!'

'You ruined my chance!'

'I was winning!'

'You were not!'

'Was so!'

Liska pulled them close and breathed deep the smell of clean hair and microwave popcorn. 'I love you guys. I love you so much!'

'You're cold!' R.J. exclaimed.

Kyle gave her a speculative look. 'Do you love me enough to let me stay over at Jason's house tonight? He called and asked.'

'Tonight?' Liska said, hugging him tighter. She closed her eyes against silly, sudden tears of relief and joy. 'Not a chance, Sport. Tomorrow, maybe. Not tonight. Not tonight.'

The sitter saw herself home. Liska played with the boys until they couldn't keep their eyes open anymore, then shepherded them off to their beds and lingered at the door, watching them sleep.

Calmer, reassured they were safe and sound, she checked all the locks, then drew a bubble bath – a rare, feminine treat. The warmth penetrated muscle, easing out the tension, the anxiety, the feeling of toxicity that always lingered after working a murder scene, as if evil hung in the air. She closed her eyes and rested her head on a rolled-up towel, a steaming cup of tea on the edge of the tub. She tried to clear her mind of everything and just drift, just *be* for a few minutes. What a luxury.

When she was completely relaxed, she opened her eyes, dried her hands, and reached for the stack of mail she'd piled on the edge of the vanity. No bills. No junk mail. Just a small stack of what looked to be Christmas cards. Once again, she wasn't going to get her cards out until God knew what holiday.

There was a card from her Aunt Cici in Milwaukee. A photo card of cousin Phil the dairy farmer and his family all in matching 'Got Milk?' T-shirts. Hallmark's finest from a college friend who had otherwise lost touch so long ago she still addressed the envelope to Mr and Mrs; why did people like that bother? Was it really so much trouble to cull out the database?

The last of the envelopes was addressed only to her. Another computer label, no return address. Odd. Obviously a card. The envelope was red. She slipped the letter opener under the flap. A simple business-type card with 'Season's Greetings' on the front. Something fell from it as Liska opened the card, and she swore and grabbed the dark square as it hit the surface of the bathwater.

A Polaroid snapshot. No. Three photographs stuck together.

Photographs of her children.

Liska's blood ran cold. Goose bumps pebbled every inch of her skin. Her hands began to tremble. One photograph had been taken as the boys stood in line to get on the bus at school. The second showed them playing with a friend as the school bus drove away from the stop down the block. The third showed them walking up the sidewalk to the house. On each photograph, someone had drawn a circle around each of the boys' heads with a black marker.

Inside the card, the only message was a phone number typed in black.

Setting the card and photos aside, Liska hauled herself out of the tub, wrapped her dripping body in a towel, and grabbed the portable phone. She was shaking so badly, she misdialed the number twice. On the third try, the call went through, and she waited. A machine answered on the fourth ring, the recorded voice sending a bolt of fear straight through her.

'Hi. This is Ken. I'm out doing something *so* exciting, I can't take your call right now. . . .'

Yeah. He was lying in a bed in a surgical intensive care unit. Ken Ibsen.

29

Famous last words: *It seemed like a good idea at the time.*

Kovac rang the bell before he could change his mind. He knew the minute she looked out the peephole in the front door. He could feel her presence, could feel her scrutiny, her indecision. Finally, the door opened and she looked out at him.

'Yes, I do have a phone,' he said. 'I have several, and I do know how to use them.'

'Then why don't you?' Savard asked.

'You might have said no.'

'I *would* have said no.'

'See?'

She didn't invite him in. Her eyes narrowed as she stared at his forehead. 'Were you in a fight?'

Kovac touched his fingers to the spot, remembering that he'd never finished washing the blood off. 'An innocent casualty of someone else's war.'

'I don't understand.'

'No. Neither did I,' he said, recalling the scene at Steve Pierce's house. 'It doesn't matter.'

'Why did you come here?'

'Mike Fallon was murdered.'

Her eyes widened. 'What?'

'Someone killed him. I've got his son, Neil, sitting in the pokey now, reflecting on the cleansing power of confession.'

'My God,' Savard murmured, opening the door a little wider. 'What have you got on him?'

'Nothing, really. We did it with mirrors. If it weren't the weekend and if he had a clever lawyer, he'd be sitting in his bar by now,' he admitted. 'On the other hand, he had opportunity, motive, and a bad attitude.'

'You think he did it.'

'I think Neil is proof there should be a lifeguard at the gene pool. He's a small, mean, angry person, bitter over the fact that people don't love him in spite of himself. His father's son,' he added, an ironic twist to his mouth.

'I thought Mike Fallon was your friend.'

'I respected what Mike represented on the job. He was an old-time cop.'

He looked back out toward the street, where a car was going by slowly. A couple checking house numbers. Normal people looking for another Christmas party. They probably hadn't come to this neighborhood from a murder scene.

'Maybe I had a soft spot for him because I want someone to have a soft spot for me when I'm that old and that resentful.'

'Is that what you came here looking for?' Savard asked. 'Sympathy?'

He shrugged. 'I'd even settle for pity tonight.'

'I don't keep much of that around.'

He thought she was almost allowing herself to smile. There was something softer in her eyes than he'd seen before.

'How about scotch?'

'I don't keep that either.'

'Neither do I. I drink it,' he said.

'That's right, you're a stereotype. The tragic hero.'

'The twice-divorced, smoking, drinking workaholic. I don't know what's heroic about that. It reeks of failure to me, but maybe I have unrealistic standards.'

'Why *did* you come here, Sergeant? I don't see what the news about Mike Fallon has to do with me.'

'Apparently so you could make me stand in the cold while you chip away at my self-esteem with your blunt indifference.'

Almost-amusement to go with the almost-smile. 'Laying it on a little thick, aren't you?'

'I find subtlety is a waste of time. Especially when I've been drinking. I've already been indulging in that scotch we were talking about.'

'Drinking and driving? I guess I'd be doing a public service if I invited you in for a cup of coffee.'

'You'd be doing *me* a service. The only thing that overheats in my car is the radiator.'

Savard sighed and opened the door wider.

Kovac took advantage of the opportunity before she could change her mind. Winning the war of attrition. The house was warm and smelled of a wood fire and the aforementioned coffee. Homey. His house was cold and smelled of garbage.

'I think maybe *you're* developing a soft spot for me, Lieutenant.'

'Mmm ... in my head,' she said, and walked away.

Kovac toed off his shoes and followed her through a small formal dining room to a country kitchen. She was dressed for lounging in a loose, flowing outfit the color of sage. Like something an old-time Hollywood star would wear, he thought. Her hair tumbled around her head in soft, silver-blond waves. A very alluring picture, except that there was a stiffness in her back and neck as she moved that hinted of pain. He wondered again about her story of a fall. Obviously, there was no one living with her, no boyfriend hanging around on a Friday night.

'How are you feeling?' he asked.

'I'm fine.'

She took a stoneware mug from a cupboard and filled it from the pot simmering on the coffee machine. The room was lit softly by small yellow lights mounted under the cupboards and on the ceiling.

'I take it Neil Fallon doesn't have an alibi.'

'Not that stands up in court,' Kovac said, leaning against the island. 'People never believe anyone else was home alone in bed. They always suspect everyone in the world is having sex or committing crimes but them.'

'Milk? Sugar?'

'Black, thanks.'

'No physical evidence?'

'None I believe will hold up past the lab.'

'He didn't leave any prints on the gun?'

'No.'

'What made you decide it was murder, then? Something the ME came up with?'

'The scene. The position of the gun. It shouldn't have fallen where it did. Couldn't have, if Mike pulled the trigger.'

She handed him his coffee, sipped her own, and made a thoughtful sound. 'That's sad his life had to end that way. His own son . . . imagine . . .' she said, staring at the floor. 'I'm sorry.'

'Yeah. You know, he had a chance to make things right with Andy and he didn't take it. Then everything went to hell on a sled.' He tasted the coffee, a little surprised there was no exotic flavor to it. It was just coffee. 'Apparently, Andy wanted to do something with Mike in relation to the Thorne homicide. Write down Mike's story or something.'

'Really? Did Mike tell you that?'

'No. A friend of Andy's mentioned it. Mike didn't want to do it. I guess stewing in the memories and sharing them were two different things. Did Andy ever say anything about it to you?'

Savard set her cup aside and crossed her arms as she leaned back against the counter. 'Not that I recall. Why would he?'

'No reason. I thought he might have mentioned it in passing, you being friends with Ace Wyatt. That's all.'

'We're not friends. He's an acquaintance. We have people in common.'

'Whatever. I guess he must have dropped it, anyway,' Kovac said. 'I didn't see anything in his office relating to it. No file, no clippings or anything like that. Unless all that stuff is in the same place as his copy of the Curtis-Ogden file. The same place as his laptop. Wherever that might be.'

'What do you think he hoped to gain by looking into his father's past?'

Kovac shrugged. 'Understanding, I guess. What Mike was these last twenty years started the night of that shooting. Or maybe he was just a brownnoser, trying to win the old man over by pretending interest in his father's life. You could say better than I – was Andy a kiss-ass?'

She thought about it a moment. 'He needed to please. He needed to succeed. That's why he took it so hard when the Curtis-Ogden case closed. He wanted to be the one to say it was over, not just have it end because Verma copped a plea.'

'I guess I know what that's like,' Kovac said with a sheepish smile. 'I'm not supposed to be spending time asking questions about Andy Fallon's death – or his life, for that matter – but I want to know. I want to feel satisfied. It ain't over till I say it's over. That's the way I am.'

'It makes you a good cop.'

'It makes me a pain in the ass. I once had a captain tell me that I'm paid to investigate crimes, not solve them.'

'What did you say to that?'

He laughed. 'To his face? "Yes, sir." My bank account couldn't handle a suspension. Behind his back? I called him something I shouldn't say in front of a lady.'

Savard picked up her coffee again and took a sip, looking at him from under her lashes. The almost-amusement, a shade of speculation. *Sexy*, he thought, *for a lady with a beat-up eye. Beautiful, bruises or no.*

She glanced away. 'I went over the case file, by the way. Ogden was verbally abusive to Andy several times during the investigation, but that's not unusual. He made a couple of vague threats – also not unusual. Then Verma made his deal and it was over. There were no addendums to the file after the case closed. Ogden had no reason to continue contact.'

'What about Ogden's partner? Rubel?'

'Nothing about him. I don't think that was the name of his partner at the time of the incident. I think it was Porter. Larry Porter.

'For what it's worth,' she added, 'I personally believe Ogden was dirty. I believe he planted Curtis's watch at Verma's apartment. There just wasn't any way to prove it. We'd taken it as far as we could go based on what we had.'

'And after Verma copped, you would have had the union on you for harassing Ogden. And the brass on you for pissing off the union,' Kovac said. 'You're paid to investigate, not to solve.'

'And I have to live with the idea that Andy might have killed himself in part because of that,' she said quietly.

'Maybe,' Kovac conceded. 'Or maybe he killed himself because his lover wouldn't come out of the closet. Or because he thought his father might never love him again because he *had* come out of the closet. Or maybe he didn't kill himself at all.

'See, maybe it wasn't your fault at all. But you'll let the idea hurt you anyway,' he said. 'You'll punish yourself and think of a dozen ways you might have stopped it from happening – if only you'd been quick enough, sharp enough, or able to read the future in tea leaves.'

'I guess I'm an easy read.'

'No, you're not,' he said quietly, thinking she was one of the toughest people to read he'd ever come across. So guarded, so cautious. And that made her all the more intriguing to him. He wanted to know who she really was and why she had become that person. He wanted to be allowed behind the walls.

'That's just what I'd do, that's all,' he said. 'It's what my partner would do too. I try to tell myself it's proof we haven't entirely detached from the human race. Though sometimes I think I'd be better off if I did.'

The weight of the evening rolled up against him, the emotions pressing against his own walls. He had successfully kept it at bay for a little while: the image of the street full of emergency vehicles; of the child's small body and the bloodstained snow.

He wandered to a set of French doors that looked out on a deck. A security light illuminated a wedge of backyard. The moon brightened what lay beyond, reflecting off the snow in a way that gave the landscape a blue cast. Dreamscape. Trees edged the property, keeping the neighbors from looking in.

'I lost one tonight,' he confessed. 'The child of a witness to an assault I was working. A little girl shot to death just to send a message to the neighborhood.'

'How is that your fault?'

He could see her edging closer. The filtered light from outside fell across her face, a gossamer veil that made her skin look pearly. *Softness*, he thought. Soft skin, soft hair in soft waves, lips that looked as soft as satin. He didn't try to see the walls and sharp edges; he wanted to pretend they didn't exist.

He shook his head. 'It's not. Not really. You look at a situation like that, an innocent child shot dead in the street. The shooter's probably fourteen and got the job handed to him on account of he's a juvenile, and he took it because a kill makes him with the gang. They shoot the little girl to scare people who are already on the edge of thinking life's too damn hard to care about anything but their own hide. They do it to scare the mother who didn't want to see a drug dealer getting his head beat in and wouldn't have testified anyway 'cause her first concern is to stay alive long enough to raise her children not to be sociopaths.

'You look at all that and there's plenty of blame to go around. But I'm a part of that picture too. I'm supposed to protect people, not get them killed. And I had to stand there tonight and look in that woman's face and offer an apology, like that would make it all right.'

'Blaming yourself won't make it right either,' Savard said.

She stood just to his right. She could have taken his hand in hers. He held his breath as if she were some wild creature who would bolt at his slightest movement.

'We do the best we can,' she said softly, looking inward. 'And punish ourselves for it. I've tried to make my choices with the idea that I've made those choices for the greatest good. Sometimes someone suffers in the process, but I made the decision for the right reason. That should count for something, shouldn't it?'

Kovac turned slowly to face her, a part of him still afraid she might run away. The need for reassurance was so clear in her eyes, it hurt him to see. A glimpse over the wall.

'It should,' he said. 'What is it inside us that doesn't let it?'

'I'm afraid to know,' she confessed, eyes bright with tears.

'Me too, I guess.'

She stared at him for a moment, then whispered, 'You're a good man, Sam Kovac.'

Half a smile curved his mouth. 'Would you say that again?'

'You're –'

He touched a forefinger to her lips. They felt exactly as he had imagined. 'No. My name. Say it again. Just so I can hear how it sounds.'

He moved his hand to cup her face. A single tear slid down her face, silvered by the light. The word slipped from her lips on a trembling breath. 'Sam . . .'

He bent his head and captured the word in his mouth as he touched his lips to hers. Hesitantly. Asking. Holding his own breath tight in his lungs, even as desire swept through his veins in a warm rush.

Her hands came up slowly and rested on his forearms, not to push him away but to connect. Her mouth trembled beneath his, not out of fear but out of need. Accepting. Wanting. Her tongue touched his.

The kiss went on. Time suspended. He lifted his mouth a scant inch from hers and whispered her name. He took her into his arms as carefully as if she were made of glass. When he raised his head again and looked into her eyes, she said one word:

'Stay.'

Except for the pounding of his heart, Kovac went absolutely still. 'Are you sure?'

She leaned up and touched her lips to his again. 'Stay . . . Sam . . . Please . . .'

He didn't ask again. Maybe her life was as empty as his. Maybe their souls recognized the same pain in each other. Maybe she just needed to be held, and he needed to hold, to care for. Maybe it didn't matter why.

She led him up the stairs to a bedroom that carried a ghost of her perfume in the air and on the sheets. Pieces of her lay scattered on the dresser: earrings, a watch, a black velvet hair band. The lamp on the nightstand glowed amber, the light bathing her skin as he undressed her.

He'd never seen anything so exquisite, had never been so moved by a woman's gift of herself to him.

She handed him a condom from a drawer in the nightstand; he tore open the package and offered it back to her. They didn't speak. Everything was said with a touch, with a look, a shuddering breath, a trembling sigh. She guided him to her. He entered her and thought his heart had stopped. They moved together, and it beat like a drum.

Need. Heat. Passion. Immersion. Languor. Urgency. One melded into the next and back again. The tastes of salt on skin, coffee on tongues. The feel of warm and wet, hard and soft. When she came, it was on a crescendo of hard-caught breaths and the wordless, desperate sounds of need. Release for him came like a bolt of lightning. His body jumped and jerked, and he thought he cried out but he wasn't sure.

He never stopped kissing her. Even after. Even as she fell asleep in his arms, his lips moved over hers, against her cheek, on her hair. In his heart was the fear the chance might not come again and he had to get his fill now, tonight. Then exhaustion swept over him like a blanket, and he closed his eyes and fell asleep.

When Kovac came around, he thought he'd had one hell of a dream. Then he opened his eyes.

Amanda.

She lay on her side, curled toward him, sleeping quietly. He pulled the covers up over her bare shoulder, and she sighed. The lamplight fell across her face, drawing his attention to the raw burns and bruises around her eye and cheekbone. His stomach clutched at the thought that he might have – must have – touched those places as they'd made love, and caused her pain. The idea of hurting her made him sick. If he ever found out a man had made those marks on her, he would track the guy down and beat him.

He rubbed a hand against his sternum, feeling as if he'd been kicked. Jesus, he'd slept with a lieutenant.

He'd fallen for a lieutenant.

You sure know how to pick 'em, Kovac.

What was she going to think when she opened her eyes? That she'd made a mistake? That she'd lost her mind? Would she be embarrassed or angry? He didn't know. What he did know was that what they had shared was pretty damn special and he wouldn't regret it.

He slipped from the bed carefully, pulled on his pants, and went down the hall in search of a bathroom, not wanting the sound of running water to wake Amanda. He found a guest bath with fancy towels and decorative soaps that were probably not intended for use. He used them anyway. The reflection that stared back at him in the mirror looked tough, beat-up, showing age and the effects of a life with more disappointment than fulfillment. What the hell would a woman see in that and want? he wondered.

He washed up and went back into the hall, catching the smell of burning coffee wafting up from downstairs. They'd left the pot on.

He went down to the kitchen and turned it off, pouring himself half a cup of what was left. Sipping at the coffee, he began to wander through the house, turning off lights as he passed through the rooms.

Amanda Savard had created a nice retreat for herself. The furniture looked comfortable, inviting. The colors were soothing and quiet. Odd, though, that there was nothing of her – no family photos, no snapshots of friends or of herself. A lot of framed black-and-white photographs of empty places. He remembered seeing some of those in her office, and he wondered what they meant to her. He wanted to see something that spoke about her life. But maybe that *was* what he was seeing. God knew there wasn't much evidence of who he was in his house. A stranger would have learned more about him in his cubicle at work.

In the living room, he took a poker and stabbed at the dying embers of the fire, breaking them up, pushing them apart. He closed the glass doors and went to turn out the ginger jar lamp on the end table by the sofa. A book lay on the table. Stress management.

Beyond the living room, beyond a pair of open French doors was another room with lights on and a stereo playing softly. It sounded like the same light jazz station Steve Pierce had been listening to.

Kovac went in to turn it off. Her office. Another lovely oasis of cherry furnishings and photographs of nothing. He'd seen a desk this neat once in an office supply store. That kind of fastidiousness spoke of a need for order and control. No big surprise there. The cubbyholes of the shelves above the desk held a few mementos that made him smile. A small carving of a mother tiger and her cub rolling together. A collection of colored glass paperweights that were more works of art than tools. A stress relief toy that was a little rubber creature whose eyes popped out when squeezed. A badge.

Curious, he picked up the badge and looked at it. It was an old style. One he recognized from when he had first come on the force half a million years ago. Certainly before Amanda's time, which meant it had to have belonged to someone who meant something to her.

City of Minneapolis. Badge number 1428.

The first thing he'd seen in her home that hinted at her past, and it had to do with the job. Maybe her life really was as empty as his.

He put the badge back in its place, turned off the lights and stereo, and left the room, the light falling from the second story guiding his way. He climbed the stairs, thinking of sliding back under the covers with her, feeling her warm, soft body next to his. It had been so long since he'd known that kind of comfort, he'd forgotten what it was like.

'No!'

The cry came as he was halfway up the stairs. Kovac bolted up the rest and ran for the bedroom.

'No! No!'

'Amanda!'

She sat upright in the middle of the bed, eyes wide open, arms swinging at nothing, engaged in a battle with something only she could see inside her mind.

'No! No! Stop it!'

'Amanda?'

Kovac stood beside the bed, not knowing what to do. It was an eerie sight. She appeared to be awake, but she didn't seem to see him standing there. Slowly, carefully, he eased a hand out to touch her shoulder.

'Amanda? Honey, wake up.'

She jerked at his touch, shying toward the other side of the bed, wild-eyed. Kovac caught hold of her arm as gently as he could and still hold on to her.

'Amanda, it's me, Sam. Are you awake?'

She blinked at him then, whatever horrible spell she had been under shattering. She tipped her face up and looked at him, seeing him, and the confusion in her face was enough to break his heart.

'It's all right, honey,' he said softly, sitting down on the edge of the bed. 'It's all right, sweetheart, you had a bad dream. You're all right now. It's all right.'

He drew her to him and she curled against him like a child. Her whole body was shaking. Kovac held her with one arm and pulled a blanket up around her with the other hand.

'I'm sorry,' she whispered. 'I'm sorry.'

'Shhh . . . There's nothing to be sorry about. You had a bad dream. You're all right now. I won't let anything hurt you.'

'Oh, God,' she whispered, miserable, embarrassed.

Kovac just held her. 'It's okay.'

'No,' she said, pulling away. Head down, not looking at him. 'No, it's not. I'm sorry.'

She got up from the bed, finding a silk robe among the covers and pulling it on, covering herself as if she were ashamed to have him see her.

'I'm very sorry,' she said, still not looking at him.

Kovac said nothing as she hurried across the room and disappeared into the bathroom. There came that feeling again: that there wouldn't be a second chance with her, that tonight was it. He had seen her at her most vulnerable. Amanda Savard would have a very hard time dealing with that.

He sighed heavily and got up, finding his shirt and pulling it on. Knowing exactly how little good it was going to do, he went to the door of the bathroom and knocked.

'Amanda? Are you all right?'

'Yes, thank you. I'm fine.'

He winced at the formality in her tone, recognizing it as one of her favorite defenses, a way to keep people at arm's length. He deliberately took the other route.

'Honey, you don't have to be embarrassed. The line of work we're in, we all have bad dreams. You ought to catch some of mine.'

The water ran, then shut off. There was no other sound. He could imagine her staring at herself in the mirror, the way he had done earlier. She wouldn't like what she was seeing: the marks on her face, the pallor of her skin, the look in her eyes.

He stepped back as the doorknob turned. She came out and stopped, arms wrapped around herself, her gaze just missing him.

'This really wasn't a very good idea –'

'Don't say that,' Kovac said.

She closed her eyes for a second and went on. 'I think we both just needed something tonight, and that was fine, but now –'

'It was better than fine,' he said, moving into her space, willing her to look at him. She wouldn't.

'I want you to leave now.'

'No.'

'Please don't make this more awkward than it already is.'

'It doesn't have to be awkward at all.'

'I don't see people from work.'

'Oh, really? Who do you see?'

'That's none of your business.'

'Uh – yes, I think it is,' he argued.

She sighed and looked away. 'I don't want a relationship. It's best I say that now, so we can just let this go and move on.'

'I don't want to let this go,' Kovac said, putting his hands on her, taking gentle hold of her upper arms. 'Amanda, don't do this.'

She turned her face away and stared at the floor. 'Please leave.'

She couldn't hide the emotion that trembled in her voice. He heard it plainly: pain, sadness. He felt the same things for her in his own heart.

'Please . . . Sam . . .' she whispered.

He bent his head and touched his lips to her cheek. He brought up a hand to stroke her hair. 'I'm sorry.'

She closed her eyes tight against the threat of tears. 'Please . . .'

'All right,' he murmured. 'All right.'

He stepped away from her, seeking out the rest of his clothes. She didn't move. When he was ready, he went to her again and touched her cheek with the back of his hand.

'Come lock up behind me. I need to know you're safe.'

She nodded and went with him.

In the entry hall, he pulled on his shoes and coat, and hunted his gloves up out of the pockets. She never met his eyes once. He tried to wait her out, just standing there by the door like a dope, but she wouldn't look up and she wouldn't say anything. He wanted to shake her and pull her into his arms and kiss her. But men weren't allowed to make a point that way anymore, and it probably wasn't the way to play Amanda anyway. She needed care and time; enough space not to feel threatened, but not so much that she could retreat.

Like you really think you can pull this off.

'Whatever you decide,' he said at last, 'this wasn't a mistake, Amanda.'

She said nothing and he let himself out, the cold slapping him in the face.

Here's your reality, Kovac, he thought as the door shut and locked behind him. *Out in the cold, alone.*

It wasn't anything less than he'd had before, but it was worse now because he'd had a taste of what could be.

He drove back into the city on empty roads, went back to an empty house and an empty bed, and lay awake the rest of the night staring inward at the emptiness of his life.

30

Liska pulled into the driveway, barely sparing a glance at the dashboard clock. Saturday morning in her house meant youth hockey. Kyle and R.J. started the day on the ice at six A.M. She had left them under the watchful charge of a buddy who worked sex crimes for the St Paul PD and had two boys of his own in the same league. No adult would come within ten feet of those children with Milo watching them.

Barely seven-thirty now, and the sun was just coming up. Most of Eden Prairie was probably still sleeping off the eggnog hangovers from the Friday night Christmas parties. Liska didn't care. She'd spent the forty-five minutes driving out here stoking her anger like a blast furnace. She didn't care if she had to kick the door in and drag his hairy ass out of bed. She was going to speak with Cal Springer, and he was going to listen.

She stormed to the front door of the too-nice house and leaned on the bell, then stabbed at it over and over. She could hear it ringing inside, and no other sound. The cul-de-sac was still. Cars parked overnight in driveways had windows thick with frost. The toothpick-young trees in the yards were flocked with white. Liska's breath silvered the air. It was so cold, it hurt to breathe.

The door opened and Mrs Cal, dressed in a flannel nightgown, stared out at her, her little mouth a round O of surprise.

'Where is he?' Liska demanded, walking in uninvited.

Patsy Springer stepped back. 'Calvin? What? What do you want at this hour? I don't –'

Liska gave her a look that had cracked confessions out of hardened criminals. 'Where is he?'

Cal's voice came from the direction of the kitchen. 'Who is it, Pats?'

Liska moved past the wife, digging a hand down into her purse as she homed in on her target. Cal sat at the oak table in the breakfast nook wearing the same clothes he'd had on the day before, a soft-boiled egg and a bowl of Malt-O-Meal in front of him. He gaped like a fish when he saw her.

'What are you doing here?' he demanded. 'This is my home, Liska –'

She pulled the Polaroids from her purse and slapped them down on the table beside his plate. Springer started to move his chair back. She grabbed a handful of his hair and held him in place, close at her side, ignoring his howl of pain.

'These are my children, Cal,' she said, working to keep from shouting in his face. 'Do you see them? Are you looking at these?'

'What's the matter with you?'

'I'm angry. These are my boys. Do you know who sent me these pictures, Cal? I'll give you two guesses.'

'I don't know what you're doing here!' he said, trying to get up again.

Liska yanked his hair and wound her fingers into it even tighter. Mrs Cal hovered at the archway to the front hall, her hands fluttering at her chest.

'She's crazy, Calvin! She's crazy!'

'Rubel and Ogden sent me these,' Liska said, grabbing one of the snapshots with her free hand. She stuck it in Cal Springer's face. 'I can't prove it, but they did. These are the people you're dealing with, Cal. This is what shitbags they are. They would threaten little children. And you're protecting them. That makes you the same as one of them, as far as I'm concerned.'

'Calvin?' the wife shrieked. 'Should I call nine-one-one?'

'Shut up, Patsy!' he shouted.

'If anyone harms a hair on the head of one of these boys,' Liska said, 'I'll kill that person. I mean that, Cal. I'll fucking kill them, and no one will ever find all the pieces. Do you understand me?'

He tried to get away from her. Liska yanked his hair and hit him in the forehead with her knuckles.

'Owww!'

'You stupid son of a bitch!' she yelled, and hit him again. 'What's wrong with you? How can you get in bed with them?'

She shoved him away from her abruptly and he fell off the chair and scrambled backward across the floor like a crab.

'You're despicable!' Liska shouted.

She grabbed the cup with the soft-boiled egg and threw it at him. He brought his arms up to protect himself and fell backward, hitting his head on a cabinet. It sounded like a gunshot. Mrs Springer screamed.

'You go to Castleton, you spineless worm,' Liska ordered. 'Tell him where you *weren't* Thursday night. You go to IA. They don't love anything more than they love a sniveling, worthless piece of shit like you. You turn these animals in or I'll make the rest of your career a misery Job couldn't survive! Nobody. *Nobody* threatens my children and gets away with it!'

She threw the Malt-O-Meal at him as a final exclamation point, then gathered up the Polaroids and stuffed them back into her bag. Springer stayed where he was, Malt-O-Meal running down his cheek.

Liska took a couple of fast, deep breaths to compose herself, and looked at Patsy Springer. 'I'm sorry to have interrupted your breakfast,' she said, her voice still trembling with rage.

Mrs Cal made a little cry in her throat and ran into a corner of the room.

'I'll see myself out,' Liska said, and left the house, shaking so hard she felt as if she was having a seizure.

When she got in the Saturn, she let go of a sigh.

'Well,' she said aloud as she cranked the key and started the engine. '*I feel better.*'

Why did you have to tell? I could have made it right. . . .

What the hell had Jocelyn Daring meant by that?

Kovac sat on a small chair in one corner of Andy Fallon's bedroom, staring at nothing. He replayed the memory of Jocelyn Daring walking into Pierce's study. The look on her face. The fury in her eyes. If he hadn't been there to stop her, what kind of damage might she have done to Pierce?

He probably should have arrested her for what she *had* done. Minnesota laws had zero tolerance for domestic abuse. Even if the victim didn't want to press charges, the state did. But he hadn't taken that step. Mitigating circumstances, a lawyer might argue. Poor Jocelyn. Upon hearing her fiancé's confession of a homosexual relationship, she lost her mind for a moment and struck out. Why add insult to her injury?

Because she might decide to finish the job.

She had left the house willingly, silently, dragging an overflowing suitcase to the waiting car of her maid of honor. Steve Pierce had gone by cab to the nearest ER to claim he'd slipped on the ice and cracked his head.

Love American style.

Love . . .

Kovac tried to shake off that thought and focus instead on the scene of Andy Fallon's death. That was part of the reason he had come here: to get his mind on something other than the big tumble he might have actually taken for a lady with lieutenant's bars and some deep dark trouble on her mind. He was trying not to wonder at the source of her nightmare, trying not to think that what had happened wasn't an isolated incident, and that was why she'd asked him to go – because she was afraid it would happen again and he would want to know why. Those were the thoughts he had come here to avoid. Those thoughts he kept thinking and then reminding himself not to.

Nor did he want to think about how it had felt to make love to her or the incredible sense of protectiveness that had come over him as he'd held her after the nightmare. He would put his mind on work, which was the only thing he was really very good at anyway. The job never told him to take a hike.

The corpse smell lingered in the room. Kovac stuck his nose over a steaming cup of Caribou dark roast and breathed deep.

I guess I'd be doing a public service if I invited you in for a cup of coffee. . . .

He blinked out the image of Amanda standing at her front door, peeking out at him. He needed to consider a different blonde.

Question: Could Jocelyn Daring have killed her fiancé's gay lover? Yes.

Had she had the opportunity? He didn't know and couldn't ask her. The case was officially closed; he had no right to question anyone. Had Pierce mentioned being with her the night of Andy Fallon's death? If she'd had the opportunity and taken it, how had she pulled it off? How would she have gotten Fallon to bed? No one had suggested Andy Fallon had flipped the switch both ways. Everyone had spoken too highly of him to imagine he might go to bed with his lover's girlfriend. So, there was that problem.

He thought of the sleeping pills, of the wineglasses in the dishwasher. Maybe . . .

Next question: If she had drugged him, knocked him out, could she have hung him? Could she have lifted a man's deadweight?

He stared at the bed, then at the beam the rope had hung from. He got up from the chair and went to sit on the edge of the bed, then rose and stood approximately where the body had been hanging. The full-length mirror was positioned exactly as it had been; the word *Sorry* appeared scrawled across his belly. The mirror had been dusted for prints but hadn't been confiscated as evidence because no crime had been committed. Kovac looked in it now and tried to picture Jocelyn Daring on the bed behind him.

It might have been possible to get the victim into a sitting position on the edge of the bed, put the noose around his neck, then hoist him up with the rope and tie the rope off on the bedpost. Maybe. What had Andy Fallon weighed? One-seventy-five? One-eighty? One hundred eighty pounds of unconscious, uncooperative weight. Jocelyn was strong, but . . .

While a woman might have struggled to accomplish what he had just imagined, a man would have been able to pull it off more easily.

Could Neil have followed that same basic plan? Killed his brother for not loaning him money, or for not being a loser like him, or because he was jealous, or because he wanted to punish their father before he did him in too?

Kovac went back to his chair and sat again. He looked at how tidy the room was, remembered how perfectly made the bed had been. It had struck him odd that Andy wouldn't have sat on the bed before he did the deed. And that there were sheets in the washing machine.

Who did their laundry, then killed themselves?

He thought of Neil Fallon's place as they had executed the search warrant. The kind of frat-house filth and disorder that gave single guys a bad name. Pierce had said it: *Neil's the messy type, don't you think? . . . devastation at the scene, fingerprints everywhere . . .*

Neil Fallon hadn't changed a sheet in his life. There was no evidence in his own home that he had any idea how to run a dishwasher.

Who then? Who else had motive? Ogden's beef with IA was over. Unless Fallon had come up with something new. And they might never know that unless they found Fallon's personal notes on the case. And how could that ox Ogden pull off something with this much finesse? It wouldn't be his nature. Beating someone with a pipe was his nature. How would Ogden even have gotten in the front door? Fallon wouldn't have let him in the house. Maybe at gunpoint.

There was no denying Liska had stirred the hornet's nest looking at the Curtis-Ogden angle. . . .

As for Steve Pierce, Kovac felt he had done his confessing. He didn't see Pierce killing his lover in cold blood, the way Fallon had died. If he had loved Andy the way he seemed to, he couldn't have humiliated him that way. And the sex-game angle didn't play, according to Kate Conlan.

Kovac sighed. 'Speak to me, Andy.'

It didn't take Sherlock Holmes to figure out most murders. A true whodunit was the exception rather than the rule. Most people were killed by someone they knew, for a reason that was simple.

Calls to the friends in Andy's address book had turned up nothing. He hadn't been that close to that many people. Too many years of living a secret life. Only Pierce had mentioned having seen him recently with another man. Another lover?

Most people were killed by someone they knew, for a reason that was simple.

Private life: family, friends, lovers, ex-lovers.

Professional life: coworkers, enemies made on the job or because of the job.

He didn't know what other cases Andy had had in the hopper. Savard wouldn't give that out, especially since his death had been ruled something other than homicide. She didn't seem concerned that any of his current caseload might be harboring a murderer. And so Kovac came back to the only case he knew anything about: Curtis-Ogden.

No. That wasn't exactly true. According to Pierce, Andy might have been looking into the Thorne murder. But what could have come of a case closed twenty years ago – besides resentment from his father?

Which brought Kovac back to suicide. Maybe a guy like Andy – a guy who dotted all his *i*s and crossed all his *t*s, a guy who needed approval and control . . . Maybe a guy like that *would* change his sheets before he stretched his neck.

Most people were killed by someone they knew, for a reason that was simple. Themselves. Suicide. Depression.

Death didn't get more simple than that.

Too bad he couldn't make himself buy it.

The homicide office was quiet on Saturday. Leonard never came in on weekends. Shift detectives were primarily on call. People sometimes came into the office to catch up on paperwork. Kovac spent most of his Saturdays here because he had no life.

He hung his coat up and wondered what Amanda was doing with her Saturday. Was she thinking about him, about what had happened? Was she reliving the moment he'd walked out the door, rewriting it in her head so that she asked him to stay?

He fell into his chair and stared at the telephone.

No. No, he wouldn't call. But he snatched up the receiver to check his voice mail. On the off chance... There was nothing. He sighed, flipped through the Rolodex, and dialed a number.

'Records, Turvey.' The voice on the other end rattled with gravel and phlegm.

'Russell, you old mole. Why don't you get a fucking life?'

'Ha! What the hell would I want with that? J. Christ. If I had to interact with regular people...' The old man made a gargling noise. 'Argh. I'd sooner hump a monkey.'

'Yeah, there's an image.' Russell Turvey: sixty-whatever years old with a face like Popeye, a cigarette hanging on his lip, a stomach like a basketball, doing it with a monkey.

Turvey laughed and coughed and hacked. His lungs sounded like a couple of plastic bags half-full of Jell-O.

Kovac picked up the pack of Salems he'd bought on the way in and threw it in the garbage.

'What'd you need, Sam? Is it legal?'

'Sure.'

'Well, shit. You're no fun. Getting dull in your old age. Hey, that was too bad about Iron Mike, huh? I heard it was you found him. It's always those hard-ass guys that eat their guns.'

'Yeah, well, he might not have. I'm looking into it.'

'J. Christ! You're shittin' me! Who'd waste a bullet on a moldy old turd like him?'

'I'll keep you posted,' Kovac promised. 'Listen, Russ, I came across an old badge the other day in a junk shop. I'm curious who might have worn it. Can you find something like that?'

'Sure. If I don't have it, I know who does. I got nothing else to do here but sit around with my thumb up my ass.'

'You're killing me with the visuals here, Russell.'

'Argh. Come on down and take a picture for your scrapbook. What's the badge number?'

'Fourteen twenty-eight. Looked like a seventies issue. I was just curious.'

'I'll dig it up.'

'Thanks. I owe you one.'

'Catch the bastard that capped Mike. We'll call it even.'

'I'll do what I can.'

'I know you, Sam. You'll do nine times more than that, and some brass cocksucker'll take all the credit.'

'The way of the world, Russ.'

'Argh. Fuck 'em.' He hacked into the phone and hung up.

Kovac dug the cigarettes out of the garbage, bent the pack in two, and tossed it back in.

He turned the computer on and spent the next hour getting to know Jocelyn Daring. Through one source, he found out she had graduated cum laude from Northwestern, where she had been a standout field hockey player. Athletic. Strong – he already knew that. Aggressive – he'd seen that for himself. She was fourth in her class at the University of Minnesota law school. Ambitious. Hardworking. Through DMV records he discovered she had a lead foot and did a poor job feeding parking meters. That could suggest a certain disregard for rules . . . or so would say John Quinn and his profiler pals.

But he discovered no criminal record, no newspaper stories about her flipping out in a restaurant or anything of the sort. He hadn't really expected to. Even if Jocelyn had a history of irrational behavior, her family had the bucks to cover it up.

Not so the Fallon clan, Kovac could see as he went through the file Elwood had put together on Neil. Neil's life foibles were a matter of public record. The assault conviction, a couple of DUIs, tax problems, health code violations at the bar, run-ins with agents of the Department of Natural Resources for taking more than his legal limit of damn near every living creature that had a season on it.

The pattern was one of wanting more than what he was entitled to. A man with resentment for authority. The complete opposite of his brother – something Neil undoubtedly blamed Andy for, though it had most likely happened the other way around. Andy had watched Neil screw up and cause trouble, and he had gone a hundred eighty degrees in the other direction to please his father. And he'd done it right up to the end, with the unforgivable exception of telling the old man the truth about his sexuality.

Poor kid. Even going so far as to try to understand Mike through his life experiences. What was to understand? There weren't that many layers to guys like Mike Fallon. That was where Neil had the edge on Andy: he had understood Mike perfectly.

'I've got nothing to say to you, Kovac. Not without having my lawyer present.'

Neil Fallon glared at him and paced by the door to the interview room. He looked natural in the orange jailhouse jumpsuit, except it should have had dirt and grease on it. He had had to cuff the pants legs to keep from tripping over them.

'This isn't about you, Neil,' Kovac said, sitting in the plastic chair and squaring an ankle over a knee. Mr Relaxation.

'Then why are you here? I got nothing to say to you.'

'So you've said. So I guess you don't want a chance to help yourself out.'

'How can I help myself out if it isn't about me?'

'Good faith.'

Fallon's eyebrows climbed his forehead. 'Good faith? Stick it up your ass.'

'For a guy who claims to be straight, you're awful big on wanting me to stick something up my ass,' Kovac observed.

'Fuck you!' Fallon snapped, catching himself too late. He growled and paced some more. 'I'm suing you, Kovac. Suing this rotten police department.'

Kovac sighed his boredom. 'Look, Neil, you tell me you're innocent. You tell me you wouldn't kill your old man.'

'I didn't.'

'So help me understand some things. That's all I'm asking. Understanding is the key to enlightenment. You know, the policeman is your friend,' he said as if he were talking to a four-year-old. 'And if he's not, you're fucked. Make me like you here, Neil.'

Fallon leaned against the wall beside the door and crossed his arms, thinking.

'My lawyer says not to talk to you without him present.'

'Once you've engaged counsel, nothing you say without him present can be used against you. You can't get hurt here. You can only help yourself. I never wanted us to be enemies, Neil. Hell, we shared a bottle. You're a decent, hardworking guy. So am I.'

Fallon waited, lower lip sticking out.

'I brought you some cigarettes,' Kovac said, holding up the pack.

Fallon came over and took it, making a face. 'They're all bent!'

'Hey, they still burn.'

'Jesus,' he grumbled, but took one out and tried to straighten it. Kovac handed him a lighter.

'I'm just curious about some things with Andy – and no, I don't think you killed him. I don't know if anybody did. Everybody says he was depressed. I just want a clearer picture of that, that's all.'

Behind the haze of smoke, Fallon narrowed his eyes, thinking: *trick question.*

'See, I'm a homicide cop,' Kovac went on. 'I look sideways at everybody when somebody's suddenly dead. It's nothing personal. If my old man turned up dead, I'd look at my mother, for chrissake. But there's another picture here to look at. Say, what if Andy wanted to get close with your dad again. He wanted a chance to win him back, so to speak. So he tries to do some things with Mike, talk to him, spend time with him. Maybe he buys him that big-ass TV in the living room –'

'Wyatt bought that,' Fallon said, matter-of-fact. He took a seat and considered the crooked cigarette.

'What?'

'Ace Wyatt. The old man's guardian angel,' Fallon said sarcastically. 'It was always that way since the shooting. Wyatt helped with hospital bills, bought stuff for the house, for Andy and me. Mike always said that's how it was – cops looking out for cops. That's what it's all about, he said, obligation. And that's what it was. Wyatt never wanted to spend any time with the old man, or with any of us. He'd come into the house and act like he thought he was getting fleas. Big asshole.'

'Yeah, that's pretty rotten, buying you stuff like that.'

'I always figured he felt guilty 'cause Mike caught that bullet. Wyatt living right across the street from Thorne and all. Him being the one that Thorne called for help. It should have been him in that wheelchair. But Mike beat him to it.'

Kovac digested the theory, thinking Fallon probably had a pretty good handle on it. Mike had caught that bullet instead of Ace Wyatt, and he'd never let Wyatt forget it. The fading image of the noble legend washed away by the acid rain of reality.

'Mike needed something, he'd call Wyatt,' Neil went on, puffing on the L-shaped cigarette. 'And don't think he didn't throw that up in my face every chance he got. I should have been taking care of him. The oldest son and all that bullshit. Like he ever did shit for me.'

'How old was Andy at the time of the shooting?'

'Seven or eight, I guess. Why?'

'Someone told me he had wanted to sit down with Mike and talk about what happened. To try to get a better understanding of your father.'

Fallon laughed and coughed and puffed on the crooked cigarette. 'Yeah, that was Andy. Mr Sensitivity. What's to understand? Mike was a bitter old son of a bitch, that's all.'

'I guess Mike didn't want to talk about what happened. Had Andy said anything to you?'

He thought about it for a moment, looking as if he was trying to remember. 'I guess he said something about it one of those last times I saw him. Mentioned it in relation to Mike not wanting him poking at old wounds. I didn't pay much attention. What was the point digging all that up?' He studied Kovac for a moment. 'Why do you care?'

Kovac turned the information over in his mind, mixing it into what he already had, trying to recall something he thought Mike had said in the last few days of his life.

'I'm just thinking,' he said, just to fill airtime. 'Andy had some problems with depression. If it meant a lot to him to get back with the old man, and Mike wouldn't cooperate, then maybe he really did hit bottom and check out. And maybe Mike blamed himself. . . .'

'Well, that would be a first.' Fallon finished the cigarette and crushed the butt out on the sole of his shoe. 'Never blame yourself when you can blame someone else. That was Mike.'

Kovac checked his watch.

'So if you're on the suicide angle now, how long before I get outta here?'

'It's out of my hands, Neil,' Kovac said, pushing to his feet. He went to the door and pushed the buzzer for the jailer. 'Not my fault. It's those rotten lawyers. I'd help you if I could. Keep the cigarettes. It's the least I can do.'

31

The *Minneapolis Star Tribune* printed Ace Wyatt's shooting schedule for *Crime Time* in the entertainment news every Thursday. Part of the show's gimmick was Wyatt's interaction with the audience. It was like a fucking infomercial, Kovac had thought the few times he'd watched it. Or something from the Food Channel. Ace Wyatt: the Emeril Lagasse of law enforcement.

The crime du jour was being reenacted in a hockey rink in the suburb of St Louis Park. Murder by curling stone: a cautionary tale of poor sportsmanship. Kovac badged the security bruiser standing at the roped-off section of bleachers and walked into the thick of Ace Mania.

A twelve-by-twelve red carpet had been spread on a section of the ice. The camera stood at one corner of it, along with a bored videographer who looked like Gandhi in a down jacket. Another videographer, this one on skates and with a handheld camera, leaned against the frame of the hockey goalie's net. Four lucky fans had been chosen to sit in the penalty boxes. Another hundred sat behind them. Lots of large women and wimpy-looking older men in red *PROActive!* sweatshirts.

'We need quiet now, people!' shouted a thin, rawboned woman in black-rimmed glasses and a coat that looked as if it had been made from olive-green shag carpeting. She clapped her hands precisely three times and the crowd obediently went silent.

The director, a fat guy gnawing on a Slim-Fast bar, shouted at the two actors: 'Places! Let's get it right this time!'

One of the actors, a fiftyish guy in a Nordic patterned sweater and what looked like blue tights, slipped and slid across the ice, arms working like spastic propellers at his sides.

'It's bothering me, Donald,' he complained. 'How can I think like a curler when there's a hockey goal sitting there?'

'Tight shots, Keith. No one's going to see the net. Think small. If you have to think at all.'

The actor went to find his mark. The director gave the God-spare-me-from-actors shake of the head.

Kovac spotted Wyatt sitting away from the audience, having his makeup retouched. Hugging themselves against the cold of the arena, a couple of Hollywood mover-shaker types stood behind him, smiling gamely while Gaines snapped a Polaroid. An anorexic young woman with brilliant red hair sculpted into a hedge on top of her head, and a twenty-something guy in a black leather coat and tiny rectangular spectacles.

'One more for the scrapbook,' Gaines said. The flash burst, and the camera spat out its product.

'The audience doesn't seem to mind the cold,' the guy said.

Gaines gave them the engaging grin. 'They love Captain Wyatt. We turn away droves at every taping. They're so excited to be here. What's a little chill?'

The girl bounced up and down and rubbed her hands over her arms. 'I've never been so cold in my life! I haven't been warm one minute since I got off the plane. How do people live here?'

'You think this is cold?' Kovac said, and huffed his disgust. 'Come back in January. You'll think you died and went to Siberia. Colder than a grave-digger's ass.'

The girl looked at him the way she might look at some odd creature in the zoo. Gaines lost the grin.

'Sergeant Kovac. What a pleasure,' he said flatly.

'For me too,' Kovac said, giving the scene the disdainful once-over again. 'I don't get to the circus every day. I have a real job.'

'Yvette Halston,' the redhead introduced herself. 'Vice president, creative development, Warner Brothers television.'

The guy stuck his hand out. 'Kelsey Vroman, vice president, reality programming.'

Reality programming.

'Kovac. Sergeant. Homicide.'

'Sam!' Wyatt came up out of his chair, shooing the makeup woman away. He pulled the paper-towel bib out of the neck of his double-breasted navy Italian suit and tossed it aside. 'What brings you here? Did you get the lab results back on the Fallon evidence?'

The WB VPs pricked up their ears at the sound of real cop talk.

'Not yet.'

'I made a couple of phone calls. They're on it today.'

'Yeah, thanks, Ace,' he said without appreciation. 'Actually, I came to ask you about something else. Have you got a minute?'

Gaines came to Wyatt's side, clipboard in hand, and tried to show him a schedule. 'Captain, Donald wants to get through this section before one. The rest of the curling people were told to be here no later than one-thirty for the interview portion. We'll be cutting lunch by thirty minutes as it is. The union people will have a fit.'

'Then break for lunch now,' Wyatt ordered.

'But they're ready for the shot.'

'Then they'll be ready after lunch, won't they?'

'Yes, but –'

'Then what's the problem, Gavin?'

'Yeah, Gavin,' Kovac goaded. 'What's the problem?'

Gaines gave Kovac a cold look. 'I believe you're the one who pointed out that Captain Wyatt is retired from the force,' he said. 'He has other obligations than to solve your case for you, but he's too decent a man to tell you to go away.'

'Gavin . . .' Wyatt chided. 'I don't have any obligations more important than a murder investigation.'

The VPs both got wet on that one.

'Ace,' the redhead purred, 'you're consulting on a case? You didn't tell us! That could be very exciting! What do you think, Kelsey?'

'We could get something set up with various law enforcement agencies for a weekly segment. Police, DEA, FBI. Have the consultation at the end of the show. Five minutes, *mano a mano*, detective to detective. Ace offers the benefit of his no-nonsense wisdom. I like it. It adds a sense of immediacy and vitality. Don't you think so, Gavin?'

'It could work very well,' Gaines said diplomatically. 'I'm just concerned about our schedule today.'

'We'll deal with it, Gavin,' Wyatt said dismissively, then turned to Kovac again. 'Let's go upstairs, Sam. You can have a bite while we talk. Our caterer is fabulous. Gavin found him. Makes the best little quiches.'

Wyatt led the way up the concrete steps to a room overlooking the rink through a long window. Food had been artistically arranged on a long table draped in red with the *Crime Time* scrapbook as a centerpiece. Wyatt didn't go near the spread, but gestured Kovac to.

'I don't like to eat when we're shooting,' he explained, opening a bottle of water. 'I stay sharper that way.'

'Gotta stay on your toes for this.' *And not bust the girdle,* Kovac thought. Wyatt looked as if he hadn't taken a full breath in five hours.

'I know you don't think much of it, Sam,' he said, 'but we're serving a real purpose here. Helping solve crimes, helping people stand up for themselves and prevent crime.'

'Making a bundle.'

'That's *not* a crime.'

'No. Never mind me,' Kovac said, paging idly through the scrapbook, slowing at the pages from Wyatt's retirement party. Posed and candid – if there could be such a thing as a candid shot of Ace – Polaroid shots of the great man in his glory. A shot of Wyatt pumping Kovac's hand, Kovac looking as if he'd just grabbed hold of an eel. A posed shot with a Channel Five reporter. A candid of Wyatt speaking to Amanda Savard. His gaze lingered.

'I don't like game shows either,' Kovac said, trying to remember having seen her there that night, but he'd been too busy feeling sorry for himself.

'I'm told I'm getting cranky in my old age, but that's bullshit. I've always been cranky.'

'You're not old, Sam,' Wyatt pointed out. 'You're younger than me, and look where I am now. A great second career. On top of the world.'

'I'll probably just stick with the one career until someone shoots me,' Kovac said. 'Which reminds me why I'm here.'

'Mike.' Wyatt nodded. 'Do you have anything more on the son, on Neil?'

'I'm more here about Andy, actually.'

Wyatt's brow furrowed. 'Andy? I don't understand.'

'I'm curious as to the why of it all,' he said in vague explanation. 'I know he'd been looking into the Thorne murder, thinking maybe Mike would want to reminisce, maybe they could get closer through it.'

'Ah . . .'

'He talked to you.' He put it as if it were a statement of fact, as if he'd seen the notes, leaving little room for denial, even though he knew no such thing.

'Yes,' Wyatt said. 'He mentioned it to me. I know Mike didn't want any part of it. Painful memories.'

'For you too.'

Wyatt nodded. 'It was a terrible night. Forever changed the lives of everyone involved.'

'Tied you to the Fallons like you were family.'

'In a way, yes. You don't go through something like that with another officer and not come away with a bond.'

'Especially with the circumstances.'

'What do you mean?'

'With you living right across the street. With the Thornes calling you for help, but Mike getting there ahead of you. You had to feel a little like Mike took that bullet instead of you, huh? Mike probably felt that too.'

'The tricks of fate,' Wyatt said with a dramatic sigh. 'My number wasn't up. Mike's was.'

'There must have been a little guilt though. You went above and beyond the call helping Mike out all these years.'

Wyatt stood silent for a moment. Kovac waited, wondering what the makeup was hiding. Surprise? Anger?

'Where are you going with this, Sam?'

Kovac shrugged a little and picked a baby carrot from a tray on the table. 'I know Mike took advantage all these years, Ace,' he said, snapping the carrot in two. 'I'm just wondering . . . With you making the big move to Hollywood . . . Making big dough . . . I'm just wondering if he might have tried to squeeze you for a little more.'

Kovac could see the color rise in Wyatt's face now.

'I don't like the direction you're taking,' he said quietly. 'I tried to do right by Mike and his family. And maybe he did take advantage and play on my guilt for not being the one in the chair. But that was between Mike and me, and that's how it should stay. We both deserve better than what you're thinking.'

'I'm not thinking anything, Ace. I don't get paid to think. I'm just wondering, that's all. You know me, I've gotta take things apart and see how they work.'

'The job's made you too cynical, Sam. Maybe it's time you got out.'

Kovac narrowed his eyes a little, studying Wyatt, trying to decide if that was a threat. Wyatt could make a couple of his famous phone calls, and that'd be it. Kiss the career good-bye or spend eternity down in Records listening to Russell Turvey hawk up lugies. And for what? To reveal the awful truth that Ace Wyatt felt guilty for being alive and whole? Even if Mike had tried to squeeze a little extra something out of him, the notion of Wyatt killing over that was ludicrous.

Unless the reason he had paid Mike Fallon off all these years had to do with some other kind of guilt altogether.

'How well did you know the Thornes?'

Gaines rapped on the open door and came into the room then, eyebrows raised at Wyatt. 'Excuse me, Captain. Kelsey and Yvette have gone to buy parkas. Everyone is breaking for lunch. Will you be joining the audience, or is this going to take longer?' he asked, emphasizing the word *this* with a look at Kovac. He pulled a small lint brush from a jacket pocket and gave Wyatt's lapels a quick swipe.

'No,' Wyatt said. 'We're finished here.'

Kovac popped the carrot in his mouth and chewed thoughtfully as Wyatt walked away. He followed at a distance and watched as Ace Wyatt worked the crowd of people who had so little going on in their lives they would waste a Saturday watching this bullshit.

Like me, he thought with a smirk, and walked out.

The on-line archives of the *Minneapolis Star Tribune* went back only to 1990. Kovac spent the afternoon in a room in the Hennepin County library, straining his eyes looking at microfiche, reading and rereading the articles written about the Thorne murder and Mike Fallon's shooting. They laid out the story as he remembered it.

The drifter-cum-handyman, Kenneth Weagle, had done some work for Officer Bill Thorne's wife and had apparently taken a shine to her. He had come to the house that night knowing Bill Thorne was on patrol. He'd been in the neighborhood long enough to scope out the comings and goings of residents. He had attacked Evelyn Thorne in her bedroom, raped her, slapped her around, then started looting the house. By chance, Bill Thorne had stopped back home and walked into the house, unsuspecting. Weagle shot him with a gun of Thorne's he had found in the house. At some point Mrs Thorne had phoned Ace Wyatt across the street. But before Wyatt could arrive, Mike Fallon did.

Bill Thorne was given a hero's funeral with all the trimmings. There were photographs with that article. The long motorcade of police vehicles. A grainy shot of the widow in dark glasses, being consoled by friends and family.

According to the article, Thorne had been survived by his wife, Evelyn, and an unnamed seventeen-year-old daughter. In the photo, Evelyn Thorne looked a little like Grace Kelly, Kovac thought. He wondered if either of them was still in the area. He wondered if any of Bill Thorne's old cronies would know. Evelyn Thorne had been a relatively young woman at the time of the incident. Chances were she had remarried. She would be fifty-eight now, the daughter thirty-seven.

If Andy Fallon had been looking into the case, wanting to come to some kind of understanding, he might already have done the legwork. But there was no file. Kovac wondered if Amanda could be talked into letting him look around Fallon's office, check out his work computer. The Thorne murder wasn't an active IA case. She might not care.

You don't even know if she'll ever speak to you again, Kovac.

There was that.

'Sir?' The librarian's voice startled him. He jerked around to find her standing too close.

'The library is closing,' she said apologetically. 'I'm afraid you'll have to leave.'

Kovac gathered the copies of articles he'd run off, and went back out into the cold. Afternoon had surrendered to night, though it was barely five. The homeless who had spent their day in the warmth of the library had been shooed out along with him. They milled around on the sidewalk, instinctively shying away from Kovac, smelling cop. The librarian had probably thought he was one of them. He hadn't shaved, had spent the afternoon pulling at his hair and rubbing his eyes. He felt like one of them, standing on the cold street in this bleak, gray part of town. Alone, disconnected.

He tried to call Liska on his cell phone and got her voice mail; debated paging her, then let it go. He drove home so he could feel alone and disconnected in a warmer setting.

The neighbor had added to his lawn display a painted plywood cutout of Santa bending over, showing three inches of butt crack. Hilarious. It was positioned directly toward Kovac's living room window. Such class.

Kovac contemplated taking out his gun and blasting Santa an asshole. *See the humor in that, cocksucker?*

The house still smelled of garbage, even though he had taken it out. Like the corpse smell at Andy Fallon's. He tossed the copies of the Thorne murder articles on the coffee table and went into the kitchen. He burned some coffee grounds on the stove to get rid of the odor – a trick he'd learned at death scenes. See if Heloise put that in her helpful hints column. *What to do in the event of putrid corpse decay.*

He went upstairs, took a shower, pulled on some jeans and wool socks and an old sweatshirt, and went back down in search of supper, even though he had no appetite to speak of. He needed calories to keep the mind going. If keeping his mind going was what he really wanted tonight.

The only edible food in the house was a box of Frosted Flakes. He ate a handful, dry, and poured some of the scotch he'd picked up on the way home. Macallan. What the hell.

On the stereo, he found the faux jazz station playing a faux jazz tune, and he stood at the window listening to it and sipping the Macallan and staring at Santa's ass.

This is my life.

He didn't know how long he'd been standing there when the doorbell rang. The sound was so unfamiliar, it took three rings before he responded.

Amanda Savard stood on the front step, the black velvet scarf swathing her head, hiding her wounds. Some of them anyway.

'Well,' Kovac said, 'you must be a detective too. I'm unlisted.'

'May I come in?'

He stood back and waved her in with the scotch glass. 'Don't expect much. I get so many tips from the Home and Garden channel, but I just don't have the time.'

She went to the middle of the living room, pushed the scarf off her head, but didn't remove her gloves or the long black coat. She didn't take a seat.

'I came to apologize,' she said, looking just past his right shoulder. Kovac wondered if she could see Santa's moon, but if she did, she didn't react.

'For what?' he asked. 'Sleeping with me? Or throwing me out after?'

She looked as if she wanted to be anywhere but there. She held her hands together, then brought one up to touch her hair near the burns. 'I – I wasn't – I didn't mean –' She stopped and pressed her lips together and closed her eyes for a moment. 'I'm not – I don't easily . . . share my life . . . with other people. And I'm sorry if I . . .'

Kovac set his glass on the coffee table as he stepped close. He touched her cheek, his thumb brushing just below the wound. Her skin was cold to the touch, as if she must have been sitting out front for a long time before she worked up the courage to come to the door.

'You don't have to be sorry, Amanda,' he said softly. 'Don't be sorry about me, or for me.'

She met his gaze. Her lower lip was quivering ever so slightly.

'I'm not good at this,' she said.

'Hush.' He bent his head and touched his mouth to hers. Not with passion, but with something gentler. Her lips warmed, and softened, and opened to him.

'I can't stay,' she whispered, her voice tight with whatever conflict she was battling internally.

'Shh . . .'

He kissed her again. The scarf fell to the floor. He trailed the kiss down her neck and slipped her coat off her shoulders.

'Sam . . .'

'Amanda . . .' His lips brushed the shell of her ear. 'I want you.'

A delicate shiver ran through her. He felt it pass beneath his hands as he slid them down her back. She turned her head and her mouth found his. A trembling kiss. Hesitant, but anxious. Needing, but afraid. She opened her eyes and looked at him through tears.

'I don't know what we can have,' she said. 'I don't know what I can give you.'

'It doesn't matter,' he answered, the truth of the moment. 'We can have this. We can have now.'

He could feel her heart beat against his chest, marking the passing of time. Even now he couldn't read her, didn't know what questions she asked or answered within herself. He could feel the sadness in her, the emptiness, the loneliness, the conflict. He recognized those qualities, responded to them, lost himself in them as they sank down onto the sofa.

They could have this. They could have now. Even if that was all they ever had, he didn't have anything else that was worth a damn by comparison.

'I can't stay,' Savard said softly.

She lay in Kovac's arms, the pair of them on his sofa, covered by her coat. His skin was warm against hers. She liked the feel of his body pressed to hers, of her legs tangled with his; the feeling of being wrapped up with him, the suggestion of being inseparable. But it was a suggestion she couldn't fulfill. That knowledge left her feeling empty, hollow, isolated.

He touched the back of her head and pressed his lips to her forehead. 'You don't have to, but you can . . . if you want. I might even have clean sheets.'

'No,' she said, forcing herself to move, to sit up. She pulled her clothes together and covered herself. 'I can't.'

Kovac levered himself up on one arm and gently combed out the tangles he'd put in her hair. 'Amanda, I don't care where the nightmares come from. Do you understand what I mean by that? It doesn't matter. It doesn't scare me that you have them.'

It matters to me. It scares me, she wanted to say, but she didn't.

'You can share them with me if you need to,' he said. 'Believe me, there's nothing I haven't heard.'

Of course, that wasn't true, but she didn't point that out to him either. She had learned long ago when to argue and when to be silent.

Kovac sighed behind her. 'The bathroom's down the hall on the right.'

Kovac watched as she walked out of the room, half dressed. If this was all he could have of her, it was better than anything he'd ever dared hope for. Let her keep her secrets. He was oh-for-two with deep relationships, why try again? But he knew better. Amanda was a mystery, a puzzle. He would never rest until he got to the heart of her. As guarded as she was, she would resent the intrusion, and he would ultimately destroy what they did have.

He pulled his clothes on, rubbed a hand over his hair, and sat on the arm of the couch, sipping at his scotch while he waited for her to emerge. She came back into the room looking just as she had when she arrived. Beautiful, reserved, disguised.

'I don't know what to tell you,' she said, addressing the empty aquarium.

'Then don't tell me anything. You brass types,' he said, making a face. 'There doesn't have to be a master plan.'

She looked worried about that.

He went to her and touched her face with the back of his hand.

'Sometimes we just need to follow a trail and see where it goes,' he said. Sam Kovac, sage. 'Listen to me. Like I know what I'm talking about. I'm a two-time loser. Every trail I take ends up in a dark tunnel with a train coming my way. I should stick to just being a cop. I'm good at that.'

She found half a smile for him. It faded as her gaze fell on the coffee table. Her brows drew together.

'What's this?'

'The Thorne murder. Mike Fallon's shooting. Andy was looking at it. I'm just turning over rocks, see what crawls out.'

'Follow the trail and see where it goes,' she said absently. She spread out some of the pages, not picking them up, just looking at them.

'Sad story. You're too young to remember.'

'Sad,' she murmured, staring at the bad copy of the photograph of Bill Thorne's widow being consoled by her family.

'Life turns on a dime,' Kovac said.

'Yes, it does.'

She straightened and adjusted the velvet scarf, took a deep breath, looking past his shoulder again.

'Just say, "I'll see you around, Sam," ' he told her. 'It beats the hell out of good-bye.'

She tried to smile but failed, then rose up on her toes and kissed his cheek, her hands tightening on his shoulders. 'I'm sorry,' she whispered.

Then she was gone, and all he had left to keep him warm was a fifty-dollar bottle of scotch.

'You're not as sorry as me,' he said as he stood in the open door and watched her drive away.

Next door, the Saint-O-Meter was counting down the minutes.

The phone rang, and he actually hurried to pick it up. It didn't even matter who it was.

'Lonely Hearts Club,' he said. 'Join now. Misery loves company.'

'Do you take masochists?' Liska.

'Two for one if you join with a sadist.'

'What are you doing, Kojak? Sitting home feeling sorry for yourself?'

'I don't have anyone else to feel sorry for. My life is an empty shell.'

'Get a dog,' she said without sympathy. 'Guess who partnered with Eric Curtis until about a year before he was murdered?'

Kovac took a sip of the Macallan. 'If you tell me Bruce Ogden, I'm walking out of this movie, Jodie.'

'Derek Rubel,' she said. 'And guess who was at HCMC yesterday having a blood test, then lying about it?'

'Derek Rubel.'

'Give the man a cigar.'

'I'll be damned,' Kovac murmured.

'No,' Liska said. 'But I have a feeling Derek Rubel will be.'

32

Steele's was the kind of gym where sweating and grunting were required. There were no jazz dance aerobic classes, no yoga. It was all iron, hard-bodied hard-asses, heavy metal blasting from the stereo. It had the ambience of a machine shop, and the stench of people with too much testosterone was enough to make a normal person's eyes water.

Liska badged the bored biker chick working the desk and went into the main weight room. She stood at the edge of the action for a moment, scanning the small crowd, secretly awestruck by the male bodies. Amazing to think what an ordinary human could become through well-applied obsessive behavior and, in some cases, the miracles of modern chemistry. Every third guy in the gym was built like the Incredible Hulk.

Rubel stood in a corner, spotting someone on a bench. He wore a black T-shirt with the sleeves cut off to accommodate upper arms as thick as Virginia hams. The muscles were so perfectly defined, he could have been used as a live model for a human anatomy class.

Liska wove her way through the maze of people pumping iron, knowing the instant Rubel became aware of her, even though he didn't look right at her. She could sense the energy change in the air. She walked up to the bench and looked down into Bruce Ogden's ugly face. He was straining beneath a barbell loaded with iron plates the size of truck wheels, red in the face, squawling.

She cut a look at Rubel. 'Does he make this much noise in bed?'

'I wouldn't know.'

'I'd ask his girfriend, but he's never had one as far as I've been able to find out.' She leaned over Ogden again and made a face of apology. 'Whores don't count. Sorry.'

Ogden let out a roar and shoved the barbell up.

'What do you want, Sergeant?' Rubel asked. 'We're in the middle of something here.'

'I'll say you are,' Liska said, deadly serious, showing some of her hatred for these two men. 'You're up to your necks in it. And note how I came here in person to tell you to your faces. No anonymous call from a pay phone. No photographs in the mail. I've got bigger balls than both of you put together.'

Ogden racked the barbell and sat up, grunting, sweat running off his face like rainwater. 'Yeah? We heard that about you.'

Liska rolled her eyes. 'Now with the lesbian innuendo. You're too much, Ox. Maybe if you stopped trying to make yourself look like a big bad heterosexual male animal and exercised your brain instead, you wouldn't be in this shit. But it's too late for you to get smart now. You crossed the line when you decided to involve my children. There's no going back from that. And, since it's not legal for me to rip your beating hearts from your chests and show them to you while you die, I'm going to see you both in prison.'

'I don't know what you're talking about,' Rubel said without emotion.

Liska looked him in the eye and made him wait. 'I've got Cal Springer. He's mine. I turned him. And now the fun begins,' she said with malicious relish. 'First one to the prosecutor gets the deal. Cal and I are sitting down with someone in Sabin's office tomorrow at noon.'

Ogden's mouth curved in a pout. 'You're full of shit, Liska. You don't have anything or you'd be pulling out cuffs.'

'There's nothing to have,' Rubel said, still cool. 'There's no case.'

Liska smiled up at him. 'You keep thinking that, sweetheart. And why don't you also spend some time thinking about what happens in prison to good-looking boys like you? I hear it gets rough. Then again, maybe you like it that way.'

She reached up and patted his cheek. 'Too bad Eric's not alive to fill us in.'

Bang! Right between the eyes. Rubel didn't flinch, didn't change his expression, but he felt the hit as surely as if he'd taken a bullet. Liska felt the shock wave roll off him, and he knew she knew. She savored the moment. Maybe a thousand moments like that would make up for what she'd felt when she'd seen those photographs of Kyle and R.J.

Maybe not.

She turned to go and pulled up short. Just for a heartbeat. Rubel and Ogden probably didn't even notice. She doubted she faltered longer than a split second. But in that split second, eye contact was made. Standing ten feet away, taking a break from squats on the Smith machine, was Speed.

'Are you sure the voice activation thing works?' Springer whined. 'What if it doesn't turn on?'

Barry Castleton knelt on the floor in front of him, duct-taping the microcassette recorder to Springer's squishy midsection. As the lead on the Ibsen case, Castleton had deserved a heads-up when Springer broke. Liska wanted the collar herself – for personal reasons more than for what it would put in her jacket – but she couldn't cut him out and live with herself. Castleton – forty-something, African American, a tendency to dress like an

English professor – was a good cop and a good guy. If she had to share, she didn't mind sharing with him.

'Don't worry about it,' he said to Springer. 'It's foolproof.'

Kovac snorted. 'Nothing is foolproof to a talented fool.'

They occupied Springer's kitchen. Springer, Castleton, Tippen from the SO – because they were out of their jurisdiction and wanted to cover their asses with the county people – Liska, and Kovac. Mrs Springer had gone to stay with a sister. Liska wondered if she would come back after this was all over. Probably. Then again, it remained to be seen if Cal would escape jail time and be here for Mrs Cal to come back to.

Springer's first part in the drama had been to look the other way when Ogden planted evidence in Renaldo Verma's house. In doing that, Ogden had him on the hook. It was one thing for a uniform to do something stupid, but the lead detective on a homicide investigation was a much bigger target and stood to lose much more. Cal Springer, with the high waters of his lifestyle already coming up around his head, couldn't afford to lose.

'I'm not feeling well,' Springer complained.

'Yeah, we can all smell that, Cal,' Castleton grumbled, getting to his feet.

Liska broke the pattern of her pacing, went over to Springer, and kicked him.

'Ouch!' He bent over and grabbed his shin.

'A man might die because of you, and you're complaining you don't *feel well*?' she said with utter disgust. 'My children were threatened because you weren't man enough to say no to Bruce Ogden.'

'He could have cost me my job,' Springer defended himself.

'And now you're going to prison. Great choice, Cal.'

'You don't understand.'

She stared at him, incredulous. 'No. I don't understand. I will *never* understand. You let Ogden plant evidence so you could close a case and get a big one in your win column.'

'What was the difference with Verma?' he argued. 'The guy was a killer. We knew he did it! And – and – the vic was one of ours. We couldn't let him walk for that!'

'How dare you pretend an interest in justice!' Liska spat the words at him. 'That wasn't your motivation, that's your rationalization. Your motivation to look the other way on Verma was for your own advancement.'

'Oh, and *you've* never done anything to get ahead,' Springer sneered.

'I've never contaminated an investigation. Did it ever occur to you that maybe Verma *didn't* do Curtis – an HIV-positive gay cop who'd changed patrol partners three times in five years and had lodged formal complaints of harassment.'

'When I had Verma cold on the Franz murder? No.'

'Hey, fuck that, Springer,' Castleton jumped in. 'Bobby Kerwin got Verma on Franz. You weren't even in the picture.'

Springer clenched his jaw. 'It was a figure of speech. Verma was good for an identical murder and how many robberies? Why shouldn't I take him?'

'The fact that you didn't have any physical evidence might have weighed in there,' Tippen suggested.

Springer scowled at him. 'Why should I suspect another cop, for God's sake? We spoke with all of Curtis's ex-partners. There were no red flags.'

'Then you weren't listening,' Liska said. 'Curtis's last partner, Engle, told me – and he doesn't know me from anyone – he thought something had gone on between Curtis and Rubel. He didn't tell you when you were looking into Curtis's murder?'

'It didn't pan out,' Springer said. 'I mean, look at Rubel. He's not queer. And – and why would he kill Curtis? They hadn't been partners for a long time.'

'Because of the HIV, you moron. If Curtis infected Rubel with an incurable, terminal disease, I would call that motive, wouldn't you?'

Springer inhaled and exhaled.

'And it didn't strike you odd that a couple of months after Curtis was murdered, Derek Rubel, who had been one of Curtis's partners, suddenly became partners with the guy who tampered with the evidence in the case?' Liska asked.

Springer looked ready to have a temper tantrum but was too afraid of Liska to do it. Red in the face. Shaking. 'People get reassigned all the time. Besides, the case was closed by then.'

'Oh, well, the case was closed. So what if you hung it on someone who didn't do it? He'd done something else just as bad. And you were already way on the meat hook, as far as Ogden was concerned. He could have sold you to IA in a heartbeat,' Liska said. 'Sure, it would have cost him. But it would have cost you more. So when Ogden and Rubel needed an alibi for Thursday night, all Ogden had to do was pick up the phone.'

'Ogden would have ruined me.'

'Bad cops ruin themselves,' Liska said quietly, remembering Savard telling her that when she had gone into IA after Andy Fallon's body had been discovered. It seemed like a year ago.

'It didn't matter to you what they did to Ken Ibsen?' she asked.

Springer turned his face away in shame. He hadn't cared enough to put himself on the line, and someone else had nearly paid with his life.

'I wish I could drag your sorry ass to the hospital and make you stand next to Ken Ibsen's bed when his doctors come to examine him,' she said. 'I wish I could take his memories of what those two animals did to him in that alley, and permanently implant them in your brain so that you would have to relive that attack over and over every day of your miserable life.'

'I'm sorry!' Springer shouted.

'Yes, you are.'

Kovac stepped between them and took Liska by the arm. 'Come on, Tinks. They'll be here soon. Let's go hide for the surprise party.'

He led her into the Springer pantry, a narrow closet of a room lined with shelves of canned foods and extra china. Liska leaned back against one set of shelves, Kovac the other.

'You got 'em, Tinks,' Kovac said quietly.

'They're on the hook, not in the net. I want them bludgeoned and on my stringer.'

'Then maybe you shouldn't chew the shit out of the one person who's going to get them there for you.'

'He deserves worse.'

'He deserves exactly what you said – to relive Ken Ibsen's attack every day of his life. But we'll have to settle for his career being ruined and his sorry butt in jail.'

'They threatened my boys, Sam,' she said, trembling again at the thought. 'You know, I kept thinking all week, what homophobe would beat a gay man to death in a manner that exposed him to so much blood? It didn't follow. Every guy I know like that is terrified of AIDS. They think they can get it from toilet seats, a handshake, breathing the air. It had to be someone who was either completely ignorant of the risk, or someone who was already infected. Then I saw Rubel at HCMC. . . .'

'Rubel didn't hate Curtis because he was gay,' Kovac said. 'He killed him because Curtis infected him. Revenge.'

'And Ogden put the evidence on Verma to protect Rubel because they're lovers.'

'They're bad guys, Tinks. And you got 'em.' He reached across and touched her shoulder. 'I'm proud of you, kiddo.'

'Thanks.' She looked away and chewed on her lip. 'You think Springer can get them to cop to Andy Fallon?'

'Maybe. If they did it.'

Tippen stuck his head in the pantry. 'The party guests have arrived. Places, everybody.'

Liska drew her weapon and checked it. Kovac did the same. The game faces went on. They would stay where they were while Cal Springer tried to get Ogden and Rubel to incriminate themselves on tape. When they'd heard enough, the trap would be sprung with Ogden and Rubel in the kitchen. Meanwhile, radio cars from the SO would roll in as backup.

The doorbell rang. There was the sound of voices, though Liska couldn't make out the words. She visualized Springer greeting his guests, inviting them in, assuring them he was on their side. But the tone of the voices changed abruptly, and Cal Springer started to shout *no!* The word was cut short by a gunshot.

'Shit!' Kovac yelled and bolted from the pantry.

Liska was right behind him.

'Freeze, police!' Castleton shouted.

Three more shots.

Kovac dashed for the living room, crouching low.

Liska went out the service door to the garage, and to the door that opened onto the driveway.

Rubel and Ogden were running for Rubel's truck, a dozen feet in front of Liska, guns out.

'Rubel!' Liska shouted, and discharged her weapon, then ducked back behind the door.

Two quick shots answered her, one splintering the door frame at the top. Three shots came from somewhere, and a man screamed.

The truck engine roared to life and spun backward out of Springer's driveway. Liska swung the door open to see Rubel sticking an arm out the truck window, and fire flashed from the end of his gun.

Lights and sirens running, a pair of radio cars were screaming toward the bottleneck of the cul-de-sac. Rubel never slowed down, splitting the space between the noses of the cars. One clipped the rear passenger side of his truck with a *bang!* Rubel kept going, speeding away as one of the sheriff's cars swung around to give chase.

Bruce Ogden lay sobbing on the driveway, rolling like a beached seal, trying in vain to grab at his back.

Liska ran toward him, leading with her weapon, and kicked his gun out of reach. Kovac ran up from the sidewalk, cursing a blue streak.

'Springer's dead!'

'Help me! Help me!' Ogden squealed. A dark stain spread on the ice-packed driveway beneath him. Liska stared down at him, thinking of Ken Ibsen.

A radio car from the Eden Prairie PD roared up, and two uniforms bailed out and came running.

'Don't touch him without gloves,' Liska ordered, stepping back. 'He's a health risk.'

'Whose bright idea was this?' Leonard asked, looking right at Kovac.

'We had to move fast, Lieutenant,' Liska said. 'We wanted Ogden and Rubel on tape before they had a chance to lawyer up.'

They stood in Cal Springer's living room with the cold fireplace and unlit Christmas tree. Cal was at that very moment being zipped into his own personal gift bag to be delivered to the morgue. He had taken a shot point-blank in the middle of the chest.

'We sure as hell never thought this would happen,' Kovac said.

'I could see Rubel and Ogden trying to get him out the door,' Castleton said. 'Probably to take him somewhere and make him disappear. Springer knew it. He tried to pull back. Rubel shot him before I could do anything.'

'Jesus H.' Leonard stared in disgust at the body bag on the gurney as the ME's people wheeled it out the front door. 'The press is going to have a field day with this.'

And, oh yeah, Mrs Springer, sorry for your loss, Liska thought.

'Every cop in the metro area and surrounding counties has the BOLO on Rubel,' Castleton said.

'He'll probably ditch his truck and steal some wheels,' Kovac said. 'He's got nothing to lose now. We catch him and he goes down for two murders and an aggravated assault. He'll never see the light of day.'

The Eden Prairie police chief stepped into the foyer from outside. 'Lieutenant Leonard? We have members of the press waiting.'

Leonard cursed under his breath and went away.

Liska went into the Springers' kitchen, pulling out her phone to call and check on the boys. Speed came in through the laundry room, stopped in the doorway, and stared at her.

'Are you okay?' he asked.

'No.'

Liska dropped her head and punched in Milo Foreman's phone number. Speed waited, listening as she explained the situation briefly and asked if the boys could stay until Sunday. She closed the phone and dropped it in her coat pocket.

'I'd ask what you're doing here,' she said, 'but –'

'I heard it on the scanner.'

'Really? You didn't just follow Ogden and Rubel out here from that gym you don't belong to?'

He rubbed the stubble on his jaw and looked away.

'What were you doing there, Speed?'

The big sigh. 'I've been on loan to Minneapolis narcotics. They were aware of a steroid problem within the department. They needed an unfamiliar face.'

'How long?' she asked, feeling the anger, the hurt, the frustration building inside her.

He hesitated again before confessing. 'The last two months.'

Liska laughed and shook her head. *Why should it hurt this much?* she asked herself. She shouldn't have even been surprised. Maybe she wasn't surprised. But she had to admit, there had been that sliver of hope, that tiny little spark. . . . After all these years, he still hadn't managed to kill it. She couldn't understand how it hadn't died of its own accord.

'So your sudden renewed interest in my life and the boys –'

'Is genuine, Nikki.'

'Oh, please.'

He moved toward her. 'I knew you had run into Ogden and Rubel. They were at the gym that afternoon you caught the Fallon thing.'

'And what was your purpose in watching me deal with that?' she asked. 'And you never saying one fucking word to me –'

'I can't talk about a case, Nikki. You know that.'

'Oh, but it's fine for you to pump me for information about my case,' she said. Every question he'd asked her this week bubbled up in her memory. 'You are such an asshole.'

He came toward her again, backing her toward the counter, trying to look sad and concerned and hurt by her low opinion of him. Liska ducked away, cringing away from any contact with him.

'Nikki, I was looking out for you, for the boys –'

'How were you looking out for us?' she demanded. 'By not filling me in? By not letting me know you were there for us?'

'You didn't exactly ask me to stick around.'

'Don't try to put this on me!'

He spread his hands and took a step back. 'I thought I could keep an eye on you without compromising my investigation or yours.'

'So that I wouldn't blow your collar if mine didn't pan out,' Liska said. 'Or were you planning to swoop in at the end, like Superman, and save the day for everyone? That would have been a nice feather in your cap, wouldn't it? Get the bad guys, get the girl –'

Speed was losing patience, as he always did when charm and false sincerity failed him. 'If that's what you really think, Nikki . . .'

Liska took a deep breath and willed her own emotions down. 'I think you need to go. I have a job to do.'

He bit back another sigh, regrouped mentally, tried to come again with the concerned-friend routine. 'Look, I know this isn't the time or the place. I just wanted to make sure you were okay. Maybe I'll stop by the house later –'

'Don't do that.'

'I can take the boys for the afternoon tomorrow if you want.'

'What I want,' Liska said, pointing her gaze toward the laundry room because it was hurting her to look at him, 'is not to see you for a while, Speed.'

It finally sunk into him that he wasn't going to win this one. Charm and looks could take him a long way in his day-to-day world, but he had run out of disguises with her. At least until the next time she felt weak enough to believe in him.

'Take the boys tomorrow if what you want is to be with them. But don't do it to get to me.'

He hesitated for a moment, as if he had something more to say, but he didn't say it. He went back out the way he'd come.

Liska stood there, staring at the floor, trying to clear her mind, get back to work mode, shake it off, suck it up, be tough. Again. She could see Kovac standing in the archway to the main part of the house.

'Why do I never learn?' she asked.

''Cause you're a hardhead.'

'Thanks.'

'Takes one to know one.' He came in and hooked an arm around her shoulders. 'Come on, Tinks. Unless you decide to run out and put a couple in that asshole's head, our work here is done. Call it a night. Go home. I'll put a radio car in front of your house.'

She made a face. 'I don't need –'

'You *do* need. You're the one who found Rubel out, kiddo. And he knows where you live.'

A chill went down her back like an icy finger.

'You know,' she said, putting her head on his shoulder, 'some days I wish I was a waitress.'

33

By six A.M. news of the manhunt for Officer Derek Rubel had brought in reporters from every major network. Minneapolis was crawling with camera crews. Kovac, Liska, Tippen, and Castleton had all been ordered to speak to no one regarding the murder of Cal Springer. Interviews were being handled by Leonard, the Hennepin County sheriff, and the Eden Prairie chief.

The FBI had been called in on the case, along with the Minnesota Bureau of Criminal Apprehension. The Minnesota and Wisconsin State Highway Patrols both had helicopters in the air, doing a grid search for Rubel's black Explorer, a tedious job sparking one false alarm after another. Minnesota was full of black Ford Explorers. None of the ones stopped and searched belonged to Rubel.

Neighbors and known associates of his were questioned as to his habits in order to try come up with a list of likely hiding places. Deputies were dispatched to eighty acres of hunting land in the scrub near Zimmerman, property owned jointly by half a dozen officers. There was no sign Rubel had been to the crude cabin.

Ogden, who had taken two bullets in the shoot-out, had been airlifted by chopper to the Hennepin County Medical Center, where he was listed as stable after three hours of surgery. He had yet to be questioned, and already the union had staked out a lawyer at the door to his hospital room.

Kovac worked KOD duty all night, preferring knocking on the doors of perfect strangers to spending the night in his empty house. By morning, his social skills were running on empty. He passed the baton to Elwood and went home.

The neighbor was out in the frigid sunshine wearing his plaid bomber cap, digging bits of snow from his yard with a spade.

'Goddamn dogs,' Kovac heard him grumble as he got out of the car. At the slam of the door, the old man's head came up and he drew a bead on Kovac through his cockeyed glasses.

'Hey, we heard about that manhunt!' he called, his excitement overriding his dislike for Kovac. 'A killer cop, huh? Are you in on that?'

'I'm the guy they're looking for,' Kovac said. 'Driven mad from sleep deprivation caused by my neighbor's garish light display.'

The neighbor couldn't decide whether to show offense or pretend good humor.

'Quite a story, this guy,' he said. 'It's all over the television. They're even doing a special *Crime Time* on it.'

'Another good reason to read a book,' Kovac grumbled.

The neighbor paid no attention. 'Best goddamn show on television.'

'Reality programming.'

'You know that guy? Ace? He's something. He's a *real* cop.'

'He used to be a woman,' Kovac said, unlocking his door.

The neighbor gave a little jolt of surprise. He narrowed his beady eyes to the size of BBs. 'You're sick!' he announced, and went back to the other side of his yard to hunt for dog shit and yellow snow.

Kovac went into the house. His gaze went directly to the couch, and he stood there for a moment before it hit him.

Someone had been there.

The articles he'd brought home from the library were strewn all over the coffee table. His briefcase had been pried open and now lay on the floor, half hidden behind a chair. The television screen had been kicked in.

The air in the room seemed to thicken and crackle with electricity. Kovac could feel it on his skin. His pulse jumped. He opened his coat and discreetly reached inside, slipping his gun from the holster. With his other hand, he dug his cell phone out of his pocket and hit 911.

He reported the break-in as he crept through the house, room by room, taking in the damage, looking to see if the perpetrator was still in the building. The drawers had been pulled from his desk. His dresser had been gone through. Cash he had left on top of the dresser was gone, along with an expensive watch he'd won in a raffle at a law enforcement conference. That said burglary. Probably a junkie looking for stuff to pawn.

He checked his bedroom closet, relieved to find his old .38 in its shoe box on the shelf.

Back downstairs, he found that the intruder had broken in through the kitchen door. A task that looked to have been embarrassingly easy. He would take some ribbing for his lack of home maintenance, Kovac thought as he turned and saw the basement door ajar.

He flipped the light switch and listened. Nothing. He descended the first few steps, then crouched down to look, still fairly well concealed by wall.

The basement wasn't finished space. He kept a dehumidifier going to fight the damp of the concrete walls and floor. There was no furniture, nothing that would be of any interest to a thief; only half-empty paint cans and boxes and boxes of old case files.

Boxes that had been pulled from the shelves and dumped all over the floor.

His cell phone trilled in his pocket.

'Kovac.'

'Liska. They've found Rubel's truck. In Lake Minnetonka. Went off the road, down an embankment and through the ice.'

'So he's dead?'

'I said they found the truck. Rubel wasn't in it.'

The atmosphere on the banks of Lake Minnetonka was not unlike that on the first day of fishing season. Cars and news vans lined the narrow strip of road. People wandered up and down, waiting for something to happen. Deputies had established a perimeter beyond which only law enforcement personnel were allowed. Just before that line, various representatives of the media had staked out their territories. The largest of the sideshows, by far, was *Crime Time*. The same crew from the ice rink had set up as near to the yellow crime scene tape as possible.

Kovac stared. Ace Wyatt, bundled into a heavy parka, stood on his trademark red carpet before a crowd of spectators. Beyond him, beyond the yellow tape, Derek Rubel's Explorer had been pulled ashore by a tow truck and stood with all doors open as the crime scene unit from the Minnesota Bureau of Criminal Apprehension went over every inch of it. They would look it over here, at the scene, then the vehicle would be transported to their garage in St Paul and every piece of hair and lint in the thing would be cataloged and held under a microscope.

Kovac took a moment to assess the scene, trying to imagine it without the crowd. They were on a narrow finger of the lake that had been deemed beneath the efforts of development. A couple of small houses were within sight, near enough to walk to on a cold night, but not so near for a witness to see a man leaping from a vehicle as it ran into the lake.

Tippen came over in his Dr Seuss hat, hands stuffed in the pockets of a fat parka.

'They checked the houses. One is vacant. The other isn't, but nobody's home and there's no vehicle. They're trying to track down somebody who might know where the owner is – or rather, where the owner is supposed to be. No luck so far.'

'Rubel's probably riding around with the owner's body in the trunk of the owner's Buick,' Kovac said. 'What a nightmare.'

'It's that. Minnesota hasn't gotten this kind of attention since Andrew Cunanan.'

'Andrew Cunanan wasn't a cop. This has Hollywood written all over it.'

Kovac spotted the WB VPs just at the corner of Wyatt's carpet, right behind Fat Donald, the director. The redhead had bought herself a parka that looked made from aluminum foil. Gaines came over to them and seemed to be explaining something, pointing one arm toward the lake, where, in the distance, ice fishing houses dotted the snowscape.

Kovac looked around again, trying to get his bearings – hard to do for a city boy tossed out into the maze around Minnetonka. But he didn't think they were far from Neil Fallon's place. Where Gaines was pointing might have been it, though one ice fishing hut looked pretty much like the next to Kovac.

Wyatt was having his makeup done again while some toady held a light meter next to his head and called out numbers.

'Can you believe this guy?' Kovac said.

'His people were here staking out that spot practically before we were,' Tippen said. 'It pays to have friends in high places, even at a freak show like this.'

'Especially at a freak show like this. Reality programming.'

A gust of wind came up off the lake, blowing Wyatt's red muffler across his face. The director swore, then turned and swore again at the woman in the shag carpet coat, then announced everyone should take ten, and stalked off toward the official *Crime Time* motor home parked on the road.

The videographers dug out cigarettes. Shag Coat went onto the carpet to adjust Wyatt's scarf, the WB VPs right behind her. Gaines paused en route to accept a steaming cup of coffee from another minion.

Kovac joined the cadre, giving the eye to the bouncer who stepped toward him at the edge of the carpet. The bouncer stepped back.

'Johnny-on-the-spot here, aren't you, Ace?' Kovac said.

'Too bad we can't say the same for you, Sam.' Wyatt stood perfectly still while Shag Coat arranged the offending scarf in an artful and clever way. 'I understand you and your partner were in on the fiasco last night.'

'Yeah, well, I'm a real cop, I don't just play one on TV. As you know, in the real world, with real bad guys, shit happens.'

'And you step in it?' Gaines suggested as he put the coffee cup into Wyatt's hand.

'I swim through it, Slick. If that's what I have to do to get what I'm after. You should know how that tastes, you being a professional kiss-ass. Do they give college degrees for that now?'

'We're very busy here, Sergeant,' Gaines said tightly.

'I understand, and I'll let you get back to finding the cure for cancer in a minute. I just have a question for Captain America here.'

Wyatt huffed a sigh. 'You're starting to get on my nerves, Sam.'

'Yeah, I have a talent,' Kovac said. 'After our chat yesterday, I was curious, so I went back and read over the articles from the Thorne murder. That's a hell of a dramatic story, Ace. I'd forgotten. You ought to do a special on that. A movie of the week maybe. The network could run it to hype the new show.'

'The show will succeed on its own merits,' Wyatt said tightly. 'I have no intention of capitalizing on that night.'

Kovac laughed. 'You've done it your whole career. Why stop now?'

'No!' Wyatt barked. 'That was *never* my intent. What happened with my career at the time was out of my hands.'

He turned and snapped at the shag coat woman, who was still fussing with his clothes. 'Leave the goddamn scarf alone!'

The WB VPs looked at Wyatt, then at each other, then at Gaines, panicked at having been left out of the loop.

'It's a tragic story,' Kovac explained.

'Which is precisely why the captain doesn't want to bring it up,' Gaines said, putting himself between Kovac and Wyatt. He spoke to the VPs. 'A friend of the captain's was killed, another was left a paraplegic. You can understand why he wouldn't want to dredge up the trauma.'

'No, they can't,' Kovac said. 'That night made the Ace here a hero. He saved another cop's life. It's a story made for Hollywood. Ace makes it big with the show, everybody in America's gonna want to hear it.

'I'm just wondering, Ace,' he continued, cocking his head to look around Gaines. 'Have you kept in touch with Bill Thorne's widow over the years? It occurred to me she might appreciate hearing about Mike's passing.'

'No,' he said. 'We lost touch.'

Kovac raised his brows. 'As close as you stayed with Mike, you lost touch with Evelyn Thorne? After all you went through?'

'Because of all we went through,' Wyatt murmured.

'When Andy Fallon talked with you about the case, did he mention if he'd spoken with her? Or with Thorne's daughter?'

'I don't recall.'

'Well, I'm sure it's in his notes,' Kovac said. 'I just haven't found them yet. I'll let you know. In case you want to reach out.'

'We need to clear the set, Sergeant,' Gaines said, trying to back him away. 'We're airing this tonight. Trying to help bring this mess to a conclusion for you.'

'That's big of you, Junior,' Kovac said. 'Frees me up to concentrate on something else. Thanks.'

Kovac walked away, shooting a glance up at the bouncer. 'You should have gone into wrestling. Better class of people.'

34

'Once again, citizens, this is a photograph of the known *murderer* at the heart of this manhunt tonight.'

Wyatt had what was often described as 'the look of eagles.' Steely-eyed. Hard-jawed. A face that inspired fear and trust.

'This is the face of Officer Derek Rubel. Known to have *murdered* a fellow police officer. Suspected in several more *brutal* crimes. This man is at large in our country tonight, and it's going to take the courage and diligence of citizens to bring this *animal* to justice.

'If you see Derek Rubel, do *not* under *any* circumstances approach him. This man is *extremely* dangerous. What *do* you do, Citizen Jane?'

'*Do* go to the nearest telephone and call the police,' the woman says.

Another member of the audience is called on.

'*Do* write down a license number!'

On cue, the audience shouts in unison, '*Be PROActive!*'

The hot-line number and Web site address appear on the screen.

The television goes black.

Admirable.

A testament to the powers of redemption and penance.

A service to the community. Empowering to the powerless.

The agitation returns.

A fear burning in the pit of the stomach and radiating outward.

Fear of discovery.

Fear of death.

Fear of the inner knowledge of one's own capabilities when threatened.

There is the sense that the world is turning faster and faster, growing smaller and smaller, making discovery inevitable.

It is only a matter of time.

The thought repeats endlessly as the gaze scans the photographs of death.

It is only a matter of time.

Kovac must die.

35

'I love that show,' Liska said as she hung up the phone.

Across the cubicle, Kovac scowled. He had his computer on and the telephone receiver wedged between his shoulder and ear.

'The hot-line phones rang off the hook after the show ran last night.'

'With how many legitimate leads?' he asked.

'All it takes is one. What's your problem with it, anyway?' she asked.

'I hate –'

'Besides that you hate Ace Wyatt.'

Kovac pouted. 'That'd pretty much be it.'

'Look what that show does. It teaches people who feel they have no power to stand up and make something happen. If Cal Springer had paid attention to that message, Derek Rubel wouldn't be running loose now.'

'It's the whole reality programming thing.'

'You love *America's Most Wanted.*'

'That's different. What Wyatt has is a game show. What's next? Interactive court trials? People can log on and vote guilty or not guilty?'

'They've already got that on *Dateline.*'

'Great. And next season they can televise the executions from Texas. Maybe they can get Regis Philbin to host,' he crabbed.

'Who are you on the line with?' Liska asked, finally noticing that he had yet to speak into the receiver.

'Frank Sinatra.'

'Kojak, he's dead.'

'I'm on hold. Donna at the phone company. Anyway, what if the show gives someone a false sense of power, and they do something stupid and end up dead?'

'What if someone ends up dead because they're spineless and stupid and they don't watch the show?'

'I hate Ace Wyatt.'

'The WB is promoting him as Captain America.'

Disgust made a strangled sound in his throat. 'Aw, jeez, those fucking VPs. They stole that from me!'

'Call your agent, Hollywood.'

'You're the one who wants that, Tinker Bell, not me.'

'Just so I get my fame for catching Rubel, not for being killed by him.'

Kovac drew breath to ask her how she was doing – really doing – when, finally, a human being picked up on the other end of the line.

'Sorry to keep you on hold, Sam. What can I do you for?'

'Hey, Donna. I need the LUDS on a Minneapolis number.'

'You have the paperwork?'

'Not exactly.'

'That would mean no.'

'Well ... yes. But the guy's dead. Who will care?'

'How about his family?'

'Dead and in jail.'

'How about the county attorney?'

'I just need to shake something loose here, Donna. It doesn't have to stand up in court.'

'Mmm ... You didn't get it from me.'

'I never have, but I live in hope.'

Donna cracked up at that. Classy broad. Kovac gave her Andy Fallon's phone number and hung up.

'What are you after?' Liska asked.

'I'm not exactly sure,' he admitted. 'I want to go through Andy's phone records and see if something jumps out. Andy was poking around in the Thorne murder, trying to connect to Mike through his experiences. When I did some of that same poking, I got a rise out of Wyatt. I want to see –'

'You're obsessed, Sam,' Liska said. 'You don't like Rubel for Andy's murder? If it *was* a murder.'

'No. It doesn't fit. Andy's scene was too neat. Look what Rubel did – beat a guy to death with a ball bat, beat a guy near to death with a pipe, shot a guy point-blank in the chest. Where's the finesse?'

'But you said Pierce told you he'd seen Andy with another guy. What if it was Rubel? That might track. Andy was looking at Ogden for being dirty. No one knew Ogden and Rubel were an item. Through his connection to Curtis – having once been a patrol partner – Rubel gets close to Andy to keep an eye on the case from the inside, so to speak. Andy gets too close to some truth. . . . See?'

'No way. Rubel was Ogden's partner –'

'Not at the beginning of the investigation. There was no connection between them at the time, none that anyone knew of. Rubel had been patrol partners with Curtis, but Curtis swore none of his former partners harassed him.'

'Until he infected one.'

'And if Andy somehow found out about Rubel's HIV status . . .' She left Kovac to finish the thought for himself, then added, 'I'm putting Rubel in a photo array and showing it to Pierce.'

'Have at it,' Kovac said. 'Meanwhile, who broke into my house? Why would Rubel? It's not like I've got the one piece of evidence that can hang him.'

'That could have been anybody, for any reason. Probably a junkie looking for your secret cash stash. Or maybe it was some other scumbag you're looking at for something else. It doesn't necessarily have anything to do with Fallon.'

The possibility had crossed Kovac's mind. He had other cases ongoing. . . . He grabbed his phone on the third ring.

'Homicide. Kovac.'

'Kovac, Maggie Stone. I looked over that case – Fallon, Andy.'

'And?'

'Is he in the ground yet?'

'I don't think so. Why?'

'I'd like to have him back for a visit. I think he might have been murdered.'

Maggie Stone's office at the Hennepin County morgue always made Kovac think of those news stories about crazy old people whose bodies were found mummified among the stacks of newspapers and magazines and garbage they had not thrown out in nine years. The room was a maze of papers and professional journals and books on forensic medicine and motorcycle magazines. Stone rode a Harley Hog in good weather.

She waved Kovac into the office with one hand, holding a sugared jelly doughnut in the other. The doughnut was oozing red from its center, and bore a little too much resemblance to some of the stuff in the photographs spread out on the desk.

'Do you ever read any of this?' Kovac asked.

She peered down at a photo through a pair of funky reading glasses and an illuminated magnifying glass. 'Read what?'

Her hair was a peculiar toffee shade this month, cut in a pixie style and slicked to her head with goo. Most days she looked as if she hadn't remembered to use a comb since the eighties.

'What did you find?'

'Okay.' She swung the magnifying glass on its swivel arm so that Kovac could look through it from the other side of the desk. 'What I look for on the neck in a hanging death is a V-shaped bruising or abrasions, obviously following the angles of the noose. We see that clearly here,' she said, pointing out the marks. 'And you found him hanging. We know he was hung. However, I also see what looks to be some shadows of a straight-line bruise around the neck here.'

'You think he was strangled, then hung?'

'The bruising isn't clear. Anyone looking at this case with a foregone conclusion of suicide wouldn't even notice it. But I feel that it's there. If I'm right, I suspect the killer might have put protective padding between the ligature and the victim's neck. If we're lucky and the funeral home did a poor job of preparing the body, I may still be able to get some fibers off the throat. And, if the bruising *is* there, I'll bet there's more at the back of the neck.'

She sat back, made two fists, and held them out in front of her to demonstrate. 'If the killer tightens the ligature with his hands, the knuckles press into the back of the neck, leaving several bruises. If you're looking at a garrote, then the pressure at the point where the ligature crosses and tightens creates a significant single bruise.'

'There aren't any photographs of the back of his neck?'

'No. I admit this wasn't the most thorough of autopsies. But it came in looking like a slam-dunk suicide, and apparently there were calls from your end of things to move it through quickly for the family's sake.'

'Didn't come from me,' Kovac corrected her, frowning as he looked at the photographs. He stared at the barely discernible bruises on Andy Fallon's throat, just below the vivid marks the noose had made. The nerves in his stomach came to life like a tangled pile of worms. 'I'm on the ass-end on my end of things. That pressure came from higher up the food chain.'

That pressure had come from Ace Wyatt.

Kovac leaned over the counter and caught Russell Turvey sitting back in the corner paging through *Hustler*.

'Jesus, Russell. Do me a favor and don't offer to shake my hand.'

Turvey barked and growled, his chest sounding like thunder in the distance. 'Kojak! J. Christ! You'd be back here too, if you got the chance.'

'Not with you.'

Turvey laughed again, tossing the magazine under his chair. He grabbed hold of the counter and rolled himself into position without getting up.

'I hear Springer bought it,' he said, fixing his squint eye on Kovac. The other one looked off to the left. 'I never liked him.'

Like that had made Cal Springer's demise inevitable.

'You were there too,' Turvey said.

'I swear I didn't pull the trigger. Liska can vouch for me.'

'Ha! Argh . . . Liska,' he purred, his expression a postcard for the word *lascivious*. 'Is she a dyke?'

'No!'

'Not even . . .' He waggled a hand.

'No,' Kovac said emphatically. 'Can we move on, please? I came down here for a reason.'

Turvey waved a hand at him. 'What?'

'I need to look at an old file. The Thorne murder. I don't have a case number but I've got the dates –'

'Don't matter,' Turvey said. 'It's not here.'

'You're sure?'

'I'm here every goddamn day. You think I don't know the place?'

'But –'

'I know it's gone because someone from IA came down and asked for it a couple of months ago. Mike Fallon's kid. It wasn't here then. It ain't here now.'

'And you don't know where it is?'

'Nope.'

Kovac sighed and started to turn away, wondering who might have it or have a copy.

'Funny you should ask for that one,' Turvey said.

'Why is that?'

''Cause I found that badge number you asked for the other day. It belonged to Bill Thorne.'

Amanda Savard had Bill Thorne's badge sitting on her desk in her home.

Kovac just stood there, trying to get his brain around that idea.

'I remember Bill Thorne,' Turvey said, rubbing his knobby chin. 'I rode patrol in the Third Precinct back then. He was the meanest son of a bitch I ever knew.'

'You're sure?' Kovac asked.

Turvey's brows went up. 'Sure? I once saw him knock a prostitute's teeth out for lying to him.'

'You're sure it's Thorne's badge?'

'Yeah. I'm sure.'

Kovac walked away, Russell Turvey's words blurring into white noise. Amanda Savard had Bill Thorne's badge on her desk.

He went into the men's room, ran the cold water and splashed his face, then stood there with his hands braced on the sink, staring into the mirror.

His mind scanned back over the days, flashing on images of her, of the two of them. He thought back to Saturday night. They'd made love on his couch. And when she was getting ready to leave, she'd looked down at the coffee table and had seen the articles he had gathered at the library.

What's this?

The Thorne murder. Mike Fallon's shooting. Andy was looking at it. I'm just turning over rocks, see what crawls out.

Life turns on a dime, he'd said.

And gives back change.

He went to the first floor, where traffic was heavier than usual, the hall busy with cops and with reporters looking for scraps on the Rubel manhunt. No one seemed to see him. He stood at the edge of the scene, looking past the crowd, toward Room 126.

She was likely in her office. IA would be busy digging up dirt on Rubel and Ogden, going through any reports of prior problems with either of them. Savard would likely be called on the carpet by a captain who would demand to know why the investigation into Ogden and the Curtis murder had died out. Why hadn't any mention been made of Rubel at the time?

If he went down there right now, he might catch her between calls. And

... what? Confront her like some cheated husband? He could see the scene in his mind. He could feel the humiliation. No.

One of the reporters spotted him, and life snapped back into fast-forward mode.

'Hey, Kovac,' the guy said, coming over, trying to keep his voice down so as not to tip off his competition. 'I hear you were on the scene Saturday night. What happened?'

Kovac held up a hand and turned away. 'No comment.'

He ducked into the anteroom, pushed past the crowd trying to circumvent the receptionist, and keyed his way into the main office. Liska was gone. Donna from the phone company had come through with Andy Fallon's phone records for the past three months. Distraction. He could do this while his brain tripped and stumbled over the subject of Amanda. He turned on his computer, brought a reverse phone directory up on-line, and started in.

Too many of the numbers were unlisted. Nowadays, everyone wanted anonymity – and to avoid telemarketers. Those numbers that were listed were not of much interest. Mike, Neil, take-out restaurants. There were several calls to something called the Hazelwood Home. Kovac looked it up in the on-line Yellow Pages and found the place discreetly described as a 'care facility'. Care of what? A rest home for Mike, maybe? Though Mike Fallon hadn't really seemed in need of anything like that. A housekeeper, yes. A nursing home? No.

When he had gone through the list with the reverse directory, Kovac started with the cold calls, dialing the unlisted numbers and, for the most part, getting answering machines.

One of the machines belonged to Amanda Savard. Fallon had called her at home several times in the last few days of his life.

Andy Fallon had been looking into the Thorne murder. Amanda Savard had Bill Thorne's badge on her desk.

She had very coolly denied Andy's mentioning his private investigation into the Thorne case.

God *damn*! If only he had Fallon's notes. There had to be files somewhere ... and his laptop ...

Or he could walk down the hall and ask Amanda point-blank about Thorne's badge.

His gut told him not to ask.

Or maybe it wasn't his gut at all.

She had Bill Thorne's badge. She had seen Andy Fallon on the night of his death. She had been to his house. Andy had phoned her house frequently just before he died.

I love a puzzle, he thought, a vicious feeling cracking through him like a whip.

Amanda Savard had gone to bed with him. Twice. He was poking around in the death of Andy Fallon. Andy Fallon had been poking around in the death of Bill Thorne. Amanda had Bill Thorne's badge.

He grabbed the telephone receiver and punched in the number for the Hazelwood Home.

The Hazelwood Home was a psychiatric care facility.

Kovac grabbed his coat and hat and bolted.

The wind skimmed over the snow, lifting a fine powder into the air so that, from the end of the driveway, the Hazelwood Home appeared shrouded in mist. A former private residence, the home was a sprawling, overdone homage to Frank Lloyd Wright. Long, low, horizontal lines gave the impression that the building was crouching into the ground. Huge old trees studded the snow-covered lawn. Beyond the grounds, the landscape looked open and marshy, which was much of the landscape west of Minneapolis.

Kovac parked under the carport at the entrance and went in past dueling holiday displays. Christmas on one side of the foyer, Hanukkah on the other. The overwhelming impression of the entry hall was darkness. A low beamed ceiling seemed too close overhead.

He looked for the youngest, least-experienced staff member working around the front desk, and homed in on her. A cherubic girl with natural blond curls clipped like a poodle's. Her name tag read 'Amber'. Amber's eyes went wide as Kovac showed her his badge, using it to lure her away from the older woman answering the phone.

'Is he near *here*?' the girl asked, worried.

'Excuse me?'

'That guy,' she answered in a hushed whisper. 'That *killer*. Are you here looking for him?'

Kovac leaned toward her. 'I'm not at liberty to say,' he whispered back.

'Oh, my gosh.'

'I need to ask you a couple of questions, Amber,' Kovac said, pulling out a snapshot of Andy Fallon he had taken from Mike's place. 'Have you seen this man around here?'

She seemed disappointed the photograph wasn't of Derek Rubel, but she recovered gamely.

'Yes. I've seen him. He's been here a couple of times.'

'Lately?'

'In the past few weeks. He's a police officer too,' she said, narrowing her eyes. 'At least, he *claimed* to be.'

'What was he doing here? Who did he speak to?' Kovac kept one eye on the older woman at the other end of the desk. At a place like Hazelwood, discretion would be the rule. Amber looked too innocent of sin to understand the meaning of the word.

'He came to visit Mrs Thorne,' she said simply, eyes blinking.

'You have to understand, Sergeant, Evelyn lives in her own world,' the doctor said as they walked down the long hall toward Evelyn Thorne's room. 'She'll acknowledge your presence. She'll interact with you. But the conversation will be her own.'

The psychiatrist was a large, soft-looking woman with a thick mane of long blond hair.

'I just want to ask her a couple of questions about the cop who came to see her a couple of times,' Kovac said. 'Sergeant Fallon. Did he speak with you?'

The doctor looked troubled. 'I spoke briefly with Mr Fallon. I wasn't aware he was here on police business. He told me he was Evelyn's nephew. He asked me if she ever speaks about her husband's murder.'

'Does she?'

'No. Never. She had her breakdown shortly after his death.'

'And she's been like this ever since?'

'Yes. Some days she's better than others, but she pretty much stays in hiding in her mind. She feels safe there.'

The doctor looked in the glass set in the center of Evelyn Thorne's door, then rapped twice before going in.

'Evelyn, you have a visitor. This is Mr Kovac.'

Kovac stopped just inside the room, feeling as if he'd taken a fist in the belly. Evelyn Thorne sat in an upholstered armchair, looking out her window, dressed in a blue track suit. She was thin, the kind of thinness that came from nerves. Her hair had gone gray. She wore it swept back from her face with a velvet headband. In the newspaper photograph he'd thought she looked a little like Grace Kelly. In reality she looked too much like someone else.

She turned her head to see him, her eyes a little vacant but her mouth curved in a pleasant smile.

'I know you!'

'No, ma'am, you don't,' he said, walking toward her.

'Mr Kovac needs to ask you some questions about the young man who came to see you, Evelyn,' the doctor said.

She paid no attention to the doctor. 'You were a friend of my husband,' she said to Kovac.

The doctor gave him the I-told-you-so look and left them.

The room was spacious, with normal-looking furniture except for the hospital bed, which was draped with a pretty flowered spread. *Not a bad place to while away the hours locked inside your own reality*, Kovac thought. It had to cost some major bucks. He wondered if Wyatt was footing the bill for this as well. No wonder he needed to go Hollywood.

'So nice of you to come,' Evelyn Thorne said with formality. 'Please have a seat.'

Kovac took the chair across from her and held out the photograph he'd shown Amber. 'Mrs Thorne, do you remember Andy Fallon? He came to see you recently.'

She took the photograph, still smiling. 'Oh, isn't he handsome? Your boy?'

'No, ma'am. He's Mike Fallon's boy. Do you remember Mike Fallon? He was a police officer. He came to your house the night your husband died.'

He didn't know if she heard a word he said. She seemed not to.

'They grow up so fast,' she said, getting up from her chair and going to a little bookcase that held a lot of magazines and a Bible.

'I have pictures too,' she said, digging for a magazine at the bottom. *Redbook.* 'She thinks she took them all. She doesn't like having photographs out, not of family. But I had to keep a few.'

She pulled a manila envelope from the magazine and extracted a couple of snapshots.

'My daughter,' she said proudly, holding them out to Kovac. He didn't want to touch them, as if not touching them, not looking at them, would keep their truth at bay. But Evelyn Thorne pushed them into his hands.

She was younger in the photograph. A little thinner. Her hair was different. But there was no mistaking Evelyn and Bill Thorne's daughter: Amanda Savard.

36

Amanda Savard was Bill Thorne's daughter.

He remembered the only hint in the newspaper articles from all those years ago: *Thorne is survived by his wife and one daughter.* That was it. No name, no photo.

Savard was Evelyn's maiden name. He had been able to get that much out of her. Amanda must have taken the name for her own after the murder. Otherwise, she never could have come on the job without people making something of it.

Andy Fallon worked for Amanda Savard, Bill Thorne's daughter. He'd been looking into Bill Thorne's murder, the night Mike Fallon was shot, the night Ace Wyatt became a hero. Ace Wyatt had been paying off Mike Fallon for years. Andy Fallon was dead. Mike Fallon was dead. . . .

Kovac sat in the dark parking lot of the building that housed the Wyatt Productions offices. On his third cigarette in two hours, his head was pounding. Hell of a day. He felt beat up. He felt old. He felt hollow. Funny, he'd thought he was too cynical to be disillusioned or disappointed. *The joke's on you, Kovac.*

The building was nondescript. A brick two-story like a thousand others in the western suburbs. The parking lot had emptied in the last hour as the business day had come to a close and the CPAs and attorneys and orthodontist who shared the building had climbed into their cold vehicles and rolled down the street in a fog of exhaust to edge their way into the rush hour crawl on 494.

Wyatt was expecting him. Had expected him ten minutes ago. Kovac let him wait, let the office staff leave. The Lincoln was parked in a reserved spot near the front of the building. Kovac had parked three rows back, alone. His pager trilled and he checked the display. Leonard. Fuck 'em.

He turned off the car and walked across the lot and into the building, tossing his cigarette just outside the door, not caring where it landed. The circular reception desk was deserted, the telephone ringing. A directory board on the wall showed Wyatt Productions to be on the second floor.

Kovac walked past the elevator, went up the stairs, and slipped into the outer office unnoticed. Like the rest of the building, everything was gray –

the carpet, the walls, the upholstery on the square furniture. The walls were covered mainly with photographs of the great man being given commendations for this and that remarkable feat, being honored for his selfless service to the community. Photographs of him with local celebrities, with legends in law enforcement, with movie stars buttonholed on the sets of pictures being shot in the metro area.

The man had never met a camera he wouldn't turn his good side to. Evelyn Thorne's included.

Kovac sniffed and shook his head.

The knob turned on the door to Wyatt's office and the sound of voices spilled out in dribs and drabs, the volume rising and falling.

'. . . that kind of publicity . . . unacceptable, Gavin.' Wyatt.

'. . . situation can be defused . . . denials . . .' Gaines.

'Goddammit, you have to . . . image . . . my audience is Middle America, for God's sake.'

'I'm sorry –'

The door closed tight again. Kovac moved closer, straining to hear. Then Gaines came out, looking flushed and angry.

'What's the matter, Slick?' Kovac asked. 'Hard day on your knees?'

'I realize you have no appreciation for what I do, Sergeant,' he said. 'There's really no need for you to make the point every time we meet.'

'But I like the way it makes your nostrils flare, Gavin.'

Gaines looked ready to bend an iron bar with his teeth. 'Captain Wyatt has been waiting for you.'

'Good. I'm a busy man.' Kovac went to the door, then looked back at Wyatt's right hand. 'You can go, Gaines. The captain won't be needing you. We're just going to talk about old times.'

Wyatt stood looking out a window at nothing. Darkness had fallen like an anvil an hour before. He watched Kovac's reflection in the window.

'No word yet on Rubel,' he said. A statement of fact.

'You'll hear it before I will.'

'Shouldn't you be out on the search?'

'With all your citizens beating the bushes? They'll bring him to you hogtied. He can be the special guest on your next show.'

Wyatt went for the straight line. 'Maybe. I like the idea of the occasional interview with a bad guy. Let the public see how twisted minds work.'

He'd been spending too much time with the WB VPs.

'I have other cases ongoing,' Kovac said. 'Mike's murder. Andy's murder . . .'

Wyatt looked straight at him then.

'No one called you?' Kovac said, feigning shock. 'Stone believes Andy was strangled before he was hung.'

The color drained from his face. 'What?'

'Marks on the throat,' he said, running a finger around his own to demonstrate. 'Faint but there. The doc who did the autopsy missed them. I asked Dr Stone to personally go back over the autopsy, just in case the new guy missed something – having had pressure on him from higher up. Good thing, huh? Or he might have been buried with that little secret.'

'Why . . . ?' Kovac could see Wyatt scrambling mentally, trying to get his legs back under him, trying to sound intelligent and ignorant at once. 'Do you think it had to do with Rubel?'

'Personally, no,' Kovac said. 'I think it's a pretty damn strange coincidence that first Andy dies and it looks like suicide, then his old man buys it and it's made to look like suicide. Don't you find that strange?'

Wyatt furrowed the famous brow. 'So you like Neil for both murders?'

Kovac ignored the question, feeling too raw and wrung out emotionally to dance the mental minuet. 'I found Evelyn Thorne. Andy found her too. You think I'll end up the same as he did, or the same as Mike?'

'I don't know what you're talking about.'

'Jesus Christ, Ace,' Kovac said, the impatience burning through. 'I don't have time for this bullshit! It goes back to Thorne! Andy found something about what happened that night, something no one else saw at the time, because they didn't want to see it, or they buried it because it was all in the family. It was cops. Thorne was a cop, you, Mike. The only one dead not a cop was that poor bastard Weagle.'

'Weagle attacked Evelyn!' Wyatt said. 'He – he beat her. He raped her. He shot Bill. Killed him. He shot Mike.'

'Did he?' Kovac asked. ''Cause I'm wondering here, Ace, why people interested in that case, connected to that case, are suddenly dead if it happened the way we all heard back then.'

Wyatt walked away, went behind his desk. Retreating, or taking cover . . . Kovac never took his eyes off the man, every muscle in his body taut, ready to move. He positioned himself so he could see both Wyatt and the door.

'What did Evelyn say to you?' Wyatt asked. 'She's not a well woman. I'm sure the doctors told you she's often delusional.'

'You told me you'd lost touch with her. You told me you didn't know where she was.'

'I was trying to protect her. Evelyn never recovered from what happened. She was always . . . fragile. Something broke in her mind that night. The doctors have never been able to fix it. She retreated to a safe place, a world of her own. She seems to be happy there most of the time.'

'She showed me photographs,' Kovac said. 'Pictures of the old neighborhood, barbecues, friends. You know, she didn't have one photograph of Bill. Not one photograph of her husband.'

'Painful memories.'

'How painful?' Kovac asked.

Wyatt closed his eyes and drove his hands back over his hair. 'What's the point of this, Sam? It was twenty years ago.'

Kovac stared at him, looked around the plush executive office, thought of the career Ace Wyatt had made for himself since the night someone had shot and killed Bill Thorne. What if it was all a lie? A house of cards. A legend born of blood. With Wyatt's show poised to go national, what if Andy Fallon had found the answer to that question?

'There's a body count, Ace,' he said. 'If you don't see the point of that, you're in a bad place.'

Wyatt pulled down the game face, a granite mask. 'You haven't shown me any evidence that these deaths are tied to one another, or tied to the past. I don't believe it.'

'I'll admit, at this point, I'm still fishing,' Kovac said. 'Probably the same as Andy was fishing. But I think he found something – which is why he's dead – and I think I know where he put it. If it's there, Ace, it's mine. Better for everyone to get out in front of it now. You know what I'm saying? You. Savard. I know she's Thorne's daughter.'

Wyatt looked through him. 'You're saying you think I've done something wrong,' he said flatly. 'I haven't. I didn't. There's nothing to be gained in stirring up old dust, Sam. People, careers, reputations could be damaged. For nothing.'

'I think two people are dead because of it,' Kovac said. 'That's something, Ace. I don't give a damn about any of the rest of it.'

He went to the door and put his hand on the knob, looking back at the legend. A man he'd never liked, and still there was a place deep inside him where he felt sorry.

'Evelyn sends her love,' he said quietly, and let himself out.

She was so tired. . . .

The workday had come and gone. Savard remained sequestered in her office. Hiding. Avoiding the press, avoiding having to go home. She had turned the lights off, except for her desk lamp, and sat, letting the silence envelop her. What a relief to be still, she thought, staring at the photograph she had taken and developed and framed herself years ago. A winter landscape.

This was why she shot landscapes rather than people: the stillness. If she could find stillness in her surroundings, she could hope to achieve it within herself . . . if only for a little while. If only while she was lost in the stark beauty of the picture. For those few moments, she could successfully ease the tension that quivered at the core of her.

The stillness didn't last tonight. A cacophony of sound invaded her brain. Angry questions, blunt questions, demands, directives. All that and the message from Hazelwood on her voice mail. She was so tired.

Kovac knew.

It had been just a matter of time. In the back of her mind, she'd always known that. In her heart, she had hoped for something more: a fold in time where events could be trapped, contained, separated, isolated. What a lovely idea. If only. But the past was poisonous and difficult to restrain, seeping around the edges of the boundaries she erected.

She closed her eyes and conjured an image, the fleeting memory of feeling safe and cared for. She had wanted so badly to accept it. She didn't want to carry the weight anymore. She was so tired. . . .

When she opened her eyes again, he was standing there. Panic clenched like a fist in her chest as she wondered if this moment was real or surreal. The nightmares came so frequently lately, it was becoming more difficult to tell.

He stood there in the shadows, expressionless, silent, the collar of his coat turned up. A sense of dread began to build deep inside her.

'You're Bill Thorne's daughter,' he said, and raised a gun.

37

Kovak took his time driving, playing it all through in his mind, trying to sort into chronological order the things he had learned today, patching the gaps with educated guesses. Trying not to react to any of it in an emotional way. Trying not to feel the sense of betrayal. Trying not to remind himself that he'd been right all along: that it was better not to want something more.

Neil Fallon's bar was closed, looking abandoned. The whole place looked like a shantytown that even the bums had forsaken – the crude cabins, the ice fishing houses, the work shed, the shed where Fallon stored the boats – all dark and empty of life, save for the rats. The only lights were a couple of security lights on poles and the Coors sign buzzing in the tiny window of the bar.

Kovac parked under the light and got out. He dug his Maglite out from under a pile of junk on the floor behind the driver's seat, then went to the trunk and rummaged through paper bags and evidence kits, finally coming up with the tire iron.

The wind had not let up. The temperature had dropped. It wasn't a night for a walk in the moonlight. Kovac took one anyway, going down to the boat shed. Senses sharp, he was hyper-aware of the cold, of the way it felt in his nose, in his lungs; hyper-aware of the sound of his shoes on the packed snow. He stopped near the shed and looked down the bank and down the shoreline.

In the moonlight, he couldn't see to where Derek Rubel's truck had gone through the ice, but it wasn't far. Standing among the empty buildings in the middle of nowhere, Kovac thought this was the kind of place where a man might vanish from one dimension into another and never be seen again.

There was a secret worth knowing. He filed it away for future reference. He had a feeling escape was going to look like a fine option after this was all over.

The gun went off with a deafening *bang!*

Amanda jerked back, up and out of her chair, arms flinging out to the sides.

And then she was awake.

The office was empty.

She stood behind the desk, her heart racing, lungs pumping as if she'd run a mile. She could smell her own sweat. Her clothes were damp with it. The emotions built and built and built inside her, choking her. Crushing her. A ragged sob tore from her throat and she flung herself at the desk, swinging her arms, knocking down the lamp, sending everything scattering, tumbling, falling, crashing. She pounded her fists on the desktop, crying, fighting, furious, terrified.

When the adrenaline ebbed and the outburst died, she sat back down in her chair and forced her mind to work.

No matter how she might have deluded herself all these years, it had always been only a matter of time.

Time was up.

She pulled open the desk drawer and took out the gun.

With the tire iron, Kovac pried loose the latch plate from the old door. The latch, complete with padlock, flopped to the side, and he went into the shed. He clicked on the flashlight in order to find the light switch.

Half a dozen boats of various sizes and types had been parked for the winter. Kovac walked around them, looking at the names. *Hang Time*, *Miss Peach*, *Azure II*. He chose one called *Wiley Trout* and climbed the ladder. When he climbed back down, he held a large, heavy backpack by one padded strap.

'Put it down, Kovac.'

Kovac held the bag out to one side and breathed a sigh. 'Put it down or what?'

'Or I'll kill you where you stand.'

'As opposed to killing me later and making it look like suicide? You weren't kidding when you said you did whatever the captain needed.'

'No, I wasn't kidding,' Gaines said. 'Put the bag down.'

'I guess you think there's something in it worth having.'

'It doesn't matter what's in it. Put it down.'

'Ah,' Kovac said, turning his head, trying to see what Gaines had pointed at his back. ''Cause you see, there's nothing in it but a ream of scrap paper. But you'll kill me first and worry about the evidence later. I know this is going to sound like a cliché, but you won't get away with it, Gaines. It's too late. Too many people know too much.'

'I don't think so,' Wyatt's assistant said with confidence. 'You suspect, you don't know. You're just fishing, and you're on your own. You don't have an official investigation. You haven't spoken with Leonard about your suspicions. You don't have any evidence as of now. The only people aware of what Andy Fallon was looking into are people who stand to lose. Neil

Fallon was arraigned today for his father's murder. The ME won't change the ruling on Andy's death.'

'You sound pretty damn sure of all that,' Kovac said. 'Did Wyatt tell you he'd make it happen that way?'

'Wyatt doesn't know.'

'He doesn't know you've killed for him, that you've gotten rid of the people who could ruin his image with the American public? That's selfless of you, Gavin. He should be giving you a bonus.

'Or does that come later? When he's established, when the show's a hit and the big money rolls in? Is that when you show him the pictures or the videotape or whatever evidence you've squirreled away? Show him how much you love him.'

'Shut up.'

'And how do you explain my death?' Kovac asked, shifting his feet, shifting his position subtly. He still couldn't see what Gaines had in his hands. 'I'll tell you right now, Slick, I ain't gonna let it look like no suicide. If I'm going down, I'm going down kicking.'

'I have some ideas. Put the bag down.'

'It was easy with Andy, wasn't it?' Kovac said. 'He comes to Wyatt to ask some innocent questions. You see it makes Ace nervous. Maybe you decide to dig a little yourself, try to find out what Andy's got. Maybe he doesn't even realize what he's got, so he's got no worries. You're a good-looking guy, he's a good-looking guy. You go out a couple of times. He doesn't think much of it when you drop by with a bottle of wine....'

'I didn't want to kill him,' Gaines said, and Kovac could hear the emotion in his voice, a strange mix of regret and relish. 'I'm not a killer.'

'Yes, you are. You thought he had something that might ruin your future. You planned it out. You drugged him. You strangled him unconscious so he couldn't fight. Then you hung him from a beam and let the noose do the last of the job.'

'I didn't want to.'

'And I'll bet you stood there and watched while he kicked and twitched. It's amazing how fast it happens, isn't it?'

'I told him I was sorry,' Gaines said. 'I was. But he would have ruined everything. He would have ruined Captain Wyatt. I've worked too hard for this chance. It's right there, in reach. It's happening – the show, the network deal. He would have taken it away. For nothing. For something that was over twenty years ago. For something that can't be changed. I couldn't let that happen.'

'You know what happened that night?' Kovac asked.

'I know Mike Fallon knew. He'd kept his mouth shut all this time because Wyatt paid him off. Andy had figured that out. If he had gotten his father to talk ... I couldn't let that happen.'

'Wyatt has to suspect, Gavin. You think he's gonna keep you around if he knows you're a murderer? He's a cop, for chrissake. It's a law enforcement show. If he's smart, he'll put the collar on you himself and save his own ass. Think of the network special that would make.'

'Drop the fucking bag!'

'You're a murderer,' Kovac said again. 'He finds out –'

'So is he!' Gaines screamed. 'Drop the fucking bag!'

Kovac had no time to digest the revelation. He caught the motion of Gaines's arm in his peripheral vision and dove forward. The claw hammer just grazed the back of his head, his shoulder taking the brunt of the impact. Even through the thickness of his coat, the pain was a hard, hot ball, burning into the muscle.

Kovac rolled onto his back as Gaines swung wildly for his head again, burying the head of the hammer in the dirt floor.

'Drop it, Gaines!' Liska shouted. 'You're under arrest!'

'Gun!' Kovac yelled as Gaines drew from inside his open coat and ran.

Kovac rolled to the side and half under the boat. But Gaines's purpose now was escape, and he was already running, the backpack in his left hand, gun in his right. He swung his arm back and let a shot go. Liska answered back. Gaines kept running, heading for the lake-end door of the boat shed.

Liska charged past as Kovac pushed to his feet and pulled his weapon. Gaines ducked around the side of the last boat for cover and fired two more shots. Liska ducked right, the second of the shots splintering the fiberglass hull she used for cover, the bullet coming through two inches from her head. Then Gaines was out the door.

Kovac went out a side door and crouched behind several fifty-five-gallon oil drums, straining to hear, to get some bearing on which way Gaines had run. He couldn't hear anything but the wind.

'Elwood's got his vehicle,' Liska said, dropping down behind him, breathing hard. 'Tippen'll have radio cars on the way by now.'

They had set up the trap on the fly. No time to take the plan to Leonard. No desire to. Kovac admitted there hadn't been much to use as bait, but he'd heard enough and pieced together enough to float a hunch. If they kept the plan between themselves and no one bit, nothing was lost. If they had taken it to Leonard and Leonard had nixed it, nothing could have been gained.

Kovac pulled off a glove, touched the back of his head, and came away with bloody fingers. He swore under his breath. 'Which way did he go? He gets off the property and we have another Rubel on our hands, you and I are gonna be on duty at the county landfill.'

'We'll be *in* the landfill. Leonard will have us killed.'

Kovac moved to the last of the drums and scanned as much as he could see of the yard. No sign of Gaines, which meant he could have taken refuge in any one of the buildings on the property and they could end up with a standoff situation. Then suddenly the angry buzz of a small motor split the air, and there was no time to think.

The snowmobile burst out the end door of Neil Fallon's work shed, roaring straight for Kovac. Kovac planted his feet and squeezed off a shot, hitting the nose of the machine, then dove out of the way, rolled, and came up running.

Gaines had the throttle wide-open, heading for the lake, heading for the open area to the east of the ice fishing houses. The machine bucked hard over wind-packed drifts. Kovac ran after it, hoping just to keep Gaines in sight. He squeezed off two shots on the run with no real hope of hitting anything.

The snowmobile hit the bank and flew, Gaines coming up off the seat. The machine twisted out from beneath him in midair, ass-end dropping down, Gaines still hanging on to the handlebars.

Kovac ran harder. He could see Liska coming on his left.

The snowmobile hit the ice on end, driving into it. The sound of the lake's surface breaking was like a crack of thunder. Gaines landed beside the machine and went still for an instant.

'Watch the ice! Watch the ice!' Liska shouted as Kovac ran down the length of the old boat dock.

Gaines was already shaking off the impact, struggling to get to his feet, the backpack strapped around his shoulders. The snowmobile was going down, the ice around the point of impact cracking and popping. Another *pop* and the machine was gone.

'Give it up, Gaines!' Kovac shouted. 'There's nowhere to go!'

Gaines came up with the gun and pulled off another round. Kovac dropped flat to the dock. Gaines's scream brought his head back up.

'He's in the water!' Liska yelled.

Gaines made a strangled squealing sound, one arm flailing above the surface. Kovac stepped off the dock, testing the ice.

'Hang on, Gaines! Don't move!'

But Gaines was in panic mode, bobbing down in the water, then coming up and attempting to throw himself out of the hole, only breaking more ice and sending himself under again.

Kovac got down on all fours, spreading his weight over more of the surface, moving toward the crumbling edge inches at a time.

'Gaines! Don't fight!' he shouted.

He could hear Gaines gasping, wheezing. The water temperature would send the body into shock quickly, shutting systems down. The weight of wet clothing would pull at him like a suit of armor. The backpack would be like an anvil strapped to his shoulders. His muscles would cramp and the panic would worsen.

'Let me grab your arm!' Kovac yelled, reaching out. Beneath his body he could hear the ice cracking.

Instead of allowing Kovac to take hold of him, Gaines clawed at him wildly but couldn't catch hold, couldn't grip. Another few inches of ice gave way and an animal sound of fear wrenched out of him.

'Hold still! Goddammit! Hold still!' Kovac screamed.

He focused on Gaines's arm and lunged forward, grabbing hold. The ice beneath his chest gave way, and his upper body went face-first into the water.

The cold was so intense, it was like hitting a brick wall at full speed. Instinctively, he beat at the water with his hands, as if it were solid and he could push himself up against it. He felt Gaines's hands on him, pushing him, pulling him, trying to drag him in. Another force pulled at him from behind, anchoring his legs, pulling him backward.

Kovac jerked his head back, came up coughing, choking, kicking, trying to scuttle backward to gain safer ice.

'Sam!' Liska shouted.

She was behind him, flat on the ice, still hanging on to one of his legs. Kovac went still. His fingers were already half numb with cold. Coughing, choking on the water he'd taken in, he stared at the hole in the ice.

Gaines was gone. The water was still and black in the moonlight.

For just an instant Kovac flashed on what drowning would be like: that brief instant beneath the water, blind, trying to come up for air and feeling nothing but ice above your head.

Then he closed the door on that part of his mind and crawled back toward the dock.

38

'And you think *I'm* ambitious,' Liska said. 'I've never actually murdered anyone for career advancement.'

They sat together in Kovac's car. The SO units had made the scene and Tippen was walking them through. One of the deputies had loaned Kovac a dry sweater. He'd borrowed a filthy hunting coat from Neil Fallon's workshop to put over it. The sleeves came halfway up his forearms, and it smelled like a wet dog.

'You've talked about it,' Kovac said. Someone had brought coffee. He drank it without tasting the coffee or the scotch Tippen had come up with.

'That doesn't count.'

They were silent for a moment.

'How much do you think Wyatt knows?' Liska asked.

Kovac shook his head. 'I don't know. He has to suspect by now. It all goes back to Thorne. He sure as hell knows everything about that night.'

'And it's been a secret all these years.'

'Until Andy Fallon started digging around. That must have been what Mike was talking about when he said he couldn't forgive Andy for what he was doing, that Andy had ruined everything, that he'd told Andy just to let it go. I thought he was talking about Andy coming out. . . . Jesus, all these years.'

'You think Wyatt killed Thorne?' Liska asked.

'That's where I end up. Evelyn Thorne was in love with him.'

'But how would Gaines have found out?'

'I don't know. Maybe Andy had made the same connection and said something to Gaines. Maybe he'd seen Andy's notes. I don't know.'

'Where does the guy who got pinned for the murder fit in?'

'I don't know.'

There was a hell of a lot of story to what happened that night all those years ago, Kovac thought. Aside from Ace Wyatt, there was one other person living who might be able to tell it. Amanda.

'You want to talk to Wyatt alone?' Liska asked. 'I'll ride along if you need me –'

'No,' he murmured. 'I need to do it. For Mike. Whatever else he was, he meant something good to me once.'

Liska nodded. 'I'll go back to the office, then get a jump on the paperwork for this adventure.'

'Why don't you go home, Tinks? It's late.'

'The boys are staying with my mother because of Rubel. I got nothing to go home to but a radio car with a couple of assholes sitting in my driveway.'

'No word on Rubel yet?'

'Lots of tips. Lots of false alarms. I hope something flushes him out, if he hasn't blown for Florida by now.'

'Are you scared?' Kovac asked, looking at her.

She met his gaze and nodded. 'Yes. For myself. For the boys. I just have to keep thinking we'll get him first.'

They fell silent again.

'I feel really old, Tinks,' Kovac said at last. 'Tired.'

'Don't think about it, Sam,' she advised. 'If you stop moving long enough to think about it, you won't get up again.'

'That's cheery.'

'Hey, I've lost my shot at a career in Hollywood,' she said with a false scowl. 'What do you want from me? Mary Fucking Sunshine?'

He found enough energy to chuckle, then coughed. His lungs still hurt from the cold water.

'Hey.' Liska reached across and patted his cheek. 'I'm really glad Gaines didn't kill you, partner.'

'Thanks. Thanks for saving my life, partner. I could have been under that ice with him.'

'That's what friends are for,' she said simply, and got out of the car.

Somehow, even in the middle of the night, all legal on-street parking spaces around city hall were taken. Liska pulled into the emergency zone smack in front of the building and left it there. The hell if she was parking in a ramp tonight.

She was secretly glad for the chance to come back to the office. She had always liked being here at night, while most of the city was asleep. Tonight it beat going home. If she went home, she would have too much quiet time to think about the sorry state of her personal life, too much time to miss the boys.

The hallways were quiet. The feds had set the Rubel task force in their own building on Washington Avenue. The action would be there tonight.

She paused in front of the door to the IA offices, thinking how strange the circles of life could be. A week before, she would have spat on the ground at the mention of Internal Affairs. In a matter of days she had seen enough bad cops to last her a lifetime.

No one noticed her as she went into the CID offices. Maybe she would just stay the night, she thought as she stowed her purse in the drawer, sleep in the space under her desk, like the homeless people who sought out hiding places in the skyway system after everything had closed.

She clicked the computer on, turned to take her coat off ... and found Derek Rubel standing at the end of the cubicle, holding a gun.

'Tell the story. From the beginning.'

The room was so quiet, Savard could feel the silence as a pressure against her eardrums.

Wyatt sat behind his desk, staring at her, staring at her gun. She had placed a small tape recorder on the desk in front of him. They were in his home. Just the two of them. Wyatt had married once in the years since the night of Bill Thorne's murder. It hadn't lasted.

'Tell the story,' she insisted. 'Don't waste my tape.'

He looked hurt. 'Amanda ... why are you doing this?'

'Andy Fallon is dead. Mike Fallon is dead.'

'I didn't kill them,' he said.

'All these years,' she whispered. 'All these years, I couldn't tell ... because of Mother. Because of what she did that night. That man was already dead. I couldn't save him. I thought I could make it up somehow, make it right some other way ...'

For a long time she had let herself believe that was penance enough: stopping other bad cops from hurting people. Keeping the dirty secret of her family, the dirty secret of the family of cops her father had been a part of. At the same time, she dedicated her life to breaking the secrets of the people in the MPD, not allowing the cops in her department to get away with what Bill Thorne had gotten away with, with what Ace Wyatt had done.

Wyatt had done his own penance. But it hadn't mattered. Her father was still dead ... except in her nightmares. Weagle was still dead ... except in her nightmares. Now Andy ... Now Mike Fallon ...

'I can't live with all these corpses in my head,' she said, voice quavering. She made a motion with the gun. 'You tell the story. Tell it now.'

'Amanda ...'

His voice was like a razor on her nerves: condescending, patronizing. She shifted the gun two inches to the right and put a bullet into the wall behind his head.

'I said tell the story!' she screamed.

Wyatt went white, then red. Sweat ran down his face. The strong ammonia smell of urine burned the air.

'I ... can't ... take ... this ... any ... more,' she said through her teeth. There was a part of her brain that recognized her behavior as irrational. But then, that was part of the problem, wasn't it? She had been too rational, too practical for too long, suppressing the horror, the fear, the knowledge that what had happened was wrong and that she could have stopped it all.

'I'll begin for you,' she offered, then announced herself and the date and the place, beginning the tape in the way she would any police interview. She introduced the subject, stated the date of the incident. Wyatt stared at her.

'I loved your mother,' he said. 'What I did, I did for her, to protect her. You know that, Amanda.'

Tears filled her eyes. 'She's protecting herself now. No one can hurt her. I can't let any more people die and not do anything about it. That's wrong. I became a cop to keep that from happening. Do you understand that? Because of that night, I am what I am. I became a cop to police the police, so what happened that night wouldn't happen to someone else. But then it did.'

'I didn't kill them, Amanda. Andy. Mike. I didn't –'

'Yes, you did. Don't you see? Tell the story.'

'They killed themselves,' he said, but there was no conviction in his voice. He couldn't even tell the lie to himself.

Tears rolled down Wyatt's face. He was shaking visibly. He looked at the tape recorder, probably wondering if she wanted the story on tape because she was planning to kill him after he had finished telling it.

'Bill Thorne was the cruellest man I ever knew,' he began, his voice trembling. 'He tormented your mother, Amanda. You knew that. Nothing she did was good enough for him. He took his anger out on her. He beat her. He didn't hurt you, though, did he, Amanda?'

'No,' she whispered, trembling too. 'He never hit me. But I knew. I saw. I hated him for it. I wanted someone to stop him, but no one ever did ... because he was a cop. You saw what he did to her – the black eyes, the bruises. You saw. The other cops saw. They all looked the other way. I could never understand that,' she said. 'The others, maybe ... but you. She loved you. How could you have let that go on?'

'Your mother didn't want –'

'Don't. Don't even pay lip service to that excuse. That she didn't want the embarrassment, that she didn't want to make trouble. She was a battered woman.'

He looked away, ashamed.

'Because he was a cop,' she said. 'You let it all come to what happened that night because you couldn't rat out a rotten son of a bitch like Bill Thorne.'

Wyatt didn't answer. There was no answer.

'On the night in question . . .' she said.

'I got a call from her that something was wrong. She was hysterical. Bill had come home unexpectedly. He'd been drinking. Bill would do that – drink on the job. He had no regard for any rules but his own. He –' He broke off and started again, the emotions of that night coming back. 'He raped her. He beat her.

'Evelyn had had enough,' he said, staring down at the desktop, tears falling faster. 'She got hold of a gun, and she shot Bill twice in the chest. Then she called me.

'I couldn't let her be punished for what Bill had done to her. I couldn't trust that the courts would take her side. What if it came out she and I had been seeing each other? A prosecutor would have seen it as motive. She might have gone to prison.'

'And so you found Weagle –'

'He was there. In the neighborhood. He was on the street as I went to your house. I didn't know what he might have seen or heard.'

Wyatt put his head in his hands and began to sob. 'I got him to come into the house. And I shot him ... with Bill's thirty-eight. Oh, Jesus ... Then Mike came ... and I was there with the body. I panicked. . . .'

'Jesus Christ,' Kovac said, pushing the office door open. He stared at Wyatt, who was crying and choking and did not look up. 'You shot Mike Fallon.'

Liska stood frozen. A thousand things went through her mind in a heartbeat. To rush him, to scream, to throw something, to try to take cover. Thank God she had called the boys earlier and told them she loved them.

'Put the gun down, Rubel,' she said in a tone that was remarkably, ridiculously conversational.

'You bitch.'

He wore the mirrored shades. She couldn't see his eyes. Not good.

'You're smart to give it up here,' Liska said. 'No one will hurt you. You're with family.'

'It was none of your fucking business.'

'You killed a man,' she said. 'That's all my business.'

Behind him, Liska could see Barry Castleton moving in slowly, his eyes huge, gun in hand.

'Put the gun down,' she said. 'You won't leave this building, Derek.'

'What do I care?' he said. 'I knew that when I came in. I'm a dead man walking. I've got nothing to lose. Better to die now, fast. And what a bonus – I get to take you with me, bitch.'

'You put Mike Fallon in that chair,' Kovac said, coming into the room. 'All these years you let everyone think you were the big hero. You put him in that fucking chair.'

Wyatt cried harder, blubbering through his hands. 'I didn't mean to! I panicked. When I realized ... I did what I could to keep him alive. Thinking all the while that my career was over, that he would tell. But still I kept him alive –'

'And became a hero because of it.'

'What could I do? I tried to make it up to him.'

'Yeah, I'm sure having a big-screen TV made all the difference,' Kovac said. 'Did he know it was you that shot him?'

'He claimed he never remembered all of it. And yet ... there were times ... comments he made ... I thought maybe ...'

'And no one ever checked the ballistics beyond seeing all the slugs were thirty-eights,' Kovac said. ''Cause you were all cops except the dead mutt with the record. And besides, you had a witness – Evelyn. Or were there two?' he asked, looking to Savard.

Savard never took her eyes off Wyatt. 'I was told to stay in my room, to say I hadn't seen anything. I did that because of Mother, because she would have taken the blame.'

'Jesus.' Kovac took a breath, feeling sick.

'Mike was the hero,' Wyatt insisted. 'Mike was the hero.'

'Mike is dead. Gaines killed him. Because of you. And he killed Andy,' Kovac said. 'You knew Andy was asking about that night. He came to you. Then he turns up dead. You had to know –'

'No! I thought he killed himself!' Wyatt insisted. 'Really –'

'You could have stopped it all,' Savard said, tears running down her face. '*I* could have stopped it. Andy had come to me too. After he found Mother. I should have stopped it then. I'm a cop.

'I could have stopped it,' she said, looking inward. The gun was in her hand, her hand was shaking badly. 'I'm sorry. I'm so sorry, Andy. . . .'

'You didn't kill him, Amanda,' Kovac said gently, his anger shifting to fear as he watched her look at the weapon in her hand. 'Let me have the gun. We'll stop it now, tonight. I'll help you.'

'It's too late,' she murmured, looking inward. 'I'm sorry. I'm so sorry.'

'Give me the gun, Amanda.'

She looked at the weapon in her hand and raised it, turning the barrel toward herself.

'Drop the gun, Rubel!' Castleton called. 'We're on you.'

Rubel pointed the nine-millimeter at Liska's chest and screamed, an animal roar, his face going red, the cords in his thick neck standing out like ropes beneath the taut skin.

'Give me the gun, Amanda,' Kovac said, stepping toward her. Everything inside him was shaking. 'It's over now, honey.'

'I could have stopped it,' she said.

Kovac took another step. 'Amanda, please . . .'

She looked into his eyes. 'You don't understand.'

'Amanda.'

'It's all my fault.'

'No,' Kovac whispered, reaching out slowly. His hand was shaking like a drunk's.

'Yes,' she said softly, nodding her head. Her finger stroked the trigger. 'They're all dead because of me.'

Castleton roared back, screaming, moving on Rubel.

Liska jammed her hand into her coat pocket.

Rubel turned his head, just for a second. A second was all she needed.

The tactical baton snapped to full length, and Liska moved in and to the side, swinging it overhand as hard as she could. The bones in Rubel's forearm snapped as the gun went off, and the shot went into a wall. Then Rubel crumpled to the floor, screaming, writhing.

Liska dropped the baton and walked out of the cubicle.

'Amanda . . .' Kovac whispered. He would later look back on that single instant in time, and know that what he'd seen in her eyes at that moment was a reflection of his own dying hope.

'Amanda . . . give me the gun.'

'No,' she said softly. 'No, Sam. Don't you see? I could have stopped it twenty years ago. My mother didn't shoot Bill Thorne. I did.'

Kovac would never have any memory of the sound the gun made when it went off. He would never remember the screams – Ace Wyatt's, his own. The memory would forever be in images only:

The spray of blood and bone and brain matter.

The split second of surprise in Amanda's eyes before they went blank.

Himself, sitting on the floor, holding her body, as if his consciousness had detached from his own body and pulled away to try to escape the horror.

But there was no escape. There never would be.

39

'Tippen called,' Liska said.

She looked like hell. Tinker Bell on heroin. Pale, purple smudges under her eyes, hair sticking up in all directions. Who knew the last time she'd slept. Kovac could barely remember the last time *he'd* slept. Yet, exhausted as he was, the last thing he wanted to do was go home. The job was his refuge. Liska's too.

And so they had gone on instead of going home. A new day had dawned, bright and cold. They stood on the front steps of Gavin Gaines's town house for the execution of the search warrant, looking for whatever they could find to tie him to the murders of Andy and Mike Fallon. Looking for anything that might suggest Ace Wyatt had knowledge of those murders.

Kovac looked at the sun, a pale orange ball in the palest of blue skies, a halo around it. Sundog. Meant it was cold.

No fucking lie.

'He said they found Andy's files,' Liska said. 'In his boat. Good hunch.'

'Neil told me Andy had been out there Sunday afternoon,' Kovac said. 'The files weren't anywhere else. Gaines didn't have them, or he wouldn't have followed me out there last night. Though I'll bet he grabbed the laptop and got rid of that the night he killed him.'

'Why do you think Andy hid the files and then let Gaines into his house?'

'I don't know. Maybe he just didn't want Gaines to get a look at them. I'm sure he didn't think Gaines would kill for them.'

'What's going to happen to Wyatt?'

Kovac shrugged. 'There's no statute of limitations on murder. We've got the tape with his confession to killing Weagle and shooting Mike.'

'And his lawyer will say it was given under duress, and he hadn't been Mirandized, and blah, blah, blah.'

'Yeah. I'd say there's no justice,' he said. 'But there is. Sometimes it just takes a while to come around. And sometimes when it does, it's not quite what we had in mind.'

They said nothing for a moment, just stood there watching the street.

'I'm sorry about Savard,' Liska said.

Kovac hadn't told her about his feelings for Amanda. What was the point in anyone hearing that? Bad enough that he had to deal with it at all. Worse to have sympathy. Worse yet, pity. But he'd told her the tale of what had happened in Wyatt's house. He'd told her what he knew, what he'd pieced together, what Wyatt had told him in the aftermath.

He could too easily picture Amanda, seventeen and vulnerable and afraid; in need of justice, not getting it from the people she should have been able to rely on. She'd done the only thing she thought would save her mother: she'd shot her father dead. Then Evelyn Thorne had done the only thing she believed would save her daughter: assumed culpability. Then Wyatt had come into the picture, and the tragedy spiraled on.

He remembered now what Amanda had said to him Friday night as they stood in her kitchen. *I've tried to make my choices with the idea that I've made those choices for the greatest good. Sometimes someone suffers in the process, but I made the decision for the right reason. That should count for something, shouldn't it?*

'I'm sorry too,' he murmured at last, glad for the sunglasses that hid his eyes and the emotions in them.

'There's nothing left for Wyatt,' he said, digging a cigarette out of his pocket and hanging it on his lip. 'He's over. There's nothing left . . .'

For me, he thought, but he didn't say it.

He had the job, the only thing he'd ever been any good at.

Somehow it didn't feel like enough now. He didn't think it would fill the hole inside him. Maybe nothing ever would.

'How are you doing?' he asked.

Liska shrugged and put on her shades. 'Okay for having stared into the face of death. I wouldn't want to do that every day.' She gave him the elbow and a smirk. 'See? That Hollywood job would have been the way to go. Money for nothing.'

They were quiet again for a moment, then she said, 'I was scared. I'm still scared. I don't want to think about the boys growing up without me. Someone sticks a gun in my face and I make a joke of it. But it's not funny.'

'You're not gonna leave me, are you, Tinks?'

She didn't answer him right away, and when she did, it wasn't really an answer at all. 'I'm gonna take a vacation. Take the boys somewhere fun. Get a tan.'

Elwood came to the door and stuck his head out. 'You'll want to see this.'

They went into the town house and followed him through a maze of cops, up the stairs to the master bedroom and into a walk-in closet.

Gaines had been a clotheshorse. The closet was hung with rods of suits and shirts. Shelves were stacked with sweaters and shoes. Someone had pushed aside the clothes on the rod that extended across the back of the closet to reveal a secret work of art.

'Jesus,' was all Kovac could say.

Gaines had filled the wall with photographs and news clippings of Wyatt. Articles about the man, about the show, about the deal with the WB network. Polaroids of Wyatt in fifty different settings, shaking hands, posing with officials and fans. Photographs of the two of them in various social settings. In the center: Wyatt's eight-by-ten glossy. A shrine.

'Eew,' Liska said, wrinkling her nose. 'Does anyone besides me want to go take a shower?'

'I found these in an envelope on the shelf,' Elwood said, handing Kovac a stack of Polaroids.

Andy Fallon hanging from the beam in his bedroom. Full body shot. Naked. Freshly dead. A close-up of his face. Mike Fallon sitting dead in his chair.

'Something for the scrapbook,' Kovac said, echoing Gaines's own words as he had shot pictures at Wyatt's party and at the ice rink with the WB VPs.

'You think he took them to blackmail Wyatt later on?' Elwood said.

Kovac looked from the Polaroids to the collage and back.

'No,' he said, handing the photographs back. 'I don't.'

EPILOGUE

Amanda Savard's funeral was Thursday. A week to the day after Andy Fallon's. Kovac attended alone, one of two dozen people in the small chapel at the funeral home. She had lived a confined, controlled life within the walls of her defenses. Kovac suspected he was one of the few people who had ever had a glimpse inside those walls.

Evelyn Thorne was there with her doctor. Whether or not she knew what was happening was anyone's guess. She sat quietly through the service, staring at the photograph she had brought with her. Amanda at the age of five. Bright-eyed and very serious. Her hair in a ponytail with a blue velvet bow. She showed it to Kovac three times. A part of him wanted to ask to keep it, but he didn't.

The service was simple, the basic closing on earthly existence. Ashes to ashes and dust to dust. Such an inadequate distillation of life: you're born, you live, you die. There were no eulogies. There was no service graveside. She was not buried next to her father.

The details of Amanda's involvement in Bill Thorne's death had been kept from the press. Her funeral was not considered newsworthy. Mike Fallon's funeral drew a thousand law enforcement professionals from all over the upper Midwest, and made the front page of the *Star Tribune*. Kovac did not attend.

He slipped back into the chapel after the service had ended, after the rest of the mourners had gone. He sat for a long time, staring at the closed casket, not quite allowing himself to wonder what might have been. The funeral home director came in and gave him that same hopeful look as waitstaff in a bar at closing.

'Take your time,' the man said with a polite smile, backing away toward the potted palms along the side of the room.

Kovac stood and dug a hand into his coat pocket. 'Can I leave something with her? Is it too late for that?'

'Certainly.' He came forward again, his eyes kind. 'I can take care of that for you.'

Kovac pulled out the badge he had carried as a patrolman when he'd first come on the job too many years ago. He looked at it, ran his thumb over it, then handed it to the funeral director.

'I'd like her to have this.'

The man took it, nodded, and offered a gentle smile. 'I'll see that she gets it.'

'Thanks.'

There were just two cars left in the side lot. His and Liska's. She stood leaning against his driver's side door, arms crossed.

'You okay?' she asked, eyes narrowed.

Kovac looked back at the building. 'Naw, not really . . . I broke one of my own rules. Expected too much.'

Liska nodded. 'I broke that one too. . . . So, I guess we can be morose together.'

He shoved his hands into his pockets and hunched his shoulders against the cold. One corner of his mouth twitched up. 'I'm not morose, I'm bitter.'

For a moment she just looked at him, not with the cop eyes, but with the eyes of a friend. Then she came away from the car and put her arms around him and held him. Kovac hugged her back, eyes squeezed tightly against the need to cry. They held each other that way for a minute, maybe two.

When she stepped back, Liska popped him on the arm and tried to grin. 'Hey, we've got each other, huh? Come on, partner, I'll buy you a cup of joe.'

Kovac smiled softly. 'You're on . . . friend.'

Dark Horse

This book was inspired by the adventurers of Tess and Mati. May there be many more, and may they live to tell the tales.

Acknowledgments

As always, I have several people to thank for sharing with me their professional expertise as I wrote this story. Lieutenant Ed Serafin, Palm Beach County Sheriff's Office, Robbery/Homicide division. Robert Crais. Eileen Dreyer. Jessie Steiner. Mary Phelps. And most of all, Betsy Steiner, true friend and partner in international intrigue.

Author's note

Welcome to my other world.

In my life away from my desk, I am a competitive equestrian. In fact, I've been a rider longer than I've been a writer. Over the years horses have been my joy, refuge, therapy, salvation, and comfort. I've ridden in nearly every equestrian discipline, from barrel racing to jumping. When I was thirteen and my girlfriends were baby-sitting to earn spending money, my father was bringing home young horses for me to break to saddle.

Several years ago I settled on the equestrian sport of dressage as my out-of-office passion. Dressage is all about control and precision and the mastery of imperceptible cues between rider and horse. The ultimate result is something like equine ballet, which appears elegant and effortless but requires the same physical and mental fitness as power yoga.

I began competing in dressage in 1999. Being me, I didn't ease into the sport. I have one gear in everything I do: full-on. I bought a wonderful – if difficult – horse named D'Artagnon from Olympic rider Guenter Seidel, and within a year's time went from my first dressage competition to being nationally ranked amateur rider in the US Dressage Federation. At the end of my first season, my coach, trainer, mentor, and great friend, Betsy Steiner (a world-class rider herself), encouraged me to bring D'Artagnon along with several other horses from her stable to Florida for the winter season.

Every year top equestrians from the East Coast, Midwest, Canada, and Europe migrate to Wellington in Palm Beach County to spend three months in constant training and competition in some of the most prestigious dressage and jumper shows in the country. Thousands of horses and hundreds of riders converge to create a fascinating world, a world driven by the thrill of victory, the agony of defeat, and lots of money. A world populated by the ultrarich and the very poor; celebrities, royalty, and ordinary people who scrimp and save year-round in order to 'do the season'; philanthropists, dilettantes, professionals, amateurs, con men, and criminals. People who love horses, and people who love to exploit people who love horses. A world with a glamorous surface and a rough underbelly. Yin and yang. Positive and negative.

By the end of that first season in Florida, my imagination was running wild with story ideas that would blend my two worlds. The result is *Dark Horse*, a classic private-eye novel set against the backdrop of international show jumping. I hope you enjoy this glimpse into the dark side of my other world.

If you come away from this book thinking the horse business is all bad, I'll tell you that's not so. Some of the finest, kindest, most generous people I have ever known have been in the horse business. But on the flip side of that coin, some of the most vile, vicious, loathsome people I have ever known have been in the horse business. The horse world can be a world of extremes and amazing adventures. I've had horses drugged, horses stolen. I've been stranded in a foreign country with a sociopathic horse dealer who canceled my transportation home. I've masqueraded as a groom and flown in the belly of a cargo plane with a horse bent on killing me. But these adventures don't happen every day. Every day I go to the stables and find friendship and partnership and calm within my soul.

My own horses appear in this book, in Sean Avadon's stable. But, in answer to the inevitable question, Elena is not me (if my life were so exciting, when would I write a book?). However, I do agree with her when she says, 'On the back of a horse I felt whole, complete, connected to that vital place in the center of me . . . and the chaos within me found balance.'

Act One

SCENE ONE
FADE IN:
EXTERIOR: PALM BEACH EQUESTRIAN CENTER — SUNSET

Flat, open fields of scrub stretching to the west. A dirt road running north onto equestrian center property and south toward small horse farms some distance away. No one around. The fields are empty. No people, no horses. Sunday night: everyone has gone home.

Erin stands at the back gate. She's waiting for someone. She's nervous. She thinks she's here for a secret purpose. She thinks her life will change tonight.

It will.

She looks at her watch. Impatient. Afraid he won't show. She's not aware of the camera filming her. She thinks she's alone.

She's thinking: maybe he won't come, maybe she's wrong about him.

A rusted white van approaches from the south. She watches it come toward her. She looks annoyed. No one uses this back road this time of day. The gate to the show grounds has already been chained shut for the night.

The van stops. A masked assailant leaps out.

ERIN No!

She starts to run toward the gate. He catches her arm from behind and spins her around. She kicks him. He backhands her across the face, knocking her sideways. She wrenches free of his grasp as she stumbles, and she tries to run again but can't get her feet under her. The assailant knocks her down from behind, coming down on top of her, his knee in her back. He pulls a hypodermic needle from the pocket of his jacket and rams the needle into her arm. She makes a sound of pain and starts to cry.

659

He pulls her to her feet and shoves her into the van. He slams the door shut, gets in the van, the van turns around and drives away.

Life changes in a heartbeat.

FADE OUT

1

Life can change in a heartbeat.

I've always known that. I've lived the truth of that statement, literally from the day I was born. I sometimes see those moments coming, sense them, anticipate them, as if they have an aura that precedes their arrival. I see one coming now. Adrenaline runs through my bloodstream like rocket fuel. My heart pounds like a piston. I'm ready to launch.

I've been told to stay put, to wait, but I know that's not the right decision. If I go in first, if I go in now, I've got the Golam brothers dead-bang. They think they know me. Their guard will be down. I've worked this case three months. I know what I'm doing. I know that I'm right. I know the Golam brothers are already twitching. I know I want this bust and deserve it. I know Lieutenant Sikes is here for the show, to put a feather in his cap when the news vans arrive and to make the public think they should vote for him in the next election for sheriff.

He stuck me on the side of the trailer and told me to wait. He doesn't know his ass. He doesn't even know the side door is the door the brothers use most. While Sikes and Ramirez are watching the front, the brothers are dumping their money into duffel bags and getting ready to bolt out the side. Billy Golam's four-by-four is parked ten feet away, covered in mud. If they run, they'll take the truck, not the Corvette parked in front. The truck can go off-road.

Sikes is wasting precious time. The Golam brothers have two girls in the trailer with them. This could easily turn into a hostage situation. But if I go in now, while their guard is down . . .

Screw Sikes. I'm going in before these twitches freak.

It's my case. I know what I'm doing.

I key my radio. 'This is stupid. They're going to break for the truck. I'm going in.'

'Goddammit, Estes —' Sikes.

I click the radio off and drop it into the weeds growing beside the trailer. It's my case. It's my bust. I know what I'm doing.

I go to the side door and knock the way all the Golam brothers' customers knock: two knocks, one knock, two knocks. 'Hey, Billy, it's Elle. I need some.'

*Billy Golam jerks open the door, wild-eyed, high on his own home cooking –
crystal meth. He's breathing hard. He's got a gun in his hand.*

Shit.

The front door explodes inward.

One of the girls screams.

Buddy Golam shouts: 'Cops!'

Billy Golam swings the .357 up in my face. I suck in my last breath.

And then I opened my eyes and felt sick at the knowledge that I was still
alive.

This was the way I had greeted every day for the past two years. I had
relived that memory so many times, it was like replaying a movie over and
over and over. No part of it changed, not a word, not an image. I wouldn't
allow it.

I lay in the bed and thought about slitting my wrists. Not in an abstract
way. Specifically. I looked at my wrists in the soft lamplight – delicate, as
fine-boned as the wing of a bird, skin as thin as tissue, blue-lined with veins
– and thought about how I would do it. I looked at those thin blue lines and
thought of them as lines of demarcation. Guidelines. *Cut here.*

I pictured the needle-nose point of a boning knife. The lamplight would
catch on the blade. Blood would rise to the surface in its wake as the blade
skated along the vein. Red. My favorite color.

The image didn't frighten me. That truth frightened me most of all.

I looked at the clock: 4:38 A.M. I'd had my usual fitful four and a half
hours of sleep. Trying for more was an exercise in futility.

Trembling, I forced my legs over the edge of the bed and got up, pulling
a deep blue chenille throw around my shoulders. The fabric was soft,
luxurious, warm. I made special note of the sensations. You're always more
intensely alive the closer you come to looking death in the face.

I wondered if Hector Ramirez had realized that the split second before he
died.

I wondered that every day.

I dropped the throw and went into the bathroom.

'Good morning, Elena. You look like shit.'

Too thin. Hair a wild black tangle. Eyes too large, too dark, as if there was
nothing within to shine outward. The crux of my problem: lack of
substance. There was – is – a vague asymmetry to my face, like a porcelain
vase that has been broken, then painstakingly restored. The same vase it was
before, yet not the same. The same face I was born with, yet not the same.
Slightly skewed and strangely expressionless.

I was beautiful once.

I reached for a comb on the counter, knocked it to the floor, grabbed a
brush instead. Start at the bottom, work upward. Like combing a horse's
tail. Work the knots out gently. But I had already tired of looking at myself.
Anger and resentment bubbled up through me, and I tore the brush

through my hair, shoving the snarls together and tangling the brush in the midst of the mess.

I tried maybe forty-five seconds to extricate the thing, yanking at the brush, tearing at the hair above the snarl, not caring that I was pulling hair out of my head by the roots. I swore aloud, swatted at my image in the mirror, swept the tumbler and soap dish off the counter in a tantrum, and they smashed on the tile floor. Then I jerked open a drawer in the vanity and pulled out a pair of scissors.

Furious, shaking, breathing hard, I cut the brush free. It dropped to the floor with a mass of black hair wrapped around it. The pressure in my chest eased. Numbness trickled down through me like rain. Calm.

Without emotion, I proceeded to hack away at the rest of my mane, cutting it boy-short in ten minutes. The result was ragged with a finger-in-the-light-socket quality. Still, I'd seen worse in *Vogue*.

I swept up the mess – the discarded hair, the broken glass – tossed it in the trash, and walked out of the room.

I'd worn my hair long all my life.

The morning was cool, shrouded in a thick, ground-hugging fog, the air ripe with the damp scents of south Florida: green plants and the murky canal that ran behind the property; mud and manure and horses. I stood on the patio of the little guest house I lived in and breathed deeply.

I had come to this farm a refugee. Jobless, homeless, a pariah in my chosen profession. Unwanted, unloved, abandoned. All of it deserved. I had been off the job two years, most of that time spent in and out of hospitals as doctors repaired the damage done to my body that day at the Golam brothers' trailer. Piecing together shattered bone, patching torn flesh, putting the left side of my face together like a three-dimensional puzzle. They had been less successful with my psyche.

Needing something to do until I could make up my mind about reaching for that boning knife, I had answered an ad in *Sidelines,* a locally based, biweekly magazine for the horse industry: GROOM WANTED.

Life is strange. I don't want to believe anything is preordained. To believe that, one would have to accept the existence of a viciously cruel higher power in order to explain things like child abuse and rapists and AIDS and good men being shot dead in the line of duty. But the occasional twist of fate always makes me wonder.

The phone number in the ad belonged to Sean Avadon. I'd known Sean a hundred years ago in my riding days, when I was a spoiled, sulky, Palm Beach teenager and he was a spoiled, outrageous twenty-something spending his trust fund on horses and mad flings with pretty young men from Sweden and Germany. We had been friends, Sean always telling me I needed him to be my surrogate sense of humor and fashion.

Our families lived a couple of mansions down from one another on the Lake Worth side of the narrow island, Sean's father a real estate magnate, mine an attorney to the wealthiest crooks in south Florida. The slumlord and the shyster, each of them sire to ungrateful offspring. Sean and I had bonded in parental disdain and our love for horses. Wild child times two.

All that had seemed so long ago as to be a dream I could barely remember. So much had happened since. I had left Palm Beach, left that world. I had metaphorically lived and died in another life. Then I answered that ad: groom wanted.

I didn't get the job. As bad a shape as I was in, even I could see the pity in his eyes when we met for drinks at The Players. I was a dark shadow of the girl Sean had known twenty years past, so pathetic I didn't have the pride to fake mental health. I guess that might have been rock bottom. I might have gone home that night to the apartment I was renting and tried to find that boning knife.

Instead, Sean took me in like a stray cat – a recurring theme in my life. He put me in his guest house and asked that I work a couple of his horses for the winter season. He claimed he needed the help. His ex-trainer/ex-lover had run off to Holland with his groom and left him in the lurch. He made it sound like he was giving me a job. What he was giving me was a stay of execution.

Three months had passed. I was still fantasizing about suicide, and every evening I took a bottle of Vicodin out of my nightstand, emptied out the pills, and looked at them and counted them and thought how one pill would ease the physical pain that had been with me every day since 'the incident', as my attorney called it. (How sterile and neat that sounded. A small segment of unpleasantness that could be snipped from the fabric of life and isolated. How in contrast to my memories.) One pill could ease the pain. Thirty could end it. I had a stockpile of three hundred and sixty pills.

Every evening I looked at those pills, then put them back in the bottle and put the bottle away. I had never taken one. My evening ritual.

My daily ritual for the past three months was the routine of Sean's barn and time spent with his horses. I found both rituals comforting, but for very different reasons. The pills were a connection to death, and every night I didn't take them was a victory. The horses were a connection to life, and every hour spent with them was a reprieve.

Early on in my life I came to the conclusion that my spirituality was something uniquely and privately my own, something I could find only deep within a small quiet space in the very center of my being. Some people find that place through meditation or yoga or prayer. I find that place within me when I am on a horse. My Zen religion: the equestrian art of dressage.

Dressage is a discipline born on the battlefield in ancient times. Warhorses were trained in precision movements to aid their masters in battle, not only to evade enemies, but to attack them. Over the centuries the training went from the battlefield to the showring, and dressage evolved into something like equine ballet.

To the untrained eye it appears graceful and elegant and effortless. A skilled rider seems to be so quiet, so motionless as to virtually blend into the background. In reality, the sport is physically and mentally demanding on both horse and rider. Complex and complicated. The rider must be attuned to the horse's every footfall, to the balance of every inch of the horse's body. The slightest shift of the rider's weight, the smallest movement of a hand, the lightest tensing of a calf muscle will affect the quality of the performance. Focus must be absolute. Everything else becomes insignificant.

Riding was my refuge as a teenager, when I felt I had little control over any other aspect of my life. It was my stress release when I had a career. It had become my salvation when I had nothing else. On the back of a horse I felt whole, complete, connected to that vital place in the very center of me that had otherwise closed itself off, and the chaos within me found balance.

D'Artagnon and I moved across the sand arena through the last wisps of the morning ground fog, the horse's muscles bulging and rolling, his hooves striking the ground in perfect metronome rhythm. I massaged the left rein, sat into his back, tightened my calves around him. The energy moved from his hindquarters, over his back; his neck rounded and his knees came up into the stylized, slow-motion trot called *passage*. He seemed almost to float beneath me, to bounce like a huge, soft ball. I felt he might take wing if only I knew the one secret word to whisper to him.

We halted in the center of the ring at the place known as X. In that moment I felt joy and peace.

I dropped the reins on his neck and patted him. He lowered his head and started to walk forward, then stopped and came to attention.

A girl sat on the white board fence that ran along the road. She watched me with a sense of expectation about her. Even though I hadn't noticed her, I could tell she'd been there, waiting. I judged her to be about twelve. Her hair was long and brown, perfectly straight, and neatly held back from her face with a barrette on each side. She wore little round black-rimmed glasses that made her look very serious. I rode toward her with a vague feeling of apprehension that made no sense at the time.

'Can I help you?' I asked. D'Ar blew through his nostrils at her, ready to bolt and save us from the intruder. I should have let him.

'I'm here to see Ms Estes,' she said properly, as if she'd come on business.

'Elena Estes?'

'Yes.'

'And you are ... ?'

'Molly Seabright.'

'Well, Molly Seabright, Ms Estes isn't here at the moment.'

'*You're* Ms Estes,' she declared. 'I recognize your horse. His name is D'Artagnon, like in *The Three Musketeers*.' She narrowed her eyes. 'You cut your hair.' Disapproval.

'Do I know you?'

'No.'

'Then how do you know me?' I asked, the apprehension rising up like bile through my chest to the base of my throat. Maybe she was a relative of Hector Ramirez, come to tell me she hated me. Maybe she'd been sent as a decoy by an older relative who would now pop out of nowhere to shoot me or scream at me or throw acid in my face.

'From *Sidelines*,' she said.

I felt like I'd walked into the middle of a play. Molly Seabright took pity on me and carefully climbed down from the fence. She was slightly built and dressed neatly in sensible dark slacks and a little blue T-shirt with a small daisy chain embroidered around the throat. She came up along D'Artagnon's shoulder and carefully held the magazine out to me, folded open to an interior page.

The photograph was in color. Me on D'Ar, riding through thin ribbons of early-morning fog. The sunlight made his coat shine as bright as a new penny. My hair was pulled back in a thick ponytail.

I had no memory of being photographed. I had certainly never been interviewed, though the writer seemed to know things about me I didn't know myself. The caption read: *Private investigator Elena Estes enjoys an early-morning ride on D'Artagnon at Sean Avadon's Avadonis Farm in Palm Beach Point Estates.*

'I've come to hire you,' Molly Seabright said.

I turned toward the barn and called for Irina, the stunning Russian girl who had beat me out for the groom's job. She came out, frowning and sulky. I stepped down off D'Artagnon and asked her to please take him back to the barn. She took his reins, and sighed and pouted and slouched away like a sullen runway model.

I ran a gloved hand back through my hair, startled to come to the end of it so quickly. A fist of tension began to quiver in my stomach.

'My sister is missing,' Molly Seabright said. 'I've come to hire you to find her.'

'I'm sorry. I'm not a private investigator. This is some kind of mistake.'

'Why does the magazine say that you are?' she asked, looking stern and disapproving again. She didn't trust me. I'd already lied to her once.

'I don't know.'

'I have money,' she said defensively. 'Just because I'm twelve doesn't mean I can't hire you.'

'You can't hire me because I'm not a private investigator.'

'Then what are you?' she demanded.

A broken-down, busted-out, pathetic ex-sheriff's detective. I'd thumbed my nose at the life I'd been raised in, been ostracized from the life I'd chosen. What did that make me?

'Nothing,' I said, handing the magazine back to her. She didn't take it.

I walked away to an ornate park bench that sat along the end of the arena and took a long drink from the bottle of water I'd left there.

'I have a hundred dollars with me,' the girl said. 'For a deposit. I expect you have a daily fee and that you probably charge expenses. I'm sure we can work something out.'

Sean emerged from the end of the stable, squinting into the distance, showing his profile. He stood with one booted leg cocked and pulled a pair of deerskin gloves from the waist of his brown breeches. Handsome and fit. A perfect ad for Ralph Lauren.

I headed across the arena, anger boiling now in my stomach. Anger, and underlying it a building sense of panic.

'What the fuck is this?' I shouted, smacking him in the chest with the magazine.

He took a step back, looking offended. 'It might be *Sidelines*, but I can't read with my nipples, so I can't say for certain. Jesus Christ, El. What did you do to your hair?'

I hit him again, harder, wanting to hurt him. He grabbed the magazine away from me, took another quick step out of range, and turned to the cover. 'Betsy Steiner's stallion, Hilltop Giotto. Have you seen him? He's to die for.'

'You told a reporter I'm a private investigator.'

'They asked me who you were. I had to tell them something.'

'No, you didn't have to. You didn't have to tell them anything.'

'It's only *Sidelines*. For Christ's sake.'

'It's my name in a goddam magazine read by thousands of people. Thousands of people now know where to find me. Why don't you just paint a big target on my chest?'

He frowned. 'Only dressage people read the dressage section. And then only to see if their own names are in the show results.'

'Thousands of people now think I'm a private investigator.'

'What was I supposed to tell them? The truth?' Said as if that were the most distasteful option. Then I realized it probably was.

'How about "no comment"?'

'That's not very interesting.'

I pointed at Molly Seabright. 'That little girl has come here to hire me. She thinks I can help her find her sister.'

'Maybe you can.'

I refused to state the obvious: that I couldn't even help myself.

Sean lifted a shoulder with lazy indifference and handed the magazine back to me. 'What else have you got to do with your time?'

Irina emerged from the barn, leading Oliver – tall, elegant, and beautiful, the equine version of Sean. Sean dismissed me and went to his teak mounting block.

Molly Seabright was sitting on the park bench with her hands folded in her lap. I turned and walked to the barn, hoping she would just go away. D'Artagnon's bridle hung from the ceiling on a four-pronged hook near an antique mahogany cabinet full of leather-cleaning supplies. I chose a small damp sponge from the work table, rubbed it over a bar of glycerine soap, and began to clean the bridle, trying to narrow the focus of my mind on the small motor skills involved in the task.

'You're very rude.'

I could see her from the corner of my eye: standing as tall as she could – five-feet-nothing – her mouth a tight little knot.

'Yes, I am. That's part of the joy of being me: I don't care.'

'You're not going to help me.'

'I can't. I'm not what you need. If your sister is missing, your parents should go to the cops.'

'I went to the Sheriff's Office. They wouldn't help me either.'

'*You* went? What about your parents? They don't care your sister is missing?'

For the first time Molly Seabright seemed to hesitate. 'It's complicated.'

'What's complicated about it? She's either missing or she's not.'

'Erin doesn't live with us.'

'How old is she?'

'Eighteen. She doesn't get along with our parents.'

'There's something new.'

'It's not like she's bad or anything,' Molly said defensively. 'She doesn't do drugs or anything like that. It's just that she has her own opinions, that's all. And her opinions aren't Bruce's opinions . . .'

'Who's Bruce?'

'Our stepfather. Mom always sides with him, no matter how asinine he is. It makes Erin angry, so she moved out.'

'So Erin is technically an adult, living on her own, free to do whatever she wants,' I said. 'Does she have a boyfriend?'

Molly shook her head, but avoided my eyes. She wasn't so sure of that answer, or she thought a lie might better serve her cause.

'What makes you think she's missing?'

'She was supposed to pick me up Monday morning. That's her day off. She's a groom at the show grounds for Don Jade. He trains jumpers. I didn't have school. We were going to go to the beach, but she never came or called me. I called her and left a message on her cell phone, and she never called me back.'

'She's probably busy,' I said, stroking the sponge down a length of rein. 'Grooms work hard.'

Even as I said it I could see Irina sitting on the mounting block, face turned to the sun as she blew a lazy stream of cigarette smoke at the sky. Most grooms.

'She would have called me,' Molly insisted. 'I went to the show grounds myself the next day – yesterday. A man at Don Jade's barn told me Erin doesn't work there anymore.'

Grooms quit. Grooms get fired. Grooms decide one day to become florists and decide the next day they'd rather be brain surgeons. On the flip side, there are trainers with reputations as slave masters, temperamental prima donnas who go through grooms like disposable razors. I've known trainers who demanded a groom sleep every night in a stall with a psychotic stallion, valuing the horse far more than the person. I've known trainers who fired five grooms in a week.

Erin Seabright was, by the sound of it, headstrong and argumentative, maybe with an eye for the guys. She was eighteen and tasting independence for the first time . . . And why I was even thinking this through was beyond me. Habit, maybe. Once a cop . . . But I hadn't been a cop for two years, and I would never be a cop again.

'Sounds to me like Erin has a life of her own. Maybe she just doesn't have time for a kid sister right now.'

Molly Seabright's expression darkened. 'I told you Erin's not like that. She wouldn't just leave.'

'She left home.'

'But she didn't leave *me*. She wouldn't.'

Finally she sounded like a child instead of a forty-nine-year-old CPA. An uncertain, frightened little girl. Looking to me for help.

'People change. People grow up,' I said bluntly, taking the bridle down from the hook. 'Maybe it's your turn.'

The words hit their mark like bullets. Tears rose behind the Harry Potter glasses. I didn't allow myself to feel guilt or pity. I didn't want a job or a client. I didn't want people coming into my life with expectations.

'I thought you would be different,' she said.

'Why would you think that?'

She glanced over at the magazine lying on the shelf with the cleaning supplies, D'Artagnon and I floating across the page like something from a dream. But she said nothing. If she had an explanation for her belief, she thought better of sharing it with me.

'I'm nobody's hero, Molly. I'm sorry you got that impression. I'm sure if your parents aren't worried about your sister, and the cops aren't worried about your sister, then there's nothing to be worried about. You don't need me, and believe me, you'd be sorry if you did.'

She didn't look at me. She stood there for a moment, composing herself, then pulled a small red wallet from the carrying pouch strapped around her waist. She took out a ten-dollar bill and placed it on the magazine.

'Thank you for your time,' she said politely, then turned and walked away.

I didn't chase after her. I didn't try to give her her ten dollars back. I watched her walk away and thought she was more of an adult than I was.

Irina appeared in my peripheral vision, propping herself against the archway as if she hadn't the strength to stand on her own. 'You want I should saddle Feliki?'

Erin Seabright had probably quit her job. She was probably in the Keys right now enjoying her newfound independence with some cute good-for-nothing. Molly didn't want to believe that because it would mean a sea change in her relationship with the big sister she idolized. Life is full of disappointments. Molly would learn that the same way as everyone: by being let down by someone she loved and trusted.

Irina gave a dramatic sigh.

'Yes,' I said. 'Saddle Feliki.'

She started toward the mare's stall, then I asked a question for which I would have been far better off not having an answer.

'Irina, do you know anything about a jumper trainer named Don Jade?'

'Yes,' she said casually, not even looking back at me. 'He is a murderer.'

2

The horse world is populated by two kinds of people: those who love horses, and those who exploit horses and the people who love them. Yin and yang. For every good thing in the world, there is something bad to counterbalance. Myself, I've always felt the bad far outweighs the good, that there is just enough good to buoy us and keep us from drowning in a sea of despair. But that's just me.

Some of the finest people I've known have been involved in the horse business. Caring people who would sacrifice themselves and their own comfort for the animals who relied on them. People who kept their word. People with integrity. And some of the most loathsome, hateful, twisted individuals I've ever known have been involved in the horse business. People who would lie, cheat, steal, and sell their own mother for a nickel if they thought it would get them ahead. People who would smile to your face, pat you on the back with one hand, and stab you in the back with the other.

From what Irina told me, Don Jade fit into that second category.

Sunday morning – the day before Erin Seabright didn't show to pick up her little sister to go to the beach – a jumper in training with Don Jade had been found dead in his stall, the victim of an allegedly accidental electrocution. Only, according to gossip, there was no such thing as an accident where Don Jade was involved.

I went on-line and tried to learn what I could about Jade from articles on horsesdaily.com and a couple of other equestrian sites. But I wanted the story in full, uncensored, and I knew exactly who to call.

If Don Jade defined my second category of horse people, Dr Dean Soren defined the first. I had known Dr Dean for a lifetime. Nothing went on in the horse world Dean Soren didn't know about. He had begun his veterinary career in the year naught on the racetrack, eventually moving on to show horses. Everyone in the business knew and respected Dr Dean.

He had retired from his veterinary practice several years before, and spent his days holding court in the café that was social central of the large stable he owned off Pierson. The woman who ran the café answered the phone. I told her who I was and asked for Dr Dean, then listened as she shouted across the room at him.

Dr Dean shouted back: 'What the hell does she want?'

'Tell him I need to ask him a couple of questions.'

The woman shouted that.

'Then she can damn well come here and ask me in person,' he shouted back. 'Or is she too goddammed important to visit an old man?'

That was Dr Dean. The words *charming* and *kindly* were not in his vocabulary, but he was one of the best people I had ever known. Whatever softer elements he lacked, he more than made up for in integrity and honesty.

I didn't want to go to him. Don Jade interested me only because of what Irina had said about him. I was curious, but that was all. Curiosity wasn't enough to make me want to interact with people. I had no desire to leave my sanctuary, especially in light of the photo in *Sidelines*.

I paced the house, chewing at what was left of my fingernails.

Dean Soren had known me off and on most of my life. The winter season I was twelve, he let me ride along with him on his rounds one day a week and act as his assistant. My mother and I had moved to a house in the Polo Club for the season, and I had a tutor so that I could ride every day with my trainer, and not have a school schedule interrupt my horse show schedule. Every Monday – rider's day off – I would bribe the tutor and slip off with Dr Dean to hold his instrument tray and clean up used bandages. My own father had never spent that kind of time with me. I had never felt so important.

The memories of that winter touched me now in an especially vulnerable place. I couldn't remember the last time I had felt important. I could hardly remember the last time I had wanted to. But I could remember very clearly riding beside Dr Dean in the enormous Lincoln Town Car he had tricked out as a rolling vet clinic.

Perhaps it was that memory that made me pick up my car keys and go.

The prime property Dr Dean owned was populated by hunter/jumper people in one large barn and by dressage people in the other. The offices, Dr Dean's personal stable, and the café were all located in a building between the two large barns.

The café was a simple open-air affair with a tiki bar. Dr Dean sat at the centermost table in a carved wooden chair, an old king on his throne, drinking something with a paper umbrella in it.

I felt light-headed as I walked toward him, partly afraid to see him – or rather, for him to see me – and partly afraid people would come out of the woodwork to stare at me and ask me if I was really a private investigator. But the café was empty other than Dean Soren and the woman behind the counter. No one ran over from the barns to gawk.

Dr Dean rose from his chair, his piercing eyes on me like a pair of lasers. He was a tall, straight man with a full head of white hair and a long face carved with lines. He had to be eighty, but he still looked fierce and strong.

'What the hell's wrong with you?' he said by way of a greeting. 'Are you in chemotherapy? Is that what happened to your hair?'

'Good to see you, too, Dr Dean,' I said, shaking his hand.

He looked over at the woman behind the counter. 'Marion! Make this girl a cheeseburger! She looks like hell!'

Marion, unfazed, went to work.

'What are you riding these days?' Dr Dean asked.

I took a seat – a cheap folding chair that seemed too low and made me feel like a child. Or maybe that was just Dean Soren's effect on me. 'I'm riding a couple of Sean's.'

'You don't look strong enough to ride a pony.'

'I'm fine.'

'No, you're not,' he pronounced. 'Who is Sean using for a vet now?'

'Paul Geller.'

'He's an idiot.'

'He's not you, Dr Dean,' I said diplomatically.

'He told Margo Whitaker her mare needs "sound therapy". She's got headphones on the poor horse two hours a day, playing the sounds of nature.'

'Gives Margo something to do.'

'The horse needs not to have Margo hovering around. That's what the horse needs,' he growled. He sipped his umbrella drink and stared at me.

'I haven't seen you in a long time, Elena,' he said. 'It's good you're back. You need to be with the horses. They ground you. A person always knows exactly where they stand with horses. Life makes more sense.'

'Yes,' I said, nervous under his scrutiny, afraid he would want to talk about my career and what had happened. But he let it go. Instead, he quizzed me about Sean's horses, and we reminisced about horses Sean and I had ridden in years past. Marion brought my cheeseburger and I dutifully ate.

When I had finished, he said, 'You said on the phone you had a question.'

'Do you know anything about Don Jade?' I asked bluntly.

His eyes narrowed. 'Why would you want to know about him?'

'A friend of a friend has gotten mixed up with him. It sounded a little sketchy to me.'

His thick white brows bobbed. He looked over toward the jumper barn. There were a couple of riders out on the jump field taking their mounts over colorful fences. From a distance they looked as graceful and light as deer bounding through a meadow. The athleticism of an animal is a pure and simple thing. Complicated by human emotions, needs, greed, there is little pure or simple about the sport we bring the horses into.

'Well,' he said. 'Don has always made a pretty picture with some ragged edges.'

'What does that mean?'

'Let's take a walk,' he suggested.

I suspected he didn't want anyone showing up to eavesdrop. I followed him out the back of the café to a row of small paddocks, three of them occupied by horses.

'My projects,' Dr Dean explained. 'Two mystery lamenesses and one with a bad case of stomach ulcers.'

He leaned against the fence and looked at them, horses he had probably saved from the knackers. He probably had half a dozen more stashed around the place.

'They give us all they can,' he said. 'They do their best to make sense out of what we ask them to do – *demand* they do. All they want in return is to be cared for properly and kindly. Imagine if people were like that.'

'Imagine,' I echoed, but I couldn't imagine. I had been a cop a dozen years. The nature of the job and the people and things it had exposed me to had burned away any idealism I might ever have had. The story Dean Soren told me about Don Jade only confirmed my low opinion of the human race.

Over the last two decades, Jade's name had twice been connected to schemes to defraud insurance companies. The scam was to kill an expensive show horse that hadn't lived up to potential, then have the owner file a claim saying the animal had died of natural causes and collect a six-figure payout.

It was an old hustle that had come into the spotlight of the national media in the eighties, when a number of prominent people in the show-jumping world had been caught at it. Several had ended up in prison for a number of years, among them an internationally well-known trainer, and an owner who was heir to an enormous cellular phone fortune. Being rich has never stopped anyone from being greedy.

Jade had lurked in the shadows of scandal back then, when he had been an assistant trainer at one of the barns that had lost horses to mysterious causes. He had never been charged with any crime or directly connected to a death. After the scandal broke, Jade had left that employer and spent a few years in France, training and competing on the European show circuit.

Eventually the furor over the horse killings died down, and Don Jade came back to the States and found a couple of wealthy clients to serve as cornerstones for his own business.

It might seem inconceivable that a man with Jade's reputation could continue on in the profession, but there are always new owners who don't know about a trainer's history, and there are always people who won't believe what they don't want to believe. And there are always people who just plain don't care. There are always people willing to look the other way if they think they stand to gain money or fame. Consequently, Don Jade's stable attracted clients, many of whom paid him handsomely to campaign their horses in Florida at the Winter Equestrian Festival.

In the late nineties, one of those horses was a jumper called Titan.

Titan was a talented horse with an unfortunately mercurial temperament.

A horse that cost his owner a lot of money and always seemed to sabotage his own efforts to earn his keep. He earned a reputation as a rogue and a head case. Despite his abilities, his market value plummeted. Meanwhile, Titan's owner, Warren Calvin, a Wall Street trader, had lost a fortune in the stock market. And suddenly one day Titan was dead, and Calvin filed a $250,000 claim with his insurance company.

The official story pieced together by Jade and his head groom was that sometime during the night Titan had become spooked, had gone wild in his stall, breaking a foreleg, and had died of shock and blood loss. However, a former Jade employee had told a different tale, claiming Titan's death had not been an accident, that Jade had had the animal suffocated, and that the horse had broken his leg in a panic as he was being asphyxiated.

It was an ugly story. The insurance company had immediately ordered a necropsy, and Warren Calvin had come under the scrutiny of a New York State prosecutor. Calvin withdrew the claim and the investigation was dropped. No fraud, no crime. The necropsy was never performed. Warren Calvin got out of the horse business.

Don Jade weathered the rumors and speculation and went on about his business. He'd had a convenient alibi for the night in question: a girl named Allison, who worked for him and claimed to have been in bed with him at the time of Titan's death. Jade admitted to the affair, lost his marriage, but kept on training horses. Old clients either believed him or left him, and new pigeons came to roost, unaware.

I had learned pieces of this story from my research on the Internet, and from Irina's gossip. I knew Irina's opinion of Jade had been based on the stories she'd heard from other grooms, information that was likely grounded in fact and heavily flavored with spite. The horse business is an incestuous business. Within the individual disciplines (jumping, dressage, et cetera) everyone knows everyone, and half of them have screwed the others, either literally or figuratively. Grudges and jealousies abound. The gossip can be vicious.

But I knew if the story came out of Dean Soren's mouth, it was true.

'It's sad a guy like that stays in business,' I said.

Dr Dean tipped his head and shrugged. 'People believe what they want. Don is a charming fellow, and he can ride the hell out of a jump course. You can argue with success all you want, Elena, but you'll never win. Especially not in this business.'

'Sean's groom told me Jade lost a horse last weekend,' I said.

'Stellar,' Dr Dean said, nodding. His ulcer patient had come to our corner of the paddock and reached her nose out coyly toward her savior, begging for a scratch under the chin. 'Story is he bit through the cord on a box fan hanging in his stall and fried himself.'

The mare stepped closer and put her head over the fence. I scratched her neck absently, keeping my attention on Dean Soren. 'What do you think?'

He touched the mare's head with a gnarled old hand, as gentle as if he were touching a child.

'I think old Stellar had more heart than talent.'

'Do you think Jade killed him?'

'It doesn't matter what I think,' he said. 'It only matters what someone can prove.' He looked at me with those eyes that had seen – and could see – so much about me. 'What does your friend's friend have to say about it?'

'Nothing,' I said, feeling sick in my stomach. 'She seems to be missing.'

On Monday morning Don Jade's groom, Erin Seabright, was to have picked up her little sister to take her to the beach. She never showed and hadn't been in contact with her family since.

I paced the rooms of the guest house and chewed on the ragged stub of a thumbnail. The Sheriff's Office hadn't been interested in the concerns of a twelve-year-old girl. It was doubtful they knew anything about or had any interest in Don Jade. Erin Seabright's parents presumably knew nothing about Jade either, or Molly wouldn't have been the only Seabright looking for help.

The ten-dollar bill the girl had given me was on the small writing desk beside my laptop. Inside the folded bill was Molly's own little homemade calling card: her name, address, and a striped cat on a mailing label; the label adhered to a little rectangle of blue poster board. She had printed her phone number neatly at the bottom of the card.

Don Jade had been sleeping with one of his hired girls when the horse Titan had died half a decade past. I wondered if that was a habit: fucking grooms. He wouldn't have been the first trainer with that hobby. I thought about the way Molly had avoided my eyes when she'd told me her sister didn't have a boyfriend.

I walked away from the desk feeling anxious and upset. I wished I'd never gone to Dr Dean. I wished I had never learned what I'd learned about Don Jade. My life was enough of a mess without looking for trouble. My life was enough of a mess without the intrusion of Molly Seabright and her family problems. I was supposed to be sorting out the tangle of my own life, answering inner questions, finding myself – or facing the fact there was nothing worth finding.

If I couldn't find myself, how was I supposed to find someone else? I didn't want to fall down this rabbit hole. My involvement with horses was supposed to be my salvation. I didn't want it to have anything to do with people like Don Jade, people who would have a horse killed by electrocution, like Stellar, or by shoving Ping-Pong balls up its nostrils, cutting off its air supply, like Warren Calvin's Titan.

That was how suffocation was accomplished: Ping-Pong balls in the nostrils. My chest tightened at the dark mental image of the animal panicking, throwing itself into the walls of its stall as it desperately tried to escape its fate. I could see the eyes rolling in terror, hear the grunt as it flung itself backward and hit a wall. I could hear the animal scrambling, the terrible sound of a foreleg snapping. The nightmare seemed so real, the sounds blaring inside my mind. Nausea and weakness washed through me. My throat felt closed. I wanted to choke.

I went outside onto the little patio, sweating, trembling. I thought I might vomit. I wondered what it said about me that in all the time I'd been a detective, I'd never gotten sick at anything I'd seen one human being do to another, but the idea of cruelty to an animal undid me.

The evening air was fresh and cool, and slowly cleared the horrible images from my head.

Sean had company. I could see them in the dining room, talking, laughing. Chandelier light spilled through the tall casement windows to be reflected in the dark water of the pool. I had been invited to dinner, but turned him down flat, still furious with him for the *Sidelines* fiasco. He was probably, even as I stood there, telling his pals about the private investigator who lived in his backyard. Fucking dilettante, using me to amuse his Palm Beach pals. Never giving a thought to the fact that he was playing with my life.

Never mind he had saved it first.

I didn't want the reminder. I didn't want to think of Molly Seabright or her sister. This place was supposed to be my sanctuary, but I felt as if half a dozen unseen hands were grabbing at me, plucking at my clothes, pinching me. I tried to walk away from them, going across the damp lawn to the barn.

Sean's barn had been designed by the same architect who designed the main house and the guest house. Moorish arches created galleries down the sides. The roof was green tile, the ceiling teak. The light fixtures hanging down the center aisle had been taken out of an art deco era hotel in Miami. Most humans don't have homes that cost what his stable cost.

It was a lovely space, a place I often came to at night to calm myself. There are few things as quieting and reassuring to me as horses browsing on their evening hay. Their lives are simple. They know they are safe. Their day is over and they trust the sun will rise the next morning.

They trust their keepers absolutely. They are utterly vulnerable.

Oliver abandoned his food and came to put his head out over his stall door to nuzzle my cheek. He caught the collar of my old denim shirt between his teeth and seemed to smile, pleased with his mischief. I hugged his big head and breathed in the scent of him. When I stepped back, extricating my collar, he looked at me with eyes as kind and innocent as a small child's.

I might have cried had I been physically able to do so. I am not.

I went back to the guest house, glancing in again at Sean's dinner party as I passed. Everyone looked to be having a grand time, smiling, laughing, bathed in golden light. I wondered what I would see if I were to walk past Molly Seabright's house. Her mother and stepfather talking around her, preoccupied with the details of their mundane lives; Molly isolated from them by her keen intelligence and her worry for her sister, wondering where to turn next.

When I went inside my house, the message light on my phone was blinking. I hit the button and braced myself to hear Molly's voice, then felt something like disappointment when my attorney asked me to please return his call sometime this century. Asshole. We'd been waging the battle for my disability pay since I had left the Sheriff's Office. (Money I didn't need, but was entitled to because I had been injured on the job. Never mind that it had been my own fault, or that my injuries were insignificant compared to what had happened to Hector Ramirez.) What the hell didn't he know about the situation after all this time? Why did he think he needed me?

Why would anyone think they needed me?

I went into my bedroom and sat on the bed, opened the drawer of the nightstand. I took out the brown plastic bottle of Vicodin and poured the pills out on the tabletop. I stared at them, counted them one by one, touching each pill. How pathetic that a ritual like this might soothe me, that the idea of a drug overdose – or the thought that I wouldn't take them that night – would calm me.

Jesus God, who in their right mind would think they needed me?

Disgusted with myself, I dumped the pills back in the bottle, put the bottle back in the drawer. I hated myself for not being what I had always believed myself to be: strong. But then I had long mistaken being spoiled for being strong, being defiant for being independent, being reckless for being brave.

Life's a bitch when you find out in your thirties that everything you ever believed to be true and admirable about yourself is nothing but a self-serving lie.

I had painted myself into a corner and I didn't know how to get out of it. I didn't know if I could reinvent myself. I didn't think I had the strength or the will to do it. Hiding in my own private purgatory required no strength.

I fully realized how pathetic that was. And I had spent a lot of nights in the past two years wondering if being dead wasn't preferable to being pathetic. So far I had decided the answer was no. Being alive at least presented the possibility for improvement.

Was Erin Seabright somewhere thinking the same thing? I wondered. Or was it already too late? Or had she found the one circumstance to which death was preferable but not an option?

I had been a cop a long time. I had started my career in a West Palm Beach radio car, patrolling neighborhoods where crime was a common career choice and drugs could be purchased on the street in broad daylight. I had done a stint in Vice, viewing the businesses of prostitution and pornography up close and personal. I had spent years working narcotics for the Sheriff's Office.

I had a head full of images of the dire consequences of being a young woman in the wrong place at the wrong time. South Florida offered a lot of places to get rid of bodies or hide ugly secrets. Wellington was an oasis of civilization, but the land beyond the gated communities was more like the land that time forgot. Swamp and woods. Open, hostile scrubland and sugarcane fields. Dirt roads and rednecks and biker meth labs in trailer houses that should have been left to the rats twenty years past. Canals and drainage ditches full of dirty black water and alligators happy to make a meal of any kind of meat.

Was Erin Seabright out there somewhere waiting for someone to save her? Waiting for me? God help her. I didn't want to go.

I went into the bathroom and washed my hands and splashed water on my face. Trying to wash away any feelings of obligation. I could feel the water only on the right side of my face. Nerves on the left side had been damaged, leaving me with limited feeling and movement. The plastic surgeons had given me a suitably neutral expression, a job so well done no one suspected anything wrong with me other than a lack of emotion.

The calm, blank expression stared back at me now in the mirror. Another reminder that no aspect of me was whole or normal. And I was supposed to be Erin Seabright's savior?

I hit the mirror with the heels of my fists, once, then again and again, wishing my image would shatter before my eyes as surely as it had shattered within me two years ago. Another part of me wanted the sharp cut of pain, the cleansing symbolized in shed blood. I wanted to bleed to know I existed. I wanted to vanish to escape the pain. The contradictory forces shoved against one another inside me, crowding my lungs, pushing up against my brain.

I went to the kitchen and stared at the knife block on the counter and my car keys lying beside it.

Life can change in a heartbeat of time, in a hairsbreadth of space. Without our consent. I had already known that to be the truth. In my deepest heart I suppose I knew it to be true in that moment, that night. I preferred to believe I picked up the keys and left the house to escape my own self-torment. That idea allowed me to continue to believe I was selfish.

In truth, the choice I made that night wasn't safe at all. In truth, I chose to move forward. I tricked myself into choosing life over purgatory.

Before it was all over, I feared I might live to regret it – or die trying.

3

Palm Beach Polo Equestrian Center is like a small sovereign nation, complete with royalty and guards at the gates. At the front gates. The back gates stood open during the day and could be reached from Sean's farm by car in five minutes. People from the neighborhood regularly hacked their horses over on show days and saved themselves the cost of stabling – ninety dollars a weekend for a pipe-and-canvas stall in a circus tent with ninety-nine other horses. A guard making night rounds would lock the gate at some point late in the evening. The guard hadn't made his rounds yet that night.

I drove through the gates, a yellow parking pass stolen from Sean's Mercedes hanging on my rearview mirror, just in case. I parked in a row of vehicles along a fence opposite the last of the forty big stabling tents on the property.

I drove a sea-green BMW 318i convertible I bought at a sheriff's auction. The roof sometimes leaked in a hard rain, but it had an interesting option that hadn't come from the factory in Bavaria: a small, foam-lined metal box hidden in the driver's door panel, just big enough to hold a good-sized bag of cocaine or a handgun. The Glock nine millimeter I kept there was tucked into the back of my jeans, hidden by my shirttail as I walked away.

On show days the show grounds are as busy and crazy as the streets of Calcutta. Golf carts and small motorcycles race back and forth between the barns and showrings, dodging dogs and trucks and trailers, heavy equipment, Jaguars and Porsches, people on horses and children on ponies, and grooms walking charges done up in immaculate braids and draped in two-hundred-dollar cool-out sheets in the custom colors of their stables. The tents look like refugee camps with portable johns out front, people filling buckets from pump hydrants by the side of the dirt road, and illegal aliens dumping muck buckets into the huge piles of manure that are carted away in dump trucks once a day. People school horses on every available open patch of ground, trainers shouting instructions, encouragement, and insults at their students. Announcements blare over the public address system every few minutes.

At night the place is a different world. Quiet. Almost deserted. The roads are empty. Security guards make the rounds of the barns periodically. A groom or trainer might drop by to perform the ritual night check or to tend an animal with a medical problem. Some stables leave a guard of their own posted in their elaborately decorated tack room. Baby-sitters for horseflesh worth millions.

Bad things can happen under cover of darkness. Rivals can become enemies. Jealousy can become revenge. I once knew a woman who sent a private cop everywhere with her horses after one of her top jumpers was slipped LSD the night before a competition offering fifty thousand dollars in prize money.

I'd made a couple of good busts at this show grounds when I'd worked narcotics. Any kind of drug – human or animal, remedial or recreational – could be had here if one knew whom and how to ask. Because I had once been a part of this world, I was able to blend in. I had been away from it long enough that no one knew me. Yet I could walk the walk and talk the talk. I had to hope Sean's little joke in *Sidelines* hadn't taken away my anonymity.

I made the dogleg turns from the back area known euphemistically as 'The Meadows', the tent ghetto where show management always sticks the dressage horses that ship in for only several shows each season. From those back tents it takes twenty minutes to walk to the heart of the show grounds. Earth-moving equipment sat parked at one corner, backed into freshly cleared land amid the scrubby woods. The place was being expanded again.

Lights glowed in the tents. A woman's melodic laugh floated on the night air. A man's low chuckle underscored the sound. I could see the pair standing at the end of an aisle in tent nineteen. Elaborate landscaping at the corner of the tent set the stage around a lighted stable sign with one golden word on a field of hunter green: jade.

I walked past. Now that I had found Jade's stalls, I didn't know what I was going to do. I hadn't thought that far ahead. I turned on the far side of tent eighteen and doubled back around, coming up through the aisles of nineteen until I could hear the voices again.

'Do you hear anything?' The man's voice. An accent. Maybe Dutch, maybe Flemish.

I stopped breathing.

'Gut sounds,' the woman said. 'She's fine, but we'll go through the drill with the vet anyway. Can't be seen looking careless after Stellar.'

The man gave a humorless laugh. 'People have made their minds up about that. They believe what they want.'

'The worst,' the woman said. 'Jane Lennox called today. She's thinking of putting Park Lane with another trainer. I talked her out of it.'

'I'm sure you did. You're very persuasive, Paris.'

'This is America. You're supposed to be innocent until proven guilty.'

'Innocent always if you're rich or beautiful or charming.'

'Don is beautiful and charming, and everyone believes he's guilty.'

'Like O.J. was guilty? He's playing golf and fucking white women.'

'What a thing to say!'

'It's true. And Jade has a barn full of horses. Americans ...' Disdain.

'I'm an American, V.' An edge to the tone. 'Do you want to call me stupid?'

'Paris ...' Smarmy contrition.

'Stupid Americans buy your horses and line your pockets. You should show more respect. Or does that just prove how stupid we are?'

'Paris ...' Smarmier contrition. 'Don't be angry with me. I don't want you angry with me.'

'No, you don't.'

A Jack Russell terrier came sniffing around the corner then and stared at me while he raised his leg and peed on a bale of hay, considering whether or not to blow my cover. The leg went down and the dog went off like a car alarm. I stood where I was.

The woman called out: 'Milo! Milo, come here!'

Milo stood his ground. He bounced up and down like a wind-up toy every time he barked.

The woman rounded the corner, looking surprised to see me. She was blond and pretty in dark breeches and a green polo shirt with a couple of gold necklaces showing at the throat. She flashed a thousand-watt toothpaste-ad smile that was nothing more than jaw muscles flexing.

'Sorry. He thinks he's a Rottweiler,' she said, scooping up the Russell. 'Can I help you?'

'I don't know. I'm looking for someone. I was told she works for Don Jade. Erin Seabright?'

'Erin? What do you want with her?'

'This is kind of awkward,' I said. 'I heard she was looking for another job. I have a friend in the market for a groom. You know how it is during the season.'

'Do I ever!' She gave a dramatic, put-upon sigh, rolling the big brown eyes. An actress. 'We're looking too. Erin quit, I'm sad to say.'

'Really? When was that?'

'Sunday. Left us high and dry. Found something more interesting up in Ocala, I guess. Don tried to talk her out of it, but he said her mind was made up. I was sorry to hear it. I liked Erin, but you know how flighty these girls can be.'

'Huh. I'm surprised. The way I understood it, she wanted to stay in the Wellington area. Did she leave an address – to have her paycheck sent?'

'Don paid her before she left. I'm Don's assistant trainer, by the way. Paris Montgomery.' Keeping the dog tucked against her, she held a hand out and shook mine. She had a strong grip. 'And you are ... ?'

'Elle Stevens.' A name I had used undercover in my past life. It fell off my tongue without hesitation. 'So, she left Sunday. Was that before or after Stellar went down?'

The smile died. 'Why would you ask that?'

'Well . . . a disgruntled employee leaves and suddenly you lose a horse –'

'Stellar bit through an electrical cord. It was an accident.'

I shrugged. 'Hey, what do I know? People talk.'

'People don't know shit.'

'Is there a problem here?'

The man stepped into the picture. Mid-fifties, tall and elegant with silver temples highlighting a full head of dark hair. He wore a stern, aristocratic expression, pressed tan slacks, a pink Lacoste knit shirt, and a black silk ascot at his throat.

'Not at all,' I said. 'I was just looking for someone.'

'Erin,' Paris Montgomery said to him.

'Erin?'

'Erin. My groom. The one that left.'

He made a sour face. 'That girl? She's good for nothing. What would you want with her?'

'Doesn't matter,' I said. 'She's gone.'

'What's your friend's name?' Paris asked. 'In case I hear of someone.'

'Sean Avadon. Avadonis Farm.'

The man's cold blue eyes brightened. 'He has some very nice horses.'

'Yes, he does.'

'You work for him?' he asked.

I supposed I did look like hired help with my hacked-off hair, old jeans, and work boots. 'He's an old friend. I'm leasing a horse from him until I can find what I'm looking for.'

He smiled then like a cat with a cornered mouse. His teeth were brilliantly white. 'I can help you with that.'

A horse dealer. The third-oldest profession. Forerunners of used-car salesmen the world over.

Paris Montgomery rolled her eyes. A truck pulled up at the end of the tent. 'That's Dr Ritter. I've got to go.'

She turned the big smile back on and shook my hand again. 'Nice meeting you, Elle,' she said, as if we'd never had that moment of unpleasantness at the mention of Stellar's death. 'Good luck with your search.'

'Thanks.'

She set the Russell down and followed the barking beast around the corner as the vet called for her.

The man held his hand out to me. 'Tomas Van Zandt.'

'Elle Stevens.'

'My pleasure.'

He held my hand a little too long.

'I'd better be going,' I said, drifting back a step. 'It's getting late for a wild-goose chase.'

'I'll take you to your car,' he offered. 'Beautiful women shouldn't go around unescorted here in the dark. You don't know what kind of people might be around.'

'I have a pretty good idea, but thanks for your concern. Women shouldn't get into cars with men they've only just met either,' I said.

He laughed and placed a hand over his heart. 'I am a gentleman, Elle. Harmless. Without designs. Wanting nothing of you but a smile.'

'You'd sell me a horse. That would cost me plenty.'

'But only the best horses,' he promised. 'I will find you exactly what you need and for a good price. Your friend Avadon likes good horses. Maybe you could introduce us.'

Horse dealers. I rolled my eyes and gave him half a smile. 'Maybe I just want a ride to my car.'

Looking pleased, he led the way out of the tent to a black Mercedes sedan and opened the door for me.

'You must have a lot of satisfied customers if you can rent a car like this for the season,' I said.

Van Zandt smiled like the cat that got the cream *and* the canary. 'I have such happy clients, one gave me the loan of this car for the winter.'

'My goodness. If only my ex had made me so happy, he might still be considered in the present tense.'

Van Zandt laughed. 'Where are you parked, Miss Elle?'

'The back gate.'

As we started down the road toward The Meadows I said, 'You know this girl, Erin? She's not a good worker?'

He pursed his lips like he'd gotten a whiff of something rotten. 'Bad attitude. Smart mouth. Flirting with the clients. American girls don't make good grooms. They're spoiled and lazy.'

'I'm an American girl.'

He ignored that. 'Get a good Polish girl. They're strong and cheap.'

'Can I get one at Wal-Mart? I've got a Russian now. She thinks she's a czarina.'

'Russians are arrogant.'

'And what are Dutchmen?'

He pulled the Mercedes in where I pointed, alongside my Beemer.

'I am from Belgium,' he corrected. 'Men from Belgium are charming and know how to treat ladies.'

'Slick rascals, more like,' I said. 'Ladies should be on their guard, I think.'

Van Zandt chuckled. 'You are no pushover, Elle Stevens.'

'It takes more than a smile and an accent to sweep me off my feet. I'll make you work for it.'

'A challenge!' he said, delighted at the prospect.

I got out of the car without waiting for him to come around and open the door, and dug my keys out of my hip pocket. The back of my hand brushed over the butt of the gun tucked in my waistband.

'Thanks for the ride,' I said.

'Thank you, Elle Stevens. You brightened an otherwise boring evening.'

'Don't let Ms Montgomery hear you say that.'

'She's all gloom, talking about the dead gelding.'

'Losing a horse worth that kind of money would bring me down too.'

'It wasn't her money.'

'Maybe she liked the horse.'

He shrugged. 'There's always another.'

'Which I'm sure you'll be happy to supply to the grieving owner for a price.'

'Of course. Why not? That's business – for me and for her.'

'You sentimental fool, you.'

In the harsh glow of the security light from above I saw the muscles of Van Zandt's jaw flex. 'I am in this business thirty years, Elle Stevens,' he said, a thread of impatience in his voice. 'I am not a heartless man, but for professionals horses come and horses go. It's a shame the gelding died, but with professionals a sentimental fool is just that: a fool. People have to move on with their lives. Owners too. The insurance will pay for the dead horse, and his owner will buy another.'

'Which you will be happy to find.'

'Of course. I know already a horse in Belgium: clean X-rays and twice as good as that one over the fences.'

'And for a mere one-point-eight million he can belong to some lucky American and Don Jade can ride him.'

'The good ones cost, the good ones win.'

'And the rest can bite through electrical cords in the dead of night and fry themselves?' I asked. 'Careful who you say that to, Van Zandt. Some insurance investigator might hear you and think the wrong thing.'

He didn't shrug that off. I sensed him tense.

'I never said anyone killed the horse,' he said, his voice tight and low. He was angry with me. I wasn't supposed to have a brain. I was supposed to be the next American with too much money and too little sense, waiting for him to charm me and sweep me off to Europe on a buying trip.

'No, but Jade has that reputation, doesn't he?'

Van Zandt stepped closer. My back pressed against the frame of my car's roof. I had to look up at him. There wasn't a soul around. There was nothing but a lot of open country beyond the back gates. I slipped one hand into the back of my waistband and touched my gun.

'Are you that insurance person, Elle Stevens?' he asked.

'Me?' I laughed. 'God, no. I don't work.' I said the word with the kind of disdain my mother would have used. 'It's just a good story, that's all. Don Jade: Dangerous Man of Mystery. You know us Palm Beachers. Can't resist a juicy scandal. My biggest concern in life at the moment is where my next good horse is coming from. What goes on with this show-jumping crowd is nothing but good gossip to me.'

He relaxed then, having decided I was sufficiently self-absorbed. He handed me his card and dredged up the charm again. Nothing like greed to rally a man. 'Give me a call, Elle Stevens. I'll find you your horse.'

I tried to smile, knowing only one side of my mouth moved upward at all. 'I may take you up on that, Mr Van Zandt.'

'Call me V.,' he suggested, his tone strangely intimate. 'V for Very Good Horses. V for Victory in the showring.'

V for vomit.

'We are friends now,' he announced. He leaned down and kissed my right cheek, then the left, then the right again. His lips were cold and dry.

'Three times,' he said, Mr Suave again. 'Like the Dutch.'

'I'll remember that. Thanks again for the ride.'

I got into my car and backed out of the line. The back gate was locked. I turned and went back down the road past tent nineteen. Van Zandt followed me to the truck entrance. The lights blazed in the four big permanent barns to the right. A guard stood in the little booth between traffic lanes before the main gates, reggae music blasting from a radio on the counter. I waved at him. He waved me past without a question, his attention on the eighteen-wheel commercial horse van pulling in. I could have had a trunk full of stolen saddles. I could have had a body back there. I might have been anyone, may have done anything. An unsettling thought for the ride home.

I turned right on Pierson. Van Zandt turned right on Pierson. I watched him in the mirror, wondering if he hadn't believed me when I'd said I wasn't an insurance investigator. I wondered what his reaction would be if he saw the photo in *Sidelines* and put two and one together.

But people are funny that way, more easily fooled than the average person might like to believe. I didn't look like the woman in the photo. My hair was short. I hadn't given the name of the woman in the photo. The only real connection was Sean. Still, the words *private investigator* would set off alarms. I had to hope Sean was right: that only dressage people read the dressage section.

I turned right on South Shore. Van Zandt turned left.

I cut my lights, pulled a U-turn, and followed at a distance, past the polo stadium. He turned in at The Players club. Wining and dining. Part of a horse dealer's job. A new best friend at the bar in a place like that could turn out to have deep pockets and no self-restraint.

Van Zandt stood to make a tidy profit selling the Belgian jumper to Stellar's owner, who stood to collect a fat insurance payoff on a horse with no real future. And Don Jade – who had trained and shown Stellar, and would train and show the next one – stood in the middle of them, taking money at both ends of the deal. They might have all been in Players together right then, drinking to Stellar's timely demise.

Erin Seabright hadn't been heard from since the night Stellar died.

I dismissed the idea of going into the club. I wasn't prepared. I gunned my car's engine, turned it around, and headed home.

I was about to become a private investigator.

4

I wonder why I'm still alive.

Billy Golam had pointed that gun right in my face. In countless nightmares I have looked down the barrel of that .357 and sucked in what should have been my final breath. But Golam had turned and fired in another direction.

Was living my punishment, my purgatory? Or was I supposed to have chosen to end it myself to pay for my recklessness? Or was I just damn lucky and unwilling to believe it?

Four-thirty A.M.

I was lying in bed, staring at the blades of the ceiling fan go around. The guest house had been decorated by a Palm Beach interior designer who had gone amok with delusions of Caribbean plantations. It seemed a cliché to me, but no one had ever paid me to pick out paint chips and pillow shams.

At four I went out and fed the horses. By five I had showered. It had been so long since I'd had to introduce myself to people and care about what they thought of me that I couldn't remember how to go about it. I couldn't shake the idea that I would be rejected on sight, or if not on sight, on reputation.

What a strange conceit to believe everyone in the world knew all about me, all about what I'd done and what had happened to end my career. I had been a story on the evening news for a couple of days. A sound bite. Something to fill the airtime before the weather came on. The truth was probably that no one not directly involved with what had happened, no one not living in that world of cops, had given the story more than the most cursory attention. The truth is that people seldom really care about the catastrophic events of someone else's life beyond thinking, 'Better her than me.'

I stood in my underwear, staring at myself in the mirror. I put some gel in my hair and tried to make it look as if it had an intentional style. I wondered if I should attempt makeup. I hadn't worn any since the surgery to put my face back together. My plastic surgeon had given me the card of a woman who specialized in postsurgical makeup. The Post-Traumatic Avon Lady. I had thrown the card away.

I dressed, discarding a dozen different choices and finally settling on a sleeveless silk blouse the color of fresh-poured concrete and a pair of brown trousers that were so big around the waist, I had to pin them shut to keep them from sliding down my hips.

I used to care about fashion.

I killed some time on the Internet, chewed my nails, and made some notes.

I found nothing of interest on Tomas Van Zandt. His name did not appear even on his own Web site: worldhorsesales.com. The site listed on his business card showed photos of horses that had been brokered through Van Zandt's business. Phone numbers were listed for a business office in Brussels, a number for European sales, and for two US subagents, one of whom was Don Jade.

I found several articles about Paris Montgomery in the *Chronicle of the Horse* and *Horses Daily* describing recent wins in the showring, talking about her humble beginnings riding ponies bareback in the Pine Barrens of New Jersey. According to the propaganda, she had worked her way up the ranks from groom to working student to assistant trainer; succeeding on hard work and raw talent. And charm. And the fact that she could have been a model.

She had been Don Jade's assistant trainer for three years and was so grateful for the opportunity, blah, blah, blah. So few people realized what a great guy he really was. He'd been unfortunate to do business with some people of questionable ethics, but shouldn't be condemned by association, et cetera, et cetera. Jade was quoted as saying Paris Montgomery had a bright future and the ambition and talent to attain whatever she set her sights on.

Photographs with the articles showed Montgomery going over a fence on a horse called Park Lane, and close-ups of her flashing the big smile.

The smile irritated me. It was too bright and came too easily. The charm seemed insincere. Then again, I'd only just met her for ten minutes. Maybe I didn't like her because I couldn't smile and wasn't charming.

I flipped the screen shut on my laptop and went outside. Dawn was a pale notion on the edge of the eastern sky as I let myself into Sean's house through the French doors into the dining room. He was alone in bed, snoring. I sat down beside him and patted his cheek. His eyelids pulled slowly upward, revealing a lot of red veins. He rubbed a hand over his face.

'I was hoping for Tom Cruise,' he said in a voice full of gravel.

'Sorry to disappoint. If a horse dealer named Van Zandt comes around, my name is Elle Stevens and you're looking for a groom.'

'What?' He pushed himself upright and shook his head to clear the cobwebs. 'Van Zandt? Tomas Van Zandt?'

'You know him?'

'I know of him. He's the second-biggest crook in Europe. Why would he come here?'

'Because he thinks you might buy horses from him.'

'Why would he think that?'

'Because I pretty much led him to believe it.'

'Uh!!'

'Don't look offended,' I said. 'That expression emphasizes the lines around your mouth.'

'Bitch.'

He pouted for a moment, then caught himself and rubbed his hands over his face – outward and upward from his mouth. The ten-second face-lift. 'You know I already have a European connection. You know I only work with Toine.'

'Yes, I know. The last honest horse dealer.'

'The only one in the history of the world, as far as I know.'

'So let Van Zandt think he's wooing you away from Toine. He'll have an orgasm. If he comes around, pretend you're interested. You owe me.'

'I don't owe you that much.'

'Really?' I said. 'Thanks to you, I now have a client and a career I didn't want.'

'You'll thank me later.'

'I'll exact my revenge later.' I leaned over and patted his stubbled cheek again. 'Happy horse dealing.'

He groaned.

'And, by the way,' I said, pausing at the door. 'He thinks I'm a Palm Beach dilettante and that I'm leasing D'Artagnon from you.'

'I'm supposed to keep this all straight?'

I shrugged. 'What else have you got to do with your time?'

I was almost out the bedroom door when he spoke again.

'El . . .'

I turned back toward him, one hand on the door frame. He looked at me, uncharacteristically serious, a certain softness in his expression. He wanted to say something kind. I wanted him to pretend this day was like any other. We each seemed fully aware of the other's thoughts. I held my breath. One side of his mouth lifted in a smile of concession.

'Nice outfit,' he said.

I waved at him and left the house.

Molly Seabright lived in a two-story stucco house on the edge of a development called Binks Forest. Upscale. Backyard on a fairway. A white Lexus in the drive. There were lights on in the house. The hardworking upper middle class preparing to face another day. I parked down the street and waited.

At seven-thirty kids in the neighborhood began drifting out of their homes and wandering past me toward the school bus stop at the end of the block. Molly emerged from the Seabright house pulling a wheeled book bag behind her, looking like a miniature corporate exec on her way to catch a plane. I got out of my car and leaned back against it with my arms crossed. She spotted me from twenty feet away.

'I've reconsidered,' I said as she stopped in front of me. 'I'll help you find your sister.'

She didn't smile. She didn't jump for joy. She stared up at me and said, 'Why?'

'Because I don't like the people your sister was mixed up with.'

'Do you think something bad has happened to her?'

'We know something has happened to her,' I said. 'She was here and now she isn't. Whether or not it's something bad remains to be seen.'

Molly nodded at that, apparently pleased I hadn't tried to falsely reassure her. Most adults speak to children as if they're stupid simply because they haven't lived as many years. Molly Seabright wasn't stupid. She was smart and she was brave. I wasn't going to talk down to her. I had even decided not to lie to her if I could help myself.

'But if you're not a private investigator, what good are you?' she asked.

I shrugged. 'How hard can it be? Ask a few questions, make a few phone calls. It's not brain surgery.'

She considered my answer. Or maybe she was considering whether or not to say what she said next. 'You were a sheriff's detective once.'

I might have been that stunned if she had reached up and hit me in the head with a hammer. I who wouldn't talk down to a child. It hadn't occurred to me Molly Seabright would run home and do her own detective work on-line. I felt suddenly naked, exposed in that way I had earlier convinced myself was unlikely to happen. Blindsided by a twelve-year-old.

I glanced away. 'Is that your bus?'

A school bus had pulled up to the curb and the children gathered there were clambering aboard.

'I walk,' she said primly. 'I found a story about you in the computer archives of the *Post*.'

'Only one? I'm offended.'

'More than one.'

'Okay, so my dirty secret is exposed. I was a detective for Palm Beach County. Now I'm not.'

She understood to leave it at that. Wiser than most people I've known three times her age.

'We need to discuss your fee,' she said. Ms Business.

'I'll take the hundred you offered and we'll see what happens.'

'I appreciate that you're not trying to patronize me.'

'I just said I'd take a hundred dollars from a kid. Sounds pretty low to me.'

'No,' she said, those too-serious eyes staring at me through the magnifying lenses of the Harry Potter glasses. 'I don't think so.' She put her hand out. 'Thank you for accepting my case.'

'Jesus. You make me feel like we should sign a contract,' I said, shaking her hand.

'Technically, we should. But I trust you.'

'Why would you trust me?'

I had the feeling she had an answer, but that she thought it might be too much for me to comprehend and so thought better of sharing it with me. I began to wonder if she was really from this planet.

'Just because,' she said. A child's pat answer to people who aren't really paying attention. I let it go.

'I'll need some information from you. A photograph of Erin, her address, make and model of her car, that sort of thing.'

As I was asking, she bent down, unzipped a compartment of her book bag, and withdrew a manila envelope, which she handed to me. 'You'll find everything in there.'

'Of course.' I shouldn't have been surprised. 'And when you went to the sheriff's department, who did you speak with?'

'Detective Landry. Do you know him?'

'I know who he is.'

'He was very rude and condescending.'

'So was I.'

'You weren't condescending.'

A black Jag backed out of the Seabright garage, a suit at the wheel. Bruce Seabright, I assumed. He turned away from us and drove down the street.

'Is your mother home?' I asked. 'I'll need to speak with her.'

The prospect didn't thrill her. She looked a little nauseated. 'She goes to work at nine. She's a real estate agent.'

'I'll have to speak with her, Molly. And with your stepfather, too. I'll leave you out of it. I'll tell them I'm an insurance investigator.'

She nodded, still looking grim.

'You should leave for school now. I don't want to be arrested for contributing to the delinquency of a minor.'

'No,' she said, heading back toward the house, head up, her little book case rattling along on the sidewalk behind her. We should all have so much character.

Krystal Seabright was on a cordless phone when Molly and I walked into the house. She was leaning over a hall table, peering into an ornate rococo mirror, trying to stick down a false eyelash with a long pink fingernail while she chattered to someone about an absolutely fabulous town house in Sag Harbor Court. No one would have picked her out of a lineup as Molly's mother. Having met Molly first, I might have pictured her mother as a buttoned-up attorney or a doctor or a nuclear physicist. I might have, except that I knew firsthand children and parents didn't always match.

Krystal was a bottle blonde who'd used one too many bottles in her thirty-some years. Her hair was nearly white and looked as fragile as cotton candy. She wore just a little too much makeup. Her pink suit was a little too tight and a little too bright, her sandals a little too tall in the spike heel. She glanced at us out of the corner of her eye.

'. . . I can fax you all the details as soon as I get to my office, Joan. But you really need to see it to appreciate it. Places like this just aren't available now during the season. You're so lucky this just came up.'

She turned away from the mirror and looked at me, then at Molly with a *what now?* expression, but continued her conversation with the invisible Joan, setting up an appointment at eleven, scribbling it into a messy daybook. Finally she set the phone aside.

'Molly? What's going on?' she asked, looking at me, not her daughter.

'This is Ms Estes,' Molly said. 'She's an investigator.'

Krystal looked at me like I might have beamed down from Mars. 'A what?'

'She wants to talk to you about Erin.'

Fury swept up Krystal's face like a flash fire burning into the roots of her hair. 'Oh, for God's sake, Molly! I can't believe you did this! What is the matter with you?'

The hurt in Molly's eyes was sharp enough that I felt it myself.

'I told you something bad's happened,' Molly insisted.

'I can't believe you do these things!' Krystal ranted, her frustration with her younger daughter clearly nothing new. 'Thank God Bruce isn't here.'

'Mrs Seabright,' I said, 'I'm looking into a case at the equestrian center which might involve your daughter Erin. I'd like to speak with you in private, if possible.'

She looked at me, wild-eyed, still angry. 'There's nothing to discuss. We don't know anything about what goes on over there.'

'But Mom –' Molly started, desperately wanting her mother to care.

Her mother turned a withering, bitter look on her. 'If you've told this woman some ridiculous story, you're going to be in such hot water, young lady. I can't believe the trouble you're making. You don't have any consideration for anyone but yourself.'

Two red dots colored Molly's otherwise paste-pale cheeks. I thought she might start to cry. 'I'm worried about Erin,' she said in a small voice.

'Erin is the last person anyone needs to worry about,' Krystal said. 'Go to school. Go. Get out of this house. I'm so angry with you right now . . . If you're late for school you can just sit in detention this afternoon. Don't bother calling me.'

I wanted to grab a handful of Krystal Seabright's overprocessed hair and shake her until the hair broke off in my fist.

Molly turned and went outside, leaving the front door wide open. The sight of her wheeling away her little book bag made my heart ache.

'You can leave right behind her,' Krystal Seabright said to me. 'Or I can call the police.'

I turned back to face her and said nothing for a moment while I tried to wrestle my temper into submission. I was reminded of the fact that I had been a terrible patrol officer when I'd first gone on the job because I lacked the requisite diplomatic skills for domestic situations. I have always been of the opinion that some people really do just need to be bitch-slapped. Molly's mother was one of those people.

Krystal was trembling like a Chihuahua, having some control issues of her own.

'Mrs Seabright, for what it's worth, Molly has nothing to do with this,' I lied.

'Oh? She hasn't tried to tell you her sister has vanished and that we should be calling the police and the FBI and *America's Most Wanted*?'

'I know that Erin hasn't been seen since Sunday afternoon. Doesn't that concern you?'

'Are you implying I don't care about my children?' Again with the bug-eyes and the practiced affront – always a sign of low self-esteem.

'I'm not implying anything.'

'Erin is an adult. At least in her own mind. She wanted to live on her own, take care of herself.'

'So you're not aware that she was working for a man who's been involved in schemes to defraud insurance agencies?'

She looked confused. 'She works for a horse trainer. That's what Molly said.'

'You haven't spoken with Erin?'

'When she left she made it very clear she wanted nothing more to do with me. Living a decent life in a lovely home was just all too boring for her. After everything I've done for her and her sister . . .'

She went to the hall table, glanced at herself in the mirror, and dug her hand into a big pink and orange Kate Spade purse. She came out of the bag with a cigarette and a slim lighter, and moved toward the open front door.

'I've worked so hard, made so many sacrifices . . .' she said, more or less to herself, as if it comforted her to portray herself as the heroine of the story. She lit the cigarette and blew the smoke outside. 'She's done nothing but give me grief since the night she was conceived.'

'Does Erin's father live in the vicinity? Might she have gone to spend time with him?'

Krystal burst out laughing, but not with humor. She didn't look at me. 'No. She wouldn't have done that.'

'Where is her father?'

'I wouldn't know. I haven't heard from him in fifteen years.'

'Do you know who Erin's friends are?'

'What do you want with her?' she asked. 'What's she done now?'

'Nothing I'm aware of. She may have some information. I'd just like to ask her some questions about the man she's been working for. Has Erin been in trouble in the past?'

She leaned way out the door, took another hard drag on the cigarette, and exhaled the smoke at a hibiscus shrub. 'I don't see that my family is any business of yours.'

'Has she ever been involved with drugs?'

She snapped a look at me. 'Is that what this is about? Is she mixed up with drug people? God. That's all I need.'

'I'm concerned about where she's gone,' I said. 'Erin's disappearance happened to coincide with the death of a very expensive horse.'

'You think she killed a horse?'

I thought my head might split in two. Krystal's concern seemed to be about everyone except her daughter. 'I just want to ask her some questions about her boss. Do you have any idea where she might have gone?'

She stepped outside, tapped her ash into a plant pot, and hopped back into the house. 'Responsibility isn't Erin's thing. She thinks being an adult means doing whatever you damn well please. She's probably run off to South Beach with some boy.'

'Does she have a boyfriend?'

She scowled and looked down at the tiled floor. Down and to the right: a lie. 'How would I know? She doesn't check in with me.'

'Molly said she hasn't been able to reach Erin on her cell phone.'

'Molly.' She puffed on the cigarette and tried to wave the smoke out toward the street. 'Molly is twelve. Molly thinks Erin is cool. Molly reads too many mystery novels and watches too much A&E. What kind of child watches A&E? *Law and Order, Investigative Reports*. When I was twelve I was watching *Brady Bunch* reruns.'

'I think Molly has reason to be concerned, Mrs Seabright. I think you might want to speak with the Sheriff's Office about filing a missing person's report.'

Krystal Seabright looked horrified. Not at the prospect that her daughter might have been the victim of foul play, but at the idea of someone from Binks Forest having to file a police report. What would the neighbors say? They might put two and two together and figure out her last house was a double-wide.

'Erin is not missing,' she insisted. 'She's just . . . gone somewhere, that's all.'

A teenage boy emerged through a door into the upstairs hall and came thudding down the stairs. He looked maybe seventeen or eighteen and hungover. Gray-faced and glum, with platinum-tipped dark hair that stood up in dirty tufts. His T-shirt looked slept in and worse. He didn't resemble Krystal or her daughters. I made the assumption he belonged to Bruce Seabright, and wondered why Molly had made no mention of him to me.

Krystal swore under her breath and surreptitiously tossed her cigarette out the door. The boy's eyes followed it, then went back to her. Busted.

'Chad? What are you doing home?' she asked. A whole new tone of voice. Nervous. Obsequious. 'Aren't you feeling well, honey? I thought you'd gone to school.'

'I'm sick,' he said.

'Oh. Oh. Uh . . . Would you like me to make you some toast?' she asked brightly. 'I have to get to the office, but I could make you some toast.'

'No, thank you.'

'You were out awfully late last night,' Krystal said sweetly. 'You probably just need your sleep.'

'Probably.' Chad glanced at me, and slouched away.

Krystal scowled at me and spoke in a low voice. 'Look: we don't need you. Just go away. Erin will turn up when Erin needs something.'

'What about Erin?' Chad asked. He had come back into the hall, a two-liter bottle of Coke in one hand. Breakfast of champions.

Krystal Seabright closed her eyes and huffed. 'Nothing. Just – nothing. Go back to bed, honey.'

'I need to ask her some questions about the guy she works for,' I said to the boy. 'Do you happen to know where I can find her?'

He shrugged and scratched his chest. 'Sorry, I haven't seen her.'

As he said it, the black Jag rolled back into the driveway. Krystal looked stricken. Chad disappeared down a hall. The man I assumed to be Bruce Seabright got out of the car and strode toward the open front door, a man on a mission. He was stocky with thinning hair slicked straight back and a humorless expression.

'Honey, did you forget something?' Krystal asked in the same tone she'd used with Chad. The overeager servant.

'The Fairfields file. I've got a major deal going down on a piece of that property this morning and I don't have the file. I know I set it on the dining room table. You must have moved it.'

'No, I don't think so. I –'

'How many times do I have to tell you, Krystal? Do not touch my business files.' There was a condescension in his tone that couldn't have been categorized as abusive, but was, in a subtle, insidious way.

'I'm – I'm sorry, honey,' she stammered. 'Let me go find it for you.'

Bruce Seabright looked at me with a hint of wariness, like he suspected I might have a permit to solicit charitable donations. 'I'm sorry if I interrupted,' he said politely. 'I have a very important meeting to get to.'

'I gathered. Elena Estes,' I said, holding my hand out.

'Elena is considering a condo in Sag Harbor,' Krystal hurried to say. There was a hint of desperation in her eyes when she looked at me in search of a coconspirator.

'Why would you show her something there, darling?' he asked. 'Property values in that neighborhood will only decline. You should show her something at Palm Groves. Send her to the office. Have Kathy show her a model.'

'Yes, of course,' Krystal murmured, swallowing down the criticism and the slight, allowing him to take away her sale. 'I'll go find that file for you.'

'I'll do it, honey. I don't want anything dropping out of it.'

Something on the stoop caught Seabright's eye. He bent down and picked up the cigarette butt Krystal had thrown out. He held it pinched between his thumb and forefinger and looked at me.

'I'm sorry, but smoking is not allowed on my property.'

'Sorry,' I said, taking the thing away from him. 'It's a filthy habit.'

'Yes, it is.'

He went into the house to find his errant file. Krystal rubbed at her forehead and stared down at her slightly too flashy sandals, blinking like she might have been fighting tears.

'Just go, please,' she whispered.

I stuck the butt in the plant pot and went. What else could I say to a woman who was so under the thumb of her domineering husband, she would sooner abandon her own child than displease him?

Over and over in my life I've found that people are amazing, and seldom in a good way.

5

We never know the quality of someone else's life, though we seldom resist the temptation to assume and pass judgment. Plenty of women would have looked at Krystal Seabright's situation through the filter of distance and assumed she had it made. Big house, fancy car, career in real estate, land developer husband. Looked good on paper. There was even a Cinderella element to the story: single mother of two swept out of her lowly station in life, et cetera, et cetera.

So too with the apparently well-heeled folks who owned the four thousand expensive horses at the equestrian center. Champagne and caviar every day for a snack. A maid in every mansion, a Rolls in every five-car garage.

The truth was more checkered and less glamorous. There were personal stories full of nasty little plot twists: insecurities and infidelities. There were people who came to the Florida season on a dream and a shoestring, saving every dime all year so they could share a no-frills condo with two other riders, take a few precious lessons from a big-name trainer, and show their mediocre mount to anonymity in the amateur arena just for the love of the sport. There were second-tier professionals with second mortgages on farms in East Buttcrack, hanging on the fringes of the big stables, hoping to pick up a real client or two. There were dealers like Van Zandt: hyenas prowling the water hole, in search of vulnerable prey. The lush life has many shades of gray beneath the gold leaf. It was now officially my job to dig up some of those darker veins.

I thought it would be best to put in as much time as possible near the Jade stable before someone attached to Don Jade went into the bathroom with a copy of *Sidelines* and came out with a revelation. I'd spent enough time working undercover as a narc to know the chances of that were small, but there nonetheless. People see what they're programmed to see, they seldom look for anything else. Still, a cop's life undercover is never without the fear of being made. It can happen any second, and the deeper under, the worse the timing.

My strategy working undercover had always been to get as much information as possible, as fast as possible; to sketch my illusion boldly and

698

quickly. Dazzle the mark, draw them in close, then hit with the sucker punch and get out. My superiors in the Sheriff's Office had frowned on my methods because I'd borrowed my style from con artists rather than cops. But they had seldom frowned on the outcome.

Sean's parking pass still hanging from my rearview mirror, I rolled past the guard at the gatehouse and into the maelstrom of the Wellington show grounds day shift. There were horses everywhere, people everywhere, cars everywhere, golf carts everywhere. A show was under way and would run through Sunday. Horses and ponies would be jumping over fences in half a dozen competition rings. The chaos would work in my favor, like running a game of three-card monte on a corner in Times Square. Difficult to keep your eye on the queen when you're in the middle of a circus.

I parked in the second lot, cut past the permanent barns and the vet clinic, bypassed the concession stands, and found myself on the show grounds' version of Fifth Avenue: a row of mobile tack shops and pricey boutiques in tricked-out fifth-wheel trailers. Custom jewelers, custom tailors, antiques dealers, monogramming shops, cappuccino stands. I hit a couple of the boutiques to pick up trappings for my role as dilettante. Image is everything.

I purchased and put on a wide-brimmed straw hat trimmed with black grosgrain ribbon. Men never take seriously a woman in a hat. I chose a couple of silk blouses and long wraparound skirts made from vintage saris. I made sure the clerks went overboard with the tissue paper, making the shopping bags look full to bursting. I bought some impractical sandals and trendy bracelets, and put them on. When I thought I looked frivolous enough, I went in search of Don Jade.

There was no sign of him or of Paris Montgomery at his stalls. An underfed Guatemalan man was mucking out a stall, head down, trying not to attract attention lest the next stranger be an INS agent. The front of another stall had been removed to create a grooming bay. In it an overfed girl in a too-revealing tank top was grudgingly brushing a dappled gray horse. The girl had the mean, narrow eyes of someone who blames everyone but herself for the shortfalls in her life. I caught her looking at me sideways, her expression sour.

I tipped my head back and regarded her from under the brim of the ridiculous hat. 'I'm looking for Paris. Is she around?'

'She's riding Park Lane in the schooling ring.'

'Is Don with her?' Don, my old pal.

'Yeah.' And did I want to make something of it?

'And you are . . . ?'

She looked surprised I would bother to ask, then suspicious, then determined she would take advantage of the opportunity. 'Jill Morone. I'm Mr Jade's head groom.'

She was Mr Jade's only groom by the look of it, and by the anemic way she was wielding that brush, she defined the position loosely.

'Really? Then you must know Erin Seabright.'

The girl's reactions were so slow, her brain might have been in another time zone. I could see her every thought move sluggishly through her mind as she tried to decide on an answer. She dragged the brush along the horse's shoulder. The horse pinned its ears and rolled an eye at her.

'She doesn't work here anymore.'

'I know. Paris told me. Do you know where she went? A friend of mine wanted to hire her.'

Jill shrugged, eyes sliding away. 'I dunno. Paris said she went to Ocala.'

'You guys weren't friends, I guess. I mean, you don't seem to know very much.'

'I know she wasn't a very good groom.' The pot calling the kettle.

'And I can assume you are?' I said. 'Are you interested in moving?'

She looked pleased with herself, like she had a naughty little secret. 'Oh, no. Mr Jade treats me *very* well.'

Mr Jade probably barely knew her name – unless she was his latest alibi, which I doubted. Men like Don Jade went for girls who were pretty and useful. Jill Morone was neither.

'Good for you,' I said. 'I hope you still have a job to keep after that business with Stellar.'

'That wasn't my fault.'

'A horse dies like that. Suspicious circumstances. Owners get nervous, start making phone calls to other trainers . . . Business can go downhill fast.'

'It was an accident.'

I shrugged. 'Did you see it happen?'

'No. I found him, though,' she admitted with a strange spark of pride in her beady little eyes. The chance celebrity. She could be on the fringe of a dark spotlight for a week and a half. 'He was just laying there with his legs straight out,' she said. 'And his eyes were open. I thought he was just being lazy, so I slapped him on the butt to make him get up. Turned out he was dead.'

'God. Awful.' I looked down the row of Jade's stalls – a dozen or more – each of them hung with a box fan outside the bars of the stall fronts. 'I'm surprised you still have the fans up, considering.'

She shrugged again and swiped the brush over the gray a couple more strokes. 'It's hot. What else should we do?'

The horse waited for her to drift back a step, then whipped her with his tail. She hit him in the ribs with the brush.

'I wouldn't want to be the person who was careless enough to let that electrical cord hang into Stellar's stall,' I said. 'That groom would never work in this business again. I'd see to that if I had anything to do with it.'

The little eyes went mean again in the doughy face. 'I didn't take care of him. Erin did. See what kind of groom she was? If I was Mr Jade, I would have killed her.'

Maybe he had, I thought as I walked away from the tent.

I spotted Paris Montgomery some distance away in a schooling ring, golden ponytail bobbing, sunglasses shading her eyes as she guided her mount over a set of jumps. Poetry in motion. Don Jade stood on the sidelines, filming her with a camcorder, as a tall, skinny, red-haired, red-faced man spoke at him, gesturing angrily. He looked like a giant, irate Howdy Doody. I approached the ring a short way down the fence from the two men, my attention seemingly directed at the horses going around.

'If there's so much as a hint of something rotten in those test results, Jade, you'll face charges,' the red-faced man said loudly, either not caring or else craving the attention of everyone in the vicinity. 'This won't just be about whether or not General Fidelity pays out. You've gotten away with this crap for too long as it is. It's time someone put a stop to it.'

Jade said absolutely nothing, nothing in anger, nothing in his own defense. He didn't even pause in his filmmaking. He was a compact man with the rope-muscled forearms of a professional rider. His profile looked like something that should have been embossed on a Roman coin. He might have been thirty-five or he might have been fifty, and people would probably still be saying that about him when he was seventy.

He watched his assistant go over a combination of fences with Park Lane, and frowned as the horse rapped his front ankles and took a rail down. As Paris cantered past, he looked up at her and called out a couple of corrections for her to make to get the horse to bring its hindquarters more fully under itself in preparation for takeoff.

The other man seemed incredulous that his threats had not elicited a response. 'You're a real piece of work, Don. Aren't you even going to bother to deny it?'

Jade still didn't look at him. 'Why should I bother, Michael? I don't want to be blamed for your heart attack on top of everything else.'

'You smug bastard. You still think you can get people to kiss your ass and convince them it smells like a rose.'

'Maybe it does, Michael,' Jade said calmly, still watching his horse. 'You'll never know the truth because you don't want to. You don't want me to be innocent. You enjoy hating me too much.'

'I'm hardly the only one.'

'I know. I'm a national pastime again. That doesn't change the fact that I'm innocent.'

He rubbed the back of his sunburned neck, checked his watch, and sighed. 'That's enough for her, Paris,' he called, clicking the camera off.

'I'll be on the phone with Dr Ames today,' the other man said. 'If I find out you've got connections at that lab —'

'If Ames tells you anything about Stellar, I'll have his license,' Jade said calmly. 'Not that there's anything to tell.'

'Oh, I'm sure there's a story. There always is with you. Who were you in bed with this time?'

'If I have an answer to that, it's none of your business, Michael.'

'I'm making it my business.'

'You're obsessed,' Jade said, turning toward the stables as Paris approached on Park Lane. 'If you put as much energy into your work as you do into hating me, maybe you could actually make something of yourself. Now, if you'll excuse me, Michael, I have a business to run.'

Michael's face was a twisted, freckled mask of bitter emotion. 'Not for long if I can help it.'

Jade walked off toward the barn, seemingly unaffected by the exchange. His adversary stood for a moment, breathing hard, looking disappointed. Then he turned and stalked off.

'Well, that was ugly,' I said. Tomas Van Zandt stood less than ten feet from me. He'd watched the exchange between Jade and the other man surreptitiously, same as I had, pretending to watch the horses in the ring. He glanced at me in a dismissive way and started to walk off.

'I thought men from Belgium were supposed to be charming.'

He pulled up short and looked at me again, recognition dawning slowly. 'Elle! Look at you!'

'I clean up good, as they say down at the trailer park.'

'You've never been to a trailer park,' he scoffed, taking in the hat, the outfit.

'Of course I have. I once drove a maid home,' I said, then nodded after the man Jade had argued with. 'Who was that?'

'Michael Berne. A big crybaby.'

'Is he an owner or something?'

'A rival.'

'Ah ... These jumper people are so dramatic,' I said. 'Nothing this exciting goes on in my neck of the equestrian woods.'

'Maybe I should then sell you a jumper,' Van Zandt suggested, eyeing my shopping bags, pondering my credit card limit.

'I don't know if I'm ready for that. Looks like a tough crowd. Besides, I don't know any of the trainers.'

He took my arm. The courtly gentleman. 'Come. I'll introduce you to Jade.'

'Swell,' I said, looking up at him out the corner of my eye. 'I can buy a horse and collect the insurance. One-stop shopping.'

Like flipping a switch, Van Zandt's face went from courtly to stormy; the gray eyes as cold as the North Sea, and frighteningly hard. 'Don't say such stupid things,' he snapped.

I stepped away from him. 'It was a joke.'

'Everything with you is a joke,' he said in disgust.

'And if you can't take one, Van Zandt,' I said, 'fuck you.'

I watched him struggle to put Mr Hyde back in his box. The mood swing had come so quickly, I couldn't believe it hadn't given him whiplash.

He rubbed a hand across his mouth and made an impatient gesture.

'Fine. It's a joke. Ha ha,' he said, still clearly angry. He started toward the tent. 'Forget it. Come.'

I didn't move. 'No. Apologize.'

'What?' He looked at me with disbelief. 'Don't be silly.'

'Keep digging that hole, Van Zandt. I'm stupid *and* silly, and what else?'

The muscles in his face quivered. He wanted to call me a bitch or worse. I could see it in his eyes.

'Apologize.'

'You shouldn't have made the joke,' he said. 'Come.'

'And you should apologize,' I countered, fascinated. He seemed incapable of performing the act, and amazed that I was insisting.

'You are being stubborn.'

I laughed out loud. '*I'm* being stubborn?'

'Yes. Come.'

'Don't order me like I'm a horse to be moved from one place to another,' I said. 'You can apologize or you can kiss my ass.'

I waited, expecting an explosion, not sure what would happen after it came. Van Zandt looked at me, then looked away, and when he turned back toward me he was smiling as if nothing had happened.

'You're a tigress, Elle! I like that. You have character.' He nodded to himself, suddenly enormously pleased. 'That's good.'

'I'm so glad you approve.'

He chuckled to himself and took my arm again. 'Come along. I'll introduce you to Jade. He'll like you.'

'Will I like him?'

He didn't answer. He didn't care what I liked or didn't like. He was fascinated that I had challenged him. I was sure he didn't get much of that. Most of his American clients would have been wealthy women whose husbands and boyfriends had no interest in horses. Women who gave him undue credit simply because he was European and paid attention to them. Insecure women who could be easily charmed and manipulated, impressed by a little knowledge, a little Continental elegance, and a big ego with an accent.

I had witnessed the phenomenon firsthand many times over the years. Women starved for attention and approval will do a lot of foolish things, including parting with large sums of money. That was the clientele that made unscrupulous dealers a hell of a lot of money. That was the clientele that made dealers like Van Zandt snicker and sneer 'stupid Americans' behind the client's back.

Park Lane came out of the tent with Jill the groom in tow just as we were about to step into the aisle. Van Zandt snapped at the girl to watch where she was going, muttering 'stupid cow' only half under his breath as the horse dragged her away.

'D.J., why can you not find any girls with brains in their heads?' he asked loudly.

Jade stood at the open door to a tack stall that was draped in green and hung with ribbons won in recent shows. He calmly took a drink of Diet Coke. 'Is that some kind of riddle?'

Van Zandt took a beat to get it, then laughed. 'Yes – a trick question.'

'Excuse me,' I said politely, 'but do I look like I'm standing here with a penis?'

'No,' Paris Montgomery said, coming out of the tack stall. 'A couple of dicks.'

Van Zandt made a growling sound in his throat, but pretended good nature. 'Paris, you're the quick one with the tongue!'

She flashed the big grin. 'That's what all the fellas say.'

High humor. Jade paid no attention to any of it. He was looking at me. I stared back and stuck out my hand. 'Elle Stevens.'

'Don Jade. You're a friend of this character?' he asked, nodding at Van Zandt.

'Don't hold it against me. It was a chance meeting.'

The corner of Jade's mouth flicked upward. 'Well, if there's a chance, Tomas will be right there to take it.'

Van Zandt pouted. 'I don't wait for opportunity to come and knock on the door. I go and invite it politely.

'And this one came to steal your groom,' he added, pointing at me.

Jade looked confused.

'The cute one. The blonde,' Van Zandt said.

'Erin,' Paris said.

'The one that left,' Jade said, still looking at me.

'Yes,' I said. 'Apparently someone beat me to her.'

He gave no kind of reaction at all. He didn't look away or try to express his sadness that the girl had left. Nothing.

'Yeah,' Paris joked. 'Elle and I are going to start a support group for people without grooms.'

'What brought you looking for Erin in particular?' Jade asked. 'She didn't have very much experience.'

'She did a good job, Don,' Paris said, defending the missing girl. 'I'd take her back in a heartbeat.'

'A friend of a friend heard your girl might be looking to make a change,' I said to Jade. 'Now that the season has started, we can't be too fussy, right?'

'True enough. You have horses here, Elle?'

'No, though Z. here is trying to remedy that.'

'V.,' Van Zandt corrected me.

'I like Z. better,' I said. 'I'm going to call you Z.'

He laughed. 'Watch this one, Jade. She's a tigress!'

Jade hadn't taken his eyes off me. He looked beneath the stupid hat and past the chic outfit. He wouldn't be easily fooled. I found I didn't want to look away from him either. Magnetism hummed from within him like electricity. I thought I could feel it touching my skin. I wondered if he had control of it; could turn it on and off, up and down. Probably. Don Jade hadn't survived at his game without skill.

I wondered if I was up to matching him.

Before I had to answer that question, a more imminent danger swaggered into the picture.

'God in heaven! What kind of sadist put my class at this uncivilized hour of the day?'

Stellar's owner: Monte Hughes III, known as Trey to friends and hangers-on. Palm Beach playboy. Dissolute, debauched drunk. My first big crush when I'd been young and rebellious, and had thought dissolute, debauched, drunken playboys were romantic and exciting.

Sunglasses hid undoubtedly bloodshot eyes. The Don Johnson *Miami Vice* haircut was silver and wind-tossed.

'What time is it, anyway?' he asked with a lopsided grin. 'What day is it?'

He was drunk or on something or both. He always had been. His blood had to have a permanent alcohol level after all the years of indulgence. Trey Hughes: the happy drunk, the life of every party.

I held myself very still as he came toward us. There was little chance he would recognize me. I'd been a young thing when last he'd seen me – twenty years before – and the term 'pickled brain' didn't mean preservation of any kind. I couldn't say he'd ever really known me, though he had flirted with me on several occasions. I remembered feeling very impressed with myself at the time, ignoring the fact that Trey Hughes flirted with every pretty young thing to cross his path.

'Paris, honey, why do they do this to me?' He leaned into her and kissed her cheek.

'It's a conspiracy, Trey.'

He laughed. His voice was rough and warm from too much whiskey and too many cigarettes. 'Yeah, I used to think I was paranoid, then it turned out everyone really was out to get me.'

He was dressed to ride in buff breeches, a shirt and tie. His coat bag was slung over his shoulder. He looked exactly the same to me as he had twenty years ago: attractive, fifty, and self-abused. Of course, he'd been thirty at the time. Too many hours in the sun had lined and bronzed his face, and he'd gone gray at an early age – a family trait. He had seemed dashing and sophisticated to me back when. Now he just seemed pathetic.

He leaned down and peered at me under the brim of my hat. 'I knew there had to be a person under there. I'm Trey Hughes.'

'Elle Stevens.'

'Do I know you?'

'No. I don't think so.'

'Thank God. I've always said I never forget a beautiful face. You had me thinking I might be getting Old Timer's.'

'Trey, your brain is too drenched in alcohol for it to contract anything,' Jade said dryly.

Hughes didn't so much as glance at him. 'I've been telling people for years: I drink for medicinal purposes,' he said. 'Maybe it's finally paying off.'

'Never mind me, darling,' he said to me. 'I never do.' His brows drew together. 'Are you sure ... ?'

'I'm a new face,' I said, almost amused at my own joke. 'Have you ever been to Cleveland?'

'God, no! Why would I go there?'

'I was sorry to hear about Stellar.'

'Oh, yeah, well ...' he rambled, making a dismissive gesture with his hand. 'Shit happens. Right, Donnie?' The question had a barb to it. He still didn't look at Jade.

Jade shrugged. 'Bad luck. That's the horse business.'

C'est la vie. C'est la mort.

Such is life. Such is death.

His grief was underwhelming.

'God bless General Fidelity,' Hughes said, raising an imaginary glass. 'Provided they cough up.'

Again, there was a bite to his words, but Jade seemed unaffected.

'Buy the Belgian horse,' Van Zandt said. 'You'll then say: Stellar who?'

Hughes laughed. 'It's not enough I've given you my Mercedes. Now you're spending my money before it even gets into my pocket, V.?'

'That seems wisest, knowing you, my friend.'

'All my dough's going into the new barn,' Hughes said. 'Casa de Money Pit.'

'What good is a fancy stable with no horses to put in it?' Van Zandt asked.

'Let someone like Mr Jade here come in with a truckload of clients to pay the mortgage and buy me a new speedboat,' Hughes answered. 'Like half of Wellington.'

True enough. A great many Wellingtonians paid a year's mortgage with the exorbitant rents they charged for the three or four months the winter people were in town.

'Trey, get on your horse,' Jade ordered. 'I want you sober enough to complete the course.'

'Hell, D.J., booze is the only thing that gets me around. I couldn't do it sober.' He looked around, searching. 'Erin, my peach,' he called. 'Be a doll and bring my noble steed along.'

'Erin doesn't work here anymore, Trey. Remember?' Paris said, taking his coat bag and handing him his hard hat.

'Oh, right. You got rid of her.'

'She left.'

'Huh.' He looked off into the middle distance, smiling to himself. 'Seems like I just saw her.' He glanced around to see that the coast was clear and said to Paris in a stage whisper: 'Honey, why couldn't you lose the little heifer instead?'

Paris rolled her eyes. 'Get on your horse, Trey.'

She called to the Guatemalan man in Spanish to bring the gray horse, and the entourage began to move out of the aisle. I turned to follow. Jade was still standing there, still watching me.

'It was nice meeting you, Elle. I hope we see you around – whether V. sells you a horse or not.'

'I'm sure you will. I'm intrigued now.'

'Like a moth to a flame?' he said.

'Something like that.'

He shook my hand, and I felt that current pass through me again.

I watched the pack of them make their way toward the schooling ring. Van Zandt walked alongside the gray, bending Hughes's ear about the jumper in Belgium. Hughes listed to one side on the horse's back. Paris glanced backward, looking for Jade to catch up.

I started the hike back to my car, wishing I had time to go home and take a shower, to wash off the taint. There was a slick oiliness to Jade's crowd that should have had a smell to it, the same way I've always believed snakes should have a smell to them. I didn't want to have anything to do with them, but the wheels were turning now. The old familiar buzz of anxious excitement in my head. Familiar, not altogether welcome.

I'd been on the sidelines a long time. I lived one day to the next, never knowing whether I would decide I'd lived one day too many. I didn't know if I had my head together enough to do this. And if I didn't, Erin Seabright's life could hang in the balance.

If Erin Seabright still had a life.

You got rid of her, Trey Hughes had said. An innocent enough statement on the face of it. A figure of speech. And from a man who didn't even know what day it was. Still, it struck a nerve.

I didn't know if I should trust my instincts, they'd been so long out of use. And look what happened the last time I trusted them, I thought. My instincts, my choice, and the consequences. All bad.

But it wouldn't be my action that did the damage this time. It would be inaction. The inaction of Erin Seabright's mother, of the Sheriff's Office.

Someone had to do something. These people Erin Seabright had known and worked for were far too dismissive when it came to the subject of her, and far too cavalier when it came to the subject of death.

6

The address Molly had given me as Erin's was a three-car garage some entrepreneurial sort had converted into rental property. Geographically, it was only a few miles from the Seabright home in Binks Forest. In every other respect it was in another world.

Rural Loxahatchee, where the side roads are dirt and the ditches never drain; where no one had ever met a building code they wouldn't ignore. A strange mix of run-down places, new middle-class homes, and small horse properties. A place where people nailed signs to tree trunks along the road advertising everything from 'Make $$$ in Your Own Home' to 'Puppies for Sale' to 'Dirt Cheap Stump Grinding'.

The property where Erin had lived was overgrown with tall pines and scrubby, stunted palm trees. The main house was a pseudo-Spanish ranch style, circa mid-seventies. The white stucco had gone gray with mildew. The yard consisted of dirty sand fill and anemic, sun-starved grass. An older maroon Honda sat off to one side on the driveway, filthy and dotted with hardened gobs of pine sap. It looked like it hadn't gone anywhere in a long while.

I went to the front door and rang the bell, hoping no one would be at home in the middle of the day. I would have been much happier letting myself into the garage-cum-guest house. I'd had enough human interaction to last me the day. I swatted a mosquito on my forearm and waited, then rang the bell a second time.

A voice like a rusty hinge called out: 'I'm around the back!'

Small brown geckos darted out of my path and into the overgrown landscaping as I walked around the side of the garage. Around the back of the house was the obligatory pool. The screened cage that had been erected to keep bugs out of the patio area was shredded in sections as if by a giant paw. The door was flung wide on broken hinges.

The woman who stood in the doorway was long past the age and shape anyone would care to see her in a two-piece swimming suit, but that was what she was wearing. Flab and sagging skin hung on her bent frame like a collection of half-deflated leather balloons.

'What can I do for you, honey?' she asked. A New York transplant in giant Jackie-O sunglasses. She must have been pushing seventy, and appeared to have spent sixty-eight of those years sunbathing. Her skin was as brown and mottled as the skin of the lizards that lived in her yard. She was smoking a cigarette and had two hugely fat ginger cats on leashes. I was momentarily stunned to silence by the sight of her.

'I'm looking for my niece,' I said at last. 'Erin Seabright. She lives here, right?'

She nodded, dropped her cigarette butt, and ground it out with the toe of her aqua neoprene scuba diver's boot. 'Erin. The pretty one. Haven't seen her for a couple of days, darling.'

'No? Neither has her family. We're getting kind of worried.'

The woman pursed her lips and waved my concern away. 'Bah! She's probably off with the boyfriend.'

'Boyfriend? We didn't know she had a boyfriend.'

'What a surprise,' she said sarcastically. 'A teenage girl who doesn't tell her family anything. I thought they were on the outs, though. I heard them fighting out in the yard one night.'

'When was that?'

'Last week. I don't know. Thursday or Friday maybe.' She shrugged. 'I'm retired. What do I know from days? One's the same as the next. I know I came out to walk my babies the next morning and someone had run a key down the side of Erin's car and ruined the paint. I have a gate to keep the riffraff out, if my lazy son would come and fix it. He could care if I'm raped and killed. He thinks he inherits.'

She chuckled and looked down at the ginger cats, sharing a joke telepathically. One of the cats lay on its back in the dirt with its hind legs stretched out. The other pounced at her foot, ears flat.

'Bah! Cecil! Don't bite Mommy's toe!' she scolded. 'I got an infection the last time. I thought I would die of it!'

She swatted at the cat and the cat swatted back, then scuttled to the end of its leash and growled. It had to weigh twenty-five pounds.

'Could I possibly take a look in her apartment?' I asked politely. 'Maybe I can get an idea where she's gone. Her mother's worried sick.'

She shrugged. 'Sure. Why not? You're a relative.'

The kind of landlady we all want. Fourth Amendment? What Fourth Amendment?

She tied the cat leashes to the handle of the broken screen door and dug in the fanny pack slung around her waist, coming out with a set of keys, a cigarette, and a hot pink Bic lighter. She fired up as we went around to the front of the garage, where two doors flanked windows that had been set into the plywood wall where the original garage doors had once been.

'When I did the guest house I had them put in two apartments,' the woman confided. 'One bath. You can get more rent that way. Semiprivate. Seven-fifty a month per.'

Seven hundred and fifty dollars a month to live in a garage and share a bathroom with a stranger.

'I'm Eva by the way,' she said, sliding her sunglasses on top of her head. 'Eva Rosen.'

'Ellen Stuart.'

'You don't look like family,' Eva said, squinting at me as we went into the apartment.

'By marriage.'

The apartment was a single room with dingy vinyl flooring and an assortment of hideous thrift store furniture. An efficiency kitchen setup was tucked into one corner: a small sink full of dirty dishes crawling with ants, two burners, a microwave, and a mini-fridge. The bed was at the back, unmade.

There was no other sign anyone lived there. There were no clothes, no shoes, no personal effects of any kind.

'It looks like she's moved out,' I said. 'You didn't see her packing stuff in her car?'

Eva turned around in the middle of the room, mouth agape, cigarette stuck to her lower lip and bobbing precariously. 'No! No one said anything to me about moving out. And left me dirty dishes, no less! You give people a nice place and this is how they treat you!'

'Have you seen anyone else coming in and out in the past few days?'

'No. Just that other one. The chubby one.'

'Jill Morone?'

'She's a mean one. Those beady little eyes. I'd never leave my babies with that one.'

'She lives in the other half?'

'Someone is going to have to answer to me,' Eva muttered. 'They rented for the season. They have to pay.'

'Who pays the rent?'

'The checks are from Jade Farms. That nice girl, Paris, always brings the check herself. She's so nice. I can't believe she would let this happen.'

Puffing angrily on the cigarette, she went to the sink and turned the water on. The pipes kicked and spat. When the water finally ran, it looked brown. 'People can't just move out in the middle of the night and think they don't have to pay. My no-good son is good for one thing: he's a bail bondsman. He knows people.'

I followed as Eva opened a door and went through the shared bath to Jill Morone's side of the garage. The floor was piled with wet towels, the walls of the shower stall orange and black with rust and mildew.

'This one's still here,' Eva muttered. 'The little pig. Look at this mess.'

The place looked like it had been tossed, but I suspected that was simply the girl's mode of housekeeping. Clothes and magazines were strewn everywhere. An ashtray heaped with butts sat on the coffee table. I spotted the issue of *Sidelines* with my photo in it lying on the floor, and surreptitiously toed it under the sofa.

'I wouldn't let dogs live like this,' Eva Rosen muttered, freely pawing through Jill Morone's things. 'Where does she get all this? Clothes from Bloomingdale's. The tags still on. I bet she steals. She's the type.'

I didn't argue. I browsed through the tangled mess of jewelry on the girl's dresser, wondering if any of it might have walked over from next door. An even trade for a stack of dirty dishes.

'Were you around here Sunday, Mrs Rosen?'

'It's *Miz*. I was here all day.'

'What about Sunday night?'

'Sunday nights I go with my friend Sid to A-1 Thai. I had the chicken curry. So spicy! I had a heartburn for days.'

'What time did you get home?'

'That would be none of your business.'

'Please, Ms Rosen, it could be very important. Erin is missing.'

She pretended to be stubborn for a moment, then tipped her head on one side and shrugged. 'Sid is a special friend, if you know what I mean. I didn't get home until Monday. Noon, maybe.'

Ample time for Erin to have packed up her own stuff, or for someone to have done it for her.

'She's run off with a boy, that's what,' Eva said, finishing off her smoke and adding it to the heap in the ashtray. 'No offense to your family, but she had that look with the tight shirts and the bare belly button.'

This from a seventy-year-old in a bikini.

'What can you tell me about her boyfriend?' I asked. 'Do you know what kind of car he drives?'

'Sixty-seven years I lived in Queens. I should know from cars?'

I tried to breathe slowly. Another of my shortcomings as a cop: lack of diplomacy with the general public. 'Color? Size? Anything I could give to the police?'

'Black, maybe. Or dark blue. I only saw it the one time, and it was night.'

'What about the boy? What does he look like?'

'What's with the third degree?' she asked, pretending indignation. 'I'm on *Law and Order* now? You're Miss District Attorney or something? Is Sam Waterston going to come out of the closet now?'

'I'm just concerned about my niece, Ms Rosen. I'm afraid something might have happened to her. She didn't tell anyone she was moving. Her family doesn't know anything about this boyfriend. How can we be sure she went with him willingly?'

Eva thought about that, her eyes brightening for a second at the possibility of intrigue, then she waved a hand, pretending indifference. 'I didn't get a good look. I heard arguing, I looked through the blinds, I saw the back of a head.'

'Could you tell if he was tall or short? Younger or older?'

She shrugged. 'He was average. His back was to me.'

'Have you ever met the man Erin worked for?' I asked.

'What man? I thought she worked for Paris.'

'Don Jade. Middle-aged, on the slight side, very good-looking.'

'Don't know him. I only know Paris. She's such a nice person. Always takes the time to ask after my babies. I have to think she doesn't know Erin ran off, or she would have spoken to me about it.'

'I'm sure that's true,' I said. 'Did you notice anything at all about the boyfriend, Ms Rosen? Anything.'

Eva Rosen shook her head. 'I'm sorry, darling. I would help if I could. I'm a mother too, you know. Do you have children of your own?' she asked, looking suspiciously at my haircut.

'No, I don't.'

'They drive you crazy with worry. And then there's the disappointment. It's a trial.'

'Did you ever hear Erin call the boyfriend by name?' I asked.

She searched her memory. 'Maybe. I might have heard her mention a name that night. Yes. It was something like it was from a soap opera. Brad? Tad?'

'Chad?'

'That's it.'

Chad Seabright.

Forbidden love. I wondered if that Shakespearean story line had contributed to Erin's defection from the Seabright home. I couldn't imagine Bruce Seabright would have approved of his son and his stepdaughter dating, regardless of the fact they weren't blood relatives. And if Bruce didn't like it, Krystal wouldn't like it.

I wondered why Molly hadn't told me about Erin and Chad, why she hadn't told me about Chad at all. Maybe she believed I would disapprove too. If that was the case, she overestimated me. I didn't care enough to have an opinion on her sister's morality. My only interest in Erin's love life was as motive in her disappearance.

I drove back to the Seabright home. Chad the Invalid was in the driveway, washing his black Toyota pickup. The all-American boy in khakis and a white T-shirt. He glanced up at me through a pair of mirrored Oakley shades as he rinsed the soap off his wheel rims.

'Nice ride,' I said as I walked up the driveway. 'Eva Rosen told me about it.'

'Who's Eva Rosen?'

'Erin's landlady. She doesn't miss a trick, old Eva.'

Chad stood up, the hose and the wheels forgotten. 'I'm sorry,' he said politely. 'I didn't get your name.'

'Elena Estes. I'm looking for your stepsister.'

'Like I told you this morning, Ms Estes: I haven't seen her.'

'That's funny, because Eva tells me you were in her yard just the other night. She seems to know some pretty interesting things about you,' I said. 'About you and Erin.'

He shrugged and shook his head, then added a boyish grin to complete the whole Matt Damon look. 'I'm sorry. I don't know what you're talking about.'

'Come on, Chad,' I cajoled. 'I've been around the block a few times. It doesn't matter to me if you and Erin are involved. A boy fucking his stepsister isn't going to make me turn a hair.'

He frowned at the accusation.

'That's why Erin left the house, isn't it?' I said. 'Your father wouldn't put up with the two of you doing it under his nose.'

'We're not involved,' he insisted.

'Eva tells me the two of you had a fight the other night in her driveway. What happened, Chad? Did Erin dump you? Let me guess: you weren't nearly so interesting as a boyfriend once her mommy and stepdaddy weren't watching anymore.'

He looked away from me, trying to decide how to play this. Respond with the truth, with outrage, stick with denial, stay calm? He had chosen the latter tack to start, but my bluntness was beginning to irritate him.

'I'm not sure who you are, ma'am,' he said, still trying to hang on to the false good humor, 'but you're crazy.'

I found a dry patch along the front fender of the pickup, leaned back against it, and crossed my arms. 'Who'd she dump you for, Chad? An older man? Her boss, maybe?'

'I don't know who Erin is seeing,' he said curtly. 'And I don't care.'

He dumped the wash water on the driveway and carried the bucket into the garage. I followed.

'Okay. Maybe I'm way off base. Maybe the fight was about something else altogether,' I offered. 'If that hangover you had this morning is anything to go by, you're a guy who likes to party. From what I've heard, Erin might like a wild time. And there she is at the equestrian center, a whole new world of drug dealers and users. Maybe that's what you fought about in Eva Rosen's driveway: drugs.'

Chad slammed the bucket onto a shelf where car care products were arranged like a display at Pep Boys. 'You're way out of line, lady.'

'She try to cut you out of a deal, Chad? Is that why you came back later and keyed her car?'

'What's with you?' he demanded. 'Why are you here? Do you have a warrant or something?'

I was standing too close to him. He wanted to back away. 'I don't need a warrant, Chad,' I said quietly, my eyes steady on his. 'I'm not that kind of a cop.'

He didn't know quite what that meant, but it made him nervous. He put his hands on his hips, shuffled his feet, crossed his arms over his chest, looked out at the street.

'Where's Erin?' I asked.

'I told you, I don't know. I haven't seen her.'

'Since when? Since Friday? The night you fought with her? The night you keyed her car?'

'I don't know anything about that. Talk to that fat cow she works with,' he said. 'Jill Moron. She's nuts. Ask her where Erin is. She probably killed her and ate her.'

'How do you know Jill Morone?' I asked. 'How would you know anything about the people Erin works with if you haven't been in touch with Erin?'

He went still and looked out the door.

Gotcha. It was nice to know I still had the touch.

'What did you fight about Friday night, Chad?' I asked again, then waited patiently while he struggled to decide on an answer.

'I dumped her,' he said, turning toward the shelves again. He selected a white cotton towel from a stack of white cotton towels, all neatly folded. 'I don't need the trouble.'

'Uh-huh. Bullshit. You don't dump a girl, then come back and key her car. There's no point if you're not the dumpee.'

'I didn't key her car!'

'I don't believe you.'

'Well, that's your problem, not mine.'

'I don't see you dumping her, Chad. Erin might have been off the hook with Krystal and Bruce because she moved out, but you could still pull your old man's chain by staying involved with her.'

'You don't know anything about my family.'

'Don't I?' I looked around the garage with its place for everything and everything in its place. 'Your old man is a tight-ass control freak. His way is the only way. His opinion is the only opinion. Everyone else in the house is there to serve his needs and validate his superiority. How am I doing so far?'

Chad went to his truck in a huff and started trying to towel off the water spots that had already dried on the finish.

'He'll ride you if you don't get those spots out, won't he, Chad?' I said, following him around the truck. 'Can't have spots on the cars. What would the neighbors think? And imagine if they found out about you and Erin. What a disgrace, doing it with your stepsister. It's practically incest. You really found Dad's hot button, didn't you?'

'Lady, you're pissing me off.'

I didn't tell him that was the idea. I followed him around the hood to the other side of the truck. 'Tell me what I want to know and I'll leave.'

'There's nothing to tell. I don't know where Erin is, and I don't give a shit.'

'I bet you'll give a shit when you've got a cop tailing you. Because maybe there's a drug angle to Erin's disappearance. I can tell you from experience, there are few things a narc likes better than getting his hooks into a kid with money and connections. And how about when your father gets questioned about your involvement? I guess you might enjoy that –'

He turned on me, hands up, as if I was holding him at gunpoint. 'All right! All right. Jesus, you're something, lady,' he said, shaking his head.

I waited.

'All right,' he said again, letting out a sigh. 'Erin and I used to be together. I thought it meant something, but it didn't mean anything to her. She dumped me. That's it. That's the whole story. There's nothing to do with drugs or deals or anything else. That's it. She dumped me.'

He shrugged and his arms fell back to his sides, limp, the admission taking all the starch out of him. The male ego is a fragile thing at seventeen or seventy.

'Did she give you a reason?' I asked quietly. 'I wouldn't ask,' I added as his tension level came back up. 'But something has happened where Erin was working, and now she's nowhere to be found.'

'Is she in trouble?'

'I don't know.'

He thought about that for a minute. 'She said there was someone else. "A man," she said. Like I'm twelve or something.' He shook his head in disgust.

'Did she say who?'

'I didn't ask. I mean, why should I care? I know she had a thing for her boss, but he's like fifty or something . . .'

'Did she tell you she was going anywhere? Did she say anything about changing jobs or moving?'

He shook his head.

'She never said anything about going to Ocala?'

'Ocala? Why would she go there?'

'Her boss says she quit her job and moved to Ocala to take another.'

'That's news to me,' he said. 'No. She wouldn't do that. It doesn't make any sense.'

'Thanks for the info.' I pulled a card from my pocket, my phone number scribbled on it. 'If you hear from her, would you call this number and leave a message?'

Chad took the card and stared at it.

I went back to my car and sat at the end of the Seabright driveway for a moment. I looked around the neighborhood. Quiet, lovely, expensive; golfers lining up a tee shot beyond the backyard. The American dream.

I thought about the Seabrights. Well-off, successful; neurotic, contentious, seething with secret resentments. The American dream in a fun house mirror.

I parked on the street in front of the school, the soccer moms and me. I would have felt less out of place in a chorus line. Kids began to pour out the doors and head for the buses or the car-pool line.

There was no sign of Krystal Seabright, not that I had expected to see her. It seemed quite clear to me that Molly was just a small person who happened to live in the same house as Krystal. Molly had turned out the way she had turned out by luck or self-preservation or watching A&E. She had probably watched all the drama and rebellion and parental conflict of Erin's life, and consciously turned in the other direction in order to win approval.

Funny, I thought, Molly Seabright was probably exactly who my little sister would have been, had I had a little sister. My parents had adopted me and called it quits. I was more than enough to handle. Too bad for them. The child learning from my mistakes might have been exactly the daughter they had wanted in the first place.

I got out of the car as I saw Molly come out of the school. She didn't spot me right away. She walked with her head down, pulling her little black case behind her. Though she was surrounded by other children, she seemed alone, deep in thought. I called out to her as she turned and started down the sidewalk. When she saw me, her face brightened with a carefully tempered expectation.

'Did you find her already?' she asked.

'No, not yet. I've spent the day asking a lot of questions. She may be in Ocala,' I said.

Molly shook her head. 'She wouldn't have moved without telling me, without calling me.'

'Erin tells you everything?' I asked, opening the car door for her. I glanced around to see if anyone had me pegged as a child molester. No one was paying any attention at all.

'Yes.'

I went around to the driver's side, got behind the wheel, and started the engine. 'Did she tell you she and Chad were involved with each other?'

Her gaze glanced off of mine and she seemed to shrink a little in the seat.

'Why didn't you tell me about Chad?'

'I don't know,' she mumbled. 'I would rather not acknowledge Chad's existence.'

Or that Erin had shifted from sister to sexual being, I thought as I drove back toward the cul-de-sac where Molly lived. Erin had been her idol and protector. If Erin abandoned her, then Molly was all alone in the land of dysfunctional Seabrights.

'Chad was at Erin's apartment Friday night,' I said. 'They had an argument. Do you know anything about that?'

Molly shrugged. 'Maybe they broke up.'

'Why would you think that? Was Erin interested in someone else?'

'She had a crush on her boss, but he's too old for her.'

That was a matter of opinion. From what I had learned about Erin so far,

I wouldn't have been at all surprised to find out she had her sights set on a man old enough to be her father. And if past history was anything to go by, Jade wouldn't draw that line for her.

'Anyone else?'

'I don't know,' Molly said irritably. 'Erin liked flirting with guys. I didn't pay attention. I didn't want to hear about it.'

'Molly, this is very important,' I said as I pulled to the curb at the end of her street. 'When I ask you questions about Erin, or about anything, anyone, you have to tell me the absolute truth as you know it. No glossing over details you don't like. Got it?'

She frowned, but nodded.

'You have to trust me,' I said, and a bolt of white-cold fear ran through me.

Molly looked at me in that steady, too-wise way and said, 'I already told you I do.'

This time I didn't ask her why.

7

I stand at the side of the Golam brothers' trailer. I've been told to stay put, to wait, but I know that's not the right decision. If I go in first, if I go in now, I've got the brothers dead-bang. They think they know me. I've worked this case three months. I know what I'm doing. I know I'm right. I know the Golam brothers are already twitching. I know I want this bust and deserve it. I know Lieutenant Sikes is here for the show, to put a feather in his cap. He wants to look good when the news vans arrive. He wants to make the public think they should vote for him in the next election for sheriff.

He's stuck me on the side of the trailer and told me to wait. He doesn't know his ass. He didn't listen to me when I told him the side door is the door the brothers use most. While Sikes and Ramirez are watching the front, the brothers are dumping their money into duffel bags and getting ready to bolt out the side. Billy Golam's four-by-four is parked ten feet away, covered in mud. If they run, they'll take the truck, not the Corvette parked in front. The truck can go off-road.

Sikes is wasting precious time. The Golam brothers have two girls in the trailer with them. This could easily turn into a hostage situation. But if I go in now . . . They think they know me.

I key the button on my radio. 'This is stupid. They're going to break for the truck. I'm going in.'

'Goddammit, Estes —'

I drop the radio into the weeds growing beside the trailer. It's my case. It's my bust. I know what I'm doing.

I draw my weapon and hold it behind my back. I go to the side door and knock the way all the Golam brothers' customers knock: two knocks, one knock, two knocks. 'Hey, Billy, it's Elle! I need some.'

Billy Golam jerks open the door, wild-eyed, high on his own home cooking — crystal meth. He's breathing hard. He's got a gun in his hand.

Shit.

The front door explodes inward.

One of the girls screams.

Buddy Golam shouts: 'Cops!'

Billy Golam swings the .357 up in my face. I suck in my last breath.

He turns abruptly and fires. The sound is deafening. The bullet hits Hector

*Ramirez in the face and blows out the back of his head, blood and brain matter
spraying Sikes behind him.*

The image faded slowly from my brain, and the building I had worked
out of slowly came into focus before me.

The Palm Beach County Criminal Justice Complex is tucked away on a
patch of landscaped acres off Gun Club Road near Lake Lytal Park. The
complex houses the Sheriff's Office, the medical examiner's offices, the
morgue, the county courts, and the jail. One-stop shopping for lawbreakers
and their victims.

I sat in the parking lot looking at the building that held the Sheriff's
Office, feeling sick in my stomach. I hadn't been through those doors in a
long time. There was a part of me that believed everyone in the building
would recognize me on sight and that all of them nursed a virulent hatred
of me. Logically, I knew that wasn't true. Probably only half of them would
know and hate me.

The clock was ticking toward change of shift. If I didn't catch James
Landry now, it would have to wait until the next day. I wanted Erin
Seabright's name in his mind, a mental thorn to rub at all night.

My legs felt weak as I walked toward the doors. Jail inmates in dark gray
uniforms were working on the landscaping, overseen by a black guard in
camo pants and a painted-on black T-shirt, a trooper's hat perched on his
head. He exchanged bullshit with a couple of cops standing on the sidewalk
smoking cigarettes. None of them looked at me.

I went inside to the desk. No one called out my name or rushed to assault
me. Maybe it was the haircut.

The receptionist behind the bulletproof glass was a round-faced young
woman with three-inch purple lacquered fingernails and a Medusa's head of
intertwined black braids.

'I need to speak with Detective Landry,' I said.

'What is this regarding, ma'am?'

'A missing persons case.'

'Your name?'

'Elena Estes.'

There was no flicker of recognition. No scream of outrage. I didn't know
her, she didn't know me. She called Landry on the phone and told me to
wait in the chairs. I stood with my arms crossed and stared at the door to
the stairwell, barely breathing. It seemed an hour before the heavy gray door
opened.

'Ms Estes?'

Landry held the door back by way of invitation.

He was a compact, athletic-looking man, mid-forties, with a meticulous
quality about him. There was still starch in his shirt at nearly four P.M. His
hair was cropped almost military-short; black, heavily salted with gray. He
had a stare like an eagle's: penetrating and slightly disdainful, I thought. Or
perhaps that was my paranoia showing.

I had known several of the seventeen detectives in Robbery/Homicide, the major case squad, but I hadn't known Landry. Because of the nature of their work, narcotics detectives usually keep – or are kept – to themselves, their paths crossing with the other detectives only over dead bodies.

We went up the stairs to the second floor without speaking. There was no one behind the glass in the small vestibule that led to the Robbery/Homicide squad room. Landry let us in with a card key.

Steel desks grouped together made islands across the expanse of the room. Most of the desks were empty. I recognized no one. The gazes that flicked my way were hooded, flat, and cold. Cop eyes. The look is always the same, regardless of agency, regardless of geography. The look of people who trust no one and suspect everyone of something. I couldn't tell what they were thinking. I knew only that some of the gazes lingered too long.

I took the seat Landry indicated beside his desk. He smoothed a hand over his tie as he settled into his chair, his eyes never leaving my face. He clicked his computer on and settled a pair of reading glasses on the bridge of his nose.

'I'm Detective Landry,' he said, typing. 'I'll be taking your statement. I understand you want to report someone missing.'

'She's already been reported missing. Erin Seabright. Her sister spoke with you a couple of days ago. Molly Seabright. She told me you were rude and condescending and of no help to her.'

Another chapter from *The Elena Estes Guide to Winning Friends and Influencing People.*

Landry pulled his glasses off and gave me the stare again. 'The kid? She's twelve.'

'Does that somehow change the fact that her sister is missing?'

'We don't take complaints from children. I spoke on the phone with the mother. She didn't want to file. She says the daughter isn't missing.'

'Maybe she killed the girl,' I said. 'You're not going to look for her because her murderer doesn't want to file a complaint?'

His brows pulled together. 'You have reason to think the mother killed her?'

'No. I don't think that at all. I'm saying you didn't know differently and you blew the girl off.'

'So you came here to pick a fight with me?' he said, incredulous. 'Are you mentally ill? What have you got to do with these people? Are they relatives of yours?'

'No. Molly is a friend.'

'The twelve-year-old.'

'She asked me to help her. I happen to believe she has good reason to think her sister is missing.'

'Why is that?'

'Because her sister is missing. She hasn't been seen since Sunday.'

I filled him in on the Don Jade saga and the death of Stellar. Landry was angry with me. Impatience hummed in the air around him. He didn't like that I'd done his job for him, even if he didn't believe he'd had a job to do. Cops can be territorial that way.

'You think something happened to this girl because of a dead horse.' He said it as if it were the most ludicrous theory he'd ever heard.

'People are killed for their shoes,' I said. 'People are killed for turning down the wrong street. This dead horse by himself is worth a quarter of a million dollars in insurance money, and the sale of his replacement to his owner is probably worth nearly that much in sales commissions alone. I don't find it hard to believe someone would resort to violence for that kind of money, do you?'

'And the trainer says the girl quit her job and moved to Ocala.'

'The trainer who probably had the horse killed and stands to profit handsomely by the next deal.'

'Do you know that she didn't move to Ocala?' Landry asked.

'No. But it seems unlikely.'

'Have you been to her apartment? Were there signs of a struggle?'

'I've been to her apartment. There's nothing there.'

'Nothing. As if she moved out?' he suggested.

'Maybe. But we won't know if someone doesn't look for her. You could put a call in to Ocala.'

'Or you could drive up there and look for her.'

'Or you could call the local PD or SO or whatever they have in Ocala.'

'And tell them what? That this girl might have moved up there and taken a job? She's eighteen. She can do whatever the hell she wants.'

'Give them a heads-up on her car.'

'Why? Has it been stolen?'

I stood up. I was angrier than he was and glad he couldn't see it on my face. 'Okay, Landry. You don't give a shit this girl has vanished, couldn't care less that she might be dead, and you have no interest in a six-figure fraud case. What am I paying taxes for?'

'Insurance fraud isn't insurance fraud until the insurance company says so. And the girl isn't missing if she's eighteen and willingly moved elsewhere – unless her family reports her missing.'

'Her family did report her missing. Her sister reported it. That fact aside, you're saying if she's estranged from her family and something happens to her, only she could report her own disappearance. That's absurd. You're going to let God-knows-what happen to this girl because her mother is a self-absorbed airhead who's just happy to be rid of her.

'I guess I can see that,' I said sarcastically. 'After all, it might take an hour or two out of your busy day investigating purse snatchings to make a couple of phone calls, do some background checks, ask a few questions –'

Landry stood now too. His face was growing red beneath his tan. Everyone in the office was watching us. In my peripheral vision I could see one of the sergeants had come out of his office to watch. In the background a phone rang unanswered.

'Are you trying to tell me how to do my job, Estes?'

'I've done your job, Landry. It's not that hard.'

'Yeah? Well, I don't see you working here now. Why is that?'

The phone stopped ringing. The silence in the room was the silence of outer space: absolute.

Half a dozen valid answers trailed through my head. I gave none of them. Only one answer counted – to the people in this room and to me. I didn't work here anymore because I'd gotten one of our own – one of *their* own – killed. Nothing trumped that.

Finally, I nodded. 'All right. You win,' I said quietly. 'Cheap Shot of the Day Award goes to Landry. I figured you'd be a big asshole, and I was right. But Erin Seabright is missing, and someone has to care about that. If it has to be me, so be it. If that girl ends up dead because I couldn't find her quickly enough and you could have, that one will be on your head, Landry.'

'Is there a problem here?' the sergeant asked, coming over. 'Oh, yeah,' he said, stopping in front of me. 'I'm looking at it. You've got a hell of a nerve coming into this building, Estes.'

'Sorry. I didn't realize crime fighting had become by invitation only. Mine must have gotten lost in the mail.'

The path to the door seemed to elongate as I walked away. My legs felt like columns of water. My hands were shaking. I went out of the squad room, down the hall, and into the ladies' room, where I slumped over a toilet and vomited.

A handful of moments passed as I leaned against the wall of the stall, closed my eyes, and held my face in my hands. I was hot, sweating, breathing hard. Exhausted. But I was still alive, literally and metaphorically. I had bearded the lions in their den and survived. I probably should have been proud of myself.

I pushed myself to my feet, went and washed my face and rinsed my mouth with tap water. I tried to concentrate on my small victory. James Landry wouldn't be able to put Erin Seabright so easily out of his mind tonight, if for no other reason than that I had challenged him. If confronting him resulted in one phone call that turned up one lead, it would have been worth the effort and what it had cost me emotionally.

As I walked out to my car, I wondered dimly if I was developing a sense of purpose. It had been so long since I'd had one, I couldn't be sure.

I got into the BMW and waited. Just when I was ready to decide Landry had made his exit while I was hugging the porcelain life preserver, he came out of the building, sunglasses hiding his eyes, a sport coat folded over one arm. I watched him get into a silver Pontiac Grand Am and roll out of the parking lot. I pulled into traffic two cars behind him, wanting to know who I was dealing with. Did he go straight home to a wife and kids? Could I play that parental angle on him? He hadn't been wearing a ring.

He drove straight to a cop bar on Military Trail. Disappointingly predictable. I didn't follow him inside, knowing my reception would probably be openly hostile. This was where the rank and file blew off steam, complained about their superiors, complained about civilians, complained about their ex-spouses. Landry would complain about me. That was all right. I didn't care what James Landry thought of me . . . as long as thinking of me made him think of Erin Seabright too.

8

Unlike me, Sean still enjoyed embarrassing his proper Palm Beach family by occasionally showing up at the charity balls that are the life of Palm Beach society during the winter season. The balls are lavish, over-the-top affairs that cost nearly as much to put on as they raise for their various causes. The net for the charity can be shockingly low, considering the gross, but a good time will be had in the process. If one goes for that sort of thing – designer gowns, designer jewels, the latest in cosmetic surgery, the posturing and the catty mind games of the ridiculously rich. Despite having been raised in that world, I had never had the patience for it.

I found Sean in his closet – which is larger than the average person's bedroom – in an Armani tuxedo, tying his bow tie.

'What's the disease du jour?' I asked.

'It starts with a P.'

'Pinkeye?'

'Parkinson's. That's a hot one with the celebs these days. This will be a younger crowd than some of the more traditional diseases.' He slipped his tux jacket on and admired himself in the three-way mirror.

I leaned against the marble-topped center island and watched him primp. 'One of these years they're going to run out of afflictions.'

'I've threatened my mother I'm going to put on a ball for genital herpes,' Sean said.

'God knows half the population of Palm Beach could benefit.'

'And the other half would catch it at the after-party parties. Want to be my date?'

'To catch herpes?'

'To the ball, Cinderella. Your parents are sure to be there. Double your scandal, double your fun.'

The idea of seeing my mother and father was less appealing than going into the Sheriff's Office had been. At least facing Landry had the potential for something good to come of it.

My mother had come to see me in the hospital a couple of times. The maternal duty of a woman without a maternal bone in her body. She had pushed to adopt a child for reasons that had nothing to do with a love of children. I had been an accessory to her life, like a handbag or a lapdog.

A lapdog from the pound, my heritage was called into question by my father every time I stepped out of line – which was often. He had resented my intrusion on his life. I was a constant reminder of his inability to sire children of his own. My resentment of his feelings had only served to fuel the fires of my rebellion.

I hadn't spoken to my father in over a decade. He had disowned me when I'd left college to become a common cop. An affront to him. A slap in his face. True. And a flimsy excuse to end a relationship that should have been unbreakable. He and I had both seized on it.

'Gee, sorry,' I said, spreading my arms wide. 'I'm not dressed for it.'

Sean took in the old jeans and black turtleneck with a critical eye. 'What happened to our fashion plate of the morning?'

'She had a very long day of pissing people off.'

'Is that a good thing?'

'We'll see. Squeeze enough pimples, one of them is bound to burst.'

'How folksy.'

'Did Van Zandt come by?'

He rolled his eyes. 'Honey, people like Tomas Van Zandt are the reason I live behind gates. If he came by, I didn't hear about it.'

'I guess he's too busy trying to sweet-talk Trey Hughes into spending a few million bucks on horses.'

'He'll need them. Have you seen that barn he's building? The Taj Mahal of Wellington.'

'I heard something about it.'

'Fifty-box stalls with crown molding, for God's sake. Four groom's apartments upstairs. Covered arena. Big jumping field.'

'Where is it?'

'Ten acres of prime real estate in that new development next to Grand Prix Village: Fairfields.'

The name gave me a shock. 'Fairfields?'

'Yes,' he said, adjusting his French cuffs and checking himself out in the mirror again. 'It's going to be a great big gaudy monstrosity that will make his trainer the envy of every jumper jockey on the East Coast. I have to go, darling.'

'Wait. A place like you're saying will cost the earth.'

'And the moon and the stars.'

'Can Trey really live that large off his trust fund?'

'He doesn't have to. His mother left nearly the entire Hughes estate to him.'

'Sallie Hughes died?'

'Last year. Fell down the stairs in her home and fractured her skull. So the story goes. You really ought to keep up with the old neighborhood, El,' he scolded. Then he kissed my cheek and left.

Fairfields. Bruce Seabright had just that morning been on his way to close a deal at Fairfields.

I don't like or trust coincidence. I don't believe coincidence is an accidental thing. In college I had once attended a lecture by a well-known New Age guru who believed all life at its most basic molecular structure is energy. Everything we do, every thought we have, every emotion we experience, can be broken down to pure energy. Our lives are energy, driving, seeking, running, colliding with the energy of the other people in our small worlds. Energy attracts energy, intent becomes a force of nature, and there is no such thing as coincidence.

When I feel like believing strongly in my theory, I then realize I have to accept that nothing in life can truly be random or accidental. And then I decide I would be better off believing in nothing.

Considering the people involved in Erin Seabright's life, whatever was going on was not positive. Her mother seemed not to have known who Erin was working for, and I could believe that was true. Krystal wouldn't have cared if Erin had been working for the devil himself, so long as her little world wasn't rocked because of it. She probably preferred not to think Erin was her daughter at all. But what about Bruce Seabright? Did he know Trey Hughes? If he knew Hughes, did he then also know Jade? And if he knew either or both of them, how did Erin fit into that picture?

Say Bruce wanted Erin out of his house because of her involvement with Chad. If he knew Hughes – and via Hughes had a connection to Don Jade – he might have gotten her set up with Jade as a means to that end. The more important question was whether or not Bruce Seabright cared about what happened to Erin once she was out of his house. And if he cared, would his caring be a positive or a negative thing? What if he wanted her gone permanently?

These were the thoughts and questions that filled my evening. I paced the guest house, chewing the stubs of my fingernails. Quiet, smooth jazz seeped out of the stereo speakers in the background, a moody sound track to the scenarios playing through my head. I picked up the phone once and dialed Erin's cell phone number, getting an automated voice telling me the customer's mailbox was full. If she had simply moved herself to Ocala, why wouldn't she have picked up her messages by now? Why wouldn't she have called Molly?

I didn't want to waste a day going to Ocala on what my gut told me would be a fool's errand. In the morning I would call a PI up there and give him the pertinent information, along with instructions. If Erin was working at the Ocala show grounds, I would know it in a day, two at the most. I would have the PI page her from the show office, say that she had an important phone call. If someone answered the page, he could verify whether or not it was, in fact, Erin Seabright. A simple plan. Landry could have done the same utilizing local law enforcement.

Asshole. I hoped he was lying awake.

It was after midnight. Sleep was nowhere in sight for me. I hadn't had a real night's sleep in years – partly because of my state of mind, partly because of the low-level chronic pain the accident had left me with. I didn't wonder what the lack of sleep was doing to my body or to my mind, for that matter. I didn't care. I'd gotten used to it. At least tonight I wasn't dwelling on thoughts of the mistakes I'd made or how I should pay for those mistakes.

I grabbed a jacket and left the house. The night was cool, a storm blowing across the Everglades toward Wellington. Lightning backlit the clouds to the far west.

I drove down Pierson, past the truck entrance to the Equestrian Club, past the extravagant stables of Grand Prix Village, made a turn and found the stone entrance gates of Fairfields. A sign showed the layout of the development in eight parcels ranging in size from five to ten acres. Three parcels were marked 'Sold'. Gracious beauty for exclusive equestrian facilities was promised, and a number was listed for Gryphon Development, Inc.

The stone columns were up, and a guardhouse had been constructed, but the iron gates had yet to be installed. I followed the winding drive, my headlights illuminating weeds and scrub. Security lights glowed white at two building sites. Even in the dead of night I had no trouble identifying which of the two properties belonged to Trey Hughes.

The stable was up. Its silhouette resembled a big K-mart. A huge, two-story rectangle that ran parallel to the road, flaunting its size. It stood back maybe thirty yards from the chain-link construction fence. The gate was chained and padlocked.

I pulled into the drive as far as the gate allowed and sat there trying to take in as much as I could. My headlights bathed a piece of earth-moving equipment, and revealed torn ground and mounded piles of dirt. Beyond the stable on the near end I could just make out what must have been the construction boss's office trailer. In front of the stables, a large sign advertised the construction company, proud to be building Lucky Dog Farm.

I could only ballpark the cost of the place. Ten acres this near the show grounds was worth a fortune with nothing on it. A facility the likes of what Trey Hughes was putting up had to go two, maybe three million just for the buildings. And that would be for horse facilities alone. Like Grand Prix Village, there would be no stately homes in Fairfields. The owners of these stables had posh homes at the Polo Club or on the island or both. The Hughes family had a beachfront estate on Blossom Way, near the exclusive Palm Beach Bath and Tennis Club. Trey himself had had a mansion in the Polo Club when I'd last known of him. Now he had it all, thanks to Sallie Hughes taking a wrong step on the stair.

Lucky dog, indeed. Rid of the woman Trey used to call The Domina-triarch, and unfettered access to an obscene fortune in one simple fall. That idea writhed in the back of my mind like a snake in the shadows.

After speaking with Sean, I had gone online to find any stories on Sallie Hughes's death, and found nothing but her obituary. No story of any investigation.

Of course, there wouldn't be a story. How unseemly to allow such things in the papers, my mother would have said. The newspaper on the island was for social news and announcements. Not for such dirty business as death and police investigations. The newspaper my mother read was printed on glossy stock with ink that wouldn't rub off on the reader's hands. Clean in fact and in content.

The *Post* – printed in West Palm Beach (where the common folk live) – reported Sallie Hughes had died in her home at the age of eighty-two.

However it had happened, Trey Hughes was now a very fat golden goose. There were sure to be a few people willing to do him a little favor like getting rid of a jumper with more heart than talent. It didn't matter how much money Trey already had. Another quarter of a million was always welcome.

Don Jade had to be at the head of that list of helpful hopefuls. What a sweet deal for Jade, or any trainer: walking into a barn like this one, the kind of place that would give him legitimacy again and draw still more clients with bottomless pockets.

I wondered about the tension I'd sensed between the two men that morning. Trey Hughes could now afford to put nearly any big-name trainer he wanted in his stable. Why had he gone with Don Jade – a man whose reputation was based more on scandal than on success? A man with a reputation for doing bad deeds and getting away with them . . .

Whatever had put him there, Don Jade was in the catbird seat. That had to make him the envy of a lot of bitterly jealous people.

Michael Berne came to mind. I had recognized the name as soon as Van Zandt had blabbed it that morning. Berne had been mentioned in Stellar's obituary in the on-line magazine *Horses Daily*. He'd had the ride on Stellar before Jade, with only limited success in the showring. Then Jade got the horse. Got the horse, got the owner, got the Taj Mahal of Wellington. No wonder Berne was angry. He hadn't just lost a paycheck when Stellar had been led out of his barn. He'd lost a big-time meal ticket.

He wasn't just Jade's rival, as Van Zandt had said, he was an enemy.

An enemy could be a valuable source of information.

I drove back to the equestrian center, wanting time to prowl without having to worry about any of Jade's crowd seeing me. I wanted to find Berne's stable. If I could get a phone number off his stalls, I would be able to set up a meeting somewhere we weren't likely to be caught by any Jade confederates.

The guard came out of the gatehouse looking bored and unhappy.

'It is very late,' he said in heavily accented English.

I heaved a sigh. 'Tell me about it. We've got a horse with colic. I drew the short straw.'

He frowned at me as if he suspected I might have just insulted him.

'A sick horse,' I explained. 'I have night watch, like you.'

'Oh, yes.' He nodded then. 'I understand. I am very sorry to hear. Good luck with that, miss.'

'Thank you.'

He didn't bother to ask my name or what barn number this phantom horse was in. I had a parking pass and a believable story. That was enough.

I parked back in The Meadows, not wanting anyone's attention on my car. With my Maglite in hand and my gun in the back of my jeans, I walked the aisles of the tent barns, looking for Michael Berne's name, hoping not to run afoul of someone's groom or a roving security guard.

The storm was rolling closer. The wind was coming up, making tent tops billow and flap, making horses nervous. I kept my light low, looking at stall cards and emergency numbers, and still managed to spook some horses, sending them spinning around their small quarters, eyes rolling white. Others nickered at me, hoping for something to eat.

I cut the light as I walked the dogleg from The Meadows to the next set of tents. If I was lucky, Berne's horses were stabled relatively near Jade's. Their run-in had taken place at the schooling ring nearest Jade's barn. Maybe that was Berne's schooling area too. If I was unlucky, Berne had gone out of his way to pick a fight with Jade, and I would have to walk forty stables before I found what I wanted.

A gust swept in from the west, shaking the trees. Thunder rumbled overhead. I ducked into tent twenty-two and started checking names.

A quarter of the way down the first row I stopped and listened. The same sounds as in the other tents: horses moving, nickering, kicking against the pipes that framed the stalls. Only these sounds weren't coming from the horses around me. The disturbance was a couple of rows over. The creak and groan of a stall door opening. The shuffling sound of hooves moving through deep bedding. A horse whinnied loudly. The horse in the stall nearest me rushed its door and whinnied back.

I flicked the light up at it to see a bay, head high, ears pricked, white-rimmed eyes focused past me, past the horse across the aisle. The horse whinnied again and spun around. Another down the row followed suit.

I doused my light and crept down the aisle to the back end of the tent, the Maglite held like a club in my hand. The flashlight weighed three pounds. When I'd been in uniform I had once used this flashlight to defend my life against a 270-pound biker on PCP. He'd ended up in the hospital with a concussion.

I didn't draw my weapon. I wanted to see, not confront. The Glock was my last line of defense.

The wind howled and the tent top swelled upward like a balloon wanting to take flight. The thick ropes holding the tent stakes squeaked and groaned. I slipped around the end stalls, staying close to the wall. The land behind the tent dropped off sharply to ground that had been cleared and burned over the summer, being made ready for more tents, more schooling rings. It looked like a moonscape. The smell of ash flavored the air.

As I started to ease around the end stall to the next aisle, I heard a door swing back on its hinges, and there was a sharp, distinct sound that didn't register until the next thing had already happened.

Like a specter running from the otherworld, a huge, ghostly gray horse barreled down the aisle straight at me. He was nearly on top of me before I could react, knocking me backward. I scrambled to keep my feet moving, to throw myself out of his way. A tent spike caught my right ankle and jerked my leg out from under me, dumping me to the ground with a jarring thud. I tried to cover my head and pull myself into a ball, every inch of me braced for the horrible strike of steel-shod hooves and the driving weight of a half-ton animal coming down on soft tissue and fragile bones. But the gray leapt over me, then soared over the edge of the embankment. I scrambled to my knees and watched in horror as he stumbled hard down the bank, going down on his knees, hind legs still running. He squealed in fright, flailing to right himself, dragging himself up and running on into the night.

Pushing to my feet, I turned back toward the tent as another horse ran out. Dark with a blaze. Whinnying as it ran after the gray. I dove to the side as he bolted past.

A slap on the ass.

The sound I'd heard before: the flat of a hand slapping a horse's rump.

I ran back into the tent. The rest of the barn was in an uproar by now, horses screaming and banging in their stalls. The flimsy pipe-and-canvas stalls shaking and rattling. The tent walls shuddering as the wind kicked at them. I shouted, hoping to frighten the perpetrator with discovery and send him running.

Another horse pranced out of an open stall, saw me, snorted and bolted past, knocking me into the door of the stall behind me. Then that door shoved forward, pushing me with it, knocking me to my knees.

I scuttled ahead like a crab, reaching for the door across the way to pull myself up. The horse came out of the stall behind me like a rodeo bronc, a raw bellow coming from it as it bucked and kicked out at me. I felt the air whoosh past my ear as the hoof just missed its mark.

Before I could start to turn around, a smelly, suffocating blackness engulfed my head and upper body and I was shoved forward against a stall. I tried to claw at the blanket, but couldn't get my arms up. I wanted air. I wanted what little light there was. I wanted to be free to fight my assailant, who jerked me backward, then sideways, one way and then the other.

Dizziness swirled through my head and I staggered and stumbled and went down on one knee. Then something struck hard, hitting me across the back with enough force to make me see stars.

On the third blow I fell forward and lay still. My breath was a hot rasp in the shallowest part of my lungs. I couldn't hear anything but a roaring in my head, and I wondered if I would know what was happening before the next loose horse ran over me, crushing me beneath its hooves. I tried to push myself up and couldn't. The messages scattered somewhere between my brain and my nerve pathways. Pain kicked me in the back and I choked and coughed, needing air, unable to take a deep breath.

A moment passed. No horses trampled me. No pitchfork impaled me. I figured my attacker had run, which left me in a very bad place at a very bad time. Horses were running loose. If someone came rushing into this barn and found me ...

I tried again to gather my strength and managed to shove the horse blanket off my head. Gulping air, fighting nausea, I grabbed hold of the stall door and dragged myself to my feet. Dizzy, the ground seeming to pitch beneath me, I stumbled out the back of the tent and fell down again.

The Maglite lay on the ground where it had landed when the first horse had hit me, its beam a yellow beacon in the dark. I scooped it up, grabbed hold of a tent rope, and pulled myself up.

Horses were running in the cleared ground down the slope. Some were running between this tent and the next. The wind was blowing harder, carrying the first pelting drops of rain. I heard someone shout in the distance. Time to go.

I stepped inside the tent just far enough to flick the beam across the front of an open stall.

In Case of Emergency Phone Michael Berne ...

'Don't move. Drop the flashlight.'

The voice came from behind me on a beam of light that spilled around my shoulders. I kept the Maglite in my hand, but held my arms away from my body.

'I heard a commotion,' I said, turning slightly. 'Someone was in here opening stall doors.'

'Yeah, right,' he said sarcastically. 'Guess who. Drop the flashlight.'

'It wasn't me,' I said, turning a little more. 'I tried to stop them. I've got the bruises to prove it.'

'I'm not gonna tell you again, lady. Drop the flashlight.'

'I want to see who you are. How do I know you're not the person who did this?'

'I'm with security.'

I didn't find that reassuring. Security for the show grounds was contracted out to a private company that lowballed the bid for the job. The staff was probably as reliable and well trained as the people who let lunatics get on commercial airliners with guns and knives. For all I knew, half of them were convicted felons. With my back to him, I couldn't be sure he was even wearing the uniform.

'Let me see you.'

He huffed an impatient sigh. Before he could say no, I turned around and hit him full in the face with the beam from the Maglite.

I noted his clothes second. I noted his gun first.

'Is that part of the uniform?' I asked.

'It's part of *my* uniform.' He made a motion with it. 'Enough with the questions. Cut the light and give it to me. Let's go.'

I did as instructed, more than willing to get out in the open where I knew there were other people around. I considered and rejected the idea of making a break for it. I didn't want people looking for me, my description and sketch on the front page of the newspaper. Nor did I want to get shot in the back. Playing along for the moment could offer an opportunity to learn something.

Outside, people were calling, horses were whinnying. I could hear hoofbeats on the hard-packed road. The guard herded me to a golf cart parked on the side of tent nineteen – Jade's barn.

I wondered how long the cart had been parked there. I wondered how easy it would be to buy a guy like this to open some stall doors. Working nights for peanuts guarding horses worth more than the average man would make in a lifetime might alter a person's perspective of right and wrong.

I slid onto the passenger's side of the bench seat, the seat wet and slippery as the rain came harder. The guard kept his gun in his left hand as he started the cart and backed it around. I shifted positions, turning slightly toward him, and surreptitiously touched the Glock, still secure in the back of my jeans, beneath my jacket and turtleneck.

'Where are we going?'

He didn't answer. A walkie-talkie crackled on his belt. Other guards radioing about the loose horses. He didn't get on the air to tell anyone he'd apprehended me. I didn't like that. We started down the road toward the main part of the show grounds, a ghost town at two in the morning.

'I'll want to speak to your supervisor,' I said with authority. 'And someone will need to call Detective James Landry with the Sheriff's Office.'

That turned his head.

'Why?'

I took my turn not answering. Let him wonder. We passed other guards, other people running through the rain to join in the fun of trying to catch half a dozen hot-blooded horses drunk on freedom.

We drove through the maze of tents and down a row of deserted retail shops. The rain came now in sheets. We drove farther and farther away from any source of help. My heart rate increased a beat. Adrenaline was like a narcotic in my bloodstream, the prospect of danger intoxicating and exciting. I stared at the security guard and wondered what he would think if he knew that. Most people would find it disturbing.

He pulled the golf cart alongside one of the big trailers that housed the various show grounds management offices and cut the engine. We clattered up the metal stairs and the guard ushered me inside. A heavyset man stood beside a metal desk, listening to the noise coming over a walkie-talkie the size of a brick. He had a throat like a bullfrog: a sack of flesh wider than his head, spilling over the collar of his shirt. He wore the blue security uniform too, with a couple of extra pins on the chest. Decorated for meritorious ass-sitting and delegating above and beyond the call, I guessed. He scowled at me as I stood dripping water all over the floor.

'She's the one,' the guard said. 'I caught her opening stall doors.'

I looked him in the face and said with just enough point to make my meaning crystal clear: 'Any more little surprises like that in your pocket?'

He had stuffed the gun. I could see him struggle with the notion that he'd blown it showing me the thing. I had something to use against him. He wasn't supposed to be carrying on the job. He probably didn't have a permit for it either. If that was true and I reported him to the police, there was a good chance he'd lose his job at the very least. I could see on his face all these things were just now occurring to him.

If he'd been overly bright he wouldn't have been working dog watch in a rent-a-cop uniform.

'You caught me standing in a barn with a flashlight,' I said. 'I was trying to help. Same as you.'

'You got something against Michael Berne?' the bullfrog asked. He had the thick drawl of a panhandle Floridian, where the Sunshine State and the Deep South rub loins, as it were.

'I've never met Michael Berne, though I did see him having a loud, threatening argument with Don Jade this morning. You might want to find out where Mr Jade is right now.'

The supervisor stared at me. 'Berne is on his way,' he said. 'And a couple of deputies. Have a seat, Miss ... ?'

I didn't answer and I didn't sit, though my back was aching like a son of a bitch from the beating I'd taken.

'You'll need to tell the deputies to treat that stall area as a crime scene,' I said. 'In addition to letting the horses loose, your perp assaulted me when I tried to run him off. They'll find a pitchfork or a broom – something with a long handle – that may have his prints on it. I'll want to press charges. And I'll want to go to the emergency room for an examination, and to have them take photographs of my bruises. I may sue. What kind of management does this place have if they can't keep people or animals safe?'

Bullfrog looked at me as if he'd never seen one of my kind before. 'Who are you?'

'I'm not telling you my name.'

'I need your name, miss. I have to make a report.'

'That's a problem then, because I'm not telling you,' I said. 'I don't have to tell you anything. You're not an officer of the court or of the government, and therefore you have no right to demand information of me.'

'Deputies are on the way,' he said by way of a threat.

'That's fine. I'll be happy to go with them, though they have no grounds to arrest me. Standing in a barn aisle is not a crime that I'm aware of.'

'Bud says you let them horses loose.'

'I think you should ask Bud again what he saw.'

He looked at Bud. 'Was she letting them loose or not?'

Bud looked constipated, unable to tell the lie he wanted to tell either to cover his own ass or to grab a little glory with his boss. 'She was right there.'

'So were you,' I pointed out. 'How do we know you didn't open those doors?'

'That's ridiculous,' Bullfrog said. 'Why would he do something like that?'

'I could only speculate. Money. Maliciousness. Mental illness.'

'Maybe those motives all apply to you.'

'Not in this particular instance.'

'You have horses here on the grounds, Miss – ?'

'I'm through speaking with you now,' I announced. 'May I use your phone to call my attorney?'

He squinted at me. 'No!'

I sat then in a straight chair beside the desk. Bullfrog's radio crackled. The gate guard announcing the arrival of the sheriff's deputies. A stroke of luck. I didn't want to meet Michael Berne in these circumstances. Bullfrog instructed the gate guard to send the radio car to the security office.

'Letting them horses loose is a serious crime,' he said to me. 'You could do time for that.'

'No, I couldn't, because I didn't let the horses loose. The perpetrator might be charged with malicious mischief, which is a misdemeanor. There would be a fine and maybe community service. It's nothing compared to, say, illegally carrying a concealed weapon,' I said, looking at the scowling Bud.

'I thought you said you were through talking,' he said.

I smoothed my wet hair back with my hands and stood up as a car door slammed outside the trailer. The deputy came in looking like he'd been awakened from a sound sleep to answer the call.

'What's up, Marsh? Somebody let some nags loose? This her?'

'She was in the vicinity,' Bullfrog said. 'She may have information about the crime.'

The deputy looked at me, unimpressed. 'Do you, ma'am?'

'I'll speak directly to Detective Landry,' I said.

'What's your name, ma'am?'

I moved past him, going to the door, checking out his name tag as I passed. 'We'll talk in the car, Deputy Saunders. Let's get going.'

He looked at Bullfrog, who shook his head and said, 'Good luck with that, son. She's a pistol.'

9

'You got me out of bed for this?' Landry looked from Deputy Saunders to me with the kind of disgust usually reserved for spoiled food.

'She won't talk to anyone else,' Saunders said.

We walked down the hall toward the squad room, Landry muttering, 'Aren't I the lucky one. I don't see what any of us are doing here. You could have handled this in the field in half an hour. Jesus.'

'I was assaulted,' I said. 'I think that warrants a detective.'

'Then you take whoever is up. You know that.'

'But I've already established a relationship with you regarding this case.'

'No, you haven't, because there isn't any case. What you talked to me about yesterday isn't a case.'

We went into the division offices through reception. Landry handed his badge and his weapon to the security officer through the drawer beneath the bulletproof glass. Saunders followed suit. I pulled the Glock out of the back of my jeans, put it and my car keys in the tray. Landry stared at me.

I shrugged. 'I've got a license.'

He turned to Saunders. 'You fucking idiot. She could have blown your empty head off in the car.'

'Now, Detective,' I cooed, slipping past him as the security officer buzzed the door open. 'I'm not that kind of girl.'

'Get out of here, Saunders,' he snapped. 'You're about as useful as a limp dick.'

We left Saunders looking forlorn in the outer office. Landry stalked past me, the muscles in his jaw working. We went past his desk to an interview room. He pushed the door back.

'In here.'

I went in and gingerly took a seat. The pain in my back wouldn't let me draw a full breath. I had begun to wonder if maybe I really should go to an ER.

Landry slammed the door. 'What the hell were you thinking?'

'That's rather a broad question, so I'm just going to take my pick of moments,' I said. 'I went to the equestrian center to look for some hint of what might have happened to Erin Seabright.'

735

'But you weren't in the barn where she worked, right? She worked for some guy named Jade. So how is it you were in this other barn?'

'Michael Berne is an enemy of Don Jade. This morning I witnessed Berne threaten Jade.'

'Threaten him how?'

'In that if-I-find-out-you-killed-that-horse-I'll-ruin-you kind of way.'

'So this Jade sneaks in and turns the guy's horses loose. Big deal.'

'It's a big deal to the man whose livelihood depends on the soundness of those horses. It's a big deal to the trainer who has to explain to owners how a horse worth a quarter of a million or a half a million dollars came to break a leg running around loose in the dead of night.'

Landry heaved a sigh and turned his head at an odd angle, as if to pop a vertebra in his neck. 'And you'd drag me out of bed for this?'

'No. I did that just for fun.'

'You're a pain in the ass, Estes. Not like you haven't been told that before.'

'That and worse. It doesn't bother me. I don't have a very high opinion of myself either,' I said. 'I suppose you think I'm being flip, and that's all right. I don't care what you think of me. I want you to be aware there are bad things going on that all seem to center on Don Jade. Don Jade is the man Erin Seabright was working for. Erin Seabright is missing. Do you see the connection here?'

He shook his head. 'So I'm told you're caught standing there in this other guy's barn. How do I know you didn't let these nags loose just to get attention? You want people looking at Jade, so you orchestrate this little opera –'

'Nice turn of phrase. And did I beat myself with a pitchfork handle too? I can assure you, I'm not that flexible.'

'You're walking around. You don't look any worse for wear to me.'

I slipped my jacket off and stood up. 'All right. I don't usually do this on the first interrogation, but if you promise not to call me a slut . . .'

I turned my back to him and pulled my sweater up to my neck. 'If those marks look anywhere near as bad as they feel –'

'Jesus.'

He spoke the word softly, without anger, without energy, the wind knocked out of his sails. I knew it probably didn't have as much to do with the marks my assailant had left on me as it did with the patchwork of skin grafts I'd worn for the past two years.

That wasn't what I had wanted. Not at all. I had lived with those scars a long time now. They were a part of me. I had kept them to myself because I kept to myself. I didn't dwell on them. I didn't look at them. In a strange way, the damage that had been done to my body was unimportant to me, because I had become unimportant to myself.

Suddenly the damage was very important. I felt naked emotionally. Vulnerable.

I pulled the sweater down and picked up my jacket, my back still to Landry.

'Forget it,' I said, embarrassed and angry with myself. 'I'm going home.'

'You want to press charges?'

'Against whom?' I asked, turning to face him. 'The asshole you're not going to bother to look for, let alone question, because nothing that goes on with that horse crowd is of any interest to you? Unless, of course, someone turns up murdered.'

He couldn't think of anything to say to that.

The corner of my mouth moved in what passed for a bitter smile. 'Imagine that: You at least have the humanity to feel sheepish. Good for you, Landry.'

I stepped past him, going to the door. 'How do you like my odds that Saunders is sitting in the parking lot catching twenty? Pretty good, I think. See you around, Landry. I'll call you when I find a body.'

'Estes. Wait.' He didn't want to meet my eyes when I turned again and looked at him. 'You should go to an ER. I'll take you. You might have busted a rib or something.'

'I've had worse.'

'Jesus Christ, you're a hardhead.'

'I don't want your pity,' I said. 'I don't want your sympathy. I don't want you to like me or care what happens to me. I don't want anything from you but for you to do your job. And apparently, that's too much to ask.'

'I'll show myself out. I know the way.'

He followed me back to reception. Neither of us spoke as we retrieved our weapons. I pretended he had ceased to exist as we walked down the hall and down the stairs.

'I'm good at what I do,' he said as the front doors came into view.

'Really? What's that? You have a second career as a professional asshole?'

'You're a piece of work.'

'I'm what I have to be.'

'No, you're not,' he said. 'You're rude and you're a bitch, and that somehow makes you feel superior to the rest of us.'

The rain was still coming down. It looked white as it passed through the beams of the security lights in the parking lot. Saunders and his radio car were gone.

'Great,' I said. 'I guess I have to take you up on that ride, after all.'

Landry looked at me sideways as he flipped up the collar of his jacket. 'Fuck you. Call a cab.'

I watched him get into his car, and stood there in the rain until he'd backed up and driven away. Then I went back inside to use the phone.

I couldn't say I hadn't asked for it.

When the cabbie finally showed, he wanted to chat, curious about why I needed a ride from the Sheriff's Office at 3:45 in the morning. I told him my boyfriend was wanted for murder. He didn't ask any more questions after that.

I propped myself up in the back of the cab and spent the ride home wondering how Erin Seabright was spending the night.

Act Two

SCENE ONE
FADE IN:
INTERIOR: OLD TRAILER HOUSE

Night. A single lightbulb in a lamp with no shade. No curtains at the filthy window. A rusty old iron bed frame. Stained mattress with no sheets.

Erin sits on the bed, huddled against the headboard, frightened, naked. She is chained to the bed by one wrist. Her hair is a mess. Mascara rings her eyes. Her lower lip is split and bloody.

She is very aware of the camera and the director of the scene. She tries to cover as much of herself as she can. She is crying softly, trying to hide her face.

DIRECTOR   Look at the camera, bitch. Say your line.

She shakes her head, still hiding.

DIRECTOR   Say it! You want me to make you?

She shakes her head and looks at the camera.

ERIN   Help me.

FADE OUT

10

Landry didn't sleep for shit, and it was Estes's fault. Her fault he'd been dragged out of bed in the first place. Her fault he couldn't get back to sleep once he'd finally gotten back home. Every time he closed his eyes he saw her back, crisscrossed with lines where new flesh had been stitched into old. The bruises just coming to the surface from her run-in at the equestrian center were insignificant, pale shadows beneath the old damage.

Damage. He thought of Estes and what he knew about her. Their paths hadn't crossed when she was on the job. Narcs ran their own way. They spent too much time undercover, as far as he was concerned. It made them edgy and unpredictable. An opinion borne out in the incident that had ended her career, and ended the life of Hector Ramirez. What he knew about that incident was what everybody knew: Estes had jumped the gun, gone against orders to make the bust herself, and all hell had broken loose.

He had never given any thought to Estes, beyond thinking she'd gotten what she deserved, losing her job. He knew she'd been wounded, hospitalized, was suing the SO for her disability pay – which seemed pretty damned nervy, considering – but it had nothing to do with him, and he didn't give a shit about her. She was trouble. He had figured it, and now he knew it for a fact.

Pushy bitch. Telling him how to do his job.

He wondered about what had happened to her at the equestrian center, wondered if it really did have anything to do with this girl she said was missing . . .

If the girl was missing, why would a twelve-year-old child be the only one to report it? Why not her parents? Why not her employer?

Her parents who maybe wanted to be rid of her.

Her boss who maybe had a major scam going, and maybe beat Estes across the back with a broom handle.

He saw her back, a patchwork of mismatched flesh stretched taut over bone.

At five-thirty he got out of bed, pulled on a pair of running shorts, stretched, did a hundred sit-ups and a hundred push-ups, and started his day. Again.

I stand at the side of the Golam brothers' trailer. I've been told to stay put, to wait, but I know that's not the right decision. If I go in first, if I go in now, I've got the brothers dead-bang. They think they know me. I've worked this case three months. I know what I'm doing. I know I'm right. I know the Golam brothers are already twitching. I know I want this bust and deserve it. I know Lieutenant Sikes is here for the show, to put a feather in his cap. He wants to look good when the news vans arrive. He wants to make the public think they should vote for him in the next election for sheriff.

He's stuck me on the side of the trailer and told me to wait. He doesn't know his ass. He didn't listen to me when I told him the side door is the door the brothers use most. While Sikes and Ramirez are watching the front, the brothers are dumping their money into duffel bags and getting ready to bolt out the side. Billy Golam's four-by-four is parked ten feet away, covered in mud. If they run, they'll take the truck, not the Corvette parked in front. The truck can go off-road.

Sikes is wasting precious time. The Golam brothers have two girls in the trailer with them. This could easily turn into a hostage situation. But if I go in now . . . They think they know me.

I key the button on my radio. 'This is stupid. They're going to break for the truck. I'm going in.'

'Goddammit, Estes –'

I drop the radio into the weeds growing beside the trailer. It's my case. It's my bust. I know what I'm doing.

I draw my weapon and hold it behind my back. I go to the side door and knock the way all the Golam brothers' customers knock: two knocks, one knock, two knocks. 'Hey, Billy, it's Elle! I need some.'

Billy Golam jerks open the door, wild-eyed, high on his own home cooking – crystal meth. He's breathing hard. He's got a gun in his hand.

Shit.

The front door explodes inward.

One of the girls screams.

Buddy Golam shouts: 'Cops!'

Billy Golam swings the .357 up in my face. I suck in my last breath.

He turns abruptly and fires. The sound is deafening. The bullet hits Hector Ramirez in the face and blows out the back of his head, blood and brain matter spraying Sikes behind him.

I go for my weapon as Billy bolts out the door and knocks me off the stoop. He's running for the truck as I scramble to get my feet under me.

The engine roars to life.

'Billy!' I scream, running for the truck.

'Fuck! Fuck! Fuck!' The cords in his neck stand out as he screams. He throws the truck into reverse and hits the gas.

I throw myself at the driver's door, grab hold of the side mirror and the window frame, and get one foot on the running board. I don't think what I'm doing. I just act.

I'm screaming. He's screaming.

He brings the gun up and points it in my face.

I hit the gun, hit his face.

He cranks the wheel around as the truck runs backward. One of my feet slips off the running board. He throws the truck into drive and gravel spews out behind it.

I struggle to keep from falling. I try to grab the wheel.

The truck catches hold of pavement. Golam cranks the wheel hard left. His face is a contorted mask, mouth wide, eyes wild. I try to grab for him. He shoves the door open as the truck spins around in the road.

I'm hanging in space.

I'm falling.

The road slams against my back.

My left cheekbone shatters like an egg.

Then the black shadow of Billy Golam's four-by-four sweeps over me, and I die.

And I wake.

Five-thirty A.M. After two hours of fitful dozing, waiting for a rib fragment to deflate one or both of my lungs, I oozed over the side of my bed and forced myself to attempt stretching.

I went into the bathroom, stood naked in front of the mirror, and looked at my body. Too thin. Rectangular marks on both thighs where the skin grafts were taken. Gouges into the meat of the left leg.

I turned and tried to look over my shoulder at my back in the mirror. I looked at what I had shown Landry, and called myself stupid.

The one useful thing my father had ever taught me: never show a weakness, never appear vulnerable.

The bruises from my beating were dark maroon stripes. It hurt when I breathed.

At 6:15 – after I'd fed the horses – I drove myself to the ER. The X-rays showed no broken bones. A bleary-eyed resident, who'd had even less sleep than I, questioned me, clearly not believing my story of having fallen down a flight of stairs. All the staff looked at me askance with jaded eyes. Twice I was asked if I wanted to talk to a cop. I thanked them and declined. No one forced the issue, which led me to wonder how many battered women were allowed to simply walk out of the place and back into their own private hell.

The resident vomited up a big load of medical terms, trying to intimidate me with his expensive education.

I looked at him, unimpressed, and said, 'I have bruised ribs.'

'You have bruised ribs. I'll give you a prescription for painkillers. Go home and rest. No significant physical activity for forty-eight hours.'

'Yeah, right.'

He gave me a scrip for Vicodin. I laughed when I looked at it. I stuffed it in the pocket of my windbreaker as I left the building. My arms worked, my legs worked, no bones were protruding, I wasn't bleeding. I was ambulatory,

I was fine. As long as I knew I wouldn't die of it, I had places to go, people to see.

My first call was to Michael Berne, or rather, to Michael Berne's assistant – the phone number on the stall doors. Michael was a busy man.

'Ask him if he's too busy to speak to a potential client,' I said. 'I can always take my business to Don Jade, if that's the case.'

Miraculously, Michael's time suddenly freed up and the assistant handed off the phone.

'This is Michael. How can I help you?'

'By dishing some dirt on your friend, Mr Jade,' I said quietly. 'I'm a private investigator.'

11

I dressed in black from head to toe, slicked my hair back with a handful of gel, put on a pair of narrow black wraparound sunglasses, and stole Sean's black Mercedes SL. I looked like a character from *The Matrix*. Serious, mysterious, edgy. Not a disguise, but a uniform. Image is everything.

I had asked Berne to meet me in the parking lot at Denny's in Royal Palm Beach, a fifteen-minute drive from the show grounds. He had groused about the drive, but I couldn't take the risk of being seen with him near the equestrian center.

Berne arrived in a Honda Civic that had seen better days. He got out of the car looking nervous, glancing around. A private eye, a clandestine meeting. Heady stuff. He was dressed to ride in gray breeches with a couple of stains and a red polo shirt that clashed with his hair.

I buzzed down the Mercedes's side window. 'Mr Berne. You're here to meet me.'

He squinted at me, doubtful, uncertain, unable to get any kind of a read on me. An agent for a shadow organization. Maybe he'd been expecting Nancy Drew.

'We'll talk out here,' I said. 'Please get in the car.'

He hesitated like a child being offered a ride by a stranger. He looked around the parking lot again as if he expected something bad to happen. Masked operatives creeping out of the shrubbery to ambush him.

'If you have something to tell me, get in the car,' I said impatiently.

He was so tall, he had to fold himself in to fit into the Mercedes, as if he were getting into a clown car. What a contrast he was to Jade's handsome, elegant image. Howdy Doody on growth hormones. Red hair and freckles, skinny as a rail. I'd read enough about Michael Berne to know he'd been a minor contender in the international show-jumping world in the early nineties, when he had ridden a horse called Iroquois. But the biggest thing he'd done was a tour of Europe with the second string of the US Olympic team. Then Iroquois's owners had sold the stallion out from under him, and he hadn't had a big winner since.

When Trey Hughes had come into his barn, Berne had been quoted in an interview saying that Stellar was his ride back into the international spotlight. Then Stellar went to Don Jade's barn, and Michael Berne's star dimmed again.

'Who do you work for again, Ms Estes?' he asked, taking in the pricey car.

'I didn't say.'

'Are you with the insurance company? Are you with the police?'

'How many cops do you know drive a Mercedes, Mr Berne?' I asked, allowing the barest hint of amusement to show. I lit one of Sean's French cigarettes and blew the smoke at the windshield. 'I'm a private investigator – *private* being the operative word. There's nothing for you to be concerned about, Mr Berne. Unless, of course, you've done something wrong.'

'I haven't done anything wrong,' he said defensively. 'I run an honest business. There aren't any stories going around about me killing horses for the insurance money. That's Don Jade's territory.'

'You think he had Stellar killed?'

'I know he did.'

I watched him from the corner of my eye, and when I spoke I used a flat, monotone, business voice. 'You have something to back that up? Like evidence?'

His mouth turned down in a sour pout. 'Jade's too smart for that. He always covers his tracks. Last night, for example. No one will ever connect Don Jade to it, but he had my horses turned loose.'

'Why would he do that?'

'Because I confronted him. I know what he is. It's people like Jade that give the horse business a bad name. Crooked deals, stealing clients, killing horses. People turn a blind eye as long as they aren't the victims. Someone has to do something.'

'Did Trey Hughes ever approach you about doing something to Stellar?'

'No. I had Stellar on track. He was making progress. I thought we had a shot at the World Cup. I would never have anything to do with a scheme like that anyway.'

'Why did Hughes take the horse away from you?'

'Jade poached him. He steals clients all the time.'

'It didn't have anything to do with the fact that you weren't winning?' Berne glared at me. 'We were getting there. It was only a matter of time.'

'But Hughes wasn't willing to wait.'

'Jade probably told him he could do it faster.'

'Yeah, well, now Stellar is going nowhere.'

'What about the autopsy?'

'Necropsy.'

'What?'

'It's called a necropsy when it's a horse.'

He didn't like being corrected. 'So what did it show?'

'I'm not at liberty to divulge those details, Mr Berne. Were there any rumors going around before the horse died? I heard he wasn't sound.'

'He was getting older. Older horses need maintenance – joint injections, supplements, things like that. But he was tough. He had a big heart and he always did his job.'

'No one was hinting anything hinky was going on in Jade's barn?' I asked.

'There are always rumors about Jade. He's done this before, you know.'

'I'm familiar with Mr Jade's background. What kind of rumors lately?'

'The usual. What drugs his horses are on. Whose clients he's after. How he's got Trey Hughes by the balls – pardon my language.'

'Why would anyone say that?'

'Come on,' he said, defensive again. 'He must have something. How else is he getting that barn Hughes is building?'

'Through merit? Good deeds? Friendship?'

None of my suggestions appealed.

'You worked for Trey Hughes,' I said. 'What could Jade have on him?'

'Take your pick: his drug du jour, whose wife he's been sleeping with –'

'How he came to inherit so suddenly?' I suggested.

Berne tried to sit back and study me for a moment, his expression not unlike Jill Morone's when she'd been trying to decide how to play me. 'You think he killed his mother?'

'I don't think anything. I'm just asking questions.'

He considered something and laughed. 'Trey would never have the nerve. He stuttered whenever he talked about Sallie. She scared the crap out of him.'

I didn't point out that Trey only needed nerve enough to hire someone else for the job. Delegating was something I was sure came quite easily to a man who had spent his entire life shirking any kind of responsibility.

'You haven't heard any rumors up that alley?' I asked.

'People make jokes behind his back. No one really thinks it. Trey has all he can do getting himself through the day. He couldn't organize his wallet, let alone plan a murder and get away with it. Anyway, he was with someone the night he got the call about his mother.'

'Really? Who?'

He looked away. 'What difference does that make?'

'It makes a difference if that person is in fact an accessory to murder.'

'It's nothing like that.'

'I'll get the answer one way or another, Mr Berne. Do you want me asking all around the show grounds, opening up old wounds, stirring up old gossip?'

Berne stared out the window.

'Should I start guessing?' I asked. 'Maybe it was you. That would put a fresh spin on an old story, wouldn't it?'

'I'm no fruit!'

'It's hardly a stigma in the equestrian community, is it?' I said on the verge of boredom. 'From what I've seen, maybe every third guy is straight.

Think of all the new friends you'll have if you come out of the closet. Or maybe you already have. I could look for an old boyfriend –'

'It was my wife.'

Who he gave up in a heartbeat rather than have a perfect stranger think his switch clicked the other way.

'Your wife was with Trey Hughes the night his mother died? With him in the biblical sense?'

'Yes.'

'With or without your consent?' I asked.

Berne turned purple. 'What the hell kind of question is that?'

'If you thought you were on the verge of losing a client, maybe you and the missus cooked up a little incentive plan for him to stay.'

'That's sick!'

'The world's a twisted place, Mr Berne. No offense to you, but I don't know much about you as a person. For instance: I don't know if you're trustworthy. I need my name and my job description kept out of the public forum. I find people to be more closemouthed if they themselves have a secret they'd like kept. Are you getting my drift here, Mr Berne? Or do I need to be more direct?'

He looked incredulous. 'Are you threatening me?'

'I prefer to think we're reaching a mutual understanding on the importance of confidentiality. I'll keep your secret if you keep mine.'

'You don't work for General Fidelity,' he mused. 'Phil would have said something.'

'Phil?'

'Phil Wilshire. The claims adjuster. I know him. He would have said something about you.'

'He's talked to you about this case?'

'I want Jade caught once and for all,' he said, screwing up some self-righteous indignation. 'He should be run out of the business. If there's anything I can do, I will.'

'Anything?' I asked pointedly. 'I'd be careful with my mouth if I were you, Mr Berne,' I cautioned. 'A case could easily be made that you so hated Don Jade, you killed Stellar and you're trying to hang it on Jade in order to ruin him. There goes his career. There goes his position with Trey Hughes. You patch things up with Hughes, maybe you slip right back into the picture.'

Berne exploded. 'You asked me to come here so you could accuse me?! What are you? Crazy?'

'My, what a temper you have, Mr Berne,' I said calmly. 'You should try anger management counseling. Rage is bad for your health.'

He wanted to scream at me. I could see him almost choke on it.

'To answer your earlier question: No. I'm not crazy,' I said. 'I'm blunt. I have to cover all the bases, and I don't have time to screw around. I don't make friends doing it, but I get the answers I need.'

'Maybe you're not guilty of a thing, Mr Berne. Like I said, I don't know you. But in my experience, most crime is underpinned by three motives: money, sex, and/or jealousy. You score in all categories. So let's clear you right now, and I can concentrate on Jade. Where were you when Stellar died?'

'Home. In bed. With my wife.'

I took a last long drag on the cigarette and exhaled through half a smile. 'She's going to have to change her name to Alibi.'

Berne held up his hands. 'That's it. I'm through here. I came out of the goodness of my heart to help –'

'Put the violin away, Berne. We both know why you came here. You want Jade ruined. That's fine with me. I have my own agenda.'

'Which is what?'

'My client's interest. Maybe we can both end up with what we want. How long after Sallie Hughes died did Trey take his horses to Jade?' I asked.

'Two weeks.'

'And when did you hear Hughes had bought the property in Fairfields?'

'A month later.'

My head felt like it had been put in a vise. I didn't want to know the sordid details of Trey Hughes's life or Michael Berne's life or Don Jade's life. I wanted to find Erin Seabright. My luck she lived in Pandora's box.

I pulled her photograph out of the inside pocket of my jacket and handed it to Berne. 'Have you ever seen this girl?'

'No.'

'She worked for Jade up until last Sunday. She was a groom.'

Berne made a face. 'Grooms come and go. I have all I can do to keep track of my own.'

'This one vanished. Look again, please. You never saw her with Jade?'

'Jade always has women around him. I don't see the attraction, myself.'

'Jade has a reputation in that area, doesn't he? Sleeps with the help?'

'The help, the clients, other people's clients. There's nothing he won't stoop to.'

'That's what I'm afraid of, Mr Berne,' I said. I handed him a plain white card with a number printed on it. 'If you have anything useful to tell, please call this number and leave a message. Someone will contact you. Thank you for your time.'

Landry parked his car among the giant four-by-four trucks, BMWs, and Jaguars, and got out, already scanning the ground so he wouldn't step in anything. He'd grown up in a city. All he knew about horses was that they were huge and smelled bad.

The day was bright and warm. He squinted even through the lenses of his aviator shades as he surveyed the scene. It looked like a goddamn refugee camp – tents and animals everywhere. People on bicycles and motor scooters. Dust billowed in clouds as trucks rumbled past.

He saw Jade's sign, went into the tent, and asked the first person he saw where Mr Jade was. An Hispanic man with a pitchfork of shit in his hand nodded to the side of the tent and said, 'Outside.'

Landry went in the direction of the nod. Halfway between Jade's tent and the next a man in riding clothes was sipping from a Starbucks cup, listening impassively as an attractive blonde talked at him. The blonde seemed upset.

'Mr Jade?'

The pair turned and looked at him as he approached and showed them his badge.

'Detective Landry, Sheriff's Office. I'd like to ask you a few questions.'

'Oh, my God!' the blonde laughed, flashing a big smile. 'I knew you'd get caught! You never should have torn the tag off that mattress.' She turned the smile on Landry. 'Paris Montgomery. I'm Mr Jade's assistant trainer.'

Landry didn't smile back. Three hours' sleep didn't supply enough energy to waste on phony charm. He looked past the woman. 'You're Mr Jade?'

'What's this about?' Jade asked, striding into the tent and past Landry, trying to draw him back away from where passersby might see them.

'Are you aware of what happened here last night?' Landry asked. 'Some horses were set loose a couple of tents down the row.'

'Michael Berne's,' Paris Montgomery supplied. 'Of course we know. It's terrible. Something has to be done about security. Do you have any idea what these animals are worth?'

'Their weight in gold, apparently,' Landry said, bored hearing about it. Why in hell should a horse be worth a million bucks if it wasn't on a racetrack?

'He's going to come after you, Don,' she said to her boss. 'You know Michael will be telling everyone who'll listen you did the deed – or had it done.'

'Why would you say that, Ms Montgomery?' Landry asked.

'Because that's how Michael is: bitter and vindictive. He blames everything but his lack of talent on Don.'

Jade looked at her with hooded eyes. 'That's enough, Paris. Everyone knows Michael is jealous.'

'Of what?' Landry asked.

'Of Don,' the woman said. 'Don is everything Michael is not, and when Michael's clients see that and leave him, he blames Don. He probably turned those horses loose himself just so he could publicly blame Don.'

Landry kept his eyes on Jade. 'That must get old. You ever want to do something to shut him up?'

Jade's expression never changed. Calm, cool, controlled. 'I learned a long time ago to ignore people like Michael.'

'You should threaten to sue him for libel,' Paris said. 'Maybe that would shut him up.'

'Slander,' Jade corrected her. 'Slander is spoken. Libel is written.'

'Don't be such a prick,' Paris snapped. 'He's doing everything he can to ruin your reputation. And you walk around like you think you're in some kind of isolation bubble. You think he can't hurt you? You think he isn't in Trey's ear every chance he gets?'

'I can't stop Michael from spewing his venom, and I can't stop people from listening to him,' Jade said. 'I'm sure Detective Landry didn't come here to listen to us complain.'

'I'm not here about the horses either,' Landry said. 'A woman was assaulted in the attempt to stop whoever set them loose.'

Paris Montgomery's brown eyes widened in shock. 'What woman? Stella? Michael's wife? Was she hurt?'

'I understand there was a scene yesterday between you and Mr Berne, Mr Jade,' Landry said. 'Would you care to tell me where you were around two A.M.?'

'No, I would not,' Jade said curtly, going to stand beside the horse that was tied in an open stall. 'Now, if you'll excuse me, Detective, I have a horse to ride.'

'Maybe you'd rather discuss it at length at the Sheriff's Office,' Landry suggested. He didn't like being dismissed like a servant.

Jade gave him a look. Haughty – even through the shades. 'Maybe you'd rather take it up with my attorney.'

'Save your money and my time, Mr Jade. All you have to do is tell me where you were. It's only a trick question if you were here.'

'I was with a friend. We were not here.'

'Does this friend have a name?'

'Not as far as you're concerned.'

He tightened a strap on the saddle. The horse pinned its ears.

Landry looked for a place to jump in case the beast went nuts or something. It looked mean, like it would bite.

Jade unsnapped the ties that held the animal in the stall.

'Our conversation is over,' Jade announced. 'Unless you have something that connects me to what happened, other than the hearsay that Michael and I don't get along – and I know that you don't – I don't intend to speak to you again.'

He led the horse out of the stall and down the aisle. Landry pressed back against a wall, holding his breath – a good idea regardless, in this place. The smell of manure and horses and Christ-knew-what hung in the air like smog. When the horse was out of range to kick him, he followed.

'What about you, Ms Montgomery?'

The blonde caught a look from her boss, then turned to Landry. 'Ditto. What he said. With a friend.'

They went out into the sunshine and Jade mounted the horse. 'Paris, bring my coat and hat.'

'Will do.'

Jade didn't wait for her, but turned the horse and started down the road.

'With each other?' Landry asked, walking back into the tent with Montgomery.

'No. God no!' she said. 'I take orders from him all day. I'm not interested in taking them all night too.'

'He's got an attitude.'

'He's earned it. People don't cut him a lot of breaks.'

'Maybe that's because he doesn't deserve any.'

He followed her into a stall draped in green with an oriental carpet on the floor and framed art on the walls. She opened an antique wardrobe and pulled out an olive green jacket and a brown velvet-covered helmet.

'You don't know him,' she said.

'And you do. Who do you think he was with last night?'

She laughed and shook her head. 'I'm not privy to Don's private life. This is the first I heard he's seeing anyone.'

Then it seemed unlikely he was, Landry thought. From what he'd gathered, these horse people practically lived in each other's pockets. And proximity aside, they were all rich, or pretended to be rich; and the only thing rich people liked better than fucking each other over was gossiping.

'He's very discreet,' Montgomery said.

'I guess that's what's kept him out of prison: discretion. Your boss has toed the wrong side of the line a couple of times.'

'And has never been convicted of anything. Now, if you'll excuse me, I'd better get up to the schooling ring or he'll kill me.' She flashed the bright smile. 'Then you'll have a job to do.'

Landry followed her out of the tent. She climbed behind the wheel of a green golf cart with the Jade logo on the nose, folded the coat, and put it on the seat beside her. The helmet went into a basket behind the seat.

'What about you, Ms Montgomery? Does your mystery pal have a name?'

'Yes, he does,' she said, batting her eyes coyly. 'But I don't kiss and tell either, Detective. A girl could get a reputation that way.'

She started the golf cart and drove away, calling and waving to people as she went past the tents. Ms Popularity.

Landry stood with his hands on his hips for a moment, aware there was a girl watching him from inside the tent. He could see her from the corner of his eye: chubby, unkempt, tight T-shirt showing off curves and rolls better left to the imagination.

Landry wanted to get back in the car and leave. Estes was right: he didn't give a shit what these people did to each other. But he'd had to account for what had gone on in the office in the middle of the night with Estes demanding to see only him, and no paperwork being filed, and what a fucking nightmare. His lieutenant wouldn't take that Estes wasn't filing charges and leave it at that. He had to follow up.

He sighed and turned, drawing a bead on the girl.

'You work here?'

Her small eyes widened. She looked like she didn't know whether to shit her pants or have an orgasm. She nodded.

Landry went back inside, pulling his notebook out of his hip pocket. 'Name?'

'Jill Morone. M-O-R-O-N-E. I'm Mr Jade's head groom.'

'Uh-huh. And where were you last night around two?'

'In bed,' she said, smug with a secret she was dying to spill. 'With Mr Jade.'

12

The offices of Gryphon Development were located in a stylish stucco wanna-be-Spanish building on Greenview Shores across the street from the Polo Club's west entrance. I parked in a visitor's slot next to Bruce Seabright's Jaguar.

A poster-sized ad for Fairfields filled the front window of the office, Bruce Seabright's photo in the lower right-hand corner. He had the kind of smile that said: I'm a big prick, let me sell you something overpriced. Apparently that worked for some people.

The offices were professionally done to look expensive and inviting. Leather couches, mahogany tables. There were photographs of four men and three women on the wall, each with professional accolades etched in brass on the picture frames. Krystal Seabright was not among them.

The receptionist looked a lot like Krystal Seabright. Too much gold jewelry and hair spray. I wondered if this was how Krystal and Bruce had met. The boss and the secretary. Trite but true too much of the time.

'Elena Estes to see Mr Seabright,' I said. 'I have some questions about Fairfields.'

'Wonderful location,' she said, giving me a saleswoman-in-training smile. 'There are some spectacular barns going up in the development.'

'Yes, I know. I've been past.'

'The Hughes property,' she supplied with a look of near euphoria. 'Is that to die for?'

'I'm afraid so.'

She buzzed Seabright. A moment later, the door on the far side of the reception area opened and Bruce Seabright stepped out, hanging on to the doorknob. He wore a crisp tan linen suit with a regimental striped tie. Very formal for south Florida, land of loud aloha shirts and deck shoes.

'Ms Estes?'

'Yes. Thank you for seeing me.'

I walked past him into his office and took a position on the opposite side of the room, my back to a mahogany credenza.

'Have a seat,' he offered, going behind his desk. 'Can we get you anything? Coffee? Water?'

'No, thank you. Thank you for seeing me without an appointment. I'm sure you're a very busy man.'

'I'm glad to say I am.' He smiled the same smile from the photo on the Fairfields poster. 'Business is booming. Our little jewel of Wellington is being discovered. Property here is as hot as any in south Florida. And the land you're asking about is a prime example.'

'Actually, I'm not here to buy property, Mr Seabright.'

The smile faded to mild confusion. His features were small and sharp, like a ferret's. 'I don't understand. You said you had questions about Fairfields.'

'I do. I'm an investigator, Mr Seabright. I'm looking into an incident at the equestrian center that involves a client of yours: Trey Hughes.'

Seabright sat back in his chair, unhappy with this turn of events. 'Of course I know Trey Hughes. It's no secret he bought in Fairfields. But I certainly don't go around talking about clients, Ms Estes. I have my ethics.'

'I'm not after personal information. I'm more curious about the development. When the land came up for sale. When Mr Hughes bought his parcel.'

'That's a matter of public record,' Seabright said. 'You could go to the county offices and look it up.'

'I could, but I'm asking you.'

Suspicion had overtaken confusion. 'What's this about? What "incident" are you investigating?'

'Mr Hughes recently lost a very expensive horse. We have to cross all the *t*s and dot all the *i*s. You know.'

'What does the property have to do with this horse?'

'Routine background information. Was the owner in financial straits, et cetera. The property Mr Hughes is developing was expensive, and the development of the property itself –'

'Trey Hughes doesn't need money,' Seabright said, offended by the suggestion. 'Anyone will tell you he came into a large inheritance last year.'

'Before or after he bought the Fairfields property?'

'What difference does that make?' he asked irritably. 'He'd been interested in the property for some time. He purchased last spring.'

'After the death of his mother?'

'I don't like what you're implying, Ms Estes. And I'm not comfortable having this conversation.' He rose from his chair, a heartbeat from throwing me out.

'Are you aware your stepdaughter has been working for Mr Hughes's trainer?' I asked.

'Erin? What's Erin got to do with this?'

'I'd like an answer to that myself. But she seems to be missing.'

Seabright's level of agitation went up a notch. 'What are you – Who exactly do you work for?'

'That's confidential information, Mr Seabright. I have my ethics too,' I said. 'Did you have anything to do with Erin getting that job?'

'I don't see how that's any of your business.'

'Are you aware no one has had any contact with Erin in nearly a week?'

'Erin isn't close to the family.'

'Really? I was told she was quite close to your son.'

Bruce Seabright turned burgundy and jabbed a forefinger at me. 'I want your license number.'

I raised the one eyebrow I could and crossed my arms over my chest, sitting back against the credenza. 'Why are you so upset with me, Mr Seabright? I would think a father would be more concerned about his daughter than his client.'

'I'm not –' He caught himself and closed his mouth.

'Her father?' I supplied. 'You're not her father, therefore you don't have to be concerned about her?'

'I'm not concerned about Erin because Erin is responsible for herself. She's an adult.'

'She's eighteen.'

'And no longer lives under my roof. She does as she pleases.'

'That's been a problem, hasn't it? What pleases Erin doesn't please you. Teenage girls . . .' I shook my head as if in commiseration. 'Life is easier without her around, isn't it?'

I thought I could see his body vibrate with the anger he was trying to contain. He stared at me, burning my image into his brain so he could visualize and hate me when I'd gone.

'Get out of my office,' he said, his voice tight and low. 'And if I see you on this property again, I'm calling the police.'

I moved away from the credenza, taking my time. 'And tell them what, Mr Seabright? That I should be arrested for caring more about what's become of your stepdaughter than you do? I'm sure they'll find that to be very curious.'

Seabright yanked the door open and called out loudly to the receptionist: 'Doris, call the Sheriff's Office.'

Doris stared, bug-eyed.

'Ask for Detective Landry in Robbery/Homicide,' I suggested. 'Give him my name. He'll be happy to make an appearance.'

Seabright narrowed his eyes, trying to decide if I was bluffing.

I left the Gryphon offices at my own pace, got in Sean's car, and drove away – just in case Bruce Seabright wasn't.

13

'My God, El, you look like one of Robert Palmer's all-girl eighties' bands.'

I had put the top down for the drive home, hoping the air would clear my head. Instead, the sun had baked my brain, and the wind had swept my hair up into a 'do from a fashion shoot for the tragically hip. I wanted a drink and a nap in the sun by the pool, but knew I would allow myself neither.

Sean leaned down and kissed my cheek, then scolded me peevishly. 'You stole my car.'

'It matched my outfit.'

I got out of the Mercedes and handed him the keys. He was in breeches and boots, and a tight black T-shirt with the sleeves rolled up to show off biceps the size of grapefruits.

'Robert must be coming to teach you,' I said.

'Why do you say that?' he asked, irritated.

'The muscle shirt. Darling, you're really so transparent.'

'Well, meow, meow. Aren't we catty today?'

'A good beating will do that to me.'

'I'm sure you deserved it. Invite me next time. I'd love to watch.'

We walked together across the stable yard toward the guest house. Sean looked at me out of the corner of his eye and frowned.

'Are you all right?'

I gave the question undue weight and consideration, instead of tossing off the usual meaningless answer. What an odd moment to be struck by insight, I thought. But I stopped and acknowledged it within myself.

'Yes,' I said. 'I am.'

As tangled and trying as this case was becoming, as unwilling a participant as I'd been, it felt good to use the old skills. It felt good to be necessary to something.

'Good,' he said. 'Now go powder your nose and transform yourself again, Cinderella. Your alter ego has company coming.'

'Who?'

'Van Zandt.' He spat the name out as if it were a bitter thing with a pit in it. 'Don't say I never sacrificed for you.'

'My own mother wouldn't do as much.'

'You'd better believe that, honey. Your mother wouldn't let that slimebag in the service entrance. You've got twenty minutes to curtain.'

I took a shower and dressed in one of the outfits I had purchased at the show grounds: a jewel-red wraparound skirt made from an Indian sari, and a yellow linen blouse. An armload of bracelets, a pair of thick-soled sandals, and tortoiseshell shades, and I was Elle Stevens, Dilettante.

Van Zandt had just arrived as I cut through the stables to the parking area. He was dressed to impress in the uniform of the Palm Beach patriarch: pink shirt, tan slacks, blue blazer, his signature ascot at his throat.

As he spotted me, he came toward me with his arms outstretched. My long-lost old friend.

'Elle!'

'Z.'

I suffered through his cheek-kissing routine, bracing my hands against his chest so he couldn't embrace me.

'Three times,' he reminded me, stepping back. 'Like the Dutch.'

'Sounds to me like an excuse to grope,' I said with half a smile. 'Clever lech. What other cultures do you steal from in order to cop a feel in the guise of good manners?'

He smiled the smarmy/suave smile. 'That all depends on the lady.'

'And I thought you'd come to see my horses,' Sean said. 'Am I just a beard?'

Van Zandt looked at him, puzzled. 'Are you a beard? You don't even have a beard.'

'It's a figure of speech, Z.,' I explained. 'You have to get used to Sean. His mother sent him to drama camp as a child. He can't help himself.'

'Ah. An actor!'

'Aren't we all?' Sean said innocently. 'I've asked my girl to saddle Tino – the gelding I was telling you about. I'd like to get eighty thousand for him. He's talented, but I've got too many that are. If you have any clients looking . . .'

'I may have,' Van Zandt said. 'I've brought my camera. I'll make a video to send to a client I have coming down from Virginia. And when you're ready to look for something new, I'll be happy to show you the best horses in Europe. Bring Elle along with you. We'll have a wonderful time.'

He looked at me, taking in the skirt. 'You are not riding today, Elle?'

'Too much fun last night,' I said. 'I'm recuperating. Sean and I went to the Pinkeye Ball.'

'Elle can't resist a worthy cause,' Sean said. 'Or a glass of champagne.'

'You missed all the excitement at the show grounds,' Van Zandt said, pleased to have the gossip. 'Horses being turned loose. Someone was attacked. Unbelievable.'

'And you were there?' I asked. 'In the dead of night? Might the police want to speak with you?'

'Of course I wasn't there,' he said irritably. 'How could you think I would do a thing like that?'

I shrugged. 'Z., I have no idea what you might or might not do. I do know you can't take a joke. Really, these moods of yours are getting tedious, and I've only known you two days,' I said, letting my irritation show. 'You expect me to want to ride around Europe in a car with you and your multiple personalities? I think I'd rather stay home and hit my thumb with a hammer over and over.'

He splayed a hand across his chest as if I'd wounded him. 'I am a sensitive person. I want only good things for everyone. I don't go around accusing people for a joke.'

'Don't take it personally, Tomas,' Sean told him as we neared the barn. 'Elle sharpens her tongue on a whetstone every night before bed.'

'All the better to fillet you with, my dear.'

Van Zandt looked at me, pouting. 'It's not a sharp tongue that attracts a husband.'

'Husband? Why would I want one of those?' I asked. 'Had one once. Threw him back.'

Sean grinned. 'Why be a wife when you can have a life?'

'Ex is best,' I agreed. 'Half of the money, none of the headache.'

Van Zandt wagged a finger at me, trying to rally a sense of humor. 'You need taming, Miss Tigress. You would then sing a different song.'

'Bring a whip and a chair for that job,' Sean suggested.

Van Zandt looked like he'd already imagined that and then some. He smiled again. 'I know how best to treat a lady.'

From the corner of my eye I saw Irina coming. A flash of long bare legs and clunky hiking boots. I saw she had something in her hand. She looked angry, and I assumed – wrongly – angry with Sean for being late or upsetting her schedule, or one of the fifty other transgressions that regularly put Irina in a snit. She stopped five feet from us, shouted something nasty in Russian, and flung the thing in her hand.

Van Zandt cried out in surprise, just managing to bring an arm up and deflect the flight path of the steel horseshoe before it struck him in the head.

Sean jumped back in horror. 'Irina!'

The groom launched herself at Van Zandt like a missile, screaming: 'Pig! You filthy pig!'

I stood, flat-footed, watching in amazement as Irina pummeled him with her fists. She was slender as a reed, but strong as a teamster, the muscles in her arms clearly delineated. Van Zandt staggered backward and sideways, trying to shake her off, but she clung to him like a limpet.

'Crazy bitch!' he shouted. 'Get her off! Get her off!'

Sean jumped to, grabbing hold of the girl's blond ponytail with one hand and catching a wildly swinging arm with the other. 'Irina! Stop it!'

'Son of bitch! Stinking son of bitch!' she shouted as Sean peeled her off Van Zandt and pulled her backward down the aisle. She rattled off another slur in Russian and spat violently at the Belgian.

'She's crazy!' Van Zandt shouted, wiping blood from his lip. 'She should be locked up!'

'I take it you two have met,' I said dryly.

'I've never seen her before in my life! Crazy Russian cunt!'

Irina lunged against Sean's hold on her, the look on her face venomous with hate. 'Next time I tear out your throat and shit in your lungs, cur! For Sasha!'

Van Zandt backed away looking stricken, his perfect hair standing up in all directions.

'Irina!' Sean shouted, appalled.

'Why don't we ladies retire for a moment?' I suggested, taking Irina by the arm and steering her toward the lounge.

Irina snarled and made a rude gesture in the direction of Van Zandt, but came with me.

We went into the lounge, a room paneled in mahogany and fitted with a bar and leather-upholstered chairs. Irina paced, muttering expletives. I went behind the bar, took a bottle of Stoli from the freezer, and poured three fingers in a heavy crystal tumbler.

'Here's to you, girlfriend.' I raised the glass in a toast, then handed it to her. She drank it like water. 'I'm sure he had it coming, but would you care to fill me in?'

She fumed and called Van Zandt more names, then heaved a sigh and calmed herself. Just like that: instant composure. 'That is not a nice man,' she said.

'The guy who delivers feed is not a nice man, but you've never gone to such an effort for him. Who is Sasha?'

She took a cigarette from a box on the bar, lit it, and took a long, deep drag. She exhaled slowly, her face tilted at an elegant angle. She might have been Greta Garbo in a past life.

'Sasha Kulak. A friend from Russia. She went to work for that pig in Belgium because he made all kinds of big promises. He would pay her and let her ride good horses and they would be like partners and he would make her a star in the horse shows. Stinking liar. All he wanted was to have her. He got her to Belgium and thought he owned her. He thought she should fuck him and be grateful. She said no. She was a beautiful girl. Why would she fuck an old man like him?'

'Why would anyone?'

'He was a monster to her. He kept her in a gypsy camper with no heat. She had to use the toilet in his stables and he spied on her through holes in the walls.'

'Why didn't she leave?'

'She was eighteen and she was afraid. She was in a foreign country where she knew no one and could not speak their stupid language. She didn't know what to do.'

'She couldn't go to the police?'

Irina looked at me like I was stupid.

'Finally, she went to bed with him,' she said, shrugging in that way Americans can never mimic. 'Still he was terrible to her. He gave her herpes. After a while she stole some money and ran away when they were looking for horses in Poland.

'He called her family and made threats because of the money. He told them lies about Sasha. When she came home, her father threw her out into the street.'

'He believed Van Zandt over his daughter?'

She made a face. 'They are two alike, those men.'

'And what became of Sasha?'

'She killed herself.'

'Oh, God, Irina. I'm sorry.'

'Sasha was fragile, like a glass doll.' She smoked a little more, contemplating. 'If a man did this thing to me, I would not kill myself. I would cut off his penis and feed it to the pigs.'

'Very effective.'

'Then I would kill him.'

'A little luckier in your aim with that horseshoe and you might have,' I said.

Irina poured another three fingers of the Stoli and sipped at it. I thought about Van Zandt abusing his authority over a young girl that way. Most adults would have had a difficult time dealing with his mercurial temperament. An eighteen-year-old girl would have been in way over her head. He deserved exactly what Irina had imagined for him.

'I'd like to say I'll hold him down while you kick him,' I said. 'But Sean will expect you to apologize, Irina.'

'He can kiss my Russian ass.'

'You needn't be sincere.'

She thought about that. If it had been me, I would still have told Sean to kiss my ass. But I couldn't afford to alienate Van Zandt, especially not in the light of what Irina had told me. Her friend Sasha was dead. Maybe Erin Seabright was still alive.

'Come on,' I said before she could have a chance to set her mind against it. 'Get it over with. You can kill him on your day off.'

I led the way out. Sean and Van Zandt were standing on the grass near the mounting block. Van Zandt was still red in the face, rubbing his arm where the horseshoe had struck him.

Irina unhooked Tino from the grooming stall and led the gelding out.

'Sean, I apologize for my outburst,' Irina said, handing him the reins. 'I am sorry to have embarrassed you.' She looked at Van Zandt with cold disdain. 'I apologize for attacking you on Mr Avadon's property.'

Van Zandt said nothing, just stood there scowling at her. The girl looked at me as if to say, *See what a swine he is?* She walked away, climbed the stairs to the gazebo at the end of the arena, and draped herself on a chair.

'The czarina,' I said.

Van Zandt sulked. 'I should call the police.'

'But I don't think you will.'

'She should be locked up.'

'Like you locked up her friend?' I asked innocently, wishing I could stick a knife between his ribs.

His mouth was trembling as if he might cry. 'You would believe her lies about me? I have done nothing wrong. I gave that girl a job, a place to live –'

Herpes . . .

'She stole from me,' he went on. 'I treated her like a daughter, and she stole from me and fucked me in the ass, telling lies about me!'

The victim yet again. Everyone was against him. His motives were always pure. I didn't point out to him that in America if a man treated his daughter the way he had treated Sasha, he would go to prison and come out a registered sex offender.

'How ungrateful,' I said.

'You believe her,' he accused.

'I believe in minding my own business, and your sex life is not and never will be my business.'

He crossed his arms and pouted, staring down at his tasseled loafers. Sean had mounted and was in the arena warming up.

'Forget about Irina,' I said. 'She's only hired help. Who cares what grooms have to say? They should be like good children: seen and not heard.'

'These girls should know their place,' he muttered darkly as he unzipped his camera case and took out a video camera. 'Or be put in it.'

A shiver ran down my spine like a cold, bony finger.

As we stood and watched Sean work the horse, I knew neither of us had our mind on the quality of the animal. Van Zandt's mood had gone to a very dark place. He had to be thinking about damage control to his reputation, probably believing Irina – and maybe I – would spread the Sasha story around Wellington and he would lose clients. Or maybe he was simply fantasizing about strangling Irina with his bare hands, the bones in her throat cracking like small dry twigs. Irina sat in the gazebo smoking, one long leg swinging over the arm of the big wicker chair, never taking her glare off Van Zandt.

My thoughts were running in another direction. I wondered if Tomas Van Zandt had thought Erin Seabright should be glad to accept his advances, or if he had 'put her in her place'. I thought about my feeling that Erin had dumped Chad, and wondered if Van Zandt or someone like him might have made her promises, then broken them in the most terrible way.

And I wondered again if all these terrible possibilities had been made possible by Bruce Seabright.

Erin hadn't fit his idea of the perfect daughter, and now she was out of his way. If she turned up dead, would he feel a moment's guilt? If she never turned up at all, would he feel a second's responsibility? Or would he be pleased for a job well done?

I thought about my own father and wondered if he would have been relieved to have his ungrateful daughter simply disappear. Probably. I had loudly opposed everything he was, everything he stood for. I'd thumbed my nose at him and taken up a profession putting away the people he defended in court, the people who provided for the lifestyle I'd grown up in. Then again, maybe I *had* disappeared for him. I hadn't seen or spoken to him in years. For all I knew, I had ceased to exist in his mind.

At least my father hadn't set me up for doom. That had been my own doing entirely.

If Bruce had set Erin up with Trey Hughes, and Hughes had set her up with Jade, and via Jade she had been exposed to Van Zandt, Erin had never really had any say in her destiny. The irony was that she had thought she was gaining independence, taking control of her life. But the longer she was missing, the longer the odds were she would come out of this with a life at all.

By the time Sean had finished showing Tino, Robert Dover had arrived to teach him, leaving me to see Van Zandt off the property.

'Do you think your client from Virginia will be interested?' I asked.

'Lorinda Carlton?' He gave the Continental shrug. 'I will tell her to be, so she will be,' he said. The word of Van Zandt, amen. 'She's not a talented rider, but she has a hundred thousand dollars to spend. All I have to do is convince her this horse is her destiny and everyone will live happily ever after.'

Except the woman who bought a horse she couldn't handle. Then Van Zandt would convince her to sell that one and buy another. He would make money on both deals, and the cycle would begin again.

'You shouldn't reveal your trade secrets,' I said. 'You'll disillusion me.'

'You are a very smart woman, Elle. You know the ways of this horse world. It's a hard business. People are not always nice. But I take care of my clients. I am loyal to them and I expect them to be loyal to me. Lorinda trusts me. She gives me the use of her town house while I am here for the season. See how grateful my friends are to me?'

'That's one word for it,' I said dryly.

And he would blithely betray the trust of his grateful friend so he could foster a more lucrative relationship with Sean Avadon. He told me without batting an eye, as if it were nothing to him, and in the next breath he spoke of loyalty as if he were the poster boy for personal virtue.

'Are you free for dinner, Elle?' he asked. 'I'll take you to The Players. We can talk about what kind of horse I want for you.'

I found the suggestion revolting. I was exhausted and in pain and fed up to my eyeballs with this nauseating character and his bipolar mood swings. I wanted to do what Irina had done, jump on him and pummel him and call him every vile name I could think of. Instead, I said, 'Not tonight, Z. I have a headache.'

He looked hurt and angry again. 'I am not a monster. I have integrity. I have character. People in this business, they get angry, they spread rumors. You should know better than to believe them.'

I held up a hand. 'Stop. Just stop, will you? Jesus. I'm tired. My head hurts. I want to spend my evening in the jacuzzi with no one talking at me. As impossible as this might be for you to grasp, it's not about you.'

He didn't believe that, but he changed tack at least. He stood straighter and nodded to himself. 'You will see, Elle Stevens. I will do for you. I will make you a champion,' he said. 'You will see what kind of man I am.'

In the end, that was the one prophecy he made that actually came true.

14

Jill stood in front of the cheap full-length mirror wearing nothing but makeup, a black lace bra, and a thong. She turned this way and that, practicing her various looks. Shy, coy, sexy. She liked sexy best. It went with the bra.

The bra was too small by a couple of sizes and dug into her sides, but it made her boobs look all the bigger, which she thought was a good thing. Like the women in *Hustler,* her tits seemed to swell up out of the cups. She could easily imagine Jade burying his face in her cleavage. The idea gave her a tingle between her legs, which drew her attention to the thong.

It also was too small for her, the skinny little straps cutting into the fat on her hips. Pubic hair sprouted out on either side of the scrap of black lace at the front. She twisted around and looked at her butt, bare and white, wide and dimpled. She didn't like the way the thong felt going up her crack, but she thought she'd better get used to it. The thong was sexy. Men went for a thong. She just wished that bitch Erin hadn't been so fucking skinny. Maybe if the thong was for a normal-sized person it wouldn't be so uncomfortable.

Oh, well. It was free. And it kind of turned her on that it belonged to someone else. She was taking Erin's place – in the barn, in the world. With Erin gone, Jill could be the flirty one. Jill could be the clever one.

But she would still be in the shadow of Paris Montgomery.

That cunt.

Jill scowled at the reminder. It was not a pretty reflection that looked back at her.

She hated Paris. She hated her smile, hated her big eyes, hated her blond hair. She hated Paris more than she had hated Erin. And she had hated the two of them together more than anything. Together they had been like the popular girls in school: too cool to be friends with someone like Jill, full of private jokes and catty looks. At least she didn't have to put up with that shit anymore. But there was still Paris.

Men fell all over themselves for Paris. She could get anybody to do anything for her. Nobody seemed to see that she was just a big phony. Everyone thought she was so funny and sweet and nice. She wasn't nice at all. When people weren't looking she was bossy and bitchy and mean. She was always making snide remarks about Jill eating too much and Jill needing to exercise and Jill not knowing how to dress.

Jill looked at herself head to toe in the mirror and suddenly saw exactly what Paris Montgomery saw. Not a sexy woman in sexy lingerie, but a fat face with small, piggy eyes and a sour, downturned mouth; arms inflated with fat; fat legs with dimpled knees; a body she hated so much she often fantasized taking a knife and slicing off big slabs of it. Ugly and pathetic in her stolen, too-small underwear.

Tears squeezed out of her eyes and her face turned mottled red. It wasn't her fault she was fat. Her mother had let that happen when she was a kid. So she couldn't help it now that she ate the wrong things. And it wasn't her fault she didn't exercise. She was tired at the end of the day — never mind that bitch Paris was always accusing her of not working hard enough.

Why would she work any harder for Paris? Paris didn't give her any incentive to work hard, so if she wasn't getting as much done as Paris wanted, it was Paris's fault. And it wasn't her fault she didn't have nice clothes. She didn't get paid enough to buy nice things. She had to shoplift to get nice things. And she deserved them as much as anybody — more, really, considering people were so mean to her.

Well, she would show Paris Montgomery, she thought, digging through the pile of clothes tangled in the sheets of the unmade bed. She was going to take Paris Montgomery's place, just like she'd taken Erin's place.

Jill knew she could be just as good a rider as Paris if only someone would give her the chance. She had never had a good enough horse, that was all. Her father had bought her a crummy, cheap Appaloosa to ride. How was she supposed to get anywhere in the jumping world on that? She had once written a letter to her mother's brother to see if he wouldn't buy her a real horse. She couldn't see why he wouldn't. He was rich, after all. What was seventy or eighty thousand dollars to him? But she had never heard a thing from him. Cheap bastard.

She'd show him too. She'd show everybody. She was going to be rich, and she was going to ride the best horses and go to the Olympics. She had it all planned. All she needed was a break, and she knew right where she was going to get it.

She pulled a see-through white stretch lace blouse out of the pile of clothes Erin had left behind. Jill had claimed the stuff for herself. Why not? It wasn't even stealing if the other person just left it. She struggled into the top. Even with the stretch, the front gapped open between the buttons. She undid the top three, showing cleavage and black bra. That helped. And it was sexy. It was just the kind of thing Britney Spears wore all the time. That was why Erin had bought it. Erin always dressed that way: crop tops and hip huggers. And guys had always had their eyes on her — including Don.

Jill rummaged through another pile. She came up with a purple stretch miniskirt she'd stolen from Wal-Mart. It had been on clearance, anyway. The store wasn't out that much. She stepped into it and wriggled and pushed and pulled until she had it in place. She had a serious panty line from the too-small thong, but she figured that was a good thing. It was like advertising.

A pair of big hoop earrings and a necklace from the pile of jewelry that had belonged to Erin, and the bangle bracelets she'd lifted from Bloomingdale's, and she was set. She squeezed her feet into a pair of platform sandals, grabbed her purse, and left the apartment. She was going to show everybody, and she was going to start tonight.

Landry sat at his desk feeling like an asshole, scrolling through pages on the computer screen. Friday night, and this was what he had going on in his life.

It was Estes's fault, he thought, scowling. He had let that become his mantra for the day. Like a thorn, she'd gotten under his skin to irritate him. Because of her he was sitting at his desk reading old newspaper stories.

The squad room was mostly empty. A couple of the night-shift guys were doing paperwork. Landry's shift was long over, and the other four guys he worked with had gone home to girlfriends or wives and kids, or were sitting in the usual watering hole drinking and bitching, as cops are wont to do.

Landry sat at his desk trying to dig something up on the horse people. Neither Jade nor his assistant had a criminal record. The groom who was allegedly fucking Jade had been picked up a couple of times for shoplifting, and once on a DUI. She had struck him as trouble, and he'd been right about that. He didn't believe she'd been with Jade Thursday night, but she'd felt compelled to give the guy an alibi just the same. Landry had to wonder why.

Did the girl know Jade had been involved in letting Michael Berne's horses loose? Had she done the job herself, and by giving Jade an alibi, given herself one as well? Maybe Jade had put her up to it. He seemed too sharp to risk pulling a stunt like that himself. If the girl got caught, he could always deny knowledge of what she'd been up to. He could say it was a misguided attempt to gain his approval.

Michael Berne certainly believed Jade had been behind the incident. Landry had interviewed him in the afternoon, and he'd thought Berne was going to cry or choke as he blamed Don Jade for all the problems in his life. What had Paris Montgomery said? That Berne blamed Jade for everything except his own lack of talent. Berne seemed to think Jade was the Antichrist, responsible for all evil in the horse business.

Maybe he wasn't all wrong.

Estes had told Landry about Jade's past the first time she'd come in, the schemes to kill horses for the insurance money. No one had touched the guy for any of that. Jade had slipped out from under it all like a greased snake.

Insurance fraud, killing horses – what might Erin Seabright know about any of that, Landry wondered. And why wasn't she around to ask?

He had put a call in that afternoon to the Ocala authorities to see if they could locate the girl up there, and he had put out an alert for all law enforcement officers in Palm Beach County to be on the lookout for her car. She had probably split town for a new job or a new boyfriend, but in case she hadn't, it wouldn't hurt to cover the bases.

And if anyone asked him what the hell he was doing, he would say it was all Estes's fault, he thought irritably.

He sipped his coffee and glanced over his shoulder. The night guys were still into their paperwork. Landry tapped a couple of keys and brought up a newspaper account of the Golam brothers' bust, two years prior. He had read it earlier in the day, knew what was in it, knew exactly the paragraph his eyes would go to: the paragraph that described narcotics detective Elena Estes hanging on the door of Billy Golam's truck, then falling beneath it. She had been dragged fifty yards down Okeechobee Boulevard, and was hospitalized in critical condition at the time the story had been written.

He wondered what she must have gone through since that day, how many weeks, months she'd lain in a hospital bed. He wondered what had possessed her to jump on that truck and try to wrestle control of it from Billy Golam.

Narcs. Cowboys, every last one of them.

Two years had passed. He wondered what she'd been doing all that time, and why she'd come out of the shadows for this case. He wondered why her life was crossing paths with his.

He sure as hell didn't want the trouble that came with her. But there it was. He'd taken the bait. He was on the case now.

It was all Estes's fault.

Jill ran out the front door of The Players, huffing and hiccuping, fat tears spilling down her cheeks with a dirty stream of black mascara. She swiped the back of her hand under her running nose, then scraped a stringy strand of hair back out of her eyes.

The valets stood off to the side, staring at her, saying nothing. They didn't ask if they could get her car, because they knew by looking at her, she wouldn't have a car worth letting them park. They parked cars for beautiful people, rich people, thin people.

'What are you looking at?' Jill snapped. They looked at each other, smirking. 'Fuck you!' she shouted and ran, crying, across the parking lot, falling off one platform sandal and turning her ankle. Stumbling, she dropped the beaded handbag she'd stolen at Neiman Marcus, and the contents spewed out of it across the pavement.

'Goddammit!' Crawling on her hands and knees, she broke a fingernail as she scraped at a tube of lipstick and a pack of condoms. 'Fuck! Fuck!'

Spittle and tears and snot ran from her face onto the concrete. Jill folded herself over into a ball and sobbed, a wrenching, ugly noise. She was ugly.

Her clothes were ugly. Even her crying was ugly. Pain swelled inside her like a blister and burst with another wave of tears.

Why? She had asked the question a million times in her life. Why did she have to be the fat one, the ugly one; the one nobody liked, much less loved? It wasn't fair. Why was she supposed to have to work hard to change herself when bitches like Erin and Paris just had it all?

She wiped her face on the sleeve of the white lace blouse, gathered her stuff together, and struggled to her feet. An elegant older couple walking away from a Jaguar stared at her with something like horror. Jill gave them the finger. The woman gasped and the man put his arm around her protectively and hustled her toward the building.

Jill opened her car and flung her purse and the things that had come out of it in the direction of the passenger's seat. She flung herself behind the wheel, slammed the door, and burst into tears again. She pounded her fists on the wheel, then against the window, then hit the horn by accident and startled at the blast of sound.

Her big plan. Her big seduction. What a fucking joke she was.

She'd gone into Players, knowing Jade would be there, thinking he would invite her for a drink, and she could flirt with him and let him know how she'd helped him out with that cop. He was supposed to have been thankful and impressed with her quick thinking, and grateful for her loyalty. And they were supposed to have ended up at his place, where he would fuck her brains out. Phase one in her plan to get rid of Paris.

But everything had gone wrong, because she could never get a break. The whole stupid world was against her. Jade hadn't arrived yet when she got there, and the maître d' had wanted to throw her out. She could tell by the way he looked her up and down, like he thought she was some cheap hooker or something. He hadn't believed her when she told him she was meeting someone. And the waitress and the bartender had put their heads together and snickered at her as she sat at a table, waiting like an idiot drinking Diet Coke because they wouldn't go for her fake ID and serve her booze. Then that creep Van Zandt had showed up, half-drunk, and invited himself to sit with her.

What a jerk. All the mean, rotten things she'd heard him say about her, and he thought he could just suddenly pretend to be nice to her and charm his way into her pants. He'd never taken his eyes off her cleavage for the first fifteen minutes. And when she told him she was waiting for someone else, he had the nerve to be offended. Like she'd ever want to have sex with an old guy like him. So what he'd slipped her a couple of drinks? That didn't mean she owed him a blowjob, which was what he had wanted. If she was going to suck dick tonight, it wasn't going to be his.

And then Jade had finally walked in. And he'd looked at her with such disgust, she had wanted to shatter like a piece of glass. His angry words rang in her ears as if he'd screamed them at her, when in reality he'd asked her out into a quiet hall and had never raised his voice above a near whisper.

'What were you thinking, coming in here dressed like that?' he demanded. 'You're my employee. The things you do in public reflect on me.'

'But I was just –'

'I don't want the words *street whore* associated with my barn.'

Jill had gasped as if he'd slapped her. That was when Michael Berne had come into the hall. She had seen him from the corner of her eye, pretending to make a phone call, watching them.

'I see clients here,' Jade went on. 'I conduct business here.'

'I j-just w-wanted to see you,' she'd said, her breath hitching in her throat as tears welled up. 'I w-wanted to tell you about –'

'What's the matter with you? Thinking you can come here and interrupt my evening?'

'B-but I have t-to tell you – I know about Stellar –'

'If you need to speak with me about something, we'll do it at the barn during business hours.'

'B-but –'

'Is everything all right here?' Michael Berne asked, butting in like it was any of his business, the skinny freckled dork.

'This doesn't concern you, Michael,' Jade said.

'The young lady seems upset.' But when he looked at her, Jill had known he didn't care whether or not she was upset. He had looked at her the same way every other man had looked at her tonight – like she was selling it and she ought to be cutting her prices.

She had glared up at him through a wavy sheen of tears and said, 'Butt out! We don't need you around here or anywhere else!'

Berne had moved away. 'You ought to take your personal business somewhere private, Jade,' he said like a prissy fruit. 'This is really unprofessional.'

Jade had waited until Berne was out of sight, then turned on her again, angrier than before. 'Get out of here. Get out of here before you embarrass me any more than you already have. We'll talk about this tomorrow, first thing in the morning. If I can stand the sight of you.'

He might as well have cut her with a knife. The pain had gone as deep inside her as if he had.

Fuck him, Jill thought now. Don Jade was her boss, not her father. He couldn't tell her how to dress or where she could and couldn't go. He couldn't call her a whore and get away with it.

All the hard work she did for Don Jade, and this was the way he treated her. She would have been his partner – in bed and out. She would have been loyal to him. She would have done anything for him. But he didn't deserve her or her loyalty and devotion. He deserved to have people betray him and stab him in the back. He deserved whatever happened to him.

An idea slowly began to take shape in Jill's mind as she sat there in her car. She didn't have to put up with being treated like dirt. She didn't have to stand for being called names. She could get a job with any stable she wanted. Fuck Don Jade.

She drove out of the parking lot and took a left on South Shore, heading for the equestrian center, paying no attention to the car that pulled out behind her.

15

Molly could hear Bruce and her mother arguing. She couldn't make out all the words, but the tone was unmistakable. She lay on the floor of her bedroom, near the air-conditioning duct. Her room was right above Bruce's office, where he often summoned her mother or Chad or Erin to shout at them for their latest sin against him. Molly had learned long ago to make herself inconspicuous to the men her mother dated. She made no exception for Bruce, even if he was technically now her father. She didn't think of him that way. She thought of him as someone whose house she happened to live in.

The argument was about Erin. Her sister's name had stood out in the rise and fall of the conversation. Something was definitely up. Her mother had already been upset when Molly had gotten home from school, pacing, nervous, darting out the back door to smoke one cigarette after another. Dinner had been delivered from Domino's. Krystal hadn't eaten any of it. Chad had bolted down enough to choke a wolf, then beat it out of the house before Bruce got home.

And when Bruce walked in the door, Krystal had immediately asked to speak to him in his office.

Molly's stomach was churning with worry. She had made out Erin's name and had heard the word 'police'. Her mother's tone had gone from urgent to angry to hysterical to tears. Bruce just sounded angry. And intermingled with the voices was a mechanical sound, like the VCR going on, going off, rewinding. Molly couldn't imagine what it meant. Maybe Krystal had found a porno tape in Chad's room. But then, why had she heard Erin's name, not Chad's?

Heart pounding, Molly left her room and crept down the back staircase. The house was dark except for the light coming from the office. She made her way down the hall on her tiptoes, holding her breath. If the office door opened, she was caught. The family room was adjacent to the office. If she could just slip in there . . . She ducked into the corner behind the ficus tree and crouched down against the wall.

'We are not calling the police, Krystal,' Bruce said. 'First of all, I don't believe it's real. It's some kind of hoax –'

'But what if it isn't?'

'They said don't call the police.'

'My God, I can't believe this is happening,' Krystal said, her voice trembling.

'I don't know why not,' Bruce said. 'She's your daughter. You know she's never been anything but trouble.'

'How can you talk that way?'

'Easily. It's true.'

'You can be so fucking cruel. I don't believe it. Ouch! You're hurting me! Bruce!'

Tears welled up in Molly's eyes. She hugged her knees to her chest and tried not to shake.

'I've asked you not to use foul language, Krystal. You can't be a lady with the mouth of a sailor.'

Krystal rushed to apologize. 'I'm sorry. I'm sorry. I'm upset. I didn't mean it.'

'You're irrational. You have to get control of yourself, Krystal. Think this through logically. The tape says no police.'

'What will we do?'

'I'll handle it.'

'But I think —'

'Has anyone asked you to think?'

'No.'

'Who makes the decisions in this house, Krystal?'

Krystal drew a shaky breath. 'The person who is best equipped to make them.'

'And who is that person?'

'You.'

'Thank you. Now leave it to me. Go take a pill and go to bed. There's nothing we can do tonight.'

'Yes,' Krystal said softly. 'I think I will do that.'

Molly knew from past experience her mother would take more than one pill, and she would wash it down with vodka. She would retreat into her own little world and pretend everything in her life was lovely and fine. Molly, meanwhile, felt sick to her stomach. Everything she'd heard frightened her. What had Erin done now? Something terrible, if Krystal wanted to call the police.

'I'm going for a drive to clear my head,' Bruce said. 'I had a terrible day. Now this.'

Molly held very still, praying neither of them would come into the family room for any reason. She heard her mother's heels on the tile in the hall. Krystal always went up the main staircase because it was beautiful and she had always dreamed of living in a beautiful house. Bruce walked past the family room on his way to the kitchen. Molly stayed still until she heard him go out the door to the garage. She waited to hear his car start and for the garage door to close, and then she waited a little longer. When she was sure he had gone, she crept out of her hiding place and went into his office.

No one was allowed in Bruce's office when Bruce wasn't there. He expected everyone to respect his privacy even though he regularly invaded everyone else's. This was his house, and he never let any of them forget it.

Molly turned on the desk lamp and looked around at the bookshelves and the walls covered with photographs of Bruce shaking hands with important people, with Bruce's awards for this and that having to do with his job and with his service to the community. Everything in the room was placed exactly as Bruce wanted it, and he would know if one little thing got moved a fraction of an inch.

Molly checked over her shoulder as she picked up the remote for the television and VCR. She hit the play button and waited, so nervous she was shaking all over.

The movie started without any credits or titles or anything. A girl standing by a gate on a back road. Erin. Molly watched in horror as a van pulled up and a man in a mask jumped out and grabbed her and threw her into the van.

A strange mechanical voice came out of the speakers: 'We have your daughter. Don't call the police –'

Tears flooding her glasses, Molly hit the stop button, hit eject, scrambled onto a chair, and reached up to snag the video out of the machine. She wanted to cry out loud. She wanted to throw up. She did neither.

Clutching the tape, she ran through the house to the laundry room and grabbed her jacket off the hook. She wrapped the tape in the jacket and tied the jacket around her waist. She was shaking so badly, she didn't know if she would have the strength to do what she had to. All she knew was that she had to try.

She opened the garage door, climbed on her bike, and took off, pedaling as hard as she could down the street and into the night.

16

Despite the fact that every law enforcement agent in Palm Beach County hated me, I did still have contacts in the profession. I called an FBI agent I knew from the field office in West Palm. Armedgian and another agent had coordinated with PBSO narcotics on a case that involved heroin dealers in West Palm Beach and a connection in France. Armedgian had handled all the work between our respective offices, the FBI liaison in Paris, French authorities, and Interpol. The case had lasted six months, and in that time, Armedgian had become not only a contact, but a friend – the kind of friend I could call and ask for information.

I called him at the end of the day and reintroduced myself. *It's Estes. Remember me? We'll always have Paris . . .* Of course, he said, though there was a pause first, and a tension in his voice.

I asked him to get me what he could on Tomas Van Zandt and World Horse Sales from Interpol. Again the pause. Was I back on the job? He thought I'd left the profession, after . . . well, after . . .

I explained to him I was helping out a friend who had gotten mixed up with this character in a business deal, and I'd heard the guy was a crook. I wasn't asking for anything but to find out if he had a record. That didn't seem too much, did it?

Armedgian made the customary noises of complaint and fear of discovery and censure. Federal agents were the kids in school who really did worry that going to the lavatory without a hall pass would put a black mark in their permanent records that would ruin their lives. But in the end he agreed to do the deed.

Tomas Van Zandt hadn't become what he was overnight. It wasn't unreasonable to assume if he had terrorized one girl, he had terrorized others. Maybe one of them had dared to go to the authorities. Then again, part of his control over Sasha Kulak had been the fact that she was a stranger in a strange land, and probably there illegally.

It made me furious to think about it. He was a predator preying on vulnerable women, whether they were his employees or his clients. And the truly infuriating thing about that was the fact that vulnerable women often either refuse to see the danger in a man like Van Zandt, or convince themselves they have no recourse but to suffer through. And a sociopath like Van Zandt could smell that a mile away.

I picked up his business card and looked at it. It was late, but I could still call him on his cell phone, apologize again for Irina's behavior, ask to meet him for a drink . . . Maybe I'd get lucky and have to kill him in self-defense at the end of the evening.

I was reaching for the phone when something hit my front door with force. My hand went for the Glock I'd laid on the table to clean. My mind raced through scenarios in the blink of an eye. Then the pounding started and a small voice penetrated the wood.

'Elena! Elena!'

Molly.

I pulled the door open and the girl fell inside as if she'd been blown to the house by a hurricane. Her hair was matted with sweat. She was as pale as parchment.

'Molly, what's wrong? What's happened?'

I guided her to a chair and she melted into it like a limp noodle, so out of breath she was panting.

'How did you get here?'

'My bike.'

'God. It's the dead of night. Why didn't you call me if you needed to see me?'

'I couldn't. I didn't dare.'

'Have you heard something from Erin?'

She pulled off the jacket she'd worn tied around her waist and fumbled through the folds of cloth. Her hands were shaking violently as she fished out a videotape and thrust it at me.

I took the thing to the VCR, rewound it, and hit the play button. I watched the drama unfold as I knew Molly had, but with a quality to my sense of dread I knew she didn't have because she hadn't lived as long as I had or seen the things that I had seen. I watched her sister knocked to the ground and shoved into the white van. Then came the voice, mechanically altered to disguise or to frighten or both: 'We have your daughter. Call the police, she dies. Three hundred thousand dollars. Directions later.'

The picture went to static. I stopped the VCR and turned to look at Molly. Molly the Mini-Exec was gone. Molly the adult in disguise was nowhere in sight. Sitting at my table, looking small and fragile, was Molly the child, twelve years old and terrified for her big sister. Tears trapped behind the lenses of her Harry Potter glasses magnified the fear in her eyes.

She was trying very hard to be brave as she waited for something from me. That almost frightened me more than the video had.

I crouched in front of her, my hands braced on the arms of the chair. 'Where did you get this, Molly?'

'I heard Mom and Bruce fighting about Erin,' she said quickly. 'When they went out of his office, I went in, and I found it.'

'They've seen it.'

She nodded.

'What did they do?'

The tears rolled out the sides of the glasses and down her cheeks. She spoke in a very, very small voice. 'Nothing.'

'They didn't call the police?'

'Bruce said he would handle it. Then he sent Mom to bed.' She shook her head in disbelief. I could see the anger rise up inside her, bringing color to her face. 'And he went for a drive to clear his head, because he had a *bad day*! I hate him!' she cried, slamming a small fist on the table. 'I hate him! He won't do anything because he doesn't want her back! Erin's going to die because of him!'

The tears came in earnest now, and Molly fell against me, throwing her arms around my neck.

I've never known how to comfort people. Perhaps because I wasn't taught by example. Or perhaps I had always taken my own personal pain so deeply within me, I wouldn't allow anyone to touch it. But Molly's pain was overflowing, and she gave me no choice but to share it with her. I closed my arms around her and stroked her hair with one hand.

'It won't be up to him, Molly,' I said. 'You've got me, remember?'

In that moment I knew real fear. This was no longer a case I didn't want with a probable outcome of no big consequence. It wasn't a simple matter of working a job. I had a connection to this child in my arms. I had made a commitment. I who had wanted nothing more than to hide with my misery until I could find the nerve to check out.

I held her tighter, not for her, but for me.

I made a copy of the videotape, then we put Molly's bike in my trunk and headed for Binks Forest. It was nearly midnight.

17

Jill let herself into Jade's tack room and turned on the small lamp that sat on an antique chest. She grabbed a jug of leather oil from the supply shelves, twisted off the top, pulled open the drawer with Jade's show breeches in it, and doused the pants with oil. She knew from looking in the catalogs those breeches cost at least two hundred dollars each. She threw open the armoire, pulled out his two custom-made jackets, and soaked them both, then did the same with his freshly pressed, custom-made shirts.

It didn't seem enough. She wanted more satisfaction.

She was supposed to have cleaned the stalls at the end of the day because Javier, the Guatemalan guy, had to leave early. But Jill didn't like pitching shit, and so she had simply stirred the bedding around to cover it. She snickered now as she went to the first stall and took out Trey Hughes's gray horse. She put the horse in the empty stall where Stellar had lived, then took a pitchfork into the gray's stall and uncovered the piles of manure and the spots wet with urine. The smell of ammonia burned her nose and she smiled a malicious smile.

Setting the fork aside, she went back to the tack stall and grabbed up the pile of clothes.

Jade would have a fit when he found this mess. He would know she had done it, but he wouldn't be able to prove it. And he was supposed to be in the showring in the morning. He wouldn't have any clothes. His horses wouldn't be ready. And Jill would be busy lying on the beach, getting a tan and looking for a hot guy.

She spread the clothing out in the stall, over the piles of shit and spots of pee, then went around and around the stall, stomping on Don Jade's expensive clothing, grinding it into the mess. This would teach him not to treat people like servants. He couldn't humiliate her and get away with it. Big asshole. He was going to regret what he'd done to her. She could have been his ally, his spy. Instead, he could rot.

'Fuck you, Don Jade. Fuck you, Don Jade.' She chanted the words as she marched around the stall.

She had no fear of being caught by Jade. He was back at that snotty club, trying to impress some client or some woman. Paris was supposed to have night check, but Jill knew for a fact she hardly ever did it when it was her turn.

It didn't occur to Jill that someone from another stable might come through the barn, or that a security guard might be making rounds. She almost never got caught doing stuff. Like keying stupid Erin's car. Everyone assumed Chad did it because Chad had been there that night and he and Erin had argued. And Jill had once had a job at a Wal-Mart where she had stolen all kinds of stuff, right under her manager's nose. It served the store right, getting ripped off, if they were stupid enough to hire a guy as dumb as that guy had been.

'Fuck you, Don Jade. Fuck you, Don Jade,' she chanted, happily grinding his clothes into the muck.

And then the stable lights went out.

Jill stopped marching and stood very still. She could feel her heart beating. The sound of it in her ears made it impossible to hear if someone was coming. As her eyes adjusted she could make out shapes, but the stall she was in was too far to the back of the tent to get much light from the big light pole out by the road.

Some of the horses turned around in their stalls. Some nickered – nervously, Jill thought. She felt around the wall blindly, trying to find the pitchfork. She'd left it on the far side of the stall. She turned her back to the door as she groped for it.

It happened so fast, she couldn't react. Someone rushed in behind her. She heard the rustle of the stall bedding, felt the presence of another person. Before she could scream, a hand was over her mouth. Her own hands closed desperately on the handle of the pitchfork, and she twisted around, trying to wriggle from her captor's grasp, breaking the hold, stumbling backward, swinging the pitchfork in a wide arch, hitting something. Her grip on the handle was too near the end of it, giving her little control or strength in her swing, and it flew out of her hands and thumped against the canvas wall.

She tried to scream then, and couldn't. As in a nightmare, the sound died in her throat. In that split second she knew she was going to die.

Still, she tried to run for the door. Her legs felt as heavy as lead. Her feet tangled in the clothes on the floor of the stall. Like a lasso around her ankles, the clothes pulled her feet out from under her. She fell forward, heavily, knocking the wind from her lungs. Her attacker came down on top of her from behind.

There was a sound – a voice – but she couldn't hear it above the pounding in her ears and the wrenching sound from her own throat as she tried to breathe and sob and beg. She felt the miniskirt being pulled up over her butt, a hand digging between her legs, tearing at the too-small thong.

She tried to pull herself forward. There was a terrible pressure in the middle of her back, then against the back of her head, forcing her head down, pushing her face into the manure she was supposed to have cleaned out of the stall that day. She couldn't breathe. She tried to turn her head and couldn't; tried to suck in air and her mouth filled with shit; tried to vomit and felt a terrible burning in her chest.

And then she didn't feel anything at all.

18

The Seabrights' neighborhood was silent, all the big lovely homes dark, their inhabitants blissfully ignorant of the dysfunction next door. There were still lights on downstairs on one end of the Seabright home. The second story was dark. I wondered if Krystal really was sleeping.

Bruce had 'sent her to bed,' Molly had said. As if she were a child. Her daughter had been abducted and her husband told her to go to bed. He would handle it. If Krystal hadn't seen the tape, I wondered if Bruce would have simply thrown it in the trash like a piece of junk mail.

Molly let us in the front door and led the way to Bruce Seabright's home office, the source of the lights. The office door stood open. Bruce was inside, muttering under his breath as he searched the bookcases near the television.

'Looking for this?' I asked, holding up the video.

He spun around. 'What are you doing here? How did you get into my house?'

His glare hit on Molly half hiding behind me. 'Molly? Did you let this person in?'

'Elena can help –'

'Help with what?' he said, choosing denial even while I stood there with the tape of his stepdaughter's kidnapping in hand. 'We don't need her help for anything.'

'You think you can handle this on your own?' I asked, tossing the tape on his desk.

'I think you can leave my home or I can call the police.'

'That threat doesn't work with me. I thought you learned that lesson this morning.'

His mouth pulled into a tight knot as he stared at me with narrowed eyes.

'Elena used to be a detective with the Sheriff's Office,' Molly said, moving out of my shadow. 'She knows all about those people Erin worked with, and –'

'Molly, go to bed,' Seabright ordered curtly. 'I'll deal with you tomorrow, young lady. Eavesdropping on conversations, coming into my office without permission, bringing this person into my home. You've got a lot to answer for.'

Molly kept her chin up and gave her stepfather a long look. 'So do you,' she said. Then she turned and left the room with the dignity of a queen.

Seabright went to the door and closed it. 'How did she know to call you?'

'Believe it or not, the people living in *your* house do have lives and minds of their own, and allow themselves to think without asking your permission. I'm sure you'll put a stop to that, now that you know.'

'How dare you criticize the way I run my house? You don't know anything about my family.'

'Oh, I know all about your family. Believe me,' I said, hearing an old bitterness in my tone. 'You're the demigod and the mortals revolve around you like planets around the sun.'

'Where do you get off, speaking to me this way?' he asked, advancing toward me, trying to get me to back away literally and figuratively. I didn't move.

'I'm not the one who has explaining to do, Mr Seabright. Your stepdaughter has been kidnapped and Molly is the only person who seems to care whether she's ever seen alive again. What do you have to say about that?'

'I don't have anything to say to you. None of this is any of your business.'

'I've made it my business. When, where, and how did this tape arrive?'

'I don't have to answer your questions.' He walked past me as if to dismiss me, going back to the bookcases to close the doors on his television.

'Would you rather answer the questions of a sheriff's detective?' I asked.

'They said no police,' he reminded me as he moved a bookend two inches to the left. 'Do you want to be responsible for the girl's death?'

'No. Do you?'

'Of course not.' He straightened a stack of books, his eyes already moving in search of the next piece of his kingdom out of place. Nervous, I thought.

'But if she simply never came back, you wouldn't exactly mourn her loss, would you?' I said.

'That's an obnoxious thing to say.'

'Yes, well . . .'

He stopped rearranging and put on a face of high affront. 'What kind of a man do you think I am?'

'I don't think you'd really like me to answer that right now. When did this tape arrive, Mr Seabright? Erin hasn't been seen or heard from in nearly a week. Kidnappers usually want their money ASAP. It's rather the point of the thing, you see. The longer they hang on to a victim, the shorter the odds of something going wrong.'

'The tape just came,' he said, but he didn't look at me when he said it. I was willing to bet he'd had it for a couple of days.

'And the kidnappers haven't called.'

'No.'

'How did the tape arrive?'

'In the mail.'

'To the house or to your office?'

'The house.'

'Addressed to you or to your wife?'

'I – I don't recall.'

To Krystal. And he'd kept it from her. He probably screened all her mail, the controlling prick. And when she'd finally seen it, he'd sent her to bed and gone out for a drive.

'I'd like to see the envelope,' I said.

'I threw it out.'

'Then it's in your trash. Let's go get it. There could be fingerprints on it, and the postmark could provide valuable information.'

'It's gone.'

'Gone where? Your trash was at the curb yesterday. If the tape arrived today . . .'

He had no answer for that, the son of a bitch. I heaved a sigh of disgust and tried again.

'Have they called?'

'No.'

'God help you if you're lying, Seabright.'

His face flushed purple. 'How dare you call me a liar.'

'You are.'

We both turned toward the door to find Krystal standing there looking like an aging crack whore. Her face was drawn and pale. Mascara ringed her eyes. Her bleached hair stood up like a fright wig. She wore a short pink robe trimmed with feathery flounces around the neck and cuffs, and matching high-heeled mules.

'You are a liar,' she said, glassy eyes fixed on her husband.

'You're drunk,' Bruce accused.

'I must be. I know better than to speak to you out of turn.'

I watched Seabright. He was furious, trembling with anger. If I had not been there, I don't know what he might have done. But then, if I hadn't been there, Krystal would never have had the nerve to say anything. I turned to her, taking in the dilated pupils and the smudged lipstick.

'Mrs Seabright, when did you first see the tape of your daughter's kidnapping?'

'I had seen the box. It had my name on it. I didn't know why Bruce hadn't given it to me. I thought it was something I had ordered through the mail.'

'Krystal . . .' Bruce growled.

'What day was that?'

Her mouth trembled. 'Wednesday.'

Two days.

'I didn't see any point in upsetting you with it,' Seabright said. 'Look at you. Look what it's done to you.'

'I found it today,' she said to me. 'My daughter's been kidnapped. Bruce didn't think I should know about that.'

'I told you, I will handle it, Krystal,' he said through his teeth.

Krystal looked at me, tragic, pathetic, terrified. 'In our family, we leave the decisions to the person best equipped to make them.'

I looked hard at Bruce Seabright. He was perspiring. He knew he could intimidate a woman like Krystal, but he could not intimidate me.

'I'm going to ask you one last time, Mr Seabright. And before you answer, know that the Sheriff's Office can pull your local usage details from the phone company and verify the information. Have the kidnappers called?'

He put his hands on his hips and looked up at the ceiling, weighing the pros and cons of denial. He wasn't the type to openly defy the cops. If he took my word on the phone records, and thought about what would happen if the Sheriff's Office became involved . . . his public image could be damaged . . . I held my breath.

'Last night.'

A strange sound of anguish wrenched out of Krystal Seabright and she doubled over the back of a fat leather chair as if she'd been shot.

Seabright puffed himself up like a furious pigeon as he tried to justify his behavior. 'First of all, I think the whole thing is a hoax. This is just Erin trying to humiliate me –'

'I'm up to my back teeth with men and their persecution theories today,' I said. 'I don't want to hear yours. I saw the tape. I know the kind of people Erin has been mixed up with. I wouldn't be willing to bet her life against your fear of embarrassment. Who called? A man? A woman?'

'It sounded like the voice on the tape,' he said impatiently. 'Distorted.'

'What did it say?'

He didn't want to answer. His mouth pulled into that pissy little knot I wanted to slap off his face.

'Why should I tell you any of this?' he said. 'I don't know anything about you. I don't know who you're working for. I don't know that you're not one of them.'

'For God's sake, tell her!' Krystal cried. She slipped around the side of the leather chair and crawled into it, curling herself into a fetal position.

'And how do I know you're not?' I returned. 'How does your wife know you're not?'

'Don't be ridiculous,' Seabright snapped.

'*Ridiculous* isn't the word I'd use to describe it, Mr Seabright. Erin has been a source of considerable irritation to you. Maybe you saw a way to eliminate the problem.'

'Oh my God!' Krystal cried, putting her hands over her mouth.

'That's absurd!' Seabright shouted.

'I don't think the Sheriff's Office will think so,' I said. 'So you'd better start coming up with the details.'

He heaved another sigh, the put-upon patriarch. 'The voice said to put the money in a cardboard box and leave it in a specific spot at the Equestrian Estates horse-show grounds out in Loxahatchee somewhere.'

I knew the area. Twenty minutes from Wellington, Equestrian Estates was an as-yet-undeveloped development. More or less wide-open spaces with a show ground used only several times a year.

'When?'

'Today. Five o'clock.'

'And did you leave the money?'

'No.'

Krystal was sobbing. 'You killed her! You killed her!'

'Oh, for God's sake, Krystal, stop it!' he snapped. 'If she's really kidnapped, they aren't going to kill her. What would be the point?'

'The only point is to get the money,' I said coldly. 'They'll try to get it whether she's alive or not. Did they promise you would see Erin at the drop site? Did they say you'd be able to pick her up somewhere else if you came through with the cash?'

'They didn't say.'

There was no guarantee Erin wasn't already dead. If the kidnapper was ruthless enough, she might have been killed in short order after the abduction to eliminate her as a possible witness later, and simply to make the kidnapper's life easier. Or that might have been the point all along – to eliminate her – with a dummied-up kidnapping plot thrown over it for camouflage.

'Have they called since?'

'No.'

'I find that hard to believe. If I was expecting three hundred thousand at five in the afternoon and it didn't show, I'd want to know why.'

He lifted his hands and walked away to a window where half-opened plantation shutters let in the darkness. I watched him and wondered just how cold a man he was. Cold enough to knowingly throw his stepdaughter to a sexual predator? Cold enough to have her killed? Maybe.

The one thing I had difficulty accepting was the idea of Seabright relinquishing control in any kind of collaborative scheme that would leave him vulnerable. But his only other choice would have been to dirty his hands himself, and that I didn't see at all. Conspiracy was the lesser of evils. Conspiracy could always be denied.

My gaze fell on Seabright's desk, immaculate in its organization. Perhaps I would see a file lying there labeled: KIDNAP ERIN. Instead, I stopped at the telephone, a Panasonic cordless with a caller ID window on the handset. The same phone I had in Sean's guest house. I went behind the desk, sat down in the leather executive's chair, and picked up the phone. The caller ID light on the base was blinking red.

'What are you doing?' Bruce demanded, hurrying back across the room.

I pressed the search button on the handset, and a number appeared in the display window. 'I'm taking advantage of the miracle of modern technology. If the kidnapper called you on this line from a phone that wasn't blocked, the number will be stored in the memory of this unit and can be checked against a reverse directory. Isn't that terribly clever?'

I jotted the number on his spotless blotter, scrolled to the next stored number, and noted it. He wanted to snatch the phone out of my hand. I could see the muscles working in his jaw.

'My clients and business associates call me here,' he said. 'I won't have you harassing them.'

'How do you know one of them isn't the kidnapper?' I asked.

'That's insane! These are wealthy and respectable people.'

'Maybe all but one.'

'I don't want people dragged into this mess.'

'Do you have any enemies, Mr Seabright?' I asked.

'Of course not.'

'You've never pissed anybody off? A man in land development in south Florida? That would be astonishing.'

'I'm a reputable businessman, Ms Estes.'

'And you're about as likable as dysentery,' I said. 'I can't believe you don't have a list of people who would be pleased to see you suffer. And I'm only thinking of your immediate family.'

He hated me. I could see it in his small, mean eyes. I found the notion satisfying, the feeling mutual.

'I will have your license number,' he said tightly. 'I have every intention of reporting you to the proper authorities.'

'Then I would be stupid to give it to you, wouldn't I?' I said, making note of another call. The phone reported having stored thirteen numbers since last having been cleared. 'Besides, I don't see that you're in any position to complain about me, Mr Seabright. I know too much you'd rather not read about in the newspapers.'

'Are you threatening me?'

'I'm always amazed when people have to ask that question,' I said. 'Do you owe money to anyone?'

'No.'

'Do you gamble?'

'No!'

'Do you know a man named Tomas Van Zandt?'

'No. Who is he?'

'Did you arrange for Erin to get the job working for Don Jade?'

I noted the last of the stored phone numbers and looked up at him.

'What difference does that make?' he asked.

'Did you?'

He seemed nervous again. He straightened a humidor on the desktop a sixteenth of an inch.

'It would be quite a coincidence if Erin had simply stumbled into a job with the trainer of the client you sold a hugely expensive property to.'

'What does this have to do with anything?' he demanded. 'So I might have mentioned she was looking for a job with horses. So what?'

I shook my head, tore the page of numbers off the blotter, and stood. I looked at Krystal, still huddled in the leather chair, eyes glassy, locked in her own private hell. I wanted to ask her if she thought it was worth it – the house, the clothes, the car, the money – but she was probably suffering enough without me accusing her of selling out her own child. I gave her one of the cards with my phone number on it, and laid one on the desk.

'I'll run these numbers and see what I come up with,' I said. 'Call me immediately if you hear from the kidnappers. I'll do what I can. In my professional opinion, you should call the Sheriff's Office, the detective division, and ask to speak directly to Detective James Landry.'

'But they said no police,' Seabright said, a little too happy to comply with that demand.

'Plain clothes, plain car. No one will know he isn't a Jehovah's Witness.'

Seabright pouted. 'I don't want other people making decisions for my family.'

'No? Well, contrary to your egomania, you are not best equipped to make these decisions,' I said. 'You need professional help with this. And if you don't want to accept it, I'll cram it down your throat.'

19

Two-forty A.M. Bruce Seabright couldn't sleep. He didn't try. He had no desire to share a bed with Krystal tonight, even though he knew she was unconscious. He was too agitated to sleep, or even to sit. He had spent an hour cleaning his office: polishing the fingerprints from the furniture, wiping down every item on the desk, spraying the telephone with Lysol. His inner sanctum had been breached, contaminated.

Krystal had come in here without his knowledge and pawed through the mail on his desk, even though he had told her very specifically never to do that. He always handled the mail. And Molly had come in and taken the videotape. He had expected better of both of them. The disappointment was bitter in his mouth. The order of his world had been upset, and now that bitch private investigator was trying to take over. He wouldn't stand for it. He would find out who she was working for, and he would make sure she never worked again.

He paced the room, breathing deeply the scents of lemon oil and disinfectant, trying to calm himself.

He never should have married Krystal. That had been a mistake. He had known her eldest daughter would be a problem he would end up having to deal with, and here he was.

He opened the television cabinet, pulled a video from the shelf, and popped it in the VCR and hit play.

Erin, naked, chained to a bed, trying to cover herself.

'Look at the camera, bitch. Say your line.'

She shakes her head, tries to hide her face.

'Say it! You want me to make you?'

She looks at the camera.

'Help me.'

Bruce ejected the tape and put it in its cardboard sleeve. He went to the small secret wall safe hidden behind a row of books on real estate law, opened the safe, put the tape inside, and locked it away. No one else would see the tape. That was his decision. He was best equipped to make it.

20

I have never been hindered by the belief that people are basically good. In my experience, people are basically selfish, and often cruel.

I slept for three hours because my body didn't give me a choice. I woke because my brain wouldn't let me rest. I rose and fed the horses, then showered and went to my computer in a T-shirt and underpants and started tracing the phone numbers from Bruce Seabright's phone using a reverse directory on the Internet.

Of the thirteen numbers, six were unlisted with a Wellington prefix, four came back with names, one came back to Domino's Pizza, and two calls had come from the same Royal Palm Beach number, also with no listing. Seabright claimed the kidnapper had called only once, but I didn't believe him. He'd been a no-show for the drop. I couldn't believe he wouldn't have gotten a call after that.

I dialed the Royal Palm number and listened to it ring unanswered. No cheerful greeting: Kidnappers R Us.

I dialed the unlisted numbers, one by one, getting answering machines and maids, and waking up a couple of very cranky people who would no doubt be calling Bruce Seabright's office to complain about his new assistant.

I dialed the Sheriff's Office, wending my way through the various receptionists to get to Landry's voice mail, at the same time checking my e-mail for word from my FBI contact on the inquiry to Interpol. Nothing yet. As I listened to Landry's message and jotted down his pager number, I considered calling Armedgian to hasten a response, but decided not to press my luck. Any info from abroad would just be corroboration. I already knew Van Zandt was a world-class sleaze.

Was he bold enough to try kidnapping? Why not? He'd been just a step away from it with Irina's friend, Sasha Kulak. If Bruce Seabright had set up Erin's job through Trey Hughes, it stood to reason Van Zandt could have found out Erin was connected to the Fairfields developer. Developers take in a lot of money, he might have reasoned. Why shouldn't he be entitled to some? Motive: greed. He knew the girl, knew the show grounds, knew when people would be around and when they wouldn't. Opportunity.

Means? I knew Van Zandt had a video camera, so he could have made the tape. The distortion device would have disguised his accent. What about the white van? Where had it come from, and if Van Zandt had been running the video camera, then who was the guy in the mask?

Scum finds its own level. There were plenty of people skulking in the shadows of the show grounds who could have been persuaded to do just about anything for money. Decent people might not have been able to find them, but Tomas Van Zandt was not a decent person.

The truly disturbing possibility of Van Zandt as the kidnapper was his possible connection to Bruce Seabright and Seabright's lack of action on the ransom demand. But if Seabright was connected, then why would the videotape have been addressed to Krystal? And why would he have tried to hide it from her? If the projected outcome was in fact to get rid of Erin but make it look like a kidnapping gone wrong, Seabright needed corroboration on his end. It didn't make sense for him to keep it to himself.

His lack of action couldn't be denied, whatever his motive. I was willing to bet he had yet to act, despite my threat.

I dialed Landry's pager and left my number. Avadonis Farms would come up in his caller ID. That gave me a better shot for a return call. He would have taken one look at my name and hit the erase button.

While I waited for the phone to ring, I poured a cup of coffee, paced, and considered other angles. The fact that Erin had cared for Stellar and Stellar was dead; the possible connections to Jade, with his shadowy past. The fact that Erin had been involved with Chad Seabright; the fact they had been seen arguing two days before her disappearance. She'd dumped him – for an older man, Chad said. She'd had a thing for her boss, Molly said.

The phone rang. I scooped it up and answered.

'This is Detective James Landry. I received a page from this number.'

'Landry. Estes. Erin Seabright has been kidnapped. Her parents received a videotape and a ransom demand.'

Silence on the other end as he digested that.

'Do you still think it's not a case?' I asked.

'When did they get the demand?'

'Thursday. The stepfather was supposed to make the drop yesterday. He took a pass.'

'Excuse me?'

'It's a long story. Let's meet somewhere. I'll fill you in, then take you to them.'

'That won't be necessary,' he said. 'I'll get the details from the parents. Thanks for the tip, but I don't want you there.'

'I don't care whether you want me there or not,' I said flatly. 'I'll be there.'

'Hindering an official investigation.'

'So far, hindering has been your area of expertise,' I said. 'There wouldn't be an investigation but for me. The stepfather doesn't want to do anything.

He'd be happy to say "oh well" and hope the perps dump the girl in a canal with an anchor around her waist. I've got a three-day jump on you and an in with the people the girl worked for.'

'You're not a cop anymore.'

'And I needed you to remind me of that. Fuck you, Landry.'

'I'm just saying. You don't call the shots, Estes. You want to lord it over somebody, hire a minion. I don't work for you or with you.'

'Fine. Then I'll keep what I know to myself. See you there, asshole.'

I hung up and went to dress.

There are few creatures on earth more pigheaded than cops. I can say this with surety, because I am one. I may no longer have carried a badge, but that isn't what being a cop means. Being a cop is in the nature, in the bones. A cop is a cop, regardless of status, regardless of uniform, regardless of agency, regardless of age.

I understood Landry because we were related by calling. I didn't like him, but I understood him. I suspected he understood me on one level as well as anyone could. He wouldn't admit to it, and he didn't like me, but he knew where I stood.

I pulled on a pair of tan slacks and a black sleeveless T-shirt. The phone rang again as I was strapping on my watch.

'Where do you live?' he asked.

'I don't want you coming to my house.'

'Why not? Are you selling crack? Fencing stolen goods? What are you afraid of?'

I didn't want my sanctuary breached, but I wouldn't tell him that. Never willingly reveal a vulnerability to an adversary. My reluctance was telling enough. I gave him the address and cursed myself for giving him that tiny victory.

'I'll be there in thirty,' he said, and hung up.

I buzzed him through the gate in twenty-three.

'Nice digs,' Landry said, looking at Sean's house.

'I'm a guest.' I led the way from the parking area near the barn toward the guest house.

'It pays to know people who don't live in cardboard boxes and eat out of Dumpsters.'

'Is that your social circle?' I asked. 'You could aim a little higher. You live at the marina, after all.'

He gave me the look – suspicious, offended I would have knowledge of him without his permission. 'How do you know that?'

'I checked you out. Idle hands and the World Wide Web . . .'

He didn't like that at all. Good. I wanted him to know I was smarter than he was.

'Your blood type is AB negative, and you voted Republican in the last election,' I said, opening my front door. 'Coffee?'

'Do you know how I take it?' he asked sarcastically.

'Black. Two sugars.'

He stared at me.

I shrugged. 'Lucky guess.'

He stood on the other side of the kitchen peninsula with his arms crossed over his chest. He should have been on a recruiting poster. Starched white shirt with thin burgundy stripes, blood-red tie, the aviator shades, the military posture.

'You look like a fed,' I commented. 'What's up with that? Agency envy?'

'Why are you so curious about me?' he asked, irritated.

'Knowledge is power.'

'So this is some kind of game to you?'

'Not at all. I just like to know who I'm dealing with.'

'You know me as well as you're going to,' he said. 'Fill me in on the Seabrights.'

I played the videotape for him and told him what had happened the night before at the Seabright house. He didn't bat an eye at any of it.

'You think the stepfather has some kind of angle on this?' he asked.

'There's no question how he feels about Erin, and it's certainly strange the way he's handled things so far. I don't like his connections. But if this kidnapping is staged and he's a party to it, why be secretive with the tape? I don't get that.'

'Control, maybe,' Landry said, running the tape back and playing it again. 'Maybe he waits until it's over and the girl is dead, then he shows the tape to the wife and tells her how he was protecting her from the awful truth and he handled the situation as he thought best.'

'Ah, yes. The decisions in the family are left to the person best equipped to make them,' I muttered.

'What?'

'The family motto. Bruce Seabright is a serious control freak. Pathological. Egotistical, a bully, psychologically abusive. The family is something out of Tennessee Williams.'

'Then it fits.'

'Yes,' I agreed. 'The thing is, this girl existed in a veritable snake pit. I can name three other legitimate suspects.'

'Then do.'

I told him about Chad Seabright, and told him again about Don Jade.

'And I'm waiting to hear from a connection to Interpol about priors on Tomas Van Zandt. He has a history of bad behavior toward young women, and by all accounts he's as crooked as a dog's hind leg.'

'Charming crowd these horse people,' Landry said.

'The horse world is a microcosm. The good, the bad; the beautiful, the ugly.'

'The haves and have-nots. That's what keeps the prisons full,' Landry said. 'Jealousy, greed, and sexual perversion.'

'Make the world go round.'

Landry sighed and backed the tape up again. 'And what's your stake in this mess, Estes?'

'I told you. I'm helping out the little sister.'

'Why? Why did she come to you?'

'It's a long story that doesn't really matter. I'm in it now, and I'm staying in it to the end. Do you have a problem with that?'

'Yeah, I do,' he said, his attention on the television. 'But I'm sure that won't stop you.'

'No, it won't.'

He hit the pause button and squinted at the screen. 'Can you make out that tag number?'

'No. I tried. I couldn't make it out on Seabright's tape either. You'll need a technical wizard.

'Look, Landry, I'm already on the inside with Jade's people,' I said. 'I'm more than willing to work with you. You'd be stupid to take a pass on that. You're a lot of things, I'm sure, but I don't think stupid is one of them.'

He gave me a long look, trying to see something beyond what I would allow him to see.

'I've done my homework too,' he said. 'You're a loose cannon, Estes. You always were, the way I hear it. I don't like that. You think this Seabright guy is a control freak. I consider that a virtue. When I'm on a case, I own it. Period. I don't want to be in this thing and wondering what the hell you're going to pull next. And I can guarantee no one else in the SO is going to stand for that either. My lieutenant finds out you've got your fingers in this, he'll have my ass.'

'I can't do anything about that. I am in it, and I'm staying in it. I said I'll work with you, but I don't work for you. You don't control me, Landry. If that's your focus, we have a problem. There's only one goal here: getting Erin Seabright out alive. If you think it's some kind of contest, you can keep your dick in your pants. I'm sure yours is bigger than anybody's, but I don't want to see it. Thanks anyway.

'Now can we get on this?' I asked. 'We're burning daylight.'

Landry took a beat, then motioned toward the door. 'Lead the way. I hope I don't regret this.'

I returned his look and his sentiment. 'That makes two of us.'

Bruce Seabright was not happy to see me. He came to the door himself – no doubt having forbidden everyone else to – dressed for golf in khakis and a tangerine polo shirt. He had the same tasseled loafers as Van Zandt. It was now 8:15 A.M.

'Mr Seabright, this is Detective Landry with the Sheriff's Office,' I said. Landry held up his shield. 'He tells me he hasn't heard from you.'

'It's Saturday,' Seabright said. 'I didn't know how early I could call.'

'So you thought you'd get eighteen in before you tried?' I asked.

'Ms Estes tells me your stepdaughter has been abducted,' Landry said.

Seabright glared at me. 'The kidnappers said no police, so I didn't call the police. I certainly hope Ms Estes hasn't put Erin in greater danger by bringing you here.'

'I don't think this trumps blowing off the ransom drop,' I said. 'May we come in?'

He stepped back reluctantly, and closed the door behind us lest the neighbors see.

'Have you received any further communication from the kidnappers?' Landry asked as we followed Seabright to the inner sanctum. There was no sign of Krystal. The house was as silent as a mausoleum. I spied Molly crouched in the upstairs hall, peering down at us through the balusters.

'No.'

'You last heard from them when?'

'Thursday night.'

'Why didn't you pay the ransom, Mr Seabright?'

Seabright closed the doors of his office and turned around to go behind his desk. Landry had already taken a position there, standing behind the desk chair with his hands resting on the chair back.

'I'm sure Ms Estes has told you, I'm not convinced this whole thing isn't a hoax.'

'You're convinced enough not to call the Sheriff's Office for fear of what might happen to Erin, but not enough to pay the ransom?' Landry said. 'I'm not sure I understand that, Mr Seabright.'

Seabright paced the end of the room with his hands on his hips. 'I'm sorry I don't know the protocol for kidnapping victims. This is my first time.'

'Do you have the money?'

'I can get it.'

'On a Saturday?'

'If I have to. The president of my bank is a personal friend. I do an enormous amount of business with him.'

'Good,' Landry said. 'Call him. Tell him you may need to ask him a favor later today. You need three hundred thousand dollars in marked bills. He'll need some lead time to get that together. Tell him someone from the Sheriff's Office will meet him at the bank to assist him.'

Seabright looked shocked. 'B-but we're not actually going to give them the money, are we?'

'You are if you ever want to see your stepdaughter alive again,' Landry said. 'You do want that, don't you, Mr Seabright?'

Seabright closed his eyes and huffed a sigh. 'Yes. Of course.'

'Good. I'll have people out here within the hour to put a tap on your phone. When the next call comes in we'll be able to trace its origin. You'll set up the drop. You'll tell them you'll show with the money, but Erin has to be there where you can see her or it's a no-go. They already know you're not a pushover. If they haven't already killed her, they'll bring her. They want the money, not the girl.'

'I can't believe any of this is happening,' Seabright muttered. 'You'll be there? At the drop?'

'Yes. I've already spoken with my lieutenant about your situation. He'll be calling shortly to speak with you himself.'

'What about the FBI?' Seabright asked. 'Don't they always get involved with kidnappings?'

'It's not automatic. They can be called in if you like.'

'I don't. This is way out of hand already. They said not to call the police, now my home is going to be crawling with them.'

'We'll be very discreet, Mr Seabright,' Landry said. 'I'll want to speak to everyone living in the house.'

'My wife is sedated. Other than Krystal, it's just myself, my son Chad, and Krystal's younger daughter, Molly.'

'Detective Landry is aware of the sexual relationship between Erin and Chad,' I told him. Color spread up Seabright's neck like the red in a thermometer. 'He'll definitely want to speak with Chad.'

'My son has absolutely nothing to do with this.'

'Because you say so?' I challenged. 'Your son had plenty to do with Erin. He was seen at her apartment two nights before she disappeared, arguing with her.'

'That was all her doing,' Seabright said bitterly. 'Erin goaded him into a relationship just to spite me.'

'You don't think Chad would want to spite you for his own sake?'

Seabright came over and stuck a finger in front of my face. 'I've had it with you and your accusations. I don't care who you're working for, I don't want you here. The Sheriff's Office is involved now. I'm sure they don't have any use for a private investigator either. Do you, Detective?'

Seabright looked to Landry. Landry looked at me, his face as unreadable as mine.

'Actually,' Landry said. 'Ms Estes's cooperation in this is very important, Mr Seabright. I wouldn't be here if not for her.'

Good cop, bad cop. I almost smiled.

'Perhaps you'd like to explain *that* to Detective Landry's lieutenant,' I said to Seabright.

He wanted to put his hands around my throat and choke me. I could see it in his eyes.

'I'm sure he'll be very interested to hear all about how you didn't want to be bothered with your stepdaughter's kidnapping,' I went on, walking away from him. 'You know, Detective Landry, maybe you *should* call in the FBI. I've got a friend in the regional office I could reach out to. After all, this could have international implications if one of the foreign nationals at the equestrian center is involved. Or it could involve some out-of-state client of

Mr Seabright's. If Erin has been taken across a state line, it automatically becomes a federal case.'

All I had to do was mention his business dealings and Seabright's sphincter curled into a French knot.

'I don't like being threatened,' he pouted.

I walked past him again, leaning toward his ear as I murmured, 'That would be the point.'

'Your focus needs to be on your stepdaughter, Mr Seabright,' Landry said. 'Complaining about the people who seem to care more about this girl than you do isn't going to stand you in very good stead. Do you understand what I'm saying?'

'You're making me feel like I should call my attorney,' Seabright said.

'Feel free to do that if you have concerns about talking to me.'

That shut him up. He rubbed his hands over his face and looked up at the ceiling.

'Do you consider *me* a suspect?' he asked.

'Investigations of this type of crime are always of a two-pronged nature, Mr Seabright. We have to consider possibilities both outside the family and within it,' Landry said. 'I'd like to speak with your son now. Is he home?'

Seabright went to an intercom panel on the wall and pressed a button. 'Chad, would you come to my office, please?'

I imagined being elsewhere in the Seabright home, Bruce Seabright's voice ringing out of the walls. All he needed was a remote-control burning bush and his image would be complete.

'Has Chad been in any kind of trouble with the law, Mr Seabright?' Landry asked.

Seabright looked offended. 'My son is an honor student.'

A polite knock sounded against the door and Chad Seabright stuck his head in the room, then slipped inside with the expression of a shy, hopeful puppy. He was dressed neatly in khakis and a navy Tommy Hilfiger polo. He looked ready to hit the links with the Young Republicans.

'Chad, this is Detective Landry and Ms Estes,' Bruce Seabright said. 'They want to ask you some questions about Erin.'

Chad put on big eyes. 'Wow. Sure. I've already spoken with Ms Estes. She knows I haven't seen Erin. I wish I could be more helpful.'

'You and Erin had a relationship,' Landry said.

Chad looked embarrassed. 'That was over. I admit that was wrong. It just sort of happened. Erin is very persuasive.'

'You had an argument with her last week. What was that about?'

'We broke up.'

'Chad!' Bruce Seabright snapped. 'You told me it was over months ago! When Erin moved out.'

Chad looked at the floor. 'It was . . . mostly. I'm sorry, Dad.'

'Chad, where were you last Sunday between four and six P.M.?' Landry asked.

Chad looked around as if the answer might be pasted on the walls. 'Sunday? Um ... I was probably –'

'We were at the movies,' Bruce Seabright said. 'Remember, Chad? Wasn't it Sunday we went to that new Bruce Willis movie?'

'Was that Sunday? Oh, yeah.' Chad nodded and looked at Landry. 'At the movies.'

'Which movie?'

'*Hostage.* It was great. Have you seen it?'

'I don't go to movies,' Landry said.

'You don't happen to have a ticket stub, do you?' I asked.

Chad flashed a goofy smile with a little laugh. 'Who keeps those things? Anal-retentives?'

'Then I'll ask you, Mr Seabright. You strike me as a man who would keep his stub and have it laminated.'

'No, I'm not.'

'You're just the kind of man who would encourage his child to lie to a sheriff's detective,' I said.

'Did you go with friends?' Landry asked. 'Anybody who could say they saw you there?'

'No,' Bruce said. 'It was a father-son outing.'

'Which theater?'

'The big one on State Road Seven.'

'What time did the movie start?' I asked.

Seabright was on the verge of losing his temper again. 'The late matinee.' He glared at Landry. 'Why are you standing here grilling us? If someone has taken Erin, they probably knew her from the equestrian center. Aren't there all kinds of lowlifes involved in the horse business? Shouldn't you be speaking with them?'

'Have you?' I asked. He looked at me blankly. 'You set her up for that job through Trey Hughes. Have you spoken with him? Asked him if he's seen Erin, if he knows anything, if he's heard anything?'

Seabright's mouth moved, but nothing came out.

'After you saw the tape and knew Erin had been taken from the show grounds, you didn't call the one person you knew who had a connection to her?'

'I – well – Trey wouldn't know anything about it,' he stammered. 'Erin was just a groom.'

'To Hughes. She's your stepdaughter.'

Landry's cell phone rang and he excused himself from the office, leaving me and the Seabright males looking at each other. I thought they both should have been strung up by their scrotums and beaten with canes, but that isn't proper procedure even in south Florida.

'I've dealt with a lot of cold, rotten people in my time,' I said to Bruce. 'But you, Mr Seabright, really must be crowned king turd on the shit pile.

I'm going to step out for a moment now. I'm having anger management issues.'

Landry was standing near the front door, brows drawn together as he spoke quietly into the phone. I looked upstairs and saw Molly, still sitting against the railing. She looked small and forlorn. She had to feel absolutely alone in this house. Krystal was of no help to her, and Bruce and his spawn were the enemy.

I wanted to go up the stairs and sit with her, and put my arm around her shoulders, and tell her I knew how she felt. But Landry had finished his call.

The look on his face made my stomach clutch.

'What is it?' I asked quietly, braced for the worst. And that was just what I heard.

'A girl's body has been found at the equestrian center.'

21

There is nothing so humbling to a self-proclaimed cynic than to be so deeply affected by something as to be knocked breathless by it.

I literally felt the blood drain from my head when Landry told me about the body. He left me standing in the hall and went to tell Bruce Seabright.

Was it Erin? How had she died? Had she died because I'd failed her? What a selfish thought. If Erin was dead, the blame went first to the perpetrator, second to Bruce Seabright. In terms of culpability, I ranked way down the list. I thought perhaps it wasn't Erin, and in the next microsecond thought it couldn't be anyone else.

'What's happened?'

Molly suddenly appeared at my side. My tongue, which was usually quicker than my brain, was stuck in my mouth.

'Is it about Erin?' she asked, frightened. 'Did somebody find her?'

'We don't know.' It was the truth, but it tasted like a lie, and it must have sounded like one too. Molly took a step back from me.

'Tell me. I deserve to know. I'm not some – some stupid child everyone has to talk around and hide things from,' she said angrily.

'No, you're not, Molly,' I said. 'But I don't want to scare you without knowing all the facts.'

'You already have.'

'I'm sorry.' I took a breath to buy a moment so I could think through my delivery of the news. 'Detective Landry just had a call from his captain. A body has been found at the equestrian center.'

Her eyes went huge. 'Is it Erin? Is she dead? It's because of the police. On the tape they said no police!'

'We don't know who it is, Molly,' I said, taking hold of her by the shoulders. 'But I can tell you, no one has killed Erin because Landry is here. The kidnappers have no way of knowing who he is or that he's from the Sheriff's Office.'

'How do you know?' she demanded. 'Maybe they're watching the house. Maybe the house is bugged!'

'That's not what's happened. The house is not bugged. That only happens in the movies. In real life, criminals are lazy and stupid. And whoever this dead body is, she's been dead longer than Landry has been in this house,' I said. 'I'm going to the show grounds now. I'll let you know as soon as I find out what's what.'

'I'm coming with you,' she said stubbornly.

'Absolutely not.'

'But she's my sister!'

'And I'm doing my job. I can't have you there, Molly, for a whole list of reasons. And I don't want you there for a whole list of reasons.'

'But I hate just sitting here,' she argued. 'Erin's in trouble. I want to help.'

'If you want to help, keep your eyes open for any kind of a delivery. If the kidnappers send another video, we need to know about it the second it lands. That's your assignment. All right?'

I understood her frustration. She was the one person who had taken action to find Erin, and now she was being made to feel helpless.

'All right,' she said on a sigh. I started to turn away. 'Elena?'

'What?'

She looked up at me with wide eyes. 'I'm really scared.'

I touched her head as if I were giving some kind of benediction, wishing I had that kind of power, and knowing too well that I didn't. 'I know. Hang in there. We're doing everything we can.'

Landry came out of the office. Bruce Seabright did not emerge. I wondered if he was giving Krystal the news over the intercom.

'I'll call as soon as I know anything,' I said to Molly, and went out the door, Landry right behind me.

'Do you know where barn forty is?' he asked.

'Yes. It's at the rear of the property. Follow me. I'll take you in the back way. It'll be much faster. Do you have any details?'

He shook his head. 'Not that made any sense to me. The lieutenant said somebody dug her up. I don't know what that means – if it's a fresh body or a skeleton or what.'

'We'll find out soon enough,' I said, going around the front of my car. That sounded like a lie too. Every minute I didn't know felt like an hour. Because of Molly. I didn't want to have to tell her her sister was dead.

I took a route from Binks Forest through Aero Club – a housing development for people with their own planes – on to Palm Beach Point, to the dirt road that led to the back gate of the equestrian center. The gate where Erin Seabright had been snatched nearly a week before. Barn forty was in The Meadows, just beyond that gate.

As it was every weekend during the season, the area was bustling with riders and grooms and dogs and kids; cars and trucks and golf carts and motorbikes. The biggest crowd, however, was gathered around a rusty yellow front-end loader and a dump truck parked near one of the three-sided muck pits out in front of the tents. I could see a number of blue shirts. Security. A white and green county cruiser had parked in the mud at the edge of the road.

I pulled into a parking spot opposite the excitement, grabbed a hat out of my backseat, and got out of the car. Landry stopped in the road and opened his window. I leaned down and said, 'You don't know me.'

He rolled his eyes. 'My fondest wish.'

He drove ahead and pulled up alongside the radio car.

My heart was thumping as I neared the scene. I asked a girl with a ponytail sticking out the back of a baseball cap if she knew what had happened.

She looked excited. 'They found a dead body.'

'God. Does anybody know who it is?'

'Someone said a groom. I don't know.'

I moved past her and threaded my way around the crowd. The security guards were telling people to go back to what they had been doing. The driver of the dump truck was sitting on his running board, blank-faced, hands hanging down between his knees. The driver of the front-end loader was standing beside his machine, gesturing as he spoke with a security guard, the deputy, and Landry.

I had reached the front of the mob. Beyond the loader, the muck pit was half dug out. Sticking out of the pile was a human arm. Female, purple fingernails, a cuff of bracelets sparkling in the blazing sun. A horse blanket had been thrown over whatever other body parts had been exposed.

'Miss?' Landry said, coming over to me. 'The guard said you might be able to help us. If you could . . .'

'Oh – I don't know. I'm sure I couldn't,' I said for the benefit of the spectators who were looking at me and wondering who the hell I was.

Landry took me by the arm and led me, protesting, toward the muck pit. When we were out of earshot of the crowd, he said, 'The guy was cleaning out this pit and dug her up. Buried in shit. There's respect for the dead. He says this pit hasn't been cleaned out since Thursday, but it was emptied to the ground then.'

'If it's Erin, I want ten minutes alone with Bruce Seabright and a large serrated knife.'

'I'll hold him down, you cut his heart out.'

'Deal.'

Making a face at the smell of manure and urine, he leaned over the body and lifted the edge of the horse blanket.

I steeled myself for the worst. The body was white and stiff. Smudged mascara, blue eye shadow, and berry-red lipstick gave the face the impression of a macabre work of art. There was a thumb-sized bruise on the cheek. Her mouth was partially open, crumbled chunks of old manure spilling out.

I let go of my held breath, relieved and sickened at once. 'It's Jill Morone.'

'You know her?'

'Yes. And guess who she worked for.'

Landry frowned. 'Don Jade. She told me yesterday she was sleeping with him.'

'Yesterday? What were you doing out here?' I asked, forgetting the audience, forgetting the role I was supposed to be playing.

He looked perturbed and wouldn't meet my eyes. 'Following up on your assault.'

'Gee. And I thought you didn't care.'

'I care that you caused me paperwork,' he complained. 'Get out of here, Estes. Go play dilettante. Make yourself useful.'

I put on a tragic face for the onlookers and hurried away to my car, where I called Molly Seabright to tell her her sister wasn't dead . . . as far as I knew. Then I set off to Don Jade's barn in search of a killer.

22

When I arrived at the Jade stalls there was a major clean-up under way. Paris was supervising as the Guatemalan man carried articles of clothing out of a stall and dumped them into a muck cart. She alternated snapping at the man with snapping at someone on the other end of her cell phone.

'What do you mean clothing isn't covered? Do you know what this stuff is worth?'

I looked at the pile in the muck cart. White and buff show breeches; an olive green three-season wool jacket, probably custom-made; custom-tailored shirts. All of it worth a lot of money. All of it stained with manure.

'What happened?' I asked.

Paris clicked her phone shut, furious, dark eyes burning with anger. 'That rotten, ugly, stupid, fat girl.'

'Your groom?'

'Not only has she not shown up, not gotten the horses groomed, did not clean the stalls yesterday when Javier was gone; she did *this*.' She thrust a finger at the pile of ruined clothing. 'Spiteful, hateful, little –'

'She's dead,' I said.

Paris pulled up mid-tirade and looked at me like I'd sprung a second head. 'What? What are you talking about?'

'Haven't you heard? They found a body in the manure pile at barn forty. It's Jill.'

She looked at me, then looked around as if there might be a hidden camera somewhere. 'You're kidding, right?'

'No. I drove in the back way. The cops are there now. I'm sure they'll be here soon enough. They know she worked for Don.'

'Oh, great,' she said, thinking about the inconvenience, not the girl. I saw her catch herself mentally and put on an appropriate expression of concern. 'Dead. That's terrible. I can't believe it. What happened to her? Did she have an accident?'

'I don't suppose she accidentally buried herself in horseshit,' I said. 'She must have been murdered. I wouldn't move anything around here if I were you. God knows what the detectives will think.'

'Well, they can't think any of us would kill her,' she said huffily. 'She's the only groom we had left.'

As if that was the only reason not to kill her.

'Why do you think she made this mess?' I asked, pointing at the clothes.

'Spite, I'm sure. Don said he saw her at The Players last night and he reprimanded her for something. Oh, my God,' she said, eyes widening. 'You don't think she was killed here, do you?'

I shrugged. 'Where else would she have been?'

'I don't know. She might have been meeting a guy in one of the other barns or something.'

'She had a boyfriend?'

Paris made a face. 'She talked about guys like she was the village slut. I never believed she had one.'

'Looks like she had one last night,' I said. 'You jumper people have all the excitement. Murder, mayhem, intrigue . . .'

Javier asked her in Spanish if he should keep cleaning the stall. Paris looked in through the bars. I looked too. The stall was a mess of churned-up muck and pine shavings and leather oil.

'Is that blood?' I asked, pointing. There were some drops that might have been blood splashed on curls of white pine bedding. It might have belonged to the dead girl. It might have belonged to her killer. It might have belonged to the horse that normally occupied the stall. Only a lab would tell us for sure. Who knew what else had already been dug out of the stall and hauled away.

Paris stared. 'I don't know. Maybe. Oh, this is just too creepy for words.'

'Where's Don?'

'Off buying clothes. He has to show today.'

'I wouldn't count on that. He saw Jill last night. She came here and did this, and now she's dead. I think the cops are going to want to talk to him.'

Paris found her way to a director's chair with JADE embroidered on the seat back. 'Elle, this is just horrible,' she said, sitting down, as if she suddenly didn't have the strength to stand. 'You don't think Don could have . . . ?'

'It doesn't matter what I think. I barely know the man. What do you think? Is he capable of something like that?'

She stared off into the middle distance. 'I want to say no. I've never seen him violent. He's always so in control . . .'

'I heard he'd been in trouble for killing horses for the insurance money.'

'Nothing was ever proven.'

'What about Stellar?'

'That was an accident.'

'Are you sure? What did the claims adjuster say?'

She put her head in her hands for a moment, then smoothed them back over her golden hair. On her right hand she wore an antique emerald and diamond ring that looked to be worth a fortune.

'The company will look for any reason not to pay,' she said with disgust. 'Because Don's involved. It's fine for owners to pay thousands in premiums, but God forbid they actually file a claim.'

'But if it was an accident . . .'

'The adjuster called this morning and claimed the postmortem on Stellar turned up a sedative in the horse's bloodstream. It's ridiculous, but if they can deny the claim, I know they will. Trey is going to be furious when he hears.'

And there goes the million-dollar stable, I thought. Even if Hughes had wanted the horse dead, he didn't want to be caught involved with insurance fraud. He would blame Jade and fire him.

'Was there any reason the horse would have had anything in his system?' I asked.

Paris shook her head. 'No. We have the stuff around, of course. Rompun, acepromazine, Banamine – every stable has that stuff on hand. A horse colics, we give him Banamine. A horse is difficult having his feet worked on by the farrier, we give him a little ace. It's no big deal. But there wasn't any reason for Stellar to have anything in his system.'

'Do you think Jill might have known something about it?' I asked.

'I can't imagine what. She barely did her job. She certainly wouldn't have been here in the middle of the night when Stellar died.'

'She was last night,' I pointed out.

Paris looked to the end of the aisle as Jade came into the tent. 'Well. I guess we never really know the people we work with, do we?'

Jade held shopping bags in both fists. Paris jumped out of the chair and went into the tack room with him to break the news about Jill. I strained to hear, but couldn't make out more than the urgent tone and the odd word, and Jade telling her to calm down.

I looked at Javier, who was still standing at the door of the stall waiting for instructions, and asked him in Spanish if this was a crazy business or what. More than you know, señora, he told me, then he took his pitchfork to a stall farther down the row.

Landry's car pulled up at the end of the tent. He had had to wait for the crime scene unit and the medical examiner's people to arrive at the dump site, and he had probably called in extra deputies to canvass the grounds, looking for anyone who might have seen Jill Morone the night before. He came in with another plainclothes cop at the same time Michael Berne stormed into the tent from the side, red-faced.

Berne stopped at the tack room door, sweeping the curtain back with one hand. 'You're through, Jade,' he said loudly, his voice full of excitement. 'I'm telling the cops what I saw last night. You can get away with a lot of things, but you're not getting away with murder.'

He seemed almost gleeful at the idea that someone had died.

'What do you think you saw, Michael?' Jade asked, annoyed. 'You saw me speaking with an employee.'

'I saw you arguing with that girl, and now she's dead.'

Landry and the other detective arrived to hear the last of Berne's declarations. Landry flashed his badge in Berne's face.

'Good,' Berne said. 'I definitely want to talk with you.'

'You can speak with Detective Weiss,' Landry said, moving past him into the tack room. 'Mr Jade, I need you to come with me.'

'Am I under arrest?' Jade asked calmly.

'No. Should you be?'

'He should have been a long time before now,' Berne said.

Landry ignored him. 'We believe an employee of yours has been found dead. I'd like you to come with me to identify the body and answer some routine questions.'

'Ask him what he was doing with her at The Players last night,' Berne said.

'Ms Montgomery, we'll need to speak with you as well,' Landry said. 'I think we'll all be more comfortable at the Sheriff's Office.'

'I have a business to run,' Jade said.

'Don, for God's sake, the girl is dead,' Paris snapped. 'She may have been killed right here in our barn for all we know. You know she was here last night, busy ruining your wardrobe, and now –'

'What was she doing here last night?' Landry asked.

Jade said nothing. Paris got an oh shit look on her face and clamped her pretty mouth shut.

Landry stared at her. 'Ms Montgomery?'

'Uh ... well ... someone came in late last night and vandalized some things. We assumed it was Jill because she knows the combination to the lock on the tack room door.'

Landry looked at Weiss, communicating something telepathically. Weiss went out to the car. Calling the CSU to come to Jade's stalls when they finished at the dumping site. Calling deputies to come secure the area until the CSU could get here.

Berne pointed at Jade. 'I saw him fighting with the dead girl last night at The Players.'

Landry held up a hand. 'You'll get your turn, sir.'

Perturbed by Landry's lack of interest in him, Berne stepped back out of the stall and turned to me. 'They were in the bar together,' he said loudly. 'She was dressed like a hooker.'

He looked back into the tack stall.

'You're not getting out of this noose, Jade. I heard that girl say she knew about Stellar. You killed her to shut her up.'

'That's completely ridiculous. I did nothing of the sort.'

'Let's go, Mr Jade,' Landry said. 'The medical examiner's people are going to want to move the body.'

'You don't want me to look at her here, do you?' Jade said. 'I won't be the centerpiece of a sideshow.'

Bad for business. Don Jade seen peering at his dead groom.

'We can meet them at the morgue.'

'Can't we do this later? After I've finished my day?'

'Mr Jade, a girl is dead. Murdered. I think that's a little more serious than your average day's work,' Landry said. 'You'll come with us now, voluntarily or not. How do you think it would be for your reputation to be seen in handcuffs?'

Jade heaved a big put-upon sigh. 'Paris, call the clients and let them know what's going on. I don't want them hearing the news from unreliable sources,' he said, glaring at Michael Berne. 'Then stop at the show office and scratch our rides for the day.'

'Scratch them for the rest of his life,' Berne said with a sneer. 'And I couldn't be happier.'

I watched them walk out of the tent: Landry, Jade, and Paris Montgomery; Michael Berne bringing up the rear, mouth flapping. I thought about what Berne had said. I had punched his buttons the day before, suggesting he might have killed Stellar himself in order to ruin Jade. But maybe there was something to it. To Berne's way of thinking, Jade had robbed him of a dream life when he'd taken Trey Hughes away from him. What would it have been worth to get that dream back, to get revenge? The life of an animal? The life of a human? Jealousy can be a powerful motivator.

Stellar had had a sedative in his system when he died. Like Paris had said: those kinds of drugs were in every tack room on the grounds – Berne's included, no doubt.

The horse had died of electrocution – the method of choice among equine assassins, because it left no obvious signs and mimicked death by colic, a common and sometimes fatal illness in horses. The murder was easily accomplished by one person with a couple of wires and a power source. Done correctly, it was difficult to prove the death was anything other than natural.

If the rumors about his past were true, Jade certainly knew that. But having a sedative show up in the postmortem was a big red flag, and Jade knew that as well. If he had killed the horse, he never would have put anything in the animal's system that would show up in the tox screen.

For that matter, if Jade had killed Stellar, why wouldn't he have claimed the horse died of colic? Why wouldn't he have simply said he didn't know what happened? Why the story about the accidental electrocution? There must have been some kind of evidence. Too bad the person who had found the horse dead was no longer around to tell us what that evidence might have been.

'I heard her say she knew about Stellar.'

Berne had said it to further implicate Jade, but if Berne had killed the horse and Jill Morone knew and had been about to tell Jade ... Motive.

Berne had seen the girl at The Players. He could have seen her leave. He could have followed her here ... Opportunity.

I sank back into the chair Paris had occupied and wondered how Erin Seabright's kidnapping figured into any of this.

'This is some glamorous business you're involved with,' Landry muttered as he came back. 'A girl gets murdered, and all these people can think about is the inconvenience of it all.'

'Take a good look at Berne,' I said quietly as he stopped beside me. 'If the girl's death is connected to the horse's death, he could be as much a suspect as Jade. He lost a big opportunity when the owner moved his horses to Jade's care.'

'All right. You can explain that to me later. I don't even know these people ten minutes and I can believe they might be capable of anything. What about the Belgian guy?'

'Haven't seen him, but he's sure to turn up. There might be some blood in this stall,' I said, tipping my head in that direction. 'You'll want to give the CSU a heads-up.'

He nodded. 'Okay. I'm running Jade in for questioning. Weiss has Berne. The techno-geeks and my lieutenant are at the Seabrights' hooking up the phones.'

'I hope to God it isn't too late.'

An uneasy feeling crept down my right side, then Van Zandt came into focus in my peripheral vision. I didn't know how long he'd been standing there.

'Really, I don't know anything, Detective,' I said. 'I knew the girl by sight, that was all.' I turned toward Van Zandt. 'Z., did you see Jill last night?'

He looked like he had a sour stomach and a bad disposition. 'Jill who?'

'Jill. The groom. Don's groom.'

'Why would I see her?' he snapped irritably. 'He should fire her. She's good for nothing.'

'She's dead,' Landry said.

Van Zandt looked perturbed. 'Dead? How is she dead?'

'That's for the medical examiner to find out. My job is to find out why she's dead and who killed her. Did you see her last night?'

'I don't pay attention to grooms,' Van Zandt said with disdain, and went into the tack room.

'Sir, I have to ask you not to touch anything,' Landry said.

Van Zandt had the mini-fridge open. He closed the door and gave Landry an imperious look. 'And who are you to ask anything of me?'

'Detective Landry. Sheriff's Office. Who are you?'

'Tomas Van Zandt.'

'And what's your connection to Don Jade?'

'We are business associates.'

'And you don't know anything about this girl Jill? Except that she was good for nothing.'

'No.'

The deputies came in then to secure the scene, and herded us out of the tent into the blinding sun. Landry got in his car with Jade and drove away.

'They are arresting Jade?' Van Zandt said. He looked pasty and ill in the daylight. He was wearing a blue and red ascot at the throat of his blue dress shirt. Perhaps it was cutting off the blood supply to his brain.

'No. Routine questioning,' I said. 'His employee was murdered. Don't you find that shocking?' I asked. 'I've never known anyone who was murdered.'

Van Zandt shrugged. He didn't seem disturbed in the least. 'The girl was a slut, always talking about this boy and that boy, dressing like a whore. It's no surprise she would come to a bad end.'

'Are you saying she was asking for it?'

'I am saying if you lie down with the dogs, sometimes they bite.'

'Well, there you go. A lesson to us all.'

'This fucking sun,' he complained, putting on his shades, changing the subject as if a girl's violent death was of no more consequence than a bad round in the showring. Less.

'What's your story, Z.?' I asked. 'You look like death, yourself. Were you out partying last night without me?'

'Bad food. I don't get a hangover,' he said stubbornly. 'I never become drunk.'

'Is that from lack of trying or are you superior to the rest of us?'

He mustered a thin smile. 'The second, Elle Stevens.'

'Really? And I thought the Germans were supposed to be the master race.'

'It is only Germans who think that.'

'You've got it all figured out, Z. Come on,' I said, taking him by the arm. 'I'll buy you a Bromo-Seltzer and you can tell me all about the New World Order.'

23

'You saw her at The Players last night. You had an argument.'

'It wasn't an argument,' Jade said calmly. 'She was dressed inappropriately –'

'What's it to you? Was she there with you?'

'No, but she's my employee. The way she conducts herself in public reflects on me.'

'You weren't there to meet her?'

'No. She worked for me. I didn't socialize with the girl.'

Landry raised his brows. 'Really? That's funny, because she told me yesterday you were sleeping with her.'

'What? That's a lie!'

Finally, a human reaction. Landry had begun to suspect Jade didn't have a nerve in his body. They sat on opposite sides of a table in an interview room, Jade – until that moment – perfectly composed, every hair in place, a crisp white shirt accentuating his tan, his monogram on the cuff of the sleeve.

Michael Berne was next door with Weiss. The blonde was cooling her heels in the reception area. Jill Morone was on a slab in the morgue with an assortment of contusions but no obvious fatal injuries. Landry figured strangulation or suffocation. She appeared to have been sexually assaulted.

Landry nodded as he took a bite out of his tuna salad sandwich. 'She told me she was with you Thursday night when Michael Berne's horses were being turned loose.'

Jade rubbed his hands over his face and muttered, 'Oh, that stupid girl. She thought she was helping me.'

'Helping you, as in giving you an alibi? Why would she think you needed one? She was right there when you told me you were with someone that night. Did she know otherwise?'

'Of course not. Jill didn't know anything about anything. She was a dim, pathetic girl with a vivid fantasy life.'

'She had a thing for you.'

He let go a long sigh. 'Yes, I suppose she did. That was why she was at the club last night. She was waiting for me, apparently with ideas to seduce me.'

'But you didn't want to see her.'

'I asked her to leave. She was embarrassing herself.'

'And you.'

'Yes,' Jade admitted. 'My clients are wealthy, sophisticated people, Detective. They want to be represented in a certain way.'

'And Jill didn't fit the bill.'

'I wouldn't take Javier to The Players either, but I didn't kill him.'

'He hasn't claimed you were fucking him,' Landry said, reaching again for his sandwich. 'That I know of.'

Jade looked annoyed. 'Do you need to be so crude?'

'No.'

Landry sat back and chewed on his lunch, more to be irritating than out of hunger.

'So,' he said, making a show of running the facts through his head as he formed a thought, 'she got all dolled up and went to The Players to meet you . . . just on the off chance maybe you'd be interested?'

Jade made a gesture with his hand and shifted positions on his chair. He was bored.

'Come on, Don. She was around, she was hot for it, it was free. You're telling me you never took advantage?'

'That suggestion is repugnant.'

'Why? You've fucked your help before.'

The zinger hit its mark. Jade twitched as if at a small electrical shock. 'I once had an affair with a groom. She was not Jill Morone. Nevertheless, I learned my lesson, and have made it a policy ever since not to become involved with the help.'

'Not even Erin Seabright? She's no Jill Morone either, if you get my drift.'

'Erin? What's she got to do with this?'

'Why isn't she with you anymore, Don?'

He didn't like the familiarity. His eyes narrowed ever so slightly every time Landry used his name.

'She quit. She told me she took another job elsewhere.'

'So far as I've been able to find out, you're the only person she actually told about this big change in her life,' Landry said. 'Taking a new job, moving to a new town. She never even told her family. I find that strange. She only told you. And no one has seen or heard from her since.'

Jade stared at him for a moment, speechless, or knowing the wisdom of holding his tongue. Finally, he stood up. 'I don't like the direction this conversation is taking. Are you charging me with something, Detective Landry?'

Landry stayed in his seat. He leaned back in the chair and rested his elbows on the arms. 'No.'

'Then I'd like to leave now.'

'Oh. Well . . . I just have a few more questions.'

'Then I'd prefer to have my attorney present. It's becoming clear to me you have an agenda that isn't in my best interest.'

'I'm just trying to get a clear picture of the things going on in your business, Don. That's part of my job: to map out the victim's world, put all the pieces in place. You don't want me to get to the truth behind Jill Morone's death?'

'Of course I do.'

'Do you feel you need an attorney present to do that? You're not under arrest. You've told me you don't have anything to hide.'

'I don't.'

Landry spread his hands. 'So ... what's the problem?'

Jade looked away, thinking, considering his options. Landry figured he was maybe good for another five minutes, tops. A sergeant supervisor sat in a room down the hall watching the interview via closed-circuit TV, watching the readout of a computer voice-stress analysis machine, looking for lies.

'Feel free to call your attorney if you like,' Landry said generously. 'We can wait for him ...'

'I don't have time for this,' Jade muttered, coming back to the table. 'What else?'

'Mr Berne said he heard Jill tell you she knew something about Stellar – this horse that died. What did she know?'

'I have no idea what she was talking about. The horse died accidentally in the middle of the night. There was nothing for her to know.'

'There was plenty to know if it wasn't an accident.'

'But it *was* an accident.'

'Were you there when it happened?'

'No.'

'Then you don't really know what happened. If it was an accident, why did the horse have a sedative in its system?'

Jade stared at him. 'How do you know that?'

Landry looked back at him like he was an idiot. 'I'm a detective.'

'There was nothing criminal in Stellar's death.'

'But the owner stands to pick up a big check from the insurance, right?'

'If the insurance company decides to pay, which is unlikely now.'

'Would you have gotten a cut of that money?'

Jade stood again. 'I'm leaving now.'

'What time did you leave Players last night?'

'Around eleven.'

'Where did you go?'

'Home. To bed.'

'You didn't swing by the show grounds, check on your horses?'

'No.'

'Not even after what went on the night before? You weren't worried?'

'Paris had night check last night.'

'And she didn't notice anything wrong? She didn't see the vandalism?'

'Obviously, she was there before it happened.'

'So, you went home to bed. Alone?'

'No.'

'Same friend as Thursday night?'

Jade sighed again and looked at the wall.

'Look, Don,' Landry confided, rising from his chair. 'You need to tell me. This is serious business. This isn't just some nags running around in the middle of the night. A girl is dead. I realize in your world, she might not have counted for much, but in my world, murder is a big deal. Everyone who knew her and had a problem with her is going to have to account for their whereabouts. If you have a corroborating witness, you'd better say so or I'm going to end up wasting a lot more of your valuable time.'

He thought Jade might let his arrogance get the best of him and just walk out. But he wasn't a stupid man. Landry imagined the guy's mind sorting information like a computer. Finally he said, 'Susannah Atwood. She's a client. I would appreciate if you didn't mention this to any of my other clients.'

'Everybody wants to be the trainer's pet?' Landry said. 'That's quite a gig you've got going, Don. Ride the horses, ride the owners too.'

Jade went for the door.

'I'll need her address and phone number, and the name and number for Jill Morone's next of kin,' Landry said.

'Ask Paris. She takes care of my details.'

His details, Landry thought, watching him go. That was what a young girl's life came down to for Don Jade: details.

'Thank you for your time, Mr Jade.'

'Jade needs to run his business differently,' Van Zandt pronounced.

We stood alone along the rail of one of the competition rings, watching a pint-sized rider take her pony over a course of small, elaborately decorated fences. Both girl and pony wore expressions of absolute concentration, eyes bright with determination and the fire of competitive spirit. They were a team: girl and pony against the world.

I remembered that feeling well. Me and a bright copper pony called Party Manners. My very best friend and confidant. Even after I had outgrown him, I had taken all my troubles to Party and he had listened without prejudice. When he died at the ripe old age of twenty-five I mourned his loss more deeply than the loss of any person I had known.

'Are you listening to me?' Van Zandt asked peevishly.

'Yes. I thought you were making a rhetorical statement.' I had offered to buy him lunch, he had declined. I had offered to buy milk shakes and he had told me they would make me fat. Asshole. I bought one anyway.

'Yes,' I agreed. 'Murder puts off potential clients.'

Van Zandt scowled. 'I am in no mood for your sense of humor.'

'You think I was joking? One groom disappears. One turns up dead –'

'Disappears?' he said. 'That one left.'

'I don't think so, Z. The detective was asking about her.'

He turned sharply and looked down his nose at me. 'What did you tell him?'

'Nothing. I've never even met the girl. I'm just letting you know. He'll probably ask you too.'

'I have nothing to say about her.'

'You had a lot to say the other night. That she flirted with clients, that she had a smart mouth – Come to think of it, pretty much the same things you said about Jill. You know, you shouldn't speak ill of the dead, Z. Especially not when there's a detective in earshot.'

'They have no right to question me.'

'Of course they do. You knew both girls. And frankly, you didn't have a very good attitude toward either of them.'

He puffed up in offense. 'Are you accusing me?'

'Oh, for God's sake,' I said, rolling my eyes. 'Behave this way with the cops and they'll pin the murder on you out of spite. And I'll volunteer to push the plunger when they stick the needle in your arm.'

'What are you talking about? What needle?'

'This is a death penalty state. Murder is a capital offense.'

'That's barbaric,' he said, highly offended.

'So is burying a girl in a pile of horseshit.'

'And you think I could do such a terrible thing?' Now he put on his expression of hurt, as if he were being betrayed by a lifelong friend.

'I didn't say that.'

'This is all because of that Russian whore –'

'Watch it, Van Zandt,' I said, giving him a little temper back. 'I happen to be fond of Irina.'

He huffed and looked away. 'Are you lovers?'

'No. Is that your attempt to offend me? Accuse me of being a lesbian?'

He made a kind of shrugging motion with his mouth.

'That's pathetic,' I said. 'I'll bet you say every woman who won't fuck you is a lesbian.'

A hint of red came into his face, but he said nothing. The conversation was not going his way. Again.

'Not that it's any of your business,' I informed him as the girl and the pony concluded their round and the spectators applauded, 'but as it happens, I am happily heterosexual.'

'I don't think happily.'

'Why? Because I haven't had the pleasure of your company in my bed?'

'Because you never smile, Elle Stevens,' he said. 'I think you are not happy in your life.'

'I'm not happy with you trying to get inside my head – or my pants.'

'You have no sense of purpose,' he announced. He was thinking he was back in control of the situation, that I would listen to him the way too many weak, lonely women listened to him. 'You need to have a goal. Something to strive for. You are a person who likes a challenge and you don't have one.'

'I wouldn't say that,' I muttered. 'Just having a conversation with you is a challenge.'

He forced a laugh.

'You have a nerve, making presumptions about me,' I said calmly. 'You don't know a thing about me, really.'

'I am a very good judge of people,' he said. 'I am a long time in the business of assessing people, knowing what they need.'

'Maybe I should set solving Jill's murder as my goal,' I said, turning the tables around on him again. 'Or solving the disappearance of the other girl. I can start by interviewing you. When was the last time you saw Erin Seabright alive?'

'I was more thinking you need a horse to ride,' he said, unamused.

'Come on, Z., play along,' I needled. 'You might start me on the path to a career. Did you hear her say she was going to quit, or is that just D.J.'s story? Inquiring minds want to know.'

'You are giving me a headache.'

'Maybe she was kidnapped,' I said, pretending excitement, watching him carefully. 'Maybe she's being held as a sex slave. What do you think of that?'

Van Zandt stared at me, his expression blank. I would have paid a fortune to know where his mind was at that moment. What was he imagining? Was he thinking about Erin, hidden away somewhere for his own perverse pleasure before he cashed in? Was he remembering Sasha Kulak? Was he considering me as his next victim?

His cell phone rang. He answered it and started conversing in fluent French. I sucked on my milk shake and eavesdropped.

Europeans generally make the correct assumption that Americans can barely speak their own language, let alone anyone else's. It never occurred to Van Zandt that I had an expensive education and a talent for languages. From listening to his side of the conversation, I gleaned that Van Zandt was cheating someone in a deal and was pissed off that they weren't being entirely cooperative pigeons. He told the person on the other end of the call to cancel the horse's transportation to the States. That would teach them they couldn't fuck with V.

The conversation segued then into arrangements for several horses being flown to Florida from Brussels via New York, and two others being sent on the return flight to Brussels.

The horse business is big business in Europe. As a teenager I had once flown back home from Germany with a new horse, traveling in a cargo plane with twenty-one horses being shipped to new owners in the States. Flights like that one land every week.

Van Zandt ended the conversation and put the phone back in his pocket. 'My shipping agent, Phillipe,' he said. 'He is a stinking crook.'

'Why do you say that?'

'Because it's true. He is always wanting me to send things to him from the States. Pack it in with horse equipment and ship it with the horses. I do it all the time,' he confessed blithely. 'No one ever checks the trunks.'

'And you're angry because he's cheating customs?'

'Don't be stupid. Who pays customs? Fools. I am angry because he never wants to pay me. Five hundred dollars' worth of Ralph Lauren towels, for which he still owes me. How can you trust a person like that?'

I didn't know what to say to that. I might have been standing with a serial sex offender, a kidnapper, a killer, and his biggest concern was getting stiffed for five hundred bucks of smuggled towels.

I disentangled myself from him when another dealer came by and they started talking business. I slipped away with a little wave and a promise that I was off in search of the meaning of my life.

A sociopath's stock-in-trade is his ability to read normal humans in order to see their vulnerabilities and take advantage of them. Many a corporate CEO hit the Fortune Five Hundred on those skills, many a con man lined his pockets. Many a serial killer found his victims . . .

Van Zandt wasn't smart, but he was cunning. It was with that cunning he had lured Irina's friend to Belgium to work for him. I wondered how he might have used that instinct on Erin, on Jill. I didn't like the way he had turned it on me when he'd said he didn't believe I was happy. I was supposed to be the carefree dilettante to him. I didn't like to think he could see anything else. I didn't like to think anyone could see inside me, because I was embarrassed by what little there was to see.

He was wrong about one thing, though. I had a goal. And if I found him in my crosshairs on my way to that goal, I was going to be all too happy to take him down.

I made my way back to Jade's barn on foot. Yellow tape blocked off the stalls from either end of the aisle. Despite the warning printed on the tape, Trey Hughes had crossed the line and was sitting in a chair with his feet up on a tack trunk, a beer in one hand and a cigarette in the other.

He squinted and grinned. 'I know you!'

'Not really,' I reminded him. 'Are you part of the crime scene?'

'Honey, I'm a one-man walking crime scene. What's going on around here? It's like a goddam morgue.'

'Yes, well, that would be because of the murder.'

'But that was days ago,' he said.

'What was days ago?'

His thoughts were tripping over each other in his beer-soaked brain. 'I think I missed something.'

'I think *I* missed something if there was a murder here days ago. Who are you talking about? Erin?'

'Erin's dead?'

I ducked under the tape and took a seat across from him. 'Who's on first?'

'What?'

'What's on second.'

'I dunno.'

'Third base.'

Hughes threw his head back and laughed. 'God, I must be drunk.'

'How could you tell?' I asked dryly.

'You're a quick study. Ellie, right?'

'Close enough.'

He took a drag on his cigarette and flicked a chunk of ash onto the ground. I'm sure it never entered his head that he might start a fire in a tent full of horses. 'So, who died?' he asked.

'Jill.'

He sat up at that, sobering as much as he probably could. 'You're joking, right?'

'No. She's dead.'

'What'd she die of? Meanness or ugliness?'

'You're a kind soul.'

'Shit. You never had to be around her. Is she really dead?'

'Someone murdered her. Her body was found this morning over by barn forty.'

'Jesus H,' he muttered, running the hand with the cigarette in it back through his hair. Despite his comments, he looked upset.

'So far, no one misses her,' I said. 'Poor thing. I heard she was hot for Don. Maybe he'll miss her.'

'I don't think so.' Hughes leaned his head back and closed his eyes. 'He'd have gotten rid of her a long time ago if he'd known it was that easy.'

'She was a problem?'

'She had a big mouth and a little brain.'

'Not a good combination in this business,' I said. 'I heard she was at The Players last night saying she knew something about Stellar.'

One bleary blue eye tried to focus on me. 'What could she know?'

I shrugged. 'What is there to know?'

'I don't know. I'm always the last to know.'

'Just as well, or you might end up like Jill.'

'Somebody killed her,' he said to himself. Leaning forward, he put out his cigarette on the toe of his boot and sat there with his head down and his hands dangling between his knees, as if he was waiting for a wave of nausea to pass.

'The cops are questioning Don,' I said. 'Do you think he could kill a person?'

I expected a quick denial. Instead, he was silent so long, I thought he might have gone into a catatonic state. Finally he said, 'People can do the goddamnedest things, Ellie. You just never know. You just never know.'

Paris Montgomery sat staring at him with her big brown eyes wide and bright. Not a deer in the headlights, Landry thought. The expression was more focus than fear. She had brushed her hair and put on lipstick while he'd been interviewing Jade.

'When did you last see Jill yesterday?' he asked.

'Around six. She was complaining about having to stay so late. She'd been dropping hints all day that she had big plans for the evening.'

'Did you ask her what those plans were?'

'No. I hate to speak ill of the dead, but I have to admit I didn't like the girl. She had a bad attitude and she lied all the time.'

'Lied about what?'

'Whatever. That she'd done a job she hadn't, that she knew people she didn't, that she'd trained with big-name people, that she had all these boyfriends –'

'Did she name names of these boyfriends?'

'I didn't want to hear about it. I knew it wasn't true,' she said. 'It was just creepy and pathetic. I was looking for someone to replace her, but it's hard to find good help once the season has started.'

'So, she left around six. Were you aware of anything going on between her and your boss?'

'Don? God, no. I mean, I know she had a crush on him, but that's as far as it went. Don had been after me to get rid of her. He didn't trust her. She was always flapping her mouth to anyone who would listen.'

'About what?'

She blinked the big eyes and tried to decide how much she should tell him. 'About everything that went on in our barn. For instance, if a horse was a little lame or –'

'Dead?' Landry suggested.

'This is a very gossipy business, Detective,' she said primly. 'Reputations can be made or lost on rumors. Discretion is an important quality in employees.'

'So if she was running around shooting her mouth off about the horse that died, that would probably piss you off.'

'Yes. Absolutely.'

'And Don?'

'He would have been furious. Stellar's death has been a nightmare for him. He didn't need his own employee adding fuel to the fire.' She stopped herself and frowned. 'I'm not saying he would have hurt her. I won't believe that. I just won't.'

'He doesn't have a temper?'

'Not like that. Don is very controlled, very professional. I respect him enormously.'

Landry leaned over his notes and rubbed at the tightness in his forehead. 'You didn't see Jill later last night?'

'No.'

'You had night check last night. What time –'

'No, I didn't,' she said. 'Don did. I offered, but he insisted. After what happened in Michael Berne's barn the other night, he said it wasn't safe for a woman to wander around out there at night.'

'He told me you had the job last night,' Landry said.

Paris Montgomery's pretty brow furrowed. 'That's not right. He must have forgotten. God, if one of us had been there last night, maybe we could have prevented what happened.'

Or one of them *had* been there and caused what had happened.

'What time would he have done the check – if he had remembered?' Landry asked.

'Normally, one of us will check the horses around eleven.'

Jade had said he'd been at The Players. If he'd gone to the barn later, he would surely have seen the vandalism, might even have caught the girl in the act. It wasn't a stretch to think they might have argued, things might have gotten out of hand ...

'Where were you last night?' he asked.

'Home. Doing my nails, doing my bills, watching TV. I don't like to go out when we've got horses showing in the morning.'

'You were alone?'

'Just me and Milo, my dog. We fight over the remote control,' she said with a flirtatious smile. 'I hope we didn't keep the neighbors up.'

Landry didn't smile back. He'd been at this job too long to be swayed by charm. It was a form of dishonesty, as far as he was concerned.

That should have meant Estes was the girl for him. He'd never known anyone as blunt as Elena.

'Have you noticed anyone strange hanging around your stalls?' he asked.

Paris made a face. 'There are plenty of strange people around the equestrian center. I can't say that I've noticed anyone in particular.'

'So, you're fresh out of grooms now,' he said. 'I hear you lost one a week ago.'

'Yes. Erin. Boom. Just like that. Quit and went somewhere else.'

'Did she give you any explanation as to why?'

'She didn't talk to me about it. Never even said she was thinking about it. End of the day Sunday she told Don she was leaving, and off she went.'

'No forwarding address?'

She shook her head. 'I have to say, that really hurt, her just dumping us that way. I liked Erin. I thought she would be with us a long time. She talked about how cool it was going to be when we moved into the new barn. She was looking forward to going with us to show in Europe in the spring. I just never expected her to leave.'

'You last saw her when?'

'Sunday afternoon. I left the equestrian center around three. I had a migraine.'

'And Erin seemed fine when you spoke with her?'

She started to give an automatic answer, then stopped herself and thought about it. 'You know, I guess she'd been distracted the last week or so. Boyfriend blues. She had broken up with some guy her own age and had her eye on someone else. I don't know who. Someone who wasn't a child, she said. Then some jerk keyed her car a couple of nights before. She was upset about that. My money's on Jill for that. She was horribly jealous of Erin.'

She stopped herself again, looking confused. 'Why are you asking about Erin?'

'She seems to be missing.'

'Well, I think she went to Ocala –'

'No. She didn't.'

The big brown eyes blinked as she took that in. 'Oh, my God,' she said quietly. 'You don't think – Oh, my God.'

Landry slid a business card across the table to her and rose to his feet. 'Thank you for your time, Ms Montgomery. Please call if you think of anything that might be helpful.'

'We're finished?'

'For now,' Landry said, going to the door. 'I'll need you to call with a number for Ms Morone's next of kin.'

'Yes, of course.'

'Oh – and a number for a Susannah Atwood and the rest of your clients, but first and foremost for Ms Atwood.'

'Susannah? Why Susannah?'

'Seems Mr Jade was performing a night check of his own last night,' he said, curious to see her reaction. He expected jealousy. He was disappointed.

Paris raised her eyebrows. 'Don and Susannah?' she said, amusement turning one corner of her mouth. 'I learn something new every day.'

'I would think it'd be hard to keep a secret in such a small world.'

'Oh, you'd be surprised, Detective Landry,' she said, standing too close to him, her hand just below his on the edge of the open door. 'There are two things the horse world is full of: secrets and lies. The trick is telling which is which.'

24

People can do the goddamnedest things.

Words of insight from Monte Hughes III. Perhaps there was a scrap of substance beneath the self-absorbed, alcohol-soaked narcissist after all. Certainly there was something lurking beneath his well-worn surface, something that had penetrated the fog enough to trouble him.

' . . . *that would be because of the murder.*'

'*But that was days ago.*'

I had to think he'd been referring to Stellar, and in that, admitting the horse had been killed. But at the same time, I couldn't get the image of Jill Morone's corpse out of my mind. The connection between Jill and Erin made me anxious. If one could be murdered, why not the other?

I hated that all of this was happening in the world that had been my refuge. But people are people. The setting doesn't change basic human emotions – jealousy, greed, lust, rage, envy. The players in this drama could have been plucked from this particular stage and placed on any other. The story would have been the same.

I left Trey Hughes and went in search of the one person no one had questioned who I thought might have something relevant to contribute. The one person in Jade's barn who was ever-present, but practically invisible. Javier.

His inability to speak English did not render him blind or deaf or stupid, but it did give him a cloak of anonymity. Who knew what he might have witnessed among the staff and clients of Jade's operation? No one paid any attention to him except to order him around.

But Javier had vanished that morning when Landry had come down the barn aisle, and I had no luck finding him. The Hispanic workers in the neighboring barns had nothing to say to a well-dressed woman asking questions, even if I did speak their language.

I felt at loose ends. For the first time that day I admitted to myself that I wished I still had a badge and could have been sitting in an interview room, pushing the buttons and pulling the strings of the people who had known and disliked Jill Morone, the people who had known Erin Seabright and may have held the key to her whereabouts. I knew those people and understood them in a way the detectives interviewing them never would.

At the very least I wanted to be there putting questions in Landry's ear. But I knew I would never openly be allowed that near an active investigation. And, despite my threats to Bruce Seabright, I would now be held completely outside the kidnapping investigation. I couldn't bully my way into that house with half the Palm Beach County detective division involved. I couldn't even call Molly on the phone because the calls would be traced and recorded.

I had been relegated to the role of informant, and I didn't like it – even though I had been the one dragging Landry into it in the first place.

I who had wanted no part of this case.

Grinding my teeth on my frustration, I left the show grounds and drove to a strip mall, to a cell phone store, where I purchased a prepaid, disposable phone. I would get it to Molly somehow so we could stay in contact without the Sheriff's Office listening in.

I thought about the caller who had rung Bruce Seabright twice in that long list of numbers from his home office phone, and wondered if the kidnappers had been smart enough to do what I was doing. Did they have a phone they could ditch? Had they bought it with cash, given a phony ID?

I had given the list of phone numbers to Landry, who would be able to get a line on all of them through the phone company. I doubted we would be lucky enough to have one of the numbers come back listed to Tomas Van Zandt or Don Jade or Michael Berne. Landry would know by the end of the day. I wondered if he would tell me. Now that he was in this mess up to his neck, I wondered if he would include me at all. A small hollow ball of fear had taken up residence in my stomach at the thought that he might not.

Sean waved me to the barn as I drove into the yard. The afternoon was slipping away in the west. The sky was orange with a drift of black smoke billowing along the horizon. Farmers burning off the stubble of their sugarcane fields. Irina was feeding the horses their dinner. I breathed in the scent of animals and molasses and grass hay. Better than a Valium to me. D'Artagnon stuck his head out over the door of his stall and nickered to me. I went to him and stroked his face and rested my cheek against his and told him that I missed him.

'Just in time for cocktails, darling. Come along,' Sean said, leading the way to the lounge. He was still in breeches and boots.

'Sorry I haven't been any help the last few days,' I said. 'Are you going to fire me and throw me out into the street?'

'Don't be silly. You've embroiled me in international intrigue. I'll dine out on this for years to come.' He went to the bar and poured himself a glass of merlot. 'Want some? Blood red. That should appeal to you.'

'No, thanks. I'll be giddy.'

'That will be the day.'

'Tonic and lime sounds nice.'

He fixed the drink and I crawled onto a barstool, tired and body sore.

'I spoke today with friends in Holland,' he said. 'They had already heard Van Zandt had been in my barn.'

'That's some grapevine.'

'Apparently, Van Zandt didn't waste any time putting the word out that I might be buying and selling horses with him.'

'I'm sure he didn't. You're a plum catch, my peach. Great taste and lots of money. I'm sure he wanted that news to get to your longtime agent as soon as possible.'

'Yes. Thank Christ I had called Toine ahead of time and warned him I was sacrificing myself for a noble cause. He would have been on the first plane over from Amsterdam to rescue me from Van Zandt's evil clutches.'

'And what did your other friends have to say about the evil Z.?'

'That he's a pariah. He's been banished from the best farms in Holland. They simply won't do business with him.'

'But plenty of other people will.'

He shrugged. 'Dealers always manage to find clients, and people with horses to sell need clients to sell them to. If no one did business with shady characters like Van Zandt, not much business would get done.'

'I'll tell him you said so over dinner tonight.'

He made a face. 'You're having dinner with him? You'll want to buy a case of liquid Lysol.'

'To drink?'

'To bathe in afterward. Seriously, Elle,' he said, frowning at me, 'be careful with that creep. Irina told me what he did to her friend. And now there's been a murder at the show grounds. Is he involved in that? That's where you were all day, isn't it?'

'I don't know if he was involved. Other people may have had reason to want the girl dead.'

'Jesus, Elle.'

'I know what I'm doing. And the cops are involved now.'

'Is that who was here this morning?' he asked, a sly look coming into his eyes. 'Mr Very Good-Looking in the silver car?'

'Detective,' I corrected. 'Is he good-looking? I hadn't noticed.'

'Honey, you need an optometrist if you haven't noticed that.'

'His personality leaves something to be desired.'

'So does yours,' he said, trying not to grin. 'Could be a perfect fit.'

'Could be you need your head examined,' I complained. 'This mess I'm involved in – thanks to you, by the way – involves a lot of ugly stuff. Romance is not on the agenda even if I was interested – which I'm not.'

He hummed a note to himself, thinking something I was certain I didn't want to know. I was uncomfortable with the idea of anyone thinking of me as a sexual being, because I had ceased to think of myself in that way two years before.

Deeper than the scars on my body, my sense of self had been stripped down to nothing that day in rural Loxahatchee when Hector Ramirez had been killed and I had gone under the wheels of Billy Golam's truck.

Despite the fact that surgeons had spent the last two years repairing the physical damage to my body – mending broken bones, patching skin burned away by the road, rebuilding the shattered side of my face – I didn't know that I would ever feel whole again. Essential parts of me were missing – parts of my soul, of my psychological self. Maybe the layers would fill in eventually. Maybe that process had begun. But I had a very long way to go, and most days I doubted I had the strength or the will for the journey. I did know I didn't want anyone close enough to watch the process. Certainly not James Landry.

'Never say never, darling.' Sean finished his wine and went off to ready himself for a night on the town in Palm Beach. I went to the guest house and checked my e-mail.

Special Agent Armedgian, my contact with the FBI field office in West Palm, had come through with the Interpol info.

According to Armedgian, Van Zandt had no arrest record, but Interpol had a file on him, which said something. He had dabbled in a lot of business pies, always skirting the line of what was legal and what was not, but never quite crossing over it – or not getting caught, at any rate.

There was no mention of him coming under scrutiny for anything of a sexual nature. I was disappointed, but not surprised. If there were other victims of his dubious charms, they were probably like Irina's friend: young, inexperienced, alone in a foreign country, afraid to tell anyone.

Needing to clear my head before the evening's mind games, I changed into a swimsuit and went to the pool to let the warm, silky water soothe my body and clean the layers of grit from my brain.

The sun was gone, but the pool shimmered midnight blue, lit from within its walls. I thought of nothing at all as I swam lazy laps with slow-motion underwater turns at the end of each. The tension washed away, and for a short time I was simply a sleek, aquatic animal, bone and muscle and instinct. It felt good to be something that fundamental and uncontrived.

When I'd had enough, I rolled over onto my back and floated, looking up at the pinpoint stars in the black velvet sky. Then Landry came into view, standing at the water's edge.

I dove under and came back up, shaking the water from my head.

'Detective. You got the drop on me,' I said, treading water.

'I'm sure that doesn't happen very often.'

He was still in his work clothes, though he had jerked the tie loose and rolled up the sleeves of his shirt.

'My fault for giving you the gate code,' I said. 'Hard day turning the thumbscrews?'

'Long.'

'Sorry I missed it. No one makes a better bad cop than me.'

'I have no doubt about that,' he said with half a smile. 'Aren't you going to invite me in? Say the water's fine?'

'That would be a cliché. I abhor predictability.'

I swam to the ladder and climbed out, forcing myself not to rush to cover my body with my towel. I didn't want him to know how vulnerable I felt. Somehow I thought that even in the dim light around the pool he would see every scar, every imperfection. It made me angry that I cared.

I toweled myself off, rubbed my hair dry, then wrapped the towel around my waist like a sarong to hide the pitted, scarred flesh of my legs. Landry watched, his expression unreadable.

'Nothing about you is predictable, Estes.'

'I'll take that as a compliment, though I don't think you consider unpredictability a virtue. Do you have any good news?' I asked, leading the way to the guest house.

'The deputies found Erin Seabright's car,' he said. 'Parked under about six inches of dust in a corner of that first lot at the truck entrance of the equestrian center.'

I stood with my hand on the doorknob, holding my breath, waiting for him to tell me Erin had been found dead in the trunk.

'The CSU is going over it for prints, et cetera.'

I let go a sigh at the initial sense of relief. 'Where was it?'

'In the first parking lot as you come in the truck entrance, over by the laundry place.'

'Why would it be there?' I asked, not expecting an answer. 'She would have parked near Jade's barn, not half a mile away. Why would it be there?'

Landry shrugged. 'Maybe she had dropped stuff off at the laundry.'

'Then walked all the way to Jade's barn? And then walked to the back gate to meet whoever she thought she was meeting? That doesn't make sense.'

'It doesn't make sense for the kidnappers to move it there either,' Landry said. 'They kidnapped her. Why would they care where her car was parked?'

I thought about that as we went into the house. 'To buy time? Monday would have been Erin's day off. If not for Molly, no one would have missed her until Tuesday morning.'

'And no one would have missed her then, because Jade claimed she'd quit and moved to Ocala,' Landry finished the theory.

'How did he take the questioning?'

'It was an inconvenience to him. The interview and the murder.'

'Any nerves?'

'Not worth mentioning.'

'Well . . . the guy makes a living riding horses over fences taller than I am. It's not a game for the faint of heart.'

'Neither is murder.'

A game. It would be difficult for the average person to consider murder and kidnapping a game, but in a macabre way it was a game. A game with very serious stakes.

'Any word from the kidnappers?'

Landry sat against the back of a chair, hands in his pockets. He shook his head. 'No. The phones are rigged at the Seabright house. I've had a couple of guys checking out the neighbors. That's a dead end.'

'There's a bar in that armoire under the TV,' I said, pointing into the living room. 'You look like you need it. Help yourself while I change.'

I made him wait while I took a quick shower, then stood in front of the mirror for five minutes, staring at myself, trying to read my own inscrutable expression.

I didn't like the anxious feeling lingering in my belly. The bubble of fear had been replaced by something I almost didn't recognize: hope. I didn't want it to mean so much that Landry had come back, that he was filling me in, including me.

'You told Seabright you're a private investigator,' he said. His voice was strong and clear. He must have been standing just on the other side of the bedroom door. 'Are you?'

'Not exactly.'

'That's fraud.'

'No. It's a lie,' I corrected. 'It would only be fraud if I were misrepresenting myself and accepting money from the Seabrights based on that misrepresentation. I'm not.'

'You'd make a hell of a lawyer.'

So my father had always said, which was the reason I had become a cop. I hadn't wanted to be like him, bending the law like it was made of wire, bending it to suit the needs of corrupted people, corrupted wealth. I hadn't realized at the time that as a cop I would end up bending it as many ways myself and excusing my actions because I believed my cause was just. I still wasn't like him. That was the important thing.

'I checked the Seabright kid's record,' Landry said. 'He's never been in any trouble. Good student, lots of extracurricular activities.'

'Like screwing his stepsister?'

'And the math club.'

'I don't like that he's lying about where he was Sunday,' I said.

'Like father, like son.'

I pulled on black underwear, checking over my shoulder, half-expecting to see Landry standing in the doorway. He wasn't.

'Seabright's going to stick by his own flesh and blood,' I said. I put on a white tuxedo shirt and a pair of black cigarette pants. 'He isn't going to allow for the possibility Chad might be involved somehow.'

'That's assuming the father is the one providing the alibi. It works the other way too.'

I tied the shirt at the waist and escaped the bedroom. Landry stood leaning back against the kitchen counter, a scotch in hand. He took in the outfit with hooded eyes.

'You didn't have to dress up for me,' he said.

'I didn't. I can't see Bruce Seabright actively participating in the kidnapping. Even if he wanted Erin gone, he wouldn't get his hands dirty. Too risky. So why would he need an alibi?' I asked. 'Chad was the one involved with Erin.'

'And Erin is the one with the juvie record,' Landry said. 'Shoplifting. Possession.'

'Of what?'

'Ecstasy. Busted at a party. She got a slap on the wrist. I've got someone in the Juvenile Division checking out the pals she was arrested with,' Landry said. 'And I reached out to a guy I know in Narcotics to get a line on the dealer.'

'Who in Narcotics?'

'Brodie. You know him?'

I looked at my feet and nodded. I stood across from Landry, leaning back against the other counter, my arms crossed over my chest. The room was so small, my bare feet were nearly toe-to-toe with his shoes. Good quality, brown leather oxfords. No tassels for Landry.

Matt Brodie had been a friend once. Or so I had thought. I wished I hadn't asked the question. Now Landry was waiting for me to elaborate. 'He's good enough,' I said.

'I'm sure he'd be happy to have your approval,' Landry said with a dry edge of sarcasm.

I wondered what Brodie might have said about me, not that it mattered. Landry would think what he wanted.

'Jade is the one who claims the girl just up and left,' he said. 'He's the last one who saw her. I think it goes this way: Erin knew something about the dead horse. Jade wanted her out of the way. He set up the kidnapping to make some extra money for his trouble. The girl is probably as dead as the one in the shit pile.'

'I'll hope you're wrong about the last part,' I said, knowing he could well be right. I'd had the thought myself.

'Look, Estes, I owe you an apology,' he said. 'That's why I'm here. Maybe if I'd listened to you the first time you came in, Jill Morone wouldn't be dead. Maybe we'd have Erin Seabright back by now.'

I shrugged. 'I don't know what to say to that.'

He was right and we both knew it. I wasn't going to offer platitudes like some good wife excusing a husband's minor transgressions. Nor was I going to grind the truth in his face. He had made a judgment call, a bad one. I was the last person with a right to criticize on that count.

'It's not all about you,' I said. 'I was there ahead of you. I didn't stop that girl getting killed. I didn't find Erin. Sometimes things just play out the way they play out.'

'You believe that?'

'I have to. If I didn't, then I'd be to blame for every rotten thing that ever happened, and I know for a fact I'm only to blame for two-thirds of them.'

He looked at me for a moment that stretched on. I wanted to turn away or move, but I didn't.

'So, did Jade have an alibi for last night?' I asked.

'A woman. A client. Susannah Atwood.'

'She confirmed?'

He nodded.

'And did she have anyone to corroborate *her* story?'

He rolled his eyes. 'Sure. Jade. Why? Do you know her?'

'I know of her. Sean knows her. She has a reputation as a social dragonfly.'

'Don't you mean butterfly?'

'No.'

He raised his brows.

'I know her type,' I said. 'Susannah might just think providing an alibi to a murderer is the oral sex of the new millennium. I wouldn't trust her. Then again, I don't trust anyone.'

I checked my watch and moved away from the counter. 'I'm going to throw you out now, Landry. I've got a dinner date with the devil.'

'Which one?'

'Van Zandt.'

As I went in search of a pair of shoes, I told him what I'd learned through Sean and through Interpol via Armedgian. I had told Van Zandt I would meet him at The Players at eight. I had wisely declined his offer to pick me up.

Landry stood staring into the closet, hands on his hips. 'You're telling me you think this guy could be a sexual predator, but you're going out to dinner with him?'

'Yes.'

'What if he killed Jill Morone? What if he's got Erin stashed somewhere?'

'Hopefully, I'll learn something to help nail him.'

'Are you on crack?' he asked, incredulous. 'Are you stupid?'

'He won't try to pull anything with me,' I said, coming out of the closet one heel on, one in hand. 'First: He knows he doesn't scare me and can't control me. Second: He thinks I'm worth money to him as a client, not as a victim.'

'And if he's just a fucking pervert who wants to rape you and slit your throat?'

'Then I will have made a gross misjudgment of his character – which I haven't.'

'Estes, he may have killed that girl last night, for all you know. He lied about seeing her. He was there at The Players. The bartender and the waitress said he was there, drooling all over the girl. We'd have hauled him in by now, but we don't know where he is.'

'What time did he leave the bar?'

'No one could say for certain.'

'So pull him in and rake him over the coals if you want,' I said. I stepped into the bathroom and looked at my hair. There was nothing to be done about it. 'I'll gladly spend the evening in the tub reading a book. But if he's got Erin stashed somewhere, he's sure as hell not going to tell you about it.'

'And you think he'll just up and tell you?' Landry asked, blocking the doorway. 'Like that's some kind of smooth line: wanna come back to my place and see the girl I kidnapped? Jesus Christ!'

'So tail us! What are you getting so upset about?'

He shook his head and turned around in a circle, moving back into the bedroom. 'This is why I don't want you involved in this,' he said, pointing at me as I came out of the bathroom. 'You've got your own agenda, you run off half-cocked –'

'So look the other way,' I said, pushing his finger out of my face, my temper rising. 'I'm a private citizen, Landry. I don't need your permission and I don't need your approval. If I turn up dead, you'll know who to arrest. I'll make your fucking case for you. You'll be a hero in the Sheriff's Office – getting rid of me and catching a killer all in one fell swoop.'

'It's not my job to let you get yourself killed!' he shouted.

'Believe me, if I haven't done the job myself by now, I'm not about to let some hump like Van Zandt do it for me.'

We were nearly nose to nose, the air in the scant inches between us charged with electricity. Landry held whatever it was he wanted to say tight in his chest. Maybe he was counting to ten. Maybe it was all he could do to keep from strangling me with his bare hands. I didn't know what he was thinking. I was thinking I was standing too damn close to him.

'I was good too, Landry,' I said quietly. 'On the job. I know that's not what anyone wants to remember about me, but I was good. You'd be a fool not to take advantage of that.'

Another eternity came and went. We stood there staring at each other like a couple of angry porcupines – all defenses up. Landry blinked first and took a step back. I thought I should have been proud of that, but what I felt was more like disappointment.

'Van Zandt wants to impress me,' I said. I went back into the closet and found a small clutch purse to stash my microcassette recorder in. 'He wants to come across like a hotshot, but his mouth is bigger than his brain. I can get him to say things he shouldn't. I'll tape the conversation. I'll call you after.'

'After what?' he asked pointedly.

'After coffee,' I said. 'I draw the line at prostituting myself. Glad you have such a high opinion of me, though.'

'I'm glad you have a line,' he muttered.

He pulled his cell phone out of his pocket, dialed a number, and stood staring at me while he waited for someone to pick up on the other end. I knew what he was doing. A part of me wanted to ask him not to, despite what I'd said earlier. But I wouldn't allow it. I had come as close to begging as I was going to.

'Weiss. Landry. Van Zandt is at The Players. Pick him up.'

Never taking his eyes off me, he put the phone back in his pocket. 'Thanks for the tip.'

I wanted to tell him to go to hell, but I didn't trust my voice. It felt like I had a hard, hot rock stuck in my throat. I much preferred feeling nothing, caring about nothing but getting from one day to the next – and not caring very much about that. If you have no expectations, no purpose, no goal, you can't be disappointed, you can't feel hurt.

Landry turned and walked out, taking the information I'd given him, taking my plans for the evening with him, taking my hope to make a break in the case. I felt like a fool. I thought he had come to me to include me, but all he had wanted was to absolve his conscience. The case was his case. He owned it.

'Thanks for the tip.'

I paced the house, trying to shove back the emotions crowding in on me. I needed to do something. I needed a new plan. I wasn't going to sit home with all these feelings to contemplate, and I didn't have a good book to take to the bathtub.

An idea began to take shape in my mind. Before it was more than an embryo, I had changed clothes and was out the door.

My life would have been easier if I had gone to Barnes & Noble.

25

Lorinda Carlton's Wellington address was a town house on Sag Harbor Court. Unless Van Zandt made a revelation during his interview with Landry, there was not probable cause for a warrant to search the premises. But if Van Zandt had been involved in Erin's kidnapping or Jill's murder, and had kept a souvenir, there was a good chance he would get rid of it as soon as he came back to the town house.

I parked in a visitor's slot at the end of the block of buildings where Carlton's unit was located. Half the places on the block had lights on, but there was no activity going on outdoors. No friendly neighbors sitting on their front stoop, watching Saturday night go by.

Because of the nature of Wellington and the winter show season, rentals experience a big turnover of tenants every year. While some of the horse people own homes, many find themselves in a different apartment every winter. The nature of horse people being what it is, the accommodations for their horses are arranged first, accommodations for themselves often wait until the last minute. The town house and apartment complexes consequently do not have a strong feeling of community.

Carlton's unit was on the far end of the dead-end street and completely dark. I peered in the sidelight at the front door, looking for a security system panel. If there was one, it was located out of my limited range of sight. If there was an alarm and I tripped it, I was in a bad position to get back to my car. I would have to find a way to make my escape through or over the tall hedge that ran along the end of the complex, hoping that no one would see me, then double back around later to get my car.

With that much of a plan in mind, I slipped a couple of picks out of my coat pocket and went to work on the front door lock. Any casual passerby would be far less suspicious of someone unlocking a front door than trying to sneak in the back. I could always shrug and say I'd lost my key, make up a story about how I was in for the weekend to see my friend Van Zandt, who had rudely forgotten about me.

I held my breath as I worked the picks in the lock. Lock picking is not a skill taught at the police academy. I learned it from a groom when I was eleven years old. Bobby Bennet had spent many years working the south

Florida racetracks until an unfortunate misunderstanding about a burglary had landed him in prison for three to five. He claimed to have mended his wicked ways after he got out, but he had retained his old skills and passed them on to me because I was a pest and he got a kick out of me.

I thanked God for Bobby Bennet as the lock's tumblers fell into place. My heart was still thumping as I opened the door and went inside. Many security systems allow entry with a key, but then require the proper code to be entered on the keypad within a minute or two or the alarm sounds both within the house and with whatever agency the system is connected to, whether it be a private security company or the Sheriff's Office.

I found the system control panel on the wall adjacent to the hinged side of the door. A small green light declared the system unarmed.

Relieved, I moved on about my business. I flipped on a table lamp in the living room. Any neighbors bothering to notice the lights on would simply assume the person in the town house was the person who was supposed to be in the town house, because what thief would turn the lights on?

The place was vaguely shabby and smelled of stale dog. The carpet had been white once. So had the fake leather sofas that were now cracked and dingy. Van Zandt needed to get a wealthier client to put him up free of charge. He probably had Sean in mind for that. He was probably already scheming to get the guest house next season.

I passed through the galley kitchen, doing a cursory check of drawers and cupboards. Nothing but the usual assortment of mismatched utensils, cereal boxes, and laundry soap. He liked Heineken beer and orange juice with extra pulp. There were no amputated body parts in the refrigerator or freezer. A small load of laundry lay clean, dry, and wrinkled in the dryer. Slacks, socks, and underwear. As if he had undressed and thrown everything into the washing machine together. Except that there was no shirt. I wondered why.

The living room offered nothing of interest. A collection of videos in the TV cabinet. Science fiction and romances. Lorinda Carlton's, I assumed. I couldn't picture Van Zandt sitting through *Titanic*, weeping as Leonardo DiCaprio went under for the third time. There was no sign of the video camera he had brought to Sean's.

I climbed the stairs to the second floor, where the bedrooms were located – one small and decorated with dog toys, one a master with cheesy laminated furnishings. This room smelled of Van Zandt's cologne. The bed was made, his clothes were put away neatly in the closet and in the drawers. He might have made some woman a good husband if not for those unfortunate sociopathic and misogynistic tendencies.

The video camera was in the closet, sitting on the floor beside a row of shoes. I opened the leather case and looked through the tapes, all of them labeled with the names of sale horses. Van Zandt would tape the horses, then copy the tapes (judiciously edited to show only the best traits of each horse) for prospective buyers to preview. I popped one of the VHSC cassette tapes into the camera, rewound it, and hit the play button. A gray horse appeared on the viewing screen, going over a series of jumps. Good form. The tape fuzzed out, then refocused, and a chestnut came into view. I hit the stop button and swapped tapes. More of the same. Van Zandt managed to get not only film of the horse in question, but also a smiling shot of some sweet young thing attached to the horse in some way or another. Rider or groom or owner. Cause for an eye roll, not alarm.

On the third tape I found Paris Montgomery astride a black gelding with a white star on his forehead. Stellar.

It broke my heart to watch him perform. He was a handsome animal with a mischievous sparkle in his eye and a habit of flipping his tail up like a flag as he jumped. He went to the fences with enthusiasm, but there wasn't a lot of spring in his jump and he didn't always get his hind legs out of the way in time to miss brushing the top rail of the fence. But I could see the will in him, the heart Dr Dean had spoken of. When Stellar knocked a rail he pinned his ears and shook his head as he landed, as if angry with himself for not doing better. He had a lot of 'try', as horse people say, but it took more than try to win at the elite level or be sold at an elite price.

Behind the camera, Van Zandt clearly became bored with the horse. There were far too many close-ups of Paris and her model's smile. I wondered just how close they were, whether or not Paris Montgomery drew the same line I did when it came to getting what she wanted from a man.

Then came one long shot of a girl holding Stellar by the reins, posing the riderless animal for a side view. Erin Seabright in a skin-fitting T-shirt and a pair of shorts that showed off slender, tan legs. Just as she got the horse positioned to best show him off, he butted her with his head and sent her staggering backwards, laughing. Pretty girl, pretty smile. She took hold of the horse's head and planted a kiss on his nose.

The tough, mouthy, bad girl. Not in this scene. I could see Erin's connection to the horse. I could see it in the way she spoke to him, the way she touched him, the way her hand lingered on his neck as she moved him. Knowing her family situation, it wasn't hard to imagine Erin felt closer to the horses she cared for than she did to most of the Seabright household. The horses didn't judge her, didn't criticize her, didn't let her down. The horses didn't know or care if she had broken rules. They only knew whether or not she was kind and patient, whether or not she brought them treats and knew where they liked to be scratched.

I knew these things about Erin Seabright because I had been Erin Seabright a lifetime ago. The girl who didn't fit the family mold, didn't want to live up to family expectations; the girl who chose acquaintances based on their objectionable qualities. Her only true friends lived in the stables.

The tape revealed more to me about Erin than it did about Van Zandt. I rewound it and watched Erin's part again, hoping I would have the opportunity to see her smile like that in person, though I knew even if I could get her out of this mess, it could be a very long time before she felt like smiling.

I swapped the tape for another and zoomed fast-forward through three more horses, then Sean and Tino popped up, and I let the tape play. The pair made a lovely picture as they moved around the arena. Sean was an excellent rider, strong, elegant, quiet and centered in his body. The brown gelding was lean and leggy and had a stylish way of going. The camera followed as they moved laterally across the ring toward the gazebo, diagonal pairs of legs crossing with the grace of a ballet dancer, the horse's body curving like a bow around Sean's leg. And then they went out of the frame.

The camera lingered on the gazebo, zooming in on Irina. She stared out of the picture with an expression of cold hatred, brought her cigarette to her lips, and blew the smoke right at the glass eye. It didn't seem to unnerve her that Van Zandt was watching her. It made my skin crawl. I wanted to go to Irina's apartment and lecture her on locking her door at night.

Elena Estes, Mother Hen.

I put the camera back where I had found it and went back into the bedroom, to the TV stand that housed another television and VCR. And a collection of porn. Multiple girls with one guy. Multiple guys with one girl. Lesbian sex. Lots of lesbian sex. Gay men. Some of the movies looked like they might have been violent, most didn't.

An equal opportunity perv, our Mr Van Zandt.

I searched the drawers of the dresser and nightstands. I looked under the bed and found dust bunnies and some petrified dog turds. Van Zandt's patron needed a new cleaning person.

I found no tapes related to Erin's kidnapping. I knew the kidnapper had to have them. The tape that had been sent to the Seabrights was a full-sized VHS tape. Most modern camcorders were either digital or recorded on eight millimeter or a small VHSC cassette like the ones in the closet. The tape would then have been copied via VCR onto the larger tape. The kidnapper had also had access to more sophisticated audio equipment than any I had seen in the town house. The voice on the tape had been mechanically altered. If Van Zandt was involved in the kidnapping, he had the tapes and recording equipment stashed elsewhere.

Disappointed, I turned out the lights and went back downstairs. My internal clock was telling me it was time to go. I had lingered too long over the videotapes of the horses. I knew Landry would try to keep Van Zandt in the interview room as long as he could, but there was always the possibility Van Zandt would just get up and leave. He wasn't under arrest – that I knew of. He didn't even think the laws of the United States should apply to him.

I looked at the front door, but didn't move toward it. The idea of striking out had never appealed to me. I wanted to find something more incriminating than a porn habit, something – anything – that, even if it didn't tie him directly to the murder or the kidnapping, could at least be used as leverage against him in a future interview.

I went through the kitchen and let myself into a garage just large enough for one car and some storage lockers along one wall. The locker doors had padlocks on them. I didn't have the time to pop them. On top of the lockers were precarious piles of junk: a Styrofoam cooler, pool toys, cases of Diet Rite soda, a twelve-roll package of cheap toilet paper. In other words: nothing.

Plastic trash cans and recycling bins sat along the wall at the far end of the garage. I wrinkled my nose and went to them.

A criminal's garbage can be a treasure trove of evidence. Egg-coated, stinking evidence in most cases, but evidence nonetheless.

I pulled the lid off the first can and peered down into it. The only lightbulb in the garage was on the wall beside the kitchen door. The wattage wasn't enough to be of any real help to me. I wished I had brought my flashlight from the car, but there wasn't time to go get it.

I dug through the trash, having to get much too close to see what I was looking at. Junk mail, boxes and microwave trays from frozen dinners, egg cartons, egg shells, egg goo, Chinese take-out cartons, pizza boxes. The same garbage anyone might have. No credit card receipts, no to-do list that included murder and kidnapping.

I found a note that listed names of horses, a date, a departure time from Palm Beach, an arrival time in New York, flight number and times for a flight to Brussels. The horses he was shipping to Europe. I slipped the note into my jeans pocket. If Van Zandt was shipping horses out of the country, he could ship himself out of the country with them. He could fly with the horses and be gone from Landry's jurisdiction like a thief in the night.

Then I pulled the lid off the second trash container, and adrenaline rushed through my system like a drug.

The only item in the can was a shirt. The shirt that hadn't been run through the wash with the pants and socks and underwear – clothes taken off in haste and thrown in the machine together.

I had to lean down into the container to pick the shirt off the bottom. The smell of the can assaulted me, made my eyes water, turned my stomach. But I came back up with the shirt in hand and took it over by the light for a closer inspection.

Fine Egyptian cotton in a warm French blue. I held the shirt up to the light, looking for a monogram, wanting some positive ID the shirt belonged to Van Zandt. I found none, but there was something on the left side of the collar that might just as positively identify the owner: dark stains that looked like blood. The left front panel of the shirt had a large tear in it about halfway down with more blood.

My heart was racing.

Van Zandt might have cut himself shaving, a defense attorney would argue. And did he stab himself shaving too, a prosecutor would ask. The evidence suggested he might have been injured in a struggle, the prosecution would say.

I could easily picture Jill Morone fighting her attacker, arms flailing, fingers curled into claws, raking at him. She might have caught him on the neck, scratched him, he bled on the shirt. If the autopsy revealed skin beneath her fingernails . . . If Van Zandt had corresponding wounds on his neck . . . I hadn't noticed any, but he could have hidden them with his ever-present ascot. I thought of the stall in Jade's barn, of what I had thought might be blood on the pine bedding. Maybe from the second injury. She might have struck him with something, cut him with something. Maybe it wasn't liquor that accounted for Van Zandt's pallor that morning after all.

My heart was pounding so hard, my hands were shaking. I'd hit the jackpot. In the old days, I would have bought a round for the house after a find like this. Now I couldn't even claim the victory, and I wouldn't be welcome in the cop bars even if I could have. I stood there in the dim light of the garage, trying to temper my excitement, forcing myself to think through the next crucial steps I had to take.

Landry needed to find the shirt. As much as I would have enjoyed throwing it in his face, I knew that if I took it to him, it would never make it into a trial. As a private citizen, I didn't need a warrant to search someone's house. The Fourth Amendment protects us from agents of the government, not from each other. But neither could I be in that house illegally. If Van Zandt had invited me over, and during the course of my visit I had found the shirt, that would have been a different story. And still there might have been complications. Because I had once been a law enforcement agent, and because I had had contact with the Sheriff's Office about this case, a good defense attorney would argue that I should be considered a de facto agent of the Sheriff's Office, thereby blowing my status as an innocent citizen and rendering the evidence I had found inadmissible.

No. This had to be done by the book. Chain of custody had to be established. The SO needed to come into the garage with a warrant. An anonymous tip, along with Van Zandt's history and his connection to Jill Morone, might be enough to get it.

Still, I didn't want to put the shirt back into the trash container. I couldn't trust that something wouldn't go wrong; that Van Zandt wouldn't spook after his chat with Landry, come back here and get rid of the evidence. I needed to hide it somewhere Van Zandt wouldn't find it.

No sooner had that thought crossed my mind than came the sound of a car pulling into the drive, and the garage door opener started to growl.

The door was already a third of the way up as I turned and ran for the kitchen door, the car's headlights illuminating the wall like spotlights on a prisoner escape.

The car horn blasted.

I bolted into the kitchen, slammed the door, and locked the dead bolt, buying a few precious seconds. Frantically, I looked around the room for a place to hide the shirt.

No time. No time. Ditch it and run.

I stuffed the shirt into the back of a lower kitchen cupboard, shut the door, and ran on as the key turned in the dead bolt.

Jesus Christ. If Van Zandt recognized me . . .

Running through the dining area, I caught a chair with my hip, tripped, stumbled, struggled to stay on my feet, my eyes on the sliding door to the screened patio.

Behind me I heard a dog barking.

I hit the patio door, yanked the handle. The door was locked.

A voice – a woman? 'Get him, Cricket!'

The dog: growling. I could see him coming out of the corner of my eye: a small, dark missile with teeth.

My thumb fumbled at the lock, flipped it up. I yanked the door back on its track and went through the opening as the dog hit my calf with its teeth.

I jerked my leg forward and the dog yelped as I tried to slam the door on his head.

I dove across the small patio for the screen door, fell against it, then through it as it swung open. I was in the backyard.

Lorinda Carlton's town house was the last on its row. A tall hedge bordered the development. I needed to be on the other side of that hedge. On the other side of the hedge was an open, undeveloped space owned by the village of Wellington, and at the far end of that property, the Town Square shopping center.

I ran for the hedge. The dog was still coming behind me, barking and snarling. I took a hard right and sprinted along the hedge, looking for an opening to the other side. The dog was snapping at my heels. I pulled my jacket off as I ran, wrapped one sleeve of the windbreaker tight around my right hand, and let the rest of it trail the ground.

The dog lunged for and caught the jacket between his jaws. I grabbed hold of the one sleeve with both hands, planted one foot, and pivoted around, swinging the dog around on the end of the jacket. Around once, twice, like a hammer thrower in the Olympics. I let go.

I didn't know how far the dog's weight and momentum would carry him, but it was far enough to buy me a few seconds. I heard a crash and a yelp just as I caught sight of a way over the hedge.

A pickup sat parked beside another of the end unit town houses. I scrambled up onto the hood, onto the roof, and over the hedge.

I landed like a skydiver – bent knees, drop and roll. The pain that went through my body was sharp and shattering, starting in my feet and rocketing through all of me to the top of my head. For a moment I didn't try to move, I simply lay in a heap in the dirt. But I didn't know if anyone had seen me go over the hedge. I didn't know that horrid little mongrel wasn't going to come tearing, teeth bared, through the foliage like the shrunken head of Cujo.

Cringing, I pulled my feet under me, pushed myself up, and moved on, staying as close to the hedge as I could. Twin lightning bolts of pain shot from my lower back down my sciatic nerves to the backs of my knees, making me gasp. My bruised ribs punished me with every ragged breath. I would have been cursing, but that would have hurt too.

Another fifty yards and I would be at the shopping center.

I broke into a jog, fell back to a quick walk, and tried to will myself along. I was sweating like a horse, and I thought I smelled of garbage. I could hear a siren in the distance behind me. By the time the deputies arrived at Lorinda Carlton's/Van Zandt's town house and got the lowdown on the break-in, I would be safe. For the moment, anyway.

Of all the rotten luck. If I had left the house two minutes sooner ... If I hadn't spent too much time looking at the horse tapes or marveling at Van Zandt's porn collection ... If I hadn't stayed those extra few minutes and gone into the garage to dig through Van Zandt's garbage ... I would never have found the shirt.

I had to call Landry.

I walked into the lights of Town Square. It was Saturday night. People were on the sidewalk in front of the Italian place, waiting for a table. I walked by, head down, trying to look casual, trying to regulate my breathing. Music spilled out the door of Cobblestones, the next restaurant on the row. I passed China-Tokyo, breathing in the deep-fried MSG, reminding me I hadn't eaten.

Normal human beings were having a lovely evening eating kung pao chicken and sushi. There probably wasn't a woman in the place who had ever broken into a house to search for evidence in a murder.

I've always been different.

I wanted to laugh and then cry at that thought.

In Eckerd's drugstore, I bought a bottle of water, a Power Bar, a cheap denim shirt, and a baseball cap, and got change for the pay phone. Outside, I tore the tags off the shirt and put it on over my sweat-soaked black T-shirt, broke in the bill of the ball cap and pulled it on.

I pulled a couple of scraps of paper out of my jeans pocket – one: the note from Van Zandt's garbage, the other: Landry's numbers. I rang Landry's pager, left the pay phone number, and hung up. While I waited, I tormented myself wondering how clearly the woman at Van Zandt's had seen me, wondered who she was, wondered if Z. had been with her.

I didn't think she'd gotten a very good look. She had told the dog to get 'him'. She'd seen the short hair and assumed, as most people would, that burglars are men. The cops would be looking for a man – if they looked at all. A simple B&E, nothing taken, no one hurt. I didn't think a lot of effort would go into it. I hoped to hell not.

Even if they bothered to dust the place for prints, mine weren't in any criminal database, and no other database was checked as a matter of routine. Because I had been in law enforcement, my prints were on file with Palm Beach County, but not with the prints of the common bad folk.

Still, I should have worn gloves. If nothing else, they would have been nice to have while I was digging through the trash.

I kept the wrapper around the Power Bar as I ate it.

They would have my jacket – or what was left of it when the dog finished with it – but nothing about the jacket connected it to me. It was a plain black windbreaker.

I tried to think if there had been anything in the pockets. A Tropicana lip sunblock, the end of a roll of Breathsavers, a cash receipt from the Shell station. Thank Christ I hadn't paid with a credit card. What else? When had I last worn that jacket? The morning I went to the emergency room.

The bottom dropped out of my stomach.

The prescription. The prescription for painkillers, which I'd had no intention of filling. I had stuffed it in my pocket.

Oh, shit.

Had I taken it out? Had I thrown it away and forgotten? I knew I hadn't. I felt sick.

I leaned back against the wall and tried to remember to breathe, to think. My name was on the scrip – Elena Estes, not Elle Stevens. The name wouldn't mean anything to Van Zandt. Unless he had seen the photograph in *Sidelines*. The photograph with the caption that identified me riding at Sean's farm. And if that happened, how long before all the puzzle pieces fell into place?

Stupid, careless mistake.

If the deputies came knocking on my door, I would deny having been on Sag Harbor Court. I would say I'd lost that jacket at the show grounds. I wouldn't have a witness to corroborate the lie that would be my alibi, but why would I need an alibi, for heaven's sake? I would say with indignation. I was no criminal. I was a well-brought-up citizen with plenty of money. I wasn't some crack addict forced to steal to buy my next fix.

And they would show my photograph to Van Zandt and ask him if he recognized me, and I would be fucked.

Dammit, why wasn't Landry calling back? I called his pager again, left the pay phone number with 911 after it, hung up, and started to pace.

The worst of this mess wasn't going to be explaining my way out of charges. The worst of this was going to be if Van Zandt found that shirt before Landry could get there with a warrant.

Damn, damn, damn. I wanted to bang my head against the concrete wall.

I didn't dare go back to Van Zandt's. Even if I could have cleaned up and changed clothes, showed up as Z.'s abandoned dinner date in the hopes of finding him there, I couldn't risk that woman recognizing me – or Van Zandt himself identifying me as the person in his garage, if Van Zandt had been in that car too. At this point I didn't even dare go back to the complex to get my car.

What a fuckup. I'd had the best of intentions, but there was a real chance my actions were going to result in the loss of a potentially crucial piece of evidence, and a chance I'd blown my cover with Van Zandt – and thereby with all of Jade's crowd.

This was why I shouldn't have gotten involved in the first place, a nasty little voice inside told me. If a killer got away because of this, it was on my conscience. Another weight pressing down on me. And if Erin Seabright ended up dead as a result –

Why didn't Landry fucking call?

'Screw him,' I muttered. I picked up the phone and called 911.

26

The phone on the other end of the line rang unanswered. Landry swore and hung up. He didn't recognize the number. The 911 on the end of it made him think it was Estes. Up to her pretty ass in God knew what. It was a sure bet she hadn't stayed home and gotten into the tub with a book.

She was something. Going off to dinner with a possible sex killer like it was no big deal. Landry supposed he had overreacted to the plan. She was a cop, after all – had been. And she was the last woman any man should have felt compelled to protect, but he had just the same. There was something about her lack of a sense of self-preservation that got to him, that made her seem, of all things, vulnerable. He kept thinking of her jumping on the running board of Billy Golam's truck, trying to wrench the wheel out of his hands ... going under the goddamn thing ... being dragged down the pavement like a rag doll.

She didn't know enough – or care enough – to take care of herself. And it was a safe bet she didn't appreciate him doing the job for her. He could still see the look in her eyes when he'd called Weiss and told him to pick up Van Zandt. Anger, hurt, disappointment – all just beneath a scrim of tough indifference.

He stood in the hall outside an autopsy suite in the medical examiner's building. He had run straight from interviewing Van Zandt to catch the ME at the tail end of Jill Morone's slice-and-dice.

Van Zandt had provided nothing but frustration, mouthing off for fifteen minutes about the inferiority of the United States justice system, then exercising his right to an attorney. End of interview. They hadn't had anything solid to back up an arrest warrant. As had been pointed out to him recently, being an asshole was not against the law.

He had really screwed the pooch with this move. If he had waited until after the autopsy to bring in Van Zandt, he would have had some facts to play off, to twist around, to use against the man, maybe get him scared, get him to say something he would never say now.

Landry told himself again he had needed to maintain control of the situation, not have a wild card – Elena – adding to the mayhem.

He wondered what she was tangled up in right that moment. Nothing good, he was sure.

She would want to hear all about the autopsy. She would want to know Jill Morone had been pushed facedown into the floor of a horse stall. There had been pieces of wood shavings and horse manure lodged in her throat and in her mouth and nose. She had died from suffocation. A hand had gripped her neck from behind, exerting enough pressure to leave finger marks on the skin. At some point she had struggled with her assailant, breaking off several fingernails in the process. But there had been no skin or blood or anything else under her remaining nails.

That didn't make sense to Landry. If she'd fought hard enough to break fingernails, there should have been something to find. She had been held facedown in filth. There should at least have been traces of the stall bedding and the manure under her remaining nails, wedged there as she tried to struggle to push herself up. But there was nothing.

And while her clothes had been torn in a way that suggested a sexual assault, there had been no semen present in or on the body. In fact, evidence of rape was minimal. Some scratches on the thighs and labia, but no vaginal bruising or tearing. Could have been Jill's attacker had worn a condom, or he'd lost his erection and hadn't been able to close the deal. Or the attempted rape was an afterthought, staged to make a straight murder look like something else.

Landry could have used all this information against Van Zandt before the man had demanded an attorney, particularly the apparently failed attempt at rape. He could have gone straight at Van Zandt's ego with that, taunted him, mocked him. Van Zandt would have blown up. The man was too arrogant to stand for having his masculinity questioned, too arrogant to control his temper. He was smart enough to ask for a lawyer, though, and now there would be no questioning, no taunting, no mocking, without that lawyer present.

Who was too arrogant?

Landry cursed himself as Weiss came out of the autopsy suite. Weiss, a transplant from New York, was a small man who spent too much time in the gym and consequently had an upper body that looked like it had been inflated to the point of discomfort. Little man syndrome. His arms could not lie entirely flat at his sides.

'What do you think?'

'I think it's pretty goddamn strange her fingernails were clean,' Landry said. 'What kind of perp kills a girl in what is essentially a public place, then takes the time to clean under her fingernails?'

'A smart one.'

'One who's been caught before – or learned by doing,' Landry mused.

'One who watches the Discovery Channel.'

'One who knows there would have been evidence.'

'Meaning she scratched him,' Weiss said. 'Did Van Zandt have any marks on him?'

'Not that I could see. He was wearing a turtleneck. I couldn't see anything on Jade either. We're not going to get a good look at either of them unless we have some pretty strong evidence to hold them on. Any word back on whether or not that was blood in the stall?'

Weiss shook his head and rolled his eyes. 'It's Saturday night. If Dr Felnick didn't have his in-laws staying at his house, we wouldn't have gotten the autopsy tonight.'

'I think we would have,' Landry said. 'The management at the equestrian center have friends in high places. They want this thing solved and swept away ASAP. Murder is bad for morale among the patrons.'

'People don't get murdered in Wellington.'

'No. You have to come to West Palm for that.'

'What about that assault the other night?' Weiss asked. 'When the horses got turned loose. Think they're connected?'

Landry frowned, remembering the bruises on Estes's back that night, though at the time the bruises had hardly registered in his mind. He'd been too stunned by the old scars and lines of demarcation where skin had been grafted over tissue.

She had taken a beating Thursday night, but she hadn't said anything about a sex angle. She had surprised someone in the act of letting the horses loose. Wrong place, wrong time. Now he wondered if she'd come off lucky. Jill Morone had been in the wrong place at the wrong time too. Just two tents over.

'I don't know,' he said. 'What did the security people have to say?'

'Nothing. According to them, the place is virtually crime-free. The odd theft here and there. Nothing serious.'

'Nothing serious. They've got serious now. Estes said she didn't like the guard she ran into that night. I spoke with him the next day. I didn't like him either. I meant to run a check on him, then –'

'Estes?' Weiss looked at him as if he was certain he had heard wrong.

'The vic,' Landry qualified.

'What's her first name?'

'What's it matter?' Landry said defensively.

'Not *Elena* Estes?'

'What if it is?'

Weiss turned his head, and his thick neck made a sound like heavy boots on crushed shell. 'She's a problem, that's what. Plenty of people would be happy if she was the one on that table in there,' he said, looking at the door to the autopsy suite.

'Are you one of them?' Landry asked.

'Hector Ramirez was a hell of a guy. That bitch got his head blown off. I have a problem with that,' Weiss said, puffing up, his arms raising another inch from his sides. 'What's she doing in this? I heard she'd gone off and crawled into a bottle.'

'I don't know anything about that,' Landry snapped. 'She's in the middle of this mess because she's helping somebody out.'

'Yeah? Her kind of help I don't need,' Weiss said. 'Does the lieutenant know she's in it?'

'Oh, for Christ's sake. What is this, Weiss? Kindergarten? Are you gonna tell on her?' Landry said sarcastically. 'She got the crap beat out of her Thursday. Be happy about that and get your head where it belongs. We've got a dead girl here and one kidnapped.'

'Why are you defending her?' Weiss demanded. 'Are you fucking her or something?'

'I'm not defending her. I barely know her, and what I do know, I don't like,' Landry said. 'I'm doing my job. Are we picking and choosing vics now? Did I miss that briefing? Can I just go sit on my boat every goddam day until we get a vic I feel is worthy of my services? I've gotta say that's going to cut my hours by a lot. No more crack whores, no more white trash —'

'I don't like that she's involved in this,' Weiss declared.

'So? I don't like that I just watched a dead girl get carved up like a side of beef. If you don't like the job, go drive a cab,' Landry said, turning away and starting down the hall. 'If you don't think you can work this case, tell the boss and get the hell out of the way for someone who can.'

His pager went off again. He swore, checked the display, then went back to the phone and dialed.

'Landry.'

He listened as he was told about an anonymous tip stating the exact location of evidence in the murder of Jill Morone. A kitchen cupboard in a town house occupied by Tomas Van Zandt.

'Make up your mind, Weiss,' he said as he hung up the phone. 'I've got to go see about a search warrant.'

I had no real way of knowing what happened to my 911 call. The operator had given me a hard time, clearly thinking I was trying to pull a hoax, and keeping me on the line so she could send a radio car to my location. I was as adamant as I could be that I knew Van Zandt had murdered 'my friend' Jill Morone at the equestrian center, that Detective Landry could find Van Zandt's bloody shirt in the kitchen cupboard of the town house owned by Lorinda Carlton at the specific address on Sag Harbor Court. I described the shirt in as much detail as I could, then I hung up, wiped my prints off the phone, and went to sit on a bench outside the Chinese place. A deputy cruised by shortly after.

I hoped the message had gotten to Landry. But even if it had and he had decided to do something about it, a lot of time was going to pass before he made it to Van Zandt's.

A search warrant isn't something a detective can just run off his computer. He can't simply go to his boss and get one. He has to write an affidavit, substantiating the reasons for his request, specifying probable cause for the search, and specifying in detail what he intends to search for. If he wants to execute the search at night, he needs to make a convincing argument that there is imminent danger of evidence being destroyed or of another crime being committed, otherwise executing a search at night can be considered grounds for harassment charges. The affidavit has to go to a judge, who decides whether or not to issue the warrant.

It all takes time. And during that time the suspect might do anything – ditch evidence, bolt and run.

Had Van Zandt been in the car with the woman? I couldn't say. I knew the car was a dark color, but I hadn't taken the time to register make and model. It might have been the Mercedes Trey Hughes had given Van Zandt to use for the season, or not. I assumed the woman was Lorinda Carlton.

Whoever had seen me, if they had seen the shirt in my hands, I had to hope it would be assumed I had taken it with me.

I checked my watch and wondered if there were uniforms knocking on doors in the neighborhood around my car. If I nonchalantly showed up with the key to a BMW in my hand, would I be questioned? I walked to the Chevron station, used the bathroom and washed up, checked my watch again. More than an hour had passed since my escape.

I took the long way back to Sag Harbor Court. There were no cops, no searchlights. Van Zandt's black Mercedes was sitting in the drive at Lorinda Carlton's unit.

He did not come running down the street to accost me. Things seemed as quiet on Sag Harbor Court as they had when I had arrived. I wondered if Carlton had called in the break-in after all, or if the siren I had heard had gone elsewhere. I wondered where in that time frame Van Zandt had shown up, and if he might have dissuaded her from calling because he didn't want a bunch of deputies in the house.

Unable to get answers to those questions, still twitching with the idea of being found out, I drove out of Sag Harbor Court and headed toward home with a detour through Binks Forest.

There were a couple of cars parked on the street on the Seabrights' block. Probably surveillance from the SO. The house was lit up.

I wanted to be inside, assessing the level of strain among the natives. I wanted to see Molly, to let her know she wasn't all alone. She had me on her side.

And I had just made the fuckup of the century, compromised my cover, and compromised evidence that might have linked Van Zandt to a murder.

Yeah. That would be a comfort to her. Me on her side.

Depressed and upset, I went home to regroup and wait for the worst to happen.

*

'This is an outrage!' Van Zandt ranted. 'Is this now a police state?'

'I don't think so,' Landry said, opening a cupboard door and peering in. 'If the police ran the state, I'm pretty sure I'd be making more money.'

'I can't believe anyone would think Tommy could do such a horrible thing!'

Lorinda Carlton had that look of someone who wished she had been a hippy once, but had probably gone to boarding school. She was forty-something with long dark hair in braids, and she wore a T-shirt with some kind of New Age bullshit saying on it. She would probably claim to be descended from Indian shamans or reincarnated from the ancient Egyptians.

She stood beside Van Zandt, trying to cling to him. He shrugged her off. *Tommy.*

'This is not even my home,' Van Zandt said. 'How can you come into Lorinda's house this way?'

Weiss showed him the warrant again, tipping his head back so he could manage to look down his nose at a man half a foot taller than he was. 'Can you read English? It has her name and address right on it.'

'He lives here, right?' Landry said to the woman.

'He's my friend,' she said dramatically.

'Yeah. You might want to rethink that.'

'He's the kindest, most honest man I know.'

Landry rolled his eyes. This one needed 'Victim' tattooed on her forehead. Her rotten little shit-ass dog circled her feet, growling and barking. He was built like a little torpedo with hair and teeth. No question he'd bite if he got the chance.

'I don't know what you think you are going to find,' Van Zandt said.

Weiss looked under the sink. 'Bloody shirt. Torn, bloody shirt.'

'Why would I have such a thing? And why would I keep it in a kitchen cupboard? It's ridiculous. Do you think I am stupid?'

Neither detective answered.

Landry reached up to move a stack of phone books off the refrigerator, and dust rained down in a thick cloud. The tip had specified the shirt was in a cupboard, but he had expanded the scope of the warrant to include the entire property, on the chance that Van Zandt had moved it. It was looking like he had. They had been through all the kitchen cupboards. A deputy was upstairs going through the cabinets and dresser drawers.

'On what grounds did you get this warrant?' Van Zandt asked. 'Or are you allowed to persecute just anyone who is not a citizen?'

'A judge determined we have probable cause to believe this item is in your possession, Mr Van Zandt,' Landry said. 'We have a witness. How's that for grounds?'

'Lies. You have no witness.'

Landry arched a brow. 'And how would you know that if you weren't there and didn't kill that girl?'

'I haven't killed anyone. And who could know what I have in this house? I have had no one here but a burglar. I'm sure you don't care about that.'

'When did you have a burglar?' Landry asked casually as he looked in the closet that housed the washer and dryer.

'Tonight,' Lorinda said. 'Just as I got here from the airport. There was someone in the garage. Cricket chased him through the house, but he got away.'

The dog started barking again at the mention of his name.

'Was anything taken?'

'Not that we've been able to see. But that doesn't change the fact that someone broke in.'

'Was there a sign of forced entry?'

Carlton frowned.

'Did you call nine-one-one?'

Van Zandt pulled a face. 'What would you have done? Nothing. Nothing was taken. You would say to be more careful locking the doors. A waste of time. I told Lorinda not to bother.'

'You'd had your fill of law enforcement for one evening?' Landry said. 'That's great. For all you know, this person killed someone last week, and now they're still running around loose thanks to you.'

'Then you should have caught that person when they killed someone,' Van Zandt pronounced.

'Yeah. We're working on that,' Weiss said, bumping Van Zandt as he passed him to go into the living room.

'Did you get a good look at this person, Ms Carlton?' Landry asked, thinking he was going to have to lock Estes in a cell for the duration of this mess. And if Lorinda Carlton had called 911, that job might already have been taken care of.

'Not really,' she said, squatting down to catch hold of her dog. 'It was dark.'

'Man? Woman? White? Hispanic? Black?'

She shook her head. 'I couldn't say. White, I think. Maybe Hispanic. I'm not sure. Slight build. Dark clothes.'

'Nnn,' Landry said, chewing his lip. Jesus Christ. What had Estes been thinking?

That she might find a bloody shirt. But she'd gotten caught in the act, and Van Zandt had ditched the evidence in the time it had taken to get the warrant.

'Do you want to file a report?' Weiss asked.

Carlton kind of shrugged, kind of shook her head, her attention on her dog. 'Well ... nothing was taken ...'

And Van Zandt didn't want the cops going over the place with a fine-tooth comb. That was why they hadn't called it in. And what the hell was this woman thinking? How could she listen to him tell her not to call the cops after a break-in and not think he had something to hide?

The rationale of the serial victim never ceased to amaze him. He was willing to bet Lorinda had a rotten ex-husband or two in her background, and this asshole had somehow managed to convince her he was a good guy – while he lived off her largesse.

'That person might have been here *planting* evidence,' she said. And now Landry knew how Van Zandt had explained away a bloody shirt.

'The evidence we're not finding?' Weiss asked.

'We can dust the place for prints, see if we get a hit on a known criminal,' Landry said, looking at Van Zandt. 'Of course, we'd have to fingerprint both of you for elimination purposes. You know, the guy might have been a serial killer or something. Wanted all over the world.'

Van Zandt's eyes were narrow and hard as flint. 'Fucking assholes,' he muttered. 'I'm calling my attorney.'

'You do that, Mr Van Zandt,' Landry said, moving past him to go into the garage. 'Waste your money – or the money of whatever sucker you've got supplying you with a lawyer like Bert Shapiro. There's nothing he can do about us searching this house. And you know, even if you've gotten rid of that shirt, we have blood evidence from the stall where Jill Morone died. Not her blood. Yours. We'll nail you on it eventually.'

'Not mine,' Van Zandt declared. 'I wasn't there.'

Landry stopped with his hand on the doorknob. 'Then you would be willing to submit to a physical exam to prove your innocence?'

'This is harassment. I'm calling Shapiro.'

'Like I said' – Landry smiled a nasty smile – 'it's a free country. You know what's funny about this murder, though? It looked like a rape, but there wasn't any semen. The ME didn't find any semen. What happened, Van Zandt? You didn't want to do her after she suffocated? You like 'em kicking and screaming? Or could you just not get it up?'

Van Zandt looked like his head would explode. He grabbed at the phone on the wall and knocked the receiver on the floor. He was shaking with anger.

Landry went out the door. At least he'd gotten in a shot.

They searched the premises for another forty minutes – and ten of those were just to annoy Van Zandt. If there had been a bloody shirt, it was gone. All they found was a video porn collection and that no one in the house ever bothered to clean. Landry was certain he could feel fleas biting his ankles through his socks.

Weiss sent the deputy on his way, then looked at Landry like *what now?*

'So this burglar,' Landry said as they stood in the foyer. 'Did you see which way he went?'

'Through the patio and that way through the yards, along the hedge,' Lorinda said. 'Cricket went after him. My brave little hero. Then I heard a terrible yelp. That awful person must have kicked him.'

The dog looked up at Landry and snarled. Landry wanted to kick him too. Filthy, flea-ridden, vicious mutt.

'We'll take a look,' he said. 'Maybe the guy dropped his wallet on the way out. Sometimes we get lucky.'

'You won't find anything,' Van Zandt said. 'I already have looked.'

'Yeah, well, you're not exactly playing on our team,' Weiss said. 'We'll see for ourselves. Thanks anyway.'

Van Zandt went off in a huff.

Weiss and Landry went to the car and got a flashlight. Together, they walked around to the back of the town house, shining the light on the shrubbery, on the grass. They walked in the direction Lorinda Carlton had pointed until they ran out of real estate, and found not so much as a gum wrapper.

'Pretty strange coincidence Van Zandt's place gets broken into while he's being interviewed,' Weiss said as they walked.

'Crime of opportunity.'

'Nothing was taken.'

'Thievery Interruptus.'

'And then we happen to get that tip.'

Landry shrugged as they reached their car and he opened the driver's door. 'Don't look a gift horse in the mouth, Weiss. They bite.'

27

The call came at 3:12 A.M.

Molly had taken the handset from the portable phone in the living room, snuck it upstairs, and hidden it under a magazine on her nightstand. She wasn't allowed to have her own telephone, even though practically every girl in her class did. Bruce believed a girl and her own phone were a recipe for trouble.

He didn't let Chad have a phone either, though Molly knew Chad had a cell phone *and* a beeper so he and his stupid loser friends could send text messages back and forth, and page each other like they were important or something. Bruce didn't know about that. Molly kept the secret because she disliked Bruce more than she disliked Chad. According to Bruce, everyone in the house – except him – was supposed to make calls from the kitchen, where anybody could hear the conversation.

The phone rang three times. Molly stared at the handset she clutched in one hand, holding her breath, holding her microcassette recorder tight in her other small, sweating hand. She was afraid Bruce was going to sleep through the call. He didn't care what happened to Erin. But just as she decided she would answer, the ringing stopped. She bit her lip and punched the on button on the phone and the record button on the tape recorder.

The voice was that terrible, creepy, distorted voice from the video, like something from a horror movie. Every word drawn-out and deliberate, metallic and ominous. Molly's eyes filled with tears.

'You broke the rules. The girl will pay the price.'

'What are you talking about?' Bruce asked.

'You broke the rules. The girl will pay the price.'

'It wasn't my choice.'

'You broke the rules. The girl will pay the price.'

'It wasn't my fault. I didn't call the cops. What do you want me to do?'

'Bring the money to the place. Sunday. Six P.M. No police. No detective. Only you.'

'How much?'

'Bring the money to the place. Sunday. Six P.M. No police. No detective.

849

Only you. You broke the rules. The girl will pay the price. You broke the rules. The girl will pay the price.'

The line went dead.

Molly clicked the phone off, clicked the recorder off. She was shaking so hard, she thought she might get sick. *You broke the rules. The girl will pay the price.* The words played over and over, so loud, she wanted to slam her hands over her ears to drown them out, but the sound was inside her head.

It was all her fault. She had thought she was doing the right thing, the smart thing. She had thought she was the only one who would do anything to save Erin. She had taken action. She had gone for help. Now Erin could die. And it was her fault.

Her fault and Elena's.

You broke the rules. The girl will pay the price.

28

In the uncertain hour before the morning
Near the ending of the interminable night

Strange the things we remember and the reasons we remember them. I remember those lines from a T. S. Eliot poem because at eighteen, as a headstrong freshman at Duke, I had an obsessive crush on my literature professor, Antony Terrell. I remember a passionate discussion of Eliot's works over cappuccino at a local coffeehouse, and Terrell's contention that *Four Quartets* was Eliot's exploration of issues of time and spiritual renewal, and my argument that Eliot was the root cause of the Broadway musical *Cats* and therefore full of shit.

I would have argued the sun was blue just to spend time with Antony Terrell. Debate: my brand of flirtation.

I didn't think of Antony as I sat curled in the corner of the sofa, chewing on my thumbnail, staring out the window at the darkness before dawn. I thought about uncertainty and what would come at the end of the unending night. I didn't allow myself to contemplate issues of spiritual renewal. Probably because I thought I may have blown my chance to hell.

A tremor went through me and I shivered violently. I didn't know how I would live with myself if my getting caught at Van Zandt's caused the loss of evidence that could prove him to be a murderer. If he was somehow tied to Erin Seabright's disappearance, and I had blown the chance for him to be charged with something, and in charging him pressure him to give up Erin . . .

Funny. Before I had ever heard of Erin Seabright, I hadn't known how I would live with myself because Hector Ramirez had died as a consequence of my actions. The difference was that now it mattered to me.

Somewhere in all this, hope had snuck in the back door. If it had come knocking, I would have turned it away as quickly as I would turn away a door-to-door missionary. *No, thanks. I don't want what you're selling.*

'Hope' is the thing with feathers
That perches in the soul

And sings without the words
And never stops – at all
EMILY DICKINSON

I didn't want to have hope for myself. I wanted to simply exist.

Existence is uncomplicated. One foot in front of the other. Eat, sleep, function. Living, truly living, with all the emotion and risk that entails, is hard work. Every risk presents the possibility of both success and failure. Every emotion has a counterbalance. Fear cannot exist without hope, nor hope without fear. I wanted neither. I had both.

The horizon turned pink as I stared out the window, and a white egret flew along that pink strip between the darkness and the earth. Before I could take it for a sign of something, I went to my bedroom and changed into riding clothes.

No deputies had come knocking on my door in the dead of night to question me about my jacket and the break-in at Lorinda Carlton's/Tomas Van Zandt's town house. My question was: if the deputies didn't have my jacket, who did? Had the dog dragged it back to Lorinda Carlton? His trophy for his efforts. Had Carlton or Van Zandt followed my trail and found it? If ultimately Van Zandt had possession of the prescription with my name on it, what would happen?

Uncertainty is always the hell of undercover work. I had built a house of cards, presenting myself as one thing to one group of people and something else to another group. I didn't regret the decision to do that. I knew the risks. The trick was getting the payoff before I was found out and the cards came tumbling down. But I felt no nearer to getting Erin Seabright back, and if I lost my cover with the horse people, then I was well and truly out of it, and I would have failed Molly.

I fed the horses and wondered if I should call Landry or wait to see if he would come to me. I wanted to know how Van Zandt's interview had gone, and whether or not the autopsy had been performed on Jill Morone. What made me think he would tell me any of that after what he had done the night before, I didn't know.

I stood in front of Feliki's stall as she finished her breakfast. The mare was small in stature and had a rather large, unfeminine head, but she had a heart and an ego as big as an elephant's, and attitude to spare. She regularly trounced fancier horses in the showring, and if she had been able to, I had no doubt she would have given her rivals the finger as she came out of the ring.

She pinned her ears and glared at me and shook her head as if to say, what are *you* looking at?

A chuckle bubbled out of me, a pleasant surprise in the midst of too much unpleasantness. I dug a peppermint out of my pocket. Her ears went up at the crackling of the wrapper and she put her head over the door, wearing her prettiest expression.

'Some tough cookie you are,' I said. She picked the treat delicately from my palm and crunched on it. I scratched her under her jaw and she melted.

'Yeah,' I murmured, as she nuzzled, looking for another treat. 'You remind me of me. Only I don't have anybody giving me anything but grief.'

The sound of tires on the driveway drew my attention out the door. A silver Grand Am pulled in at the end of the barn.

'Case in point,' I said to the mare. She looked at Landry's car, ears pricked. Like all alpha mares, Feliki was ever on the alert for intruders and danger. She spun around in her stall, squealed and kicked the wall.

I didn't go out to meet Landry. He could damn well come to me. Instead, I went to D'Artagnon, took him out of his stall, and led him to a grooming bay. Out of the corner of my eye, I watched Landry approach. He was dressed for work. The morning breeze flipped his red tie over his shoulder.

'You're up bright and early for someone who was out prowling last night,' he said.

'I don't know what you're talking about.' I chose a brush from the cabinet and started a cursory grooming job that would have made Irina scowl at me and mutter in Russian if it had not been her day off.

Landry leaned sideways against a pillar, his hands in his pockets. 'You don't know anything about a B&E at the town house of Lorinda Carlton – the town house where Tomas Van Zandt is living?'

'Nope. What about it?'

'We got a nine-one-one call last night claiming there was a piece of evidence there that would lock Van Zandt into the murder of Jill Morone.'

'Terrific. Did you find it?'

'No.'

My heart sank. There was only one piece of news that would have been worse, and that would have been that they had found Erin's body. I hoped to God that wasn't the next thing coming.

'You weren't there,' Landry said.

'I told you I was going to bed with a book.'

'You told me you were getting in the tub with a book,' he corrected me. 'That's not an answer.'

'You didn't ask a question. You made a statement.'

'Were you at that town house last night?'

'Do you have reason to believe I was? Do you have my fingerprints? Something that fell out of my pocket? Video surveillance tapes? A witness?' I held my breath, not sure which answer I feared most.

'Breaking and entering is against the law.'

'You know, I kind of remember that from when I was on the job. And there was evidence of forcible entry at this town house?'

He didn't look amused by the clever repartee. 'Van Zandt made it back to his place before I could get the warrant. If that shirt was there, he got rid of it.'

'What shirt is that?'

'Goddammit, Estes.'

He grabbed my shoulder and pulled me around, startling D'Artagnon. The big gelding scrambled and pulled back against the cross-ties, jumped ahead, then sat back and reared.

I hit Landry hard in the chest with the heel of my hand. It was like punching a cinder block. 'Watch what you're doing, for Christ's sake!' I hissed at him.

He let me go and backed away, more leery of the horse than of me. I went to the horse to calm him. D'Artagnon looked at Landry, uncertain that calming down was the wisest choice. He would have sooner run away.

'I've had zero sleep,' Landry said in lieu of an apology. 'I'm not in the mood for word games. You haven't been properly Mirandized. Nothing you say can be used against you. Neither Van Zandt nor that goofy woman wants to pursue the matter anyway, because, as I'm sure you know, nothing was stolen. I want to know what you saw.'

'If he got rid of it, it doesn't matter. Anyway, I have to think you had an accurate description of whatever it was or you wouldn't have gotten the warrant. Or did he give you grounds during your interview? In which case you should have been smart enough to hold him while you got the warrant and executed the search.'

'There was no interview. He called a lawyer.'

'Who?'

'Bert Shapiro.'

Amazing. Bert Shapiro was on a par with my father in terms of high-profile clients. I wondered which of Van Zandt's grateful pigeons was footing that bill.

'That's unfortunate,' I said. And doubly so for me. Shapiro had known me all my life. If Van Zandt showed him that prescription slip, I was cooked. 'Too bad you didn't wait until the autopsy was done to pull him in. You might have had something to rattle his cage with before he used the L word.'

I struck a nerve with that. I could see it in the way his jaw muscles flexed.

'Was there anything in the autopsy?' I asked.

'If there was, I wouldn't be standing here. I'd be in the box busting that asshole's chops, lawyer or no lawyer.'

'It's hard to imagine he's clever enough to get away with murder.'

'Unless he's had practice.'

'He hasn't been caught at it,' I said.

I chose a white saddle pad with the Avadonis logo embroidered on the corner and tossed it on D'Artagnon's back, lifted his saddle off the rack, and settled it in place. I thought I could feel Landry's inner tension as he watched me. Or maybe the tension was my own.

I moved around the horse, adjusting the girth – a job that had to be done gradually and in ridiculously small increments with D'Ar because he was, as

Irina called him, a delicate flower. I tightened the girth one hole, then knelt to strap on his protective leg boots. I watched Landry shuffle his feet as he shifted positions restlessly.

'The Seabrights had another call,' he said at last. 'The kidnapper said the girl would be punished because Seabright broke the rules.'

'Oh, God.' I sat back on my heels, feeling weak at the news. 'When did the call come?'

'Middle of the night.'

After my screw-up at Van Zandt's. After Landry had executed the search warrant.

'Do you have someone sitting surveillance on Van Zandt?'

Landry shook his head. 'The LT wouldn't approve it. Shapiro was already screaming harassment because of the search. We don't have a goddamn thing on him. How do we justify surveillance?'

I rubbed at the tension in my forehead. 'Great. That's great.'

Van Zandt was free to do as he pleased. But even if he wasn't, we knew he wasn't in the kidnapping alone. One person had run the camera, one had grabbed the girl. There was nothing stopping the partner from hurting Erin even if Van Zandt was under twenty-four-hour guard.

'They're going to hurt her because I brought you into it,' I said.

'First of all, you know as well as I do, the girl could already be dead. Second, you know you did the right thing. Bruce Seabright wouldn't have done anything at all.'

'That's not a lot of comfort at the moment.'

I pushed myself to my feet and leaned back against the cabinet, crossing my arms tightly against my body. Another tremor rattled through me, from my core outward, as I thought of the consequences Erin Seabright was going to suffer for my actions. If she wasn't dead already.

'They set up another drop,' Landry said. 'With luck, we'll have the accomplice by the end of the day.'

With luck.

'Where and when?' I asked.

He just looked at me, his eyes hidden by his sunglasses, his face like stone.

'Where and when?' I asked again, moving toward him.

'You can't be there, Elena.'

I closed my eyes for a moment, knowing where this conversation was going to end. 'You can't shut me out of this.'

'It's not up to me. The lieutenant will run the show. You think he's going to let you ride along? Even if it was my call, you think I'd let you in after that stunt you pulled last night?'

'That *stunt* netted a torn, bloody shirt from a murder suspect.'

'Which we don't have.'

'That's not my fault.'

'You got caught.'

'None of that would have happened if you hadn't had to flex your muscles last night and take Van Zandt in when you did,' I argued. 'I might have gotten something out of him over dinner. You could have had him afterward, after the autopsy. You could have held him, gotten the warrant, found the shirt yourself. But no. You couldn't play it that way, and now this guy is running around loose –'

'Oh, it's *my* fault you broke into that house,' Landry said, incredulous. 'And I suppose it was Ramirez's fault he walked in front of that bullet.'

I heard myself gasp as if he had slapped me. My instinct was to step back. Somehow, I managed not to.

We stood there staring at each other for a long, horrible moment, the weight of his words hanging in the air. Then I turned, very deliberately, and went back to D'Artagnon to put on his other boot.

'Jesus,' Landry murmured. 'I'm sorry. I shouldn't have said that.'

I didn't say anything. My focus was on tightening the boot straps just so, aligning them perfectly.

'I'm sorry,' he said again as I stood. 'You just make me so goddam mad –'

'Don't put this on me,' I said, turning to face him. 'I'm carrying enough guilt without taking on yours too.'

He looked away, ashamed of himself. I could have done without the small victory. The price for it had been too high.

'You're a son of a bitch, Landry,' I said, but not with any strong emotion. I could have as easily said, you have short hair. It was a simple statement of fact.

He nodded. 'Yeah. I am. I can be.'

'Don't you have a ransom drop to arrange? I've got a horse to ride.'

I took D'Ar's bridle down from the hook and went to put it on him. Landry didn't move.

'I have to ask you a question,' he said. 'Do you think Don Jade could be Van Zandt's partner in this? In the kidnapping?'

I thought about that. 'Van Zandt and Jade were both connected to Stellar – the horse that was killed. They both stand to make a lot of money if Trey Hughes buys this jumper from Belgium.'

'So, they're partners of a sort.'

'Of a sort. Jade wanted rid of Jill Morone – maybe because she was lazy and stupid, or maybe because she knew something about Stellar. Erin Seabright was Stellar's personal groom. She might have known something too. Why? Do you have something on Jade?'

He debated whether or not to tell me. Finally, he drew a deep breath and let it out, and lied to me. I could feel it. I could see it in the way his eyes went flat and blank. Cop eyes. 'I'm just trying to connect the dots,' he said. 'There are too many coincidences for this not all to be tied together.'

I shook my head and smiled my bitter, ironic half smile, and thought of Sean's matchmaking talk. Oh, yeah. Me and Landry. A match made in hell.

'So what came out in the autopsy?' I asked again. 'Or is that a state secret too?'

'She suffocated.'

'Was she raped?'

'My personal feeling: he tried to rape her and couldn't get the job done. He had her facedown in that stall, and she suffocated while he was trying. She aspirated vomit and horse manure.'

'God. Poor girl.' To die like that, and not one person she'd known here mourned her.

'Or the rape attempt was staged,' Landry said. 'No semen anywhere.'

'Anything under her nails?'

'Not so much as a flake of skin.'

I finished doing up the buckles on the bridle, turned and looked at him. 'He *cleaned* her fingernails?'

Landry shrugged. 'Maybe he's not as dumb as he seems.'

'That's a learned behavior,' I said. 'That's not: oops, I've accidentally suffocated this girl and now I have to panic. That's an MO. He's done this before.'

'I'm already running it as an MO through the VICAP database, and I've got a call in to Interpol and to the Belgian authorities for similar cases.'

My thoughts were already on what it could mean for Erin if she was in the hands not of a kidnapper whose only motive was money, but of a serial killer whose dark motive was his own.

'That's why they have a file on him,' I said more to myself than to Landry. 'That bullshit about his business practices – I knew that didn't add up to Interpol involvement. Armedgian, you son of a bitch,' I muttered.

'Who's Armedgian?'

The Interpol information had been filtered through him. If I was right, and Van Zandt had a documented history as a predator, my good friend at the FBI had kept that information to himself. And I knew why. Because I wasn't part of the club anymore.

'Have the feds been in contact with your office?' I asked.

'Not that I'm aware of.'

'I hope that means I'm wrong, not just that they're assholes.'

'Oh, they're assholes,' Landry pronounced. 'And if they try to horn in on my case, they'll each have a new one.'

He looked at his watch. 'I've got to go. We're executing a search warrant at Morone's and Seabright's apartments. See if there's anything that might point us in a direction.'

'You'll find a lot of Erin's personal effects in Jill's apartment,' I said, taking my horse by the reins.

'How do you know that?'

'Because in the photograph I have of Erin, she's wearing the blouse Jill Morone died in. That's why it looked like Erin had moved out – Jill stole everything.'

I led D'Artagnon out of the barn to the mounting block, leaving Landry to see himself out. From the corner of my eye, I could see him just standing there with his hands on his hips, looking at me. Behind him, the door to the lounge opened and Irina emerged in ice blue silk pajamas, coffee mug in hand. She gave Landry a scathing look as she glided past on her way to the stairs to her apartment. He didn't notice.

I got on my horse and we walked away to the arena. I don't know how long Landry stayed. As I took up the reins, I cleared the detritus of our encounter from my mind. I breathed in the scent of the horse, felt the sun warm my skin, listened to the jazz guitar of Marc Antoine coming over the arena speakers. I was there to cleanse myself, to center my being, to feel the comfort of familiar muscles working and the trickle of sweat between my shoulder blades. If I hadn't earned a moment of peace, I was going to take one anyway.

By the time I had finished, Landry was gone. Someone else had come to call.

Tomas Van Zandt.

29

'So she was the dead person they found at the show grounds?'

Landry looked sideways at the old lady. She was wearing pink tights, an off-the-shoulder sweater, and furry bedroom slippers. She held a hugely fat orange cat in her arms. The cat looked like it would bite.

'I really can't say, ma'am,' Landry said, looking around the tiny apartment. The place was a dump. And filthy. And it looked like it had been tossed. 'Has anyone been in here since Friday evening?'

'No. No one. I've been here the whole time. And my friend Sid has been staying,' she confided with a coy blush. 'Since I found out the other one disappeared, I figure a girl can't be too careful.'

Landry motioned to the room at large. 'Why does it look this way?'

'Because she's a little pig, that's why! Not that I would speak ill of the dead, but . . .' Eva Rosen looked at the nicotine-stained ceiling to see if God was watching her. 'She was mean too. I know she tried to kick my Cecil.'

'Your what?'

'Cecil!' She hefted the cat. It growled.

Landry moved to pick through a pile of clothes left on the unmade bed. Many items that looked too small for Jill Morone. Many items with price tags still attached.

'I think she stole,' Eva said. 'So how did she die?'

'I'm not at liberty to comment on that.'

'But someone murdered her, right? They said on the news.'

'Did they?'

'Was it a sex crime?' Clearly, she was hoping it was. People were amazing.

'Do you know if she had a boyfriend?' Landry asked.

'This one?' She made a face. 'No. The other one.'

'Erin Seabright.'

'Like I told your little friend in the other room. Thad Something.'

'Chad?' Landry said, moving on to a coffee table littered with candy wrappers and an overflowing ashtray. 'Chad Seabright?'

Eva was horror-stricken. 'They had the same last name? They were married?'

'No, ma'am.' He picked through a stack of magazines. *People, Playgirl, Hustler.* Jesus.

'*Oy vey.* Under my own roof!'

'Did you ever see anyone coming in and out?' Landry asked. 'Friends? Their boss?'

'The boss.'

'Don Jade?'

'I don't know him. Paris,' she said. 'Blond, pretty, a very nice girl. She always takes time to chat. Always asks after my babies.'

'Babies?'

'Cecil and Beanie. She was the one who paid the rent – Paris. Such a nice girl.'

'When was she last here?'

'Not lately. She's very busy, you know. She rides those horses. Zoom! Over the fences.' She swung the fat cat in her arms as if she meant to toss him. The cat flattened its ears and made a sound in its throat like a siren.

Landry went to the nightstand beside the bed and opened the drawer.

Bingo.

He took a pen from his pocket and gingerly moved aside a hot-pink vibrator, then lifted out his prize. Photographs. Photographs of Don Jade sitting astride a black horse with a winner's ribbon around its neck. Pictures of him jumping another horse over a huge fence. A photo of him standing beside a girl whose face had been scratched out of the picture.

Landry turned the photograph over and looked at the back. The first half of the inscription had been scratched over with a pen that had been pressed so hard it had carved a groove into the paper, but so carelessly it could still be read.

To Erin.

Love, Don.

30

'He must be rounder, softer in the downward transitions.'

Van Zandt had parked along the road – a dark blue Chevy, not the Mercedes – and stood leaning on the fence, watching me. My stomach flipped at the sight of him. I had hoped to next see him – if not on the news, being taken into custody by the authorities – at the equestrian center in a throng of humanity.

He climbed carefully over the board fence and came toward the ring, his eyes hidden by mirrored sunglasses, his expression flat and calm. I thought he still looked ill, and wondered if it was killing that upset his system, or the danger of being caught. Or perhaps it was the idea of having a loose end dangling. Me.

I glanced at the parking area adjacent to the barn. Irina's car was gone. She had left while I'd been engrossed in my ride.

I hadn't seen any sign of Sean. If he had returned home from his night out, he was sleeping late.

'You must be looser in your back so that the horse may be looser in his back,' Van Zandt said.

I wondered if he knew, and knew in a fatalistic corner of my soul that he did. The possibilities ticked through my mind as they had every hour since my blunder at the town house: He had found the prescription and recognized my name from *Sidelines,* or Lorinda Carlton had recognized the name. The magazine might have been in the town house somewhere. They might have looked at the photograph together. Van Zandt might have recognized the horse, or my profile, or put the puzzle pieces together from the mention of Sean's farm. He might have found the jacket and the prescription, assumed Elena Estes was a cop conducting a search while he'd been in the interview room with Landry; called his attorney and asked to have the name checked out. Shapiro would have recognized my name.

It didn't matter how he might have found me out. What mattered was what he was going to do about it. If he knew I had been in his home Saturday night, then he knew I had seen the bloody shirt. I wished now I had kept the thing and damned the admissibility consequences. At least he would be in jail for the moment, and I would not be alone with a man I believed to be a murderer.

'Try again,' he said. 'Pick up the canter.'

'We were just finishing for the day.'

'Americans,' he said with disdain, standing at the edge of the ring with his hands on his hips. 'He is hardly warm. The work is only just beginning. Pick up the canter.'

My natural inclination was to defy him, but staying aboard the horse seemed preferable to a level playing field where he had six inches and sixty pounds on me. At least until I could get a better read on him and what he may or may not know, it seemed best to humor him.

'On the twenty-meter circle,' Van Zandt instructed.

I put the horse on a circle twenty meters in diameter, tried to breathe and focus, though my hands were so tight on the reins, I thought I could feel my pulse in them. I closed my eyes for two strides, exhaling and sinking into the saddle.

'Relax your hands. Why are you so tense, Elle?' he asked in a silky voice that made a chill go down my back. 'The horse can sense this. It makes him also tense. More seat, less hand.'

I made an attempt to react accordingly.

'What brings you out so early?'

'Aren't you happy to see me?' he asked.

'I would have been happy to see you at dinner last night. You stood me up. That doesn't win you any points with me.'

'I was unavoidably detained.'

'Taken to a desert island? A place with no phones? Even the police let you make a phone call.'

'Is that where you think I was? With the police?'

'I'm sure I don't know or care.'

'I left word with the maître d'. I couldn't call you. You have not given me your number,' he said, then changed tones in the next breath. 'Collect, collect, collect!' he demanded. 'More energy, less speed. Come! Sit into him!'

I gathered the horse beneath me until I held him nearly on the spot, his feet pounding the sand in three-beat time. 'Are you trying to make up to me with a free riding lesson?'

'Nothing is free, Elle,' he said. '*Carry* him into the walk. Like setting down a feather.'

I did as instructed – or tried to, rather – and failed because of my tension.

'Don't let him fall out of the gait that way!' Van Zandt shouted. 'Is your horse to be on its forehand?'

'No.'

'Then why did you let this happen?'

The implied answer was that I was stupid.

'Again! Canter! And more energy in the transition, not less!'

We went through the exercise again and again. Each time, something was not quite worthy, and that something was glaringly my fault. Sweat became lather on D'Artagnon's massive neck. My T-shirt was soaked through. My back muscles began to cramp. My arms were so tired, they trembled.

I began to question my wisdom. I couldn't stay on the horse all day, and by the time I got off, I was going to flop on the ground, limp, boneless, like a jellyfish washed ashore. For his part, Van Zandt was punishing me, and I knew he was enjoying it.

'. . . and make him float into the walk like a snowflake landing.'

Again I brought the horse to the walk, holding my breath in anticipation of another outburst.

'Better,' he said grudgingly.

'Enough,' I said, letting the reins out to the buckle. 'Are you trying to kill me?'

'Why would I do such a thing to you, Elle? We are friends, are we not?'

'I thought so.'

'I thought so too.'

Past tense. Intentional, I thought, not a misuse of the language that was probably third or fourth on his list.

'I called the restaurant later in the evening,' he said. 'The maître d' told me you never came.'

'I was there. You weren't. I left,' I lied. 'I didn't see the maître d'. He must have been in the men's room.'

Van Zandt considered the story.

'You are very good,' he said.

'At what?' I watched him as I walked D'Artagnon on the circle, waiting for the gelding's breathing to slow.

'At the dressage, of course.'

'You just spent half an hour screaming at me to get one decent transition.'

'You need a strong coach. You are too willful.'

'I don't need to be abused.'

'You think I am abusive? An asshole?' he asked with a lack of emotion that was more disturbing than his usual attitude. 'I believe in discipline.'

'Putting me in my place?'

He didn't answer.

'What brings you out so early?' I asked again. 'It couldn't be to apologize for last night.'

'I have nothing to apologize for.'

'You wouldn't recognize the occasion if it slapped you in the face. Did you come to see Sean about Tino? Is your client down from Virginia yet?'

'She arrived last night. Imagine her shock when she arrived at the house to interrupt an intruder.'

'Someone broke into your house? That's terrible. Was anything stolen?'

'Oddly, no.'

'Lucky. She wasn't hurt, was she? I saw a story on the news just the other night about an elderly couple being robbed in their home by two Haitians with machetes.'

'No, she was not injured. The person ran away. Lorinda's dog gave chase through the lawns, but came back with only a jacket.'

My stomach rolled again. My arms pebbled with goose bumps despite the heat.

'Where is your groom?' Van Zandt asked, looking toward the barn. 'Why is she not here to take your horse?'

'Taking a coffee break,' I said, wishing that were true. I watched Van Zandt's gaze go to the parking area where my BMW sat alone.

'A good idea, coffee,' he said. 'Put the horse in the cross-ties. We can have a cup of coffee together and make new plans.'

'He needs to be hosed off.'

'The Russian can do it. That's her job, not yours.'

I considered picking up the reins and running him down. Easier said than done. He would be a moving target, and D'Ar would try to avoid hitting him. Even if I could knock him down, then what? I would have to go over a fence to get off the property. I didn't know if D'Artagnon would jump. He might as easily refuse at the fence and throw me.

'Come,' Van Zandt ordered. He turned and started for the barn.

I didn't know if he had a weapon. I knew I did not. If I went into the building with him, he would have a big advantage.

I gathered the reins. My legs tightened around D'Artagnon's sides. He danced beneath me and blew through his nostrils.

A flash of color near the fence caught my eye and my attention. Molly. She had propped her bike and climbed through the fence, and was now running toward me.

I raised a finger to my lips in the hopes of keeping her from calling out my name. As if it mattered. My training as the child of a defense attorney: never admit anything. Even in the face of overwhelming evidence: deny, deny, deny.

Molly pulled up, looked at me, looked at Van Zandt, who had just noticed her. I climbed off D'Artagnon and held my hand out toward the girl.

'It's Miss Molly the Magnificent!' I exclaimed. 'Come to call on her Auntie Elle.'

Uncertainty filled her eyes, but her expression was a blank. Too much practice with volatile situations between Krystal and the men in her life. She came to me, breathing hard, her forehead shiny with sweat. I put my arm around her narrow shoulders and gave her a squeeze, wishing I could make her invisible. She was here because of me, and now because of me, she was in danger.

Van Zandt looked at her with something like disapproval. 'Auntie Elle? You have family nearby?'

'Honorary Auntie,' I said. My fingers tight on her arm, I said to Molly, 'Molly Avadon, this my friend Mr Van Zandt.'

I didn't want Van Zandt to associate her with Erin. And I also thought it might be one thing for Van Zandt to make me disappear, but he might think twice about killing a relative of Sean's. He had to believe with the conceit of a sociopath that he had a good chance of getting away with what he'd done so far. Otherwise I thought he would already have been on a plane to Brussels or places unknown. If he still believed he could come away unscathed, he could still have a business here, could still hobnob with the rich and famous.

Molly looked again from me to Van Zandt, and said hello with cool reserve.

Van Zandt smiled a brittle smile. 'Hello, Molly.'

'I promised Molly we'd go to the horse show today,' I said. 'I'd better take a rain check on that coffee, Z. I don't see Irina, and I have to get this horse put away.'

He frowned at that, considering his options.

'Let me help you, then,' he said, taking D'Artagnon's reins.

Molly looked up at me with worried eyes. I thought I should tell her to slip away, to run for help. Van Zandt turned back toward us before I could do it.

'Come, Miss Molly,' he said. 'You are interested in horses? Like your Uncle Sean?'

'Kind of,' Molly said.

'Come, then, and help with taking off this horse's boots.'

'No,' I said. 'If she gets stepped on, it's my fault.' I looked at Molly, trying to will her to read my mind. 'Molly, honey, why don't you run to Uncle Sean's house and see if he's up?'

'He is not home,' Van Zandt said. 'I called as I was driving here. I got his machine.'

'That only means he didn't answer,' Molly said. Van Zandt frowned and continued on toward the barn with the horse.

I bent as if to brush a kiss against Molly's cheek and whispered in her ear, 'Call nine-one-one.'

She turned and ran for the main house. Van Zandt glanced over his shoulder and watched her go.

'Isn't she a doll?' I said.

He didn't comment.

We went into the barn and he put D'Artagnon into the grooming stall, removing his bridle and putting on his halter. I went to the opposite side of the horse and crouched to pull one of his boots off, keeping my feet under me and one eye on Van Zandt.

'You owe me dinner,' I said.

'You owe me for a lesson.'

'Are we even then?'

'I don't think so,' he said. 'I don't believe I'm through teaching you, Elle Stevens.'

He came around the front of the horse. I moved behind the horse to the other side and bent to pull off another boot.

'You are if I say so.'

'There are many kinds of lessons,' he said enigmatically.

'I don't need a mentor. Thanks anyway.'

I moved to the cabinet with the grooming supplies and surreptitiously pulled out a pair of scissors. I wouldn't hesitate to stab him with them if he made a wrong move.

Maybe, I thought, I should stab him anyway – the best defense being a good offense. He was a murderer. Why run the risk of him hurting me, hurting Molly? I could step in close, shove the scissors to their hilt in his stomach at his navel. He would bleed out before he could do more than realize I'd killed him.

I would plead self-defense. The 911 call would establish I had felt in danger. Van Zandt was already known to the Sheriff's Office as a murder suspect.

I could call on my father to defend me. The press would eat it up. Father and prodigal child reunited as he fights to save her from the death chamber.

I had never purposefully taken a life. I wondered if I would feel remorse, knowing what I knew about Van Zandt.

'We could have made a good team, you and I,' he said.

He moved back around the front of the horse.

I palmed the scissors and watched him come toward me.

My arms were trembling with fatigue and nerves. I wondered if I would have the strength to drive the blade into his body.

'You make it sound as if I'm never going to see you again,' I said. 'Are you going somewhere? Am I?'

He still had the sunglasses on. I couldn't see his eyes. His face was without expression. I didn't think he would kill me here, now. Even if he was willing to kill Molly too, he couldn't know for certain Sean wasn't in the house.

'I am not going anywhere,' he said, stepping closer.

'Tomas!' Sean's voice rang down the aisle. Relief washed through me like a tidal wave, taking my strength with it. 'I thought you might never come back! No one has tried to injure you this time, have they?'

'Only his pride,' I said, leaning against the cabinet, setting the scissors aside. 'I've denied him the joy of becoming my coach.'

'Oh, my God!' Sean laughed. 'Why would you want that job? She eviscerated the last one and served his remains in a spaghetti sauce with fava beans and a fine Chianti.'

'She needs taming,' Van Zandt said, finding a thin smile.

'And I need to be twenty again, but that's never going to happen either,' Sean said, coming to me. He kissed my cheek and gave my arm a reassuring squeeze. 'Darling, Molly is waiting impatiently. Why don't you run? I'll see to D'Artagnon.'

'But I know you need to get going too,' I said. 'You have that luncheon today, don't you?'

'Yes.' He gave Van Zandt a look of apology. 'Riders Against Rheumatoid Rumps, or some equally worthy cause. Sorry to give you the bum's rush, Tomas. Call me tomorrow. We'll do dinner or something. Maybe when your client from Virginia arrives we could all go out.'

'Of course, yes,' Van Zandt said.

He came to me, put his hands on my shoulders, and kissed my cheeks. The right one, the left one, the right one. Like the Dutch. He looked at me and I thought I could feel the hate in his gaze, even through the mirrored lenses. 'Until later, Elle Stevens.'

31

I started to shake as I watched Van Zandt drive away. He might have killed me. I might have killed him.

Until later . . .

'What the hell was that about?' Sean demanded. 'Your little friend came running, telling me to call nine-one-one.'

'I told her to. I didn't think you were home. Did you make the call?'

'No. I beat it out here to save you! For God's sake, I'm not waiting in the house for the fucking deputies to get here while some maniac is dismembering you.'

I put my arms around him and hugged him. 'My hero.'

'Explanation, please,' he said firmly.

Moving away from him, I glanced out to make sure the devil hadn't changed his mind and come back.

'I have pretty good reason to believe Van Zandt murdered that girl at the show grounds.'

'Jesus, Elle! Why isn't he in jail? What was he doing here?'

'He's not in jail because he ditched the evidence. I know that because I saw it and called the cops. But when Landry got there it was gone. I think Van Zandt knows I know.'

Sean stared at me, shocked, trying to process it all. Poor boy. He really hadn't known what he was in for when he'd taken me in.

'I'm going to take advantage of this moment of silence to remind you: you got me into this,' I said.

He looked at the ceiling, looked down the aisle, looked at D'Artagnon, who stood waiting patiently in the cross-ties.

'This is supposed to be a genteel sport,' Sean said. 'Lovely animals, lovely people, polite competition . . .'

'Every business has an underside. You've seen it.'

He shook his head, sober, sad. 'Yes, I've seen people cheated, I know people who've gotten conned in a horse deal, I know people who've gotten away with some questionable practices. But my God, Elle. Murder? Kidnapping? You're talking about a world I don't know anything about.'

'And I'm up to my chin in it.' I reached up and gently patted his handsome cheek. 'You wanted me to be something interesting.'

'If I'd had any idea ... I'm sorry, honey.'

'No. I'm sorry,' I said, not knowing quite how one apologized for visiting a murderer upon one's friends. 'I could have said no. Or I could have bailed when the Sheriff's Office took the case. I didn't. My choice. But I shouldn't have dragged you into it.'

We stood there, both of us shell-shocked, feeling drained. Sean put his arms around me and hugged me, and kissed the top of my head.

'Please be careful, El,' he murmured. 'I didn't save you so you could get yourself killed.'

I could hardly remember the last time anyone had held me. I'd forgotten how good it felt to be enveloped by another person's warmth. I'd forgotten how precious and fragile was the genuine concern of a real friend. I felt very lucky – another first time in too long a time.

The corner of my mouth turned up as I looked up at him. 'No good deed goes unpunished,' I said.

From the corner of my eye I saw Molly peek around the corner of the barn, eyes wide.

'He's gone, Molly,' I said. 'It's okay.'

She composed herself as she came down the aisle, shaking off the traces of the frightened child who had run for help.

'Who was that?' she asked. 'Is he one of the kidnappers?'

'I can't say yet. He might be. He's a bad guy. I know that for certain. I was lucky you showed up when you did, Molly. Thank you.'

She glanced at Sean, said, 'Excuse me,' then looked up at me with her Junior Businesswoman expression. 'I need to speak with you in private, Elena.'

Sean raised his brows. 'I'll see to D'Ar,' he offered. 'I need to do something to calm my nerves. It's too early in the day to drink.'

I thanked him and took Molly into the lounge. The scent of the coffee Irina had made filled the room. I wondered absently why she had come down from her apartment to make it. She had a small kitchen of her own. It didn't matter. Grateful for what was left in the pot, I poured myself a cup, took it to the bar, and dropped a healthy shot of whiskey into it.

Too early my ass.

'Would you like something?' I asked Molly. 'Water? Soda? Double-malt scotch?'

'No, thank you,' she said politely. 'You're fired.'

'Excuse me?'

'I'm sorry, but I have to terminate our arrangement,' she said.

I gave her a long, hard look, trying to see where this was coming from. Landry's news came back to me, cutting through the smog of Van Zandt's veiled threats.

'I know about the latest call, Molly. Landry told me.'

Her earnest little face was white with fear. Tears rose up in her eyes behind the lenses of her glasses. 'They're going to hurt Erin, because of me. Because I hired you and you brought in the sheriff's detectives.'

I had never seen anyone look so forlorn. Molly Seabright stood in the middle of the room in red pants and a navy blue T-shirt, her small hands clasped in front of her as she tried valiantly not to cry. I wondered if I had looked half that despondent when I had said basically those same words to Landry earlier.

Coming around from behind the bar, I motioned her to one of the leather chairs and took another for myself.

'Molly, don't blame yourself for what was said in that call. You did the right thing getting help. Where would Erin be if you hadn't come to me? What would Bruce have done to get her back?'

The tears were falling now. 'B-but they s-said no police. Maybe if – if it was only you –'

I took hold of her hands and squeezed them. They were as cold as ice. 'This isn't a job for one person poking around, Molly. We need every resource available to us to try to get Erin back and to catch the people who took her. The Sheriff's Office has access to phone records, criminal records; they can tap phones, analyze evidence. It would have been a mistake not to call them in. You didn't do anything wrong, Molly. Neither did I. The only ones doing wrong here are the people who have your sister.'

'B-but the voice kept saying over and over sh-she's going to pay the price because we b-broke the rules.'

She pulled her hands away from me to dig in the fanny pack she had strapped around her waist, coming out with a microcassette recorder.

She held it out to me. 'You have to listen.'

'You recorded the call?'

She nodded and dug around in the fanny pack for a scrap of paper, which she handed to me. 'And I wrote down the number from the caller ID.'

I took the recorder and the slip of paper from her and punched the play button on the machine. The metallic, machine-altered voice came out of the tiny speaker: *You broke the rules. The girl will pay the price.* Over and over, separated by Bruce Seabright's terse comments. Then: *Bring the money to the place. Sunday. Six P.M.* No police. No detective. Only you. You broke the rules. The girl will pay the price. You broke the rules. The girl will pay the price. You broke the rules. The girl will pay the price.

Molly pressed a hand over her mouth. Tears rolled down her face.

I wanted to rewind the tape and play it again, but I wouldn't do it in front of her. She was going to be hearing that voice in her nightmares as it was.

I thought about the things that had been said, the way they had been said. *No police. No detective.*

Did they mean Landry? Did they mean me? How had they known either way? No marked cars, no uniforms had been sent to the Seabright home.

There had been no direct contact with the kidnappers. If they were watching the house from a distance, they would have seen a few different men in and out of the house Saturday.

No police. No detective.

Landry and Weiss had spoken with most of Jade's crowd, asking about Jill Morone and about Erin. All of those people would know the Sheriff's Office was involved in investigating the murder. But I was willing to bet no mention had been made of the kidnapping, only that Erin was missing and had anyone seen or heard from her.

No police. No detective.

Why differentiate if the detective – singular – was Landry? Who knew we were both involved?

'What time did this call come?' I asked.

'Three-twelve A.M.'

After my fiasco at Van Zandt's town house.

Aside from Van Zandt, who knew about my involvement? The Seabrights themselves, Michael Berne, and Landry. Eliminate Molly. Eliminate Krystal. Bruce had taken the call, therefore couldn't have made it. That didn't absolve him of involvement, since we knew there was more than one kidnapper, and knew that Bruce had lied about his whereabouts at the time of the kidnapping.

It seemed doubtful Van Zandt would have made the call from the town house, knowing the cops were already looking at him for the murder and asking questions about Erin. He might have gone out of the house to make the call. Or I supposed he could have made the call from the comfort of his bedroom, using a cell phone while watching one of his porn videos. Lorinda Carlton in the next room with her horrible little dog.

'I wanted to call the number back, but I was afraid,' Molly said. 'I knew the sheriff's detectives would be listening. I thought I would get in trouble.'

I got up and went to the phone on the bar, dialed the number, and listened to it ring unanswered on the other end. I looked at Molly's note, her careful, girlish printing. What a kid – taping the call, getting the number. Twelve years old and she was more responsible than anyone else in her family.

I wondered what Krystal was doing as Molly was here saving my life and trying to save her sister's.

'Come with me,' I said.

We went to the guest house and I pulled the list of numbers from Bruce Seabright's phone out of my notes for comparison. The number matched the two calls that came in to Bruce's phone. The Royal Palm Beach prefix.

I had given Landry the list of numbers. He had names to go with all of them by now – if there were names to be had for all of them.

Do you think Don Jade could be Van Zandt's partner in this? In the kidnapping?

871

Had Landry traced this number to Jade? Was that the thing he had decided to keep to himself?

It didn't make sense to me that Jade would be so careless as to use a traceable phone number to make ransom demands. Any fool would know enough to make that kind of call from a pay phone or from a disposable cell phone.

If the call had come from a disposable phone, like the one I had purchased the day before, and the SO had been able to trace the number to a phone sold at a particular store, they might have been able to get an ID on Jade from a salesperson.

'What happens now?' Molly asked.

'First, I'm giving you this,' I said, handing her the phone I'd bought for her, along with a slip of paper with my numbers on it. 'This is for you to contact me. It's prepaid for one hour of time, then it quits working. These are my numbers. You see or hear anything regarding Erin, call me right away.'

She looked at the cheap phone like I'd handed her a gold brick.

'Do your folks know you're out of the house?'

'I told Mom I was going for a ride on my bike.'

'Was she conscious at the time?'

'Mostly.'

'I'll drive you home,' I said. 'We don't need the deputies out looking for you too.'

We both started for the door, then Molly turned and looked up at me.

'Will you go to the place for the ransom?' she asked.

'I won't be allowed, but I have other leads to follow. Do I still work for you?'

She looked unsure. 'Do you want to?'

'Yes,' I said. 'I do. And even if you fired me, I would stay in this to the end. When I start something, I finish it. I want to see Erin back safe.'

Phone still clutched in her hand, Molly came and put her arms around my waist and hugged me tight.

'Thank you, Elena,' she said, more serious than any twelve-year-old should ever be.

'Thank you, Molly,' I returned, more serious than she knew. I hoped I would prove worthy of her trust and her gratitude.

'You're a very special person,' I said as she stepped back. 'It's a privilege to know you.'

She didn't know what to say to that, this special child I knew went unnoticed by the people who should have treasured her most. In a way, I supposed it was just as well. Molly had done a far better job raising herself than her mother could have done.

'I wish I didn't have to be special,' she confessed softly. 'I wish I could just be normal and have a normal family and live a normal life.'

Her words hit home with me. I had been twelve once, wishing I had a normal family, wishing I wasn't the sore thumb, the outsider. Unwanted by the man who was supposed to be my father. A burden to the woman who was supposed to be my mother. At twelve I had long since lost my value as an accessory to her life.

I said the only thing I could: 'You're not alone, Molly. Us special chicks stick together.'

32

'Do we pull him in?' Weiss asked.

They had crammed into the lieutenant's office – Landry, Weiss, and two other detectives: Michaels and Dwyer; and an unwelcome newcomer to the party – Special Agent Wayne Armedgian, FBI. Robbery/Homicide lieutenant William Dugan stood behind his desk, hands on his hips, a tall, tanned, gray-haired man who aspired to retire and go on the Senior PGA tour.

Dugan looked to Landry. 'What do you think, James?'

'I think what we've got is too thin and circumstantial, unless Jade's blood type happens to match what we got out of the stall where Jill Morone was killed. Even that would be a stretch to hold him on. *If* we had a clue what his blood type is. He sure as hell isn't going to tell us. We'd need a court order to get a sample. Besides, we know that blood is likely Van Zandt's, anyway.'

'You think,' Weiss challenged. 'Jade was seen arguing with the girl at Players. And he lied about not going back to the equestrian center.'

'He lied about not *having* to go back,' Landry corrected. 'No one at the guard gate saw him come through. No one in the barn area saw him.'

'No one saw Van Zandt either,' Weiss said.

Landry shrugged. 'They both know the back way in. Van Zandt was all over Jill Morone at Players before Jade got there. And we had the tip about the bloody shirt.'

'The shirt we don't have,' Weiss reminded him. 'We don't even know that it really exists. We do know Jill Morone vandalized a couple of grand's worth of Jade's stuff. If he walked in and caught her . . . He could have killed her in the heat of the moment, then made it look like a rape attempt to try to put it on Van Zandt. Maybe he planted the shirt and made the nine-one-one call.'

'Let's say they both did it,' Landry offered. 'I could be happy with that. They can have side-by-side executions.'

'What do we know about the nine-one-one?' Dugan asked.

'It came from a pay phone outside Publix in the Town Square shopping center, half a block from the town house Van Zandt is staying in,' Weiss said, watching Landry.

'Van Zandt's lawyer is screaming harassment and conspiracy,' Dugan said.

Landry shrugged. 'Judge Bonwitt said we had sufficient grounds for the search. Bert Shapiro can kiss his ass *and* mine.'

'Conspiracy with whom?' Armedgian asked.

'Someone broke into Van Zandt's place last night while we had him here,' Weiss explained. 'And then we got the tip about the bloody shirt.'

'Just as well you didn't find it,' Armedgian said. 'It probably would have gotten tossed out of court. Shapiro would have argued the shirt could have been planted.'

'Van Zandt could move to Miami. Him and O.J. could become golf partners,' Weiss suggested. Everyone but Landry chuckled politely at the bad joke.

'Or we could have that cocksucker dead to rights on a murder, locked up in jail while we nail the case down,' Landry said, 'instead of running around loose, free to get on a plane and leave the country anytime he wants.'

'You think Van Zandt and Jade are in the kidnapping together?' Armedgian asked.

'Could be. Van Zandt's the pervert, Jade's the mastermind. Or it's Jade and someone else.'

'Motive?'

'Money and sex.'

'And what have you got on him?'

'Jade was last to see Erin Seabright. He claims she quit her job and left town, but she never told anyone else she was quitting,' Landry explained.

Dwyer picked up. 'Phone calls made from the kidnappers to the Seabright house came from a prepaid cell phone. With the phone number, we were able to get the name of the company that produced the phone, and from them we were able to get a serial number on the phone the calls came from. The phone was purchased at the Radio Shack on Okeechobee in Royal Palm Beach.

'The store has records of sales, but not of the serial numbers of the individual phones sold. They sold seventeen cell phones in the week prior to Erin Seabright's abduction. We've tracked three buyers through credit cards. The rest were cash transactions.'

'We showed Jade's picture to the staff,' Michaels said. 'No one could ID him, but one of the clerks thought the name rang a bell.'

'Why would Jade use his own name?' Armedgian asked.

'We could bring him in and ask him,' Landry said. 'But he's already threatened to call a lawyer, and if he pulls in the same breed of lawyer Van Zandt did, he's out of here in three minutes, and we've blown the ransom drop with nothing to show for it. This close to the appointed hour, they could panic and kill the girl – or kill her just because we pissed them off.'

'Or you could hold Jade and try to get him to turn on his partner,' Armedgian suggested.

Landry gave him the did-anybody-ask-you? look. 'Do you know these people? Have you talked with Don Jade?'

'Well, no –'

'Ice wouldn't melt in his asshole. He's not copping to anything. We go near him, he's calling the dogs. It's a waste of time. Our best bet is to tail Van Zandt and Jade from a good distance, see if one of them goes to the girl, or if we can nail one or both of them at the drop. Then we've got real leverage and the lawyers will want to talk deal.'

Armedgian fussed with the knot in his tie. 'Do you really believe they're going to carry through with the drop?'

'Do we have a choice?' Landry said. 'What do you want to do, Armageddon? Blow it off and go eat clams at Chuck and Harold's?'

'Landry,' Dugan growled.

'What? What did I say?'

'The attitude . . . Special Agent *Armedgian* is here to assist us.'

'I know what he's here for.'

Armedgian raised his eyebrow. He appeared to have only one. A thick black caterpillar that crawled from one side of his bowling ball head to the other. 'And what's that?'

Landry leaned toward him. 'You're here because of the Belgian – through no fault of your own. And if you'd coughed up the goods on him the first time you were asked, maybe Jill Morone would still be alive.'

Armedgian hung his eyelids at half-mast. 'I don't know what you're talking about.'

'Neither do I,' Dugan said. 'What are you talking about, James?'

'I'm talking about the feds wanting a little international feather in their cap. Van Zandt turns out to be a serial killer, they want the bust.'

'The only thing we have on Van Zandt,' Armedgian said, 'is some speculation from an agency in Europe. That's all. He's had a couple of minor charges dismissed. You should have learned the same thing just by asking Interpol, Detective Landry.'

Landry wanted to get in his face and point out that someone *had* asked, but this asshole would bring Estes's name into it, and then all hell would break loose. As it was, Weiss was giving him the eye.

'Didn't you contact them?' Dugan asked. 'I thought you contacted them.'

'Yeah, I contacted them.' Landry kept his attention on the fed. 'All right, I'll play. What are your people doing here? I don't want them underfoot, fucking up the drop.'

Armedgian held his hands up. 'It's your show. I'm here to consult and advise.'

My ass, Landry thought.

'I've worked kidnappings,' Armedgian said. 'Have you checked out the drop site?'

Landry made his eyes wide. 'Gee, should we do that?'

'Landry . . .'

'I understand it's very open,' Armedgian said.

'I've got a man out there keeping an eye on the place,' Dugan said. 'It's a difficult location for surveillance. He's hiding in a horse trailer across the road from the show grounds.'

'There's one road that circles through Equestrian Estates,' Michaels said. 'And a dirt side road that can be accessed through a gate near the drop site. We can't have cars cruising through there.'

He gave the fed the hard stare too.

'My people can tail Van Zandt, Lieutenant,' Armedgian offered. 'That way your people are clear of any harassment charges.'

'Fucking magnanimous,' Landry muttered.

Dugan scowled at him. 'That's enough out of you or I'll feed you to Bert Shapiro myself.'

Landry kept his eyes on Armedgian. 'Lawyers or feds. We get fucked over either way.'

He just hoped Erin Seabright didn't end up paying the ultimate price.

33

Bring the money to the place. Sunday. Six P.M.

Since there had been no further instructions, I had to assume the location of the drop was the place the kidnappers had originally chosen.

The Horse Park at Equestrian Estates show grounds had been in existence only since the 2000 show season, when it had been the site of the US Equestrian Team Olympic team trials for dressage. Unlike the show grounds in Wellington, it was a compact and simple place, with four sand competition arenas used specifically for dressage, and three warm-up rings set in a U around the perimeter of a large grass field. Like most of the stabling at the equestrian center, the barns consisted of several huge tents with portable stalls, all situated at the front of the property. The stalls were occupied during shows only. The rest of the time, the place was a big empty playground in the middle of nowhere.

At the back and center of the property stood the only permanent structure: a grand-looking two-story stuccoed building with huge white columns out front. The building housed the show secretary's office on the first level, and the announcer's electronic control center on the second floor.

From the second floor one could survey the entire grounds. It was the perfect surveillance and sniper's perch if it could be accessed undetected.

The building sat at the very back of the property. Behind it ran a canal, the bank on the far side thick with trees. On the other side of the trees ran a trail used by dirt bikes and all-terrain vehicles, much to the dismay of people showing high-strung horses. If a person were to take the trail and get across the canal, they could use a staircase that ran up the back side of the building.

Certainly the kidnappers knew all of these things. They had chosen the spot. A strange choice, I thought. There weren't a lot of ways in and out. They would see the enemy coming from a distance, but so too would the enemy see them. Trapping and catching them was only a matter of manpower. Why not choose a busy place with lots of commotion, lots of people, lots of escape routes?

No police. No detective. You broke the rules. The girl will pay the price.

No way this was going to go well.

The kidnappers knew the Sheriff's Office was involved now. They couldn't risk showing up with Erin at such an open place. I couldn't see why they would risk showing up themselves. My conclusion was that they wouldn't.

Six P.M. Sunday. A week from the day Erin Seabright had been taken. I wondered if the timing was significant. I wondered if all the cops would be at Equestrian Estates in rural Loxahatchee while the kidnapper dumped Erin's body at the back gate of the equestrian center in Wellington – the spot where she had been grabbed.

I played the videotape of the kidnapping, wanting to see something I hadn't seen before, wishing for some sudden epiphany.

Erin standing outside the gate. Waiting. For who? A friend? A lover? A drug connection? Don Jade? Tomas Van Zandt? She doesn't seem nervous as the white van approaches. Does she recognize the van? Does she think this is the person she's supposed to meet? *Is it* the person she's supposed to meet?

Landry had told me he had contacted Narcotics to see about Erin Seabright's drug connections, if the bust for possession of Ecstasy wasn't just a one-time thing. I wondered what they had come up with. I would have known exactly who to look at for information two years before, when I'd been a part of the narcotics team. But two years is a long time in the drug business. Things change fast. Dealers go to prison, they go to Miami, they get killed. The turnover of personnel is especially swift regarding dealing drugs to high school kids. The dealers need to be at or around the age of their customers or they won't be trusted.

It was difficult for me to give very much credence to the drug angle anyway. If she was into a coke dealer or a heroin dealer for a lot of money, maybe. But it would take a hell of a lot of Ecstasy to run up a three-hundred-thousand-dollar tab that would hatch a desperate kidnap for ransom scheme. Erin's crime had warranted nothing more than a slap on the wrist by the juvenile court. She hadn't been charged with dealing, just possession.

I wondered what Chad Seabright, honor student, knew about Erin's drug use. I wondered how complete Erin's corruption of him might have been. He had no believable alibi for the night of the kidnapping.

But Landry hadn't asked me about Chad.

Do you think Don Jade could be Van Zandt's partner in this? In the kidnapping?

Landry hadn't asked that question for no reason. Had Erin been there to meet Jade? Was Jade the older man in her life? A good bet the answer was yes. But if that was true, then Jade would have had control over Erin, and she wouldn't have been a threat, even if she had known what had really happened to Stellar.

I thought again about the horse and the way he had died, and the fact there had been a sedative in his system. Paris hadn't pinpointed the drug. She had listed several possibilities: Rompun, acepromazine, Banamine.

The consensus was that Jade had killed horses before and gotten away with it. But if that was true, he would have known better than to sedate the horse first. He wouldn't have taken the chance of anything showing up in the necropsy.

What if the jab I had thrown at Michael Berne to rattle him was true? I wondered. What if Berne hated Jade enough to ruin him, hated him so much he would sacrifice an animal he himself had loved in order to frame Jade?

Berne would know as well as anyone a sedative in the horse's system would be a big red flag to the insurance company. The death would be ruled the result of foul play. The company wouldn't pay out. Trey Hughes would lose a quarter of a million dollars. Jade would lose his career, and possibly go to jail.

If what Erin had known about Stellar's demise was that Berne had orchestrated it, then Berne had a motive to get rid of the girl. But why risk the kidnapping plot? Was he that desperate for money? The chances of getting caught seemed far too great – unless he had a way to hang the kidnapping on Jade as well, but I couldn't see how he would pull that off. And if Van Zandt was a part of the kidnapping, I had seen no connection between him and Berne.

I got up from my chair and walked around the house, trying to separate the tangled strands of truth and speculation.

I knew in the marrow of my bones Tomas Van Zandt was a sociopath, a criminal, a murderer. It stood to reason: if he was responsible for one girl dying, he was responsible for another disappearing. He had the arrogance to think he could pull off a kidnapping for ransom. But who would he trust for a partner? And who would trust him?

All of it seemed too risky for Jade. He may well have been a sociopath too, but there was a world of difference between Van Zandt and Don Jade. Van Zandt was unpredictable. Jade was controlled and methodical. Why would he concoct a scheme that made him look like a crook and a killer? Why would he kill Stellar in a way that would make everyone jump to the conclusion he was guilty of the crime? Why would he risk kidnapping Erin for ransom?

If he had needed to be rid of her, why wouldn't he just make her disappear? If he was going to claim she had moved out of town, why wouldn't he ditch her car? Why leave it parked at the show grounds on the off chance that no one would ever look for it?

It didn't make sense to me. But Landry thought Jade was connected. Why?

Erin's connection to Stellar.

Erin had allegedly told Jade she was quitting. Told him and no one else. Jade was the last person to see her.

He said she'd gone to Ocala. She hadn't.

Why would Jade make up a story like that – a story that could be easily checked out and discounted as untrue.

It didn't make sense to me. But somehow it made sense to Landry. What other information did he have that I didn't? What small thread that could tie Don Jade to the crime?

The phone numbers of the calls to the Seabright house.

I hated the idea that Landry had details I wasn't privy to. I was the one who had given him those numbers, but he was the one who could check them out. And I was the one who had given him the videotape of the kidnapping, but he had access to the technicians who could enhance the tape. I was the one who had tried to reach out to Interpol, to check out Van Zandt. But I knew that if Landry had made first contact with Interpol, no one would have held back from him the information about Van Zandt's past history as a possible sexual predator.

The frustration built inside me like a thunderhead. I was on the outside. It was my case. I was the one who had cared enough to try to help this girl. I was the one who had done all the dog work. Yet I was the one being shut out, information kept from me. Information available on a need-to-know basis, and it had been decided I had no need to know.

And whose fault was that?

Mine.

It was my fault I wasn't a cop anymore. It was my fault I'd brought Landry into the picture. I'd done the right thing and pushed myself out of the picture in the process.

My case. My case. The words pounded in my head like a drumbeat as I paced. *My case. My case.* The case I hadn't wanted. *My case. My case.* The thing that had reconnected my life to the real world. The world I had retreated from. The life I had given up on.

The conflicting emotions sparked off each other like stone and flint, igniting my temper. Unable to contain the pressure, I grabbed up one of the decorator's objets d'art and threw it as hard as I could against the wall.

The motion felt good. The crash was satisfying. I picked up another piece – some kind of heavy wooden ball from a collection in a bowl – and threw it like a baseball. A wild, animal sound ripped up my throat and exploded from my mouth. A deafening shout that lasted so long, my head was pounding from the sheer effort of it. And when it ended, I felt spent, as if a demon had been exorcized from my soul.

I leaned against the back of the sofa, breathing hard, and looked at the wall. The wallboard had two large dents about head-high. Looked like a good place to hang a picture.

I sank into a chair and held my head in my hands, and I didn't think at all for a good ten minutes. Then I got up, grabbed my keys and my gun, and left the house.

The hell if I would let James Landry cut me out. This was my case. I was in it to the end.

The end of the case or the end of me – whichever came first.

34

There is no surer way to tell which direction the wind is blowing than to spit into it.

Sunday is the marquee day at a horse show in Wellington. During the Winter Equestrian Festival, the big grand prix jumping competitions are held on Sunday afternoon. Big money, big crowds.

Just down the road from the polo stadium, where an international match would be going on at the same time, the stands and banks around the Internationale arena fill with hundreds of fans, owners, riders, grooms – all come to watch the best of the best jump a massive course of fences for prize money upward of a hundred grand.

Camera crews from Fox Sports dot the landscape. Vendor stands line the walkway on the high bank between the Internationale arena and the hunter rings below, teeming with people eager to part with their money for everything from ice cream to diamond jewelry to a Jack Russell puppy. At the same time the grand prix is going on, there are lesser events taking place in half a dozen smaller arenas around it.

I drove in the exhibitors' gate and down the row of tents, backing my car into a spot about three tents before Jade's. I had no way of knowing whether Van Zandt had ratted me out to the Jade camp. Fine if he had, I thought. My patience was too thin to play any more games.

I had not come dressed as the dilettante. Jeans and sneakers. Black T-shirt and baseball cap. Belt holster and Glock nestled in the small of my back under the loose shirt.

Circling around the back of Jade's tent, I entered as I had the first night I'd come there. Down the aisle of some other trainer's stalls where people I didn't know were talking, laughing, shouting at each other as they prepared for their classes. Horses were being groomed and braided, tack cleaned, boots polished.

Farther down the row, directly behind Jade's stalls, another trainer's horses stood bored in their stalls. Two had already gone that day, their short manes were still curly from having their braids let down after their rides. The others hadn't seen a brush that day. There was no sign of a groom in the vicinity.

Cap pulled low, I picked up a pitchfork and dragged a muck cart to one of the stalls, let myself in. The occupant of the stall barely spared me a glance. Head down, I picked through the bedding with the fork, working my way to the back of the stall, and peered between the iron frame of the stall and the canvas that made the wall.

In the stall behind, a girl with spiky red hair stood on a step stool, braiding Park Lane. Her fingers worked quickly, expertly. She sewed the braids in place with heavy black thread, every braid perfect and flat against the horse's neck. Her head bobbed as she worked, keeping time to a tune only she could hear on her headphones.

One of the many cottage industries of the winter show season is braiding manes and tails. With four thousand horses on the grounds, most of them needing full braids for the showring, and not enough grooms to go around, a tidy sum can be made every day of a show by a good braider. There are girls who do nothing but go from stable to stable, starting before dawn, braiding manes and tails until their fingers give out. A good braider can clear several hundred dollars a day – cash if the clients are willing to do business that way.

The girl braiding for Jade kept her eyes on her work and her fingers flying. She didn't notice me.

Paris paced in the aisle in front of the grooming stall, talking on her cell phone. She was dressed to show in buff breeches and a tailored sage green blouse. There was no sign of Jade or Van Zandt in the immediate area.

I doubted Landry had hauled either of them in. He wouldn't make a move before the ransom drop. If there was still a chance of them getting the money, the kidnappers had an incentive to keep Erin alive – provided they hadn't killed her already. Unless what Landry had on Jade was ironclad, taking him into custody was too risky. He still had nothing solid on Van Zandt. If he pulled in one suspect, the other kidnapper would still be free to do as he pleased to Erin. If he knew his partner was in custody, he might panic, kill the girl, and bolt.

Landry had to play the odds on the drop, hoping against hope the kidnappers would show up with Erin in tow, even if he knew the odds were against him.

I couldn't quite make out the conversation Paris was having. She didn't seem upset. The tone of her voice rose and fell like music. She laughed a couple of times, flashing the big smile.

I tossed a couple of forkfuls of manure into the muck cart, moved to the next stall, and repeated the process. Looking between the canvas and the post, I watched Javier emerge from the Jade tack stall with Park Lane's tack in his arms.

'Excuse me? Excuse me?'

I started at the sound of the voice behind me, and turned to find an older woman peering in at me. She wore a helmet of starched-stiff apricot hair, too much makeup, too much gold jewelry, and the severe expression of a society matron.

I tried to look confused.

'Can you tell me where to find the Jade stables?' she asked.

'Jade stables?' I repeated with a heavy French accent.

'Don Jade's stables,' she repeated loudly and with very precise diction.

I pointed at the wall behind me and went back to digging through the shit.

The woman thanked me and went out the end of the tent. A moment later, Paris Montgomery's voice rang out: 'Jane! It's wonderful to see you!'

Jane Lennox. Park Lane's owner. The owner who had called after Stellar's death, talking about moving the horse to another trainer.

Through my spy hole, I watched the two women embrace – Paris bending down to put her arms around the older woman, unable to get too near because of the size of Jane Lennox's bosom.

'I'm so sorry, Don's not here, Jane. He's tied up with something related to that poor girl's murder. He called to say he won't be back in time to show Park Lane. I'll be filling in for him. I hope that's not too disappointing for you. I know you flew all the way down here from New Jersey to watch Don ride her –'

'Paris, don't apologize. You ride her beautifully. I won't be disappointed watching you take her in the showring.'

They went into the tack stall, and their voices became muffled. I moved to the stall directly behind them to listen through the wall. Their voices went from whisper to murmur and back, the volume increasing with emotion.

'. . . You know I love how you handle Parkie, but I have to tell you, Paris, I'm very uncomfortable with what's going on. I thought he'd put his past behind him when he went to France . . .'

'I understand what you're saying, but I hope you'll reconsider, Jane. She's such a good horse. She's got such a bright future.'

'So do you, dear. You have to consider your own future in this. I know you're loyal to Don, but –'

'Excuse me?' A voice behind me asked sharply. 'Who are you? What are you doing in there?'

I turned to face a woman with thick gray hair and a face like a wizened golden raisin.

'What do you think you're doing?' she demanded, opening the stall door. 'I'm calling security.'

I went with confusion again, shrugged, and asked in French if these were not the stalls of Michael Berne. I was asked to clean the stalls of Michael Berne. Was I not in the right place?

Berne's name was the only part the woman understood. 'Michael Berne?' she said, her face pinched tight. 'What about him?'

'I am to work for Michael Berne,' I said haltingly.

'These aren't his horses!' she snapped. 'What's the matter with you? Can't you read? You're in the wrong barn.'

'Wrong?' I asked.

'The wrong barn,' the woman said loudly. 'Michael Berne. That way!' she shouted, waving her arm in the general direction.

'I am so sorry,' I said, slipping out of the stall and closing the door. 'I am so sorry.'

I set the pitchfork aside, shrugged, spread my hands, tried to look sheepish.

'Michael Berne,' the woman said again, waving like a demented contestant in charades.

I nodded and backed away. *'Merci, merci.'*

Head ducked, shoulders hunched, hat pulled low, I stepped out the end of the tent. Paris was walking away on Park Lane, looking like a cover girl for *Town and Country*. The Jade golf cart trailed behind, Jane Lennox and her cotton-candy balloon of apricot hair perched behind the wheel.

I slipped back into the tent on Jade's row. Javier, who had apparently been promoted, was leading Trey Hughes's gray into the grooming stall. I waited for him to start working on the horse, then slipped unnoticed into the tack stall.

The crime scene unit had been through everything the day before. The sooty residue of fingerprint dust clung to the surfaces of the cabinets. The remains of yellow crime scene tape hung on the door frame.

I didn't like that Jade was absent, with the ransom drop only a couple of hours away. What detail of Jill Morone's death would he see to personally? He hadn't wanted to take time out of his life to answer questions about her when the cops had dug her corpse out of the manure pile. He wouldn't want to be bothered with details when he should have been on a horse. Details were Paris Montgomery's job as his assistant. The details, the scut work, the PR, the day-to-day. All of the nitty-gritty and none of the glory. The lot of the assistant trainer.

Not today. Today Paris would ride the star of the stables in the showring while the wealthy owner looked on. Lucky break.

I wondered how loyal to Jade Paris Montgomery really was. She was quick to pay lip service, but her compliments to and defenses of Don Jade always seemed to have a backside to them. She had spent three years working in Don Jade's shadow, running his operation, dealing with his clients, schooling his horses. If Jade left the picture, Paris Montgomery might have a hell of an opportunity. On the other hand, she had no reputation in the international show-jumping ring. Her talent in the arena had yet to be realized. It would take the support of a couple of wealthy patrons to make that happen.

And in a little while she would ride Park Lane into the ring in front of Jane Lennox, who was on the verge of jumping the Jade ship.

I looked around the stall, one eye on the door, waiting to be found out.

Paris had left the armoire open. Clean shirts and jackets hung neatly on the rod. Jeans and a T-shirt had been tossed on the floor. A leather tote bag was carelessly half-hidden by a discarded blouse on the floor of the cabinet.

Checking the door again, I squatted down and dug through the bag, finding nothing of interest or value. A hairbrush, a show schedule, a makeup case. No wallet, no cell phone.

On the right-hand side of the cabinet, at the bottom of a bank of drawers, was a small plastic lockbox bolted to the floor of the cabinet. I tried the door. The simple keyed lock was in place, but the box was cheap with flimsy plastic hinges that wobbled as I pulled on the door. A casual thief would leave it alone and move on to one of the many open stalls where purses were carelessly left in plain sight.

I was not a casual thief.

I glanced at the stall door again, then worked the door of the lockbox, jiggling and pulling at the hinged side. It moved and gave, tantalizing me with the possibility of coming open. Then a cell phone rang, playing the William Tell overture. Paris Montgomery's cell phone. And the sound was coming not from the lockbox in front of me, but from a drawer above my head.

With the tail of my T-shirt, I wiped my prints off the lockbox door, then rose and started opening the drawers above it. The caller ID window in the phone displayed the name: Dr Ritter. I turned the phone off, clipped it to the waistband of my jeans, and let my T-shirt fall to cover it. I closed the drawer and slipped out of the stall.

Javier was in the grooming stall with the gray, his attention on his work as he plied a rubber currycomb over the horse's hide. The horse dozed, enjoying the process the way one might enjoy a good massage.

I stepped into the doorway of the stall, properly introduced myself in Spanish, and asked politely if Javier knew where I might find Mr Jade.

He looked at me out of the corner of his eye and said he didn't know.

A lot of very bad things going on lately, I said.

Yes, very bad.

Terrible about what happened to Jill.

Terrible.

Had the detectives asked him questions about what he might know?

He wanted no business with the police. He had nothing to say. He was with his cousin's family that night. He didn't know anything.

It was too bad Señor Jade had not come by for night check that night and stopped the murder from happening.

Or Señora Montgomery, Javier said as he kept working the brush.

Of course, some people thought Señor Jade was the guilty one.

People always like to think the worst.

I also knew the detectives had spoken with Van Zandt. What did he think of that?

Javier thought only of his work, of which he had too much with both girls gone.

Yes, the other girl was gone too. Had he known Erin Seabright very well?

No, he didn't. He was nothing to those girls because he could not speak English very well.

That makes things hard, I said. People don't respect you. It never occurs to those people that you could feel the same way about them because they don't speak Spanish.

Young girls think only of themselves and the men they want.

Erin had her eye on Señor Jade, yes?

Yes.

Did Señor Jade have his eye on her?

No answer.

Or maybe Van Zandt was the one?

Javier only did his job. He didn't mind the business of other people.

That was the best way to be, I agreed. Why borrow trouble from others? Look at Jill. She said she knew something about Stellar's death, and look what happened to her.

The dead tell no tales.

His gaze flicked past me. I turned to find Trey Hughes coming up behind me.

'By golly, Ellie, you're a woman of many talents,' he said. He seemed subdued, not his usual drunken, jovial self. 'Speaking in tongues.'

I lifted a shoulder. 'A language here, a language there. It's nothing every girl in boarding school doesn't get.'

'I've got all I can do with English.'

'You're not riding?' I asked, taking in his casual attire. Chinos, polo shirt, deck shoes.

'Paris is taking him today,' he said, reaching past me to touch the gray's nose. 'She can undo all the confusion I wreaked on him in the last go-round Friday.'

He looked at my outfit and lifted a brow. 'You don't exactly look yourself today either.'

I spread my hands. 'My disguise as one of the common folk.'

He smiled a sleepy kind of smile. I wondered if he had taken the mood elevator down with a little chemical assistance.

'I heard a little rumor about you, young lady,' he said, watching me out of the corner of his eye as he fed a stalk of hay to his horse.

'Really? I hope it was juicy. Am I having a flaming affair with someone? With you?'

'Are you? That's the hell of getting old,' he said. 'I'm still having fun, but I can't remember any of it.'

'Then it's always new and fresh.'

'Always look on the bright side.'

'So what did you hear about me?' I asked, more interested in whom he had heard it from. Van Zandt? Bruce Seabright? Van Zandt would spread the news to turn people against me for his own sake. Seabright would have told Hughes because he valued his client more than he valued his stepdaughter.

'That you're not who you seem to be,' Hughes said.

'Is anyone?'

'Good point, my dear.'

He came out of the stall and we walked to the end of the aisle to stand looking out. The sky had gone gray with the threat of rain. Across the road the water of the lagoon rippled silver under the skimming breeze.

'So, who am I supposed to be – if I'm not who I seem?' I asked.

'A spy,' he said. He didn't seem upset, but strangely calm. Perhaps he was tired of playing the game too. I wondered just how key a player in all this he was, or if he had simply allowed himself to be swept along by someone else's current.

'A spy? That's exciting,' I said. 'For a foreign country? For a terrorist cell?'

Hughes gave an elaborate shrug, tipping his head to one side.

'I knew that I knew you,' he said quietly. 'I just couldn't quite place the face. The old brain doesn't fire like it used to.'

'A mind is a terrible thing to waste.'

'I'd get a transplant, but I keep forgetting to call.'

It was a terrible thing, I thought as we stood there side by side. Trey Hughes had had it all going for him: good looks, quick wit, money to do or be anything. And this was what he had chosen to become: an aging alcoholic wastrel.

Funny, I thought, people who had known me along the way might say a similar thing: *She had every advantage, came from such a good family, and she threw it all back in their faces. For what? Look at her now. What a shame.*

We can never know another person's heart, what gives them strength, what breaks them down, how they define courage or rebellion or success.

'How do you think you know me?' I asked.

'I know your father. I've had occasion to call on his services over the years. The name made it click. Estes. Elle. Elena Estes. You had the most glorious mane of hair,' he reminisced. He had a faraway look as he stared through the haze of his memory. 'A friend tells me you're a private eye now. Imagine that.'

'It's not true. Call the licensing board and ask. They don't know me by any name.'

'Good business to be in,' he said, ignoring my denial. 'Christ knows there's never any shortage of secrets around here. People will do anything for a dime.'

'Kill a horse?' I asked.

'Kill a horse. Kill a career. Kill a marriage.'

'Kill a person?'

He didn't seem shocked by the suggestion. 'The oldest story in the world: greed.'

'Yes. And it always ends the same way: badly.'

'For someone,' he said. 'The trick is not to be that someone.'

'What character do you play in this story, Trey?'

He tried a weary smile. 'The sad clown. All the world loves a sad clown.'

'I'm only interested in the villain,' I said. 'Can you point me in a direction?'

He tried to laugh, but didn't have the energy for it. 'Sure. Go into the hall of mirrors and take a left.'

'A girl is dead, Trey. Erin Seabright's been kidnapped. It's not a game.'

'No. It's more like a movie.'

'If you know something, now's the time to tell it.'

'Honey,' he said, staring out at the water. 'If I knew anything, I wouldn't be where I am today.'

He walked away from me then, got in his convertible, and drove slowly away. I watched him go, thinking I had been wrong at the start of this, when I had said everything led back to Jade. Everything led back to Trey Hughes – the land deal with Seabright, Erin getting the job with Jade, Stellar. All of it came back to Trey.

And so, the big money question was: was he at the center of the storm because he was the storm, or had the storm blown up around him?

Trey had an eye for the girls. That was no secret. And scandal was his middle name. God knew how many affairs he'd had in his lifetime. He'd had an affair with Stella Berne while Michael was his trainer. He'd been with her the night his mother died. It wasn't hard to imagine him having his eye on Erin. But kidnapping? And what about Jill Morone?

I couldn't imagine any of it. I didn't want to. Monte Hughes III, my first big crush.

I know your father. I've had occasion to call on his services over the years.

What the hell had he meant by that? Why would he have needed the services of a defense attorney the caliber of my father? And how would I find out? Call my father after all these years of bitter silence and ask him?

So, Dad, never mind that I defied you at every turn and dumped my education to become a cop. And never mind that you were always a lousy, distant, uninvolved parent, disappointed in me for the simple fact that I was not a child of your own making. Water under the bridge. Tell me why Trey Hughes has needed your esteemed expertise.

My father and I hadn't spoken in a decade. It wasn't going to happen now.

I wondered if Landry had interviewed Trey. I wondered if he'd run his name through the system as a matter of routine. But Landry hadn't asked me any questions about Trey Hughes, only about Jade.

I went to my car and climbed in to sit and wait. Paris would be getting on Hughes's gray soon. Trey would come back to the barn after for the postmortem of the ride. And when he left the show grounds afterward, I would be behind him.

Trey Hughes had just become the center of the universe. It all revolved around him. I was going to find out why.

Act Two

SCENE TWO
FADE IN:
EXTERIOR: THE HORSE PARK AT EQUESTRIAN ESTATES —
SUNSET

Wide open spaces on three sides. Trees and a canal at the back of the property. A paved road curves past the front. No one in sight, but the cops are there, hidden.

A black car approaches and parks at the gate. Bruce Seabright gets out of the car and looks around. He looks pissed off and nervous. He thinks it's a trap.

He's right.

He opens the trunk and takes out two large blue duffel bags. He heaves the bags over the gate, then climbs over, picks the bags up, and looks around again. He's looking for a sign, for a person. Maybe he's even looking for Erin, though he would be just as happy if he never saw her again.

He starts walking up the drive toward the building, reluctantly. He has the expression of a man who will wet his pants at the first sudden loud noise.

Halfway to the building he stops and stands and waits. Slowly he turns around in a circle. He wonders what will happen next. He sets the bags down and checks his watch.

6:05 P.M.

Darkness is closing in. The security light comes on with a loud humming sound. The voice, the same mechanically altered voice from the phone calls, comes over the loudspeakers.

THE VOICE   Leave the bags on the ground.

BRUCE   Where's the girl?

THE VOICE   Leave the bags on the ground.

BRUCE   I want to see Erin!

893

THE VOICE   In the box. Ring one. In the box. Ring one.

BRUCE   What box? Which ring?

He is agitated, doesn't know which way to turn. He doesn't like not having control. He doesn't want to leave the money. He looks at the two rings nearest the building and chooses the one to his right. He takes the bags with him and goes to stand at the corner of the ring.

BRUCE   What box? I don't see any box!

He stands there, impatient. It's getting darker by the second. He stares for a moment at the judge's booth – a small wooden shelter – at the end of the ring, then goes toward it.

BRUCE   Erin? Erin!

He circles the booth cautiously. Someone might jump out and shoot him or stab him. Erin's body might fall out onto the ground.

Nothing happens.

He inches toward the door, pulls it open, jumps back.

Nothing happens.

BRUCE   Erin? Are you in there?

No answer.

Slowly, he sets the bags on the ground and inches toward the booth again, eventually stepping inside. There is no one in the booth. A videotape cassette has been left on the floor. Written in black block letters on a white label on the tape: PUNISHMENT.

THE VOICE   You broke the rules. The girl has paid the price.

Cops come out of the woodwork. Several charge up the stairs of the building. They pry the lock off the door, kick the door in, burst into the room shouting with guns drawn. The beams of their flashlights bob and sweep around the room. There is no one there.

As they approach the console of audio equipment situated under the bank of windows that allow full view of the grounds, they spot the simple timer that turned the machines on at precisely 6:05 P.M.

The tape is still playing.

THE VOICE   You broke the rules. The girl has paid the price.
You broke the rules. The girl has paid the price.

The voice echoes across the emptiness of the night.

FADE OUT

35

Trey Hughes never came back to Don Jade's barn.

I waited in my car, checking my watch it seemed every three minutes as the time ticked on toward six. Javier led the gray, draped in a Lucky Dog cooler, away from the barn and came back leading Park Lane. Paris and Jane Lennox returned in the golf cart, then Lennox climbed into a gold Cadillac and drove away.

I checked my watch again: 5:43.

At another show grounds some few miles away, Landry and his team from Robbery/Homicide would be in place, waiting for the kidnappers to show.

I wanted to be there to see how the drop played out, but knew I wouldn't be allowed anywhere near the place. I wanted to know where Jade and Van Zandt were, what they were doing, who was watching them. I wanted to know where Trey Hughes had gone. I wanted people reporting these facts to me. I wanted to be running the case.

The old rush of adrenaline was there, speeding up my metabolism, making me feel a hum of electricity running just under my skin. Making me feel alive.

Paris emerged from the barn in street clothes, climbed into a money-green Infiniti, and drove toward the truck exit. I started my car and followed, leaving a pickup truck between us. She took a left on Pierson and we began winding through the outskirts of Wellington, passing through Binks Forest.

Molly would be in the Seabright house, tucked away in a corner like a mouse, eyes wide, ears open, breath held, waiting desperately for any word of Erin and what had happened at the ransom drop.

I wish I could have been there for her, as much as for myself.

I hung back as Paris brought her car to a stop at Southern – a busy east-west drag that led to Palm Beach one way or the rural county the other. She crossed to the Loxahatchee side of the road and continued down B Road, into the wooded darkness.

I kept my eyes on the Infiniti's taillights, very aware that we were traveling in the direction of Equestrian Estates.

A creepy sense of déjà vu crawled down my back. The last time I'd driven these side roads at night, I'd been a narcotics detective. The Golam brothers' trailer wasn't far away.

The Infiniti's brake lights came on. No blinker.

I slowed and checked my rearview as headlights glared through my back window. My heart rate picked up a beat.

I didn't like having someone behind me. This was not a heavily traveled road. No one came out here unless they had to, unless they lived here or worked at a nursery or a mulch-grinding place.

I was revisited by the sick feeling I'd gotten in the pit of my stomach that morning when Van Zandt had shown up at the farm and I had thought I was alone with him.

Until later, he had said when he kissed my cheek.

Ahead of me, Paris had turned in at a driveway. I went past, catching a quick glimpse. Like most of the places out this way, the house was a seventies vintage ranch style with a jungle for a yard. The garage door went up and the Infiniti rolled inside.

Why would she live out here? I wondered. Jade had a good business. Paris should have been making decent money. Enough that she could have lived in Wellington near the show grounds, enough to afford an apartment in one of the many complexes that catered to riders.

It was one thing to stick the grooms out here in the sticks. Rent was cheap – relatively speaking. But Paris Montgomery with her money-green Infiniti and her emerald and diamond heirloom ring?

The lights in the rearview brightened as the car behind me closed the distance between us.

Abruptly, I hit the brakes and turned hard right onto another side road. But it wasn't a road at all. It was a cul-de-sac ringed by several freshly cleared lots. My lights caught on the frame skeleton of a new home.

The headlights turned into the cul-de-sac behind me.

I gunned the engine around the curve of the drive, beating it back toward the main road, then hit the brakes and skidded sideways, blocking the exit.

The hell if I would let that son of a bitch stalk me like a rabbit.

I pulled the Glock out of its box in the door.

Kicked the door open as the other car pulled alongside and the passenger's window went down.

I brought the gun up into position, dead aim on the face of the driver: eyes wide, mouth open.

Not Van Zandt.

'Who are you?' I shouted.

'Oh, my God! Oh, my God! Don't kill me!'

'Shut the fuck up!' I yelled. 'I want ID. Now!'

'I just – I just –' he stuttered. He looked maybe forty, thin, too much hair.

'Out of the car! Hands where I can see them!'

'Oh, my God,' he whimpered. 'Please don't kill me. I'll give you my money →'

'Shut up. I'm a cop.'

'Oh, Jesus.'

Apparently, that was worse than if I had been ready to rob and kill him. He climbed out of the car with his hands held out in front of him.

'Are you right-handed or left-handed?'

'What?'

'Are you right-handed or left-handed?'

'Left.'

'With your *right hand,* take out your wallet and put it on the hood of the car.'

He did as he was told, put the wallet on the car and slid it across to me.

'What's your name?'

'Jimmy Manetti.'

I flipped the wallet open and pretended I could see in the faint backwash of the headlights.

'Why are you following me?'

He tried to shrug. 'I thought you were looking too.'

'Looking for what?'

'The party. Kay and Lisa.'

'Kay and Lisa who?'

'I dunno. Kay and Lisa. Waitresses? From Steamer's?'

'Jesus Christ,' I muttered, tossing the wallet back on the hood. 'Are you an idiot?'

'Yeah. I guess.'

I shook my head and lowered the gun. I was trembling. The afterglow of an adrenaline rush and the realization that I had nearly shot an innocent moron in the face.

'Keep your distance, for God's sake,' I said, backing toward my car. 'The next person whose ass you run up might not be as nice as I am.'

I left Jimmy Manetti standing with his hands still up in the air, pulled out of the cul-de-sac, and went back in the direction I had come. Slowly. Trying to regulate my heartbeat. Trying to get my head back where it belonged.

The lights were on in the house Paris Montgomery had gone to. Her dog was chasing its tail in the front yard. There was a car parked in the drive.

A classic Porsche convertible with the top down and personalized plates: LKY DOG

Lucky Dog.

Trey Hughes.

36

'Obviously, they went in there and set up the tape and the timer before they even made the last ransom call,' Landry said.

They had gathered in a conference room: himself and Weiss; Dugan and Armedgian. Major Owen Cathcart, head of the Investigations Division, had joined the gathering and would act as liaison to Sheriff Sacks. Completing the group were Bruce and Krystal Seabright, and a woman from Victim Services whose name Landry hadn't caught.

The Vic Services woman and Krystal Seabright sat off to the side of the group, Krystal shivering like a Chihuahua, her eyes sunken, her hair a bleached fright wig. Bruce had been none too happy to see her there, insisting she go home and let him handle things. Krystal pretended not to hear him.

'There hasn't been an event at that facility in the last three weeks,' Weiss said. 'The place is kept locked up, but we're talking padlocks. Security has never been an issue because of the location. But it wouldn't be hard to break in.'

'Any fingerprints?' Cathcart asked.

'A few hundred,' Landry said. 'But none on the audiotape, none on the videotape, none on the timer, none on the tape deck . . .'

'And is someone trying to get that tape to sound like a real human being?'

'They're working on it,' Dugan said.

'And what's on the videotape? Let's see it.'

Landry hesitated, glancing at Krystal and the Vic Services woman. 'It's pretty rough, sir. I don't know that the family –'

'I want to see it,' Krystal said, speaking up for the first time.

'Krystal, for God's sake,' Bruce snapped as he paced behind her. 'Why would you want to see it? The detective just told you –'

'I want to see it,' she said with more force. 'She's my daughter.'

'And you want to see some animal attack her? Rape her? That's what you're saying, aren't you, Landry?' Bruce said.

Landry moved his jaw. Seabright set his teeth on edge. If he got through this case without popping the guy in the face, it was going to be a miracle.

'I said it's pretty rough to watch. There's no rape, but Erin takes a beating. I wouldn't recommend you watch it, Mrs. Seabright.'

'There's no reason, Krystal –' Bruce started. His wife interrupted him. 'She's my daughter.'

Krystal Seabright stood up, her trembling hands clasped in front of her. 'I want to see it, Detective Landry. I want to see what my husband has done to my daughter.'

'Me?' Bruce turned red in the face and made a choking sound in his throat like maybe he was having a heart attack. He looked at the cops in the room. 'I am nothing but a victim in this!'

Krystal turned on him. 'You're as guilty as the people who took her!'

'I'm not the one who brought the cops into this! They said no cops.'

'You wouldn't have done anything,' Krystal said bitterly. 'You wouldn't even have told me she was gone!'

Seabright looked embarrassed. His mouth quivered with bad temper. He stepped closer to his wife and lowered his voice. 'Krystal, this is neither the time nor the place to have this discussion.'

She ignored him, looking instead at Landry. 'I want to see the tape. She's my daughter.'

'As if you ever cared,' Bruce muttered. 'A cat is a better mother than you.'

'I think it's important for Mrs Seabright to see at least part of the tape.' The Vic Services woman put her two cents in. 'You can always ask them to stop it at any point, Krystal.'

'I want to see it.'

Krystal walked forward, teetering unsteadily on leopard print stiletto heels. She looked as fragile as a glass ornament, as if one tap would shatter her into a million gaudy-colored slivers. Landry moved to take her by the arm. The Vic Services woman then finally got up off her wide ass to help, to come and stand beside Krystal Seabright and offer support.

'This is against my better judgment, Mrs Seabright,' Dugan said.

Krystal looked at him, eyes bugging out. 'I want to see it!' she shouted. 'How many times do I have to say it? Do I have to scream? Do I have to get a court order? I want to see it!'

Dugan held up a hand in surrender. 'We'll play the tape. Just tell us when to stop it, Mrs Seabright.'

He nodded to Weiss, and Weiss fed the tape into the VCR that sat with a twenty-one-inch TV on a cart at the front of the room.

Everyone was silent as the video image faded in to a scene inside a bedroom in what looked to be a trailer house. The window gave it away: a cheap aluminum frame around filthy glass. Someone had taken a finger and written on the dirty pane: HELP, the letters backward so the word could be read from outside the trailer.

It was night. One lamp with a bare lightbulb lit the scene.

Erin Seabright sat naked on a filthy, stained mattress with no sheets, chained to the rusty iron frame of the bed by one wrist. She was hardly recognizable from the girl Landry had seen only in a photograph. Her lower lip was split and crusted with dried blood. Mascara ringed her eyes. There were red welts and bruises on her arms and legs. She sat with her knees pulled up, trying to cover as much of her nakedness as she could. She looked directly at the camera, tears streaming down her face, her eyes glassy with terror.

'Why won't you help me? I asked you to help me! Why can't you just do what they say?' she asked, a thread of hysteria quivering through her voice. 'Do you hate me that much? Don't you know what he's going to do to me? Why won't you help me?!'

'Oh, my God,' Krystal murmured. She brought a hand up to cover her mouth. Tears welled up in her eyes and spilled down her cheeks. 'Oh, my God, Erin!'

'We warned you,' the metallic voice said, the words drawn-out, low and slow and slightly garbled. 'You broke the rules. The girl will be punished.'

A figure dressed in black from head to toe stepped into the frame from behind the camera – black mask, black clothes, black gloves – and moved toward the bed. Erin began to whimper. She shrank back on the bed, huddling against the wall, trying to hide, trying to cover her head with her free arm.

'No! No!' she screamed. 'It's not my fault!'

The figure struck her with a riding whip. Landry felt himself flinch at the sound of the whip connecting with bare flesh. The whip came down again and again with vicious force on her arms, her back, her legs, her buttocks. The girl screamed again and again, a horrible piercing shriek that went through Landry like an ice pick.

Dugan stopped the tape without being asked.

'My God,' Bruce Seabright muttered. Turning away, he rubbed a hand over his face.

Krystal Seabright fell against the Victim Services woman, trying to cry, but no sound coming out of her open mouth. Landry caught hold of one of her arms, Weiss caught the other, and they moved her toward a chair.

Bruce Seabright stood where he was, the asshole, staring at this woman he had married, looking like he was wondering if he could call it quits on that deal right there and then.

'I told you it would only upset you,' he said.

Krystal sat on the chair, doubled over, her face in her hands, her pink skirt halfway up her thighs.

Landry turned his back to her, stepped up to Bruce, and said in a low voice, 'If you could crawl out of your own asshole for three seconds, a little faked compassion would be a good thing right now.'

Seabright had the gall to be offended.

'I'm not the villain here! I'm not the one who called you people in when the kidnappers said not to.'

'No,' Krystal said, lifting her head. 'You didn't call anyone! You didn't do anything!'

'Erin would be home by now if not for that detective sticking her nose into it,' Bruce said angrily. 'I was handling it. They would have let her go. They would have known I wouldn't give in to their terrorism, and they would have let her go.'

'You hate her!' Krystal shrieked. 'You want her dead! You never want to see her again!'

'Oh, for Christ's sake, Krystal. Neither do you!' Seabright shouted. 'She's nothing but a nasty little piece of white trash, just like you were before I found you! That doesn't mean I want her dead!'

'That's it!' Landry declared, moving toward Seabright. 'You're out of here.'

'I've given you a life you never would have gotten any other way,' Seabright said to his wife. 'You didn't want Erin messing it up. You threw her out of the house yourself.'

'I was afraid!' Krystal cried. 'I was afraid!'

Sobbing again, she fell off the chair onto the floor, and curled into a ball.

'Out!' Landry said, shoving Seabright to the door.

Seabright shrugged him off and went out into the hall. Landry followed, with Dugan coming behind him.

'I'm pressing charges!' Seabright shouted.

Landry looked at him like he'd lost his mind. 'What?'

'I want that woman brought up on charges!'

'Your wife?'

'Estes! None of this would be happening if not for her.'

Dugan looked at Landry. 'What's he talking about?'

Landry ignored him and advanced on Seabright. 'Your stepdaughter was kidnapped. That wasn't Estes's doing.'

Seabright stuck a finger in his face. 'I want her license. And I'm calling my attorney. I never wanted you people involved, and now look what's happened. I'm suing. I'm suing this department and I'm suing Elena Estes!'

Landry batted his hand to the side and backed him up against the wall. 'Think twice before you start throwing threats around, you fat prick!'

'Landry!' Dugan shouted.

'I find one thing that ties you into the kidnapping, you can bend over and kiss your ass good-bye!'

'Landry!'

Dugan grabbed him roughly by one shoulder. Landry shrugged him off and stepped aside, his glare still on Seabright.

'Take a walk, Detective Landry,' Dugan said.

'Ask him what she meant,' Landry said. 'Ask him what Erin meant when she said she had asked him to help her. When did she ask? Why didn't we hear about it? I want a warrant for that house and for that bastard's office too. If he's withholding evidence, he can rot in jail.'

'Go,' Dugan said. 'Now.'

Landry went down the hall, into the squad room to his desk, and dug through the pencil drawer for a pack of Marlboro Lights he kept there. He had quit smoking as a rule, but certain moments were exceptions, and this was one of those moments. He shook out one cigarette, took the lighter, and went out of the building to pace on the sidewalk and smoke.

He was shaking. He wanted to go back into the building and beat Bruce Seabright unconscious. The son of a bitch. His wife's daughter kidnapped and his solution was to do nothing. Let her rot. Let them rape her, kill her, throw her in a canal. Jesus H.

I asked you to help me! Why won't you help me? Do you hate me that much?

Seabright hadn't said anything about having spoken with Erin directly. Landry was willing to bet his pension Seabright had another tape stashed somewhere. A tape where Erin begged for help. And Bruce Seabright hadn't done a goddam thing.

But that wasn't why Erin was being punished, was it? She was in that filthy place, chained naked to a bed, being beaten with a whip because the rules had been broken and the Sheriff's Office had been called in.

It could have been that Estes had poked at the wrong hornet's nest. She'd spoken with everyone involved with Erin Seabright. Maybe Van Zandt had figured out she wasn't what she seemed to be.

All of Jade's crowd had been interviewed Saturday regarding Jill Morone's death. Erin's name had been raised. Jade might have been tipped off that way.

Someone in the neighborhood might have been watching, but Landry didn't believe it. He'd looked over the reports on the neighbors: their families, their professions, their connections to the Seabrights. Nothing.

Maybe the kidnappers had had the house bugged, but that seemed a long stretch. This wasn't some multibillionaire they were trying to shake down.

Or the kidnappers had inside information. That kid of Seabright's. Or Seabright himself.

What better way to distance himself from suspicion than to cooperate with the cops, then blame it on them when things went south. He would never have done a thing to help Erin if Estes hadn't stuck her nose in it.

He would have done exactly what Landry had said in the beginning: kept all the info to himself until the girl turned up dead – if she turned up at all. And he would have told his wife he'd done everything he could, everything he'd thought best. Too bad it hadn't worked out, but what the hell, Erin was just a white trash liability anyway.

The cigarette was gone. Landry dropped it on the sidewalk, ground the butt out, picked it up and threw it in the trash.

And how did Don Jade fit into the picture?

Estes had told him: Seabright sold land to Trey Hughes, Don Jade worked for Trey Hughes. Bruce got Erin the job with Jade through Hughes. The girl would have been better off running away from home to live on the street in Miami.

Everything goes back to Jade, Estes had said in the beginning. But that wasn't quite true. Everything went back to Trey Hughes.

Landry dug his cell phone out of his pocket and dialed Dwyer, who had the tail on Jade.

'Where is he?'

'Having dinner at Michael's Pasta. Specials of the night: penne putanesca and seafood risotto.'

'Who's he with?'

'Some tiny old broad with big fake tits and orange hair. Can we pick him up?'

'No.'

'What happened at the drop?'

'It was a setup. They knew we'd be there.'

'How?'

'I've got a hunch.'

'They've got medication for that now.'

'Yeah, it's called an arrest. Do you know where the feds are?'

'Sitting with their thumbs up their asses. They say Van Zandt hasn't left the town house. The Mercedes is sitting in the driveway.'

'And where's the Carlton woman's car?'

'Don't ask me. I'm doing *my* job.'

'Great.'

Landry wished for a second cigarette as he watched Dugan come out the door behind Bruce Seabright. Seabright went across the parking lot to his Jaguar, got in, and drove away. His wife was noticeably absent from the passenger's seat. Dugan turned and came down the sidewalk.

'I've gotta go,' Landry said to Dwyer, and snapped the phone shut.

'What do you know about Elena Estes?' Dugan asked.

'She used to be a narc.'

'What do you know about her being a private investigator?'

'I know she's not.'

'Why does Seabright think otherwise?'

Landry shrugged. 'Why does he think anything? He's a fucking asshole. He thinks it's a good idea to let perverts have an eighteen-year-old girl so they can beat her with a whip.'

'What do you know about Estes in relation to this case?' Dugan asked. His face was tight with temper.

'I know there wouldn't be a case if she hadn't come into this office and told me what was going on,' Landry said.

'She's involved in this.'

'It's a free country.'

'It's not that free,' Dugan snapped. 'Get her in here.'

37

Suddenly living in rural Loxahatchee made sense. Secluded, away from the throng of horse people, it was the perfect place to conduct a clandestine affair.

Apparently, Don Jade wasn't the only one in his barn willing to play bedroom games to further his cause. If Trey Hughes was in that house for something other than a discussion of how his horse had gone in the ring that day, then Paris Montgomery had snagged Jade's most affluent patron. With malice aforethought.

Or maybe Jade knew. Perhaps she had his blessing. Perhaps she was Jade's insurance policy for keeping Trey's attention.

My gut said no. I had witnessed no overt displays of affection between Paris and Trey. Their interaction at the barn had appeared to be nothing more than client and trainer.

Paris was a smart, ambitious girl. If Paris made Trey happy, Trey could certainly make Paris happy.

As I drove back to Wellington, I wondered if Paris knew Hughes had been involved with Michael Berne's wife before her. That certainly hadn't insured Michael a place in the posh new stables – or Stella Berne either, for that matter.

I wondered how long the affair had been going on. Hughes had taken his horses to Jade about nine months previous, meaning they had gone up to Jade's barn in the Hamptons for the summer. Trey had likely spent the summer there, soaking up the social swirl. A relationship might have sparked.

Turning these things over in my mind, I drove back to Wellington and swung by Sag Harbor Court.

The Mercedes Trey Hughes had loaned to Van Zandt was parked in the driveway. In the visitor parking spots down the street, two men in shirts and ties sat in a dark Ford Taurus.

Feds.

I parked a couple of slots down from the sedan and approached the vehicle from the front. The guy in the driver's seat rolled his window down.

'FYI guys,' I said, 'I saw him this morning driving a dark blue Chevy Malibu.'

The driver stared at me with cop eyes. 'I'm sorry?'

'Tomas Van Zandt. That's who you're supposed to be sitting on, right?'

They looked at each other, then back at me.

'Ma'am? Who are you?' the driver asked.

'I used to be a friend of that prick Armedgian. Tell him I said that.'

I left them sitting there like a couple of assholes, watching a car that probably hadn't left the driveway all day.

Tomas Van Zandt was a free man.

Until later . . .

I put my gun on the passenger seat of my car and drove home to wait.

There was no obvious sign of an intruder in the area of Sean's farm. I knew Sean would not have given Van Zandt the gate code. But my senses were humming just the same.

I parked my car at the barn and checked on the horses, walking down the aisle with gun in hand. I stopped to pet each horse, feeling my tension lessen a fraction at each stall. Oliver wanted to eat the gun. Feliki pinned her ears at me, to remind me who the alpha mare was, then expected a treat. D'Artagnon wanted only to have his neck scratched.

I thought of Erin Seabright as I performed the task, of the way she had laughed at Stellar in the video I'd found in Van Zandt's bedroom. I wondered if she let memories like that one comfort or torment her wherever she was, whatever was happening to her.

I wanted to call Landry and find out what had happened at the drop, but I wouldn't. He wasn't my friend or my confidant. He wouldn't appreciate my need to know. I hoped Molly would have called, but knew she wouldn't be the first to hear whatever news there was. Bruce would have been sent to the drop. Regardless of what transpired, there would be a postmortem of the operation at the Sheriff's Office. And during that time, no one would think or have the courtesy to let Molly know what was going on.

Nothing to do but wait, I thought, then remembered I had Paris Montgomery's cell phone in my car. I retrieved it on the way to the house and sat down with it at the writing desk.

The phone was a Nokia 3390. The voice mail icon indicated she had messages, but I had no way to retrieve them because I didn't know her password. I did know from experience, however, this model of phone automatically stored the last ten numbers dialed.

I scrolled to the last number dialed. 'Voice mailbox' appeared in the screen. I scrolled to the next call: Jane L – Cell. The next: Don – Cell.

Headlights flashed in the drive.

It wasn't Sean. I never saw Sean's lights when he drove in because he always went directly into the garage, which was on the far side of the main house.

Irina, perhaps.

Perhaps not.

I set the phone aside, picked up the Glock, turned off the only light I had on in the house, then went to look out the window.

The security light on the end of the stable didn't quite reach the car. But as the driver got out and came toward my house, I could tell by the way he carried himself it was Landry.

My heart beat faster. He would have news. Good or bad, he would have news. I opened the door before he made it to the patio. He stopped and put his hands up, his eyes on the gun still in my hand.

'Don't kill the messenger,' he said.

'Is it bad news?'

'Yes.'

'Is she dead?'

'Not that we know.'

I leaned against the door frame and let go a sigh, feeling relieved and sick at once. 'What happened?'

He told me about the drop, the taped message rigged with a timer, the videotape of Erin being beaten.

'My God,' I mumbled, rubbing my hands over my face, feeling it on only one side. In that moment, I wished all of me could have been numb. 'Oh, my God. That poor kid.'

You broke the rules. The girl will pay the price.

Breaking the rules had been my idea. I'd spent my entire life breaking rules and never thinking twice until it was too late. I never seemed to learn that lesson. Now Erin Seabright was paying the price.

I should have done something differently. If I hadn't been such a bully with Bruce Seabright, if I hadn't insisted on bringing the SO into the picture . . .

If I hadn't been me. If Molly had gone to someone else.

'Don't beat yourself up, Estes,' Landry said quietly.

I laughed. 'But that's one of the few things I do really well.'

'No,' he murmured.

He was standing very close to me. Our shadows overlapped on the flagstone as the front door light washed down over us. If I'd been a different woman, I might have turned to him in that moment. But I couldn't remember the last time I had offered my vulnerability to anyone. I didn't know how. And I didn't trust Landry not to hand it back.

'It's not all about you,' he said. 'Sometimes things just play out the way they play out.'

I had used those same words with him just twenty-four hours before. 'Anything I say can and will be used against me.'

'Whatever works.'

'Did it work when I fed it to you?'

He shook his head. 'No. But I liked the sound of it.'

'Thanks.'

'You're welcome.'

We looked at each other for a little too long, then Landry rubbed the back of his neck and looked past me into the house.

'Can I help myself to your scotch? It's been a hell of a day.'

'Sure.'

He went to the cabinet and poured himself a couple of fingers of whiskey as old as I was, and sipped at it.

I sat on the arm of a chair and watched him. 'Where was Jade during the drop?'

'In West Palm, meeting with Jill Morone's parents. They flew down from Buttcrack, Virginia, this afternoon and demanded he meet with them personally.'

'And Van Zandt?'

He shook his head, the line of his jaw tightening. 'Good call this morning about your FBI friend.'

'Armedgian? He's no friend of mine – or yours, I imagine.'

'He's suddenly here to "consult and advise". His people are sitting on Van Zandt.'

'His people are watching a car in a driveway. Van Zandt was out here this morning driving a Chevy.'

Landry gave me the eagle eye. 'What was he doing out here?'

'Serving me notice, I think.'

'He knows it was you in his place last night?'

'Yes. I think so.'

'I don't like that.'

'Imagine how I feel.'

He sipped his scotch and thought. 'Well ... he wasn't at the drop. We know that.'

'That doesn't mean he's not connected to the kidnapping. Or Jade either, for that matter. I'm sure that was half the point of rigging the tape with a timer: so the bad guys could make airtight alibis for the time of the drop.'

'That and to punish Seabright.'

'They had to know you'd be there. They never had any intention of showing up with or without Erin.'

'We still had to go through with it.'

'Of course,' I said. 'But I don't like what it means for Erin. They know now they're not going to get the money. What do they have to gain by keeping her alive? Nothing.'

'Fun and games with the riding whip,' Landry said. He stared at the floor and shook his head. 'Jesus. You should have seen him go at her. If he beat his horses like that, the SPCA would have him locked up.'

'Jade?' I said. 'I'm sure you know something about him I don't, but I'm having some serious doubts he's our guy.'

'You're the one who told me everything came back to him.'

'In a way, it does. But in a way that doesn't add up for me. He's sitting pretty professionally with Trey Hughes putting him into that new facility, buying expensive horses for him. Why would he risk that by doing something so outrageous as kidnap Erin?'

'Erin knew something about that horse he killed.'

'So why not just get rid of her?' I asked. 'This is south Florida. It's the easiest thing in the world to get rid of a body. Why get embroiled in a messy kidnapping plot?'

Landry shrugged. 'So he's a psycho. He thinks he's omnipotent.'

'I could go for that explanation regarding Van Zandt. But I don't see Jade risking everything on some scheme, and I don't see him partnering with a loose cannon like Van Zandt.'

Landry took another sip of the scotch. Trying to decide whether or not to share with me, I thought.

'One of the phone numbers you gave me from Seabright's incoming calls belonged to a prepaid cell phone we traced to the Radio Shack in Royal Palm Beach. We couldn't get an ID from the clerks off Jade's photo, but one of them thinks he took a phone call from a man named Jade, asking him questions about the phones, and asking him to set a phone aside for him.'

'Why would Jade do something so stupid?' I said. 'He wouldn't.'

Landry shrugged. 'Maybe he figured a disposable phone would be untraceable, so it wouldn't matter who he talked to.'

I got up to pace, shaking my head. 'Don Jade hasn't gotten where he is by being an idiot. If he wanted a phone held for him, why not give a phony name? Why not give them just his first name? No. This doesn't make any sense at all.'

'It's the lead we have,' Landry said defensively. 'I'm not going to ignore it. You know as well as I do, criminals fuck up. They get careless. They make mistakes.'

'Yeah, well maybe someone made this mistake for him.'

'What? You think someone's trying to frame him?'

'It looks that way to me. Jade has more to lose than to gain by any of this.'

'But he's done it before – the insurance scam with the dead horses.'

'Yes, but things were different then.'

'Tigers don't change their stripes.'

'Look,' I said, 'I'm not trying to defend him. I just think there are more rotten apples in this barrel than Don Jade. What did Michael Berne have to say for himself about the night Jill was murdered?'

'He was at Players for drinks with a client, the client was a no-show. Berne went out into the hall to call the client, and witnessed the scene between Jade and the girl.'

'And after that?'

'Went home and spent the evening with his wife.'

I rolled my eyes. 'Ah, yes, the accommodating Ms Alibi.'

'What?' Landry said, looking irritated. 'You think Berne masterminded the whole thing? Why?'

'I'm not saying that. I still don't see why anyone would risk getting caught at the kidnapping scheme. But Michael Berne hates Don Jade with a vengeance – and I mean that literally. Berne lost a lot when he lost Trey Hughes as a client. He's the definition of bitter. He might have killed the horse. Maybe he thinks if Jade was out of the way, he would get back in with Hughes. Even if that didn't happen, he would have the satisfaction of ruining Jade's life.'

'And where does Van Zandt fit in with Berne? You still believe he killed Jill, don't you?'

'Yes, but maybe he doesn't fit in. Maybe he killed Jill and it didn't have anything to do with anything but sex,' I said. 'Or maybe he's partners with Berne, or he's partners with Paris Montgomery – who's screwing Trey Hughes, by the way – but I don't believe he's partners with Don Jade. And then there's Trey Hughes. This whole nightmare is revolving around him.'

'Jesus, what a fucking mess,' Landry mumbled. He finished his scotch and set the glass on the coffee table. 'I wouldn't mention any of this to Lieutenant Dugan, if I were you.'

'Why would I?'

Landry's pager went off. He checked the display, then glanced up at me. 'Because he wants you in his office ASAP.'

Landry held the door for me as we entered the building. I didn't have the manners to thank him. My mind was on the meeting ahead. I needed a strategy going in or Dugan and Armedgian would run me off the case on a rail.

They were waiting in the lieutenant's office: Dugan, Armedgian, and Weiss. Weiss gave me the glare as I entered the room, the flat cop eyes with a mountain of pent-up anger behind them. I dismissed him and went straight to Dugan, looking him in the eye, offering my hand.

'Lieutenant. Elena Estes. I'd say it's a pleasure, but I'm sure it won't be.' I turned to Armedgian. 'Wayne. Thanks for the info on Van Zandt. The whole truth would have been more helpful, but what the hell? Nobody liked Jill Morone anyway.'

Armedgian's round face colored. 'I can't give sensitive information to a civilian.'

'Sure. I understand. And that's why you called Lieutenant Dugan here straightaway, right? To warn him, so he could have someone keep an eye on the guy, right?'

'We had no reason to believe Van Zandt was an immediate danger to anyone,' Armedgian defended himself. 'I hadn't been made aware of the Seabright girl's kidnapping.'

'I'm sure that will be a comfort to Jill Morone's family.'

'Your concern for the family is touching, Ms Estes,' Dugan said. 'And surprising, considering the way you've treated the Seabrights.'

'I've given due courtesy to the Seabrights.'

'Not according to Bruce Seabright.'

'He wasn't due any, as you've probably found out for yourself by now. Frankly, I'm not convinced he isn't involved in the kidnapping.'

'I'm not interested in your theories, Ms Estes,' Dugan said.

'Then why am I here?'

'The Seabrights want to lodge a complaint against you. Seems you've misrepresented yourself to them.'

'Not so.'

'You are not a private investigator,' Dugan said.

'I never told anyone that I was. The Seabrights have made an erroneous assumption.'

'Don't try to bullshit me with semantics. If you want to play word games, become a lawyer.'

'Thanks for the career advice.'

'Too bad she couldn't have taken it before she got one of ours killed,' Weiss muttered behind my back.

I kept my focus on Dugan. 'I got into this to try to help a little girl who believed her sister was in trouble when no one – including this office – believed her. That's my only purpose in this, Lieutenant. If Bruce Seabright somehow feels threatened by that, you might want to have a hard look at why.'

'We've got it under control,' Dugan said. 'I want you out of it. Now.'

I looked around the room. 'Gee, did I miss something? Have I been rehired by this agency? Because, if I haven't been, then I'm pretty certain you can't tell me what to do or where to go or with whom I might have a conversation. I'm a private citizen.'

'You're impeding an official investigation.'

'There wouldn't be an investigation if not for me.'

'I can't have a citizen running loose, breaking and entering homes, tampering with evidence –'

'Breaking and entering is a crime,' I said. 'If you have some kind of proof I've committed a crime, then you should arrest me.'

'Say the word, Lieutenant,' Weiss offered. 'I'll do the honors.'

'Van Zandt is our business now, Elena,' Armedgian said. 'The sheriff's and the FBI's.'

I looked at him, bored. 'Uh-huh. Great job. He came to my house this morning and threatened me. Where were you then, Wayne? And you know what? I'll bet a hundred dollars you don't know where he is right now. Do you?'

The look on his face spoke for him.

'The Seabrights intend to file a restraining order against you, Ms Estes,'

Dugan said. 'If you go near them, their home, Mr Seabright's place of business, we'll have to pick you up.'

I shrugged. 'You could have sent a deputy to tell me that. Unless you really want to talk about this case, Lieutenant, you're wasting my time.'

Dugan arched an eyebrow. 'You have pressing business somewhere?'

I pulled my cell phone out of my jacket pocket, scrolled through a few numbers, and hit the call button. I kept my gaze on the lieutenant as the phone rang on the other end.

'Van Zandt? Elle. Sorry I had to rush off this morning. Especially after you took all that time to scream at me and make me feel like I couldn't ride a bicycle, much less a horse.'

There was a pause on the other end of the line. Only background noise. He was in a car. I figured to proceed with the conversation even if Van Zandt hung up on me. I wanted Dugan to know he didn't own me, and at the same time know that I could be an asset, whether he liked the idea or not.

'You think I was too tough on you?' Van Zandt asked.

'No. I like it rough,' I said suggestively.

Another pause, and then he chuckled. 'I don't know anyone like you, Elle.'

'Is that a good thing or a bad thing?'

'I think that remains to be seen. I'm surprised you are calling me.'

'The moth to the flame,' I said. 'You exercise my brain, Z. Sean and I are going to Players for a late dinner and a drink or three. Are you free?'

'Not at the moment.'

'Later?' I suggested.

'I don't think I should trust you, Elle.'

'Why not? I don't have any power. I'm the odd one out.'

'You don't trust me,' he said. 'You think bad things about me which are not true.'

'So convince me you're a good guy. It's never too late to make friends. Besides, it's only drinks, for God's sake. Bring your friend Lorinda. You can sell her Sean's horse over dessert. See you later. *Ciao.*'

I ended the call, put the phone back in my pocket.

'Yes,' I said to Dugan. 'I have pressing business. Seems I have a date with Tomas Van Zandt.' I turned to Wayne Armedgian. 'Do you think you can pick up the tail from a dead standstill in a parking lot?'

I didn't wait for an answer.

'It's been real, guys,' I said, and with a wave of my hand, I left the room.

I felt dizzy. I felt like I had walked up to a giant and spit in his eye. I'd managed to alienate the head of Robbery/Homicide and a regional supervisory special agent of the FBI in one fell swoop.

What the hell. I'd been the alien going in. They had excluded me, not the other way around. I would have happily told them anything about the case I could, but they didn't want me. I had just put them on notice I couldn't be bullied. I knew my rights, I knew the law. And I knew I was right: They wouldn't have had a case if I hadn't badgered Landry into it, if I hadn't called Armedgian looking for information. I wouldn't let them pat-pat me on the head now and send me to the sidelines.

I walked up and down on the sidewalk outside the building, breathing in the thick, warm night air, wondering if I'd played it right, wondering if it would even matter or if it was already too late.

'That's some set you've got on you, Estes.'

Landry came toward me with a cigarette in one hand and a lighter in the other.

'Yeah, it's a wonder my pants fit.'

'Think Van Zandt will show at Players?' he asked, lighting up.

'I think he will. He likes the game too much. And it's not as if he's in imminent danger of arrest. He knows you don't have anything on him or he'd be in jail already. I think he'll show to rub your face in it – and mine.'

On impulse I took the cigarette from his fingers and took a drag. Landry watched me, inscrutable.

'You smoke?' he asked.

'No,' I said on a trail of smoke. 'I quit years ago.'

'Me too.'

'Desk pack?' I asked.

He took the cigarette back. 'It's this or a flask. I can't get suspended for this. Yet.'

'Weiss has a real bug up his ass.'

'He's short,' Landry said by way of explanation.

'I know I'm not welcome in this,' I said. 'But it was my case first, and I can still serve a purpose.'

'Yeah, I know. You just slapped my lieutenant in the face with it.'

A hint of a smile pulled at his mouth. His approval meant too much to me.

'Subtlety is overrated and it takes too long,' I said. 'We don't have time to fuck around.'

I took the cigarette for one last puff, my lips touching where his had been. I didn't want to let myself think there was anything erotic in that, but of course there was, and Landry knew it too. Our gazes locked and held, a current running between us.

'I've got to go,' I said, backing down the sidewalk.

Landry stayed where he was. 'What if Dugan wants you back inside?'

'He knows where I'm going. He can come and buy me a drink.'

He shook his head in wonder. 'You're something, Estes.'

'Just trying to survive,' I said as I turned and went to my car.

As I pulled around past the sidewalk on my way out of the lot, my headlights flashed on Weiss standing in the doorway to the building. Little prick. I figured he would make trouble for Landry sharing his smoke with me, but that was Landry's business. I had problems of my own. I had a date with a killer.

38

Women. Stupid, ungrateful bitches. Van Zandt spent most of his life courting them, flattering them – no matter what they looked like – carting them around to look at horses, giving his advice and counsel. They needed him to tell them what to do, what to think, what to buy. And were they grateful? No. Most of them were selfish and silly and didn't have a brain in their heads. They deserved to be cheated. They deserved whatever happened to them.

He thought of Elle. He still thought of her by that name, even though he knew it to be false. She was not 'most women'. She was clever and devious and bold. She thought with the hard logic of a man, but with a woman's slyness and sexuality. He found that exciting, challenging. A game worth playing.

And she was right: there was nothing she could do to hurt him. There was no evidence against him, therefore he was an innocent man.

He smiled at that, feeling happy and clever and superior.

He snatched up his cell phone, punched the speed-dial number for the town house, and listened to it ring unanswered on the other end. His mood spiraled back down. Another ring and he would get the machine. He didn't want to speak to a fucking machine. Where the hell was Lorinda? Off somewhere with that obnoxious dog of hers. Horrible, flea-ridden beast.

The machine picked up and he left a curt message for her to meet him at The Players later.

Angry now, he ended the call and threw the phone onto the passenger's seat of the cheap piece-of-shit car Lorinda had given him to drive. He hadn't wanted to tolerate the police following him around. Following him for no good reason, he had told her. He was the innocent victim of police harassment. She had believed him, of course, despite the fact that she had seen the bloody shirt. He had excused that away, and she had believed him in that too.

Stupid cow. Why she didn't rent a better car when she traveled was beyond him. Lorinda had money she had inherited from her family in Virginia. Tomas had taken it upon himself to do the research. But she wasted it on charities for abandoned dogs and broken-down horses, instead of using it for herself. She lived like a gypsy on the farm that had belonged to her grandmother, renting out the grand plantation house and living herself – with a pack of dogs and cats – in an old clapboard farmhouse that she never cleaned.

Tomas had told her she needed to get a face-lift and a boob job, and fix herself up or she would never get a rich husband. She laughed and asked him why she should get another husband when she had Tomas to look out for her best interests.

Stupid creature.

Women. The bane of his existence.

He drove east on Southern Boulevard, thinking about the woman he was to meet. She thought she could blackmail him. She told him she knew all about the dead girl, which, of course, she did not. But she had already become a problem before that, because of the lies she told the Americans about him. Bitter, vindictive cunt. That was the Russians. A more vicious race of people had never lived.

The death of this one would be, of course, the fault of Sasha Kulak. Tomas had taken her in, given her a roof over her head, a job, an opportunity to learn from him and take advantage of his vast knowledge – in the barn and in the bedroom.

She should have worshiped him. She should have wanted to please and service him. She should have thanked him. Instead, she had stolen from him and stabbed him in the back and spread stories about him.

He had, at great cost to himself, called any clients she might have known, might have contacted after she had left him, to warn them this girl was trouble, that she was a thief and probably on drugs; to tell them of course he hadn't done anything wrong.

And now he had to deal with her friend, Avadon's Russian girl. Avadon should have fired her on the spot Friday when the girl had tried to kill him in Avadon's own stable. Incredible what these Americans would tolerate.

He'd had his fill of Florida. He was ready to go back to Belgium. He had a flight already lined up. A cargo plane traveling to Brussels with a load of horses. Going as a groom, he never had to pay. One more day he would do business here, showing everyone he had nothing to hide, no reason to worry about the police. Then he would return to Europe for a time, and come back when people had better things to gossip about than him.

He slowed the car as he looked for the sign. He had suggested meeting at the back of the show grounds, but the girl had refused, insisting on a public place. This was the place she had chosen: Magda's – a shitty bar in an industrial part of West Palm Beach. A clapboard building that even in the dark looked as if it needed paint and had termites.

Van Zandt pulled in the drive alongside the bar and drove around back to find a parking place.

He would find the girl in the bar, buy her a drink. When she wasn't looking, he would slip her the drug. It was a simple thing. They would talk, he would try to assure her there had been a misunderstanding about Sasha. The drug would start to take effect. When the moment was right and she was incapable of protest, he would assist her outside.

She would appear to be drunk. He would put her in the car and drive away to a place where he could kill her and dispose of her body.

He found a spot to park, backing in along a chain-link fence that separated the bar's property from an auto salvage yard. The perfect place. Out of sight. This problem would be dealt with quickly and neatly, and then he would go to The Players to have a drink with Elena Estes.

I went into The Players alone. If Van Zandt showed with Lorinda Carlton, I would make Sean's excuses, but I wouldn't drag Sean any further into the drama than I already had.

The club was busy. Celebrants from the showring and losers drowning their sorrows. Most stables are closed on Mondays so everyone can recuperate from the weekend's competition. No reason to go to bed early on Sunday.

The place was a stage with a hundred players. Women showing off the latest in Palm Beach fashions and the newest plastic surgery. Swarthy polo players from South America hitting on every rich thing in a skirt. Minor celebs in town for a long weekend. Saudi Arabian royalty. Every pair of eyes in the place sliding to the next most promising conversation partner in the room.

I found a small table in the corner of the bar and settled in with my back to the wall and a view of the room. I ordered tonic and lime and fended off an ex-baseball star who wanted to know if he knew me.

'No,' I said, amused he had singled me out. 'And you don't want to.'

'Why is that?'

'Because I'm nothing but trouble.'

He slid into the other chair and leaned across the table. His smile had lit up many an ad for cheap long-distance service and colorful underwear. 'Wrong thing to say. Now I'm intrigued.'

'And I'm waiting for someone.'

'Lucky guy. What's he got that I haven't?'

'I don't know,' I said with a half-smile. 'I haven't seen him in his underwear yet.'

He spread his hands and grinned. 'I have no secrets.'

'You have no shame.'

'No. But I always get the girl.'

I shook my head. 'Not this time, Ace.'

'Is this character giving you a hard time, Elle?'

I looked up to find Don Jade standing beside me with a martini in hand.

'No, I'm afraid I'm giving him a hard time,' I said.

'Or something,' Mr Baseball said, bobbing his eyebrows. 'You're not waiting for this guy, are you?'

'As a matter of fact, yes.'

'Even after you've seen me in my underwear?'

'I like surprises. What can I say?'

'Say you'll ditch him later,' he said, rising. 'I'll be at the end of the bar.'

I watched him walk away, surprised at myself for enjoying the flirtation.

'Don't look so impressed,' Jade said, taking the empty seat. 'He's all hat and no cattle, as they say in Texas.'

'And how would you know that?'

He gave me a steady look that belied the drink in his hand. He was sober as a judge. 'You'd be surprised at the things I know, Elle.'

I sipped my tonic, wondering if he knew about me; wondering if Van Zandt had told him, or Trey, or if he had been left out of that loop on purpose.

'No, I don't think I would,' I said. 'I'm sure there isn't much that gets past you.'

'Not much.'

'Is that why you were with the detectives so long yesterday?' I asked. 'Because you had so much to tell them?'

'No, I'm afraid Jill's murder is a subject I don't know anything about at all. Do you?'

'Me? Not a thing. Should we ask someone else? Van Zandt is coming later. Shall we ask him? I have a feeling he could tell us some stories to make our hair stand on end.'

'It's not difficult to get someone to tell you a story, Elle,' Jade said.

'No. The hard part is getting them to tell the truth.'

'And that's what you're looking for? The truth?'

'You know what they say: the truth shall set you free.'

He sipped his martini and looked away at nothing. 'That all depends on who you are, doesn't it?'

The girl was waiting under the back-door light. Her hair stood out around her head like a lion's mane. She wore black tights that clung to her long legs, and a denim jacket, and her mouth was painted dark. She was smoking a cigarette.

At least Van Zandt thought it was Avadon's girl. They never looked the same, these girls, away from the stables.

Van Zandt opened the car door and got out, wondering if he should simply lure her away from the building, shove her in the car, and go. But the threat of a possible witness coming out the back door of the bar was too big a risk. Even as he thought of it, the door opened and a large man stepped out under the light. He took a position there, feet apart, hands clasped in front of him. The girl glanced up at him, smiled bewitchingly, and said something in Russian.

Halfway between the car and the building, a sense of apprehension crawled over Van Zandt's skin. His step slowed. The big Russian had something in his hand. A gun perhaps.

Behind him, car doors opened and shoe soles scuffed the cracked concrete.

He'd made a terrible mistake, he thought. The girl was near enough that he could see she was looking at him and smiling wickedly. He turned to try to go back to the car. Three men stood in front of him, two built like plow horses standing on either side of a smaller man in a fine dark suit.

'Are you thinking you should not have come, Mr Van Zandt?' the small man said.

Van Zandt looked down his nose. 'Do I know you?'

'No,' he said as his associates moved to take hold of Van Zandt, one on each arm. 'But perhaps you know my name. Kulak. Alexi Kulak.'

'Do you believe in karma, Elle?' Jade asked.

'God, no.'

Jade was still nursing his martini. I was on my second tonic and lime. A couple of cheap dates. We'd been sitting there fifteen minutes with no sign of Van Zandt.

'Why would I want to believe in that?' I asked.

'What goes around comes around.'

'For everyone? For me? No, thank you.'

'And what have you ever done that you'd have to pay for?'

'I killed a man once,' I confessed calmly, just to see the look on his face. It was probably the first time in a decade he'd been surprised. 'I'd rather not have that come back around on me.'

'You killed a man?' he asked, trying not to look astonished. 'Did he have it coming?'

'No. It was an accident – if you believe in accidents. How about you? Are you waiting for your past deeds to ambush you? Or are you hoping someone else will have their markers called in?'

He finished the martini as Susannah Atwood came in the room. 'Here's what I believe in, Elle,' he said. 'I believe in me, I believe in now, I believe in careful planning.'

I wanted to ask him if it had been in his plan for someone to murder Jill Morone and kidnap Erin Seabright. I wanted to ask him if it had been in his plan for Paris Montgomery to have an affair with Trey Hughes, but I had already lost his attention.

'My dinner companion has arrived,' he said, rising. He looked at me and smiled with a cross between amusement and bemusement. 'Thanks for the conversation, Elle. You're a fascinating person.'

'Good luck with your karma,' I said.

'And you with yours.'

As I watched him walk across the room, I wondered what had prompted his sudden philosophical turn. If he was an innocent man, was he thinking this sudden turn of twisted bad luck was payback for the things he'd gotten away with in his past? Or was he thinking what I was thinking? That there was no such thing as bad luck, that there are no accidents, no coincidences. If he was thinking someone was hanging a noose around his neck, who did he like for a candidate?

From the corner of my eye I could see the baseball player homing in on the seat Jade had vacated. I got up and left the room, my patience for flirtation worn thin. I wanted Van Zandt to show up for no other reason than to rub Dugan's and Armedgian's noses in my obvious usefulness.

I believed he would show. I believed he wouldn't be able to resist the opportunity to sit in a public place, relaxed and pleased with himself, conversing with someone who believed he was a murderer and couldn't do anything about it. The sense of power that would give him would be too intoxicating to pass up.

I wondered what his business of the evening entailed, if it had anything to do with the kidnapping. I wondered if he was the man in black Landry had described viciously beating Erin Seabright with a riding whip. Sick bastard. It wasn't hard to imagine him getting off on that kind of thing. Control was his game.

As I stood outside the front doors of The Players, I pictured him in prison, suffering the ultimate lack of control, every minute of his life dictated to him.

Karma. Maybe I wanted to believe in it after all.

The beating wasn't the worst of it. The worst thing was knowing that when the beating was over, so too would be his life. Or perhaps the worst thing was knowing he had no control in the situation. All the power was held by Alexi Kulak, cousin of that Russian cunt who had now ruined his life.

While the Russian stationed at the back door kept anyone from coming out to witness the act, Kulak had personally slapped a wide swatch of duct tape over Van Zandt's mouth and taped his hands together behind his back. They shoved him into the backseat of Lorinda's rental car, which they drove through an open gate onto the grounds of the auto salvage yard behind the bar. They then parked the car inside a cavernous, filthy garage and dragged him from it.

He tried to run, of course. Awkward with his arms behind him and panic running like water down his legs, it seemed the door grew no closer as he ran. The thugs caught him with rough hands and dragged him back onto a large black tarp laid out on the concrete floor. Tools had been lined up on the edge of the tarp like surgical instruments: a hammer, a crowbar, pliers. Tears flooded his eyes and his bladder let go in a warm, wet rush.

'Break his legs,' Kulak instructed calmly. 'So he cannot run like the coward he is.'

The largest of the henchmen held him down while another picked up a sledgehammer. Van Zandt kicked and writhed. The Russian swung and missed, cursing loudly as the hammerhead connected with the floor. The second swing was on target, hitting the inside edge of his kneecap and shattering the bone like an eggshell.

Van Zandt's screams were trapped by the duct tape. The pain exploded in his brain like a white-hot nova. It ripped through his body like a tornado. His bowels released and the fetid stench made him gag. The third blow hit squarely on the shin below his other knee, the force splintering the bone, the head of the hammer driving through the soft tissue beneath.

Someone ripped the tape from his mouth and he flopped onto his side and vomited convulsively, again and again.

'Defiler of young girls,' Kulak said. 'Murderer. Rapist. American justice is too good for you. This is great country, but too kind. Americans say please and thank you and let killers run free because of technicalities. Sasha is dead because of you. Now you murder a girl and the police cannot even put you in jail.'

Van Zandt shook his head, wiping his face through the mess on the tarp. He was sobbing and panting. 'No. No. No. I didn't . . . accident . . . not my fault.' The words came out in gasps and bursts. Pain pulsed through him in searing, white-hot shocks.

'You lying piece of shit,' Kulak snapped. 'I know about the bloody shirt. I know you tried to rape this girl, like you raped Sasha.'

Kulak cursed him in Russian and nodded to the thugs. He stood back and watched calmly while they beat Van Zandt with thin iron rods. One would strike him, then another, each picking his target methodically. Occasionally, Kulak gave instructions in English so Van Zandt could understand.

They were not to hit him in the head. Kulak wanted him conscious, able to hear, able to feel the pain. They were not to kill him – he did not deserve a quick death.

The blows were strategically placed.

Van Zandt tried to speak, tried to beg, tried to explain, tried to lay the blame away from himself. It was not his fault Sasha had killed herself. It was not his fault Jill Morone had suffocated. He had never forced himself on a woman.

Kulak came onto the tarp and kicked him in the mouth. Van Zandt choked on blood and teeth, coughed and retched.

'I'm sick of your excuses,' Kulak said. 'In your world, you are not responsible for anything you do. In my world, a man pays for his sins.'

Kulak smoked a cigarette and waited until Van Zandt's mouth stopped bleeding, then wrapped the lower part of his head with the duct tape, covering his mouth with several layers. They taped his broken legs together and threw him in the trunk of Lorinda's rented Chevy.

The last thing he saw was Alexi Kulak leaning over to spit on him, then the trunk was closed. Tomas Van Zandt's world went dark, and the awful waiting began.

39

I watched the world come and go from The Players that night, but Tomas Van Zandt never showed. I heard a woman ask for him at the bar, and thought she might be Lorinda Carlton: the hard downside of forty with a low-rent Cher look about her. If it was her, then Van Zandt must have called her about meeting for drinks. But there was no sign of Van Zandt.

I saw Irina come in with some girlfriends around eleven. Cinderellas on the town, just in time to blow five bucks on a drink and flirt with some polo players before their coaches turned into pumpkins and they had to go back to their rented rooms and stable apartments.

Around midnight Mr Baseball tried his luck again.

'Last call for romance.' The winning smile, the eyebrows up.

'What?' I asked, pretending amazement. 'You've been here all evening and no sweet young thing on your arm?'

'I was saving myself for you.'

'You have all the lines.'

'Do I need another one?' he asked.

'You need to take a hike, spitball.' Landry stepped in close on him and flashed his shield.

Mr Baseball looked at me.

I shrugged. 'I told you I'm trouble.'

'She'd eat you alive, pal,' Landry said, smiling like a shark. 'And not in a good way.'

Baseball gave a little salute of resignation and backed away.

'What was *that* about?' Landry asked, looking perturbed as he settled into the other chair at the table.

'A girl has to pass the time.'

'Giving up on Van Zandt?'

'I'd say I'm officially stood up. And I officially look like a fool. Did Dugan call off the dogs?'

'Five minutes ago. He was betting on you. That's something.'

'Never bet on a dark horse,' I told him. 'You'll tear up the ticket nine times out of ten.'

'But you can make it all back when one comes in,' he pointed out.

'Dugan doesn't strike me as a gambling man.'

'What do you care what Dugan thinks? You don't have to answer to him.'

I didn't want to admit that it mattered to me to gain back some of the respect I'd destroyed when my career ended. I didn't want to say that I had wanted to show up Armedgian. I had the uncomfortable feeling I didn't need to say it. Landry was watching me more closely than I cared for.

'It was a gutsy move, calling Van Zandt the way you did,' he reminded me. 'And it might have paid off. What'd he say when you asked him if he was free?'

'He said he had some business to take care of. Probably dumping Erin's body somewhere.'

'I saw Lorinda Carlton,' Landry said. 'I stopped her on her way out.'

'Long braid with a feather in it?' I asked. 'Stalled on the shoulder of the fashion highway?'

He looked amused at the description. 'Meow.'

'Hey, any woman stupid enough to fall for Van Zandt's act gets no respect from me.'

'I'm with you there,' he said. 'That one got an extra helping of stupid. A hundred bucks says she saw that bloody shirt, even helped Van Zandt get rid of it, and she still thinks he's a prince.'

'What did she have to say tonight?'

He huffed. 'She wouldn't call nine-one-one if I was on fire. She thinks *I'm* evil. She had nothing to say. But I don't think she came here trolling for men. Strikes me her idea of a good time would be burning incense and reading bad poetry aloud.'

'She asked the bartender if he'd seen Van Zandt,' I said.

'Then she came here expecting him to be here. See? You weren't such a long shot after all.'

The bar was closing down, wait staff putting chairs up and carrying glasses back to the bar. I stood up slowly, body aching and stiff from my adventures of the last few days. I dropped a ten on the table for the waitress.

Landry arched a brow. 'Generous.'

I shrugged. 'She's got a shit job and I've got a trust fund.'

We walked out together. The valets had already gone for the night. I could see Landry's car sitting opposite mine in the lower parking lot.

'I don't know any cops with a trust fund,' he said.

'Don't make a big thing out of it, Landry. Besides, as you are so fond of reminding me, I'm not a cop anymore.'

'You don't have a badge,' he qualified.

'Ah, do I flatter myself or was that a backhanded compliment?' I asked as we arrived at the cars.

'Don't make a big thing out of it, Estes,' he said with a slight smile.

'Well, I'll be a lady and say thank you, anyway.'

'Why'd you become a cop?' he asked. 'You could have been anything, or done nothing.'

I looked around as I thought about how to answer him. The night was almost sultry, the moonlight glowing white through the humidity. The scents of green plants and wet earth and exotic flowers perfumed the air.

'A Freudian would yawn and tell you my choice was an obvious rebellion against my father.'

'Was it?'

'Yes, but there was more to it than that,' I admitted. 'Growing up, I watched my father bend lady justice like a Gumby doll and sell her to the highest bidder. I thought someone needed to tip the other side of the scale, make an effort to even things out.'

'So why not become a prosecutor?'

'Too much structure. Too much politicking. You might not have guessed this, but diplomacy and ass-kissing are not on my list of talents. Besides, prosecutors don't get to do neat things like get shot at and beat up.'

He didn't laugh. He watched me in that way he had that made me feel naked.

'You're something, Estes,' he murmured.

'Yeah, I'm something.'

I didn't mean it the way he did. In the span of a week I had lost hold on just what I was. I felt like some creature emerging from a cocoon, not quite knowing what the metamorphosis had changed me into.

Landry touched my face, the left side – where feeling was more a vague memory than it was real. That seemed fitting somehow, that he couldn't really touch me, that I couldn't allow myself to feel it in the acute, nerve-shattering way I might have once. It had been so long since I had let anyone touch me, I don't know that I could have taken it any other way.

I lifted my chin and looked in his eyes, wondering what he could see in mine. That I felt vulnerable and didn't like it? That I felt anticipation and it unnerved me? That I didn't quite trust him, but felt the pull of attraction just the same?

Landry leaned closer and settled his mouth on mine. I allowed the kiss, participated, though with a timidity that may have seemed out of character. But the truth of it was that the Elena standing there at that moment in time had never been kissed. The experiences of the pre-exile me were so distant as to seem like something I'd once read in a book.

He tasted like coffee and a hint of smoke. His mouth was warm and firm. Purposeful, I thought. Nice. Exciting.

I wondered what he felt, if he thought me unresponsive, if he wondered at the way my mouth worked – or didn't work. I felt self-conscious.

The flat of my hand rested on his chest. I could feel his heart beating and wondered if he could feel mine racing.

He raised his head and looked at me. Waiting. Waiting. Waiting...

I didn't fill the silence with an invitation, though a part of me certainly wanted to. For once, I thought before acting. I thought I might live to regret it, but while I was bold enough to toy with a murderer and defy the authority of the FBI, I wasn't brave enough for this.

The corners of Landry's mouth turned upward as he seemed to read all of these things I couldn't sort out in my own mind. 'I'm going to follow you home,' he said. 'Make sure Van Zandt isn't waiting for you.'

I glanced away and nodded. 'Thanks.'

I was afraid to look at him, afraid I would open my mouth and ask him to spend the night.

I turned away from him and got in my car, feeling more scared now than I had that morning when I had thought I might have to stab a man to save my own life.

The drive to Sean's farm was uneventful. The main house was dark. A single light burned in the window of Irina's apartment above the barn. Van Zandt was not there lying in wait for me.

Landry came into the house and looked around. Then he went to the door like a gentleman and waited again for me to say something.

I fidgeted, chewed my thumbnail, crossed my arms. 'I'd – ah – I'd ask you to stay, but I'm kind of in the middle of this kidnapping thing . . .'

'I understand,' he said, watching me, his gaze very dark and intense. 'Some other time.'

If I had an answer for that, it stuck in my throat. And then he was gone.

I locked the door and turned out the lights, went into the bedroom and undressed. I took a shower, washing the scent of cigarette smoke out of my hair. After I'd toweled off, I stood for a long time in front of the mirror, looking at my body, looking at my face; trying to decide who I was seeing, who I had become.

For the first time in two years, I felt aware of myself as a woman. I looked at myself and saw a woman, instead of an apparition, instead of a mask, instead of the shell of my self-loathing.

I looked at the scars on my body where asphalt had stripped away skin and new skin had filled the gaps. I wondered what Landry's reaction would be if I were to allow him to see the full extent of the damage up close in good light. I disliked feeling vulnerable with him. I wanted to believe that he would look at my body and not be shocked, not say a word.

The fact that I was even contemplating these thoughts was amazing to me. Refreshing. Encouraging. Hopeful.

Hope. The thing I hadn't wanted. But I needed it. I needed it for Erin, for Molly . . . for me.

Maybe, I thought, just maybe I had been punished enough, that perhaps to drag it on any further failed to serve a purpose and became simple self-destructive self-indulgence. I hadn't done everything right in this case, but I had tried my best for Erin Seabright, and I had to let that count for something.

I went into the bedroom, opened the drawer in the nightstand, and took out the bottle of painkillers. With a strange mix of giddiness and fear, I took the pills into the bathroom and spilled them out on the counter. I counted them one by one, as I had nearly every night for two years. And one by one, I dropped them into the toilet and flushed them all away.

Act Three

SCENE ONE
FADE IN:
EXTERIOR: LATE NIGHT — EDGE OF SHOPPING CENTER PARKING LOT

The parking lot is mostly empty. A few cars in the rows near the supermarket, which is open twenty-four hours. The rest of the businesses are dark.

The girl runs toward the store. Her legs are weak and tired. She's crying. Her hair is a tangled mess. Her face is bruised. Her arms are striped with red welts.

She spots a pair of Palm Beach County cruisers parked together and veers toward them. She tries to cry out for help, but her throat is dry and parched, and hardly any sound comes out.

A few feet from the car, she stumbles and falls on her hands and knees.

GIRL   Help. Help me. Please.

She knows the deputy can't hear her whispered pleas. She is only a few yards from the car, but she doesn't have the strength to get up. She lies sobbing on the concrete. The deputy spots her and gets out of his car.

DEPUTY   Miss? Miss? Are you all right?

The girl looks up at him, sobbing in relief.

The deputy kneels down beside her. He calls to the other deputy.

DEPUTY   Reeger! Call for an ambulance! (*Then, to the girl*) Miss? Can you talk to me? Can you tell me your name?

GIRL   Erin. Erin Seabright.

FADE OUT

927

40

'What kind of shape is she in?' Landry asked as he walked into the Palms West Hospital ER. The deputy who had brought Erin Seabright in hustled alongside him.

'Someone beat the hell out of her, but she's conscious and talking.'

'Sexual assault?'

'The doc's doing the rape kit now.'

'And where did you find her?'

'Me and Reeger were in the Publix lot down the street. She came running out of nowhere.' He motioned Landry toward an exam room.

'Did she say how she got there?'

'No. She was pretty hysterical, crying and all.'

'Did you see anyone in the vicinity? Any vehicles?'

'No. We've got a couple of cars cruising the area now, looking for anything unusual.'

Landry rapped on the door and showed his badge to the nurse who stuck her head out.

'We're almost done,' she said.

'How's it look? Anything?'

'Inconclusive, I'd say.'

He nodded and stepped away from the room, pulling his phone out of his pocket. Dugan himself had gone to notify the Seabrights. Weiss had yet to show up.

He punched Elena's number into the phone and listened to it ring on the other end. He tried not to picture her in bed. The taste of her mouth still lingered in his memory.

'Hello?' She sounded more wary than weary.

'Estes? Landry. Are you awake?'

'Yes.' Still wary.

'Erin Seabright is in the Palms West ER. The kidnappers let her go or she escaped. I don't know which yet.'

'Oh, my God. Have you seen her? Have you spoken with her?'

'No. They're doing the rape kit now.'

'Thank God she's alive. Has the family been notified?'

'Lieutenant Dugan is with them. I expect they'll be here soon. Look,' he said as he spotted Weiss looking lost at the reception desk. 'I've gotta go.'

'Okay. Landry?'

'Yeah?'

'Thanks for the heads-up.'

'Yeah, well, it was your case first,' he said. He ended the call and clipped the phone on his belt, his eyes on Weiss.

'Was that Dugan?' Weiss asked.

'He's with the family.'

'You talk to the girl yet?'

Before Landry could answer, the doctor came out of the exam room, looking. Landry showed her his badge.

'Detectives Landry and Weiss,' he said. 'How's she doing?'

'She's quite shaken, as you might imagine,' she said. She was a small Pakistani woman with glasses that magnified her eyes about three times. 'She has a great many minor cuts, abrasions, and contusions, though no evidence of broken bones. It looks to me as if she has been struck with something like a wire or a whip of some kind.'

'Signs of rape?'

'Some vaginal bruising. Marks on her thighs. No semen.'

Like Jill Morone, Landry thought. They would have to hope for some other source of DNA from the attacker, maybe a pubic hair.

'Has she said anything?'

'That she was beaten. That she was frightened. She keeps saying she can't believe he could do such a thing.'

'Did she give a name?' Weiss asked.

The doctor shook her head.

'Can we talk to her?'

'She is mildly sedated, but she should be able to answer your questions.'

'Thank you, Doctor.'

Erin Seabright looked like an escapee from the set of a horror movie. Her hair was a tangled blond mass around her head. Her face was bruised, her lip split. She looked at them with wide, haunted eyes as Landry and Weiss entered the room.

Landry recognized the expression. He'd done a couple of years working Sex Crimes. He had discovered quickly he didn't have the temperament for it. He couldn't keep a lid on his anger dealing with suspects.

'Erin? I'm Detective Landry. This is Detective Weiss,' Landry said quietly, pulling up a stool beside the bed. 'You're a sight for sore eyes. A lot of people have been working hard to find you.'

'Why didn't he just pay them?' she asked, bewildered. She held a plastic bottle of water in her hands, and kept turning it around and around, trying to find some comfort in the repetitive motion. 'That was all he had to do. They kept calling and calling him, and they sent him those tapes. Why couldn't he just do what they said?'

'Your stepdad?'

Tears spilled down her cheeks. 'He hates me so much!'

'Erin? We need to ask you some questions about what happened to you,' Landry said. 'Do you think you can do that now? We want to be able to get the people who did this to you. The sooner you tell us about it, the sooner we can do that. Do you understand?'

She didn't answer. She didn't make eye contact. That wasn't unusual. Landry knew she didn't want to be a victim. She didn't want any of this to be real. She didn't want to have to answer questions that would require her to relive what had happened. She felt angry and embarrassed and ashamed. And it was Landry's job to drag it all out of her anyway.

'Can you tell us who did this to you, Erin?' he asked.

She stared straight ahead, her lip quivering. The door to the examination room opened and she started to cry harder.

'He did,' she said, glaring at Bruce Seabright. 'You did this to me! You son of a bitch!'

She sat up in the bed and flung the bottle at him, water spraying everywhere as Bruce Seabright brought his arms up to deflect the object from his head.

Krystal screamed and rushed toward the bed. 'Erin! Oh, God! Baby!'

Landry stood up as the woman tried to fling herself on the bed. Erin pulled herself into a ball at the head of the bed, cringing away from her mother, looking at her with hurt and anger and something like disgust.

'Get away from me!' she shouted. 'All you've ever done is side with him. You never cared about me!'

'Baby, that's not true!' Krystal cried.

'It *is* true! Why didn't you make him help me? Did you even do *anything*?'

Krystal was sobbing, reaching out to her daughter, but not touching her, as if one or both of them were contained inside a force field. 'I'm sorry! I'm so sorry!'

'Get out!' Erin screamed. 'Get out of here! Both of you!'

A hospital security guard came in from the hall. Landry took hold of Krystal by the arms and moved her toward the door.

Weiss rolled his eyes and muttered, 'Nothing like a family reunion.'

41

Molly's call came on the heels of Landry's. I was already pulling on clothes. I told her I would go to the hospital, though I knew I wouldn't get anywhere near Erin's room. If Bruce Seabright caught sight of me, I would end up being escorted from the building. If he had the right kind of pull with the right people, and had gotten a restraining order from a judge on a Sunday night, I could end up taking a ride to the county accommodations. I had been warned, after all.

All that said, I didn't think twice about going.

When I walked into the waiting room, Molly came running to me. She was pale with fear, eyes bright with excitement. The contradiction was the difference between relief that her sister was safe and apprehension about what might have happened to her that she had to be in a hospital.

'I can't believe Bruce let you come along,' I said.

'He didn't. I rode with Mom. They're having a fight.'

'Good for Mom,' I muttered, steering her to the couches in the waiting area. 'What are they fighting about?'

'Mom blames Bruce for Erin being hurt. Bruce keeps saying he did what he thought was best.'

Best for Bruce, I thought.

'Will you get to talk to her?' Molly asked.

'Not anytime soon.'

'Will I get to?'

Poor kid. She looked so hopeful, yet so afraid of disappointment. She didn't have anyone in this mess but me. In her mind, the big sister she loved so much was her only real family. And who knew what resemblance there would be in Erin now compared to the Erin whom Molly had idolized just a week ago. Knowing what I had learned about Erin over the last few days, I had to think Molly's perception had been a dream even before Erin had been taken.

I remembered thinking, the day Molly had first come to me, that Molly Seabright was going to learn that life is full of disappointments. I remembered thinking she would have to learn that lesson the way everyone did: by being let down by someone she loved and trusted.

I wished I could have had the power to shield her from that. The only thing I could do was not be another someone who let her down. She had come to me when no one should have, and bet on that dark horse I had tried to lecture Landry about.

'I don't know, Molly,' I said, touching her head. 'You probably won't get to see her tonight. It might be a day or so.'

'Do you think she's been raped?' she asked.

'It's a possibility. The doctor will have examined her and taken certain kinds of samples —'

'A rape kit,' she said. 'I know what it is. I watch *New Detectives*. If she was raped, they'll have DNA samples to match to a suspect. Unless he was particularly meticulous and used a condom, and made her take a shower afterward. Then they won't have anything.'

'We have Erin,' I said. 'That's all that matters right now. Maybe she can identify the kidnappers. Even if she can't, we're going to get these guys, Molly. You hired me to do a job. I won't quit until it's over. And it's not over until I say so.'

It was a good line at the time. In the end, I would come to wish that I hadn't meant it.

'Elena?' Molly said, looking up at me with her earnest face. 'I'm still scared. Even with Erin back, I still feel scared.'

'I know you do.'

I put my arm around her shoulders and she leaned her head against me. It was one of those small moments that I knew would remain stamped in my memory forever. Someone turning to me for comfort, and me being able to give it.

From somewhere in the ER came a crash and a scream and a lot of shouting. I looked down the hall that ran behind where Molly and I were sitting, and saw Bruce Seabright backing away from a door, looking stunned. Then Landry came out of the same room pushing a sobbing, hysterical Krystal along ahead of him.

'I'll find out what I can,' I told Molly, knowing it was time to make myself disappear. 'Call me in the morning.'

She nodded.

I went past the reception desk to the ladies' room and ducked inside, betting Krystal wouldn't be far behind me. She came in half a minute later, crying, mascara striping her face, her lipstick smudged.

I felt sorry for her. In some ways Krystal was more a child than Molly. All her life she'd dreamed of having a respectable husband and a nice home and all the trappings. She had never imagined living the Barbie Doll life would have the same pitfalls as living poor. I'm sure it had never occurred to her that making bad choices in men crossed all socioeconomic borders.

She leaned against the counter, hanging her head over the sink, her face distorted with emotional anguish.

'Krystal? Can I help?' I asked, knowing I couldn't.

She looked up at me, swiping tears and snot from her face with her hands. 'What are you doing here?'

'Molly called me. I know Erin is back.'

'She hates me. She hates me, and I don't blame her,' she confessed. She looked at herself in the mirror and spoke to her reflection. 'Everything's ruined. Everything's ruined!'

'You've got your daughter back.'

Krystal shook her head. 'No. Everything is ruined. What am I going to do?'

I would have started by taking Bruce Seabright to the cleaners in the divorce court, but then I'm the bitter, vindictive type. I chose not to offer that advice. Whatever decisions this woman would come to, she would have to come to them herself.

'She blames Bruce,' she said.

'Don't you?'

'Yes,' she whispered. 'But it's my fault really. It's all my fault.'

'Krystal, your life is none of my business,' I said. 'And God knows you probably won't listen to me, but I'm going to say this anyway. Maybe it is all your fault. Maybe you've made nothing but bad choices your whole life. But your life is not over, and Erin's life is not over, and Molly's life is not over. You still have time to do something right.

'You don't know me,' I went on, 'so you don't know that I'm an expert on the subject of fucking up one's own life. But I've recently discovered that every day I get another shot at it. So do you.'

Ladies' room psychology. I felt like I should have offered her a linen hand towel and hoped she would leave a tip for me in a basket on the counter.

A large woman in a purple Hawaiian mumu came in the door and gave Krystal and me the glare, like she thought we were hogging the room to have lesbian sex. I glared back at her and she turned sideways and waddled into a stall.

I went out in the hall. Bruce Seabright was in the waiting area near the exit, having an argument with Detective Weiss and Lieutenant Dugan. Landry was nowhere in sight. I wondered if anyone had let Armedgian know about Erin's escape. He would want in on the interview in the hopes that Erin would finger Van Zandt as one of her kidnappers.

There seemed to be nothing for me to do but wait until the hostile forces left. I would hold out in the parking lot, stake out Landry's car. If I could get a moment alone with him, I would.

I turned and went down the hall in search of a cup of bad coffee.

The doctor offered Erin Seabright a stronger sedative. Erin snapped at the woman to leave her alone. The fragile flower flashing her thorns, Landry thought. He hung back in the corner, saying nothing as he watched the girl order the doctor from the room. She turned then and looked at him.

'I just want it to be over,' she said. 'I just want to go to sleep and wake up and have it be over.'

'It won't be that easy, Erin,' he said, coming forward to take his seat again. 'I'll be straight with you. You're only halfway through the ordeal. I know you want it to be over. Hell, you wish it had never happened. So do I. But you've got a job now to help us catch the people who did this to you so they can't do it to someone else.'

'I know you've got a little sister. Molly. I know you wouldn't want to imagine what happened to you happening to her.'

'Molly.' She said her sister's name, and closed her eyes for a moment.

'Molly's a pretty cool kid,' Landry said. 'All she's wanted from the beginning of this is to have you back, Erin.'

The girl dabbed at her swollen eyes with a tissue and breathed a shaky sigh, preparing herself, settling herself to tell him her story.

'Do you know who did this to you, Erin?' Landry asked.

'They wore masks,' she said. 'They never let me see their faces.'

'But they spoke to you? You heard their voices. And maybe you recognized a voice or a mannerism or something.'

She didn't answer yes, but she didn't answer no either. She sat very quietly, her eyes on her hands neatly folded in her lap.

Landry waited.

'I think I know who one of them was,' she said softly. Fresh tears filled her eyes as the emotions welled up inside her. Disappointment, sadness, hurt.

She touched a hand to her forehead, partly shielding her eyes. Trying to hide from the truth.

'Don,' she whispered at last. 'Don Jade.'

42

Weiss came out of the hospital first, running for his car. As he drove past me, I could see he was on his cell phone. Something was going down.

Ten minutes later, Armedgian finally arrived and went into the hospital, then came back out a minute later with Dugan. They stood on the sidewalk, Armedgian angry and animated. Their voices rose and fell, the gist of the conversation drifting my way as I sat in my car with the windows down. Armedgian felt he'd been left out, should have been notified immediately, blah, blah, blah. Dugan was short with him. Not the FBI's secretary, get over it, all on the same page now, et cetera, et cetera, et cetera.

They went to their individual vehicles and drove away, dash lights flashing.

I got out of my car and went back into the ER, going down the hall toward the examination room Erin had been in. Landry came out of the room with a large brown paper evidence bag in hand: Erin's clothes, which would go to the lab to be examined for DNA evidence.

'What's going on?' I asked, changing direction and hustling to keep up with him.

'Erin says Jade was one of the kidnappers.'

'Positive ID?' I asked, not believing it. 'She saw him?'

'She says they wore masks, but she thinks it was him.'

'How? Why does she think it was him? His voice? A tattoo? What?'

'I don't have time for this, Elena,' he said impatiently. 'Weiss and some uniforms are on their way to pick him up. I've got to get back to the station.'

'Did she say anything about Van Zandt?'

'No.'

'Who else then?'

'She didn't say. We don't have the whole story yet. But we're grabbing Jade before he can split. If he knows she's gotten away, he knows he's gotta get out of Dodge. If we can snag him now, we'll get him to roll on his partner.'

The doors swooshed open and we went outside, headed for Landry's car. I wanted everything to stop, for time to stop right then so I could think before anything more happened. The plot had taken a hard left turn, and I was having a difficult time making the corner. Landry, however, had no intention of slowing down.

'Where did they have her?' I asked. 'How did she get away?'

'Later,' Landry said, getting into his car.

'But –'

He fired the engine and I had to jump back as he pulled out of the parking space and drove away.

I stood there like an idiot, watching him go, trying to digest what had just happened. It just didn't make sense to me that Jade would take the risk of kidnapping someone – or that he had the temperament for it. I couldn't see Jade as a team player in a thing like this.

Landry had developed Jade as a suspect, had circumstantial evidence against Jade. He had a vested interest in Jade being the perpetrator.

I wanted to know what Erin had said. I wanted to hear her story from her lips. I wanted to ask the questions and interpret her answers from my own perspective, with my own knowledge of the case and the people involved.

An ambulance came screaming toward the hospital, screeching to a halt in the bay as hospital staff ran out to meet it. A huge woman screaming blue murder came out of the vehicle on the gurney, calling for Jesus as arterial blood sprayed in a geyser from what looked like a compound fracture of her left leg. Someone shouted something about a victim from the second car coming in.

I slipped back into the hospital behind the mob as they rushed the woman toward a trauma room. Staff were running everywhere in the chaos of the moment. I went directly to the room where Erin had been and slipped inside.

The bed was empty. Erin had already been taken to a regular room. The exam room had not yet otherwise been cleared. A steel tray sat with suture equipment and bloody cotton balls. A speculum lay in the small sink, discarded after the rape exam.

I felt like the party was over and no one had invited me in the first place. Landry had Erin's clothes and the rape kit. There was nothing here for me to find.

I sighed and stepped back from the table, my absent gaze dropping to the floor. A small silver bracelet lay half-hidden under the table. I bent to pick it up. Made of silver, the links were fashioned in the shape of stirrups, one interlocking with the next. A couple of tiny charms hung from it – one a horse's head, one the letter E for Erin.

Just the thing for a horse-crazy teenager. I wondered if it had been a gift. I wondered if the gift-giver was a man, and if that man had betrayed her in the most terrible way.

The door swung open and I turned around to face a deputy.

'Where did they take my niece?' I asked. 'Erin Seabright?'

'Fourth floor, ma'am.'

'Will she have a guard?' I asked. 'I mean, what if one of the men who took her comes here –'

'We've posted someone outside her room. You won't have to worry, ma'am. She's safe now.'

'What a relief,' I said without enthusiasm. 'Thank you.'

He held the door for me as I left the room. I walked away, disappointed. I couldn't get to Erin. I couldn't get to Jade. I didn't know where Van Zandt was lurking. It was three in the morning and I was locked out of the case again.

I slipped the bracelet in my pocket and headed home to sleep.

The calm before the storm.

43

'What do you have to say about this, Mr Jade?'

Landry placed the photographs on the table in front of Don Jade, side by side by side. Jade astride a horse, smiling at the camera. Jade standing beside a colorful fence in a showring, in breeches and boots, profile to the camera as he pointed to something. Jade on another horse, going over a fence. Jade with his arm around Erin, her face scribbled over in ink by a jealous Jill Morone.

'I don't have anything to say about them.'

Landry reached out and turned the last picture over like a blackjack dealer flipping an ace.

'Until someone drew a line through it, the inscription on this was: To Erin. Love, Don. Do you have something to say now?'

'I didn't write it.'

'We can have an expert compare handwriting samples.'

'Don't even start the battle of the experts with me, Detective,' Bert Shapiro said, sounding like he might die of boredom. Landry wished he would. 'I've got bigger clubs in my bag than you do.'

Bert Shapiro: walking, talking, designer-dressed prick.

Landry looked at the attorney with hooded eyes. 'What's your connection to these people, Counselor?'

'This should be self-evident, but we are dealing with the Sheriff's Office, after all,' Shapiro said to the room at large, amused with himself. Stubby little cocksucker. 'I'm Mr Jade's attorney.'

'Yeah, I caught on to that. And Van Zandt's attorney.'

'Yes.'

'And who else in that little rat's nest? Trey Hughes?'

'My client list is confidential.'

'Just trying to save you some time,' Landry said. 'Hughes will be in here next, talking to us about Mr Jade. So, if he's one of yours too, you can just hang out with us morons at the Sheriff's Office all day. Enjoy our hospitality and bad coffee.'

Shapiro frowned. 'Do you have some legitimate reason for wasting Mr Jade's time here, Detective?'

Landry looked around the room, the same way Shapiro had. 'That should have been self-evident when Mr Jade was Mirandized. He's charged with the kidnapping of Erin Seabright.'

Jade pushed his chair back from the table and got up to pace. 'That's absurd. I haven't kidnapped anyone.'

'What evidence do you have to support the charge, Detective?' Shapiro asked. 'And before you answer, let me point out to you that it's not illegal to have one's photograph taken by an ardent fan or employee.'

Landry looked at Jade, letting the anticipation gain some weight. 'No, but it is against the law to hold a young woman against her will, chain her to a bed, and beat her with a riding whip.'

Jade exploded. 'That's ridiculous!'

Landry loved it. The cool cat was in a corner now. Now the temper came out. 'Erin didn't seem to find it amusing at all. She says you were the mastermind.'

'Why would she say such a thing?' Jade demanded. 'I've never been anything but kind to that girl.'

Landry shrugged just to be annoying. 'Maybe because you terrorized her, abused her, raped her –'

'I did no such thing!'

Shapiro put a hand on his client's arm. 'Have a seat, Don. Clearly, the girl is mistaken,' he said to Landry. 'If she's been tortured, as you say, who knows what kinds of things the kidnappers put into her head. They might have convinced her of anything. They might have had her on drugs –'

'Why would you say that?' Landry asked.

'Because clearly the girl isn't in her right mind if she thinks Don had anything to do with this.'

'Well, somebody's misunderstood something,' Landry said. 'When last we spoke, Mr Jade denied having had anything other than a working relationship with Erin Seabright. Maybe he misunderstood the meaning of "working relationship". That doesn't generally involve sex between employer and employee.'

Jade blew out a breath. 'I told you before: I have never had sex with Erin.'

Landry pretended not to be listening. He fingered the photographs on the table. 'You know, we found these photographs this morning – Sunday morning – in the apartment shared by Jill Morone – victim of murder and sexual assault – and Erin Seabright – victim of kidnapping and sexual assault. Jill Morone was last seen alive having an argument with you, and you yourself admit you were the last person to see Erin before she disappeared.'

'She came to tell me she was quitting,' Jade said. 'I had no idea she'd gone missing until you brought it up.'

'Employee relations are not your strong suit, are they, Don?' Landry said. 'Erin wants to leave you, so you chain her to a bed. Jill disappoints you, so you shove her face in a pile of shit and suffocate her –'

'My God,' Jade said, still pacing. 'Who could believe I would do any of that?'

'The same people who believe you electrocuted a horse for the insurance money.'

'I did nothing of the kind.'

'Erin knew, Jill knew. One's dead, one's lucky not to be.'

'This is all speculation,' Shapiro said. 'You don't have a shred of evidence against him.'

Landry ignored him. 'Where were you a week ago Sunday, Don? Sunday late in the day, say around six o'clock.'

Shapiro gave his client a look of warning. 'Don't answer that, Don.'

'Let me speculate,' Landry said. 'With your friend Ms Atwood, who has the amazing ability to be in two places at once?'

Jade glanced down. 'I don't know what you mean.'

'You told me Ms Atwood was with you Thursday night when Michael Berne's horses were being set loose and a woman was being assaulted not fifty yards from your barn.'

Shapiro held a finger up. 'Don't say anything, Don.'

Landry went on. 'The night Ms Atwood was also seen in attendance at a charity ball in Palm Beach. Did you think we'd just take your word for it, Don? Or the lady's, for that matter?'

'We got together after her event.'

'Don, don't –'

'Oh.' Landry nodded. 'You mean the same time she was also partying with friends at Au Bar?'

Jade sank back into his chair and rubbed his temples. 'I don't remember the time exactly –'

'You would have been smarter picking Jill for your alibi for Thursday night, after all,' Landry said. 'She was willing to lie for you, and she was probably home alone at the time.'

Shapiro was up now, hovering behind his client. He leaned forward and said, 'Mr Jade has nothing to say to you on this subject or any other. We're through here.'

Landry gave the lawyer a look. 'Your client can still help himself out here, Mr Shapiro. Don't get me wrong. He's in deep shit, but maybe he can still climb out of it and take a shower. His partner is still out there, running around loose. Maybe Don here wasn't the one with the whip. Maybe the whole scheme was the partner's idea. Maybe Don can help himself out giving us a name.'

Jade closed his eyes for a moment, inhaled and exhaled, composing himself. 'I'm trying to be cooperative, Detective Landry,' he said, still struggling to be calm. 'I don't know anything about a kidnapping. Why would I risk doing something so insane?'

'For money.'

'I have a very good career. I have a very good situation with Trey Hughes at his new facility. I'm hardly desperate for money.'

Landry shrugged. 'So maybe you're just a psycho. I once knew a guy killed a woman and cut her tongue out just to see how far back it went in her throat.'

'That's disgusting.'

'Yes, it is, but I see that kind of thing all the time,' Landry said reasonably. 'Now I see this deal: one girl dead, one girl missing, and a horse killed for the insurance money; and it all revolves around you, Mr Jade.'

'But it doesn't make sense,' Jade insisted. 'I would have made good money on Stellar as a sales horse –'

'Provided you could get him sold. I understand he had some problems.'

'He would have sold eventually. In the meantime, I collected my training fee every month.'

'And you'll collect your training fee for his replacement, too. Right?'

'Trey Hughes doesn't have to wait to sell one horse to buy another.'

'That's true. But I've learned over the years there are few people greedier and less patient than the rich. And you stand to make a big commission on the replacement horse. Isn't that right?'

Jade sighed and closed his eyes for a moment, trying to gather himself. 'I intend to have a long and happy working relationship with Trey Hughes. He's going to buy and sell a lot of horses in that time. I'll profit on all of them. That's how the business works. So, why would I risk that by kidnapping someone? The risk would far outweigh any possible gain.'

'If, on the other hand, I live a law-abiding life,' he went on. 'I'm set to move into a beautiful new facility to train horses for people who will pay me a great deal of money. So you see, Detective Landry, you simply don't have a case against me.'

'That's not quite true, Don,' Landry said, pretending sadness.

Jade looked at Shapiro.

'What do you think you have, Landry?' Shapiro asked.

'I have ransom calls placed to the Seabright home on a prepaid cell phone purchased by Don Jade two weeks ago.'

Jade stared at him. 'I don't know what you're talking about.'

'And do you have a witness who can positively identify Mr Jade purchasing this phone?' Shapiro asked.

'I never purchased any phone,' Jade said, peeved with his attorney for making it sound like he had.

Landry kept his gaze on Jade. 'I've got Erin Seabright, beaten and bloody and scared to death, telling me you're responsible. It doesn't get any more real than that, Don.'

Jade turned away and shook his head. 'I had nothing to do with it.'

'You got greedy,' Landry said. 'If you wanted her out of the way because she knew something about Stellar, you should have just killed her and dumped her body in a canal. You hold a hostage, things go wrong. People are unpredictable. You maybe wrote the script, but not everybody takes direction as well as a girl chained to a bed.'

Jade said nothing.

'Do you own property in the Wellington area, Mr Jade?'

'That would be a matter of public record,' Shapiro said.

'Unless he put it in a partnership or a blind trust,' Landry pointed out. 'Will you share that information with us or make us dig for it? Or should I ask Ms Montgomery, who keeps track of all your little details?'

'I fail to see what this has to do with anything,' Shapiro said.

Again, Landry ignored him, his focus on Jade, watching every nuance of his expression. 'Have you ever had any dealings with Bruce Seabright or Gryphon Development?'

'I know Gryphon Development is in charge of Fairfields, where Trey Hughes's barn is going up.'

'Have you personally had any dealings with them?'

'I may have spoken with someone from their office once or twice.'

'Bruce Seabright?'

'I don't recall.'

'How did Erin Seabright come to work for you?' Landry asked.

'Trey knew I was in need of a groom and told me about Erin.'

'How long have you been associated with Mr Hughes?'

'I've known Trey for years. He brought his horses to me last year.'

'Shortly after the death of his mother?'

'That's it,' Shapiro announced. 'If you want to go on a fishing expedition, Detective Landry, I suggest you hire a boat. Come on, Don.'

Landry let them move for the door to the interview room, speaking only as Shapiro reached for the doorknob.

'I own a boat, Counselor,' he said. 'And once I get a trophy on the line, I reel him in, fillet him, and fry him. I don't care who he is or who his friends are or how long it takes.'

'Good for you,' Shapiro said, pulling open the door.

Dugan was standing on the other side with Armedgian and an assistant district attorney.

'You're free to go, Mr Shapiro,' Dugan said. 'Your client, however, will be enjoying the county's hospitality for what's left of the night. Bail hearing tomorrow.'

44

'He told me to meet him at the back gate,' she said quietly, her eyes downcast.

Landry had slept on a bunk at the station and come back to the hospital at the crack of dawn to wait impatiently for Erin Seabright to wake up. Jade would be arraigned later that morning. Landry wanted the state's attorney to have every scrap of ammunition possible to keep Jade in the tank.

'People gossip – especially about Don,' Erin said. 'He said he didn't want them talking about us. I totally understood that. I thought it was kind of exciting, really. Our secret affair. Pathetic.'

'Had you had sex with him prior to that?' Landry asked. He kept his voice matter-of-fact. No accusation, no excitement.

She shook her head. 'We flirted. We were friends, I thought. I mean, he was my boss, but . . . But I wanted it to be more, and he did too. At least, that's what he told me.'

'So he asked you to meet him at the back gate. You knew no one would see you there?'

'There weren't any horses in those last two barns that weekend. That's where the dressage horses are stabled when they come to Wellington for a show, but there wasn't a show for them. Plus it was Sunday night. No one hangs around.'

'You hadn't told Mr Jade you were quitting your job, moving to Ocala?'

'No. Why would I? I wanted to work for him. I was in love with him.'

'What happened then, Erin? You went to the back gate to meet him . . .'

'He was late. I was afraid he had changed his mind. Then this van pulled up and a guy in a mask jumped out and – and – he grabbed me.'

Her voice died out as another bout of tears came. Landry handed her a box of tissues and waited.

'Did you recognize him, Erin?'

She shook her head.

'Did you recognize his voice?'

'I was so scared!'

'I know you were. It's hard to remember details when you're afraid and something awful like that is happening. But you need to try to slow it all down in your mind. Instead of seeing it all happen so fast, you need to try to see individual moments, like snapshots.'

'I'm trying.'

'I know you are,' he said quietly. 'Take your time, Erin. If you need a break, just let me know and we'll take a break. Okay?'

She looked at him and tried to smile. 'Okay.'

'If you never saw their faces, why do you think Jade was one of the kidnappers?'

'He's the one who told me to be there at the back gate.'

'I know, but did you recognize anything in particular about one of the kidnappers that made you think it was him?'

'I know him,' she said, frustration showing. 'I know his build. I know how he moves. I'm sure I heard his voice different times.'

'What about the other guy's voice? Did he sound familiar? Did he have an accent?'

The girl shook her head and rubbed a hand across her eyes, exhausted. 'He didn't talk much. And when he did, he whispered and mumbled. He never talked to me.'

'Do you know where they were holding you?' Landry asked. 'Could you take us there?'

Erin shook her head. 'It was a trailer house. That's all I know. It was horrible. It was filthy and old.'

'Could you tell if you were near a busy road? Were there any particular sounds you heard regularly?'

'I don't know. Cars, I guess, in the distance. I don't know. They kept me drugged most of the time. Special K.'

'How do you know that was the drug?'

She glanced away, embarrassed. 'I've had it before. At a party.'

'What happened last night? How did you get away?'

'One of them – the other one – he dragged me out of the trailer and put me in the van. I thought he was going to kill me and dump my body somewhere, and no one would ever find me!'

She paused to catch a ragged breath and try to compose herself. Landry waited.

'He just drove around. I don't know how long. He had given me a shot of K. I was pretty out of it. I just kept waiting for the van to stop, knowing that when it did, he would kill me.'

'You couldn't see out the windows?'

She shook her head. 'I was on the floor. And then we stopped, and I was so scared! He opened the door and dragged me out. I was dizzy. I couldn't stand up. I fell on the ground, a – a – dirt road. And he just got back in the van and drove away.'

Thrown on the side of the road like a sack of garbage. Something they had used and didn't need anymore. Still, she was damn lucky, Landry thought.

'I don't know how long I was laying there,' Erin said. 'Then finally I got up and started walking. I could see lights. Town. I just started walking.'

Landry said nothing for a moment. He let Erin's story sink in. He turned it over a few times in his mind, more questions shaking loose.

So, Jade and company figured out they weren't going to get the ransom. They dumped the girl rather than face a murder rap. Only, the way Landry saw it, Van Zandt was Jade's accomplice, and he was already under the lights for one murder. Why risk Erin Seabright identifying them? Because they knew she couldn't do so positively? Because they had taken pains to make certain there was no physical evidence to tie them to her?

That remained to be seen, of course. The clothes Erin had been wearing were at the lab being scrutinized under microscopes and fluorescent lights, swabbed and stained and picked over with tweezers.

Maybe letting Erin go was just part of the game for them. Let the victim live, and let her live with the knowledge that she can't put them away. Let the vic live, and let the cops live with the knowledge of their guilt, but no evidence to prove it. Power trip.

The problem with that theory was that Landry had no intention of letting anyone get away with anything.

'Erin, did they ever talk about why they singled you out?'

She shook her head, her eyes on Landry's microcassette recorder sitting on the bed tray, tape rolling. 'I was so drugged up most of the time. I know they wanted money. They knew Bruce has money.'

'Did they call him Bruce?'

'They called him I don't know how many times –'

'When they talked about him,' Landry clarified, 'did they use his first name? Did they call him Bruce?'

Erin nodded, though he thought she didn't get the significance of her answer.

'Did you tell them his name?'

'No. They just knew it.'

It struck Landry odd the perps would call Seabright by his first name. Familiar. Like a friend.

'I could have died because of him,' Erin said bitterly. 'I can't believe my mother stays with him. She's so weak.'

'People are complicated,' Landry offered, out of his element.

Erin just looked at her lap and shook her head.

'Erin, how many videotapes did they make of you while you were in the trailer?'

'I don't know. Three or four. It was so humiliating. They made me beg. They did things to me. They hit me.' She started to cry again. 'It was horrible.'

That son of a bitch, Landry thought. Three or four tapes. Seabright had handed over one besides the tape he had picked up at the ransom drop.

'Erin, did either of the men have sex with you?'

The tears came harder. 'They k-kept drugging me. I couldn't do anything about it. I c-couldn't stop them. I c-couldn't d-do anything.'

'We're going to try really hard to do something about it now, Erin. We'll work together – you and me – to build the case against them. Deal?'

She looked up at him with tear-filled eyes and nodded.

'Get some rest,' Landry said as he started for the door.

'Detective Landry?'

'Yes?'

'Thank you.'

Landry walked out hoping he would be able to really give her something to thank him for sooner rather than later.

I was waiting down the hall when Landry came out of Erin's hospital room. He didn't look surprised to see me. He stopped outside her door, took out his cell phone, and made a call that lasted about three minutes. When he ended the call, he glanced in the opposite direction down the hall, toward the nurses' station, then came toward me.

'What's she saying?' I asked as we walked toward the emergency exit.

'She says it was Jade, but that the kidnappers wore masks the whole time and they kept her doped up on ketamine. She never actually saw Jade. She can't identify the other guy at all. She says he rarely spoke.'

'That doesn't sound like Van Zandt,' I said. 'I've never met anyone who liked the sound of his own voice better than Tomas Van Zandt.'

'But she'd know his voice, because of the accent,' Landry said. 'Maybe he's smarter than he looks.' He sighed and shook his head. 'She won't make a good witness.'

He was frowning, and I could tell I had only a fraction of his attention. He was mentally replaying what Erin had told him, trying to find a way to work it into a lead or lead him to a piece of evidence.

'She doesn't need to be a good witness, yet,' I reminded him. 'You've got enough for Jade to be arraigned. Maybe you'll come up with some forensic evidence.'

'Yeah. Don't strain yourself in your enthusiasm,' he said sarcastically.

I shrugged. 'What do you have on him I don't know about? Have you come up with anything from his condo?'

He said nothing.

'Anything from the girls' apartment?'

'Some snapshots of Jade. One of him and Erin together. Someone wrote on the back: "To Erin. Love, Don." Jill had the pictures stashed. She had scratched out Erin's face and name with a ballpoint pen.'

'All the girls love Donnie.'

'I don't see it, myself,' Landry muttered.

'Have you found whether or not he owns or rents property other than the condo?'

'He wouldn't be stupid enough to hold Erin on property that could be traced back to him. And I couldn't get that lucky.'

'How did she get away?'

'She says they let her go. They figured they weren't getting the money, so they tossed her in the back of the van, drove her around, and dumped her like an old rug.'

'So, she can't say where they held her.'

'No. A trailer house. That's all she knows.'

'Could you tell anything from the last videotape? Any background sounds?'

'There was some noise in the background. The techno-geeks are trying to figure it out. Sounded like heavy machinery to me.'

'What did Erin say about it?'

He looked out the window. 'That she wasn't sure. That they kept her drugged. Special K, she says. It's easy to come by,' Landry said. 'Especially for people who work around veterinarians.'

'But it's not a sedative we use on horses,' I told him. 'It's commonly used on small animals.'

'Still, the access is there.'

'What about Chad?'

'He never left the Seabright house last night,' Landry said, opening his phone again. 'Besides, Erin and Chad had an intimate relationship. You think she wouldn't recognize him while he was raping her?'

'Maybe he was the silent one. Maybe he just watched the partner do her. Maybe they had her so drugged up, she wouldn't have recognized Santa Claus if he was bending over her.'

Landry scowled at me while he checked his messages. 'You know what? You're a pain in the ass, Estes.'

'Yeah, like *that's* news.' I slipped down from the ledge. 'Well, what the hey, Landry. Just kill them all and let God sort 'em out.'

'Don't tempt me. Half the people involved in this girl's life belong in prison, if you ask me,' he muttered as he listened to the phone. 'We'll be executing a search warrant at the Seabright house in a couple of hours. I'll be sure Dugan includes drugs as part of the warrant inventory.'

'What else are you looking for?'

'Erin keeps saying the kidnappers called Bruce Seabright multiple times, and that they made more than one video in the trailer. Three or four, she says.'

'Jesus God, what's he doing with them?' I asked. 'Selling them on eBay?'

'Yeah, and he'll claim he was just trying to defray the cost of the ransom,' Landry muttered. 'Asshole.'

I sat down on the deep window ledge, the early morning sun hot on my back, and thought about Bruce Seabright's possible involvement. 'So, let's say Seabright wanted Erin gone. He sets up the kidnapping scheme with no intention of ever bringing the cops in, or ever bringing Erin home. Why wasn't she killed right away? They could have made the tapes in an hour, killed her, and dumped her.

'Then I get involved and bring you in,' I went on. 'Now Bruce has to play along. Again, why not just have the accomplice get rid of her?'

'Because now we're watching him, asking questions. The accomplices see cops nosing around and they get scared.'

'So they let Erin go so she can help you build a case against them?' I shook my head. 'That doesn't make any sense.'

'I'm playing with the cards I've got, Estes,' Landry said impatiently. 'Erin says it was Jade. I'm going with that. It'd be stupid not to. If the thing tracks back to Bruce Seabright, I'll go with that too. Felony makes strange bedfellows.'

I didn't say anything. Occasionally, I do realize the value of discretion. Landry had his suspect and his circumstantial evidence. He had a half-sure victim and doubts of his own.

'I've got to go,' he said, closing his phone. 'The state's attorney wants a meeting before Jade's arraignment.'

I thought I might be able to slip into Erin's room after he'd gone, but I could see the deputy assigned to the post had already come back from his coffee break.

'Landry?' I asked as he started down the hall. He glanced back at me. 'Any sign of Van Zandt yet?'

'No. He never came back to the town house.' He started to turn away and I called him back a second time.

I took Erin's bracelet from my pocket and held it out to him. 'I found this on the floor of the examination room Erin was in last night. Ask her about it. Maybe it was a gift from Jade.'

He took it from me, his fingers brushing mine. He nodded.

'Thank you,' I said. 'For filling me in.'

Landry tipped his head. 'Your case first.'

'I thought you didn't share.'

'First time for everything.'

He looked at the bracelet in his hand, then walked away.

I left the hospital and took a drive around the parking lot with an eye peeled for a navy blue Chevy, but Van Zandt wasn't there. Nor was Krystal Seabright's white Lexus or Bruce's Jaguar. Ever the loving parents. Erin had told them to go, so they'd gone. Off the hook.

I have never understood people who have children but don't raise them, don't nurture them, don't help them become human beings. What other reason is there? To carry on the family name? To get a welfare check? To preserve proof of a relationship? Because that was what one was supposed to do at a particular time in one's life: get married, have kids. No one ever explained why.

I didn't know much about Erin Seabright's upbringing, but I knew she hadn't gotten where she was by being loved. She was, by her own sister's account, an angry, bitter girl.

I didn't like her sketchy tale. I knew from personal experience that angry, bitter girls want the people who hurt them most to pay for their sins. I wondered if she might blame whom she wanted to blame. Perhaps Jade hadn't loved her. Perhaps he'd broken her heart. And, in pain, in terror, under the influence of drugs, she might have projected his identity onto her tormentor.

Or perhaps the tormentor had put the idea there for her to believe.

I thought of Michael Berne again. It would have been simple for him to call Radio Shack and ask for that cell phone to be set aside. He could have sent a minion in to get the thing. If he had known about Erin's attraction to Jade, he could have played on that during Erin's captivity.

But who would Michael's partner be? He had no connection to the Seabrights I was aware of. He was on the wrong side of the relationship with Trey Hughes.

Trey Hughes, who kept my father's phone number in his wallet. Trey with his eye for the girls and his connection to every aspect of this sordid tale.

I didn't want to believe he could be a part of something so vicious as what had been done to Erin Seabright. I was still putting money on Van Zandt.

But it seemed to me I had pieces from three different puzzles. The trick would be coming up with a final picture that wasn't an abstract.

45

The assistant state's attorney seemed unperturbed by the fact that Erin Seabright had not seen the faces of her captors. As Elena had said, they had enough evidence to hold him on the charges, to arraign him and make a strong argument for high bail or no bail. They would then, by Florida law, have 175 days to bring Jade before a jury. Ample time to put the case together, provided the additional evidence was there to find.

The blood that had been found in the stall where Jill Morone had died had been typed. If they could match it to Jade, they were on their way to a murder indictment to add to the kidnapping charge. They had put Jade's alibi for the night of Jill's death in doubt. He had no alibi for the night the horse had been killed, the event Estes believed had kicked everything into motion.

Landry thought of Elena as he left the prosecutor's office. He didn't like that she had doubts about Jade's involvement, and he didn't like that it mattered to him what she thought. She had dragged him into this mess, and he wanted it to lay out as simply as her original theory had. Most crimes were like that: straightforward. The average murder was about money or sex, and didn't require Sherlock Holmes to solve. Kidnapping for ransom – the same. Good basic police work led to arrests and convictions. He didn't want this case to be any different.

And maybe the reason Estes's doubts bothered him so much was that some of those same doubts were chewing at the back of his mind. He tried to shake them off as he walked down the hall. Weiss came out of the squad room to meet him.

'Paris Montgomery is here. Asking for you,' he added with an eye roll.

'Did you find anything at the Seabright house?'

'Jackpot,' Weiss said. 'We found a videotape stashed on a shelf in Seabright's home office. You won't believe it. It actually shows the girl being raped. We've got Seabright in the conference room. I'm on my way now.'

'Wait for me,' Landry said, fury burning in his gut. 'I want a crack at that son of a bitch.'

'There'll be a line,' Weiss assured him.

Paris Montgomery was pacing behind the table as Landry walked into the interview room. She looked upset and nervous, though her emotional state had not prevented her from putting on makeup or styling her hair.

'Ms Montgomery. Thank you for coming in,' Landry said. 'Have a seat. Can I get you anything? Coffee?'

'God, no,' she said, sitting down. 'If I have any more caffeine I'm going to start spinning around the room like a top. I can't believe any of this is happening. Don in jail. Erin *kidnapped*. My God. Is she all right? I just tried calling the hospital, but they wouldn't tell me anything.'

'She's been roughed up,' Landry said. 'But she'll recover.'

'Will they let me see her?'

'Immediate family only, for the time being. Maybe later today.'

'I feel terrible about what happened. I mean, she worked for me. I should have looked out for her.' Tears filled the big brown eyes. 'I should have done something. When Don said she'd quit and gone – I should have tried harder to contact her. I should have known something was wrong.'

'Why is that? Did you have reason to be suspicious?'

She glanced away; her expression seemed to have the kind of glazed look people get when they are watching memories run through their minds.

'Erin had seemed happy with the job. I mean, I knew she was having boyfriend trouble, but what girl her age doesn't? I just – I should have questioned her leaving so suddenly. But you have to understand, grooms come and go during the season. There's too much opportunity. Someone offers more money or health insurance or an extra day off and they're gone.'

Landry offered no platitudes, no absolution. Someone sure as hell should have been paying closer attention to what was going on with Erin Seabright. He wasn't inclined to let anyone off the hook.

'Were you aware of any relationship between Erin and Don?' he asked.

'Erin had a crush on him.'

'To your knowledge, did he act on it?'

'I – well – Don is very charismatic.'

'Is that a yes or a no?'

'He's a magnetic kind of person. Women are drawn to him. He enjoys that. He likes to flirt.'

'With Erin?'

'Well ... sure ... but I didn't think he would take advantage of her. I don't want to believe that he did.'

'But he might have.'

She looked uncertain, which was answer enough.

'Did Erin say anything to you about the death of the horse?'

'She was upset. We all were.'

'Did she hint that she knew something about what happened?'

She looked away again and pressed two fingers against the small crease digging in between her eyebrows. 'She didn't believe it was an accident.'

'She took care of the horse, right?'

'Yes. She was very good with him – with all the horses. She put in extra time with them. She would come and check on them after hours sometimes.'

'Had she checked on them that night?'

'Around eleven. Everything was fine.'

'Why did she think it wasn't an accident?'

Paris Montgomery began to cry. She looked around the room as if looking for a crevice to disappear into.

'Ms Montgomery, if Don Jade did what we believe he did, you don't owe him any loyalty.'

'I didn't believe he'd done anything bad,' she said in a small voice, making the excuse for herself, not for Jade.

'What happened?'

'Erin told me Don was at the barn already when she got there that morning. Early. Really early. We had horses showing that day, and Erin had to get there early to braid manes and get the horses ready. She told me she saw Don in Stellar's stall, doing something with the cord of the electric fan. She went over to the stall to ask him why he was there so early.'

She stopped and tried to compose herself, her breath catching. Landry waited.

'She saw Stellar was down. Don told her the horse had bitten through the cord of the fan, and he held the cord up. But Erin said he had something in his other hand. Some kind of a tool.'

'You think he cut the cord to make it look like an accident.'

'I don't know!' she sobbed, covering her face with her hands. 'I don't want to believe he could have killed that poor animal!'

'And now that might be the least of what he's done,' Landry said.

He sipped his coffee impassively while Paris Montgomery cried for her sin of omission. He turned the new facts over in his mind. Erin could have fingered Jade for staging the accident. That might logically have led to her death, he thought, as it may have led to Jill Morone's death. But the evidence regarding the cell phone purchase indicated the kidnapping had been planned in advance of the horse murder. Therefore, the one thing had nothing to do with the other.

'What did you do when Erin came to you with this information?' he asked.

Paris dabbed at her eyes with a tissue. 'I got angry. I told her of course it was an accident. Don wouldn't –'

'Despite the fact that Don *had* on several occasions previous.'

'I never believed that was true,' she said adamantly. 'No one ever proved anything.'

'Except that he's clever and adept at evading the consequences of his actions.'

Even now, she rose to Jade's defense. 'In three years I have *never* known Don to do one cruel thing to a horse in his care.'

'What was Erin's reaction when you didn't believe her?'

'She was upset at first. We talked some more. I told her what I just told you about my experience working for Don. I asked her if she could believe him capable of hurting anyone. I made her feel ashamed for even thinking it.'

'So, when Jade told you she had quit later that day –'

'I wasn't that surprised.'

'But you didn't try to call her.'

'I tried to call her, she didn't answer. I left a message on her voice mail. I went to her apartment a couple of days later, but it looked like she had moved out.'

She sighed dramatically and looked at Landry with the big eyes, looking for forgiveness. 'I would give anything if I could go back to that day and change what happened.'

'Yeah,' Landry said. 'I'll bet Erin Seabright would too.'

46

I went back to the day it all began. The day Stellar was found dead in his stall. The day Erin Seabright was snatched from the back gates of the Palm Beach Polo Equestrian Center. I laid it all out in black and ecru on sheets of expensive stationery I found in the writing desk. A time line. When Jade had allegedly purchased the cell phone. When Erin and Chad had argued. When Stellar had been found dead. When Erin had been taken. Everything I knew about the case, I wrote down and I spread the sheets out in order on my bedroom floor.

I had become focused on the idea that everything had come out of the death of Stellar, but looking at the time line, reflecting on what I knew, I realized that it wasn't so. The kidnapping plan was already in motion when Stellar died. Someone had purchased the disposable cell phone. Someone had lined up the trailer where Erin had been held, had gathered the video and audio equipment, had procured the ketamine to drug Erin and found the van used in the abduction. An elaborate plan with at least two people involved.

I wanted to know everything that had transpired that Sunday, the day of Stellar's death and Erin's abduction. I wanted to know what had gone on between Erin and Jade that day and prior to it. I wanted to know where Trey Hughes had been that day, and Van Zandt.

I looked at my time line and all the things I did know. No matter how many times I went over it, the simplest explanation was not the best. But I knew plenty of people would have been happy to stop there. Landry among them.

I have never been able to do things the easy way.

I went back into the living room, pulled out the tape of the kidnapping, and shoved it into the VCR.

Erin standing at the back gate, waiting. She watched the van approach. She stood there as the masked man got out. She said, 'No!' Then she ran. He grabbed her.

I rewound the tape and played it again.

I thought about the things she had told Landry, and the things she had not told him.

I thought about who had come under suspicion and who had not.

Don Jade was sitting in jail. Bruce Seabright was under a microscope. Tomas Van Zandt, known predator, suspected murderer, was nowhere to be found.

I went back to the writing desk and dug through the mess I'd made to find the piece of paper I had taken from Van Zandt's trash. The flight schedule of horses being shipped to Brussels. The plane was scheduled to leave that night at eleven. I would have to give that information to Landry. And Landry would have to pass it on to Armedgian.

Screw that. I wasn't giving Armedgian anything. If I could find a way to make him look like an idiot, I would. God knew, after the fiasco at The Players, neither Armedgian nor Dugan was going to have anything to do with me anyway.

I decided, when the time came, I would go to the airport and wait for Van Zandt myself, then call in Landry. If Tomas Van Zandt thought he could get away with murder in my country, he could think again.

47

He had no idea how long he had been in the trunk of the car. Night had become day. He knew that because of the heat. The fucking Florida sun was beating down on the car, the temperature in the trunk becoming unbearable.

He was going to die in this horrible place because of that Russian cunt. Two of them. Their faces blended together in his brain. He went in and out of delirium from the pain and the heat.

He would have tried to break out, but he couldn't move. He didn't know how many of his bones were broken. He would have tried to scream, but the lower half of his face was encased in tape. Many times in the hours past he had feared he would vomit and choke to death.

Like the fat groom. Stupid little whore. She had been ready to have sex with Jade. She should have been willing to have sex with him. Some of his beating was her fault. Kulak had known about her death.

An accident. Not murder. If he had gotten rid of her body the way he had wanted, no one would ever have known. No one would have asked questions about where was Jill. Who in the world could give a shit about that one?

If he hadn't been talked into dumping the body into that manure pit, plenty of what had happened wouldn't have. And maybe he would not now be waiting to die.

He could hear sounds outside the car. Machinery running, men's voices. Russians speaking Russian. Fucking Russians.

Something struck the car, rocking it, then it began to move forward. The noise of the machinery grew louder, like a beast from hell devouring everything in its path. The noise grew deafening – the roaring of the beast, the crunching of metal as the front end of the car collapsed.

He knew what was coming. He knew, and he started screaming, even though the sound could not escape his own head. He screamed the names of every woman who had turned against him.

Women. Stupid, ungrateful bitches. The bane of his existence. Many times he had said women would be the death of him. As always, he was right.

48

The scene was as nightmarish as anything Landry had ever watched. Erin Seabright, tied spread-eagle on the bed, screaming and crying as one of her captors violated her.

Dugan, Weiss, Dwyer, and he stood in a half-circle, arms crossed, watching the tape play, their faces like stone. At the top of the half-circle, Bruce Seabright sat on a chair, his complexion the color of putty.

Landry punched the power button off and slammed a fist against the side of the television. He wheeled on Seabright.

'You sick son of a bitch.'

'I've never seen that before in my life!' Seabright shouted, coming to his feet.

'Landry . . .' Dugan warned.

Landry didn't hear him, he didn't hear Weiss's phone ring. He was hardly aware anyone else was in the room. He saw only Bruce Seabright, and he wanted to beat him to death with his bare hands.

'What? You were saving it for later?' Landry said. 'Planning your own little film festival?'

Seabright shook his head vehemently. 'I don't know how that thing got in my office.'

'You put it there,' Landry said.

'I didn't! I swear!'

'The kidnappers sent it to you, just like they sent the first one.'

'No!'

'And if it had been left up to you, no one would have seen either of them.'

'That – that's not true –'

'You lying sack of shit!' Landry shouted in his face.

Dugan tried to step between them, shoving at Landry's chest. 'Detective Landry, step back!'

Landry stepped around him. 'It wasn't bad enough you wanted rid of her? You wanted to see her tortured too?'

'No! I –'

'Shut up!' Landry shouted. 'Shut the fuck up!'

957

Seabright stepped back, small eyes popping with fear. The backs of his legs hit the folding chair he'd been sitting on, and he stumbled and fell awkwardly back down onto it.

'Landry!' Dugan shouted.

Dwyer stepped in front of him, holding up a hand. 'James –'

'I want a lawyer!' Seabright said. 'He's out of control!'

Landry stilled himself, slowed his breathing, stared at Bruce Seabright.

'You'd better call God, Seabright,' Landry said tightly. 'It's going to take more than a lawyer to get your sorry ass out of this crack.'

Jade's bail hearing took twenty minutes. Five minutes for business and fifteen minutes for Shapiro to hear himself talk. For what a guy like that charged by the hour, Landry supposed he ought to at least give the appearance of being worth more than the average suit.

Landry stood at the back of the courtroom, taking roll of the attendees. He was still trembling from the adrenaline and rage that had burned through him in the conference room. Like counting sheep, he counted heads. Shapiro's entourage of lawyers-in-waiting, the assistant state's attorney, a small pack of reporters, and Trey Hughes.

The prosecutor, Angela Roca, stated her intention to take the case before the grand jury and asked for bail in the amount of a million dollars.

'Your Honor,' Shapiro whined. 'A million dollars! Mr Jade is not as wealthy as his clients are. For all intents and purposes, that would amount to denying bail altogether.'

'Fine by us, Your Honor,' Roca said. 'Mr Jade has been identified by his victim as a kidnapper and rapist. Additionally, the Sheriff's Office considers him a suspect in the brutal murder of one of his employees.'

'With all due respect, Your Honor, Mr Jade can't be penalized for a crime for which he has not been charged.'

'Yeah, I caught that one in judge school,' the Honorable Ida Green said sarcastically. Ida, a tiny redheaded New York transplant, was one of Landry's favorite judges. Nothing impressed Ida, including Bert Shapiro.

'Your Honor, the prosecution's case –'

'Is none of my business. This is a bail hearing, Mr Shapiro. Need I enlighten you as to basic proceedings?'

'No, Your Honor. I remember vaguely from law school.'

'Good. You didn't waste your parents' money. Bail is set at five hundred thousand, cash.'

'Your Honor –' Shapiro began.

Ida waved him off. 'Mr Shapiro, your client's clients spend that much on a horse without batting an eye. I'm certain if they are as devoted to Mr Jade as you are, they'll help him out.'

Shapiro looked pissed.

Roca took the inch and went for the mile. 'Your Honor, as Mr Jade has lived in Europe and has many contacts there, we consider him to be a flight risk.'

'Mr Jade will surrender his passport. Anything else, Ms Roca?'

'We request Mr Jade be required to submit to a blood test and give a hair sample for the purposes of comparison to evidence in custody, Your Honor.'

'Make it so, Mr Shapiro.'

'Your Honor,' Shapiro argued. 'This is a gross invasion of my client's person –'

'A colonoscopy is a gross invasion, Mr Shapiro. Hair and blood samples are so ordered.'

The proceedings ended with a bang of the gavel. Trey Hughes got up, went to the front of the courtroom, wrote a check for the clerk, and Don Jade was a free man.

49

I rewound the tape again.

I wondered if Landry's people had found any of the other videotapes Erin had spoken of in Bruce Seabright's possession. If they had, I hoped he would be arrested and charged with something – hindering, withholding evidence, conspiracy, something, anything. Regardless of the outcome of Erin's ordeal, regardless of the origin or motive of what had happened, Bruce Seabright had exhibited a depraved indifference to human life.

I thought about the tape of Erin's beating, which I had not seen, but which Landry had described to me as brutal. An eye for an eye, Bruce, I thought.

I hit the play button for the one tape I had.

How many times had I watched this? I didn't know. Enough that I should have seen every detail there was to see, yet I felt compelled to play it again and look for things I hadn't, couldn't, wouldn't see. Again and again, and still something bothered me, a feeling that nagged at the edge of my consciousness, and another I as yet could not put a finger on.

The van approaches. Erin stands there.

The van stops. Erin stands there.

A masked man jumps out. Erin says, 'No!'

She tries to run.

I hit pause, freezing the image. A thick band of snow ran across the faces of Erin and her pursuer as they ran toward the gate. Without seeing her expression or his mask, the shot might have taken on any meaning. Out of context, the two people might have been lovers chasing each other out of joy. They might have been people running from a disaster or to the rescue of others. Without expression, they were two torsos in faded jeans.

The sluggishness of Erin's reactions bothered me. Was it disbelief? Was it fear? Or was it something else?

I let the tape run forward, watching the man catch her roughly from behind and spin her around. She kicked him hard. He backhanded her across the face with enough force to knock her almost off her feet.

Horrible. Absolutely horrible. Violence that was completely real. I couldn't deny it.

I watched him shove her down from behind and drive her face-first into the dirt. I watched him jab a needle into her arm. Ketamine. Special K. Drug of choice of rave-goers, date rapists, and small animal vets.

Erin had used party drugs in the past. She herself had told Landry it was the drug that had been used on her. How would she have known that unless her captors graciously filled her in, unless she had a working knowledge of the drug herself?

I thought about the things Erin had told Landry, the things she had not told Landry, the pieces of her story that didn't all fit the same puzzle.

She was sure Jade was one of the kidnappers, but she had never actually seen him. She was sure it was him – the man she'd had a thing for, the man she had supposedly dumped Chad for. Yet, without ever seeing his face, she could believe he would brutalize her. Why? Why would she think it? Why would he do it?

And while she was dead certain Jade was one of her captors, she didn't have a clue about his partner.

Then, after raping her, beating her, drugging her, and not getting the ransom for which they had gone to such elaborate lengths, her abductors simply drove her around and let her go. Just like that. And not only had they let her go, they had given her clothes back to her, even her bracelet.

I didn't believe her. I didn't believe her story, and I would have given anything to change that gut feeling. I wanted to doubt my own instincts as I had doubted them every day since Hector Ramirez had been killed. What irony that through this case I had gained back a belief in myself, and yet, I wanted nothing more than to be wrong.

I thought of Molly and wished I could have cried.

I would have prayed to be wrong, but I have never believed any higher power ever listened to me.

Feeling ill, I rewound the tape and forced myself to watch it again, this time in slow motion, so that I might even more closely scrutinize it, looking for something I was afraid I wouldn't find.

The quality of my equipment was average. Landry would have a much better look at the tape with all the high-tech equipment at the lab. Still, as I watched the tape second by second, I had a good view. Throughout the filming, the camera had remained focused fairly tightly on Erin, she appeared to be no more than eight or ten feet away. I could see that her hair was pulled back in a clip, she was wearing a tight red T-shirt that showed off her flat belly. Her jeans had a little white spot on one thigh.

As her assailant caught her by the arm, I could see she was wearing a watch. But I didn't see the one thing I wanted desperately to see.

Prowling the guest house like a caged cat, I thought of the people involved in Erin's life: Bruce, Van Zandt, Michael Berne, Jill Morone, Trey Hughes, Paris Montgomery. I wanted Bruce to be guilty. I knew Van Zandt was a murderer. Michael Berne had a motive to ruin Don Jade, but kidnapping made no sense. Jill Morone was dead. Trey Hughes was the center of all their universes. And then there was Paris Montgomery.

Paris and her backhanded loyalty to Don Jade. She had as much to gain by Jade's ruination as Michael Berne – even more. She had labored in Jade's shadow for three years with her cover-girl smile and her love of fine things and her hunger for the spotlight. She had run his life, run his barn, run interference.

I thought of the small, destructive 'truths' Paris had confessed to me about the death of Stellar, even as she defended Don Jade. If she would say those things to me, what slivers of doubt was she putting into Trey Hughes's mind every time she slept with him?

On the morning Jill Morone's body had been found, Paris had been supervising Javier's clean-up of the crime scene. Even as she called their insurance adjuster about the damage to Jade's clothing and personal effects, she'd had Javier cleaning up the mess. I wondered now if news of Jill's murder had been a surprise to her at all.

I thought of the supposed rape and Landry's feeling that it might have been staged. I thought of Jill's body buried in the manure pit at barn forty, where it would surely be found. And when it was found, who would be the first suspect? Don Jade.

His clients might tolerate a few scandals, but the murder of a girl? No. Kidnapping? No. And with Jade out of the picture, and few wealthy patrons to believe in him, who would benefit most? Paris Montgomery.

I called Landry and left a message on his voice mail. Then I turned off the television and left the house.

At one end of the barn Irina was stretched out in a lounge chair in a bikini top and short shorts, dramatic black sunglasses shading her eyes.

'Irina,' I called on my way to my car. 'If Tomas Van Zandt comes by, call nine-one-one. He's wanted for murder.'

She raised a hand lazily to acknowledge me, and rolled onto her stomach to tan her back.

I went to the show grounds, to Jade's barn, for a second shot at Javier. There was less chance on a Monday of his being caught speaking to me. The stables were closed. There was no reason for Trey Hughes to show up, or Paris. Perhaps he would feel more free to tell me what he knew.

But there was no one at Jade's stalls. The stalls had not been cleaned and the horses were clamoring for lunch. It appeared they had been abandoned. The aisle was an obstacle course of forks, rakes, brooms, and overturned muck buckets. As if someone had come through in a very big hurry.

I raided Jade's feed stall and tossed each horse a flake of hay.

'Don't tell me. Now you're pretending to be a groom?'

I looked out the back of the tent to find Michael Berne standing there in jeans and a polo shirt. He looked as happy as I had seen him since this mess had begun. Relaxed. His rival was in jail and all was right with the world.

'I'm a multitalented individual,' I said. 'What's your excuse for being here?'

He shrugged. I noticed for the first time he held a small box in his hand. Something from a vet's office.

'No rest for the weary,' he said.

'Or the wicked.'

Rompun. One of the sedatives used commonly on horses. Everybody has the stuff around, Paris had said as she spoke of the drug found in Stellar's bloodstream.

'Having a party?' I asked, looking pointedly at the box.

'I've got one that's hard to shoe,' Berne said. 'He needs a little something to take the edge off.'

'Was Stellar hard to shoe?'

'No. Why do you ask?'

'No reason. You haven't seen Paris today, have you?'

'She was here earlier. Just in time to watch the INS cart her last groom away.'

'What?'

'There was a raid this morning,' he said. 'Her Guatemalan guy was one of the first rounded up.'

'Who tipped them off? You?' I asked bluntly.

'Not me,' he said. 'I lost a guy too.'

The INS rolled in for a surprise raid, and a man in barn nineteen was one of the first to go. The one person left in Jade's camp who might have been persuaded to tell the truth – if he knew it – gone just as the case seemed to be breaking.

Trey had seen me speaking with Javier. He might have told Paris. Or perhaps Bert Shapiro had wanted the Guatemalan out of the country in the event he might know something about Jade.

'I hear he's in jail,' Michael Berne said.

'Jade? Yes. Unless he's made bail. Kidnapping charges. Do you know anything about it?'

'Why would I?'

'Maybe you were here the night it happened. A week ago, Sunday, late in the day at the back gate.'

Berne shook his head and started to walk away. 'Not me. I was at home. With my wife.'

'You're a very devoted and forgiving husband, Michael,' I said.

'Yes, I am,' he said smugly. 'I'm not the criminal here, Ms Estes.'

'No.'

'Don Jade is.'

No, I thought as he walked away, *I don't believe that either.*

50

My phone rang as I walked back to my car.

'Meet me for lunch,' Landry said.

'Your telephone etiquette is sorely lacking,' I pointed out.

He named a fast-food place ten minutes away and hung up.

'Erin Seabright caught Jade in the stall with the dead horse,' Landry said. We sat in his car. A sack of food lay on the seat between us, filling the car with the aroma of charbroiled meat and french fries. Neither of us touched it. 'She caught him doctoring the electrical cord on the fan.'

'Erin told you that?'

'I'm on my way to ask her about it now. We didn't get into the whole dead horse saga this morning. I only asked her for details about her abduction. Paris Montgomery came in on her own and told me. There was a story on the morning news about Erin's escape from the kidnappers. Apparently, that put the fear of God in Ms Montgomery.'

'More like a vulture circling a dying animal,' I said. 'She smells opportunity.

'She says Erin caught Jade, and at the end of the day Jade kidnapped her? It doesn't track, Landry.'

'I know. The kidnapping plot was already in motion.'

'If that's what it was,' I said. 'Have the technical wizards enhanced that first videotape?'

'Yes, but I haven't had a chance to look at it. Why?'

'Look for the bracelet I handed you this morning.'

'What about it?'

'Do you think the kidnappers gave it to her as a parting gift?' I asked. 'I've watched that tape fifty times. I don't see a bracelet, but she was wearing one last night.'

Landry looked incredulous. 'Are you trying to say the girl is in on it? You're out of your mind. Estes, you haven't seen her. She's had the shit kicked out of her. You didn't see that tape of the perp going at her with the whip. And this morning Weiss and Dwyer found another tape in Seabright's office. It shows the girl being brutally raped.'

That brought me up short. 'He had it in the house? In his office?'

'Stuffed behind some things on a shelf.'

I didn't know what to say to that. It was what I had been hoping for – for Seabright to be made to pay a price. But news of the taped rape was something else.

'It looked genuine?' I asked.

'Made the hair on the back of my neck stand on end,' Landry said. 'I wanted to take Seabright and choke him till his eyes popped out.'

'Where is he now?'

'He's sitting in a holding cell. The state's attorney is trying to decide what to charge him with.'

'What happened at Jade's arraignment?'

'Trey Hughes posted bail.'

'I wonder if Paris knows about that.'

'I'd bet he's paying for Bert Shapiro too.'

'Have you interviewed him yet? Trey?'

'He's been asked to come in. Shapiro won't allow it.'

'Run his name through the system,' I said. 'Trey has a checkered past. He told me yesterday he has a past professional acquaintance with my father. People don't hire Edward Estes for traffic mishaps.'

Landry shook his head in disgust. 'It's like a goddam bag of snakes, this bunch.'

'Yes,' I said. 'Now we get to find out how many of them are poisonous.'

Nothing breeds contempt more virulent than unrequited devotion. I drove toward Loxahatchee, thinking of Paris Montgomery walking into the Sheriff's Office to give up her boss on the horse murder and insurance fraud. Paris was a first-chair kind of girl who had been playing second fiddle to Don Jade for three years. She had helped him build his clientele.

She had defended him with one hand and dug the foundation out from under him with the other.

I wondered if it had been Paris who dropped the dime to the INS regarding Javier. She had been with Trey the night before. He might have told her he believed me to be a private investigator, and that he had found me conversing in fluent Spanish with the one Jade employee left who might have known something valuable.

Or perhaps Trey had called them himself. For reasons of his own. I tried to picture him as one of the kidnappers. Had the years of debauchery so warped him that he might consider kidnapping a girl to be a game?

The afternoon was already half-gone as I turned down the road to Paris Montgomery's house. In the dense woods of rural Loxahatchee, much of the light had already fallen victim to the long shadows of tall thin pine trees.

I drove past the house Paris lived in to the cul-de-sac where I had nearly shot Jimmy Manetti the night before. The half-built houses had been abandoned by their work crews for the day. I parked my car, took the Glock out of its hiding place, and made my way back down the road, ducking into the cover of trees as quickly as I could.

The house was much like Eva Rosen's: a pseudo-Spanish seventies rambler with mildewed white stucco and a cedar shake roof crusted with moss. I let myself in a side door to the garage, which was stacked with the property owner's lawn equipment and Christmas decorations. The money-green Infiniti was not there.

The door into the house was locked, and the lights on the security system panel showed that the system was armed. I walked around the exterior of the house, looking for an unlocked door, a partially open window. No luck.

Through the living room windows I could see a nasty once-white shag carpet and a lot of cheesy 'Mediterranean' furniture no one from the Mediterranean would ever have laid claim to. The TV looked almost as tall as I was and had every kind of symbiotic machine hooked up to it – VCR, DVD, Dolby sound system with a bank of stereo equipment that looked like something from NASA.

I went around the side yard to the back, where a big redwood hot tub sat inside the requisite caged patio, along with an assortment of tacky patio furniture and sun-starved plants. The screen door was not locked, but the sliding glass door into the dining room was secure. I could see mail on the dining room table: magazines, bills.

A second sliding glass door at the far end of the patio led into a bedroom with orange shag carpeting. The drapes were pulled back, revealing a king-sized bed with a red velvet spread. A painting of a naked woman with three breasts and two faces hung above the ornate, fake wood headboard. A TV sat on an open-sided stand at the end of the room. I checked the titles on the stack of videos on the bottom shelf and wondered if I was the only person in south Florida without a collection of porn.

Somewhere beyond the yard, the engine of a piece of heavy machinery had fired up with a throaty growl. My luck someone had come back to the construction site down the road and was about to bulldoze my car.

The backyard was dim with shadows, but the sky above the treetops was still an intense blue. The racket was not coming from the direction of the new houses down the road, but from beyond those trees, beyond Paris Montgomery's backyard, to the west.

A large motor grumbled constantly, the intermittent crunching and chewing of materials being fed through some big machine. A mulch grinder, I guessed, and I almost turned away. Then I paused.

Landry had said there was a sound of heavy machinery in the background of the video showing Erin being beaten by her captors. A sound Erin hadn't been able to remember when he'd asked her about the place where she was held.

I walked toward the back of the property. Dense with young trees and wild bamboo, vines knitting all of it together, the back border of the yard was a jungle that would have eventually swallowed up the yard and the house if allowed.

The thump and grind of the machine grew louder. A truck engine revved and the beep-beep-beep of warning sounded as it backed up.

Trying to see through the curtain of greenery to the property on the other side, I almost missed it. The thing sat in the tangled growth like an ancient ruin. Gray and rusted, once an alien thing that had become almost an organic part of the landscape over the course of time. A trailer. What might have been a construction boss's office once, with a window on the end of it that was coated with dirt on the inside. Someone had scratched through the filth with their fingertip, writing a single word: HELP.

51

Life can change in a heartbeat.

I had nearly missed it. I had been a heartbeat from turning and walking away. Then, there it was: the real reason Paris Montgomery had taken this shitty house too far from the show grounds. I had thought she had come here to be away from prying eyes, and I was right. But her affair with Trey Hughes was not the only thing she had wanted to hide.

The trailer squatted in the overgrowth like something from a bad dream. The sight of it evoked memories I wished I didn't have.

Adrenaline runs through my bloodstream like rocket fuel. My heart pounds like a piston. I'm ready to launch.

I pulled my gun and moved in close along the side of the trailer. Only when I was right on top of it could I see the path where someone had walked around the end to get to the twisted, rusted metal stairs that hung off the back side of the trailer.

Despite the fact that the sun hadn't touched this yard in an hour or more, and the temperature was in fact cool, I was perspiring. I thought I could hear myself breathing.

I've been told to stay put, to wait, but I know that's not the right decision . . . wasting precious time . . . It's my case. I know what I'm doing . . .

I felt the same push now. My case. My discovery. But a hesitation, also. Apprehension. Fear. The last time I had made that decision, I had been wrong. Dead wrong.

I leaned back against the side of the trailer, willing my pulse to slow, trying to slow my thought process, trying to shut out the emotions that had more to do with post-traumatic stress than with the present.

Paris would have rented this property months ago, I reasoned. If this place had been chosen because of the privacy, because of the trailer, that extended the period of premeditation to before the season had begun. I wondered if Erin had been chosen for her job because of her potential as a groom or as a victim.

My hand was shaking as I pulled out my phone with my left hand. I dialed Landry's pager number, left my number and 911. I called his voice mail, left Paris Montgomery's address, and told him to get here ASAP.

And now what? I thought as I closed the phone and stuck it in my pocket. Wait? Wait for Paris to come home and find me in her backyard? Let opportunity and daylight pass, waiting for Landry to call me back?

It's my case. I know what I'm doing ...

I knew what Landry would say. He would tell me to wait for him. Go sit in my car like a good girl.

I've never been a good girl.

It's my case. I know what I'm doing ...

The last time I had thought that, I had been very wrong.

I wanted to be right.

Slowly, I went up the metal stairs that over time had sunken into the sandy earth and settled away from the trailer, leaving a gap of several inches between the two. Standing to the side of the door, I knocked twice, and called out 'Police.'

Nothing happened. I couldn't hear any movement within the trailer. No shotgun blasts came through the door. It occurred to me Van Zandt might be inside, hiding out until he could catch his plane to Brussels. He might have been Paris Montgomery's partner in it all, helping her to oust Jade and secure her place in Trey Hughes's life, while Van Zandt indulged himself in his hobby of dominating young girls. Perhaps the ransom was to have been his fee for helping to ruin Don Jade.

And Erin's role in the game? I wasn't sure now, in light of what Landry had told me about the videotapes of her being raped and beaten. The tape of her abduction, which I had watched a dozen times, made me question whether Erin was truly a victim. Perhaps Paris had lured her into the plot with the opportunity to punish her parents, and once the plan was in motion had given her over to Van Zandt. The idea sickened me.

Standing to one side, I held my breath as I opened the door a crack with my left hand.

Billy Golam jerks open the door, wild-eyed, high on his own home cooking – crystal meth. He's breathing hard. He's got a gun in his hand.

A bead of sweat ran down between my eyebrows and skittered off my nose.

Leading with the Glock, I ducked into the trailer and swept the barrel of the gun from left to right. There was no one in the first room. I took in only the swiftest impression of the furnishings: an old steel desk, a pole lamp, a chair. All of it covered in dust and cobwebs. Piles of old newspapers. Discarded paint cans. The stale, musty smells of dust and cigarettes and mildew growing beneath the old linoleum floor assaulted my nose. The sounds of the machinery outside seemed to resonate and amplify inside the tin can trailer.

Cautiously, I moved toward the second room, still leading with the gun.

I hadn't seen the video of Erin's beating, but I knew from Landry's description this was where it had taken place. A bed with a metal-framed headboard sat against the back wall. A filthy, stained mattress with no sheets. Bloodstains.

I pictured Erin there as Landry had described her: naked, bruised, chained by one arm to the headboard, screaming as her assailant beat her with a whip. I pictured her as a victim.

A few feet from the foot of the bed stood a tripod with a video camera perched atop it. Behind the tripod a table littered with empty soda cans, half-empty water bottles, opened bags of chips, and an ashtray full of butts. There were a couple of lawn chairs, one with a copy of *In Style* magazine left on the seat, the other with clothes tossed carelessly over the arm and back and dropped on the floor beside it.

A movie set. The stage for a twisted drama with a final act yet to be played out.

The roar of the machines outside had ceased. I felt the silence like a presence that had just come through the door. The skin on my arms and the back of my neck prickled with awareness.

I moved to stand beside the wall next to the doorway into the first room, the Glock raised and ready.

I could hear, but not see the exterior door open. I waited.

Movement in the front room. The sound of shoes scuffing and thumping on the old linoleum. The rattle of the old paint cans knocking together. The smell of paint thinner.

I wondered, if I stepped through the doorway, who I would confront. Paris? Van Zandt? Trey Hughes?

I moved into the doorway and leveled my gun on Chad Seabright.

'You're going to lose your seat on the student council for this.'

He stared at me as paint thinner puddled on the floor around his shoes.

'I'd ask what you're doing here, Chad, but that seems obvious.'

'No,' he said, shaking his head, eyes wide. 'You don't understand. It's not what you think.'

'Really? I'm not watching you prepare to destroy evidence of a crime?'

'I didn't have anything to do with it!' he said. 'Erin called me from the hospital. She begged me to help her.'

'And you – a complete innocent – just dropped everything to commit a felony for her?'

'I love her,' he said earnestly. 'She screwed up. I don't want her to go to prison.'

'And what would she go to prison for, Chad?' I asked. 'She's supposed to be the victim in all this.'

'She is,' he insisted.

'But she told you to come here and burn the place? She told the detectives she didn't know where she'd been held. How is it you knew to come here?'

I could see the wheels spinning in his mind as he scrambled for an explanation.

'Why would Erin be in trouble, Chad?' I asked again. 'Detective Landry has the videotapes of her being beaten and raped.'

'That was her idea.'

'To get beaten? To be raped? That was Erin's idea?'

'No. Paris. It wasn't supposed to be real. That's what Erin said. It was supposed to be like a hoax. That's what Paris told her. To ruin Jade so she could take over his business. But everything got way out of hand. Paris turned on her. They almost killed her.'

'Who are "they"?'

He looked away and heaved a sigh, agitated. Sweat greased his forehead. 'I don't know. She only talked about Paris. And now she's scared Paris will try to take her down with her.'

'So you'll burn the crime scene and everyone calls it even. Is that it?'

His Adam's apple bobbed as he swallowed. 'I know how it looks.'

'It looks like you're in it up to your eyeballs, Junior,' I said. 'Up against the wall and spread 'em.'

'Please don't do this,' he said, blinking back tears. 'I don't want any trouble with the cops. I'm supposed to go to Brown next fall.'

'You should have thought of that before you agreed to commit arson.'

'I was only helping Erin,' he said again. 'She's not a bad person. Really, she isn't. She just – It's just that – She always gets a raw deal. And she wanted to get back at my father.'

'And you didn't?'

'I'll graduate soon. It won't matter what he thinks. Erin and I can be together then.'

'Up against the wall,' I said again.

'Can't you have a little sympathy?' he asked, crying now, taking a step toward the wall.

'I'm not the sympathetic sort.'

I moved farther into the room as Chad moved toward the wall that divided the spaces. A slow dance of unwilling partners trading places. I kept the gun on him. My gaze darted to the side as I stepped past the open door.

Paris Montgomery was coming up the steps.

As I turned my head, Chad turned and charged me, his face twisted with rage.

My gun went off as he hit my forearms and deflected my aim. I stumbled backward, his weight coming against me, paint cans and stacks of old newspapers tripping me. My breath went out of me as we hit the floor, the back of my head banging so hard I saw stars.

The Glock was still in my right hand, my finger jammed through the trigger guard. The gun was out of position, my trigger finger bent at an unnatural angle. I couldn't shoot, but brought the gun up and slapped the body of it as hard as I could against Chad Seabright's head. He grunted, and blood ran from a gash in his cheek as he tried to get a hand around my throat.

I swung and hit him again, the barrel of the Glock tearing across his right eye. The eyeball exploded, fluid and blood raining out of the collapsing tissue. Chad screamed and threw himself off me, hands over his face.

I rolled away from him, trying to get my legs under me, slipping through paint thinner, clawing at anything that might give me purchase.

'You bitch! You fucking bitch!' Chad screamed behind me.

Grabbing the leg of the metal desk, I pulled myself up. I glanced back to see Chad, one hand pressed against his ruined eye, the other swinging a paint can. The can caught me on the left jaw and snapped my head sideways.

I fell across the desktop, grabbed the edge with one hand, and dragged myself over as Chad struck at me with the empty can again and again.

Hitting the floor on the other side, I fumbled to pull my gun free of my broken finger. Adrenaline blocked the pain. I would feel it later – if I was lucky.

I expected Chad to come over the desk, but instead as I looked up I saw the translucent flash of orange and blue across the room as the paint thinner was ignited and the gases exploded upward.

Gripping the Glock, my left forefinger on the trigger, I pushed myself to my feet and fired as Chad went out the door and slammed it shut behind him.

The far side of the room was in flames, the fire licking hungrily up the cheap paneled wall to the ceiling, catching on the piles of paper on the floor. It burned toward me. It burned toward the second room. The trailer would be fully engulfed in a matter of minutes. And as far as I could see, there was no way out.

Landry could see the glow of the fire a mile away, though he hoped against hope – even as he stepped on the gas and went with lights and sirens – that the source of the blaze would be something else, somewhere else. But as he neared the address Elena had given him, he knew it wasn't. The county dispatcher was calling the code over the radio.

Landry pulled in the yard, jumped out of the car, and ran to the back of the property.

The walls and windows of a small house trailer were silhouetted against the backdrop of orange.

'Elena!' He screamed her name to be heard above the roar. 'Elena!'

Jesus God, if she was inside . . .

'Elena!'

He ran toward the trailer, but the heat pushed him back.

If she was inside, she was dead.

Coughing, I ran for the second room, flames chasing me, flames already shooting up the wall around the doorway. I could smell the paint thinner that soaked my shirt. One lick of a flame and I would be swallowed whole.

Another exit door was located in the far back corner of the second room. The smoke was so thick, I could barely see it. Stumbling over chairs, I ran for it, hit it running, turned the doorknob and shoved. Locked. I twisted the dead bolt and tried again. Locked from the outside. The door wouldn't give.

The fire rolled into the room like a tide on the flimsy ceiling.

Jamming the gun in the back of my jeans, I grabbed the video camera off the tripod, tossed the camera on the bed and swung the tripod like a baseball bat at the window where Erin Seabright had written the word HELP in the dust. Once. Twice. The glass fractured but stayed in the frame.

I slammed the end of the tripod against the glass, trying to knock the glass out, afraid that when I did the flames would rush to the fresh oxygen. It would char my skin and melt my lungs, and if I didn't die instantly, I would wish that I had.

I saw the flames coming and thought of hell.

Just when I'd thought I might redeem myself . . .

One last time I rammed the tripod against the glass.

'Elena!' Landry screamed.

Once more he tried to approach the trailer and was knocked flat as something inside the place exploded. Flame rolled out the broken windows in billowing clouds of orange. In the distance he could hear sirens coming. Too late.

Shaken, sick, he pushed himself to his feet and stood there, unable to do anything or think anything.

My first thought was that it was Chad standing in the yard, watching his handiwork, thrilled with the idea that he had killed me. Then he started toward me and called my name, and I knew it was Landry.

Clutching the video camera against me, I tried to run toward him, my legs like rubber, weak from effort and relief.

'Elena!'

He grabbed me by the shoulders and pulled me along with him, dragging me away from the burning trailer toward Paris Montgomery's patio.

'Jesus Christ,' he breathed, sitting me in a chair, going over me with his eyes, with his hands. His hands were trembling. 'I thought you were in there.'

'I was,' I said, coughing. 'Chad Seabright set the fire. He's in this with Paris and Erin. Did you get him? Did you get them?'

He shook his head. 'No one in the house but her dog.' The Jack Russell was at the patio doors bouncing up and down like a ball as it barked incessantly.

Sirens screamed at the front of the house. A deputy came running around the side of the garage. Landry went to meet him, holding up his shield. As I sat coughing the smoke out of my lungs, I watched him motion toward the house. The deputy nodded and drew his weapon.

'Are you hurt?' he asked me as he came back and crouched down in front of me again. He touched my cheek where the paint can had struck me. I couldn't feel it, didn't know if any damage had been done. I guessed not as Landry moved on, inspecting me.

'I broke my finger,' I said, holding up my right hand. He took the hand gently and looked at the finger. 'I've had worse.'

'You goddamn knothead,' he muttered. 'Why didn't you wait for me?'

'If I had waited for you, Chad would have burned the place –'

'Without you in it!' he said, standing. He paced a little circle in front of me. 'You never should have gone in there, Elena! You could have compromised evidence –'

'We would have ended up with nothing!' I shouted back, pushing to my feet.

'We?' he said, stepping into my space, trying to intimidate me.

I stood fast. 'It's my case. I brought you into it. That makes *we*. Don't even think of trying to shove me out again, Landry. I'm in this for Molly, and if it turns out her sister was a willing participant in this thing, I'm going to strangle Erin Seabright with my own two hands. Then you can put me in prison and I'll be out of your way for the next twenty-five years.'

'You were almost out of my way permanently!' he yelled, swinging an arm in the direction of the fire. 'You think that's what I want?'

'It's what everybody in the SO wants!'

'No!' he shouted. 'No! Me. Look at me. That's not what I want.'

We were toe to toe. I glared up into his face. He stared at me, his expression slowly, slowly softening.

'No,' he whispered. 'No, Elena. I don't want you out of my life.'

For one rare moment, I didn't know what to say.

'You scared the hell out of me,' he said softly.

Likewise, I thought, only I meant in the present tense. Instead, I went back to the other topic. 'You said you'd share. My case first.'

Landry nodded. 'Yes . . . Yes, I did.'

Trucks from the Loxahatchee fire department arrived, the lead truck barreling into the backyard. I watched the firemen leap to action as impassively as if they were on a movie screen, then looked down at my hands. I still held the video camera. I held it out to Landry.

'I saved this. You'll get fingerprints.'

'This was where they held her?' he asked, looking back at the trailer.

'Chad said Erin was in on it at first, but that Paris turned against her. But if Paris turned against her, why isn't she dead?'

'I guess we'll have to ask Paris that question,' he said. 'And Erin. Do you know what Paris is driving?'

'A dark green Infiniti. Chad has a black Toyota pickup. And he's missing an eye. He might turn up at a hospital.'

Landry arched a brow. 'Missing an eye? You gouged out his eye?'

I shrugged and looked away, the horrible image still so strong in my mind it turned my stomach. 'A girl's gotta do what a girl's gotta do.'

He rubbed a hand over his mouth and shook his head. 'You're some kind of tough, Estes.'

I'm sure I didn't look tough in that moment. The weight of the emerging truth of the case was weighing down on me. The adrenaline rush of the near-death experience had passed.

'Come here,' Landry said.

I looked up at him and he touched my face with his hand – the right side, the side that I could feel. I felt it all the way to the heart of me.

'I'm glad you didn't die,' he murmured. I had the feeling he wasn't talking about now, about the trailer.

'Me, too,' I said, leaning my head against his shoulder. 'Me, too.'

52

Landry put an APB out for Paris Montgomery and Chad Seabright. All county and state units on the road would be on the lookout for the money-green Infiniti and Chad's Toyota pickup. Additional alerts had gone to the Coast Guard, and to the West Palm Beach and Fort Lauderdale airports, as well as to all small airports in the vicinity.

One of the reasons south Florida has always been a conduit for drugs is the fact that there are many ways in and out, and a quick exit can take you to another country in short order. Paris Montgomery knew a lot of people in the horse business, a lot of very wealthy people, people who owned planes and boats.

And she knew one who was shipping horses to Europe that very night: Tomas Van Zandt.

'Has he been located?' I asked Landry. We sat in his car in the front yard of Paris Montgomery's rented house.

'No. Armedgian's guys scored the fuckup of the century there.'

I told him about the horses flying to Europe. 'My bet is they both try getting out of the country tonight.'

'We've alerted the airlines,' Landry said.

'You don't understand. Flying cargo is a whole different ball game. If you ever want a good scare thinking about terrorism, fly transatlantic with a bunch of horses sometime.'

'Great. Weiss and the feds can go sit on the cargo terminal.'

The Loxahatchee fire chief approached the car as Landry reached for his cell phone. He was a tall man with a heavy mustache. Out from under the gear, I imagined he would be slender as a post.

'Treat it as a crime scene, chief,' Landry said out the window.

'Right. Arson.'

'That too. Have you located the owner of the property?'

'No, sir. The owner is out of the country. I've contacted the property management company. They'll get in touch with the owner.'

'Which property management company?' I asked.

The chief leaned down to look across at me. 'Gryphon Property Management. Wellington.'

I looked at Landry as his cell phone rang. 'Time to have another chat with Bruce. Is he still in custody?'

'No. They cut him loose. Landry,' he said into the phone. The muscles in his face tightened and his brows pulled low. 'What the hell do you mean, gone? Where was the fucking guard?'

Erin, I thought.

'When?' he demanded. 'Well, that's just fucking fantastic. Tell that deputy when he gets his head out of his ass, I'm gonna rip it off his shoulders and shout down the hole!'

He snapped the phone shut and looked at me. 'Erin's gone. Someone set a fire in a trash can on the other side of the nurses' station and the deputy at her door left his post. When he came back, she was gone.'

'She's with Chad.'

'And they're running.' Landry started the car. 'I'll drop you at the emergency room. I've got to roll.'

'Leave me at my car,' I said. 'I'll drive myself.'

'Elena . . .'

'It's a finger, Landry. I'm not going to die of it.'

He heaved a sigh and closed his mouth.

It was a slow night in the ER. My finger was X-rayed and found to be dislocated rather than broken. The doctor shot my hand full of lidocaine and manipulated the finger back into a straight line. I refused the cumbersome splint in favor of taping the finger to its neighbor. He handed me a prescription for painkillers. I gave it back.

On my way out I stopped at the desk and asked if anyone had come in with a severe eye injury. The clerk told me no.

I checked my watch as I walked out of the hospital. Five hours until Van Zandt's plane left for Kennedy Airport, then on to Brussels.

Every uniform in Palm Beach County was looking for him, looking for Paris, looking for Chad and Erin. Meanwhile, Don Jade was out on bail, and Trey Hughes had written the check.

It all revolved around Trey Hughes – the land deal, Stellar, Erin – and to my knowledge, no one was looking for him. I went in search. If he was at the center of it all, maybe he held the key.

Last I'd known, Trey had a house in the Polo Club, a gated community near the show grounds that caters to horse people with money. I headed in that direction, taking the back streets that would swing me past Fairfields on the way.

The gate stood open at Lucky Dog Farm. I could make out the shape of a car near the construction boss's trailer. I turned in and my headlights washed over the back of Trey's classic Porsche. I killed the engine and got out, the Glock in my left hand.

The only light I could see was the big security light on the pole, but somewhere nearby Jimmy Buffett was singing a song about the joys of irresponsibility.

I followed the sound, walking the length of the huge, dark stables, and around the end. A second-story balcony ran the length of the building, overlooking the jumping field. Candles and lanterns illuminated the scene. I could see Trey dancing, the end of his omnipresent cigarette a glowing orange dot in the dark.

'Come on up, honey!' he called. 'I thought you'd never get here! I started the party without you.'

I climbed the stairs, keeping my eyes on him. He was high. On what, I couldn't know. Cocaine had been his thing in the eighties. It was making a comeback when I'd checked out of the Narcotics division. Nostalgia among the tragically hip.

'What are we celebrating, Trey?' I asked as I stepped onto the balcony.

'My illustrious and stellar life,' he said, still dancing. He held a bottle of tequila in one hand. His aloha shirt hung open over a pair of khaki pants. He was barefoot.

'Stellar,' he said, and started to laugh. 'What a bad joke! Shocking!'

The song ended and he fell back against the railing and took a long pull on the bottle.

'Were you expecting me?' I asked.

'No, actually I was expecting someone else. But you know, it doesn't really matter, does it?'

'I don't know, Trey. I think it might – depending on your reasons. You were expecting Paris?'

He rubbed his face, tiny embers of cigarette ash floating around his head like fireflies. 'That's right. You're the private eye, now. The gumshoe. The private dick – or is that politically incorrect? It really should be private pussy, shouldn't it?'

'I don't think Paris will be here tonight, Trey. She's been unavoidably detained.'

'Yeah? What's she up to?'

'Running from the law,' I said. 'She and Chad Seabright tried to kill me today.'

He squinted at me, waiting for the punch line. 'Honey, what have you been smoking?'

'Come on, Trey. You've been to her place a hundred times. I know about your affair. Don't try to tell me you don't know anything about the trailer, about Erin.'

'Erin? Somebody kidnapped her. The whole fucking world's going to hell on a sled.'

I shook my head. 'It was all a play. Didn't you know? A play for you.'

I could see his face in the candlelight. He was trying to find his way through the fog in his brain. Either he didn't know what I was talking about, or he wanted to convince himself he didn't know.

'A three-act play,' I said. 'Deceit, double-crosses, sex, murder. Shakespeare would have been proud. I don't know the whole script yet, but it begins with a quest for the holy land – Lucky Dog Farm – and its king – you.'

The last of his puzzled smile faded away.

'Here's what I know so far: The story opens with a girl named Paris who wants very much to be queen. So much so that she plots to ruin the one person standing between her and the fulfillment of her dreams: Don Jade.

'It shouldn't be that hard to do, she thinks, because he's already got a bad reputation. People are ready to believe the worst about him. They'll believe he would kill a jumper who wouldn't bring top dollar. Insurance fraud? He's done it before and gotten away with it.

'His groom disappears. He's the last person to see her. Turns out she's been kidnapped. And when she gets away, who does she name as one of her abductors? Don Jade.

'Surely, Paris thinks, now Trey will dump him. Jade will be in prison soon, at any rate. And she'll become queen of Lucky Dog Farm.'

'That's not a very funny story,' Trey said. He put his cigarette out on the cast stone railing and flicked the butt out into the night.

'No. It isn't. And it's not going to have a happy ending either,' I said. 'Did you think that it would?'

'You know me, Ellie. I try not to think. I'm just a Dixie cup on the sea of life.'

He sniffed and rubbed his face again. A round patio table squatted like a mushroom in front of an open set of French doors that led into a dark room. A dozen candles burning on the table spilled their light over a glass tray of cocaine that had been cut into lines. Near the tray lay a .32 caliber Beretta pistol.

'What's the gun for, Trey?' I asked, reassured by the weight of my own weapon – even if it was in the wrong hand.

'Rats,' he said, digging another cigarette out of his pocket. He flicked a lighter and took a drag, exhaling into the night sky. 'Maybe a little Russian roulette later.'

'That'll be a very short game,' I said. 'That's an automatic weapon.'

He smiled and shrugged. 'The story of my life: stuck in a rigged game.'

'Yeah, you've got it hard. How much did you inherit when Sallie died? Eighty million? A hundred?'

'With a string attached to every one,' he said.

'They don't seem to be holding you back from spending.'

'No.'

He turned and looked out at the property, nothing to see but a patchwork in varying shades of black.

'Why did you bail Jade out, Trey? Why did you get him Shapiro?' I asked, moving to stand down the railing from him.

He flashed a smile. 'Because your father was unavailable.'

'You've never been more loyal than a tomcat your whole life. Why stick by Don Jade?'

'He made me what I am today,' he said with another crooked smile.

'He killed Sallie, didn't he?' I said. 'You were with Michael Berne's wife, fucking your alibi, and Jade was at the house, hiding in the shadows . . . And now you can't walk away.'

'Why would I walk away from all this?' he asked, spreading his arms wide. The cigarette bounced on his lip. 'I'm king of the world!'

'No, Trey,' I said. 'You were right the first time. You're the sad clown. You had it all. And you're going to end up with nothing.'

'You know a little something about that, don't you, Ellie?' he said.

'I know all about it. But I'm climbing out of that hole, Trey, and you're going to end up buried in it.'

I pulled my phone off the pocket of my jeans and tried to dial Landry's number, my right hand awkward, still half-numb and under the numbness a hot, throbbing pain waiting to come fully to life. Landry needed to know Trey had been expecting Paris. She had probably thought to come to him for a car the cops wouldn't be on the lookout for. Perhaps she thought to come to him for money to live on in Europe. Or perhaps she would try to convince Trey to go with her. Wealthy fugitives on the lam in Europe's glamour capitals.

I took a couple of steps back from Trey, switching hands with phone and gun, my eyes on him, the pathetic playboy, Peter Pan corrupted utterly by time and self-indulgence.

Landry's line was ringing as Paris Montgomery came out of the darkness beyond the open French doors. Without hesitation, she scooped the Beretta off the patio table and pointed it right at my face.

53

'We manage a lot of properties, Detective,' Bruce Seabright said. 'I have nothing to do with most of them.'

'I only care about what you have to do with this one,' Landry said.

They stood in Seabright's home office. Seabright turned around in a circle and heaved a sigh up at the ceiling. 'I don't have anything to do with it!'

'We both know that's not true.'

'I don't know where that videotape came from,' he said. 'Someone planted it.'

'Yeah, right. You stick with that story. I'm asking you about the property in Loxahatchee.'

'I have an attorney,' Seabright said. 'Talk to him.'

'This is an unrelated line of questioning.'

'And I told you, I don't have anything to do with the rental property.'

'You expect me to believe that someone involved in Erin's kidnapping just happened to rent that property from your company? The same way these people you sent Erin to for a job just happened to turn out to be killers and rapists and Christ knows what all.'

'I don't care what you believe,' Seabright said, reaching for his phone. 'I had nothing to do with any of this, nor did my son. Now get out of my office or I'm filing harassment charges.'

'File it up your ass, Seabright,' Landry said. 'You and your rotten kid are both going to jail. I'll see to it personally.'

Landry left the office, thinking he just wanted to drive the lot of these people out to Lion Country Safari and dump them inside the pen with the big cats.

Krystal Seabright was standing in the hall a few feet from the office door. For once, she didn't look stoned, but stricken. She held a hand out to stop him from passing her, her mouth opening to form words that didn't come out.

'Can I help you, Mrs Seabright?'

'I did it,' she said.

'I'm sorry?'

'That woman came to me, to my office. I rented her that property. I remember her name. Paris. I've always wanted to visit Paris.'

She didn't know quite how she should be reacting to the news, Landry thought. With guilt? With shock? With outrage?

'How did she happen to come to you?' he asked.

'She told me a friend sent her.' Tears shone in her eyes. She shook her head and looked toward her husband's office. 'Was it him? Do you think it was him?'

'I don't know, Mrs Seabright,' Landry confessed. 'I guess you have to ask him.'

'I guess I do,' she murmured, staring at the office door. 'I have to do something.'

Landry left her there in the hall, glad he was just a cop. He could walk away from this mess when it was over. Krystal Seabright wouldn't be so lucky.

54

I stared at the barrel of the gun in Paris Montgomery's hands. Jimmy Buffett was still singing in the background.

'Put down the phone and the gun,' Paris said to me.

I now held the Glock in my weak and damaged right hand. I could have tried to raise it up and call her bluff, but I couldn't have done it convincingly. I couldn't have pulled the trigger if I needed to. I weighed my options as Landry's voice-mail message came on the line.

Paris came toward me. She was angry and she was afraid. Her neat little scheme was fraying at the edges like a cheap rag.

'It seemed a simple plan, didn't it, Paris?' I said. 'You got Erin to help you frame Jade. She and Chad got to ruin Bruce Seabright in the process. It would have worked like a charm if Molly Seabright hadn't come to me for help.'

'Put down the phone and the gun,' she ordered again.

I clipped the phone onto my jeans and glanced at Trey, who stood flat-footed and expressionless.

'Why did you let Van Zandt in on it?' I asked. 'Or did he force his way in?'

'I don't know what you're talking about.'

'Then why are you pointing a gun in my face, Paris?'

She glanced at Trey. 'This is all Don's doing,' she said. 'He killed Stellar. He kidnapped Erin. He killed Jill. It's all Don, Trey. You have to believe me.'

'Why?' he asked. 'Because it's part of your plan?'

'Because I love you!' she said emphatically, though her eyes were on me, sighting down the barrel of a gun. 'Erin saw Don kill Stellar. Don did horrible things to her, to punish her. And he killed Jill.'

'No, he didn't, honey,' Trey said wearily. 'I know he didn't.'

'What are you saying?'

'You had night check the night Jill was killed. You left my bed to go do it. Just like you did the night before, when Berne's horses were turned loose.'

'You're confused, Trey,' Paris said, an edge in her voice.

'Generally, yes. Life's easier that way. But not about this.'

She took another step toward me, her patience wearing thin. 'Put the fucking gun down!'

I heaved a sigh and slowly crouched down as if to set the gun on the floor, then ducked and rolled sideways.

Paris fired twice, one of the bullets hitting the floor near me and spitting up shards of travertine marble.

I switched my gun to my left hand, trying to steady it with my right, came to my feet, and rushed her before she could adjust her position to fire at me a third time.

'Drop it, Paris! Drop it! Drop it!'

She turned and bolted for the stairs at the far end of the balcony. I ran after her, pulling up short as she turned the corner and fired off a shot behind her.

Cautiously, I peered around the corner, looking down on an empty stairwell faintly illuminated by the glow of the security light. She could have been waiting beyond the landing, tucked against the wall, waiting for me to charge after her. I could see myself turning the corner on the landing and the bullet hitting me square in the chest, my blood the only color in a black-and-white scene.

I went instead to the end of the balcony and looked down. She was gone. I ran down the stairs. The engine of Trey's Porsche roared to life as I hit the ground. The headlights blinded me as the car leapt toward me.

I brought my gun up and put a round through the windshield, then dove to the side.

Paris tried to swing the Porsche around, tires spinning, dirt and gravel spraying out behind it. The car skidded sideways and slammed violently against the side of the concrete building, setting off the horn and alarm system.

Paris shoved the door open, fell out of the vehicle, got up and started to run down the driveway, a hand pressed to her left shoulder. She stumbled and fell, got up and ran another few steps, then stumbled and fell again. She lay sobbing on the ground within sight of the sign proudly announcing construction of Lucky Dog Farm.

'No, no, no, no, no!' she whimpered over and over as I reached her. Blood ran between her fingers from the bullet wound in her shoulder.

'The game is over, Paris,' I said, looking down at her. 'You're out of luck, bitch.'

55

Molly sat curled up in a little knot on her bed, knees pulled up beneath her chin. She was trembling and trying hard not to cry.

She listened to the fight going on below her, their voices coming up through her floor. Bruce shouting. Things crashing. Hateful and angry, her mother shrieking like something from a nightmare, like nothing Molly had ever heard. An eerie, high-pitched tone that rose and fell like a siren. She sounded insane. Bruce called her insane more than once.

Molly feared he might be right. That maybe the tight band that had held Krystal together all this time had just broken, and everything she had held repressed inside her had come bursting out.

As the shrieking rose again, Molly jumped off the bed, locked her door, and struggled to shove her nightstand in front of it. She grabbed the phone Elena had given her, scrambled back to her spot against the headboard, and dialed Elena's cell phone.

She listened to the phone ring unanswered. Tears spilled down her cheeks.

Below her the noise abruptly stopped and a strange, horrible silence took its place. Molly strained her ears for any kind of sound, but the silence pressed in on her until she wondered if she'd gone deaf.

Then came a small, soft voice drifting up through the vent as if from another dimension. 'I only ever wanted a nice life . . . I only ever wanted a nice life . . .'

56

Landry arrived on the heels of the ambulance that had been called for Paris. My shot through the windshield had clipped her shoulder. She had lost some blood, but she would live to see another day, and another and another – all of them from a prison cell, I hoped.

Landry got out of his car and came directly to me, holding a finger up at the deputy who had secured the scene, warding him off for the moment. Deputy Saunders, my escort from the night Michael Berne's horses had been turned loose, stood watching me, not willing to accept my word for my innocence.

Landry dismissed him, his focus on me.

'Are you all right?'

I gave him the half-smile. 'You must be tired of asking me that. I'm fine.'

'You've got more lives than a cat,' he muttered.

I filled him in on what had happened, what had been said, my take on it all.

'What made you come here in the first place?' he asked.

'I don't know. I thought Paris might try to get to Trey. It all revolved around him – around Trey, around his money, around this place.'

I looked back at the barn, the massive walls washed in the colored lights from the ambulance and county radio cars. Trey was being escorted in handcuffs to one of the cruisers.

'I believe Trey and Jade cooked up a scheme to kill Sallie Hughes so Trey could inherit and build this place. I confronted Trey about it. He didn't even bother to deny it. That's why he's stayed loyal to Jade. He didn't have a choice. Paris wanted Jade out of the way so she could have it all. And in the end, none of them will end up with anything,' I said. 'All the deceit, all the scheming, all the pain they caused – it's all for nothing. Everybody loses.'

'Yeah,' Landry said as the ambulance rolled out with a cruiser behind it. 'Cases like this one make me wish I'd listened to my old man. He wanted me to be a civil engineer.'

'What did he do for a living?' I asked.

His mouth quirked. 'He was a cop. What else? Thirty years on the Baton Rouge PD.'

'No sign of Van Zandt yet?' I asked as we walked back toward our cars.

'Not yet. The guy at the cargo hangar told us Van Zandt's horses arrived by commercial shipper a while ago, but they haven't heard from Van Zandt all day. You think he was in it with Paris?'

'I still believe he killed Jill. But Trey said Paris got out of his bed to go check the horses that night. Jill's body was left to be found, and whoever put it there knew everyone would connect it to Jade. That furthers Paris's plan.'

'We know Van Zandt was at The Players that night,' Landry said. 'He was all over the girl. Say he followed her out, thinking to pick up the pieces after Jade had broken her heart. Maybe she said no and he didn't want to hear it. She ends up dead.'

'Paris comes on the scene and convinces Van Zandt to dump the body in the manure pit,' I speculated. 'Was he involved in the rest of it? I don't know. Chad tried to tell me someone had actually raped Erin, that Paris had let things get out of hand. Maybe Van Zandt came into it and took over.'

'If that's what happened, I'm sure she'll spill it,' Landry said. 'She's in custody, he's not. Nothing ruins a partnership faster than threat of jail time. Good work, Estes.'

'Just doing my civic duty.'

'You should still have a badge.'

I looked away. 'Oh, well, don't you say the sweetest things? I wouldn't express that opinion around the SO, if I were you.'

'Fuck 'em. It's true.'

I felt embarrassed that his compliment meant so much to me.

'Any news of Chad and Erin?' I asked as my phone rang.

Landry shook his head.

'Estes,' I said into the phone.

'Elena?'

The tremulous sound of her voice sent fear through me like shards of glass. 'Molly? Molly, what's wrong?'

I was already hustling toward Landry's car. I could see the concern on his face as he kept pace with me.

'Elena, you have to come. Please come!'

'I'm on my way! What's happening?'

In the background I could hear pounding, like someone banging on a door.

'Molly?'

And then a strange and terrible keening sound that ended with her name.

'Hurry!' Molly said.

The last thing I heard before the line went dead was an eerie voice: 'I only ever wanted a nice life ... I only ever wanted a nice life ...'

57

'Okay,' Landry said. 'Here's how we're playing it. I'm going in first with the uniforms.'

I let him talk, not caring what he said, not caring what his plan was. All I could think of was Molly.

If someone had harmed that child . . .

I thought of Chad and Erin running at large. If they had come back to the house –

'Elena, did you hear me?'

I didn't answer him.

He turned in at the driveway and ran the car onto the lawn. A radio car turned in behind us. I was out of the car before it was stopped.

'Dammit, Estes!'

The front door was open. I went through it without a care to what danger might be on the other side.

'Molly!'

Landry was right behind me. 'Seabright? It's Landry.'

'Molly!'

I took the stairs two at a time.

If someone has harmed that child . . .

Landry went toward Seabright's home office. The house was eerily silent, except for a small, faint sound coming from beyond the office doors.

'Seabright?'

Landry moved along the wall, gun drawn. In his peripheral vision, he saw Elena bolt up the steps.

'Seabright?' he called out again.

The sound was growing more distinct. Singing, he thought. He sidled along the door, stretching his arm as long as he could to reach the doorknob.

Singing. No, more like chanting. 'All I ever wanted was a nice life.'

'Molly!'

I had no idea which of the closed doors belonged to her. I stood to the side and opened the first one I came to. Chad's room.

If someone has harmed that child . . .

I shoved open another door. Another unoccupied bedroom.

'Molly!'

If someone has harmed that child . . .

The third door opened an inch and hit something. I shoved at it.

'Molly!'

If someone has harmed that child . . .

The doors to the study fell open, revealing a gruesome tableau. Krystal Seabright stood behind her husband's desk, covered in blood. Blood streaked her bleached hair, her face, the pretty pink dress she had been wearing when Landry had seen her earlier. Bruce Seabright was slumped over his otherwise immaculate desk, a butcher's knife sticking out of one of perhaps fifty stab wounds in his back, neck, and head.

'Jesus God,' Landry murmured.

Krystal looked at him, her eyes glassy and wide.

'I only ever wanted a nice life. He ruined it. He ruined everything.'

If someone has harmed that child . . .

I pulled back, took a deep breath, and rammed the door with my shoulder as hard as I could.

'Molly!'

The block on the other side of the door gave a few inches, enough for me to wedge into the opening and shove it a few inches more. Someone had piled half the furniture in the room as a blockade.

'Elena!'

Molly ran into me full force. I fell to my knees and caught her in my arms and held her as tightly as I had ever held anyone in all my life. I put my arms around Molly Seabright and held her while she cried, and held her for a long time after that.

For her . . . and for myself.

58

All I could say to Molly as I hugged her tight was that it was over. *It's over. It's over. It's over.* But that was a lie of such grand proportions, all lies that had come before it were dwarfed in comparison. Nothing was over for Molly, except having a family.

Krystal, fragile in the best of times, had shattered under the pressure. She blamed her husband for what she believed had happened to Erin. The kidnapping, the rape. Landry told me she had suspected Bruce of sending Paris Montgomery to her to rent the Loxahatchee house where the whole drama had been staged.

She had reached her limit. In the end, one might have tried to put a nobler face on it and said Krystal had defended her daughter, had taken revenge for her. Sadly, I didn't believe that at all. I believed killing Bruce had been punishment not for ruining her daughter, but for ruining her fairy tale.

I only ever wanted a nice life.

I wondered whether Krystal would have stayed with Bruce if she had found out that what they had all been put through had been orchestrated at least in part by her daughter. I suspected she would have put the blame squarely on Erin and no one else. She would have found a way to excuse Bruce's sins and keep her pretty life intact.

The human mind has an amazing capacity for rationalization.

Landry sent Krystal to the Sheriff's Office in a cruiser, then drove Molly and me to Sean's farm. Not a word was said about calling Child Protective Services, which was standard operating procedure in a case like Molly's.

We rode in silence most of the way, drained of our emotions and our energies, weighed down by the magnitude of what had gone on. The only sound in the car was the crackle of Landry's radio. An old familiar noise for me. For a moment I felt as nostalgic for it as I ever had for any song from my adolescence.

As we turned in at the Avadonis gate, Landry used his cell phone to call Weiss at the airport. There was still no sign of Van Zandt, and the plane was ready to taxi onto the runway.

Exhausted, Molly had fallen asleep leaning against me in the backseat.

Landry scooped her out and carried her into the guest house. I led the way to the second small bedroom, thinking what an odd family unit we made.

'Poor kid,' he said as he and I walked back outside onto the little patio. 'She'll grow up in a hurry.'

'She's already done that,' I said, sitting down sideways on a delicate iron chaise with a thick cushion. 'That one was a child for a minute and a half. Do you have kids?'

'Me? No.' Landry sat beside me. 'You?'

'Always seemed like a bad idea to me. I've watched too many people screw it up. I know how badly that hurts.'

I knew he was watching me, trying to read into me, into my words. I looked up at the stars and marveled at the vulnerability I had just shown him.

'Molly's great, though,' I said. 'Figures. She raised herself watching the Discovery Channel and A&E.'

'I was married once,' Landry offered. 'And I lived with a woman for a while. It didn't work out. You know: the job, the hours, I'm difficult. Blah, blah, blah.'

'I never tried. Go straight to "I'm difficult. Blah, blah, blah." '

He smiled wearily and produced a cigarette and a lighter from his pocket.

'Car pack?' I asked.

'Gotta get that corpse taste out.'

'I used to drink,' I confessed. 'To cleanse the palate.'

'But you quit?'

'I gave up everything that could dull pain.'

'Why?'

'Because I believed I deserved to hurt. Punishment. Penance. Purgatory. Call it what you like.'

'Stupid,' Landry proclaimed. 'You're not God, Estes.'

'A welcome relief to all true believers, I'm sure. Maybe I thought I should beat Him to the punch.'

'You made a mistake,' he said. 'I don't believe the Pope is infallible either.'

'Heretic.'

'I'm just saying, you've got too much good in you to let one bad mistake shut it all down.'

The half-smile tugged at the corner of my mouth. 'I know,' I said. 'I know that now. Thanks to Molly.'

Landry glanced back over his shoulder at the house. 'What are you going to tell her about Erin?'

'The truth,' I said on a sigh. 'She won't stand for anything less.'

The prospect drove me to my feet. As exhausted as I was, still I was restless, frustrated at the injustices of Molly Seabright's life and the inadequacy of my people skills. Crossing my arms against the damp night air, I walked to the edge of the patio.

'On the first day of this, I remember thinking Molly was about to get a lesson in life. That she would learn the way everyone learns that she can't count on anyone but herself in this world: by being let down by someone she loved and trusted. I wish now I could change that for her.'

Landry came to stand beside me. 'You can,' he said. 'You have. She trusts you, Elena. You haven't let her down. You won't.'

I wished I could have been that certain of myself.

His pager went off. He checked the number, pulled his phone off his belt, and returned the call.

'Landry.'

I watched his face, sensed his tension.

When he ended the call he turned to me and said, 'Erin and Chad were picked up on Alligator Alley, halfway to Venice. She's claiming Chad abducted her.'

59

'You're eighteen,' Landry said. 'In the eyes of the law, you're an adult. You made bad choices that have big consequences, and now you're going to pay. The question is, are you going to take the big fall, or are you going to try to make life easier for all of us?'

Chad Seabright stared at the wall. A heavy gauze patch covered the socket where his left eye had been. 'I can't believe any of this is happening,' he muttered.

A state trooper had spotted Chad's pickup speeding on the highway known as Alligator Alley, the road that connected Florida's east coast with the Gulf Coast. A chase had ensued. A roadblock had eventually stopped them. The pair had been returned to the gracious accommodations of the Palm Beach County justice system, where both of them had been seen and treated in the infirmary.

Now they sat in back-to-back interview rooms, each wondering what story the other was telling.

Had Bruce Seabright survived, Landry did not doubt that Chad would have had a lawyer the caliber of Bert Shapiro sitting at his elbow. But Bruce Seabright was dead, and Chad had taken the first public defender out of the pool.

Assistant State's Attorney Roca tapped her pen on the table impatiently. 'You'd better start talking, Chad. Your girlfriend has been telling us quite a tale in the other room. How you kidnapped her to extort money from your father. We have the videotape of you beating her.'

'I think I should see that tape,' the public defender said.

Roca looked at him. 'It's quite convincing. She'll be a very sympathetic witness.'

'That's a lie,' Chad said, sulking, petulant, scared. 'Erin wouldn't do that to me.'

'Wouldn't do what?' Landry asked. 'Tell us how you grabbed her out of the hospital while the guard was trying to put out the fire you set?'

Chad shook his head emphatically.

'You don't think Erin would tell us how you raped her and kept her doped up on ketamine?' Roca said.

The public defender sat there like a toad, his mouth opening and closing, no words coming out.

Landry sighed and stood up. 'You know, I've just about had it with this,' he said to Roca. 'This little shit wants to take the fall. Fine. Let him rot. His father was an asshole. He's an asshole. Get him out of the gene pool. Go make a deal with the girl. You know a jury will get out the hankies for her.'

Roca pretended to consider, then looked to the PD. 'Talk to your client. The charges are going to be a potpourri of felonies: kidnapping, rape, attempted murder, arson —'

'I never raped anybody,' Chad said. 'I only went to that trailer yesterday to help Erin.'

'To destroy evidence for her because she was the mastermind of the whole plot?' Roca said.

Chad closed his eye and tipped his head back. 'I *told* you: Erin told me she was in it to start, but Paris turned on her. I didn't have anything to do with it! None of this is my fault. I was just trying to help Erin. Why should I be punished for that?'

Landry leaned across the table, looming over him. 'People are dead, Junior. You tried to kill a friend of mine. You're going away.'

Chad put his head in his hands and started to cry. 'It wasn't my fault!'

'And what about the tape we took out of your father's home office, Chad? The tape showing the alleged rape. The tape that was conveniently left on a bookshelf. How did it get there?'

'I don't know!'

'I do,' Landry said. 'You put it there.'

'I didn't! I didn't have anything to do with it!'

Landry sighed in disgust. 'Well, you know what, Chad? I know for a fact that you did. You can either take responsibility and do yourself a favor here, or you can dig that hole deeper with every lie that comes out of your mouth.'

He went to the one-way mirror in the wall, raised the blinds, and flicked a switch on the intercom.

Roca stood up. 'Think about it, gentlemen. The best deal goes first. He who hesitates loses.'

'Why would Chad take you from the hospital, Erin?' Landry asked.

'He must have been the other one,' the girl said in a voice as weak as a kitten's. She kept her eyes downcast, as if she were afraid or ashamed. Tears fell like tiny crystal beads down her cheeks. 'He must have been the other kidnapper. That must be why he never talked. He knew I would know it was him.'

'And so he walked into your hospital room in broad daylight, and kidnapped you a second time so you couldn't tell anyone how you couldn't identify him in the first place?' Landry said.

She put a trembling hand over her mouth and cried. Her public defender, a plump motherly woman named Maria Onjo, patted her on the shoulder.

Landry watched impassively. 'Chad tells us you and he are in love. That you went with him willingly.'

Erin's jaw dropped. 'No! That's not true! I – We – had a relationship for a while. Before I moved out of the house.' She shook her head at her own stupidity. 'We only did it to make Bruce crazy. He couldn't stand the idea of his perfect boy involved with me,' she said bitterly. 'Chad was furious when I broke it off with him. He told me. He told me he wouldn't let me go.'

Maria Onjo offered her a box of tissues.

'Erin,' Roca said. 'Chad claims you were in on the kidnapping, not him. That the whole thing was a play to discredit Don Jade, and to embarrass and extort money from your stepfather, and that things got out of hand.'

'Out of hand?' Erin said, incredulous and angry. 'They raped me!'

'And you didn't notice that one of them was Chad?' Landry said. 'The guy you'd been involved with, slept with.'

'They kept me drugged! I told you that. Why won't you believe me?'

'It might have something to do with the fact that the doctor who examined you the night you came in couldn't conclusively say you'd been raped.'

'What? But – but – You saw the tape.'

'Oh, I saw it,' Landry said. 'It was horrible, brutal, vicious. And if it was real, you should have had massive bruising and tearing in your vagina. You didn't.'

Her expression was that of someone trapped in a nightmare. 'I can't believe this is happening to me,' she murmured to herself. 'They beat me. They raped me. Look at me!'

She shoved her sleeves up to show the red welts the whip had left.

'Yeah,' Landry said. 'That's very convincing. So, you're telling us Don Jade and Chad were partners in your kidnapping, along with Paris Montgomery. How does Chad know Don?'

'I don't know.'

'And why would he be partners with the man who stole you away from him?' Landry asked. 'I don't get that.'

He could see her frustration level rising. Her breathing was becoming shallow and rapid.

The PD gave Landry a glare. 'You can't expect Erin to make your entire case for you, Detective. She can't know the minds of the people involved in this.'

'I don't know about that, Ms Onjo. Erin was intimate with Chad, worked for Don Jade, claimed to be in love with him. Seems to me if anyone could know the answer to these questions, it would be Erin.'

Onjo patted the girl on the back. 'Erin, you don't have to do this at all –'

'I haven't done anything wrong!' Erin said to her. 'I don't have anything to hide. It wasn't my fault!'

Landry looked at Roca and rolled his eyes. 'So how did Chad hook up with Jade, Erin? As far as I can see, the only thing Don Jade and Chad Seabright have in common is knowing you. I can't picture them being friends.'

'Ask them!' she snapped. 'Maybe they fell for each other. I wouldn't know.'

'And they were both in on it with Paris Montgomery, right? They held you in a trailer in her backyard.'

Erin put her face in her hands. 'I don't know!'

'Erin is the victim in this,' Onjo said. 'She's the last person who should be sitting in jail.'

'That's not what Chad is saying,' Roca said. 'That's not what Paris is saying. They're both saying the kidnapping was Erin's idea. Paris came up with the plot to kill the horse and implicate Jade. Erin pushed her to fake the kidnapping to extort money from her stepfather and drive a wedge between Seabright and her mother, as well as to implicate Jade in a crime that would ruin his career.'

'And you know what?' Landry said. 'That story makes a lot more sense to me than Chad and Jade as sociopathic secret bisexual lovers.'

'This is a nightmare!' Erin sobbed. 'They *raped* me!'

Landry sighed, got up, stretched his shoulders, rubbed his face. 'I'm just having a hard time with that, Erin.'

Onjo pushed her chair back and stood up. She was no taller standing than sitting. 'This is barbaric, and it's over.' She called to the guard outside the door.

'You're not going to stay for the movie?' Landry asked, gesturing toward the television and VCR on a metal cart in a corner of the room.

Onjo scowled at him. 'What are you talking about? What movie?'

'They made videos,' Erin said. 'They made me do things. It was horrible.'

'I don't think they made this one for public consumption,' Roca said. 'You may want to reconsider your strategy, Erin. I tend to give the best deal to the person telling me the fewest lies.'

Landry pushed the play button on the VCR.

'You're a very talented actress, Ms Seabright,' he said. 'If you hadn't turned to a life of crime, you might have made it all the way to triple-X porn.'

The tape was a copy of the one that had been in the video camera Elena had saved from the trailer. Behind the scenes of the alleged kidnapping. Outtakes. The actors rehearsing.

The image that filled the television screen was of Erin posing suggestively on the bed, smiling seductively at the camera. The same bed she had been chained to in the videos that had been sent to Bruce Seabright. The same bed she had huddled into in the video that showed her taking a beating so brutal, even hardened cops had been shocked to see it.

Maria Onjo watched the tape, the color in her face draining away with her defense.

Erin looked from her attorney to Landry. 'They made me do that. I had to do exactly what they said or they beat me!' she cried. 'You think I *wanted* to do that?'

Her own image stared out at her from the television screen as she touched herself between her legs, then licked her fingers.

'Yeah,' Landry said. 'I do.'

A male voice in the background on the tape mumbled something, then he and Erin both laughed.

Erin shoved her chair back from the table and got up to pace. A caged, cornered, angry little animal. 'I had to play along,' she said. 'I was afraid they would kill me! What is wrong with you people? Why won't you believe me? It was Chad. I know that now. He was punishing me.'

Something struck the one-way mirror from the back side. Erin and Onjo jumped. Landry looked at Roca.

On the screen, Chad Seabright walked around in front of the video camera and joined Erin on the bed. They kneeled face-to-face on the stained mattress.

'How do you like it, baby?' he asked.

Erin looked up at him and smiled like a vixen. 'You know how I like it. I like it rough.'

They both started to laugh. Two kids having fun. Actors rehearsing.

Landry glanced over at the one-way mirror, nodding to someone on the other side, then went to the door and opened it on the excuse of telling something to the guard outside.

'You fucking bitch!' Chad Seabright screamed into the room as a deputy pulled him past in handcuffs. Seabright tried to jerk away, lunging toward the interview room. 'I loved you! I loved you!'

He tried to spit at her from ten feet away. Landry stepped to the side, frowning in distaste.

'Some people just aren't well brought up,' he commented as he closed the door.

Onjo puffed up. 'This is outrageous! Terrorizing my client with her attacker –'

'Give it up, Counselor,' Roca said wearily. 'A jury takes one look at this tape, and your client can kiss her movie future good-bye.'

'I want a deal!' Chad shouted. 'I want a deal!'

Erin jumped up from her chair. 'Shut up! Shut up!'

'I did it for you! I loved you!'

Erin glared at him with venomous disdain. 'You stupid fucking idiot.'

Landry went out onto the sidewalk to stand in the hot afternoon sun and smoke a cigarette. He had to get the taste of other people's lies out of his mouth, burn out the stink of what they had done.

Chad Seabright had copped to everything, giving up his claims of innocence in order to hurt Erin. He claimed Erin had come to him with the plan. They would fake her kidnapping, and collect the ransom from Bruce Seabright. If he didn't pay one way, he would pay another: with his reputation, with his marriage. At the same time, Don Jade would be implicated and ruined, and Paris Montgomery would get what she wanted – Jade's business and Trey Hughes's stables.

A simple plan.

The three of them had sat down together and come up with the scripts for the videotapes as if they were shooting a movie for a film class. According to Chad, the beating had been Erin's idea. She had insisted he actually strike her with the whip for the sake of realism.

It was Erin's idea. It was Paris Montgomery's idea. It wasn't Chad's fault. Nothing was ever anybody's fault.

Chad had been deceived and used by Erin. He was an innocent. Erin's mother hadn't raised her right. Bruce Seabright didn't love her. Paris Montgomery had brainwashed her.

Paris Montgomery had yet to be questioned, but Landry would eventually have to listen to her while she cried and told him how her father made her play the skin flute when she was three, and how she lost out on being the homecoming queen in high school, and how that all warped her.

Chad claimed not to know anything about Tomas Van Zandt or about the death of Jill Morone. Landry figured that would turn out not to be anyone's fault either.

What Landry wanted to know was: If nothing was ever anybody's fault, then how was it people ended up murdered, orphaned, lives destroyed? Paris Montgomery and Erin Seabright and Chad Seabright had made decisions that had ruined people's lives, ended people's lives. How was all that nobody's fault?

60

In the uncertain hour before the morning
Near the ending of the interminable night ...

I recalled those lines again as I sat tucked up against the back of the chaise on my patio, watching the sunrise the day after Chad Seabright had cut a deal with the state's attorney.

Chad had turned on Erin. Erin had turned on Paris Montgomery. Paris had fingered Van Zandt as Jill Morone's killer, trying to win herself points with the state's attorney. They all deserved to rot in hell.

I thought of Molly, and tried to apply T. S. Eliot's words as a caption to what she was going through, and to the journey of her life. I tried not to dwell on the irony that it had been Molly who had fought to bring her family back together by hiring me to find her sister, and at the end of it, Molly was the only one left.

Bruce Seabright was dead. Krystal's mind had shattered. If she had ever been of any real support in Molly's life before, it was doubtful she ever would be again. And Erin, the sister Molly had loved so much, was lost to her forever. If not by a prison term, by Erin's betrayal.

Life can change in a heartbeat, in an instant, in the time it takes to make a wrong decision ... or a right one.

I had given Molly the news about Erin's involvement in the plot the night before and held her in my arms while she cried herself to sleep.

She came out onto the patio then, wrapped in an enormous green blanket, climbed onto the chaise, and curled up beside me without saying a word. I stroked a hand over her hair, and wished I had the power to make that moment last a long, long time.

After a while I finally asked, 'So what do you know about this Aunt Maxine person?'

The Sheriff's Office had located Krystal Seabright's only living relative in the area, a sixty-something widow in West Palm Beach. I was to drive Molly to her in the afternoon.

'She's okay,' Molly said without enthusiasm. 'She's ... normal.'

'Well, that's highly overrated.'

We were silent for a time, just looking off across the fields at the sunrise. I searched awkwardly for words.

'You know I'm terribly sorry for everything that happened in the end, Molly. But I'm not sorry you came to me that day and asked me to help you. I'm a better person for knowing you.

'And if I don't like this Maxine broad,' I added in my crankiest tone. 'You're coming straight home with me.'

Molly looked up at me through her owlish little glasses and smiled for the first time since I'd known her.

Great-aunt Maxine lived in a nice complex of apartments, and seemed as advertised: normal. I helped Molly in with her things and stayed for a cup of coffee and a fresh oatmeal cookie. Normal.

Molly walked me out, and we suffered through good-bye.

'You know, you can call me anytime for anything, Molly,' I told her. 'Or even for nothing at all.'

She smiled a soft, wise smile and nodded. Behind the lenses of her glasses, her earnest blue eyes were shimmering with tears. She handed me a small card cut out of a piece of stationery. She had printed her name and new address and phone number beside a tiny sticker of a purple pansy.

'You have to send me your final bill,' she said. 'I'm sure I owe you quite a lot of money. I'll have to pay you in installments. We can work something out.'

'No,' I murmured. 'You don't owe me anything at all.'

I hugged her tight for a long while. If I could have, I would have cried.

By the time I returned to the farm, the day was slipping away, the sun pouring molten orange along the flat western horizon. I parked my car and wandered down to the barn.

Irina had Feliki in the cross-ties, dressing her legs with witch hazel and alcohol, and wrapping them for the night.

'How's tricks?' I asked.

'Is fine,' she said, her concentration on making the right front bandage match perfectly with the left.

'I'm sorry, I haven't been much help lately,' I said.

She looked up at me and smiled softly. 'Is fine, Elena. It doesn't matter. I know the things that matter.'

I was tempted to ask her the meaning of life.

She moved to the mare's hind legs and sprayed on the alcohol concoction.

'Have the police yet found the Belgian?' she asked.

'No. It seems he simply vanished with Lorinda Carlton's rental car. They'll get him eventually.'

'He pays for his crimes, I think,' Irina said. 'I believe in karma. Don't you?'

'I don't know. Maybe.'

'I think yes.'

She was singing when I left the barn.

Landry had parked himself in a lounge chair by the pool. He was watching the sun set through his shades. I sat down beside his legs and blocked his view.

'What do you know, Landry?'

'People are scum.'

'Not all of them.'

'No. I like you, Estes,' he said. 'You're a good and decent human being.'

'I'm glad you think so. I'm glad I think so too,' I confessed, though I didn't think he probably understood the depth of what that really meant to me.

Or perhaps he did.

'Trey Hughes rolled on Jade today,' he said. 'He says it was Jade's idea to off the old lady so Trey could inherit. Not his fault the guy followed through with it.'

'Of course not. And what does Jade have to say?'

He just shook his head. 'Did you get Molly settled in?'

'Yes. She'll be all right. I miss her,' I confessed.

Landry reached out and touched my hand. 'You'll be all right too.'

'I know. Yes. I will be. I will be. I am.'

'You are,' he agreed, his hand squeezing mine. 'What do you say we get to know each other?'

I smiled the half-smile and nodded, and we walked toward the guest house hand in hand.

Life can change in a heartbeat.